# THE
# VEILED
# THRONE

KEN LIU is the winner of the Nebula, Hugo,
World Fantasy, Locus, and Sidewise awards. He
is the author of short story collections *The Paper
Menagerie and Other Stories* and *The Hidden Girl
and Other Stories,* as well the epic series The
Dandelion Dynasty. A former programmer and
lawyer, he speaks and consults on futurism,
technology history, and sustainable storytelling.

## WRITTEN BY KEN LIU

**The Dandelion Dynasty**
*The Grace of Kings*
*The Wall of Storms*
*The Veiled Throne*

**Short story collections**
*The Paper Menagerie and Other Stories*
*The Hidden Girl and Other Stories*

## TRANSLATED BY KEN LIU

*The Three-Body Problem* (by Cixin Liu)
*Death's End* (by Cixin Liu)
*The Redemption of Time* (by Baoshu)
*Waste Tide* (by Chen Qiufan)
*Vagabonds* (by Hao Jingfang)

## EDITED BY KEN LIU

*Invisible Planets*
*Broken Stars*

# THE VEILED THRONE

## KEN LIU

HEAD
ZEUS

An Ad Astra Book

First published in the United States of America in 2021
by Saga Press, an imprint of Simon & Schuster, Inc.

First published in the United Kingdom in 2021 by Head of Zeus Ltd
An Ad Astra book

9 7 5 3 1 2 4 6 8

A catalogue record for this book is available
from the British Library.

ISBN (HB) 9781784973292
ISBN (The Broken Binding HB) 9781803283753
ISBN (XTPB) 9781784973308
ISBN (E) 9781784973285

Interior design by Kathryn A. Kenney-Peterson

MIX
Paper from
responsible sources
FSC
www.fsc.org
FSC® C020471

Printed and bound by CPI Group (UK) Ltd, Croydon, CR0 4YY

Head of Zeus Ltd
First Floor East
5–8 Hardwick Street
London EC1R 4RG

WWW.HEADOFZEUS.COM

*For my grandfather, who lived a life*
*grander than any story I could tell*

Écofi

Arulugi

Karo Peninsula

Lake Toyemotika

Müning

Amu Strait

Canfin

Napi

Dimushi

Tan Adü

PORIN PLAINS

Dimu

GÉFICA

AMU

The
ISLANDS
of
DARA

Kiesa

Zudi

COCRU

Er-Mé Mountains

Mt. Kana

Laru River

Pan

Wisoti Mountains

Tiro Cozo

Çaruza

Mt. Ra

Tunoa

Farun

Rana Kida

Gonlogi
Desert

GAN

Sonaru
Desert

Sonaru River

Itunti Peninsula

Maji Peninsula

Nasu

Nokida

Kishi Chann

Toa

0          75          150

Miles

Crescent
Island

XANA

Dasu
Daye

Mt. Kiji

Rui

Kigo Yezu

Kriphi

*Gaing Gulf*

Big Island

*ke Tututika*

*Miru River*

HAAN

Lutho Beach

Ginpen

*mu Mountains*

Mt Fithowéo

Temple of
Peace

RIMA

Na Thion

Zathin Gulf

Silkworm Eggs

FAÇA

HIGHLANDS

Boama

Shinané Mountains

Rufizo Falls

*Tazu
Whirlpool*

Ogé

Big Toe

Wolf's Paw

W

S        N

E

# UKYU and GONDÉ

Lower Peninsula

Luan Zya's
Landing Site ⚓

Upper
Peninsu...

Péa's
Sea

Admiral Krita's
Landing Site ⚓

Taten
*(Pékyu Tenryo Roatan...)*

## GONDÉ

Sliyusa Ki

Tenryo & Diaman
⚔

*Lurodia Tanta*
*(The Endless Desert)*

Sea
of
Tears

*Blood River*

The
Barrows

*Ghost River*

Wing
*(Agon)*

Foot
*(Lyucu)*

Tail
*(Lyucu)*

Atnler
*(Agon)*

Kiri Valley

# CONTENTS

## RAIN-LASHED SAPLINGS

## SUN-KISSED BOUGHS

# A NOTE ON PRONUNCIATION, TRANSLITERATION, AND TRANSLATION

Many names in Dara are derived from Classical Ano. The transliteration for Classical Ano in this book does not use vowel digraphs; each vowel is pronounced separately. For example, "Réfiroa" has four distinct syllables: "Ré-fi-ro-a." Similarly, "Na-aroénna" has five syllables: "Na-a-ro-én-na."

The *i* is always pronounced like the *i* in English "mill."

The *o* is always pronounced like the *o* in English "code."

The *ü* is always pronounced like the umlauted form in German or Chinese pinyin.

Other names have different origins and contain sounds that do not appear in Classical Ano, such as the *xa* in "Xana" or the *ha* in "Haan." In such cases, however, each vowel is still pronounced separately. Thus, "Haan" also contains two syllables.

The notion that Classical Ano is one fixed language, unaltered for millennia, is attractive and commonly held among the less erudite in Dara. It is, however, false. As the (primarily) literary language of learning and officialdom, "Classical" Ano has continued to evolve, influencing and influenced by the vernacular as well as contact with new peoples, new ideas, new practices.

Scribes and poets create neologisms based on Classical Ano roots, along with new logograms to write them with, and even novel grammatical forms, at first deemed solecisms, become accepted over time as stylists adopt them with little regard to the carping of Moralist grammarians.

The changes in Classical Ano are most readily seen in the logograms themselves. However, it's possible to see some of the changes even through transliterations (we leave aside, for now, the problem of how even the way Classical Ano is spoken has changed over time). The Classical Ano in which Kon Fiji wrote most of his observations is not the same language in which Vocu Firna wrote his poems.

To emphasize the different register that the language evokes for the people of Dara, Classical Ano words and phrases are always italicized in the text.

The representation of Lyucu and Agon names and words presents a different problem. As we come to know them through the people(s) and language(s) of Dara, the scrubland words given in this work are doubly mediated. Just as English speakers who write down Chinese names and words they hear with Latin letters will achieve only a rough approximation of the original sounds, so with the Dara transliteration of Lyucu and Agon.

Lyucu and Agon do not pluralize nouns in the manner of English. For the benefit of the anglophone reader, certain words, such as "pékyu" and "garinafin," are pluralized in this book as though they have become "naturalized" English words. On the other hand, other words and phrases, less common, retain the character of their non-English origins.

"Dara," "Lyucu," and "Agon" can refer to a language, the people who speak that language, the culture of that people, or even a single individual of that culture—a practice closer to the way these languages represent such concepts natively.

Also, in contrast to Classical Ano, Lyucu and Agon words and phrases are not (with very few exceptions) italicized in the text. For the people who speak the language(s), they are not foreign.

Like most matters involving translation, transliteration, assimilation, adaptation, and migration, these practices represent an imperfect compromise, which, given the nature of the tale re-remembered here, is perhaps appropriate.

# LIST OF MAJOR
# CHARACTERS

## THE CHRYSANTHEMUM AND THE DANDELION

KUNI GARU: Emperor Ragin of Dara, who died during the Battle of
Zathin Gulf, though his body was never recovered.

MATA ZYNDU: deceased Hegemon of Dara, worshipped by some
cults in Tunoa and among the common soldiers as the pinnacle
of martial prowess and honor.

## THE DANDELION COURT

JIA MATIZA: Empress and Regent of Dara; a skilled herbalist.

RISANA: an illusionist and accomplished musician; posthumously
given the title Empress of Dara.

KADO GARU: Kuni's elder brother; holds the title of King of Dasu
without the substance; father of Prince Gimoto.

COGO YELU: Prime Minister of Dara; one of the longest-serving
officials at the Dandelion Court.

ZOMI KIDOSU: Farsight Secretary; prized student of Luan Zyaji
and a noted inventor in her own right; Princess Théra's lover;
daughter of a Dasu farming-fishing family (Oga and Aki Kidosu).

GIN MAZOTI: Marshal of Dara and Queen of Géjira; the greatest
battlefield tactician of her time; posthumous victor at the Battle
of Zathin Gulf; Aya Mazoti is her daughter.

THAN CARUCONO: First General of the Cavalry and First Admiral
of the Navy.

PUMA YEMU: Marquess of Porin; noted practitioner of raiding
tactics.

SOTO ZYNDU: Jia's confidante and adviser; aunt of Mata Zyndu.

WI: leader of the Dyran Fins, who serve Empress Jia.

SHIDO: a Dyran Fin.

LADY RAGI: an orphaned girl raised by Jia; serves the empress on special missions.

GORI RUTHI: nephew of the late Imperial Tutor Zato Ruthi and husband of Lady Ragi; a noted Moralist scholar.

## CHILDREN OF THE HOUSE OF DANDELION

PRINCE TIMU (NURSING NAME: TOTO-*TIKA*): Emperor Thaké of Ukyu-taasa; Kuni's firstborn; consort of Tanvanaki; son of Empress Jia.

PRINCESS THÉRA (NURSING NAME: RATA-*TIKA*): named by Kuni as his successor and once known as Empress Üna of Dara; yielded the throne to her younger brother Phyro in order to journey to Ukyu-Gondé to war with the Lyucu; daughter of Empress Jia.

PRINCE PHYRO (NURSING NAME: HUDO-*TIKA*): Emperor Monadétu of Dara; son of Empress Risana.

PRINCESS FARA (NURSING NAME: ADA-*TIKA*): an artist and collector of folktales; youngest of Kuni's children; daughter of Consort Fina, who died in childbirth.

PRINCESS AYA: daughter of Gin Mazoti and Luan Zyaji; given the title of Imperial Princess by Empress Jia to honor the sacrifices of her mother.

PRINCE GIMOTO: son of Kado Garu, Kuni's elder brother.

## SCHOLARS OF DARA

LUAN ZYAJI: Kuni's chief strategist; Gin Mazoti's lover; he journeyed to Ukyu-Gondé and discovered the secret of the periodic openings in the Wall of Storms; known during life as Luan Zya.

ZATO RUTHI: Imperial Tutor; leading Moralist of modern times.

KON FIJI: ancient Ano philosopher; founder of the Moralist school.

POTI MAJI: ancient Ano philosopher; the most accomplished student of Kon Fiji.

RA OJI: ancient Ano epigrammatist; founder of the Fluxist school.

ÜSHIN PIDAJI: ancient Ano philosopher; the most renowned student of Ra Oji.

NA MOJI: ancient Xana engineer who studied the flights of birds; founder of the Patternist school.

GI ANJI: modern philosopher of the Tiro states era; founder of the Incentivist school.

MIZA CRUN: renowned scholar of the silkmotic force; once a street magician.

### UKYU-TAASA

TENRYO ROATAN: seized position of Pékyu of the Lyucu by murdering his father, Toluroru; conqueror of the scrublands; leader of the Lyucu invasion of Dara; died at the Battle of Zathin Gulf.

VADYU ROATAN (NICKNAMED "TANVANAKI"): the best garinafin pilot and current pékyu of Ukyu-taasa; daughter of Tenryo.

TODYU ROATAN (NURSING NAME: DYU-*TIKA*): son of Timu and Tanvanaki.

DYANA ROATAN (NURSING NAME: ZAZA-*TIKA*): daughter of Timu and Tanvanaki.

VOCU FIRNA: a thane close to Timu; a poet.

CUTANROVO AGA: a prominent thane, commander of the Capital Security Forces.

GOZTAN RYOTO: a prominent thane; rival of Cutanrovo.

SAVO RYOTO: Goztan's son; also known by the Dara name Kinri Rito.

NAZU TEI: a scholar; teacher of Savo.

NODA MI: a minister at the court of Tanvanaki and Timu; betrayed Gin Mazoti at the Battle of Zathin Gulf.

WIRA PIN: a minister at the court of Tanvanaki and Timu; once tried to persuade Prince Timu to surrender to the Lyucu under Pékyu Tenryo.

OFLURO: a skilled garinafin rider.

LADY SUCA: one of the few non-Lyucu to learn to ride a garinafin; wife of Ofluro.

## THE SPLENDID URN AND THE BLOSSOM GANG

RATI YERA: leader of the Blossom Gang; an illiterate inventor of ingenious machines.

MOTA KIPHI: member of the Blossom Gang; a man rivaling Mata Zyndu in pure strength; survivor of the Battle of Zathin Gulf.

ARONA TARÉ: member of the Blossom Gang; an actress.

WIDI TUCRU: member of the Blossom Gang; a paid litigator.

WIDOW WASU: head of the Wasu clan; she knew Kuni Garu as a youth.

MATI PHY: sous-chef at the Splendid Urn.

LODAN THO: head waitress at the Splendid Urn; Mati's wife.

TIPHAN HUTO: the youngest son of the Huto clan, rival of the Wasu clan.

MOZO MU: a young chef employed by Tiphan Huto; granddaughter of Suda Mu, legendary cook in the time of the Tiro kings.

LOLOTIKA TUNÉ: Head girl of the Aviary, Ginpen's leading indigo house.

KITA THU: head of the Imperial laboratories in Ginpen; once led the effort to discover the secret of garinafin fire breath during the war against the Lyucu.

SÉCA THU: a scholar; nephew of Kita Thu.

## DARA AT LARGE

ABBOTT SHATTERED AXE: head of the Temple of Still and Flowing Waters in the mountains of Rima.

ZEN-KARA: a scholar; daughter of Chief Kyzen of Tan Adü.

RÉZA MÜI: a troublemaker.

ÉGI AND ASULU: a pair of soldiers in the city garrison of Pan.

KISLI PÉRO: a researcher at one of the Imperial laboratories.

## THE CREW OF DISSOLVER OF SORROWS

RAZUTANA PON: a scholar of the Cultivationism school.

ÇAMI PHITHADAPU: a Golden Carp scholar; an expert on whales.

MITU ROSO: an admiral, commander-in-chief of the expedition to Ukyu-Gondé.

NMÉJI GON: captain of *Dissolver of Sorrows*.

TIPO THO: former air ship officer; commander of the marines aboard *Dissolver of Sorrows*.

THORYO: a mysterious stowaway.

## THE LYUCU

TOLURORU ROATAN: unifier of the Lyucu.

CUDYU ROATAN: leader of the Lyucu; son of Tenryo; grandson of Toluroru.

TOVO TASARICU: Cudyu's most trusted thane.

TOOF: a garinafin pilot.

RADIA: a garinafin rider.

## THE AGON

NOBO ARAGOZ: unifier of the Agon.

SOULIYAN ARAGOZ: youngest daughter of Nobo Aragoz; mother of Takval.

VOLYU ARAGOZ: youngest son of Nobo Aragoz; Chief of the Agon.

TAKVAL ARAGOZ: pékyu-taasa of the Agon; husband of Théra.

TANTO GARU ARAGOZ (NURSING NAME: KUNILU-*TIKA*): eldest son of Théra and Takval.

ROKIRI GARU ARAGOZ (NURSING NAME: JIAN-*TIKA*): second son of Théra and Takval.

VARA RONALEK: an old thane who refuses to give up riding garinafins into battle.

GOZOFIN: a warrior, skilled in the crafting of arucuro tocua.

NALU: Gozofin's son.

ADYULEK: an aged shaman, skilled in the taking of spirit portraits.
SATAARI: a young shaman.
ARATEN: a thane trusted by Takval.

## THE GODS OF DARA

KIJI: patron of Xana; Lord of the Air; god of wind, flight, and birds; his *pawi* is the Mingén falcon; favors a white traveling cloak; in Ukyu-taasa he is identified with Péa, the god who gave the gift of garinafins to the people.

TUTUTIKA: patron of Amu; youngest of the gods; goddess of agriculture, beauty, and fresh water; her *pawi* is the golden carp; in Ukyu-taasa she is identified with Aluro, the Lady of a Thousand Streams.

KANA AND RAPA: twin patrons of Cocru; Kana is the goddess of fire, ash, cremation, and death; Rapa is the goddess of ice, snow, glaciers, and sleep; their *pawi* are twin ravens: one black, one white; in Ukyu-taasa they are identified with Cudyufin, the Well of Daylight, and Nalyufin, the Pillar of Ice and the hate-hearted.

RUFIZO: patron of Faça; Divine Healer; his *pawi* is the dove; in Ukyu-taasa he is identified with Toryoana, the long-haired bull who watches over cattle and sheep.

TAZU: patron of Gan; unpredictable, chaotic, delighting in chance; god of sea currents, tsunamis, and sunken treasures; his *pawi* is the shark; in Ukyu-taasa both he and Lutho are identified with Péten, the god of trappers and hunters.

LUTHO: patron of Haan; god of fishermen, divination, mathematics, and knowledge; his *pawi* is the sea turtle; missing from Dara when he became mortal to hitch a ride on *Dissolver of Sorrows*.

FITHOWÉO: patron of Rima; god of war, the hunt, and the forge; his *pawi* is the wolf; in Ukyu-taasa he is identified with the goddess Diasa, the she-wolf club-maiden.

# BURIED SEEDS

# CHAPTER ONE

# A NIGHT RUN

TATEN, THE SEAT OF THE PÉKYU OF THE LYUCU IN
UKYU-GONDÉ: THE FIFTH MONTH IN THE TWELFTH
YEAR AFTER STRANGERS FROM AFAR ARRIVED IN
THEIR CITY-SHIPS, CLAIMING TO SERVE SOMEONE
NAMED "MAPIDÉRÉ" (BY DARA RECKONING, THIS
IS THE FIFTH MONTH IN THE FIRST YEAR IN THE
REIGN OF FOUR PLACID SEAS, WHEN KUNI GARU
PROCLAIMED HIMSELF EMPEROR RAGIN AND
ESTABLISHED HIS CAPITAL IN REBUILT PAN).

The stars pulsed in the firmament like glowing jellies in a dark sea.
The eternal surf sighed in the distance as the almost-full moon's pale
light illuminated a field of tents as far as the eye could see, each as
white as the belly of a corpse-plucker crab.

Goztan Ryoto staggered out of one of the larger tents, a thin pelt
tunic draped over her shoulders and a skull helmet dangling from
her hand. The tent's garinafin-hide flap fell back heavily against
the frame, muffling the angry curses and din of clashing bone clubs
inside. She swayed on her feet as she tried to regain her balance.

"Steady, votan!" One of the two guards standing by the tent opening rushed up to support her lord. Casting a glance back at the tent
flap, the guard asked, "Do you want us to—"

Goztan shoved her away. "No. Let 'em fight. I've had enough of
them slinging insults at each other over dinner like children—can't
even have a drink in peace." She struggled to pull the skull helmet
over her clean-shaven head.

"I'm guessing you won't summon any of them to your bed tonight?" asked the other guard. "It's too bad. Kitan took a bath earlier today"—she lifted her eyebrows suggestively—"and he made sure we knew it."

Both guards laughed.

Goztan glared at them through the eye sockets of the skull helmet. "I'd love to see either of you try maintaining a peaceful household with four husbands."

Something crashed to the ground inside the tent; a furious howl of pain followed.

The guards looked at each other but remained where they were.

Goztan shook her head in exasperation. The cool breeze had cleared her head of kyoffir-haze, and after a moment, she said, "I'm taking a walk. The audience with the pékyu is first thing tomorrow, and I need to plan out what I want to say. Keep an eye on them; intervene only if Kitan's head is about to be bashed in."

"It *is* a very handsome head," said one of the guards.

They lifted the tent flap and ducked in, eager to witness the domestic drama among the chief's consorts.

Goztan strode aimlessly through the wide avenues between the tent-halls of Taten, her face flushed from rage and embarrassment. Despite the bright moonlight and the cool breeze, few of the thanes and warriors gathered in the Thanes' Quarter were walking about, for evening was a time reserved for the fire pit and ancestral portraits, for family and kyoffir. For a tiger-thane like Goztan, the chief of the Five Tribes of the Antler, roaming alone through the tent-city at this hour instead of spending time with her spouses was a choice bound to rouse gossip. Although the skull helmet covered her face, it was still too distinctive to make her completely anonymous.

Goztan was beyond caring.

She began to run, her legs pumping faster as her breath deepened and steadied. The skull helmet isolated her from the world at large, and her breathing resonated in her ears like the crash of the distant surf. At twenty-nine, she was in prime fighting shape, stronger and deadlier than she had been during the years when she had fought most of her battles. The sensation of boundless strength coursing through her limbs and the rhythmic slapping of her bare, calloused feet against the ground calmed her until, gradually, she fell into a trancelike state. She imagined herself soaring freely through the air on the back of a garinafin—instead of being stuck here on the ground, plodding through a morass of competing obligations that threatened to trip her with every step.

She should be swooping through the sky and scattering her enemies with the flame tongue of her mount, getting drunk on their terrified shrieks, taking delight as cattle and sheep and hide tents and waybones and earthen storage pits turned to ash and roasted flesh.

She was meant to be a fighter, not a mediator for petty power struggles among her consorts: aloof Ofta; hotheaded Kyova; crafty Finva-Toruli; and sweet, sickly, paranoid Kitan. Ofta's tribe had the most cattle; Kyova's tribe laid claim to the most extensive grazing rights; Finva-Toruli's tribe had the least amount of everything except an overabundance of ambition; and Kitan's tribe resisted her in everything, yearning to return to the days before the Five Tribes were united, before she was in charge.

Each had his own agenda, pushed for by his tribe's council of elders; each presented a different claim on her time and affections; each was trying, in subtle and not-so-subtle ways, to maneuver himself into the position of being the father of her firstborn. The Five Tribes might be united as one in name, but in reality they were more like five eels forced to share the same narrow cave in the coral reef.

The pékyu's peace had brought many benefits, but it wasn't suited to her temperament. She had journeyed almost a thousand miles to Taten for the first time in six years ostensibly to plead the Five Tribes of the Antler's case for grazing rights by Aluro's Basin, but the truth was that she wanted to get away from all the elders and chieftains and clan heads who hounded her to settle minor disputes in their favor, pestered her to make trivial decisions, nagged her about why she still refused to bear an heir, years after she had become the chief of the Five Tribes and had been elevated to the rank of tiger-thane.

*If only I had also left my husbands behind.*

Darkness. The flickering torches and flapping war banners, made from the tails of foxes, wolves, and tigers, faded like wisps of dreams. Without intending it, she had run beyond the limits of Taten, the pékyu's roving tent-city. The pale beach spread before her, glistening in the moon's silvery glow, inviting her to dive into this earthly reflection of the celestial river of stars. She ordered her imaginary mount to slow its beating wings as her heels sank into the yielding sand.

What had happened to those exhilarating first days of her marriage, when she had thought that five hearts could beat as one, that betrayals and plots were behind her, and that the Five Tribes of the Antler could finally take their rightful place as the model of a new Lyucu, a united people no longer terrorized by Agon raiders or invading strangers from beyond the sea, no longer riven by bloody internecine warfare, a proud race whose bloodlust would be channeled into war against winter storms and summer plagues, against starvation and flood and drought, against heaven, earth, and sea?

She had taken all her husbands in a single ceremony to show that they were all equal, despite their differences in age. To celebrate the act of union, she had ordered the tribes' best bone-crafters to fashion a new weapon: a magnificent axe replete with symbolism. She was the blade of the axe, made from a tusked tiger's fang, and her husbands were the handle, four yearling garinafin ribs tied together with twisted bundles of horrid-wolf sinew. She had given it the name Gaslira-sata, the Peace-Bite. Closing her eyes, she imagined the way the handle dug into her palms as she wrapped her fingers around it. A perfectly balanced weapon, equally suited to be thrown through the air to decapitate an Agon pilot's head as to be swung on the ground to cleave in halves the torso of a Dara barbarian.

The Peace-Bite, long starved of blood, now lay dormant in her tent, wrapped in a sheath of sharkskin, while her jealous consorts raged and plotted and argued and jostled and fought to be invited to her bed.

*What am I going to say to the pékyu tomorrow?*

*The truth?*

*"For ten years, the Tribe of the Four Cacti have driven their herds to the land promised to us on the shores of Aluro's Basin ahead of our arrival in*

*spring, leaving us with nothing but roots and dung. Since we can no longer press our claim by force, the elders have been sitting in front of my tent day and night, wailing for me to do something. My first husband thinks I should offer you our store of Dara jewels to persuade you to rule for us. My second husband counsels against it because he thinks his tribe would have to sacrifice more treasure than the others. My third husband thinks I should imitate the elders and kneel before you to move you with my tears. And my fourth husband tells me at every opportunity that my other husbands are plotting to kill him. I want to lose myself in drink because it's impossible to think with all four of them bickering and screaming without cease. . . ."*

In her mind, she could already see the pékyu's eyes glaze over, and then he would dismiss her with a pitying but resolute wave of his arm. Her jaw clenched with the imaginary humiliation.

"Who goes there?" A man's voice woke her from her fantasy. Two male guards stood in her way, bone clubs resting over their shoulders.

She saw that she had wandered so far from the edge of Taten that she was approaching Victory Cove, where the city-ships from Dara were anchored. The massive hulls, still breathtaking despite years of neglect, blotted out the stars and gently undulated in the sparkling sea, their silvery masts and spars reminding her of the conifer forests near her homeland in the foothills of the mountains at the edge of the world, or perhaps the bleached skeletons of sea monsters whose flesh had rotted away.

*Cities of ghosts,* she thought, and shuddered at the memories they brought.

On the other side of the beach, away from the water, were the pens for adolescent garinafins, separated from their families so that they could be drilled in the flight patterns necessary for warfare. The sleek bodies of the slumbering beasts glinted in the moon like a herd of cattle, albeit far larger.

Directly ahead of her, far in the distance, she could see a bonfire and dancing figures around it. The breeze brought occasional snatches of laughter.

"Answer!" the guard shouted again. "Come no closer."

She didn't remember the city-ships or garinafin pens being so

heavily guarded the last time she was in Taten. The chances of an
Agon raid or slave rebellion now were remote, more than twenty
years since Pékyu Tenryo had united the Lyucu and conquered the
Agon.

*What are they guarding?*

Half turning so that her face was in the moonlight, she lifted the
skull helmet off her head and cradled it in the crook of her arm. The
breeze cooled the sweat off her brow as she intoned imperiously,
"Are you blind?"

Only a thane of her rank could wear a helmet made from the
skull of a juvenile tusked tiger. She didn't want to say her name—
announcing her lineage and tribe seemed shameful when she had
come to Taten to beg the pékyu to help her feed cattle, when she
couldn't even keep her husbands in line, when she had to find a
moment of peace by running away from her own tent-hall.

"Votan." The guards nodded their heads respectfully. But they
made no move to get out of her way.

She took two steps forward. The guards remained where they
were, blocking her.

Heat rose into Goztan's face. The exertion of the night run had
made her feel better, but now the frustration and sense of powerless-
ness had returned with a vengeance.

"Why do you keep me from the merriment beyond?" she asked.
In truth, she had little interest in whatever revelry was going on by
the bonfire—she far preferred to be alone at this moment—but she
disliked the insolent attitude of the guards.

"Thanes and chiefs, great and small, come to Taten every day
with their retinues," said one of the guards in an even tone, "and
most are strangers to us. We're sworn to keep strangers away from
the Road-to-the-City-Ships, so unless you have the pékyu's talisman,
please return to the safety of Taten."

Goztan glared at the guards. They were so young, barely more
than boys. She was certain they had never killed anyone except perhaps defenseless slaves. When Goztan was facing down Agon garinafins and Dara swords, these boys hadn't even been old enough to
be allowed out of the sight of their grandmothers.

Rage erupted from her throat in the form of an unnatural guffaw. "I wonder if you'd dare speak this way to the Thane of the Four Cacti, with his retinue of dozens always around him. I wonder if you'd bar the way of the Thane of the Sixteen Tribes of the Boneyard, borne everywhere on a cattle-litter. Just because my followers are few and my tribe remote, you dare to bark at me like ill-mannered curs. Sworn to protect the road to the ships, are you? I'm the one who captured those ships!"

The guards looked shaken but didn't back down. "We don't care who you are. We serve only the pékyu and will do whatever has been ordered by the hand that wields Langiaboto. You can't pass without his talisman."

Goztan let the helmet fall from her hand and dropped into a fighting stance, her fists up and ready. She regretted leaving in such a hurry that she was without her weapon, but she wasn't going to let a couple of boys with unscarred faces turn her away from where she wanted to go.

The guards tensed their grips on their clubs and glanced at each other nervously. Goztan was taller than they were, and clearly a seasoned fighter, judging by the scars over her arms and face. But before they could decide on a coordinated response, Goztan lunged at the guard on the left, her right fist aimed at his nose.

Surprised, the guard tilted his head back and stumbled three steps rearward, looking rather foolish as he dragged his club through the sand. Goztan's punch just missed.

Having seized the initiative, she pressed her advantage, striding forward quickly to punch with her left fist, not giving the guard a chance to raise his club for defense or counterattack. Once more, the guard dodged back clumsily, looking even more flustered.

Instead of coming to the aid of his partner, the other guard circled further to Goztan's right, and her aggressive assault left him behind. Goztan stepped forward and punched again with her right fist at the first guard. But this time, instead of retreating, the guard dug his heels in and brought up his club in a long swing at the thane's midsection, apparently willing to trade punch for blow.

The young man smiled even as Goztan's fist closed in on his

nose—his retreat hadn't been the result of desperation, but a part of the two guards' trained routine. Goztan's punch would no doubt sting or even stun, but as she wasn't wearing armor, a single, solid strike from the guard's club would bring her down. In fact, Goztan was trapped. Even if she dodged back at this point instead of taking the bait to punch him, she would fall straight into the path of the swinging club of his partner, who was attacking from her blind spot.

But Goztan's follow-up punch turned out to be only a feint. Her right fist opened to grab the tip of the swinging club and pushed it down as she easily stepped to the right, planted her right leg, and kicked her left leg behind her without looking. Her foot seemed to have eyes of its own as it connected solidly with the wrists of the guard behind her, and with an agonized shriek, he dropped the club.

Meanwhile, the guard in front of her had been thrown off balance by the missed swing as the tip of his club thwacked into the sand. Before he could recover, Goztan had leapt forward and landed a solid chop against the back of his left elbow as she seized the club and twisted it out of his hands.

She twirled the club as she surveyed her disarmed opponents, one nursing an elbow, the other two wrists. "Am I allowed to pass now or would you rather dance some more?"

To their credit, neither of the young guards showed any sign of fear. They moved close together, barring her way. "You'll have to kill us if you want to get by," one of them said. His hands hung limply— at least one of his wrists was probably broken—and he winced as he spoke. The other guard picked up a shell whistle dangling on a sinew cord around his neck and blew into it, letting forth a loud, shrill alarm.

Answering whistles sounded in the dark; Goztan could see on the beach beyond shadowy figures closing in as the whistling grew louder.

Now that her fighting instinct had cooled slightly, Goztan regretted her impulsive choice. There was no reason to lash out against these guards. Pékyu Tenryo was sure to look unfavorably upon a thane who injured his guards, even if they had insulted her first. How was she to plead her people's case to an angry lord? But it was too late to back down. She lifted the club, preparing to take on dozens of guards if necessary.

Loud beating wings approached from behind her, and a young girl's crisp voice called out. "Stop, all of you!"

Goztan whipped around just in time to see a juvenile garinafin, about twenty feet long from nose to tail, thump down into the sand. The garinafin was clearly untrained, as it staggered forward a few paces, knelt down, and folded its leathery wings against its heaving body, the turbulence filling Goztan's nostrils with the familiar scent of garinafin musk. A ten-year-old girl sat on its back, the moonlight reflecting off the blond tresses haloing her pale, flawless face.

"Pékyu-taasa," said the guard who had sounded the alarm as he lifted both arms and crossed his wrists in salute. "The pékyu said no one is allowed near the ships except those who have been purified. This stranger tried to—"

"I know my father's orders," said the young girl. She caressed the shoulders of her mount, and the garinafin curled its long neck around to place its head on the sand right next to its shoulder; the pilot climbed down, using the head as a stepping-stone. The beast was breathing very fast and loud, sounding like a muffled conch-shell trumpet.

The girl turned to Goztan and saw that the woman was staring at the garinafin and frowning. A look of worry flitted across the girl's face.

"Reveal to them your name," she said in a tone that brooked no disagreement.

From the guard's address, Goztan gathered that the girl was a daughter of Pékyu Tenryo, and judging by her age, she must be Vadyu, said to be her father's favorite. She had been barely more than a toddler the last time Goztan was in Taten.

There seemed little point in continuing to conceal her identity. "I am called Goztan Ryoto, daughter of Dayu Ryoto, son of Péfir Vagapé. I serve the pékyu as the Thane of the Five Tribes of the Antler."

Vadyu turned to the guards. "Call off the alarm. The thane is my guest."

"But we don't know she is who she claims—"

"I know exactly who she is," interrupted Vadyu.

"Even so, she has broken—"

"You can explain your injuries as the result of a training accident," said Vadyu, "or tomorrow everyone will know that you were so ignorant that you dared to challenge one of the most renowned veterans of the Agon Wars, who was forced to teach you a lesson. It's your choice, but I do think a lie is easier maintained if there are fewer witnesses."

Goztan's heart swelled with pride. The insults she had endured all evening seemed to melt away. *One of the most renowned veterans of the Agon Wars.* But then, as she continued to observe the girl and her mount, the frown returned to her brow.

The pair of guards looked at each other and seemed to come to a decision. The man with the whistle blew a series of quick toots. A few moments later, receding answering whistles told them that the reinforcements were returning to their stations.

"Go get your elbow and wrists taken care of," said Vadyu. "I know you were trying to carry out my father's orders faithfully, and your loyalty will not be forgotten."

The dejected guards nodded at her gratefully and departed, leaving the thane and the pékyu-taasa alone.

Goztan turned to Vadyu. "You aren't supposed to be out here, are you?"

The girl's face froze in startlement. "How . . . how did you know?"

Goztan chuckled. "You were even more eager to get rid of those guards than I was."

"I simply didn't want them to bring shame to a great warrior I know and admire," retorted the girl.

"Is that so? What did I accomplish in the Agon Wars? What was my proudest moment?"

The girl hemmed and hawed, and then sheepishly said, "I've heard of your name."

"You almost had me fooled—clever of you to appeal to my vanity. But I haven't been in Taten in six years, so you couldn't have remembered me from my last visit to Taten. Why did you lie and claim to know me?"

The girl pressed her lips together and said nothing.

Goztan took a menacing step closer. "Helmets can be stolen. I could be an Agon slave in disguise plotting sabotage."

Vadyu refused to back away, but Goztan could see that her right hand had darted to the bone dagger she wore on her belt. But then, deliberately, she moved her hand away from the dagger. "Then you wouldn't have only disarmed the guards instead of killing them, which you were clearly capable of."

Goztan was impressed by the girl's cool and quick wit. She could see why the pékyu favored the young pékyu-taasa. She continued to stride toward the girl, and Vadyu's whole body tensed. But at the last moment, Goztan veered away, dropped the club she had seized from the guard, and knelt down next to the young garinafin. Gently, she lifted the garinafin's head and cradled it in her lap. The garinafin, a young female who had probably just learned to fly, was foaming at the mouth, her body trembling violently.

"What's wrong with Korva?" Vadyu asked anxiously.

"Quick, give me all the tolyusa on you."

A frightened Vadyu reached into her waist pouch and brought out handfuls of the fiery berries, dumping them in Goztan's cupped hands. The kneeling woman fed them to Korva a few at a time. After a while, the garinafin calmed down and closed her eyes. But even in sleep, her eyes seemed to move rapidly under the lids.

"Will she be all right?" asked Vadyu, agitated.

"She's just dreaming," said Goztan. "The tolyusa makes garinafins see visions, the same as us. She's overheating, and the tolyusa slows down her heart, dilates her arteries, and relaxes her muscles so she can rest."

"I *knew* you could help her," said Vadyu. "I was so scared because we were sinking in the air, and I had to land. Then I saw how you looked at her like you knew what was wrong, so I decided—"

"Garinafins this young shouldn't be ridden at all!" Goztan raised her voice, and her words came in a rapid torrent. "They don't have the endurance for sustained flight, and their families may even have to carry them on long journeys. It takes time for them to learn how to conserve lift gas and to master their own bodies. You were pushing her too hard."

"I didn't know—"

"I know you didn't know! The way you raise these war garinafins in massive corrals—" Goztan took a deep breath and forced herself to calm down. Voicing her criticisms of the pékyu's methods for raising large garinafin armies to his daughter was not going to gain her any favors. "I'm an old-style garinafin pilot, probably one of the best in your father's army, even though he hasn't needed my services for years now. I can't stand seeing these fine beasts mishandled."

"Korva's not from the corrals," objected Vadyu. "I'm trying to bond with her the old-fashioned way."

Goztan's eyes narrowed as she caressed the garinafin's smooth antlers. "She has no marks of bonding. . . . Did you steal her? You were told you shouldn't ride her, and you decided to disobey, didn't you?"

Vadyu bit her bottom lip, her chin jutting forward defiantly. "She's a gift to Father from the Thane of Windless Mesa. Her dam was supposed to be the fastest garinafin who ever fought for the thane—"

Goztan's voice softened just a hint. "And so you wanted to see if she inherited her dam's speed? She's not going to be fully developed—"

"I *know* she's too young to reach her full speed! You don't even listen! Do you take me for an ignorant child?" Vadyu sputtered, her eyes wide with the rage of being misunderstood.

Goztan knew better than to answer that. "All right, Pékyu-taasa, please go on. I promise not to interrupt."

Vadyu took a deep breath. "Even though I saw her first and begged Father to give her to me, he wants to offer her to my brother instead. 'I need a war mount,' I told him. 'But this little beast has quite a temper,' he said. 'So do I!' I said. 'Cudyu has more experience,' he said. 'From riding cattle? I bet I can outlast Cudyu on any bucking bull,' I said. 'Cudyu is older and will need a war mount sooner,' he said, and that was the end of the discussion. Well, that's not fair! I never get what I want just because I'm younger. So I decided to take her on a long ride first so she would be bonded to me."

Goztan laughed. "So I was right. You *are* a thief."

"I am *not*! Until a garinafin bonds to a pilot, she doesn't belong to anyone."

"How can you call yourself a pilot when you don't even know how to take care of your mount properly?"

Tears threatened to spill from Vadyu's eyes. "I . . . I should have learned more, but don't tell me you always did exactly as you were told when you were my age."

Goztan sighed. Her voice softened when she spoke again. "You do have me there. My mother, who was thane before me, was bonded to a big bull garinafin, incredibly bad-tempered. He was supposed to be impossible to ride. Of course I decided that I had to try, even though his saddle was so wide that when I finally climbed up, my legs were horizontal, like I was doing a split. . . ."

As Goztan reminisced, she gently caressed Korva's head, gazing affectionately at the young garinafin's fluttering eyelids.

Thus, she didn't notice the sudden change in Vadyu's expression as she listened to Goztan's story, nor did she see the young girl slowly reach for the club lying at her feet, and she certainly was not prepared when the girl reared back and slammed the club into the back of her head.

# CHAPTER TWO

# A SECRET EXPEDITION

VICTORY COVE, UKYU-GONDÉ: THE FIFTH MONTH
IN THE TWELFTH YEAR AFTER STRANGERS FROM
AFAR ARRIVED IN THEIR CITY-SHIPS (KNOWN IN
DARA AS THE FIRST YEAR IN THE REIGN OF FOUR
PLACID SEAS).

She came to.

Stars swimming in water filled her vision.

Gradually, she realized that the stars were not in water, but shimmering in heated air. Sparks from a roaring bonfire shot into the dark heavens like fireflies. The smell of burning dung and the aroma of roasted meat filled her nose. There was also a trace of the acrid tang of smoked tolyusa, consumed only at big feasts and celebrations. The back of her head hurt so much that she groaned.

A hypnotic chant filtered into her consciousness.

> *Brave warriors of Lyucu, heed my words,*
> *A tale as rich as the pékyu's vast herds.*
> *Though I am still a stranger in your land,*
> *I've beheld divine beauty with my hand.*

The way the speaker pronounced a few of the words revealed that he hadn't grown up speaking the language of the Lyucu, and the solecisms were telling—whoever heard of beholding beauty with the hand instead of the eye?—yet there was a compelling grace to the verse, a different rhythm and cadence that made the images stand out, that forced the listener to savor them, as though plain roasted wild marrow tubers had been spiced with tolyusa juice.

She thought the voice and accent both sounded familiar, though she couldn't quite place the speaker. She tried to turn her head toward the voice and found that her arms and legs had been bound tightly with thick ropes of twisted sinew. She was a captive.

*. . . Now you've all heard the old tale of the Agon herder who took in a starving puppy one winter and nurtured it back to health with the milk of his sheepdogs. When the puppy grew up, it turned out to be a wolf. One day, the herder caught the wolf with its jaws around a newborn calf's neck.*

"*Why have you repaid my kindness with such treasury?*" *asked the herder.*

"*I can't help it,*" *said the wolf.* "*It's my nature.*"

Laughter and loud shouting interrupted the tale.

"Serves him right!"

"Foolish Agon herder."

"Even an Agon bitch's milk is full of betrayal and 'treasury'!"

A childish face hovered into Goztan's still-fuzzy field of view: the pékyu-taasa, her hair glowing golden in the firelight.

"Why?" Goztan croaked. She squeezed her eyes shut and opened them again in an attempt to clear her vision. The back of her head throbbed. She hoped nothing was broken.

Vadyu leaned down to whisper into her ear, "Who *are* you, really?"

*. . . in my land, there is a familiar saying that probably shares the same wisdom in diffident words. We say,* "*A cruben begets a cruben, a dyran begets a dyran, and an octopus's daughter can crack eight oysters all at the same time.*"

More guffaws and shouts.

"More kyoffir!"

"More tolyusa!"

"I wouldn't mind some raw octopus right now."

"I think you meant 'different words,' old man. Get that tongue untwisted!"

"Oh, shush. The slave talks a fair bit better than you do. I wouldn't mind if you were more 'diffident.'"

No one seemed to be paying attention to the captive tied up by the fire, or the girl interrogating her.

Goztan couldn't understand why Vadyu was asking her a question whose answer she'd already given. Despite the pounding headache, her mind churned quickly. Somehow the girl was convinced that Goztan was not who she said she was and posed a threat, and until Goztan figured out the cause, she needed to take a different approach. "I'm impressed you managed to move me here all by yourself."

The girl looked away in embarrassment. "I tried to, but you're much too heavy for me to move by myself. I had to get a few of the naros here to help me. They were surprised to see me, but I told them that my father sent me to take note of their courage. They were grateful that I caught a saboteur along the way."

"Aren't you worried that your helpers will tell your father about Korva?"

Vadyu giggled. "Just about everyone here is going to sail off first thing in the morning to find the northwest passage to Dara. They won't see my father again for years, if ever."

Goztan craned her stiff neck to look at the sea. By the glow of the roaring bonfire, she could just make out a fleet of massive coracle-rafts resting upon the beach. These were an innovation of the pékyu. By lashing together multiple circular bone-and-hide coracles, the traditional watercraft of the coastal tribes, and adding a stiffening bone lattice with numerous flotation bladders, the Lyucu managed to construct novel seagoing vessels without dependence on Dara shipbuilding techniques. They didn't have the load capacity of the city-ships, necessary for a full invasion force, but could carry an exploratory expedition into the open ocean.

Finally, the heavy security around the cove and the sentries that had barred her way earlier made sense. For years, Pékyu Tenryo had been obsessed with finding a way to Dara, the land of origin of the city-ships, so that he could launch an invasion against it. However, the remote location of the islands and the awe-inspiring Wall of Storms described by Dara captives presented seemingly insurmountable obstacles. Multiple expeditions had been launched to find a way to Dara, but most of the ships were never heard from again, and the crew of one of the few ships that had managed to return had been so frightened by their experience that they insisted Tenryo give up a mad dream of conquest. The pékyu had to have them executed lest they infect and corrupt the morale of the Lyucu.

As wreckage of failed expeditions occasionally washed up on the coast, carried there by the great belt current in the ocean, the pékyu had grown wary that support for these overseas adventures was waning. Perhaps the present expedition, in contrast to previous voyages, was shrouded in secrecy in order to minimize the possibility that ambitious thanes and recalcitrant elders who had lost children in previous expeditions would make a scene.

Goztan looked around some more but didn't see the young garinafin.

"Where's Korva?"

"Still sleeping. She'll be safe enough, this close to the pens for the garinafins in training. I didn't like leaving her alone, but it's more important that I make sure a spy like you doesn't harm my father's brave naros."

"If you'd just go find one of the older warriors who fought with me—"

"Ha, nice try. But you can't fool me that easily. No one here is old enough to have fought the Dara barbarians to seize the city-ships. You were counting on that, weren't you? That's why you stole the identity of a hero from an obscure tribe who rarely visits Taten, knowing that no one here would be able to definitively say that you aren't the person you claim to be."

*Of course,* Goztan thought, *only the young are foolish enough to volunteer for an expedition to find a scattering of remote islands in the boundless sea. It's as mad as blindly leaping off the back of a garinafin swooping over the scrublands and hoping to land in a water bubble in the grass sea.*

"You could go back to the Great Tent—"

"Do you think I'm five? I'm certainly not going to bring one of my father's old retainers here so they can run into Korva on the way—"

"You could take them the long way around and approach the cove from the other side—"

"Right. *Of course* you'd want me to take the long way around so you'd have more time alone to escape and carry out some evil scheme. I may not know your plan yet, but I'm going to figure it out."

Goztan wanted to laugh and scream at the same time. Like all children who seized upon an idea, the girl's logic for defending her conviction was unassailable.

"So what are you going to do with me?"

Vadyu pointed to her eyes with two fingers and then jabbed them at Goztan, looking fierce.

"Until when?"

"Until the fleet sets sail in the morning and Korva has recovered. Then I'll . . . I'll get Korva and escort you back to Taten. Since I caught you, a dangerous spy, I won't get in trouble for stealing Korva. In fact, Father may even give Korva to me as a reward. It is *all* going to work out for the best."

*. . . Tonight, the pékyu has ordered me to recite for you an account of my voyage here so that your dreams may be filled with visions of the whale's way. I, not being born of this land, cannot speak to your gods as clearly as you do, but perhaps the gods will examine your dreams and descry a way across the pathless main and keep you safe.*

*So let me entertain you for a while with a few tales, some of them factual, and some merely possible—and I'm not telling you which is which—though all of them are true. . . .*

Only a few chuckles now, and those soon faded away. The audience quieted. The cadence of the storyteller cast a hypnotic spell over the crowd as they wondered if perhaps one of the tales would indeed illuminate the dark sea like a brilliant shooting star, guiding them over the unknown expanse.

Goztan had to admire the girl for her audacity. Hers was a preposterous plan, but it actually had a chance of working—if Goztan were really a spy.

As it was, of course, when Vadyu marched Goztan into Taten in the morning, the pékyu was going to be so furious that the pékyu-taasa might not even be able to sit on her bottom without wincing for some time, much less ride a garinafin. She *would* enjoy seeing the surprise on Vadyu's face . . .

. . . except that if Vadyu kept Goztan here all night, Goztan would miss her audience with Pékyu Tenryo, scheduled at the crack of dawn. It would do no good for Tenryo to know the truth behind her tardiness. If the pékyu would look unkindly upon thanes who were too weak to solve their own problems at home and had to come beg him for help, he certainly would despise even more a thane who couldn't even escape from a ten-year-old girl, and he would be positively furious with a thane whose lack of resourcefulness brought ridicule upon his favorite daughter and, by association, himself.

Goztan might as well say good-bye forever to those grazing rights by Aluro's Basin.

*. . . The whale's way is turbulent and wild, and the wonders to be found in it as innumerable as the stars in the welkin.*

*One time, as we passed through a warm patch of water, the sails flapped and then drooped as the wind died. We had no choice but to drift along in the great oceanic current that had carried us away from Dara like dandelion seeds upon the wind.*

*A pod of dolphins swam next to the fleet along the starboard side. We could hear the finned air-breathers chatting in their whistling, joyful language, which offered some re-life from the boredom.*

*A sharp-eyed lookout shouted, "A shark! A shark!"*

*We rushed to the gunwale and found the words to be true. There, amidst the leaping and dancing dolphins, one fish stood out like a rat among mice. Instead of the sleek bottle-form snout, there was a wide toothy grin; instead of the pair of horizontal flukes that flexed like a man's legs, there was a vertical, asymmetrical tail that waved like a caudal fin; instead of a blowhole on top of the head that sprayed mist in the air, there were gill slits next to the cheeks open to the brine. . . .*

The headache and vertigo had subsided enough for Goztan to turn and focus her eyes on Vadyu without feeling like she was going to throw up. She had to convince the girl to let her go. "What if you're wrong and I really am who I say I am? How can you be so sure I'm a spy?"

Vadyu looked at her smugly. "Tell me again your lineage."

"I am called Goztan Ryoto, daughter of Dayu Ryoto, son of Péfir Vagapé. I serve the pékyu as the Thane of—"

"Liar!" Vadyu shouted. "You *almost* had me. Almost. But you're just like that wolf pup in the old tale. You can't hide your true nature."

Goztan was utterly confused. "You must be mis—"

"When we were with Korva, you said your mother was thane before you."

"She was."

"And yet you just named your father in your birthright lineage, not your mother," Vadyu said triumphantly. "So either you are an imposter who didn't prepare your lies well enough or you are a *usurper*, and my father would never have tolerated a usurper as one of his trusted thanes."

*. . . We expected to see bloodshed; we expected to see the dolphins turn on this killer fish, this ancient enemy of the cetacean race.*

*But there was no fight, no ramming of the intruder. The lumbering gray shark, twice as large as the largest dolphin, was acting just like a member of the pod. Though it could not leap as gracefully as the dolphins, it dove below the surface, accelerated with powerful strokes of the wrongly oriented tail, and heaved itself out of the water in imitation of its unfamilial family. And as it crashed back into the ocean, the dolphins let out a cheer of whistles and squeaks, celebrating the accomplishment as though the shark were an indulged child. . . .*

Goztan couldn't help but chuckle. Given how Pékyu Tenryo himself had come to power, the idea that he would have no tolerance for usurpers was absurd, but she wasn't sure that the pékyu-taasa had experienced enough of the world to understand the reasons behind her "lie."

"Stop laughing! What's so funny?"

"Eh, you really are mistaken, but where do I begin—"

The sentence stuck in her throat, unfinished, because she had finally caught a glimpse of the gesticulating figure of the storyteller by the bonfire, and she realized why his voice seemed so familiar.

# CHAPTER THREE

# THE MESSAGE
# ON THE TURTLE SHELL

UKYU-GONDÉ: THE YEAR THE CITY-SHIPS ARRIVED
FROM DARA (KNOWN IN DARA AS THE FIRST YEAR
IN THE REIGN OF RIGHTEOUS FORCE, WHEN
EMPEROR ERISHI ASCENDED TO THE THRONE
AFTER THE DEATH OF EMPEROR MAPIDÉRÉ).

Goztan's mother, Tenlek Ryoto, chieftain of the Third Tribe of the Antler, had been one of the first thanes of Pékyu Toluroru Roatan to pledge allegiance to Tenryo after the disfavored son murdered his father to usurp the position of pékyu. And as a little girl, Goztan watched with admiration as Tenryo bound the loose Lyucu tribes of the scrublands into a divine hammer with himself as its head and pounded the hated Agon, the ancient enemy and oppressor of the Lyucu, into submission. When she was old enough, she joined his army as a garinafin pilot. There, she studied Tenryo's cold tactics, emulated his hot passions, and slaughtered so many that she ran out of room on her helmet for the little cross marks that she used to record the Agon corpses she left behind.

The Third Tribe of the Antler prospered. Though she was too young to be a mother herself, Goztan watched with pleasure as the tribe's mothers grew fat and beautiful from the meat and milk yielded by the herds of long-haired cattle and flocks of knob-horned sheep she captured, their children cared for by the Agon slaves she abducted. Though her own parents were still young and vigorous, Goztan sighed with relief as feeble elders of the tribe no longer had to say farewell to their families and walk into winter storms—sure, that meant more aged Agon starved in their stead, but that was the way of life on the scrublands.

"You're better than any of your sisters and brothers," Tenlek said, her voice full of pride. "You're just like me."

And then, in the same year that she reached the age at which she could take a husband and have her own children, strangers from across the sea arrived in monstrous city-ships.

Despite the cautious welcome given to them by the Lyucu under the direction of Pékyu Tenryo, the strangers soon revealed their bestial natures and slaughtered scores of Lyucu with their fantastic metal weapons.

The barbarians from Dara were powerful. They killed from a distance with little spears launched from half-moon-shaped frames, far more accurate and deadly than Lyucu slingshots and slings; they dressed in wisps of clouds, which were much more colorful and comfortable against the skin than the hide and leather and fur worn by the Lyucu; their city-ships rode confidently over towering waves that would have capsized Lyucu coracles, propelled by enormous vertical wings that yoked the power of the wind like the wings of a garinafin; they seemed completely immune from the mysterious new plagues that swept through the Lyucu ranks.

Their pékyu, a man by the name of Admiral Krita, declared that he intended to enslave the people of the scrublands and bind them in chains from which they could never escape, even unto the seventh generation. Many cried out in confusion and terror to the All-Father and the Every-Mother, wondering why such darkness had been allowed to descend upon their mortal children.

Instead of riding forth with his warriors mounted on garinafins to fight these barbarians to the death, Pékyu Tenryo called for women, thanes and naros, to volunteer to be sexual companions for the men who styled themselves the Lords of Dara. Many of the thanes seethed at the pékyu's weakness, including Goztan's mother. But Goztan, having witnessed Tenryo getting the better of his enemies time after time, volunteered, trusting instinctively that the pékyu had in mind some grander scheme.

The pékyu held a banquet for the women warriors on the night before they were to be sent to the city-ships, asking them to keep their eyes and ears open for the ways of Dara, but to reveal as little of the Lyucu way of life as possible.

"There is a long winter ahead," the pékyu said. "The clever wolf wags her tail and drinks the offered milk, adopting the guise of the domesticated dog. But her true nature is held deep inside, like a sheathed bone dagger."

She endured the barbarians' vile caresses and lewd gazes and acted the part of the humiliated captive, gradually gaining the trust of Dathama, captain of one of the city-ships, to whom she had been gifted. She fed him his meals, bathed his body, slept in his bed. Word by word, phrase by phrase, she learned to speak his language; hour by hour, day by day, she studied how he fought and how he thought; square foot by square foot, deck by deck, she memorized the layout of the city-ship and the caches of weapons and food.

One early spring day, Captain Dathama, who usually spent all his time on his ship and had grown ever more flabby and lethargic on the rich food and idleness made possible by the Lyucu servants, decided that he wanted to take in some fresh air. He demanded that a team of Lyucu men be sent to bear himself and his native mistress—whom he had renamed "Obedience" for he could not be bothered to learn her "barbarian" name—on a large litter fashioned from whale ribs and woven seagrass, its cushions covered in smooth Dara silk and stuffed with soft yearling cattle hair.

As if to make up for his unimpressive physique—weedy, uncoor-dinated, with a high-pitched voice and a face that reminded one of a scavenging prairie vole—Dathama stuffed the litter with supplies catering to his creature comforts: two jugs of wine, eight baskets of food to snack on, sea-chilled stones to soothe his hemorrhoids, a bucket of flower-scented water that Goztan was supposed to sprin-kle over him to keep him cool. . . . As the Lyucu warriors huffed and labored to carry the litter at a jog up and down the desolate sand dunes of the beach, indolent Dara soldiers followed along with a few servants and maids, all entertaining themselves with anecdotes that supposedly demonstrated the lack of intelligence among the men of the scrublands and speculating aloud whether some ancestral sin had doomed the Lyucu to a squalid existence. Luckily, as the Lyucu men could not understand the speech of Dara, the insults deflected off them like water off a tidal tern's back.

But Goztan seethed. She had thought she was inured to such insults, yet seeing her people treated like beasts of burden by the Lords of Dara made her scabbed-over heart bleed anew. She struggled to smile coquettishly and to ply Dathama with more cups of aged wine the way the vile man had taught her.

And then, one of the litter-bearers stumbled, and a corner of the litter sank, almost tossing the ungainly captain out. Only by grabbing for Goztan did he avoid an embarrassing fall, but the wine in one of the jugs spilled all over his fine silk robe.

Enraged, Dathama halted the procession and ordered all the litter-bearers whipped. As bloody streaks crisscrossed the backs of the kneeling Lyucu men, Goztan could see the fire of rage and humiliation build in their eyes. The Dara soldiers stood vigilantly to the side, their swords unsheathed, waiting for any sign of resistance to give them the excuse for slaughter. Desperately, she pleaded with the captain to show mercy upon the litter-bearers, and the captain slapped her hard across the face. It was all she could do not to leap up and strangle him right then and there.

*The clever wolf,* she spoke to herself through the blinding fury. *I must be the clever wolf.*

"A sign! A sign!" a voice cried out a few paces away from the foot of the litter.

Everyone turned.

The speaker was a wiry, long-limbed man of Dara dressed in a mix of woven hemp rags and rough-cut pelt like many of the barbarian servants. The long sea voyage had left their clothes in tatters, and they did not yet know how to make proper garments the native way (or perhaps didn't want to learn). Goztan couldn't recall ever seeing him, which meant that he was probably a sailor or deckhand rather than a personal servant attending to Dathama. The Dara man's tanned face was dominated by large, intelligent eyes, and his hands and exposed arms were covered by scars. Goztan thought his scraggly beard made him resemble a placid but watchful ram. He was kneeling in the sand and cradling a turtle shell as though it were the greatest treasure in the world.

"Oga Kidosu," Dathama said, "what are you babbling about?"

The soldiers observed this unexpected development with interest, temporarily halting the whipping of the Lyucu litter-bearers.

Oga lifted the turtle shell, which was the size of a small coconut, above his head with both hands. "A most auspicious portent, Captain!"

The captain awkwardly climbed off the litter, took a few clumsy steps forward, and plucked the shell out of Oga's hands. It was from a young turtle, and so weathered that the bones inside the shell had long since disintegrated. In addition to the regular seams between the plates, a strange series of markings covered both the carapace and the plastron.

On the carapace were a set of irregularly shaped blobs outlined in white that the captain immediately recognized as a map of the Islands of Dara. On the plastron, on the other hand, appeared five human figures. An older man, a woman, two younger men holding long weapons, and a swaddled baby in the older man's arms. From the woman's raised hand trailed a rope, the other end of which was attached to a suspended horizontal stick, but not at the stick's center. A fish dangled from the short end of the stick while a small bell-shaped weight hung from the long end—it was a scale for weighing things, used by everyone in Dara from petty fishmongers to jewelry appraisers. All the figures had Dara hairstyles and clothing.

The drawings were etched into the surface of the shell, but didn't show the sharp turns and angular streaks characteristic of knife carving. Indeed, as the captain's fingers ran over the marks, they were so smooth that they seemed natural, part of the shell itself.

"Where did you find this?" asked Dathama.

"When that foolish litter-bearer stumbled, I saw him kick something from the sand. I retrieved it, thinking it a rock or a conch shell. But when I saw what was on it, I realized that it's a sign from Lutho, a message borne by his *pawi*."

Dathama's glance flitted between the shell in his hand and the kneeling figure of Oga Kidosu. The man's story was ridiculous,

and he was certain that the markings had not come about naturally. Clearly, Oga, an unlettered fisherman-peasant, was presenting
some kind of forged "supernatural" artifact in the hopes of being
rewarded. He was just about to order the man whipped for lying
when his eyes took in the Dara soldiers nearby, who were staring at
the shell in his hand with a mixture of curiosity and awe.

"The admiral said there might be omens," a soldier whispered to
his companion.

"I heard Captain Talo was purifying himself so he could meditate
and seek divine guidance," whispered another.

*Omens.*

Dathama swallowed the order and reviewed the political situation.

Admiral Krita's harsh treatment of the natives had drawn plenty
of objections from his own people, especially among the Moralist
scholars brought along for the purpose of persuading the immortals
to return to Dara for the glory of Emperor Mapidéré. Many scholars
denounced Krita's policies as inhumane and contrary to the teachings of the One True Sage. They peppered him with flowery Classical
Ano quotations at every turn, insisting that he had to treat the natives
with more compassion. To the admiral, these naive scholars were
fools whose heads had been stuffed with useless ideals like "mutual
respect" and "common humanity." They had no understanding that
harsh militaristic policies were absolutely necessary for the expedition to survive in a hostile land.

Krita was sick of the Moralists and would have buried them alive,
the way the emperor had silenced their outspoken colleagues back
in Dara. But the common soldiers and sailors, illiterate themselves,
revered these men of learning. Killing the scholars would have sent
an unmistakable signal that the military commanders had given up
on the expedition's primary objective: the search for immortals to
be brought back to Dara for Emperor Mapidéré. And the common
soldiers, once they realized that Krita and his top commanders had
no interest in returning home, would surely mutiny. Thus, the military leadership had no choice but to tolerate the scholars' wagging
tongues to sustain the legitimacy of their authority.

But the common soldiers and sailors were also a superstitious lot, and there was a long tradition in Dara of clever leaders invoking signs of the supernatural to enhance their own standing and to defang their political opponents among the elite. Leaders of peasant rebellions during the era of the Tiro states often rallied men to their cause by claiming authority from inscrutable oracles, and even Mapidéré himself justified the disarming of the populace by melting down weapons to construct gigantic statues of the gods. Krita had been dropping hints that he wished to be thought of as a divinely inspired representative, sent here by the gods of Dara to rule over the benighted natives.

The shell's markings could be readily interpreted to support Krita's claim. To have a map of Dara appear on a native turtle shell was to symbolically suggest that this unenlightened land needed to be remade in the image of Dara. Under that reading, the older male figure in the picture, the one holding the baby, was obviously a reference to Admiral Krita as the giver of life and source of protection, safety, stability. The woman holding the fish and scales was likely a reference to a native consort—though Krita seemed to prefer a large harem—as a synecdoche for all the Lyucu, charged with the duty of feeding her lord and extracting the full value of the bounty of this land. The whole image could thus be interpreted to mean that Krita was not just a lord of Dara, but fated to produce many strong descendants—those young men holding weapons—in this new homeland and become the progenitor of a new race.

Even Dathama was impressed by the planning and thought that had obviously gone into the picture.

The scholars' moral objections would be powerless against such a divine vision, and once they found their authority waning, they'd surely find a way to rationalize themselves into supporting the vision to secure their own positions. Forget about Emperor Mapidéré; Krita would be emperor himself!

And if Dathama presented the turtle shell with its prophecy to the admiral, the captain was sure to gain favor and would be elevated into the highest rank of the new emperor's court.

*I'm not the only one sensing an opportunity—that sneaky Talo, always*

*sniffing the political winds with his rat-like nose, must be crafting his own*
*"omen" right now. I'd better act quick.*

To be sure, there were risks to such a course of action. The other
captains, jealous of Dathama's success, might choose to question
the authenticity of the "omen," but they would then have to explain
how the marks came to be on the turtle shell. The natives obviously
could not be the source of the drawing since they knew nothing of
Dara—indeed, Captain Dathama doubted they had any notion of
art or geography at all. And there was no known method of carving or etching in Dara that could produce such smooth results on
bone or shell. Besides, what foolish man would dare to question the
authenticity of such an object if Admiral Krita was pleased by it?
Their efforts would be better spent in finding their own portents to
present in hopes of currying favor.

A lie became the truth when enough people had reasons to pretend it was true.

*Is this a risk worth taking?*

"If I recall correctly, you were rescued by the fleet after almost
losing your life in a terrible storm before we left Dara and passed
through the Wall of Storms," said Dathama, gazing at the kneeling Oga. He had to test this man, a likely forger and the biggest
unknown in his calculations. "It's clear that Lutho, god of those lost
at sea, favors you. As the discoverer of this marvel, I imagine you'll
be richly rewarded."

"I picked it up only because the gods smile upon *you*, Captain,"
said Oga Kidosu as he touched his forehead to the ground. Then he
looked up, careless of the sand grains stuck to his brow. "Without
your magnificent presence, the gods would not have made that barbarian stumble. Without that fortunate fall, who knows how long
this divine wonder would have remained hidden? I am but the witness of your grace and the hand by which *you* discovered the portent.
I am at most like a treasure-hunter's probing stick: helpful perhaps,
but hardly where the credit is due."

Dathama nodded, satisfied. The man might speak like a groveling fool who learned his ideas of elevated speech from traveling
folk opera troupes, but his answer indicated that he understood the

stakes. He was yielding to Captain Dathama all the credit for the discovery—though that was so obviously the right thing to do that it hardly merited remarking on—and more importantly, he had tied his fate to the captain's. By publicly reaffirming his belief in the divine origin of the carved shell, he was also making a promise never to reveal the truth—whatever *that* was—lest he be executed for sacrilege and attempting to deceive his superiors.

"Even a treasure-hunter's stick may be gilded and sheltered in a pouch of silk for the good luck it has brought its master," the captain said.

Oga said nothing but touched his forehead to the sand again.

The captain laughed and tossed the shell into the lap of Goztan, sitting on the litter. "Behold the reason why even the gods have decreed that it is right for the Lords of Dara to rule over you and your people."

Goztan examined the turtle shell. The marks presented no mystery at all to her—the Lyucu had long etched decorative figures onto shells and bones with the concentrated, fermented juice of the gash cactus, whose oozing sap produced a prickling, tingling sensation against the tongue and skin. Lyucu artisans would cover a shell in a thin layer of animal fat mixed with sand, and then scrape figures into the mixture with a cactus spine or a bone needle. The shell was then soaked in gash cactus juice for a few days to allow the caustic fluid to eat into the exposed bony surface where the protective layer of fat had been scraped away. When the shell was finally retrieved and the fat layer cleaned off, the figures carved by the artisan would be etched into the surface, smooth and shiny, as though they had grown in the shell naturally.

But she could not tell why the human figures on the plastron were dressed like the Lords of Dara or what the odd shapes on the carapace were. And she certainly could not understand why Dathama treated the artifact as a message from his gods. Surely he had seen etchings just like this one. They were all over the ceremonial skull cups and shamans' headdresses that the Lords of Dara had seized from the Lyucu as trophies and then distributed to the captains and officers to decorate their cabins. Indeed, Dathama himself had an etched garinafin skull that he used as a stool in his quarters, though he had never bothered to ask her what animal the skull was from.

She looked thoughtfully at the kneeling figure of Oga Kidosu.

With the turtle-shell interlude concluded, the Dara soldiers prepared to resume their whipping of the Lyucu litter-bearers. But Oga once again interrupted.

"Captain Dathama, you may show more piety if you forgive these clumsy slaves their error. After all, they stumbled only because they were in the presence of divinity. If you bring them back to the fleet as men who have carried out the will of the gods of Dara—albeit inadvertently—you may provide yet more evidence for the power of the portent."

Dathama held up a hand; the soldiers' whips hung in the air. The Lyucu men looked up, their eyes defiant. Goztan clutched the shell so tightly that her knuckles turned white. At that moment, she locked eyes with Oga Kidosu, and two minds seemed to touch briefly, exchanging an understanding that could not be put into words. They nodded at each other, barely perceptibly.

"Oh, pity the All-Father!" she shouted in Dara, her eyes bulging out of her skull as she stared at the turtle shell. "What strength must your gods have to breath-burn word-scars into the back of a turtle?"

"The word you're looking for is *writing*," said Dathama indulgently, "not *word-scars*." He liked to instruct her, constantly criticizing her accent and pointing out her mistakes. He enjoyed teaching her the civilized language of Dara, sculpting her into a proper lady. "There's no writing on this thing anyway, just pictures. But I don't expect you to understand the difference."

"Oh, such fl-flower! Such mighty breath to make the dead turtle's shell blossom!" she cried.

"The word you're looking for is *power*," said Dathama, "and breathing has nothing to do with it. Our gods are indeed mighty, beyond your understanding."

"Yes, such power—" She seemed to choke on the Dara word. Gasping, she fell back on the litter and convulsed, as though in the feverish grip of a tolyusa-inspired trance. The turtle shell fell from her trembling fingers.

"What's wrong?" asked Dathama, alarmed. He rather liked this barbarian girl. She was pretty, pliant, and quick to learn what pleased him. He did not want to have to train another. "Are you ill, my little Obedience?"

Goztan was now at the edge of the litter, curled up in the fetal position. She struggled to get as far away from the turtle shell as possible, as though it were a flame whose heat she could not withstand. *"Toa-tolyusa. Tento! Tento!"* she screamed, as though the language of Dara had deserted her.

She stopped abruptly. A gurgling noise emerged from her throat, and white foam spilled from between her lips. Her eyelids fluttered, revealing only the whites of her eyes.

The Dara soldiers looked on in consternation, the whips in their hands forgotten.

The still-kneeling Lyucu litter-bearers stiffened at Goztan's shouts. A few exchanged quick looks, then, almost at once, they started to shake and convulse uncontrollably, pointing at the turtle shell and yelling incomprehensibly. A few fell down and touched their foreheads to the sand in the direction of the litter.

"By Kiji's beard!" Dathama swore. "Help her! Get that turtle shell away from her!"

Two servants ran up and tried to calm Goztan down, wiping her face with a cool washcloth and whispering comforting words. Oga Kidosu ran up and removed the shell from the litter, and once again returned to kneeling before Captain Dathama, holding up the magical object.

"The Lyucu do not understand writing," said Oga. "Even an illiterate man of Dara like me feels a sense of awe at the magic of the written word, so imagine how much greater that awe must be in the hearts of these barbarians!"

"There's no writing on the turtle shell," objected Dathama.

"But they don't know that. To them, all the symbols of Dara are indistinguishable. Seeing a human design grown in a product of nature must be utterly shocking. Look at how they've all been seized by religious fervor. This was probably why the litter-bearing slave had stumbled. This is *proof* of the portent!"

Dathama had his doubts over Oga's interpretation of events. To be sure, he could readily see how his concubine and the Lyucu slaves, being ignorant primitives, would be so terrified of this portent that they descended into hysterics. But he did not quite believe that a glance at a shell in the sand would cause a dull-witted barbarian to stumble—and why had they started convulsing only after Obedience reacted like that? Was there, perhaps, some kind of deception?

But he brushed his doubts aside. After months of living with Obedience and being served by the other Lyucu, he had come to the conclusion that the natives were strong in limb but simple in mind, incapable of planning beyond their next meal. It was enough to know that the artifact could awe and shock the natives, adding even more to its value for Admiral Krita. And Oga's interpretation did make for a better story, which was all that mattered.

"Wash the blood from their bodies and dress their wounds," intoned Dathama as he surveyed the litter-bearers. The Lyucu men gradually stopped convulsing as the soldiers dropped their whips and approached with washcloths. After a moment, he added, "Send for fresh clothes. Get them changed when we're closer to the fleet. Oil their bodies and spray them with perfume so that their sweaty odor doesn't offend the admiral. We need to make a proper presentation of this omen."

"It would show more honor to bear the shell on the litter," suggested Oga, his head bowed. "Though your august personage would have to suffer the burden of a hike back on foot."

"Ah! . . . Good idea."

*This Oga Kidosu has an instinct for theater.* Dathama looked at the middle-aged former fisherman with pleasure. There was no better way to ensure that this "message from the gods" would be properly received than to elaborate upon every detail and present the admiral with a perfect tableau. If he was going to gamble, he had to go all in.

Later—after a panting and sweating Captain Dathama had finally made it back to the anchored fleet, his arm draped over Goztan's shoulder so that the Lyucu woman practically carried him like an invalid; after the excited captain had recounted his miraculous discovery and presented the turtle shell to the admiral; after Admiral Krita had declared Dathama was henceforth to be known as "First Comber of the Immortal Shore, the Most Pious and Loyal Lord of Dara"; after Dathama's men had carried the trunks filled with jewels and gold and bundles of silk—originally intended as gifts for the immortals but now repurposed as rewards for those who pleased the admiral—to the captain's quarters; after the other Lords of Dara, their eyes brimming with envy as well as reluctant admiration, had streamed past Dathama's seat on the banquet deck to toast him for his good fortune; after the celebration and revelry that lasted late into the night and then early into the morning; and after all the captains had retired to their own ships and Dathama, asleep in a drunken stupor, had been carried back to his cabin—Goztan crept quietly through the ship's winding and narrow passageways, climbed down steep ladders and up dimly lit stairs, and finally emerged onto the upper deck under the last starlight before dawn.

There, she found the hunched-over figure of Oga Kidosu gutting and cleaning fish.

"Why?" she asked in Dara. There was no need to say more.

"We have some old words in Dara—" he began, enunciating each syllable with care.

It was as though a peal of thunder had exploded over her head. He was speaking Lyucu.

She had never heard Dathama or any of his lieutenants, courtiers, maids, cooks, laundresses, servants, or soldiers speak a single word of her own language. Pékyu Tenryo had admonished the Lyucu who came to serve the Lords of Dara to learn but not to teach, and none of the men and women of Dara had ever seemed to want to learn her tongue. Why bother speaking like the barbarians if the barbarians were so eager to learn to talk like civilized people?

"Before the sea, all are—" He struggled, unable to come up with the right word. Then he switched to Dara. "Brothers." He looked at her expectantly.

"Votan-ru-taasa," she said, teaching him the Lyucu word, knowing that she was breaking Pékyu Tenryo's order yet not caring.

He nodded, his face breaking into a smile. "Ah, 'older-younger,' or maybe 'grander-smaller.' That makes sense." He switched back to Lyucu. "Before the sea, all are brothers."

She could see now how he had managed to learn her language. He had a pure curiosity that made you want to give him the answer, and he showed such joy in learning that you felt elated just watching him, as though the gods had warmed you on a winter's night by exhaling on you.

"We have a saying as well," she said, sticking with Lyucu. "A horrid wolf doesn't care if you're Lyucu or Agon. You taste the same."

She had to repeat herself a few times and mime the snapping jaws and wild flowing mane of the horrid wolf before he understood.

He laughed, a deep and resonant guffaw that made her think of the warm springs near Aluro's Basin. "The horrid wolf today was very loud. Very scary." He saw that she was confused, so he turned and lifted up the back of his pelt vest to show the whipping scars on his back. "Even a peasant of Dara tastes the same to the horrid wolf."

Oga managed to say the whole thing in Lyucu save for a single word, a word that she had heard before but didn't understand. *"Peasant?"*

He mimed digging in dirt. She couldn't comprehend what he was trying to show her. Perhaps in Dara there were people who made a living by digging things out of the earth. It was hard to imagine, but so many things about this people were hard to believe.

She found it unsettling to see those scars on Oga's body, as vivid and as raw as the ones on the bodies of the Lyucu litter-bearers. She had seen Dara servants being whipped for minor infractions before, but until now, she had not truly thought of them as being akin to her, men and women at the mercy of the Lords of Dara. Perhaps being a *peasant* was like being a Lyucu.

He pointed at her and then at himself, and then said, "Votan-ru-taasa?"

She shook her head. His face fell.

She laughed. Then she pointed at herself and mimed the curves of her body. "Votan-sa-taasa," she said. Only a few moments earlier, she would never have believed that she would ever say that to a man of Dara.

He grinned as the first rays of dawn lit up the eastern sky over the scrublands. "Sister-and-brother," he said, in Dara.

They continued to converse in a mix of two languages as the world emerged gradually from the darkness.

"Why does Dathama beat you and tell you what to do?" she asked.

"Ah, that is perhaps the hardest question of all," he said.

Oga explained to her the ranks in Dara. He sketched a pyramid in the air, like the shape of the top of the Great Tent. There was the mighty emperor at the apex, and just below him stood the grand nobles and generals and officials who served at his pleasure. Below them were the scholars who knew the magic of writing and the wisdom of the sages, the merchants who slept on silk and ate with silver eating sticks, the landowners who drew lines on sheets of paper and counted their coins. At the very bottom were the peasants who owned nothing except themselves—and sometimes not even that—and dug for food out of both land and water.

"Some are born Lords of Dara, and some are born peasants," Oga said, pointing to the top and bottom of the imaginary pyramid. "It just is."

She didn't understand everything—there were just too many words whose meaning eluded her—but she was struck by how much it sounded like life on the scrublands, at least the way it was after the final defeat of the Agon. At the top was the pékyu, and below him stood the garinafin-thanes and tiger-thanes and wolf-thanes who served at his pleasure. Most of the thanes were chieftains of small tribes, composed of a few clans, or chiefs of bigger, multi-homed roaming tribes, formed by aggregating the territories and peoples of several ancient tribes. Below them were the naros-votan, who owned large herds of cattle and sheep and slaves, and the naros, who owned smaller herds and fewer slaves. Warriors from these ranks fought in Pékyu Tenryo's army as commanders and garinafin riders. Below them were the culeks, who owned nothing and received their meat and milk by caring for the naros' herds and fighting as foot soldiers. At the very bottom were the Agon slaves, who didn't even own their own bodies and lived only as long as the Lyucu allowed them to.

Some were born thanes, and some were born as slaves. It was the nature of things.

Or was it? Didn't Pékyu Tenryo turn the old pyramid upside down, and make the Agon lords into slaves? Now these strangers from Dara were here, seeking to stand on top of her people. Who knew what the future held?

"Was it a portrait of your family that you etched into the turtle shell?" she asked.

"Yes," he said, his face filled with anguish and longing. "I was hoping . . . to have something to let them know that I've never stopped thinking about them for a single day."

He told her about his life as a fisherman-farmer on the shore of the island of Dasu. He told her about his wife and two grown sons, and the great storm that had accompanied the birth of his infant daughter. He told her about the even greater storm in the form of the temperamental magistrate whose whims had separated him from his family, cast him away from home through the Wall of Storms.

"The Lords of Dara really treat you no better than us!" exclaimed Goztan.

"The sea laps the shores of Dara as well as of Ukyu," agreed Oga.

"I once thought you were one herd, one flock."

"And I once thought you were one school, one pod."

"What were your sons like?"

The way his voice caught when he spoke of his children reminded her of her father, Dayu, who was born with one leg shorter than the other and was thus deemed unfit to be a warrior. But he had the gift of reading the signs of Diasa, the club-maiden and huntress, and was unerring in his interpretation of the movements of horrid wolves and wild aurochs from droppings and tracks. Hunters who followed his directions always had great success.

But whenever she went out on a hunt or raid with him, he spent more time fasting and praying to Diasa than helping her track down wandering mouflon and moss-antlered deer. He was no help to her at all.

"Why won't you help me?" she had asked once, exasperated.

"When you were in your mother's belly," he had told her, "I

promised Diasa that I would offer her my portion of the hunt for
the rest of my life if she would keep you healthy and safe. When
you were born, I must have counted all your fingers and toes and
measured your legs and arms twenty times over before I believed
that the goddess had accepted my pledge. That is why I never eat
the meat and marrow you bring me from your hunts, daughter,
and I must remind the goddess of her promise whenever you're in
danger."

She had not known what to say then. The nascent understanding
of a father's love and mortality by a daughter who was no longer a
child and not yet a woman could not be expressed in words. Turning
away from him so he would not see her moistening eyes, she had
raced after what she claimed was a fleet-footed mouflon.

He was probably praying for her now.

To distract herself from the tears that now also threatened to spill
from her eyes, she asked hurriedly, "Who taught you to etch with the
juice of the gash cactus?"

"Can't say I learned it from any single person. Like your language,
I've had to pick up bits and pieces of your ways from whoever was
willing to teach me. When I go onshore to bring supplies back to the
ship, I watch and listen, and sometimes I find an opportunity to ask
a question. It hasn't been easy to get to know any of you."

"That tends to happen when your people want to make us slaves
and kill whoever dares to say no," she said.

After an awkward pause, he said, "Some of us just want to go
home."

She thought of the scars on his body, and her voice softened.
"Maybe Dathama will treat you better now that you've brought him
a miracle."

Again, his deep, warm, infectious laugh. "Dathama gave me
nothing except a promise of jewels and my own cabin, but I best stay
out of his sight and never bring up the promise again. Men like him
do not like to be reminded of who has done them service."

"But how can your lords be so foolish? Have they never seen
Lyucu children play with etched sheep bones or maids and lads
fetch water in waterskins with etched-shell spouts?"

"The world looks very different through the eyes of a Lord of Dara than a peasant."

She shook her head, still not understanding. That word again, *peasant*.

He elaborated. "Dathama's eyes are so attuned to the flow of power that he is blind to everything else. Because he expected to see nothing of beauty or use from the Lyucu, he passed by Lyucu children with etched shell jewelry and Lyucu dwellings with etched bone posts without noticing them. When I employed a Lyucu skill to make a map on that shell turtle, he saw only what he needed and wanted to see. He could no more see the arts of the Lyucu than a dome-headed whale diving after a giant squid could see the cities built by the skittering shrimp on a nearby coral reef."

"Cities built by shrimp?" She was confused.

"Let me tell you a story."

# CHAPTER FOUR

# STORYTELLERS

UKYU-GONDÉ: THE YEAR THE CITY-SHIPS ARRIVED
FROM DARA (KNOWN IN DARA AS THE FIRST YEAR
IN THE REIGN OF RIGHTEOUS FORCE, WHEN
EMPEROR ERISHI ASCENDED TO THE THRONE
AFTER THE DEATH OF EMPEROR MAPIDÉRÉ).

Long ago, when the gods were young and humans even younger, Lutho and his brother Tazu, the two gods of the sea, debated the wisdom of the mortals.

"The mortals cannot ever be as wise as we are," said Tazu. "While we were gifted with Moäno's divine insight from the moment of our birth, the mortals are born knowing nothing. How can they ever hope to know what we know?"

"But the mortals have the gift of growth and change," said Lutho. "They are born ignorant, yet that also makes them ideal vessels for understanding the world. They are blank pages upon which their feeble senses etch the truth, bit by bit, like a child pricking out her future upon oracle bones with the spine of a cactus. They may yet, through nurture, become as wise as the gods."

"Your faith in nurture is misplaced," said Tazu. "The mortals emerge through the veil of oblivion into this world with natures that cannot be altered. They are bits of foam carried upon waves, their understanding of the world constrained by their natal forms and stations in life."

To resolve their dispute, they each picked a soul and watched their incarnated progress through the mortal sphere. And then, just as the two souls were about to shed their earthly bodies and cross the

River-on-Which-Nothing-Floats to enter the afterlife, the gods asked them to tarry and answer a few questions.

"What is the ocean?" asked Lutho of the soul he had picked, who had lived a life as a dome-headed whale.

"The ocean is a vast, boundless realm of desolation in which massive, sleek lords career, each as lonely as a star in heaven," said the dome-headed whale. "When they meet, the only language spoken is that of battle. Every day, I dove into the inky abyss to pursue the many-tentacled, sharp-beaked squid, and let me tell you:

> "O scaled fish, O tooth-skinned shark, all kith and kin of the
>       finny tribe,
> O turtle, O nautilus, all armored denizens of the deep,
> Hear the bone-breaking beak tear into battle-scarred flesh,
> Watch the bright blade-barbed teeth cleave off arm and tentacle!
> One is a water-guzzling demon with lantern-bright eyes,
> The other a thick-helmeted warrior who quaffs air.
> Will the ever-tightening limbs crush the whale's skull like the
>       vise of Fithowéo?
> Or will the snapping jaws fling the head-full-of-feet into
>       Rapa's eternal sleep?

"I have seen all there is to be seen of the ocean, Lord Lutho and Lord Tazu. It is a briny dominion of warfare and stratagem, where all mortals contest for supremacy in a dance on the precipice of death and oblivion."

The two gods nodded. Then Tazu asked the same question of the soul he had picked, who had lived a life as a skittering shrimp in the coral reefs off the shore of the Big Island.

"The ocean is a warm, inviting cloud of living water that surrounds the rainbow-hued terraces of my city, the capital of the Crustacean Kingdom. We made our homes in reef caves, whose walls were studded with jewel-like shells, the bones and crusts of animals who had staked their homesteads there before us. During the day we strolled through gardens of anemones of every hue and variety, and during the night we slept on beds of the softest sponge. We dined on the spicy algae grown along the wide avenues of our colorful conurbation, and devoted our time to the contemplation of the finer things in life.

*"Once, my friend, a hermit crab, visited me, and as we neared nightfall, I said:*

*"'The crushed green kelp is brewing, the white cowry cups*
    *salted and crisp.*
*A hint of chill in the evening tide; tarry for another sip?'*

*"We drank kelp tea and admired the dancing jellyfish who glowed and pulsed in the liquid empyrean like the legendary fireworks spoken of by hallucinatory poets. We spent the whole night discussing contemporary philosophy and the elegant compositions of the classical Thalassa Poets. It was my favorite night."*

*"Do you recognize the ocean described by the skittering shrimp?"* Lutho asked the dome-headed whale.

The whale heaved his failing body to the surface, and as sunlight refracted through the spray from his blowhole, a rainbow-hued reef city appeared briefly. *"Not at all,"* he said with wonder and regret. *"I've soared over countless coral reefs in my life, but never have I imagined the beauty of the sights described by her. How I wish I had lingered to look closer."*

*"Do you recognize the ocean described by the dome-headed whale?"* Tazu asked the skittering shrimp.

The shrimp, too old to dance anymore with grace, swayed and tumbled in the ocean currents. *"No. I have never imagined that the world outside the reef is so vast and dreadsome, full of titans warring in the darkness like gods in primordial chaos. How I wish I had been bold enough to explore."*

*"I was wrong and you were also wrong, brother,"* said Lutho to Tazu. *"The mortals cannot ever become as wise as we are, but it isn't because of their lack of divine insight. The world is infinite, but the lives of the mortals are finite. Nurture and nature are both powerless before all-devouring Time. Look at how disappointed these souls are at learning how little they knew. It's impossible for the finite to ever discern the truth of the universe in its infinite multitudes."*

*"To the contrary, I was right and you were also right, brother,"* said Tazu to Lutho. *"Do you not see the wonder in the eyes of these dying bodies or hear the awe in their fading voices as they imagined the world through each other's stories?"*

*"What good is a story that comes at the end of a life?"*

*"Though each individual mortal experiences life for but a score of years, they can draw upon a store of stories left by all their forbearers. The race of humankind grows toward infinity, even as the nature of each individual is limited. Nature may describe tendencies and circumscribe potentialities, but it is within the power of each soul to nurture itself for another life, to imagine a course not taken, to strive for a different view. Through that yearning by the finite for the infinite, the portraits painted by all the mortal eyes may yet piece together a grander truth than our divine understanding."*

*"If I didn't know you better," said Lutho, "I would almost say you're turning kindhearted toward the mortals. Will you nurture them by my side?"*

*"I am the Lord of Chaos," said Tazu. "I am neither kind nor unkind. It is my lot to introduce chance into the lives of the mortals, and watch as their natures unfold."*

*And this was why, from then on, Lutho asked remoras to attach themselves close to the eyes of dome-headed whales, so that the little fish could clean parasites and dead skin off the giant eyelids, so that the small might share their stories with the grand as brother and sister, so that the magnificent finned lords of the ocean might see realities with more care and clarity.*

*And this was why, from then on, Tazu's storms periodically tossed the tiny inhabitants of coral reefs onto distant and strange shores filled with alien leviathans and antipodal krill, so that they could see what they never would have seen, so that they could hear stories they never would have heard and tell stories they never would have told, so that their natures could be nurtured by new experiences.*

"You must have so many stories about the gods and heroes of Dara," said Goztan, imagining that unimaginable life the man had led and trying to understand his strange deities.

"And some of them may even be true," said Oga, chuckling. "But it's not fair to hear a story without telling one in return. Would you share a story with me?"

"I'm no storyteller," she demurred.

"Everyone is a storyteller," he said. "That's how we make sense of this life we live. Misfortune and affliction test us with one blow after another, most of which we don't deserve. We have to tell ourselves a story about why to make all the random manipulations of fate and fortune bearable."

She had never thought of it that way. After a pause, she said, "All right. I will tell you a story, an old story passed down the genera-tions, from mother to daughter, father to son, grandparent to toddler, votan to taasa."

*Long ago, before there were Lyucu or Agon, before there were gods or land or sky or sea, the world was a milky soup, where light was not separated from darkness, nor life from un-life.*

*One day, a gigantic long-haired cow drank the universe. In the last of her stomachs, the universe began to curdle, much as we make cheese in the stomach-pouches of calves.*

*As the pieces of the universe separated from each other, a wolf was born. The wolf cried silently in that churning chaos, trapped and suffocating. He lashed out with his teeth and claws and ruptured the cow's stomach.*

*Pieces of the universe spilled out. The solids turned into land, the liquid turned into the sea, and the vapors, full of flavors and spices, turned into the sky. The wolf sucked in the first breath in the whole universe, and then howled until the sky vibrated in sympathy.*

*The wolf was Liluroto, the All-Father, and the cow was Diaarura, the Every-Mother. This is why every birth is accompanied by pain, and every breath of life sustained by an act of slaughter.*

*The All-Father and the Every-Mother roamed over the newborn world, devoid of life. They coupled and fought, fought and coupled—and this is why there is no distinction between the pleasures felt during sex and the pleasures felt during battle. They spilled blood into the soil, seed into the sea, and their howling and moaning and panting and growling stirred the skies. Plants and fish and beasts and birds sprang up from these shreds of the divine, and the world was now full of life.*

*The All-Father animated every living thing by pricking it with a strand of his hair, and this is why all of us, from humans to voles, share the same base nature. The Every-Mother then fed each living thing a drop of milk, and this is why all of us, from garinafins to slisli maggots, yearn for some-thing more than mere existence.*

*They also bore children, who were the first gods. The gods had no form* and every form, for they were both of this world and not of it, much as a reflected image seen in the calm water of Aluro's Basin is both true and not true. There was Cudyufin, the Well of Daylight, the first-born. The sun was her eye, and she was both the voice of judgment and the offerer of praise. There was Nalyufin, the Pillar of Ice, the hate-hearted. The moon was her mouth, and she was the reaper of the weak and the numbing comfort for those near death. There was Kyonaro-naro, the Many-Armed, the dissatisfied. He had a thousand limbs, each with a will of its own, like an octopus gone mad. He was constantly at war with himself, and when one limb ripped off another, ten more limbs sprang up in its place. Eventually, Kyonaro-naro ripped himself into a thousand-thousand-thousand pieces, and each piece climbed up and found a place in the heavens as a star. But some of the smaller pieces had lost so much of the All-Father's and Every-Mother's strength that they could not ascend the dome of heaven at all. They became humans, remnants of a broken god stripped of divinity, and full of strife and discontent.

And there were many other gods besides these, each an aspect of the thousand-eyed, thousand-thousand-hearted, thousand-thousand-thousand-limbed Will that animated the milk of the universe. They loved, fought, and bred, with one another and with the All-Father and Every-Mother. Each day the world was transformed anew because new gods were born.

While the All-Father and Every-Mother roamed over the world, satisfied with the results of their labor, the young gods tested out their strength by playing in the sea, through the air, and over land, much as young children of the people of the scrublands act out their dreams with grass-woven armor and charred-bone weapons. Some decided to hold a peeing contest, and that is how we have lakes and rivers. Some wrestled and tumbled, and the muddy tracks thrown up by their kicking and thrashing turned into mountains and ridges. Some, more patient in nature, colored the fruits and flowers with bits of paint taken from the brilliant clouds at sunset and sunrise. Some caught animals and took them apart, reassembling the pieces into new creatures: mounting a walrus's tusks inside a catamount's mouth produced the tusked tiger; slotting the lungs of a star-snout bear into the body of a fish yielded the whale; and putting together the neck of a serpent, the feet of an eagle, the head of a moss-antlered deer, the wings of a bat, and the torso and stomachs of a cow led to the garinafin.

Then the All-Father and the Every-Mother called all the gods together for a council.

"The humans are your votan-sa-taasa," said the All-Father.

"But the breath of divinity has left them," said the Every-Mother. "They sit upon the land like rocks that have fallen from the sky, their once-bright glow fading into obscurity. They complain to the All-Father and me constantly."

"You must do something to provide for them," said the All-Father.

And so the gods set about trying to create a homeland for their less-fortunate siblings. In that process, they reshaped the landscape of Ukyu and changed its fauna and flora, all to find a way for the humans to be more satisfied with their lot, and to praise the gods rather than complain.

So came the Ages of Mankind. The gods tried everything, sometimes turning Ukyu into a desert, sometimes flooding it with the deluge of a thousand-thousand storms. Sometimes they coddled the humans, and sometimes they punished them with trials and tribulations, hoping to craft their character to be closer to the gods'. Even the form of the humans themselves had to be changed to fit with the new world. But no matter what the gods did, the first four Ages all ended in failure. The humans would not stop complaining.

And so came the Fifth Age of Mankind, when the gods used all their power to turn one corner of Ukyu into a paradise. This was when humans finally began to look much as they do now, and they lived in a world that was neither too wet nor too dry, neither too cold nor too hot. Water sweeter than kyoffir flowed freely over the earth and animals willingly lay themselves at the feet of the people for slaughter. There were no seasons, no storms, no years of drought and starvation. The gods thought of everything, and they couldn't imagine any reason the humans would not be satisfied.

But it was not to be. Instead of treasuring the gift of the gods, the humans set to despoiling it. Instead of simply taking what the land gave willingly, they tried to tame the land to force it to yield more. Instead of praising the gods for their generosity, they fought amongst themselves, striving to claim to be gods themselves. Instead of working together as one people, they celebrated division and discord, and as they warred with one another, they forgot about the gods.

The All-Father and the Every-Mother had had enough. "If they cannot be satisfied by us, then let them find their own satisfaction."

*They sent monsters of every description into paradise and destroyed it. They cast the people out of their homeland, stripped them of all the signs of their vanity, and scattered them to every corner of Ukyu. The gods then decided to give free rein to their own impulses, to play and romp as they wished. The world was again plunged into chaos, almost like it had been in the first days after Liluroto had eaten his way out of Diaarura.*

*Once again, the All-Father and the Every-Mother called a council. The gods agreed to impose some order to their play. They set up the seasons and the tides, established cycles of growth and decline, gave the fleet-footed mouflon and the sharp-tusked tiger both their time and place.*

*And that was how Ukyu became the scrublands at the beginning of the Sixth Age.*

*The chastised humans gathered into small tribes, their life one of endless toil and terror. Hairless, weak, without the teeth of the wolf or the claws of the eagle, they survived on carrion and cactus fruit, huddling in the bushes whenever the sky cracked with thunder. Summer heat killed them with thirst, and the storms of winter felled them with starvation. They had no tools, no clothing, no knowledge of how to live in this new world. They were the All-Father and Every-Mother's least favorite children, failed gods who survived but could not thrive.*

*Two friends, Kikisavo and Afir, decided that they had to do something to relieve the suffering of the people. Kikisavo, who had six fingers on each hand, had the strength of ten bears and his voice was as loud as thunder. Afir, who had six toes on each foot, had the endurance of ten spiral-horned mouflon and her feet were quick as lightning. The two were such good friends that they thought of themselves as votan-sa-taasa. They called each other "my breath."*

*They vowed to find the All-Father and Every-Mother. "We shall wander the earth, neither of us taking mates nor having children until we come face-to-face with the World-Makers and demand that they return us to paradise."*

*Kikisavo and Afir turned west and dove into the sea. They asked every fish and crab, "Have you seen Liluroto and Diaarura?"*

*A great whale swam toward them, intent on swallowing them in its yawning maw. But the companions showed no fear and went straight for the whale's tail, tying it into a knot so that the whale could not slap them with his flukes. They wrestled in the airless, lightless deep. The whale was* not only strong but also clever, and whenever it seemed that the humans were going to win, the whale transformed into something else and fought again. He slipped from Kikisavo's grasp as a slippery eel; he evaded Afir's hands by hiding among the corals as a giant clam; he faded into the lit water near the surface as a transparent jellyfish. But Kikisavo and Afir would not yield, and always they managed to find the whale and begin the fight anew.

For ten days and ten nights they fought in the ocean, and the waves from their struggle wrecked the coast. On the tenth day, the creature transformed back into the shape of a whale and tried to drown Kikisavo by trapping his legs with his jaws and diving deep. But Kikisavo stuck his hands into the whale's blowhole to keep him from breathing, and Afir swam to the surface, where she gulped down big lungfuls of air that she carried down to Kikisavo and fed him mouth-to-mouth. Finally, the whale yielded.

"I am Péten, the sly trickster," said the whale. "But I must admit that you're cleverer."

"How can humans return to paradise?" asked Kikisavo and Afir.

"Though I know the answers to a thousand riddles and the truth behind a thousand-thousand lies, I don't know the answer to that," said Péten. "But I will teach you how to build traps and plot ambushes so that you can hunt for more food. Take my sinews, with which you can weave nets and make slingshots."

Kikisavo and Afir thanked him and went on their way.

They turned south and trekked into the endless desert of Lurodia Tanta, where the oases were far apart and sandstorms changed the landscape every hour. For ten days and ten nights they wandered in the wilderness until they came into a lush oasis guarded by a giant she-wolf, who would not allow them to come near and drink the water.

Although Kikisavo and Afir had no weapons and no armor, they were not afraid. He jumped onto the back of the wolf and would not let go, and she led the wolf on a wild chase around the oasis, through the water and over the dunes. Although the wolf leapt and bucked and snapped her jaws, she could neither dislodge the resolute Kikisavo nor catch the fleet-footed Afir. Finally, the wolf tired and begged for a respite.

"If you promise not to bite me, I will lead you to a safe place where you can lie down and rest," said Afir. The wolf agreed.

Afir led her into a copse near the oasis, and pointed to a flat part of the ground where the grass was tamped down to make an inviting bed. The wolf staggered toward it, but she kept an eye on Afir, thinking to leap unexpectedly and catch her by surprise.

But just as the wolf stepped over the bed and tensed her legs, the ground gave way, and she fell into a pit Afir had dug ahead of time. Kikisavo jumped into the pit and wrapped Péten's whale sinew around the wolf's muzzle. The wolf yielded and lay flat on the floor of the pit, her tail between her legs.

Kikisavo and Afir unmuzzled her.

"I am Diasa, the vigorous huntress," said the wolf. "But I must admit that you're stronger."

"How can humans return to paradise?" asked Kikisavo and Afir.

"Though I can rip apart a thousand mouflon and crunch the bones of a thousand-thousand aurochs, I don't know the answer to that," said Diasa. "But I will teach you how to fight with the weapons of defeated enemies, their teeth and claws, and defend yourself with the armor of vanquished foes, their skulls and head-tents. Here, take my foreleg and my teeth, and make them into a war club and pellets for a slingshot."

Kikisavo and Afir thanked her and went on their way.

They trekked toward the center, the heart of the scrublands. There, they met a long-haired bull who pawed the ground and snorted and would not let them pass. For ten days and ten nights Kikisavo and Afir wrestled the bull, throwing him to the ground by his horns only to have the bull get up again to charge them. Finally, Afir blinded the bull with well-placed shots of wolf's teeth, and Kikisavo slammed the war club made from the wolf's leg right into the bull's nose, stunning him. They staked him to the ground with the sinew-rope.

"I am Toryoana, the patient healer," said the bull. "But I must admit that you're more persistent."

"How can humans return to paradise?" asked Kikisavo and Afir.

"Though I can run a thousand miles from the shore of the Sea of Tears to the placid mirror of Aluro's Basin, and I can chew the toughest grass a thousand-thousand times until it turns into nourishing food, I don't know the answer to that," said Toryoana. "But I will teach you how to herd cattle and sheep so that you can drink their milk and eat their flesh. Here, take this pouch, made from my stomach. You can fill it with milk and ferment it into cheese and yogurt, which cure a thousand-thousand-thousand ailments."

*Kikisavo and Afir thanked him and went on their way.*

*They turned to the north and approached the frozen ice fields, where pure white star-snout bears hunted seadogs. There, a giant bear stopped them and demanded to eat one of the pair because she was hungry.*

*"You'll have to catch us first," said Kikisavo and Afir.*

*The two leapt from floe to floe across the frigid sea, and the white bear roared and followed. For ten days and ten nights they traversed that no-man's-land, where every breath froze instantly into blossoms of delicate icy tendrils and drifted away on the howling wind. Only by drinking kyof-fir did the companions manage to survive the deadly cold, and finally, they ensnared the bear with ropes of whale sinew and tipped her into a hole in the ice. Every time the bear tried to climb up onto the ice, Kikisavo smacked her head with the war club and Afir shot at her delicate nose with wolf's teeth, forcing the bear to lift her paws for protection and therefore slip back into the deadly water. The bear yielded.*

*"I am Nalyufin, the hate-hearted," said the bear. "But I must admit that you're more ruthless."*

*"How can humans return to paradise?" asked Kikisavo and Afir.*

*"Though I can swim for a hundred days in the icy sea, keeping my breath warm by the blood of a thousand seadogs, I don't know the answer to that," said Nalyufin. "But I will teach you how to make clothing and shelter out of the skins and hides of animals, and to fashion tent poles and stakes from their bones. Here, take my skin and skull, wear them to ward off both the cold wind and blows from your enemies."*

*Kikisavo and Afir thanked her and went on their way.*

*They turned to the east and hiked until the land became shrouded in mist, as though it had not fully emerged from the primordial milk. The companions became lost, and for ten days and ten nights they wandered through the thick fog, unable to tell which way was east or west, up or down.*

*Where had the mist come from?*

*As Kikisavo and Afir defeated god after god, they also grew stronger. Humans had now learned to hunt and fish and herd, to drink milk and make cheese, to seek comfort in kyoffir, to protect themselves from the elements with clothing and shelter, to fight with weapons and wield tools. They were almost as powerful as the gods, and if they also became gods, was there enough room in the sky to hold all the new stars?*

"Can you give them paradise again?" asked the All-Father and Every-Mother.

"It's too late now," lamented the younger gods. "We've already destroyed it in our wild rumpus."

The All-Father and the Every-Mother and their divine children decided to hide far in the east, away from humans, and to bar their way with a sea of impenetrable fog produced by garinafins.

For you see, back then garinafins did not breathe fire. They could only drink water and spray mist. The gods had made the fog wall by tying all the world's garinafins to stakes in the ground in a row, and then stomping on their tails to make them spit and spray.

Inside the fog there was no day or night, no rain or sunshine, only a perpetual grayness that muffled all sound and obscured all sight. No matter how hard Kikisavo swung his war club, he could not smash through the billowing mist, which flowed back and filled any gap as soon as it was created. No matter how quickly Afir worked her slingshot, she could not strike another creature, person, or god.

The heroes Kikisavo and Afir huddled under the bearskin and drank the last of their kyoffir, but they knew that if they couldn't find their way out of the fog, they were doomed. For a hundred days and a hundred nights they fought against that lightless, shadowless, changeless, mindless mist of despair, an absence of all strife and action that deadened all feeling.

But then, a ray of sunlight parted the mist and lit up the bearskin tent. A golden-feathered eagle descended on this beam of light and landed before the tent, where she turned into a beautiful maiden, with hair as bright as the sun and skin as fair as purest snow.

"I am Cudyufin, the Well of Daylight," said the maiden. "I have come to bring you a gift."

"But we haven't defeated you," said Kikisavo and Afir. The two companions were wise, for unlike tributes from defeated enemies, gifts could not be trusted, and those from gods even less so.

"Never mind that," said Cudyufin. "I bring you the gift of fire, which will allow you to eat that which had once been inedible, to destroy that which had once been indestructible, to be warm in the heart of winter, to see in the depth of the night. With fire, you can reshape the land, clear the scrubs, and bring the tender long-ear grass that will fatten your herds and invite more game. With fire, you can harden your weapons and crack stone and rock. It will allow humans to live almost as gods."

Despite their misgivings, Kikisavo and Afir were tempted. This wasn't paradise, but it sounded so much better than what they had.

"Come with me so that you can take the seed of fire back to your people," said Cudyufin, and the two companions followed her.

As the goddess walked through the mist, a path opened immediately before her but quickly filled in after her passing. The two humans had to follow very closely. And then, abruptly, the goddess dashed forward, and the mist closed up behind her, stranding the two companions.

"Wait!" cried out Kikisavo and Afir, but the goddess did not reappear.

The two humans ran forward, and suddenly, the ground gave way beneath their feet. As they fell, the mist cleared around them, and they plunged into a lake of burning fire.

The gods had planned this trick. Because they could not defeat the heroes with despair, they decided to lure them with false hope, which was even more deadly.

Kikisavo and Afir fought in the sea of fire, but fire was not an enemy that you could wrestle or shoot or muzzle or crush. The bearskin went up in smoke; the skull helmet cracked and fell away; the pouch of kyoffir burst; the war club and slingshot turned into torches; the sinew rope shriveled and charred. Fire scarred their naked bodies and singed their hair.

Worst of all, they could not breathe or speak. Smoke filled their lungs and mouths and nostrils, and like Liluroto inside Diaarura, without breath, without voice, there is no life.

Just as they were about to abandon all hope, a garinafin swung his long neck over the pit of fire and spoke to the heroes.

"Do you want me to free you?" asked the garinafin.

"What will you ask in return?"

"That you free me," said the garinafin. And the two humans saw that the garinafin was tethered to the shore of the fire lake with thick bundles of sinew.

"We swear by the lives of our unborn children that if you save us, we will free you and be friends forever."

And the garinafin opened his mouth and sprayed water like a thunder-storm. The fire around the companions hissed and went out.

Kikisavo and Afir climbed out of the charcoaled pit and worked at the sinew binding the garinafin. They had lost all the trophies they obtained from the defeated gods, so they tore at the thick bundles with their nails and bit the ropes with their teeth. Blood seeped from their fingers and gums as their teeth cracked and their nails were torn from their roots. But they would not relent. A promise was a promise, especially a promise for freedom.

Only when the heroes had lost their last tooth and nail did they finally break the last sinew rope. The garinafin asked them to climb up on his back, and then he dipped his head to swallow the embers smoldering in the pit. With the two humans secure on his back, the garinafin took off.

The gods, amazed that their plan had been foiled again, chased after the garinafin, trying to bring him down to the ground. But the garinafin was too strong and swift, and he managed to carry Kikisavo and Afir back home. The garinafin spat out some fire on the ground.

"The gift of Cudyufin!" the two companions exclaimed in astonishment.

"You should always take what is yours," said the garinafin, "even if it was offered with ill intentions."

And this was how the humans learned all the secrets that would allow them to thrive on the scrublands.

The gods would not give up, though, and they brought back the monsters that had driven the people out of paradise and sent them after the humans. There were sharks who walked on land, horrid wolves with twenty jaws, garinafins with seven heads, tusked tigers whose silent roar flattened thousands in a single moment. Once again, elders and children cried out in terror and men and women died in the onslaught.

Kikisavo and Afir were too injured to fight, but the garinafin spoke to them, "You have freed me and I you. We are friends unto eternity. We have defeated the gods before, and we will do so again."

And the garinafin took off again and met the tide of monsters without fear. He spat fire against the hordes and ripped apart any who slipped through with his talons, and for ten days and ten nights, no monster dared to emerge from the mist to set foot in the scrublands, so fierce was this defender.

But in the end, the garinafin was too exhausted to stay aloft, and with an earth-shattering moan, he fell from the skies.

*Where he fell, he turned into a giant mountain range. A thousand-thousand monsters were crushed by his weight, and the rest scattered into the mist on the other side. Even in death, the garinafin was ready to defend his friends.*

*And that was how the alliance between humans and garinafins was forged. They had freed each other from enslavement, and they would stand together, even against the gods.*

*The people honored Kikisavo and Afir in a great victory celebration.*

*"What is there for them to celebrate?" asked the jealous gods of one another. "Kikisavo and Afir haven't found the way back to paradise."*

*"No," said Diaarura, the Every-Mother. "They brought back to their people the most precious gift of all."*

*"What is this gift?" asked the gods. "Herding and trapping?"*

*Diaarura shook her head.*

*"Milk and kyoffir?"*

*Diaarura shook her head.*

*"Weapons and skull helmets?"*

*Diaarura shook her head.*

*"Clothing and shelter?"*

*Diaarura shook her head.*

*"Fire?"*

*"The friendship of garinafins?"*

*Diaarura shook her head. "No, the most precious gift of all is the indomitable spirit of the warrior. Though the breath of divinity has left the humans, they now understand that there is nothing to be feared so long as they are willing to fight."*

*And that is why even the gods gaze upon the spirit portraits of great warriors and cross their wrists to show respect.*

"Did the gods ever make their peace with humans?" asked Oga, when it seemed that Goztan would say no more.

"Yes," said Goztan. "Eventually Péten convinced the gods to stop fearing the people, and he had to use many tricks to do so. But that's a different story."

"What happened to Kikisavo and Afir after their victory?" asked Oga.

"Oh, I don't like the rest of the story as much. They fought with each other over who should get the bigger share of credit for stealing fire from the gods, and sundered their friendship in pride."

She did not add that there were many versions of this story, varying from tribe to tribe. She did not add that in some variations, Afir betrayed Kikisavo and killed him by drowning him in a water bubble in the grass sea. She did not add that in other variations, Kikisavo betrayed Afir and killed her by sneaking up on her from behind to bash in her skull. She did not add that the Roatan clan, the lineage of Pékyu Tenryo, traced their ancestry back to Kikisavo, or that the Aragoz clan, the lineage of Pékyu Nobo, traced their ancestry back to Afir. She did not add that wars had been fought to determine which version was the truth, and more wars might be fought still.

Much as she liked this man of Dara, she did not think he would understand a story of how two people, as close as votan-sa-taasa, could stand together against adversity yet could not share the fruits of their rebellion against the gods in peace. She did not think he would understand how a people who loved freedom in the deepest part of their souls could contemplate the enslavement of the Agon or shackle young garinafins to compel the obedience of vast armies composed of their elders. Indeed, sometimes she scarcely understood these changes herself. The stories of her people were complicated and contradictory, and she was protective of their delicate beauty, afraid that the stranger would find them wanting, would judge her people harshly.

With a start, she realized that she cared what he thought. Why? Wasn't he a man of Dara, an enemy?

"Ah," said Oga. "That is sad. Even in fighting for freedom, humans can't seem to . . . be better than human."

"That is true," she said, her voice full of relief. He had not attributed the faults of Kikisavo and Afir to some essence of the Lyucu, but to human nature. "You should hear this story told by a shaman through a voice painting dance. There are songs and dances and much lore that I can't even remember. This is barely an outline."

"I liked the way you told it just fine."

"I wish I could tell stories the way you do, with poems and

gestures and banging against the deck of the city-ship so it sounds
like the thrashing of a whale's tail," she said, thinking of the difficulty of articulating what one truly meant—to friends, loved ones,
but especially to foes.

"Oh, you're talking about performance," he said, waving his
hand through the air dismissively. "What I did was nothing. I think
you put on the much better act during that turtle-shell story for
Dathama."

She laughed nervously. "I was just following your lead."

"You added some nice touches. That trick with the 'word-scars'
was inspired."

She tensed. "What do you mean?"

"You speak Dara far better than you let on to Dathama."

She said nothing.

"All this time we've been talking, you haven't made any mistakes
like the ones you made on the beach, when we put on that show. I
think you made those errors on purpose."

"And what purpose is that?"

"You wore those mistakes like a disguise, a way to make him see
what he wants to see. I think you're telling an elaborate story, a very
long story. I just don't know the ending you have in mind yet."

She regretted talking to him for so long. He had such a disarming
demeanor that it was easy to become complacent, to forget that he
was her enemy. She was risking everything the pékyu and the other
Lyucu women had worked so hard to accomplish.

She had to change the subject.

"You give me too much credit," she said. "I was nervous, and
perhaps Dathama and you both simply saw and heard what you
wanted to see and hear. Neither the whale nor the shrimp can see
the sea urchin crawling across the barren seafloor the way she sees
herself."

He smiled and then looked wistful. "I was hoping that we could
speak as friends, as votan-sa-taasa rather than a man of Dara and a
woman of Ukyu."

For a moment, thinking of the scars he had shown her, she almost
felt guilty. She thought of the story he had told about the whale and

the shrimp—*is it truly impossible to imagine the life of another, to strive for a different view?*

But then, the details in his story came into focus, like the way the world emerged out of the dawn mist after a winter storm on the scrublands.

"You were not speaking as a brother," she said, "but as a seducer with a mask."

"What?" he asked, sounding genuinely shocked.

"That story you told me about your gods," she said. "It wasn't a story you learned in Dara, was it?"

She recalled the little details in his story that seemed to be inspired by her homeland: the etching spine of the cactus, dwellings made from bones and hides, the hint of an ethos of dauntless courage and warfare as a way of life.

Oga had probably thought they would make the story more appealing to her, make her think well of him. Without the arrogance of the other Dara barbarians. Respectful to her and her people. To gain her trust.

She was alarmed by how close he had come to succeeding.

It was like seeing a shaman's face before she had painted on the mask of Péa or Diasa. The very thought that he had been trying to manipulate her was revolting. But more than that, something about the way he had marshaled the details of what he knew about her people into his tale bothered her. She felt a rising fury that she could not explain, not even to herself.

"Parts of it I *did* learn in Dara," he said, speaking carefully, watching her face. "But I changed some parts and added new parts."

"Why?"

He seemed at a loss. "I guess it's a habit. I used to love going to the folk operas and listening to traveling storytellers as they stopped in the village. After we had children, my sons begged me for stories. So I took what I could recall from the operas and storytellers, tales told by my father when I was a boy, gossip from the neighbors, histories recounted by the village tutor, and whatever I saw out at sea or in the fields that day, and mixed everything into a big stew, and sprinkled some spices I made up."

"So you never try to tell a story about the gods just the way you learned it? Never try to pass on the truth?"

He looked even more confused. "Well, there are different kinds of stories . . . lots of stories told by the folk operas were just for fun, never claiming to be true. And I didn't like the way some of the stories were told, so I made them better. I certainly wouldn't tell the same story intended for the late-night crowd at a pub to my boys." He smiled ingratiatingly. "Stories have to change for the teller and the audience, right? My sons certainly liked my tales, but you should hear my wife. She's the real storyteller in the family."

Goztan could not keep the deep sense of revulsion from her face. So this man had been telling her *lies*. Stories about gods and heroes were not sacred to him, were not the repository of truth. While she had shared with him one of the most important, unchanging truths in the world, he had been fooling her with something he *made up*. He saw no shame in hearing a story about his gods and then repeating it with changes; he was arrogant enough to think he could make the truth *better*, or, worse yet, make something *new* better than the truth.

The men of Dara were more alien to her than garinafins.

"What's wrong?" Oga said. "Do you not change your stories? But stories are as alive as we are, and surely they change with each retelling. All my stories grow and learn, just as I grow and learn."

She closed her eyes, thinking about the story of her own life. She thought about her girlhood, when the Agon had enslaved all the Lyucu, and portions of every hunt had to be turned over to the hated overlords. She remembered her father teaching her how to etch a drawing of a young woman holding a club, the goddess Diasa, into the scapula of the first mouflon ram she had ever brought down herself— though she didn't get to eat any of the meat, which had to be turned over to the Agon thane's daughter to show her tribe's submission. Unfamiliar with the acid-etching process, she had burned her hand as she wrapped the bone inside layers of moss soaked in fermented gash cactus juice. She could still see the scars against her palm.

"Maybe you'll teach me more of your ways," Oga said, sounding conciliatory. "I've been very curious about how your tents are pitched."

She thought about the hard winters and dry summers, when the Five Tribes of the Antler had fought one another over the little grazing that could be had in their territories at the foot of the World's Edge Mountains. She remembered her grandmother walking into the storm one winter night so that there would be one less mouth to feed in the clan, and more of the meager stores could be saved for her and her cousins. She recalled the noise of the wind howling against the flap of hide that was the door to the tent, and how her mother had told her to stop crying so as not to dishonor the love and sacrifice of her grandmother.

"Not all of us think like Admiral Krita or Captain Dathama," Oga said. "Some of the captains and most of those who were peasants don't agree with what has been done to your people."

She thought about Pékyu Tenryo's daring rebellion against the Agon, and the all-too-brief years of joy that had followed its success. She thought about the catastrophes that accompanied the landing of the city-ships, and the horrors her people continued to endure from the people of Dara. She thought about the blindness of the arrogant Lords of Dara and the admonition from Pékyu Tenryo to bide her time. She thought about the pain and heartache of watching companions and kin die in battle, but she also thought about how the All-Father and Every-Mother had crafted the Lyucu to be dedicated to war: against the harsh landscape, against the vicissitudes of nature, against death-dealing monsters and trickster gods, against false hope and despair, against enemies who would enslave and murder and rape and *tell stories that sounded sacred but were in fact lies.*

"If we can't go home," Oga said, "we'd like to live together, in peace, and teach you everything you want to learn so that you could live a better life. Paradise may not exist, but we can try to build it, side by side."

Finally, she understood the full extent of her rage at Oga.

It wasn't just that he had made up a story that sounded like a myth. That was between him and his gods. The ease with which he admitted his lying simply showed how little the story mattered to him.

Into this made-up story he had incorporated bits of what he knew about the Lyucu—the craft of shell- and bone-etching, the art of using the skin and bone of the dead for shelter, the joy of affirming one's existence in battle.

These were strands of her way of life, as inseparable from her as her arteries and sinews. Together, they told the most sacred story of them all, the story of who the Lyucu were.

Yet Oga had stolen these things, just like how he had stealthily spied on her people to learn her language, just like how he had sneakily copied the art of cactus-etching, and placed them into his story like bits of decoration, like baubles to entertain children, like the treasures of her people seized by the Lords of Dara to add a dash of "primitive" color to their cabins.

He had stolen them, but he had not understood them, not really. He had not even a babbling baby's grasp of the honor of being descended from Kikisavo, of the grace of her people, of the sanctity of the scrublands way of life. Instead, he had reduced them to twisted, meaningless caricatures in his story—*sprinkled some spices*, as he put it—and he had been arrogant enough to think that she would be pleased.

She gazed at him, her face flushed but her breathing deliberately measured. He had intervened on behalf of the Lyucu litter-bearers, it was true, but he had done so for his own gain. He had *used* the art of the Lyucu to etch a map of Dara, to tell a story that belonged to him and his, not her and hers. He had spoken of teaching her, of giving her and her people a *better* life, as though he belonged to a race of gods, not a group of refugees who had turned on their hosts and enslaved them. He might be a peasant of Dara, but in his eyes, he felt infinitely superior to her, the daughter of a thane, a great warrior.

He was, at heart, not really that different from Dathama.

And she had almost fallen for his slippery words and crafty plot. She had almost seen him as a friend, a brother. The Lords of Dara were horrid wolves, but Oga was a wolf too, even if he also cowered before Dathama.

She could never be votan-sa-taasa with this man. He was Dara, and she was Lyucu. He was the enemy, and there was a gulf between their natures that could not be bridged.

"Good-bye," she said, and turned away, leaving a stunned Oga Kidosu behind. "You are not my ru-votan."

"Wait!" he called out. "I'm sorry—I don't know what I said—"

She did not stop or turn around. She also had been tossed by a storm away from home, into the midst of a strange people, and she would nurture her nature until it unfolded into a deadly blossom.

# CHAPTER FIVE

# BIRTHRIGHT

UKYU-GONDÉ: THE YEAR THE CITY-SHIPS ARRIVED
FROM DARA (KNOWN IN DARA AS THE FIRST YEAR
IN THE REIGN OF RIGHTEOUS FORCE, WHEN
EMPEROR ERISHI ASCENDED TO THE THRONE
AFTER THE DEATH OF EMPEROR MAPIDÉRÉ).

For a few days, she worried that Oga would report his suspicions that she was plotting treachery to Captain Dathama. When no such report seemed forthcoming, she gradually relaxed. She blamed herself for almost jeopardizing the pékyu's grand plan, and she vowed never to let her guard down before a crafty Dara barbarian—peasant or lord—again.

In fact, she never saw Oga after that day. Perhaps Dathama had promoted him in gratitude for his discovery of the "portent" so that he no longer needed to clean fish or trot along next to Dathama's litter. Perhaps Admiral Krita's new favorite had decided that it was better to send Oga to another ship so that he would never have to be reminded of how he had come by his good fortune.

Sometimes she wondered if she had been wrong about him. She recalled his pure joy at learning her words; his sorrow as he thought of his family; his mischievous laughter when comparing Dathama to a horrid wolf; his look of concentration as the two of them worked together to save the litter-bearers from torture. Maybe he really wasn't like the others; maybe she had been too harsh with him, too quick to blame him for the sins of his people, too impatient to attribute to him an ill intent—yet, what did the intent of an individual matter when two peoples were locked in a bitter contest for their very survival?

But there was no time to dwell on such thoughts. Other portents turned up: sandcastles that were purportedly sculpted by the waves and the winds to resemble the grand palaces and awe-inspiring towers of Pan, the Immaculate City; a sheep's liver that, when seen from the right angle, resembled Admiral Krita's profile; a kitchen maid who was scalded by boiling water, leaving behind a large scar on her back shaped just like the sitting form of Admiral Krita, with smaller scars that resembled a crowd of kneeling Lyucu subjects.

Admiral Krita stroked his beard in pleasure and held banquet after banquet. No one pointed out to him the suspicious footprints found near the sandcastles or the rumors of two servants who claimed to have heard the scalded woman screaming in a locked cabin for half the night before the day of her supposed accident.

One of the captains, drunk at a celebration, boasted that he could nibble a piece of liver into a portrait of any of the Lords of Dara. "I've done . . . done . . . done it!" The other captains scattered from him as though he had vomited. Admiral Krita walked past the drunken man impassively, as though he had heard nothing.

The next day, evidence came to light that the liver-chewing captain had been plotting against the admiral with Lyucu servants. He was promptly disemboweled so that his liver could be retrieved and examined. It was said to be shaped like the logogram for "guilt."

Another portent.

Lies begot more lies, and it was no longer clear who was fooling whom.

Then came the day when Pékyu Tenryo finally gave the order.

Preparations for Admiral Krita's coronation as the Emperor of New Dara had exhausted everyone in the fleet. Even the guards charged with keeping an eye on the native servants had drunk too much and snored loudly. The Lyucu servants aboard the city-ships had little trouble securing the armories, the cockpits, the officers' quarters.

She took great pleasure in laying Dathama flat on the ground with one well-placed kick to the back of his knees, and, holding his neck against the floor with one foot, she easily dispatched his guards with his sword.

Overnight, the Lyucu became the masters of the city-ships. The tail-wagging pups had revealed their fierce wolf-nature.

Pékyu Tenryo, after reserving to himself the weapons and books and navigational instruments of the captives, heaped all the treasures of the Lords of Dara in an open field to be divided among the Lyucu thanes, with the women who had done the most to bring about the invaders' ruin getting first pick.

Instead of paying any attention to the bundles of silk and chests of malleable gold and colorful corals, which the other thanes fought over, Goztan took her time sorting through the plundered Lyucu artifacts so that every carved whalebone ancestor pole, every stomach-lining spirit portrait, every vellum voice painting, and even every single cactus-etched arucuro tocua toy could be returned to the family from whom it had been taken.

She picked up the "miraculous" etched turtle shell that had started it all and gazed at the portrait of the family on the carapace. She didn't know where to find the man who had once saved those young Lyucu litter-bearers from the lash but who had also sought to reduce bits of her way of life into decorative beads in his stories. He had wanted to call her sa-taasa, as if the gulf between them could be bridged simply by a man belonging to the fleet of enslavers extending a hand to a slave. He was foolish, but he was also not unkind. He was like the other men of Dara, but he was also different.

The shell felt heavy in her hand. She held on to it.

By then, she was also several months into her pregnancy—she could hardly have made Dathama wear a lambskin sheath, after all.

The growing life in her was a source of unending stress. She could not sort through her own tangled feelings. It was a constant reminder of the humiliation and rapes she had endured from Dathama, but it was also her first opportunity to be a mother, to bring another voice into the world.

The child quickened. She felt it move.

Other Lyucu warriors in her position would have long since taken the bitter brew that cleansed the unwanted fetus from her womb. It was not uncommon on the scrublands for the children of nonconsensual couplings to be slaughtered when the captive partner finally freed themselves, and shamans were skilled with abortifacients, sometimes needed to preserve the lives of mothers or to ready a tribe for war.

But Goztan hesitated. She could not even explain to herself exactly why. The very thought of Dathama made her skin crawl, but she could not bring herself to end the pregnancy. Could the sins of the father be attributed to the child, who was also of her flesh, sustained by her blood and breath?

*They are blank pages upon which their feeble senses etch the truth, bit by bit, like a child pricking out her future upon oracle bones with the spine of a cactus.*

But then she woke up one morning and suffered the worst back pain she could remember. There was bleeding between her legs, the stains on the sheepskin sleeping mat dark and thick. She no longer felt the movement inside her.

She recognized the symptoms of a miscarriage and went to the shamans of the Third Tribe of the Antler. They gave her a brew that purged the remnants of the dead fetus.

Had the gods chosen to intervene to do what she could not do herself? Did the gods work like that?

She remained bedridden for several days, both from the physical ordeal as well as the psychic strain. She felt empty, but not clean.

(Years later, she would wonder whether this experience was also partly responsible for her reluctance to become pregnant again. The scars left in minds were invisible, but they dictated the course of lives as much as physical disfigurements.)

At least she was finally ready to resume her old life.

Tenlek Ryoto, her mother and the chieftain of the tribe, who had not visited earlier during Goztan's recovery, showed up one afternoon as Goztan was taking a walk around the camp. Stone-faced, the thane explained that it was the consensus of the elders and shamans that Goztan could never be her heir.

"Why?" Goztan managed, her voice rasping in her throat.

The pregnancy had tainted her, her mother explained. How could the elders trust that she would be true to the interests of the tribe and the Lyucu after she had first allowed the seed of Dara to be planted in her womb and then refused to purge herself at the first opportunity? It was proof that her nature was weak.

The accusation struck Goztan hard—as though voicing aloud the doubt in her own heart. She *had* wanted to keep the child. She *had* almost befriended a barbarian. She *had* found beauty in some of the stories of Dara, even wisdom, hadn't she?

But even in her shocked state, her mind remained keen. Her mother's reasoning was absurd. *Allowed the seed of Dara to be planted . . .*

"You think I'm . . . weak? Because of my *womb*?"

"You've spent too much time among the invaders."

Goztan suspected the real, unspoken reason. She had willingly yielded up her share of the gold, silk, corals, and other baubles captured from the city-ships. She would have preferred to see these *foreign* things, these barbaric artifacts, consigned to garinafin fire or the briny deep. What good were they for life on the scrublands? She couldn't even understand why Pékyu Tenryo had insisted on protecting the navigation instruments and books. No Lyucu knew how to decipher the wax logograms on silk scrolls, so what was the point of saving them?

"They contain the secrets of the invaders' magic," the pékyu had said when she confronted him.

"But we don't *want* any of their magic," she had said.

"In war, we become more like our enemies," the pékyu had said, "whether we want to or not."

Though she had not wanted to believe him, his prediction had turned out to be true. The baubles from the city-ships had become the most desired treasures on the scrublands, and the tribes fought over them. Even though silk was inferior to fur and hide as protection from the elements, a two-pace length of silk was sometimes enough to be bartered for five heads of long-haired cattle. It was as though the people had gone mad, coveting these Dara objects solely because they were rare.

Goztan had heard the grumblings of the elders, blaming her for the Third Tribe of the Antler's lack of wealth. She had hoped that the elders would understand that she had fought for something far more valuable; she had fought for *who they were*.

"You're the one who's weak," she said to her mother, her heart convulsing in pain. "You can't even look me in the eye and tell me the truth, instead of making up that ridiculous excuse about my *womb*."

Her mother refused to meet her gaze. "The elders have spoken."

Tenlek explained that Goztan had two choices: exile herself to the scrublands and live alone, looking only to the gods for aid; or stay with the tribe but give up all claims to her birthright, including changing her name so that she was no longer counted as a member of Clan Ryoto. She would be known by the single name of Goztan, like one of the culeks or low-status naros, without cattle, without sheep, without even kin who acknowledged her.

Goztan stood rooted to the spot, unable to comprehend how, after all she had endured and borne, her mother and the elders could turn on her like this.

"Let me know of your choice by sundown," her mother said. She turned and strode away without a second glance at her.

A limping figure appeared out of nowhere and knelt in Tenlek's way. Goztan saw that it was her father, Dayu Ryoto.

"It wasn't her fault," he pleaded. "She's a true daughter of the Lyucu, and everything she did was for love of the tribe and our people. If you must punish anyone, punish me. I know it's my weak nature that you despise. Take away my name and exile me in her stead."

"*I* gave you the name Ryoto when you married into *my* family, thereby elevating your lineage," said her mother coldly, "so it's hardly *your* name. My father should never have agreed to have me marry a cripple who can't even climb onto the back of a yearling garinafin. What good is the ability to speak to the gods when your prayers couldn't even keep our daughter pure from barbarian seed?"

"I know you want the son of your younger husband to succeed you," Dayu said. "But there will never be another leader like Goztan for our people. You're making a terrible mistake."

"It's hardly your place to tell me who should succeed me in my lineage."

She tried to step around him, but he wrapped his arms around her knees and hung on. "I won't let you go until you agree to accept our daughter back and give her her birthright."

Enraged by this display of defiance, her mother struggled to free herself. She finally twisted out of his embrace and kicked him in the face. He fell, and the back of his skull made a sickening sound as it struck a rock on the ground. He lay very still.

Her mother knelt by his head, saying nothing. After a long while, she stood up and walked away, never looking back.

Goztan ran up to the body of her father and howled. In her mind, she seemed to hear a voice.

*. . . eyes so attuned to the flow of power that she is blind to everything else . . .*

Goztan left before sunset.

She built her own tribe.

Alone on the scrublands, she could have given up all hope and joined the tanto-lyu-naro, tribeless bands of wanderers who had renounced all warfare so that they could live on handouts and pray to their weak, useless god, an aspect of the god of healing called Toryoana of Still Hands. She could have pleaded to be adopted by another tribe, to become one of the culeks without lineage or pride, little better than an Agon slave.

But she refused to submit to those lesser fates. By dint of her prowess as a fighter, she gradually gathered around her other exiles from the Five Tribes of the Antler. Some were younger siblings driven away from home to enlarge the inheritance of elder siblings; some were naros and culeks who had broken tribal laws or offended powerful clans; still others were warriors who simply didn't fit into the places others wanted to assign to them. Under her leadership, they lived as robbers and thieves, raiders who preyed upon lone herdsmen and caravans.

When she felt strong enough, she approached the other thanes of the Five Tribes, seeking contracts of marriage and alliances to bolster her claim as successor to the thane of the Third Tribe. She learned to see the flow of power and to manipulate it, to promise this elder better grazing rights and that chieftain's son her support in his own succession bid, to trade one favor for another, to plot and cajole and lie and threaten.

By the time she challenged her mother, enough shamans had been paid off with tolyusa and garinafin stomach lining to give her the prophecies she needed, and enough herds of cattle and flocks of sheep and bars of gold and bundles of silk had changed hands for the tribes' elders to declare neutrality. When she finally landed in her mother's camp, she was at the head of a garinafin force composed of contributions from all her four fiancés. Her mother offered to go into exile, but Goztan refused her terms. There was only one thing Tenlek had that she wanted.

And so, after the shamans took Tenlek's spirit portrait, Goztan plunged a bone dagger into her mother's heart and received her last breath, as though they weren't related by blood. She even made sure that the whole ceremony was performed outside, so that her mother's shame of not dying in battle would be fully exposed to the sun, the Eye of Cudyufin.

She went to Taten to see Pékyu Tenryo and to seek his confirmation of her thanage.

"Declare your lineage," the pékyu said.

"I am called Goztan Ryoto, daughter of Dayu Ryoto, son of Péfir Vagapé. I wish to serve you as the Thane of the Five Tribes of the Antler."

To deny her mother's name in her lineage was the greatest revenge she could have.

The pékyu nodded and that was so.

# CHAPTER SIX

# IT'S MY NATURE

VICTORY COVE, UKYU-GONDÉ: THE FIFTH MONTH
IN THE TWELFTH YEAR AFTER STRANGERS FROM
AFAR ARRIVED IN THEIR CITY-SHIPS (KNOWN IN
DARA AS THE FIRST YEAR IN THE REIGN OF FOUR
PLACID SEAS).

Recovering from her recognition of the storyteller performing by the bonfire, Goztan told Vadyu an abbreviated version of the history of how she had come to be the Thane of the Five Tribes of the Antler.

She did not mention her encounter with Oga. She did not describe her rage and sorrow when she witnessed her father's death. She did not linger on the details of greed and power or emphasize the parallels between her tale and the experience of Pékyu Tenryo. She stuck to only the essential parts.

Vadyu stared at her, dumbfounded.

Goztan turned to regard the figure of Oga, the slave in the middle of his tale.

*. . . The three new sharks swam around the pod in large circles, grinning in grim determination. Beckoned by the steady whistles of their matriarch, the dolphins retreated to the center in a tight huddle, their heads pointing outward vigilantly. After that bloody initial skirmish, the two sides now settled into a tense standoff.*

*Any dolphin that strayed from the huddled pod was sure to meet a fate as grisly as the two hotheaded dolphins who had lost their lives to rows of daggerlike teeth, but if any of the three sharks made a foolhardy attempt*

*to break into the pod, it was sure to meet deadly resistance from the agile*
*dolphins as well. . . .*

She saw that his face had grown more lined and scarred in
the intervening dozen-odd years. His beard, now rather long and
unkempt, was peppered with gray streaks. A collar made from a
bull's ribs was locked around his neck, and a long leash of twisted
sinew dangled from the collar to a stake pounded into the ground
about twenty feet away, giving him freedom to move only within the
circle described by the leash.

The Lyucu audience was completely absorbed by the scene
painted by Oga's words as they sipped kyoffir and occasionally clapped at an exciting moment. No one paid attention to the
pékyu-taasa and her captive.

Vadyu recovered from her shock. "Your mother *blamed* you for
bearing the seed of Dara? But that only happened because you were
doing what the pékyu asked you to do to bring victory to the Lyucu!"

Goztan let out a long puff of breath. She seldom brought up this
part of her life with anyone, but somehow trying to explain it to a
young girl who believed that anyone who did what her father asked
must have been right made the task easier.

"She saw my pregnancy as a sign of my weak nature, of the part
of me that came from my father, whom she despised. Perhaps it was
also a way for her to show disapproval of the pékyu's method of
gaining victory over the Lords of Dara, which she found beneath her
ideals."

Hadn't someone once told her that stories had to change for the
teller and the audience? In the years since, she had come to reluctantly embrace that wisdom.

"You weren't being weak at all, and neither was my father. My
father says that only the truly strong dare to use their weakness as a
weapon."

"Argh—" Goztan moaned. "My head . . ." She was certainly not
above using her weakness as a weapon. "Now that you know my
story, will you let me go?" She looked pleadingly at the pékyu-taasa.

Vadyu bit her bottom lip as she weighed her choices.

*. . . What will the shark-who-thinks-it's-a-dolphin do? we wondered.*

*It swam in tight, agitated circles in the middle of the dolphin pod. Its eyes darted from one shark to another, utterly fascinated.*

*"Do you think it has ever seen another shark?" my friend Pama asked me. He was an old salt, and had seen more of the ocean than even I, who made a living from the fruits of the sea. It was said that he had hooked more than fifty species of sharks in his life, including the ice sharks who lived for hundreds of years and moved as slowly as drifting icebergs.*

*I shook my head, uncertain of the answer. . . .*

The thane could almost see the struggle inside the girl's head. Should she believe the thane? She was proud of the fact that she had deduced that Goztan was a spy, and believing Goztan now meant she had to give up that triumph. No one liked having their own cleverness taken away.

"No," the pékyu-taasa finally said. "You spun a good tale, but you've offered no proof. Let's wait until morning, after Korva's recovered, and I'll have her watch you while I go back to Taten to check out your story. If you're telling the truth, I'll come back and have you ride back with me on Korva—"

"Ride back with you on Korva?!"

"Exactly so. And we'll tell people that . . . that . . . Korva escaped and got lost, but I recaptured her so she wouldn't injure any roguish children who tried to ride her." The pékyu-taasa's eyes shone with excitement as she went on. "Of course, despite my undaunted courage, the beast proved too much for me, and just then you came to my aid—"

"Wait a—"

"This way, I won't get in trouble, and my father will be grateful to you for saving me. I'm sure the pékyu's gratitude can be useful to a thane, even a tiger-thane and hero of the campaign to humble the Dara barbarians."

Goztan sucked in her breath. The pékyu-taasa's mind was supple and quick. For a brief moment, she even considered going along with Vadyu's absurd plan, but then she remembered that she was the Thane of the Five Tribes of the Antler. How could she live with herself if she succeeded only by going along with the lies of her lord's minor daughter?

"That's not even close to what actually—"

"It's *pretty close* to what happened. On the other hand, if I find out you aren't telling the truth, I'll get Korva to bite you as a traitor, which was my first plan."

Goztan shook her head.

"Suit yourself, but I'm not letting you go tonight."

Goztan sighed. Vadyu, despite her young age, was as headstrong as her father. Explaining to her that Goztan needed to see the pékyu first thing in the morning would do no good. Even if Vadyu were to believe her, she was now committed to the thought of using Goztan as part of her own scheme to get out of trouble for stealing Korva.

Goztan had to get out of this mess herself.

The captive and the pékyu-taasa, each deep in her own thoughts, listened halfheartedly to the tale spun by the bonfire. Oga was now leaping about, tethered to the end of his leash, his dancing, elongated shadow sweeping over the faces of his rapt audience, his voice rising and falling like waves in a stormy ocean.

*. . . one of the circling sharks lunged for the dolphin that had wandered too far from the pod, and the water instantly erupted into a confusion of flapping fins and flashing teeth.*

> *The grinning demon snapped its jaws on the unwary gray arc.*
> *The azure surface turned carmine, first blood drawn by the*
>   *sly shark.*
> *Six bottle-nosed briny battlers, their spear-snouts steadied*
>   *with pride,*
> *Aimed at the killer: Wham! Slam! Bam! In the belly, the soft side.*
> *Thrashing, leaping, snapping, bashing. Fluke meets fin; spine*
>   *parries tail.*
> *Bloodier than wolves hounding a tiger, this fight-ring of sail.*

*With coordination and determination, a team of six dolphins managed to flip the much larger shark onto its back. And as was the wont with those dagger-jawed fish, the shark fell into a stupor, its sail-fin slacking. The*

pod of dolphins celebrated with a symphony of chirps and whistles and
squeaks.

The dolphin-shark, meanwhile, stared at the catatonic shark with
unblinking eyes. It was not celebrating with the rest of the pod, but neither
did it make a move to help its fellow fish.

Meanwhile, the dolphins tried to finish their assault on the shark, but
since their teeth were far less fearsome than the shark's, they could only nip
at the lolling torso and draw spurts of blood, unable to open up a fatal gash
in the shark's belly.

With little warning, the other two sharks abandoned their careful orbit
around the pod and headed straight for the dolphins in a frenzied dash, heedless of their own safety. With a series of clicks and high-pitched whistles, the
matriarch of the pod ordered her warriors to retreat for a final stand.

The only one who didn't obey was the dolphin-shark. Still gazing at the
upside-down shark that was bobbling gently with the waves, blood streaming from its wounds like the tendrils of some deformed sea jelly, the dolphin-
shark drifted farther and farther from the pod, no matter how loudly the
matriarch squeaked. Its tail thrashed wildly in the water, as though it was
having trouble keeping its body under control.

"It's the blood," Pama said. "It's all that blood in the water."

I understood. With the wounded shark and the dolphin carcasses in the
area, the turbulent seawater must have inundated the noses of the sharks
with the scent of blood. That was why those two sharks had abandoned their
careful plan and charged at the dolphins, mad and senseless. They couldn't
help it. It was their nature.

"I don't know if that shark who thinks it's a dolphin had ever felt the
blood-madness," said Pama.

"Is he going too?" Goztan asked abruptly.

"What?"

"The storyteller from Dara. You said that everyone around the
bonfire is leaving on the expedition to Dara in the morning. So . . . is
he going with them as a guide?"

"You mean Oga the Re-rememberer? Father *was* going to keep
him around, but he turned out to be too sly to be trusted."

Goztan thought she heard a mixture of anger and disappointment in the pékyu-taasa's voice. There was probably a more complicated relationship between Vadyu and this slave. "The re-rememberer?" she asked cautiously.

"He's a . . . strange one. At first, Father kept him around to interpret the wax logograms, but he turned out to be illiterate. But then he discovered that Oga knew many stories from Dara, including some that weren't even known to the Lords of Dara."

Goztan nodded. She was certainly familiar with Oga's narrative skills.

"And of all the slaves from Dara, he learned our language faster than anyone else. He has a gift for learning our stories and retelling them in the fashion of the Dara poets. Father realized that he was probably an example of an odd kind of shaman they have in Dara called *historians*—though Oga denied it—whose job is to observe the deeds of the great lords, shape them into stories, and recount them."

"Like the shamans who record the deeds of the pékyu with voice paintings or the elders who memorialize treaties with knotted ropes?" asked Goztan.

"It's not quite the same thing. Historians in Dara don't just recall facts, but must explain them," said Vadyu.

"With the aid of their gods, surely?" asked Goztan.

"Actually, no," said Vadyu. "Father thinks the historians of Dara prefer to explain everything without ever invoking the gods. I told you they were odd shamans."

Goztan nodded. The irreverence of the people of Dara toward their gods was something she had noted herself.

"Father described the historian's work as a kind of re-remembering, and he found it amusing. Father wanted Oga to teach all the pékyus-taasa the language and stories of Dara so that we could understand our enemies better."

There was no mistaking the wistfulness in Vadyu's tone. She respected the old storyteller. "That sounds like a nice position," Goztan said.

"Of course it was. He was saved from heavy labor and had double the rations given the other slaves. But the insolent fool kept on telling me and my siblings false stories filled with messages from their sages about how it was wrong to kill and how living a better life meant not conquering your enemies. Father grew tired of his attempts at weakening our resolve, and so he's been stripped of his post and sent here to go along on the expedition as a guide."

The bitterness in her voice surprised Goztan. "So you've heard many of his fables, then?" she asked, keeping her voice neutral.

"I have," said Vadyu begrudgingly. "They can be quite fun, even if they have unbecoming morals."

*So he's still not given up on the idea of "teaching" us, barbarians in his mind*, thought Goztan.

She had done everything the pékyu had demanded of her; she had fought in whichever direction he had thrown Langiaboto, his battle axe, without question; she had killed and maimed for him, first to overcome the Agon and then the invaders of Dara; she had believed his promises that everything would be better after just one more battle.

Yet, after so many years, all she had to show for it was a tentful of squabbling, petty men; ambitious rivals who plotted against one another, unified only in their desire to bring her and her naros and culeks under their dominion; and the pékyu's ever more elaborate dreams of the conquest of distant lands. The tribes of the scrublands had more meat and children, but why did she feel so little . . . satisfaction?

Oddly, she didn't find the idea of Oga's "teaching" nearly as revolting this time.

*Instead of heading straight for the pod of tightly clustered dolphins, the two charging sharks veered away from each other, describing two long arcs in the foamy sea.*

*"Are they trying to approach the pod from opposite sides? To ensure that the dolphins can't concentrate their defenses?" I asked.*

*Pama shook his head. "It's impossible to know what the sharks are thinking. When in the grip of the blood-madness, they act more out of instinct than thought."*

*Indeed, the sharks did not turn to attack as they passed on each side of the pod. The dolphins turned their heads to follow, as baffled as we were.*

The sharks turned again, now converging on a single spot.

I finally understood what they were after. These living jaws, these finned death-dealers, these demonic creatures were without sympathy or natural feeling. They were headed for the drifting body of their wounded companion.

One of the two sharks lunged at the comatose shark and ripped off a chunk of flesh the size of a man's torso from its side. The victim convulsed and thrashed its tail, but its movements were lethargic, uncontrolled.

"They need to be constantly moving to replenish their strength with fresh water flowing past their gills," said Pama. "If it doesn't get turned right side up soon, it's going to drown."

The idea of a shark drowning would have been funny at another time. But the bloody scene aroused my sympathy, even for such a monster. Did its soulless eyes look pleading and full of pain, or was I merely imagining it?

The eyes rolled inward and turned into featureless white orbs. I would never know my answer.

The dolphin-shark could no longer hold itself back. With powerful side-to-side strokes from its tail, it headed for the scene of carnage like a bolt loosed from a bow, like a missile launched from a catapult. More chirps and whistles of shock and concern came from the rest of the pod, but none of the dolphins moved to stop it, knowing that it was useless.

It was heeding the call of its nature. It was going to join in the cannibalistic feast.

The second of the two frenzied sharks reached the dazed shark from the other side. Opening its terrifying jaws as it neared, it plowed right into the convulsing body and snapped its teeth into the exposed belly. Blood spurted like wine from a tapped cask. The attacking shark shook its head violently and ripped away a long strip of flesh, as though undressing its victim. As the seam widened, the victim's body cavity yawned open like a bloody maw, disgorging the fish's innards to the merciless brine. Crimson froth churned around the dying shark.

I averted my eyes, unable to watch this carnage.

"O gods," whispered an incredulous Pama. "She's a mother."

My eyes snapped back. I saw a scene I wish I could unsee. Two shark pups, each about the size of a grown man, had spilled into the bloody water along with the fish's coiled intestines and massive liver. The baby sharks, still partially wrapped in their mother's womb, struggled in the tangled *offal, utterly bewildered by the shock of their untimely emergence into the world.*

*The two attacking sharks had by now swallowed their first mouthfuls, but their hunger and blood-madness had barely been sated. They turned and headed for the baby sharks, intent on ending these lives before they had a chance to even live.*

*But there was a new arrival on the scene.*

*The dolphin-shark's erect dorsal fin divided the bloody, churning water like a knife through pig's-blood curd. It headed straight for the baby sharks. Would it begin its life as a true shark with a cannibalistic meal of babies?*

*Wham! It slammed into the shark on the left. The force of the impact lifted the other shark into the air. And before the shocked shark had even fallen back into the water, the dolphin-shark had smashed its powerful tail into the face of the other shark, stunning it with the strength of its blow.*

*Before the two attackers could recover from this unexpected assault, the dolphin-shark disappeared from sight and dove. The bloodstained water undulated over the spot where it had disappeared, undisturbed by telltale bubbles from an air-breathing creature like a dolphin.*

*The two remaining sharks circled warily, the bloody mother shark carcass and still-writhing pups momentarily forgotten. They stayed underwater, and constantly adjusted their depth as they surveyed the inky deep below. It was the habit of sharks to dive below their victims, rising suddenly to attack the underbelly. The two sharks seemed to anticipate such a maneuver as the dolphin-shark's likely next move.*

*Seconds ticked by, but the dolphin-shark did not re-emerge. The two circling sharks slowed down and swam nearer to the surface. Perhaps the dolphin-shark, after that initial surprise attack, had thought better of taking on two sharks larger in size and far more experienced in shark-to-shark combat. Maybe it decided that it was time to assume its fated life as a solitary hunter, and it had departed this bloody battlefield to seek out its own hunting grounds.*

*A few scattered chirps and whistles from the observing dolphin pod to the side. They sounded lamenting and regretful.*

*The two sharks poked their noses and eyes out of the water. It was time to finish what they had started. The dolphin pod tensed and readied themselves.*

With a thunderous clap, the sea parted about forty feet away from the circling sharks. A dark-gray shadow emerged out of the water, like a garina-fin taking off at dawn, like a great cruben breaching at dusk, like the scarlet Phaédo bird calling forth the rising sun. The powerful, sleek body traced a graceful arc through the air, echoed by the rainbow that appeared in the misty rivulets cascading off its back. . . .

The two sharks watched this astounding sight, slack-jawed. They could never have anticipated such an aerial assault. Their enemy looked like a shark, but it was moving like a dolphin, except that no dolphin possessed such muscular power or such deadly weapons.

Like Diasa's divine club, crowned by rings of razor-sharp teeth, the missile landed against one shark and bit into another. The nearer shark sank below the waves from the force of the blow while the more distant shark disappeared in a bloody explosion as those massive jaws snapped into its torso. Unlike a similar scene on land, when a tusked tiger rips into a garinafin calf or a horrid wolf brings down a spiral-horned mouflon, there were no screams, no howls, no roars, only the incessant background murmuring of the sea. That none of the three participants in this horrible scene could vocalize their pain and terror and bloodlust only made the sight even more terrifying.

Grimly, the battle raged on. Here a crescent-shaped slice was ripped out of a fin; there a man-sized chunk was gouged out of a back. The crimson water churned like a frenzied tornado, and the three silent combatants enacted that most ancient epic of all, a tale older than all the gods of Dara and Ukyu and Gondé, the very bass line of the chorus of life, of living being but the manifestation of the ceaseless need to kill.

With an urgent series of trills, the matriarch of the pod made her will known. The dolphin naros left their protective formation and rode to the rescue of their gilled ru-taasa. In twos and threes, they slammed into the sides of the two thrashing stranger sharks and smacked their flukes into their unblinking eyes, creating opportunities for their scaled kin to deal the death blow.

Perhaps it was due to the loss of blood, or else the accumulating layers of pain, but gradually, the blood-madness seemed to cool in the two sharks, and they decided that retreat was the better part of valor. All at once, both stranger sharks retreated from the battle and fled from the scene, leaving bloody trails in their wake. One shark now sported a flabby, misshapen dorsal fin that hung limply, missing most of its flesh like a war-torn sail. Another swam with a jerky motion that tilted to the right, having lost one of its pectoral fins. They reminded me of defeated dogs running away with tails held between their legs.

Only the dolphin-shark was left, with a bloodied face and bite wounds all over its formerly porpoise-smooth body. Slowly, it swam through the water, gazing at its departed foes with those large, expressionless eyes, as though daring them to return. Blood gradually faded from the azure water, much as the sky clears after a storm. The dolphins huddled nearby, chirping anxiously, uncertain whether their ru-taasa was too far gone in the blood-madness to ever return to them.

The dolphin-shark turned sharply in the water, its gore-filled maw wide open. The dolphins whistled in alarm, and a few reared out of the water, baring their tiny teeth in warning.

However, the dolphin-shark ignored them. Instead, it turned to the floating carcass of the mother shark and the mess of floating entrails.

I sighed. The dolphin-shark was a savage cannibal, after all.

But the fish had one more surprise in store. Keeping its deadly jaws open, it drifted near the deceased mother shark, and wielding its dagger teeth like the birthing knife of a midwife, it gently severed the tangled intestinal cords and sliced away what was left of the membranous womb, loosening the wriggling pups into the warm sea.

The two pups, finally free to swim, headed straight for the body of their mother. Their little jaws snapped hungrily at the floating mess of warm flesh and cooling organs, still steaming in the sun.

"Are they really going to eat their mother?" I asked in disbelief.

"Unborn shark pups feed on the other eggs and pups in their mother's womb before they're born," said wise Pama. "It's only natural now that they should feed upon their mother. Indeed, when shark pups are born they must flee as quickly as possible from their dam, lest she turn on them and make of them a meal."

"How could the gods have created such unnatural creatures!" I exclaimed.

"There are many types of nature," said Pama. "The gods have decreed one set of feelings for mankind, and another for sharks. Don't deem your sentiments universal."

*The dolphin-shark approached the pups and gently bumped them with its nose to drive them away from their mother. Then it interposed itself between the pups and the shark carcass to keep them from moving back in.*

"What's it doing?" I asked.

"I have no idea," said Pama. "Perhaps it wants to hoard the carrion all for itself."

*The dolphin-shark stuck its nose even farther out of the water, opened its jaws wide, and seemed to swallow. I could see its pink insides clearly through the yawning maw—it was sucking air into its belly!*

*Then it snapped its jaws shut, and I heard the most incredible noises issue from its grinning mouth: a loud bark that changed in pitch and rhythm, like a grosser version of the trilling whistle of dolphins.*

*I looked at Pama, whose jaw hung open in an echo of our subject. "By the Twins!" he whispered. "This shark knows how to talk like a dolphin—is it Lord Tazu incarnate?"*

*Whatever the dolphin-shark said, the dolphins acted thunderstruck. After a while, the matriarch answered it in a series of confident whistles. A few dolphins instantly dove out of sight. Moments later, they resurfaced and approached the dolphin-shark, who was swimming in slow circles around the shark pups in an effort to keep them calm. The dolphins lifted their snouts and vomited, and a mess of fish, some chewed and half-digested, some still whole, floated before the pups.*

*The dolphin-shark nudged the pups with one of its pectoral fins, like a father urging his children to a meal. The pups, after a moment of hesitation, dove into the regurgitated meal with gusto.*

*The matriarch trilled a few more bars, and the dolphin-shark answered with its unique bark. A chorus of whistles and chirps then filled the air, and I dearly wished I knew what was being said in this marine council.*

*The wind picked up again, and our sails filled. We felt the power of a greater force pushing us along to the next stop in our grand adventure. All of us remained at the gunwale, watching the dolphin-shark, the feeding pups, and the tribe of dolphins until they disappeared below the horizon.*

"Do you think that was how the shark came to be a member of the tribe in the first place?" I asked Pama later. "Was it an orphan who had been rescued by the dolphins and brought up as one of them?"

*"We can speculate as we like upon the mysteries of the past," said Pama, "but they would only be just-so stories."*

With a start, Goztan realized that no one had interrupted Oga in quite some time. All the gathered naros and culeks held their breath, the cups of kyoffir in their hands forgotten. Even she and Vadyu were no longer conversing with each other, transported to the fantastic realm crafted by Oga out of words.

He went on, his words now flowing smoothly, the solecisms and errors of his opening forgotten like the shallows and rough rapids of a surging stream's early tributaries.

*"Who knew that a shark could defy its instincts and live according to the rules of its adopted tribe?" Undeterred by Pama's refusal to conjecture, I gave my imagination free rein. "The dolphins must have given it nourishment just like those pups, and that was why it thought of itself as a dolphin. As it witnessed the deadly power of the other sharks, shark-nature must have warred with dolphin-nurture within its heart."*

*"I don't think that was what happened at all," said Pama.*

*"Oh?"*

*"We speak of fixed natures and the uplifting influence of nurture, as if we understand all there is to know. But what is shark-nature or dolphin-nurture? What is godhead or human civilization? Tazu, the least caring of the gods, who rules over the heartless sea, once lived as a human girl and rescued a village from ruin; Kon Fiji, the gentlest of sages, who counseled against violence, once picked up a sword and fought off a gang of thieves. It is error to reason from the general to the specific."*

*"You sound like a Moralist sage in one of the folk operas!" I exclaimed. I didn't agree with Pama, but wondered if he had perhaps been privy to knowledge I lacked. "They say that you know the language of the dolphins. What did the dolphin-shark say to the matriarch?"*

*Pama looked at me. "What do you think it said?"*

*"I can't even begin to guess. I know not the code."*

*"But you saw what happened," said Pama. "There are more ways to speak than mere voice, and what is said may not be as important as what is done."*

"I want to know the meaning of those trilling barks!" Pama, it seemed to me, was deliberately obfuscating. "Old fishermen tell us that the cetaceans have their own civilization, though it is different from ours. I've fished the northern seas all my life, and I know when dolphins are warning each other of danger or when a bull is courting a cow, but I cannot interpret the subtler shades of meaning."

Pama chuckled. "You fish for a living, yet you don't seem to understand how to listen to the sea."

"What do you mean?"

"A lobsterman who winches up a string of traps and finds only scuttling crabs inside is going to be disappointed, but his daughter is delighted by the swimming legs, which she has never seen before. A fishwife gutting a beaknose boarfish is delighted to find it full of golden roe, but her toddler is disappointed to see that the 'fish pearls' are not beautiful jewels. They were presented with the same catch, so what's the difference?"

I pondered his question. "One of expectations."

"That's right," said Pama. "Before you cast your net, you've already filled it with hope and fear, and the measure of the catch depends on the weight and quality of your anticipation. Whether you're listening to a language you're born into or a language you barely comprehend, every utterance is first filled by expectations before it is parsed for meaning. You and I have different expectations, and so we will never understand the dolphin-shark's trilling barks the same way."

"Enough of this mysticism," I said. "Just translate what it said!"

Oga stopped.

He turned in place to survey his audience, grinned, and slowly walked over to the leather beverage pouches hanging on a rack to the side, trailing his leash on the ground. He lifted one of the bags, removed the antler-moss stopper, and tilted the spout to take a drink. The prominent bump in his throat moved up and down above his bone collar as he quaffed. It was a very long drink.

Vadyu fidgeted, as anxious as everyone else. Even Goztan, who was still tied up, found herself straining to lean forward so that she would not miss the next word.

Oga pushed the spigot of the drinking pouch away from his

mouth, took a deep, satisfied breath, and went back to drinking again.

Vadyu cursed. Goztan smiled.

The other Lyucu warriors could no longer hold back.

"Come on! You can drink when you're done with the story."

"What did the dolphin-shark really say?"

"Let Pama talk!"

Finally, having drunk his fill, Oga wiped his lips on the back of his hand and hung the drinking pouch on the rack. He walked back next to the bonfire, stopping once to untangle his leash, which had caught on a rock protruding from the ground. After surveying his audience once more, he said, "Pama sighed, and then said to me, 'The dolphin-shark's speech can be boiled down to a single sentence, "It's *my* nature."'"

Oga lifted his arms to the sides like the wings of a crane and bowed deeply toward the fire, a gesture that traditionally marked the end of a storyteller's tale.

A long while later, after the angry shouts and banging of bone clubs against the ground had finally subsided somewhat, Oga added, "That really is the end of the tale. I never saw the dolphin-shark again. It's the re-rememberer's curse to know that there are no endings to most stories.

"May our journey to my homeland be as open-ended."

A wolf-thane stood up. "Votan-ru-taasa, votan-sa-taasa, the stars have spun half of their course through the night, and the kyoffir is running dry. We should go to sleep now on the soil of our homeland one last time and absorb all her strength. It may be a long time before we get to kiss her again."

The other warriors assented, and soon everyone had wrapped themselves up in hide blankets and settled down for the night. A few naros came by to make sure that the pékyu-taasa had all she needed, and the girl nodded at them reassuringly and sent them away.

Oga looked around, a wistful expression on his face. Then he sat down where he was and prepared himself for a night in the open. There were no blankets or bedding provided for him, and no one came to release him from his restraints.

Goztan called out, "Peasant of Dara, do you remember an old acquaintance?"

Oga, startled, sat up and looked in her direction uncertainly.

Vadyu tensed. "What are you doing?"

"He was there during the war against Admiral Krita," said Goztan. "Even if you refuse to fetch one of your father's old retainers, surely you won't mind exchanging a few words with a man of Dara who remembers me?"

Vadyu hesitated. "He tells stories. Who knows which are true and which are not?"

Oga approached them, the leash attached to his collar growing taut.

"A great leader must be able to tell true stories apart from false ones," said Goztan. "Pékyu Nobo Aragoz of the Agon couldn't, and that is why your father deceived and then defeated him. Are you telling me you wish to emulate Nobo the Herder, instead of Tenryo the Wolf-Pup?"

This had the intended effect. "I emulate no one; I *am* the wolf-pup," Vadyu said. "Fine. Summon him, and let's see what he has to say."

*So she dreams of being the pékyu one day, despite not being the eldest,* Goztan mused. *This little night adventure may turn out to be more useful than I thought.*

"But we have to make this fair," Vadyu muttered. "I'll test the truth of his words my way. If you try to talk and guide him, I won't believe a word he says." Her eyes glinted with excitement. "Open up," she ordered, hiding her right hand behind her back.

Goztan shook her head. "Ipromiseiwontsayanything," she spat out in one quick breath, and then clamped her lips shut. *Who knows what the willful pékyu-taasa has in mind as an appropriate gag?*

Vadyu pinched Goztan's nose shut with her left hand. Goztan struggled to free herself, but her bound state made the effort futile. After a few seconds, she gave in and opened her mouth, and Vadyu shoved something hard about the size of a fist into her mouth, wrapped a length of sinew around her head a few times, and tied it off.

Oga's leash had forced him to stop about five paces away from the pair. He said nothing as he watched the brief, fierce exchange between Vadyu and Goztan. When Vadyu had finished gagging her captive, Oga bowed to her respectfully.

"Do you recognize this woman?" Vadyu asked. "Be careful how you answer."

Oga gazed at Goztan, and Goztan couldn't tell what thoughts vied for dominance behind those dark, expressionless eyes in the fading firelight.

Goztan didn't dare draw Vadyu's wrath with any attempt at giving Oga hints. This was her last chance to get out of this predicament and make it to the audience with the pékyu in the morning on time. She felt carefully around the gag with the tip of her tongue. It was smooth and hard with a depression in the center that tasted of ashes—likely a cow's talus bone used as a fire starter when combined with a drill. She relaxed. It wasn't anything dangerous or humiliating; the pékyu-taasa had simply grabbed what was at hand near the bonfire.

"Suppose," said Oga placidly, "that my answer is no. What will happen to her?"

Vadyu's eyes narrowed. "Are you telling me your answer will *change* depending on what will happen to her?"

"Pékyu-taasa, you told me to answer carefully. How can I take care without knowing how my answer will be used?"

While Oga conversed with Vadyu, Goztan took the time to examine the man more closely. She noted where the skin on Oga's neck was bleeding under the collar, the long welts and scars that covered the backs of his hands and his cheeks, the hint of tension in his posture even though all the Lyucu warriors of the expedition, his masters, were asleep.

The image of those litter-bearers seething under the weight of Dathama's overloaded pleasure vehicle came to her mind unbidden.

"All right," said Vadyu, a rather cruel grin curving the corners of her mouth. "I'll tell you what's going to happen to her based on your answer. If you tell me you don't know her, then you will have confirmed my suspicion that she is a spy, and I will bash her skull in with this club. But if you tell me you *do* know her, then you must also tell me her name and lineage and the deeds she performed during the war against your people. If your story deviates even one whit from what she told me, I will bash *your* skull in for lying to me."

"Mmmfff—" Goztan's eyes bulged as she strained against her bonds, though the gag blocked her voice most effectively. Cold sweat broke out on her back. The pékyu-taasa had struck her as ambitious, spoiled, devious, perhaps a bit reckless, but she'd never expected the girl to be so hotheaded and willful that she would risk erroneously murdering one of her father's thanes simply because she didn't recognize her.

Goztan's plan had failed spectacularly. Instead of proving her identity to the pékyu-taasa, Oga was going to get her killed. Even if he recognized her, they hadn't parted on the best of terms. He had also been mistreated by his Lyucu masters for so long that there was little reason for him to want to save one of them. He could easily exact a measure of revenge upon the Lyucu simply by stating that he didn't know her. Since he was going to depart in the morning with the expedition, there would be no consequences for him when the pékyu found out what had happened.

The way Vadyu had phrased the question practically demanded him to do exactly that.

Goztan stared into Oga's scarred, placid face, and closed her eyes in despair.

"I do know her," Oga said.

Goztan's eyelids snapped open.

"What is her name and lineage, and what deeds had she done?"

"I don't know her name or lineage, for when I knew her she wasn't called by her true name. But I can tell you we once fought together against a cruel Lord of Dara, who had imposed on her the false name 'Obedience.'"

"Liar!" Vadyu scoffed. "The strongest muscle in that gangly body of yours is probably your wagging tongue. You're no warrior."

"Battles don't have to be fought with weapons that cleave or bash," Oga said. And he proceeded to recount how he and Goztan had managed to save the litter-bearers from Captain Dathama's whips.

"Though I haven't seen her since, I do know that she is wily as the ice-furred snow fox and resolute as the fire-breathing garinafin," Oga said. "Like all the warriors who overcame the Lords of Dara, she is valiant, wrathful, and above all, true to the spirit of the Lyucu. Though I wanted to befriend her and call her sa-taasa, she never forgot that I was her enemy."

Goztan stared at Oga, unable to sort out the mix of emotions roiling in her chest.

"Why didn't you simply tell me what I wanted to hear?" The pékyu-taasa's face was hidden in shadow, and her voice trembled with restrained fury. She pointed her chin at the bound Oga. "This woman doesn't think of you as a friend. Why try to save her when you don't even know her name?"

"Because it would be wrong to harm the innocent for the pleasure of the powerful, to take the easy road out of cowardice," said Oga. "Don't you remember the stories I told you and your brothers and sisters, pékyu-taasa? The tall tree that refused to bend before the storm saved the chicks huddling under its protection, though at the end of the storm it lay dead and broken. I may not be able to read the books of the great sages of my land, but I still must live in accordance with what I've learned of their wisdom."

"Is that really all?" asked the pékyu-taasa, sounding disappointed.

Oga took a deep breath. "I didn't just want to save her, pékyu-taasa. I didn't want you to lose favor in the eyes of your father, either."

"What do you mean?"

"If you had harmed or killed this woman, who has done your people great service, your father would never have forgiven you."

"And why do you care about what happens to me? I was the one who reported you to my father for telling stories that would have made us weak."

"You were doing what you thought was right. In that devotion to duty there is the spark of hope for your people—if only you could be persuaded to see the right path to follow—"

"Don't try to fool me with more of your lies! You don't care about the Lyucu. *Why do you care about what happens to me?*"

Oga stared at her for a long moment. When he spoke again, his voice was gentle, composed, like that of a patient tutor. "In Dara there is a sacred bond between a teacher and a student. Though I am your slave, I am also your teacher. It's my duty to protect you from the consequences of bad choices, and that duty is not dissolved just because you didn't like my lessons."

"Out of devotion to your homeland's ideals, you'd rather risk your own death than have the satisfaction of vengeance, of seeing me humiliated and cast away by my father?"

"It's my nature."

Vadyu stared at Oga, jaw clenched and eyes narrowed. A moment later, she let out a long sigh. "All right. I see you can still be trusted."

Oga tilted his head and gave Vadyu an appraising look. "So . . . you were testing *me*, not her."

Vadyu nodded. "I knew she was telling the truth as soon as she demanded that I speak with you."

"How?"

"A pékyu must be able to tell true stories apart from false ones," said Vadyu. "You may have been granted more privileges than most slaves, but you were also watched closer than most. No spy would have been able to conspire with you."

"Ah."

"I decided to use the opportunity to probe the color of your heart and see if you believed in your own stories."

"And if I hadn't passed your test?" asked Oga.

Vadyu swung the club overhead in a wide circle, and the turbulent air she whipped up brushed against Oga's and Goztan's faces. That was all the answer she was going to give.

Vadyu turned to Goztan and loosened the ties that secured the gag in her mouth as well as the sinews that bound her arms and legs. Goztan worked her sore jaw and rubbed the welts in her wrists and ankles. She was going to make the audience with the pékyu in time after all.

"You can release him from his collar," said Vadyu, tossing a notched key-bone to Goztan. "Take him back to Taten when you're ready."

"I thought he was supposed to leave with the expedition."

"I've changed my mind," said Vadyu in a haughty tone. "I got him into this expedition, and I can certainly keep him out of it as well. *I* get to decide."

Goztan looked over at Oga, expecting him to argue—she remembered how much Oga had wanted to go back to his family in Dara—but the man simply bowed to Vadyu. When he straightened his back, a look of relief flashed across his face. When he saw Goztan's questioning expression, he shook his head almost imperceptibly.

Goztan swallowed what she was going to say. Disappointment washed over her heart like a sudden, cold downpour.

*Another lie.*

"I will ask Father to make you his personal re-rememberer," said Vadyu. "You will no longer teach us. Instead of the dreamlike past of Dara, you will re-remember the living present of the Lyucu. Tell the story of my father, Oga the Re-rememberer, and tell it well. Shape the facts of Father's life into a powerful tale to awe the people of Dara when we conquer them. Don't make another mistake and let your talent be wasted."

Vadyu turned and strode away.

"Pékyu-taasa, wait!" Goztan called to the receding figure.

Vadyu didn't slow down. "I told you, you can come back with him when you're ready. I'm going home now to face my father."

"What happened to your plan of bringing me to the pékyu with a tale of how I saved you from Korva?" asked Goztan.

"Oga reminded me that my father can tell a true story apart from a false one. There's nothing worse than losing his trust if I want to be the one to sit in his place one day. Perhaps going to him with my error—my weakness—will only strengthen his affections.

"I am not as hopeless a student as you think, Oga."

She faded into the darkness.

Goztan unlocked Oga's bone collar and watched as the Dara man massaged his neck.

"After all these years, you're as slippery-tongued as the day I met you," she said.

Oga froze. A moment later, he turned to face Goztan, taking a deep breath as if preparing to launch into a long speech.

Goztan spoke before he could. "Even if we can't be votan-sa-taasa, I'm tired of an endless series of lies within lies. I think we owe each other something approaching the truth."

Oga sighed. "I spoke the truth to the pékyu-taasa."

"Not the whole truth," said Goztan. "I know how much you miss your family, and this expedition is your best chance to go home. Yet, you made no objection at all when Vadyu dashed those hopes. In fact, you looked almost joyful to be kept behind. Is the expedition to Dara truly as hopeless as that?"

"To those who have not seen the Wall of Storms, it's impossible to explain its power. I want to see my family, but with my living eyes, not as an oblivious ghost who has crossed the River-on-Which-Nothing-Floats. Without the favor of the gods of Dara, the expedition has no chance of surviving the passage."

Looking at all the men and women lying about the dying embers of the bonfire in deep slumber, secure in their own invincibility, Goztan was overwhelmed by an urge to wake all of them and march to the Great Tent to make Tenryo reconsider his mad scheme. But she could readily imagine how the pékyu would look at her, a thane who spread defeatism among the warriors he had chosen to accomplish his grandest dream.

With her gone, the Five Tribes of the Antler would fall back into internecine warfare. The naros and culeks around the bonfire would still have to go on their hopeless expedition, and if they refused, the pékyu would execute them and ask for more volunteers. She could save no one, after all.

"When there is nothing you can do to stop a tsunami, all you can do is to run to higher ground with your loved ones," Oga said.

Goztan laughed bitterly. "How do you square that aphorism with the one concerning the unbending tree you spouted to your young master but a moment ago? Which is more reflective of your true nature?"

"Aphorisms can't help you survive, but the ability to hold in mind competing ideals just might," Oga said. "I can't stop you from perceiving my deeds through your expectations; all I can do is be grateful each dawn that I get to see another sunrise."

Once again, Goztan noted the scars over Oga's body and the blood that seeped from the wounds around his neck.

*In war, we become more like our enemies. What right do I have to demand honesty and consistency from him?*

He had once saved a few strangers—barbarians really, by his reckoning—with a bold-faced lie to his lord; he had saved her tonight by telling the truth at great personal risk; he had once seen through her act for the benefit of Dathama, but he did not report what he saw, thereby dooming his people to the pékyu's plots; he had lied by omission tonight in order to save himself, thereby dooming an expedition full of Lyucu warriors to a storm-riven fate.

She couldn't tease apart the complex mix of admiration, curiosity, guilt, hatred, and attraction she felt toward him. It was not easy to understand the nature of anyone, much less a man of Dara like Oga.

"The last thing I said to the pékyu-taasa wasn't a lie," Oga said. "I've come to truly care for her as a student. She is ambitious and clever, and she has the capacity to take on the perspective of another."

Surprised, Goztan asked, "You think she is sympathetic to you?"

"No, not quite sympathy," Oga said. "She is . . . empathetic. She is good at gaining and holding the favor of her father and the powerful thanes, and that requires the ability to see the world from their vantage point. Perhaps, one day, when Pékyu Tenryo has ridden a cloud-garinafin beyond the mountains at the edge of the world, she will succeed him and see the wisdom in my stories, thus freeing me and the other captives. Maybe the gods of Dara will then open a passage through the Wall of Storms so that we may go home in peace."

"That's a lot of hope riding on a single person," Goztan said.

"Why not hold on to hope, when the alternative is living death in despair?"

*Why not?* Goztan asked herself. *Oga is no prophet. How can he know that the expedition will not survive the passage? The pékyu has never believed in fate. Even the gods of Dara may be no match for the might of Lyucu warriors. The pékyu is right: For the Lyucu to ever renew themselves, they must look outward, not be content with what has been accomplished. Her own listlessness was proof of that.*

She gazed at the lanky form of Oga, at his fair skin glowing in the dying firelight, and an irresistible urge to dominate him, to probe into him, to truly *know* him seized her.

She shivered. *Is this a sign? Is this what a whisper from the gods feels like? Is this what Kikisavo and Afir felt the moment before they climbed onto the garinafin, realizing that the future was never going to be the same?*

He was a stranger to the complex web of politics that entangled her. He was powerless and alone, unconnected to the web of competing clan interests baying at her, threatening to tear the Five Tribes apart. Relatively rare among the people of Dara, his complexion was almost as pale as the Lyucu. There would be few questions should she go through with her plan.

But above all, she found him beautiful. He didn't possess the virility of her youthful husbands, but her desire for them could not be disentangled from their ambitions and private agendas. She wanted him just for *him*, just for *herself*.

He was, perhaps, the solution to the problem that had plagued her for years.

"Come, we're going back to my tent."

Obediently, Oga followed her.

# FRESH SPROUTS

CHAPTER SEVEN

# A CHASE
# BEYOND THE STORMS

JUST BEYOND THE WALL OF STORMS: THE FIFTH
MONTH IN THE FIRST YEAR OF THE REIGN OF
SEASON OF STORMS (HALF A YEAR AFTER THE
DEATHS OF EMPEROR RAGIN AND PÉKYU TENRYO
DURING THE BATTLE OF ZATHIN GULF).

Ten ships from Dara bobbed gently on calm waves, surrounded by the floating hulks of crubens like whale calves in the middle of a pod. Men and women danced on the decks, whooping and laughing, unable to believe that they had passed under the legendary Wall of Storms unscathed.

To the south, the meteorological wonder loomed like a mountain range sculpted out of cyclones, typhoons, sheets of rain so dense that they might as well be solid water, and roiling clouds lit up from within by bolts of lightning, each the size of Fithowéo's spear. From time to time, small cyclones—each capable of devastating an island in isolation, but here, next to the sky-scraping storm columns, as insignificant as a rock formation in a scholar's garden would be next to Mount Kiji—departed from the wall to wander over the open ocean, gradually dissipating as their peregrinations took them too far from the fabled marvel that was the Wall.

All signs of the Lyucu city-ship fleet had been erased, swallowed up by the Wall like a mouthful of krill by a dome-headed whale. It was a stark reminder that before the power of nature, the works of humans were mere vanity.

Sailors detached thick towing cables from the tails of the crubens. The majestic scaled whales sprayed mist from their blowholes in unison and covered the Dara fleet in rainbows, a good omen. They bellowed their farewell, the resulting deep rumble through the water making the ships' tightly fitted hull planks tremble and squeak against one another. Slapping their massive flukes against the water, the crubens turned to the north in unison, their long horns swaying steadily like the compass needles of the gods, and soon vanished beneath the waves.

Aboard *Dissolver of Sorrows*, flagship of the modest fleet, two figures stood on the elevated stern deck above the aftercastle.

"Thank you, Sovereign of the Seas," whispered the woman who had once been known as Empress Üna and was now again called Princess Théra. She bowed in *jiri* to the wakes left by the crubens.

"I wish we could mandate and command these creatures," said Takval Aragoz, would-be pékyu of the Agon and Théra's fiancé. "They would greatly comfort and aid our cause."

The princess suppressed a smile at the prince's not-quite-right attempt at formal Dara speech. After months of living in Dara, Takval's speech was fluent—except when he tried to sound impressive. "The Fluxists say that there are four powerful forces whose aid can only be petitioned for but not commanded: the strength of a cruben, the favor of the gods, the trust of the people—" She paused.

"And what is the fourth thing?" asked Takval.

"The heart of a lover," said Théra.

The two smiled at each other tentatively, uncertainly, hesitantly.

Thinking of Zomi Kidosu, the brilliant, beautiful woman who had been her first love, Théra's heart ached. She still woke up some mornings expecting to find Zomi beside her in bed; she still saved up stories, expecting to share them with her someday; she still found it jarring when she got ready to write and found the writing knife's edge dulled—Zomi used to sharpen it for her without her noticing.

But she hardened her resolve and put Zomi's smile out of her mind. She had to focus on the present, on the future.

"A ship!" cried a lookout in the crow's nest above the main mast, breaking the awkward silence. He pointed toward the horizon in the east, and his voice quavered as he continued. "*A city-ship.*"

As lookouts on the other ships confirmed the sighting, the celebration on the decks soon turned to consternation. How could there be another city-ship when the Lyucu fleet had just been overwhelmed by the Wall of Storms?

Théra and Takval ran to the mizzenmast and climbed up the rigging. Halfway up, they could already see the massive ship on the horizon, from this distance a mere sliver darkening the boundary between sea and sky, with multiple masts sticking up out of the horizontal hull like the long hairs poking up from the back of a caterpillar.

"Incoming garinafin! Incoming garinafin!" cried the lookout.

It was true. A familiar winged shape could be seen hovering above the distant ship like a childish scrawl against the smooth empyrean. From so far away, it was hard to tell if the figure was indeed heading for them, but then where else could it be going?

"Did you see how the garinafin took off?" asked Takval of the two lookouts on the main mast. "How keen—prickly—no, *sharp* was the rising angle?"

Instead of answering, the pair of lookouts continued their conversation with each other, shading their eyes and pointing at the distant garinafin excitedly.

"Report on the garinafin's angle of ascent on takeoff, if you saw it," said Théra, her voice not any louder than Takval's had been.

"*Rén*—Your Highness!" Instantly, both lookouts turned to her. "We didn't see. By the time we noticed the ship, the garinafin was already in the air."

Théra could see Takval seething with resentment and frustration. Other than Princess Théra, he had no friends among the thousand-plus members of this expedition. Although he was nominally a coequal leader of the fleet with Princess Théra, the Dara crew either pretended that he didn't exist or expressed contempt for his presence in a thousand small ways. This didn't bode well for the Dara-Agon alliance.

"The angle of ascent could have told us the condition of the garinafin," Takval whispered to her sullenly. "It's like how a cow with soupy shit can't run very fast."

Théra put a hand on his shoulder to reassure him. She had already told the captains and commanders that they were to treat orders from Takval as though they had come from her, and she tried to consult Takval on every decision. But prejudices against the people of the scrublands ran deep after the Lyucu invasion, and though the Agon were the enemies of the Lyucu, the crew distrusted Takval. She could not manufacture respect out of thin air. This was a problem that Takval had to solve himself.

"Why didn't that ship attempt to sail through the Wall with the rest of the fleet?" asked Théra, trying to stay focused on the problems of the moment.

"I think it must have been kept behind by the Lyucu fleet commander, Garinafin-Thane Pétan Tava, out of care and caution," said Takval. "I learned about him on the way here, before I escaped from the city-ships. He had a reputation for holding back a reserve in every battle, instead of committing everything to the initial assault."

Théra's heart pounded so hard that her chest hurt. The memory of their nearly fatal encounter with the lone garinafin that had survived the destruction of the Lyucu fleet during the passage through the Wall of Storms was fresh in her mind. Now that they were without the protection of the crubens, the chances of surviving another garinafin assault seemed remote.

"Maybe we should go underwater again?" asked Takval. "When caught in the open by garinafins with no garinafins of our own, the Agon way is to hide."

"That's not going to work," said Théra. "Once we dive, we won't be able to move except drifting with the current, and the city-ship, under full sail, will catch us shortly. We can't stay under forever, either. When we're forced to resurface, we'll be sitting ducks."

"Then we'll have to leave two ships behind to fight," said Takval. "They die so that the other ships can live."

Théra looked at him. "This is our first encounter with the Lyucu, and you're proposing we sacrifice a fifth of our fleet?"

"This is what Agon warriors must do to save the tribe, and I would be happy to lead those willing to stay behind to forge a wall with our bones that will rival this Wall of Storms in future bonfire recountings." Takval took off the leather cord around his neck. "This pendant, made from the stones found in a garinafin's liver-pisspot, will let my people—"

"Wait, wait. A 'liver-pisspot' . . . Do you mean the pouch-shaped organ under the liver, a gallbladder?"

"Yes, that's the word: 'gallbladder.' The gallbladder stones will let my people know that you've been invested and divested with my authority. It won't be perfect, but when you get to Gondé—"

"Oh, stop it!" chided Théra. She wasn't sure whether to scream or cry or laugh at some of Takval's ideas—it didn't help that Takval's Dara, originally acquired from both nobles and peasants in Mapidéré's fleet, was peppered with incongruous locutions. "Where does this obsession with living on in song and story instead of thriving in this world come from? The world right *here*, right *now*, between the Veil of Incarnation and the River-on-Which-Nothing-Floats, is where we can make the most difference. Every single person on this expedition is irreplaceable, with unique experiences and skills. We're *not* going to jump to sacrifice as the first solution to every problem. That's the easy way out. I intend to get every ship and every member of our crew to Gondé, you included."

Takval was taken aback—this was definitely not how an Agon leader would have reacted. "How do you intend . . . to live through the garinafin assault then?"

"By doing the most interesting thing, of course," said Théra, a look of determination and defiance on her face. "We've got about an hour, so tell me everything you know about what happens to garinafins on long journeys."

Throughout a thirty-year career as a fighting man, first under the wily Pékyu Tenryo and then under the exacting Pékyu-taasa Cudyu, Toof had piloted a dozen garinafins and fought in hundreds of engagements. By rights, he should have been able to face any threat with complete equanimity.

But on this scouting mission, he felt as scared as on his very first mission as a fifteen-year-old boy, when he had been told to take care of an ambush of tusked tigers all by his lonesome self.

Toof's mount, a ten-year-old female named Tana, trembled beneath his saddle as she flexed and stretched her long-unused wings, as if sharing his unease. His crew, reduced to only four to conserve garinafin lift gas after so much inactivity at sea, clung to the webbing draped over Tana's torso quietly, not engaging in their habitual banter or singing heart-lifting battle songs.

Who could blame them for being afraid? Never in the history of the peoples of the scrublands had there been a garinafin flight like this.

To his left loomed the Wall of Storms, an impenetrable, shimmering mountain of water and lightning that had just swallowed thousands of his comrades like an insatiable monster. Beneath him was the endless ocean, over which the Lyucu fleet had sailed for months without sight of land. He felt as though he was flying through a scene ripped from the ancient myths or a shaman's tolyusa-fueled nightmare, a primordial time when the gods of the Lyucu had not taken human form, but endlessly transformed themselves and their surroundings, sculpting the world like so much tallow.

As Toof approached his targets—ten small ships huddled on the sea like a pod of sunning dolphins—his nervousness only increased as he guided Tana to fly lower. He swallowed hard to moisten his parched throat as he began to plot a course that would take Tana directly over the Dara fleet, giving her a chance to strafe the crew and rigging with fire breath.

Truth be told, Toof's trepidation was partly the result of his uncertainty that the ships from Dara were even crewed by humans at all. How else could these tiny ships, bobbing over the ocean like arucuro tocua toy boats, have survived a passage through the Wall of Storms? Either these ships were crewed by ghosts and spirits, or they had unimaginable powers that mere mortals could not hope to withstand. Who knew if a garinafin's fire breath would even be effective at all?

As if in answer to his fervid imagination, giant, flat shapes lifted off from the decks of the little ships and rose into the air to meet Tana and her riders. Were these the fabled airships of Dara that Pékyu Tenryo had warned them about? Or were they some new kind of engine of war that the barbarians had invented to bring ruin to the Lyucu? Nothing was impossible after what he had just witnessed a few hours ago.

Tana moaned and veered sharply to the right, away from the flying objects, her nostrils flaring in alarm. Instead of swooping over the fleet, she was using up her precious lift gas to maneuver in a wide circle around the fleet, too far for her to have any opportunity of attacking it.

"Ah . . . ah . . ." The port slingshot scout, Radia, who was in the best position to observe the targets from her perch on the webbing over Tana's left shoulder, seemed at a loss for words.

"Ttt . . . tusss . . ." Toof wasn't doing any better.

"What in the world are you two babbling about?" asked the starboard slingshot scout, Voki. Having heard no further clarification, he and Oflyu, the spearhand as well as tail lookout, climbed up the webbing over Tana's right shoulder and back to get a better look.

"Ttt . . . tusss . . ." "Fffff . . . ffflyyy . . ." "Ah . . . ah . . ." "Bu . . . bu . . ."

Tana sneezed and flapped her wings vigorously to get farther away. She was even more frightened and shocked than her human crew by the spectacle above the Dara fleet: ten brightly colored tusked tigers, each almost twenty-five feet long and twelve feet tall at the shoulders, leaping and swooping through the air.

Tusked tigers were among the few predators of the scrublands that could strike fear into the heart of a garinafin. These tawny-colored giant cats, typically the size of several long-haired cattle, sported a pair of curved tusks that could puncture tough garinafin hide. While male tusked tigers tended to wander far over the scrublands and hunt alone, females lived in large groups called ambushes with their cubs, hunting cooperatively. With their sharp claws, keen tusks, and muscular bodies, tusked tigers posed a great threat to young garinafins who hadn't the endurance for long flights, and even adult garinafins could be overcome by large ambushes. Although the tusks didn't inject any venom, wounds inflicted by these foul-breathed creatures festered. Some ambushes of tusked tigers were known to deliberately injure a garinafin's leathery wings during an initial attack before tracking their prey for multiple days and nights, across hundreds of miles through the trailless scrublands, until, weakened by the infection from that initial bite, the garinafin finally succumbed.

Worst of all, tusked tigers had the terrifying ability to shock their prey with silent roars. Experienced elders spoke of witnessing tusked tigers chasing after herds of wild aurochs and opening their maws when close. Although no sound emerged from those fetid throats, the straggling members of the herd fell down as though paralyzed by some unseen force. The tusked tigers' magic was not well understood, and hunting parties generally avoided them unless a fight was absolutely necessary.

Thus, an ambush of larger-than-life tusked tigers *who could fly* was without a doubt the most frightening thing that a garinafin could imagine.

By now, Tana's crew had spent enough time marveling at these nightmarish creatures to realize that they weren't real. In fact, they appeared to be constructed from some kind of translucent material—possibly silk, which they were familiar with from the spoils of Admiral Krita's expedition—stretched over a rigid frame, tethered to the ships below by long, thin cords, which the Dara crew used to guide them to dive, soar, roll, and pounce through the air.

The contraptions looked absolutely worthless as weapons—a single blow from one of Tana's talons would no doubt send one of these kites careening into the sea in pieces. Indeed, as Tana stayed cowardly at a distance, the crew could see the tail of one of the "tigers," apparently constructed in haste, detach from the body and fall into the sea like a withered leaf.

But no matter how hard Toof kicked at the base of her neck with his bone spurs, Tana refused to fly any closer to the false tusked tigers. She even twisted her head around on her long, sinuous neck and gazed at her pilot reproachfully, baring her long, sharp upper canines as she lowed.

Toof was confounded and had no idea what to do. For a well-trained and experienced war garinafin to show such defiance was almost unheard of. Even during bloody battles where the stench of singed flesh filled the air and garinafins tumbled out of the sky like flaming meteors, he could not remember any of his mounts reacting this way.

"She's in the same state as the rest of us," said Radia, who was almost as experienced with garinafins as Toof himself. "Dizzy, confused, exhausted. Even harmless silk tusked tigers at this point are too much."

Toof looked at Radia and realized that the slingshot scout was right. A year's journey over the trackless ocean, fed only on rations of hard pemmican and stale water that never seemed enough, meant the crew was always hungry and tired. Every single person on the city-ship looked like skin wrapped around bones, and he was already feeling out of breath even with the minimal exertion of this short flight.

Tana was in even worse shape. To conserve feed, the few adult garinafins carried by the fleet were kept on rations of thornbush and blood-palm grass hay as strict as the regimen applied to the human crew. Such a diet not only made the garinafins emaciated, but also left them with very little lift gas to sustain flight. Indeed, of the three adult war garinafins on their city-ship, the other two could not fly at all, and Tana's takeoff had been so shallow and flat that Toof's crew was certain at first that the garinafin was going to fall into the sea.

Besides a few on-deck airings during the journey, the garinafins had been mostly kept belowdecks. This flight was thus the first time in a year that she had been able to really spread her wings. Shaken by the destruction of the Lyucu fleet and surrounded by strange, impossible sights, the garinafin was likely on the verge of a total mental breakdown. No wonder she was spooked by these decoy tigers.

"Let's head back." Toof had made up his mind. "Tana can't take the stress."

"Nacu isn't going to like that excuse."

"At least we can inform Nacu that these barbarian ships don't seem to be very fast, and he can catch them on the open sea."

The garinafin circled the fleet once from afar before heading back toward the city-ship. As it receded into the distance, crews on the Dara fleet once again broke into cheers.

A celebration was held on *Dissolver of Sorrows* that evening. Officers from the entire fleet congregated on the deck of the flagship, sharing a feast of freshly caught fish and crabs as well as warm rice beer and sea-chilled plum wine. A few sheep had been slaughtered, and Prince Takval oversaw their roasting after the manner of the people of the scrublands, in which the only flavoring used was sea salt (of which they had an abundance) and a dash of tolyusa juice (of which they had none).

Although a few of the officers, still suspicious of Takval, stood awkwardly at the edge of the crowd, most of the attendees came by the roaring bonfire in the bronze firebowl to accept a cut of roast mutton from the Agon prince. Takval taught them to eat with their hands, tearing off pieces of juicy meat, rather than relying on eating sticks. After a while, everyone grinned as their greasy lips and fingers glistened in the firelight.

"You know wha' wou' go well wi' di'?" mumbled Tipo Tho, commander of the marines on *Dissolver of Sorrows*. She swallowed the mouthful of succulent meat before continuing. "A compote of wild monkeyberries and ice melon. My home village in Wolf's Paw is famous for it."

"That sounds like a very sweet dish," said Takval. "And wouldn't it be too mushy?" Before this, the marine commander had probably spoken all of two words to him.

"That's why it will taste good. You want a good mix and contrast of flavors so that the sweetness isn't cloying and the salty savoriness doesn't parch the tongue." She tore off another strip of meat with her teeth and chewed, closing her eyes in satisfaction.

"I'm sure we'll have a chance to mix more of Agon and Dara cooking," said Takval, smiling. "We'll create flavor mixtures undreamed of by the gods or men."

Food had a way of bringing people together like nothing else.

Elsewhere, the talk was more formal. "Modifying our signaling kites to resemble tusked tigers was pure genius, Your Highness," said Çami Phithadapu. She had been one of the Golden Carp scholars elevated by Emperor Ragin, and Princess Théra had recommended her to the secret laboratory in Haan, where she had played a role in the dissection of garinafin carcasses to reveal their secrets. Grateful for the princess's recognition of her talent, she had volunteered to come on this mission to Gondé.

"The real credit should go to the pékyu-taasa," said Théra. She was trying to learn as much of the Agon language in as short a time as possible, and tried to use some Agon words in her daily speech to set an example for the rest of the crew. Takval had explained to her that although the Agon and the Lyucu tribes all spoke local topolects that were largely mutually intelligible, there were differences that clearly marked one people from another—mainly because the topolects spoken by the Roatan clan and the Aragoz clan had become the prestige topolects of the Lyucu and the Agon, respectively. Fluency in the language of their allies as well as enemies was critical to the ultimate success of their mission.

Théra paused to bow in *jiri* to Takval and held the pose. After a few beats, the others emulated her gesture of respect. Takval, standing next to the firebowl, grilling spit and fork in hand, smiled awkwardly and wiped the sweat from his brow.

A grin flashed across the princess's face before she continued. "Without Takval's knowledge concerning the debilitating effects of transporting garinafins across the ocean and their natural fear of tusked tigers, we wouldn't have been able to scare the attackers away. Now that the creature has exhausted what little lift gas it had kept in reserve, it won't be available for another flight for some time."

Çami nodded and raised her cup to the Agon prince. Setting down the grilling implements, Takval lifted his cup in return and drained it in one gulp. Turning to the rest of the crowd, he said, "Théra and I might have come up with the idea, but we couldn't have succeeded if the kite-crafters hadn't been able to modify the signal kites so quickly. Let me raise a cup to everyone who helped bend a bamboo hoop, sew a silk strip, or paint a tusked tiger stripe today."

The crew raised their cups in return, murmuring words of thanks to the prince.

"He makes it sound so organized and impressive," one of the marines in the crowd whispered to another. "It was pure chaos on deck. I had no idea what to do."

"It's a wonder that we got those things up in the air at all," her friend whispered in response. "I hope we do things with more *planning* in the future."

"Shhh!" Commander Tipo Tho gave the two a withering look.

Takval's face reddened slightly. But he went on as though he hadn't heard. "A garinafin crew is more intelligent and fearsome than any of its members alone. So long as we hold one another as brother and sister, we can only fight better in the future."

Théra was pleased. Takval might be young and inexperienced as a leader, but he clearly had the right political instincts. She had deliberately emphasized his contribution to today's events, and he had immediately understood it to be an opportunity for sharing credit more widely. This was a small step toward making the Agon and the Dara expedition feel like members of a single family, a unified tribe.

"But we aren't out of danger yet," said Théra, injecting a somber note into the feast. "Under full sail, the city-ship is faster than we are. If we keep running, they'll eventually catch us—and we can't hope to scare away rested garinafins with silk-and-bamboo tigers again. Our small ships don't have the armaments to take on a city-ship head-on. For now, we remain the prey and they remain the hunter. Let's all put our minds to finding a way to reverse the situation."

Nacu Kitansli, Thane of the Tribe of the Second Toe, commander of *Boundless Pastures*, the sole Lyucu city-ship to survive the ill-fated attempt to penetrate the Wall of Storms, was having trouble sleeping.

His crew was on the verge of mutiny.

Initially, the Lyucu warriors had been grateful that they had survived while the rest of the fleet foundered, thinking it a sign of favor from the gods of both Ukyu and Dara—or whoever was in charge in these waters. But news that the sole garinafin capable of flight after the arduous voyage across the ocean had been turned back by some decoy tusked tigers had plunged morale to the nadir.

He needed some way to rouse their spirits, but there weren't a lot of good choices.

Increasing rations for the skittish garinafins so that they could attempt another assault shortly with a belly full of lift gas and confidence was out of the question—as known to everyone from the scrublands, where starvation was just one bad winter storm away, humans and beasts needed time to recover after a long period of hunger. Besides, after the yearlong voyage across the ocean, there wasn't even enough food left on *Boundless Pastures* to feed the crew for the one additional year needed to sail back to Ukyu, let alone to indulge the garinafins.

That, ultimately, was Nacu's biggest problem. It was impossible to see how the meager provisions could last even if the crew was put on a starvation diet of one-sixteenth rations. The expedition had been provisioned with the expectation of a welcoming base in Dara established by Pékyu Tenryo, not to wander fruitlessly around the ocean for two years. The prospect of cannibalism and worse loomed in the not-too-distant future.

Already, Nacu had had to have some crew members whipped and dunked in the sea after they were caught trying to break into the ship's supply of tolyusa and pemmican. "A feast! A final feast before we join the cloud-garinafins!" the leader of the troublemakers had hollered. "Let us die at least with bellies full of meat and heads full of visions."

The Dara fleet was the only ray of hope left to the tiger-thane. The Dara ships that had sailed out of the Wall of Storms could have had only one destination in mind: the Lyucu homeland. If Nacu and his crew could seize the rich stores aboard the Dara ships, they would have a chance to make it back home. The Dara fleet was a flock of plump sheep, and the Lyucu city-ship a hungry wolf that needed to eat before the coming of winter.

Nacu Kitansli ordered all the spare battens and sails brought out and rigged. The forest of masts on *Boundless Pastures* sprouted new branches and leaves to catch every scrap of breeze. A whole panoply of skysails, moonrakers, cloudcombs, butterfly sails, even "autumn cocoons"—giant, balloon-like sails that had no battens and rigged only on stays, suitable solely for off-wind or downwind sailing in calm seas—eked out every last bit of speed to aid the city-ship's westward pursuit of the Dara fleet. Using such a top-heavy sail plan so close to the Wall of Storms made even old-time sailors, who had learned the craft of managing these man-made isles directly from Emperor Mapidéré's original crew, sweat in their palms, but at least with every passing day, *Boundless Pastures* drew closer to its prey.

∾

As the city-ship loomed larger behind them with each dawn, Théra and Takval anxiously debated possible courses of action.

"We have to fight them," said Takval.

"How?" asked Théra. "Even the largest stone-throwers we have on board won't make a dent against those thick planks."

It was true. The city-ship was so much bigger and taller that a naval engagement between it and the Dara fleet would resemble assaulting a walled city with a few horse wagons.

Théra summoned the most experienced marine officers and ship captains to *Dissolver of Sorrows* for a council of war.

"Can we do something with the kites?" Takval tossed out the first idea. He had developed a fixation on battle kites after the ploy with the decoy tusked tigers.

Takval elaborated. He thought that the numerous flapping sails that had turned the city-ship into a moving aspen stand presented tempting targets for archers strapped to kites and armed with fire arrows.

"But if we're in range to deploy fire arrows, they'll also be in range to send out coracles and skiffs to board us," said Admiral Mitu Roso, the commander-in-chief of the fleet's armed forces, second in military authority only to Princess Théra (and in theory, required to seek the advice and counsel of Prince Takval). "Not to mention they'll be able to deploy their stone-throwers—I'm sure the Lyucu have learned to wield the weapons on the captured vessel. They'll have the range advantage due to the city-ship's height." He gave Takval a look of contempt. "This is the kind of idea that shows little understanding—"

"As the Ano sages would say," interrupted Théra, " 'Sometimes a paving stone is essential on the path to mine pure jade.' Even an impractical idea may spark a better plan down the road."

Mitu Roso grumbled but said nothing more.

Encouraged by Takval's first try, the captains and marine officers brainstormed other suggestions. Théra purposely kept herself largely out of the discussions so that the officers would feel freer to debate.

But none of the suggestions could pass muster when examined and discussed in more detail.

Takval tried again. "I'd like to quote an ancient Agon proverb: 'A trapped wolf may bite off his paw—'"

"No." Théra cut him off. "I know what you're going to suggest: divide the fleet in half and dispatch one-half of the ships to use fire kites to disable or slow down the city-ship while the other half escape. I need a plan that will save *everyone*."

"If we can't outrun them and we aren't allowed to make a stand and fight them, what else can we do?" Takval complained.

"I didn't say we *can't* fight," said Théra, "but it must not be a head-to-head naval battle—win or loss, the cost will be too high."

"I have an idea," said a new voice. "I've been observing the whales swimming near us in the belt current."

The war council turned as one and saw that the speaker was Çami Phithadapu.

The Phithadapu clan were prominent whalers from Rui. As a little girl, Çami had sailed all around the coast of Rui and beyond with her uncle, a whaling captain, as they pursued the dome-headed whale and the combing whale for profit. Close observation of the majestic, intelligent creatures had eventually made Çami more interested in studying their habits than killing them. For one of her essays at the Imperial examinations, in order to avoid retreading the same few topics favored by most examinees, she had discussed evidence of midwifery being practiced among the ceta-ceans. Once she had placed among the *firoa*—the top one hundred scorers at the Grand Examination in Pan—she had advocated that the Throne encourage fleets throughout Dara to adopt a new style of whaling invented in Gan, in which harpooners tired out dome-headed whales to get them to vomit up the valuable living amber without killing them.

The Wall of Storms, the boundary that had played such an impor-tant role in the fate of Dara, appeared not to constrain the migration of whales at all. The barnacle-encrusted whales that greeted the fleet in these uncharted waters were indistinguishable from those seen among the Islands. Thus, no one had been paying much attention to them—except Çami.

It took Çami some time to explain her cetacean-inspired plan. She even had to illustrate it with a bulky writing wax block and some slender ink brushes, serving as models of the ships.

The captains and marine officers sat in stunned silence, trying to digest Çami's plan.

"It's a completely untested tactic," said Captain Nméji Gon, *Dissolver of Sorrows*'s commanding officer. "I don't even know if this ship could handle what you'd be asking of her."

"Just about any tactic taking advantage of the unique features of these ships will be untested," countered Çami. "This is actually the most orthodox one of the several plans I've devised. If you want to hear a really innovative—"

"Maybe later, Çami," said Théra. "Let's talk through this one first."

"Even if the idea works in principle, there won't be enough time to drill the marines and sailors in such a novel method of war," objected Admiral Mitu Roso.

"Marshal Gin Mazoti always said that there's never enough time to prepare the soldiers adequately. You always go to war with the army you have, not one you wish you could have had," said Théra. "The benefit of unorthodoxy is that the Lyucu won't be expecting anything like it either, despite their deep study of Dara tactics from the captives taken from Krita's expedition. I note that you didn't object to the plan as fundamentally flawed."

"To be honest, I'm both awed by it and a little terrified," admitted Mitu Roso. "It has potential, but there are a lot of unknowns."

"And that makes it interesting," said Takval. He and Théra exchanged a quick smile. "In fact, the more I think about this plan, the more I like it!"

"Easy for you to say," said Captain Nméji Gon. He had once commanded one of the mechanical crubens that had played such a crucial role in Kuni Garu's rise from the tiny island of Dasu. "You won't be the one who has to make this ship do what she was never meant to do."

"I agree with the prince. On an expedition like this, we all have to do what we thought we weren't meant to do," said Tipo Tho, commander of the marines. Before volunteering to come with Princess

Théra, she had been an experienced airship captain. As there was no airship corps in the fleet—maintaining a few expensive airships for a voyage to a faraway land with no known source of lift gas was deemed impractical—she, like the other air force veterans on the expedition, had been reorganized into the marines. "Don't tell me that your ship won't be up to the challenge."

"Oh, the ship will be up to the challenge," Captain Gon said through gritted teeth. Insulting his ship got his hackles up far faster than insulting him. "I'm just worried that a thin-boned swallow like you, used to the luxurious accommodations and stately pace of an Imperial airship, won't be able to take the rough sailing. You'll be vomiting up your dinner, lunch, *and* break—"

"If you think sitting in a waterlogged wooden tub that can dip a few yards below the surface is even one-tenth as rough as flying—"

"Please!" interrupted Théra. "If you want to carry on the ridiculous rivalry between aviators and submariners, play a game of *zamaki* after this mission. I just want to know if you can do what Çami is asking of you."

"Absolutely."

"Count on it."

"I'll have the ship sailing so smoothly you'll think you're out picking lotus seeds on Lake Tututika—"

"Even without my airship, I'll lead our troops on an assault so fast and deadly that our enemies—"

"Instead of all this strutting and posturing," pleaded Théra, rubbing her temples with a pained expression, "why don't you each try to poke holes in the part of the plan the *other* is supposed to carry out, and let's see if Çami's idea really is workable?"

Captain Nméji Gon and Commander Tipo Tho worked through Çami's plan step by step, arranging and rearranging the wax block and ink brushes through different configurations on the floor. Each tried to outdo the other by coming up with new ways that every step could fail, and both furrowed their brows as they refined the plan in response.

Admiral Mitu Roso edged up to Princess Théra. "I served under Emperor Ragin in campaigns against the Hegemon, Duke Théca

Kimo's rebellion in Arulugi, and the Lyucu," he whispered. "Your father was always skilled at using rivalries among his lieutenants to perfect a plan. Seeing shadows of your father's style in you makes my heart leap in joy."

Théra nodded to acknowledge the compliment, but her heart roiled at being reminded of her dead father. *It is a ruler's job to find a way to balance,* Kuni Garu had taught her. She hoped she could find a way to harmonize competing factions, jealousies, mutual distrust, all the forces that threatened to spill out of control in this alliance, and convert all that energy into forward motion. She prayed that her dead father would watch over her and help her find the wisdom needed to succeed.

Nméji and Tipo were slowing down, as each pondered the other's challenges for minutes at a time to come up with the perfect response. They were like two *cüpa* or *zamaki* players locked in the final stages of a hard-fought game, where every move had the potential to alter the outcome. Other officers and captains, like onlookers to an exciting match, offered a cacophony of advice.

"Shouldn't you be the one devising and revising the plan?" whispered Takval in Théra's ear. "Your followers will lose faith in you if you don't take charge."

Théra shook her head almost imperceptibly. "I'm no warlord nor tactician," she whispered. "It would be the height of foolish arrogance for me to lead where I'm blind. Knowing when to be resolute in my own will and when to take counsel is the most important thing my father taught me."

Takval was taken aback. It was practically unheard of among the Agon as well as the Lyucu for a leader not to be an expert at war—or at least not to pretend to be one. Yet again, he was seized by a bout of doubt as to whether he had done the right thing to place the future of his people in the hands of a Dara princess who saw no shame in admitting that she was no skilled warrior.

But wasn't the fact that the Dara were *not* of the scrublands why he had sought their help? Their ways were not the ways of the Agon and the Lyucu, and it was that very foreignness that offered the promise of change. Théra was *interesting*.

In any event, his fate was entwined with hers now, and he could only wait and watch.

Finally, Nméji and Tipo concluded their game. They set down the wax block and ink brushes and stared at each other solemnly.

The other officers held their breaths, waiting for them to announce the outcome.

"Err . . ." Admiral Mitu Roso could no longer tolerate the suspense. "Who won? Who broke the plan?"

Smiles cracked the faces of both Nméji Gon and Tipo Tho as they gripped each other by the arms and laughed heartily.

"We both lost," said Tipo.

"And so we both won," said Nméji.

"Bring in the rice beer!" Tipo called out. "I'll drink with this salty bastard. It's the only way to deal with that fish-gut breath—"

"Let's see if you drink as well as you plan a city-ship assault," said Nméji. "Given that sticklike frame, I have my doubts—"

"Um . . . does this mean," Théra asked, "that you think the plan will work? You trust each other to carry it out?"

Nméji and Tipo turned to her, as if insulted by her question.

"Oh, I'd sail with this man to the palace of Tazu at the bottom of his whirlpool—"

"I'd follow this woman in an assault on the castle of Mata Zyndu—"

"If he had only a boat made out of paper, I'd wager on him—"

"If she had only a hairpin for a weapon, I'd pity her foes—"

"I think the point has been amply made," a smiling Théra said, gesturing for them to stop.

Relief and joy were visible on everyone's face. Flasks full of warm rice beer were brought out and cups filled and drained.

"Don't be too cocky," said Théra. "Making a plan is only the first step; executing the plan will be ten times harder."

The council worked until the stars had spun their nightly course. At dawn, skiffs brought the officers and captains back to their own ships, but none of them went to bed. There was a lot that needed to be done in the next few days.

# CHAPTER EIGHT

# SHADOW PLAY

ALONG THE BELT CURRENT TO UKYU-GONDÉ: THE
SIXTH MONTH IN THE FIRST YEAR OF THE REIGN
OF SEASON OF STORMS.

Pékyu Tenryo had warned his thanes repeatedly not to underestimate the Dara. They were weak and morally corrupt, but they had a kind of cowardly craftiness that led to the invention of fanciful engines (like the city-ships) and elaborate plots (as recounted by their historian-shamans).

Terrified that the sly barbarians of Dara would come up with some new stratagem against him, Nacu Kitansli ordered lookouts to keep the Dara fleet under constant observation, whether night or day.

The sun was settling slowly into the sea ahead of *Boundless Pastures*. From the crow's nest atop the foremast—really just a simple platform on which a couple of sailors could perch and look about with an unimpeded view—Radia jabbed her elbow into her dozing partner's ribs. "Hey, what do you think they're doing?"

Startled awake, Toof cursed in terror as he swayed and stumbled, his arms windmilling to keep the balance as he teetered hundreds of feet above the sea.

Radia chuckled. "Serves you right for falling asleep." She wasn't worried about Toof tumbling to his death. Above the platform of the crow's nest, at chest height, were four large, horizontal iron hoops arranged around the mast like the petals of a flower. Toof, like Radia, was standing in one of these hoops and secured to it by a harness.

"I'm getting too old for lookout duty," complained Toof. Normally, garinafin riders, pilot and crew alike, were exempt from the unpleasant task of climbing into rickety crow's nests to be lashed by the wind and the rain, swaying hundreds of feet above the turbulent waves. But Thane Nacu had been so displeased by the crew's performance during Tana's aborted attack on the Dara fleet that they had all been stripped of that privilege.

"Be glad you still get to be a lookout. If you keep on falling asleep, you're going to be assigned to the same duties as the Agon slaves."

"At least they are allowed to see Tana during dung-shoveling duty," said Toof. "I hope she's all right."

Nacu blamed Toof's crew for Tana's "cowardice" and had assigned other pilots to take over the care and feeding of the garinafin. In addition, Toof and the others were forbidden to go anywhere near the garinafins. Under Tenryo, close bonds between pilots and war garinafins were discouraged so that riders and mounts could be treated as interchangeable parts in a more professional army, but old habits died hard. Toof was very attached to Tana, having raised her from a hatchling.

"Forget about Tana; she can take care of herself. And never mind your carping." Radia pointed to the horizon with an outstretched arm. "Look! Look!"

Toof squinted. The Dara fleet was miles away, sailing in two parallel columns. The combined height of the city-ship and the mast, however, gave the Lyucu lookouts excellent visibility. A billowing, rectangular piece of white cloth, at least a hundred feet tall and several times as long, hung between the mainmasts of the two ships at the ends of the columns. The massive screen hid the rest of the fleet from view.

"What kind of sail is that?" Toof asked, his brows knitted in puzzlement.

"They're trying to sail faster to get away from us," Radia offered.

"But it's so unwieldy! And whoever heard of a sail tying together two ships?" Toof tried to think if anyone had ever seen such a contraption. "I don't think it's going to help them at all. It will slow them down."

"Maybe they are preparing to launch another ambush of painted tusked tigers?" Radia suggested.

Toof shook his head uncertainly.

The barbarians of Dara were *definitely* up to something.

Toof climbed down the mast to report the unusual activities to Nacu Kitansli. The thane looked as befuddled as Toof felt, and ordered more observation.

Soon, Lyucu warriors climbed into the rigging and filled the foredeck as they stretched their necks for a better view. Even those who were supposed to be asleep belowdecks had woken up and joined their shipmates.

By now, only a sliver of the sun remained above the waves, and the screen, catching the dying light of the sun behind it, glowed brightly as it billowed smoothly between the tall masts of the two trailing Dara ships.

Giant shadows appeared on the screen and began to move.

A flat city of sweeping, angular, curved roofs and towering, blocky walls appeared on the left side. A gigantic winged creature constructed out of sharp triangles and a sinuous chain of circles, evidently a stylized representation of a garinafin, approached from the upper right-hand corner. The garinafin swooped over the city, letting out a triangular orange tongue of flames. But after the fire-tongue lashing, the city stood proudly unbowed.

Soon, pulsating shadows that resembled swimming jellyfish with feathery tentacles appeared above the city and attacked the garinafin with flame tongues of their own, forcing it to retreat. Excited Lyucu naros and culeks whispered to one another, guessing that these were representations of the fabled airships of Dara.

Back and forth, the two sides fought an epic war on the screen. As the sky darkened and the first stars peeked out, the screen somehow glowed even brighter, a shining rectangle of light over the wine-dark sea, compelling everyone's attention. The protagonists of the drama, made out of simple geometric shadows—crude, flat, and largely uncolored save for dabs of bright accents—seemed to take on lives of their own that were every bit as momentous as life in this solid realm.

The air cooled; faint sounds of music—drums, horns, even clanging bells of different pitches—drifted over the water, adding an aural dimension to the spectacle on the screen. The horns bellowed like an injured garinafin; the clanging bells beat out a martial tune; the rhythm of the drums accelerated or slowed in accordance with the action on the screen, drawing the emotions and the heartbeats of the enraptured Lyucu audience in sync.

"How are they doing that?" whispered an awed Toof.

Radia shook her head, too absorbed by the shadow play to answer.

About ten yards behind the massive screen, thick cables stretched between the masts of *Dandelion Seed* and *Drifting Lotus*, forming a complex web of rope bridges and bamboo-planked platforms. Teams composed of the strongest men and women from the crews of all ten ships scrambled over these catwalks, manipulating long bamboo poles attached to giant shadow puppets—modified kites—against the screen.

In order to balance the two ships against the weight of the lopsided cabling between them, almost everything heavy had been moved to the outer sides of the two ships: ballast stones, barrels of drinking water, casks of dried and smoked meat, live sheep and cattle, bags of rice and sorghum flour, the stoves used for heating and cooking. Even the anchors had been shifted to one side and draped over the gunwales.

On the forecastles of the two ships, roaring fires danced merrily from thick hemp wicks dipped in barrels of whale oil—as much as Çami loved whales, nothing else provided a fire as bright. Polished bronze mirrors arranged in parabolic formation reflected the light back onto the screen, providing the necessary illumination to cast strong shadows for the puppet show.

Aboard *Dissolver of Sorrows*, which was sailing just ahead of the two shadow puppet ships, the crew rushed about over the deck and inside the hold, preparing for the next phase of the plan.

A group of senior advisers and officers stood on the elevated stern deck atop the aftercastle of the flagship, with Takval and Théra in the middle, gazing over at the towering screen that hid them from Lyucu sight. From this vantage point, they could discern every detail of the bustling organized chaos that made the shadow play possible.

Every time someone missed a cue or collided with a fellow pup-peteer, Théra cringed. Even with several days of intensive rehearsals, the players were still not fully in sync, like the crew of a new ship on its shakedown cruise. Théra could hardly blame them. So much had to be compressed into so little time; everyone was working on just a couple of hours of sleep each night. To avoid giving away the scheme, the players couldn't even rehearse with the real screen, but had to make do with the sails of ships near the front of the fleet (during the day only, hidden by the sails of the ships behind them). And they, unlike those entrusted with other parts of the complex plan, at least had the luxury of *rehearsals*.

She felt like she was dancing on the edge of a blade. So much had to go *exactly* right. Yet, what choice did they have? This was what it meant to do the *interesting* thing.

"There's nothing like this among the Agon or Lyucu," marveled Takval, who was standing next to her. He was grinning like a kid at his first experience with the theater. "Our shamans will love this art."

"When we were little, my siblings and I used to sneak out of the palace to hear storytellers and watch shadow plays," said Théra wistfully. "Now we're scattered to the ends of the world like wind-blown seeds from a dandelion ball, and the memories of those times grow ever sweeter."

"I can't replace what you've sacrificed," said Takval, and he placed a hand against the small of her back reassuringly. "But my family shall be your family, and my people your people."

Théra nodded but did not speak. The warmth of Takval's hand was comforting, but she wasn't quite ready to be comforted.

As she watched the outsized shadows dancing against the screen, she worried about her siblings: bookish Timu, sword-happy Phyro, and little Fara, who loved romantic stories. In fact, as a way to honor her little sister, she had based the designs of some of the shadow puppets on Fara's unique drawing style, with an emphasis on clean, abstract geometric shapes that captured the spirit of the characters more than their exact form. Would she ever see any member of her family again? Or would they fade in her memories until they were barely more than geometric outlines?

And what about Zomi, clever, brave, beloved Zomi? Théra thought of that magical night in the bedroom in the Three-Legged

Jug, which she and Zomi had spent together, not doing much sleeping. Instead of words of farewell, they had made finger shadow puppets on the wall by the light of the candle, pressing them together until it was impossible to tell which hand belonged to whom.

*Will my heart be grand enough to contain multiple loves? Will I be true to them all?*

The puppet crews on the rope catwalks made the garinafin dive into two airships, but the two airships somersaulted to dodge out of the way and circled around to clip the garinafin's wings with flame-lances. Of course no real airship could do any of that, but fantasy physics had its advantages.

It had been Théra's idea to use such an outsized spectacle of music and shadows to disguise the true intent of the Dara fleet, and since she had put herself in charge of penning the script for the show, she decided to have some fun with it.

*We each have a role in the grand shadow play that is politics and war. Who can tell if it will be a tragedy or a comedy?*

A quick series of martial drumbeats broke into her reverie.

"This may be my favorite music from Dara," said Takval. "Much of the music I've heard in Dara is . . . like a rich meal that puts me to sleep, but this . . . this I can dance to!"

"Are you sure they can hear this all the way back there on the city-ship?" Théra asked. "I hope we aren't going to a lot of trouble for nothing."

"Don't worry," said Çami. "Sound carries well over water, and even more so at sundown. It's well-known to old whalers that the best time to pass messages from ship to ship by talking trumpet is at dawn and dusk, though I don't know exactly why it works. Good thing you picked this time for the assault."

"At sundown and sunrise?" Théra mused. "I wonder if it has to do with the temperature of the air? As the sun goes down, the air cools near the surface of the ocean, but up above it remains warm. Perhaps sound can be deflected down and rebound along . . ." Her voice faded away as she mumbled to herself, again lost in thought.

"What are you talking about?" asked Takval. "You speak of sound like pebbles tossed by a child bouncing along the ground."

"Never mind," said Théra. "Now isn't the time to delve into the why. I picked sundown to maximize the impact of the visuals of the shadow play, but I'm glad it has this fortuitous aural benefit. We're lucky you came along, Çami. My mother said that when you learn enough about the world, even a blade of grass can be a weapon. You've turned knowledge of your passion, the whales, into a shield of disguise as well as a spear of cunning."

Çami smiled but did not give the expected response of downplaying her expertise, as so many Dara scholars were wont to do. She was proud of her hard-earned knowledge, and excessive humility always felt to her like a cloying sort of boast.

"Now that we're near the climax of the show," said Théra, "let's set in motion the heart of your interesting plan."

She turned to the officers and mates on the stern deck. "Inform Admiral Mitu Roso on *Drifting Lotus* via flag signals that he has the command of the fleet. Lower the masts and secure the hatches. Prepare to dive!"

"Fight! You cud-chewing gasbag, you featherless prairie partridge, you squishy oversized caterpillar! Fight!" screamed Radia at the distant flickering shadows on the silvery screen, waving her arms and stomping the deck for emphasis. She and Toof had been relieved from their posts in the crow's nest, but the pair, like everyone else from the watch, had no desire to go belowdecks. There was a show!

The tide in the fight between the shadow-born garinafin and the geometric Dara city had turned several times. The latest twist was that the garinafin was going on a long journey to seek the help of a legendary pilot while the crafty people of Dara harassed the garinafin with a series of kite attacks. Blocky scenery made of triangular mountains, double-stacked-triangle sea waves, and triple-stacked-triangle forests passed below the garinafin in an endless scroll while the garinafin struggled to escape the pursuing kites.

Meanwhile, in the real world, a few giant kites had launched from the Dara ships, carrying drummers, bell ringers, and horn players aloft so that their auditory accompaniment could be better appreciated by the audience on the city-ship. The music that drifted over the sea at the moment was lugubrious and despondent, as if the imaginary garinafin had lost the will to fight.

Other Lyucu warriors shouted and whistled in agreement with Radia. They couldn't wait to see the legendary pilot join forces with the garinafin to teach these sneaky barbarians a lesson.

However, Nacu Kitansli, Thane of the Tribe of the Second Toe, watched the show with growing unease.

*What in the world are the barbarians doing? This makes no sense.*

He was certain that there was some trick behind this display. The most obvious conclusion was that the shadows served as a distraction. He barked at the lookouts to keep their eyes peeled, especially in other directions, away from the Dara fleet. But all around him was the endless sea. They were miles and miles from Dara; any barbarian reinforcements were trapped behind the Wall of Storms.

Though he couldn't figure out the barbarian plot, he was sure he had to do something.

"Tell everyone to get belowdecks except the sailors on watch," he said to the naro-votan who was the watch officer.

"Votan, I don't know if that's such a good idea," said the woman. "The warriors haven't had anything to entertain them in a long while, and morale is low after . . ."

Nacu pondered this. It was true that the ill-fated garinafin attack had damaged morale and his own reputation. He had been so concerned about a possible mutiny that he dared not reduce the crew's rations, justifying the decision by telling himself that the capture of supplies from the Dara fleet was imminent.

The surprise show from the barbarians really was having a positive effect. He hadn't seen his crew so excited and energized in a long while.

"We know that sheep will often lie down and bleat for mercy when they feel the wolf's breath right behind their ears," said the naro-votan.

*Perhaps the Dara are trying to curry favor with us with this show, knowing that they will soon be our captives.*

Nacu nodded. The Dara were wily, but they were also devoid of courage. They probably thought a good show that flattered their pursuers was their best option.

"Let's make this a proper celebration then," Nacu declared.

The thane gave the command to let the dwindling supply of water and kyoffir flow freely among the crew. Even the few Agon slaves on the city-ship, normally consigned to the most backbreaking, unpleasant tasks, were allowed to carry the water casks and food barrels out of the hold to get some fresh air.

Naros and culeks cheered wildly.

"The gods favor Thane Nacu!"

"He is truly a generous kyoffir-giver!"

"Votan! Votan! Votan!"

Pleased with the reception, Nacu ordered that some of the precious tolyusa be brought out and distributed to naros-votan and naros who had done distinguished service. Though tolyusa was usually consumed only at grand feasts and festivals, this seemed an occasion to maximize the boost to morale.

As kyoffir was imbibed and tolyusa leaves were smoked, the crew grew more raucous and jubilant. The shadow garinafin on the distant screen had triumphed over the worthless Dara pursuers and was dancing in celebration, wiggling its sinuous circle-chain body from side to side. The music from the kite-musicians, meanwhile, was brassy, arrogant, full of swagger. It fit the mood of the Lyucu crew perfectly.

Toof and Radia, unfortunately, had received no kyoffir or tolyusa leaves. Everyone knew that they were out of Nacu's favor, and the naros-votan in charge of distributing the rare treats bypassed them entirely.

Radia sighed and tried to breath in the tolyusa smoke exhaled by a nearby naro. The naro glanced at her disdainfully and moved away.

Toof, completely absorbed by the show on the screen, was unperturbed by this latest sign of his declining status on the ship. He whooped in delight at the garinafin's exultant aerial dance, an invitation for the legendary pilot.

"It's unbelievable how much I'm feeling for these shadows," he muttered. "This must be some kind of witchcraft."

"Nah," said Radia. "In your case it's just because you care about garinafins—even one made of shadows—more than you care about people."

Toof grinned. Some other ambitious garinafin pilot would have probably taken Radia's comment as an insult, but Toof had long accepted his own station in life. A simple naro with no clan name and no prominent lineage to boast of, he had long been more concerned with the well-being of his mounts than kill ratios and victories—not exactly a recipe for success in Tenryo's army, where garinafins were viewed as little more than interchangeable living weapons. That was why, even after decades of fighting, long after he had aged beyond being a desirable prospect for marriage, he had never even been promoted to naro-votan.

"If I were riding that garinafin," he began. "Whoa—"

He felt a tremor in the hardwood gunwale he was leaning against, as though the city-ship had struck something in the water. He looked down into the choppy waves at the bow of the ship but saw nothing.

"Did you feel that?" he asked Radia.

"What are you talking about?" Radia was busy trying to get downwind of another naro smoking tolyusa.

"I don't know . . . Something bumped against the ship, I think. I should go tell the thane."

Radia grabbed him. "Leave it be. Do you really want to go grab the tusked tiger's whiskers now? He hates us!"

Toof hesitated.

"Look! There's the legendary pilot! Doesn't he look like Pékyu Tenryo?"

Toof squinted at the screen. Indeed, the squarish head of the human figure that had just appeared on screen, a massive claw-shaped battle-axe slung over his shoulder, bore a certain resemblance to the great pékyu. Even the Dara barbarians held a measure of respect for the Lyucu leader, it seemed, for his shadow puppet was almost as large as the garinafin itself, no doubt a reflection of his awesome reputation.

The tremor he had felt earlier was forgotten as all the Lyucu warriors held their breath, their hearts beating as quickly as the distant drumbeats, waiting to see how the legendary pilot would lead the garinafin to victory over the barbarians of Dara.

Hidden by the shadow-play screen, *Dissolver of Sorrows* sank beneath the surface.

Anxiously, Théra stood in the captain's quarters with Takval, under the stern deck. Since *Dissolver of Sorrows* was also the fleet's flagship, Admiral Mitu Roso and Captain Nméji Gon had moved into cabins aft to bunk with the other officers, leaving the captain's quarters to the princess and her intended.

These were the most comfortable accommodations in the whole ship, and the row of thick glass windows in the transom, caulked watertight and strengthened against water pressure, turned the place into a kind of observation lounge when the ship was underwater.

At the moment, no lights were on in the cabins lest the glow through the windows and the water give up their presence. The darkness inside was reflected outside. The windows showed nothing but inky twilight, punctuated here and there by the pale flash of a jellyfish or some other luminescent denizen of the deep, their pulsing light the only illumination in this realm of gloom, like twinkling stars studding the featureless empyrean.

*Flash. Glimmer. Spark.* The pulses dimly limned the tense faces squeezed in front of the windows.

"Wish we could see more," whispered Théra. "I feel so helpless, unable to move the ship at all. We can't even see the city-ship approaching. Maybe I should have scheduled the attempt at dawn rather than dusk."

Although Zomi Kidosu had modified the ships in Théra's fleet to have the mechanical cruben's diving ability, there had been no time to retrofit the ships with a means of submerged propulsion. They had to be towed by something to move at all. Right now they were simply adrift in the current, kept on the right heading by what little momentum remained from their surface speed and the rudder.

"Don't doubt yourself," said Takval. He kept his voice low so as not to be overheard by the semicircle of officers and mates behind them. "I think you were absolutely right that a daytime attempt would have risked lookouts spotting *Dissolver of Sorrows*. Once a garinafin has begun to dive, the pilot must commit wholeheartedly to the venture lest the whole crew tumble to their deaths."

"I can't help it," whispered Théra. "People may die because of my choice. How can I know if I'm doing the right thing?" Though she had been taught the lessons of power all her life by Emperor Ragin, and she had worked closely with Zomi in research during the war against the Lyucu, she had never been in a position to make the final decision to send people to die.

"You won't ever know," said Takval. "And I can't tell you it will ever feel easier—for I have never known the weight of wielding the war club of a pékyu either. But I have heard many stories of great Agon pékyus of generations past, and their wisdom guides us. You can never let doubt show on your face. That is the burden of a leader, whether in Dara, Gondé, or under the sea."

"It's time," said Admiral Mitu Roso, standing behind Théra and Takval.

"Come back to me safely," Théra whispered to Takval. She squeezed his hand, hard, and then let go. "Go up and join the boarding party," she said aloud as she forced her face to show no emotion.

Takval had insisted on taking up one of the most dangerous jobs on this mission—it was the only way he knew to be a leader, and Théra couldn't dissuade him.

The semicircle of observers parted to make a path for Takval. He turned, felt his way through the captain's quarters, and climbed up the interior ladder into the conning tower protruding above the aftercastle, the tallest part of the ship's superstructure (now that the masts were lowered to lie flat against the deck). This was intended to serve as a secondary command post when the ship was mostly submerged, with only the conning tower sticking out of the water.

Ten marines—counting Commander Tipo Tho—picked for their agility and compact physiques were squeezed into the conning tower, ready for the next step. They barely nodded at the Agon prince who joined them, their faces lit harshly from below by the pure white light of a whale-oil lamp. As they were away from any portholes or windows, lighting here was safe.

They could feel *Dissolver of Sorrows* slowing in the water, gradually losing its momentum. They could imagine themselves falling behind the rest of the fleet, unseen beneath the waves. They could imagine the Lyucu city-ship catching up to them, closer and closer.

Like miners trapped underground watching the air tubes connecting them to the surface, the marines and Takval stared at the thin bamboo poles in the middle of the conning tower and listened intently for any thumps or scrapes. They were drifting blind into the path of the Lyucu city-ship, and the only dimension they had control over was their depth.

The engineers in the hold had to maintain the ship's depth very carefully. The success of the mission depended on it. Too shallow and *Dissolver of Sorrows* might be broken apart by the thick prow of the city-ship on collision; too deep and they might miss the city-ship altogether.

With a muffled *thwack* that nevertheless seemed deafening in the enclosed space, the bamboo poles in the conning tower began to vibrate, emitting a series of crisp, rhythmic snaps.

The poles were designed to act like the antennae of a lobster or insect. Protruding above the conning tower, they slapped against the underwater portion of the city-ship's hull and allowed the crew of *Dissolver of Sorrows* to know when they were directly under the enemy vessel.

"We have contact!" Commander Tipo Tho shouted down into the aftercastle.

"Reduce depth. Steady as she goes," ordered Captain Nméji Gon, standing on the bridge directly below the conning tower.

His orders were passed via a series of urgent whispers down a line of sailors stationed between the bridge and the hold, where engineers tended to the ballast tanks that adjusted the depth of the ship. The deck tilted slowly as *Dissolver of Sorrows* began to rise.

This was again a delicate and highly complex maneuver. Ascending too slowly risked having the ship pop up in the wake of the city-ship, missing the target entirely, but rising too fast risked slamming into the city-ship, giving themselves away and possibly damaging their own vessel. The engineers had only been able to practice this maneuver a few times before *Dissolver of Sorrows* set sail from Dara, and once they were under the watchful eyes of the Lyucu, they couldn't practice with the real ship at all lest they give away the ship's secret diving capability. In order to make sure that they could perform the maneuver under pressure, Captain Gon had to run numerous simulated drills where the crew touched the controls without actuating them. To give the crew a better intuition of the ship's maneuvering characteristics, he built a scale model of *Dissolver of Sorrows*, submerged it in a tub of water, and then demonstrated how minute buoyancy adjustments trimmed the ship by having his engineers blow air into the model ballast tanks with straws.

In the dim interior of the captain's quarters, Théra's masklike impassive face disguised the roiling emotions in her heart. Her fate was entirely in the hands of the men and women stationed at the ballast controls, pumping air into the tanks to lighten the ship under the coordinating, rhythmic thwacks from wooden clappers controlled by cables leading to the bridge, from which Captain Gon issued orders. The amount of air pumped into each tank and the speed at which the air was pumped had to be carefully calibrated to keep the ship properly trimmed.

With a loud thump that rattled the teeth of the crew and even threw a few sailors who weren't properly braced to the deck, the conning tower struck the bottom of the city-ship. Then, as the conning tower slid and bumped along the ship's keel, a series of loud, staccato thumps filled their ears.

"May Lutho and Tazu protect us," whispered Admiral Roso in the captain's quarters. "Let's hope no one up there noticed that!"

Théra said nothing. The shadow-puppet show, besides distracting the Lyucu crew from realizing that the escaping Dara fleet had been reduced in number by one ship, was also intended to draw all the Lyucu sailors onto the deck and into the rigging, as far away from the bottom of the city-ship as possible. They had timed it so that the climax of the shadow play would occur just as *Dissolver of Sorrows* drifted beneath the city-ship, maximizing the chances that no crew member would notice the moment of contact.

Théra squeezed her fists so hard that her nails drew blood against her palms. No matter how much they planned, there was always an element of unpredictability: What if someone were sick and stayed belowdecks? What if the Lyucu commander had worked out that the Dara ships could dive because it was the only way to bypass the Wall of Storms? There was nothing she could do except to wait and trust that the conning-tower crew would accomplish their jobs as quickly as possible.

*But . . . is there really nothing I can do?*

She turned to the side. "Çami, let's check the trumpet and bamboo reeds one more time."

"Don't you want to see if—"

"Waiting and wishing aren't going to help Captain Gon and Commander Tho," Théra said resolutely. Doing something, any-thing, would have a steadying effect on her nerves. She turned to the others in the cabin. By the faint glimmer of bioluminescence outside the transom windows, she saw the anxious faces of the other officers.

She turned to Admiral Roso and whispered, "Çami can stay with me. But there's no need for everyone to worry themselves sick here."

Admiral Roso understood. He began to bark out orders. "I need a team in the aftercastle under the conning tower to man the pumps; I also need damage control teams and people to relieve the engineers. . . ."

As *Dissolver of Sorrows* continued to ascend and pressed the con-ning tower tighter against the bottom of the ship, the heart-stopping thumps slowed, and then eventually, stopped. Sharp hooks installed fore and aft of the conning tower's hatch cover had sunk into the worm-ridden wood at the bottom of the city-ship's hull, some-where to the starboard side of the keel. However, the hooks were not designed to hold on for long.

The marines in the conning tower sprang into action.

"Screws!" whispered Commander Tipo Tho. Now that they were attached to the city-ship directly, it was even more important to keep noise to a minimum, as sound could be carried far through the struc-ture of the ship.

Four pairs of marines jumped to the four handwheels suspended from the corners of the conning-tower ceiling, each two feet in diameter, and began to crank them.

For this mission, the top of *Dissolver of Sorrows*'s conning tower had been modified. Instead of the typical cylindrical handrails above the hatch that offered the watch officer some measure of stability against turbulent seas, ironsmiths had installed a short, chimneylike tube with a slanted lip that could be rotated to fit against either the port or starboard side of the bottom of the city-ship. Around the lip of this tube were coils of rope that made the end of the tube resemble the sucker at the end of an octopus's tentacle. The tube had some flex in it so that once affixed, the motion of the vessels in the unceasing waves wouldn't simply wrench it free.

As teams of marines cranked their handwheels, four thick and long screws extended from the top of the conning tower, around the short sucker-tube, bit into the bottom of the city-ship, and bore in. As the crew continued to crank the wheels, the screws raised the sucker-tube and pressed its lip tight against the bottom of the ship, compressing the coils of rope to form a seal.

When the crew could crank their wheels no more, they jumped away and rested their weary arms. *Dissolver of Sorrows* was now attached to the bottom of the gigantic Lyucu city-ship like a remora attached to a whale—or more precisely, a barnacle, the original image that had inspired Çami Phithadapu to come up with this plan.

"Ready?" asked Commander Tho.

The other marines and Takval nodded and backed up against the walls of the conning tower, some of them holding stakes and mallets, others cradling in their arms bundles of oakum—soft, fluffy hemp fiber treated with tar.

Commander Tho took a deep breath, reached above her head, and cranked the large central handwheel that sealed the hatch to the conning tower.

As soon as the circular hatch opened, water fell through in torrents, instantly drenching everyone in the conning tower and continuing to flow below into the aftercastle and the bridge.

"Pump!" shouted Commander Tho as she squatted next to the

access ladder and looked down into the aftercastle. Captain Gon's crew was already hard at work bailing the water into the bilge.

Meanwhile, the other marines in the conning tower, with Takval in the lead, battled the gushing water to plug the leaks. No matter how tightly they had cranked the screws, it was impossible to form a complete seal between the lip of the sucker-tube and the barnacle-encrusted bottom of the city-ship. Now they had to work as fast as they could to make the seam between the sucker-tube and the city-ship's hull watertight before the sea overwhelmed their efforts.

In order to make this job manageable, the sucker-tube had been made wide enough to admit only one person at a time. Tipo Tho had picked Takval as the lead worker for the task because he was slender and tall and could reach high into the sucker-tube, despite the fact that he wasn't an experienced sailor or shipwright. Two of the marines squatted and used their locked arms to form a platform to hoist the Agon prince into the tube.

Cold seawater poured down all around him, mimicking the sensation of drowning. But the hours of unrelenting practice under the tutelage of experienced sailors paid off as Takval fought off panic and pounded oakum into the seams between the bottom of the city-ship and the lip of the sucker-tube methodically. When he needed to take another breath, he jerked his knees in a certain pattern so that the marines supporting him would know to lower him. When a stake broke or he ran out of oakum, the other marines under him handed him replacements right away.

Gradually, the torrents of water slackened to trickles, and then ceased. Buckets of hot pitch were then passed up to Takval to be poured over the oakum to make the connection between the conning tower of *Dissolver of Sorrows* and the hull of the city-ship completely watertight and secure.

Takval was set down, and he heaved heavy breaths of relief. Smiling marines around him clapped him on the back and gave a low cheer of celebration. The good news was passed on to the rest of the ship. This was going far better than anyone had dared to hope.

"*Almost* there," said a grinning Takval. "We're heading into the belly of the beast." Cradling the shaft and bit of a large drill in his

arms, he was once again hoisted up to the new ceiling of the conning tower: the worm-ridden, barnacle-covered bottom of the city-
ship. Holding his breath against the powerful stench of wood long
immersed in the brine, he pressed the drill bit into the city-ship's
hull, and the rest of the marines began to push-pull the bow that
turned the bit.

"What a dirty trick!" screamed Radia. "The All-Father will punish all
of you!" The other Lyucu warriors gathered in the rigging and at the
bow of the city-ship howled in approval and knocked their clubs and
axes against each other.

The shadow garinafin, now united with the legendary pilot, had
returned to the angular shadow city of the Dara barbarians. But the
oversized pilot turned out to be more of a burden than a help, as the
garinafin labored to stay aloft with such a disproportionate passenger. Moreover, the Dara barbarians kept on flying various delicacies
up to the pilot with their kites: baskets of circular fruit, pigs fashioned
from pairs of circles, a flock of globulous sheep, even the inflated silhouette of an entire cow. The gluttonous pilot gobbled everything
sent up, and the shadow puppet swelled like a bloated bag of gas.

The music accompanying the show now turned playful and
mocking, with tinkling bells that sounded like laughter and horn
toots that imitated farts and lethargic drumbeats that suggested a
stomach that had been stuffed too full.

The enraged Lyucu warriors watched as the shadow garinafin,
weighed down by its useless passenger, slowed down even further,
and war kites from the city, squares trailing long, flapping tails,
attacked the buffoon pilot and his hapless mount like a flock of
swooping vultures pecking at a stupid, helpless, dying bull.

The horns on the kites played a mournful *wah-waaah* that mocked
this greedy, insatiable shadow Tenryo.

The anger of the Lyucu crew was now palpable. The shadow-
puppet play that had begun as an epic narrative about the glorious
struggles of a lone garinafin had by now morphed into a farce ridi-
culing Pékyu Tenryo—and by extension, the Lyucu people. The denigrating metaphor was too crude to be missed. Emotions swelled in

the crowd, and curses rang out all over the deck and in the rigging. Some of the Lyucu warriors tossed what they could get their hands on—cups, platters, food, bits of garbage—toward the faraway flickering screen. Others pounded their clubs and axes against the masts and deck of the city-ship, as if attacking their own ship would lend strength to the struggling fantasy pékyu. Still others climbed the rigging and tried to break the spars and battens. The torches that illuminated the deck flickered, as if frightened by the shift in the crew's mood.

Nacu Kitansli watched the growing chaos on his ship in disbelief.

The general revelry, combined with the intoxicating effects of the libations, chewed berries, and smoked leaves, had made the crew giddy and vulnerable to the emotional twists in the play. The thane deeply regretted allowing the crew to watch this performance, much less encouraging it.

It was too late. A group of culeks picked up a barrel of pemmican on deck and tossed it overboard, whooping and stomping their feet as though they had accomplished something grand and helpful. One naro smashed her fist into the nose of another—a combination of drunkenness and carelessness—and a brawl involving dozens soon spread across the deck. The shadow-puppet show in the distance was forgotten—only the sense of humiliation, of rage, of guilt at the deaths of so many comrades unavenged, remained.

Nacu shouted for the brawling, smashing, rioting crew to restore discipline, to behave. "Stop this! Calm down! We must watch the Dara with care!"

But he was met only with even more defiance.

"Why did you get picked to be left behind?" one of the brawling naros yelled.

Nacu's face darkened. This was a question that he had asked himself many times. Why had the fleet commander, Garinafin-Thane Pétan Tava, picked *him* to be the rear guard, the last ship to sail into Dara through the Wall of Storms? Was it a punishment? A lack of faith in his abilities? Did it show a kind of contempt for the Tribe of the Second Toe? The crew of *Boundless Pastures* had always felt that the crews of the other city-ships looked down on them because their thane had inherited his tiger-thanage rather than earned it in battle. And Nacu himself had always worried that his vacillation over whether to support Tanvanaki or Cudyu to be the designated successor to Pékyu Tenryo had earned him distrust among the other garinafin-thanes and tiger-thanes.

In the wake of the disaster that had befallen the rest of the fleet, Nacu had congratulated himself for being so fortunate as to escape their watery demise. But no matter how many times he told himself that his survival was a sign of the favor of the gods, the fact that he had been told to stay behind while the rest of the fleet pressed ahead to conquest rankled. To stay behind at the camp while the rest of the tribe went to war was the province of the aged, the crippled, mere children—it was what happened to those who were not great warriors at all.

"Sheepdog" was the nickname the other thanes used for Nacu Kitansli in private, in contrast to the wolf, the idealized image of every Lyucu thane.

"Is being *disciplined* and *calm* and *watching with care* how you intend to avenge our comrades?" shouted another warrior, this one a mere culek. "This is why the barbarians have put on that show! They are mocking us because they see the true color of your liver."

The words stung. The crew's earlier praise for the thane had been forgotten like so much sea-foam whipped away by the uncertain wind of passion. Thane Nacu understood that he was facing the most dangerous challenge to his authority on this voyage.

"Send the rioters into the hold!" he barked at the naros-votan around him, most of them from the Tribe of the Second Toe instead of the other tribes that had been forced to contribute warriors for this mission. "No food and water for three days!"

The naros-votan hesitated, uncertain that they wanted to fight the incipient mutiny for the benefit of a thane who appeared to have lost the respect of the crew. A big Lyucu tribe like the Second Toe was an aggregation of smaller tribes, each of which consisted of multiple clans. The naros-votan were all either chieftains of the small tribes or clan heads, and some of the rioters were their own relatives.

"If this turns into a real mutiny, do you think you'll escape unscathed?" Thane Nacu hissed. "Does anyone here harbor the fantasy of replacing me? Remember, there are warriors from seven different tribes here, and they obey me *only* because Pékyu-taasa Cudyu put me in charge. With me gone, this city-ship will revert to the state of the scrublands before the unification, and the Second Toe will be outnumbered."

The naros-votan looked at one another, then turned to the agitating crew and raised their clubs.

The rioting naros and culeks bellowed with rage. Fueled by kyof-fir and tolyusa and the blood-boiling excitement of smashing their fists and clubs into anything, anyone, they rushed at the naros-votan and other warriors still loyal to the thane. Soon, the deck had turned into a battlefield; howls, screams, groans, and the muffled thwacks of club meeting flesh spread across the ship.

"This is madness," said Radia, inching away from the spreading melee. Whenever a red-eyed combatant came too near, she shoved them away.

"I told you there's witchcraft involved," said Toof. Their involuntary sobriety had saved them from descending into the general mania.

"We have to get away from here," said Radia, jumping out of the way of a bone club tumbling end over end through the air. It ended its flight with a thump against the chest of an unwary culek, instantly felling him to the deck.

They weren't the only ones with that idea. Across the deck, naros and culeks who had no interest in participating in a spontaneous mutiny or its suppression inched their way toward the hatches leading belowdecks, seeking shelter from this man-made storm. Singly or by twos and threes, they gathered at the hatches and climbed down the ladders into the interior of the ship, where the provisions were stored and most of the crew had their quarters.

As Radia and Toof descended into the ship, away from the tumult on deck, they heard a muffled *boom* somewhere deep inside the ship, followed moments later by the panicked lowing of a garinafin.

# CHAPTER NINE

# THE BARNACLE
# AND THE WHALE

ALONG THE BELT CURRENT TO UKYU-GONDÉ: THE
SIXTH MONTH IN THE FIRST YEAR OF THE REIGN
OF SEASON OF STORMS.

After what seemed like an eternity of backbreaking labor, Commander Tho's boarding party breached the outer planking, climbed through the gap in the city-ship's ribs—they were lucky that the sucker-tube happened to attach to a spot on the hull between ribs—and drilled through the inner planking. In this effort they were aided not only by a good supply of fresh drill bits that could be swapped in as old ones were dulled, but also by a foul-odored mixture prepared by the fleet's alchemists, designed to quickly rot and weaken wood.

Slimy bilgewater from the city-ship poured through the hole into the conning tower, requiring yet more pumping and bailing by the crew. For a few tense moments, there was some concern that the large bilge of the city-ship would overwhelm the relatively small volume inside *Dissolver of Sorrows*. Though Admiral Roso, an expert on the history of shipbuilding, had reassured everyone that the city-ships were internally partitioned into watertight compartments and the boarding party would be dealing only with a small portion of the bilge, not the whole thing, when the slimy, filthy torrent finally stopped, everyone aboard heaved a sigh of relief.

Takval climbed through the hole in the inner hull into the dark interior of the city-ship, a spelunker entering an unexplored cave. Light beams from the conning tower shot up into the cavernous space and dissipated in the murk before they could strike the ceiling far above. For a moment he stayed still on the slimy floor, listening for signs that the Lyucu had discovered their entrance. But the only noise that greeted him was the muffled pounding of the waves against the hull.

"All clear," he called into the conning tower below him.

"Go, go!" ordered Commander Tho. There was no telling for how long *Dissolver of Sorrows*, the outsized barnacle attached to the bottom of the city-ship, would remain undiscovered.

One by one, marines, sailors, and even some civilian volunteers climbed through the narrow passage, carrying whale-oil lanterns that lit up the dank, smelly, enormous bilge. A small hole like the one they had drilled in the bottom of the ship was not enough to sink a city-ship. It was only an opening in the skin of the apple to let in the caterpillars. Next, they had to tunnel through the apple's flesh to maximize the damage.

Silently, stealthily, marines fanned out through the decks to find choke points where they could hold off anyone coming down to investigate. As long as the shadow-puppet play continued to distract the Lyucu crew and kept them on the top deck, there shouldn't be a large-scale response. But it was important to prevent any straggling Lyucu going about the ship from raising an alarm.

Meanwhile, other members of the boarding party climbed into neighboring compartments in the bilge and higher decks to drill more holes where the inner planking had already been weakened through normal wear. Once the holes were made, slender-figured dancers, acrobats, kite-scouts, former aviators—and even a few noodle-armed scholars who wanted to contribute with their bodies as well as their minds—clambered into the space between the ribs in the ship's frame, where they slithered through the claustrophobic gap between the inner and outer planking. Their goal: places below or near the waterline where the outer planking also felt particularly weak or rotten.

At these locations, they installed the wall-buster bombs—small ceramic cylinders filled with firework powder designed to burst open like a blossoming flower when set off. These were originally intended as siege weaponry against earthen walls and tools of sabotage against enemy airships in dock, but they would serve equally well against wooden ship hulls if properly planted. The long fuses were then run back into the interior of the city-ship, to be lit when the boarding party was ready to evacuate.

Earlier that week, one of the scholars in Théra's fleet, a young Cultivationist named Razutana Pon, had complained to Princess Théra about the military arm of the expedition.

"They're nigh insufferable!"

"What exactly have they done now?" asked Théra. The Cultivationists followed one of the smaller branches of philosophy among the Hundred Schools. Their primary interest was in the histories and practices of farming, breeding, stock and varietal improvement, and similar subjects. Théra had specifically wanted some Cultivationists along, hoping their expertise would be of use in the new land.

"The marines, submariners, and former aviators strut across the decks and swagger through the narrow passageways, unwilling to yield to oncoming scholars." Razutana gestured passionately, moved by his own accounting of the insults he had suffered. "They act as if they own the place!"

"Since we're preparing for a military operation," explained Théra patiently, "the fighters have to carry out lots of orders in very little time. I'm sure they were just in a hurry to get to where they needed to be, and no insult was intended."

"Your Highness, you make too many excuses for them! If I were part of this military operation, would I also be granted the privilege of peacocking around the ship like a champion rooster and glaring at everyone who doesn't get out of the way?"

"But you're a scholar, not a warrior," said Théra, rather befuddled by Razutana's conflicting avian imagery.

"Who says that only muscle-bound soldiers have a monopoly on courage? Emperor Ragin himself was a scholar, too. In fact, I think it could be argued that he was a Cultivationist like me. He did plant rice in the Palace Garden."

"Er . . ." Théra had to suppress a giggle. She could only imagine the face of her father upon learning that he had been claimed by one of the minor schools of philosophy as a role model. "I mean no disrespect to my own father—or the learned Cultivationists—but it is well known that the emperor belonged to no school and was not particularly studious."

"It's true that the emperor never attained the rank of *firoa*—"

"—or even *toko dawiji*. In fact, I doubt my father had any scholastic ambition—"

"Your Highness, please let me *finish*. The emperor's school affiliation or academic accomplishments are *not* the point. The point is, as a child, the emperor was once inspired by the words of Kon Fiji to defend his friend Rin Coda from arrows raining out of the sky, an incident well-known by every teahouse storyteller. From this, we can infer that scholarship is directly correlated with courage. The more books read, the greater the warrior."

"You know, I think my father would have enjoyed chatting with you," Théra said, straining to maintain a serious face. "You show . . . certain patterns of mind that he would have appreciated."

By the time Razutana finally left, he had somehow convinced Théra to make him a member of the boarding party.

Razutana had volunteered for this assault on the city-ship to prove his mettle, but the reality of a military assault was nothing like what he had imagined. There was so much chaos and confusion! Nothing was happening on schedule. True, he had been told that he would have to help with pumping water, but he had never imagined that the inside of the city-ship's bilge would smell so bad—worse even than a latrine that hadn't been cleaned for a week! And climbing through the sucker-tube was horrible: He discovered that he had a fear of tight spaces. As he panicked, his hair bun caught against the inner surface of the narrow tube and prevented him from moving forward. When those behind him pushed impatiently, he had to bite his tongue from screaming with pain as he was shoved forward in the tube, clumps of hair being ripped out by the roots in the process.

But that wasn't all. His turn came to crawl between the inner and outer planking to plant a wall-buster.

"There might be . . . ra-ra-rats in there!" he wailed, staring at the tiny, dark opening as if expecting monsters to leap out of it at any moment.

A sailor who had been a dancer in her former life in Dara laughed, shaking her head. "I'll do this one, Pon-*ji*," she said, adding the honorific for great teachers in mockery. She slid easily into the hole without a second look. The marines who had drilled the hole chuckled as they stole glances at Razutana out of the corners of their eyes.

Humiliated, Razutana slunk away. He couldn't bear to remain in the presence of his comrades any longer. Concealing his face behind an upheld sleeve, he backed out of their sight and fled down the nearest corridor. He kept on climbing and running until his flushed cheeks had cooled down enough for him to contemplate his next move.

*Since I'm already in the upper decks, I might as well investigate the rest of the ship.*

Perhaps he could redeem himself by discovering some interesting secret. And by the time he was ready to return to the bilge, the shameful incident would have been forgotten.

Holding a whale-oil lantern, shuttered so that only a narrow beam of light shot from the front, he wandered through the deserted passageways of the massive vessel. He wasn't too concerned that he would run into a Lyucu barbarian—they were all up on the top deck, watching the play that Princess Théra had written to ensnare them.

A series of staterooms opened off both sides of one long passageway. At the time of Emperor Mapidéré's original expedition, these had been quarters for the craftspeople and skilled artisans traveling with the fleet. Each stateroom, though small, had been equipped with a sliding door and partitioned into social and private spaces by internal screens. The arrangement gave the occupants some privacy and the freedom to decorate the space as they liked, providing a spiritual refuge on the long and uncertain voyage across the sea.

But the sliding doors and internal partitions had long been ripped out. Now Lyucu warriors were packed into the cabins, four to a room.

Bones and refuse littered the floors, and the walls showed disrepair and damage. Some rooms had been so wrecked—it was hard to tell whether from planned weapons practice or kyoffir intoxication—that they had been abandoned and converted into midden heaps. Rats skittered into the shadows as Razutana's footsteps approached, and maggots wriggled in the beam from his lamp like living grains of rice.

The Lyucu were treating these rooms not as homes, but as a temporary campsite to be abandoned as soon as better pastures and hunting grounds were found. Would they do the same to the Islands of Dara?

Razutana shuddered, no more willing to follow these unsettling thoughts than he was to chase after the rats. There was nothing he could do to directly help his aged parents or newborn nieces, who were still facing the Lyucu threat inside the Wall of Storms. He had to do what he could to contribute to Princess Théra's expedition into the Lyucu heartland and cut off further reinforcements for the enemy.

He turned a corner and found himself in a tall passageway at least three decks in height. The end of the passageway opened into a wide bay, and there was a set of massive sliding doors in the wall on the right. The doors weren't shut fully, and there was a narrow crack down the middle. Given the size of the doors, Razutana guessed that the compartment behind had likely originally been intended as a warehouse for stage equipment and war machinery that could be used to impress any immortals Mapidéré's expedition happened upon.

*But what is being stored in there now? Some kind of secret war engine?*

Curious, Razutana crept up to the seam between the sliding doors. A powerful animal stench emanated from within. Razutana shielded his nose with one sleeve, held up his lamp with the other, and peeked in.

He stared directly into the eye of a garinafin. The size of a dinner plate, the pupil-less orb glistened in the light of the whale-oil lamp like a malevolent negative sun, absorbing rather than giving off light. The creature, clearly surprised, snorted through its sewer-pipe nose, and the eruption of fetid air blasted Razutana with a spray of slimy snot.

Razutana stumbled back and fell onto his bottom. Terror suffused every inch of his body, dulling his senses as he envisioned himself being incinerated by garinafin breath. Instinctively, he scooted rearward on the floor, and cried out as something hard pressed into the small of his back. He reached behind and wrapped his fingers around a ceramic cylinder tucked into his belt. In his hurry to get away from the scene of his humiliation, he had forgotten to hand back the wall-buster to the marines.

The gigantic beast lowed, a deep rumble that made the hairs on his back stand up. Then it glared at him balefully with a single eye. The seam between the sliding door panels widened as the beast pressed against them, straining to pop out of their grooves.

*I'm going to die. I'm going to die. I'm going to . . .*

Almost without thinking, the terrified Razutana fumbled with the cylinder, lit the fuse, and tossed it into the crack between the massive door panels, straight into the face of the curious garinafin. The bomb struck the garinafin on the nose, fell to the ground, and rolled until it came to a stop somewhere under the beast. Razutana's vision contracted into a narrow tunnel whose end was the sputtering fuse.

The monster dipped its head to examine the sparkling object on the floor more closely.

Razutana scrambled onto his feet and ran back into the passageway he had come from, too terrified to even scream. As he turned the corner, a loud explosion behind him shook the deck like an earthquake. He kept on running.

A moment later, he heard an enraged bellow of pain and shock, and the passageway behind him lit up like dawn, throwing his stark, quivering shadow ahead of his pumping legs.

"What was that thunder-like noise?" exclaimed Radia.

"Whatever it was, it spooked the poor garinafins!" said Toof.

"Listen. More noises!"

The very frame of the ship thrummed with rhythmic thuds, as

though someone were striking at it with an enormous mallet. The Lyucu warriors trying to escape the turmoil on the top deck froze, unsure what was going on.

The thumping stopped.

More moans, screeches, long mournful lowing.

There were only three adult garinafins aboard *Boundless Pastures*. Amidst the distressed lowing from the two other garinafins, Toof and Radia could also hear the angry howls and screams of Tana, their erstwhile mount.

Toof grabbed a torch near the ladder leading down from the open hatch and ran toward the noise.

"What are you doing?" demanded Radia. "We have no idea what's going on down there!"

"Tana is my tribe!" shouted Toof, not slowing down at all.

Radia stomped her foot in frustration. But she couldn't just leave her partner to face the danger alone, and after only a moment of hesitation, she took off after him. The other Lyucu warriors followed close behind, uncertain what was going on.

Through a maze of mostly dark passageways, hatches, ladders, and narrow stairs—the rationing of torches and lighting tallow had led to much of the city-ship being kept in perpetual darkness—Toof directed the motley gang toward a wide passageway that led to Tana's stable. Originally intended as a loading bay for the warehouse that had been converted to a garinafin stable, the passageway featured a ceiling that opened to an enormous hatchway in the top deck. When the giant hatch doors were flipped open, the garinafins could use the wide space as a runway to take off from the city-ship.

Toof pushed through the last set of doors leading to the loading bay and skidded to a stop, and Radia and the others almost collided into him. No explanation was necessary as a wall of heat struck them in the face, and across the open space of the bay, roaring flames burned in the stable, whose sliding doors had been smashed apart. Smoke was quickly filling the bay, making it impassable. Already the Lyucu warriors were breaking into hacking coughs.

"What in the All-Father's name happened!?" exclaimed Radia.

Toof shook his head. "Something must have really frightened Tana."

"She's not in there, bless Péa, and neither are the other garinafins. I can hear her moaning. . . . She must have smashed her way deeper into the ship."

"We have to find her," said Toof.

"But how are we going to get down there through all this smoke?"

"We've got to get the hatch open to clear the smoke."

Normally, the heavy hatch had to be winched open from the deck above. But in case of emergencies, it was possible to open it from the inside by cranking two capstans that raised the doors on thick poles. While his companions waited by the capstans, Toof climbed up the tall ladder at the side of the bay. Fighting against the thickening smoke, he finally got to the bulky cables at the top lashing the hatch doors shut. Taking out his flint dagger from an arm-sheath, he hacked and slashed at the cables.

The air in the room was so hot that the doors popped open as soon as the last cable was cut. The thick smoke swirled out, clearing the air, but the fire in the stable on the opposite side of the bay, suddenly fed by a gust of fresh wind, also leapt higher with a *fwump*.

Toof squinted against the bright light from the fire and peered into the gloom of the open space below, and his jaw dropped as a column of Dara barbarians emerged into the bay from a side passage.

As soon as she heard the muffled explosion above, Commander Tipo Tho knew that the boarding party had run out of time. There was no way that the Lyucu wouldn't know that something had gone wrong.

She held out a hand to Takval.

"It's time," she said.

"Surely we can keep at it a little longer," pleaded the Agon prince.

Tipo shook her head. "The princess was clear that we must not take unnecessary risks."

Reluctantly, the Agon prince handed her his massive war club. Unlike the bone-and-teeth weapons traditionally wielded by the people of the scrublands, this one was made from ironwood, with a bronze-sheathed head and two curved metal spikes that resembled the scrubland tiger's tusks. It had been a betrothal gift from Princess Théra—and a way to show how knowledge of metalworking in Dara could benefit the Agon in their war against the Lyucu.

Wielding the club with both arms, Tipo slammed it three times against the nearest rib of the ship like a mallet, pausing in between. She waited a few seconds and slammed the club against the rib five more times in quick succession. Another few seconds. Another three strikes with pauses in between.

She handed the club back to Takval.

The sound reverberated through the city-ship's thick wooden skeleton. This was a common technique for crew members spread out across the vast frame of an airship to communicate with one another. The pattern she had tapped out was the prearranged signal for everyone in the crawl space between the inner and outer planking, as well as those who had gone up to scout and hold choke points, to *get out*.

Like rats emerging from their warrens, the dancers, acrobats, scholars, former aviators, and kite-scouts crawled out of the holes in the hull of the ship, trailing fuses behind them. They raced to the compartment above the bilge, the emergency rallying point, where dozens of fuses were gathered into a single spot.

"Well done, everyone!" shouted Commander Tipo Tho. "I'll light the fuses as soon as the boarding party is safely back on *Dissolver of Sorrows*."

"Wait," said Takval. "Have we planted enough bombs to sink the ship? When you drilled us on this, we had planned for a lot more time."

"It can't be helped," said Tipo. "Even the best-made battle plans never survive an encounter with the enemy. We just have to hope that what we've done is enough."

"How long does it take for the bombs to go off?" asked Takval, who had no intuitive understanding of the Dara ways of making war.

"With some of the longer fuses, as long as it takes to boil an egg."

"So there's plenty of time for the Lyucu to put them out if they get down here," said Takval. "And rising water may also extinguish some of the fuses."

"Captain Gon and I have gone through all these scenarios," said Tipo impatiently. "We expect some of the bombs to be duds, yes."

"But with the reduced number of bombs we've been able to plant, will our plan still work?"

Tipo Tho said nothing.

"Even if the bombs do go off, if the compartments flood slowly, the Lyucu crew can plug them, can't they?" Takval persisted.

Tipo Tho gritted her teeth. "Yes, there is such a possibility. A skilled Dara crew could probably shore up the leaks made by a few wall-busters, if discovered in time. But the Lyucu are not expert sailors—they didn't even build these ships." Only out of respect for Princess Théra was Tipo Tho tolerating these questions. What little goodwill the prince had built up with her during the last few days was quickly dissipating. The barbarian noble seemed not to have any understanding of the urgency of their situation.

"Don't underestimate the 'barbarians,'" said Takval. "I know you think little of the people of the scrublands, Lyucu or Agon. But Pékyu Tenryo's army managed to seize the city-ships from your people and sailed all the way across the ocean and through the Wall of Storms. They're *not* stupid."

Tipo Tho's face flushed. "What do you expect to do about that *now*? Can't you hear that?" She pointed above her.

Everyone quieted. Ponderous, slow footsteps thumped on some distant deck above them, punctuated now and then by a low moan or a long screech.

"A garinafin is loose," muttered Takval. "Why would they do such a thing?"

Razutana, who had just staggered back into the assembly spot, looked shamefaced at this.

"We have to get out," said Tipo Tho. "Pray what we've done is enough."

"No!" said Takval. "We can do more. I'll go up there and cause as much chaos as possible and fight off anyone trying to come down here to investigate. The longer I can hold them off, the longer the bombs have to do their work and the more water can flood through any leaks. Every extra second increases the chance of success."

"That's not the plan. The princess specifically said that no one is to—"

"The princess doesn't command me," said Takval, a wolfish grin on his face. "She has her way of doing things, and I have mine." He turned to the other marines, who had stopped climbing down the ladder into the bilge to watch this exchange. "Anyone want to join me?"

The marines immediately shouted their assent.

"You won't be able to get back to *Dissolver of Sorrows*," warned Tipo Tho. "And you may not be able to get off this ship at all, at least not alive."

The marines made no acknowledgment that they had heard. They climbed back up the ladder to stand next to Takval.

"I can knock you out right now and drag you back to the ship," said Tipo Tho, glaring at Takval and holding tight to the hilt of her sword. "The princess doesn't need sacrifices. *You* are needed for the future."

"The princess knows when she needs counsel and when she must be resolute in her will, as do I," countered Takval. "Her planning and cunning, the hard work by everyone in the fleet the last few days, the lives of the men and women on this expedition, the fate of my people—all depend on this moment, on the success of *today*."

They stared at each other, and after a moment, both seemed to find in the eyes of the other what they were looking for.

Takval turned and jogged toward the stairs leading to the upper decks, a lantern in one hand and his war club held over his shoulder, never looking back.

Tipo Tho took a step forward, but she did not draw her sword.

"You'll have to show me how to make that monkeyberry and ice melon compote," Takval called out as he ascended the stairs. "I'm holding you to that promise."

The other marines who had volunteered looked at one another and turned to Tipo. "Sorry, Commander."

Tipo Tho waved her hand. "Go." And after a moment, she added, "May the gods of Dara . . . and of Gondé watch over you."

∾

Nacu Kitansli wasn't sure whether to be grateful to the gods or to curse them for buffeting him with surprise after surprise on this day. His mood had risen and fallen so many times that he felt like a ship seized by the Wall of Storms looming on the port side: lifted on the crest of a mountainous wave one moment; plunged into an abyssal trough the next.

The instant the forward hatch of the ship blew open and thick smoke poured out, the brawling mutineers as well as the naros-votan and warriors still loyal to the thane jumped back and stopped their fighting. The shocking sight was like a thundershower on the scrublands, drenching both sides and washing away the haze of intoxication and battle-lust, leaving only confounded silence. All stood frozen, uncertain why they had even been fighting.

Even the distant shadow play on the giant screen hung between the Dara ships stopped, as if the barbarians weren't sure what to make of the thick column of smoke rising above the city-ship, glowing from the smoldering fire in the ship's bowels like a volcano about to erupt.

The screeching and bellowing of a rampaging garinafin stumbling through the decks below, however, brought Thane Nacu back to life.

"Save the ship!" he shouted. "Put out that fire now if you want to live!"

The crew scrambled into action. An out-of-control garinafin was one of the worst disasters that could befall a Lyucu ship at sea. If they didn't get the beast and the fire under control as quickly as possible, they were all doomed.

Warriors who had only moments earlier been at each other's throats now jostled to work together, attaching hoses to barrels stacked on deck, hauling water in tubs up from the sea, passing buckets from hand to hand to drench the deck before the fire made its way up from the hold into the rigging and sails.

Nacu, his heart leaping wildly with joy that the gods had seen fit to strangle this mutiny—albeit with an equally dangerous threat to his ship—rushed to the hatch and looked down. Through the smoke and shimmering heated air, he saw a group of Lyucu warriors fighting against—could it be?—strangers dressed in the garb of Dara.

"Barbarians! Spies! We've been boarded!" he screamed, not caring how shrill his voice had grown or that he was flapping his arms like a child who had seen a scrubland snake for the first time.

"Votan!" One of the culeks ran up to him. "What horror! What cunning! May Cudyufin's blessed light preserve us! What deceit! What witchcraft! May Nalyufin—"

The fact that someone was even more panicked than he served to calm the thane down. "What is it? Spit it out!"

"I . . . we were"—the terrified culek gestured at a group of Lyucu warriors standing by the starboard gunwale, pointing and jabbering excitedly—"hauling up a tub of seawater to help put out the fire. We . . . we thought we saw a whale—"

"What are you babbling about?" screamed Nacu. "This isn't the time to worry about whales. Get down there and fight the barbarian boarders—"

"That's where they're coming from!" The culek hopped and gesticulated wildly. "There's a Dara ship down there, *under the water*! It's biting into the bottom of the ship!"

*Dissolver of Sorrows* had latched onto the bottom of the city-ship on the starboard side of the keel. As the city-ship rolled and pitched in the waves, the bow hooks had come undone, swinging the much smaller Dara ship into view if sailors on the city-ship looked directly down over the side.

Ever since *Boundless Pastures* had begun to chase the Dara fleet, Nacu had been sleeping poorly, haunted by nightmares of barbarian warriors who rode on magical ships that could bypass the Wall of Storms by materializing out of thin air. That these vague hunches were becoming *true* was simply too much. "Kill the whale-ship! *Kill them!*"

The culek stared at him. "How?"

"*I don't care.* Chop down the mast and spear their ship with it if you have to. But *kill them now!*"

A thunderous crash. *Dissolver of Sorrows* shook from stern to bow like a speared fish.

"What happened?" Princess Théra struggled to get up from the floor in the darkness that permeated the captain's quarters.

"We've been hit!" cried Captain Nméji Gon. "Something struck us directly over the bow from above."

"We've been sighted," said Çami Phithadapu. She pointed outside the transom windows. Indeed, a reddish glow suffused the water—bright torches had been lit above and were being held over the gunwale of the city-ship.

"Damage?" asked Théra.

"A crack in the forecastle, and we're taking on water," said Captain Nméji Gon. "But the hole isn't big and can be plugged. Looks like they were dropping whatever they could find on hand over the side." He paused as footsteps boomed in the conning tower above him. "The boarding party is returning. They say that a garinafin is loose aboard the city-ship, and we have to detach as soon as possible."

"Get some lights!" ordered Théra. "No point in staying in the dark when they already know we're here."

Another thunderous crash, and the ship shook again. Théra braced herself against a bulkhead so that she didn't fall.

"Another hit on the forecastle," said Captain Nméji Gon. "We're lucky the aim was off and the missile bounced off the side. Given the height of the city-ship, if they drop a stone in the right place, we'll be stove-in."

Théra stumbled onto the bridge in the aftercastle and anxiously watched as men and women clambered down the ladder from the conning tower one by one, rushing forward to the front of the ship to help with plugging the leak and bailing.

"Is everyone aboard?" asked Théra when the ladder was clear. "Where's Takval?"

"He's not coming," said Tipo Tho, the last member of the boarding party to descend from the conning tower, poking her head down from the conning tower. "He went into the upper decks with a team of marines to try to slow down the Lyucu and give the bombs more time to do damage."

"I told him *not* to always look for an excuse to play the hero!" Théra was enraged. "Get back up there and drag him back."

"We won't survive another hit," said Captain Nméji Gon. "And lookouts in the forecastle report coracles being lowered into the water from the city-ship. If they board us and pry open the hatches, it's all over."

"I've already lit the fuses," said Commander Tipo Tho. "If we don't get out of here when the wall-busters blow, the sinking city-ship is going to crush us."

Théra closed her eyes and cursed the gods under her breath. The plan had called for the boarding party to be safely back aboard *Dissolver of Sorrows*, and for the ship to sail away under cover of darkness, before the wall-busters blew. Somehow everything had collapsed into a tangled mess, and nothing was working the way it had been planned.

And everyone was looking to *her* to decide what to do.

"Your Highness," said Admiral Roso, "you must honor the wishes of Prince Takval and the other marines who went with him. The best-laid plan in the world is no match for the unpredictable storms of reality. He tried to adapt to the winds, and so should you."

The other officers nodded and murmured their assent.

Théra felt very, very alone.

*Are they offering me counsel or are they telling me what to do? Is this a challenge to my authority? Damn you, Takval! Why did you defy me? It's hard enough to know the right thing to do in calm waters, much less in the midst of a storm of doubt in your heart.*

"And if I tell you to stay here until Takval and his marines are rescued?" asked Théra, her eyes narrowed. Though she was straining hard, she couldn't keep the tremors out of her voice.

There was a moment of silence as the officers looked back at her, shadows flitting across their faces in the flickering torchlight.

"Then I will organize a new boarding party and lead it myself," said Admiral Roso. "*Rénga*, you may be called princess now, but in my heart you'll always be Empress Üna, the rightful heir to your father."

"Then *Dissolver of Sorrows* will hold fast to this anchorage," said Captain Gon, puffing his chest out. "Even if this ship is smashed to smithereens, I will stay here, clinging on to the city-ship with my teeth and nails."

"Then I will fight up through the burning decks to find Prince Takval," said Commander Tho. "I care not if I must slay man, garinafin, or even a god. Men and women must be willing to die for great lords who recognize their talent. Emperor Ragin elevated me from a farmer's daughter to command an airship. To die for his daughter would not repay a tenth of the debt I owe him."

Théra looked at the resolute faces around her. Was Takval's decision the right one after all? Was she so angry with him because she truly believed that it was possible to succeed without losing anyone, or was it merely because he had defied her? She needed to assert her authority, but was this the right way? Her mother, Empress Jia, had always said that she wanted the best for the people of Dara, and rode roughshod over everyone else's ideas. Her father, on the other hand, had always been known to listen to the counsel of his advisers. Should she take her cue from her mother or father?

Whatever she decided, someone was going to die.

*These people are ready to die for me because I am my father's daughter, not because they believe I'm right. Who can blame them? I don't even trust myself.*

"Detach from the city-ship," she ordered, her tone flat. "Surface and get us out of here."

Captain Gon barked a series of orders as Commander Tho went back up into the conning tower with a few marines to close the hatch and to detach the screws that held *Dissolver of Sorrows* fast to the city-ship.

An eternity of a few minutes later, *Dissolver of Sorrows* was free from the Lyucu vessel. As the city-ship continued to sail forward, the underwater Dara ship dove lower to slip beneath its wake. Once it was completely behind the city-ship, it would be able to surface and get away before the wall-busters blew.

Another thunderous crash, louder than any that had come before, and the ship shook from side to side like a quivering arrow. The deck tilted violently until the bow of the ship was pointed downward at a sharp angle. Everyone tumbled to the deck.

"Report!" shouted Théra before she had even climbed back up.

"They dropped a large stone directly through the forecastle," said

Captain Gon after he had had a chance to assess the situation. "Four sailors are dead and six wounded. The forecastle is flooded. We are losing buoyancy."

"Surface now!" ordered Théra. Even she, no expert sailor, understood the gravity of the situation.

Captain Gon issued another series of urgent orders through the system of wooden clappers. As damage-control teams rushed at the forecastle with wooden planks and sandbags and long nails in a desperate bid to slow down the flooding, engineers at the buoyancy controls pumped the bellows to drive all remaining water out of the ballast tanks to give the ship a chance at escaping the clutches of Lord Tazu's deadly realm.

The deck tilted at an even steeper angle as the stern of the ship, where the captain's quarters, bridge, and aftercastle were located, rose up and shot for the surface. Everything slid off the tables, shelves, and other horizontal surfaces. The floor turned into a sheer cliff as everyone, from sailors to marines to the princess herself, grabbed onto anything that could serve as a handhold to stop sliding into the bow of the ship.

With a booming eruption, *Dissolver of Sorrows* shot out of the sea, stern-first, like some kind of reverse-breaching whale, and then settled back onto the turbulent waves. Water gushed out of the forecastle in cascading sheets as sailors fought to patch the jagged hole.

Just as Théra heaved a sigh of relief and was about to climb up from the floor, the ship shook with another loud crash. The sound of splintering wood filled the bridge, and Captain Gon's face blanched.

"We've been dismasted," he said after another series of damage reports. "The Lyucu have gotten to their stone-throwers and destroyed the main mast. They've doused the sails to keep pace with us. There's no way we can get the other two masts up or the sails rigged as long as they can cover the deck with their slingshots and stone-throwers. Anyone we send onto the deck will be slaughtered."

"So we have no way to move, even though we're on the surface?" asked Théra.

Captain Gon nodded. "We can't deploy oars, either. Same problem. One more direct hit from a stone-thrower will likely doom the ship."

Théra slammed her fist into the nearest bulkhead. Her hesitancy had cost them precious time, allowing the Lyucu to land a killing blow. And now they had lost their only means of escape.

"When are those wall-busters going to blow?"

As a garinafin groom for Pékyu Tenryo, Takval had witnessed plenty of bloody and confusing battles in his life, but for sheer strangeness, the battle aboard the Lyucu city-ship surpassed them all.

Through the smoke, Takval rushed at the first Lyucu warrior he saw, the man who had slid down the ladder leading up to the now-open loading-bay hatch doors. The man's eyes were red and tear-filled from the billowing smoke, and Takval thought he made a tempting target.

But the man nimbly dodged out of the way, and Takval's Dara war club thunked into the floor, where one of the metal spikes bit into the wood and held. The Lyucu fighter was quick and sure-footed, despite the heated air, the swirling smoke, and the fact that he had just dropped down the equivalent of multiple decks. Takval was sure that he was a garinafin rider.

Takval struggled to free his club. Since Agon slaves in Taten weren't allowed weapons at all, Takval had to practice fighting in secret with bones picked out of the middens. He had little actual battle experience and was unfamiliar with the characteristics of metal weapons.

Meanwhile, the Lyucu had pulled his own weapon, a war club of cattle-bone and wolf's teeth, off his back. Takval managed to free his club and lunged at him, and metal and bone clashed in midair. The wolf's teeth embedded in the head of the Lyucu's club shattered and one of the bones making up the handle broke.

Takval's heart leapt wildly, and he laughed out loud. He, an inexperienced fighter at best, had just disarmed a Lyucu garinafin rider. This was what metal weapons could do against bone and teeth. *This* was the point of the Agon alliance with Dara.

~

Toof jumped back after parrying the stranger's blow, his arm numb from the impact. After a shocked glance at what remained of his ruined weapon, he examined his opponent carefully: Though the tall man wore the armor of Dara, his loose hairstyle, his pale skin, and his fighting style all spoke of the scrublands.

"What are you doing?" he shouted at the man. "You're Lyucu!"

The Lyucu warrior's exclamation caused an unexpected surge of emotion in Takval's heart. As an enslaved Agon, there should have been nothing more insulting than to be mistaken for a member of the hated Lyucu. Yet, his first reaction had been a raw burst of joy . . . a sense of familiarity and of being home.

For months he had been alone among the Dara, a strange people with powerful machines and arcane knowledge, but who also looked down upon the people of the scrublands, though some of them tried to conceal their contempt. He had not been able to speak his own language to anyone except in lessons with Princess Théra, and she was far too busy with leading the expedition to devote the necessary attention to speaking it well.

Hearing the familiar syllables of the speech of the scrublands, even in the accent of a Lyucu topolect, felt shockingly beautiful. He had not realized how much he missed home until now, and he wanted to hear more.

"I'm Takval," he said. "An Agon, actually."

"Oh? I'm Toof."

It was so bizarre to make introductions in the middle of a pitched battle that for a moment, both men hesitated, unsure whether "Well met" or "It's an honor" was in order.

Toof was the first to recover. He tossed away his ruined club, backed up to the wall of the loading bay, and picked up a shovel from one of the hooks. The handle was thick and solid, and Toof hoped the iron blade would stand up against Takval's club better than his bone club. Originally intended as a demonstration of Dara's farming techniques for the benefit of the immortals Krita's expedition was supposed to locate, it had been re-appropriated by the Lyucu crew to clean garinafin dung.

Takval, recovering his wits in turn, lunged after Toof. Though Takval was taller and stronger—he had, after all, been well fed and rested in Dara during the months when the Lyucu were on rations on the open sea—he deliberately fought with less than full strength.

"How did you come to fight with these barbarians?" asked Toof.

"Wouldn't you like to know?"

They danced and parried in the firelight from the burning stable, as smoke swirled around them, as sweat glistened on their skin, as their hair singed in the heat. Club struck shovel like a tiger's tusk colliding with a garinafin claw.

"How many of you are here?"

"Hundreds," boasted Takval. "Your ship is lost."

Toof didn't know what to think. The idea that the Lyucu's ancient enemy had somehow managed to cross the ocean to join forces with the Dara barbarians was too absurd to contemplate. But then again, was it any more absurd than the idea of Dara barbarians teleporting across miles of open sea to board *Boundless Pastures*?

The two opponents snarled at each other and clashed again. Lunging, leaping, feinting, quickstepping, sweeping, kicking, smashing, the two seemed evenly matched, and both realized this was going to be a long fight.

But Takval's marines were another story. As many of them had been former aviators chosen for this boarding mission on account of their smaller physiques and quickness rather than brute strength, they were gradually overwhelmed by the relentless assault of the Lyucu warriors, who, despite the long journey across the sea, were generally physically stronger and more practiced with hand-to-hand combat. The slender swords the marines carried also had trouble parrying the heavy bone clubs. The marines retreated into a huddle with their backs to each other to better defend against the Lyucu fighters, who not only outnumbered the Dara marines but whose ranks continued to swell as reinforcements arrived from the top deck.

A marine screamed as two Lyucu warriors found an opening in her defenses and smashed her wrist, her sword clattering to the floor. Before the marine could retreat or her companions could come to her aid, two war clubs bashed into her skull from opposite directions, and bloody brains and skull fragments rained over all the combatants.

Takval's heart sank. He had led the marines here, but this wasn't a style of fighting that his Dara allies could win. He had to improvise.

Takval jumped back, out of the reach of Toof's shovel.

"Do you yield?" shouted Toof.

"Hardly," said Takval. "What's so impressive about winning when you have the advantage of numbers here? If you're truly brave, come and fight us farther down in the ship, where my Agon brothers and sisters are ready for you."

He dove into the circle of Lyucu warriors surrounding the Dara marines like a wolf tearing into a pack of dogs and managed to smash open a bloody path with his metal-sheathed club. Then he led the retreating marines back into the passageway that they had emerged from earlier.

Radia and the other Lyucu warriors gathered around Toof, their impromptu leader. "What if it's a trap?"

Toof considered the situation. He wasn't worried about the Dara marines after seeing them fight, but what if the Agon fighter wasn't bluffing about having backup?

More deck-shaking moans and screeches echoed from deep in the interior of the ship.

Tana had lost her way and was in pain.

"We have to get to her," said Toof.

"Our advantage in numbers won't matter in those narrow passageways," warned Radia.

"We have to get to her," repeated Toof stubbornly. He sent one of the culeks back up to report to Thane Nacu what had happened, and then assigned half of the remaining warriors to help put out the fire in the stable. The rest he led down the dark passageway in pursuit. "Let's just press ahead cautiously."

The Lyucu crew advanced against Takval and his marines methodically, compartment by compartment, deck by deck. From time to time, the Dara marines turned back and put up a fight, but soon fled again deeper into the ship.

"We have to slow down the Lyucu advance," said Takval to his marines. "The bombs need more time!"

Withdrawing into the mazelike warren of rooms and narrow passageways, Takval and his marines started fires wherever they went, set booby traps, and when cornered, fought like ferocious wolves who had nothing to lose.

In this they were aided by the rampaging garinafins. Tana's distress had panicked the other two garinafins, and they also broke out of their stables and roamed through the ship, increasing the confusion tenfold. The lumbering beasts crashed through bulkheads as though they were nothing more than the silk-and-bamboo screen partitions in Dara homes.

Toof and Radia tried to calm down the frenzied beasts with whistles and toots from their bone trumpets, but they were too far from the garinafins to be effective.

"This isn't working," said Radia, panting. "We're advancing too slowly to get to Tana."

Toof nodded in agreement. The Dara boarding party was treating the city-ship like the streets and alleyways of a city and fighting an urban battle—a style of warfare that the Lyucu had little experience with.

"She must be badly hurt and confused," said Radia. "Otherwise I don't know why she hasn't found a way up to the top deck."

"We should break off and find her by ourselves," said Toof. "There are enough fighters here to take care of the Dara barbarians. We have to focus on Tana."

And so, instead of leading the Lyucu pursuit, Toof and Radia gradually fell back. The next time a side passageway presented itself, the two snuck into it. Abandoning the battle between the Lyucu crew and the boarding party, the two garinafin riders quickly closed in on their suffering mount.

Suddenly, the passageway they were in buckled and the wooden walls groaned, and Toof and Radia fell down. Powerful booms rattled their bones even as they plugged up their ears.

Like peals of thunder in the still-looming Wall of Storms, the wall-busters' muffled detonations, deep inside the thick planking and frame of the city-ship, shook every part of the vessel like a series of earthquakes.

# CHAPTER TEN

# THE CALL OF THE TRIBE

ALONG THE BELT CURRENT TO UKYU-GONDÉ: THE
SIXTH MONTH IN THE FIRST YEAR OF THE REIGN
OF SEASON OF STORMS.

Watching through portholes and light-bending mirror tubes, the crew of *Dissolver of Sorrows* cheered as the featureless hull of the looming city-ship abruptly blossomed into a tapestry of brilliant firework flowers. Red, white, orange, purple—the explosions above the waterline sketched a brief tableau reminiscent of a wildflower-filled spring in the valleys of the Damu Mountains, and those below the waterline reminded observers of glowing jellyfish or sea anemones relaxing their beautiful, varicolored tentacles.

The firework flowers and anemones quickly faded, replaced by jagged, smoking holes through which the merciless sea gushed.

The Lyucu crew staggered away from their stone-throwers and dropped their slingshots and spears, giving in to full panic. The city-ship, its sides torn and open to the cold sea, its interior smoldering with garinafin fire, was dying. Théra climbed onto the aftercastle and watched as the magnificent city-ship began to settle into the water.

"The gods are watching over us," whispered the sailors and marines as they stared at the unfolding tragic scene.

Théra ordered Captain Gon to begin repairing the ship. "Get that mast back up. We need mobility!"

"But we can use oars," said Captain Gon. "Shouldn't we try to get as far away from here as possible while they're too busy to shoot at us?"

Théra shook her head. "Stay close to the city-ship. We have to rescue the marines who stayed behind."

Once they got up from the still-swaying deck, the boarding party whooped with delight. The sound of gushing water below sounded to their ears like the refreshing music of the Rufizo Falls.

"Let's get topside," Takval urged. "There's still a chance we can get off this ship before it sinks."

They heard the retreating footsteps of their pursuers. No one was coming after them now. The only thought in the mind of every terrified Lyucu warrior was to go *up*, to get as far away from the deadly rising water as possible.

As the column of marines climbed a ladder, Takval, taking up the rear, looked down a passageway to the side and saw two figures at the other end climb *down*, deeper into the ship.

He stopped.

It was possible that the two were just stragglers trying to find another way up, but it was also possible that they were heading down to try to save the ship.

Curiosity and the desire for survival fought in Takval's heart. It was almost inconceivable that two individuals could save a doomed city-ship, but it had also been almost inconceivable that a small band could sink the ship in the first place.

So many things in life depended on seizing the slimmest of chances. That was how he had managed to survive in the belly of a whale to reach Dara, and who knew what gods or monsters could be invoked to save this ship?

"Keep going," he shouted to the marines, who had reached the deck above. "I have to check on something first."

"We'll come with you."

"No. The rest of you need to get up there and secure a way to leave the ship," said Takval. "Find a coracle or a boat. I'll join you as soon as I'm done. That's an order."

He wasn't sure that the marines would obey him. After all, he was not Théra. He wasn't Dara at all. But to his surprise, the marines saluted him and said, "Yes sir. We'll wait for you up there. Good hunting and stay safe."

As Takval started down the passageway to find those two descending figures, he felt like a true pékyu-taasa of the Agon for the first time.

Thane Nacu, who had been hysterically jumping up and down on the top deck, demanding that his naros-votan find some way to destroy the magical Dara ship, had fallen to the deck as the explosions rocked the ship. His head struck the hard wood, and he lost consciousness.

"Wake up! Wake up!"

He came to and found himself staring into the face of a naro-votan, caked with blood and streaked with soot. "Votan, we're sinking! You need to get to a lifeboat!"

Nacu struggled to sit up. The deck seemed tilted, and he wasn't sure if that was really the case or only because he was still feeling dizzy.

"A lifeboat?" Nacu's head throbbed and everything sounded muffled. He didn't even realize that he was screaming. "What good is a lifeboat when we are trapped between the Wall of Storms and the endless sea? Plug the leaks! Shore up the holes! What are you standing here for?"

"We can't get down there," said the despondent naro-votan. "The garinafin fires have sealed off most of the passageways to the lower decks, and the boarding party—they must have more than a hundred traitorous Agon slaves with them—are killing anyone who dares to attempt the few open paths!"

The ship lurched again, and by now it was obvious that the deck was closer to sea level. Sails flapped and the rigging was in disarray. *Boundless Pastures* was no longer riding with the wind but drifting aimlessly with the current. Warriors emerged from the open hatches of the loading bays like terrified rats, running for coracles and lifeboats. Once again, naros and culeks fought one another, punching, cursing, smashing, biting—all for the chance to get into a few rickety bone-and-hide floats that would take them away from the island that was slowly descending into the sea.

Thane Nacu's eyes glowed with terror and rage. Yet, even as he surveyed the chaos on deck, the primal, animal-like panic drained out of them. The incredible run of bad luck seemed to have a transformative effect on him. Since the worst of his nightmares had come true, there was nothing left to be afraid of anymore.

Holding on to the faithful naro-votan, he struggled up, grabbed his garinafin-bone trumpet, the instrument that launched the winged beasts into the air and presaged an all-out assault, and blew it with all his strength.

The long, bone-chilling blast stopped the commotion on deck. Naros and culeks paused their pushing and shoving and cursing and fighting to gaze at their almost-forgotten thane in wonder.

"Votan-ru-taasa, votan-sa-taasa," said Thane Nacu, "this is the moment we've been waiting for. The cunning barbarians of Dara, through deceit and illusion, have boarded our ship and sown discord, but they've also handed us the chains by which we will bring them to heel.

"Our home for the past year, *Boundless Pastures*, is sinking, but the enemy's ship is right off the starboard side. Look at how it's painted a distinct color from the other ships. Observe how it has a broader beam. This is their flagship, where the leader of this flock of sheep resides. If we can capture this ship, we'll have the hostages necessary to force the other Dara ships to surrender.

"Imagine the food and drink we'll plunder from their holds! Imagine the slaves we'll capture and use for our pleasure! Imagine the heroes' welcome we'll receive back at home—for Pékyu-taasa Cudyu, this victory will assuage some of the pain of the untimely death of our comrades.

"Illusions and witchcraft can never match the indomitable Lyucu spirit. We've triumphed over the loathsome Agon; we've seized the city-ships from the Dara invaders. Let this new Dara ship be a miniature of the war between our races—we'll take her as a prize to prefigure the ultimate victory of the great Lyucu people. Pékyu Tenryo is watching. Let's make him proud!"

The speech was crude but effective. The warriors milling about the deck realized that Thane Nacu was right. Rather than eking out a few more days on the high seas in rickety lifeboats and unseaworthy coracles, the better choice by far was to take the Dara ship, which was now drifting just behind and to the side of the great city-ship. The smashed forecastle and broken masts and the deserted deck all suggested an easy prey that could neither get away nor fight back.

Once again, the Lyucu warriors rushed about the deck with some semblance of order. As they prepared the lifeboats and coracles for an assault on the Dara vessel, a few alert naros noticed something curious. Soon, excited whispers buzzed around the deck.

"We're not sinking!"

"The city-ship will survive!"

"Diasa is with us! The Club-Maiden has saved the ship."

"Pékyu Tenryo has come to our aid because we're acting like wolves again!"

Indeed, the city-ship had stabilized.

A few brave Lyucu scouts managed to dodge the Dara assassins and spreading flames until they found a way down into the dark interior of *Boundless Pastures*. They returned to report that the water, which had flooded the lower decks, was no longer rising. In fact, with the top deck now closer to sea-level, it was even easier to launch the coracles and lifeboats to go after the Dara ship.

Like a gang of bloodthirsty pirates, the Lyucu warriors chanted their praise to the gods of Ukyu and oared their little vessels toward the helpless Dara ship, ready to capture the hated Dara barbarians who had been responsible for so much misery.

"They've stopped sinking," said Admiral Roso, who had kept an eye on the city-ship through a mirror tube even as the rest of the crew celebrated.

"What happened?" asked Théra, alarmed. To come so close to victory only to have it snatched away at the last second felt even worse than an outright failure. "How could they have plugged so many holes so quickly?"

"I don't think that's what happened," said Admiral Roso. "My best guess is that this has to do with the construction of the city-ships. Emperor Mapidéré's shipwrights were among the best ship-builders in Dara, and no expense was spared in outfitting the fleet to find the immortals. Remember how I said the hulls were constructed from multiple watertight compartments with thick interior bulk-heads such that a breach in one place would not be fatal?"

"Why wasn't this accounted for?"

"It was! Part of the plan was for the boarding party to spread out and plant the wall-busters through the length of the ship."

"But we didn't have enough time," said Commander Tipo Tho, her voice tinged with regret.

"It appears that most of the explosions were concentrated in just one or two compartments," said Admiral Roso. "The ship took on some water but the rest of the compartments, still intact, are keeping it afloat."

Théra looked up helplessly at the stars through the open forecas-tle hatch. They had been defeated by the ingenuity of Dara's own shipbuilders from the past. Were the gods truly watching out for these cruel barbarians?

But there was no time for her to wallow in regret.

"They're launching small boats to board us," said Commander Tho. "Your Highness, please go back into the safety of your quarters. We'll fight for every inch of this ship. You can be certain that every sailor and marine will do their duty. No one will surrender."

"I'll begin preparations to scuttle *Dissolver of Sorrows*," said Captain Gon. "They mean to take us as a prize, but I'll ensure that they get nothing, not even a single grain of rice."

"I'll find a way to signal the rest of the fleet to continue their escape," said Admiral Roso. "At least we've damaged the city-ship enough that it probably won't be able to catch the other ships now."

Théra closed her eyes. Had it really come to this? Should she, like her father on the island of Rui, order everyone to cease resistance to preserve their lives? Should she, like her mother during the Battle of Zathin Gulf, face the Lyucu slaughter defiantly in a final dramatic gesture? After all the planning and sacrifices, were their only choices to be enslaved or die?

*I can't live in the shadow of my parents. They've fought their battles, but this one is mine.*

"Captain Gon, how much of the repairs have you completed?" she asked.

"The leak in the forecastle has largely been patched. But the main mast is beyond repair. We can get rowers onto the deck, but they'll be exposed—"

"We're not running. Can the ship dive?"

Surprised by the question, Captain Gon took a moment to consider. "Yes, though I don't advise going very deep. With all the leaks, we have to pump constantly to maintain buoyancy. We can't stay down long."

"Dive!" ordered Théra. "Stay at the depth where the breathing tubes will be effective. But keep them retracted unless we have no other choice."

"That won't buy us much time, and once we're surrounded by Lyucu coracles and boats, we'll be trapped!"

Théra looked beyond him to the face of Çami Phithadapu. "We're going to try something else."

"Halt!" Takval called out in the dark passageway. He had doused his torch so that while he was hiding in the shadows, the two Lyucu warriors he pursued were illuminated by the torches they held aloft as they stood at the top of a ladder leading down deeper into the ship.

He could have simply snuck up on them and bashed in their skulls with his war club. But that yearning to hear the familiar syllables of the speech of the scrublands had again sprouted in his heart, and he decided to honor these two with a proper death, one that allowed them to face their enemy, their weapons in hand.

"You again!" Toof blurted. The man emerging from the darkness was the tall, slender Agon he had fought earlier. He tried to raise his shovel, but it was awkward with one hand.

"I guess Maiden-of-the-Wind wanted us to meet again," said Takval. "Unfortunately, this will be the last time. We won't all leave here alive."

"There are two of us here and only one of you," said Radia as she switched the bone club to her right hand.

"That'll make it more interesting, won't it?" said Takval.

But Toof lowered his shovel. "We don't have to fight. You're alone, and no one knows the two of us are down here," he said. He whispered urgently to Radia, and after a moment of hesitation, she lowered her club as well.

"What are you getting at?" asked Takval, his eyes narrowing suspiciously.

A long, pained moan echoed up from the vertical shaft next to them. It spoke of loneliness, terror, and despair.

"We raised Tana from a hatchling," said Toof.

"She was an orphan," said Radia. "Both her parents died in battle, and none of the other mother garinafins would accept her. We stole the milk meant for kyoffir and fed her in secret."

Takval was astonished. While bigger tribes kept a small population of garinafins for herding and as the personal mounts of thanes and senior naros-votan, most garinafins, as beasts of war, belonged to Pékyu Tenryo. Among the Lyucu (and the Agon as well, back when they were masters of the scrublands), the modern practice was to slaughter orphan garinafins who could not be adopted into a new garinafin family. Without family ties, it was impossible to ensure the loyalty of war garinafins by holding their relatives hostage. For Toof and Radia to secretly raise such a dangerous beast amounted to treason.

"Why did you do such a thing?" he asked.

"I've never felt right about what happened to Kidia," Radia said.

Kidia was Pékyu Tenryo's personal mount, the orphan garinafin who had helped a young Tenryo escape from the Agon as a hostage. Later, Tenryo had had Kidia killed as a demonstration of his willingness to sacrifice even those he loved in order to achieve the dream of uniting the scattered Lyucu tribes.

"Saving Tana felt like a small way to appease the gods for what the pékyu had done," Radia finished.

"I've never liked this new way of raising garinafin armies," said Toof. "The garinafins are creatures who feel, just like you and me, and it isn't right to treat them like inanimate arucuro tocua."

Takval was silent. The "new way" that Toof referred to had in fact been first devised by Pékyu Nobo Aragoz of the Agon, his own revered grandfather. Nobo's innovation of de-emphasizing the personal bond between pilot and mount, and replacing it with a system of bondage maintained by threats and punishments directed at the war garinafins' aged and immature relatives, had been instrumental in the conquest of the Lyucu. Pékyu Tenryo had simply adopted his old enemy's system and then expanded upon it. But having cared for these creatures for years as an enslaved garinafin groom himself, Takval felt conflicted about his grandfather's invention.

Another pained moan echoed up the shaft.

"She's scared, and she can't find her way out," said Radia. "We have to help her. We're her only family. Can we postpone this fight . . . until after we've found her?"

He should hate these two, Takval knew. But now that he had heard their story, it didn't feel right not to grant them their last wish.

"Let's get going," Takval said, "before she stumbles too low in the ship and drowns."

Quietly, like a wounded whale having trouble staying afloat, the Dara ship sank beneath the waves. The pursuing Lyucu in coracles and lifeboats cursed and rowed faster, but the lookouts on the city-ship reassured them that the barbarians weren't going anywhere. The Dara ship didn't dive out of sight; instead, it was hovering just beneath the surface.

In the distance, the Dara fleet seemed to have recognized that their assault had gone awry. The glowing screen, now empty of shadow players, hung limp. Instead of taking advantage of the fact that the city-ship had stopped to escape, the Dara ships had reefed their sails to drift along in the current. Perhaps they also realized that their flagship was in trouble, and weren't sure what to do next.

"You're watching, are you?" muttered a satisfied Thane Nacu aboard *Boundless Pastures*. "Good, good. It's always better to have the flock watch when we butcher a troublesome ram. Don't worry, after we're done with all the fat and meat from this one, we'll start on the rest of you."

The ragtag flotilla of small craft assembled around the submerged form of the Dara ship like a whaling fleet, and torches and lamps lit up the sea. Most of the Lyucu warriors, not being from coastal tribes, had no whaling experience, and they weren't sure what to do now that they had trapped their prey. Boarding a submerged ship seemed beyond their means.

Some suggested using hook-ended ropes and nets to ensnare the ship and prevent it from running away, just in case; others suggested using long spears to poke through the glass portholes, forcing the ship to surface by flooding it.

Their debate and chatter ceased as a strange music emanating from the submerged boat filled the air and the water. At once mournful and defiant, it sounded like singing, but not singing by any human voice. Above a deep, throbbing bass line was overlaid a melody formed from pulsing whistles and tremulous trills, an expressive, plaintive voice chanting in a language that no one could understand.

The thin shells of the coracles and lifeboats vibrated in sympathy to the otherworldly music. The very sea seemed to tremble with its power as the sound traveled far into the darkness, reaching miles and miles beyond the bubble of light formed by the burning Lyucu torches.

Abruptly, the underwater darkness was pierced by a bright beam that shot out of the transom windows of the Dara ship and probed far into the ocean like a ray from a miniature sun. The beam swept from side to side, settled on this coracle or that boat for a moment, blinked, and moved on, as though putting on a mesmerizing light show.

"What in the world is that?"

"More witchcraft?"

"How are they making that sound?"

"It's beautiful."

"Look at that light. It's like the Eye of Cudyufin is swimming."

Other than awed whispers amongst themselves, the Lyucu aboard *Boundless Pastures* and those in the flotilla of coracles were uncertain how to react. The ethereal music seemed to fill the ocean and evoke feelings that did not belong to this sublunary world. They didn't know what exactly the Dara were planning, and that was worrisome, but all felt it was a moment of wonder that they were lucky to witness.

Inside *Dissolver of Sorrows*, a team of engineers under the direction of Princess Théra worked the bellows that normally pumped air into the ballast tanks of the ship, but now were connected to a set of tubes that pushed the compressed air past a series of bamboo strips, which vibrated like the reeds of musical instruments, producing a low, thrumming tone with complex harmonies. The bamboo reeds were attached to a large cast-iron pot that was normally used to cook for the crew, but now acted as a resonant chamber.

A set of mirrors and smooth planks—taken from the paneling and cabins of the captain's quarters—were placed around the pot in a parabolic shape to deflect the booming bass line into the bow of the ship, from where it emanated into the sea.

Meanwhile, Çami Phithadapu wiped the sweat from her brows, took a deep breath, and blew into the mouthpiece of a bronze trumpet. By altering the shape of her lips and working the trumpet keys, Çami was essentially singing with the trumpet. This melody, amplified by another resonant chamber jury-rigged from a washbasin, was combined with the bass line and projected into the ocean as well.

Back at the stern of the ship, Captain Gon directed another team of sailors in the captain's quarters to concentrate the light from a handful of whale-oil lamps into a tight beam with a parabolic dish assembled from the small personal grooming mirrors carried by some of the marines and sailors. By turning and tilting the dish, they directed this beam of light, like a giant's baleful gaze, out of the transom windows to point at the various Lyucu boats drifting above.

"Blind the bastards," muttered Captain Gon. "Shine the light right in their eyes."

The apparatus and method for producing and projecting music into the sea were based on Çami's knowledge of whale anatomy—in particular, how they sang—but Princess Théra, herself an accomplished musician, had helped her devise a way to mechanically replicate the workings of nature. Théra had some facility with aural engineering because, intrigued by an experiment with *moaphya* slabs during the war against the rebels of Tunoa, she had continued to experiment on her own with various means of sound production.

The apparatus was so crude and the execution so haphazard because there hadn't been enough resources or time for refinement. Théra and Çami had used moments stolen from here and there to work out this plan as a kind of thought experiment that they were both interested in, but one they never thought they'd have to put into practice.

*"This is actually the most orthodox one of the several plans I've devised. If you want to hear a really innovative—"*

*"Maybe later, Çami,"* said Théra. *"Let's talk through this one first."*

Théra had indeed followed up with Çami after the war council, and one of her wilder ideas had seized Théra's imagination.

She had wondered what to do about it.

Kuni Garu had spoken to Théra of an exchange between himself and Luan Zyaji, the great scholar and one of the first to believe in his vision of a transformed Dara. Luan and Kuni had been in Pan, preparing to storm Emperor Erishi's palace after a daring surprise attack with captured airships. Luan offered to stay at the airships with a detachment of soldiers just in case the assault failed.

*"Do you always plan for failure even when success is within reach?"* Kuni asked.

*"It's the prudent thing to do."*

*"Sometimes prudence is not a virtue,"* said Kuni. *"I gambled a lot when I was younger. I can tell you that Tazu is more fun than Lutho. If you're going to gamble, you'll have more fun if you don't hold anything back."*

Over the years, Théra had pondered the meaning of this lesson. Did it really mean that prudence itself was *not* a virtue? Her father had believed in taking interesting leaps of faith when circumstances called for such, trusting that the universe would conspire to reward him and his.

Yet she was not her father, and she would take away a different meaning. Prudence was sometimes required because plans did not always work out the way we wanted them to. However, the best way to overcome the fickleness of the gods wasn't to cower and hold on to false security, but to be prepared to leap even farther.

It's fine and good to do the most interesting thing, but sometimes it's even better to be ready to do the outrageous thing.

The dome-headed whales began their lives as calves surrounded by mothers and aunts and grandmothers and sisters and little brothers. Here, immersed in the songs and myths of a culture even older than humanity, they learned the language of head-singing and the ethos of the open seas.

In pods of a handful to a hundred, they glided through the ocean, diving deep into the aphotic abyss to catch the many-tentacled giant squids and octopuses they prized. In that inky darkness, lit only by the cold glow of creatures who made their own light and knew not what the sun was, the whales and their prey engaged in titanic struggles that rivaled the legendary battle between Mata Zyndu and Mocri Zati. Here, jaws full of teeth slashed and parried against the daggerlike beak, the coppery blue blood of the cephalopod commingling with the bright crimson life-wine of the cetacean; there, a sucker arm ripped out chunks of flesh where the milk-giving fish wasn't armored with barnacles.

An eternity of violence was bounded by the length and breadth of a held breath.

When females grew older, they carried on the traditions of their tribe, singing songs that passed on the lore and faith of their ancestors. The males, on the other hand, left home to wander the wild oceans as single hunters, loneliness and the memories of their home pod their sole companions. Only once in a while, when the urge to couple seized them, did they head for civilization to look for pods of females to sing the songs of courtship.

The whales knew of ships and boats, and most of the time they left these non-creatures alone. But lately, some of the ships had grown dangerous, killing mothers and aunts and desecrating their bodies. The gangly-limbed creatures who lived in the ships were barbaric half-octopuses impossible to reason with. That they were armed with spears sharper than a cruben's horn and winches more powerful than a bull whale's tail did not prove that they had the morals of even a one-year-old calf.

So when the strange, half-submerged little ship lying next to the gigantic island-ship began to sing in the language of the whales, the matriarch of the nearby pod was suspicious. The accent was strange and the articulation lacking—there was no beauty to the song at all. But there was, nonetheless, a rough sketch of the map of an alien mind, the first signs of the presence of not mere intelligence in these shipbound air-remoras, but also an emotional life.

Such a thing had never happened in the memories of the pod, and the matriarch wasn't sure what to make of it. Whales did not intrude on the affairs of ships, no more than migrating turtles interfered in the councils of coral-reef shrimp. But the song of the ship-whale grew louder, more insistent, and in its tremolo notes the matriarch could sense death and suffering, terror and grandeur.

An eternity of violence was bounded by the length and breadth of a pocket of air, a dying ship filled with defiant souls.

She was finally convinced to be involved, however, by the sight that greeted her ancient eyes when she approached the strange ship-whale to take a closer look. The island-ship had sent out dozens of tiny boats to surround the ship-whale, who lay just under the water, as still as a beached bull.

The matriarch recognized the scene and knew what would happen next: harpooners would get up on the bows of the tiny boats and hurl their deadly barbs at the ship-whale. It was how many members of the pod had been killed, their carcasses slowly falling into the abyss after being stripped of blubber.

A beam of light emerged from the ship-whale, pointing at the small boats that had trapped her, pointing at danger. To the matriarch, the beam of light was a warning as well as an accusation: *Will you do what is right?*

It was the nature of whales not to be involved in matters they did not understand, but the matriarch felt the stirring of a deep and unfamiliar emotion: the anticipation of sorrow, of anguish, of regret.

Something had to be done.

*Sisters, daughters, nieces, granddaughters, heed my song . . .*

"Whales! Whales!" cried a few lookouts high in the rigging of *Boundless Pastures*.

In the pale light of the moon, a few telltale sprays misted over the ocean, drenching the crew of the few coracles nearest the periphery.

Whales were a common sight in and along the giant oceanic current that had brought the Lyucu city-ships to Dara. The crew of *Boundless Pastures*, even if they weren't from the coast, had long grown used to the presence of these large but gentle and harmless creatures. That they would come so close to the Lyucu boats was unusual, but none of the Lyucu felt fear as they gazed into the sea, hoping to catch a glimpse of the visitors.

The ocean erupted as a whale shot up, directly under a cluster of boats. Broken planks and shattered oars flew through the air, along with screaming Lyucu warriors. The massive whale traced a long arc above the surface and crashed into another lifeboat, breaking it into two halves.

Another whale breached at the other end of the flotilla, capsizing and smashing coracles.

And another.

The strange music from the underwater Dara boat continued unabated, but it was now answered by more voices: some deep, some shrill, liquid clicks like wooden clappers in an underwater cave, lingering whistles like the compositions of cowherds deep in an echoey valley.

The submerged boat's beam of light pointed upward like a slanted sword piercing the gloom of the sea, shining a spotlight on clusters of Lyucu craft. Wherever the beam of light pointed, a whale struck, smashing boats, breaking coracles, mangling limbs, shattering bones. The screams of terrified Lyucu warriors filled the air as the rest desperately oared their way back to the city-ship.

Takval, Toof, and Radia found themselves in waist-deep water. Torchlight revealed the remnants of broken bulkheads and smashed decks all around them. The garinafin had crashed through here like a tornado, paying no mind to the human-sized design at all.

The last moan they heard had come from some distance ahead, on this level. They sloshed forward through the cold water, brushing aside the flotsam with their weapons and arms.

"I have to say," said Toof, "setting loose a frenzied garinafin on the ship was a brilliant ploy from you and your Dara friends."

Takval gave him a wry smile. "You allow me too much credit. I'm as much in the dark as you are. All we wanted was to sneak around the ship planting bombs. She caught us by surprise too."

"Listen to him," muttered Radia, shaking her head. She mimicked Takval's voice, "'All we wanted to do was to kill you without you noticing.' You sound just like a Dara barbarian."

"I think Tana got loose in order to warn us about you," said Toof.

Takval laughed. "That's wishful thinking."

"You don't know her like I do," insisted Toof.

The deck under their feet slanted downward, and now the water was up to their chests.

"What's that?" asked Radia.

They stopped to listen to the whale song reverberating through the ship.

"Sounds like somebody howling at the moon."

"More like blowing a trumpet."

"More like crying and sneezing."

Cold spray drenched them as something large and heavy slammed into the water a few dozen yards in front. A terrible howl of pain filled the space. Radia's torch was doused.

Toof waded forward and raised his torch high. "Tana!" he screamed.

The garinafin was lying in the water, her massive head half-submerged. Where her left eye had been there was now a crater-like wound from which gore oozed.

"Oh, you poor thing!" Radia said, her voice trembling. "What happened to you?"

Toof and Radia sloshed through the water toward the giant beast, their progress agonizingly slow. "Let me take a look at your . . . face,"

Toof said. "Wish we had some tolyusa to take the edge off the pain," he muttered.

Tana growled and lifted her head out of the water. Frigid seawater cascaded off her antlers in sheets. She turned her head to regard the approaching figures with her one remaining, pupil-less eye. There was no sense of recognition in it.

"Don't!" shouted Takval. "Back away!"

It was too late. The beast reared back her head, snapped her jaws shut, and lunged forward—

The three humans ducked under the water, and the last torch went out—

A tongue of fire lanced over the surface, lighting up the broken interior of the ship in a false dawn—

Underwater, Takval gestured at the other two. Toof and Radia looked at each other and followed Takval as the three swam away from the raging garinafin.

Çami Phithadapu had spent years cataloging and interpreting whale song, going so far as to develop a notation modeled on music to record samples. When the princess asked her for alternatives to the "barnacle plan," she had proposed the idea of singing to the whales that could often be seen in the vicinity of the fleet.

"Whalers tell stories of pods of dome-headed whales attacking whaling ships in a coordinated fashion," said Çami.

"But are these *reliable* reports?"

Çami shrugged. "The stories are told by drunken sailors and mates in taverns between whaling voyages. In wine and beer there is truth, but also much else."

The idea was too experimental and uncertain to gamble the fleet's lives on as the primary plan, but the princess had decided that it was worth looking into as an outrageous backup, a prayer to Tazu when all else failed. After all, this was the Year of the Whale on the folk calendar of Dara, and that had to mean an extraordinary amount of cetacean luck, right?

As the Lyucu flotilla scurried back to the city-ship, leaving only wreckage and the dead and dying behind, *Dissolver of Sorrows*'s crew was too stupefied by the carnage wreaked by the whales to celebrate. There was no time for it either. All hands were scrambling to deal with the worsening leaks throughout the ship. Their breathing was becoming labored as the air inside the ship grew increasingly foul.

Captain Gon came to the princess, his face grave. "We can't—"

"I know," said Théra. "Surface!"

The bellows wheezed as everyone pumped to get as much air as possible into the ballast tanks. But the ship, instead of surfacing, continued to sink slowly. Soon, the breathing tubes would be submerged, and there would be no way to halt the descent of *Dissolver of Sorrows* toward her watery grave.

"I'm useless," said Captain Gon to the princess, his head hanging in shame. "The ship has taken on too much water."

"It isn't your fault," said Théra. She turned to offer a wan smile to Çami. "We tried."

Çami held up a hand, gesturing for her to stop talking. Her brows were knotted in thought. Suddenly, she ran back toward her trumpet.

"What are you doing?" Théra called after her.

"My essay for the Grand Examination!" Çami said, without turning back.

The officers looked at one another in confusion, but Théra's eyes widened in understanding. She laughed. "Go get the bellows pumping into the bow again," she ordered Captain Gon.

Once more, the artificial whale song of bamboo reeds and resonating trumpet filled the sea.

"Do you intend to call upon the whales for one more attack against the Lyucu boats?" asked Admiral Roso. There was a defiant smile on his face. "You truly are a worthy heir to your parents. We'll die fighting."

Théra shook her head. "Never speak of death if there's even a glimmer of hope left."

As Çami's song continued, some of the whales in the pod turned and swam for *Dissolver of Sorrows*. The crew tensed, but instead of attacking the ship, the whales gently came alongside and bumped into the hull.

The ship's descent stopped. More gentle bumps. The crew held their breath.

Slowly, *Dissolver of Sorrows* began to ascend.

"Whale pods often do this for injured whales or young calves," said Çami, gasping as she took her lips away from the trumpet's mouthpiece. "*Dissolver of Sorrows* is a bit big, but I've convinced them that we're just a really well-fed calf."

Çami had written her essay for the Grand Examination on the subject of midwifery being practiced among whales. It was, in fact, that very essay that had drawn Théra's attention during the war against the Lyucu invasion, when the princess sought scholars of talent to help study the garinafins.

"We're not out of danger yet," warned Captain Gon. "Once the Lyucu are back on the city-ship, they may decide that if they can't capture us, they may as well sink us."

Çami put her lips back to the trumpet and began to sing harder than ever.

The Lyucu warriors returned to the city-ship and climbed up the rope ladders. Some went back to the stone-throwers; others hurled spears and axes at the whales diving and surfacing near the ship. There was little coordination as Thane Nacu was too shocked by the latest setback to come up with a new speech or plan to rally his fighters.

While confusion and chaos reigned throughout the city-ship, the eight surviving Dara marines fought their way to the top deck. There, they made their way to an unattended coracle. If they could lower the coracle into the water and climb down, they would have a chance to escape the city-ship.

"But the city-ship has stopped sinking—"

"There's nothing we can do—"

"Maybe we should go back down and sabotage—"

"Where's Takval?"

. . .

The debate cost them precious time. The leaderless Lyucu warriors milling about like a swarm of flies finally noticed the strangers by the gunwale. With bloodcurdling cries, they converged on the spot.

"Get into the coracle!" shouted one of the marines to her comrades. "I'll wait behind for Prince Takval."

"How can we live with the shame if we left now?" countered another marine. "We promised to wait for him."

The marines knew that Takval was likely long dead, but no one would get into the coracle. In the end they raised it as a barricade and fought behind it against the Lyucu onslaught.

The marines were illiterate and none could recite an inspiring quote from one of the Ano sages; instead, they chanted, "There was never doubt in my heart" as Mata Zyndu, Hegemon of Dara and a demigod to all soldiers, was reported to have done as he made his last stand by the sea.

Blood and gore drenched their armor and faces and slicked the deck beneath their feet.

Thirty-six Lyucu warriors lay dead before the last Dara marine fell.

The matriarch surveyed the sea in satisfaction: capsized boats and drowning humans everywhere, and the remaining boats were rowing away.

She ordered her pod to rescue the ship-whale, to keep it afloat like a young calf that had not yet learned how to breathe. But the ship-whale didn't chirp with relief. Instead, it sang even louder, and its accusing beam of light pointed at the giant ship.

The matriarch hesitated. It was one thing to capsize a few small boats, but to attack an island-ship that dwarfed the whales as much as the whales dwarfed mere remoras? Her instinct was to lead the pod away, hoping never to see this floating wooden island of death again.

The call of the ship-whale was insistent, urgent. *Kill it. Kill it. Kill it.*

Tiny figures were running across the island-ship, setting up engines of death. The ship-whale was wounded. It wouldn't be able to get away.

The matriarch tried to recall lore about the crubens, the great scaled whales who ruled the seas. Wasn't there a tale about a contest between two great crubens? About how it was important to finish what was begun? To destroy the foe when he was down?

She seemed to be in the lightless abyss again, surrounded by the tentacles of foes who insisted on death. There was no way out of the thicket but to cut through. Her blood began to boil with an ancient rage that she had not felt for many years.

She sang a long and intricate song, a timeworn epic about heroism and courage, about the need to defend the tribe, even when tribe was only a memory so dim that it felt like a myth. Her daughters, granddaughters, and even great-granddaughters, mere calves, joined the chorus.

In the distant darkness, a bull whale hunting alone heard the ancestral voices prophesying war.

Like Langiaboto arcing over the scrublands, hurled by the arm of Pékyu Tenryo, the bull whale, twice the length of the matriarch, accelerated toward the ship that loomed ahead like an island.

He circled the ship once, trying to find a weak spot. Axes, clubs, broken spars rained down around his head, glancing harmlessly off his barnacle-armored skin. The bull whale wasn't afraid. He had survived countless encounters with whalers, and he had the scars to prove it. When harpooned, instead of running away, he had headed for the whaleboats, forcing the whalers to cut the cables attached to the harpoons, much like he might escape a particularly devious giant squid who attempted to drown him in the abyss by severing its tentacles. The harpoons had remained embedded in his body, piercings around which the flesh had healed, stronger than before, like so many war trophies.

The matriarch was asking him to fight for the tribe, to go to war, a concept that intrigued him. Never before had he thought to attack the whale ship itself instead of the whaleboats, but why not?

Stones arced from the whale ship, splashing into the sea around the bull whale in tall spumes. The bull whale was too nimble to be caught by the thrown stones, but the attack hardened his resolve. He dove.

The island-ship seemed to sense something was wrong. Sails were being rigged across the masts, and the ship was now moving ahead, trying to get away.

This was exactly what the bull whale had wanted. He doubted that even at full speed, he could ram through the thick planking of a whaler. But it was a different story when the ship itself was moving. Bull whales sometimes fought each other, and he knew, from experience, that there was much more force in an impact when both combatants were moving.

He sped ahead of the ship, turned around, and aimed straight for the bow. His thick dome-shaped head, filled with oil, accelerated through the parting waves.

From the spot where they'd found Tana, deep at the stern of the ship, Takval, Toof, and Radia climbed, ran, swam, jumped, always staying just a few steps ahead of the lumbering beast that crashed through behind them.

They emerged into the cavernous cattle-stable.

This was a vault in the middle of the city-ship that ran the whole width of the ship, making it one of the largest compartments in the vessel.

High up, near the ceiling, a series of narrow windows let in air and light. This was where Emperor Mapidéré's expedition had kept pigs and sheep to provide a source of fresh meat for the officials and nobles, and where Pékyu-taasa Cudyu had stocked living cattle for his warriors. By now, of course, all the cattle had been slaughtered and eaten, and the open space was filled only with scattered bedding straw and the stench of dung and piss.

The three humans ran across the wide-open space until they reached a thick wall of oak that doubled as one of the structural bulkheads that divided the ship into watertight compartments. The only way forward was a small door high up near the top, accessible by a set of zigzagging catwalks and ladders. The opening led into the feed storeroom on the other side. In an emergency, the small opening could be plugged to isolate the watertight compartments from each other.

The three dashed over to the base of one of the ladders and began to climb. If they could escape into the opening through the thick bulkhead, they'd be safe for a while. It would take a very long time for Tana to find a way through—she'd have to either climb to the top deck or bash her way through a solid wall of thick oak.

The tall doors to the stable crashed open as Tana lumbered in.

It was a race now. Would the three humans climb to the small opening in time? Or would the frenzied garinafin catch them before they made it?

The whole ship lurched, as though Fithowéo had slammed his spear into the hull like a battering ram. The hull vibrated, planks buckled and squeaked and cracked under the strain, and the very cattle-stable itself seemed to deform under the pressure.

The bamboo ladders sprang away from the wall, their anchoring screws popping off. The three humans fell to the floor, stunned by the impact.

Even the pursuing garinafin was thrown to the deck.

"Did we hit a reef?" croaked Radia.

Neither Takval nor Toof replied. Water gushed out of seams in the floor. The city-ship was sinking again.

With difficulty, the three managed to struggle up and look around. All the ladders had been shaken loose from the wall by the impact, and now lay across the floor in a jumble like eating sticks at the end of a meal. The catwalks leading to the opening to the other side had been ripped off their anchor points. Some pieces dangled uselessly from the wall, only loosely attached. Others were heaped at the foot of the wall.

Tana got to her feet, screeched, and took a step forward. The weakened deck groaned under her weight.

The three ran and found the longest, still intact ladder and tried to erect it under the opening. "Radia and I will hold the ladder steady," said Takval. "Toof, you're the lightest. Climb up there and find a rope to bring us up. Hurry!"

As the floor quaked with every approaching step the garinafin took, Takval and Radia struggled to hold the ladder steady. Toof climbed up the rickety contraption, clinging to every rung with all his strength.

He was at the top. The opening was fifteen feet away. "I can't reach it!" he screamed down.

"We can try to lift the ladder," called Takval.

"It's not enough!" cried Toof. "It's just too far."

"Maybe we can extend the ladder with sections—"

Another crash, and despite the best efforts of Takval and Radia, the unsteady ladder would not hold. Toof lost his grip, tried to slow his fall with desperate grabs at the rungs of the ladder, failed, and collapsed into a heap with the other two at the ladder's foot.

They struggled to their feet, their backs against the wall.

Tana lumbered toward them, her pupil-less eye red with fury. The garinafin panted.

One more step.

Thane Nacu could not believe what he was seeing: The malignant bull whale, its eyes glinting mercilessly, was headed straight for his ship. He shouted for the naro at the wheel to turn the ship away, out of the path of this mad creature. He screamed at his warriors to stand their ground, to fight back, to chop down the mast of the ship and wield it like a spear so that the crazed whale could be destroyed.

But there was no response. When Nacu looked around, he saw that he was alone at the prow of the ship. All his naros-votan and naros and culeks had deserted him. Through the thick columns of smoke that swirled around the deck, he saw his crew huddled at the back of the ship like so many terrified children.

Nacu knew that he was doomed. Unknown weapons and magical underwater ships and frenzied whales and foes who popped out of thin air were all things he could fight against. But he was helpless when the spirit of his warriors was broken.

He would not be able to go home after all.

He laughed maniacally and hurled his axe at the massive head of the bull whale charging through the water. The axe flipped end over end, glinting in moonlight and torchlight.

It bounced off the head of the whale, a pebble bouncing off a mountain.

The whale slammed into the ship like a flesh battering ram, and broken pieces of timber exploded in every direction. One jagged piece went straight through Nacu's neck.

The crew of *Dissolver of Sorrows* watched the bull whale continue his relentless assault on the Lyucu city-ship.

After each impact, he seemed stunned, and floated in the water for some time before recovering his senses. But he didn't give up. He swam away from the ship in a long arc, turned around, and accelerated for the floating island again.

A series of jagged holes were punctured around the city-ship. Water gushed in. The city-ship stopped moving and settled lower.

Lifeboats and coracles tumbled into the sea like dumplings falling into a boiling pot. Desperate Lyucu jumped into the ocean from the burning deck, swimming for the boats.

"Signal the fleet with a lamp sent aloft by kite," ordered Théra. "Patch up the ship as well as you can. We'll row in and look for our comrades."

Although Captain Gon thought there was little hope of finding Takval or the other marines, he complied.

Takval stood, a smile on his face. He took his war club off his back. To die facing one's enemy, weapon in hand, was the greatest honor an Agon warrior could have, and especially fitting for one who would be pékyu.

Radia and Toof, however, had long lost their weapons during the escape through the ship.

"Find bamboo ladder legs and wield them like bone-spears," advised Takval.

The two Lyucu garinafin riders ignored him.

"Come on," cooed Radia. "Good girl. Don't you remember your Radia? You can smell me, can't you? We're not here to hurt you."

"I know you're scared," said Toof. "I know you want to lash out and hurt someone. But I'm not your enemy. Let's try to get out of here. There's still time."

Tana's lone eye seemed to clear for a minute, but she snorted and the cloud of pain-rage once again covered the dark orb. She only remembered that it was a human just like these who had blinded her left eye. Her head was filled with a throbbing agony that was worse than anything she had endured in her life of suffering. It was hard for her to judge how far away she was from the three figures in front of her, so she took a tentative step forward, stretched out her neck, and growled. The boards under her talons groaned. She was even heavier than normal now, having exhausted all her reserves of lift gas from breathing fire throughout the ship.

Radia and Toof closed their eyes and opened their arms. They had known Tana since they could cradle her in their arms. They didn't want her to die feeling alone, feeling like an orphan.

To be killed by a creature they had raised was a risk that every garinafin rider faced, but that didn't make this any easier.

The city-ship shuddered from another powerful impact. Overhead, the ceiling cracked and broke. Through the jagged hole the stars twinkled behind a haze of smoke.

Planks under Tana's clawed feet broke and collapsed as water gushed out of the fresh opening. Repeated assaults from the bull whale had weakened the structure of the frame supporting the cattle-stable flooring, and the concentrated weight of the lift-gas-deprived Tana was finally too much for the strained columns. She fell partway into the yawning gap below her, flapped her wings desperately, and barely managed to cling to the still-solid part of the floor with her claws.

A gulf of roiling and rising seawater now divided the garinafin from the humans. Once again, the three humans had been tossed to the ground by the impact.

Tana moaned piteously. She was again the hatchling that had emerged from the shelter of the egg into the cold, pitiless air under the stars. Seawater rose around her, as salty as the amniotic fluid that had covered her at her birth. She was again the motherless child who no family wanted to take in. The pain in her head threatened to drown her as much as the water around her.

Toof began to sing.

> *The stars are colder than a lone tusked tiger's tears.*
> *The wind is more bitter than a dead wolf's liver.*

*Lie against my chest, my darling, my dearest child,*
*You're never alone when you hear the tribe's lungsong.*

"She's a beast," said Takval, sighing. "The nature of the beast will always be revealed."

"The All-Father created all of us as beasts," countered Radia, "but the Every-Mother gave us all hope that we can be more."

Tana stretched out her neck, listening to the song.

Torrents poured into the stable, widening the gulf between Tana and the three humans. As the garinafin was pulled away, Takval rushed to erect another ladder against the bulkhead and scrambled onto it. Toof sang even louder over the sound of the waves.

*Tents sprout across the scrublands like mushrooms after rain,*
*People roam the endless grass like stars through the cloud-sea.*
*Feel my arms around you, my eyes on you;*
*Feel my breath against you, my voice through you.*
*You're never alone when you hear the tribe's lungsong.*

The haze in Tana's single eye faded. In the faint starlight her gaze found the three figures on the other side of the water. She sniffed the air, and a moan of joy escaped her throat that sounded like a baby lamb bleating for her mother.

Another loud crash as the planks fell away from the skeleton of the ship to reveal more of the stars dancing through smoke. A wave toppled the ladder, the deck tilted, and the three humans were thrown into the rising water.

With another moan, Tana climbed out of the hole in the deck, waddled forward, and leapt into the sea, stretching her neck toward her family.

Incredulously, Takval followed Toof and Radia and climbed onto the neck of the garinafin, and as the ship broke apart around them, the garinafin swam for the stars.

The waterlogged wooden island broke apart. The back half, mostly intact, turned vertical and sank stern-first, creating a giant whirlpool.

The two other garinafins, unable to take off, were pulled down into the vortex. The Lyucu still afloat struggled to crawl up that roiling, churning, swirling, liquid surface.

Tana swept her tail from side to side, kicked her feet, flapped her wings through this thick, turbulent medium, so different from air, her natural realm. There was no lift gas left in her body; her lungs were filling with water. Her limbs moved slower, more stiffly. Still, she stretched her neck up, holding her riders above the turbulent water.

With a final, wheezing apologetic groan, the garinafin stopped struggling against the relentless sea. She began to sink, and the three humans riding on her jumped off to swim next to her head.

"Tana! Tana! Don't give up!" Toof cried.

She gazed at Toof with her lone eye, and it didn't close even as she sank beneath the waves.

"Is there anyone alive?" a faint cry came over the winds.

It was the speech of Dara.

*Dissolver of Sorrows* cut through the flotsam and jetsam. Everything gleamed golden in the rising sun. The pod of whales, along with the bull nursing a headache, had departed for new feeding grounds. Far to the south, the Wall of Storms continued its inhuman display of arrogant power. Nature seemed to care nothing for the battle that had been fought here, nor the lives that had been lost. The dappled waves erased all.

"Why are we looking for Lyucu survivors?" asked Takval, who had been pulled out of the water along with Toof and Radia.

"Because before the sea, all men are votan-ru-taasa," said Théra. Her voice was cold.

Takval knew that Théra's joy at his survival was deep and heartfelt—the look of relief on her face as he was brought aboard, shivering and limbs so numb that he couldn't even sit up, told him everything. He suspected that some of it was out of practical political considerations: Without him, he couldn't imagine how she would convince the Agon in Gondé to trust her and her people in an alliance. But he wondered if some of it was also because she had genuinely come to care for him in the brief time they had spent together—she had rushed over to wrap another blanket around him, trying to warm him with her own body heat.

However, as soon as it was clear that he would be all right, she had turned formal and stiff, leaving him to supervise the work of searching for more survivors.

Takval knew that she blamed him for the deaths of the marines. He sighed. He didn't explain that had he and the marines not stayed behind to harass and delay the Lyucu scouting parties inside the city-ship until the wall-busters had gone off, the whole assault might have failed. What-ifs could advocate for any side in an argument, and there was simply too wide a gulf between him and the princess on the necessity of sacrifice and the wisdom of mercy.

Still, he didn't suggest that they toss Toof and Radia back into the ocean. It wasn't just because he knew Théra would disagree. He found that he could not . . . hate them as he would have liked. It was a confusing feeling.

In the end, Radia, Toof, and Takval were the only ones to be rescued. Dead bodies drifted all around them in the morning sun, glowing gold like a field of chrysanthemums.

After the other ships of the fleet reunited with *Dissolver of Sorrows*, they spent a day to search for and recover the bodies of the dead marines so that they could be given a proper burial at sea after a solemn funeral. Toof and Radia, bound prisoners, sat mutely in shock on deck, silently mourning their dead mount and companions.

Takval also convinced Théra to salvage some fragments of wreckage. Although much of the foodstuffs from the city-ship were spoiled by the sea, many of the storage chests and pouches adrift contained raw materials and finished Lyucu artifacts that would be useful once they reached Gondé: garinafin bone, skull bowls, waterskins, tent poles, bladders, and so on.

It would take days for the damage to *Dissolver of Sorrows* to be repaired. A sturdy bamboo framework replaced the screen that had been strung between *Dandelion Seed* and *Drifting Lotus*, and with the aid of this makeshift gantry, the flagship was hoisted as high out of the water as possible so that the leaks could be properly patched. The crew went deep into the bilge and climbed all over the exposed hull.

Théra was standing on the aftercastle of *Dandelion Seed* when Admiral Roso came to her, looking anxious.

"Your Highness, we've found a stowaway."

# CHAPTER ELEVEN

# THE STOWAWAY

*Sing, memories. Sing.*

The Islands sparkled like a handful of jewels scattered across the wine-dark sea. Around them rose a shimmering veil of storms, a silk mask draped around the rim of a crown to keep the wearer's visage a mystery. In the grandness of the world, Dara was but a tiny corner, no more significant than one star in the endless empyrean, or one whale spout in the vastness of the ocean.

But to tarry at this height will freeze the blood-belt-current and to keep such a distant perspective will sicken the heart-mind with loneliness; therefore, let's descend, get close, and listen.

Tinkling pitter-patter, like spring rain on bamboo leaves.

- *What do you hope to find by undertaking this unprecedented journey, my brother?*

An ancient laugh, leathery, sandy, wise, filled with as much texture and color as the tidal pools on the black beaches of old Haan.

- *If I knew the answer to that, last born of the gods, my baby sister, I wouldn't bother going at all. It is into terra incognita that I plan to sail.*

Two voices now: bubbling lava and slow-gliding glacier, hissing steam where fire met ice.

- *We don't approve. Our charge was to guide and protect Dara—*

*—not to abdicate our responsibility when things are hard.*

A wild cackle, like the stormy waves battering the cliffs of Wolf's Paw.

*- I vote yes! Let Lutho take on mortal form—trust me, it's every bit as bad as you think, but don't let that stop him. Let the old turtle seek the immortals beyond the Wall of Storms like Mapidéré's fools. These Islands— not to say this god-shape the Lyucu have brought with them—is too small for the both of us.*

The tidal pool again: hundreds of creatures, a microcosm in strife, a miniature world in dynamic balance, a million crisscrossing ripples sketching out a billion thoughts, self-generating, self-reflective, self-critical.

*- We're not voting. My immortal siblings, let's never thwart the nature of any of us by force or compulsion. My nature is to be drawn to new knowledge like the sunflower to the golden orb. In following that original divine spark, implanted in me by our parents, high-minded Thasoluo and grand-hearted Daraméa, I no more abdicate my duties as a guardian of Dara than Théra is abdicating her duties as the heir to the throne by pursuing those who would harm her people across an ocean.*

The howling of winds—like the cries of a thousand Mingén falcons—and the gentle bubbling of hot springs—like the bleating of a thousand newborn lambs.

*- Will you remember us when you're in mortal form?*

*- Will you remember the sights and sounds of Dara beyond the Wall?*

*- Do you have any words of wisdom you wish us to remember, brother?*

*- Do you have any unfinished tasks you wish us to complete, brother?*

*- When and how will you return?*

The roar of rising tides in the distance, bearing new forms, new smells, new tastes, new life, a deluge that would destroy this pool as it had been but also refresh it, like an aged dyran that dove into a subterranean volcano to be rejuvenated.

*- Though I'm the god of knowledge, I know not what the future holds, brothers and sisters. I have no answers for you. But . . . there is one thing I want to share with you before my departure. We were charged by our parents to protect Dara and its people, but I have grown ever more doubtful of our methods.*

*- What do you mean, wise brother?*

*- There was a time when we interfered directly in the affairs of the mortals, waging war among them like outsized champions. There was a time when we guided and instructed, offering salvation through miracles and castigating with omens. These methods sometimes worked, but failed just as often. I wonder if we've been misunderstanding the intent of our parents.*

*- Oho, this ought to be good. So what do you think we should do, old turtle?*

*- A good parent sees the nature of the child and tends to it rather than thwarting it. A good guardian ought to do no less for their charge. It is the nature of mortals to ever enlarge their realm of understanding and to seek mastery over their own fate. Perhaps we should let them.*

*- What? You think we should do nothing?*

*- No. But perhaps we can withdraw our presence further and manifest our divine nature through patterned regularity in our respective domains. Rather than corralling them ineffectively with blunt force and unsolvable mysteries, let's step back and let the mortals weigh the fish and discover the wonders of a universe that is knowable. With enlarged souls, they may guard themselves better than we're able.*

Noises of outrage and objection: thunder, lightning, howling storms, volcanic eruptions . . .

But there was no answer from Lutho.

The gods of Dara were not allowed to leave their realm. To follow Princess Théra across the Wall of Storms, he had to become mortal. And mortal ears were not attuned to divine voices.

The varied sounds of weapons clanging, armor plates grinding, shields bashing gradually fused into the metallic music of the *moaphya*, bronze slabs struck with a mallet. The music reverberated against the mountains and the sea, bouncing back to craft in the musician an echoey image until sound and light were indistinguishable.

*- You have our blessing, brother. May you find what you desire, though you know not what you seek. I had to become blind before I could see, and perhaps you must be bathed in oblivion before you can learn new wisdom.*

The song of memories was a chaotic jumble of sound that failed to cohere into syllable. Her thoughts consisted of light and shadows that failed to coalesce into shapes and objects. She was without language, a creature of sensations and instincts.

She was in a dim place that she did not know was labeled the hold of a ship. Her feet were immersed in something wet and cold that she did not know was called seawater. She felt a need that she did not know was termed hunger. She felt a craving that she did not know was named thirst. There was not even the shadow of a memory of these sensations in her mind, because in her previous life she had not experienced them.

A door opened above her. Light flooded into the darkness, revealing angles and edges and surfaces. Footsteps above her. She held still. The footsteps receded. The door closed. The light went out, and darkness swallowed the universe.

Movement. More light and shadows. Scuttling beyond the edge of vision.

Creatures with long tails and reddish eyes came to her, and she felt neither revulsion nor fear because she did not know that they were called rats.

The creatures regarded her with curiosity; they turned and dropped the objects held in their jaws onto the ledge on which she sat. She picked them up and placed them into her mouth, chewed; they were stringy, salty. She swallowed and felt the emptiness in her stomach replaced by fullness.

She tried to put her mouth into the cool liquid at her feet, thinking that the gentle, yielding medium would unstick her swollen tongue from the roof of her mouth. But the bitter liquid only made things worse. She had to learn to lick the droplets dripping from the ceiling of the dark space she was in, which seemed to lack the bitterness that had made her gag.

The creatures returned with more things for her. This time they were round and succulent. She bit into them, and her tongue tingled with the delight of first sweetness. She felt the fire in her throat be quenched.

She tried to understand the world through her senses. She did not know why except a vague memory of the idea of weighing, of measuring, of trying to grasp the slippery, cold truth that flitted through the darkness like the scaled creatures that touched her feet from time to time.

She studied surfaces, and caressed the rough boards around her until her hands bled. She gazed at the wounds in her skin, fascinated. The sensation of pain was novel. She liked it at first, and then found how it darkened, lingered, and grew unpleasant. It would not stop. She learned to avoid pain.

She began to understand that vision could not penetrate into the interior of things, and she started to associate images with textures, with weight, with heat and cold.

As she slept, she saw visions of black and white ravens, of sharks and turtles, of doves and fish, of birds winging their way through the sky. She did not know their names, much less why she was dreaming of them.

The creatures returned, this time with something soft and bulky. She tried to eat it, but did not like the taste. She tried wrapping it around herself. She felt warm, and stopped shivering. *What a delightful sensation!* she thought, but without words. She had not known that she was cold until she was no longer cold. Change was what made knowledge possible.

She indulged in smells and tastes, in the briny odor of the sea, the sour flavor of worm-ridden stale bread, the fragrant aromas that seeped into the hold from unknown sources, redolent of mysteries. She studied how it was possible to know the truth of something without seeing or touching.

But it was the sense of hearing that most moved her. Sounds were not like light or touch: They did not come only from surfaces. Sounds came from the insides of things, the insides of the skin of the world that enveloped her.

Chirps, moans, plaintive cries. She did not know this was called music or song, but she felt her body move in sync with it, felt her breath and heart meld with it. Song was not memory, but it lifted her spirits. For the first time, she felt the urge to sing herself, and she opened her mouth and learned to breathe a new way, to shape throat and tongue and folds in her neck to imitate the music she heard. She discovered her voice.

Thumps, bumps, loud crashes. The gurgling and splashing of water. Screams. Terrified babbles. She tried to imagine the sources of the new sounds and could not.

More water came into the hold. Those long-tailed furry creatures fell into the water and swam to the walls, trying to scrabble their way up the slippery surfaces. The world lurched, tilted, and the water rose in a giant wave that washed the creatures off the wall, that pushed her off her bench and held her under.

She was not afraid because she did not know what there was to be afraid of.

The water filled her nostrils and mouth. She coughed. The water burned against her throat and lungs. She realized she could not breathe.

A sensation that she did not know was called panic seized her. She thrashed and flailed, trying to push herself out of the water by any means necessary. But the yielding, cold medium gave no purchase, and she made no headway. She felt light-headed, as though thought were slowing down, as though her very self were being shut away like the light that from time to time created the universe out of darkness.

One of her flailing hands grabbed something. The thing wriggled in her grasp—one of the long-tailed creatures. She squeezed her fingers tighter. The creatures had given her gifts that had helped her before, and surely they would help her again? The creature in her hand kicked wildly, and then she felt a sharp, piercing pain as its tiny jaws bit into her finger. She opened her mouth to scream and more bitter, cold water flooded in. She refused to let go. Somehow, clutching the creature was the only way to save herself; she was sure of it. She squeezed even harder and felt the tiny, delicate bones snap. The creature stopped struggling.

The world lurched and tilted again, the other way.

As quickly as the wave had overwhelmed her, it now retreated. She found herself on a ledge, with water cascading off her in sheets. She coughed, gagged, gasped. She clung to the ledge with every fiber of her being.

She sat up and uncurled her fingers. She looked at the creature in her hand. It did not move. She tilted her hand, and it flopped softly onto the ledge. She leaned down, placing her cheek at the tiny snout. There was no breath. She picked it up and dropped it into the receding water at her feet, hoping somehow it would revive. It had been swimming earlier, hadn't it?

But the creature drifted along with the other flotsam in the hold. It was not different from the broken pieces of wood, not different from the bobbing cork plugs, not different from the empty coconut-husk ladle.

*Lifeless.* The concept came to her in a flash of terror. It was *dead*.

It would never again experience sweetness and sourness, never again crave water or yearn for food, never again dance across the rough boards on its scrabbling feet, never again know the world's aromas and flavors through panting breath, never again be enveloped in a universe of delightful, terrifying, mysterious sensations.

She picked the creature up out of the water and stared at it. A pain that she had not known before began to fill her, starting at the thumping in the middle of her chest, moving up until it stabbed her behind the eyes. Her vision blurred, and her breathing became shallow and fast. That was how she learned of sorrow, of regret, of death. She began to sing the only song she knew, the song that had taught her she had a voice. It was mourning; it was memory; it was a defiant affirmation of life. So long as she could sing, she could breathe.

She was unaware that death had been a stranger to her in her previous state of existence, but she understood now that in this life, death would be her constant companion and teacher.

Théra examined the stowaway.

The girl was about twelve, dark-skinned and long-limbed, with the bright green eyes common among the people of Haan. Instead of looking back at Théra, her eyes scanned the sea, darting from one piece of wreckage to another. Her gaze seemed to linger on the floating dead bodies, and she made terrified mewling noises in her throat.

The way she huddled against the hulking figure of Admiral Roso, who stood protectively behind her, and the manner in which she squinted against the bright sunlight and held her arms up defensively, reminded Théra of a frightened rat.

"We found her in the ship's hold, in a chilled storage compartment for produce. Good thing she's dressed for it," said Admiral Roso, indicating the thick, bulky winter coat wrapped around the girl. "The room was locked and she couldn't get out, and I guess the cooks didn't find her the few times they went in for supplies."

"Does anyone recognize her?" asked Théra.

"No one on *Dissolver of Sorrows.* I've sent skiffs to the other ships with sketches and a description of the girl, but I doubt anyone knows her."

Théra kept her voice soft and kind as she approached the girl. "Little sister, what's your name?" The girl was just about Fara's age.

"We've tried," said Admiral Roso. "She doesn't speak."

"Oh, you mean she's deaf and mute?"

"No. She can hear just fine, and she can sing. In fact, that was how we found her: singing like a whale in the hold. She just doesn't seem to know human language."

Théra was taken aback. "How is that possible? Is she an orphan abandoned in the wilderness? What the common people call a child of the gods?"

"A child of the gods," the girl said suddenly, a perfect copy of Théra. She had lowered her arms and regarded Théra with a look of intense curiosity.

Théra was startled, and then chuckled.

"Why, you lying tadpole!" Admiral Roso roared. "You broken barnacle! Slippery eel! Trying to fool me into thinking you can't talk, do you? How dare—"

"We've tried! Fool me into?! Lying tadpole! What's your name? Deaf and mute. How is that possible?" the girl said, imitating Théra and Mitu Roso by turns. Her voice was crisp and musical, reminding the listener of an unsullied brook.

Admiral Roso's face turned red as a ripe monkeyberry, but before he could explode, Théra waved him off. "I don't think she's playing a trick on you."

"How do you know, Your Highness?" asked Roso.

Théra turned to Takval, who was standing by, watching quietly. "Can you say a tongue twister in Agon?"

"A tongue twister?"

"Something that is hard to say without tripping your tongue over it," said Théra, "even if you were born speaking Agon."

"Ah." Takval thought for a second. "Dia dia diaara culek, ally ally allyuri rupé."

The girl, who was watching Takval and Théra intently, waited a few moments before speaking. "Even if you were born speaking Agon. Ah. Dia dia diaara culek, ally ally allyuri rupé."

Théra tried to do the same. "Dia dia dia a a—dia-a-ra-ra—forget it. You'll have to say that again, slower."

Takval went on speaking Agon to the girl excitedly. The girl responded and the two seemed to be carrying on a conversation, but Théra could tell that she was only repeating certain phrases from what Takval had said. Gradually, the excitement faded from Takval's face, replaced by bewilderment.

"Does she pronounce the words strangely?" asked Théra.

"Not at all. She speaks like someone from my home tribe. I've spoken to some of the old enslaved Dara captives in Gondé who have learned the language of the scrublands, and they always speak it with a strange tilt in the shapes of the sounds, much like you. But this girl . . . she sounds like she was born in Gondé."

Théra turned to Admiral Roso. "If she was only pretending and playing a trick on you, she couldn't have done the same for Takval. There's no native of Dara on this expedition who knows the language of the scrublands, much less anyone who can speak it with no accent. I think she truly doesn't know human speech, and is only imitating the sounds with perfection."

Somewhat mollified, Admiral Roso said, "I suggest we shackle her and keep her in the brig under constant watch. We don't know who she is, and we can't tell what kind of mischief she's up to. Is she a spy? Is she a sabo—"

Théra shook her head to stop him. "I can sense no threat from her. Sometimes the gods test us by sending us unexpected guests."

Light. There was so much light. So much open space. She could not believe how bright the world was, how big it was, or how many colors and shapes there were. She was overwhelmed.

Then she noticed the elongated objects floating in the water. She looked closer. They were shaped just like her, and so she knew they experienced the world the same way. But they weren't moving. They were just like the broken spars and wrecked casks, just like the bobbing jars and frothy foam at the tips of the waves, just like the long-tailed creature that had drifted in the cold water in the bottom of the hold.

They were dead.

She mourned them. She was revolted by the scene of destruction. There was no greater terror than death, and no greater evil in the world than to cause death.

And then, other creatures shaped like her. But not corpses. Alive.

They sang at her, and it was a different kind of song from the one she knew. She could hear the beauty in the songs—love, longing, understanding of the inside of things, beneath surfaces. The sounds tickled her heart, caressed her heart, made her lungs and throat and tongue tingle in sympathy. She understood then that as long as the sounds stirred her in this way, as long as she could stir others with such sounds, death would be kept at bay.

She wanted to learn to sing like that. More than anything else.

Once *Dissolver of Sorrows* was fully repaired, the fleet left behind the watery graveyard and went on its way.

As the Dara expedition sailed first to the west and then south, always going with the belt current, the language lessons for the young girl continued.

Toof, Radia, and Takval taught the girl the tongue of the scrublands. Since the girl was going to live in Ukyu and Gondé, it only made sense for her to learn to speak the topolects that would be useful there. Théra also assigned a group of learned tutors to teach her the vernacular of Dara. Among them was Razutana Pon the Cultivationist, whose reputation among the other scholars had soared after tales spread of his brave and clever plot to unleash a garinafin to rampage through the city-ship during the boarding.

"Once she learns how to speak," said Théra, "perhaps she will be able to tell us how she came to be here and what she wants."

Though Théra was curious about the girl's origins, she had far more pressing issues to attend to. The girl's presence, however, did give her an unexpected solution for a problem that had been plaguing her.

The main reason that members of the expedition had been so slow to learn the language of the scrublands was that they were already such accomplished men and women. Weighed down by the respect they thought of as their due, it was difficult for them to relieve themselves of these burdens, to risk being seen once again as silly and incompetent, to learn the names of simple, everyday things, to struggle to express themselves, to be vulnerable—in other words, to be like children.

Even Théra herself, despite her best efforts, felt the same impulse to avoid embarrassment. But without embarrassment, it was impossible to learn.

The stowaway girl, on the other hand, had none of these obstacles in her way, and as members of Théra's expedition monitored the language lessons, ostensibly meant for the girl, they could learn alongside her.

So much of learning, decided Théra, consisted of forgetting how much you already knew.

There were arguments among the teachers, of course. Takval and the Lyucu garinafin riders disagreed over which topolect of the scrublands was most proper, and the scholars assigned by Théra, being from different regions of Dara, fought over the best accent. The girl seemed to take it all in stride, learning multiple ways of saying the same thing with equanimity, imitating the vocalizations perfectly.

One of the biggest arguments occurred over her name.

"We can't always just call her 'the girl,'" said Razutana. "As Poti Maji once said, '*Réfigéruca cadaé pha thicruü co mapidathinélo,*' that is, 'A proper name is the beginning of understanding.'"

"The right to name her belongs to the people of the scrublands," said Takval, "for her condition was only understood when she first spoke our tongue. Let's call her Ryoana, after Toryoana, the merciful god of healing hands. She shall be a sign of the healing wind that will come to the scrublands."

Toof and Radia immediately voiced their support. The two Lyucu naros had come to like the Agon prince on the city-ship, and they were able to walk about *Dissolver of Sorrows* in relative freedom only because Takval had insisted that they be allowed to teach the girl to speak their (largely) shared language.

Moreover, Takval's suggestion was auspicious. Rather than making some reference to strife and warfare, which they knew were in the future of the Lyucu and the Agon as surely as the belt current pulled them toward their destination, Takval had chosen to commemorate this moment of relative peace.

But Razutana objected. "Why should we give her a barba—a name that isn't found in the Ano Classics? She is a girl of Dara. Let's name her after Lutho, the god of wisdom, and call her Yemilutho. She shall be a prefiguration of the enlightenment that will come to the people of the scrublands."

"What makes you think she's a girl of Dara?" asked Takval. A hint of anger crept into his tone in response to the barely disguised insult in Razutana's speech.

"She's . . . she's found on this ship," said Razutana. "Where else would she be from?"

"*We* are also found on this ship," said Radia, "at least as of now. By your logic, are we also from Dara then?" Toof and Radia resented Razutana for what he had done to Tana. Anything he suggested, they were sure to oppose.

"Are you telling me that she rode all the way here from Ukyu and Gondé?" asked Razutana in disbelief.

"That's no less likely than your theory," countered Radia. "We don't know where she's from, and she speaks perfect Lyucu."

"Thoryo."

Everyone turned to the young girl, who was pointing at herself. "Thoryo," she repeated.

"That's not a Dara name at all," scoffed Razutana. "I don't even know how to write it in logograms."

"That's not a Lyucu name either," said Radia. "It sounds barbaric."

"It's definitely not Agon," said Takval. "But it does . . . have a ring to it."

"Well, since we don't know her parentage or lineage, I think the only one who can name Thoryo is Thoryo," said Théra. "After all, she's not Lyucu, nor Agon, nor Dara. She must discover for herself who she is."

*My name is Thoryo. I am aboard a ship called* Dissolver of Sorrows. *I am alive.*

She said this to herself, first in both varieties of the language of the scrublands, then in the many varieties of the vernacular of Dara, and finally in a mixture of words and grammars from all of them, testing the syllables out on her tongue like she had run her hands over the textures she had found in the hold: the soft fur of the dead rat, the stinging liquid chill of seawater, the rough splinters in the unfinished wood.

What powerful magic it was, Thoryo thought, to map the world of things to names, to build ethereal structures out of names, to reason and to feel with these structures, to translate light and shadows and noises and smells and tastes and feelings into thought.

And then, to speak—to shape breath with lips and tongue, to articulate, to modulate sound into syllables, to accumulate syllables into words, to arrange words into sentences, to craft sentences into the song of speech, to play that thought-scored music with the living instrument that was her whole body.

And, even more marvelously, to listen—to have her music be understood by another, to have a different body vibrate in sympathy, to have a disparate mind see, hear, touch, taste, and smell the same things she saw, heard, touched, tasted, and smelled.

Speech was how she understood the interior of another mind, how she incorporated the world into her self, how she held on to memories—through silent recitations of the present until the present had turned into the past, had lost its vividness and color, until only the words remained; but as soon as she spoke the words again, the memory also came back to life.

The magic of speech was ephemeral, gone the very moment it was heard. Every utterance died as soon as it was born. To live was to breathe, and to be human was to think. Therefore speech, being thinking-breath, was as mortal as the speaker. No matter how hard one tried, one could not hold on to speech.

For that, she loved it all the more.

The fleet retraced the voyage taken by Luan Zya all those decades ago as it followed the great belt current around the ocean, heading for the distant shores of Ukyu and Gondé.

Each day, the scholars studied the stars, took measurements and observations, and recorded the marvels they saw around them. Çami climbed to the crow's nest to sketch spouting whales. The crew pulled up new kinds of fish, shrimp, jellyfish, sea stars, and even an occasional small whale or shark in their nets, many of which were unknown in both Dara and Ukyu-Gondé. Painters, potters, ceramicists, and carvers, searching for some way to exercise their hands, took to sketching anatomies and fashioning models. Razutana devised fanciful names for the new species in formal Ano logograms, replete with colorful classical allusions: *oné gi ofégo Ginpen zahugara* ("the drifting belt of Ginpen"—a type of jellyfish with very long tentacles), *crupa cowin* ("glaucous glare"—a rather frightening-looking fish with disproportionately large eyes), *jijimoru wi tutho ré wizétha* ("creaking loom of the wizened god"—perhaps a heretofore unknown species of seaweed, though no one was quite sure), and so on.

Most of the crew, on the other hand, preferred to admire these new fruits of the sea via gustatory means. In this endeavor, Captain Nméji Gon and Commander Tipo Tho provided ample leadership by example. They explored all sorts of ways to cook and enjoy these unfamiliar creatures, and named them by taste: stinkfish, tongue-tingling jelly, salty plum clams, and so forth.

Naturally, the gluttons' names were far more popular, causing Razutana Pon to shake his head and lament the lack of refinement among his comrades.

Thoryo's studies were progressing quickly, and by now she could converse with everyone on the ship, whether Lyucu, Dara, or Agon, with equal facility. The rest of the crew had made uneven progress as well, but none could match her skill with language acquisition, especially the uncanny way she could replicate any accent with native accuracy.

She amazed the crew with stories of her time in the hold, when she had survived on the food brought to her by rats and the occasional fish that lived in bilgewater, when she had stayed warm with a coat brought her by the furry vermin. Not everyone believed her, but sailors were used to fishing tales. Yet, she could not remember how she had come to be on the ship, her parentage, origin, or indeed, anything about her life before she had appeared in that hold, seemingly out of nowhere.

"You know what I miss the most?" asked Toof one day as the group of linguists, finished with another joint lesson, lounged about the foredeck. The sun was bright, the sky cloudless, and the sails flapped gently in the cool breeze.

"What?" asked Captain Gon. He was supervising the sailors as they set up a grill on the foredeck in preparation for the catch of the day.

"Mouflon sponge," said Toof.

"Oh, I'll second that," said Radia. Even Takval nodded and licked his lips.

"How do you make it?" asked Captain Gon. As part of the linguistic exchange around Thoryo, they were conversing in a mixture of languages at this point, with the Lyucu and Agon instructors trying to speak as much as possible in Dara, while the Dara instructors endeavored to speak in the language of the scrublands.

"Definitely hot," said Toof, "especially if cooked in the cap, without being plucked."

"Definitely cold," said Radia, "preferably sliced fresh and served with the original sauce."

"Definitely dried," said Takval, "preferably salted, though honeyed sponge is good too."

"Only an Agon would think that an appropriate way to prepare mouflon sponge," scoffed Toof.

"Only a Lyucu would think it appropriate to deny those away from the hunt the pleasures of mouflon sponge," said Takval.

Captain Gon spoke for the rest of the Dara in the group when he asked, "Err . . . just where do you find this 'mouflon sponge'?"

Toof and Radia, being relatively unskilled in speaking Dara, sometimes made memorable howlers. Captain Gon wasn't sure Toof knew the exact words he was looking for.

The three mouflon sponge aficionados turned as one to him. "You mean you don't eat the sponge of animals? It is the most delicious part," said Radia.

"Maybe we do," said an exasperated Captain Gon. "But I don't know what you're talking about!"

"The best way to enjoy sponge, whether mouflon, deer, or cattle, is to leave the sponge where it is and cook the whole skull like a pot over a banked bed of ashes," Toof said. He had to swallow a mouthful of saliva as he conjured up memories of his favorite treat. "And then, you just sprinkle in some sea salt and squirt in a few lobes' worth of gash cactus juice, and dig in with an antler spoon."

"Is this 'sponge' . . . the brains of the mouflon?" Commander Tho's face was turning white.

"Of course!" said Radia. "But you don't call it 'brains' when eating it. It is the most nourishing part of the animal. However, Toof is wrong about the best way to enjoy the dish. It's best to extract the sponge and cut it into very thin slices with a good stone knife. Then you should eat it raw so that the flavor is unspoiled by any extra seasoning, except perhaps a dipping sauce of blood. This has to be done when the sponge is very fresh, though, and ideally when the heart hasn't yet stopped beating."

"But that's barbaric!" said Commander Tho.

"How is that barbaric?" asked Takval.

"To have the heart of the animal still beating while you dine upon its brains—" Commander Tho couldn't finish as she gagged at the thought.

"Do you not kill your animals to obtain meat?" asked Radia.

"We do," said Captain Gon, his face twisted in distaste. "But we don't delight in the slaughter."

"And a gentleman of learning and virtue goes nowhere near the kitchen, especially not a Cultivationist," said Razutana. "The Moralist Poti Maji said that to *cultivate* virtue, one must stay away from the chopping block and the cleaver, the blood and gore of the slaughterhouse, as well as the smoke and oil of the frying pan. To be exposed to death in this manner corrupts the sensitive soul dedicated to growth and breeding."

"Then a virtuous and learned gentleman must starve?" asked Takval.

"Of course not! But the food should be prepared by servants into a civilized form before it may be consumed. Fish should be filleted, meat should be chopped into bite-sized chunks, and birds should not be served unless feet and heads are removed."

"Well, that's only if you could afford it," muttered Tipo Tho. "The rest of us eat fish heads and chicken feet, and are grateful for it."

"It's an ideal to aspire to," said Razutana.

"In other words, the food should be served so that it doesn't resemble food," said Takval contemptuously.

"That's not quite how I would put it—"

"That is *exactly* how you should put it," said Takval. For the moment, there seemed to be a kind of Lyucu-Agon alliance against Dara in the debate. "It sounds to me like your Moralist and Cultivationist philosophers advocate hypocrisy so that they may ignore the fact that their lives depend on slaughter. I think it's far more 'civilized' to face the reality of what we eat, to feel the blood squirting out of the dying body even as we feast on it, to be thankful for the gift of the weak to the strong by consuming every part that may yield nourishment."

"Even if all eating depends on death," said Razutana, "there is a difference between taking pleasure in the death throes of the victim and minimizing exposure to pain and suffering. Kon Fiji, the One True Sage, said that if we could all survive on dew and air, we should do so. That we cannot is a great tragedy of our mortality. We are better than beasts who know only tooth and claw, or at least we should strive to be."

"I think there is no greater barbarism than to eat meat while pretending it is something else," said Takval. His face had turned red and his voice had risen.

"That's enough, all of you," said Théra, arriving late to the argument. She didn't like how a harmless conversation about food had degenerated so quickly into mutual contempt and accusations of barbarism. It revealed just how much tension there was beneath the surface of her crew.

The others seemed unwilling to give up the fight, but in that temporary lull, the sounds of quiet weeping grabbed their attention. They turned and saw that it was Thoryo, who stood crying over the fish being grilled on the foredeck.

"What's wrong?" asked Théra.

"I think the greatest barbarism of them all is that we all have to die," she said. "You're here arguing over what way to kill and eat is more civilized, but what separates any of you from this fish? Nothing. Whether we are strong or weak, barbaric or civilized, in the end we all end up as food for something else. Why spend so much of the little time you have to show how you're superior to someone else? That is all vanity."

"But the Ano sages say that there are things more important than life—" began Razutana.

"But the gods have promised the brave and worthy a ride upon the cloud-garinafin—" began Takval.

"Why should I listen to the Ano sages and the gods?" said Thoryo. "The sages no longer breathe and the gods never speak as we do. What do they know of the bodies scattered upon the sea after a battle? What do they know of the infinite wonders of the mind extinguished upon the death of every life? What do they know of being *alive*?"

As the days grew longer and then shorter, as the sun shifted from one side of the ship to the other, as the stars changed overhead, the fleet sailed into even more eerie waters.

From time to time, lookouts announced that they sighted land in the distance, replete with shimmering cities and streaming carriages on the horizon. Knowing that they were mirages, Théra and Takval refused to steer for them.

But the fleet also sailed over vast sunken reefs, and as sunlight glinted off the colorful corals, they thought they could see cities beneath. The decision was made to have *Dissolver of Sorrows* dive beneath the surface to investigate, having first tethered her to two other ships on the surface for propulsion.

The officers stood in the captain's quarters and watched in awe as their ship glided over a sunken ruin.

"This is like being in an airship," whispered Commander Tho. And those who had flown in an airship nodded.

Beneath them, broken stone columns showed the outlines of ancient temples, and formations of corals sketched out long-inundated roads. Collapsed buildings lay open to the sea, their angular roofs in pieces at their feet. Crabs skittered across courtyards with mosaic floors whose patterns were still discernible after who knew how many millennia.

They saw piles of rubble with broken walls and lintels, through which schools of fish swam as though they were the natural heirs of the lost civilization. They saw eels dash from crumbled towers as the shadow of their underwater ship passed over them like the shadow of a cloud, as though the eels were still defending the lost city against a prophesied invasion. They saw jellyfish dance through the tiered seats of octagonal theaters, as though performing for a ghost audience.

"It was said that the Ano had escaped their homeland far to the west when it sank into the ocean," whispered Théra. "Could these be the ruins of that mystical realm?"

No one answered.

As evening fell, *Dissolver of Sorrows* surfaced, and the fleet was back on their way, but for a long time that night, no one could sleep, thinking about what they had seen.

Takval heard light scratching noises against his cabin door. He opened it and found Théra standing outside. Surprised, he asked her to come in.

"What's troubling you?" he asked.

"I don't know how to explain it," she said, hesitant. "But I fear that the ruins were an ill omen."

"Why?"

"The Ano were a wondrous people, refined and full of knowledge. But they were also riven from within by divisions. In the sagas, it was said that when their homeland began to sink into the ocean, instead of coming together to meet the common threat, they fell into internecine warfare over the dwindling land. In the end, they had no choice but to leave for new shores, refugees who found a new home in Dara."

"What does that . . . have to do with you?"

"The Ano were my ancestors, and we revere them. But what if we have inherited not just their civilization and refinement, but also their capacity for self-destruction?"

"My ancestors were also a wondrous people, and they also had stories that serve as warnings against internal strife."

And so Takval told Théra the story of Kikisavo and Afir, of their unparalleled bond, of their victories over the gods, of Kikisavo's jealousy and betrayal, and of Afir's reluctant decision to go to war against him.

"According to some shamans," said Takval. "Kikisavo and Afir were not just friends, but also lovers. She never could forgive him, but she also couldn't forget him. After Kikisavo was exiled beyond the sea after his defeat, Afir would send him food on the backs of turtles."

"A sort of care package, I suppose," said Théra, smiling. When Takval did not understand the reference, she explained the Dara custom for wives to send husbands comfortable under-tunics and warm socks they made when the men were away at war, or for parents to send homemade treats to children studying in Ginpen or taking the Grand Examination in Pan.

"Though I don't understand all the customs of Dara," said Takval, "I understand the love that endures between husband and wife, between parent and child, between brother and sister, between individuals who consider themselves one people."

"But is love enough? Will Dara survive the Lyucu invasion? Will we be able to rally your people to freedom? Or will petty jealousy and ambition destroy all that we yearn for? Have we been shown a sign today in the ruins beneath the waves?"

"We're not our ancestors," said Takval. "We can only do what we believe is best."

"I don't know if the best is enough, when weighed against human nature, fate, and the whims of the gods. I'm afraid, Takval. I'm afraid."

"Stay with me then, and we'll tell each other happier stories. I am no shaman and cannot read omens, but don't you remember how beautiful the ruins looked? How full of life? Finned and clawed, the new denizens were not troubled by tales of the past."

Théra smiled. "That's lovely. The fish did look happy, didn't they?"

"So let my thinking-breath comfort your heart and yours mine."

She nodded and leaned against him, and he embraced her, less awkwardly than before.

Thoryo's quick progress in languages never slackened. Once she was confident with her speech, she demanded her instructors tell her about the histories of the three peoples she found herself among. She learned about Dara legends as well as Lyucu myths; she listened to stories about Ano sages as well as Agon heroes. She didn't pass judgment on what she heard, seemingly soaking it all in like a sponge.

"Why do the gods seem to decline in power in all of your stories?" she asked one night as the group gazed up at unfamiliar stars and tried to make new patterns out of them.

"How do you mean?" asked Takval.

"In your stories, the gods once created the heavens and the earth, and fashioned the people and every living thing. At a whim they created new stars out of failed gods and new races out of inert matter. But now they are living beyond the mountains at the world's edge, and do not make their presence felt except to bring about a storm or guide the mouflon herds from one part of the scrublands to another."

Takval, Radia, and Toof contemplated this and were silent.

"And in your stories," Thoryo said, turning to Théra and Razutana and the others from Dara, "the gods once constructed the Islands with tears and sweat, created mountains out of valleys, brought lakes forth from the desert. They fought right next to the heroes of your sagas, slaughtering thousands at a single blow. But now they seem absent from the world, only speaking through obscure oracles that are subject to diverse interpretations, giving no clear guidance."

"I have wondered the same myself," said Théra. "The apparent withdrawal of the gods from human affairs is a question that has plagued philosophers throughout history."

"Could the gods, in fact, not exist at all?" asked Thoryo. "Are they but figments of the imagination, metaphors and allegories offered to explain what could not be explained? Are the old legends mere stories?"

Toof, Radia, Captain Gon, and Commander Tho, who were more pious, muttered prayers to their own gods and looked askance at the others. There was an uncomfortable silence.

"You ask a question that may be unanswerable." It was Razutana who eventually spoke. "The best answer I know comes from Kon Fiji, who admonished us to respect the gods but to keep them at arm's length."

"What did Kon Fiji mean, exactly?" asked Admiral Roso. "I've never quite understood that particular adage."

"I think he meant that we can't know for certain if the gods are mere metaphor and allegory," said Razutana. "But if the gods have chosen to remain mostly silent now, it's best to heed their wishes and to seek our own answers to our problems."

"So the gods are lazy?" asked Thoryo. "Having created the world and populated it, they then abandoned everything?"

"I wouldn't put it as lazy," said Razutana. "Parents must do everything for their children when they're first brought into the world, but then they stand back when the children are grown. It's possible that the gods thought fit to intervene much more in the infancy of the human race, but now that we're more mature, they've decided to let go. We can no longer rely on them for everything like a toddler still attached to the apron strings of its mother."

"I find this answer most unsatisfactory," said Thoryo. "In the legends of the Agon, Lyucu, and Dara, the gods were jealous, vain, self-serving, worse than humans in many ways. They didn't always behave as fit parents, and I cannot see why we should assume they've changed. I think the most likely answer is that the gods were constructed in the image of the humans themselves, and not real at all."

Once again, the pious members of the group looked uncomfortable, but they were not skilled in debate and hoarded their words carefully.

"That is a position that many philosophers over the years have taken as well," said Théra eventually. "Huzo Tuan, a leading voice of the Skeptic school, argued that faith in the gods is the source of all our problems. But I have felt the presence of divinity in my own life, and so I cannot subscribe to a theory of complete denial. The world is more interesting, to my mind, with the gods in it than without."

"Then why do you think the gods seem so much more distant and weaker now?" asked Thoryo.

"I'm no priest nor philosopher," said Théra, "and so I cannot say I've given this deep thought. But perhaps the gods are like children on the beach, who, having constructed wondrous cities and sculpted animals out of sand, now prefer to stand back in admiration rather than stomping through their creation, which would wreck it."

"That is an interesting interpretation," said Thoryo. "So the gods are not parents in your view, but fellow children with humanity."

"There is a wonder that comes to us after having built something beautiful," said Théra, "and I don't think the gods are immune to such charms."

"When I was little," said Takval, "the other children and I built miniature tent-cities and landscapes from grass, mud, discarded bone, and bits of skin and sinew. Sometimes we caught voles and sand lizards and populated these camps with them. We watched them fight and run and told epic tales of glory and conquest. I know of what you speak."

Théra smiled at the thought of her intended as a playful god over a domain of his creation. "I remember weaving houses out of twigs and grass in the Palace Garden as a little girl, and Fara would put a roof on each with a banana leaf. Phyro and Timu liked to pull up the flowers planted by our mothers to create wide avenues and line them with pebble-built palaces. We peopled them with ants, caterpillars, turtles from the creek that ran though the Palace Garden, and even baby birds we found hopping through the grass."

"And I certainly remember building grand houses out of mud

and sand on the beach as a boy," said Captain Gon. "I draped them with seaweed shingles and erected fences around them with scallop and clam shells. The snails were my peasants, tilling the land in long, meandering plow trails, while the crabs who skittered through were the landlords, rushing hither and yon to make their tenants work faster."

The others in the group joined in reminiscence, each describing their own childhood exploits. Even studious Razutana had apparently once made towns out of scrap paper for the mice in his teacher's house.

"But are these castles of sand on the beach and mansions of twig and grass in the garden so wonderful as all that?" asked Thoryo. "Do the creatures who live in them find them as delightful as the builders?"

The group fell silent.

"Ah, you ask another question that I've not thought about," said Théra. "I'm . . . not sure. I suppose the baby birds were more frightened than delighted, and the caterpillars and ants were eager to escape."

The others assented. Children were not always inclined to take into account the feelings of the creatures serving as props in the stories they wished to tell.

"If the world doesn't in fact suit its inhabitants, it is a shame that the gods no longer intervene in it," said Thoryo. "You all have told me many tales of strife and woe in this world, and there appears to be so much unhappiness."

"It is hard to tear down something you've built, even if it isn't perfect," said Takval.

"I've never thought of us as the crabs and birds and voles forced to live in the imagination of the gods," said Théra. "Perhaps we should emulate the animal denizens of our childhood constructions, who escaped to build homes more suited to their own dreams. Maybe that was why the Ano left their ancient homeland, seeking new shores to start anew as the ill-fitting past sank into the ocean."

"Maybe it isn't only the gods who construct such houses," said Thoryo. "In your stories, you speak of the great lords and ladies of the world as colossi who stride across the earth, viewed from the perspective of the low and base. And perhaps the great lords and ladies are so fascinated by their own creation that they hear only the story they want to tell."

The ships sailed on in the darkness, carrying as many different lives woven from thinking-breath as there were stars in the heavens above.

# LURODIA TANTA

SOMEWHERE IN LURODIA TANTA, THE ENDLESS
DESERT OF UKYU-GONDÉ: THE FIFTH MONTH
IN THE SECOND YEAR AFTER PRINCESS THÉRA
DEPARTED DARA (KNOWN IN DARA AS THE
SECOND YEAR OF THE REIGN OF SEASON OF
STORMS).

The world had shrunk down to the patch of tan earth that could be seen at her feet, framed by the black cowl of her robe.

One step. Another.

Théra had lost count. Though the sun had barely risen, they had already been walking for hours, it seemed. The heat was making it hard to think of anything beyond putting one foot in front of the other.

She had to start counting again. Every one thousand steps, she would allow herself one drink of water. That was the rule. The waterskins on her back, so full when they had set out, lay flat and empty. She hoped that she wouldn't have to change the rule to two thousand steps for each drink, though it might come to that if they didn't get to the Agon camp soon.

The strong current and winds had brought *Dissolver of Sorrows* and the rest of the fleet to the shores of Ukyu-Gondé two months ago. But instead of making landfall in Péa's Sea, where Admiral Krita had taken his city-ships, or the Lower Peninsula, where Luan Zyaji had beached his raft, the fleet had stayed in the ocean just beyond the horizon, creeping south. They could not risk discovery by landing near green pastures and well-stocked fishing grounds, all occupied by the Lyucu. Instead, they sailed south until the shore turned into the lifeless wastelands of Lurodia Tanta, into which the Lyucu had driven many of the Agon tribes.

The few horses that they had brought had died many days ago, as was expected. Théra had not liked the idea of bringing pack animals along when they were certain to die, but Takval had pointed out that it was impossible for them to carry all the water they would need on their backs, and they didn't have any garinafins or short-haired cattle, better suited to desert crossings.

"We have to drive them as far as they last and then finish the rest of the crossing on foot," said Takval. "Even with a small expedition of just ten people, this is the only way."

Théra reluctantly agreed to the plan, but she insisted on coming on the expedition with Takval. If she was going to send these horses, who had crossed thousands of miles of water, to die in a foreign desert, then she wanted to be there to look them in the eye and feel the full weight of her decision to doom them so that she might live.

Takval strenuously objected, even claiming that now that they were in his land, she had to obey him.

"How can we risk your life on this trip when keeping you safe is the foundation for the alliance?"

"You are at least as important to this marriage as I am," she said, deliberately switching away from the political. A year spent living, fighting, eating, talking together, and eventually, sharing the same bed, had brought them close. She was not yet certain that she would ever love him the same way she loved Zomi, but she was not sorry that he was her partner.

"But there is only one of you—" Takval stopped. Théra thought it was because he realized how silly he sounded, but there was a strange look in his eyes that she could not interpret. He looked away.

"There is also only one of you," she said, pointing out the obvious.

"*I* have to go because my people trust me. And I can bring back garinafins to help secure the rest of the fleet."

"*I* have to go because they won't respect their future queen if she waits by the sea to be rescued," countered Théra. "Can you imagine? A princess of Dara sitting in her comfortable ship, ordering the Agon pékyu-taasa to risk his life for her. That will confirm every terrible prejudice they already harbor about Dara after the stories about Admiral Krita."

"But I don't even know if I'll find my tribe. I last saw my mother and uncle at the oasis of Sliyusa Ki when I was a boy. I can only hope that I'll find them there still."

"There is no certainty to any of this! But it is certain that you can't tell me not to do what I've made up my mind to do."

"Why must you be so stubborn?" said Takval, grabbing his hair in frustration.

"I won't be a hypocrite," she said slowly. "If there's going to be death because of me, whether it's the horses or you or anyone else, the least I can do is not look away. That would be barbaric."

Takval locked eyes with her, and a complicated series of emotions flashed through his gaze. Then he knelt on one knee and placed both hands atop the other knee, a gesture reserved for intimates who also commanded high respect. "Princess of Dara, you are as precious to me as Afir was to Kikisavo."

Takval declared it was too hot to keep moving; they made camp in the shade of a dry gully. About three hundred paces from the camp was a patch of clenched-fist cactus, and Takval took two of the marines to collect some.

"Are you all right?" asked Théra as she spread a blanket on the ground. The blanket kept them off the scorching sand during the day and helped them stay warm at night.

Thoryo nodded as she sat down on the blanket. She had begged to come along as Théra's maid, though Théra was taking care of her more than the other way around.

"I don't want to be away from either of you," Thoryo had said, clutching Théra's hand desperately, her voice verging on panic. Théra and Takval were the first two people to treat her with kindness after she was discovered in the hold of *Dissolver of Sorrows*, and there was a bond between her and them that felt like how she thought a bond of blood must feel.

Despite Captain Gon's objection that Thoryo didn't possess any useful skills and Commander Tho's protest that she was too physically frail to survive such a journey, both Takval and Théra had agreed to have her come. They could not explain it in rational terms, but the mysterious girl felt like a talisman of good luck.

Théra noticed Thoryo's dry lips. "Have you been drinking the way I taught you?"

The girl nodded, paused, and shook her head.

Théra took the flat waterskin off the girl's back, uncapped it, and held it to the girl's lips. Nothing came out. She took her own waterskin, almost as flat, and squeezed every last drop into the girl's mouth. She drank greedily and gratefully.

"I drank too fast early on," said Thoryo softly, "so I had to take sips later."

"If you have trouble keeping count," said Théra, "drink whenever I take a drink. Remember, you have to take a deep drink each time, not sip. You'll get sick from that."

The girl nodded, and Théra stroked her finger lightly across the childish cheek. Thoryo's dependence on her brought to mind her little sister, Fara. Théra was sure that her younger brother, Hudo-*tika*, would find his own path, but how would Ada-*tika*, who liked telling stories and painting pictures more than politics, thrive or even survive in her mother's court? And there was Toto-*tika*, who had trouble distinguishing books from real life. . . .

Takval and the marines returned with grass-woven sacks filled with the cut lobes of the clenched-fist cactus. They hacked off the spines, chopped the tough lobes into chunks, and placed them back in the sacks. The sacks were then pressed between stones to squeeze out as much of the juice as possible. In the endless desert of Lurodia Tanta, this was the closest thing to a well for miles.

The juice was collected into a skull bowl. There wasn't much. All those bulging sacks of cactus lobes yielded barely enough to fill one bowl. Takval sprinkled into it a powder made from crushed blood coral. The shamans believed that the powder could remove poison, and the people of the scrublands used it to make the water obtained from cacti potable.

After the water was allowed to sit for a while, it was strained again, and the bowl passed around the camp.

Seeing Thoryo lick her lips, Théra handed her the bowl of strained cactus juice first.

"Drink slowly," she admonished, "and not too much."

The skull bowl, made from the delicate head of a seadog pup the fleet had caught for food during the voyage, still made Théra's stomach turn, but she had to agree with Takval that bone implements were lighter and more practical than irreplaceable Dara artifacts here in the scrublands.

Obediently, Thoryo drank slowly. While she refused to hunt or fish, and she wept over the slaughtering of animals, once the animals were dead, she did not resist the process of butchering and cleaning, or making use of their parts afterward.

Théra had once asked the girl if she was bothered by being surrounded by so many artifacts fashioned from animal remains when she seemed so terrified of death itself. Thoryo's answer had surprised her. "Holding on to the bones helps me keep them alive in my head."

In Dara, butchering, tanning, and all the mortuary arts were seen as necessary, but unclean and unlucky. While Thoryo spoke Dara like a native, she had none of the taboos and prejudices of Dara.

*You're lucky,* thought Théra. *You are so open to everything.*

She had wanted Thoryo to come not only because taking care of her made her feel like she was also taking care of Fara, but also because she thought the girl served as a useful reminder that there was more than one way of looking at any aspect of the world.

They rested through the heat of the day and decamped as the sun began to set. The evening march was easier than the morning one because the sun was behind them. And even after dark, starlight kept the dunes lit like a silvery sea.

The temperature dropped quickly after sunset, however, and soon it was time to rest again.

As Théra was about to drift off to sleep, bundled up in a sleeping bag with Takval, he woke her with a jab in the ribs.

"Shhh." He held a finger to his lips as her eyes snapped open and stared into his. He crawled out of the lean-to and gestured for her to follow.

When they were about a hundred paces away from the camp and their voices unlikely to be heard, Takval finally stopped.

"We're moving too slowly," he said.

Théra's heart sank. She had suspected that something was wrong from the way Takval's face had grown grimmer over the last few days. But she had tried to avoid confronting him, as if voicing a fear made it real.

"I didn't make enough adjustment for everyone's lack of experience in desert crossings," said Takval. "Even Toof . . . he hasn't had to do this."

Théra nodded in understanding. Though Toof had also been born and bred on the scrublands, he hadn't had to live in the wastelands of Lurodia Tanta. That was a fate reserved for the defeated Agon.

They had taken Toof on the expedition while leaving Radia behind with the fleet. Ostensibly, this was because Takval said he wanted another garinafin pilot with him once they had secured his tribe's aid. This wasn't entirely a lie, but Takval had also wanted to separate the two Lyucu naros so that each could act as a hostage to ensure that the other didn't cause trouble. Although the two had lived with them as fellow crew members for almost a whole year, Takval still didn't fully trust them. Théra, who had gotten to know the Lyucu captives through language lessons and had come to like them, didn't fully agree with the logic—Takval's thinking resembled the sort of paranoia that her mother was prone to—but she was glad to have Toof along.

"Even if we're moving slower than you planned, we must be close?" asked Théra.

Takval shook his head. "I'm not sure. Lurodia Tanta is as difficult to navigate as the trackless ocean. We're also running out of water."

"We can replenish the water," said Théra. "We are collecting dew every morning, and we can find more clenched-fist cacti."

"There isn't enough dew to even fill half of one waterskin," said Takval. "And we're already drinking more cactus juice than I'm comfortable with. We can't survive on it. Even with the blood coral to make the juice less poisonous, it's going to kill us if we don't get a lot more clean water."

The despair in Takval's voice frightened Théra. "Whatever it is you're about to propose, I won't have it."

Takval looked at her, his expression unreadable. "What do you think I'm about to propose?"

Théra took a deep breath. "You're going to suggest that Thoryo and I take all the remaining water and head east, leaving the rest of you behind to fend for yourselves. Since there's not enough water to get everyone to the camp, you're going to propose a sacrifice."

"Why Thoryo?" asked Takval, his voice preternaturally calm.

"If you're proposing a sacrifice, you always make yourself part of it," said Théra, her voice shaky. "And you wanted Thoryo to come along because you were prepared for exactly this scenario, where you couldn't make it to your home. Although Thoryo is no help in finding water or food, and she can't carry much of a load, she speaks Agon now like a native. Even with all my practice, I can't express myself perfectly in your tongue. She can act as my interpreter."

Takval chuckled softly.

"What's amusing about any of this?" demanded Théra, on the verge of tears.

"To know that you can think as I do makes me glad. I see in you . . . a reflection of my soul."

"Well, you can stop laughing, because I *won't* follow the plan."

"I know," said Takval. "That's why I'm not proposing it at all."

"You're not?"

"Do you think after all this time together, if you've learned how I think, I haven't learned how you think? There must be another way."

Théra didn't know what to say.

"I *am* capable of learning, you know?" said Takval. "I wanted to tell you how bad the situation is so that we can come up with a solution together."

They leaned against each other in the frigid night as the stars glared at them from the velvety black dome. They whispered and debated every possible solution they could think of, huddling against each other for warmth. Two minds, from opposite ends of the world, strove together as one.

But they found no way out of their predicament.

Before the sun had risen the next morn, Takval took two of the marines to the clenched-fist cacti again to scrape off as much of the morning dew as possible. It didn't amount to more than a few mouthfuls, but he was unwilling to let any potable water go to waste.

"Sleepyhead," said Théra as she gently rocked Thoryo's bundled-up figure. "It's time to get up. We have to try to make good time before it gets too hot again."

Reluctantly, Thoryo poked her head out of the sleeping bag. "I wish I could stay here forever."

"Silly girl," said Théra, "don't you have to pee? Come on, get up."

"If I never make water, maybe I won't need to drink it either."

"It doesn't work like that," said Théra. "Takval and the others will bring back some cactus chunks. Even if you can't get much drinkable water out of them, chewing the pieces and spitting will make your mouth feel better."

"We really can't drink our pee?" asked Thoryo.

Théra made a face. "What gave you such a disgusting idea?"

"Is it really disgusting?"

Théra was again reminded that the girl just didn't share her ideas about what was proper and what was not. "It's—"

"It's not just disgusting," answered Takval, back from the dew-collection trip. "It also doesn't work. If you try to survive by drinking your own urine, you won't last more than a couple of days. You get sick and die. There's something toxic in urine."

"Oh," said Thoryo, disappointed. Then her eyes lit up again. "There's no way to make urine safe, the way you make the cactus juice mostly safe?"

"I don't know of a way," said Takval.

"When I was in the ship's hold," said Thoryo, "I got sick from drinking the seawater at first. But when I licked the condensation from the beams overhead, I was all right. It has to be the same water, isn't it? Just somehow made safe."

Théra stared at Thoryo, dumbstruck.

"Maybe that's what dew is," continued Thoryo, oblivious to Théra's look, "just cactus juice refined by the power of the sun. I wish we could make dew."

Théra grabbed Thoryo and shook her. "I think you've just solved our problem!"

Noonday sun in the desert can be deadly. Normally, by this time Théra and Takval's expedition would already be hiding inside the shade of some gully or rocky outcrop, dozing to conserve energy and water until the evening, when they could make another sprint across the deadly wasteland.

Today, however, the expedition hadn't budged at all from their campsite since dawn.

To keep the wait from driving everyone mad, Takval took the marines and Toof to collect clenched-fist cactus. With more time, they could afford to focus only on the most tender lobes and underground roots, which tended to produce the least toxic juice.

Back at the campsite, Princess Théra and Thoryo, ensconced in the shade under a rocky overhang, stared intently at a translucent bubble in the desert, like a strange mushroom that didn't belong.

The bubble was a waterskin with the leather cover stripped off to reveal the sheep's bladder inside. It was now exposed to the intense rays of the sun and baked by the reflected heat of the tan desert all around it.

Out of sight, under the bulging sand piled on one side of it, lay a second, identical waterskin. The two pouches were connected spout to spout so that whatever vapors emanating out of the exposed skin would be collected by the one buried under the sand.

This morning, when Théra had set up the double-pouch system, the waterskin under the sand had been completely empty. The other pouch, the one now baking in the sun, had been filled.

But not with water.

"I'm not doing it!" Takval had said. "This isn't the first time someone thought drinking urine was a good idea. Trust me, every camp knows of someone who wanted to make it through Lurodia Tanta without enough water and ended up trying it. They all died horribly."

"It's not going to be like that," said Théra. "You have to trust me."

To start, Théra persuaded everyone in camp who hadn't finished their morning routines yet to pee into the first waterskin. Next, she carefully scooped out a depression in the sand so that the heat of the sun would be reflected from every direction to concentrate on the urine-filled waterskin, converting the liquid inside to vapor. The second waterskin, connected to the first spout to spout, was buried in an elevated mound. The slightly elevated position of the waterskin meant that all the vapor from the first pouch, freed of impurities, would be directed into it, and the earth mound around the second waterskin would keep it at a lower temperature, allowing the vapor to condense into purified water again. The neck of the second waterskin was bent so that the body was lower than the spigot, keeping the purified water from flowing back into the first waterskin.

"In Dara, distillation is a well-known technique for removing impurities," she said.

After he understood what Théra was after, Toof proposed that the mound around the second waterskin be augmented with tubes made from thin, hollow garinafin wing bones, originally intended as tent poles. The idea was to pierce the base of the mound with a series of thinner tubes, and to push a wider tube down the center, almost like a chimney. Inside the mound, all the tubes would be connected together.

Though skeptical, Théra followed Toof's advice. As the sun continued to rise, the tubes began to make a faint whistling sound. When Théra leaned closer, she could feel streams of warm air coming out of the thin tubes in the mound. It was as though the mound itself was breathing.

"What sort of magic is this?"

"No magic at all," explained Toof. "You want the inside of the mound as cool as possible, right? The thinner bones heat up in the sun faster than the thick bone at the center, so the hot air is pushed out and the inside cooled by fresh air coming down the chimney."

"But how did you come up with such an idea?" asked Théra in disbelief. How could a people with no Imperial academies and laboratories, no scholars, no *writing* even, have invented such a system?

"I've watched hundreds of garinafins build breathing mounds like this to keep their eggs cool until the mothers are ready to incubate—of course they do it by digging tunnels instead of using bone. And I've heard that ant mounds work the same way. The Great Tent in Taten also has cooling tubes that work similarly."

Théra looked at Toof with newfound respect. What other knowledge did the people of the scrublands possess that she could learn?

By the time the afternoon rolled around, Théra declared the experiment over. Gingerly, she and Thoryo dug out the waterskins, careful not to mix the contents of the two. The foul odor of the urine that had been left to bake in the sun was overwhelming.

"I'm *not* drinking that," said Toof, a look of revulsion on his face.

Even Takval and Théra, as they held up the other waterskin, looked reluctant to try.

But Thoryo laughed, grabbed the second waterskin from Théra, and drank her fill without a second thought.

"It tastes perfectly fresh," said Thoryo. She looked at the skeptical faces around her. "Are you too *scared* to try a little purified pee-water? I wonder who's braver: Lyucu, Agon, or Dara?"

The marines, Takval, and Toof looked at one another. Then everyone fought to be the first to grab the waterskin from her.

With the sun rising, the expedition was going to have to stop in another quarter of an hour. Takval decided that they would climb over the next dune and find shelter in the shade.

But as he crested the top, he froze.

"What's wrong?" asked Théra. As she climbed up next to him, she froze as well.

The rest of the expedition scrambled up; they whooped, jumped, and hugged one another, laughing and crying in equal measure.

On the other side of the dune, less than an hour's journey away, was an impossible vision: Green grass painted the desert floor like a velvet cloth, in the middle of which was a sparkling emerald lake. Palm trees, cactus trees, and thick, verdant shrubs crowded the shore, along with strands of reeds. Flocks of birds swooped over the lake and frolicked in its waters.

And most lovely of all, a patch of white tents like mushrooms sprouted next to the lake. Flocks of long-haired and short-haired cattle grazed farther away from the shore. Behind the flocks, a few garinafins paced, their serpentine necks craning in the expedition's direction with curiosity.

# CHAPTER THIRTEEN

# AN UNWELCOME WELCOME

THE OASIS OF SLIYUSA KI, UKYU-GONDÉ: THE
FIFTH MONTH IN THE SECOND YEAR SINCE
PRINCESS THÉRA DEPARTED DARA (KNOWN IN
DARA AS THE SECOND YEAR OF THE REIGN OF
SEASON OF STORMS).

"Princess of Dara, welcome to Sliyusa Ki, the First Oasis of the
Agon," said the gray-haired man who sat at the head of the open-
air banquet. "I am called Volyu Aragoz, son of Nobo Aragoz, son of
Akiga Aragoz, that Akiga who was once dance-drawn as the Pride of
the Scrublands. I serve my people now as the Pé-Afir-tekten. You are
a stranger alone among us tonight, far from home. May your heart
be seen as clearly as the bottom of this bowl."

"Pé-Afir-tekten" meant "Chief of the Children of Afir." It was an
old title that had been used by many legendary heroes who claimed
descent from Afir.

Eyes on Théra, Volyu raised a bull skull, full of kyoffir, and
drained it in one long gulp. Then he tilted the skull bowl to show the
princess the empty inside.

"Kyoffir! Kyoffir!" the dozens of Agon chieftains and naros-votan
sitting in an oval around the banquet-fire shouted. They drained
their skull bowls as well and showed the empty containers to those
around them.

"I thank you, Chief Volyu Aragoz of the Agon," said Princess
Théra, sitting at the opposite end of the oval from Volyu. Having
delivered her brief answer, she swallowed nervously. She was

unaccustomed to the formal register of the Agon tongue, and it required all her concentration to parse the unfamiliar words and to carefully compose her sentences. She was afraid of missing nuances, misinterpreting intentions, misapprehending directions.

*I am a princess of Dara. I can do this.*

Forcing her hands to be steady, she lifted her skull bowl in return and drank. But instead of gulping down the strong alcoholic drink, she merely sipped it before tipping the skull bowl toward Volyu. Starlight and firelight glinted off the brimming liquid.

"A delicate maiden!" exclaimed Volyu, a contemptuous smirk on his face. "That is all right. Take your time."

The other Agon chuckled at the princess's inability to drink like a warrior. At this rate, it would take a hundred sips for Théra to match Volyu's toast. They waited for her to collect herself and resume drinking.

The princess did not bring the skull bowl back to her lips.

As the wait stretched, laughter among the crowd died down. Volyu's smile froze. The faces of the chieftains turned stony.

Scattered cries of consternation erupted from the assembled warriors at the banquet. The roaring bonfire lit their lined faces and shaggy hair with deep shadows, much as the rays of the setting sun lit up the cracks in a dried gully bed in Lurodia Tanta. Some of the naros-votan whispered to one another, anxious and confused, looking askance at the young Dara princess who had just insulted their chief.

"What are you doing?" asked Takval, sitting next to Théra. He spoke in Dara and kept his voice barely above a whisper. "Drink again! You have to finish the bowl."

"Kyoffir upsets my stomach," Théra whispered back. "Most men and women of Dara can't drink kyoffir without either becoming sick or losing their senses. It was the downfall of my brother Timu."

"You can throw up later! But right now, if you don't finish this first bowl, everyone will see it as a great insult to my uncle."

"He's trying to assert dominance over me," whispered Théra. It had not escaped her notice that Volyu had emphasized in his toast that she was alone, and made no mention of the proposed alliance between Dara and the Agon.

"It's just a drink."

Théra shook her head almost imperceptibly. Years under her parents' tutelage had taught her that there was no such thing as a simple banquet among emperors and pékyus. Everything was theater, and all performances were about power. This was a truth that did not change between Dara and Ukyu-Gondé.

"You're in Gondé," whispered Takval again. "Please."

If Takval were familiar with the Ano Classics, at this point he would probably quote her the famous episode of Iluthan's blood meal. During the Diaspora Wars, the hero Iluthan once ate the heart of a slain foe on Wolf's Paw to prove to the natives of the island that he was willing to abide by their customs and follow their laws. This act of cannibalism, though widely condemned by Iluthan's own priests and allies, proved instrumental in securing him the loyalty of the berserkers of Wolf's Paw.

In Dara, the story had been cited by generations of Moralists as an example of Iluthan's lack of principles—a prefiguration of the state of moral confusion society had to endure in the absence of good Tiro kings guided by Moralist philosophers. But some Fluxist scholars, intent on arguing against the excessive rigidity of classical Moralism (particularly the extremist strain propounded by Poti Maji, Kon Fiji's most renowned student), had also used the story as an example of the lack of absolutes when it came to moral judgments. For them, Iluthan's pragmatism showed that even a taboo like cannibalism was a matter of convention and ritual, rather than something that could be derived from self-evident principles.

Being a daughter of Kuni Garu, Théra naturally disagreed with both interpretations and had drawn her own conclusions: Iluthan wasn't interested in abstract notions of ethics; he was trying to secure power for a grander goal.

"Let me handle this my way," she whispered to Takval.

Before Takval could respond, his uncle called out in a booming voice. "Princess of Dara, are you truly too delicate for the rough drink of the scrublands? Or do you hold yourself so high that you would not deign to drain kyoffir with a barbaric chief?"

There was utter silence as every pair of ears perked up for the princess's response.

Théra stared across the long elliptic space into the eyes of Takval's uncle. The man was in his early fifties, gaunt and hunched over in his posture, as though perpetually cringing from some blow that was about to be dealt. The oasis allowed his tribe to survive but not to thrive, and years of hiding in the wasteland had drained him of the warrior's vigor that he might once have inherited from his father, the last pékyu of the Agon. Though he was not ancient, his face was already so lined that it was hard to read his expression in the dim fire glow.

The princess knew better than to underestimate the man. He was the sole surviving son of the Agon royal line, and there was no doubt that his calculated performance of the role of cringing coward had been useful in his survival.

"You misunderstand my meaning, Chief Aragoz," said Princess Théra. "I took only a sip out of great respect for both our peoples."

Volyu's eyebrows lifted. "Do explain."

"Both the Agon and the people of Dara respect the gods and believe in omens," said Théra. "Tonight, we meet to celebrate the Agon-Dara alliance secured by a royal marriage. A marriage and an alliance both must be nurtured to last for the long haul, and should not be driven by short-term interests and quick profit. I sipped from the bowl because I wished to honor the gods and give them a sign that the friendship between our peoples should last as long as this bowl of kyoffir."

The assembled chieftains and warriors murmured in approval. Several of the women even saluted her by lifting both arms, crossed at the wrist.

Takval glanced at Théra in admiration, and she smiled. Since the Agon tribes were scattered to the far corners of the scrublands and many of them were living as enslaved captives of the Lyucu, the tribe at Sliyusa Ki, Volyu's own tribe, functioned like a Taten-in-exile for the Agon. The chieftains here were the equivalent of the great thanes during the time of the Agon empire, and impressing them would do much to further Théra's reputation among Takval's people.

Volyu laughed long and loud. "You're very clever, Princess of Dara. In the scrublands we call what you've just done 'trying to sell blind cattle on a moonless night.'"

Théra's face flushed. "Is it the custom of the scrublands to insult those who come in friendship? I had hoped that our peoples would be votan-sa-taasa, like Kikisavo and Afir of old."

Volyu shook his head. "You have come prepared, that is obvious. But this alliance you speak of was negotiated by my nephew without my approval. You assume we're friends when we're strangers. Overfamiliarity is *also* an insult."

"There was no insult intended—"

"You insult my intelligence with every word you speak! No matter how pretty your words or how elaborate your false reasoning, the only thing that matters is power. An alliance can only occur between peoples who can make each other stronger."

*I knew it,* thought Théra, but there was no joy in having her suspicions confirmed. "Do you doubt the power that my people can bring to the Agon? We have knowledge, skills, and weapons. Takval can tell you how much stronger your warriors will be when armed with metal weapons—"

"Do you take me for a fool?" thundered Volyu. "Takval tells me you brought a thousand men and women with you in small ships that could not carry even a single garinafin. Admiral Krita brought more than ten times as many to these shores in city-ships that resembled floating islands, laden with magical weapons, and yet Pékyu Tenryo killed and enslaved them all. Do you command more strength than Krita did? Dara has *nothing* to offer us!"

Théra closed her eyes for a moment to keep her surging panic under control. This was the worst-case scenario. The chances that Dara could train its own army of garinafins from hatchlings in just ten years to defeat the experienced garinafin riders of Tanvanaki, audacious leader of the Lyucu invasion, were remote at best. If the Lyucu were to send any more reinforcements on city-ships when the Wall of Storms opened again, all of Dara was going to fall. To be sure, the Lyucu didn't know when the Wall was going to open again—it was a secret she had revealed only to Takval, and even other members of the Dara expedition didn't know about it, thinking only that they had to defeat the Lyucu as quickly as possible—but there was no guarantee that the Lyucu wouldn't figure out the secret on their own. Cudyu, presumably, had copies of Luan Zyaji's calculations, and he might eventually break the cipher Luan had used to disguise the truth. And even if he couldn't break the code, he could simply try his luck by sending new expeditions every few years, as Tenryo had done before Luan's arrival. She had come to Ukyu-Gondé to convince the Agon to rebel in order to prevent the Lyucu from sending any more reinforcements, but that required the Agon to first believe that Dara's aid was valuable.

Volyu continued. "Oh, yes, Théra, Takval tried to tell me about the wonders of your weapons and the glory of Dara's wealth. But weapons and wealth do not equal power. Power is like water: It flows from high places to low places, and it moves in patterns that are the same whether you're in the parched wastelands of Lurodia Tanta or the mist-shrouded forests of the World's Edge Mountains. Despite the web of lies you and Takval have tried to weave, I know that Dara lies mired in the trough, and the Lyucu are poised at the crest."

"If you only understood how vulnerable the Lyucu are and how much potential there is in what Dara can offer . . ." A note of pleading was creeping into Théra's voice. She had impressed upon Takval the importance of not presenting this alliance as a measure of desperation on Dara's part, but it seemed that Volyu was too clever for his nephew. "Surely you can see—"

"Let me tell you what I see," said Volyu, his softening voice taking on a sinister tone. The chieftains and naros-votan leaned in, their breath bated. "I see a people on the verge of ruin as they face the prospect of conquest by the Lyucu, like a flock of sheep about to be slaughtered by the wolves. I see a woman desperate for one last chance to save her people. Though I never met Krita and his Lords of Dara, tales of his arrogance and confidence are known to every shaman on the scrublands. Your people *never* would have agreed to send you out here across an unknown ocean to marry someone you consider a 'savage' unless you have run out of options. You need us, Princess of Dara, but we don't need you."

Théra was speechless. Though Takval hadn't given his uncle a detailed overview of the situation in Dara, shrewd Volyu spoke as if he had been there in Pan.

Takval could no longer contain himself. "Uncle! You don't understand—"

"Silence! You are not the Pé-Afir-tekten!" shouted Volyu. "How dare you risk the lives of our people—"

"She can help us! I have seen what she can do—"

"Oh, I have no doubt you've seen what she can do . . . or imagined it. You've brought home a feral garinafin who is unbroken and unused to being ridden. I must tame her."

The chieftains and warriors guffawed, and Takval's face turned bright red. He tried to jump up, but Théra grabbed his hand and pulled him back down.

"Sit still!" whispered Théra. "You can't fight him and all his warriors by yourself—"

"You don't understand the meaning of what he just said," said Takval, voice quavering with rage. "If I don't challenge—"

"I may not understand everything that's going on, but I know that when you're an egg, you don't smash yourself against a rock—"

Takval didn't get a chance to respond, because Volyu broke in again. "Princess of Dara, I am not without sympathy for your plight. Though there will be no alliance of equals between us, another arrangement is possible."

"What other arrangement do you propose?" asked Théra.

"Give us all that you possess, and submit to us in vassalage. After tonight, you shall no longer be a princess of Dara, but only a loyal woman of the Agon."

In other words, there would be no chance to use an Agon army to disrupt the Lyucu preparations for another invasion fleet to Dara. "I can't accept that," said Théra.

"You have no choice. I insist that you learn this lesson tonight and learn it well. Drink the kyoffir. I shall enjoy seeing you vomit at my feet."

Théra took a deep breath.

*What should I do? What would either of my parents do in my position? What would Marshal Gin Mazoti do? What would Iluthan do?*

There were no answers because she was in uncharted waters. She looked to the right at Takval, who pleaded with his eyes for her to drink. She could understand his thinking: Even if she submitted tonight, as long as Volyu agreed to accept her, there would be opportunities in the future to turn things around. If she continued to defy Volyu, there was no telling what he would be capable of.

She looked to the left at Thoryo, who was sipping from her own skull bowl. A series of expressions flitted across her face in the firelight: contentment, delight, surprise, disbelief. This was her first time imbibing kyoffir, and she was luxuriating in the sensual experience without worrying about intoxication, about her body's reactions, about the political implications of each gesture. She was carefree, completely devoted to the moment.

*What fools we are to read every gesture and motion, every bite and sip like logograms carved on a page, when the very raw sensations themselves are miraculous. What fools we are to hesitate over the meaning of every step when it is a wonder just to walk, to breathe, to be free and alive.*

*A life in submission to Volyu would be like Thoryo's time in the dark hold, devoid of color, of understanding, of interesting choices. It's no life at all. It is revolting.*

*There is a time for reading, but there is also a time for simply doing.*

She lifted the bull skull full of kyoffir again. The skull hung suspended in air, the firelight limning it in crimson-gold. The assembled chieftains and warriors began to chant in praise of Volyu, and the Agon chief smiled triumphantly.

Théra moved.

Instead of bringing the skull bowl to her lips, she poured the liquid onto the ground in front of her and showed the bottom of the empty vessel to Volyu.

Cries of surprise and outrage erupted from all around the circle. Several naros-votan jumped up and pointed at the princess, shouting incoherently.

Théra began to speak. She deliberately kept her voice low, and so the assembled throng had to quiet down in order to hear her.

"I drink only with heroes, not cowards who usurp the seat of heroes."

More angry shouts and outraged cries, but the princess still refused to raise her voice.

"I call upon the spirits of the great pékyus of the past: Togo Aragoz, who first united the Agon tribes and crafted Langiaboto; Akiga Aragoz, who first dreamed that it was possible to triumph over the Lyucu; Nobo Aragoz, who fulfilled his father's dream and held the reins of a hundred-hundred garinafins. They have crossed the World's Edge Mountains on cloud-garinafins to join the gods in their eternal feast, and I now pour this kyoffir into the earth in their honor so that it may not be wasted."

She paused, and every pair of eyes turned to focus on Volyu Aragoz.

"How would drinking the kyoffir with me be a waste?" he asked, his voice dangerously calm.

"You call yourself son of Nobo Aragoz, son of Akiga Aragoz, once the Pride of the Scrublands; yet you dare not even call yourself a pékyu, despite claiming descent from Togo Aragoz, the first pékyu herself."

Volyu's face twitched, and several times he seemed on the verge of saying something, but in the end, he remained silent.

Théra went on. "You speak to me of power and subservience; you speak to me of Dara weakness and Lyucu strength. You claim to speak for the Agon, yet your people are huddled here in the desert, eking out a life of terror in the shadow of your Lyucu masters. The Lyucu roam your ancestral pastures, desecrate the lakeshores where your father once staked his Taten, and demand you offer up your youths as tribute to be enslaved by their thanes—"

"You dare to insult the courage of our people?" thundered Volyu. "Know that we have never ceased to resist the cursed Lyucu. But the clever wolf bides his time—"

"Do not attempt to clothe yourself in the courage of others," Théra broke in, her voice still even and measured. "Takval has told me of the many failed uprisings by various Agon tribes since the time of Tenryo's conquest. Yet you've never been the leader of any of these rebellions, and each time, as the courageous rebels were crushed by the Lyucu, you stood by and did nothing—"

"I must consider the welfare of all my people. A leader waits for the right opportunity—"

"No, a real leader doesn't *wait* for the right opportunity. She plans and plots and crafts until she can *seize* the right opportunity. What have you done to strengthen yourself or to weaken the Lyucu? Absolutely nothing. I didn't come here because the time is right, but because Takval dared to brave the trackless sea to find me."

Volyu sneered. "That half-formed whelp dreams of challenging me, but he is nothing—"

Théra laughed without mirth. "He is ten times the warrior you are. You have been fooling yourself that standing still is the same as making progress, that lying down in submission is the same as plotting revenge, that telling those who dare to fight that the time isn't right is the same as seeking out the opportunity for a fatal strike. You've yielded so much of your pride and strength that you dare not even call yourself by the title that is your birthright. Who are you to speak to me of courage and power? You have turned your people into a flock of sheep, with you as a sheepdog for the Lyucu."

Instead of shouting her down, the Agon chieftains and warriors looked down in silence, ashamed.

"Pé-Afir-tekten," said one of the women, "she is no delicate maiden. If her people have as much backbone as she does, they're worthy allies."

"She honors our ancestors with her speech," said one of the men, "and we'll shame them if we refuse her aid."

"We should heed her counsel," said another woman. "She may speak our language with a halting accent, but her spirit does not stutter or stumble."

More voices assented.

Volyu gestured for the chieftains and naros-votan to quiet down. "Be not concerned, votan-ru-taasa and votan-sa-taasa, I was only testing the Dara princess to see if she is a lamb or a wolf."

He refilled his skull bowl from a bladder pouch, raised it in Théra's direction, and poured out the kyoffir on the ground.

"A good ally is not afraid to speak the truth in friendship," said Volyu. "Thank you, Princess of Dara, for reminding all of us of the reality of our bondage."

Théra refilled her bowl, bracing her arms on her knees lest she reveal the wild pounding of her heart through shaking hands. *The gamble has paid off!* She poured the kyoffir on the ground in acknowledgment. "Thank you, Chief Volyu. May we never be strangers again."

The other warriors also poured out their kyoffir on the ground, in imitation of their chief and the princess.

Volyu refilled his bowl, raised it, and turned to Takval, "Thank you, Takval, for securing this alliance. You have made me proud."

"I only did what was my duty. Let us formalize—"

Volyu waved one hand for Takval to stop. "A young garinafin pilot is impulsive; that is both a good thing and a bad thing. An experienced pilot can teach his mount much that she does yet not know she needs to know."

Takval's expression was unreadable as he locked eyes with Volyu. "There always comes a time for the old to yield to the young."

Volyu's eyes narrowed. "You have been away for a long time." Almost carelessly, he looked around the bonfire, at the gathered chieftains and naros-votan, few of whom Takval knew by name.

"You insist on riding then?" Takval asked.

"I do," said Volyu. He poured the kyoffir on the ground.

Her mind still jittery from the tense confrontation with Volyu, Théra's concentration had lapsed for a few beats, causing her to miss the beginning of this new development. By the time she had recovered and refocused, the air was already crackling with a new tension.

She strained to parse what she could recall of the exchange just now between Takval and Volyu, struggling to make sense of the foreign words and the peculiar metaphors. It was as though she were a child again, eavesdropping at her father's court, where the great Lords of Dara carried on a conversation beneath the conversation through metaphors and hints. She understood there was a contest of wills between uncle and nephew, but was Takval challenging his uncle for leadership of the Agon? Surely he didn't think the time had come for *that*!

"What matters is that your uncle supports this alliance," whispered Théra in Dara to her intended. "Let him win this. Our goals can be accomplished without internecine warfare."

Takval's eyes widened. "You . . . are you sure?"

She nodded. *Of course Volyu needs to "ride" and be the pilot of the Agon people. At least for now. The time for you and I to ride will come soon enough.*

Takval kept his eyes on her, waited a long beat, and let out a held breath. He refilled his skull bowl, and, without looking at Volyu, poured it on the ground.

Volyu smiled. "May the only blood that spills from now on be the blood of our common enemy."

This last was said with conviction and strength, and the Agon warriors at the banquet cheered.

"Will there be more kyoffir?" asked Thoryo, looking worried. "It seems such a waste to pour it all on the ground."

Théra and Takval looked at each other as their hands squeezed together. Victory had been won.

But a trace of sorrow flickered through Takval's eyes as Théra looked away.

Later, as the banquet concluded, Takval told Théra to go back to their tent while he stayed behind to speak with Volyu.

"Whatever you have to discuss with him, I should be there," said Théra.

"Some things that can be said between family cannot be said in front of outsiders," said Takval.

"I *am* family."

"Not yet," said Takval.

"We have shared the same bed!"

"That is not the same as a wedding witnessed by the gods and the people of the tribe." He softened his tone. "Please. Let me talk to him."

Back at the tent that had been assigned to Takval and Théra for the night, the Agon furnishings, though unfamiliar to Théra, nonetheless showed signs of opulence: intricately carved bone ancestor poles (Théra wondered how the delicate, smooth etchings were made); ceremonial rattles made from turtle shells (they were many-days' journey from the ocean); bladder waterskins that had been so carefully oiled and scraped that they shone in the torchlight, with beautiful plugs made from soft, gleaming gold pounded into thin foil and then wrapped around mossy antlers; pots and kettles made from garinafin hide; and so on.

Some of these objects had perhaps once been found in Pékyu Nobo's Taten, and had somehow survived the Lyucu raids. They now served as physical reminders of the Agon's former glory, much as Takval's own family served as spiritual connections of the Children of Afir to their former strength.

Thoryo examined everything with interest and asked the Agon women who had been assigned to attend to the princess to explain the story behind each artifact. The women found Thoryo fun to talk to: She spoke just like an Agon, and yet she seemed to treat even the most ordinary hide-pot as an object of wonder. Her sense of enthusiasm was infectious.

"Come with us, little sister," they said. "There are lots of other fun things to see." Thoryo left with them.

Théra, on the other hand, paced back and forth anxiously in the empty tent.

It was taking Takval much too long. She hoped he wasn't challenging his uncle again to assume the reins of power. They had worked too hard to get this far to risk everything for his ambition.

Just as Théra had decided that she needed to go find Takval, the entrance flap opened, and the Agon pékyu-taasa entered the tent. Théra ran up to him. They embraced quickly and then Théra pulled back.

"Are you going to tell me what happened?"

"Soon," said Takval. "But first, let me ask you: Do you think we've made a good start?"

"We have," said Théra. She was relieved that Takval didn't look angry or despondent. Perhaps she had been paranoid. Maybe he had only wanted to catch up with his uncle after being away for so long.

Excitement filled her voice as she began to envision the next steps. "Your uncle seems open to new ideas and new ways to challenge the Lyucu. We'll have to plot out how to rally the tribes. We don't want to make him think that his opinions don't matter, of course—"

Takval held her by the shoulders to make her stop. "You mentioned 'our goals' earlier. What are they?"

Théra was baffled by the question. Why was Takval asking about the obvious? "To save Dara and to free the Agon by destroying the Lyucu, of course."

Takval looked into her eyes. "Are these goals worth sacrificing for?"

*Is he worried about my resolve?* Théra answered slowly. "I know that my style is different from yours, but I am not so naive as to think it possible to defeat the rapacious wolf with no risk to our own loved ones. I've come to accept your decision on the Lyucu city-ship—by risking the lives of the few, you saved many."

"I don't mean that," said Takval, his expression intense. "What about yourself?"

Théra's face flushed. "You doubt my courage? My father was willing to die to save the villagers of Dasu and Rui, and I am his daughter. To save Dara means everything to me. I've already given up all I had to sail across the ocean with you to come here!"

Takval flinched, but soon he was calm again. "Then remember your goals, and come what may, do what you must."

She finally realized that something wasn't quite right. "What are you talking about?"

But before he could answer, an attendant outside the tent called out, "Chief Volyu wishes to visit the Princess of Dara."

"In the middle of the night?" Théra mused. "I wonder what he wants."

"He's here to see you," said Takval. "I should not be here."

"Why shouldn't you be here?" asked Théra, wondering what sort of unusual Agon custom she was missing.

Takval shook his head. "There's no time. I must go." He left the tent by the back entrance, leaving Théra to face the Agon chief alone.

Volyu entered. "Is everything to your satisfaction, Princess?"

"I've been hiking through the desert, drinking my own pee, for days," said Théra with a smile. "Just having clean water right now feels like a luxury. I'm grateful for your hospitality."

Volyu laughed. "I like how direct you are, Théra, so different from Dara's reputation for craftiness in our stories. I will be direct in return. I hope we can be good partners."

"Of course we'll be good partners. Both Takval and I want nothing more than that."

Volyu nodded, a look of relief on his face. "Good. Then I trust that there will be no problems for the wedding to be set for tomorrow?"

Though for the last year Théra had known she was to marry Takval, the sudden announcement of a specific date nonetheless surprised her. An image of Zomi's lovely face surfaced unbidden, and she had to force herself to concentrate on the present. "I . . . I guess so. But doesn't that seem a bit rushed?"

"As you can see for yourself, Théra, this isn't Taten and we are a people in exile. We have no slaves to build a grand wedding tent and we can't afford to slaughter a thousand cattle for a grand feast. I hope you aren't insulted by the simple rites and shabby preparations. What matters is that we seal the alliance as quickly as possible and begin the grand task of the rejuvenation of the Agon."

Théra nodded. "Of course you're right. The alliance matters the most. A quick ceremony is no insult to me—if that's what Takval wants."

"It *is* what Takval wants," said Volyu. "The sooner we get the wedding concluded, the better. The return of Takval has created . . . certain instabilities."

"What kind of instabilities?"

"Ah . . . it's no surprise he hasn't explained the details to you. I will be frank: My sister and I do not get along."

Théra nodded to herself in recognition. Takval had indeed told her that Volyu had become chief of the Agon in exile over the claim of his sister, Souliyan Aragoz, though neither had been formally acknowledged by Nobo, their father. Most of the Agon warriors now seemed to accept Volyu as their leader, but it made sense that Souliyan would still have supporters—especially among those unsatisfied with Volyu. The return of Takval, strengthened by a marriage-alliance to Dara, no doubt would be seen by some as adding to the claim of his mother. No wonder Volyu was worried.

"You have nothing to fear from us," said Théra decisively. It was important to allay Volyu's concerns and show that they were here to help him, not unseat him. She hoped that was why Takval had wanted to talk to Volyu. "You're the Pékyu of the Agon. Only when the Agon are undivided and strong can the alliance benefit Dara. I won't tolerate any attempt to undermine your authority."

"Very good. That is exactly what I wanted to hear. You won't get much rest tonight, I'm afraid, since you will have to learn the rites before the ceremony tomorrow."

"Will I have to do much to prepare?" asked Théra. She was a bit dazed as she tried to wrap her head around the idea of marrying Takval the next day.

"You need not trouble yourself about the ceremony itself as long as you learn your role," said Volyu. "It is our custom for weddings to be planned by the elders of the two clans that are about to be united, not the couple themselves. I will send experienced shamans and elders with long memories to teach you what you must do and say during the ceremony."

"But to seal the alliance—"

"Though the wedding will be conducted in haste and not lavish, I won't skimp on the necessary rites to give it the required weight. It's important that we proclaim the importance of this alliance, both for our families and our peoples, to all the tribes of the Agon."

Théra nodded at this, somewhat reassured. The wedding was, above all, a political act, and she was glad to see that even among the Agon, there was the same marriage between theater and politics.

After Volyu left, Takval didn't return, and she was glad to have a little time to herself as she sorted through her own complicated thoughts.

# CHAPTER FOURTEEN

# COMMITMENT

THE OASIS OF SLIYUSA KI, UKYU-GONDÉ: THE
FIFTH MONTH IN THE SECOND YEAR SINCE
PRINCESS THÉRA DEPARTED DARA (KNOWN IN
DARA AS THE SECOND YEAR OF THE REIGN OF
SEASON OF STORMS).

Late into the night, a succession of shamans and elders came to the
tent to teach Théra what she had to do during the wedding. There
were traditional chants to memorize and recite, specific dance steps
that she had to perform to honor the gods and the heroes of the Agon
people, and rituals she had to carry out together with the groom to
demonstrate both sides' commitment to the alliance.

After returning from visiting her new Agon friends, Thoryo
stayed by Théra's side and attended all the instruction. During the
voyage to Ukyu-Gondé, Théra had taught her how to represent
speech with zyndari letters, and Takval had shown her the various
mnemonic techniques the people of the scrublands used: knots on a
rope to mark important points in a speech, dance maps made from
charcoal on hide, collections of stones of different sizes to symbolize
events in sequence. Now she used these techniques to take notes and
help Théra practice and memorize.

Later, after most of the elders had left, just as Théra and Thoryo
were about to go to bed, a woman in her late forties entered the tent.
She was dressed like the other Agon, with no obvious insignia of her
rank—at least none that Théra had learned to read. But there was a
natural air of command in her movements that drew Théra's attention.

"Leave," she said to Thoryo. The tone wasn't arrogant or rude, but it brooked no disagreement. "I wish to speak to the Princess of Dara alone."

Thoryo looked at Théra, who nodded. She bowed and exited the tent.

"I am called Souliyan Aragoz, daughter of Nobo Aragoz, son of Akiga Aragoz, once the Pride of the Scrublands," the woman said quietly. Then, after a pause, she added, "I'm Takval's mother."

Pékyu Nobo Aragoz, last pékyu of the Agon, had fathered dozens of children by his multiple wives. After the Lyucu had successfully overthrown their erstwhile masters, Pékyu Tenryo Roatan gathered all the children and grandchildren of Nobo, and, on a day chosen by the shamans as pleasing to the gods, he had them kneel down in front of the Agon Great Tent. Then, the pékyu walked behind the line of royal children, sons and daughters of the man who had raised him like a child of his own flesh, and bashed in their skulls with a blow from Langiaboto, the Self-Reliant.

Tenryo's own thanes had looked away as the kneeling young pékyus-taasa, some of them barely old enough to lift a war club, begged tearfully for their lives as their older siblings shouted at them to shut up.

"You think I'm cruel," said the pékyu, pausing in his death-dealing walk to address his thanes, "but in fact I am being merciful. Leaving them alive so that their hearts would be gnawed daily by the shame of their own cowardice—now, that would be true cruelty."

Once the Agon tribes, scattered to the ends of the scrublands, had settled into their new role as a conquered people, rumors began to spread that not all members of the First Family had died.

Two of Nobo's children, Volyu and Souliyan, had been spared because their mothers had been Lyucu slaves serving Nobo, and the Agon pékyu had never given them his clan name or lineage. As the chiefs of the various Agon tribes jockeyed for power—in exile, the struggle over a larger oasis in the wastelands or a slightly more reliable patch of waxtongue bush grew even more intense than the fights over slaves and cattle and grazing rights to the grass sea when the Agon were masters of the scrublands—many saw the two children as valuable symbols. A chief who could claim that they were "protecting" the sole heirs of the last pékyu of the Agon could be seen as the protector of the memories of the Agon people and the legitimate leader of the ruined empire.

The two children became objects of deadly raids and counter-raids among the Agon, taken from one end of the continent to the other, nominally treated as heirs to the legacy of Nobo Aragoz, but in reality little more than pawns for ambitious chiefs who sought to aggrandize themselves and their families.

When they found out that the two royal Agon children had survived, Pékyu Tenryo's thanes urged their lord to hunt them down. But Pékyu Tenryo demurred, explaining that the situation benefited the Lyucu. The game of capture-the-pékyus-taasa promoted strife among the Agon and prevented the tribes from uniting behind a new leader. As long as the Lyucu knew where Volyu and Souliyan were, they were content to let the Agon fight over these useless figureheads.

Surrounded by intrigue and deadly violence, Volyu and Souliyan came of age.

"My brother already welcomed you to Gondé and Sliyusa Ki, so I thought I should come and welcome you into the Aragoz clan," Souliyan said, but there was no joy in her voice or her eyes.

Théra bowed to her. "Takval has told me much about you."

Souliyan said nothing but looked at the Dara princess, her face unreadable.

Slightly unnerved by this cold reception from her future mother-in-law, Théra went on. "You have done much for the spirit of the Agon people."

Souliyan's face twitched. "Have I?"

"Of course. Takval told me how in the years after the Lyucu conquest, you used your status and influence to rally the defeated tribes and to stop the bloodshed that had surrounded you and your brother."

"Was that how Takval explained it all to you?" muttered Souliyan. A bitter smile flitted across her face. "I wonder if that's really the story he believes or if he was trying to make reality sound better to you than it was. Maybe he just wanted to make his family seem more impressive—how disappointing for you to find out that he is no prince, merely the son of a woman who never even learned to fight on the back of a garinafin."

"There is more to strength than the ability to kill," said Théra. "That your brother fears you tells me all I need to know."

Souliyan's eyes focused on Théra narrowly. "Maybe you're not as foolish as I thought."

Rage reddened Théra's face momentarily, but she forced herself to calm down for the sake of Takval. "I hope to prove myself an equal partner for the next Agon pékyu, and my people valued allies of the Agon people."

"I come to see you on the night before your marriage, and you speak to me of power and alliance. Are these the only things on your mind, Princess of Dara?"

"What do you mean?" Théra was befuddled. "The alliance is, after all, the entire point of this marriage."

"So cold," muttered Souliyan. "When Takval came to me, he spent the whole time talking about you: how clever you are, how capable, how compassionate, how decisive. I thought he was speaking of the goddess Aluro in human form, a woman more beautiful than a thousand sunsets, as wise as Afir herself. He was so busy telling me about you that I don't believe he even asked after my health."

*Ah, I've been speaking to her as a leader of the Agon people instead of Takval's mother,* thought Théra. *She thinks she's losing a son rather than gaining a daughter.*

"Forgive me for being unused to speaking about matters of the heart," she said awkwardly, "especially in a language with which I'm still unskilled—"

Souliyan laughed. "How convenient it is to avoid the truth by pleading a lack of skill with our language. You seemed to have no trouble with words at the banquet, when you were verbally contending with my brother for dominance."

She had not seen Souliyan earlier at the banquet, but she must have been there in the shadows, listening. Théra had had enough.

"Your brother and you have both chosen to greet a new addition to the family by insulting her. Is this an Agon custom that I'm unfamiliar with? I hope to never have to learn it."

"I want to hear you speak from your heart, not weave illusions that are as insubstantial as reflections in a water bubble in the grass sea. My son almost died to bring you here. The least you can do is to tell me the truth of how you feel about him!"

"All right," said Théra. She hated being forced this way, hated being strong-armed into revealing her feelings. It went against every instinct she had acquired in the Dandelion Court. "I've never had much use for stories about love, and thus lack the clichés others find so easy to assemble into declarations of romance. I've always been more interested in words and deeds that touch upon the grander scheme of the world, about the flow and ebb of power that changes the fates of millions."

As she spoke, the words came more easily. She didn't care about her accent, or berate herself for not knowing all the words she needed.

"But just because I don't like to talk about what's in my heart doesn't mean I don't feel. It's true that when I agreed to marry Takval, I didn't know anything about him except his courage in crossing the whale's way to come to Dara, searching for a path to free his people. My heart was filled with the presence of another, and the life I dreamed of was not the life he offered for me."

The visage of Souliyan faded from her view. She stopped performing for an unseen audience, but spoke as though to herself.

"Times change and people grow. I've now lived with him and stood with him against death and despair for more than a year. Side by side, we've faced garinafin breath and dived beneath the sea with the aid of a cruben; we've voyaged across the pathless ocean and journeyed through the waterless wastelands of Lurodia Tanta; we've disagreed and argued, and together devised plots that kept as many alive as we could. Without knowing exactly when, my heart has grown large and made room for him, and I know he has made room for me. We're not yet the mirrors for each other's soul, but we can already dimly glimpse each other's shadow in our thoughts. That is a state that many married couples yearn for but never achieve—"

"Then *why* are you agreeing to marry my brother instead of him?"

For a moment, Théra felt as though the ground had shifted beneath her feet, and she faltered. "What?"

"As Takval's senior in lineage and status, Volyu has preempted Takval's claim on you as your partner in the royal marriage. For the sake of your Dara, Takval has refused to challenge him, and agreed to go into exile instead. To assure Volyu, he'll become one of the tanto-lyu-naro and renounce all warfare forever."

"What . . . how . . . when . . . *why?*" There were so many questions in Théra's mind that she didn't know where to start. It felt like a betrayal. Not just of all that they had endured and accomplished, but of her *heart*.

Scrutinizing Théra's face until she was satisfied that the Princess of Dara was telling the truth, Souliyan sighed. "I guess you really didn't know."

"I swear to you I didn't!" Théra was both amazed and furious. Of course, now the strange behavior of both Volyu and Takval earlier made sense. All that talk about riding the garinafin; all those questions about whether she was willing to make sacrifices for their goals; all that nonsense about how certain things could only be discussed among family. She wanted to grab Souliyan's shoulders and scream in her face. "Where is Takval? He needs to come back and answer me!"

She got up, outraged beyond measure, and strode toward the tent opening.

"Stop. You won't find him in the settlement," said Souliyan. "He's already gone into exile. He didn't want me to come see you at all until after the wedding. But I'm his mother, and I don't need to listen to him."

"And I'm not some talisman to be passed around between him and his uncle!" Théra shouted. "I'm his wife, and no one is going to be in—or out of—*my* wedding without my say-so."

Souliyan's face finally broke into a grin. "You're not quite what I expected."

Théra gritted her teeth. "Explain to me just what Takval was hoping to accomplish."

"This is likely to be a long story," said Souliyan.

Théra ran to the opening of the tent and summoned Thoryo. She whispered to the young woman to tell the others in her group to quietly prepare to leave the Agon camp. She turned back to Souliyan. "You'd better make it short then; I'm not staying."

"Volyu and I didn't have happy childhoods," Souliyan said. "Our mothers were Lyucu slaves, and so among the Agon we were considered tainted, not truly the heirs of the Aragoz lineage at all. Later, after the fall of the Agon, we became symbols, little more than ceremonial weapons or talismans that an ambitious chief might possess to get better grazing rights over their neighbor."

Théra nodded. Takval had told her as much. "Your brother and you are the closest things to a pékyu for the Agon, though you don't hold that title. Tenryo was happy to let the Agon tribes fight over you as living crowns—er, garinafin helmets."

"As we grew older, however, that power attributed to us as the last living descendants of Nobo Aragoz eventually became real. As we performed the ceremonial rites wanted by whichever chief controlled us at the moment—dances for better hunting, blessings for more calves and lambs, prayers for the fertility of the women's wombs and the potency of the men's seeds—we also took care to cultivate the elders and chieftains around us. While I built support among warriors loyal to the Aragoz name and kept alive the stories of the Agon, Volyu played one faction against another until we were finally able to build a base of power. With the help of warriors loyal to us, we escaped and established our own tribe, and the other chiefs found it more advantageous to curry our favor and thereby gain prestige rather than to dominate us outright as they used to."

"And Tenryo allowed you to grow and build unmolested?" asked Théra.

"Ah, you've stabbed into the heart of the matter right away," said Souliyan approvingly. "Once we established our independence and turned from mere playing pieces into players, Volyu and I both knew that attention from the Lyucu was inevitable. How could they allow the cubs of the slaughtered wolf to gain strength and seek vengeance?

"My thought was to seek refuge far from Taten, to take those chieftains and naros loyal to us and build a new life away from the Lyucu homeland, where our distance and poverty would make it clear to the Roatan clan that we were not threats."

"You would give up the chance to seek justice for the Agon people?" asked Théra.

Souliyan sighed. "What is justice? My father slaughtered thousands to bring the Lyucu under the shadow of Agon garinafin wings, and Tenryo then slaughtered ten times as many to reverse the situation. My mother was born a Lyucu, but when the Lyucu overran her adopted tribe, they killed her for having borne an Agon child. I have neither the skill nor the interest to restore my father's domain by killing yet ten times more. I wanted only to live in peace and relative freedom. I would have advocated that we all become tanto-lyu-naro if I could be sure we'd survive the harsh winters."

Théra was silent. A pacifistic Agon pékyu was of course not the kind of ally the people of Dara needed, but she did not think this was quite the right moment to argue against Souliyan.

"My brother, however, had very different ideas," continued Souliyan. "He believed that there was nowhere we could escape to that would be safe from the flaming breath of Lyucu garinafins. 'If I were Tenryo,' he said, 'I would never let us go.'"

Théra nodded to herself, thinking that Volyu was exactly right. But any sense of sympathy with Takval's uncle was extinguished with Souliyan's next statement.

"The only way for us to survive, according to Volyu, was for the Aragoz clan to become *useful* to the Lyucu."

Théra closed her eyes and cursed silently. It was a story only too familiar.

"We settled here, in Sliyusa Ki. To the chieftains and naros-votan who followed us, he delivered many rousing speeches about how it was important to plot for the long game, to bide our time until the Agon people could rise up against the hated Lyucu overlords. But in secret, he followed another plan.

"The Lyucu exacted heavy tribute on the scattered Agon tribes: cattle, sheep, children, garinafins, game, pemmican, anything they wanted. From time to time, especially when the winter was especially harsh or the summer especially dry, the weight of the tribute became too much for some tribes on the verge of starvation. As well, the Lyucu thanes, tasked with keeping watch over the Agon tribes in their territories, sometimes humiliated those under their watch beyond reason. In those cases, the desperate tribes would decide to raise the banner of rebellion, and it was the custom for the rebelling chiefs to seek our blessing.

"Beyond appeasing the shamans, these visits also served the purpose of probing our willingness to support the rebellion. Volyu would nod in sympathy and perhaps even pledge to counsel the other tribes to rebel in support."

Théra's blood ran cold, and she shivered involuntarily as Souliyan continued her account.

"But as soon as the rebel chiefs left, grateful for the support of the Aragoz clan, Volyu would spread rumors against the would-be rebels, raising doubts about the chiefs' characters and making up prophecies that they were doomed to fail. When confronted directly by those who wondered if they should join the rebels, he would give ambivalent answers, making everyone hesitate.

"Worst of all, he would secretly dispatch messengers to Taten, reporting to Tenryo all he had learned from the rebels.

"Thus, when the rebellions finally began, the mutinous tribes found themselves devoid of allies and surrounded by Lyucu troops, who had appeared as if by magic. Volyu would then mourn the rebels and cry in front of the next gathering of the tribes at the Festival of Afir, vowing vengeance for the dead brothers and sisters, but explaining that the time wasn't yet ripe. He would then demand the tribes raise an extra-large tribute for Taten, which he collected and sent on to Tenryo after keeping a tenth of the goods for Sliyusa Ki. He explained these tributes as a way to shield the innocent from suspicion and to buy us time to plot against the Lyucu.

"But among the Agon, his reputation for wisdom and shrewdness, for being attuned to the will of the gods, grew. Nearby tribes came to join us with their flocks and herds, and more distant tribes pledged their loyalty to him and to me.

"So many times I wished I could reveal the truth of who he was and how he gained wealth and power by sowing discord among the Agon to prop up his own tent of lies," said Souliyan, her eyes closed and her voice a dry whisper. "But then I would realize that the consequence of such revelation was the deaths of everyone I loved and everyone who trusted me. Either Volyu would kill them, or the Lyucu would. So I've been forced to hold my tongue, a silent coconspirator in my brother's despicable scheme.

"This is a secret that no one knows, not even Takval. But if you're going to ally yourself with my brother, you deserve to know what sort of man he is."

In the predawn darkness, a small group of men and women approached the garinafins penned on the shore of the lake at the heart of the Agon camp.

"Who goes there?" asked one of the Agon guards, his bone axe at the ready. The advancing figures had hidden their faces under skull helmets and animal-skin cowls. With the marriage of the Princess of Dara scheduled for noon, Chief Volyu was poised to rise even higher in the estimation of the Agon tribes. He had ordered increased security against anyone who might dare to disrupt the nuptials.

"It's me," said the woman in the lead. She pulled back her hood.

"Chief Souliyan!" said the guard in surprise. "What are you doing here?"

"I require the use of one of the garinafins," Souliyan said.

The guard looked suspiciously from Souliyan to the others behind her. Souliyan was no garinafin pilot. "Why?"

"My family's sheep were spooked in the middle of the night by the clumsy Dara visitors and ran away," said a girl standing next to Souliyan. "The chief is going to help us get them back."

The guard considered the girl. She was bundled from head to toe in animal hide, a rather odd choice considering the heat, and her face was hidden under a tusked-tiger helmet, a sign of high status. Her accent was that of the First Family's, indicating that she was from a lineage close to the Aragoz clan—perhaps even one of Chief Volyu's unacknowledged daughters.

The guard was about to ask for her name and lineage—

"Those sheep are needed for the wedding feast," said the girl impatiently. "Chief Volyu specifically picked them. We have to hurry!"

The guard decided that he didn't want to risk the chief's ire.

"Take the small female at the end of the pen. She's the fastest. Are you a good pilot?"

The girl pointed to one of the other hooded figures. "My cousin is."

The man she pointed to did have the limber build and cocky attitude of a garinafin pilot—even under that bull skull helmet. The guard had no more doubts.

"Then go, and may Péa speed you."

The winging garinafin, guided by the sure hand of Toof, soon caught up to the lone figure among the dunes. Takval had carried no supplies with him. It was clear that he was expecting this walk to be his last.

Toof landed the garinafin in front of the startled Takval. Théra scrambled down as soon as she had been released from her harness while Souliyan and the others took care to secure their position.

"Don't you ever try anything like that again," said Princess Théra. "What in the world made you think *this* was a good idea?"

"Among our people, a chief or clan head has the right to preempt a subordinate's claim to the hand of a powerful prospective spouse," said Takval. "The only alternative was for me to challenge him."

"Then challenge him! Or at least explain the situation to *me*!"

Takval looked at Théra, his eyes full of longing and confusion. "But you told me to let him win. You told me that there must be no blood spilled for the sake of the alliance—"

"That wasn't what I meant at all—"

"You said that saving Dara meant everything to you! My uncle has the support of all the Agon chiefs, while I have nothing to offer you. And I had already asked you to sacrifice so much just to come to Gondé. . . ." Tears welled up in Takval's eyes.

"Oh, you fool! You dolt!" Théra was exasperated, but her rage had dissipated in a wave of tenderness. "I know I'm no good with words of the heart, but how could you think that I would be willing to give up everything we've built—you and me—to marry some stranger with a larger army?"

"But you only agreed to marry me for an alliance—"

"Don't you ever try to make decisions *for* me. We're partners in this, don't you understand? I *did* agree to marry you as a political act, but I've come to respect you, to care for you, to make room for you in my heart. We're stronger together, and sacrifices, if they must be made, should be a joint decision."

A look of joy slowly brightened Takval's face. "I wasn't sure how you felt—"

"Then you should have asked—"

"But would you have said how you felt unless you thought you were about to lose me?"

Théra tried to answer but found that she could not. Really, until the moment she found out that she could lose Takval forever, she hadn't really known how she felt about him.

"There will be enough time for this later," said Souliyan as she approached the pair. "Right now, we have to decide what to do about my brother."

"We must head back so that I can openly challenge my uncle for your hand," said Takval resolutely.

"No," said Théra. "That is going to lead to one of you getting killed, and I'm not going to start my marriage or this alliance with sister taking up arms against brother, nephew against uncle."

"There is no other way," said Takval. "This has been the tradition of the scrublands for innumerable generations."

"I've heard that kind of excuse for death and bloodshed entirely too often," said Théra. "Before Akiga Aragoz, the tribes were scattered and did not fight as one. Before Tenryo Roatan, the Lyucu did not enslave the Agon. Before the coming of the city-ships, the people of the scrublands did not dream of conquest across the seas. Even stories that have been told for millennia can change, and I'm certain that we can change this story."

By flying close to the ground and coming in from the east with the rising sun, Toof managed to disguise the figure of the approaching garinafin until it was too late for the camp guards to raise an alarm. He guided the garinafin to land right next to Volyu's big tent, and the small band led by Takval and Théra was able to fight their way in to seize Volyu, still dreaming of his big day, before he could rally a proper defense.

Souliyan, standing in front of the tent, assured Volyu's followers that everything was fine. There was simply a family matter that needed to be discussed in private. The coup, bloodless and lightning-fast, was over before most of the camp were even up.

While Souliyan continued to deflect the growing crowd of anxious elders and shamans who demanded to know what was happening, inside the tent, Takval and Théra had to decide on the fate of the deposed Volyu.

"The best thing is to kill him," said Takval. He was seething with rage after Souliyan had revealed to him the full extent of Volyu's treachery on the flight back. "It's the only way to satisfy the spirits of all the brave Agon warriors who had rebelled and died because of him. Once we publicize his crimes, the other chiefs will support us."

"No, killing him is the one thing we must *not* do," said Théra. "To begin our marriage and the alliance between our peoples with a death is a terrible omen."

"You can't always avoid spilling blood—" began Takval.

"It's more than that," said Théra. She glanced over at Volyu, who was gagged and bound in the corner of the tent with thick ropes of sinew. He glared at his nephew and would-be bride with baleful eyes. "If we kill him or depose him, news will reach Taten. Cudyu Roatan will be alarmed if his loyal hound has been removed."

"A confrontation is inevitable."

"That may be, but your uncle is right that the time for a confrontation isn't ripe yet. The Agon tribes are too weak and too disunited. We have to grow stronger before we challenge the Lyucu, and your uncle can help us if we leave him where he is."

After much discussion, they settled on a plan. There was to be an announcement that Volyu had changed his mind and decided that an alliance with Dara was too risky, voiding the marriage plans. Volyu would be left in charge in Sliyusa Ki, but Théra and Takval would leave with those warriors who believed that an alliance with Dara was worthwhile and set up a new base elsewhere, even farther away from the notice of roaming Lyucu thanes and garinafin riders.

"Where will we go?" asked Théra.

"Very far," said Takval. "As far as the World's Edge Mountains in the east. I'm afraid conditions will be even harsher than here."

"As long as we do this together," said Théra. "I'm not even afraid to drink pee anymore; how much worse can it be?"

"What makes you think I'll keep your secret?" asked Volyu, as soon as the gag was pulled from his mouth.

"Simple: survival," said Théra. "You've made it clear that's the only thing you care about—that, and gaining power for yourself. If you reported us to the Lyucu, you would be blamed. How could Cudyu trust you if he learned that your sister and your nephew had both rebelled? And that you were so incompetent that you allowed them to get away? Surely he would think you were conspiring with them."

Volyu continued to glare at her, but said nothing.

"And even if Cudyu somehow didn't blame you, your own people would not let you off easily. Remember, Souliyan is at least as respected as you are. If our departure had her blessing, and the Lyucu then caught us, no one would believe your claims about the gods not favoring us."

The sneer on Volyu's face faded.

"Thus, the most advantageous path for *you* is to keep our secret."

"You can't keep a rebellion like this a secret forever!" Volyu said. "Eventually the Lyucu will find out."

"By then we'll be strong enough to fight them," said Théra. "Think of it this way. The longer you help keep our secret, the stronger we'll get, and the better the chances the rebellion will succeed. And when that happens, you'll be a great hero and have more power than you can possibly gather here in the desert as a Lyucu sheepdog. I know you are not much of a warrior, but even you must dream of being a true pékyu of the Agon, with your name celebrated in song and story—at little risk to you."

The stick plus the honey had the intended effect. Volyu stared at her for a few more moments and then nodded slowly.

As the warriors who would follow Takval and Théra on the long journey to the Dara fleet assembled next to the lakeshore, Volyu stood in front of them and poured kyoffir on the ground, wishing the voyagers a safe journey.

Those who were leaving would be leaving without their long-haired cattle or sheep—it was impossible to keep so many alive across the desert.

This made the departure easier to swallow for the rest of the tribe. The flocks and herds were sold to the remaining naros and naros-votan for weapons, pemmican, cheese, and short-haired cattle. Those staying and those departing both felt they were getting the better end of the bargain—one group had wealth, and the other hope.

"That was not the kind of deal I would have offered my uncle," said Takval, "or would have been offered by any Agon I know."

"We'll both have to learn to think in new ways if we're to achieve our goals," said Théra.

"I'm realizing that. I'm still getting used to the idea of leaving him alive—but you were right. It really is the safest thing to do. In fact, keeping him in place will help us. The Lyucu have come to rely on him as a watchdog. So long as he doesn't bark, the Lyucu will not even look for brewing rebellions."

"It's always easy to negotiate with people like him," said Théra, "because all he cares about is himself." She reached out for Takval's hand and squeezed it. "That we care about more is both a weakness and a strength."

And as the line of Agon warriors began to march to the west, Takval, Théra, Souliyan, and a few close companions mounted two garinafins—gifts from the suddenly generous Volyu, who couldn't wait to get them out of Sliyusa Ki—and flew ahead toward the Dara fleet.

The decision to scuttle the ships was debated, but ultimately every-one agreed it was the only choice. There was no way to maintain these ships if they were to set up their base far in the east, and leaving the ships around risked exposing their arrival to the Lyucu.

Everything was unloaded from the ships and as much of the structures that could be salvaged disassembled and then removed. As the rest of the fleet crew stood mutely on shore and said good-bye to *Dissolver of Sorrows* and her sisters, a tearful Admiral Mitu Roso led Captain Nméji Gon and the other captains to torch the ships.

Théra was crying too. Until this moment, she had harbored, in some corner of her mind, the fantasy that she would be able to return to Dara soon. But the burning ships reminded her that she had made a commitment to be here, at least until her task was done.

"You're thinking of your family?" asked Takval, putting an arm around her shoulders.

She leaned into him. "I am . . . and more."

"Would you like to send a . . . care package to them?"

She looked at him, astounded.

So Takval explained.

The moon was full.

The main Agon caravan had finally arrived. The boxes and chests and bundles from the Dara fleet were loaded onto the short-haired cattle. The warriors and marines and scholars and naros were all asleep on the beach. In the morning they would begin the long trek to the east, to the World's Edge Mountains, where they would find a way to build the fire of rebellion against the Lyucu. Along the way they hoped to stop at other Agon oases, and to gather more to their cause.

Takval and Théra stood next to the surf and watched as dozens of turtles of various sizes crawled awkwardly over the sand into the lapping waves. They had been captured by a few Dara fishermen a few days ago, and they were glad to escape their strange ordeal.

"You think they'll make it through the Wall of Storms safely?" asked Théra.

"I don't know," said Takval. "The shamans don't mention if Afir ever found out whether her turtles reached Kikisavo, either. But I'd like to think love is a shelter against any storm."

The turtles dove into the water and surfaced briefly to breathe, and moonlight glinted off the strange markings on their shells. These were unlike the patterns on any other turtles found in Dara or off the shores of Ukyu-Gondé. Théra had designed the messages carefully, and Takval had then shown her and the fishermen how to use gash cactus juice to etch the messages into the living carapace of the turtles. Thoryo and Çami had been fascinated by the turtles and helped keep them calm during their brief captivity.

Once the turtles were back in the ocean, they hoped that the great belt current would carry them on their yearly migrations back to Dara, where some curious fisherman would capture one of them and perhaps bring the message to the intended recipients. Théra had crafted the carving in such a way that it would not arouse suspicion among the Lyucu in Dara should one of the turtles be caught by them, and yet the message would be unmistakable to the one person in the Islands who would understand how to read it.

"I know that you love her," said Takval. After a pause, he added, "I'm sorry."

Théra turned to him. "The heart isn't a fixed pool like a water bubble in the grass sea; it grows and swells like the ocean. Your mother has become my mother, and your people my people. I will never stop loving her, but that doesn't mean I haven't begun to love you."

"You're my breath, Théra, the mirror of my soul."

Théra leaned up and whispered something into his ear. Startled, Takval put his hand on her belly. She smiled and kissed him.

The turtles dove under the waves, leaving only the eternal sea under the bright glow of the moon.

# RAIN-LASHED
# SAPLINGS

# CHAPTER FIFTEEN

# CAMERA OBSCURA

PAN: THE SIXTH MONTH IN THE EIGHTH YEAR OF
THE REIGN OF SEASON OF STORMS (KNOWN AS
THE EIGHTH YEAR OF THE REIGN OF AUDACIOUS
FREEDOM IN UKYU-TAASA, AND THE EIGHTH YEAR
SINCE PRINCESS THÉRA DEPARTED DARA FOR
UKYU-GONDÉ).

To a common maid or day laborer going about their business in prosperous Pan, the Imperial palace was simply a sprawling compound of imposing towers and solemn halls with sweeping roofs and gleaming gold tiles, hidden behind a wall as thick and strong as the walls of the city itself.

But behind the towers and halls, beyond the Wall of Tranquility, beyond the winding stream that separated the administrative portions of the palace from the private quarters of the Imperial family, was a garden, a secret world within a world, a hidden pool of serene nature amidst the hustle and bustle of the booming capital.

Here, Emperor Ragin had once tended to a small rice paddy to remind himself of his origins as the son of farmers; Empress Risana— Consort Risana back then—had entertained the Imperial children in a winding hedge maze full of fantastical surprises conjured by her smokecraft; and Empress Jia had kept an herb garden, complete with a shed modeled after a Cocru medicine shop in which she had plotted the downfall of the great Lords of Dara who had fought to secure an empire for her husband.

The rice paddy had long since been filled in, and the hedge maze razed. In their places were more gridded plots of herbs, hothouses cared for by teams of servants around the clock, and terrariums and cages housing exotic insects and animals with medicinal properties. Empress Jia's favorite pastime had taken over the Palace Garden, much as her presence had taken over the Dandelion Court.

One particular corner of the garden, however, showed the hand of someone other than the empress. Blue orchids and poppies, cerulean hydrangeas and irises, cobalt lotuses and periwinkle peonies—special varieties that had taken generations of Dara's horticulturalists to breed true—filled the grounds like a varicolored sea. Out of this floral water rose rock formations extracted from quarries and lake bottoms all across the realm, shaped into models of the Islands.

And on these rock formations were miniature replicas of the geography and civilization of Dara: waist-high mountain ranges with salt-tipped peaks favored by squirrel mountaineers; looming cliffs weathered by paintbrush and draped in delicate ivy and morning glory vines, favored haunts of sparrows that seemed as large as garinafins in scale; shield volcanoes about the size of pot lids, sculpted out of hardened dough by the cake decorators from the Imperial kitchen; tiny porcelain versions of Pan, Ginpen, Müning, and Çaruza, each painted with such detail that it was possible to find another version of the Palace Garden inside the model of Pan, about the size of a bull's-eye.

In equal measures childish and refined, meticulously crafted and adolescently imagined, who was responsible for this shrunken version of Dara?

Dawn.

Dewdrops hung from the tips of blades of grass, and the rising sun cast long, dark shadows that enhanced the glow of the glistening flower petals, gilded with a golden light that would not last long.

In the middle of the largest rock formation, meant to represent the Big Island, was a pool shaped like Lake Tututika. In this pool lived a school of colorful carp, with graceful long tail fins that rivaled the legendary dyran's. The largest carp was golden in color, and its slow, meandering trips around the pool were endowed with as much solemnity as the fabled tours of Emperor Mapidéré.

Two large ravens, one black and one white, landed next to the pool. They gazed into the water, where the rising sun broke into a thousand pieces in the ripples bouncing from one end of the pool to the other. The golden carp swam up to them. As the ravens cawed and the carp blew bubbles near the surface, one could almost imagine they were having a conversation.

*- Little sister, what have you been doing with your charge? She spends her days painting and singing, embroidering and making up logogram riddles, strumming the zither and playing the flute, going to the theater and penning poems about actors she fancies—*

*—practicing calligraphy and working on this absurd garden, visiting new restaurants and gushing over trinkets in the market, attending parties and sampling every type of beer, gossiping about boys and reading tales of romance—*

*- Sounds to me like she's just living the life of a young lady of wealth, Rapa and Kana.*

*- But she's not* just *an average young lady, Tututika! What about preparation for war? What about the study of politics? What about honing her talents in the service of Dara? At her age, Gin Mazoti had already taken up arms against Mapidéré—*

*—and Zomi Kidosu had already distinguished herself in the Grand Examination—*

*- Why must everyone live a life of politics and war? Is the life of a coral-reef shrimp any less beautiful than that of a majestic cruben? She fills her life with the pursuit of beauty, and who's to say that isn't her destiny?*

*- Beauty, beauty, beauty! Can't you talk of anything else? There will be war! The treaty that has kept the peace in exchange for tribute to the Lyucu will last only two more years!*

*- Beauty is my domain, sisters. Besides, you have your charge, and he thinks of nothing but war and politics. I rather agree with Kiji that we should not act as though war is the only choice in the future of Dara—a self-fulfilling prophecy—and your cawing won't persuade me to change my mind. Let me guide her the way I want to, and you can devote yourselves to her brother.*

*- You're making a grave mistake, little sister. War cannot be avoided by withdrawing into art, and beauty isn't worth much when the spear-storm strikes.*

A shack of unusual design stood in the middle of the floral sea, surrounded by the miniature islands. Cylindrical in shape, it resembled nothing so much as the stalk of a gigantic mushroom. However, on top of the stalk, instead of an umbrella-like cap, was a slender chimney bent in the middle like an elbow. If one were to crawl inside the flared mouth of this horizontal chimney, as the squirrel mountaineers in the garden were wont to do, one would find a gigantic mirror nestled in the angled joint, slanted to direct the light gathered by the flared mouth down into the shack.

The chimney was an eye, constructed along the same lines as one of the light-bending mirror tubes found on a mechanical cruben.

But instead of a human observer at the end of the tube, the light gathered by the mirror was directed into a tiny hole at the base of the chimney, in which was installed a piece of polished glass bulging in the middle, and through this lens the light entered the dark, obscure interior.

The inside of the shack's cylindrical wall was carefully lined with layers of thick fabric to ward off light leaks, and in the middle of the floor was a circular table with a pristine white sheet of paper on top. A cone of light pierced the darkness within the shack, the tip of the cone at the hole in the ceiling and the base illuminating the sheet of paper like the full moon on a cloudless night. Dust motes drifted lazily through the light cone.

The lens in the ceiling projected the scene outside onto the paper screen: islands, mountains, volcanoes, harbors, and cities, everything awash in the vivid and vibrant colors of the golden dawn, with sharp angles and contrasting shadows. A solid world was reduced to a flat image, and planes and lines contorted through perspective to evoke volume, with a precision unmatched by even the greatest painters of Dara—for this was the work of the gods, a painting of light that no mortal eye or brush could ever hope to replicate.

But that didn't mean mortals wouldn't try.

Kneeling next to the screen was a young woman of eighteen. Fair-skinned and flaxen-haired, she had the appearance of a noblewoman from the highlands of Faça. Her brows were knitted in deep concentration as she wielded a wolf's-hair brush dipped in paint, trying to capture the work of the gods stroke by stroke, dab by dab.

But a series of loud thumps against the door of the shack broke her concentration. She yelped and dropped the brush on the paper. She stared at the ruined painting for a second, her expression forlorn.

"Didn't I explicitly say that no one is to disturb me in here?" she shouted.

There was no answer.

"All right," she muttered to herself. "Guess it's not meant to be. It's more fun to paint the way I want to rather than copy the work of the gods anyway."

She got up and opened the door to the cylindrical shack.

A young man stood outside, regarding her with twinkling eyes and a playful smile.

He was in his twenties. Broad-shouldered, dark-complexioned, hair straight and black, he showed more of his father's Cocru heritage than his mother's Arulugi origins. He was dressed in the armor of a Dara army commander, though as he was in the palace, the armor was ceremonial and made of paper and silk.

With a squeal, the young woman leapt into his arms. "Hudo-*tika*! You didn't write to let me know you were coming!"

The young man was indeed Phyro Garu, son of Kuni Garu and Risana, these days also known as Emperor Monadétu of Dara. But since Empress Jia, his aunt-mother, held the Seal of Dara as regent, he seldom used that name. The young woman was his little sister, Princess Fara, daughter of Kuni Garu and Consort Fina.

"I decided to come to Pan at the last minute," said Phyro. "It's because—never mind, you wouldn't be interested. What were you doing, Ada-*tika*, all shut up in that dark shack? Teké and Comé said you've been in there since before sunrise."

"I see nothing in this palace escapes the notice of the Dyran Fins," said Fara, sounding a bit miffed. Then she brightened again. "No matter—it's not as if I'm keeping a secret. This is called a camera obscura, an old Patternist invention designed for studying form and perspective, and for training painters. Here, let me show you."

She pulled her brother into the shack, shut the door, and showed him how the light-chimney at the top could be turned in different directions to project different views of the surroundings onto the painting screen.

They came back out of the shack, Phyro looking impressed. "Do you have detailed plans for the construction of this camera obscura?"

"I'm sure you can find them in the Imperial Library. I just had Aya help me—wait, don't tell me you're thinking of taking up painting?" Fara knew her brother enjoyed learning about all sorts of machinery, including stagecraft and the tricks of street magicians, but he had rarely shown much interest in art. "Praise to Tututika! My big brother is realizing that life consists of more than learning to ride fire-breathing monsters!"

"No, no! I was thinking that such a device, properly deployed from a submerged mechanical cruben, would allow a cartographer to draw accurate coastal maps in advance of an amphibious assault—"

Fara rolled her eyes. "Can't you think about anything other than war and fighting?"

"Fine. Let's discuss . . . you. So were you studying how to paint true to life? I thought your style tended to be more abstract and less representational. You gave me a whole lecture on the genius of Lady Mira's impressionistic portraits of the Hegemon the last time I visited Pan. What was it you said? *'A nimbus in the wake of a stride, a moonbow the aftermath of strife—'*"

"*'You and I, both fate misunderstood, need no shared history for this duet,'*" finished Fara.

Both went quiet for a moment. The lines, composed by Ro Taça of Rima centuries ago, described the poet's encounter with a coconut lute player after he had been demoted by the King of Rima for giving advice that rubbed the royal ear the wrong way. Fara had appropriated the lines to characterize the power of Lady Mira's abstract embroidery portraits, but Phyro had seen in them a depiction of the smokecraft art of his own mother, Empress Risana.

"If anyone can teach a beauty-blind dullard like me the meaning of art, it's you," said Phyro, to break the somber air. "Trust your own style."

Having grown up surrounded by calligraphy scrolls written by Lügo Crupo, Lady Mira's embroidery, Dasu knotwork headdresses from centuries ago, Adüan idols and masks, oversized torrent-script logograms said to have been carved by Üshin Pidaji with a sword, ancient bronze ritual vessels from the early days of the Tiro states, and all sorts of other rare art objects in the Imperial collection, Fara had always been proud of her artistic taste. "Well, I do—or rather, *did*. It's all because of Gimoto. Last week, there was a tea-tasting party at the palace with some of the younger nobles at court. They begged me to show a few of my paintings. I brought them out. . . . Everyone was complimentary, but Gimoto said they showed no craft. 'I could have done this when I was three!' he said. 'That gourd looks like a baby's behind.' It was humiliating—"

"Forget about Gimoto," said Phyro with a frown. "He's a fool. I suppose he considers himself an expert on gourds because he resembles one: a polished head with nothing inside except air."

Prince Gimoto, the eldest son of King Kado Garu, Kuni Garu's elder brother, was making quite a name for himself in Pan. He was often seen visiting the manors of various government ministers bearing gifts, and he spent lavishly to acquire rare herbs and medicines of longevity for Empress Jia, claiming that he loved her as much as he loved his own mother and wished to fulfill the duties of a son to her. Rumors ran rampant in the capital that Empress Jia was considering taking the throne away from Phyro and making Gimoto emperor.

"He *is* a fool," said Fara. "But all these princelings and ladies at the party rushed to agree with him—"

"They agreed with him only because they think he's important. Had he pointed to a stag and claimed it was a horse, they would have vied with one another to praise the smoothness of its undivided hooves and the stiffness of its antler-like mane."

Despite the lingering embarrassment from Gimoto's criticism, Fara laughed. Hudo-*tika* did always have a way of cheering her up. "Still, it stung, and I realized that I probably should pay more attention to technique. I made Aya help me build this camera obscura so I could practice."

"Shouldn't Aya be devoting herself to studying the Martialist classics if she wants to advance? How does she find the time to goof off with you?"

Fara stuck out her tongue at her brother. "She has to look all serious and studious in front of you and Zomi, but with me she can be her real self. Look at this sitting cushion she made for me. Isn't it neat?"

Fara ducked into the shack and retrieved the sitting cushion, pointing out the patterns Aya Mazoti had embroidered in glowworm silk so that Fara could find it easily even when the inside of the shack was completely dark. ("Aya actually wanted to use a lamp powered by silkmotic force, but the Dyran Fins said those things were too dangerous.") She also pointed out the clever ventilation slots that let in air but sealed out light, and the silk wrapped around the cords for controlling the light-chimney so that Fara's hands wouldn't be injured by the rough hemp.

"That's certainly a lot of effort devoted to making this painting studio comfortable," said Phyro.

"Aya has always been good with ideas for how to make things a little more comfortable. When we were girls, she used to make the most amazing furniture for our pet mice—"

"I wish she put as much effort into learning how to lead an army," said Phyro. "Comfort will be the last thing on her mind when she's out on the battlefield—"

"But it's you and Zomi who are always pushing her to lead an army. What makes you think *she* wants to?"

"Of course she wants to," said Phyro, aghast. "She's the daughter of Auntie Gin!"

Fara sighed. "Forget it. You are home so rarely that I'm not going to spend the whole time arguing with you."

"Then let's go back to art. I can assure you that I prefer your paintings to anything Cousin Gimoto can do. Why, even if he studied nonstop for eighty years, he would fail to come within one-tenth of your skill at capturing the subject's spirit—"

Fara waved him off. "Enough. Enough! You know as much about art as I do about war. I'm sure you think I'm silly to obsess over this."

"I just want you to be happy."

A look of sorrow flitted over Fara's features, but she banished it with a determined smile. "I'm fine. But you . . . hmm . . . I bet you're here to attend a session of the Inner Council. Don't let me keep you from your important business."

"There's nothing more important than family," said Phyro.

Fara looked at her big brother and couldn't stop the tears that welled in her eyes. Since Timu was trapped in Lyucu captivity and Théra was gone beyond the Wall of Storms, the two remaining children of Kuni Garu had grown even closer.

She put her arms around Phyro and pulled her brother into a tight embrace. "Do you want to go visit Father's tomb?" she asked, her face buried in his shoulder. "You weren't here for the Grave-Mending Festival."

Awkwardly, he put his arms around her. "I can't."

She stiffened, and then pulled back. Looking into his eyes, she asked, "Why not? Don't you miss him? I'm sure he wants to hear from you, even if he's on the other side of the River-on-Which-Nothing-Floats."

"I miss him every day," said Phyro. "But I vowed never to show my face at Father's grave until I've avenged him, until I've freed the people of Rui and Dasu from the Lyucu yoke. How can I face him when that promise remains unfulfilled? How can my soldiers trust me if they knew I was so weak that I went to cry at my father's grave before bringing him news of victory?"

"More politics! Does being emperor mean you must deny yourself the natural feelings of a son to his father?"

Phyro's look was determined. "That's the price of being born to the House of Dandelion, Princess Fara."

"I wish we weren't," she said.

Phyro sighed but said nothing. "There's still some time before the meeting," he added in a gentler tone. "Why don't we go visit our mothers' shrines?"

Fara wiped her eyes and nodded, and the siblings walked together deeper into the Palace Garden.

*She found herself in front of the house just outside Çaruza, the house that Phin Zyndu had settled her in while Kuni went away to war.*

*A low stone wall topped by wattle fencing surrounded the estate, and morning glory vines wound around the sticks and through the gaps, turning the fencing into a tapestry of bright pink and lavender. Through the open gate she could see a neat yard divided into patches for medicine and cooking herbs, vegetables, and some ornamental flowers. Bright dandelions bloomed along the stone path leading to the house itself.*

*The colors were more vivid than she remembered, and the flowers tickled her nose with the fragrance of nostalgia. She could hear Otho Krin's voice in the house, ordering the footmen to conduct some repairs, and through the trellis at the side, she could see Soto, her housekeeper, in the large garden in back, playing with little Toto-tika. Baby Rata-tika must be inside, taking a nap.*

*For a brief moment she wondered what had happened to the intervening two dozen years, how she had come to be in this place again, a prisoner of Mata Zyndu, the Hegemon, with her husband Kuni on faraway Dasu, unable to help her.*

*She pushed open the gate in the wall and went in.*

*A tall pagoda tree stood next to the house, its branches heavy with the sweet strings of white flowers that she had loved to eat as a little girl. Two girls, about five or six, had climbed high among the boughs, trying to pick the most tender flowers near the tips of the thin branches with bamboo poles.*

*"Be careful!" she called out to them.*

*"Don't worry, Mistress," said the older girl. "I've tied a rope between Shido and me. I'm hugging the trunk tight so if she falls I'll catch her."*

*"We're going to make you a sweet soup of pagoda tree flowers," said the younger girl. "Wi said it was her mother's favorite."*

*Jia's throat clenched. The two girls were orphans, their parents drafted or killed in the incessant wars that tore through Dara, first between the rebels and the hated Xana Empire, and then among the new Tiro states created by the Hegemon. Mata Zyndu was a mighty warrior, but he wasn't much of a ruler.*

*Jia had taken in the girls so that they wouldn't be snatched by trafficking gangs who sold children to the indigo houses or worse fates. Like some of the poorest in Dara, they didn't even have family names, but went only by a plain, single name unadorned by Classical Ano allusions. Wi and Shido were supposed to be her servants, but she took care of them more than the other way around. The girls were trying to do something nice for their mistress, and after a young life of abject poverty, pagoda flower soup, a peasant's dish, seemed to them the most wonderful treat imaginable.*

*"I'm sure it will be delicious," she called up. "Later, I'll ask Soto to make some lotus paste and we'll steam some buns. You haven't had those yet, have you?"*

*"I can't wait!" said Shido. She climbed a little farther out on the branch and reached with her bamboo pole, trying to get at the flowers at the very tip.*

*Her little legs slipped, and with a terrified cry, she fell off.*

*Jia rushed up, her arms outstretched. The "rope" between Wi and Shido, she now saw, was nothing but a string used to tie packages. The string snapped as Shido fell, barely slowing her down, and she fell into Jia's arms, both collapsing into a heap on the ground.*

*Ignoring the pain in her back, Jia scrambled up. "Shido! Are you all right?"*

*The girl was straining not to cry. Blood seeped from a scrape on her left knee. Quickly, Jia examined her. The left foot was twisted at an unnatural angle.*

*"Don't move," said Jia. "Your ankle may be broken. I have to set it."*

*Wi had climbed down the tree trunk, looking stunned. "It can't be broken."*

*Shido struggled to sit up. "It's not broken. I'm all right." But she cried in pain and fell down again.*

*"It is definitely broken," said Jia. "Stop moving!"*

*"It's not broken!" said Shido. Her voice was high-pitched, terrified.*

*"Please, Mistress, please!" Wi knelt and touched her forehead to Jia's feet. "It's not Shido's fault. I did this. Throw me out instead."*

*Jia was confused. "What are you talking about? No one is being thrown out. It's just a broken ankle. I can fix it."*

*Shido knelt up again and also touched her forehead to the ground. "Thank you, Mistress. Thank you! I will work ten times harder. You can feed me pepper water and burnt rice as punishment for being careless."*

"Punish me instead!" said Wi. "I'm as bad as my unworthy mother, who burned and broke her arm thoughtlessly in Baron Molu's kitchen. Please whip me. I won't make any noise."

Jia closed her eyes in despair, finally understanding. The brutality of life in this lawless land wasn't just limited to the battlefield. Mata Zyndu had abolished the harsh laws of Xana and replaced them with . . . nothing. Bandits and child traffickers ran amuck. With military drafts conducted like kidnappings and armies rampaging through the countryside, peasants starved and ran to the cities to become bond servants for a mouthful of rice. The grand lords and ladies in Çaruza treated these servants like property. It was cheaper to throw out an injured maid than to get her a doctor, and that was likely how Wi's mother had died.

"Neither of you is going to be punished. You didn't do anything wrong."

She cradled Shido's lower leg in her lap and began to set and bind it.

"Mistress, why are you crying?"

"Because I know how much it hurts you, Shido-tika."

"But the wound is on my leg, not yours."

"When a child is hurting, the wound in her mother's heart is deeper, even if it is unseen."

"It doesn't hurt anymore, Mistress. It doesn't."

Hot tears spilled from Jia's eyes. She could heal Shido's broken ankle, but how was she ever going to heal the girls' broken spirits?

"Mistress, is it going to be very expensive to fix Shido's leg?"

"No, of course not. A broken ankle is not a big deal at all. You'll heal in no time."

"But you're still crying even though Shido says she's not hurt anymore."

Jia pulled both girls into a fierce embrace. "I'm crying because the world is broken. This world doesn't deserve you."

The girls were quiet for a while, confused.

"I heard a storyteller say that we need a good king," said Wi.

"A good king will fix everything!" said Shido, wincing.

"A good king?" muttered Jia. "Is that all we need?"

Shido froze, as did Wi. The dangling flowers and arcing branches of the pagoda tree stopped swaying. The noises of servants in the house and the babbling toddler in the garden in back disappeared. The world became still, quiet, and the walls and fences and trees and flowers began to fade, losing their vivid colors, turning insubstantial.

Everything vanished. Jia was sitting alone in a gray fog, much like the first stage of one of Risana's smokecraft illusions.

"The people always yearn for a good king."

She whipped around. The speaker was her husband, Kuni Garu, but not as he was at the time when she had been a captive of the Hegemon. He looked the way he did when he died, decades later, as the Emperor of Dara who was willing to die for his people.

"The people have been told that a good king is all they can hope for," she said. "But it isn't enough. Even the best king eventually dies."

She wondered if she should ask after Risana—if she was well in the realm of ghosts, if she had perhaps even forgiven Jia. But didn't those who had crossed the River-on-Which-Nothing-Floats lose all memories of their mortal lives? She wondered if he was angry with her for all the young men she had taken to bed. But she did not think he would deny her the solace they could offer on lonely, cold nights. He was too grand-spirited for that. Besides, they were important props in the performance she was staging, and he understood the importance of political theater better than anyone. Maybe he even found her young playthings amusing—

And then she realized that this wasn't the real Kuni. He was just a fragment of her imagination. Still, it was good to see him. She missed his warm touch, the confident manner in which he carried his paunch, that smirk he had when he debated the Moralist scholars. He had promised her hardship, loneliness, long-flowing heartache, to make her life interesting, and even in death he was keeping up his end of the bargain.

"You seek something grander than the Grace of Kings," said Kuni. "You wish to make a Dara of lasting peace in which it no longer matters who is king or emperor."

Jia nodded. "The people of Dara deserve it."

"Someone must wield the Grace of Kings, though it is a hard instrument to master."

She shook her head. "No, the Grace of Kings is too dangerous to leave in the hand of any man or woman. There must be a design to ensure lasting peace, to prevent the kind of havoc wreaked by a tyrant like Mapidéré or the Hegemon. I have to find a way to sheathe the Courage of Brutes, the

*Ambition of Nobles,* and *the Grace of Kings—without leaving the weak at the mercy of the strong."*

"There will always be wolves howling for blood," said Kuni. "How can you hope to save the sheep without a good shepherd?"

She smiled. She missed this part of life with Kuni most of all: arguing with him, counseling him, and having his counsel. "A bad shepherd holding the slaughter knife may be a hundred times worse than wolves."

"You seek perfection. But there is often no line between perfection and evil."

"Perfection is impossible. But to say that we should thus stop trying to do better is what makes evil possible."

"You speak of grand ideals," said Kuni. "But even in the pursuit of lasting peace, blood flows and bones pile."

"You were happy to cross rivers of blood and walls of bones in your time."

"Views change with time and experience," said Kuni. "I . . . have many regrets. Do you never doubt?"

"You were happy enough to have no doubt when you left to me the dirty work of dealing with your haughty generals," said Jia, a hard edge coming into her voice.

Kuni sighed. Some debates had no answers.

After a while, he said, "You're plotting something."

Her heart clenched. What did he suspect?

"You remain the regent, refusing to yield to Phyro," continued Kuni. "You say it's because he's not ready, and the Islands, all of them, need your peace. But are you certain that you aren't moved by a less lofty reason?"

"What do you mean?"

"Timu's life will be at risk if there is war. But he's also a child of the House of Dandelion, and that comes with certain duties. Teeth on the board."

Jia relaxed. Even in a dream, it seemed, she could keep her secret. Even with the ghost of the man she loved, she could maintain her mask.

"What's wrong if a mother's private wishes happen to align with the people's needs?" she asked.

"And when they no longer align?"

"Teeth on the board, as you say."

Kuni flinched. The relationship between him and his eldest son had been *fraught, and Jia sensed guilt, regret, the helplessness of the dead to change the past.*

*"I should have made Théra heir long before . . . perhaps Timu wouldn't have gone to Rui—"*

*"We never think children are ready until it's too late," said Jia. "Théra didn't do what you wanted her to do either, did she?"*

*"No. We have raised children who want to live interesting lives."*

*"That we have."*

*They looked at each other, and each was comforted by the quiet pride seen in the face of the other. A fierce longing squeezed Jia's heart. She had the absurd wish for time to stop, for the two of them to hold on to this moment forever, outside the palace, outside the Harmonious City, outside the plots and schemes she was spinning and others were spinning around her, outside reality.*

*But Kuni began to fade. Time never stopped, not for gods, mortals, or even ghosts.*

*In a rush, Kuni said, "Be gentle with Hudo-tika. He's like me—"*

*"Perhaps too alike."*

*The translucent figure of Kuni smiled. "He wants the same thing you do, the happiness of the people of Dara; he just thinks he can achieve it in a different way."*

*"I know," Jia croaked.*

Her mind still in the lingering aftermath of her dream-haze, Jia awakened the two young men in her bed. They smiled at her ingratiatingly and shyly, and she was almost sorry that she had already forgotten their names.

"Go with Wi and have breakfast," she said, kissing each.

Wi, the First Fin, was already standing by Jia's bed. She waited expressionlessly until the two young men were dressed and led them away.

Shido, the Second Fin, slipped into the bedchamber. Her movements were as silent as a swaying pagoda tree branch, and as efficient and deadly as the thousand-hammered steel sword she wore on her back.

"Mistress, Lady Soto wishes to see you as soon as possible."

Jia arched her brows questioningly. At fifty-four years of age, naked in her bed and without any makeup on, she nonetheless looked regal and imposing. Age had taken away some of her youthful beauty and replaced it with the glamour of confidence in power and steadfastness against doubt.

Though there was no one else in the bedchamber, Shido leaned in and whispered in Jia's ear.

Jia closed her eyes and looked thoughtful for a minute. "Did he go see her first?"

Shido shook her head. "He went to see Princess Fara first, and then to the Pellucid Cocoon Shrine. Lady Soto found out he was here when she ran into Fara talking to the Imperial chef, giving orders for tonight's dinner."

Jia nodded. "Let Lady Soto know that I am occupied. I'll see her tonight at dinner."

Shido now gave her a questioning look.

Jia returned a bitter smile. "I already know what Soto is going to say. Might as well save the arguments for later."

Shido bowed in *jiri* and disappeared as silently as she had come.

*Ah, old friend,* thought Jia, *you still think it's possible to find a compromise between me and Phyro. But how do you compromise between the desire to sheathe a sword and the desire to cut down thousands with it? I hope I can hold on to your faith. . . .*

There were so many schemes within schemes that she had to keep going.

She glanced at the pillows next to her and saw that one of the young men had left behind his jade hairpin. She picked it up.

Gimoto had brought them to see her, Jia remembered, ostensibly because they were learned *cashima* who had discovered in the annals of the ancient Tiro kings yet more examples of virtuous queen-regents who carried out the wishes of the people. At the private audience, they had been dressed in tight robes that showed off their figures well and perfumed with the sort of expensive musk found in the best scarlet houses. They were so young that even the two of them added together didn't match her age.

*Most Honored and August Aunt Empress,* Gimoto had declared as he knelt before her, an expression of solemn and pious reverence on his face, *your humble child wishes you everlasting good health so you may reign over Dara in eternity. Perhaps the vigor of these young men, my friends, may contribute to that end.*

She chuckled to herself, imagining the look on the face of Tete, Gimoto's mother, if she found out her son thought this kind of "gift" was an appropriate way to demonstrate filial devotion.

With a decisive slam, she broke the jade hairpin against the side of the bed. Carelessly, she tossed the pieces aside.

They were energetic in bed and she liked them well enough, but she was never going to see them again. They were intended as distractions, not for herself, but for those who observed her. She had once advised Kuni to take on another wife to disguise his political ambition from the Hegemon, and these young men served the same purpose. No one suspected a ruler wallowing in sexual gratification of playing the long game. The liaisons fulfilled a certain expectation some people had of men and women in power, and under the fog of misdirected expectations, she could plot without notice.

Yet, distractions had wills of their own. Evidently, Gimoto had hoped that these young men would gain her favor and whisper to him what she muttered during her dreams. That could be dangerous; she had to be even more careful.

Moreover, the dream from this morning bothered her. It indicated softness and doubt, and neither were things she could afford. It was possible that some of the fumes from her experiments had affected her. She vowed to wear a better mask in the future.

Gimoto's antics were mostly harmless, but she wished he were just a little more politically savvy. To openly court the favor of ministers of the Inner Council with extravagant gifts was such a stupid thing to do that she shook her head at his lack of political finesse. Of course no one accepted the presents. Cogo Yelu, that sly old fox, had taught them all too well. Still, some of the lesser ministers not on the council were holding banquets in the prince's honor, and rumors that she was thinking of designating a new emperor had spread. That was useful.

She hoped it was enough to persuade Phyro to finally do the right thing. For the sake of the people of Dara, she hoped he would back down.

The face of her son and Phyro's brother, Timu, came unbidden into her mind. Almost unconsciously, she found herself reaching for him. She stopped herself. *Take care of yourself, Toto-tika,* she whispered. Then she turned away from his pleading face resolutely and imagined doors closing behind her, locking away distractions.

She summoned her ladies-in-waiting. "Come, dress me for court."

# CHAPTER SIXTEEN

# THE TEMPLE OF PÉA-KIJI

MEANWHILE, BY THE SHORES OF LAKE ARISUSO
ON MOUNT KIJI, RUI.

The clergy of the Temple of Péa-Kiji were busy preparing for the Imperial visit. Pékyu Vadyu, affectionately known as Tanvanaki, Protector of Dara, was coming with her consort, Emperor Thaké. They would offer sacrifices to the god and pray for a good harvest in the fall and plenty of new calves.

The head shaman, who had the largest set of rooms in the temple, moved out into the abbot's quarters so that her rooms could be cleaned out and used as the temporary abode of the pékyu's family. The abbot, in turn, displaced the senior priests from their meditation house. The lesser shamans, meanwhile, vacated their rooms so that the pékyu's thanes and guards would sleep more comfortably. They took over the best rooms in the monastics' dormitories until all the monks and nuns, regardless of seniority, had to squeeze in together, sixteen to a room that was meant for eight.

This was how the world worked, reflected the abbot sadly. Even though he served a god, he wasn't free from the need to accommodate temporal power.

He dipped his washcloth back into the pail, swirled it around, wrung it out, and began to climb the ladder to reach the face of Péa-Kiji again.

"Don't dawdle," said the head shaman, arms akimbo, legs planted wide apart. She was standing at the foot of the statue, directing teams of native monks and nuns to clean the sacrificial hall. "Make sure Péa-Kiji's eyes really shine for the pékyu."

"Absolutely. Absolutely." The abbot paused in his climb and tried to bow to the head shaman. The effort made him almost lose his balance, and as he grabbed onto the ladder again, he squeezed the washcloth and a few drops of water fell on the face of the head shaman, looking up.

The shaman jumped out of the way and cursed. "What is the matter with you? I can't abide this kind of carelessness. Half rations for you at dinner, and you better set a good example for the rest of the lazy natives!"

"You're most generous, Your Grace," said the abbot. He made sure to tuck the washcloth into the belt of his robe before trying awkwardly to bow again from the ladder.

"Just get on with it," said the shaman, waving at him impatiently.

The abbot climbed until he was at the shoulder of the gigantic statue. Even the head of Péa-Kiji was taller than he was. Gingerly, he stepped out onto the god's lips, clinging to the nose like a gecko, and began to polish the statue's eyes. Layers of grime, most of it the result of the greasy burnt offerings favored by the Lyucu thanes, soon made the white washcloth a sooty gray. He vowed not to look down lest his legs turn soft as noodles at the sight of the floor far below.

"Faster! Faster!" shouted the head shaman. "I've seen how fast you move when the dining hall serves mutton stew or a pretty widow comes here to make offerings."

The abbot worked faster. Even the gods had to accept changes, no less than members of the clergy themselves. A giant garinafin now perched over Péa-Kiji's right shoulder, mouth wide open as though in preparation to breathe fire, while a small Mingén falcon sat over the left, looking a bit intimidated. A thick cape made of long-haired cattle fur was draped over his traditional Dara clothes, and the abbot did not relish the thought of having to dust that tentlike addition, which smelled of unwashed hair and stale incense. On top of the god's bald head was a massive helmet fashioned from the skull of a full-grown garinafin, and just looking up at the terrifying upper canines, as long as swords, made him shudder.

The Lyucu conquerors were of the view that the native gods

were "misunderstandings" of the revelations of the All-Father and the gods of Ukyu. Pékyu Tenryo had found it useful to maintain the priesthood and religious of Kiji as a way to calm the jittery populace. His daughter, Tanvanaki, had continued the policy. The natives were allowed to worship Kiji and the other gods of Dara much as they had before, but she had insisted on certain changes in the rituals to emphasize the supremacy of Lyucu beliefs. Shamans were installed at the temples to watch over the clergy lest they become a source of comfort for native rebellions. The abbot, intent on protecting the temple's treasures and library, as well as centuries of accumulated prestige and influence, had acquiesced in these changes. Sometimes, though, he wondered if he really was doing the right thing.

"I don't think we'll have time for lunch today," shouted the head shaman. "You have only yourselves to blame. We still have to air out the spirit portraits of departed garinafin riders after you're finished with this hall."

Next to the placid waves of the caldera lake Arisuso, a caravan had stopped. The way up the volcano had been hard on the horses pulling the carriages, and the drivers were taking a break before the final push toward the Temple of Péa-Kiji in the distance. Lyucu guards patrolled the perimeter, while native servants and drivers rushed about to water and feed the horses.

Two children, about seven or six years of age, jumped down from one of the smaller carriages and ran to wade in the water.

"Where are the Mingén falcons?" asked the older one, a boy, shading his eyes as he surveyed the lake. He was fair-haired, slender, and with a complexion a shade darker than the Lyucu guards. There was an impatience in his movements and expression, as though he was bored by the moment he lived in and couldn't wait to get to the next. "I thought Vocu said I'd see them here." He spoke in crisp, commanding Lyucu, save for the name of the local bird of prey, which he kept in Dara, though with an exaggerated Lyucu accent. He kicked the water, as though punishing the lake for depriving him of his desire.

"The falcons live in Lake Dako," said his younger sister. In

contrast to her brother, her movements were deliberate and thoughtful. She spoke in Dara, with a courtly accent that would be admired
in Pan, though it seemed a bit out of place here in Ukyu-taasa. "We
passed it on the way up here, Dyu-*tika*."

"Don't call me that," said the boy, almost reflexively.

"We're supposed to speak Dara," said the girl, a hint of reproach
in her voice. "Father said many of the peasants will be making their
way up here to witness the sacrifice, and we should make sure they
feel comfortable."

"Who cares what he thinks?" said the boy.

"Mother is going to speak in Dara too," said the girl.

"Fine," said the boy, shifting into Dara. "But really, it's the fault of
the mud-arms that they don't speak Lyucu."

Just then, two men climbed out of the largest carriage and strolled
toward the children. The man in the lead, slender and tall, about
thirty in age, shouted, "Dyu-*tika*, Zaza-*tika*! Don't go in too deep.
There are large fish in the lake with sharp teeth!"

The older man next to him, a Lyucu thane—though he was
dressed like a native official—laughed. "*Rénga*, let the pékyus-taasa
have their fun. Once we're at the temple, they'll have to do everything the shamans and priests tell them to do, like puppets."

A trace of displeasure flickered across the younger man's face at
this, but he said nothing. The two picked up their pace and soon
reached the children.

The younger man was Timu, son of Kuni Garu and Jia Matiza,
though he was now known as Emperor Thaké of Ukyu-taasa. The
two children were from his marriage to Tanvanaki: The boy was
named Todyu Roatan, and the girl Dyana Roatan.

"Vocu Firna, do you want to spear some of the big fish with me?"
asked Todyu. He was rubbing his hands together, looking as eager
as a puppy.

The Lyucu thane chuckled. "If you really want to go fishing, you
need to find a native guide. My tribe didn't live by the sea, and even
after so many years in Dara, I still get queasy on a boat." He spoke
Dara after the fashion of the natives of Rui and Dasu, though there
was a Lyucu accent.

"Oh." Todyu sounded disappointed. "I just figured that it was like hunting. Wasn't the god Péten a fishing whale who taught people how to hunt? And you're a great hunter."

"Well, it is a kind of hunting, votan," said Vocu Firna. "We Lyucu hunt to supplement our herds, and the natives fish to flavor rice and sorghum. But hunting is an art of necessity, and learned only through experience. Just because I used to hunt mouflon and aurochs in Ukyu, it doesn't mean I know how to fish in Ukyu-taasa."

"Remember what I taught you, Dyu-*tika*," said Timu. "What did the Ano sage Kon Fiji say when the King of Amu once asked him to design him a flying tower over Lake Toyemotika?"

Everyone looked at the young pékyu-taasa. The boy said nothing. Instead, he waded deeper into the lake, his eyes focused at his feet, as though looking for crabs or clams.

"Come on, Dyu-*tika*," said his father. A hint of impatience crept into his indulgent voice. "We went over this not more than five days ago. This was in the chapter of Poti Maji's *Acts of the Master* you were supposed to memorize."

Todyu refused to meet his father's eyes. He picked up a rock from the bottom of the lake and tossed it far into the water.

An expression of annoyance appeared on Timu's face. Just as he was about to speak again, Todyu's sister, Dyana, came to her brother's rescue. "Kon Fiji asked around Müning until he found the architect everyone recommended. He brought the architect back to the king. 'But Kon Fiji,' said the king, 'I thought you were so wise! Why didn't you design the tower yourself?' And Kon Fiji replied, 'I can design a system of rites for you that will ensure a harmonious state, but I cannot design for you a tower that will withstand rain and storms. It is because I am not entirely foolish that I know when I must ask for the expertise of others. The beginning of wisdom is always to know thyself.'"

"Very good," said Timu, smiling kindly at his daughter. "And can you write the Classical Ano logograms for 'know thyself'?"

Dyana waded onto the shore and gathered some mud into two little mounds. With a stick, she carefully carved them into the Ano logograms for *gitré üthu*.

"What a clever girl!" said Vocu Firna. "Pékyu-taasa, you write like your father, with a grace far beyond your years."

Dyana blushed and bowed to him in *jiri*. "You praise me too much. I can write no more than a few hundred logograms, and I only know the bare outline of the deeds of Kikisavo and Afir. I know nothing of the world, and certainly not myself."

"Ha, when I was your age, I could barely—"

"Look at this snail!" cried Todyu. He splashed his way back to the shore, holding aloft a snail shell about the size of his fist. He stopped next to Vocu Firna, carelessly crushing under his right foot the logograms Dyana had written. "Doesn't it remind you of a skull helmet? I bet it tastes delicious."

The snail he held under Vocu's nose looked exactly the same as the hundreds of other snails perched on rocks at the lakeshore. Dyana, seeing her logograms destroyed by her brother, scrunched up her face, ready to cry, and Timu seethed with anger at his son.

"That is indeed an impressive snail," Vocu said, trying to defuse the situation.

"Do you think the snail is fierce?" asked Todyu. "Do you think it has teeth?" He poked at the snail with the stick Dyana had been using to write, oblivious to his sister's distress.

Dyana went over to her father, who picked her up and rested her against his shoulder. The little girl wrapped her arms around Timu's neck and hid her face against it.

"Err, I don't know much about the anatomy of snails," said Vocu. "But I do know that in the past, during years when crops were destroyed by locusts, people of the surrounding regions survived on fish and snails from Lake Arisuso."

"I had not realized that you made a study of local history, Tiger-Thane Vocu," said Timu, making an effort not to glare at his son.

"Oh, if the natives eat this, it's probably not very fierce," said Todyu. He dropped the snail to the ground.

"I can't claim to be a historian," said Vocu. "But as the Minister of Rituals, it behooves me to be interested in local customs. I was surprised that there are a large number of folk logograms in use in the surrounding region based on the net or hook semantic roots, since this region isn't close to the seacoast. Oh, a folk logogram is a made-up logogram constructed using the principles of Ano logograms, but not adopted by officials or learned scribes—"

"I know what folk logograms are," said a smiling Timu. "They're used by the common people, many of whom are illiterate, to communicate simple ideas or to invite good luck, as many believe logograms to be magical."

"Of course you're the expert, *Rénga*. I've just grown used to having to explain everything to the other ministers."

"If only the other ministers took as much interest as you do in the lives of the people of Dara," said Timu wistfully.

The conversation of the adults bored Todyu. Since no one was paying attention to him, he wandered grumpily away to wade in the lake again.

"I find native Dara culture so utterly fascinating," said Vocu. "I'm trying my hand at writing some Classical Ano poems."

"Really?" said Timu, raising his eyebrows. "You must share some with me . . . But you were talking about the folk logograms."

"Oh yes. I studied folk logograms with particular interest, since I was thinking perhaps they suggested a way for writing Lyucu with logograms—as you know, using zyndari letters to write Lyucu is something most thanes refuse to learn, not least because the natives view the letters as low in status. Anyway, I asked the native scholars for an explanation why so many folk logograms used near the mountain had associations with fishing, but many of them disdained the folk logograms and had no interest in them at all. In the end, I had to ask the elders of the villages, who spoke of times of starvation and fishing in Lake Arisuso, though the hike up here is strenuous. I confirmed the accuracy of their accounts with records kept by the monastics of this temple."

"The common people have to struggle mightily just to survive," said Timu. "That is something the Lyucu naros and culeks know well."

"And their wisdom helps us. Knowing that Lake Arisuso can be a backup food source may save many peasants, should the crops fail again in the future."

Timu was impressed. It was so rare for the Lyucu to care about what happened with the common native peasantry, despite his constant attempts to bring the two peoples together.

He was about to offer some praise to Vocu when Todyu splashed his way to the shore again. "Mother is coming!" he shouted, pointing toward the eastern sky. A garinafin was winging its way toward them.

A series of complicated expressions flitted across Timu's face. But in the end, he composed himself and got ready to welcome his wife.

As soon as Tanvanaki dismounted from Korva, her aged but still powerful garinafin, Todyu rushed up to her.

"Mother, Mother!" he spoke in rapid Lyucu. "Look at how many snails I killed! At first I was just smashing the ones out of the water with a rock—"

Tanvanaki regarded her son with affection but didn't hug him or pick him up. "Killing snails isn't much of a challenge," she replied in Lyucu.

"I know! But it's a little bit like smashing a skull, isn't it?"

"Only a little. Did you get scared when the gooey part came out?"

"No! I even ate one raw just to prove that I wasn't scared. I figured that it was more challenging to aim for the ones in the water. They are crafty!"

"Crafty?"

"They move . . . without moving."

"Oh, you mean because they seem to be in different places on the bottom from when you see them through the shallow water?"

"Exactly! But I got really good at it and never missed. When will you take me hunting? I'm sure I can—"

Tanvanaki saw the blood on her son's hand. "What happened there?"

"Oh, it's nothing. I sliced it on one of the broken snail shells."

It was actually a pretty deep wound. Tanvanaki whistled to summon one of the guards, who began to bandage the hand.

"Does it hurt?"

"Not at all," said Todyu, but he winced involuntarily as the cloth was wrapped around his hand.

"Good," said Tanvanaki approvingly. "A Lyucu warrior must not be afraid of the sight of blood or avoid pain. A pékyu-taasa cannot be a tanto-lyu-naro."

A few dozen paces away, Timu regarded the scene with a mixture of revulsion and confusion. He had tried to be a good father, to do things differently from Kuni, that distant, critical paternal figure of his youth. He had tried to spend as much time with Dyu-*tika* as he could, rather than abandon him to governesses or servants. But at this moment, his son seemed a total stranger, someone he could not believe was his own flesh and blood.

"Da, please put me down," whispered Dyana. "I want to go greet Mother."

"Of course," said Timu. He set her down on the ground.

The little girl ran up to her mother and brother. Tanvanaki smiled at her.

"Why couldn't you come with us?" asked Dyana in Dara.

"I had to take care of some rebels," Tanvanaki said, also in Dara. The change in language seemed to remind her of something unpleasant, and suddenly she looked tired, weighed down.

"Bad people?" asked Dyana.

"Of course they were bad people," said Todyu, still speaking Lyucu. "That's why they were rebels. Did you kill all of them?"

Tanvanaki saw the way Timu was looking at her. She sighed.

"Vocu," Tanvanaki called, gesturing for the thane, "come and take the children to the temple and get them settled. I'll join you later." Her tone made it clear that this wasn't open to discussion. Even Todyu didn't complain.

"Yes, votan."

Vocu Firna took the children to the carriage. He glanced back at Timu, who shook his head. The drivers hitched the horses to the carriages; the Lyucu guards got back on their mounts. Soon, the caravan was on its way to the temple, and only Tanvanaki and Timu were left behind.

Without lowing or moaning, Korva walked away to graze on some succulent bushes a little distance from the lake. Even she seemed to understand it was best to leave the pair alone.

A wild goose flew over the lake high above, its lonesome cry lingering in the quiet air.

Timu walked up to Tanvanaki and fell to one knee, placing both hands atop the other knee. She nodded to acknowledge the greeting. He got up.

"You never answered Dyu-*tika*'s question," he began. Try as he might, he couldn't keep the accusatory tone out of his voice.

There was a time, during the earliest years of their marriage, when he had been able to speak to her of poetry and music, of the beauty of the land and the sea seen from the back of a garinafin, of the many ways the world could be made better through love. He had thought, at one point, that the two of them shared the same dream of the Lyucu and the natives living in harmony. He had loved to touch her and be touched by her, even if that intimacy had begun with violence and deception.

Those days were long gone. But he still loved her, a complicated and agonizing love.

"Do you really want to know?" Tanvanaki's voice was sullen.

There was a time when she had been able to speak to him with tenderness, with affection, with patience. There was a time when his naïveté and foolish ideals had charmed her, even seduced her. She loved him, a simple love of gut feelings and flushed cheeks, tinged with a trace of regret over how that love had begun and strengthened by his status as the father of her children. But these days, all they seemed to do was to argue and debate.

"How many?" Timu was relentless.

Tanvanaki sighed again. "One hundred and sixty-five."

Timu felt his legs going weak. He forced himself to remain standing. "The whole village then?" he croaked.

Tanvanaki nodded. Then, after a moment, she added, "Except for two *toko dawiji*, who helped the local garrison by informing on the rebels. You'll be pleased to know that I commended them—"

Timu acted like he hadn't heard the last part. "Then where are the children? We must find good homes for the children—"

"So that they can grow up and become rebels too?" Tanvanaki's voice was cold. "I had all of them killed. I told you: Other than the collaborating *toko dawiji*, there are no survivors."

"But you promised! You said—"

"I said I would be merciful when possible," said Tanvanaki with a sudden flare of rage. "Four of the villagers killed a naro when he was asleep. They then ran into the mountains, and the rest of the village refused to yield up their hideout. I had no choice. That naro was Cutanrovo Aga's cousin. I've already done all I could to limit the reprisals to the village responsible. Cutanrovo demanded killing all the villagers within thirty miles."

Timu closed his eyes. "But the northern shore of Rui has been peaceful for years. I thought we were making progress. Such an atrocity is going to bring back all the memories of the conquest and encourage more rebellions the next time there's a drought—"

"The only reason it has been peaceful for years is because the natives still remember what it was like if they killed a Lyucu," said Tanvanaki. "Maybe this is exactly the reminder they needed."

"But what happened? What did the naro do?"

"What makes you so certain the naro did something?"

Timu simply stared at her. After a moment, Tanvanaki relented. "He raped two women in the village and killed one of them when she scratched his face. The four villagers who killed him were the dead woman's kin, led by her grandmother."

"O gods! You should have punished the naro—"

"I would have if they hadn't killed him! But unless the natives understand the price of killing a Lyucu, there can never be any real peace—"

"But what about our dream of having the Lyucu and Dara living together side by side in peace? What about our plan to dissolve the cycles of violence—"

"I have been listening to you for too long. That's the problem," said Tanvanaki. Agitated, she paced back and forth. "I've freed most of the villages, making them subjects instead of slaves. I've adopted your plan of using native officials for administration. I've allowed you to draft most of the laws of Ukyu-taasa and keep things as much like before our coming as possible. We have defaced our gods to please yours. I've even forced all the Lyucu to learn Dara. But what do I get in return? They're still escaping Rui and Dasu in rafts, leaking our secrets to your mother. They murder one of my naros and dare to hide the killers!"

"You haven't gone far enough! To divide the population into tiers—to grant someone privileges according to how much Lyucu blood they have—that isn't what we agreed on at all. Have you heard how the thanes speak of the togaten and the Dara-raaki? Have you heard how they speak of our children?"

*Togaten* literally meant "runts." It was a term used by the Lyucu to refer to the children born from the mass rapes committed by the Lyucu army against the Dara population during the initial conquest.

Tanvanaki flinched, but she didn't back down. "The supremacy of the Lyucu isn't negotiable. My father came here promising my people a better life, and I'm not going to betray that dream. Do you think I can behave as one of your despots and just wipe away the privileges my thanes and naros have earned by right of conquest? The minute we treat the Lyucu and the natives exactly alike is also the minute I'll have a coup on my hands."

"The natives are also your people! *I* am also one of your people!"

Tanvanaki was about to reply when they heard the *clop-clop* of a horse racing up the mountain toward the lake. They turned and saw a single rider dressed in the garb of a native official. The rider saw them and turned their way. A few minutes later, the rider rolled off the back of the horse and knelt before Tanvanaki, touching his forehead to the ground.

It was Noda Mi, the man who had betrayed Gin Mazoti at the Battle of Zathin Gulf, and the highest-ranking native official at the court in Kriphi.

"Go to the temple," said Tanvanaki to Timu, and again there was no room for disagreement in her tone.

Defeated, Timu hiked toward the temple alone, his figure as stark as a departing wild goose.

"That's all they delivered? Six Moralists and a litigator? May Tazu take them!" Tanvanaki took out her rage on the snails basking in the sun on the rocks by the shore, kicking them far into the water.

She turned around and saw that Noda Mi had buried his face in the mud, his body trembling like a leaf in autumn. His teeth chattered as he struggled to answer. "Most August and Merciful Pékyu, the pi-pirates also de-delivered several hundred bows and sp-spears—"

"I don't need weapons! I need people who can give me the secret of the silkmotic force!"

"They tried! They knew you wan-wanted people of learning, but it's hard to fi-find *toko dawiji* and *cashima* on the high seas—"

"No, no, no! I don't need bookworms who can recite the Ano Classics—my husband does that enough. I need skilled engineers who can build things. I need plans. I need manuals, prototypes, manufacturing secrets. I need people with knowledge that I can actually use!"

"I will try again, votan! I will try again!" Noda Mi slammed his forehead into the mud like a chicken pecking at rice, and bits of mud splashed onto Tanvanaki's boots.

The absurdity of Noda's performance had a surprisingly calming effect on Tanvanaki. She took a deep breath and considered the situation.

No, her rage wasn't just because of Noda Mi's incompetence. Perhaps she had been too hard on Timu. He had always been weak, but his advice hadn't been useless. During the early days of the Lyucu conquest, rebellion had flared up after rebellion, and most of the skilled artisans, inventors, and scholars, thinking that there was no future for them under the "barbarians," had either joined the rebels and thus been killed, or escaped from Ukyu-taasa as refugees. But the rebellions finally petered out after she had taken Timu's advice and adopted a more accommodationist policy toward the natives. Except for the most recalcitrant offenders, most natives were freed instead of enslaved, and taxation and local administration returned to the hands of Dara officials who pledged loyalty to the Lyucu. Many natives were even recruited into the army to add to the strength of Ukyu-taasa.

Timu was a good figurehead to pacify the natives into accepting their place, but he didn't understand that accommodations only worked when backed by the threat of force. This latest rebellion might be an anomaly, but unless it was put down with maximum force, the natives would be emboldened. The words of the Ano sages that Timu worshipped more than the revelation of the gods were good only as a kind of drug that dulled the fighting instinct of the natives; they were no substitute for mass executions in terms of maintaining the stability of Ukyu-taasa.

She also had to plan for the possibility of the resumption of war against the rest of Dara. Even though the tribute ships from the Big Island came on schedule every season, bearing the promised goods, she didn't trust Jia or the rest of the Dara-raaki. They were plotting something against her, she was sure of it—and the treaty of non-aggression that she had negotiated with Jia would last only another two years after this one. As much as she despised the Dara way of life—the hypocritical scholars, the supercilious officials, the degrading treatment of women, the desecration of the land with farming—she had to admit that they did possess powerful weapons. There wasn't a day that went by without her thinking of the Battle of Zathin Gulf. The Lyucu needed knowledge of Dara machinery if they were to conquer the rest of Dara and secure a future for themselves.

With the number of scholars and engineers in Ukyu-taasa decimated, she had come up with the plan to abduct experts with specialized knowledge from the core islands and force them to work for her. Many thanes, especially the hard-liners, were opposed to adopting native expertise, viewing it as a betrayal of Lyucu traditions. But she knew that sometimes change was necessary, and to thrive in a new land meant learning new ways to hunt and make war.

"Maybe we've been going about this the wrong way," said Tanvanaki. Her voice was calm, perhaps even kind. "It's not your fault that the pirates we've been working with are idiots."

Noda Mi lifted his head out of the mud, a look of hope on his muck-encrusted face.

"Instead of asking the pirates to hunt for expertise that they don't understand, it would be better to use them as intermediaries." Tanvanaki enjoyed speaking Dara in moments like these. It felt like a language designed for plots and schemes and deviousness. "The Dara-raaki are greedy and faithless—"

"They most certainly are, Most Wise and All-Seeing Pékyu!"

Noda Mi's eyes shone. The man seemed to love plotting against his own people. He shut up when he saw the look of disgust on Tanvanaki's face.

"Through the pirates, get in touch with those on the core islands who are driven by profit," continued Tanvanaki. "Have them acquire men and women of knowledge and sell them to the pirates. Focus on Dimushi and Dimu, big cities where a few missing engineers won't draw too much attention. The key is not to let anyone know who the ultimate buyers are—it could give the usurper Jia an excuse to attack."

Once again, Noda Mi slammed his forehead into the mud. "What a cunning plan! Pékyu, you're simply without compare in the annals of Dara. The Islands are blessed to have a protector with so much wisdom and foresight. I can only thank all the gods of the Lyucu . . ."

Tanvanaki, who was striding toward Korva, didn't hear the rest of his nauseating speech.

Back in the sacrificial hall of the Temple of Péa-Kiji, the gleaming statue of the god sat alone. All the monks and nuns and shamans and priests were asleep, as were the Imperial family and their guards and retinue. Long-burning whale-oil candles were lit on the altar, keeping the god company.

This high on top of the stratovolcano, the wind howled incessantly. A sudden gust pushed open the doors of the sacrificial hall, and a swirling vortex of leaves glided in. The candles flickered.

- *Oho, my brother, you're looking so shiny! Still happy with your choice? I assume you enjoyed that blood meal Tanvanaki offered you earlier today?*

- *Tazu, I really despise your irreverence. That wasn't what I wanted, and you know it.*

A grating peal of laughter, like a shark's tooth scratching through ice.

- *Sorry, I'm not like the old turtle. I just can't put on a serious face and philosophize like some second-rate mortal sage. If you can't laugh at death as a god, then you might as well become a mortal.*

- *That is what Lutho has done. He had real courage.*

- *I'd call that foolishness. Anyway, your boy's plan is working out real well, isn't it?*

A long pause. The candle flames stood still for a few moments before bending in unison, like sighing trees.

- *Timu has managed to save many lives.*

- *Is that what he tells himself to sleep at night? Is that what you tell yourself as you grow fat on the sacrifices of the Lyucu?*

- *I don't see you rejecting the burnt offerings either. And you let those pirates roam free.*

- *Let them? I'm sorry, brother, but have you forgotten that we're not allowed to intervene in mortal affairs? My job is to fill the sea with storms, and if they manage to navigate through to safe harbor, I can't do a thing about it.*

- *Then stop tormenting me with deaths I'm not responsible for!*

- *If you and Timu are tormented by doubt and guilt, it's because you grow unsatisfied with your own compromises. Don't blame me for pointing it out. I never moralize.*

- *You may play the role of the amoral gadfly, Tazu, but I've noticed how many of those rickety rafts filled with refugees have made their way safely to the other islands from these shores. You care about the people of Dara, even though you protest.*

Another long pause. The swirling vortex of leaves slowed down, as though pondering something. Then it sped up again.

- *They were heading for freedom, and freedom is my domain. To guide the refugees out of bondage does not violate our pact.*

- *You keep on telling yourself that enough times, and maybe you'll start to believe it.*

- *So what if I care maybe a little? I hate what the Lyucu have done to my sleek form, marring it with their own stories of a lumbering trickster whale. Look at yourself! Is this how you really want to be, a mishmash of myths, a figurehead for enslavement and slaughter?*

The candle flames held still again. Then there was a long, howling sigh, and the flames winked out. The swirling vortex collapsed, leaving behind only a pile of leaves.

Darkness reigned in the sacrificial hall.

# CHAPTER SEVENTEEN

# MOONBREAD

MEANWHILE, AT THE SECRET AGON BASE IN KIRI
VALLEY, IN THE FOOTHILLS OF THE WORLD'S EDGE
MOUNTAINS.

Weather in the scrublands was often unpredictable. The flat landscape offered little resistance to the winds, and so dust storms
careened for hundreds of miles like herds of stampeding long-
haired cattle, thunderstorms roamed freely across the broad plains
like yearling garinafins testing out their wings for the first time, and
powerful tornadoes sometimes blew from one end of the continent
to the other, chasing clouds across the sky like young gods racing
after shooting stars.

In the southeastern corner of Ukyu-Gondé, the northwesterly
winds, after soaking up moisture over the shimmering waves of the
Sea of Tears, dashed headlong into the Antler Range, a branch of
the World's Edge Mountains. As the winds raced up over the mountains, the air cooled, and the moisture precipitated out in the form
of frequent rain. Thus, unlike much of the rest of the scrublands, the
strip of land at the foot of the Antler Range enjoyed a warm and mild
climate, and the rain produced many fog-shrouded valleys full of
verdant forests, gentle streams, and marshland.

In Agon lore, the garinafin who befriended Kikisavo and Afir and
turned into the long mountains at the eastern edge of the known
world faced south, toward the endless desert of Lurodia Tanta. The
Lyucu shared this belief but thought of the garinafin as facing the
other way, with his head in the far north, where the frozen tundra

made even exploration by garinafin impractical, and so they called these mountains the Tail Range.

To natives of Dara, the wet, warm valleys were the parts of Ukyu-Gondé that reminded them most of home; but to the Lyucu and Agon, this was the land of the gods, veiled away from the gaze of Cudyufin by cloud cover, where the long-haired cattle didn't find enough of the rough waxtongue bushes that they loved to graze on and lowed pitifully as their hooves sank into the soft, marshy soil, unable to roam freely.

Which made it the perfect site for those who sought to rebel by establishing a secret base.

"Mama, I really can't finish this," complained six-year-old Tanto Aragoz, eldest pékyu-taasa of the Agon, as he put the moonbread biscuit back on the chipped china dish on the bone serving tray in the middle of the fur rug. Young as the boy was, he had already figured out that if he wanted to get out of some unpleasant chore or to decline food, his chances of success shot up if he spoke to his Dara mother in her native tongue.

"I don't understand you at all, Kunilo-*tika*," said a disappointed Théra, using the nursing name of her firstborn. "That one has lotus-paste filling. It's the best kind of moonbread."

She looked at the heap of biscuits in the middle of the dining rug—no one, except her, had eaten more than one—and experienced the growing frustration familiar to every parent. The biscuit that Tanto had set down, with a single bite taken out of it, peeked through the curving rib slats at the sides of the serving tray like a broken moon—not an auspicious start to the High-Autumn Festival.

She tried again. "When I was little, the lotus-paste moonbread biscuits were always the first ones to go. Your uncles, aunt, and I used to fight over them."

"Lotus paste is disgusting," said Rokiri Aragoz, Tanto's four-year-old brother, in the tongue of Agon.

"Don't you start, Jian-*tika*," warned Théra. "I worked really hard to make the moonbread, and you're going to finish every single one."

She *had* worked hard for them—all the Dara natives in Kiri Valley had. The extended dives of *Dissolver of Sorrows* during the voyage to Ukyu-Gondé had exceeded what the caulking had been designed to take, and several storage compartments had flooded, ruining many of the seeds brought by the expedition, including most of the lotus pods. It had taken years of work before the horticultural experts on Théra's staff were able to grow a sizable crop of lotus, and Théra was determined to give her children a proper High-Autumn Festival celebration for the first time since her arrival in Ukyu-Gondé.

"Why are we celebrating 'high autumn' when it's the middle of summer anyway?" asked Rokiri.

"Because the High-Autumn Festival is about harvests, and the growing season here—never mind. Don't try to distract me. Eat your biscuits."

"I don't want to eat bread," whined Tanto. "It's cattle feed."

"Who taught you that?" asked Théra, switching to Agon. She narrowed her eyes and glanced at her husband, who was hovering near the entrance to their tent, trying to look as unobtrusive as possible.

"I never said anything like that!" Takval held up his hands, a look of wronged innocence on his face. "But you know that many of the naros and culeks dislike the idea of settling and digging for food out of mud, and it's inevitable that their children will repeat the parents' complaints to Kunilo-*tika* and Jian-*tika*."

Six years after the arrival of Takval and Théra in Ukyu-Gondé, the secret settlement at Kiri Valley had swelled to about two thousand strong, about evenly divided between Agon and Dara. Takval had formally taken the title of pékyu and revived the claim of the Aragoz clan to suzerainty over all the Agon tribes, though the claim was not widely known. As far as the Lyucu were concerned, Volyu remained the figurehead of the scattered Agon tribes. From time to time, Takval sent out messengers to Sliyusa Ki, and recruited more rebels to join the secret base. So far at least, Volyu had held up his end of the bargain.

"It's not 'digging food out of mud,'" said Théra, her voice rising. "How many times do I have to fight these stubborn thanes over this point? Farming is far more efficient than pasturing—"

"'—as a way of supporting this many people in hiding,'" finished

Takval for her. "Yes, Théra, yes. And you can point to all the children who have been born since we moved into Kiri Valley and all the droughts and storms we've avoided since we abandoned the herds. I'm on your side, but you've got to understand how hard this is for them. It's not the Agon way—"

"That's the root of the problem," said Théra. "It's always the 'Agon way' this and the 'Agon way' that, but really it's about lack of trust. They don't think of me as your equal, and argue against everything I suggest with the utmost suspicion. I've tried to show them the numbers, to walk them through the strategy, to persuade them through reason. How can I make them see that I'm trying to teach them a better way—"

"They might trust you more if you didn't always act like they're barbarians in need of instruction," Takval blurted out. Instantly, he regretted it. He tried to soften his tone. "Look, my breath, I'm not saying—"

"I know very well what you're saying," said Théra, her tone colder than the snowcapped peaks of the Antler Range. "I've done all I can to take care of the delicate feelings of your people. I've ordered my smiths to share with you all their knowledge about smelting copper and iron and forging weapons without disparaging your bone-crafting traditions; I've never asked you to put one of my officers in charge of your thanes and warriors, even though they must learn how to fight with these new weapons and care for them; I've not complained about my scholars and crafters laboring in the fields to feed everyone while so many able-bodied naros and culeks are sitting around idle, disdaining to learn how to farm. I've even scaled back the attempt to teach the thanes how to write the Agon language using zyndari letters because so many of you think writing is witchcraft. But if we're to challenge the Lyucu, then you must learn new ways. It's not my fault that reality deems some ways better than others—"

"Listen to yourself!" Takval had had enough. " 'Your people'! 'My people'! How can you possibly lead them if in your heart you don't think of yourself as Agon?" He got up, threw open the tent flap, and strode out.

With great difficulty, Théra choked back a howl of rage and suppressed the urge to chase after him to give the man a piece of her mind.

She turned back to her sons and put on a big smile.

Tanto and Rokiri stared back at her with terrified eyes.

Théra sighed. The High-Autumn Festival was a time to celebrate the harvest and the fertility of the land, to honor the love between parents and sons, between grandparents and granddaughters, between husbands and wives, between siblings and cousins, between fellow members of the same clan. Like all the others from Dara, she had been too busy with building up the base in Kiri Valley the last few years to celebrate it properly. She was determined not to mar the experience for her children because of her bullheaded husband.

"Kunilo-*tika* and Jian-*tika*," she said, modulating her voice to be as gentle as possible, "be good and finish your moonbreads."

The two boys bit into their biscuits and grimaced at the sticky, unfamiliar taste of lotus paste.

Théra felt her ire rise again. "Don't look like I'm feeding you poison. This is supposed to be a treat!"

"Tusked tiger marrow is a treat," muttered Tanto. He had shifted back into Agon because there was no word for a "tusked tiger" in Dara. "Not this sticky *cud*."

"Nalu gave *you* some marrow," muttered Rokiri. "I didn't get any."

"I'm the eldest," said Tanto. "So of course I should get—"

"Kunilo-*tika*, you know that as the eldest, you're supposed to yield to your brother. Remember what Kon Fiji said in the parable of the three brothers—" Théra stopped herself as Tanto and Rokiri regarded her with blank stares. Of course they wouldn't know about the Moralist fables—they'd been running wild with the other Agon children, learning Lutho knew what.

*Never in a thousand years could I have imagined as a girl that one day I'd sound like Master Zato Ruthi. How the gods love to play jokes on us.*

She switched topics and language. "So Nalu had some tusked tiger marrow, did he? Fresh or in pemmican?"

"Fresh!" said Tanto. His eyes took on a glazed look as he savored the memory.

Théra frowned. And not just because she hated the smell of the supposed delicacy. The very availability of tusked tiger marrow meant that some of the Agon had probably gone hunting outside Kiri Valley, in direct contravention of her orders. She would have to tell Takval to—

"Ah!" Tanto yelped in surprise as he spit out a small, half-chewed leaf. "What's this doing in there?"

"That's *supposed* to be in there," said Théra. "Each moonbread biscuit has a slip of paper with a message on it for good luck. But we have too little paper to spare, so I substituted a scapula-tree leaf." In fact, including such slips of paper in moonbread was not the custom across all of Dara, but Théra felt it was too much to explain to her sons the differences between Cocru and Xana ways of celebrating the festival. *One thing at a time,* she reminded herself. "Read it."

Dutifully, Tanto unfurled the leaf and puzzled out the tiny zyndari letters his mother had scratched into the surface. Haltingly, he read:

> *The world is drunk; I alone am sober.*
> *The world is asleep, but I am awake.*
> *Within these four walls beats a scarlet heart;*
> *The barking moon will never stand apart.*

Théra waited patiently while he stumbled through the message and had to pause several times to ask her for help with unfamiliar words. Since Théra was too busy with management of the secret settlement to take up the instruction of her children herself, she had delegated teaching duties to a rotating crew of Dara scholars, who found a few hours here and there to impart the wisdom of their native land to the young pékyus-taasa.

By now, almost all the members of Théra's expedition had learned to speak Agon with some fluency, but few of the Agon had learned to speak Dara. In order to prevent the settlement from feeling like two separate peoples forced to share one land, Théra had made the decision to make Agon the common tongue in Kiri Valley. But in her tent, she tried to keep everyone speaking Dara—without much success.

As Kunilo-*tika* struggled through the poem, Théra silently congratulated herself on taking up Zomi's idea that children should
be taught the zyndari letters first so that they could at least write
and read in the Dara vernacular, as contrasted with the traditional
Dara method of drilling even toddlers predominantly in Ano logograms. Though Tanto wasn't reading with as much fluency as she
was hoping, she was glad that her eldest son wasn't illiterate like the
children of the Agon thanes, who all viewed the act of reading and
writing with revulsion and fear.

"I don't understand," said Tanto. "What did I just read?"

"It's a logogram riddle!" said Théra excitedly. As a child, devising
and guessing riddles based on Ano logograms had been a favorite
pastime for her and her siblings. She was excited to finally have a
chance to enjoy the game with her children.

"Oh, logograms," said Tanto, with about as much enthusiasm as
he had mustered for the lotus paste. His teachers had just started
introducing logograms, and he had been dreading a test from his
mother.

"So, do you have a guess?" asked Théra patiently. "Read the
poem carefully and see if you can figure out which logograms would
be the right answer."

"Ah . . . is it the logogram for my Dara name?"

"No! Your nursing name honors your grandfather! Oh, this
is supposed to be easy. It's one of the first riddles I solved when
I was five. . . . Look, you just follow each line of the riddle like a
blueprint—I guess you don't know what a blueprint is—think of it
as instructions for building . . . one of those toy bone structures you
and Nalu are always messing with."

Théra lifted the china plate with the heaping moonbread biscuits
off the bone serving tray. She wiped it so that it was as clean as one
of the practice slates she had used as a girl, spooned some of the
lotus paste from a bowl onto the tray like a block of wax, and began
to sculpt.

"The first two lines of the riddle tell you the key is 'wakefulness,'
which is represented by the 'open eyes' logogram. The next line tells
us we need to put the open eyes over a heart semantic root to make

the sub-logogram *gitré*, which means 'insight,' and then surround the whole thing with the semantic root for 'world,' which is a square enclosure."

The boys stared unblinkingly as the shape of a lotus-paste logogram emerged under her nimble fingers.

Théra slowed down to be sure they could follow along. "Since there is already a dominant semantic root, the enclosure in this case serves as a motive modifier, meaning 'constrained.' Finally, you add the sub-logogram *séntagé*, which means 'lunar eclipse' and is written as dog-biting-moon, to the side—that's what 'will never stand apart' typically means in a riddle. And because it's to the side, you know it functions here as a phonetic adapter. Are you following all this?"

The boys nodded their heads vigorously.

Théra coaxed. "So put it all together, what do we have?"

Silence.

"Come on, I know you know this. I'm sure Master Razutana Pon taught you. It's one of the most often-used logograms in Kon Fiji's treatises."

More silence.

"Is it the logogram for 'peace'?" asked Théra.

Eyes intensely focused on her face, Tanto began to tilt his head—the motion was carefully calibrated to be halfway between a nod and a shake. And as his chin dipped lower tentatively, Théra could feel a frown of disappointment contract her own features. Instantly, Tanto switched to shaking his head forcefully.

Hastily, Rokiri copied his brother.

Théra sighed. As much as she yearned for her sons to be great scholars, she wasn't going to let herself be fooled. "So what is it?"

Two pairs of childish eyes roamed desperately over her face for clues.

"A word etymologically derived from directed-and-guided insight, which sounds like *séntagé*. . . ." Théra's hands hovered over the lotus-paste logogram, which was quickly losing its shape, much like her own deflating hope. "Isn't that *mutagé*, the Ano word for 'loyalty-benefaction' or 'faith-mercy'?"

"Oh, that's *just* what I was going to say!" said Tanto.

"Me too!" said Rokiri.

"Really?" asked Théra. "Could have fooled me. I saw Master Razutana Pon teaching you this logogram just two weeks ago, but I bet you have no memory of it. You have to pay attention if you want to be better than—"

"Mama, look! That looks like a dog biting the moon." Rokiri pointed at the biscuit that Tanto had set aside. He regarded her with puppy-dog eyes and mimed panting.

Rokiri had long learned to weaponize his cuteness to get out of trouble, and Théra was helpless against the tactic. Her lecture interrupted and forgotten, the two boys were soon rolling on the ground, wrestling and growling and barking and giggling.

"I'm going to . . . eat the moon . . . arf!"

"I'd rather eat the moon . . . than lotus paste . . . ruff!"

Théra sighed again. She really couldn't get mad at her sons. How could they be expected to understand the meaning of the High-Autumn Festival when the parents of their playmates disdained farming? How could they appreciate lotus-paste filling when they'd never had it and all their friends thought roasted bone marrow the best flavor the world had to offer? How could they appreciate the beauty and intricacy of this classic riddle, with its allusion to the poem of Lurusén, its reference to the ancient Ano belief that the world was a square covered by a celestial dome, its connection to the Dara folklore of a lunar eclipse being the result of a greedy hound running amok among the stars and the gods scaring it away, its embodiment of the core of Moralist wisdom . . . when they were growing up in a barbaric land, devoid of all the culture of Dara?

The civilization of Dara was like a tapestry woven from a thousand strands of tradition, literature, art, music, philosophy, religion, and folklore, and the children of Dara grew up like baby shrimp in a rich coral reef, effortlessly absorbing all the sights and sounds around them. Here, in this impoverished land, she had to teach them one strand at a time, and she had only herself to blame if they didn't understand what it meant to be heirs of the manifold beauties of Dara.

"All right, it's not your fault that you didn't know. But you have to work harder. Enough playing now. Get up."

The boys stopped their rambunctious play reluctantly.

"Let me show you how this riddle works again in more detail. Kunilo-*tika*, go get your logogram play set."

Tanto looked confused. After a while, he brightened. "Rokiri was playing with it last."

Under his mother's impatient glare, Jian-*tika* rummaged through the woven basket that held their toys at the foot of the sleeping mat until he triumphantly held up a leather pouch and brought it back to the dining rug.

Théra untied the lace, upended the pouch, and spread the contents on the rug. Right away, all three could see that many pieces were missing from the set.

Playing blocks in the shapes of semantic roots, motive modifiers, phonetic adapters, and inflection glyphs were traditionally used in Dara to instruct children in the basics of Ano orthography. By assembling simple and moderately complex logograms from these blocks, children gained an appreciation for the structure and principles underlying the Ano system of writing. Poti Maji, renowned Moralist and something of a theorist of education, believed that these playing blocks were especially beneficial because they provided a tangible, manipulable mode of access to the wisdom of the ancient Ano. By putting the "roof" semantic root on top to complete the logogram for "house" or inserting the "heart" semantic root into the honorific form of "you," a child enacted in ritualistic form the relationships that wove the foundation of Dara society.

Indeed, it was not uncommon for even adult scholars to keep a set at hand as a relaxation aid during breaks in study or work. The wealthy children had blocks made from precious materials like jade or coral, while the merely well-to-do used porcelain or sandalwood.

Théra had made these particular blocks out of baked clay during one of the rare holidays she gave herself. Seeing the full set reduced to a handful of pieces made her feel as though she had been slapped by her sons.

"What happened to the rest of the pieces?" she asked, her tone making it clear that she was not "playful mama."

Tanto and Rokiri looked at each other, neither willing to speak.

"Just tell the truth," Théra said. "Mama won't get mad."

The boys were still too young to understand the danger behind such a promise. "Some of the pieces broke when Jian-*tika* was trying to see how tall a tower he could build," said Tanto.

Théra took a few deep breaths. "And the others?"

"Kunilo-*tika* gave them to Nalu," said Rokiri.

"Did Nalu want them because he was interested in writing?" asked Théra. Hope sprang to life in her heart. If there was interest, she would definitely re-prioritize the suspended plans for a school for the Agon children.

"Uh . . . no," said Tanto. "We were playing with his arucuro tocua, and he agreed to a trade."

"You traded the logogram blocks for some *animal bones*?"

"You said you wouldn't get mad!" said Tanto as he shrank from her shouting. "They were tusked tiger bones!"

"I made these blocks to teach you reading! And you just traded them away for garbage—"

"Logograms are boring!" Tanto blurted. "I hate reading! I don't want to read!"

Théra felt her heart break. She could not believe what she was hearing. "How can you say that? Do you know that Zomi, Mama's dearest companion back in Dara, once so yearned for knowledge of the Ano logograms that she would rather go hungry than to be denied another lesson? You don't know how lucky you are—"

"This. Is. Not. Dara." Tears flowed from Tanto's eyes as he looked at her defiantly.

Beside him, Rokiri was wailing. "Mama is mad! Mama, don't be mad!" He tried to wrap his arms about her legs.

A stunned Théra sat down, and hot tears of rage and disappointment spilled from her eyes.

"Thank you for the moonbread, Princess," said Thoryo. "The lotus paste is delicious. I've heard so many of the soldiers and scholars from Dara talk about it, but this is the first time I've tasted it."

The young woman with no origin had never lost her appetite for interesting new sensations and tastes, and she enjoyed Dara foods as much as she did Agon aromas. She never wielded the butchering knife herself, and the sight of blood still made her blanch, but she did savor the dishes that resulted from the grilling spit.

"I'm glad *someone* likes it," said Théra. "My husband and sons won't touch the biscuits."

The two were working side by side, cutting the rice stalks with scythes. The water had been drained from the paddies for the first harvest—the climate in Kiri Valley allowed two growing seasons a year—and the pungent fragrance of mud and sap promised well-stocked granaries for the winter.

"Why don't we take a break?" asked Thoryo. She straightened and wiped the sweat from her brow with a bundle of dried moss tied around her neck with twisted bit of sinew. "You should have some moonbread too."

Théra looked to the edge of the paddy, where Agon men and women sat in a circle, drinking kyoffir and sharing stories. One of the Agon thanes, a man named Araten, was evidently miming some battle.

Though Théra and Takval had given orders every year that the Agon should help with the harvest, few were willing to set foot in the muddy paddy. Instead, they all claimed to be on "guard duty." Araten was one of the worst offenders, often proclaiming that stepping in mud sapped warriors of their fighting spirit.

"All right," said Théra, dejected. "We might as well."

The two walked to the end of the field and climbed onto a roofed platform. It was where they took their lunch during the busy planting season and kept watch over the crops, shooing away birds and other animals. They looked around. In the other paddies, the only people who worked at harvesting the rice were natives of Dara.

"I just don't understand," said Théra, pausing to bite into a biscuit. She chewed, lingering over the luscious flavor before continuing. "This is the only way for us to build up our strength to challenge the Lyucu, yet they act like I'm asking them to wade into lava. I know farming is hard work—"

"The Agon say that enslaving the land is unnatural. They don't just hate it; they despise it. Besides, eating plants and grains is what the tanto-lyu-naro do—"

"That's just prejudice! They have to change if they want to win—"

"You're asking them to become like the people of Dara," said Thoryo. "But they're not."

"At least they're well fed."

Théra looked beyond the paddies to the graveyard at the edge of the settlement. Dozens of Dara men and women had died over the years since they had first come to this secluded valley. Some had died from diseases that did not exist in Dara; others had died from attacks by predators, stampeding cattle, panicked garinafins, poisonous plants and mushrooms; still more had died from smelting accidents, exploding kilns, falling timber, collapsed buildings. Bit by bit, members of Théra's expeditions had tried to re-create pieces of their homeland in this valley, to pass on their wisdom and knowledge to their allies. The headstones marked brave souls who had given their lives to this merciless land for the dream of freeing another people. They would never see their homeland again, and their spirits would never caress another Ano logogram or enjoy the offerings of incense and beer left by their children on the Grave-Mending Festival. Would they even be able to find their way to the River-on-Which-Nothing-Floats to be reunited with their ancestors?

Théra's eyes grew moist. One of the gravestones belonged to Admiral Mitu Roso, who had died to save a group of Agon children from a pack of wolves that had made its way into the valley. As he lay dying, he had whispered to her, *You are the spitting image of your father, and it has been the greatest honor for me to serve you both.* Hugolu pha gira ki. *Bring my bones back to Dara if you can,* Rénga.

But was she in fact as good a leader as her father? She had tried to give the Agon all she could, but the gifts had not always been appreciated. Sure, they took the metal-hardened weapons, but did not care to learn smelting or smithing. They complained about the tiny size of the herd each tribe was restricted to in order to reserve most of the land in the steep-walled valley for farming. They survived on the food that she and her people grew but did not want to get their legs and arms muddy. Even her children could not understand why she looked sad each time another plate from Dara broke or a Dara-made dress was torn.

Thoryo's lighthearted voice broke into her reverie.

"They say that rice and wheat bloat their stomachs and make them feel like fat cows."

"What?"

"They think of eating farmed grain as chewing cud."

"That's ridiculous."

"Is it?" Thoryo shrugged. "I can see why they feel that way. They miss the freedom of roaming across the scrublands with their herds and hunting for birds and game at the Sea of Tears. They crave the traditional winter feast, where they could serve ten different kinds of game—"

"Farming is a much more efficient use of our limited land, and hunting is dangerous because it requires sending parties out of the valley—"

"I understand the reasons," said Thoryo. "But you can't reason against the desires of the heart. It wasn't easy to grow the lotus, but you insisted that Razutana and the others try."

"That's different! I'm trying to connect my children to their heritage, while they pine after something that will threaten our survival, something primitive and backward!"

Thoryo gave her a strange look. "The people of the scrublands have survived for generations in a harsh land. And based on what you've told me, they leveled cities in Dara like a scythe swiping across rice stalks. I don't think calling them 'primitive' is quite right."

Théra knew, of course, that conditions in much of the scrublands made agriculture impractical. The Agon and Lyucu, like the hardy clenched-fist cactus, crawling waxtongue bushes, and prickly blood-palm grass, were perfectly adapted to the landscape. But this was an extraordinary time that needed extraordinary measures.

"They are as shortsighted as children. I'm asking them to make a temporary sacrifice for a greater victory in the future."

"But that's just it," said Thoryo. "They're worried about the future, about their children."

"What do you mean?"

"They worry that if they stay here much longer, living off leaves and seeds dug out of enslaved soil rather than meat fattened by the bounty of the gods and slaughtered by the strength of their arms, their children will grow up as cowards and weaklings, unable to face down a tusked tiger or ride the garinafin into the storm. They're worried that their children will not grow up to be Agon."

Théra was stunned. "But of course they'll be Agon. This is their land. They were born here."

"What does it mean to be Agon?" said Thoryo. "It isn't about parentage, for the tribes of the scrublands have always adopted strangers and child hostages into their own ranks. It isn't about land, for the people of the scrublands are not attached to any single spot and do not claim land with fixed boundaries. It's about speaking, doing, being, knowing—and that requires practice. It requires play."

Théra chewed on her biscuit thoughtfully. Thoryo, belonging to neither Dara nor Ukyu-Gondé, sometimes said things that neither the Dara nor the Agon could. She simply loved life itself, and loved all the ways to live.

"You're wise below your years," said Théra.

Thoryo cocked her head, a grin on her face. "That doesn't sound like a compliment." She took another bite of the lotus-paste moonbread and scrunched up her face in pleasure.

"Oh, it is," said Théra. "That you can see everything through the eyes of a child is what makes you worth listening to."

"In the play of children there is much truth and wisdom, no less so than in the songs of shamans or the sentiments of the Ano sages."

Théra nodded, thinking of her own childhood as she swallowed the sweet paste.

# CHAPTER EIGHTEEN

# THE VEILED THRONE

PAN: THE SIXTH MONTH IN THE EIGHTH YEAR OF
THE REIGN OF SEASON OF STORMS (KNOWN AS
THE EIGHTH YEAR OF THE REIGN OF AUDACIOUS
FREEDOM IN UKYU-TAASA, AND THE EIGHTH YEAR
SINCE PRINCESS THÉRA DEPARTED FOR UKYU-
GONDÉ).

The Grand Audience Hall was deserted.

The walls and pillars, covered in ornate carvings evoking the Hundred Flowers (the gleaming golden stylized dandelions drew the most attention), echoed with silence. The ceiling, covered in murals featuring the deeds of gods and heroes as well as crubens and dyrans cavorting among waves, looked down upon emptiness.

Empress Jia, as Regent of Dara, rarely called for formal court—perhaps once a month, if even that. She found the rituals and rites associated with formal court tedious, and since Emperor Monadétu no longer even lived in Pan, there was no point in keeping up appearances.

At the northern end of the hall was an eight-foot-tall dais, intended for the Dandelion Throne. However, since Dara was under regency, this was her seat during formal court. The Dandelion Throne itself, with an oversized golden dandelion topping the back, had been moved to the foot of the dais, in front of the civil ministers, governors, nobles, and generals who would line up in two columns on the east and west sides of the long hall during court.

Back when Phyro still attended formal court, Empress Jia had asked the boy to sit upon the throne, but with a silk veil surrounding it like the mosquito netting drawn around the beds of wealthy merchants in Wolf's Paw.

"Why?" Phyro demanded.

"Because you're here to listen and to learn," Jia responded. "If the ministers and generals could see your reactions during debate, they would craft their arguments to persuade you. Instead, they should be attempting to persuade one another and me."

Every birthday, Phyro petitioned for the regency to be terminated and the veil around the throne removed. Always Jia's answer was the same: "Your father instructed my regency to continue until the heir is ready to take the reins of power. You're not ready."

On his twentieth birthday, Phyro asked for something different. He made a plea that the Grand Audience Hall be rearranged so that the sovereign again sat facing north, as had been the custom in the time of Emperor Ragin, the direction of Unredeemed Dara and the Lyucu conquerors, instead of facing south, a change instituted by Empress Jia.

"We must never dismiss from mind the goal of rescuing the people of Dasu and Rui, suffering and dying under Lyucu predation," said Phyro. "There must be a reminder so we don't forget to avenge my father, who died without seeing Dara free."

Empress Jia refused. "War must never be the chief aim of a wise sovereign."

She had literally turned her back on Unredeemed Dara.

The next day, Phyro took his honor guard and left Pan. He went to Tiro Cozo, a secluded hamlet in the Wisoti Mountains, where the young garinafins hatched from eggs brought by Takval Aragoz were being raised, and vowed to stay there until he could properly sit on the Dandelion Throne.

And so the throne remained empty in the Grand Audience Hall, shrouded in a silk veil.

Instead of the Grand Audience Hall, Phyro headed for the Inner Council Chamber, a small room in a secluded corner of the administrative section of the palace. This was where most of the policies governing Dara were made and issued.

By the time Phyro entered, everyone was already sitting comfortably in *géüpa* in a circle, with Empress Jia presiding at one end. The Inner Council consisted of the most senior ministers of the state: Cogo Yelu, Prime Minister; Zomi Kidosu, Farsight Secretary; Than Carucono, First General of the Cavalry and First Admiral of the Navy; Doman Gothu, Head of the College of Advocates; Mi Ropha, Chief Circuit Intendant; and the ministers of carriages and boats, justice, treasury, rituals, agriculture, household registration, and so on—in all, less than twenty men and women.

Doman and Mi, as the most junior members of the Inner Council, shifted their sitting cushions to make space for Phyro.

*"Rénga,"* said Than Carucono, his voice quavering with emotion, "it's good to see you here in Pan." His hair was so white now that it resembled fresh snow. In the sunlight slanting in from the window, his eyes glistened.

Doman and Mi exchanged awkward looks. Several members of the Inner Council had fallen into the habit of addressing Empress Jia with that honorific, but Zomi, Cogo, and Than never used it. To hear Than suddenly say *Rénga* reminded them that the honorific was supposed to be used only with the emperor.

"You have the same carriage and bearing as your father in his youth—though he was never as fit," Than went on. "He would be so happy to see you—"

"I'm certain that the emperor is as busy as the rest of the council," said Empress Jia. "Why don't we leave private reminiscences until later?"

Phyro smiled at Than. He had always felt a special bond with the old general. Than and Cogo were the last survivors from Kuni's earliest group of retainers, but Cogo was a refined politician who made disguising his feelings into an art, and Phyro was much more drawn to Than's army camp manners and unabashed, open displays of affection. As a boy, Phyro had often gone to Than, begging the man to recount for him adventures from Kuni's youth in Zudi. Consciously or otherwise, the young emperor had transferred some of his filial love for his dead father to the old general.

But as the empress reminded them all, this wasn't the time to indulge one's emotions. Calming himself, he nodded at Cogo and Zomi before bowing stiffly to Jia. "Aunt-Mother, forgive me for not coming to ask after your health earlier. I've just arrived by airship this morning."

Jia nodded. "We can have tea after. I hope you stopped by your mother's shrine at least?"

"I have."

"Good." Jia sat up straighter. "You asked to come to the Inner Council and present a new proposal. Go ahead."

"My proposal is related to the garinafin force at Tiro Cozo. But first, let me speak to you of a boat. . . ."

The fact that Dara had acquired garinafins from the Agon prince Takval was a state secret known to only a select few. The training base in the Wisoti Mountains, Tiro Cozo, was in a remote valley accessible only by airship. The riders-in-training and the support staff lived there year-round, and the security around the area was so tight that even intruding birds were shot down without mercy.

Princess Théra's marriage to Takval and the departure of *Dissolver of Sorrows*, of course, were well-publicized. But when the Wall of Storms opened and then closed almost immediately to destroy the Lyucu reinforcement fleet, it was presumed that Théra and the rest of *her* fleet had perished as well. A Lyucu city-ship sent by Tanvanaki to welcome the reinforcements had witnessed the sinking of the Dara ships under the assault of a lone garinafin.

The ability of *Dissolver of Sorrows* and her sister ships to dive underwater was kept from the public, and Empress Jia made the decision to allow most in Dara proper and Unredeemed Dara to believe that the princess was dead. The thought was that if Tanvanaki and the Lyucu invaders felt threatened by the Dara-Agon alliance, they might use Théra's voyage as an excuse to break the peace treaty and attack. With the Dara fleet destroyed by the Wall, of course, the alliance was assumed to be void as well.

And so a state funeral had been held for Théra, who was posthumously granted the title of Grand Princess. A set of her court regalia was buried in an empty tomb in the Imperial cemetery, next to the empty grave of Emperor Ragin, whose body also had never been recovered.

Zomi, Phyro, and others who knew the truth believed that Théra would succeed in Ukyu-Gondé. Their faith was further strengthened when the great belt current brought turtles with a special message from across the ocean. But that still left the problem of how to defeat the Lyucu in Rui and Dasu.

". . . the refugees were picked up in the Silkworm Eggs by a merchant-man from Wolf's Paw," continued Phyro. "In accordance with Imperial policy, the refugees were processed in Boama, the nearest large port."

From time to time, desperate inhabitants of Rui and Dasu, unable to bear the harshness of Lyucu rule, escaped the islands on rafts or stolen fishing boats. The Lyucu patrolled the coasts of the two islands vigilantly, and escapees were summarily executed or worse. But the coastlines were long and winding, and it was impossible to catch everyone.

Many—perhaps even most—of the refugees died when their rickety craft capsized on the high seas. But some did manage to reach the shores of Arulugi or the Big Island. Once rescued, the refugees were brought to large port cities to be processed. Zomi Kidosu, the Farsight Secretary, was leery of the Lyucu using these refugees as a way to smuggle in spies—after all, plenty of natives collaborated with the Lyucu either out of greed or terror. Thus, she came up with the idea of settling the refugees in isolated camps so that they could be interrogated and vetted.

The refugees proved to be a rich source of intelligence on conditions in the hermetically sealed kingdom of Ukyu-taasa—the Lyucu name for Unredeemed Dara—but Zomi found her temporary solution taking on a life of its own. Unskilled with the rules of bureaucratic logic, she had not anticipated the camps becoming indefinite detention centers. Since no one wanted to risk letting a spy go free, the clerks and magistrates decided to treat everyone as perpetually suspicious. As a result, the refugees languished for years in these settlement camps, uncertain of their ultimate fate.

In the last few years, however, the number of refugees reaching

Dara proper had drastically dwindled. What this meant was a matter of intense speculation at the court.

"When this group of refugees was interrogated," said Phyro, "the magistrate discovered that their leader was a Lyucu man named Ofluro, who had married a Dara woman named Suca. He made no effort to disguise his identity and asked for asylum."

Everyone in the circle leaned forward, and a few sucked in their breaths. It was exceedingly rare for the Lyucu to be found among the refugees. Tanvanaki favored using native spies against Dara, since they tended to blend in better and were disposable. When Lyucu operatives hoped to pass as natives, something always gave them away: accent, a stray out-of-place remark, inadequate knowledge of Dara customs.

Jia looked over at Zomi Kidosu.

Zomi bowed in *jiri*. "Your Imperial Majesty, I can confirm the emperor's account. This was described in detail in the briefing I filed two weeks ago."

Jia narrowed her eyes. Phyro must have found out about this Lyucu asylum seeker from Zomi, and Zomi had deliberately chosen not to draw the empress's attention to the matter, but buried it in her voluminous routine reports.

She turned back to Phyro. "Why does he wish to seek asylum?"

"I've spoken with Ofluro extensively," said Phyro. "He is a high-ranking warrior, what they call a naro-votan. During the conquest of Unredeemed Dara, he fell in love with a noblewoman, Lady Suca Tiron, daughter of the Baron of Naza. Instead of taking her as a concubine or enslaving her, he chose to marry her as he would a Lyucu woman. For this decision he was ridiculed by the other Lyucu warriors, and gradually fell out of the trust and favor of Tanvanaki and her thanes. Enraged by the treatment he received, he sought solace in kyoffir and tolyusa, and committed multiple errors in his duties."

"A man unable to govern his passions," muttered Jia. "A drunkard."

Phyro pretended not to hear. "These led to further decline in his status, and a month ago, he found out that a rival was plotting to report him on a made-up charge of aiding a rebellion by some native villagers on the northern coast of Rui. He decided that there was no future for him in Unredeemed Dara, and rather than submitting to his fate, he decided to gather a group of native villagers being pressed into a work gang and organized a takeover of a fishing boat. Relying on his knowledge of Lyucu patrol patterns, he and his wife led the refugees to evade capture and sailed here."

"And I assume he wishes to be made into a baron or a viscount for this act of bravery?" Jia asked, a cold sneer on her face.

"To the contrary," said Phyro. "He asks for no title and no treasure."

"Then what does he want?"

"Our protection, and the right for his wife to receive the portion of the benefice she is due as the daughter of a baron. The couple intend to use this money to purchase a small ranch in Faça and maintain themselves with it."

Jia's eyebrows lifted. "That's not much of an opening demand. He must not have much to offer."

"He has offered nothing, not even claiming credit for rescuing the refugees."

"Then he is lying," said Jia. "If his story is true, which I very much doubt, he should have plenty of knowledge of the Lyucu military that he can bargain with to get himself a superior deal."

Phyro paused and regarded Jia carefully. "Aunt-Mother, are you willing to reconsider our policy of nonaggression toward the Lyucu then?"

Jia looked coolly back at him. "Of course not. But I know what you want."

This was the heart of the conflict between Jia and Phyro. Phyro advocated a surprise attack on the Lyucu to free Dasu and Rui, while Jia insisted that the treaty of nonaggression be respected, arguing that Dara was still too weak to risk an invasion of Ukyu-taasa—doomed to fail in her judgment. Phyro thus devoted his time to training the garinafins and probing for Lyucu weaknesses, waiting for the treaty to expire. But Jia seemed to hint at a desire to continue the state of peace indefinitely.

Phyro nodded. "He does have such knowledge, but he has refused to bargain with it. He will not betray his people by revealing their weaknesses to us."

Jia laughed. "Then he is the most preposterous asylum seeker I've ever heard of. Either he is a spy or he is a fool. If we hadn't outlawed torture, I'd say he should be tormented until he reveals all he knows. Even so . . . there are other methods—"

"He says he'll kill himself if we pressure him to collaborate," said Phyro. "I believe him."

"I don't," said Jia. "Perhaps we should put our theories to the test. Weigh the fish, as Secretary Kidosu is so fond of saying." She glanced at Zomi.

Zomi's face showed no emotion.

"That would be a mistake," said Phyro. "I believe there is another way in which he can help us without offending his sense of honor."

"'Offending his sense of honor'?" Jia's face was the very portrait of incredulity. "He is a Lyucu."

Phyro was unfazed. "Isn't honor the reason that you insist the treaty of nonaggression with the Lyucu be respected? I did not agree at first, but I've come to accept your view. The Lyucu have held up their end of the bargain."

"That's different! I insist on peace because it is the wisest course. They haven't attacked us only because they're still consolidating their rule. It is power, real, naked power, that determines what can and must be done, not empty abstractions like 'honor.'"

Phyro did not meet her eyes. Instead, he looked around the circle, his voice full of conviction. "It is unfairness that Ofluro despises. When I pressed him for more information about the state of military preparedness in Unredeemed Dara, he backed up to the wall and held a dagger to his own throat. I didn't know he was armed at all."

"An inexcusable lapse in security procedures," said Jia. "Tell me the name of the magistrate who allowed you to be in the same room as an armed—"

"That's not the point!" Phyro said, his cheeks flushed. He forced himself to calm down. "Don't you see, Aunt-Mother? He could have attacked me anytime during our conversation, but he didn't. He vowed to kill himself if I pressed further, and he asked only that we not mistreat Lady Suca and the unborn child she carries after his death. He hoped that the child would be treated as any other child born to Dara parents."

"We understand that children of mixed Lyucu and Dara parentage, called togaten in their tongue, are treated poorly even when acknowledged into a Lyucu lineage," added Zomi helpfully.

"He is a man of honor, and he escaped from Unredeemed Dara because he believed his children would not receive a fair chance in that land," said Phyro. "Despite his mistreatment, he would not betray his people; despite catching me off guard, he did not attack. This is a man who can be trusted."

"Or he is simply very good at manipulating you," said Jia. "How can he be of use if he refuses to reveal his knowledge?"

"He didn't say that he would not share *any* knowledge. While he won't betray the Lyucu by sharing intelligence, I believe he *can* be convinced to teach us how to fight with garinafins. As I've mentioned in my reports, training of the garinafin force has been hampered by the lack of any experience of working with these creatures. Ofluro is a skilled garinafin rider, and even Lady Suca has learned how to ride with him—by the way, teaching her garinafin riding is one of the reasons the other Lyucu despise him. They can teach us what we need to know."

"Why would he help us in that way, *Rénga*?" demanded Than Carucono. "Isn't that also working against the Lyucu?"

"I don't know. It's just a hunch," confessed Phyro. "But having studied the Lyucu for so long, and having talked to so many refugees about their experiences, I feel I have a sense of their code of honor."

"I suppose wolves also have a code of honor for how to slaughter sheep," said Jia mockingly.

Phyro again ignored her. "It's like this . . . when the Hegemon fought Mocri of Gan, he didn't attack when Mocri stumbled, saying that a great man deserved not to have his life end by chance. 'The world may not be fair, but we must strive to make it so.' If we treat him fairly and confess to him that we have garinafins but don't know how to ride them, he'll view helping us learning to ride as similar to allowing Mocri to pick up his sword, leading to a fair fight against his people."

"Oh Hudo-*tika*," said Jia despairingly. "You quote from romantic legends to justify a childish hunch. You view the bloodthirsty Mata Zyndu as a role model to emulate. Fine, if we're quoting from the past, let me offer you a quote from Poti Maji: *'Pharagirari co ri i phyhu gicaü miro pha pharagirari co ingingtho i fésgiré phyhu gidagén.'* He is Lyucu; we are Dara. Natures do not change."

The Classical Ano phrase was almost never quoted in its translated form: *Those who do not share our blood will never share our heart.* The linguistic distance of the classical tongue made the sting in that cry of despair more tolerable.

"The sages also say that within the four seas, all men are brothers. I think honor is an ideal that moves all hearts, whether Lyucu or Dara. Théca Kimo once fought against my father, but after my father chose to trust him, he brought a quarter of Dara under the Dasu banner. Gin Mazoti once fought for the Hegemon, but after my father entrusted her with his army, she became the instrument by which he triumphed over Mata. If I treat Ofluro with honor, he will not betray us. Therefore I propose that instead of confining him to the refugee camp, we grant him asylum and make him the chief trainer of the garinafins at Tiro Cozo."

"Now that is just the kind of *interesting* idea Emperor Ragin would have liked!" cried out Than Carucono. "I believe the emperor's proposal is worth a try."

But Doman and Mi, the two junior members of the council, could see that the empress was disgusted by the emperor's speech. Nothing riled her more than citing the examples of Théca and Gin, headstrong warlords who threatened the stability and peace of Dara. Indeed, despite Gin Mazoti's contributions in the Battle of Zathin Gulf, she was still officially described as a traitor to the throne who fought the Lyucu to lessen her punishment. They shared a meaningful glance at each other and jumped into the fray.

"As Head of the College of Advocates," said Doman, "I believe it's my duty to counsel against any unproven plan. Once we grant this Ofluro asylum and release him, a sign of the sovereign's trust, he cannot subsequently be punished or executed without great damage to the dignity of the Dandelion Throne. If we reveal the existence of the garinafins to him, and he turns out to be a spy, it will be an error that cannot be remedied."

"As Chief Circuit Intendant," said Mi, "I believe it's my duty to check rash and unwise decisions. Even if this Ofluro turns out not to be a spy, there is no guarantee that he won't be more loyal to the Lyucu than to us, and sabotage the garinafin force." She bowed apologetically in *jiri* to Phyro. "*Rénga*, it is commendable for you to come up with such a bold proposal, but I strenuously urge you to reconsider, and reconsider yet again."

Other ministers of the Inner Council also offered their opinions seriatim. Most were against the experiment, and several suggested that Ofluro be drugged to extract as many secrets as possible without resorting to torture. Than was the lone voice to support Phyro.

Phyro looked at the ministers who sided with Jia coolly, a disdainful smirk at the corners of his mouth. They avoided meeting his gaze.

Only Cogo and Zomi had yet to speak.

Jia looked at them.

Cogo bowed. "Both the empress and the emperor raise many excellent points," he said, his tone as even as a still bowl of water. "My learned colleagues have also looked at this issue from every possible angle. It is almost impossible for me, in my senility, to add any words of use."

Zomi had to force herself to keep a straight face. This was always Cogo's way, excessively humble, slippery, impossible to pin down.

Jia glared at him, her index finger tapping the teacup in her hand impatiently.

"Nonetheless," Cogo went on, "after hearing so many interesting and persuasive arguments, my decaying mind can't help but wander into other matters. Something this Ofluro said . . . it has just occurred to me that we should probably issue an Imperial proclamation that the children of refugees should have all the same rights and duties as other subjects of the Dandelion Throne. Now, I'm not saying we need to do anything about the parents, and I understand there are security implications. But the children . . . I apologize if this seems like a minor thing; however, we've had such children from

Unredeemed Dara coming to our shores for many years, and we can't leave their future in suspense."

This seeming non sequitur plunged everyone into confusion as they chewed over Cogo's words. The Prime Minister was known to veil what he truly thought in a maze of verbal hedges to leave himself room for maneuver.

Zomi pondered Cogo's suggestion. Many of the refugees had come with children born from the systematic rapes committed by the Lyucu, and there was some doubt whether the natives of the core islands would ever accept them as true members of the people of Dara.

Thinking of the innocent young refugees growing up in cramped settlement camps, deprived of a proper childhood, Zomi felt pangs of guilt. She had been so focused on concerns for security, for maintaining Dara's secrets, that she had neglected the well-being of these children, the unwitting victims of her own paranoia.

"I support the Prime Minister's proposal," said Zomi. "The very idea of togaten, of tainted blood, is a barbarism that has no place in Dara. The children are Dara, regardless of how they were conceived."

The other ministers quickly assented.

"Yes, of course I agree," said Jia. "Work with the Minister of Household Registration to draft an official proclamation to be issued with the Seal of Dara later. But this is very much not an urgent matter. Why did you bring it up now?"

"I do apologize," said Cogo. "In my dotage I keep on obsessing over very small things. And I thank you on behalf of the children—"

"What about the emperor's proposal regarding asylum for Ofluro? Are you for or against?" demanded Jia.

"If you will, Your Imperial Majesty, indulge me on one more minor point," said Cogo. He turned to the Minister of Household Registration. "Mapha, would you remind me of the rights of the subjects of the Dandelion Throne as laid down by Emperor Ragin?"

Mapha Ye looked at the Prime Minister, her eyes widening in confusion. "Err . . . I believe you drafted those for Emperor Ragin during the Reign of Four Placid Seas. . . ."

Cogo Yelu chuckled. "Heh, my memory isn't what it used to be."

Mapha swallowed and began to count off on her hand. "Um, first, no one is subject to corvée; all labor demanded by the state must be compensated; second, no one may be punished for speaking against officials or the court, so long as there be no act of treason; third, no one may be made to pay a tax without a receipt from the tax collector, which may be verified with the local magistrate; fourth, no one may be prevented from traveling and settling anywhere within Dara, so long as they are not accused of a crime—"

"Oh, that's it. That's the one!" said Cogo excitedly. "Freedom of movement was very important to Emperor Ragin, since he wanted to see all subjects think of themselves as the people of Dara, rather than of Xana, Cocru, Faça, and so on."

"Yes, and it promotes commerce and the flow of ideas and goods," said Mapha. "I've read your commentaries on this point. . . ."

The Proclamation on the Rights of Subjects was indeed Cogo's brainchild. The article concerning freedom of movement, however, was one that Kuni had insisted on. Having seen the benefits of integration of the former Tiro states under Mapidéré, he had wanted to ensure its continuation under his rule, and by giving people the right to express their will with their feet, he sought to provide a check on the power of enfeoffed nobles and ambitious governors, who otherwise might support oppressive policies by tying the people to their land.

A frown appeared on Jia's face. She finally saw where Cogo was going with this. But she had already agreed with Cogo on his original proposal concerning the children, and once the sovereign had spoken, it was law. She could not take back her word without damaging her authority.

"Since the children of refugees now have full freedom of movement across Dara," said Cogo, his tone still perfectly even, "unless accused of a crime, it seems no longer proper to confine them to the settlement camps. Am I right?"

Zomi and Phyro locked eyes, and while Phyro looked lost, Zomi smiled almost imperceptibly.

By now, the chance that any of the refugees who had spent years in the camps were Lyucu spies was vanishingly small. But other than overcautious camp administrators, there were other difficulties standing in the way of releasing them and integrating them into local communities. Since many of the refugees were natives of old Xana, there was some lingering prejudice against them in the core islands, whose inhabitants had suffered greatly under the Xana Conquest. And once the refugees were released, magistrates and village elders worried about them competing for the wages of local laborers and tenant farmers. The camps thus represented a hot dumpling no official was willing to bite into.

"Absolutely," said Mapha Ye. "I will work on releasing them from the camps. But . . . Prime Minister, the children are still minors, err . . ."

"Ah, I see what you mean," said Cogo, frowning as though dealing with a difficult puzzle. "It would be most inequitable and contrary to the principles of Moralism to separate children from their parents. It would, in fact, betray the spirit of the empress's proclamation to free the children while leaving their parents confined, wouldn't you say?"

"Uh . . . yes? But—"

"If you think the only solution is to also release the parents to take care of their children, I suppose I would have to agree," said Cogo. "After all, the parents have been vetted for many years and there are no criminal charges against them. I suppose, in order to carry out the intent of the empress's Imperial proclamation, we should grant them the same status as their children, to make the paperwork sensible."

"The parents—" Mapha Ye looked helplessly over at Zomi.

Zomi was fully in sync with Cogo now. "I once advocated keeping the refugees in isolation to catch spies and to gather intelligence on the Lyucu, but after they've been living in the camps for a while and we've asked them all the questions we can, keeping them there is of diminishing value. I think the Prime Minister's suggestion is sound and very much in the spirit of the Imperial proclamation."

"Thank you, Secretary Kidosu," said Cogo.

Zomi nodded in acknowledgment. Sometimes a stalemate required an unexpected move to be broken. Now that the principle had been established for refugees to be treated as full subjects of the Throne after suitable vetting, the magistrates and clerks no longer had excuses to keep them confined indefinitely. Cogo had managed to correct an error Zomi had committed years ago when she first established the camps.

And he had done so by trapping the empress into acknowledging the status of the children, before she was fully aware of the implications. It was the kind of legalistic maneuvering that Cogo excelled at, and which Zomi was still in the process of learning.

Jia seethed but said nothing.

"But back to the emperor's proposal," said Cogo in a meditative tone. "I really have no wisdom to offer. Let's keep this Ofluro confined and delay the decision on his asylum for as long as we need to reach consensus. After all—"

"You mean we wait until his child is born," said Jia, who could no longer hold back her irritation. "Let me save you some breath. At that point, by our own proclamation, the baby can no longer be confined, which means that its parents cannot be confined, which makes the question of asylum moot."

Cogo bowed. "Your Imperial Majesty is always thinking twenty steps ahead of your foolish servant—"

Jia cut him off. "Would it really kill you, Cogo, to speak plainly what is on your mind once in a while?"

Cogo kept his head bowed and said nothing.

The ministers of the Inner Council, sensing that the empress and the Prime Minister had reached consensus, began to heap effusive praise on the Imperial proclamation.

"This is the kind of grand-spirited mercy spoken of by the Ano sages!"

"I've always said that we should try to be more empathetic toward the Lyucu who forsake darkness for light—"

"If only Master Zato Ruthi were still alive! He would surely have approved of such a display of Moralist compassion. 'Heed the teachings of Kon Fiji!' he always said. 'Answer our foes' arrows with more love.' The empress shows . . ."

Zomi neither participated in nor listened to this chorus of political theater. She was nodding to herself as she admired the elegance of Cogo's solution. Asylum for an enemy combatant was an exceptional political act. The way Phyro had presented his case had turned it into a contest of wills between him and Jia, dueling sovereigns.

But Cogo had resolved the crisis by establishing a process by which *any* refugee from Ukyu-taasa could become a full subject of the Dandelion Throne after suitable vetting. Although the case of Ofluro, a Lyucu defector, was extraordinary, Cogo had managed to subsume it under a general category—parents of minor Dara children—protected by the empress's own proclamation. In this way, he defused the tension, allowed Jia to maintain control (or at least the appearance of control), while giving the emperor what he wanted.

Zomi looked at Phyro, who seemed bored by all the political maneuvering. She sighed silently. The emperor was indeed not ready.

Jia held up her hands to silence the babbling ministers. "Zomi, you might as well participate in drafting the proclamation, since the camps were established by you. You should include even refugees who do not have minor children—it's insensible to deny them freedom indefinitely on such a distinction. But make sure you come up with a reliable vetting process."

"As you wish, Your Imperial Majesty," said Zomi.

Jia continued. "Have Ofluro and his wife interrogated separately to confirm the emperor's impressions. Also interrogate the other refugees to see if there are any discrepancies in their accounts. If you discover nothing suspicious after suitable vetting, release them from the camp at Boama as free subjects of the Throne. If Phyro convinces them at that point to join him in his riding camp, then so be it. The emperor is in charge of the training of the garinafin force, and he bears the responsibility for his staff, for good or ill."

Everyone bowed. Phyro threw a grateful glance Zomi's way. Zomi tried to direct his gaze over to Cogo, but Phyro only looked away contemptuously.

The session of the Inner Council was coming to an end. As everyone got up and filed out, Jia called for Zomi to stay behind.

They waited until the chamber was deserted, save for the two of them.

"When you interrogate the refugees, there is one issue I want you to pay particular attention to," said Jia. "The number of refugees from Unredeemed Dara has drastically decreased during the last few years. See if you can find out why."

"I've already been looking into this question," said Zomi. "It's possible that the Lyucu have gotten much better at capturing escapees."

"Unlikely, given the experience of this Ofluro. He managed to evade capture with a group of untrained peasants as his crew."

Zomi nodded. "Then the other possibility is that the number of people seeking to escape has gone down."

"Which means that the Lyucu are consolidating their control over the population of Rui and Dasu."

Both were silent for a while. The idea that the Lyucu had managed to secure their foothold in the conquered islands was the worst possibility of all. In earlier years, the constant stream of refugees brought tales of repeated rebellions and brutal repressions by the Lyucu, indicating an insecure regime. But if Tanvanaki had figured out how to work with local elites to control the islands' population, that meant a far greater danger to Dara in the future.

"If only there were some way to get more information on what's happening in Kriphi!" Zomi clenched her fists. "Refugees can only tell us so much, not being in the Lyucu Great Tent. And this Ofluro, even if he were willing to cooperate, would not know much, if he was already out of favor with the court of Unredeemed Dara."

"It may be time for us to do something a little more active. . . ."

The discussion went on for some time, and several times Zomi pushed back against the empress's demands. In the end, they agreed on a plan, one that would, like so much of the Farsight Secretary's work, be concealed in shadows.

As Zomi was about to depart the council chamber, Jia called out to her once more.

"I know Théra asked you to help Phyro."

Zomi stopped, without turning around.

"But you also took an oath to serve the Dandelion Throne when you became an official. That throne is empty at the moment, its nominal occupant too obsessed with vengeance and martial glory to properly shoulder the burden that Théra passed to him. Until he learns what he must learn, I hold the Seal of Dara. You'll do well to remember that."

Still looking away, Zomi's shoulders stiffened. She worked hard to compose her face.

"I've not forgotten about the people of Dasu and Rui." A hint of weariness crept into Jia's voice, but it was almost immediately banished. "But Phyro's impatience for war is not the answer. War isn't a game of *zamaki* or *cüpa*. Above all, Dara needs peace."

After a moment, Zomi nodded reluctantly.

"One last thing. In the future, prepare a single-page summary for the most important points of your reports."

The empress sipped her tea.

Zomi left.

*Honor and trust.*

*Like that poor Zato Ruthi, Phyro and the Moralists think softheartedness is honor and naïveté is trust. He may have the courage to start a war, but he has no understanding of what it means, or the resolve to finish it.*

*Better there be no war at all then.*

*This is why I can't tell anyone the truth; this is why I must work alone.*

*If they knew what I really intend, they'd do everything in their power to stop me. But there is no place for mercy and doubt when you wield the Grace of Kings, not when Kuni sighed on the northern shore of the Liru, and not when I stood on the Moon-Gazing Tower.*

Phyro found Fara at the camera obscura.

"You're leaving already? I was hoping you could stay a few days this time. Aya and I were going to take you to our favorite new Dasu-style restaurant. And I was going to show you my new play—you always laugh at my jokes."

Phyro chuckled. "I'll try to be back for New Year's. But I've accomplished what I came for. There's a lot to do back at Tiro Cozo."

"You won't even stay the night to have dinner with me and Aunt-Mother? I told the kitchen to prepare a special menu I designed."

Phyro's face hardened. "A meal with her would be torture. I'd rather eat the mud soup you used to make when you were four—with live worms."

"But you need to spend time with her! At least act like you respect her. Haven't you heard the rumors about Gimoto?"

Phyro cocked an eyebrow. "Since when do you care about politics?"

"Do you really think I'm still that little girl who always got left behind when the three of you wanted to go on some adventure?" Fara's face was flushed. "I may sing and paint and play the zither all day, but I grew up in the palace. I am also a daughter of the House of Dandelion."

Phyro looked at his little sister with affection and newfound respect. "Don't worry about Gimoto. I know what I'm doing."

"No, you don't!" Fara looked around to be sure they were alone. "Last month, one member of the College of Advocates submitted a report describing all the reasons why a regent may choose to designate a different heir than the one the regent is supposed to help. It was full of specious quotations from Kon Fiji and Poti Maji. There was even a citation to Lügo Crupo, the faithless usurper, as though he were some kind of moral authority."

"Master Zato Ruthi would be rolling in his grave to see his beloved sages abused so."

"It's not a joke! The report was couched as a pure thought experiment, but obviously it was meant to test the waters. And you know what? Instead of lots of responses picking apart the faulty logic and the misuse of authority, there was nothing. No one spoke up. Not even Uncle Cogo."

"Perhaps no one thought such a silly report was worthy of a response."

"Don't play dumb with me. No one responded because you don't seem to *care*. You are never in Pan, and Aunt-Mother runs everything without your input—"

"She never cared for my input—"

"You can't just give up! If you come back to the palace, play the part of the dutiful son, learn how to govern, and slowly build up a web of support at court, she won't dare to replace you with Gimoto.

Don't you see? Your enemies are trying to tell a story about you, a false story in which you're the dissolute prince unfit to govern. But you can combat it with a story about who you really are."

"Let them say whatever they want. I don't care about stories."

"No! Stories matter! Father and Aunt-Mother both talked about how being emperor is a lot like being in a play, and good plays tell good stories. Stories are what move people's hearts, long after all the facts and figures have faded away. You're the rightful heir, and there's no better story than the return of the good emperor. There'll be a swelling tide of support for you if you'd only tap into it instead of butting heads with her in this way."

Phyro took a deep breath. He stepped back and bowed to his sister. "Ada-*tika*, I apologize for underestimating you. It's difficult sometimes for an elder brother to accept that his little sister is grown. Your advice isn't wrong, but it's simply not a path that I can follow."

"You *have* to—"

"No! How can I think about petty matters like gossiping ministers and tongue-wagging junior advocates when the people of Dasu and Rui are enslaved by the Lyucu? When Théra is out there alone beyond the Wall of Storms, struggling for the very fate of our people? When Timu is a puppet over in Kriphi, bewitched by that barbarian woman? When the murderers responsible for our father's death are sitting in comfort, growing fat on our tribute? An Emperor of Dara is supposed to fight for his people—"

"But how can you fight if you're no longer emperor? You *have* to worry about it."

"No, you have it backward. Father won his empire by the sword, and it is only through the sword that the empire can be held and the people of Dara saved. That fighting must come first is something Aunt-Mother has never understood. Because she doesn't have a fighter's spirit, she despises men and women who *do* instead of *talk*. Let her worry about bureaucrats and taxes and coddle musty scholars and cowardly princes. So long as I have the support of the army, I *am* emperor."

"Don't talk like that," said Fara, shaking her head. "Don't."

"She doesn't understand honor, trust, and loyalty. But that is the foundation of a fighting force, an army that cannot be defeated. Auntie Gin taught me that, and I don't ever believe she truly rebelled. Our aunt-mother schemes and plots, but in the end, she is nothing before an army with me at its head. Nothing!"

"Stop it!" Fara plugged her ears. "Stop it!"

A discreet cough from behind the rock formation that was "Arulugi."

The two siblings stopped their conversation. An old woman with snow-white hair walked around the rock formation and approached the shack.

"Auntie Soto!" said Phyro. Soto had been the governess-tutor for him and his siblings, and even after the children were grown, she stayed at the palace as Jia's friend and confidante. Not knowing how much of the conversation between him and Fara had been overhead, he was flustered. "I . . . I'm sorry I didn't stop by to visit you. I was— am—in a hurry—"

"Children go where they will," Soto said, smiling. "I heard that you were in Pan, but I figured you wouldn't stay for long. Good thing I found out from the Dyran Fins just now where you were headed in the garden."

Phyro understood the comment for what it was: a warning that he needed to watch what he said, for the eyes of the empress were everywhere. Impulsively, he went up and embraced Soto tightly, as he used to do when he was little.

Soto patted him gently, also the way she used to do when he was little and needed some comfort after a fight with Timu or after scraping a knee practicing with his sword. But he was so tall now that she could only reach the middle of his back. "I know you're no longer a child, Hudo-*tika*, but . . . for the sake of your dead mother, listen to what I have to say."

Phyro stepped back and nodded solemnly.

"I've known your father, your mother, and your aunt-mother far longer than you," said Soto. "We're shaped by our experiences, and there were things Jia went through during Kuni's wars that changed her."

"Did my aunt-mother ask you to come to persuade me to be the obedient puppet?" asked Phyro, almost sneering. "The difference between us isn't personal; it's about the future of Dara."

Soto sighed. "I guess I should have expected both of you to be angry with me. She wouldn't even see me today, knowing that I was going to plead your case. And now you shout at me like you're berating a maid."

"Auntie Soto, I'm sorry!" Phyro knelt before her. "I . . . I shouldn't have been so disrespectful. I'm listening."

Soto nodded. "You and Jia . . . All right, let me focus on your thoughts on war. Your aunt-mother saw what war did to the common people when she was the Hegemon's captive, from the perspective of someone without the power to fight back, to direct her own fate. She is no coward, but her suspicion of armies and warlords and great lords who proclaim war as an answer must be understood from that point of view."

Phyro made as if to speak, but Soto held up a hand to silence him.

"You admire my nephew; you admire Gin. Both of them fought for grand ideals. But killing is a terrible thing, and every time you kill someone, a little bit of yourself dies. In our histories, we call those who kill thousands, hundreds of thousands, even millions, great, but they are often little more than hollow shells, walking corpses into which we project our fantasies of what heroism and nobility look like. I know what an obsession with vengeance and heroism did to my nephew; I do not believe that is what your mother would want for you."

Phyro did not argue, but he also didn't meet Soto's gaze, instead looking defiantly at the ground. When it was clear that Soto was finished, he bowed stiffly. "I'm grateful for your instruction, Lady Soto."

Then he turned to Fara. "Farewell, Ada-*tika*." He strode away toward the Wall of Tranquility, looking anything but.

"Do you think he'll listen to you?" asked Fara.

Soto sighed and did not answer.

# CHAPTER NINETEEN

# SPIES

Of all the ancient Tiro state capitals, Kriphi had always had a reputation as the least impressive. It lacked the cosmopolitan liveliness of commercial Toaza of Gan and the weight of history felt in every paving stone and roof shingle in Cocru's Çaruza. It didn't have the imposing cliff-face towers of Boama, which loomed through Faça's famous fog like ships drifting in a sea of clouds, nor the exotic sandalwood-and-pumice-paved streets of Na Thion, lined with shrines to the legendary weaponsmiths and heroes of Rima. In learning it was no match for the ancient academies and modern laboratories of high-minded Ginpen in Haan, and in beauty it paled next to the ethereal spires and suspended rope bridges of Amu's Müning, as graceful as dancers leaping across the floating islands in Lake Toyemotika.

What it did have, however, was an abundance of birds.

A series of wetlands near the city, both fresh and brackish, provided plenty of nesting sites for migratory cranes and scholar's geese. The woodlands in the foothills to the north, off-limits to commoners for generations as a royal hunting preserve, boasted triple-crested pheasants and a variety of songbirds and game birds. Even the city itself, filled with stone houses with long, curved, hanging eaves, offered as many places for swallows and doves to nest as any guano-encrusted cliff.

Best of all, because Kiji, the patron of old Xana, was also the Lord of Birds, commoners were forbidden from killing wild birds. Despite the succession of kings, governors, and pékyus who took over the palace at the northwestern corner of the city, the taboo against killing birds persisted unchanged and the winged tribe continued to thrive in and around Kriphi. Indeed, the Mingén Tower at the center of the sprawling palace, constructed from blocks of rough-hewn stone so that it resembled a craggy mountain more than a castle, hosted the aeries of many raptor families.

One of these falcons, an old male long past his prime, now dove at a fish stall in the western market in the center of the city. With a loud squawk, it grabbed a small mackerel from the iced display and took off again. The fishwife shouted and shook her fist at the thief, but there was nothing she could do.

"May the offering to Lord Kiji bring you luck," one of the amused onlookers said.

"How about you buy some fish instead of just gawking?" said the fishwife, glaring at him. "*That's* the sort of good luck I'm interested in."

The falcon gained altitude with vigorous wing flaps, easily carrying the weight of the small fish. Sure, a fish-stall mackerel wasn't as fresh or tasty as one caught fresh, but at his age, a sure thing was better than risking a broken wing or claw by diving into the cold sea.

As the falcon caught the wind and glided south, he surveyed the maze of narrow paved-stone streets below winding their way between densely packed houses and tenement buildings. In some parts of the city, the old stone buildings had been replaced by fields of white tents. The falcon remembered seeing these pop up in his youth, seven or eight years ago, like patches of mushrooms sprouting in the woods after spring rain. A new kind of people who dressed differently from those who already lived in Kriphi nested in those tents. The falcon wasn't sure how exactly they were different, only that he needed to be leery of them as a few of them had tried to attack the falcons with slingshots, an unheard-of thing among the falcon clans of Kriphi.

The falcon crossed over the southeastern wall of the city and swung in a long, wide arc over the sea. Below, he could see a new addition to Kriphi that had also come into being with the tent-dwellers. A long floating bridge extended into the bay from the shore and ended in a square formed by four long, floating wharves. The inside of the square was crisscrossed by more floating wharves, forming a miniature town that gently undulated on the waves.

Today, there was an opening in one side of the large square, and a fleet of five ships was docked inside the floating town. Lines of humans congregated on the floating wharves, unloading sacks and boxes that they then carried along the long floating bridge back to the shore. The whole scene resembled a swarm of ants carrying food back to the colony.

The falcon turned north and winged his way back to the palace and the Mingén Tower, where he would enjoy this mackerel and then take a nap, unconcerned with the affairs of the humans who shared this city with him.

On the floating wharf next to one of the docked ships, a man and a woman stood next to each other, watching the unloading process unfold.

Noda Mi, First Garinafin Groom of the Pékyu, Loyal Hound of the Lyucu, Duke of Zathin Gulf, and Deputy Minister of Native Affairs, stared at the fleet from the Big Island and wondered again whether he had made the right choice eight years ago, when he had betrayed Marshal Gin Mazoti at the last minute and saved the life of Tanvanaki, thereby becoming part of the Lyucu occupation of Rui and Dasu. Sure, he had plenty of wealth and women, but was that everything one wanted out of life?

"Most Distinguished Minister," said the emissary from unoccupied Dara, Lady Ragi, bowing in *jiri*, "I trust that the inventory of trade goods is satisfactory?"

After the stalemate that resulted from the Battle of Zathin Gulf, Tanvanaki had extracted a promise of regular tribute of foodstuffs and other goods from Empress Jia in exchange for a promise not to invade the rest of Dara for ten years. Four times a year, the tribute fleet arrived from the Big Island, carrying grain, meat, silk, and bolts of cloth. In recent years, Tanvanaki had added lacquerware, ceramics, kitchen-ware, and all sorts of other manufactured goods to the list of demands. Fearful of a Lyucu invasion, the empress had always complied.

However, in an effort to make herself feel better—Noda couldn't hide a contemptuous smile at this thought—Jia called the tribute fleets "trade missions," and the Lyucu were happy to play along by sending back on the tribute ships a few crates of cattle hides, horns, bundles of sinew, and other similar raw materials from their pastures in exchange for exorbitant amounts of silver and gold.

"The goods are very much in order," Noda said. "The people of Ukyu-taasa are pleased with these gifts. Do please pass on Emperor Thaké and Pékyu Vadyu's greetings to Empress Jia and Emperor Monadétu."

"Most Honorable Duke, I will be sure to pass on the message."

Noda's face flushed as he thought he detected a hint of mockery in the manner Lady Ragi had said the word "honorable," but he couldn't exactly blow up at her. He was secretly relieved that she had not used the rest of his long string of titles. Had she done so, he would have had to grin and bear the humiliation, as there were two Lyucu thanes standing behind him to observe this exchange, and he couldn't afford to show any displeasure at being called a lapdog of the Lyucu and a garinafin shit-shoveler. Even now, after eight years, he couldn't tell if Tanvanaki had given him those titles because she genuinely thought they were complimentary or because she was taunting him about his wavering loyalties.

Lady Ragi went on. "The empress also inquires after the health and well-being of her grandchildren."

"The pékyus-taasa are strong of limb and stout of heart," Noda said, reciting the formulaic response with little conviction.

"The empress extends again the invitation for the young prince and princess to visit their family," said Lady Ragi.

Noda cursed silently. Lady Ragi was new to him. She had been appointed to head this tributary mission because the old emissary had fallen ill, and the woman was apparently determined to go through the full list of Jia's typical demands. After years of repeated rejections, other emissaries from unoccupied Dara had long learned to skip the meaningless diplomatic dance and get straight down to business. He would have to train her.

"The pékyu responds that the pékyus-taasa are very busy with their studies and cannot undertake such a long journey," said Noda. *As if the pékyu would allow wily Jia to get her hands on her children, symbols of the legitimacy of Lyucu rule in Dara. It's easy for the young prince and princess to go "visit" their grandmother, but who knows if they'll come back?* "I know that the distinguished emissary's time is very precious—"

Ragi refused to take the hint. "But the empress has gathered many renowned scholars of deep erudition for the young prince and princess. Surely such a trip would add to the education and knowledge of . . ."

The back-and-forth went on for a while. The Lyucu thanes behind Noda fidgeted impatiently and cleared their throats. Noda's face tensed.

"Lady Ragi, it's getting late," he said.

"Ah," said Lady Ragi, glancing at the sun's position as if suddenly aware of the hour. "I do apologize. But I have to make sure I convey the empress's messages accurately. Well, I guess it's time for me to retire, as I'll have a long journey back tomorrow. Farewell—"

"Wait!" said Noda Mi. *Has no one explained to you how this works?* "I'm sorry to bring this up, but I have to inspect your ships for any contraband."

"Ah, of course," said Lady Ragi. "Why don't you come aboard for the inspection now? To compensate you for the extra work, would you allow me to play host and join me for dinner, where we can discuss the empress's requests in more detail?" She looked expectantly at the two Lyucu thanes standing behind Noda. "These honored lords are also invited—"

The Lyucu thanes shook their heads vigorously. They acted as though listening to this pair go on for another hour in flavorless diplomacyese would be pure torture.

Lady Ragi stepped to the side of the gangplank and made a gesture of invitation at Noda, winking at him when she thought the Lyucu thanes weren't watching.

Noda finally relaxed. *She gets it.*

∽

Teams of native laborers under the watchful eyes of Lyucu and native guards carried crates from the fleet down to the warehouse, a large structure onshore at the end of the floating bridge. Some of the crates were so heavy that a whole team of laborers had to work together, using a long shoulder pole to spread the weight evenly.

As soon as Noda Mi and Lady Ragi had entered the Dara ship, one of the Lyucu thanes looked to the stream of laborers and blew a low but shrill whistle.

One of the laborers in the last shoulder-pole team tensed. He whispered something to his companions and ducked out of his place at the end of the pole. The rest of the team carried on, as if they hadn't noticed his absence. As the column of laborers walked away, he stood at the edge of the floating bridge facing the water, planted his legs firmly, and loosened the waist string of his pants.

The Lyucu guards laughed and pointed at him. The native guards joined in.

The laborer's face turned red as he smiled ingratiatingly and awkwardly at the guards. Then he turned around, squatted down, and pulled down his pants so that his ass hung over the water.

The Lyucu guards laughed even harder.

The commotion drew the attention of the Dara sentries on the ships. They gathered at the gunwale to look at the humiliated man. Some joined in the jeers of the Lyucu guards. Others remained silent, seething at the way the Lyucu had reduced a fellow Dara native to such a humiliating state. Did the Lyucu not even allow the laborers a proper toilet break?

While everyone's attention was drawn to the spectacle in the middle of the floating bridge, a figure silently dove into the water at the far end of the square of floating wharves, opposite the anchored fleet. Barely making a splash, the figure silently and quickly swam for the Dara ships.

"You needn't have bothered with that song and dance," said Noda Mi as he filled the two cups from the flask of plum wine. "Those two Lyucu thanes understand what's going on."

"I prefer to be cautious, given this is my first time as an emissary to occupied Dara," said Lady Ragi.

They were seated on a broad ledge along one wall, and the low table between them was laden with small dishes of delicacies cooked to the exacting standards of the palace in Pan: pan-seared bamboo shoots dipped in fish sauce, pork dumplings served with a sesame paste, lotus-seed soup flavored with eight kinds of dried fruits— one for each of the gods of Dara—and so on. The emissary of the Dandelion Court traveled in style.

Noda Mi drained his cup and burped loudly. "Oh, this really is excellent. It's impossible to find such good wine here in Ukyu-taasa. If I'm not mistaken, this vintage dates back to the Reign of One Bright Heaven?"

"I see you are a true connoisseur, Most Honorable Duke. The fourteenth year in the Reign of One Bright Heaven, to be exact."

Noda Mi and Lady Ragi both sat in relaxed *géüpa*, as if they were already old friends. As Noda Mi contemplated Lady Ragi's shapely curves, so enticingly displayed by the tight bodice of her dress, and her comely features, he had the urge to shift into *thakrido* to show that he was interested in her. But then he thought better of it. *Business before pleasure.*

"So, regarding the 'contraband'—" Noda began.

"—you'll find the specially marked crates stacked in the back of the hold, ready to be 'confiscated,'" said Lady Ragi.

"Excellent. Excellent! My Lyucu colleagues will have the pékyu's 'reprimands' and 'formal protest' ready when I disembark."

The two shared a smile and clinked their cups.

The native officials in Kriphi who served the pékyu had long found the tribute fleets an excellent way to smuggle in a few luxury goods from unoccupied Dara to give them a taste of the sophisticated life they craved: fine silk dresses and robes cut in the latest fashion of Pan, signature teas from Müning, porcelain produced by the oldest kilns of Toaza, thousand-hammered steel knives and scholar's swords from Na Thion, popular song lyrics and erotic paintings from the indigo houses of Dimushi, authorized transcriptions of famous storytellers' performances in

Boama and Dimu, ingenious toys and gadgets from Ginpen, and so on.

Over time, as Timu continued to promote the integration of native elites with their Lyucu conquerors—with Tanvanaki's support and approval—the tastes of high-ranking native officials infected their Lyucu superiors. The popularity of Dara culture among the Lyucu elite, from garinafin-thanes to wealthy naros, swelled the demand for luxury goods. This was despite an official ban on their import, since the Lyucu and Dara were still technically at war. Lyucu thanes became involved in the illicit trade, and the corrupt officials on Empress Jia's tribute ships were happy to meet the need in exchange for silver and gold.

To preserve the appearance of propriety, the smuggling had to be done under the guise of confiscation and reprimands, and the Lyucu thanes stayed studiously out of the actual transactions, preferring to use native officials like Noda Mi as their agents. Noda was only too happy to oblige. Not only did he get to make money, but he also got a chance to converse with emissaries with the refined accents of Pan—he missed the Big Island, though he knew how much he was despised by most in Dara.

Lady Ragi refilled Noda Mi's cup and began to tell him about the particular goods in the contraband crates. Noda Mi's eyes glowed as he imagined the extra profit he would make from selling the contraband on the black market after paying off his partners. He wasn't too concerned about getting caught, since he was reasonably sure that the pékyu knew exactly what he was up to but tolerated his side dealings as a way to keep her senior thanes and native collaborators happy.

Peace was good for business.

Right outside the cabin, below the porthole, a motionless figure hung onto the ship like a woodpecker clinging to a tree or a barnacle cemented to a rock. Dark, skintight clothing made him blend into the aged wooden hull.

Swimming through the water while everyone had been diverted by the performance of the native laborer had been difficult, and climbing up the hull without being detected had been harder. He didn't complain. Compared to what he was used to, these were trivial tasks.

Besides, a spy's job was to do as his votan ordered.

He had grown up as a lowly culek along the shore of Ukyu-Gondé. Even as a boy, he was an exceptionally good swimmer and a good climber of the slippery rocks at the edge of the sea, encrusted with Péten's-eyes oysters and concealing gray-feathered toddling auk nests. He thought he would one day become a great warrior, perhaps even rise into the ranks of the naros.

But something about him repelled the garinafins, who always hissed and growled at him whenever he came near. A Lyucu who couldn't be near garinafins might as well be dead. Thinking that he was bad luck, the tribe exiled him when he was only twelve. He didn't want to join the tanto-lyu-naro, and so he lived by himself, wandering aimlessly along the shore and filling his stomach with fish and clams.

One day, he found himself next to a cove filled with ships as large as islands. Though he had never seen anything like them, he knew right away that he was looking at the city-ships of the strangers who had come from across the ocean, which now stood as deserted and mute monuments to Pékyu Tenryo's glory.

Seized with an unexplainable urge, he dove into the cold sea to swim to the city-ships. He didn't know what he was looking for, except that he wanted to prove that he could do something that no one else could. The size of the ships made it hard for him to estimate their true distance, and by the time he reached the nearest ship, he was almost dead with exhaustion.

He was too far out to swim back. If he wanted to live, his only choice was to climb onto the city-ship. And so that was what he did. There were no rope ladders or dangling lines to help him. At first, he used the barnacles as handholds and footholds, and then, after these ran out, he had to make use of every tiny depression in the planking, seek out every narrow seam in the hull, scale up a wall sheerer than any cliff he had ever climbed. Several times, he almost fell, but by sheer force of will he had hung on, and blood seeped from his fingers and toes as his nails broke, making him scream and moan.

After he finally made it onto the deck, he collapsed and blanked out.

In the morning, he was discovered by a lone garinafin rider practicing maneuvers overhead. She turned out to be Tanvanaki, Pékyu Tenryo's favorite daughter. When Tanvanaki landed on the deck of the city-ship, her mount, Korva, hissed and backed up, ready to kill him with a fiery tongue-lash, but Tanvanaki had stopped her, regarding him with curiosity.

Despair seized him, and he made to leap off the side of the empty city-ship, but Tanvanaki ordered him to halt.

She asked him how he had come to be there, and he explained.

"You swam all the way here?" She was incredulous. "But the water is freezing! And you climbed up here from the sea with no bone claw, no tiger tusk, no sinew rope?"

He showed her his bloody fingers and toes.

"I've never known any Lyucu like you," she said, her look one of wonder.

He thought he knew what she meant. "I'm bad luck," he croaked. "I can never ride or be near a garinafin. There's no place for me in Ukyu-Gondé. Let me die."

"No, you're not bad luck," she said. "I don't believe in luck, good or bad. I believe in deeds. Even the Thane of the Tribe of the Scarred Whale would have drowned before she could swim halfway here from the shore in such frigid waters, and even my father's nimblest garinafin pilot couldn't have climbed onto this smooth-hulled ship. You've done something that no other Lyucu has ever done, and that is something to be praised, not feared."

He wept at that. And he was ready to do whatever she wanted him to from that point on.

Tanvanaki sent him on many dangerous missions: retrieving eggs from nests on unreachable cliffs; diving for a pin she accidentally dropped into the sea; spying on thanes she suspected of disloyalty.

Later, when Tanvanaki went with Tenryo to conquer Dara, he came along. During the journey to Dara, she sometimes sent him to bring messages to the other city-ships without the use of a boat. Swimming through the belt current and climbing up the sheer hulls of the city-ships were feats that no other Lyucu dared, and he took pleasure in the fact that she, the best garinafin pilot, trusted him though he couldn't be near a garinafin at all.

In Ukyu-taasa, he became even more useful to her. The natives of Dara led lives much more reliant on the sea, and built many more ships. He spied for her on the carpenters on the floating wharf, and kept an eye on the goings-on on the Dara ships during tribute missions. He was how she kept an eye on her enemies, and he did things for her that no one else could.

He dug his fingers and toes into the soft wood under the porthole. His digits were tipped with metal claws that kept him securely attached and had been specially made for him—these claws were some of the best things he had been given in Dara.

As the breeze passed over his wet clothes, the spy shivered. He had to suppress the urge to cough. A little discomfort was nothing.

He had finally found his place, a place that no one else could take. He pressed his ear up to the porthole.

"If you're not leaving until late tomorrow," said Noda Mi, "I can pay another visit in the morning. Have you seen the Lyucu art of wrestling? It's very impressive. I'll bring a pair of culeks to give you a demonstration."

"Watching two naked bodies rolling around could be fun, but I prefer doing to watching for entertainment," said Lady Ragi casually, a flirtatious smile on her face.

"Oh?" Noda Mi's ears perked up. He *really* liked this new emissary. "So what do you like to *do* for fun?"

"I subscribe to the Fluxists' love for nature," said Ragi. Her gaze grew dreamy. "The carpenters told me about the natural springs in the Roro Hills to the north of Kriphi. I hear that the pools are like Tututika's heavenly baths dropped on earth, and the rare crimson-tailed woodpecker performs feats of aerial acrobatics that are unparalleled in all the Islands."

Noda Mi chuckled. "I'm sorry to tell you that you've been misinformed. I've been there, and it's nothing special. The water is cold and there are sharp rocks at the bottom of the pools. As for the woodpeckers, they're very shy creatures, almost impossible to see."

A few carpenters from unoccupied Dara, maintained at the expense of the Dandelion Court, were kept year-round on the floating wharves to maintain the wooden structures, which had been built at Tanvanaki's command to prevent the tribute ships from having direct contact with the population of Kriphi. The Lyucu did not allow the carpenters onshore at all. Isolated for months in cramped huts on a few floating boards that didn't sail anywhere and wholly dependent on their Lyucu hosts for everything, they soon grew stir-crazy. Noda could easily imagine how their confinement only made nearby scenic spots that they could never experience sound even more enticing. No doubt the carpenters had filled Lady Ragi's head with their fantasies.

"Surely a dip in a secluded pool is the best way to spend a summer morning," said Lady Ragi, smiling at Noda. "I am a very good swimmer, and I have a weakness for shy but beautiful birds. A trip there in the company of a powerful duke would be so delightful. . . . Isn't there *anything* you can do?"

Noda Mi's heart sped up as he imagined Lady Ragi's unclothed body parting the water in the natural spring like a graceful dyran. . . . With some effort, he pulled himself back into reality. "I'm afraid not. The pékyu has made it clear that no Dara-raaki is allowed outside this floating wharf-town."

Lady Ragi flinched at the use of the Lyucu slur for the natives not under Lyucu rule. Literally, "raaki" meant "impure," "muddy," "filthy."

"Err . . ." Noda Mi was seized with regret. He had become so used to speaking like one of the Lyucu that he no longer felt the sting of the slur. "Forget about the natural spring. If you don't like wrestling, I could arrange for a demonstration from the garinafin riders—"

"A pity," said Lady Ragi, a hint of mockery creeping into her voice again. "I thought the duke was a powerful man in this land, but I suppose you're but a native, after all."

Noda Mi's face flushed. "That has nothing to do with it. No one, not even Garinafin-Thane Goztan Ryoto or Tiger-Thane Vocu Firna, is allowed to bring any Dara-ra—uh, visitors from the rest of Dara, onshore without a direct order from the pékyu or the emperor. This has been the rule since the beginning."

"I've heard that a dog that's fed scraps sometimes starts to think he's a person," said Lady Ragi sardonically. "But he remains a dog, and at night he's kicked outside and the door locked behind him."

Noda Mi slammed his cup down on the table. "How dare you! Such insolence . . . such gall . . . you have no—"

Lady Ragi's pose remained relaxed. "I'm not finished. Instead of dogs, let's talk more about . . . birds. As I said, I have a weakness for shy but beautiful birds. The crimson-tailed woodpecker doesn't just settle for any tree, does it?"

The seeming non sequitur confused Noda Mi. "What?"

"It is said that these rare woodpeckers prefer trees that yield just the right sound when pecked. They knock on a trunk to see if it gives a lingering ring. Trees that sound too muffled don't have enough grubs to be worthwhile, but trees that sound too loud have been hollowed out, dead or on the verge of dying. There's no shame for a woodpecker to flit from tree to tree. After all, a bird must do what makes the most sense for the bird."

"I'm impressed by your knowledge of birds," said Noda Mi. Now that he had a chance to calm down, he was beginning to grasp Lady Ragi's gambit. Some things couldn't be discussed directly, and had to be couched in metaphors to be plausibly deniable. "But surely a woodpecker who has abandoned one tree for another cannot expect to return to the first tree. The bird wouldn't have left if that tree wasn't already dying."

"Trees are resilient," said Lady Ragi. "Sometimes they recover and become stronger than ever . . . strong enough to dream about challenging other trees for space and sunlight."

*So they've recovered from the time of the Battle of Zathin Gulf, perhaps sufficiently confident of their own power to contemplate an invasion of Ukyu-taasa.* Noda Mi pondered the news. *And they want me to help them, over there in Pan.*

His heart quickened at the highly risky conversation he found himself in. Lady Ragi, he vaguely recalled, had been one of the war orphans raised by Jia when she had been the Hegemon's hostage in Çaruza. Later, she served the empress as one of her ladies-in-waiting. Of course Jia would only send someone she absolutely trusted on a mission to recruit a spy.

This wasn't the first time that he had had second thoughts since joining the Lyucu. Lady Ragi's mockery had struck closer to home than he cared to admit. No matter how much he strove to prove himself in Ukyu-taasa, he would always be an outsider to the Lyucu, always viewed with some suspicion. Maybe it was time to evaluate his options more carefully.

"But would a healthy tree have enough grubs for the returning woodpecker?"

Lady Ragi smiled. *"Datralu gacruca ça crunpén ki fithéücadipu ki lodü ingro ça néficaü.* Even here, under the noses of your pékyu and my empress, we carry on a trade that may not be acknowledged. To return to our theme, no tree is so healthy that it doesn't have some grubs to feed the worthy woodpecker."

"There may be more grubs in the trees here in Ukyu-taasa than in the core islands."

"A clever woodpecker, I understand, will test out several trees before picking one as its perch. In fact, a really clever woodpecker will continue to try out new trees even after it has made a choice for nesting, both to get a better variety of grubs and in case a better tree presents itself." Lady Ragi paused and looked at Noda intently. "Or if the tree it has chosen starts to die."

"It's easy to make wild predictions about the deaths of trees," said Noda Mi. *There's no point in appearing too eager,* he thought. *It's all fine and good to keep options open, but some reluctance will only add to my value.* "But as you said: Trees are resilient—especially when a . . . shy and beautiful woodpecker is helping to protect the tree."

"The woodpecker would know best whether its nesting tree is dying or not, of course," said Lady Ragi. "But how healthy can a tree be that requires constant feeding and care by outsiders?"

Noda Mi considered this. The amount of "gifts" the Dandelion Court brought to Rui and Dasu had increased every year, and the pékyu had been portraying this as a sign of the Lyucu's strength. *But what if it's not? What if the need for quarterly injections of food and the pékyu's tolerance for private trade conducted in the shadow of the tribute fleet only indicate weakness?*

He remembered Tanvanaki's fury-infused face as she demanded that he work harder to acquire—through kidnappings and abductions—skilled engineers from Dara. *Maybe the pékyu is more terrified than she lets on.* He resolved to look closer into the tax collection and harvest records the next time he got a chance. He had always found such information boring, but it seemed that he needed to peck at this trunk he was on to see just how sound it was.

"Thank you for this most invigorating ornithological discussion," he said. "You may let your bird-watcher know that a certain woodpecker is willing to test out other trees."

"How about a test right now?" said Lady Ragi. "I happen to have another crate aboard, filled with wines taken from the cellar of Zyndu Castle in Tunoa. Some of the bottles go back to the time of Marshal Dazu Zyndu, the Hegemon's grandfather."

Noda smiled. "Oh, that is a most generous gift for a woodpecker."

"Who said anything about a gift? The woodpecker has to work for his grub."

Noda's smile froze. "What do you mean?"

"I think the woodpecker needs to peck a little, as a demonstration of good faith."

Noda closed his eyes and thought over the situation. He definitely wanted to keep his options open, given the possibility that Ukyu-taasa was weaker, and Dara proper stronger, than he had thought. Should the Lyucu fall, he would have to face the people he'd betrayed.

But he wasn't quite ready yet to risk his life as a spy for the Dandelion Court for a crate of plum wine, no matter the vintage. He needed to give Lady Ragi something, but it couldn't be anything too important, or anything that would harm his own interests.

"I understand that some shoreline villages on the Big Island and Arulugi have been plagued by pirates," said Noda. "You might want to do something about that."

"That some of the pirates are raiding for goods to sell to the Lyucu is well known," said Lady Ragi. "I think you need to peck harder."

"Raiding for goods to sell, you say? Perhaps that isn't all they have in mind," said Noda. "Big cities, especially places like Dimu and Dimushi, may have other attractions. I think I've said more than enough."

Lady Ragi regarded him coolly. "Perhaps. As another demonstration of good faith, I'd like you to take a message from Empress Jia to Emperor Thaké."

Noda's eyes bulged. "Do you think my skull is filled with air? I'm not going to risk my life by delivering a secret message from the enemy."

"It isn't secret," said Lady Ragi. "The empress has not seen her only son in many years, and she misses him. She would like to pass on a message to him, voice to voice, ear to ear, not through the impersonal medium of a diplomatic communiqué. Surely you can understand that?"

Still suspicious, Noda asked, "What is the message?"

"The empress says, 'Remember that I love you, Toto-*tika*. Eat well and get plenty of rest. As for your duties: teeth on the board, heart open to the sky.'"

Noda mulled over the message. It seemed innocuous enough, as cloying and clichéd as most urgings from mothers to sons were. That bit at the end was a Moralist platitude often recited in the context of loyal ministers, which seemed slightly odd.

"I will not keep this secret from the pékyu," warned Noda.

"That is fine," said Lady Ragi. "The pékyu, a mother herself, would understand well that a mother's love for her son need not be concealed."

Noda nodded. "I will pass on the message. But that is all. The woodpecker is only looking. He hasn't agreed to anything."

Lady Ragi broke into a smile. "I will add your special crate to the stack in the back of the hold."

They drank, snacked, and talked of inconsequential things.

Lady Ragi spoke of two *cashima* in Ginpen, who fought over the favor of an indigo-house girl, first by writing her competing poems, and then by dueling in front of her with swords; of the discovery of a dead white snake in the central plaza of Çaruza by the priestesses of Rapa and Kana, widely seen as a good omen; of a famous actor in

Pan, who was seen leaving in the company of a wealthy merchant after a big performance and was then caught walking home in his costume the next morning, shamefaced and barefoot.

Noda Mi laughed at the gossip. Trying to impress her, he told her about his life at the court in Kriphi, the number of Lyucu thanes who cultivated him, the native officials who sought him out as a patron, the business deals he had all over Ukyu-taasa. He avoided anything having to do with the military or detailed policies, and Lady Ragi did not probe, only asking silly questions that made him laugh.

Three plum wine flasks were emptied before Noda Mi was satisfied.

After Noda Mi left, swaying on unsteady legs, Lady Ragi remained at the table. She waved away the servants who had come in to clear away the remains of the meal.

"I'd like some time to myself," she said, her voice full of exhaustion.

Dealing with the despicable Noda had taken a lot out of her. The odious traitor had taken to putting on the airs of a genteel scholar-official, though he had first risen to power as a barely literate soldier in the Hegemon's army and then scurried up a ladder of constant betrayals and conniving schemes. Somehow, his pretension to refinement, to culture, to erudition—a naked attempt at salving his deep-seated insecurity—only reminded Ragi more of the reality of his crimes, highlighted the repulsive patterns of his mind, emphasized the vileness of his character.

Every second during the encounter, she had to restrain the urge to beat him to a senseless pulp. What she wanted most now was a long bath to wash off the disgust she felt from being in his presence, but that had to wait. Though she had accomplished most of what she needed, there was still one more critical task. The right opportunity never came up with Noda Mi.

It was already dark. Whale-oil lamps kept the cabin illuminated. The cabin was utterly quiet save for the gentle noise of waves lapping the hull outside the porthole. The cries of distant falcons and gulls drifted through the porthole. She closed her eyes and listened intently. She thought she heard a suppressed cough. From the outside.

She opened her eyes and took a sip from her cup.

Footsteps approached. A man entered the cabin and took the seat opposite her. It was her husband Gori Ruthi, nephew of the late Imperial Tutor Zato Ruthi and a noted Moralist scholar himself. He was a rising star among the farseers of Dara under Zomi Kidosu, the Farsight Secretary.

"You heard everything?" asked Ragi.

"Very clearly," Gori said. "The voice tube between this cabin and mine did its job. I just finished the full transcription of the conversation based on my shorthand notes."

"What do you think?"

"I'm not sure the Farsight Secretary will trust him."

Lady Ragi got up and began to pace back and forth.

"Oh, I wouldn't trust him either," she said. "But there's potential here. There's more than one way to rot a tree from within."

"He hasn't given us any useful information. The Farsight Secretary is already aware that the Lyucu are working with pirates."

"Still, he did tell us something new. What do you think he meant by that cryptic reference to Dimu and Dimushi?"

The two batted the idea back and forth for a while without arriving at a consensus. They resolved to let the Farsight Secretary figure it out.

"He's worth cultivating over time," said Gori.

"I agree. I just wish we could do this faster."

Lady Ragi stopped next to the porthole. She took a deep breath. So far she had simply been playing the role the Farsight Secretary and Empress Jia had agreed on, but the next step required her to go further, to carry out the instructions of the empress to her in secret.

Though she wasn't one of the Dyran Fins, the orphaned girls who had chosen to stay by Jia's side instead of starting their own lives when they were grown, she viewed them as closer than sisters by blood. And like the Dyran Fins, she believed absolutely in Jia.

She didn't understand *why* the empress wanted her to do this, but she would do it without question.

She looked outside the porthole. "It's hard to know what's going on here in Ukyu-taasa. The Lyucu run the conquered islands like a military camp. Even fishing boats heading out to sea are escorted."

"They're terrified. The ten-year treaty will only last two more years. We've been growing stronger."

"They've not been idle either," said Lady Ragi. She kept her voice even, not too loud, but enunciating clearly. "Did you see how docile the labor gangs were? And some of the guards are our own people. The Lyucu have put down roots. When the war starts again, they'll be able to count on some of the natives, the people of Dara, to fight with them."

"That's why the Farsight Secretary is so anxious about stepping up the recruiting efforts for spies in Ukyu-taasa. We need more information. We're racing against time."

Continuing to gaze outside the porthole instead of looking at her husband, Lady Ragi said, "Don't you ever wonder if the gods played a role in all of this?"

"What do you mean?"

"The peace with the Lyucu is supposed to last ten years. But the end of the treaty will come just a few months before the reopening of the Wall of Storms, when another Lyucu fleet may arrive. It seems like the gods are playing a joke on us."

"We don't know if there will be another Lyucu fleet," said Gori, but there was little conviction in his voice.

"But the possibility cannot be ignored. The wreckage from the second Lyucu expedition must have made its way back to Ukyu, and we have to count on them figuring out Luan Zyaji's code. Besides, there are those turtle messages."

"Still, based on the Farsight Secretary's calculations, the Wall will open in the fifth month of the eleventh year of the current reign, while the treaty will end in the first month of the same year," said Gori. "We must do everything we can to resolve the Lyucu threat during that four-month window of opportunity."

"Are you ever afraid?" asked Lady Ragi. "We scheme and plot and strategize all we can, but there's no way to know how it will all turn out. The gods do love to mock our plans."

Gori got up and stood next to his wife, putting an arm around her waist to pull her close. "The ancient Ano sagas used the 'word-hungry animal' as a kenning for mankind, but I like to think that we're the 'future-hungry animal' instead. We can't help but plan for the course ahead, no matter how unpredictable the weather."

After making sure that the two occupants had truly left the cabin and the servants had cleaned away the plates, the spy outside the porthole scampered down the hull and dropped back into the water.

As he swam for the shore, his heart pounded wildly, and not just with exertion. The pékyu had been so wise to keep an eye on her hound. Not only had he discovered a plot to turn the hound against her, but he had also found out a secret that would change everything in Ukyu-taasa.

*The Wall of Storms will reopen in less than three years.*

*Another Lyucu fleet is coming.*

# CHAPTER TWENTY

# LIVING BONES

SECRET AGON BASE IN KIRI VALLEY, IN THE
FOOTHILLS OF THE WORLD'S EDGE MOUNTAINS:
THE NINTH MONTH IN THE EIGHTH YEAR AFTER
THE DEPARTURE OF PRINCESS THÉRA FROM DARA
FOR UKYU-GONDÉ.

When Théra first announced that she wanted to step back from some of her duties in managing the settlement in order to spend more time with her children, neither Takval nor the boys quite knew what to expect.

In fact, Tanto and Rokiri half expected the promise would come to nothing. As long as they could remember, their mother had always insisted on involving herself in every aspect of the settlement's administration. The boys suspected that she despised idleness even more than she hated the taste of raw mouflon sponge and kyoffir.

But throughout the summer, Théra gradually delegated more of her work away. She no longer insisted on daily reports from Nméji Gon and Tipo Tho on the training of Agon warriors in the use of Dara weapons; she stopped hounding Razutana Pon on developing strains of Dara crops better suited for the soil and climate of Kiri Valley and domesticating the wild berries and roots that Agon elders gathered; she didn't check in as often with Toof and Radia—who had been adopted into an Agon clan—and other pilots about the training of the garinafins and riders; she sent Çami Phithadapu in her stead to the interminable negotiations with shamans about adopting some written form of Agon and expanding Dara-style schooling for the children; she even skipped out on some of the meetings with Takval and his thanes as they debated potential plans for attacking Pékyu Cudyu's Taten.

"I thought you always said that if you wanted something done right, you had to do it yourself," said Takval, at once bemused and amused. "When did I suddenly become competent in your eyes?"

Théra chuckled at the gentle dig. "I suspect you're not the only one who resents my style—"

"'Resent' is probably too strong a word—" began Takval.

Théra held up a hand to stop him. "This is an alliance between two peoples, but I've been acting like I'm the only one with good ideas. I've been neglecting the lessons of my father: to listen to counsel, to let those with talent fly as high as they can. Besides, all work and no play leaves one dull and uninteresting, a terrible state of mind for a leader."

Takval stared at her. "You want to . . . play?"

"That is the point of having children, is it not?"

With the second harvest of the year complete, Théra was finally able to clear out some uninterrupted time in her schedule.

In the morning, after Théra explained to her sons that she was going to spend the whole day with them, Tanto and Rokiri did not exactly react with enthusiasm.

"Mama, do we have to do logograms today?" asked Rokiri. The fiasco with the moonbread biscuits was still in his mind. Tanto stood silently behind his little brother, looking sullen.

Théra smiled at them. "No, this isn't about me being the teacher. Why don't you show Mama how to play with arucuro tocua?"

Tanto and Rokiri looked at each other in disbelief.

"You're not going to ask us to build logograms out of bones, right?" asked Rokiri, still suspicious of their good luck.

"I promise. I won't mention logograms at all. We'll start right after breakfast."

"Why don't we ask Grandmother to come with us?" asked Tanto, giving his brother a look.

"Oh yeah! We should ask Grandmother!"

Théra sighed to herself. Her sons didn't quite believe that this day with Mama wasn't some trap to quiz them about the words of the Ano sages or drill them in logograms. Since Takval wasn't available, they wanted to bring Souliyan along as "protection." Grandmother always did what they wanted.

*Well, I do have a lot to learn,* thought Théra.

Souliyan and Théra stood on a small hill near the mouth of the valley, away from the fields and the tents. The northwesterly wind, coming from beyond the foothills, brought the fragrance of blooming scrubland flowers, ashes from lightning fires, and dust stirred up by herds of roaming mouflon and aurochs.

The two boys huddled together on the ground, preparing a surprise. Souliyan and Théra stepped to the side to chat.

"I wonder what Volyu has to say this time," said Souliyan.

There was a delegation visiting from Sliyusa Ki, and Takval had taken some warriors to go meet them outside the valley. They would return together in the evening.

"He rarely has any useful news to share," said Théra. "I suppose his messengers will ask for food again." In recent years, Volyu had gotten into the habit of coming to Kiri Valley before winter to ask for pemmican, dried berries, nuts, and other traditional staples of the Agon diet. The largesse of Takval and Théra's people allowed him to grow his reputation as a generous kyoffir-giver and enlarge his tribe, while Kiri Valley ended up having to rely even more on farmed food. It was a bit of a sore point.

Souliyan sighed, acknowledging the greedy nature of her brother. She tried to change the topic. "Takval tells me that the training of the warriors is going well."

"It is certainly going better than before," said Théra. "But he still hasn't settled on a plan."

She tried to keep her voice nonchalant, but in fact Souliyan's comment had awakened her suppressed anxieties.

In the early days of the settlement, the Dara and Agon had differed sharply on strategy. The Dara faction, led by Admiral Mitu Roso, had advocated for the settlement to focus on producing metal weapons and teaching the Agon to fight as the armies of Dara did. The idea was to launch a surprise attack as soon as possible on Taten, with the goal of surgically eliminating the fleet of Lyucu city-ships. The garinafins would function essentially as fast transports for delivering the strike force and as support platforms providing air cover. This made sense to the Dara military commanders, since the primary objective of the alliance, from their perspective, was to prevent another invasion fleet from reaching Dara.

On the other hand, the Agon faction, led by Vara Ronalek, an old thane who had long served the Aragoz clan, advocated using Dara learning to boost food production in order to support a larger population of Agon warriors freed from the demands of herding and gathering, and to enable more garinafins to be raised and trained. Metal would be used mainly to strengthen traditional Agon bone weapons in order to improve the prowess of warriors fighting in the style of the scrublands. The idea here was to launch multiple attacks not only on Taten, where Pékyu Cudyu held court, but also on the tribes of the most important garinafin-thanes of the Lyucu. The garinafin riders would then be the main attack force, with their Dara allies relegated to support roles. This made more sense to Vara and the other Agon thanes, since the primary objective of the alliance, from their perspective, was to defeat the Lyucu completely and re-establish Agon supremacy.

The Agon believed that Admiral Mitu Roso's plan would leave them open to reprisals by Cudyu and the Lyucu war thanes, while the Dara believed that Thane Vara Ronalek's plan would take too long and risked giving Cudyu another chance to invade Dara. Takval and Théra tried to find a compromise but could not, and for a while both strategies were carried out simultaneously.

Eventually, Théra came to realize that Admiral Mitu Roso's plan was simply too unrealistic. Without the support of Dara's established base of skilled smiths and mature industry, it was impossible for the small number of experts brought by Théra to equip a sizable force with Dara weapons, much less to teach the Agon to fight effectively with them. After Mitu Roso's death, Théra and Takval decided to fully embrace Vara Ronalek's plan of training a traditional Agon army with support from Dara learning.

But Théra fretted over this decision. Takval, Vara, Nméji, and Tipo couldn't agree on the best way to strike at multiple Lyucu sites, since they had only a limited number of garinafins. Breeding garinafins and training skilled crews took time. Even as the settlement grew stronger year after year, the date of the anticipated showdown with the Lyucu kept on being pushed back.

Other than Takval, nobody knew of the countdown that was ever-present in Théra's head.

The opening of the Wall of Storms was still almost three years in the future. However, since it would take a full year to sail from Ukyu-Gondé to Dara, any reinforcement invasion fleet would have to be launched in only about twenty months' time. As yet, there was no sign that the Lyucu were preparing an invasion fleet, or that they even knew of the upcoming opening of the Wall of Storms. But Théra couldn't help but worry that the longer they waited, the more likely her fears would come true.

No matter what, it was better to get to the city-ships earlier rather than later.

"My son and you will come up with a plan," said Souliyan, her voice full of conviction. She held Théra's hand for comfort. "You have the heart of an Agon, daughter."

Théra nodded without speaking. She wished she shared her mother-in-law's confidence.

"Grandma, Mama, come see this!" the two boys called.

When Souliyan and Théra approached, the boys proudly stepped aside to reveal their creation. But they stood protectively close, shielding their handiwork from the strong breeze.

Curious, Théra got down on her hands and knees to get a better look.

She had assumed that the arucuro tocua, made of bits of animal bone, shell, sinew, and other material destined for the midden, were just the Agon version of toy blocks. But the creation of Tanto and Rokiri was nothing like the dollhouses and fairy-tale cities she had built as a child.

The small skeletal assembly on the ground, about the size of a chicken back in Dara, resembled no earthly creature. It had the torso and rib cage of a bird, but instead of wings, it had a long, vertical sail on top that reminded her of the sails of ships in Dara—albeit this "sail" ran parallel to the spine of the creature instead of perpendicular to it. The sail was constructed from multiple fish spinal columns (the spines on top serving as the battens) and the shimmering wings of hundreds of slisli flies (playing the role of the canvas). Holding the torso up were six legs cobbled together from the tiny bones of sand lizards and the delicate phalanges of some animal, though the bones were interlocked into six- or seven-sided polygonal "wheels" instead of the shapes of feet or hooves. At the back end of the creature, a tail formed from a piece of mossy deer antler surrounded by a cluster of fish tail fins, like a thick-stemmed flower, provided balance. Finally, up front, at the end of a flexible neck made from sinew wrapped around a core of sheep horn, was the tiny skull of a fetal garinafin that had died before it had even hatched.

It reminded her of the fantastical creatures that she had seen at the Dandelion Court as a child, when one of the *pana méji* at a Palace Examination had put on a morality play involving monsters cobbled together from incongruous parts (a cruben-wolf, a falcon-carp, a stag-worm . . .) to criticize her father's policies. But unlike those incoherent creations, which had been deliberately made to be awkward and unwieldy, this was a beast of grace and beauty. Though it was assembled from the parts of a dozen different animals, the whole was harmonious and flowing. Though it was something that had never existed and could never exist, it felt like something that *ought* to exist.

"That's beautiful," said Théra, and there was both maternal pride and sheer awe in her voice. She stood up and took a step back to admire the skeletal animal in its grassy nest, as natural as a garinafin mother sitting on a batch of eggs.

"I wish your aunt Fara could see this," she said, a pang of longing striking her heart. "She always took such delight in works of art."

"You haven't seen anything yet," said Tanto, pleased with her reaction.

He stepped back and gestured for his brother to do the same. Now that the small skeleton was no longer shielded by their bodies, it began to shake and rattle in the strong wind.

Fearful that her sons' delicate creation would break apart, Théra moved to block it from the wind, but Souliyan grabbed her hand and held her back. She looked at the old woman questioningly, and Souliyan only smiled back.

Théra looked back at the little bone beast and gasped in delight and surprise.

The creature was moving.

It was a difficult motion to describe, halfway between the shambling walk of a big lizard or an earthbound garinafin, and the uneven, rhythmic rolling motion of a cart with imperfect wheels desperately needing the service of a wheelwright. As the creature moved forward, it climbed over loose pebbles and bent blades of blood-palm grass with an organic fluidity that was closer to living grace than clever mechanical engineering. The head bobbed at the end of the flexible neck, swinging from side to side every few steps, and the minuscule lower jaw opened and closed, as though the creature were regally trying to terrify miniature, invisible people.

Once again, Théra knelt down to get a better look.

As the wind passed over the fan-shaped wing-sail on the back of the skeleton animal, the long vane undulated sinuously as the spine rays flexed and straightened. The left-right motion of the spine-rays was amplified and transmitted by a set of elbow-shaped bones into the rib cage, where it was converted into forward-backward motion by a clever series of zigzag linkages built from phalanges. These bone cranks, in turn, pistoned against a set of lizard teeth glued to the insides of the six "wheels" that served as the feet of the creature. But unlike traditional, rigid wheels, these wheel-feet did not rotate around an axle. Instead, as the teeth were pushed forward and then popped back against the bone-pistons, the polygonal rim flexed and deformed into an angular claw, lifted off the ground, rocked forward, and settled down again. The six feet of the creature worked in coordinated fashion so that at any time, three feet located on opposite sides of the body were planted against the ground in a triangular formation, providing firm support, while the other three feet extended forward for the next stride.

The living skeleton was literally *walking* on these unearthly mechanical wheel-feet.

Other teeth and antler knobs connected to the bone-gear mechanism in the rib cage pulled on sinew cables attached to the front and back of the creature, causing it to swing the tail for balance and articulating the neck and jaws.

"Did you come up with the whole idea?" asked Théra in disbelief.

"I learned the basics from Nalu," said Tanto modestly. "He's the best at building arucuro tocua, but lots of other votan-ru-taasa and votan-sa-taasa taught me tricks. I just came up with a new variation."

"I helped too," said Rokiri. "Kunilo-*tika* put the bones together and I tied the knots 'cause I have smaller fingers."

"Are the living bones built by the other children as intricate?" asked Théra.

"Even more so," said Tanto. "Kikua knows how to build an arucuro tocua that can swim! And Nalu's arucuro tocua can tumble and do flips."

Théra was speaking in Dara while Tanto and Rokiri answered in Agon. For the time being, she didn't insist that they speak only in Dara to her. It felt natural.

Since their mother was showing such interest, the boys were excited to show Théra all the details of the arucuro tocua construction. They explained how the glue was made from red ochre mixed with the gum from the waxtongue bush; how the sinew strands needed to be oiled to maintain flexibility; how strong but flexible joints could be made by wrapping spun wool around two pieces of bone; how the polygonal wheel-feet were put together from the phalanges of a single foot or hand to take advantage of the different lengths of the bones; how the lizard teeth had to be polished and then drilled to be attached to the wheel-feet. . . .

"Where did you get these little bones?" asked Théra, pointing at the zigzag linkages in the rib cage and some of the delicate segments that formed the rims of the wheel-feet.

"These are the finger and toe bones of dead warriors," said Tanto.

"What?" Théra wasn't sure she had heard right.

"Nalu's father and the other hunters sometimes find the remains of Agon and Lyucu warriors from long ago on the scrublands—"

"You disturbed the rest of the dead? You desecrated—"

She stopped herself as she saw hurt and fright in the eyes of her sons.

Théra had known that the people of the scrublands did not bury the dead. The bodies of warriors fallen in battle were left on the battlefields, to be returned to the land itself via the maws of scavengers and predators—a process called "pédiato savaga"—and so that the wind could bear witness to their courage and carry their fame far and wide. The bodies of slaughtered slaves and captives, on the other hand, were piled together into terrifying mounds and heaps, left to rot, in order to break the spirit of the vanquished. As for chiefs and warriors who died natural deaths, the funereal custom was to wrap the body in a single cowhide and leave it in a high place in the scrublands, so that the Eye of Cudyufin could gaze upon the face of the deceased and offer them comfort as the body was given up to carrion-eating birds and the elements and the spirit ascended on the wings of a cloud-garinafin.

Though Théra, like many of the elite in Dara, honored the gods but kept them at a distance, she was steeped in Moralist reverence for the dead. The custom of the people of the scrublands was something she intellectually understood but could not emotionally accept with tranquility.

"I traded for some of these with the . . . logogram blocks," said Tanto.

"Hunters sometimes gather the bones of the deceased from the scrublands," said Souliyan. "They're often given to children as toys in the hopes that the strength of the great warriors of the past can continue to nourish and teach the young in play. It's how we honor the dead."

Théra nodded and suppressed her sense of revulsion. *I am no longer in Dara*, she had to remind herself again.

The amount of engineering cleverness in her sons' toy construction astounded Théra. She was sure that if Zomi were around, she would spend three whole days and three whole nights taking it apart and putting it back together just to see how it worked. The way the arucuro tocua creature took advantage of the natural materials— bone, sinew, antler, insect wings, teeth, hair, fur—was similar to the way Dara engineering took advantage of materials available in the Islands—bamboo, silk, metal, wood, paper, glass; and yet, there was a distinct flavor to the way this creature was conceived and built. The way the Agon children made something living out of the remains of the dead was at once alien to her Moralist sensibilities, but also fascinating.

"And look, Mama," said Rokiri, pointing at one of the zigzag links in the rib cage of the beast, "did you notice that's not a bone at all?"

Théra, still recovering from the shock of being presented with such a sophisticated piece of machinery based on the play of Agon children—why hadn't she seen anything like this among the Agon thanes and warriors?—looked where Rokiri was pointing.

"Is that—"

"Yes," said Rokiri. "Kunilo-*tika* wasn't able to get a bone of the right size and shape, so he took the logogram blocks for 'arm' and 'leg' and used those instead."

Théra looked closer and saw that the logogram pieces had been carefully painted to blend in with the rest of the bones, but they remained unmistakably Ano logograms.

"Nalu made fun of us for using the logogram pieces, but Kunilo-*tika* said the logograms made our beasts special," said Rokiri. "They made them *ours*."

"Oh my baby," said Théra.

Tanto turned his head away so that she would not see the tears spilling from his eyes.

Théra pulled Tanto into a fierce hug. The boy stiffened. After a few moments, Tanto relaxed and hugged her back.

Volyu had chosen to make this trip to Kiri Valley personally. It would be the first time he had been to Kiri Valley since the establishment of the secret base seven years ago.

Instead of an elaborate welcome reception, Takval asked Vara

Ronalek, his trusted second-in-command, to entertain the naros brought by Volyu as his escorts in the long tent that served as the settlement's meeting hall. He and Théra, he explained, would host a private dinner in their home tent for his uncle.

Vara quirked a brow inquiringly.

"How would Afir greet Kikisavo, if he should return from exile?" he asked her.

Vara nodded in understanding. There had been a breach between uncle and nephew, and Takval now claimed the title of Pékyu of the Agon, even though on the scrublands, everyone knew Volyu as the Pé-Afir-tekten. There was no possible way to host a public reception without highlighting the awkwardness.

Takval now sat across the low Dara-style square table from Volyu, with Théra and Souliyan between them at the other two sides. Though the garinafin-hide tent was pitched in the traditional Agon style, much of the furnishing inside was Dara: wooden tables, porcelain washbasins, hanging silk tapestries, knife-and-wax writing sets, and so on. Though everything was patched and worn, Théra had been unwilling to throw anything out.

"Look at you, living in luxury here," said Volyu, admiring the small bronze knife in his hand. He used it to cut a slice of roast beef, flavored only with salt and tolyusa juice, and chewed it noisily. "I doubt even Pékyu Cudyu could claim to own more than a dozen metal knives."

Takval and Théra looked at each other and smiled wryly. Most of the metal objects brought by her expedition had long since been melted down to be refashioned into reinforcement bands for bone clubs or edges for war axes. The small knife in Volyu's hand was in fact Théra's writing knife, kept mostly out of sentiment, as it had been a gift from Master Zato Ruthi.

"I hear you're not doing too bad yourself, brother," said Souliyan. "Your guards tell me that you've taken two more wives—very pretty girls of eighteen. How many wives do you have now? Eight? Ten?"

"The Aragoz clan must multiply and grow to keep alive the dream of our ancestors. The weight of such responsibility weighs heavy on my shoulders, but I dare not set down the load even at my age," said Volyu, his face scrunched up as though speaking of some arduous chore.

"I can imagine how hard you've been working," said Souliyan, "especially with that gut."

Théra stifled a laugh. Volyu pretended not to hear. Volyu *had* become more flabby and *limp* since the last time they'd seen him.

Done with the roast beef, Volyu picked up a moonbread biscuit. After examining it skeptically, he bit into it. "What's in here?" He chewed slowly and his eyes gradually lit up. "Mouflon sponge? . . . Tiger-eye berries and noddinghead nuts? And something else . . ."

"You're probably tasting ice melons," said Théra. "They're from Dara."

"Who knew you could flavor mouflon sponge this way!" exclaimed Volyu. "And wrapped inside this . . . plant hide?"

"It's flatbread," said Théra, not bothering with explaining the Dara word. "I'm glad you're enjoying it."

"It tastes heavenly."

"Uncle, you should know Théra made these moonbread biscuits personally."

Théra waved her hand dismissively. "It's nothing. Commander Tipo Tho should get most of the credit, along with Thoryo, for coming up with the recipe."

Tipo Tho, always pining for the tastes of her home back in Wolf's Paw, had tried for years to find native substitutes for the herbs and fruits of Dara—it helped that Nméji Gon, her husband, was willing to finish the results of her experiments, even when they didn't turn out very palatable. In the process of sampling native plants and learning from Agon cooks, she had become a proficient chef in the style of the scrublands as well.

At first, Tipo Tho had kept the styles of cooking distinct, thinking that it was best to retain the authenticity of each cuisine. But Thoryo, always unconstrained by ideas of what was proper, kept on suggesting that she create some dishes that blended the gustatory practices of the Islands and the scrublands.

"Aren't you curious to create tastes that have never been sampled by any mortal?" she had asked. "The world is so interesting. Why should we deny our senses the pleasures that come from mixing the beautiful with the beautiful?"

In fact, Tipo realized, she had already deviated from strict adherence to the recipes and practices she had learned from her parents. Without access to many Dara ingredients, she had already become used to native substitutes—e.g., using roasted gash cactus beetles in place of pickled caterpillars or swapping monkeyberries for piquant tolyusa zest. And since the two harvests of Kiri Valley made a single High-Autumn Festival impractical, she had been making moonbread all through the summer. Why not push the experiments further and do more than mere substitution?

Unable to resist her own curiosity, Tipo experimented with mixing cooking styles. She discovered that a compote of tart tiger-eye berries and ice melons, mixed with ground mouflon sponge lightly seared after the fashion of the scrublands, made an unorthodox yet delicious filling for moonbread biscuits. The recipe was eagerly taken up by the other Dara families. Théra was gratified to see that these novel moonbread biscuits were a much bigger hit with her boys, and they even fought over the baked-clay Ano logograms she buried in the filling, which could be won as additional components for arucuro tocua if the boys recognized the logograms.

Volyu examined Théra, his eyes glinting strangely. "You're a lucky man, Takval," he said, a hint of kyoffir-fever in his voice. "You eat with iron knives and porcelain dishes; you sleep on silk blankets; you have a wife who pleases you . . . with exotic fare. To think she and I almost—"

"That's enough," said Souliyan. "Don't embarrass yourself."

Théra flushed at the lecherous expression on Volyu's face, and she shifted uncomfortably away from him. She was about to make a cutting remark when she felt Takval placing a hand over hers. She looked at him, and he shook his head almost imperceptibly. For the sake of the alliance, Théra tamped down her anger.

"Perhaps enough kyoffir has been drunk for the night," she said, her voice cold but pleasant. "Why don't you tell us why you've come to visit, uncle?"

Continuing to stare at her, Volyu waited a beat, and then, as though aroused from a daydream, his face changed back to a mask of indifference. "Winter is coming, dearest niece. As the Pé-Afir-tekten, I have to think of the welfare of my people."

*Here it comes*, thought Théra. "Whatever you need, we will do our best to help. But we can't let you have too much of the meat and leave us only grain. We can only hunt occasionally to avoid the risk of discovery. However, we can give you plenty of sorghum and rice, and I can teach you how to cook with them to make 'plant hide'—"

As Théra spoke, Volyu shook his head with increasing vigor. "No, no! Dear niece, that won't do. Don't pretend to me you're weak. I've seen the strength of your warriors."

Upon arrival in Kiri Valley, Takval had taken Volyu on a tour of the settlement. Volyu had been especially impressed by the garin-afin riders and warriors who wielded weapons improved by Dara smiths: clubs strengthened with metal bands and studded with iron nails instead of teeth; axes with steel blades; slingshots with winches and triggers derived from Dara crossbows. . . . He also exclaimed over some of the more experimental weapons prepared by the Dara artisans: skin kites painted with tusked-tiger images to frighten the garinafins; iron-tipped caltrops to block fire-breathing jaws; pow-erful slingshots mounted on the antlers of the garinafins to launch exploding firework-powder bombs meant to go into the gullets of Lyucu garinafins. . . .

He had asked Takval many questions concerning the number of warriors and garinafins under his command, whistling apprecia-tively; he even tested one of the improved war clubs himself to see how it shattered unreinforced bone helmets.

"We're strong," said Takval. "But we must grow even stronger before we can challenge the Lyucu."

"Perhaps I can help you there," said Volyu. "Give me half of your warriors. Allow me to shoulder half the weight of the task you now bear up alone, and we can get to where we need to be twice as fast."

Souliyan, Takval, and Théra exchanged quick looks. This was unexpected.

"Aren't you worried that Cudyu will discover your rebellious intentions?" asked Souliyan.

"That was before I saw just how powerful Takval had grown," said Volyu. "It's time to attack."

Théra and Takval locked eyes, and both nodded in mutual understanding. Volyu had decided to come personally to evaluate Takval's preparations without the filter of messengers. What he had seen had apparently impressed him enough that he wanted a bigger share of the glory of a successful rebellion.

"Uncle, this isn't quite the time to divide my warriors," said Takval. He couldn't outright refuse Volyu, since they still needed his help as a spy against the Lyucu. "The garinafin riders and foot soldiers alike have to drill with the new weapons, and the Dara artisans and advisers must continue to refine our plans. Most important, we have to continue to recruit. Until we have enough warriors to attack all the top Lyucu thanes and Pékyu Cudyu at the same time, we can't risk revealing ourselves."

Volyu looked at Takval, and the muscles on his face twitched as though he was struggling with some difficult decision. Finally, he said, "What if I told you there is a way to get all the Lyucu war thanes at once, with the warriors and Dara fighters you already have?"

"Explain," said Takval and Théra together. They didn't even bother disguising the excitement in their voices.

"It has been five years since Cudyu formally took the title of pékyu. . . ."

For several years after Pékyu Tenryo and Tanvanaki left Ukyu-Gondé, Cudyu retained the title of pékyu-taasa while he ruled as the de facto supreme lord of the scrublands. But eventually, he felt sufficiently certain that his father and sister would never return and took the title of Pékyu of the Lyucu. To celebrate the occasion of the fifth year of his reign as full pékyu, he had called upon all the garinafin-thanes, tiger-thanes, and wolf-thanes to leave their winter territories and gather at Aluro's Basin on Winter Solstice to honor the gods. Thereafter, the thanes would go to Taten for more sacrifices, bearing gifts and tribute exacted from the Agon tribes living under each Lyucu thane's watch. As the nominal leader of the Agon in submission, Volyu had come to Kiri Valley, in part, to obtain more goods to offer as tribute to Cudyu.

"But that was the plan before I saw just what you've done," said Volyu, his voiced filled with admiration. "I've spoken of biding our time, but the time has finally arrived."

Théra's heart pounded. She saw what Volyu meant. Each thane attending this celebration at Aluro's Basin would bring only a few warriors with them, not their entire army, which meant that all the senior Lyucu leaders would be congregated in one place with only Cudyu's forces to guard them.

"Aluro's Basin was where Tenryo began his rise," said Volyu. "It's almost too perfect that it will also be where his son falls."

"No!" said Théra. "We should target Taten!"

Volyu looked at her oddly.

"But in Taten we'd have to face the entirety of Cudyu's force of garinafin riders," Volyu said. "At Aluro's Basin there would be many fewer warriors. Besides, Aluro's Basin is closer to Kiri Valley. Why wait when you'll be ready by Winter Solstice?"

Takval nodded, agreeing with his uncle.

Théra forced herself to calm down. "You're not wrong . . . but the advantages of attacking Taten outweigh the drawbacks. The thanes, intent on impressing Cudyu, will be alert and on guard when they first arrive at Aluro's Basin. By the time they get back to Taten, however, they'll be relaxed from the earlier celebration. No doubt they'll also be competing in Taten to see whose gifts and tribute to Cudyu are the most lavish, vying for his favor. The political jostling will make their security even more lax, especially since every thane will already think themselves safe in Cudyu's home territory. *That* makes Taten a far better strike site than Aluro's Basin. And the extra time will give us more time to prepare, which is never a bad thing."

Volyu nodded, reluctantly accepting Théra's analysis.

Théra sighed in relief. What she had said was reasonable, but it wasn't the entire truth. She had picked Taten over Aluro's Basin because Taten was near the anchorage of the city-ships. A single deadly strike with a small force could wipe out the Lyucu leadership *and* capture the city-ships, achieving the objectives of the Agon and

Dara factions of the alliance at once. On the other hand, an attack on the Lyucu at Aluro's Basin would leave the city-ships intact, and Théra worried that remnants of the Lyucu or even an ambitious Agon thane could seize the city-ships, leading to further trouble down the line. True, attacking Taten *was* more risky than Aluro's Basin, but she believed that the additional hazard was worth it.

In Théra's mind, it was as if the intricate pieces of a puzzle had finally fallen into place to make a coordinated whole. All the disparate interests and goals of the Agon and the people of Dara had interlocked into one living, breathing, mechanical bone beast.

The excited look on Takval's face assured her that he agreed with her plan.

But Souliyan broke in. "This doesn't feel right."

"Why?" asked Théra.

"To attack the Lyucu at a gathering where they are honoring the gods . . ." Souliyan's eyes seemed to be focused somewhere in the indefinite distance. "I'm afraid it will draw divine anger. Besides, our preparations are inadequate."

Théra, who had an intellectual respect for the gods of Ukyu-Gondé but little instinctual piety, grew concerned. It was one thing when she didn't realize there was an opportunity to achieve victory with a single blow, but now that the opportunity had been dangled in front of her by Volyu, she couldn't help but lunge at it. "Surely the gods will be pleased by our boldness and cunning. That is the law of the scrublands—"

"I was not aware that you've become a shaman," said Souliyan, her voice uncharacteristically cold. "You now speak for our gods?"

Théra was taken aback, but luckily, Takval came to her rescue. "Mother, Théra meant no disrespect. She may not speak for our gods, but the shamans have always taught us that the gods don't like to hold our hands as though we're yearlings. Afir and Kikisavo also acted boldly when opportunity presented itself, and the gods rewarded them for it."

"You think you're the equal of Afir and Kikisavo now?"

"No," said Takval. "But Afir and Kikisavo weren't certain of success before they set out into the wilderness either."

"We have been protected by the gods . . ." Souliyan said, her voice fading.

Théra now suspected that she knew what was really behind Souliyan's hesitation. The older woman had a pacifistic streak in her. She had told Théra once that her dream was to find a refuge away from the Lyucu, to live in peace, outside the cycles of vengeance and reprisals. Kiri Valley probably seemed to her just such a haven, and she didn't want to give it up.

"Mother," Théra said, trying to keep her voice kind but not yielding, "we cannot hide forever. You know this. I've never lied to you about what the goal is."

Souliyan looked from Théra to Takval and back to Théra again. At length, she sighed. "My heart is heavy with doubt, but I am not the pékyu nor the Princess of Dara."

"You're just worried about your son, like any mother," said Volyu, waving a hand dismissively. "But he and his wife both understand that the clever wolf must not hesitate when the herdsman presents his throat." He turned back to Takval. "Give me half of your forces, and combined with my warriors, we will finally reclaim the glory of your grandfather."

Théra understood that Volyu wasn't offering this out of some sudden bout of courage or pride. He saw the rebellion as certain to succeed, and he wanted to share in the spoils. Indeed, if Takval gave in, she was certain that Volyu would plot some way to challenge Takval afterward in the hopes of becoming pékyu himself.

She was about to warn Takval unobtrusively, but Takval was already shaking his head slowly.

"Why?" demanded Volyu. "Don't tell me your mother has infected you with fear. You'll never have an opportunity like this again."

"You misunderstand me, uncle. We *will* take this opportunity to attack, but you cannot take command of half the forces. Pékyu Cudyu would no doubt want your presence at this celebration as a representative of the vanquished Agon."

Théra saw instantly that Takval was right. If Volyu didn't show up at the banquet, it would arouse Cudyu's suspicion and put the rebellion at risk.

"Therefore you have to attend the banquet as though nothing out of the ordinary is going on," said Takval.

"In fact, once you're at Taten, you can tell us how Cudyu's defenses are deployed," said Souliyan.

"It would really be the greatest contribution you can make, uncle," said Théra. "Far greater than leading half of Takval's forces."

Théra and Takval exchanged another quick look, and Théra smiled inside. She was glad that her husband was thinking much along the same lines as herself. No longer was he the impulsive warrior who jumped to sacrifice as the first solution to every problem. He had learned to anticipate, to plot, to not trust the untrustworthy.

"You're asking me to assume a great deal of risk," said Volyu, his eyes hard and his voice rasping.

"If you risk nothing, how can we trust you?" asked Théra, her voice equally hard. "If you don't commit, you'll have no claim to the spoils. When the Lyucu are overthrown, you'll have nothing."

"But I *have* taken risks! I've kept your secret! I've sheltered—"

"We will do everything in our power to rescue you before the attack," said Takval.

"And your contribution will not be forgotten," said Théra, softening her own voice. Volyu was concerned above all with what he himself would lose and gain, and she needed to offer him honey along with the threatening stick. "Takval and I will honor you and consult you on every decision."

"Once the Lyucu are overthrown, your uncle will be the pékyu-votan," said Souliyan. She looked at Takval. After a moment of hesitation, Takval nodded.

Pékyu-votan was the title given to the predecessor of the current pékyu. Since the pékyus of the scrublands rarely left their posts until their deaths, it was rare to have a living pékyu-votan, though certainly not unprecedented. Théra reflected on Souliyan's suggestion and approved of its cleverness. On the one hand, Volyu's vanity should be satisfied with such a prize, as it would make him nominally senior to Takval himself. At the same time, Volyu would be deprived of any real power, since he wouldn't command the loyalty of any of Takval's warriors.

He would, in fact, be nothing more than a figurehead, a pile of living bones, a relic of a bygone age when the Agon survived by cowering under Lyucu abuse.

Evidently, Volyu understood the reality of what he was being offered. "I have brought you the information that will help you achieve victory!" he pleaded. "I think I deserve more than that."

"You've had plenty of chances in the past, brother," said Souliyan. "Takval is the one who spent years building up this base with Théra, plotting patiently for an opportunity to present itself. You can't expect to sweep in at the last minute and take away what is his and his alone."

"I thought you didn't even approve of this plan," sneered Volyu. "But now you're already trying to make sure your son gets more credit for *my* plan?"

"I remain doubtful of this plan," said Souliyan. "But I know the gods will be more pleased with Takval's piety than with yours."

Before Volyu could retort, Takval broke in. "Work with me, uncle. Let's for once act as one family and achieve the dream that breathes inside the chest of every Agon. That, I should think, would be the greatest reward of all."

Volyu looked at the three of them and sighed. "How I regret now not having gone along with you when you first arrived in Sliyusa Ki. . . ." His gaze was distant, as though imagining a vision of himself as Pékyu of the Agon, with Théra and Takval as his loyal thanes. It was an alternate future that would never be.

Despite herself, Théra felt sympathy for the old man. He was greedy and selfish, and had sacrificed the lives of those braver than himself to keep himself safe as a servant of the Lyucu. Yet, he had also kept many of the Agon alive through some of the worst periods in Tenryo's rule, and he had been of some help to her and Takval.

"I swear to all the gods of Dara and Gondé," said Théra, "that I will let all bygones be bygones, and honor you as the pékyu-votan, if you go to Taten and help us win. I know the spirit of Afir moves through you still. You once let a chance for redemption pass you by. Seize this one."

Takval poured kyoffir into two skull bowls and pushed one in front of Volyu.

"May the only blood that spills from now on be the blood of our common enemy," he said, and drained the kyoffir in a single long gulp. He showed the empty skull to his uncle.

For a long silent moment, Volyu sat there, looking back at his nephew. Complicated emotions seemed to war on his face: doubt, jealousy, fear, anger, yearning. In the end, a look of determination prevailed. "There always comes a time for the old to yield to the young." He finished the kyoffir and showed the empty skull to Théra, Takval, and Souliyan in turn.

They sat together, eating, drinking, and plotting the downfall of the Lyucu until the sun had risen again.

## CHAPTER TWENTY-ONE

# CALCULATIONS

THE RORO HILLS NORTH OF KRIPHI: THE NINTH
MONTH IN THE EIGHTH YEAR OF THE REIGN OF
AUDACIOUS FREEDOM (KNOWN AS THE EIGHTH
YEAR OF THE REIGN OF SEASON OF STORMS IN
DARA, AND THE EIGHTH YEAR SINCE PRINCESS
THÉRA DEPARTED DARA FOR UKYU-GONDÉ).

"You're absolutely certain?" asked Tanvanaki, pronouncing the Dara words dispassionately.

Nonetheless, the Dara man kneeling before her, his forehead pressed to the ground, shook like a leaf trembling in autumn. For the first time in many months, he had been allowed clothing—not so much for his own benefit, but because Tanvanaki didn't want to see the crisscrossing scars over his back and chest, evidence of what had been necessary to implant some sense of loyalty in him.

"I've ch-checked the cal-calculations many times, votan," he said.

"Show them to me," she said.

With an effort, he crawled forward and placed a scroll on the ground at her feet before crawling backward into his place. He was on his hands and knees not only out of fear, but also necessity. His last escape attempt had resulted in Tanvanaki ordering the severing of the sinews in his lower legs, hobbling him permanently.

Tanvanaki picked up the scroll and unrolled it, reading through the columns of figures carefully. She was no great mathematician, but she could follow the derivation just fine, especially since she had worked through these steps herself many times in the years she had been in Ukyu-taasa.

"So the Wall of Storms will open in just over two and a half years?" she asked.

The man lifted his head from the floor to nod, but not high enough to look into her eyes. Then he placed his forehead back on the ground again.

*Is he afraid to look at me because he's terrified I will hurt him again or because he doesn't want me to see the hatred in his eyes?* Tanvanaki wondered. She decided it didn't matter.

"Good," she said. "I already knew the answer, but it's good to have you demonstrate your loyalty."

The man visibly relaxed.

"But why didn't you discover this earlier?" she asked.

He began to shake again. Tanvanaki turned her face away, revolted. To think this man had once been a *cashima*, a scholar who arrogantly wrote essays on the best policies for the Dandelion Throne, as though he was some kind of sage who only lacked recognition for his talents! Though she was the one who had reduced him to this groveling state, barely more than a dog begging for scraps, she hated to see a scholar so debased. The reverence for learning, seeded in her by Oga Kidosu and Luan Zya, was a childhood ideal that refused to detach from her wintry heart.

"This lowly slave is sorry, votan! Luan Zya's talents far ex-exceed mine." He was careful to avoid calling Luan "master" or using the -ji suffix with his name, as was commonly done among the core islands. "This . . . this . . . this foolish Dara-raaki couldn't detect the de-deception until you suggested there was possibly a code. This idiot tried—" The smell of urine suddenly filled the tent.

"Shut up!" growled Tanvanaki, disgusted with the abject pleas. She understood, of course, that it was far easier to crack a code once you knew there *was* a code. For years, Luan Zya's old calculations had simply been assumed to be a deception. No one thought to try to approach them as a coded message.

She strode to the entrance of the tent and summoned her guards. "Take him away. Bathe him and give him plenty of water and food."

*That brain needs to be saved.*

The Battle of Zathin Gulf had confirmed for Tanvanaki that the knowledge and skills of the people of Dara posed the greatest threat to the long-term success of the Lyucu. To truly rule Dara, the Lyucu had to achieve parity with the natives in mechanical proficiency.

However, though the Lyucu had made halfhearted attempts to study and acquire Dara engineering skills since the days of Tenryo's first encounter with Mapidéré's fleet, these efforts had never amounted to much. The mechanical tradition of a people was a language, with its own idioms and grammar and syntax and morphology and phonetics. Rooted in a people's culture and history, it could not be adopted wholesale by another without a dedicated and sustained effort at adaptation, translation, imitation, fusion, and ultimately, inspired innovation. Like the process of learning any language, it required fundamental changes in habits of the mind, in way of life, in the story a people told themselves about who they were— changes that Tenryo and his thanes could not tolerate. The Lyucu artisans could no more become skilled inventors merely by learning how to maintain the city-ships than Lyucu warriors could pick up bows and instantly become skilled archers.

Tanvanaki had neither the time nor the freedom to nurture and develop Lyucu engineering into a true competitor against Dara mechanics, not when Ukyu-taasa's position was so precarious. She had to settle for the next best thing: borrowing brains instead of growing them. This prison camp among the Roro Hills had been set up by her in secret as a place to corral talented individuals captured from the core islands of Dara, to force them to serve the Lyucu. But the plan had met with little success, since Noda's pirate partners seemed to bring her mostly useless scholars of philosophy. She had been lucky to at least get this *cashima* who knew mathematics.

After the guards dragged the terrified Dara scholar away, Tanvanaki paced in the tent, trying to sort out the skein of tangled thoughts in her mind.

The mysterious messages on the backs of the turtles that had been captured years ago now finally made sense. She had not dared to trust the information her nameless spy brought her until now, after she had received independent confirmation. Her brother must have deciphered Luan Zya's code long before her, and sent the turtles to let her know to expect a reinforcement fleet.

She had been planning for the long term, to somehow find a way to coexist with the natives even after the expiration of the peace treaty, but it was obvious now that she had to rethink those plans. How would Cutanrovo and her hard-liners react once they knew that more Lyucu city-ships were coming? How could she possibly convince them to let Timu's policy of accommodation with the natives continue? She'd better make sure that news of the expected opening of the Wall of Storms remained a secret.

The extent of Luan Zya's betrayal didn't surprise her. She had always had a talent for seeing through the perspective of another. For some people of Dara, no matter how kindly or harshly they were treated, their nature compelled them to put the interests of their own people before the interests of the Lyucu. That was true of Oga Kidosu, her first teacher, and also of Luan Zya, her second. But she could hardly blame them. Indeed, she admired their fortitude and resourcefulness. Were she in their position, she only hoped that she would show the same strength of character.

*Stop it. I cannot let this admiration develop into a weakness. They are the enemy. They are not Lyucu.*

Tanvanaki rubbed her forehead, exhausted. Her father, in so many ways, had had the easier task. To conquer the bodies of the people of Dara required guile and courage, but to conquer their hearts . . . that was a problem that she had been banging her head against for years without solution.

The nameless spy, whose report had brought her down to this secluded prison in the hills north of Kriphi, entered the tent quietly.

"I've confirmed your report," she said, relaxing into the speech of Lyucu. There was no need to praise him. "It's good that you stayed after Noda Mi left the Dara ship."

"Shall I eliminate him?" he asked.

She shook her head. "No. I already know Noda can't be trusted. But a man like that remains useful. Let Jia and the rest of the Dara-raaki think they have successfully planted a spy."

He nodded and said nothing more.

Tanvanaki didn't bother explaining to him her reasons. He was a tool, utterly devoted to her, and tools didn't need to be given explanations. "Contact the pirates and inform them that I want them to focus on the area around Ginpen."

"The same ones contacted by Noda?"

"No," said Tanvanaki, after a moment of hesitation. "Let the ones Noda dealt with continue as before."

*Misdirection can be useful.*

"But impress upon the pirates that they need to get me useful people: engineers, mechanics, smiths, artisans who know how to invent machines. They won't always know how to find such people, but they should know how to find partners who will."

The nameless spy nodded and silently left the tent.

MEANWHILE, IN PAN.

In the Inner Council Chamber, Zomi Kidosu and Empress Jia pored over the reports from Lady Ragi and Gori Ruthi.

"What do you find most interesting?" asked Jia.

Zomi pondered the question for a moment before answering. "Tanvanaki has been fairly effective in her attempts at pacifying the local population. Based on the stories Noda Mi told Ragi near the end of their conversation, the Lyucu have been cultivating the native elite, letting them share in some of the benefits of the conquest. I'm impressed at how much Ragi was able to learn."

Jia nodded. "Ragi is good at getting her targets to open up without asking questions that are too obvious."

"It would seem that the wealthy and the privileged in Rui and Dasu are content with the Lyucu, though the poor are treated far more harshly. Perhaps there are fewer massacres of the civilian population, but the price is a more secure enslavement achieved through collaboration and voluntary surveillance by the native gentry."

"It's the only way," said Jia. "Since the Lyucu conquering army is so small, they have to co-opt the local elites into helping them control the rest of the population. By tolerating a certain amount of corruption and granting useful fools like Noda privileges, Tanvanaki not only buys their loyalty, but also drives a wedge between them and the peasantry."

Left unsaid between the two was the fact that some of the policies, especially those granting additional privileges to native officials and scholars, had probably been suggested by Timu. Acting out of a misguided belief that it was possible to gradually change the Lyucu through exposure to Moralist philosophy, the puppet emperor had unwittingly been helping the conquerors secure their rule in Unredeemed Dara.

"There is some latent resentment," said Zomi. "Even with all their entitlements, the local elites are subservient to the Lyucu. Noda certainly seems to want more."

"People like Noda are never satisfied," said Jia. "But that isn't something Tanvanaki needs to worry about much. Since people in Noda's class now depend on the Lyucu for their advantages, they will fight for the Lyucu against us, knowing that they're hated by the peasants and will be executed as traitors if the Lyucu lose."

"Then we can't trust anything Noda tells us, including this vague hint about Dimu and Dimushi."

"To the contrary," said the empress, "I think we can believe him on that point."

"Why?" asked Zomi in confusion.

"Noda is an Incentivist's dream come true, being moved by nothing except his own interests," said Jia, a cold smirk curling up the corners of her mouth. "This also makes him easy to understand. What do you think is behind the piracy raids?"

Zomi looked thoughtful. "They've increased in frequency this past year, and as I noted in my last report to you, there have been multiple instances of kidnapped passengers with no demand for ransom. . . . The pirates must be going beyond just raiding goods for smuggling, but also selling the abducted men and women to the Lyucu."

"And why would Tanvanaki be interested in people?"

"That's not . . . clear. The people being abducted so far don't seem to share much in common except the misfortune of being on the wrong ships, though survivors of the raids did mention that the pirates demanded to know if they knew how to read. . . ." Her eyes narrowed. "The Lyucu are trying to raid for information?"

Jia nodded. "I believe Tanvanaki is kidnapping people for their minds."

"Despicable," spat Zomi. "This is an act of war!"

"She can plausibly deny any involvement by going through the pirates as intermediaries," said Jia.

"But even if she succeeded in abducting some skilled workers, they would certainly follow the example of Luan Zyaji and never collaborate with the Lyucu!"

"Don't be so sure of that," said Jia. "As the Incentivists are always so quick to point out, there are ways to compel anyone's obedience, whether through the lure of rewards or the threat of pain. The scholars who remain in Rui and Dasu are proof of that."

Zomi was silent. She knew that the empress was right. Even her own teacher, the great Luan Zyaji, had been forced to lead the invasion force back to Dara, though he had done so to save others from torture, not himself. And Luan had gotten his revenge after death.

"The interest in acquiring people, incidentally, also explains why Noda Mi leaked the news to us," said Jia. "He measures everyone else by his own heart, which is jealous, insecure, and obsessed with status. For him, concepts such as faith and loyalty are meaningless. He is worried that at least some of the people abducted from Dara will in fact collaborate with Tanvanaki to advance themselves. And since Tanvanaki prizes their information so much more than his own, he fears his own status will be threatened. That is why he hinted to us the truth, hoping we would thwart his master's plan."

Zomi shook her head in wonder. Often, she felt inadequate to the task of being the Farsight Secretary because it was difficult for her to bend her own mind to follow the malevolent patterns exhibited by someone like Noda Mi. A new question arose in her mind. "Something still doesn't fit. . . . The kind of information most valuable to the Lyucu is our military plans. But if that's what they're after, they ought to focus on naval bases and vessels instead of merchantmen."

"Never underestimate our opponent," chided Jia. "First, having pirates attack the navy would never work. Second, what makes you so certain Tanvanaki is after military intelligence? You're the Farsight Secretary, you must see further."

"All right," said Zomi. She closed her eyes as she concentrated on what she knew. "If they're not interested in current military intelligence, they must be planning for the long term. . . . Information that they don't have and that will help over the long term . . ." Her eyes snapped open. "They must be after knowledge of the mechanical arts, especially weapons and war machinery. Now that they've secured their rule in Rui and Dasu, they intend to upgrade the capability of their forces to overcome our technical advantage—the cause of their defeat last time."

Jia nodded approvingly. "The best minds of Rui and Dasu were decimated during the Lyucu conquest, and they lack skilled engineers and mechanics. With better knowledge of engineering, they can find weaknesses in our systems and construct counters. Just as we're acquiring expertise in garinafin warfare, they want expertise in the foundation of the Dara way of war. Indeed, I fear Tanvanaki may be thinking even further than that. Acquiring expertise by abducting engineers is likely only the first step, with the ultimate goal of developing such expertise themselves."

Zomi shuddered, thinking of how much more terrifying the Lyucu could be, with a docile enslaved population to provide support and their warriors' capabilities amplified with silkmotic lances, mechanical crubens, firework powder, and other Dara inventions. Tanvanaki truly was a master warlord to be reckoned with. "I'll increase the naval patrols in Amu Strait, and warn skilled artisans and inventors in Dimushi and Dimu to travel by land whenever possible. I'll also enhance the security around all our research laboratories and academies, just in case any Lyucu spies sneak through."

"As always, Zomi, our people are our most important resource. Their protection must be our highest priority. If the Lyucu gain advanced knowledge of Dara engineering, not only will the men and women abducted suffer, but many more will die in a future Lyucu invasion. I know you and Phyro often wish I took a more hard-line position against the Lyucu; well, here it is: We must not allow them to kidnap even one person."

Zomi nodded solemnly. "If only there were a way to disrupt Tanvanaki's plans . . . to destabilize the Lyucu rule . . ."

"We can only play the game with the pieces already on the board." Jia's face was impassive. "You may go now."

Everybody understood that in the Palace Garden, the shed that looked like an old Cocru medicine shop and the gardens and hothouses surrounding it, hidden behind a dense hedge, were forbidden grounds. Years ago, Rin Coda, Emperor Ragin's childhood friend and later Farsight Secretary, sometimes snuck in here to steal herbs that yielded waking dreams and joyous mirages. But since then, security had been tightened, and no courtier, servant, maid, or lady-in-waiting was allowed inside the hedge fence. The Dyran Fins patrolled it day and night, ensuring that only Empress Jia could access it.

It was her refuge, where she could be sure to be alone with her thoughts.

A thick mask covering her nose and mouth, Jia labored among the medicine drawers, stone mortars and jade pestles, copper scales, silver knives and hammers, blood-drawing needles, bronze braziers, bunches of hanging herbs and bowls of crushed powders, and all the other accoutrements of an expert herbalist.

She stood in front of a small cauldron, bubbling over a low fire on the workbench. The fumes from the boiling decoction were acrid, as though something was burning. A silk hood over the workbench confined the fumes, and a set of bellows powered by a windmill on the roof kept the air circulating, directing the effluvium under the hood outside through a set of pipes.

She stirred the cauldron from time to time, careful to keep her face out of the fumes. The goal was to take the most volatile components, responsible for the strong smell (and taste), out of the boiling substance, but to leave the potency of the decoction largely unaffected.

Her experiments required discretion, demanded subtlety.

Some distance from the boiling cauldron was a small cage, in which crouched a white rabbit. Though there was plenty of fresh grass and water in the cage, the rabbit paid no attention to them. Instead, its nose twitched as its eyes focused on the boiling cauldron, and its paws scrabbled at the bars of the cage, as though wishing to jump into the cauldron and bask in the pungent fumes.

Jia glanced at the rabbit dispassionately. Pausing to make a few notes on a sheet of paper, she resumed stirring.

Long ago, as a young girl, when she had studied under some of the best herbalists in Faça, her teachers had impressed upon her the importance of the ancient canons governing herbalists: everything is both a medicine and a poison; that which takes away pain, when improperly used, can cause the greater pain of emptiness; an herbalist must strive to heal, not to harm.

She wondered how her teachers would react now if they understood what she was doing. She imagined the arguments she would make.

*It's not harm if I'm simply giving them what they want.*

*I'm merely encouraging tendencies already deeply rooted in the heart.*

*To fight evil with evil is no evil.*

*I am no warrior; therefore I must fight with blades of grass.*

Oh, she could come up with excuses and rationalizations like any *cashima* caught cheating at the Grand Examination. But she knew she was breaking the canons, the accumulated wisdom of her teachers and their teachers before them.

A high-pitched scream, like that of a terrified child. Jia shuddered and dropped the spoon she was using to stir. She looked over at the cage whence the scream had come.

Blood coated the bars of the cage. The rabbit had bitten its front feet to the bone, and blood spilled from its mouth as it continued to scratch and bite at the bars of the cage, seemingly oblivious to pain. Its eyes were locked on the cauldron. The food and water remained untouched, though the water dish was a dark crimson. The high-pitched cries and whimpers continued.

With trembling fingers, Jia made a few more notes on the paper.

Resolutely, she ignored the rabbit and went back to stirring the cauldron. The globules at the bottom had lost their vibrant color, and
were now more like pearls than beads of coral.

There was no oral lore or ancient tomes describing these berries
in Dara. Painstakingly, she had cultivated them in the hothouses
attached to the shed, accelerating their growth on harsh volcanic
soil. Over the years, she had studied their properties meticulously,
experimenting on animals and . . . others. Deploying all she knew
about selective breeding, she had made each generation more potent
than the previous one, as impatient as a florist yearning to create
the legendary black beach rose or the most fashionable three-colored
peony. The berries were now as different from their progenitors as a
mop-headed lap-yapper was from a wild wolf.

To take her mind off the horrible screams from the rabbit, she
thought back to her conversation with Zomi. The young Farsight
Secretary had spoken of disrupting Tanvanaki's plans, of destabilizing
the Lyucu rule in Rui and Dasu . . . but did she understand what that
required? Did she foresee the blood and iron it would consume, as horrifying as the thick red liquid congealed on the iron bars of the cage?

No, of course not. That was why she was the empress, the one
who must weigh the sacrifice of one group of stones for another, and
then commit. It was also why she must never mention what critical
bit of information she had instructed Lady Ragi to leak in Rui, and
what message she had asked Lady Ragi to take to Timu.

Her heart ached so much at the thought of Timu that she stopped
stirring and closed her eyes. She hunched over as though she had
been punched. *Oh Toto-tika, I'm so sorry. If only there were another way.*

Even as the thought entered her mind, she swatted it away like a
fly. *I can't allow myself the luxury of regret. Teeth on the board. I hold the
Seal of Dara, and this is my burden.*

A mother never liked to admit that she had a favorite among her
children, but it was true that the love she bore for Timu differed in
quality from that which she bore for Théra. Timu, though the firstborn, was always more dependent on her, more clingy. Whereas
Théra was headstrong and endowed with an unshakable faith in
herself, even as a little girl, Timu always craved approval—from

his teacher, from his father, and above all, from his mother. Rata-*tika* reminded Jia most of her younger self, and she could let her daughter go beyond the shores of Dara with some equanimity, certain that the young woman would survive and thrive. Toto-*tika*, on the other hand, always seemed to her a perpetual boy who needed her protection, held a claim to her tenderest instincts.

She imagined her own heart encased in ice. She breathed deeply. Once. Twice. Thrice.

She straightened up and realized that the baby-like screams had stopped. She forced herself to look over at the cage. The rabbit lay still, blood streaking its white fur. It had chewed off both of its front paws and broken its jaws against the cage.

Mechanically, directing her own body as though she were operating a puppet, she made her limbs move and her senses observe. She banked the fire beneath the cauldron to reduce the heat and set down the long-handled spoon. She extracted the rabbit from the cage and dissected it, peeling back skin and muscle, extricating the organs and weighing them, noting down the colors, smells, state of degeneration, degree of damage. She took her notes in code, the zyndari letters shifted and transformed and substituted and rearranged until only she could decipher the jumbled word-squares. Even the drawings were systematically distorted to be unrecognizable to anyone who didn't already know what they were looking at.

Then she began to clean. The carcass was put into the ceramic autoclave, along with bloody rags and soiled moss. She pumped the bellows until the heat inside was intense enough to turn bones to ashes. The cage was washed and washed again, then wiped down. Drawers were pushed back in, tools restored to their assigned nooks, pestles arranged to all point in the same direction, notebooks stacked and straightened, everything on the workbench at right angles. She cleaned compulsively, obsessively. No clues must be left through which someone could discern her intentions.

She stopped. Her shoulders heaved as pent-up disgust and anguish threatened to erupt past the knot in her throat. The dead rabbit's eyes persisted in her mind's eye, refusing to fade no matter where she looked. Horror, despair, empathetic pain.

She threw off her mask, grabbed a clean pollination brush, stuck the long handle between her teeth, and bit down hard, stifling any noise. Though only the Dyran Fins patrolling outside the shed were within hearing range, she couldn't risk letting them find her like this. She was the Empress of Dara, and the performance never stopped.

Eventually, her convulsions subsided. Jia returned to her cleaning until every trace of the experiment was gone, until the shed was spotless, until she was satisfied that it was as if the rabbit had never existed.

She put on the mask, returned to the cauldron, stoked the fire back to life, and began to stir again. Tears meandered down her face, soaking the mask. She told herself it was from the fumes.

The prison warden unlocked the door to the cell. Turning around, he bowed diffidently to the empress and her two companions.

"Will there be anything else . . . my lady?" he asked in a whisper, swallowing the *Rénga* at the last second. The empress always wanted to be anonymous for these occasions.

"No," said Jia. "Leave a set of keys and don't come back. I'll return them to you when I'm done."

The warden bowed again and held out a ring of keys in both hands, palms up. One of the two women standing behind Jia stepped out to take them from him.

He backed away, locking the door to the corridor with another set of keys after he passed through. As he turned the corner, out of sight of the empress and her companions, he sped up, wishing to get as far away from the cell as possible.

The cell he had unlocked held one of the most notorious criminals in all of Dara. The leader of a gang of child-traffickers and bandits, Laughing Skeleton had been responsible for the killing and maiming of dozens of victims and the disappearance of scores of children before he was caught. Pending his execution later this autumn, he was being held in isolation in Capital Prison, Dara's most secure jail, where those sentenced to death by magistrates from all across the Islands were kept so that their cases could be reviewed one last time by the Minister of Justice.

The warden wasn't worried about Jia's safety, though he had left Laughing Skeleton alone with her. The deadly Dyran Fins, the bodyguards who followed the empress everywhere, were well-known to every teahouse storyteller. Honestly, he felt a twinge of pity for the condemned criminal. The empress had visited other prisoners in the past, and he had seen the same sequence play out time after time.

The warden was too discreet to question the prisoners "favored" by the empress's attention as to what happened during the visits, but it wasn't hard to guess. As one clue, consider the fact that the empress almost always picked healthy, energetic men in their prime. As another clue, the empress's sexual appetite was the stuff of legends, and Prince Gimoto apparently supplied his aunt with lovers. The warden was used to receiving love letters written to condemned prisoners from young women in Pan and even other cities, and he understood that there was something incomprehensibly appealing about such men as sexual conquests.

Unlike the disapproving Moralists at court, who sometimes wrote petitions to the regent empress, begging her in roundabout ways to "consider the dignity of the high office of the sovereign and the august duty to be a moral exemplar," the warden was a nonjudgmental realist. Hadn't it always been the prerogative of the powerful to indulge their sexual predilections? Lady Datha, Emperor Mapidéré's mother, was supposed to have selected the most virile soldiers of the Xana army to entertain her by lifting weights with their erect organs. And even Emperor Ragin himself was rumored to have lost himself in the pleasures offered by Mapidéré's and Erishi's harems when he conquered Pan.

If Empress Jia enjoyed these visits, thought the warden, then it was his duty, as a loyal servant of the Dandelion Throne, to open the cell doors and then leave, asking no questions. Occasionally, in his reports to the Minister of Justice on the state of Capital Prison, the warden would add an offhand comment about the physique or handsomeness of some new prisoner, hoping the report would be passed up to the empress. But that was as far as he dared to go in referencing these clandestine visits.

Discretion was an important aspect of loyalty, and an even more important aspect in promotions.

Laughing Skeleton, who had never had one of these visits before, gazed out warily from his cell at the lady. Though she was older—he guessed in her fifties—she was extremely beautiful and possessed an air of command. Her jewelry and dress, though clearly expensive and well-made, revealed little of her identity. But he knew enough about the habits of the rich and idle to venture a guess.

She was likely the wife of some high-ranking official at court, perhaps a devout follower of Rufizo, the god of healing and mercy, here to pray with him in the misguided belief that she could move his stone heart and bring him to repent for his many sins. She had such a high opinion of herself that she thought she could "reform" this bad boy, turning him to the White Dove God to find a measure of peace before his death.

A sneer, the very feature that gave him his nickname, slowly took shape on his face.

Jia could see the man's muscles tense as he calculated the distance between them. Since the cell door was open, there was nothing separating them except empty air. He clearly regarded Wi and Shido as mere maids, nothing to worry about. In another second, he was going to leap at her, thinking of capturing her as a hostage or making her his last victim before execution.

Wearily, she nodded.

Laughing Skeleton exploded into motion. Like a wolf pouncing after a ewe, he shot out of his cell, his hands ready to lock around Jia's neck.

From behind Jia, two blurs swept by her sides, quicker than the flash of lightning or the peal of thunder. When the blurs took solid shape again, Shido was standing behind the bent-over Laughing Skeleton, his arms folded on his back as Shido pushed his wrists between his shoulder blades. Wi stood between her mistress and the would-be attacker, her thumbs pressed against Laughing Skeleton's eyes. Each of the two, like the other Dyran Fins, had trained for years under the fighting monks of Fithowéo, the sword dancers of Cocru, and other martial arts masters who wished to make their name known by affiliation with the Dandelion Court.

Laughing Skeleton was no longer laughing. In fact, he was screaming like a pig about to be slaughtered. His shoulders had been dislocated, and he couldn't see anything as he felt talons digging into his eyes, ready to gouge them out any second. Worst of all, he hadn't even seen his attackers.

"Mercy! Mercy!" he screamed. "O gods! In the name of Rufizo, I'll pray to whoever you want me to pray to! I can't feel my arms—"

Wi took her hands off his eyes and gave his face two crisp slaps. "Shut up," she said. "Nobody wants you to pray."

Laughing Skeleton felt his face go numb and blood fill his mouth. He couldn't see anything because stars danced before his eyes. He coughed and spat out the blood. Instead of screaming, he whimpered, held up by Shido behind him.

"I'm here to offer you some food," said Jia, quietly, calmly, as though presenting a home-cooked meal to a beggar. "If you agree to sit down quietly and finish everything, I will tell her to let you go. The alternative is to drink more blood."

Defeated, Laughing Skeleton nodded, still whimpering.

The whimpers turned into another scream as Shido let go of his wrists and pushed up on his shoulders, relocating his arms into their sockets. He dropped to the ground, sitting as he massaged his shoulders, rocking back and forth and muttering curses.

Wi brought over a basket and laid the contents before him: a dish of roast beef, cut into small strips; a rack of lamb; a bowl of some fermented drink that smelled of alcohol. All the dishes were cooked in the Lyucu style, based on descriptions by refugees from Rui and Dasu. Jia didn't bother explaining any of this to him. It wasn't important for her purposes.

Laughing Skeleton looked at the food before him, hesitating.

"Eat!" said Shido, landing a kick against his right kidney. The man, who had been known to torture his victims before killing them, fell down again, tears streaming from his eyes as he gasped for breath.

Wi held up a restraining hand. "No internal injuries, sister."

Reluctantly, Shido set down her foot. "You better start chewing.

You have no idea how lucky you are compared to some of my mistress's other guests."

She wasn't just trying to scare Laughing Skeleton. During Jia's earlier experiments, before she had settled on a cultivar and refined the dosage, she and Wi had administered the medicine for Jia in various, more violent ways: choking the prisoner until he lost consciousness and inserting a hollow needle filled with a thick paste into a vein; wrapping a skin pouch around the head of the prisoner in order to compel him to inhale smoke; force-feeding him by sticking a hollow bamboo stick down his throat.

But Jia had grown confident enough now to try more refined, realistic delivery mechanisms.

Laughing Skeleton struggled back into a sitting position and examined the food before him again. He was sure everything was poisoned. But what choice did he have? Well, the worst that could happen was he would die, and he wasn't supposed to live another month anyway. Determinedly, he grabbed a chunk of beef and began to chew.

Somewhat to his surprise, the beef was cooked to perfection, juicy and flavorful, with a hint of salt that whetted his appetite. He swallowed, grabbled a lamb rib, and sucked off the succulent flesh. It was even better. He picked up the bowl and took a big gulp of the unknown drink—it was alcoholic and tasted sweet and sour, redolent of unknown spices.

"You certainly know how to cook, Mistress," he said to Jia. "Even if I die after this, I won't complain. There's no better last meal possible."

Jia looked at him impassively.

She knew what the warden thought was happening here, and she never bothered to correct him. In fact, she positively encouraged his runaway imagination. The false rumors, like those swirling around Gimoto, were useful as a disguise. Not only did they throw off any Lyucu spies, but they also kept the Moralists from digging into the truth. They were bothered enough by her sexual liberties, but if they knew the truth of what she was planning . . .

*Enough of that.* She gestured for Wi, who laid out paper and brush and began to take notes in coded zyndari letters.

With each bite and drink, the smile on the man's face grew wider. When the bowl was empty, Shido refilled it from a jug. By now the grin on his face was ear to ear, and he was so happy that he felt compelled to get up from the ground, kicking his legs and waving his long arms about as he continued to eat.

"Now he's really living up to his name," whispered Shido.

Wi chuckled in response. "Lucky guy, who gets to taste mistress's unparalleled cooking."

Nonetheless they moved protectively closer to Jia, just in case the man was practicing a trick.

*I shouldn't be so hard on the Moralists,* thought Jia. *It's their nature to obsess over what is right, to imagine an idealized world in which the bonds of mutual respect and faith govern all. A man like Zato Ruthi would fight a war by giving his opponent every advantage, reasoning that those who did what was right would always triumph.*

*But we don't live in a world like that. We live in a world in which to save the many, sometimes the few must be sacrificed. They would condemn me for what I'm doing and what I'm about to do, and declare me devoid of the Grace of Kings. They would be right. But better that they remain alive to condemn me than for me to follow their ideals and lead all to death.*

*We all follow our natures. Timu can't help his timid and bookish devotion to the Ano sages, and neither can the Lyucu deviate from their worship of might makes right. I will encourage these natures and push them along, and rather than confrontation, savor the long, lasting victory that comes from sheathing the Grace of Kings.*

She was pulled out of her reverie because the man had begun to sing. There was such joy and ecstasy in his voice that even Shido and Wi felt compelled to smile. He seemed oblivious to the presence of the women as he danced into the cell and out, leaping on and off his bunk in a fit of frenzy.

Jia gazed at him intently and took more notes.

Outside, an autumn thunderstorm began.

A flash of lightning that sketched the outline of a leaping wolf.

*- Listen to that laugh! Has he stolen the mead of gods and become drunk on sacred nectar?*

Rumbling peals of thunder, like the cawing of ravens.

- *You'd think he's slept with Tututika—*

*—or stolen the key to Tazu's undersea palace.*

- *What is Jia doing, Rapa and Kana?*

- *How are we supposed to know? Of all the mortals we know—*

*—she's always been the hardest to read. Not even Risana could see into her heart.*

- *But she grew the berries on volcanic ash and fed them by snowmelt water. These are your elements. You ought to understand what she's making.*

- *You speak of nature, but the mortals are full of art—*

*—and art, my brother Fithowéo, is beyond the understanding of all the gods, except perhaps Lutho.*

- *How I miss him.*


The prisoner was asleep, a contented smile on his face, by the time Jia and the two Dyran Fins left.

The warden gazed down at his charge and sighed. He had heard the singing and whooping and cries of ecstasy from his office all the way down the hall. The expression on Laughing Skeleton's face told him that the man had experienced pleasures beyond the ken of mere mortals.

It always began this way, he reflected. The first few visits from the empress.

"Enjoy it while it lasts," he whispered to the sleeping figure. He checked to be sure the cell door was secure before turning to leave.

# CHAPTER TWENTY-TWO

# A GAME OF *ZAMAKI*

RUI: THE NINTH MONTH IN THE EIGHTH YEAR OF
THE REIGN OF AUDACIOUS FREEDOM (KNOWN AS
THE EIGHTH YEAR OF THE REIGN OF SEASON OF
STORMS IN DARA, AND THE EIGHTH YEAR SINCE
PRINCESS THÉRA DEPARTED DARA FOR UKYU-
GONDÉ).

Gentle waves lapped the empty beach by the village of Kigo Yezu
on this warm early autumn afternoon; the native fishermen had yet
to return from the sea on their skiffs and canoes. Seagulls and terns
circled over the surf as crabs skittered among the strands of seaweed
at the tidal line. On the other side of the rolling dunes that echoed
the shapes of the waves, native villagers labored in the taro fields. A
light breeze commingled the faint fragrance of dune roses with the
tangy scent of the sea.

Save for the distant silhouette of a circling garinafin on the horizon patrolling for pirates and Dara-raaki spies, this shoreside scene
had probably been unchanged for centuries.

In the lee of one of the dunes stood a hut—little more than
four bamboo poles holding up a roof of woven palm leaves. In its
shade, an old woman and a young man, both dressed in the robes
of Dara scholars, knelt across from each other in formal *mipa rari* on
pig's-bristle grass sitting mats, staring intently at the low tree-stump
table between them.

"Master, why are there more red tokens than black tokens?" asked
the young man. In his speech was a slight trace of the accent of Dasu,

the island to the northwest considered by the natives of Rui to be a repository of unrefined manners and backward customs.

The young man was about eighteen years of age, with fair skin, large, inquisitive eyes, and a headful of dark brown hair carelessly tied up in a single scroll-bun. His robe was of plain hemp, dyed a common sap-green, and he wore straw shoes with wooden soles. The same outfit could be found on frugal students from across Dara— both Ukyu-taasa and the core islands. Only the garinafin-tooth hair-pin sticking out of his hair bun betrayed his Lyucu heritage.

"No general ever complains of having too many soldiers, Kinri-tika," said the old woman, Nazu Tei, her tone teasing. "Zamaki is a game inspired by war, after all." Her robe, though similarly unadorned, was made of coarse silk, and her silvery hair was worn up in a double scroll-bun, indicating that she was a toko dawiji, a scholar who had passed the first level of the Imperial examinations back when Pan had ruled Rui.

Nazu's face glowed from ample exercise and hearty food, while her hands were heavily calloused, showing signs of manual labor. This was rather unusual. Emperor Thaké's reign in Ukyu-taasa had become quite comfortable for scholars, especially those who were willing to accept the legitimacy of Lyucu rule.

Carved into the tabletop between them was a grid of lines, eleven vertical and twelve horizontal. On the grid intersection points in the half of the board in front of the old woman were arranged ten small black figurines carved out of black seashells and carbonized bone, each about three inches tall; twenty similar figurines, carved out of red coral, sat on the half of the grid in front of the young man.

Nazu Tei's answer didn't satisfy Kinri. "But don't games of skill usually give the two sides the same number of playing pieces?"

"Because our skills are unbalanced, it would lead to a quick and dull game if we played with a balanced board," said Nazu. "As the Ano sages would say, 'Ofithacru ki ingrocathu doco i icapiphiki orucrua ingro pha, gin co phinoné pha kridagén.' Treating what are manifestly different the same is not true equality."

"But—"

"Be patient with your own growth," said Nazu placatingly. "I expect that we'll be playing with the evenly matched tokens within the month."

Kinri nodded reluctantly, deciding there was no dishonor in accepting an advantage she yielded to him for pedagogical reasons. He picked up the conch-shell teapot and refilled Nazu's cup; the teacher tapped the table three times with her index and middle fingers to indicate thanks.

"What is this token called?" he asked, holding up a piece of coral carved into the form of a man holding a sword. A large dandelion crest was emblazoned on his chest armor. About the man's feet lay the coiled shape of a serpent whose head had been severed. Besides adding to the character of the statue, the snake also widened the base and provided stability.

"That is your king—sometimes also called the commander—and the object of *zamaki* is to capture the opponent's king. The red king in this set is modeled on Emperor Ragin, known as Kuni Garu in his youth."

"Ah, this must refer to that legend of him slaying the white serpent before he became emperor," said Kinri.

"That's right. He was only a bandit at the time, and few people, not even Emperor Ragin himself, could have foreseen how far he would rise in the future."

"But I think most people should have foreseen what a bloodthirsty tyrant Kuni Garu would turn out to be. A bandit—not unlike those rebels my mother used to put down—is a criminal, caring only about himself and disdaining order, laws, and the lives of innocent people."

"It's more complicated than that—" Nazu stopped herself and sipped tea from her cup, swallowing beverage and words at the same time.

Kinri was used to this. His master often stopped herself midsentence. After waiting a moment to be sure she wasn't going to continue, Kinri said gently, "Perhaps you'll tell me more about that part of his life in the future."

A hint of melancholy passed over Nazu's face before she collected herself. "Perhaps." Her tone was noncommittal.

Kinri spent a few moments to admire the red king figurine in his hand, imagining the founder of the Dandelion Dynasty as a bandit, stealing and pillaging and robbing and killing. Earlier this year, at the public execution of some native rebel leaders, he had witnessed the condemned men denounce Pékyu Vadyu's court as a bunch of bandits who had stolen Rui from the natives. The accusation from the rebel bandits was obviously absurd on every level, not the least because it attempted to equate legitimate military conquest with mere lawlessness. As it turned out, the natives' own emperor, the revered founder of the House of Dandelion, had been a real bandit himself, which just went to show how the dastardly rebels, unappreciative of the gentle hand of Lyucu rule, were wont to twist history to suit their own needs.

History was one of Kinri's favorite subjects. Translated as re-remembering in the Lyucu tongue, history as practiced in Dara was very different from the stories told by shamans in the dance stories of his own people. Rather than a performance of human deeds enabled by, and interpreted in the context of, mythical cycles, a Dara historian tried to explain events by weaving facts into a story in which the prime movers were men and women, not gods. Kinri preferred histories of warfare, finding histories of philosophy and art, which Nazu Tei favored, rather dry.

In any case, he was glad that this game seemed suffused with the history of warfare in Dara. He had begged his master to teach him how to play *zamaki* only because he had wanted a break from boring Moralist and Incentivist treatises. Some of the native soldiers played the game when they didn't think Lyucu officers were watching, and he was curious about it. That this was a way to get Master Tei to talk more about recent history, which she always seemed reluctant to do, was an unexpected bonus.

Gently, he set down the red king in its assigned place at the midpoint of the board edge on his side. "Then your king must be modeled after Mata Zyndu, the Hegemon." He pointed to the figurine at the midpoint of the board edge on Nazu's side.

Carbonized whalebone was carved into the form of a powerfully built warrior whose armor was emblazoned with the chrysanthemum crest. In his hands, he held tiny versions of Goremaw and

Na-aroénna, the legendary cudgel-sword pair that had ended count-less lives. At his feet was a pile of skulls and severed heads, which functionally served the same purpose as the serpent at the red king's feet.

Nazu nodded. "The two kings are allowed to move one step at a time, horizontally, vertically, and even diagonally, but they must never leave their respective castles, which are these two three-by-four rectangular regions marked by double lines, one at each end of the board. The two kings must also never face each other directly. If they do, whoever removed the last intervening piece or moved their king into that position loses. This is known as the 'Rule of the Torn Treaty,' and some say it commemorates Emperor Ragin's betrayal of the Hegemon at the end of the Chrysanthemum-Dandelion War."

"I remember that story!" exclaimed Kinri. "By Péa-Kiji's beard, Kuni Garu really was a rascal who couldn't be trusted. He also betrayed Pékyu Tenryo at Naza Pass, where he killed many, many innocent natives to save himself. The court-appointed tutors and historians say that the pékyu-votan raged for three days over the atrocities Kuni Garu committed there, vowing to avenge the tyrant's victims and bring freedom to Dara. How could such a man with no honor have risen to claim the Seal of Dara?"

Instead of answering, Nazu picked up the conch-shell pot and refilled Kinri's cup.

Kinri was too excited to be deterred by the lack of response. "So is everything in this game modeled on the Chrysanthemum-Dandelion War?"

While Nazu continued to look tense, Kinri's index finger hovered over the board and stopped at the three horizontal rows in the middle of the grid, an otherwise empty area decorated with a few undulating lines and relief carvings of the Ano logograms for "channel" and "river."

"What is this dividing region between the two halves of the board?" he half asked, half mused. "There are no grid lines through this region, which probably means that only specialized tokens can cross it . . . is it a reference to the Liru River, which once marked the division between the territories of the Emperor of Dara and the

Hegemon? Eh, wait . . ." He pondered the board some more. "Or is it meant to represent the Gaing Gulf, which separates Dasu, Kuni Garu's first fief, from the rest of Dara, which at that point all pledged fealty to the Hegemon?"

Nazu nodded, apparently relieved by the change in topic. "You've studied the official histories well, and these are good guesses. But your deductions proceed from a false premise: The game isn't about the Chrysanthemum-Dandelion War at all."

"Oh? Then why are the kings in the forms of Kuni Garu and Mata Zyndu?"

"There are some soldiers who claim that *zamaki* was invented by Marshal Gin Mazoti, Emperor Ragin's greatest warlord, as a simulation of the battlefield to train her officers in tactical thinking. But they speak out of ignorance of history." Nazu took a long drink of tea, settling in for a long lecture. "In truth, *zamaki* is a very old game with many variations, though it did become much more popular after the Chrysanthemum-Dandelion War. By the way, remember that what I teach you here must remain a secret. This set is very different from the ones you'll see back in Kriphi. You have to be discreet—"

"Of course," said Kinri impatiently. "I've always been careful. I'll learn the game again from one of the soldiers in Kriphi, just like how I never repeat what you teach me if it's different from the court-appointed tutor's version."

Nazu smiled indulgently at him and continued. "I once saw a set of *zamaki* pieces said to be retrieved from a grave dating from six hundred years ago, and the two commanders appeared to be modeled on the Tiro kings of Xana and Amu. Players have been adapting the game to changing methods of warfare and our unceasing history of turmoil for generations—" Abruptly, she slowed down, as if regretting the direction she was headed in. "Er . . . for instance, instead of airships, that ancient *zamaki* set had pieces modeled after chariots, a long-obsolete form of warfare—"

"Oh, Master! Can you show me what these chariots looked like? How did people fight with them?"

Kinri was even more excited by the new topics—airships and chariots—brought up by his master. If there was one subject he enjoyed more than the history of warfare, it was Dara machines. Even as a young child in Ukyu, he had been fascinated by the city-ships and the curios left by Admiral Krita's people. Later, growing up in Ukyu-taasa, he had loved climbing over the captured airships and investigating the musical instruments, writing tools, cooking utensils, and other Dara machines in his mother's collection, trying to understand how they were put together and inferring their principles of operation.

Nazu Tei shook her head and smiled regretfully. "I'm not knowledgeable about the construction or use of war chariots, I'm afraid. I never did have much interest in any kind of machinery . . . except perhaps logograms."

Kinri's face fell in disappointment. He knew, of course, that his master was no engineer, but sometimes she brought up interesting tidbits from the Ano Classics: a sage's description of the fabrication of a battle kite or a historian's account of the building of a famous temple. Since she possessed few books, she could not show him accurate diagrams or recall the exact technical details of these wonders. It was too bad that there were virtually no skilled engineers in Ukyu-taasa who could teach him what he wanted to know about the mechanical creations of the natives.

But a moment later, Kinri's eyes lit up as he seized on something else she had said. "Did you say that the ancient *zamaki* set was retrieved from a grave?" he exclaimed. "Wouldn't that be an act of sacrilege in the eyes of all the people of Dara?"

Nazu sighed inwardly. Kinri had always had the gift of asking uncomfortable questions. "Reverence for ancestors is a foundational part of the teachings of the Ano sages," she admitted, "but not everyone in Dara, certainly not grave robbers, feels bound by it. Antiques can be quite valuable on the market, and profit drives men to all kinds of outrage."

"But aren't they afraid of disturbing the peace of the dead?" To be sure, Kinri didn't actually think what the grave robbers did was morally wrong. He couldn't imagine that spirits would rest well being shut up inside a dark box surrounded by earth; if the grave robbers freed the spirits to roam about in open air, it would be a mercy.

"Oh, grave robbers have all kinds of rationalizations and super-stitions," said Nazu.

"Tell me some?"

Nazu pondered how to explain the subtleties and apparent con-tradictions in this aspect of Dara culture. "Let me see . . . As you know, Kon Fiji's student, Poti Maji, believed that honoring the dead with a proper burial was a custom among even the most primitive societies—"

"I have to agree with him," said Kinri. "I think burying bodies is barbaric—it's certainly at least as primitive as . . . farming." He had always been horrified by the Dara custom of interring the dead instead of pédiato savaga, the Lyucu practice of exposing corpses to the elements and scavenging animals.

"We won't resolve that debate today," said Nazu. "But back to Poti Maji: He made a study of the burial rites of the pre-Ano natives of Dara and the Ano themselves, connecting them to Moralist prin-ciples. One of his most famous pronouncements is '*Hugolu pha gira ki*'—can you tell me what it means?"

"'Rest is found under.'"

"Right," said Nazu. "That's the literal translation. But do you know what the expression is really about?"

Kinri shook his head. "I've never been able to make heads or tails of it. It's not even a complete sentence."

"Try writing it out," said Nazu.

Obediently, Kinri set aside the *zamaki* set for the moment and began to sculpt Ano logograms out of a block of sun-softened wax he kept on the sand outside the hut just for this purpose. Though he was no skilled calligrapher, he did have a knack for Ano logograms—they reminded him of arucuro tocua, his favorite childhood pastime—and soon the four-logogram phrase sat on the table, in the empty region between the two halves of the board.

"Notice anything special?" asked Nazu.

"Hmm . . . ah, all the logograms are written with the semantic root for 'earth.'"

"Very good, and where is the 'earth' semantic root in each logo-gram?"

"At the . . . top."

"So put it all together like a logogram riddle, and—"

"*Under earth!* Since the logograms are written literally under 'earth,' the whole phrase is 'Rest is found *under* the earth'!"

Nazu nodded with approval. "Poti Maji enjoyed logogram games like that, and so some of his statements are puzzles that must be decoded semantically, aurally, and visually."

"What does this have to do with grave robbers?"

"Some grave robbers believe that they can protect themselves from the wrath of the disturbed dead by wearing hats decorated with the logogram for 'earth' as they burrow into the tombs."

"What? How does that work?"

"With the earth-logogram hats on, they think they'll appear as 'living logograms' to the dead. And because of Poti Maji, the spirits will then believe the robbers are bringing peace and rest to them and leave them alone."

"That's . . . I don't know what to say. . . ."

"In fact, once inside the tombs, the robbers will often leave a note drafted in elaborate pseudo-legal language saying that they are only 'borrowing' the grave goods, signed with a fake name. In fact, in the cant of grave robbers, the term for 'burrowing' into a grave is 'borrowing.'"

Kinri shook his head in wonder. "That seems like a lot of punning and game playing rather than spirituality or faith." Though he spoke disapprovingly of the grave robbers, he secretly found the tricks described by his teacher rather clever. The grave robbers seemed to treat gods, ghosts, and spirits as entities that could be manipulated and engineered around. The implications of the idea were thrilling.

Nonetheless, doubt remained in his heart. "Do the grave robbers really think they can deceive the gods or the dead with such tricks?"

"That's a harder question to answer than it may seem," said Nazu Tei. "For many common people, especially the illiterate, there is a kind of magic associated with logograms, and anyone can deceive themselves into thinking that performing rote rituals is the same as doing the right thing."

"It never ceases to shock me to see so much hypocrisy among the

Dara-raaki—oh master, I'm sorry!" Seeing Nazu flinch at the slur, Kinri stopped, placed his hands together, and bowed to his teacher. "Some of the thanes at court use that—I . . . I—never mind, I'm ashamed to have allowed it to slip out of me so carelessly."

Nazu composed herself. "I know that you intended no hatred. I wish it didn't affect me so, but words have great power, especially for those who treasure learning."

"That's just what I don't understand. There is so much respect for the words of the Ano sages among the people of Dara, and yet I see throughout history instances where barbaric acts are committed, contrary to the teachings of the sages. How can this be?"

Nazu gave a wry smile. "That, Kinri-*tika*, is perhaps the grandest mystery of the human heart. Adherence to the teachings of the sages or the gods both require faith. But in every age and among all peoples, the ones who live by faith alone and the ones who reject faith completely are few, while those who stand on the border between belief and disbelief, leaning toward what is convenient at the moment, make up the majority." As she spoke, her voice took on an uncertain air, as though she was troubled by her own pronouncement.

"Some of the thanes say that the trouble with Dara began with the Ano logograms," said Kinri. "They say writing is a kind of death for the truth. Once something is written down, the logograms usurp the place of the ideas they represent and are mere shadows of. While a living voice can respond and adapt, the dead logograms stand mute, unable to answer an accusation or offer an apologia. Writing breeds hypocrisy because the clever may justify any barbarism by paying the writings of the sages ritualistic obeisance."

"That's an interesting idea," mused Nazu. "I can see why the Lyucu, who had no writing before encountering Mapidéré's fleet, would feel suspicious about writing. But don't the Lyucu also have wisdom passed down the generations?"

"We do," said Kinri. "But we don't read them out of books. The Lyucu storytellers do not memorize long speeches verbatim— though some young people who are not shamans believe that is what happens. Instead, they keep only the outline of an idea in their hearts, and improvise with every retelling. Recitation, interrogation, revelation, and adaptation are how we grow the old truths and keep them alive. Because something spoken is transient, we are constantly aware that the truth cannot be captured by mere words. We don't fall to idolatrous worship of the dead logograms, and neither do we attempt to deceive our idols with meaningless performance."

Nazu was quiet for some time. Then she bowed to Kinri.

Flustered, Kinri bowed back. "I hope my words have not offended."

"Not at all," said Nazu. "I don't agree with everything you've said, but I've learned something from your words. A teacher must never cease learning, especially from her students. You've reminded me that the wisdom within the logograms is more important than the logograms themselves, especially in times when wisdom is disdained and lies prized. The gods have brought us together for a purpose, but I am still learning to read the signs."

Her eyes were wet as she looked up again.

About five years earlier, Thane Goztan Ryoto, trusted confidante of Tanvanaki, and her thirteen-year-old son, Savo Ryoto, were hunting in the hills near Kigo Yezu.

Though horses were not native to Ukyu, many of the Lyucu thanes, naros-votan, and naros had learned to ride these "miniature earthbound garinafins" as a way to sharpen their own fighting skills and to maintain control over the native population more effectively. Savo, however, was never a skilled rider, either of horses or garinafins. During a chase after a petal-rumped deer with his slingshot and spear, he became separated from his mother. While riding aimlessly about, growing more desperate and careless with each passing minute as he sought Goztan, his mount tripped and threw him to the ground, breaking one of his legs.

Nazu Tei, passing by in the woods, carried the boy home and tended to his injuries. When the thane found them and discovered that Nazu Tei was a ranked scholar living in seclusion away from Kriphi, she looked thoughtful.

After assuring herself that Savo would be all right, Goztan asked Nazu to take on her son as a pupil.

"But I already have a court-appointed tutor," Savo protested.

Nazu also said she had no intention of accepting a court-maintained life. "I'm happy to live in obscurity, votan. Please bestow the honor of instructing your child on someone more deserving."

"I have no interest in moving you to Kriphi or bringing you to the attention of the court," Goztan said. "But I want him to learn about the culture and habits of mind of Dara from someone . . . unconstrained by the rules binding scholars at court."

"That is forbidden," said Nazu Tei.

"It will be a secret."

"Why?" asked Nazu Tei, looking expressionlessly at Goztan.

Goztan looked back at her. "Dara is where he will come of age; he must feel at home here, not a perpetual guest."

"Guest?" Nazu Tei's face flushed, and a hint of heat tinged her next words. "I had not realized that the Lyucu consider themselves guests of Dara. The rules of hospitality must be very different on the scrublands."

It was now Goztan's turn to flush. But she took a deep breath, and instead of exploding, said, "I do not agree with what has been done to your people. But without a deeper understanding from both sides, our terrible past will repeat down the generations."

Coming from someone else, those words would have seemed to verge on treason to Savo. But Goztan was his mother, and the boy thought she must have had her reasons.

Nazu Tei glared at Goztan, saying nothing.

"The people of Dara believe in signs, don't they?" Goztan persisted. "I think it's a sign that you were passing by when his horse stumbled. It's a fortunate fall that brings a pupil to his teacher."

Unlike the other thanes, who spoke of the natives in contemptuous slurs, Savo's mother had always used the phrase "the people of Dara."

Nazu Tei looked over at Savo, who was examining the few silk-and-wax scrolls on her shelf with deep interest. She looked back at Goztan. After a moment, she looked away, sighed, and nodded.

Goztan said, "I understand it's customary in Dara for parents to express their esteem of the teacher—"

"I don't want any payment," interrupted Nazu. "This arrangement must be kept a secret."

"Of course," said Goztan. "But something must be given as a token to show the seriousness of the commitment between teacher and pupil."

She asked Savo to hand her his hunting spear. She broke the tip off the shaft and handed it to Nazu. "I made this for him with my own hands. Today I give this to you in the hopes that you'll show him what I cannot: how to write instead of how to kill."

Nazu examined the spear tip. It was made from a slender piece of bone, with a pattern of abstract wavy lines etched into the surface. Somehow, the smooth grooves of the patterns felt like a natural part of the bone instead of the product of craft. She pulled out the hairpin from her double scroll-bun and replaced it with the spear tip.

"Thank you," she said.

Young Savo was then instructed to kneel before Nazu and touch his forehead to the ground three times in the native fashion.

"Since I've received a gift from you, it's only right that I reciprocate," said Nazu. "It's customary for every student of the Classics to be given a formal Classical Ano name if he didn't already receive one upon reaching the age of reason. . . . How about 'Kinri'?"

"What does it mean?" the boy asked.

"'A sign.'"

He instantly liked the way the name sounded. *Is that also a sign?* he wondered. While he had not been able to capture the petal-rumped deer, he had the premonition that he had caught something much more significant.

Later, after they had studied together for a while, she began to call him Kinri-*tika*, and he liked that even better.

Though Kinri wasn't sure why his teacher had suddenly become so emotional, he waited a respectful few moments before venturing tentatively, "Shall we return to the game, master?"

"Of course," said Nazu. She dabbed at her eyes and smiled. "I'm itching to start playing. We just have to get the rules out of the way. Now that we've covered the king, which piece's movements do you want to learn next?"

The young man looked over the board and pointed at a few

smooth, egg-shaped tokens with tiny toothpick oar-legs that prevented them from rolling around the board. "Are these airships? So
I have four and you have only one?"

"Yes," said Nazu. "These may move horizontally or vertically, as
many steps as you please, in a single turn. They can even skip over
one other token barring their way, friend or foe, unless the token is
another airship. They are among the most powerful pieces on the
board."

"But what is the *most* powerful piece in *zamaki*?" asked Kinri
eagerly. "Or is the game like *cüpa*, in which no stone is more powerful than any other?"

"Well, that's not an easy question to answer. Since *cüpa* is a game
based on strategic planning, it approximates the distant perspective
of an adviser at court, to whom all soldiers on the front line are alike.
*Zamaki*, on the other hand, is a game derived from battlefield tactics seen through the eyes of a field general, where the differences
between individual playing pieces matter. However, just as the
martial prowess of an individual fighter isn't an absolute measure
of their importance to the battle—it depends on their field position,
support units, communication lines, and other factors—a *zamaki*
piece's range of movement isn't the sole determinant of its power.
For instance, a scholar-pawn begins the game with only the ability to
move forward one step at a time, but once it has advanced inside the
opposing side's castle, it's promoted to a *pana méji*, with the ability
to move just like the king. A promoted scholar can pose a far greater
threat to the king than a distant airship, just as a well-positioned
assassin—"

"I'm well aware of such tactical basics, master," interrupted Kinri,
chuckling. "I am, after all, the son of a war thane. I can see now that
in *zamaki*, the playing pieces serve similar roles as the components
of an Ano logogram. But instead of a static structure of references
and allusions, a *zamaki* army is a dynamic machine of potential and
power, changing with every move."

Nazu looked at him admiringly. "That is an excellent observation . . . one that I hadn't even thought of. See, I told you we'd be
playing with the same number and types of tokens in no time."

Kinri blushed, pleased at the compliment. To disguise his embarrassment, he coughed and asked, "Master, let me change my question. Which piece has the most moves?"

"That would be the consort," said Nazu. She pointed to two black and two red figurines, all depicting women. "Sometimes these pieces are also called companions or 'wakeful weaknesses.' The consorts in this set are modeled on Empress Jia and Consort Risana, on the red side, and on Princess Kikomi and Lady Mira, on the black side. Consorts may move horizontally, vertically, or diagonally, as many steps as you like each turn."

"How strange!" exclaimed Kinri.

"Why?"

"Why are consorts the most mobile and capable pieces on the board," said Kinri, "when women in Dara don't fight in battles or rule kingdoms? Well, at least not until Gin Mazoti."

"That depends on the historian you consult—" Nazu again stopped herself.

Kinri waited patiently. He knew that usually when his master stopped midsentence like this, it meant she wished to change the subject.

Nazu seemed to be debating herself in her mind. Her lips moved as she muttered in a voice too low for Kinri to hear. The only phrase he caught was "a sign."

Abruptly, her face relaxed, as though she had made a decision. "The court historians have not always told the whole story, either in Kriphi or Pan."

Kinri's heart started to beat faster. His master was about to tell him something unusual and interesting.

"As you know, during the Diaspora Wars, there were many princesses and heroines who fought both with and against the hero Iluthan," said Nazu, her voice unusually determined. "And during the early days of the Tiro states, many queens ruled—not just in their husbands' or sons' steads, but outright, asserting their own claims. And grand ladies attended court and gave counsel."

"I thought all that stopped after Kon Fiji declared women should be excluded from politics and war for their own protection."

"That is certainly the version most of the Moralists would like you to believe, and . . . the pékyu encourages it, as it proves that women have always been degraded in Dara, justifying the coming of the Lyucu."

Kinri now knew that something truly unusual was happening. Master Nazu Tei rarely spoke of the Lyucu invasion, and never criticized Tanvanaki. Though his instinct was to argue with his master's cynical portrait of the pékyu, he decided to hold his tongue for the moment to listen.

"But, if you pay attention to the Moralist classics, you'll find that almost all the statements attributed to Kon Fiji concerning the separate sphere allocated to women came from texts written by Poti Maji, in particular, *Acts of the Master*. But Kon Fiji taught thousands of students in his lifetime, and of those, seventy-two achieved note as advisers to kings. About a third of *these* were women."

"What?" Kinri was astonished. "I had no idea. I thought Kon Fiji didn't teach women at all."

Nazu gave a wry smile. "That is the official position of the modern Moralists and also the position of the Kriphi-approved curriculum. However, it isn't true."

"Um . . . *Acts of the Master* mentions no women studying under Kon Fiji at all."

"Poti Maji was certainly the most ambitious and well-known student of the One True Sage. He and his disciples were responsible for creating the basis of what we now think of as the canon of Moralist classics. But there were other fragments and even entire books excluded from the canon, called apocrypha, that give a more complicated and nuanced picture of Kon Fiji's views on women. For instance, based on apocryphal texts recovered from the tombs of powerful early Tiro queens, I think several of Kon Fiji's most prized students were women, though *Acts of the Master* describes them as men."

Kinri's mind reeled. The idea that Dara's history was not as he understood it was astonishing. And the implications troubling. What else did he not know? What else was untrue in the books taught by the court-appointed tutors? "How did you know about these apocrypha?"

"Like you, I'm interested in history. Before I came to Rui, I made it my personal project to recover, collect, and preserve texts that had been ravaged by Mapidéré's destructive policies. In that process, however, I found out about a far earlier and perhaps more destructive culling of texts, conducted by the first Moralists. The only way for me to recover what they erased was to buy scrolls recovered from ancient tombs by grave robbers. To save the past, sometimes it's necessary to borrow from and burrow into the past. To revere the dead properly, sometimes it's necessary to conduct an outrage against their peaceful rest. Such is the irony of existence."

Kinri nodded. This explained why his master was so familiar with the practices of grave robbers. "I would love to read some of the apocrypha."

Nazu's look grew wistful. "I donated all my scrolls to the Imperial Library in Pan out of gratefulness to Emperor Ragin for the Golden Carp program, of which I'm a beneficiary. But I've been teaching you snippets from them already, though I didn't always tell you they weren't from canonical texts."

"I really had no idea."

"It's my fault for not being courageous enough to tell you the truth earlier," said Nazu Tei, smiling tranquilly. "I'll do better in the future. All right, enough digressions. Let me quickly go over the rest of the rules with you."

She explained the movements of the rest of the tokens: ship, mechanical cruben, adviser, assassin, general, horse, kite, and marshal. She went over the movement restrictions and bonuses provided by special regions of the board labeled "island," "mountain," and "river/channel." She taught him the rules of capture and promotion, the special cases for stalemates and repeated board positions. . . .

They began to play, and while Nazu won the first two games, Kinri was able to win the third. Delighted, Kinri insisted on reducing his advantage by one airship as they set up the pieces for the next game.

"You're improving faster even than I expected," remarked Nazu. In a teasing tone, she added, "And you seem to have a lot more mental endurance today than usual."

"*Zamaki* is *much* more enjoyable than studying the deliberately obscure Ano logograms in Gi Anji's *Commentaries on Morality*," conceded Kinri, fingering the smooth surface of a red coral airship piece. "Master, you said this game is often adapted to new developments in warfare, right? I can already imagine some modifications for the modern age. For instance, garinafin pieces could be added to the game to represent advanced Lyucu tactics."

Despite the earlier promise to be more truthful with her student, Nazu looked hesitant. In the end, she chose to address only the first part of her student's comment. "I can understand how you feel about those logograms. When I first began my formal studies, my master spent a whole month on *Letter Composed from One Thousand Flower-Rooted Logograms*, can you imagine?"

"That *would* be pure torture," marveled Kinri. "There were sixteen different logograms in that awful book that all meant 'cultivate' in one sense or another, as I recall."

"Eighteen, actually. But even obscure logograms can be interesting when you see the historical context. The proliferation of cultivation-related logograms is a reflection of how advanced the ancient Ano already were in their farming techniques. In fact, two of the logograms feature the 'hemp' semantic root—"

"Master, please! I'm interested in history, but talking about farming—"

"All right, all right. I'll stick to the logograms. Despite the contempt of your thanes and your own impatience, know that they're worth knowing well. Though I learned my zyndari letters and a few common logograms as a girl, I didn't seriously study the Ano logograms until I was in my forties, when Emperor Ragin opened the Imperial examinations to women. It seemed such a chore at the time, and I would have far preferred to study music on my zither instead. Still, once you've achieved a certain level of expertise so that the wisdom of the ancient texts is fully accessible to you, you'll discover a pleasure in playing with the logograms that can't be found anywhere else. Your calligraphy really needs improvement—"

"Ah, I'm afraid I'll never be a calligrapher," said a despondent Kinri. "I just don't have the patience or interest in making wax blocks pretty." Before Nazu could object, he hurried on. "I like logograms just fine—they're like intricate machines . . . except they don't *do* anything. I'd much rather work with real, physical machines, like the amazing inventions of Na Moji, who was supposed to have built a mechanical eye to capture nature like one of the gods—"

The long, mournful sound of a garinafin-bone trumpet broke through the gentle susurrus of the surf. No music was perhaps dreaded more in Ukyu-taasa. The garinafin trumpet tune was used to summon Lyucu warriors to the battlefield.

The faces of both Nazu and Kinri changed in an instant. Kinri looked confused, then curious and excited. Nazu, on the other hand, looked stricken with terror before her features settled into an expression of determination.

Wordlessly, they got up, exited the hut, and climbed up the dune that had sheltered them from the wind and sun. From atop the dune, they looked down at the village on the other side.

About fifty soldiers—conscripts from among the Dara natives—commanded by several Lyucu officers had taken over Kigo Yezu. They had driven all the villagers, from nursing babies to cane-leaning elders, whether napping in their huts or working in the fields, into a tight huddle in the clearing around the village well. A garinafin crouched to the side like a living knoll, its wings folded on its back. The villagers gazed at this deadly beast with terror-filled eyes.

"What's happening?" exclaimed Kinri. "Have there been reports of a pirate raid?"

Nazu ignored him as she surveyed the scene with a solemn expression. "What did you tell your guards and tutor about your plans for today?"

"The same thing I always say: to hunt and fish in the countryside."

"Did you tell them where?"

"Yes. Everyone knows Kigo Yezu is a good bay for fishing."

Nazu pondered the situation, her heart leaden. The appearance of the garinafin and so many soldiers couldn't be just a coincidence. She looked at Kinri. "Think! You've told absolutely no one about learning *zamaki* from a native?"

"No . . . wait . . . I did say something to the pékyu-taasa, Dyu-tika."

"What did you say?" Nazu struggled to keep her voice calm.

"Yesterday he was bored with all the games the courtiers knew, and I said I would teach him the soldiers' game, the one with the little horses and swordsmen and crubens—"

"Those were your exact words?"

Flustered, Kinri tried to remember. "Maybe? I can't remember. But *zamaki* isn't forbidden! I know several Lyucu officers who learned how to play from native conscripts. I just thought you'd be able to tell me the history behind it. I was going to get the rules from a soldier before showing the pékyu-taasa anyway."

Nazu closed her eyes, the muscles on her face twitching as she fought to suppress her rage and regret. Kinri had been after her to teach him the game ever since he caught her a few weeks back trying to work out some *zamaki* puzzles with these pieces. Careful as he was, he hadn't realized that the version played by the native soldiers in Kriphi didn't have cruben tokens, since the Lyucu had outlawed references to the powerful scaled whales. The creatures were considered by many to be allies of the House of Dandelion and often appeared in the iconography of rebel standards.

When she opened her eyes again, she began to scramble down the dune toward the village, careless of how she slipped and slid down the steep sand slope.

"Master, wait!" Kinri called out. Nazu made no sign of having heard him, and he ran after her.

# CHAPTER TWENTY-THREE

# A LESSON ON TRUTH

RUI: THE NINTH MONTH IN THE EIGHTH YEAR OF
THE REIGN OF AUDACIOUS FREEDOM (KNOWN AS
THE EIGHTH YEAR OF THE REIGN OF SEASON OF
STORMS IN DARA, AND THE EIGHTH YEAR SINCE
PRINCESS THÉRA DEPARTED DARA FOR UKYU-
GONDÉ).

By the time they arrived at the village, native soldiers had forced all the villagers to kneel on the ground with their hands laced behind their heads. As a senior Lyucu commander paced back and forth before the kneeling villagers, soldiers under the direction of two junior Lyucu officers went into the huts, throwing open cabinets and upending trunks, smashing bowls and plates, kicking holes in the wattle-and-daub walls as if searching for secret compartments.

Two soldiers barred Nazu Tei's way at the edge of the clearing.

"Stop! Stop at once!" shouted Nazu as she was held in place by her arms, panting. "What is the meaning of this?"

Kinri (or Savo, as he was known to the Lyucu), who was some distance behind her, stopped and instinctively hid himself among some bushes. Although it wasn't exactly a secret that, in addition to lessons from his court-appointed tutor in Kriphi, he enjoyed visiting the countryside to learn more about native culture, the practice was enough of an eccentricity among the children of the Lyucu thanes that he didn't want to make an appearance just yet.

The Lyucu commander strolled up to Nazu, her eyes narrowed

suspiciously. "What are you screaming about, old woman? Can't you see we're in the middle of an investigation here?"

Nazu inclined her head to show her double scroll-bun. "My name is Nazu Tei, and I achieved the rank of *toko dawiji* in the Imperial examinations in the sixth year of the Reign of Four Placid Seas. Emperor Thaké has given all ranked scholars the right to intercede on behalf of the peasantry. I demand to know your name and what crimes these villagers have been accused of."

With Tanvanaki's approval and support, the emperor had issued a series of edicts in the last few years intended to promote a more harmonious existence between the natives and their Lyucu conquerors. The edicts relating to the elevated status of scholars had proved especially popular and gained the Lyucu regime many supporters among the learned.

Just how much the emperor's authority bound the Lyucu nobles and officers, however, was always somewhat unclear.

The Lyucu officer glared at Nazu, but she nodded at the two soldiers holding the old woman, indicating that they could let her go. "I am called Cutanrovo Aga, daughter of Vorifir Aga, son of Kiof Aga. I serve the pékyu as the Thane of the Flock of Nalyufin. By Emperor Thaké's seal, I command the Capital Security Forces. We have reason to believe that there is suspicious activity in this village."

"What suspicious activity?"

Cutanrovo opened her mouth as if to speak—

Like any court, Pékyu Vadyu's court was divided into rival factions and parties.

One faction, led by Thane Goztan Ryoto and supported by Emperor Thaké, advocated accommodation with the natives. Many of the accommodationists, like Thane Vocu Firna, had come to enjoy Dara's native culture and products, and believed that it was possible to eventually win over the natives to support the Lyucu conquest.

The other faction, composed mostly of lower-ranking thanes and without a prominent leader, advocated a harder line against the natives. It was impossible to ever trust the natives, they argued, and any accommodation only encouraged future rebellions. Cutanrovo

Aga belonged to this hard-liner faction, which had always been out of favor with the pékyu.

Cutanrovo placed most of the blame for their political misfortune on that weakling Timu, the pékyu's consort. She couldn't see why the pékyu was so solicitous of a barbarian man's feelings. Sure, he was the father of her children, but once the pékyu had produced heirs that gave the Lyucu a claim to native legitimacy, why bother keeping the sperm sack around? Still, he seemed to maintain a hold on the pékyu, and the puppet emperor sometimes acted like the puppet master. Cutanrovo could only conclude that he must be ser-vicing the pékyu exceptionally well in bed.

For years she had sought to demonstrate the dangers of being soft on the natives. Whenever a rebellion arose, she always volunteered to lead the response, hoping to find evidence of vast conspiracies to overthrow the Lyucu. When such evidence wasn't forthcoming and the natives seemed to grow ever more docile over the years—she was certain it was only a trick—she resorted to goading the natives into new rebellions. Earlier during the summer, for example, she had instructed her cousin, a naro with a violent temper and little under-standing of the bigger picture, to commit some atrocity against the native village he was supervising. The hope was to provoke some violent response from the villagers to show that the natives couldn't be trusted.

The plan had succeeded beyond her wildest dreams. Not only did the villagers rebel, but they actually killed her cousin, giving Cutanrovo an excuse to set the entire northern shore of Rui aflame and slaughter as many as possible. In Cutanrovo's view, the only good native was a dead native.

But Tanvanaki had declined Cutanrovo's offer to lead the sup-pression force. Instead, she had gone to deal with the brewing rebellion herself, claiming that the upcoming sacrificial rites to Péa-Kiji—a ridiculous bit of accommodation to native superstition, in Cutanrovo's view—was too important to risk a prolonged distur-bance. The pékyu had resolved the situation quickly by limiting the reprisal only to the village itself. Since two native scholars had even helped the Lyucu find and put down the rebels, the event was even cited as an example of the success of accommodationist policies. Cutanrovo seethed at how her plan had backfired.

Recently, however, Cutanrovo sensed a change in the pékyu. Ever since the departure of the Dara-raaki tribute ship last month, the pékyu seemed preoccupied. Whenever conflict arose at court, she no longer automatically sided with the accommodationists.

*There is an opportunity here*, mused Cutanrovo. *Has Emperor Thaké lost favor with his wife? Has Thane Goztan done something to stir up mistrust in the pékyu? Maybe Tanvanaki has finally realized the wisdom of me and other true warriors, who haven't forgotten what it means to be Lyucu.*

On a hunch, she went to the Roro Hills, where she knew Tanvanaki kept a secret camp populated by prisoners abducted from the core islands. Tanvanaki claimed that the camp was an important way to gather intelligence about the Dara-raaki, but Cutanrovo had long suspected that it was probably a corrupt place where Tanvanaki was being softened and bewitched by the flapping tongues of wily scholars in the mold of her husband.

Claiming to be there on behalf of Tanvanaki, she had interrogated the prisoners, applying torture liberally. Most of the fools had nothing useful to offer, but one did reveal a secret that had shaken Cutanrovo to the core. The Wall of Storms was going to open in less than three years, bringing with it reinforcements from the Lyucu homeland.

And Tanvanaki had kept this a secret.

Cutanrovo knew that the secret, once disclosed, would completely alter the balance of power at court. The argument the accommodationists had always relied on, that the Lyucu invasion force couldn't win without the support of the natives, would be rendered moot. With a fresh wave of warriors and garinafins from home, the Lyucu would be able to conquer the rest of Dara without any native allies. The hard-liners' dream of a true paradise of Lyucu supremacy was within reach.

But she had to be careful about how to reveal her knowledge, to force Tanvanaki to accept the hard-liner vision as the only viable one, to utterly reject her husband and the addled advice of that Goztan Ryoto.

Cutanrovo probed and watched, until an opportunity finally presented itself.

She had found Pékyu-taasa Todyu, beloved son of Tanvanaki and Timu, demanding a native palace guard find his friend Savo Ryoto.

"But votan," the guard had pleaded, "I already asked the thane-taasa's tutor. He's out hunting and fishing near the bay of Kigo Yezu."

"He said he was learning to play the swordsman-and-cruben game today! He must be with one of you in the palace guard quarters! Find him or I'll tell my mother!"

Cutanrovo had intervened. After consoling the tearful child, who was certain that his friend was playing some wonderful game in secret without him, Cutanrovo interrogated the guards about Savo Ryoto's habits. Then she pondered the meaning of what she had found out.

If Savo just wanted to learn to play *zamaki*, plenty of native soldiers or even Lyucu officers could show him right here in the palace. There was no reason for him to be out in the countryside just to find a *zamaki* player. And even if he did want to find some *zamaki* expert out there, why did he lie to the palace guard about it?

Moreover, the pékyu-taasa had called the game "swordsman-and-cruben," which she knew was an old name for the board game that no one serving the court dared to use. He could have heard the name only from Savo. Why was Savo talking about crubens, a known native code word for rebellion? Moreover, what was Savo doing, going to Kigo Yezu all the time when he had no reputation as a distinguished hunter?

*He's hiding something.*

Since Savo Ryoto was the son of Thane Goztan Ryoto, discovering an embarrassing secret about the thane-taasa had the potential to deal a serious blow to the accommodationists and push Tanvanaki, who must already be re-evaluating the wisdom of the hard-liners in light of the news about the Wall of Storms, to a real change in policy.

Cutanrovo quickly summoned her troops and headed for Kigo Yezu.

"What suspicious activity?" demanded Nazu Tei again.

Cutanrovo's mouth gaped because she hadn't the foggiest idea.

She had brought her troops here hoping to catch the thane-taasa, Savo Ryoto, in some compromising foolish act: courting a native woman like a potential wife, worshipping some idol as part of a local mystery cult, hoarding treasure that should be turned over to the pékyu, maybe even hosting an illegal *zamaki* tournament at which players dressed up as the Lords of Dara, as some of the more corrupt children of the accommodationists were rumored to do in private.

She was acting on instinct. The specifics didn't matter. She was sure she'd find *something*.

So far, things weren't working out. Her troops hadn't found any signs of the thane-taasa in the surrounding woods or in the bay, and so she had ordered the ostentatious raid against the village, hoping to chase the thane-taasa out of one of the huts the way beaters drove game out of hiding during a hunt.

Frustrated, Cutanrovo said the first thing that came to mind. "Contraband. We have reports of contraband here."

"What contraband? I can assure you that there are no weapons in Kigo Yezu. The deci-chiefs would know if anyone possessed blades longer than a kitchen knife. And you won't find any banned books here. Most of the villagers don't know how to read."

"Why should I take your word when I can find out for myself?" Cutanrovo swept her hand at the soldiers ransacking the huts.

"You can't just destroy people's homes with no evidence."

"I have all the evidence I need," declared Cutanrovo. As always, the effort of speaking Dara taxed her. She hated the fact that she had to speak to the native scholars and soldiers in their language instead of hers—another aspect of Tanvanaki's failure. She always felt tongue-tied, unable to sound as peremptory and authoritative as she liked. "I have a . . . *feeling*."

"The emperor and the pékyu have long declared vague hunches impermissible as the basis for disrupting the lives of law-abiding native villagers!"

The commanding tone used by the old native woman irked Cutanrovo. There was a time when the natives cowered before every Lyucu warrior, but things had changed. She took another step toward the old woman, hoping to intimidate her—and caught sight of the hairpin shaped like a spearhead in her double scroll-bun.

Cutanrovo's heart sped up. She readily recognized the pattern of acid-etched lines on the bone: the sign of the Five Tribes of the Antler. *So the thane-taasa was here! Even if we didn't catch him in the act, maybe we can figure out what he was doing here.*

"It's far more than a vague hunch," Cutanrovo said. Her mind churned rapidly as she tried to imagine what the old woman had to do with Goztan's son. "I have reliable reports of forbidden activity here . . . that threatens the security of Ukyu-taasa."

Nazu laughed. "What does that mean? What do you hope to find? Maps? Terrain models? Practice dummies to train rebel fighters? We have nothing like that here. These are simple people. We don't fish more than a day's distance from shore, and many have never even been to Kriphi. No strangers have been spotted in the village for months. The idea that anyone here is plotting a rebellion is absurd."

"Even a still pool can rot," retorted Cutanrovo. "If you're so sure of the innocence of the villagers, why are you so worried about a little search? Are you afraid we'll find something . . . or *someone*? Someone who shouldn't be here?"

Behind the bushes, Savo Ryoto tensed. *Is this about me? But why shouldn't I be here? I come here all the time. To "hunt."*

He was about to step out to explain that this was all a misunderstanding when he saw Nazu holding her hands behind her back, making the *stop* sign she used with him when she wanted him to take a break in one of his impassioned arguments with her over the meaning of some passage in the Classics.

Nazu was certain now that this Lyucu thane had come here because of Kinri, and though she didn't understand why, she felt that she had to keep him out of sight for both their sakes. Forcing herself to stay calm, she said, "Even if we have nothing to hide, you can't just come in here and turn the place upside down. The emperor and the pékyu have promised that the people of Rui and Dasu will be treated as loyal subjects, not slaves or spies. How can you win the hearts of the people when—"

Nazu was interrupted by an excited shout from one of the searching soldiers. He emerged from a hut, holding aloft a silk pouch. The soldier ran over to Cutanrovo and presented the pouch to her on a wooden tray. She opened it and dumped the contents into the tray: a set of figurines made of white jade and red amber.

Cutanrovo's eyes swept over the kneeling villagers. Most looked blankly back at her, but she noticed that the village chief, Elder Do Kigo, a gaunt man in his forties who was blind in one eye, kept his gaze on the ground. Next to him knelt his three children and his wife, holding a baby in her arms. She stared at Elder Kigo and saw that the sleeves of his tunic trembled.

*What secrets lie in this village?*

"Whose home is that?" Cutanrovo demanded.

"It's mine," said Nazu.

Surprised, the Lyucu thane looked from the hut to Nazu. The hut where the figurines had been found looked no different from the simple dwellings of the other villagers. In her experience, native scholars always lived in better houses, intent on showing off their superior status to the mere peasantry.

*A* toko dawiji *who doesn't live in Kriphi and isn't a court-appointed tutor . . . one who hides in obscurity in a simple fishing-farming village . . .*

She examined the figurines on the tray more closely and was disappointed not to find anything that resembled crubens. Still thinking, she extemporized. "This set would fetch at least twenty gold pieces in Kriphi. Why do you live in a leaky hut like that if you own something like this?"

"I wasn't aware that it's a crime to live frugally. That gaming set was given to me by my benefactors, who passed away a long time ago. I keep it to honor their memory, nothing more."

"What game is this?"

"Zamaki."

"This doesn't look like any *zamaki* set I've seen." Cutanrovo picked through the pieces one by one, certain that she had found the key to the puzzle. "Is this supposed to be a long-haired bull? And these—are these meant to be peasants with the wide-brimmed hats? And what is this? Some kind of fishing vessel?"

She looked to the native soldiers around her. "Any of you ever seen a *zamaki* set like this?" They shook their heads.

"My benefactors were from the Big Island. There are so many variations of this game in the Islands that it's not surprising that their version would be unknown to most here."

"*Zamaki* is a game of war, isn't it? It can be used to simulate battles."

Nazu laughed. "It's a *game* based on abstract ideas of war. True, it's most popular among soldiers, but many people who have never gone to war enjoy this game. I've heard merchants speak of how they imagine the game as a reflection of commerce and competition, and scholars speak of the game's potential as a model of political factions. It's a *game*, nothing more. Look at the pieces on the tray. Do you see anything that looks like a forbidden engine of sabotage or allusion to insurrection?"

Cutanrovo hesitated, unwilling to concede defeat. "But it doesn't make sense that you would keep such a refined war gaming set out here in a muddy village. It's suspicious."

"By that logic, the native ministers in Kriphi who enjoy *cüpa* are also rebels in disguise, and the children who play games of bandits versus soldiers are studying how to overthrow the pékyu. If a *zamaki* set is considered contraband, you'll have to arrest half the soldiers here."

"Don't be insolent, Nazu Tei."

By now the soldiers had completed their search of the huts. Everything lay in shambles, but nothing remotely questionable had been found. Cutanrovo, embarrassed by the lack of results, barked at the soldiers to form up. "I'm going to have to bring you back to Kriphi," she said to Nazu. "There are too many unanswered questions."

Nazu spread her hands carelessly. "Fine. I haven't been to the capital in a while. It'll be good to catch up with some friends."

"You're absolutely certain you've told me everything? There's nothing else in this village that might be considered contraband?"

Nazu shook her head resolutely.

Cutanrovo glanced over at the village chief. While the other villagers had visibly relaxed at hearing that the soldiers were about to leave, Elder Kigo looked as tense as ever. He had shuddered as Nazu denied owning any more suspicious objects.

Looking thoughtful, Cutanrovo strolled slowly and deliberately toward the middle-aged man. She knew that Tanvanaki, under the influence of Timu, had made protection of the scholars a priority, and inflicting pain on this old woman without more evidence didn't seem like a smart idea. This village chief, however, was no more than a peasant. Back during the conquest of Rui, she had killed men and women like him by the hundreds.

As she approached, the village chief trembled even harder. Striding up until she was looming over the kneeling man, the Lyucu commander asked, "Is the *toko dawiji* telling the truth?"

"Yes! Yes!" the man said.

"You are sure?"

The man touched his forehead to the earth in submission. "Yes!" He shook like a leaf in the wind. "We're all loyal subjects here in Kigo Yezu! No spies! No rebels! There's absolutely nothing more in any of the huts!"

Nazu clenched her fists anxiously, but she could do no more to help the situation now.

"'Nothing more *in* any of the huts,' eh? That's a funny way to declare your innocence," said Cutanrovo. "I believe you're trying to do the right thing, Do Kigo. I really do. But I think you're going to need some help to fully appreciate the duties of a loyal subject."

She reached down and grabbed the baby, not more than a few months old, out of the hands of Elder Kigo's wife. The woman screamed and struggled to get the baby back, but she dared not get up off the ground.

"Nara, don't fight!" Elder Kigo called, his voice desperate. "The honored commander won't harm our child."

Cutanrovo lifted the baby out of the mother's reach and kicked casually, her foot landing with a muffled thud against the woman's throat. Nara's screaming ended abruptly as she fell to the ground, gasping through a collapsed trachea. Her children scrambled to help her, crying. Elder Kigo slammed his forehead to the ground repeatedly, muttering the whole time, "Mercy! My daughter! Mercy!" The baby wailed in the Lyucu thane's arms.

"Bring me a bucket of water," ordered Cutanrovo. The native soldiers looked at one other, hesitating. "Now!" the commander barked. One of the soldiers scrambled to obey and soon brought back a filled water bucket from the well.

"Torture has been specifically outlawed as a method of interrogation by the emperor," Nazu said, struggling to keep her voice calm.

"You're talking about rules governing the native constables," said Cutanrovo, "not the army."

"This isn't a time of war! I will petition the magistrate; I will petition the emperor himself!"

Cutanrovo didn't bother replying as she grabbed the bucket from the soldier and set it on the ground at her feet, right in front of the parents. She flipped the baby upside down, held her by the legs, and began to dip her head into the bucket.

"O gods! Mercy! Mercy!" Elder Kigo screamed and crawled up to the Lyucu commander, blocking the bucket with his body.

Cutanrovo kicked him away. "I'm giving you one last chance to tell the truth. Where is the other contraband?"

Savo Ryoto could hold himself back no longer.

"Enough of this!" He strode out from behind the bushes. "Mas—" Savo bit off the honorific just in time. Since Nazu Tei wasn't court-appointed, she couldn't serve as his teacher officially. Tanvanaki, who knew very well the power of the master-pupil relationship in Dara, had made unauthorized teaching an offense punishable by death. In front of others, he had to remember to treat her as merely a native informer. "Thane Cutanrovo, Nazu Tei is right. This isn't a time of war, and you can't just go around acting like these people are slaves or enemies."

A few soldiers ran up to confront Savo, but he pulled the garinafin hairpin out of his bun and held it up. "I am called Savo Ryoto, son of Goztan Ryoto, daughter of Dayu Ryoto. I serve the pékyu as Thane-taasa of the Five Tribes of the Antler."

The soldiers backed off. Goztan Ryoto was one of the most powerful thanes in Kriphi, and manhandling her son would clearly not be a good career move.

Even Cutanrovo Aga hesitated. *So, you're still here!* She kept the excitement of having caught her prey off her face and nodded at the young man as she held the wailing and wriggling baby in one hand like an ensnared rabbit. "Votan, please excuse the lack of a proper salute. As you can see, I'm a bit occupied at the moment."

"It's all right," said Savo. "Nazu Tei is a . . . trusted informer and friend, and I can vouch for her character and loyalty. In fact, I'm something of a *zamaki* expert myself, and can independently confirm that the gaming pieces you've recovered are part of a gaming set, nothing more."

Savo didn't understand why Cutanrovo was acting like this, but he was utterly revolted by her behavior, which went against the letter and spirit of the pékyu's edicts to treat the natives with kindness so long as they were obedient. The uncultured Lyucu thane was making a volcano out of a roast-pit, as the natives would say, and risked damaging the reputation of the Lyucu as a warlike but fair people, here to liberate Dara from oppression by Kuni Garu the tyrant and Jia the usurper. He had to defuse the situation as quickly as possible.

He looked over at Nazu, expecting to see his teacher show gratitude at his intervention, but Nazu's face remained tense and unreadable.

Cutanrovo examined the confident young man: single scroll-bun, scholar's robe, smooth hands that had obviously spent more time playing with ivory-handled writing knives than wielding heavy bone axes or clubs. There were no scars on his face, nor any trace of a warrior's instincts in his eyes. He looked, in short, more like the spoiled child of some wealthy native barbarian than the scion of a proud Lyucu thane.

*This thane-taasa, a boy who has no idea what it means to fight for the survival of our people, who doesn't understand the cost of his comfortable, happy life of ease, who doesn't know the pain of starvation and exposure to the elements or the terror of watching his family and companions die at the hands of bloodthirsty barbarian soldiers, is now vouching for a crafty native woman.*

As the villagers wailed and pleaded, she held on to the baby dangling from her hand, thinking dispassionately. She noticed the way Savo looked at Nazu Tei.

*There is definitely something going on between these two.*

"Let that baby go," said Savo. "Elder Kigo isn't a proven traitor, and you can't apply torture just because you suspect something.
That is the emperor's decree. I'm ordering you, in the name of my
mother, to give the baby back to her parents and end this nonsense
right now."

Cutanrovo's fingers tightened around the ankles of the baby.
Hate and rage welled up in her heart like a volcano about to erupt.
Everything in her vision turned red.

Cutanrovo wasn't from a prominent tribe. The Tribe of the Flock
of Nalyufin was from the north of Ukyu, where meager resources
meant tiny herds and few warriors. As a little girl, she had witnessed
the Agon take away the food stores the tribe had been counting on
for the winter. She had held her grandmother's lifeless body in the
deep of winter, after she starved herself to death so that Cutanrovo,
the youngest in the clan, would have more to eat.

And then, Tenryo came. He was wily like Péten, brave like Diasa,
as kind to his allies as Toryoana of Healing Hands, and as merciless to his enemies as Nalyufin, the hate-hearted. He was Afir and
Kikisavo reborn, the hope of the Lyucu, the deliverer and savior of
her people.

She had fought for him as soon as she could climb upon a garinafin, and she never hesitated to do as he ordered. The day they finally
killed Nobo Aragoz, last pékyu of the hated Agon, was the happiest
day of her life.

And then the Dara barbarians had arrived under Admiral Krita,
and the battle of wits and stratagems began. She had been instrumental in Tenryo's plans as the leader of the secret garinafin teams who
traveled far east to the World's Edge Mountains to collect lumber
for Krita's ships, dropping the logs into the sea so that Tenryo could
claim the gods had delivered a miracle for the barbarian potentate in
order to win his trust. The mission, unprecedented in the memories
of the tribes, drew much opposition among the elders and engen-
dered doubt among the shamans. But Cutanrovo had not hesitated
to obey Tenryo, and took up with gusto the unfamiliar and arduous
task of felling logs and transporting them. Her firstborn, a little boy,

was killed by a log that rolled off the back of a garinafin. She sent him on pédiato savaga herself, climbing high into a tree to set his little corpse among the swaying branches.

(Cutanrovo counted herself lucky. She wasn't one of the thanes picked by Tenryo to seduce the revolting Lords of Dara. Some of those thanes never fully recovered from their ordeal—just look at Goztan Ryoto! Cutanrovo was sure that the weakling thane's accommodationist tendencies came from her sojourn among Krita's expedition. Her Lyucu spirit had been broken.)

Cutanrovo had not resented Pékyu Tenryo for the sacrifices he demanded of her. She loved him the way an eagle loved the heat of the Eye of Cudyufin, the way a moth loved the light of the Mouth of Nalyufin. She believed in him, in his vision for a better future for the Lyucu, as much as she believed in the shamans' voice paintings and dance stories.

But Tenryo's demand for sacrifices didn't stop.

She had given up the familiar and comforting open expanse of the vast scrublands with roaming herds of sheep and cattle, mouflon and aurochs, where everything was shaped by the forces of nature and the gods, where you could fly for days without seeing any sign of human habitation, to come to this strange land, where everything seemed tamed, tied down, penned in, where even the very land itself was confined by grids of field furrows and the sea was bound by shipping lanes, in order to seek a better life for her people. She had followed Pékyu Tenryo's self-reliant war axe without question across the stormy ocean, lost two husbands to native ambushes on Rui Island, and watched her daughter die on that horror-filled day in Zathin Gulf, as garinafin after garinafin plunged into watery graves from the death-dealing barbaric silkmotic lances. She had then served Pékyu Vadyu faithfully as she consolidated the Lyucu rule over the untrustworthy and restive natives, doing whatever the pékyu asked of her.

It was true that for her courage and sacrifices, she and her tribe had been amply rewarded. But she never forgot the cost of her victories, the starved grandmothers and grandfathers, the mothers forced to kill their Agon-seeded babies, the friends and family she had lost, the Agon naros and culeks and Dara-raaki barbarians who she had to kill before they killed her. Through it all, the Lyucu spirit had sustained her, the belief in ultimate victory, no matter how long the odds.

And now this little noble, this *mere child*, this wolf pup who willingly defanged himself and wrapped himself in sheepskins, was citing the orders of the native emperor, a figurehead puppet and bedtime plaything of the great Tanvanaki, to tell *her* what to do.

She understood better than anyone the nature of the threat the Lyucu faced. The natives outnumbered their conquerors by more than a hundredfold, and they had surely not forgotten the bloody slaughters the Lyucu were forced to commit against them in order to secure their foothold in these islands. Unless the Lyucu retained their wolf nature, the docile-seeming sheep would seize the first chance they had to stomp their overlords to death.

The thane-taasa was feasting on the meat she had hunted, but he didn't understand the first thing about gratitude, about how to keep himself safe, about the Lyucu spirit. She had to do what needed to be done, even if it meant ruining this idiot.

It was utterly intolerable to see Tanvanaki and Goztan throw away the legacy of the pékyu-votan and desecrate the sacrifices of the many Lyucu who had died to give their children a better chance at life, in order to seek *accommodation* with inferior Dara-raaki, a cruel and cunning people bent on the destruction of the Lyucu unless they were enslaved or killed. To see Savo Ryoto, a child for whose future she and the other thanes had sacrificed so much, cavorting with a Dara-raaki as though he was himself a native, was simply too much.

But she forced herself to suppress her fury, to not reveal the truth of her feelings on her face, to be as wily and long-thinking as Pékyu Tenryo. Again she focused on the way the thane-taasa looked at the *toko dawiji* named Nazu Tei, a combination of deference and yearning for approval. She remembered that Nazu's bun was pinned in place with a garinafin-bone spearhead etched in the sign of Savo's tribe.

"Votan," she said, holding on to the struggling baby and her voice perfectly calm, "of course I'm not doubting your friend or your expertise. But the pékyu-votan—may he enjoy the All-Father's feast in the Great Tent beyond the World's Edge Mountains—and the pékyu herself have always instructed us to be vigilant. May I know what subjects the *toko dawiji* is informing you on?"

Savo frowned, not quite sure where Cutanrovo was going with this. Court-appointed tutors—who also wore garinafin bone hairpins to mark their status—were required to submit their lesson plans in advance to ensure that they would not corrupt the minds of their Lyucu charges with forbidden topics. In practice, the requirement was largely a formality, and the censors rarely, if ever, rejected an application, at least not if the appropriate bribes were submitted along with the application. However, since Nazu wasn't supposed to be his teacher but only a native informer, she was allowed to inform him on practically any topic he wished to know.

"I question her on whatever subjects strike my fancy," Savo said, "and she informs me honestly and without reservation." He deliberately spoke in a haughty manner to emphasize that he was in charge of his own "informing sessions" with Nazu rather than being in a forbidden master-pupil relationship. Cutanrovo's question drew attention to the fact that he was engaged in an eccentric practice, but it was hardly against the rules. "I trust her completely and consider her a dear friend," he added, lingering on the word *trust*.

"Ah, I understand now," said Cutanrovo, the corners of her mouth curving up in a smirk as she winked conspiratorially. "Votan, I didn't realize you're into well-done steak! I could suggest some indigo houses in Kriphi that specialize in more mature women so that you don't have to trek—"

"How dare you!" said a red-faced Savo. It was true that some Lyucu thanes and naros-votan with jealous spouses used the excuse of seeing "native informers" to visit their kept concubines in the countryside, but he had always viewed the practice with disgust and contempt. To have his beloved teacher insulted in this manner was more than he could bear. "Nazu Tei is a respected scholar, and I value her for her wisdom. It is precisely men and women like her who can help us plant our roots in these islands."

Cutanrovo looked utterly apologetic. "I meant no offense, votan! Ah, helping us to plant our roots . . . so am I to understand that you're having this Dara-raaki slave inform you on the native practice of farming? If you'll indulge the opinion of an uninformed simple gari-nafin rider, I really don't think that farming is suited to a warrior—"

"Oh, by the club of Diasa-Fithowéo, that was just a metaphor! Of course I'm not interested in *farming* and digging in dirt. And stop using slurs against her—"

"Don't!" cried Nazu. "She's goading you—"

But the embarrassed and enraged Savo would not be deterred. "She's teaching me calligraphy and the Classics, all right? I have a court-appointed tutor, but he's boring while Master Tei's lessons are fun. And she's also teaching me about native culture, which you should try to appreciate. Spitting on everything the natives of Dara have accomplished and hold dear is not the way to secure our rule." He was really getting into the swing of things now. Chewing out this obdurate, disrespectful, paranoid brute stuck in the past felt *good*. "As the pékyu said, we should make use of native inventions if they can be helpful. For instance, I was just now learning about the history of *zamaki*—"

Abruptly, he stopped. There was a look of despair on Nazu Tei's face, in sharp contrast to the smile Cutanrovo wore, at once triumphant and pitying.

"Votan, forgive me." Cutanrovo's tone was solicitous and careful, as if speaking to a child. "Just so that I'm absolutely clear: Did you call this woman 'master'? But she's not your court-appointed tutor, is she? You've submitted to her the way a spineless barbarian pupil submits to his mud-legged teacher?"

While it was common in Dara proper to use "master" as a generic honorific, the practice had died out in Ukyu-taasa after the conquest due to the Lyucu fear of master-pupil relationships.

"I misspoke," said Savo, desperate to salvage things. "I sometimes use the word in jest, but she is at all times under my authority—"

Cutanrovo's face shifted into one of cruel determination. "An unauthorized native teacher is one of the greatest dangers the pékyu warned us about. Soldiers, seize the criminal who dared to corrupt the mind of a Lyucu thane-taasa, and be sure you protect the ensnared thane-taasa from any more of this crafty witch's influence."

"Oh, what have you done, Kinri—"

Before she could finish, two soldiers rushed up to Nazu Tei, threw her to the ground, and began to bind her arms behind her with thick ropes of twisted sinew. Savo tried to run to her defense, but two more soldiers held him in place.

"Please, votan," one of them whispered, "don't make this harder on us."

"Cutanrovo, you can't do this!" shouted Savo. "My mother will go to the pékyu herself!"

The Lyucu thane looked at him impassively. "I'm sorry, votan, but you can't command me. I'll go to Thane Goztan later to apologize in person. I believe she'll see that this is for your own protection. I also heard the witch call you by a barbarian name, which, as you recall, is also strictly forbidden."

Savo opened his mouth to protest some more, but Cutanrovo gestured for the soldiers to bind and gag him. "Your mind is addled, thane-taasa. It's best that you not say anything you'll regret later."

Cutanrovo turned back to the kneeling villagers. Her gamble had paid off beyond her wildest imaginings. The thane-taasa's indiscretion would bring down his mother and transform the political balance at court. "The discovery of an unauthorized native teacher exerting influence over a high-ranking Lyucu thane-taasa constitutes a military emergency, and all Imperial edicts applicable to peace times are hereby suspended in Kigo Yezu."

She tightened her grip around the baby's ankles and plunged her into the bucket of water. The kneeling villagers were so shocked that a few seconds passed before Elder Kigo and Nara howled like animals.

Cutanrovo pulled the baby out of the water. She coughed and sputtered, and then cried even harder. Over the baby's terrified wailing, Cutanrovo's voice rang out calmly.

"I'm going to ask one last time: Do you know of any more contraband in the village? The next time I dip this piglet in the water, I'm not going to pull her out."

Elder Kigo recovered enough to scramble up to the Lyucu thane and hugged her knees. "Oh mercy! Mercy! I'll tell you everything . . . everything! We're loyal subjects of the emperor and the pékyu!"

"You'd best speak quick." Cutanrovo lowered the dangling baby again.

"I saw the *toko dawiji* bury something under that tree"—he pointed at the pagoda tree at the western edge of the village, whose canopy spread like an umbrella—"when she first moved here five years ago. I don't know what she buried. The *toko dawiji* isn't a member of the Kigo clan. We don't pry into any of her business. That's all I know, I swear!"

Cutanrovo glanced at a few of the native soldiers, and they ran toward the tree and began to dig.

"Why didn't you inform the local garrison commander when you first saw this suspicious activity?" the Lyucu thane asked.

The elder said nothing but slammed his forehead again and again into the ground as he lay prostrate before Cutanrovo.

"Because you liked having a *toko dawiji* in the village who could intercede on your behalf with the authorities," declared Cutanrovo. "That's why you protected her, isn't it? I've always said that edict from unready Timu was trouble. And why didn't you tell me the truth earlier, when I first asked you?"

The elder said nothing but slammed his head against the ground even harder. Blood seeped from his forehead and turned the earth at Cutanrovo's feet brown.

"Because you thought I wouldn't dare to drown your piglet," whispered Cutanrovo. "Because you thought the *toko dawiji* could actually protect you. Just because things have been peaceful for a few years, you're starting to think this is your land again, you dirty little barbarian pig, fit only for rooting in the dirt." She lifted a foot and set it down on the back of the elder's neck, pressing his face into the bloody ground. "You may no longer be slaves by the laws of your emperor, but the only law that matters to me is the word of the Lyucu. Do you understand?"

The elder, whose mouth was filled with dirt, grunted.

"What a good little pig," cooed Cutanrovo. "Now doesn't it feel good to have confessed your secret? Doesn't it feel so right to embrace your race's slavish nature?"

The elder tried to nod with his face pressed into the mud. He moaned incoherently.

The native soldiers and the kneeling villagers turned their faces away from this unwatchable scene.

Savo, gagged and bound, made muffled noises of protest in his throat.

"Stop it!" Nazu Tei shouted. "Stop, Cutanrovo!" Though her arms and legs were tied, she strained to get up from the ground. Fire seemed to shoot out of her eyes.

One of the soldiers ran back from the pagoda tree, holding a box in his hands.

"Still think you can give orders, do you?" said Cutanrovo, chuckling. "Let's take a look at this great secret you buried in the middle of the night." She opened the box and dumped the contents on the ground: figurines of jade and amber, similar to the ones seen earlier in the pouch found in Nazu Tei's hut, as well as a folded-up piece of silk.

Cutanrovo lifted her foot off Elder Kigo's neck and kicked him aside. Still dangling the baby, whose struggles had grown much less vigorous, she crouched down to examine the new figurines. "Let's see, ah, these are garinafins, and these appear to be the city-ships. . . . Is this one of those witchcraft crubens you Dara-raaki are always going on about? . . . Aha, I think this is meant to represent Kriphi, and these are models of our tents. . . ."

She unfolded the silk cloth: It was a map of Rui and Dasu, with Lyucu encampments marked. The thane stood up and asked Nazu Tei, "Still want to tell me this is a *zamaki* set?"

Nazu closed her eyes. "If you look at the map, you'll see that everything is outdated. This was made back during the initial Lyucu invasion, when some resistance fighters in Rui still thought victory was possible. The figurines were used for modeling counterattack plans, but they pose no threat to you now. As I've told you, my benefactors are long dead."

"Who are these benefactors?"

Nazu Tei said nothing.

"Yet more secrets, eh?" Cutanrovo said. "It seems to be my duty today to teach all of you a lesson about truth-telling. Well, let me see if I can figure it out. The precious materials used for the figurines tell me your benefactors were prominent individuals, probably old nobles under the tyrant Kuni Garu. Am I on the right path?"

Nazu Tei said nothing.

"Please, honored commander," said Elder Kigo, who had finally sat up and spat out the dirt in his mouth, "my daughter . . . she . . . please!" His eyes were locked on the tiny person dangling from Cutanrovo's hand, now hanging limply like a sack of mussels.

Cutanrovo shook the baby, and she let out a weak cry before stopping again.

"Be quiet," said Cutanrovo. "I'm in the middle of an interrogation here." She turned back to Nazu Tei. "I imagine they had probably surrendered to the pékyu-votan and gained his trust, which was how they were able to access the jade and amber." She paced back and forth, musing. "I've seen figurines like these before. . . . Your benefactors likely had these carved by expert artisans as gifts to the pékyu-votan, ostensibly to celebrate the Lyucu victory. But in secret, they kept some to model a Dara-raaki victory over the Lyucu. Using tokens that appear to glorify the Lyucu to plot their downfall must have seemed so clever to them, am I right?"

"Please, Master Tei," begged Elder Kigo. "Please tell the honored commander what she wants to know. My daughter! My daughter! I'm sorry I told your secret, Master Tei, but I can't let her die!"

Nazu Tei opened her eyes and looked at Elder Kigo with pity. She sighed. "I don't blame you, Do Kigo. I'm an old woman who only wants to preserve a few memories, and my death will be as inconsequential as a feather in the wind. But you've doomed the whole village. Don't you understand?"

"The problem with the slaves of Dara is that you always think you're so clever," said Cutanrovo. "But what good is a sheep's cleverness when the wolf's jaws are around her neck?" She casually tossed the baby into the air like a toy and caught the flopping body as Elder Kigo's family screamed.

"Oh, I know what you're going to say, Nazu Tei. You'll tell me that the emperor has said that even suspected traitors, as long as they are ranked scholars, should not be tortured. But who said anything about torture? I intend to take care of you and invite you to a feast.

I'll cut thin slices of flesh from this child, marinate them in spicy Dasu fish sauce, and then roast them slowly over a charcoal fire. I will enjoy feeding them to you, Nazu Tei. I hear piglet flesh is most succulent."

Nazu Tei opened her mouth and spat out a spray of blood, so hard had she been clenching her jaw and biting down on her tongue. A look of madness filled her eyes as she screamed at Cutanrovo. "May Kiji tear your eyes out and a thousand vultures feed on your flesh! You are a demon, not a human!"

"Oh, calling upon a false god! Yet one more act of treason," said Cutanrovo. "You're making this much too easy for me. Surely by now you understand that everything is already lost—you've said the same to Do Kigo—so why prolong the suffering? You know I'll drag everything out of you sooner or later."

Nazu Tei strained against her bonds before suddenly stopping, collapsing onto the ground, and curling up into herself. "I thought the emperor's edicts meant something, but there's no reasoning with you. I'll tell you everything. Just let the baby go."

"You don't get to bargain with me." But Cutanrovo set the baby down on the ground. The baby coughed and began to cry weakly. Elder Kigo and Nara crawled toward her, but stopped when Cutanrovo glared at them.

"Talk, old woman," said Cutanrovo to Nazu Tei.

"I was once a nurse-tutor in the household of Governor Ra Olu and Lady Lon."

"Ah, that would explain it," said Cutanrovo. "You served that pair of Dara-raaki slaves who licked pékyu-votan's boots before turning on him. Your character was corrupted by their example."

"I left the Big Island for Dasu with Governor Ra Olu and Lady Lon, who took me in and gave me a respected position when few were willing to hire women scholars as tutors for their children. After they were executed by the pékyu-votan, I took these figurines and came to Kigo Yezu to live in seclusion. It's true that my benefactors never gave up the resistance, but there's no rebellion in my heart. The people of this village and I only want to live in peace. The figurines and map are memory only, no threat to you."

"You err," said Cutanrovo, "in thinking that only armed insurrection poses a threat. Memories, you see, can be even more dangerous. We must have your complete submission, in both body and heart. To glorify the memories of traitors is to rebel in your heart."

"You can't ever erase the truth from the hearts of the people," said Nazu Tei. "Tyrants may rule over land, air, and sea, but the heart of a man is forever free."

Savo, on the ground next to her, listened intently.

"Is that a quote from one of your Moralist philosophers?" asked Cutanrovo. "But you're wrong. It *is* possible to have the submission of your heart, to bind you to our truth, the only truth that matters. It's just a lesson that requires repetition."

She stood up, casually picked up the baby, and before anyone could react, walked the few steps to the well and tossed the baby into it. The faint echo of a distant splash marked the end of a life.

Elder Kigo jumped up and rushed at the Lyucu thane. "Why? Why? You—"

A soldier struck him in the head with the pommel of his sword. The man collapsed to the ground. The other kneeling villagers were too stunned to speak.

Savo screamed through his gag and struggled against his bonds. Nazu Tei turned her face away. She had known, deep down, that the Lyucu commander was never going to show any mercy, but she couldn't help but harbor a sliver of hope. That made it all the harder.

"The discovery in Kigo Yezu of contraband military planning equipment and a fugitive associated with the deceased rebel leaders, the Olus, is a major success in the war against Dara-raaki saboteurs," proclaimed Cutanrovo to her soldiers, who looked dazed. "Since the village knew of Nazu Tei's treachery and aided her, the entire village is guilty of conspiracy to commit treason. All villagers older than fourteen are to be executed immediately by exposure to Cudyufin's gift, and those younger reduced to slave status, with the males castrated. The village will be burned to the ground and the fields reclaimed for grazing."

The native soldiers looked at one another, hesitating. The other junior Lyucu officers looked alarmed at this sign of insubordination.

"What's the matter with you?" Cutanrovo shouted. She strode up and slapped two of the soldiers nearest her across the face. "Have you forgotten your families? Do you want to see them suffer the same fate?" To ensure the loyalty of native soldiers, their families were gathered into compounds near Lyucu fortresses as hostages—a policy suggested by Noda Mi and Wira Pin, two high-ranking native ministers.

Despair, hatred, terror, and rage warred against one another on the faces of all the soldiers.

Nara, who had lost consciousness as her daughter was dropped into the well, suddenly climbed up off the ground and staggered toward Cutanrovo. One of the junior Lyucu officers tried to stop her, but she shoved him aside as though she had the strength of ten men. Shrieking, her hands raised like the claws of an angry wolf, she rushed at the Lyucu thane. No words emerged from her throat; the air was filled only with the incoherent noise of a mother who had lost everything except the will for vengeance.

In one swift motion, Cutanrovo grabbed the bone club off her back and slammed it into the woman's skull. Brains and blood splattered all over her. Nara's body collapsed to the ground.

Savo almost fainted. During the initial invasion of Dara, he had been but a boy of nine and kept safely away from the fighting either in his mother's city-ship or camp. He had never seen anything so brutal, not even in the public executions of traitors in Kriphi.

Cutanrovo licked some of the gore from the corner of her mouth, chewed, and swallowed. She laughed heartily. "I can teach this lesson all day long. Does anyone else wish to learn?"

Reluctantly, the soldiers began to move through the kneeling villagers, separating parents from children, sibling from sibling. Their faces set into stony masks of indifference, the soldiers tied the wailing children by their wrists to a long chain so that the captives could be marched back to the capital, where the boys would be mutilated before they were sent to hard labor. The older villagers were dragged back into the huts, where they were tied to the thick structural poles holding up the roofs or staked to the earthen floor. Elder Kigo woke up and wept inconsolably over the body of his dead wife before he was also forcibly dragged away to his hut. Pitiful wailing filled the air, but by now most villagers were so drained by terror and anguish that they no longer resisted. The few that tried to fight back were quickly subdued by the armed soldiers.

One of the women condemned to die jabbered piteously at the two soldiers dragging her. They paused as they took in what she was saying and looked back at Cutanrovo, uncertain what to do with this new information.

"She should be thanking all her false gods for being blessed with the seed of the Lyucu," Cutanrovo said. "Identify her togaten boy and the two of them may be spared. Bring them back to Kriphi for service as household menials."

Finished with separating the condemned from the enslaved, the soldiers dragged the chain of captives to the side. Cutanrovo looked over at the garinafin—who had until now been crouching to the side, observing the scene placidly—and chopped her hand forcefully through the air twice.

The garinafin stood up and strode toward the huts on its clawed feet like a monstrous rooster. It reared back, opened its jaws, slammed them shut and immediately opened them again, and a stream of lava-like fire shot out of its mouth, instantly immolating the huts, along with the villagers trapped within.

According to a Lyucu legend, humans learned to use fire when Cudyufin, the goddess of the sun, dispatched a garinafin to bring the gift of the Well of Daylight to the tribes of the scrublands. Fire was a fragment of the sun's own all-seeing gaze. To die in fire, with limbs bound and unable to resist, was a humiliation reserved for captives who didn't earn the respect of their vanquishers in battle.

Savo observed this scene of carnage with tears flowing down his face. The gag in his mouth tasted of blood and ashes. This was nothing like the tales of heroism and honor in war that he had heard at the storytelling dances or read in the annals of court re-rememberers. He prayed for the dead fervently in his head, his mind unable to make sense of all he had seen and heard. *O gods. O gods.*

As she observed the destruction of Kigo Yezu with satisfaction, Cutanrovo issued more orders. "Send a detachment to the beach to arrest the fishermen when they return from the sea. Give them the same treatment as the rest of the villagers. Dispatch messengers to all the surrounding villages to announce what happened here and remind them of their duty to report suspected traitors. Let's go."

She strode resolutely away from the burning village. Behind her, the garinafin continued to reduce the village to ashes. A few soldiers marched alongside the chain of captives, and others lifted Savo Goztan and Nazu Tei to follow.

As the fire burned down, carrion-eating birds landed in the remnants of the village. Nature had little concern for the horrors that had occurred here, so long as there was food to sustain new life.

Two large ravens, one black and one white, stood apart from the others, cawing angrily at the air.

*- Brother, how much longer will you stand by and do nothing? What of your promise to our parents to watch over these Islands?*

*- Brother, do you delight in this sacrifice from your new worshippers? What of your promise to us to protect the people of Dara?*

A gust of wind howled through the village with anguish, changing direction unpredictably, but the smell of burnt flesh and charred bones lingered.

*- I wanted none of this to happen. None of it! You know as well as I do that the mortals do what they wish, and then attribute their sins to the gods.*

*- What does what you want—*

*—matter, when the deed is done?*

*- Give me a little more time. Timu will make it right.*

# CHAPTER TWENTY-FOUR

# PRISONERS

KRIPHI: THE TENTH MONTH IN THE EIGHTH YEAR
OF THE REIGN OF AUDACIOUS FREEDOM (KNOWN
AS THE EIGHTH YEAR OF THE REIGN OF SEASON
OF STORMS IN DARA, AND THE EIGHTH YEAR
SINCE PRINCESS THÉRA DEPARTED DARA FOR
UKYU-GONDÉ).

Savo pulled the bull-skull helmet lower to better hide his face. Instead of a scholar's robe, he was dressed in the hide-and-cloth outfit of a common naro. The thanes and other naros paid no attention to him, and the native pedestrians kept a respectful distance, dodging out of his way as he pressed forward. That suited him just fine. He didn't want anyone to recognize him.

Although he was supposed to be under house arrest in the custody of his mother, and Goztan had repeatedly warned him not to cause any trouble, he just couldn't stay cooped up inside. He had to go see his master, who was imprisoned in the giant stone building simply called the Pen, where traitors and rebels were kept before public executions.

Walking along Harmony Way, Kriphi's main thoroughfare, Savo quietly observed the familiar sights of the capital of Ukyu-taasa through the eye sockets of the helmet. Here, a naro was joking with a native noodle-stall proprietor; there, a *toko dawiji* was shepherding a group of children dressed in fashionable silk robes, both native and Lyucu, out of a luxurious carriage. He passed a street magician performing illusions for a large crowd, and at the edge of the crowd, he saw a Lyucu noble standing on a bench to get a better view as his native mistresses fanned him and held up a tray of rice beer and tea. On the other side of the street, he saw an antique shop, where thanes and native ministers browsed for calligraphy scrolls together. Everything was in harmony, with the Lyucu and the natives living in peace.

The sights should have been comforting, but they were not. Savo could not forget what he had seen in Kigo Yezu a few weeks ago. Was that an aberration in the gentle rule of the Lyucu in Ukyu-taasa? Or was everything around him now a mask, as hollow as the skull helmet he wore?

Remembering the many ambiguous hints Nazu Tei had dropped over the years, Savo hurried his steps. He had to find out the truth.

"Dyu-*tika*, you should not speak like that about your friend," said Timu.

"He *is* a traitor and a weakling," said the boy defiantly to his father. Resolutely, he slammed his foot down on an arucuro tocua creation, a little caterpillar-like creature made from bird bones. The delicate bones cracked and scattered across the stone floor. It had been a gift to the pékyu-taasa from Savo Ryoto, and the boy had always treasured it, not allowing anyone else to lay a finger on it.

"He's only been accused of having an unauthorized teacher," said Timu. "It is against the law, but the desire for more knowledge is not a moral failing. You should rather plead for him to your mother—"

"I would never speak up for a traitor," said Todyu, kicking at the broken bones to scatter them some more. Before his father could say anything else, he ran out of the small hall that Timu used as an office.

Timu sighed and sat down, looking lost. His hands reflexively tried to gather the broken bones, but he knew that the arucuro tocua was beyond repair; he hoped that his relationship with his son wasn't, at least not yet.

"Da, let me help," said Dyana. She ran around the hall, picking up the broken bones. It took a long while for father and daughter to gather up the pieces and place them on a silk handkerchief.

"Thank you, Zaza-*tika*," said Timu. He smiled at her and gently patted her back, but the sadness in his eyes remained.

"Dyu-*tika* is always afraid that someone will think he's weak," said Dyana. "I wish he weren't so scared."

Timu looked at her. He tried to speak but could not think of the right words. In the end, he simply said, "At least we can save these bones for him. Someday he may regret what he did today and want them back."

He leaned down to tie the corners of the handkerchief into a bundle, but the white bone fragments reminded him of something. His hands stopped, and he muttered, almost inaudibly, "Teeth on the board."

"What did you say, Da?" asked Dyana.

"Oh, just an old story that I was reminded of," said Timu.

"Tell it to me?"

Timu smiled at her again. While Todyu never cared for stories from the Ano Classics, Dyana enjoyed them as much as she liked the storytelling dances of the shamans.

Hundreds of years ago, in the time of the Tiro kings, Faça invaded Rima and took over the strip of territory at the edge of the Ring-Woods.

Rima countered. For three years, the two armies took turns pushing the other off the disputed land, but neither was able to hold it for long. Thousands of young men died, and the fields in both states had to be tilled by widows. In the end, ministers in both Na Thion and Boama petitioned their sovereigns to cease the hostilities for the sake of the people. The two kings agreed to settle the dispute in a most unusual manner: a *cüpa* match.

Each king was allowed one adviser. The King of Faça was aided by Tema Fino, widely acknowledged to be the best player of his time and the inventor of a style of aggressive *cüpa* tactics that would later become very influential all over the Islands; the King of Rima was aided by Ro Taça, a noted Moralist who had composed the essay *Treatise on the Duties of the Adviser*.

As the disputed land was occupied by Faça at the time, Rima was considered the guest and allowed to go first, playing with the white ivory stones. Faça would play with the black onyx stones. (The rule that black always went first hadn't yet become the standard in all the Islands.)

Halfway through the match, Faça clearly had the upper hand. The King of Rima was about to concede when Ro Taça pulled him aside.

"There is no point in playing out the game to the end," said the king. "We have no hope for victory, and if I were to prolong the inevitable, I would be deemed no different from a sore-losing scoundrel in the streets, devoid of the grace of kings."

"But it's *not* hopeless, Sire," said Ro Taça. "You should do this and this . . ."

After the king listened to Ro's suggestions, he closed his eyes and pondered. Then he said, "This is a most unorthodox set of tactics. Although there is a chance of catching them off guard, if I were to lose, I'd become the laughingstock of Dara for playing like a beginner who hasn't read the *cüpa* books."

"Faça will never cease its aggression against our people without a setback. It's the duty of an adviser to offer up every ray of hope, no matter how faint."

"And it's the lot of the sovereign to be blamed, if the advice doesn't work out," said the king. "But nonetheless, I will do as you say."

The king returned to the game and made several unexpected moves. The King of Faça and Tema Fino both furrowed their brows, whispering together and taking a long time with each move.

Alas, Ro Taça's gambit failed. The unexpected moves were unexpected for a reason—they didn't follow the basic principles of good *cüpa* positioning, and left Rima open to more counterattacks. Soon, the situation looked even more hopeless. Both players were down to their last few stones. If the King of Rima played his last stone without conceding, it would be considered the most humiliating way to lose. On the other side of the board, both the King of Faça and Tema Fino grinned, already imagining the victory celebration and the shame to be visited upon Rima.

Just as the King of Rima was about to concede, once again Ro Taça stopped him.

"I've already listened to you once," said the king, sighing. "Won't you allow me to preserve one shred of dignity?"

" '*Phathuii onotaüpa pha géüing gira ingro i raraé, gipzaü gira ingro i rakin ki mican gidalo.*' A bad adviser takes credit for successes and deflects blame for failures," said Ro Taça. "Sire, if you don't think me a bad adviser, then give me a chance to fix my error."

The king couldn't see what was left for Ro to do, since there were only three stones of each color left in the jade and onyx bowls. But he admired Ro Taça's character so much that he nodded, agreeing to continue to play.

Three moves later, the King of Rima placed the last white stone on the board. Black still had the advantage. There would be no next move for white.

The King of Faça laughed and played the last black stone. He was about to get up and mockingly congratulate the King of Rima for a game well played. But he never got out of *mipa rari*. The scene before him was too shocking.

For Ro Taça had picked up the heavy, empty jade bowl before Rima and knocked out one of his front teeth. Without a single moan of pain, he wiped the blood from the tooth with his robe and dropped it into the bowl. The clinking sound reverberated through the silent hall, as loud as the ringing of a *moaphya*.

"Oh, Ro!" cried the King of Rima, wincing on his minister's behalf.

"What is the meaning of this?" demanded the King of Faça.

"The bowl isn't empty," said Ro Taça placidly. Blood seeped from his mouth, though he tried to swallow it all. "We must play on."

With trembling fingers, the King of Rima picked up Ro Taça's tooth and placed it on the grid.

The position on the board still showed an overwhelming black advantage.

Without a word, Ro Taça picked up the empty onyx bowl before Faça, knocked out a second tooth from his mouth, then a third and a fourth, wiped the blood from them, and dropped them into the jade bowl in front of Rima.

The King of Faça and Tema Fino looked at each other. They looked at the onyx bowl, devoid of black stones. They looked at the gore-splattered sleeves of Ro Taça, at his determined visage, at his bloody lips pressed together, at the teeth glinting on the board and in the jade bowl.

"I concede," said the King of Faça.

"That Ro Taça is a very brave man," said Dyana.

"That he is," said Timu.

"Knocking out his own teeth!" Dyana put a hand over her own mouth in sympathy. "I can't even imagine it."

Timu nodded. "He was permanently disfigured by the act, and it was said that for that reason, he was never made Prime Minister of Rima. But I suspect that it was also because his action led to fear and jealousy from his colleagues, for none of them would have gone as far to show their conviction for their beliefs."

"But it also seems not a fair way to win," said Dyana. "Do the rules allow you to use your teeth?"

Timu chuckled. "You have a quick mind, Zaza-*tika*. I see you resist the official Moralist interpretation of this story as an example of the power of a stouthearted moral individual who never gives up faith in his ideals."

"I don't know about faith . . . but I think the Faça king probably gave up because he didn't want to see Ro Taça hurt himself anymore," said Dyana.

"Well, that's one way to understand it. Like many old stories from history, Ro Taça's victory has been given many interpretations. The Martialist strategists cite it as an example of the value of psychological warfare, with which a weaker force can overcome a stronger foe by shifting the battlefield to the mind. The Fluxists cite it as an example of the futility of strife and the hypocrisy of kings who press for victory at all costs. The Skeptics, who question everything, argue that Ro Taça was no better than a street brawler who won only by breaking the rules and taking advantage of the civility of his opponent."

"What about you? What do you think?"

"Oh, I am a Moralist, and I view Ro Taça as a hero."

"Did he do other things to help the people of Rima?" Dyana asked, knowing which quality her father admired the most in his heroes.

"His victory at the *cüpa* match, which demonstrated to Faça the steadfastness and courage of the people of Rima, led to a curbing of Faça aggression against Rima for the rest of his life, saving countless lives. He also advocated other policies, but due to his lack of influence at court, they were seldom implemented."

"It's too bad that the king didn't trust him, even after that," said Dyana.

"Ro knew that was a risk," said Timu. "He loved Rima and her people, but the king he served was neither wise nor courageous enough to fully commit to his vision. Nonetheless, his name has glowed brightly in the annals of Dara as an example to emulate for ministers and officials down the ages."

"They are all expected to . . . knock out their own teeth?"

Timu laughed. "No, no, Zaza-*tika*, not literally."

"So what are the ministers supposed to learn from him?"

"Even the Moralists don't agree. My teacher, Zato Ruthi—"

"The one my nursing name honors?"

". . . *One* of the people your nursing name honors. Master Ruthi thought Ro exemplified the dedication of a minister to his sovereign. I have a slightly different view. I think Ro's point was that an adviser must be willing to suffer the consequences of his opinions, should they turn out to be wrong."

"Oh, so that was why he was willing to endure pain, because his first advice didn't work out."

"That's right. I think willingness to suffer is the only antidote to arrogant reformers and philosophers who advocate idealized but flawed policies for the people without fear of personal consequences. In fact, King Jizu of Rima, centuries later, quoted approvingly from Ro Taça when berating his own ministers, who, in the face of Xana aggression, tried to save their own skins at the expense of the common people."

Though Dyana was a good and dedicated student, this was a heavier dose of history lesson than the little girl could bear. She stifled a yawn. Timu patted her reassuringly and sent her away to play.

Long after his daughter and son were both gone, Timu sat alone in the stone hall, thinking of ancient history and the recent past. He thought of his years of patient advocacy for the elevation of scholars in Ukyu-taasa as a way to promote Lyucu-native integration; of the massacre at Kigo Yezu; of the pending cases of Savo Ryoto and Nazu Tei; of Ro Taça and the *cüpa* board; of the message from his own mother, delivered months ago, which he could not drive from his mind.

Had he become too enamored of his own advice to Tanvanaki, for which he did not bear the harsh consequences? Had he become a prisoner of his own choosing? Had he lost sight of what was right, of *mutagé*?

The old scholar was shackled inside the cell with her hair undone, a gesture meant to humiliate. Nazu Tei was in the same robe she'd had on the day Cutanrovo declared her a traitor, and it was now ragged, dirty, full of fleas and bits of the straw that served as bedding. Nonetheless, she looked at peace as she sat in *géüpa*, her eyes shut as though she no longer cared about the affairs of this world.

"Master," whispered Savo through the bars. "Master."

Nazu's eyes snapped open, and a bright smile appeared on her face, as though sunlight had suddenly filled the dank cell. She ignored the tray of hot food he tried to offer her, but simply kept her eyes locked on his. "It's good to see you, Kinri-*tika*."

Savo set down the tray and touched his forehead to the ground. "I have failed you, Master. I tried to go see the emperor and the pékyu, but my mother is keeping me confined at home. I managed to sneak out with the aid of trusted servants, and bribed the warden. . . ." Tears of shame and rage spilled from his eyes uncontrollably, making it hard to continue.

"You haven't failed me," said Nazu Tei. "It is I who failed you."

Surprised, Savo looked up. "But . . . but I led the soldiers to you, and revealed our relationship. . . ."

"There are always a thousand causes contributing to every effect. If I hadn't chosen to keep the mementos of my benefactors; if I hadn't decided to settle in Kigo Yezu; if you hadn't seen me with my *zamaki* set—any of these would have broken the chain of causation, but that isn't how we assign blame or responsibility. Cutanrovo's heart was full of hate, and the deaths of the villagers cannot be blamed on anyone but her"—she hesitated for a moment before plunging on determinedly—"and the coming of the Lyucu to Dara."

Savo looked shocked. His teacher had never spoken against the Lyucu so directly like this. "Master! You mustn't let rage confuse you. If you draft a petition to the pékyu and the emperor declaring your loyalty, denounce the traitor Ra Olu, and pledge to cleanse your heart of false—"

"No, I'm not going to do that," said Nazu. She waited a beat and softened her voice. "When I said I failed you, I meant it. I am your teacher, and that imposes on me a duty to teach you the truth. For too long, I, and other scholars like me, have chosen to speak around the lies rather than through them. I allowed fear to silence my tongue, and in that process misled you."

"But you've taught me many forbidden topics, about the history and culture of Dara, about the philosophers and kings, about the wonders of Dara engineering—"

"I never once spoke directly against the lies you've been taught at court," said Nazu. "I despised the court historians and court-appointed tutors for wielding their talent to serve the Lyucu butchers, but I never realized that I was just as bad for not speaking up against them in order to keep myself safe."

She saw Savo's stunned face at hearing the Lyucu described as butchers, and a trace of bitterness crept into her voice. "Pékyu Tenryo committed the atrocities at Naza Pass, not Emperor Ragin. And Emperor Thaké didn't beg Tenryo to invade the Big Island to enforce his claim to the Dandelion Throne against his own mother. Massacres like the one at Kigo Yezu are not aberrations. The Lyucu are not liberators of Dara—"

"But you also told me of the despotic acts of the old Tiro kings and Mapidéré, and Kuni Garu really was a bandit—"

Nazu held up a hand. "The native rulers of Dara were never perfect, and there is always a grain of truth hidden within the best lies. But that doesn't make the lies true. There isn't enough time to teach you the truth here—"

"Then write the petition I ask, so that you can continue to teach me!"

Nazu shook her head. "I'm done with lying, by commission or omission. Besides, I cannot teach you the truth. Experience is the only teacher that will convince you."

"But . . ." Savo didn't know what to say. Nazu's declaration of the Lyucu as butchers still rankled.

As though reading his mind, Nazu continued in a gentler voice. "Whatever happens, Kinri-*tika*, know this: I hate what the Lyucu have done, and the evil they continue to do. But that doesn't mean I hate each individual Lyucu. That there is a difference between the collective and the individual, and yet they're bound up in ways that cannot be easily disentangled, is one of the hardest problems in life, one even the Ano sages could not resolve. I'm proud to have learned from you and taught you. You're a brilliant student, Kinri-*tika*, and I wish you would hold fast to the most important teaching of the Moralists: Do the right thing even if it hurts you."

Savo looked at his master, and a sudden premonition came that he would never see her again. An urge came to him to memorize her face, to ask for a memento, but he pushed the thoughts away. His mother would save the old woman; she always managed to make things work out no matter what. So, instead, he focused on his master's lesson.

"How will I know what is right?"

"No one can teach you that," said Nazu. "Not gods, nor teachers, nor parents, nor companions and lovers. Expand your heart and listen."

MEANWHILE, OUTSIDE TIRO COZO, EMPEROR MONADÉTU'S SECRET GARINAFIN TRAINING GROUNDS.

The horses stopped at the foot of the sheer cliffs.

Phyro, riding in the lead, beckoned for Ofluro and Lady Suca to join him. The other escorting soldiers stayed behind. With his whip, Phyro pointed at the unscalable mist-shrouded mountains. "Beyond those mountains lies my home, where I spend far more time than in Pan."

There was a small airship moored some distance away, and a fortress behind it garrisoned with soldiers.

Lady Suca placed a hand on her protruding belly and frowned. Ofluro looked at her with concern. She waved him off.

"*Rénga*, how long will we need to stay with you? My husband and I are eager to start our new life in Dara. I'd like to go to Faça to find a suitable ranch to purchase before the baby is born, before spring."

"We'll stay with the emperor for as long as he'll have us as guests," said Ofluro, laughing. "My brain remains a mush from all those questions at the refugee camp. I'm sure we both can use some rest to recuperate first."

Phyro hesitated. He had not yet revealed the secret that Dara possessed garinafins to the couple. Indeed, he had chosen to bring them here over land rather than by airship from Boama because he wanted to give himself more time to think.

Jia, he knew, would not have hesitated to bring the couple into the valley by force or guile, and then keep them there until they agreed to help train the garinafins.

It seemed wrong to try to learn the secret of riding the free-flying garinafins by holding the teachers hostage. It seemed wrong to achieve his dream through mistrust and coercion.

What would his mother have done?

He remembered a story that Risana had told him. Back during the Chrysanthemum-Dandelion War, Gin Mazoti had declared herself Queen of Faça and Rima, seeming to proclaim her intent to rebel against Kuni Garu.

While Kuni and his advisers debated what to do, Risana had approached.

"*If Gin were a man, would you know what to do?*"

"*Maybe. With ambitious men sometimes it's best to let them go as far as they want, so long as they're still helping you. You can't tell how high a kite can fly without being willing to let all the string out. Trust is often better than jealousy as a path to loyalty.*"

"*Does the fact that Gin is a woman make any difference? Gin has always asked simply for the right to play by the same rules as the rest of you.*"

"I must first explain something to you," said Phyro.

Lady Suca and Ofluro stopped smiling, chilled by the expression on Phyro's face.

"There is a secret beyond those mountains," continued Phyro, "one that I can only reveal to you once you're inside. But once you know this secret, you cannot leave."

"Then you intend to keep us as prisoners," said Lady Suca. "I thought you said we're free to go where we want in Dara."

"You are," said Phyro. "But this is a military camp, and there are rules. To minimize the risk of revealing the secret here, only a few are authorized to go outside. Many of my staff have lived here with their families for years. They can't leave until . . . we achieve victory over the Lyucu."

"I told you I won't give you any intelligence about Ukyu-taasa," said Ofluro.

"I know," said Phyro. "But I thought you might be willing to help me in other ways."

"I will not," said Ofluro. "I didn't risk my family's lives for us to become prisoners."

Phyro cursed himself. He wished he had the legendary charm of his father, who could rally a gang of prisoners to follow him into banditry, who could get a city to declare him their duke. He wished he had his mother's gift of looking into the hearts of men and women. But all he had was a dream that he didn't know how to achieve.

"Everyone who lives in this camp came because they believed in me, in a vision," said Phyro. "They want to see all the Islands free, to defeat our enemies with honor." He looked to Lady Suca. "They want the children of Dara to roam over these islands freely, and none shall be called togaten and be treated differently from the *Anojiti*."

"What about the Lyucu? Is there a place for people like me in your vision?" demanded Ofluro.

"I don't know," conceded Phyro. "There are those who wish to drive all the Lyucu into the sea, and others who believe the Lyucu, once defeated, may become part of the people of Dara. I think much depends on what the Lyucu themselves will choose, as you have chosen yourself."

"You're not doing a very good job of selling your vision to me," said Ofluro, almost amused.

"If we refuse to go with you, what will happen to us?" asked Lady Suca.

"The letter given to you by Secretary Kidosu entitles you to travel all around Dara unimpeded," said Phyro. "And you're free to go to Faça, as you intended. But some will give you a hard time because Ofluro is Lyucu, and you'll always face suspicion. The magistrates will protect you from physical harm, but there are other ways people can make life difficult for you that aren't against the law. All the refugees face such hardships."

"That still sounds better than being prisoners in that valley," said Lady Suca.

"You have asked for the right for you and your children to be treated no different from any other person of Dara," said Phyro, taking a deep breath. "Then I offer you the same choice I offer any soldier who I invite into this valley. If you enter, you will not be free to leave, but you will be treated as a comrade, my companion. I will not force you to do what you believe is against your conscience, and if you wish to stay away from the military camp and farm or herd sheep in the valley, that is your right. Or you may leave and take your chances in the wider world, never having anything to do with me again."

"Then we choose to leave," said Ofluro without hesitation. Lady Suca nodded.

Phyro looked despondent. He had, after all that effort, failed. He was not his father or his mother. He struggled to conceal the disappointment from his face but could not.

He could still order the soldiers to forcibly move the pair into Tiro Cozo, he realized. And for a moment he almost gave in to the temptation.

*The world may not be fair, but we must strive to make it so.*

"All right," he said quietly. "I will instruct the captain of the escorts to give you sufficient funds to get you back to Faça. I'm both glad and sorry to have met you."

He turned his face away so that they would not see his tears as he spurred his horse toward the airship.

∾

MEANWHILE, IN PAN.

The warden looked down at the body of Laughing Skeleton.

The man was lying still in his cell, facedown, his clothing torn. Signs of struggle could be seen all around him, and there was a slowly spreading pool of blood around his head.

There was a pattern to the empress's visits. With each prisoner she picked, the first few times, the man would be left in ecstasy, as if he had experienced pleasures incomprehensible to mere humans. Indeed, he would look forward to the next visit from Jia with an eagerness that felt quite obscene to the warden. But inevitably, after the next few visits, he would be left in low spirits, as if suffering from a hunger that could not be satisfied.

The empress had ceased seeing Laughing Skeleton altogether.

In response, Laughing Skeleton had literally gone insane, refusing food and water, biting and scratching himself, banging his head against the walls, blubbering and begging the prison guards to find "that goddess" to visit him again.

The level of obsession made even the warden, who had witnessed all imaginable forms of depravity in his job, shudder.

In the past, prisoners abandoned by the empress had eventually recovered—though that hunger never quite left their eyes. This was the first time that a prisoner had died from pining for the empress.

The warden spread out his portable writing desk and began to take notes. The empress's standing orders concerning the prisoners she favored were for the warden to record their conditions each night. In the morning, he would discreetly inform the Dyran Fins, who would then swoop in and whisk the body away before the prison doctors could conduct an autopsy.

Discretion made him valuable. He never forgot that.

# CHAPTER TWENTY-FIVE

# JUDGMENT

KRIPHI: THE TENTH MONTH IN THE EIGHTH YEAR
OF THE REIGN OF AUDACIOUS FREEDOM (KNOWN
AS THE EIGHTH YEAR OF THE REIGN OF SEASON
OF STORMS IN DARA, AND THE EIGHTH YEAR
SINCE PRINCESS THÉRA DEPARTED DARA FOR
UKYU-GONDÉ).

Tanvanaki, Supreme Ruler of Ukyu-taasa, the new land that would fulfill the dreams of the Lyucu people, knelt in *mipa rari* on her garinafin-bone throne on a raised dais at the northern end of the Great Hall and waited for the herald to call for the start to formal court.

Her fur cape, stitched together from the hides of ten white wolves, gleamed in the slanting light from the high windows cut into the rough-hewn stone in the inclined ceiling and made her the center of attention in the dark Great Hall. The jawbones of the ten wolves, stacked into a pyramid and woven together with golden wires, rested atop her head as her crown, giving her a fearsome and predatory aspect.

She looked around the Great Hall and wondered again if this elaborate stage, which had taken so much effort to construct, would hold up under the storm that was about to come.

To her left, on a plain wooden throne that was smaller and placed lower than hers, sat her consort, Emperor Thaké. Timu was dressed in a bright red formal silk robe embroidered with cruben and dandelion motifs. He held his slender torso very straight as he knelt in formal *mipa rari*. A crown with dangling strands of pearls and coral beads hid his face, and only the faint chiming of the strands as they trembled against each other betrayed any emotion. As Tanvanaki glanced at him, she felt a wave of pity and affection.

Along both sides of the long Great Hall, constructed during the days of the Xana kings before they had conquered the rest of the Seven States, stood two lines of officials and military leaders. To her left, on the east, stood the administrators. Each ministerial position was occupied by a Lyucu, typically a high-ranking thane past prime fighting age, and behind them stood the deputy ministers, typically native scholars who had placed well either in the old Imperial examinations or the new ones held during the Reign of Audacious Freedom. The deputies handled the day-to-day duties of the ministry or department, promulgated policies and issued regulations, appointed the hundreds of magistrates, undersecretaries, clerks, and other bureaucrats who kept the empire functioning. The Lyucu ministers themselves, lacking either the interest or ability to keep the machinery of state humming, spent most of their time hunting, wrestling, and generally seeking pleasure.

Most of the ministers wore a mix of Lyucu and native clothing: a silk robe accessorized with a fur muffler or cinched with a twisted-leather cord, a long hempen tunic showing between the lapels of a fur cape, animal-hide vest and kilt worn under flowing silk wraps. The deputies, on the other hand, were uniformly dressed in robes decorated with the symbols of their areas of responsibility: fleece and cattle horns for the Deputy Minister of Pastures, a Lyucu bone war club crossed with a native wooden stave for the Deputy Minister of Justice, leaping whitefish and nets for the Deputy Minister of Fisheries, seashells and bowls of rice for the Deputy Minister of the Treasury, and so on.

Much of this arrangement had been the work of Timu. During the chaotic days right after the Battle of Zathin Gulf, when Tanvanaki's attention had been fully occupied with courting allies among her father's old thanes and suppressing rebellions to secure her hold on power, Timu had issued a series of Imperial decrees to set up a new government to keep the taxes flowing and to maintain local order. She had carved the garinafin mark—a trapezoid with three curved lines coming out of the top—over his seal on these decrees without so much as altering a single logogram, and she was grateful that Timu's active participation had allowed her to essentially let the pacified natives govern themselves.

To her right, on the west, stood the military commanders. The Lyucu thanes stood to the north and closer to the throne. They were generally dressed in traditional Lyucu garb: animal-hide vests, short skin kilts, fur capes, bone armor, and ceremonial skull helmets. Almost all had war clubs or axes strapped to their backs—Tanvanaki had turned down Timu's proposal to adopt the native custom of forbidding weapons at formal court. At the head of this column, occupying the most prestigious position of all, was Garinafin-Thane Goztan Ryoto. She was dressed in the full battle gear of a garinafin pilot: calfskin leggings, bone spurs, leather harness over a vest and skirt made from sheepskin, slingshot and war club strapped to her back, and a juvenile garinafin-skull helmet over her clean-shaven head. Although many in the Great Hall stole glances at her, the central figure in today's proceedings, her face was completely calm, betraying no emotion at all.

Down the line to the south, farther away from the throne, stood the native generals. They were a varied bunch: some, like Noda Mi, had betrayed the Dandelion Court and joined the invaders in order to further their own ambition; others were natives of Rui and Dasu who surrendered to the Lyucu to be spared death; still others were simply mercenaries recruited from among the pirates, who served the pékyu based on promises of gold and silver. There was little trust for them as a group, and rarely were they granted independent commands.

The actual protocol at court, including the positions of the various ministers and warlords, their formal dress, and their ritual speeches, had been designed by a group of native scholars who had pledged fealty to the Lyucu immediately after the conquest. Although many scholars in Rui and Dasu, steadfast in their Moralist principles, died in defense of the people of Dara and the Dandelion Throne, Tenryo and Tanvanaki found plenty of *toko dawiji* (and even a few *cashima*) who discovered enough wiggle room in the Ano Classics to justify serving the conquerors. The leader of this group, Wira Pin, had even acted as the pékyu-votan's emissary to persuade Prince Timu to surrender, though he was rebuffed. Wira was now the Deputy Minister of Justice of Ukyu-taasa.

The herald stepped forward, lifted the long cruben-bone trumpet, and blew into it for a solid minute, until his face was bright red. The powerful sound reverberated from the ancient stone walls, and felt to the assembled like the long thunderclap that presaged a violent storm.

*Well, let it come,* thought Tanvanaki. *Flash-of-the-Garinafin fears no storm.*

"Speak, if you have anything to say," barked Tanvanaki into the silence that followed. This was not the opening line of the elaborate court protocol designed by Wira Pin, based on the protocol in Pan but infused with Lyucu elements to please his new masters.

Though Tanvanaki made a habit of ignoring protocol, she did speak in Dara, the formal language of court. It was only in part a concession for the benefit of the native administrators. Mostly, everyone found it more convenient to use a language that was already full of expressions for things like taxes and corvées and crop planting cycles and ceremonial performances that the natives needed from their rulers.

Despite the pékyu's invitation, the officials and warriors, Lyucu and native alike, remained rooted to their spots. Everyone knew that formal court today had only one purpose. The whole capital had been buzzing with rumor and gossip for a month now as factions at court jostled for allies and plotted how to make the most of this unexpected scandal involving Thane Goztan's son.

Wira Pin, the Deputy Minister of Justice, stepped forward to whisper in the ear of his boss, the Minister of Justice. The minister, an old Lyucu thane who had no interest at all in being a bureaucrat, nodded and gestured for Wira to go ahead. The man bowed ingratiatingly at the thane, stepped into the middle of the Great Hall, turned to face the thrones, and then prostrated himself, touching his forehead to the stone floor.

Tanvanaki frowned. Such excessive displays of slavish obeisance always seemed to her a kind of mockery.

"Most Honorable and Sagacious Pékyu, Most Merciful and Pulchritudinous Sovereign, Most Courageous and . . ."

The full title of Tanvanaki, also designed by Wira Pin, was something literally no one at court used except him. Normally, Tanvanaki would have long interrupted by now to tell him to get on with it, but for once, she was glad for the delay. Despite her earlier determination, she now wished she had more time to weigh her choices.

". . . Ruler of Rui and Dasu, Protector of Dara"—having finally finished reciting the pékyu's full title, Wira paused to take a breath, and then, almost as an afterthought, he turned to Emperor Thaké, the nominal head of state, and added, *"Rénga,"* before turning back to Tanvanaki again. "Your most faithful servant has a matter to report: Savo Ryoto, son of Goztan Ryoto, daughter of Dayu Ryoto, serving the pékyu as Thane-taasa of the Five Tribes of the Antler, is accused of treason."

Every ear in the Great Hall perked up. Contrary to expectation, Wira Pin, though a native, sided with the hard-liners at court. Whether his allegiance was motivated by self-hatred or some kind of political calculus was unclear. Nonetheless, at court he often acted as the mouthpiece of the hard-liner thanes.

The fact that he chose the thane-taasa rather than the native scholar as the primary subject signaled that the hard-liners had decided to go all out. Rather than picking on the powerless native, a mere scholar-pawn in this game of *zamaki*, they had decided to assault the commander of the accommodationists, Thane Goztan Ryoto, directly.

It promised to be a good show.

"Who brings the accusation?" asked Tanvanaki.

Cutanrovo Aga stepped out from the middle of the column of Lyucu warlords and turned to face the thrones. "I do."

She went on to explain the raid on Kigo Yezu, the discovery of military planning equipment traceable back to the traitorous Ra Olu and Lady Lon in the possession of one Nazu Tei, and the forbidden relationship of master-pupil between her and Savo Ryoto. As she gave her presentation, she retrieved the physical evidence and held the objects up one by one: the so-called *zamaki* figurines, the calligraphy scrolls recovered from the thane-taasa's quarters with logograms not found in the court-approved texts, and finally, the garinafin-bone hairpin found on Nazu Tei, carved with the pattern of the Five Tribes of the Antler.

Having concluded her presentation, Cutanrovo stood proudly and surveyed the assembled officials and warlords.

Tanvanaki seethed. The situation was even worse than Goztan and Timu had led her to believe. How could Goztan have been so careless?

The pékyu was determined to save Goztan's son. After all, the woman had been instrumental in Tanvanaki's rise. During the ill-fated invasion of the Big Island, Goztan had been left on Rui to watch over Timu and secure the home base. As a result, she had not been part of the disaster at the Battle of Zathin Gulf and kept her troops intact. Since Tenryo had died during battle without leaving behind a spirit portrait, Tanvanaki's succession to the position of pékyu was open to challenge. After she returned to Rui, the Lyucu army in shambles, several ambitious thanes immediately rose up to take advantage of her weakness. But Goztan had pledged support to her as the new pékyu and quelled the rebellion. In the following years, she had been a solid ally for Tanvanaki, helping to hold back the hard-liners who clamored for fewer concessions to the natives.

But the evidence in Cutanrovo's hands was ironclad and left little room for argument.

"Who wishes to speak for the accused?" asked Tanvanaki. No one in the Great Hall moved and every pair of eyes was on Goztan.

But the thane remained as still as before, her eyes slightly down-cast, as though what was happening in the Great Hall didn't concern her at all.

This was part of the plan. Tanvanaki took a breath and prepared to speak. She would redirect interest to the native scholar—

"I do."

Tanvanaki hadn't spoken.

Every pair of eyes now swung to the source of the voice—

—behind the dangling veil next to the pékyu.

Thanes and officials looked at one another in amazement.

It was extremely rare for the emperor to speak at court. Most of the time, he was mute as a statue. Since the native scholars justified their own service to the Lyucu regime by arguing that they were in fact serving the true heir to the Dandelion Throne, all decrees and proclamations from Kriphi bore his seal. But everyone understood this was merely a cover as flimsy as Timu's veil. Timu never spoke because Tanvanaki spoke for him.

Only one thought ran through everyone's mind at that moment: *The emperor is intervening directly! Does this mean he has the support of the pékyu herself?*

In fact, no one was more surprised than Tanvanaki. Timu had pleaded with her in private on behalf of Savo Ryoto and Nazu Tei. She had, after much argument, persuaded him to see that it was impossible to save them both. The fall of Goztan would have meant the complete rout of the accommodationists. Therefore, everything had to be blamed on Nazu Tei. Sacrificing a scholar-pawn to save the commander was a universal principle that applied in politics as well as in *zamaki*.

Goztan had also come to the same conclusion, and she and Tanvanaki had agreed that no one would speak up to defend the accused. Cutanrovo's goal was clearly to manufacture as much controversy as possible over this matter in order to weaken the accommodationists. The best way to thwart that plan was to meet her accusations with silence, and allow Tanvanaki to defuse the tension by scapegoating Nazu Tei as a rogue scholar. She thought Timu had agreed to this plan—until now.

She kept her feelings off her face, however, as she intoned dispassionately, "Then present your case."

His face still concealed behind the veil, Timu said, "While what the thane-taasa did was against the rules, I think that shouldn't be the focus of the inquiry today."

"Oh? What could be more important than the crime of treason by a future thane willingly prostrating himself before a native rebel-sympathizer?" asked Cutanrovo, her eyebrows lifted in mock surprise. As always, she refused to use the native honorific of *Rénga* when addressing Timu.

"Savo's error—if error it was—pales in comparison to the atrocity perpetrated by your troops at Kigo Yezu."

Tanvanaki looked at Timu and sighed inwardly. *So this is why you decided to jump in. You can't bear to see your people die. But don't you see that this is exactly what Cutanrovo wants? You've now given her a chance to air hard-liner views in open court, and I have no idea if the passions of the thanes could be cooled once she has riled them.*

She thought of stopping him before he could do more damage, but she saw how the strands in his veil shook, revealing the depth of his feelings. *Maybe it will do him some good to see just how much support the hard-liners have, so that he can appreciate my dilemma.* She held back.

"I did no more than give traitors and rebels exactly what they deserved." While she tried to look confident, Cutanrovo's eyes darted to the pékyu's face warily.

She had to assume that the emperor's unexpected intercession had the full backing of the pékyu, even though she didn't understand Tanvanaki's intentions. The best course, Cutanrovo decided, was to remain on the attack. "Mass punishment of villages in which rebels are found has always been our policy, dating back to the time of the liberation of Ukyu-taasa under the pékyu-votan."

"Policies based on history must change when times change." Timu swept aside the dangling strands before his face and looked Cutanrovo in the eyes. His cheeks flushed and his eyes burned like two pools of fire. "During the early days of the occupation, when native rebels ambushed isolated Lyucu warriors, it was perhaps justifiable to engage in mass punishment lest Ukyu-taasa degenerate into a land of terror and lawlessness. But unprovoked attacks against the Lyucu have not occurred in years—"

"That is *not* true." Cutanrovo shook her head and took several steps toward the thrones, waving her arms for emphasis. "My cousin, a brave and trusting naro, was attacked and killed earlier this summer by cowardly rebels in a most treacherous manner—"

"I said *unprovoked*!" shouted Timu. Such defiance from the timid Timu was so unexpected that all the assembled officials and warlords, native and Lyucu alike, gaped in wonder. Even Cutanrovo took a step back.

Timu took a breath and continued in a more conciliatory manner. "In any event, there was no killing of Lyucu warriors at Kigo Yezu. Punishment must be proportional to the crime."

Cutanrovo, who had recovered from the earlier shock, argued back. "There was a vast conspiracy to rebel led by the crafty native scholar Nazu Tei. Treason is a capital crime by your own decree."

"What treason? Hiding a few old figurines to remember a couple who had treated her kindly?" Timu swept his hand to point to Tanvanaki. "Under the direction of our wise pékyu, the natives now live in harmony with the Lyucu. The people go on with their lives as before, and taxes and corvées due the pékyu are rendered without protest. Scholars continue their studies, with the revived Imperial examinations offering everyone a path to serve the pékyu. To massacre ordinary villagers for a harmless scholar stuck in the past does not serve the pékyu's goals."

All the native officials and—to Tanvanaki's surprise—more than a few Lyucu thanes nodded at this speech. Tanvanaki decided to let her consort continue down this unanticipated path. Perhaps the hard-liners had less support than she had imagined.

"You're minimizing the crime committed by Savo Ryoto and Nazu Tei," objected Cutanrovo.

She wanted to slap the faces of the thanes nodding along to the emperor's words. *Have you forgotten the reality of our condition? We are surrounded by barbarians who hate us and wish us dead! The core islands may invade us at any moment—who can trust Dara-raaki's promises of peace?—and yet here you are, pleased with how far we've fallen from the ways of our ancestors.*

She had to remind them of the gravity of the offense. "The thane-taasa was in an illicit master-pupil relationship with the rebel scholar, one facilitated by his own mother!"

"But why is it a crime for the thane-taasa to seek out a master to impart knowledge to him?" asked Timu.

Stunned expressions all around the Great Hall.

*Is the pékyu thinking of rescinding the Edict Against Unauthorized Teachers? That would be a momentous shift in policy.*

"You . . . you would bypass the court-appointed tutors? You

would expose Lyucu children to the lies of crafty rebels without protection?" Spittle sprayed from Cutanrovo's lips as she shouted at Timu. "An unauthorized master-pupil relationship is a most dangerous assault upon an impressionable young Lyucu mind, even worse than a physical attack against a Lyucu warrior. The pékyu, who in her youth had to fight off a sly-tongued Dara-raaki teacher, knows this well." Cutanrovo looked to Tanvanaki, hoping to see a hint of why the pékyu was allowing her consort to spout such nonsense.

Tanvanaki did not react.

She had been caught completely off guard. Timu had gone too far, and she knew she should stop him. But she couldn't understand where he had suddenly acquired this boldness, as though he had smoked some herbs that gave him a burst of courage. As though stuck in a bad dream, she watched helplessly as he plunged recklessly ahead.

"How can practicing calligraphy and learning about the culture of Dara and the wisdom of the Ano sages be an assault?" demanded Timu. "Many thanes and naros and even culeks enjoy native arts—just go into the streets of Kriphi to see for yourself. Lessons on calligraphy, painting, and abbreviated versions of the Classics are so popular that so-called native informers can command salaries ten times what they used to earn under the . . . old regime. Some of you, in this very hall, have spent vast fortunes to acquire native antiques to decorate your homes. Indeed, so many Lyucu now can at least read and write some logograms that Kriphi today likely has a bigger literate population than before the conquest—"

Timu's voice cracked and he had to pause for a moment. Talk of time before the conquest brought to mind his father, who had never understood his willingness to surrender to the Lyucu in order to protect the lives of the people of Rui and Dasu. *Father,* he wanted to shout, *do you see? I've done good here.*

But it wasn't enough, he knew, not anywhere near enough. *Teeth on the board.* It was time for him to be the good king the people deserved, to speak the truth.

He took a deep breath and went on. "If so much of native culture has already become part of the lives of the Lyucu, why be afraid of the master-pupil relationship?"

The instruction of children, Lyucu and native, was a sensitive topic in Ukyu-taasa.

When Tanvanaki first pursued the policy of relying on native administrators to secure the fruits of the Lyucu conquest, many of the thanes expressed doubt. Pékyu Tenryo's original vision had been to kill off a large portion of the native population so that their farmlands could be converted to pasture use. Tanvanaki reversed her father's policy by leaving much of the native way of life intact, with the Lyucu as only a thin veneer sitting on top. The goal, as she had explained, was to secure the loyalty of the natives against a counterattack from unconquered Dara.

The elevation of the status of scholars—from which most of the native administrators were drawn—suited both Timu's devotion to learning and Tanvanaki's political goals. Tanvanaki shrewdly realized that it was most effective to share some of the spoils squeezed from the peasantry with the scholar class, thereby coopting their loyalty to serve the Lyucu as well as dividing them from the trust and support of the peasantry.

But Tanvanaki was also keenly aware of the reverence in which teachers were held in Dara. To prevent the re-remembering of unpleasant facts about the Lyucu conquest and to appease thanes concerned about native influence on the next generation, traditional master-pupil relationships, for both native and Lyucu children, were strictly forbidden. Only court-appointed instructors could take on students, and they had to adhere to a curriculum drafted by Wira Pin, in which the history of Dara, Lyucu, and Ukyu-taasa had been carefully re-remembered.

Timu was going to challenge this long-standing compromise.

"You know very well that it's not the teaching of calligraphy and painting that's at issue here," said Cutanrovo, staring at the emperor.

"Then maybe it's time to rethink what *is* at issue here," said Timu. "The truth. We've become terrified of the truth. Everyone here, you, me, the pékyu, the gathered Lords of Ukyu-taasa—all of us are guilty of it."

He paused. The Great Hall was so quiet that it was possible to hear a pin drop.

Despite a rising sense of impending doom, Tanvanaki didn't interrupt. She wanted the hard-liners to see that learning from Dara was the only way to defeat Dara. Maybe Timu's sudden boldness would create an opening for *that* discussion.

"What is this truth you speak of?" asked Cutanrovo, her voice a mixture of fear and contempt.

"You're terrified that your own children, once they've come to love this land and know its people, will be ashamed of the truth of the atrocities committed to obtain it and still being committed to hold it—"

"How dare you?! How dare—"

Timu shouted over her. "But that is why you're afraid to allow your children to learn history from native masters, isn't it? And you"—he pointed to the native ministers in the hall—"you are afraid of how your own children will view you when they find out that you've been teaching them lies, that you've bought your life of leisure and wealth at the cost of the lives of those who died and are still dying at Naza Pass, in Kigo Yezu, in hundreds of other hamlets and villages. Our reign is named Audacious Freedom, but both parts are lies! You have all been living as Cowardly Slaves!"

The ministers could not meet his eyes.

"And I've been afraid of the truth myself. Though I've tried to save the lives of the people, to tolerate horrors in the name of the greater good, I've been kept safe from the consequences of this regime that I've made legitimate. I've allowed the good names of my father and mother to be sullied in the service of a fantasy. Oh, how wrong I've been, how foolish! The people massacred at Kigo Yezu died believing I would protect them, and I can't even give them a decent burial. Their ghosts wander over the ashes of their homes, unable to cross the River-on-Which-Nothing-Floats."

His shoulders heaved in a body-racking sob.

"No more. If the Edict Against Unauthorized Teachers isn't rescinded, then sentence me as a prime violator. I have been teaching my children the same way—"

Finally, Tanvanaki shook herself out of her stunned stupor. Timu had botched everything. This was not the way to advance their agenda. She had to stop him now.

"Timu, you've been overexerting yourself," she said. "You know not of what you speak." She beckoned at several of the naros standing guard below the throne. "Take the emperor away and put him to bed—"

But Timu, who had always obeyed her when she demanded it, now looked at her with a brazen defiance. "But the truth cannot be wiped away. Rather than suppressing the teaching of the truth, we should embrace it. I know what you're afraid of, my breath. You're afraid of the truth that it's impossible for the Lyucu to win, that you can never fulfill your father's dream. How can you win when there are so many more natives than Lyucu? When you refuse to treat this land as your home to be cared for rather than a conquest to be exploited? When the core islands grow stronger daily under my mother—"

"Silence!" cried Tanvanaki. The naros were climbing up the dais.

"—Your only path forward is to embrace Dara, to teach our children the truth, to help both peoples find a way to live together as equals. There is no other way out. You're isolated and without reinforcements—"

The naros finally managed to climb onto the dais. They tried to subdue the emperor, but he struggled mightily against them with a strength impossible for his slender frame, his limbs flailing, his face flushed, his veiled crown askew. In the end, as they finally managed to wrestle him to the ground, the side of his face slammed against the stone dais, and his speech abruptly ceased. As the naros tied his limbs, he spat out a mouthful of blood and a few teeth on the ground. The naros gagged him.

The Great Hall was filled with astonished and confused murmurs.

Tanvanaki gestured for the naros to take the immobilized Timu away and tried to think of what to do next. At least Timu's absurd performance had completely distracted the court from the cases of Savo Ryoto and Nazu Tei. Maybe she could declare an end to court today and push the cases to the next session—

Cutanrovo's laughter reverberated through the Great Hall, stunning everyone into silence.

The sense of impending doom grew even heavier in Tanvanaki's heart.

Cutanrovo was pleased, very pleased. The emperor's outburst had given her the perfect opening, and, based on the pékyu's reaction, she was not behind her consort's strange behavior, after all.

"Votan-ru-taasa, votan-sa-taasa"—she shifted to Lyucu as she called out to the assembled warlords and ministers—"I think we should indeed speak of the truth, as the emperor urges. And let's do it in a language devoid of lies."

Every pair of eyes in the hall locked on her.

"Speak no more"—Tanvanaki had to stop and shift into Lyucu, so strong was the habit of speaking Dara in the Great Hall—"Cutanrovo, we've all said too much already today."

She regretted having sent the naros away with Timu. They should have subdued Cutanrovo instead.

"The emperor speaks of our fear of the natives, of the impossibility of our victory over all Dara, of our lack of reinforcements," said Cutanrovo, her voice deliberately low. The Lyucu language, seldom heard in the Great Hall, only made her words even more weighty. "But you've been lied to."

Tanvanaki closed her eyes. This was a nightmare coming true. She had been struggling to find a way to disclose the truth of Luan Zya's code in a controlled manner, not have it broadcast to all the thanes in a way calculated to make her appear a liar.

"Let me tell you the truth that has been kept from you: A reinforcement fleet is coming through the Wall of Storms from Ukyu—"

"Stop!" Tanvanaki shouted, knowing it was futile.

"—in less than three years!"

The Great Hall exploded into cacophony.

"Let her speak, votan!"

"Is this true?"

"Why haven't we been told?"

"How many city-ships are coming?"

"Is Pékyu-taasa Cudyu leading the reinforcements?"

Cutanrovo gestured for the shouting thanes to quiet. She stared at the pékyu, a smirk on her face.

Tanvanaki knew that she had lost control of the court. Wearily, she nodded. "Yes, what Thane Cutanrovo said is true. There will be an opening in the Wall of Storms. I was waiting for"—her voice weakened—"an auspicious occasion to announce it."

Cutanrovo strode around the Great Hall, waving her arms as she continued to speak in Lyucu.

"The moment is here! It's now! The truth, votan-ru-taasa and votan-sa-taasa, is that it is the natives who should be afraid, not us! For too long we have lived in fear, seeking to accommodate the barbarians and their ways. We have become soft. But Pékyu-taasa Cudyu is bringing us reinforcements to finish what the pékyu-votan started. All of us must rethink our position in light of this fact.

"Since the emperor brings up the education of the youth, let me start with that. Our young people now spend more time learning the arts of the natives than practicing their own war-making skills. Some thanes-taasa can recite a hundred Ano poems but quake at the idea of climbing onto the back of a garinafin.

"And the adults are no better. Some warriors eat native food at every meal and dress in native fashion, neglecting their duties to the pékyu to be ready for war.

"How do you think you'll appear in the eyes of our votan-ru-taasa and votan-sa-taasa from the homeland? How will you hold up your heads when they see you looking like a native?"

Her gaze deliberately lingered on the faces of the thanes dressed partially in native garb, and they looked away, ashamed to meet her gaze.

Tanvanaki knew this was the most powerful argument on Cutanrovo's side. When the possibility of reinforcements from the homeland had been remote, accommodation with the natives seemed reasonable, even inevitable. But now everyone had to think about the power reconfiguration that would occur after the arrival of more thanes from Ukyu. The judgment of one's peers always weighed so much more than the opinions of one's enemies.

Vocu Firna, perhaps the thane most steeped in native culture, made as if to speak, but Goztan Ryoto caught his eyes and shook her head.

Cutanrovo's voice grew more passionate as she continued. She was finally getting a chance to speak her heart, to shame these corrupt, cowardly thanes. "Many warriors take on multiple native lovers and treat them as though they were spouses, giving them property and leaving the education of their togaten to these concubines—"

Tanvanaki's face darkened at this—it was known throughout court that Timu, not her, spent much more time with Todyu and Dyana, the pékyus-taasa, and she hated to hear her children referred to by that slur—but Cutanrovo seemed not to notice.

"Open your eyes and ears, votan-ru-taasa and votan-sa-taasa, and let illusions fall away." Cutanrovo's voice cracked, and tears welled up in her eyes. "How many of you still go home to a tent? How many of you still speak to your children exclusively in Lyucu? It should shame each and every one of you that we're now more used to conversation in the language of the slaves.

"And for all that accommodation, what have you accomplished? Did you hear the words of the native emperor, our pékyu's consort? His heart is filled with hate; he prays for our destruction!

"*We* are the conquerors, but we act like the conquered. We've allowed our true nature to be corrupted by this land's loathsome nurture. We are wolves, but we act like we've put on sheep's clothing. We are Lyucu warriors who eat the flesh and drink the blood of what we kill, not Dara-raaki who subsist on what can be dug out of the soil and grown on piss and shit!

"Now do you see why what Goztan has done with her son is so dangerous and terrible? Now do you see how the accommodationists serve the sly agenda of the native emperor, who praises his mother's prowess while denigrating our courage? To the natives, a teacher is the equivalent of a parent—'parent of the mind,' they say, and expect the student to pay the teacher the same respect due the mother or father. What greater insult can there be for our children to treat the conquered slaves the same as their parents? How will our people judge us when they finally arrive from beyond the Wall of Storms and see our children paying obeisance to barbarians and calling them masters?"

Finally, there was no choice but for Goztan to speak.

Goztan was thinking of that day, long ago in Ukyu, when Oga Kidosu had spoken to her of teaching and being taught. Teaching and learning seem to always haunt her life. *How the gods love to play jokes.*

She stepped forward and spoke for the first time, also in Lyucu. "Cutanrovo, my sa-taasa, learning from the natives is a policy that dates back to the time of the pékyu-votan. It was he who encouraged all of us to learn from the people of Dara while not forcing them to speak our language—"

"How conveniently you re-remember the past!" said Cutanrovo. "You even sound like a native with the way you twist the truth. Pékyu Tenryo forbade the slaves from learning our language in order to preserve our element of surprise, and he told us to learn from the natives only to vanquish them. We have done so. It's time to act like conquerors and to force them to learn our ways or die."

"We've come to live in a new land, where our ways aren't suitable," said Goztan. "These islands are not like the scrublands of Ukyu. Unless we're willing to kill most of the natives, we can't support a population this size on pasturing alone, and who will fight for us then when Jia and Phyro invade at the end of the ten-year treaty?"

"Reinforcements are coming!"

"Even if Pékyu-taasa Cudyu sent all the city-ships at his disposal, how many more thousands of Lyucu warriors can be brought? We can't remain the same and not adapt."

"Your mind has been poisoned by defeatism," said Cutanrovo. "*That* is the problem with you accommodationists. Don't forget that with just a few thousand warriors, we've been able to conquer two islands of Dara and fought the greatest fleet they could put together to a standstill. Even their young empress, the handpicked successor of wily Kuni Garu, was killed by the Wall of Storms when she rode out to fight against our last fleet of reinforcements—"

"You can't win if you don't respect your enemies. The people of Dara had never fought against garinafins before, and yet, they managed to bring the lightning down to halt our advance at Zathin Gulf—"

"It doesn't matter if they have a thousand times our population or a hundred hundred varieties of intricate weapons. Victory is not determined by these superficial *things*, but the strength of the fire in the hearts of those at war. Sa-votan, you've forgotten the Lyucu spirit, the only thing that *matters*."

As the thanes debated, Tanvanaki's mind was all in turmoil.

*Is Cutanrovo right? Have I indeed lost too much of the spiritual fire that allowed us to overcome the forces of Mapidéré, to cross a storm-ridden ocean, to conquer these islands and shake the very throne of Dara to its foundation?*

"I have sacrificed as much as anyone here for the future of our people." For the first time, Goztan's voice lost its calmness. "I've devoted my life to the service of the pékyu, and to the pékyu-votan before her. I lost all five of my husbands in war. I'll not allow anyone to claim a monopoly on the Lyucu spirit—"

"Then act like it! Tell your son to stand up and fight with the club and axe, not soften his hands with wax blocks and coloring brushes. . . ."

Tanvanaki continued to vacillate.

*The policies advocated by the hard-liners will plunge this land back into horror and bloodshed. I may lose Timu forever if I go down that path.*

*But how will my brother and his thanes react when they find us living indistinguishably from their hated enemies? How can I retain their respect and remain the pékyu if Cudyu challenges my claim?*

Cutanrovo had worked herself into a frenzy. "Dara-raaki must be destroyed! Before the arrival of our reinforcements, we must purge ourselves of all native taint. Dara-raaki must be destroyed! We must speak Lyucu, wear Lyucu, eat Lyucu, act Lyucu. Dara-raaki must be destroyed! We must remake Ukyu-taasa into a true copy of Ukyu, and ensure that the togaten are as close to true Lyucu as possible. Dara-raaki must be destroyed! We will purify this land of false gods and false beliefs: The only truth is that the Lyucu are supreme and must rule."

Vocu Firna joined Goztan Ryoto to plead for reason, but their speeches were drowned out by a growing chorus of thanes shouting in time with Cutanrovo.

"Dara-raaki must be destroyed! Dara-raaki must be destroyed!"

All the hard-liner thanes had joined the chant, and even a few known accommodationists were with them. Many of the thanes took their war clubs and axes off their backs and slammed them against the ground in time to the chant. The noise was deafening. The Great Hall now had the wild air of a war council on the scrublands of Ukyu.

Wira Pin and Noda Mi, along with the other native deputies and generals, cowered in the back, shaking like newborn lambs, utterly terrified by the raw hatred and fury that had been unleashed.

*Even if ultimate victory depends on adopting the native expertise with engines of war, the immediate task must be to retain the loyalty of the hard-liners. There can be no other choice.*

Tanvanaki held up a hand, but it was some time before the shouting subsided enough for her to be heard.

"I've come to a decision," said Tanvanaki.

Goztan looked at her with despair, while Cutanrovo's face flushed with excitement.

"Thane Cutanrovo must be commended for her vigilance in discovering the traitors. She is hereby promoted to the rank of garinafin-thane. In preparation for the arrival of our compatriots from Ukyu, she is tasked with rooting out traitors among our ranks and restoring the ancient virtues—"

"Votan, no!" Goztan tried to stave off the inevitable.

"Silence!" said Tanvanaki. "The traitorous scholar Nazu Tei and the treasonous thane-taasa Savo Ryoto are hereby sentenced to death by exposure to Cudyufin's gift. Their executions shall be part of the celebration of the Winter Festival."

"Votan!" Goztan's voice was piteous. "I know that what my son has done is unforgivable. But I beg you to spare him on account of my years of service."

Tanvanaki shook her head sadly. "I'm sorry, old friend. Your son was doomed the day you made the decision to have him bow to a native scholar. You must also pay for this grave error. One-half of your flocks and herds are to be stripped from you and awarded to Thane Cutanrovo to fund her campaigns."

She expected Goztan to continue to plead and fight for her son's life, and she expected that she would have to order her restrained and dragged away. But after a moment of standing still, Goztan saluted her by lifting both arms and crossing them at the wrists.

"As you will, votan. I'm sorry that my son didn't serve you well in Ukyu-taasa."

She stepped back into her position at the head of the column of warlords and did not speak again.

Tanvanaki let out a sigh. Her mind lingered on Goztan's last words. They seemed so peculiar. But there was no time to focus on them now.

"Take him to the cliff cells outside Kriphi. May the music of the sea soothe his troubled conscience. Formal court is now adjourned."

Cutanrovo remained standing in the middle of the Great Hall, basking in loud cheers and congratulations. The political reconfiguration of Ukyu-taasa was complete.

# CHAPTER TWENTY-SIX

# THE WINTER FESTIVAL

SECRET AGON BASE IN KIRI VALLEY, IN THE
FOOTHILLS OF THE WORLD'S EDGE MOUNTAINS:
THE TWELFTH MONTH IN THE EIGHTH YEAR AFTER
THE DEPARTURE OF PRINCESS THÉRA FROM DARA
FOR UKYU-GONDÉ.

Even in winter, Kiri Valley, sheltered from the harsh winds that raged across the scrublands, enjoyed a relatively mild climate. The Agon used the downtime to enjoy stories and songs in their tents, while the Dara tried to catch up on the schooling and instruction that had to be put on hold during the harvest season. The small herds that could be sustained in the valley meant that kyoffir, yogurt, cheese, and milk were relative luxuries, but with all the sorghum, rice, wheat, and vegetables that had been stored up, there was plenty to eat.

A relatively mild climate didn't mean a perpetual spring. The first storm of winter had arrived in the valley the day before, burying the whole valley, including the sheep and cattle pens, the empty and fallow fields, and even the huts and tents of the settlement in a thick layer of fluffy, pristine snow. From inside the dwellings of the Agon and Dara, sheep-tallow candles and lamps burned against the dimming twilight, making the Agon tents glow like jellyfish resting against a white coral reef and the calfskin windows of Dara huts flicker like the eyes of strange, deep-sea creatures about to go to sleep.

But sleep was far from the minds of the residents of Kiri Valley. For tonight was the Winter Festival, a traditional celebration of the tribe's successful preparations against the threats of starvation. This year, the celebration promised to be even wilder. With luck, this would be the last winter they had to spend in hiding. The coming attack against Taten was all every thane and naro and soldier and scholar could think about.

Snow had been cleared from the open ground in the middle of the settlement, and a giant bonfire—built from wood rather than the traditional dung and animal bones—flared at the center. Around it, Agon and Dara families arranged fur rugs and sitting cushions, and the feast was in full swing.

Tolyusa-leaf smoke wafted from almost every sitting rug, as naros and culeks puffed on bone pipes, comical imitations of their fire-breathing garinafin mounts. Contented naros-votan and thanes, on the other hand, held chopped tolyusa berries between their lips and gums, letting the hallucinogenic juice work its magic slowly. While the berries had the stronger effect, the leaves, being more abundant, could be distributed to more celebrants. It had been some time since the shamans had authorized the distribution of tolyusa, as normally the precious substance was reserved for birthing garinafins and religious rituals. But this grand Winter Festival, a feast before an all-out assault on the hated Lyucu, warranted it.

Théra and Takval sat on a large garinafin leather rug at one end of the oval, the seat of honor. Placed in front of them were dozens of bone dishes constructed from garinafin scapula, each holding roasted strips of meat. Small bowls made from deer skulls held a variety of seasoning—tolyusa sauce, rock salt, flakes and scrapings from smoked fish and meats, mashed mixed herbs gathered from the valley, and a few Dara-inspired dipping sauces made from pickled gash cactus grubs, salted and fermented vegetables, berry compote sharpened with chopped nuts. Alongside these staples of Agon feasting sat dishes cooked in the Dara style with local ingredients: rice balls stuffed with juicy bone marrow and thrice-cooked beef, roasted venison and wild vegetable medley wrapped in flatbread, preserved prairie partridge eggs dipped in tangy red salt, cold dumplings with kyoffir sauce, snake-and-tusked-tiger soup served in garinafin skull bowls. . . .

One by one, Agon warriors came to the rug, sat down across from them, and toasted the pékyu and the princess.

A few, like Thane Araten, who had never accepted Théra's authority, deliberately kept their eyes on Takval and never addressed Théra.

Takval was about to reprimand Araten, but Théra put a hand against his back, reminding him to remain calm. After Araten left, she said, "Don't mar the occasion with anger. Save your rage for the Lyucu."

"If only everyone had your grandness of spirit."

Before Théra could answer, more celebrants arrived.

"Votan," said Gozofin, the father of Nalu, one of the pékyus-taasa's playmates, as he raised a skull bowl full of kyoffir. "May you and the princess continue to warm the hearts of all Agon like this feast in the heart of winter."

Takval raised his own skull bowl with both hands and drank first as a sign of respect. Though Gozofin was not a thane, he enjoyed high status among the Agon in the valley for being one of the band of warriors who had fought by the side of Takval's grandfather until the bitter end. Knocked unconscious when he fell from his garina-fin, he survived the subsequent massacre because the Lyucu thought him one of the corpses. The incident gave him a reputation for being favored by the gods. His support for the young pékyu early on in the history of the Kiri Valley settlement had been crucial.

Next to Takval, Théra raised a porcelain cup to the wizened Agon warrior and sipped the warm rice beer in it. "An excellent feast, Gozofin. I've never even tasted half the meats on offer tonight."

Gozofin laughed and drained his skull bowl in one gulp, not offended by Théra's refusal to share kyoffir with him. The fact that she, like most visitors from Dara, could not digest kyoffir or gari-nafin milk was well-known by the Agon now, and the Agon often teased their Dara friends about it. "Which of the ten meats is your favorite, Princess?"

"This one," said Théra, pointing to a roasted creature vaguely recognizable as a bird. It had been cooked with garinafin fire breath—an impressive sight for the Dara members of the settlement.

"I'm glad you like the salt flat redwing. The hunting party responsible for that one had to go to the Sea of Tears to get them."

"That far?" Théra frowned. "That's a lot farther than I thought—"

"Don't worry," said Takval. "The salt flats around the Sea of Tears are uninhabited, and few hunting parties would go out there in the middle of winter. The risk of discovery is nonexistent."

Théra swallowed her objections. In preparation for the assault on Taten, the Agon had convinced Takval and Théra to suspend the general prohibition against raiding and hunting outside the valley. Since fall, multiple hunting parties had left each day to gather supplies ("You can't expect Agon warriors to have the strength to fight the Lyucu scum without plenty of meat!") and to hone their fighting skills. Théra also suspected that some of the hunting parties used the excursions as an opportunity to raid small Lyucu tribes or isolated caravans. Since stopping such practices altogether was impossible, she could only hope that their plans wouldn't be revealed to the Lyucu out of carelessness.

She was somewhat comforted by the thought that the hunting parties were at least able to avoid Cudyu's senior thanes. Once the plan for the assault on Taten had been set, Volyu had gone on a tour to visit Cudyu and his senior thanes, ostensibly to show how obedient the Agon were to their Lyucu masters. He had used the opportunity to extract intelligence about the plans and movements of the Lyucu tribes prior to the gathering at Aluro's Basin and sent the information to Kiri Valley, which allowed the Agon hunting parties to plan their routes.

At this moment, Volyu should be at Aluro's Basin, putting on an act of obeisance to further lull the reveling Lyucu into complacency before their journey to Taten. Now that he was fully committed to the rebellion, Takval's uncle, Théra reflected, had turned out to be a valuable ally—at least once he realized victory was possible and that he would get something out of it. Profit and gain moved even cowards to take great risks.

"It means a lot to all the thanes and warriors to go on the hunt," said Gozofin. "Some of the young children have never experienced a festival of ten meats until now." He swept his arm at the hubbub behind him. "They're grateful to you, Théra."

Théra smiled, glad that she could do something that gladdened every heart. She picked up a small redwing drumstick and dipped it in tolyusa sauce—not too much, for she was already feeling a bit light-headed—and enjoyed the succulent, juicy flesh, which practically melted against her tongue.

She glanced over at the children's mat, next to the pékyu's sitting rug, where the sons and daughters of thanes and high-ranking Dara advisers enjoyed easy-to-chew delicacies better suited for tender jaws and less sophisticated palates: buttery bone marrow served in vole skulls, roasted mouflon kidneys on fish-bone skewers, red-wing intestines coiled like noodles (and tenderized with gash cactus sauce), honeyed berry and fruit compote, and so on. Kunilu-*tika* and Jian-*tika* were among them, as happy as children back home on New Year's. Thoryo, though far too old to be considered a child, sat at the children's mat by her own choice.

She looked over at the other side of the sitting rug, where Vara Ronalek had seated her family. Vara was the oldest thane in the valley, but she still rode the garinafin every day as though she were a teenager. She was the one who had adopted Toof and Radia into her clan, and because of her age and high reputation, none of the other Agon thanes had objected to the unusual decision. The two Lyucu were now sitting with her and her children, chatting and drinking. They nodded at Théra and smiled.

"How do you feel?" whispered Takval in her ear.

Startled, Théra took a moment to compose herself. "I'm not sure. I suppose I should feel excited. We haven't ever had such a feast. But . . . somehow I can't shake the feeling that this isn't real. I'm as nervous as they act."

She pointed to the garinafins outside the oval of sitting rugs around the bonfire. For the feast, they were also given special treats: dried long-ear grass supposedly from the shores of Aluro's Basin (Volyu had sent a shipment in late fall, a gift from one of the Lyucu tiger-thanes to reward the Pé-Afir-tekten's loyalty to the Lyucu), dethorned gash cactus lobes, and tender, tongue-tingling vines cut from the sheer cliffs of the valley. A few of the garinafins, infected by the mood of the humans in the settlement and the deviation from routine, had been lowing impatiently all evening and scratching at the ground.

After their defeat by Tenryo, the scattered Agon tribes generally reverted back to the ancient ways of rearing garinafins to be closely bonded to their pilots—largely out of necessity, since it was no longer possible for isolated tribes to field huge armies of garinafins with interchangeable pilots in the manner pioneered by Pékyu Nobo Aragoz of the Agon and later adopted by the Lyucu.

Takval, however, had taken this further, mandating that adult garinafins should not be separated from their young and that their training should emphasize reward rather than punishment. Many of these ideas had come from Toof and Radia, and the Agon pékyu's general kindness toward the garinafins had been in large part responsible for their ultimate decision to be adopted by the Agon.

"It's natural to be nervous," Takval tried to reassure her. "In a few weeks, we'll be launching the attack on Taten and avenging both our peoples."

Théra nodded, trying to look assured but failing.

"I know it's your nature to always anticipate the future, to think about the next step," said Takval. "But sometimes it's important to remember what you've done. Look around us: The warriors have new weapons and are well fed; we eat foods both grown and hunted, cooked in the manner of two lands; many children who would have died in summer drought or winter storm now sport fat cheeks and strong limbs; our two peoples are dancing and laughing around the same fire."

"But is it enough? Most of your people continue to have no interest in learning to read and write or studying the art of farming. Most of my people won't be able to ride the garinafins with you into war. I'm afraid that our children—"

"There will always be a thousand ways you think things can be better, my breath. But without you, we wouldn't have survived the chase beyond the Wall of Storms. Without you, either my uncle or I would be dead, instead of working toward the same goal. Without you, there would be no Kiri Valley, our children's home and where the Agon and the Dara are learning to become one. Your mercy and strength must not be discounted. You did this, Théra. You made the alliance work."

Tears flowed down her face silently. She wondered if the dead spirit of her father, on the other shore of the River-on-Which-Nothing-Floats, could see this scene of celebration. She wondered if her mother and brothers, weighed down with the duty to care for the people of Dara, could imagine that their salvation was at hand. She looked up at the moon and wondered if Zomi at that moment was also looking up into the sky, and whether she was thinking of Théra just as Théra was thinking of her.

She pulled Takval into a tight embrace, and he tilted her face up to give her a kiss. In the background, Agon and Dara voices cheered.

The next person to come to toast Takval and Théra was not an Agon thane at all.

"Don't overdo it, Çami," said Théra as she watched Takval and the Golden Carp scholar compete to see who could finish their skull bowl of kyoffir first. Çami Phithadapu was one of the few natives of Dara who could consume garinafin milk without any ill effects.

Çami turned her skull bowl upside down first to show that she was done, and she laughed as Takval sputtered in surprise at losing the contest.

"Show-off," said Théra with a smile. "Don't forget that he's been drinking all night, holding all the thanes at bay by himself."

Çami cocked a brow at Takval. "Pékyu, then I guess I should thank you for letting me win."

Takval shook his head. "I wasn't holding back. You have the soul of an Agon."

"I've been told that I'm a natural on the back of a garinafin," said Çami, quite pleased with herself. "Whether it's whale whispering or garinafin riding, I guess big animals just like me."

"Speaking of learning the ways of the Agon," said Théra, "how's your research into the arucuro tocua going?"

"Not great," said Çami. "The pékyu was right about the construction technique being limited to toys."

Since the startling revelation from her boys, Théra could not stop thinking about the bone beasts. She had pressed Takval and Agon elders for more information, but they had not been able to satisfy her curiosity. She had thus set Çami the task of learning all she could about the engineering technique.

"So you've found no instances where the technique was used at a larger scale?" asked Théra incredulously.

Çami shook her head. "Arucuro tocua appears to be widely known among the tribes of the scrublands, both Lyucu and Agon, and I've been shown multiple impressive toy models of artificial beasts able to move on their own with the power of wind or a swinging weight. Some of these are so clever that they rival any clockwork mechanism in Dara. Similar construction techniques are used for some objects employed in religious mysteries, but of course I didn't see any of these."

While Théra and her Dara advisers weren't opposed to worshipping the Agon gods, the shamans had refused to allow them to participate in many mystery rituals, claiming that only the children of Afir could commune with the gods and the spirits of their ancestors. This was a mild source of tension at the settlement, but Théra didn't push the matter, reasoning that the shamans likely perceived the Dara advisers, with their foreign knowledge, as a threat to their power.

"In any event, it doesn't sound like objects used in secret religious rituals are what we're looking for," said Théra. "I'm talking about something big."

"No, nothing like that," said Çami. "No one could recall any instance of seeing arucuro tocua techniques applied to build large machines."

"I just don't understand it," said Théra. "How can such sophisticated knowledge be limited solely to the realm of playthings?"

"What would we build big arucuro tocua for?" asked Takval, exasperated.

"You could make . . . mechanical beasts of burden!" offered Théra. "If you scaled it up properly."

"These beasts of bone would move slower and carry less weight than living cattle or garinafin," retorted Takval. "Worst of all, they'd move only at the whim of the wind, not under the instruction of a driver."

A few other Dara generals and scholars, seeing that Çami seemed to be engaged in some deeper conversation with the pékyu and the princess, gathered around the sitting rug to listen to the discussion.

"What about in battle?" asked Théra.

"Again, a garinafin—or even a team of well-armed warriors on foot—would make short work of them," said Takval.

Théra was stumped. She had thought the discovery of a native tradition of machinery and crafting would give her a new way of fighting against the Lyucu, but this was turning into a dead end.

"Actually, I don't think it's that unusual," said Razutana, the Cultivationist scholar. He bit into a roasted prairie partridge, chewed loudly, and smacked his lips. A loud burp followed. "By the way, I *must* have the recipe for the sauce on this partridge!"

"What would your old classmates say if they saw you like this?" said Théra, laughing. "Didn't Kon Fiji say that it is unseemly for a gentleman to show his teeth during a meal?"

"I'm paying a compliment to the chef!" said Razutana. "Kon Fiji also said that good manners change depending on whether one is dining with grand lords at the court of the King of Cocru or with peasants at a village tea shack. When in the scrublands, do as the Agon do."

*He's certainly been living up to that adage,* reflected Théra wryly. The scholar who once claimed that it was unseemly for a learned and virtuous man to sully his thoughts with implements of the kitchen had become one of the most avid cooks in the settlement, having invented numerous dishes that combined Dara and Agon techniques and ingredients. When questioned about his new hobby, Razutana had indignantly insisted that there was nothing inconsistent in a Cultivationist *cultivating* his taste buds and *growing* his appetite through the *breeding* of new recipes.

"I'm certainly not going to debate the teachings of the Ano sages against a clever tongue like yours," said Théra. "But we're running away from the topic. Do you really not find it odd that the art of making mechanical bone beasts is reserved only for playthings?"

Razutana nodded his head professorially as he went on. "Back in

Dara, though the ancient Ano knew the secret of firework powder, they didn't use it either for construction or warfare. Instead, fireworks were made only as a form of entertainment or an aid to religious celebration. It wasn't until long after the Diaspora Wars that the people of Dara began to use firework powder for excavation and in battle."

"Why didn't they use it for those purposes before?" asked Takval. He had been suitably impressed by the effects of firework powder during the battle against the Lyucu city-ship, and was enthusiastic about producing more of it. In fact, collecting guano from caves in Kiri Valley to produce saltpeter for firework powder was one of the few suggestions from Dara advisers that the Agon thanes were excited about.

"Because it wasn't suited to how wars were fought," offered Commander Tipo Tho, very visibly pregnant. Gon Nméji, her husband, stood behind her, holding their two older children by their hands. Théra offered to have Tipo recline at their sitting rug, but she laughed and shrugged off the suggestion. "Once I lie down, getting up will be much harder. I prefer standing."

"Can you explain more about why firework powder wasn't suitable for old ways of fighting?" Takval persisted.

"During the Diaspora Wars, most battles involved small skirmishes in open fields and duels between well-trained champions wielding rare and expensive bronze weapons," Tipo said. "It wasn't until much later, as the population of Dara grew and iron weapons became common, that the Tiro states began to field large armies and conduct siege warfare, at which point the explosive property of firework powder became relevant."

"A shark doesn't think about riding battle kites," said Gon Nméji, stroking his beard like some learned scholar. "And a sparrow cannot appreciate the use of a diving bell. Razutana, surely some Ano sage has said something like this, no?"

Razutana chuckled. "I'm afraid that I am not nearly learned enough to know of such a quote among the Ano sages."

Tipo punched her husband in the shoulder. "Ha, think I don't recognize a dig against aviators from a submariner? How come you get to be a shark and I'm compared to a sparrow? I'd say a Mingén falcon and a warty toad would be more apt."

Gon rubbed his shoulder, wincing exaggeratedly. "Well, count this toad lucky then, 'cause I have you."

Théra looked thoughtful. Steeped in the ways of Dara, she had imagined how the engineering principles behind arucuro tocua could be adapted to build self-locomoting machines. But the people of the scrublands had no cities and no habit of accumulating possessions. What was the point then of developing fragile, life-size bone beasts when there were plenty of living beasts about?

"I suppose arucuro tocua is a dead end," she said to Çami. "Sorry I made you chase after a mirage."

"Not at all," said Çami. "I found it a lot of fun to study the bone beasts. They are nothing like real living animals, and yet they show so many clever ideas that rival the designs of gods. I'm thinking of writing a treatise about them."

"If you do," said Théra with a wry smile, "there won't be many who can read it in the future. I can barely get my own children to study the Ano logograms, let alone interest the Agon children. The future of the Agon lies in literacy, but I cannot seem to convince anyone."

"Don't give up hope," said Çami. "It took time to convince even my parents to let a girl learn to read. I'm sure—" But she never got to finish her sentence.

"Princess of Dara, do you pretend to know the future?"

Everyone turned. The speaker was an old woman whose back was bent like the crescent moon and whose white hair was as wispy and thin as the clumps of doetail on the edge of Lurodia Tanta. As she tottered closer, leaning on a staff that was even taller than she was, made from a garinafin wing bone, she seemed so frail that the next gust of wind could blow her away. But in her severe eyes there was nothing but fiery strength and cold fury. The crowd before Takval and Théra's sitting rug parted wordlessly to make room for her. Takval and Théra stood up in deference.

"Tongue-of-the-Every-Mother," exclaimed Takval. He bent down, filled a skull bowl with kyoffir, and reverently raised it with both hands. "Please, drink with me."

The old woman was none other than Adyulek, the most senior shaman among all the shamans and god-dancers and spirit-painters who had joined the settlement of Kiri Valley. She spoke for Diaarura, the Every-Mother.

Adyulek handed her cane to a young woman named Sataari, her apprentice and assistant. With both hands, she carefully accepted the kyoffir from Takval. Takval filled another skull bowl, stood up, and drank first. Adyulek watched him with expressionless eyes, and when he was done, lifted her bowl to her lips. She drank with gusto and abandon, her leathery throat moving up and down like the neck of a swallowing tortoise, and in even less time than Takval, she held the bowl upside down to show that it was empty.

Only when Takval had humbly taken the empty skull bowl from her hand did she turn to look at the princess, her eyes as cold as Nalyufin's light.

"I never claimed to know the future," said Théra stiffly. Adyulek had made little effort to disguise her distaste and even contempt for the Dara princess, and she, in turn, had long ceased trying to win Adyulek over. "But I do know that there are things you can learn that will help the Agon people gain more control over the future. You don't understand what writing is, and so you—"

"Do *not* presume, Princess of Dara," said Adyulek. "You think me an ignorant barbarian who cannot understand the value of your supposed gift. But we paint scenes to celebrate great hunts and victories, we carve lines and circles to enumerate the births and deaths of our herds, we tie knots on strings to remember the promises of our ancestors—we know what it is to aid memory with tangible aids." She grabbed her cane back from Sataari and held it up to show Théra the strands of twisted leather dangling from the knob at the top. Various knots were tied in them, all of different shapes and colors.

"Writing is far more than that. The methods you describe can help you remember, but they aren't free from memory." She pointed at one of the strands dangling from Adyulek's cane and turned to Takval. "What does that strand mean?"

Takval looked like he would rather be anywhere but here. "I . . . I don't know. I think it records an agreement."

"The large red knot stands for Pékyu Akiga Aragoz," said Adyulek. "And this large black knots stands for Thane Taal Tori, the chief of my tribe in the time before all the Agon were united under one banner. The three knots between them show the three conditions they negotiated when my tribe agreed to join Pékyu Akiga and become part—"

"Yes, yes," said Théra impatiently, "but don't you see the meaning of these knots is tied to your mind? The knots help *you* remember, but they are meaningless to anyone else, including the new pékyu here. With writing, even a stranger who knows nothing of the re-remembering of the Agon will be able to know exactly what the terms of that agreement were, just by reading the words—"

"Why should I care if strangers know about an agreement that matters only to me and mine?"

Théra was frustrated. This was an argument she had had so many times. "But what about after you die?"

"While I'm alive, I'll teach them to Sataari and the children of my tribe, and they to theirs. The memories of the knots will live as long as there are those who claim to be of the Tribe of the Crescent Hill."

"Diaarura-Breath, everyone knows the power of your memory," said Takval placatingly. "Have you sampled—"

"But that isn't reliable," said Théra, ignoring Takval's attempt at defusing the awkward situation. Adyulek's bullheadedness only aroused her own stubborn streak. She decided to reveal a fact that she had, out of deference to the shamans, never disclosed before. "I've had scribes take notes at your storytelling sessions, transcribing sections of your performances phonetically with zyndari letters."

Adyulek looked at her, uncomprehending.

Théra took a deep breath. On the eve of the assault on the Lyucu, she suddenly no longer cared about deferring to the shamans. One way or another, all her planning was about to come to an end. Might as well speak the truth.

"Writing is an accurate and true representation of what you said— anyway, it doesn't matter. The point is, by studying the transcripts, I can see that the stories you tell are never exactly the same! Details are dropped or added, actions altered, even genealogies modified. You think memory is perfect, but—"

"Don't you think we know that?"

Théra was shocked. This was not how she imagined the shamans reacting to being revealed as frauds.

"Every living thing changes," said Adyulek. "I don't carve the same scenes into turtle shells as my mother did, and she did it differently from her mother. I don't dance the same way I learned from the shaman who taught me. We live by the voices of our ancestors, and in the fullness of time, add our voices to theirs. Just as the flowers that bloom in the scrublands change from season to season, the stories will change from telling to telling. Only those too young, inflexible, or arrogant to understand the sacred mysteries would believe otherwise."

"But how can you call the stories the truth if they change each time?" Théra felt as though she were standing on quicksand, with nothing to hold on to. "How can you claim to have history—uh, re-remembering—when you can't be sure that the story you remember is the story your mother told?"

"The wisdom of our ancestors is not dead like yours," said Adyulek. "You seek to kill the living voice by fixing it with your word-scars, but you don't understand that what you've caught with your symbols is only a corpse, not the truth. When a man or woman speaks, they express with their body the unending battle that sustains their mind. They make thinking-breath!"

Thoryo, part of the growing gathering around Takval and Théra's sitting rug, nodded silently at this.

Adyulek went on. "A speech is full of rhythm, intonation, expression, tone, emotion, movement, change—it is *alive*. How can your word-scars capture any of that? You take delight in mere droppings and footprints while the real garinafin soars over your head!"

"That is mere mysticism, of no use—"

"Your word-scars are as dead as your way of life. You think it's enough to have food to eat, but you don't see how roaming free over the scrublands is living and breathing while burrowing for tubers out of the same spot in the ground is death for both the digger and the land!"

"It's exactly prejudice like that—"

"Enough!" said Adyulek. "You make too much noise. Hold your tongue and sit down. It's time for the storytelling dance to begin."

Théra looked over at Takval, but he shook his head and indicated that she should sit down. "Please, my breath, it's not good to fill hearts with doubt and anger on a night dedicated to feasting."

Théra sighed and sat down, defeated, as she watched Adyulek walk away.

A loud and mournful melody, like the bellowing of a garinafin in battle, rang over the settlement. The sound came from a set of Péa pipes, sometimes also called storm pipes. This traditional musical instrument of the scrublands was made from a garinafin bladder—about the size of a small Agon tent—attached to a set of massive garinafin-bone pipes—each several times longer than a standing human—sticking out one end. Before the instrument could be played, several culeks had to spend hours or even days blowing into the bag to pump it up like a massive balloon. The player then blew into a tiny pipe called "the pilot," which was about the size of a flute in Dara, made from the antler of a yearling garinafin. Instead of using finger holes, the player altered the note played by the pilot pipe by pushing it deeper into the bladder or pulling it out. Meanwhile, culeks compressed the bone bag by pushing against it from both sides to force air through the large bone pipes, called "the horde." Somehow, the reedy music of the pilot pipe would then be amplified into booming notes in the horde pipes, and the resulting music could be heard for miles, much like the voice of the garinafin.

Çami, who was supposed to be sitting with Razutana and his friends, had stayed with Théra to keep her company.

"These pipes are really interesting," she began. "I looked into them—"

Théra shook her head. "These pipes always give me a headache."

She knew that Çami's interest in whales and whale song had led to an interest in music, but Théra was in no mood to listen to a lecture now. She was still seething over the debate with Adyulek and the way Takval had failed to back her.

Çami smiled. "Well, good thing then that these instruments take so much effort to prep that they're rarely used."

As the droning music continued to boom over the settlement, all the people visiting friends and relations around the bonfire returned to their own sitting rugs. Even the children at the sitting rug on Théra's right sat still in neat rows. Everyone fell silent. Théra realized that the festival had entered a new stage.

> *In the time before stories were the gods born,*
> *By their will is the world mended and re-torn.*
> *Strong bones can be crushed by stronger jaws,*
> *Every heroic cycle hews to eternal laws.*

> *Diaru diaru gozna-gozdyu,*
> *Al-vate tatate dyupéruta,*
> *Tekpéten sa-alu fir sliryodyu.*

The bonfire was burning brighter than ever, enhanced with the addition of a supply of old bones. Next to the light, Sataari was chanting hypnotically as Adyulek danced around a set of drums and struck them rhythmically with her staff. From time to time, she swept at the crowd around the fire with her staff, and they responded with the chorus in unison.

Somehow, she had lost all the signs of age in her movements. She was dancing and leaping with the grace of a yearling mouflon or a tusked tigress in her prime.

It was the drums that most attracted Théra's attention. Rather than a set of independent squat cylinders, like the drums in Dara, Adyulek's set was constructed from a number of long, hollow garinafin bones connected at odd angles to a central column, several times the shaman's height and as thick as the oldest tree in the valley, made of cowhide wrapped around a lattice-frame of thin bones. The whole assembly brought to mind a cactus with multiple branching lobes.

She could readily imagine how much of a challenge transporting such an instrument, even if disassembled into pieces, posed to a nomadic people. The drums must be extremely rare and significant.

"How come I haven't see these before?" she whispered to Takval.

"Voice painting is reserved for grand celebrations before a battle or a grand hunt," said Takval. "Until now, we haven't been able to do either—"

"Please!" said Souliyan, sitting next to them. "Save the chatter for later. Let's try to do all we can to honor the gods."

Whether out of nerves for the success of the planned attack or ambivalence about the imminent loss of their life of peace in the secluded valley, Souliyan had grown increasingly irritable in recent days. Théra clamped her lips shut and tried to concentrate.

Each of the hollow bone tubes was capped by a drumhead of thin sheepskin or cowhide. Because each of the branching drum shells was of different shape, thickness, and length, the sound made by Adyulek's staff against each drumhead was also different. As Adyulek danced around the contraption, she created a pulsing music that complemented Sataari's story: thunderous, low booms when the young shaman spoke of the gods; quick, raindrop-like patter when she described humans; a staccato tune of three percussive notes when she mentioned a hero in joy; a different arrangement of those three same notes when the hero shifted in mood.

"*During the Fifth Age of Mankind, the land overflowed with milk and fat. Oh, you've not seen such a feast upon the face of the earth, votan-ru-taasa and votan-sa-taasa. You have not.*

"*As far as the eye could see, the land was covered in lush green, like the shores of Aluro's Basin in spring. Rivers filled with fresh, clear water were never more than an hour's ride away. Flowers bloomed in every hue of the rainbow, far more beautiful than even the most opulent feather collections of the greatest pékyus in our debased Sixth Age.*

"*Fruits of every description and taste oozed out of the ground, ready to be plucked. Lambs and calves fell from the heavens into soft grass, all trussed for the slaughter. Fish leapt out of the rivers and lakes onto the grassy banks, begging to be eaten. . . .*"

The festival attendees, Agon and Dara alike, sat mesmerized by this description of an impossible golden age. Even though most of the Dara members of the community didn't profess faith in the gods of this foreign land, the appeal of a paradise of plenty and beauty was universal.

As Théra half listened to the hypnotic tale being spun by Sataari and Adyulek, she noticed something else: two young shamans wearing the skulls of moss-antlered deer and covered from head to toe in thick fur capes stood on a circular catwalk near the top of the drum set's central column. They were taking handfuls of something out of leather bags and scattering it on top of the column.

"What are they doing?" whispered Théra to Takval, pointing at the young shamans.

"Shhh!" Takval pointed at his mother.

Annoyed, Théra scooted back a bit on the sitting rug, away from Takval. He threw her a quick, apologetic glance before turning back to the performance.

"... *Firvatek, son of Cucuarte, daughter of Kyocu, Thane of the Land-Between-a-Lake-and-a-River, was not content. He coveted the lumpfish and three-lobed melon of Aratenri, daughter of Ro, daughter of Nagoz, Thane of the River-with-Six-Islands; he wanted the hoof-fruit and six wives of Diafir, son of Lipé, son of Ro, Roaming Naro of the Thane of the Horn-Shaped Hills; he desired the tongue-searing leaves and beetleberries of Kikitan, son of Ra, son of Lektan, Thane of the Red-and-White-Shored-River ...*"

Despite her best efforts, Théra's mind drifted. Sataari and Adyulek's story seemed stuck in a catalog of names and genealogies and places and mythical objects that she had no knowledge of. The language was archaic, distinct from the vernacular she had learned, full of odd phrases that she didn't understand and with even familiar words pronounced divergently. As much as she tried to absorb Agon culture, it seemed there was always more to learn. Everything was connected to everything else, and she couldn't understand how anyone was ever supposed to keep track of the stories, references, lineages, memories.

She looked around at the other attendees. Everyone appeared

absorbed by the tale, and even the Dara were at least politely paying attention (though Théra suspected more than a few were trying to stifle yawns). Çami, however, looked just as bored as she was. The two women locked gazes, and smiled knowingly. Then Çami held up a finger and pointed to the side.

Théra followed her finger. The garinafins sitting outside the oval of families were leaning over the sitting rugs with their long necks to watch the human drama. From time to time, they dipped down to grab a mouthful of dethorned gash cactus lobes, a favorite treat, piled between the sitting rugs. Çami was pointing at a young male named Riva, who belonged to the Agon family that was teaching Çami to ride. The beast was sitting on his haunches, wings folded neatly on his back, serpentine neck coiled on top, dozing listlessly. Seeming to sense Théra's and Çami's eyes, his eyelid popped open as he gazed back at them, his antlers tilted inquisitively.

Théra's heart quickened. She looked back at Çami to confirm. Çami nodded, a mischievous glint in her eyes.

"... turned away from the ancestral ways, the ways taught to the people of plenty by the gods. Firvatek bashed his fists against the land, demanding that it provide hoof-fruit and three-lobed melons in every season; he lashed the rivers with a whip woven from cow tails, demanding that they flow where he wished; he tried to hoard all the food, chasing away the birds and free-roaming beasts. It was not enough to take just what was needed from the land, but to enslave it. . . ."

Quietly, Théra and Çami stole away from their seats until they were outside the elongated circle of sitting rugs. Takval and Souliyan didn't notice. The escapees tiptoed toward Riva. Théra stifled a giggle. This was as fun as when she and her brothers used to sneak away from the palace when they were supposed to be studying with Master Zato Ruthi.

Riva's gaze followed the two women as they approached. When they reached the garinafin, Çami looked up at Riva and nodded. Riva uncoiled his neck and dipped his head, placing it on the ground at the women's feet. The two woman scrambled up, grabbing an antler each. Riva lifted his head and brought it close to his shoulder. Although some of the flashier pilots enjoyed having their mounts lift them on their heads and then straighten out their necks so that they could stride down the long neck into the saddle, most pilots actually preferred Riva's method of elevating the rider into the saddle. Certainly it didn't look as impressive, but it was faster and more practical, especially on the battlefield.

But instead of climbing onto the back of the garinafin, Çami indicated to Théra that she should wrap her legs around the right antler and hold on. She demonstrated by doing the same herself with the left antler. Gently, Çami patted Riva above the left eye.

Surprised by this unusual sitting position, the garinafin gave a low, questioning snort. Çami patted his left eyelid again reassuringly. The garinafin relaxed his shoulders, as though shrugging, and then straightened his long, sinuous neck, lifting the princess and the scholar high off the ground.

Théra tightened her grip on the antler branches, exhilarated. Takval had tried to teach her to ride a few times, but she had always been too busy to put in much practice. In any event, she had never tried to ride on the *head* of a garinafin. Even though they weren't flying, she already felt the thrilling power of the muscle and sinew under her.

Riva leaned over the family below, extending his neck so that his head was inside the oval of sitting rugs and above the level of the top of the central column of the bone drums.

"Best view in the house," said Çami. Théra chuckled.

"Good boy," said Çami, gently patting the top of Riva's head.

"Do you think he really understands you?" asked Théra.

"Radia and Toof think the garinafins understand more of what we say than we realize," said Çami. "I'm not so sure."

"I guess it doesn't hurt to talk nicely to them," said Théra. She had always been a little afraid of the garinafins, but now she wondered if she should make more of an effort. Tentatively, she imitated Çami and patted Riva's head. "Good boy."

"Watch," said Çami, pointing down.

Holding tight to the antler, Théra leaned out as though peeking out from the crow's nest of a ship.

From their new vantage point, the two women had a clear view of what was happening above the drum set. The top of the central column flared out into a large circle, and the two junior shamans were stretching a fresh piece of thin, almost translucent garinafin skin across it. Then they scattered handfuls of dust of different colors onto this surface.

"Is that paint?" asked Théra.

Çami nodded. "That's red and brown ochre, bone black, maybe some charcoal, crushed-shell white, not sure what the blue is—"

Adyulek slammed her staff into one of the drumheads below.

Çami and Théra both gasped.

The colorful dust scattered on the garinafin skin came to life and danced.

"... rivers dried up; grass wilted; the fruits of the earth disappeared; the land cracked like the back of the tortoise ..."

Adyulek slammed her staff into the drumheads again and again, beating out a mournful tune.

The colorful dust swirled and shifted, sorting into bands and stripes that moved sinuously across the translucent surface.

"... monsters emerged from the mountains and set themselves upon the people. Blood flowed as men, women, and children died ..."

The blue bands were swallowed by the brown ochre stripes; the red circles expanded like the gaping maws of monsters; white starbursts erupted with each drumbeat, every one a fresh monument of bones to the terrors that seized the people of the Fifth Age.

"... it was the Creation in reverse, the Void swallowing up the Beautiful. The Breath turned into howling storms that careened across the land in dust tornadoes; the Milk receded into Tears, leaving behind white beaches of salt; the Heartbeat thundered across the skies, but brought no relief ..."

The young shamans continued to add more handfuls of colored dust to the top of the drum set, where they fed into the moving, roiling, forming and re-forming patterns that suggested everything and nothing.

Without consciously realizing it, Théra was no longer bored. The rhythmic movements of the dancers; the changing, vibrant colors; the fragrant smoke and stomach-tickling cooking; the hypnotic drumming; the sense of connectedness between the audience and the performer—everything impressed upon and overwhelmed her senses. She had ceased listening to the *words* of the story, but lost herself to the experience of it. It no longer felt like a recitation of the deeds and relations of strangers from long ago, but a living drama in which all, including herself, were actors.

Çami broke into her reverie. "The patterns are from the vibrations of the drumbeats."

Théra focused on the top of the drum set and saw that Çami was right. The hollow central column acted as a resonating chamber for the set, and as Adyulek beat against the different drumheads below, the skin stretched across the top throbbed and quaked, sending the dust into a frenzied dance that became an abstract painting of her dance.

"*. . . and so ended the Fifth Age of Mankind in bloodbath, starvation, and thirst. People were exiled from the land of plenty, and the gods remade the world into the scrublands.*"

Sataari finished and stood still.

Adyulek twirled in place and slammed her staff into the largest of the drums one last time. Then she plunged the tip of the staff into the ground and held on to it, letting her momentum carry her once around the pole before finally stopping like a hawk swooping down to rest. She leaned against the pole, panting. Once again, she was just an old woman, not the embodiment of the Every-Mother.

The colorful swirling dust stopped moving and settled into a fixed pattern of beautiful and bleak bands, stripes, swirls, circles, starbursts.

One of the two young shamans now picked up a second piece of thin garinafin skin and held it up while the other one began to paint it with a cattle-hair brush dipped in some viscous, clear liquid. When the whole skin had been covered, the two shamans carefully laid it on top of the colorful pattern atop the drum set and rolled a thin bone pin across the top to press it against the "canvas."

Finally, the two shamans carefully peeled the skin back. The colorful pattern stuck to the lifted skin, and as the two shamans held it up and displayed it for the crowd around the bonfire, everyone cheered. A new round of the chorus broke out.

"So this is how the voice paintings are made," said Çami. "It really is a painting of sounds."

Théra nodded, too overwhelmed to speak. She had seen the voice paintings hanging in the tents of the thanes, and Souliyan had shown her several that she said dated from the time of her father. But she had never known this was how they were created.

Though the story Sataari told was too foreign for her to appreciate, Adyulek's dance, drumming, and the painting that she left behind as a record left a deep mark on her mind.

*A speech is a living being. How can your word-scars capture that?*

Dimly, she was beginning to understand the objections of Adyulek. The story that Sataari and Adyulek told, she could see now, was not meant to be written at all. It was much more than just words—it involved dance, exertion, the heat of the bonfire, the fatty grease of the ten meats, the smell of bone smoke, the call-and-answer of shaman and crowd, the feelings of family and tribe, of camaraderie and sense of belonging.

How could mere zyndari letters, so ill-suited to the Agon language that poor Razutana had to attempt to pin down the unfamiliar sounds with novel digraphs and trigraphs that were never used in Dara, ever hope to capture the beauty of this scene? Even if they were to invent an alphabet from scratch, custom-tailored to the sounds of the scrublands, how could mere writing hope to capture the nuances of tone and timbre; the sweat-drenched face and fleeting expressions of the storyteller; the sense of freedom in her dance steps and the varieties of thumping, thudding, banging, dinging, drubbing, patting, tapping, beating, rapping, tickling, caressing that she employed against the drums; the flows and blows and motions and emotions and colors and dust pillars of the voice painting— in short, the entirety of the *experience* of being *alive* here, in this moment?

The voice painting, in its abstraction, its refusal to be reduced to language, was in fact a better medium for recording this night, she could see now. The voice painting, like those knots on Adyulek's staff, could not be interpreted in the absence of memory. But that was a strength, not a weakness.

She should have known. Hadn't she, as a child, loved the performances of the oral storytellers in teahouses? Hadn't she skipped school to attend the performances of street magicians and folk opera troupes? Hadn't she watched as Risana danced with her impossibly long sleeves while Kuni, her father, accompanied her on the coconut lute and sang songs about home and away? She ought to have known that a play was far more than the script, and a speech far more than the transcript.

She had lived so long as a *reader* that she had forgotten that a culture could not be reduced to writing, that wisdom could not be imprisoned in books, that to live was to breathe, to dance, to hunt, to forget.

She was about to turn to Çami, to request that they descend from their perch on the garinafin so that she could attempt to make peace with Adyulek, to explain that she did now see that something would be lost in the transition from orality to literacy, in the transition from movement to stillness, from hunting and herding and riding and flying to a life of sedentary agriculture. She remained convinced that the transition was worth it, but she would now be sensitive to the costs.

She looked down. The two young shamans had stretched a fresh sheet of garinafin skin across the resonating central column of the bone drums and began to strew handfuls of colored dust over the top. Adyulek had recovered enough to prepare for a new dance, Sataari stood ready to chant, and the audience was starting on their third servings of meats.

Something about the dust drew her attention. She focused on the canvas and realized that the colorful grains were dancing. Slowly, rhythmically, ever so gently.

But there was no drumming. Adyulek was still leaning against her staff.

*Why is the stretched skin across the top vibrating?*

Before she had even finished asking herself the question, Théra felt a quaking in her bones as Riva began to low and moan, his whole body quivering. She looked over at Çami, perched atop the other antler, who was busy trying to calm the garinafin down.

Around them, the other garinafins were all lowing and moaning, extremely agitated.

Everyone around the fire stood up. Voices of confusion rose from every sitting rug.

Bright streaks of fire appeared in the night sky in the direction of the mouth of the valley.

*Are they shooting stars? Is the sky cracking open?*

Takval ran into the middle of the clearing, next to the bonfire.

"Get to your mounts! We're under attack!"

# CHAPTER TWENTY-SEVEN

# EXILES

MEANWHILE, IN KRIPHI.

Savo Ryoto looked at the slanted rectangle of moonlight cast on the ground of his dank cave cell through the bars at the cave mouth. Outside, the murmur of the eternal sea drowned out the noises of the world of humankind, and he tried to synchronize his heartbeat to it, to embrace his fate.

It was cold in the cave, exposed as it was to the elements. There was no fire even in winter, and he tried to burrow deeper into the rags that served as bedding, watching his breath linger in the air like smoke.

During the months of seclusion in this prison, he had imagined the horror of death by immolation in garinafin breath so many times that it no longer frightened him. *I'll finally be warm,* he thought, and smiled a ghastly smile.

He was only sad now for his mother, because she was going to lose him, and for Master Nazu Tei, who was going to share the same fate with him tomorrow, when the Winter Festival would begin.

He would not be able to repay the debt he owed either of them in this life now. He would never find out the truth that Nazu Tei hinted at, never be able to reconcile the Ukyu-taasa that he thought he knew with the Ukyu-taasa that she told him was hidden beneath the surface, between the lines of doctored re-rememberings. He would have to go beyond the mountains at the edge of the world and hope to answer their love for him in the spiritual realm.

The door to his cell grated open on its rusty hinges. He turned to it, expecting to see a guard climb down from above. The winch at the top of the cliffs was the only way to access this cell burrowed into the rocks. It was too early for the delivery of the last meal, wasn't it?

But instead, a dark figure climbed up from below and stood at the lip of the cave. The silhouetted figure was tall, gaunt, with a smooth head. Torchlight from behind and below limned it in a halo. Was it Toryoana of Healing Hands, the god of mercy?

The figure turned around, lay down at the lip of the cave, and reached down. When it stood up again, the intruder was holding a torch. It approached Savo. "Come. There's no time to waste."

It was his mother.

As though in a dream, he passively followed her, unable to voice his questions. There was a stake driven into the cliff face to which was attached a wheel and a rope. Goztan tied a harness around his chest, much like the one that garinafin pilots wore, attached it to the rope, and began to lower him into the darkness, into the raging surf below.

Instead of helplessness, he felt taken care of. He felt as though he was again a child of four, being prepared by his mother for his first garinafin ride. They were still living in Ukyu then—the homeland that he remembered only in dreamlike fragments—and as his five fathers looked on, offering conflicting advice and encouragement, the old slave Oga cinched the harness tighter so that he was secure against the chest of his kneeling mother.

*"You're a good boy," said Oga, in the language of Dara. "Keep your eyes and heart open."*

*"There's nothing to be afraid of," said his mother as she leaned down to kiss the top of his head. Then she stood up, and he felt his feet lifting off the ground as she climbed up the garinafin's head. The garinafin then hoisted them both up toward its shoulder, and he finally believed that he was going into the sky.*

He was closer to the sea now, and he could see a tiny boat bobbing among the churning waves, not much bigger than the deep-sea fishing ships that the natives sometimes took out to catch the prized marlin.

Some rough hands grabbed him and pulled him into the boat. He faltered, unsure of his footing on the swaying deck.

Later, when his mother had also joined him on the ship, she explained that these were pirates. Pirates, lawless bandits who had no home but the endless brine, had generally kept away from the shores of Rui and Dasu in recent years, terrified of the reputation of the fire-breathing garinafins that patrolled the skies. But some more enterprising pirate captains had learned to form alliances with Lyucu thanes. The pirates raided the merchant fleets of Dara and sold the coveted goods to the thanes, who could not get enough of what they wanted through the smuggling operation on the official tribute ships. Tanvanaki tolerated the liaisons between the pirates and her thanes, and sometimes even used the pirate crews to carry out missions that the Lyucu could not perform themselves.

Goztan had recruited the crew of such a pirate ship to mount this rescue. The pirates, used to attacking cliffside villages and scaling distant rocky isles for good places to hide their treasure, had developed a whole system for making handholds and footholds up a trailless cliff.

The pirates would now take him away from Rui and Dasu. Compared to immolation in garinafin flames, even life as a pirate wandering the seas was better.

"I will see you whenever you come back to trade," said Goztan. "Perhaps you'll even have a chance to see the core islands. That's what you've always wanted, isn't it? To see the strange machines you've heard so much about."

The idea of going into exile from the only home he truly knew had been thrust upon him so suddenly that Savo didn't know how to feel. Instinctively, he thought of the welfare of the people he loved.

"Can you also save Master Nazu Tei?"

Goztan shook her head. "I have only enough funds to entice the pirates to take on one addition to their crew—this way, Diasa willing, I'll still see you once or twice a year. The pirates can use a young man like you, but they have no use for an old scholar. Saving you is all I can do."

Grief struck him like a hammer blow. He shivered in the cold.

Goztan wrapped a thick coat around him, the way she used to do when he was little.

Then he realized the risk his mother had taken.

"What will happen to you?" he asked. "When they can't find me in the morning, they'll suspect you right away."

"Oh, the pékyu knows," said Goztan. "I told her I was sorry that you couldn't serve her well in Ukyu-taasa. But that doesn't mean you can't serve her, or serve all of us, outside of it."

"I don't understand," said Savo. "What are you expecting me—"

"There's no time for questions," said Goztan. "You'll learn what you need to know when you need it. Here, take this."

She handed him something.

He ran his fingers over the object in the darkness and realized that it was a turtle shell covered in smooth markings, though he couldn't tell what they were.

"What is this?" he asked.

"A map," she said. Then, after a moment, she added, "Something to guide you back to family and home."

And then she dove into the freezing water and swam away, and he didn't even get a chance to say good-bye.

"You've done well," Tanvanaki said. After a pause, she added, "You don't need to follow her anymore."

The nameless spy waited to see if the pékyu had more tasks for him. Tanvanaki had told him to follow Goztan and watch everything she did, but not to interfere. The pékyu didn't explain why, and the spy didn't ask. There was no need for questions when he believed in her like a goddess.

Tanvanaki paced back and forth in her tent, in part to think and in part to stay warm. As part of Cutanrovo's purification campaign, the pékyu and all the thanes had abandoned the palace and native mansions in Kriphi and moved back into Lyucu-style tents. The tents didn't keep out the cold winter wind as well as stone walls, and the fire pit was far more smoky than the hearth. But no one dared to complain lest they seem less dedicated to the grand task of returning to the purity of the Lyucu way of life.

*What is Goztan doing?* she seethed. Her old friend had put her in an impossible position. *When they discover Savo missing in the morning, Cutanrovo is going to demand Goztan's head. All my efforts at protecting her will come to naught.*

*Trust, but verify* had always been her motto. Even the most powerful thanes—especially them—needed to be watched. The nameless spy acted as her eyes and ears, keeping her informed.

She still had the choice of ordering a garinafin strike against the pirate ship. They couldn't have gotten very far. But as she was about to leave the tent to summon the garinafin riders, she hesitated.

Goztan's cryptic words haunted her. *What did she mean when she said Savo would serve me, or even all Ukyu-taasa, as a refugee?*

The boy was defiant and too enamored of native ways, a fault that Tanvanaki partly attributed to the fact that he had spent so much time with Oga Kidosu, her own old master, as a little boy.

*To see the strange machines you've heard so much about.*

Tanvanaki stopped, her heart racing. Savo Ryoto was one of the few young Lyucu who was old enough to carry out important missions *and* who spoke Dara with no accent. Her previous attempts at sending Lyucu spies to the core islands had all failed because the spies could not pass as natives. Savo's linguistic skills and his knowledge of local customs, gained from Nazu Tei, combined with his love of machinery, made him the perfect spy.

*Was that what Goztan had in mind?*

Goztan had spoken to her son in such a vague manner that it was hard to tell what the garinafin-thane planned. But that was understandable; Goztan couldn't disclose to the pirates her true aim lest the pirates sell her son to Empress Jia for profit. She had given her son just enough hints to let him know what he must do.

Tanvanaki laughed silently to herself. *Sly old friend! You've saved me.*

Even after two months of midnight raids in Kriphi, harangues at court, public executions and arrests throughout Ukyu-taasa, Cutanrovo's purification campaign was showing no signs of relenting. The tiger-thane had reversed most of the accommodationist policies, stripped all privileges from native scholars, added to the oversight of native temples, and discovered more traitors in Ukyu-taasa with each passing day. She was even expanding her effort into the countryside, and the harvest had been disrupted, meaning people would have to draw more stores from the granaries than usual to survive the winter. Timu was virtually a prisoner under Tanvanaki's protection, unable to even leave his own tent.

The latest casualty had been the secret camp in the Roro Hills. Cutanrovo had led a mob of Lyucu warriors, each intent on proving they were more dedicated to the Lyucu way of life than the warrior next to them, on an attack on the camp. They bashed in the skulls of all the kidnapped scholars as a demonstration of "the Lyucu spirit," and by the time Tanvanaki found out, it was too late.

The charged political atmosphere, with the hard-liners dominant in anticipation of the arrival of reinforcements, made it impractical for Goztan to meet with Tanvanaki, which could be interpreted as a sign of support for accommodation and erode the pékyu's support.

*That's why Goztan couldn't talk to me ahead of time to coordinate,* Tanvanaki realized. *And now, she's left me a bit of a mess to clean up. How I handle it will be a test.*

She beckoned to the nameless spy waiting patiently in the darkness. "Go find a corpse—an executed native will do—and place it inside the cell that held Savo Ryoto. Do this as quickly as possible."

The spy nodded, backed away, and disappeared into the darkness.

Later, closer to dawn, she would arrange for one of the garinafins— perhaps she would even ride it herself—to incinerate that cave-cell and everything within it. She would tell Cutanrovo that Savo was killed during an escape attempt. Only Goztan would understand that the pékyu had deciphered and approved her plan.

So much had to be said without speaking, understood without signing.

*What happened to the frank and open conversations we used to have, like the first time we met, when you didn't hesitate to tell me that I was a spoiled little girl who didn't know how to take care of a young garinafin?*

Tanvanaki felt a twinge of sorrow. This land was teaching all of them to engage in more subterfuges.

*If Savo learns all he can of the native expertise with machinery, he will*

*be an invaluable resource. But meanwhile, I must continue the clandestine*
*effort to abduct more skilled engineers and mechanics from the core islands*
*through the pirates. The hard-liners may rage across the land like a winter*
*storm now, but eventually, even my brother must concede that we have to*
*learn all the secrets of the natives if we're to overcome them and secure our*
*future in these islands.*

She prayed silently to Péa-Kiji to keep the pirate ship safe, and
waited for the morning.

MEANWHILE, IN PAN.

*Bright moon. Cloudless sky.*

*The ground was far below her, and for a moment she thought she was*
*about to fall, to plunge to her death. She swayed on her feet, her arms cart-*
*wheeling.*

*She managed to stumble back from the edge of the balcony atop the Moon-*
*Gazing Tower. Heart pounding, she pressed herself against the wooden wall*
*behind her, and couldn't help but let out a terrified whimper.*

*A crisp laugh.*

*She looked to her left. There was a swirling column of smoke coalescing*
*into the shape of a woman with long sleeves. Her long hair covered her*
*face so that Jia could not see her features. But she recognized that laugh*
*instantly, even though she hadn't heard it in years.*

*Jia sat down in* mipa rari. "Sister," *she croaked. She didn't know how to*
*continue.* How does one speak to a ghost?

*Smoke-Risana approached her and sat down in* mipa rari *as well, as*
*though they were about to share a pot of tea, like they used to do long ago.*

*"This is where you killed me," said Risana.*

*Jia said nothing.*

*"You claim you did it for Hudo-tika," Risana said, "but the Dandelion*
*Throne remains veiled and empty."*

*"Phyro isn't ready," Jia said.*

*"How can he be, when you hold the Seal of Dara as tightly as the Hegemon*
*once held the seals of the Tiro states, unwilling to part with power?"*

*"That isn't the reason!" Jia took a moment to calm herself. She mustn't*

lose her cool, not even in front of a ghost. "Phyro thinks of nothing but war against Unredeemed Dara, and that will lead to unspeakable death and suffering—"

"As if your actions haven't already led to those things? People are dying over there now by the hundreds, soon thousands and perhaps tens of thousands."

Jia closed her eyes. "Between two terrible choices, I chose the one less evil. Until Phyro can see that war is the wrong choice for the people, I cannot allow him to hold the Seal of Dara."

Risana said nothing. The two women sat under the bright moon, its silvery light making the smoky form of Risana glow like a jellyfish from the deep.

Risana stood up and began to sing and dance. Now unconstrained by physical form, she moved with even more ethereal grace than Jia remembered.

> The gentle ruler governs without seeming to govern.
> He honors his subjects as he honors his own mother.

Jia shuddered, and the indistinct form of Risana swam in her suddenly moist eyes.

"I feel sorry for Toto-tika," Risana said, stopping her dance. "His mother would use him like a cüpa stone or a zamaki figurine."

"I only told him to do what was already in his heart," said Jia. She sounded weak, even to herself. She had never felt the need to defend herself from anyone, but Risana was different. She couldn't help but wonder if she would have been a better empress.

Risana cocked her head. Though Jia couldn't see her face, the posture seemed to her to show a combination of curiosity and pity. "I can never see into your heart the way I could with everyone else. I can't tell if you're telling the truth or if you've deceived yourself for so long that lies have become the truth."

"Timu is dearer to me than my own life," said Jia. "But for the people of Dara, I won't shrink from what must be done. Teeth on the board."

After a moment, Risana nodded. "Then live with your choices." Her smoky form began to fade away.

*Howls, screams, moans filled the air. Jia looked about, terrified. Puffs of smoke appeared all around her, coalescing into human shapes: Rin Coda, Théca Kimo, Laughing Skeleton, the other prisoners she had experimented on, the nameless dying men and women in Unredeemed Dara she had only imagined. . . .*

*All of them dead because of her, because of her schemes.*

*They approached her, their featureless faces containing only bloody maws through which a soul-chilling wind blew. She tried to run, but they surrounded her, blocking her way back into the tower.*

*Jia covered her face with her hands and curled up on the ground, making herself as small as possible. She felt the cold breath of the ghosts on her bare arms, felt the icy drops of blood dripping on her hands. She screamed—*

Zomi followed the First Fin and the Second Fin through the winding open galleries in the Palace Garden toward the empress's bedchamber.

It was highly unusual for a minister to wish to see the empress so late, after she had gone to bed. But Zomi believed that the latest report from the tribute fleet that had just returned from Rui could not wait.

As she ran along, she looked up at the bright moon.

*Are you looking up at the moon at this moment, my beloved? Can the moon act as a mirror to let me see your figure, alone across the ocean, as it shows you mine?*

She pushed the thought away. She missed Théra so much that it was a physical ache, and it was better to lose herself in her work than to be plagued by such pain, which left her feeling helpless. But like a wound in her mouth, she could not help licking it, savoring the taste of her heartache.

They entered the building that served as the empress's private residence and turned down the long corridor that led to her bedroom.

A bloodcurdling scream.

Shido and Wi dashed ahead like two loosed arrows. Zomi ran after them, her heart in her throat.

"A nightmare, nothing more," said Jia.

Wi and Shido looked at each other, unwilling to let it go.

"Mistress—" Wi began.

"I'm fine," said Jia, in a tone that brooked no disagreement. "Leave us."

Reluctantly, the two Dyran Fins bowed to her and faded into the shadows.

"Sit," said Jia, gesturing at the small tea table. Zomi obeyed and sat down in *géüpa*.

Even dressed only in her sleeping robe, her hair undone and no makeup on, Jia exuded an air of command. The old woman that Zomi had caught sight of when she had first run into the bedchamber after the Dyran Fins, on the verge of losing her wits, her eyes filled with terror, her limbs shaking uncontrollably, was gone, as unreal as one of Empress Risana's smokecraft creations. Zomi couldn't even be sure her memory wasn't playing tricks on her.

"You wouldn't have come to me at such a late hour without important news," said Jia impatiently, sitting down in *géüpa*. "Get on with it."

Zomi brought out Lady Ragi's report from the winter tribute trip and laid it down on the table.

Jia unfolded the scroll and began to read the columns of logograms. Since only a couple of candles were lit, she ran her fingers over the logograms, using touch to assist her sight. Zomi thought she saw the empress's fingers tremble, but she couldn't be sure. She got up to light some of the whale-oil lamps.

By the time she sat back down, Jia was finished.

"What do you think?" the empress asked.

"There are several items of interest," said Zomi. "First is the revelation from Noda Mi that there have been more massacres of villagers during the last three months than in the previous three years. Second is the report from carpenters at the floating dock that multiple scholars have been publicly executed, contrary to the usual leniency with which scholars are treated."

Jia nodded. "I noted those points too. Ragi writes here that Noda Mi is more forthcoming with information than before, and he appears far more terrified of the Lyucu. Do we know anything about this Nazu Tei he mentioned?"

Zomi shook her head. "Not much, I'm afraid. I consulted with Cogo, and the Imperial examination records indicate that she was a *toko dawiji* who once donated some possibly apocryphal manuscripts to the Imperial Library."

"A Golden Carp?"

"Yes. But not a very distinguished one. She didn't advance into the later rounds of the examinations. Perhaps that was why she went to Rui during the Reign of Four Placid Seas, thinking her limited talents would be given more recognition in a less learned land."

Jia was quiet for a moment. She imagined the woman being immolated alive by garinafin fire and suppressed a shudder. Knowing the name somehow made it more real. She knew Nazu Tei would, like the other ghosts, haunt her dreams from now on.

"There's no need to speculate upon her lack of scholastic distinctions," she chided. Zomi sometimes exhibited a tendency to overvalue the examinations. "Have a tablet erected for her in the Hall of Mutagé, and make sure the court historian records her name as a martyr."

"But there's no proof that she was loyal to the Dandelion Throne," objected Zomi. "She could have been a collaborator who was simply no longer useful to the Lyucu."

Jia sighed. Zomi's parents and teacher had all died at the hands of the Lyucu in horrifying ways. Her hatred of the Lyucu and those who collaborated with them was deep and unrelenting. No matter how much Zomi tried to conceal her emotions under the guise of dispassionate reason, her prejudices showed through from time to time.

"Even collaborators sometimes manage to save lives," said Jia. "Don't argue with me on this."

"Yes, Your Imperial Majesty," said Zomi, startled by the heat in the empress's voice. She paused, thought for a moment, and said, "But none of these items is as interesting as the last thing in Lady Ragi's report: Tanvanaki's demand for an increase in our next tribute in the spring. Rather than the normal yearly increase by a tenth, she's asking for a doubling of everything except gold. And she's added a demand for cattle."

"What do you think is happening?"

"The massacres and executions could be explained as the result of some temporary power struggle at court," mused Zomi. "But such a large increase in demand for tribute doesn't feel like a test of our resolve. I suspect some crisis has occurred in Unredeemed Dara, and Tanvanaki anticipates disruptions to her food supplies."

Jia nodded. "We'll have to accede to her demands, of course. We can't let the people of Rui and Dasu starve."

"No, we cannot," said Zomi between gritted teeth. She squeezed her fists, as though wishing for something to punch. At length, she added in a cool, analytical tone, "Looks like our prayers have been answered. We were hoping for instability in Unredeemed Dara, and the gods have delivered."

"Let Cogo know right away so that he can plan for the increase in tribute goods."

After discussing the matter a little more, Zomi bid the empress a good night. Before leaving, she said, "I just wish I knew what caused the sudden change in Kriphi. Something . . . must have altered the political balance. I hope Prince Timu is all right."

Jia said nothing in response. But just as Zomi was turning to leave, the empress said, "The Grand Examination is coming. I'm thinking of putting you in charge instead of Cogo."

Zomi paused. "Why?"

"You've always had an interest in reforming the examinations, so I'm giving you a chance," said Jia.

"I'm . . . surprised that you remember."

"It's important to watch over the Lyucu, but don't neglect the creative and useful arts. As Farsight Secretary, you're also responsible for the research of new machines and the discovery of talent. Don't let obsession with the potential for war overwhelm the needs of peace. In war, one must take care not to become like one's enemies."

Zomi bowed. "I understand."

As the Dyran Fins escorted Zomi out of the palace, Zomi was already composing a letter in her head to Phyro. With just twenty-four months to go until the expiration of the treaty of nonaggression with the Lyucu and twenty-eight months until the reopening of the Wall of Storms, the emperor would see this new instability in Unredeemed Dara as a perfect chance to build up an invasion force.

*The empress is right, but so is the emperor.*

She looked up at the moon again, sighed, and hurried her steps.

Long after Zomi left, Jia remained awake.

She had to admit to herself that she was afraid to close her eyes. The ghosts would be back.

Zomi had spoken of the destabilization of the Lyucu court in Kriphi as a gift from the gods. Jia wondered how the gods would react to being given credit for such a thing by the mortals. Yes, it was necessary to prevent the Lyucu from setting down roots and imposing their caste system on all Dara, with themselves at the top, but destabilizing a government, even a brutal one, had real human costs. Only someone responsible for the costs, whose hands were stained with the blood of the innocent, could understand.

To keep herself from the lure of bed, she dug out her experimental notebooks and read over them. The new cultivar she had developed during the last few months was finally strong enough for her purpose, she saw. It would soon be time to summon the Dyran Fins to find a place to grow it on a larger scale.

Kuni had used his rice paddy and vegetable garden as a teaching aid for his children in the art of governance, but it was Jia who had dedicated her life to cultivation: to nourish the tender shoots of peace, to kill off the weeds of war, to bring to life a system in which it no longer mattered who held the Seal of Dara.

Cultivation was at the heart of her art. A good herbalist kept her own garden and learned to breed the plants to encourage the nature that was already in each herb, to bring it to its full potential. Through selective pollination and judicious grafting, it was possible to make the flowers more magnificent, the scents more alluring, the berries more potent.

That was the one skill she had always relied on: encouraging the nature that was already there. It was how she had pushed suspicious Théca Kimo to rebel, proud Gin Mazoti to overreach, insecure Rin Coda to betray his friends. It was how she had prodded the

Lyucu into revealing their true character by leaking the news of the anticipated opening in the Wall of Storms, and how she had nudged Timu into sabotaging his own misguided collaborationist project by appealing to his ideals. She didn't know exactly how her plot had succeeded, but she knew from the start that all she had to do was to cultivate the desire that was already in the hearts of men and women of ambition.

"Just a little more time," she muttered. She wasn't sure if she was pleading with the gods, with Phyro, with Timu, with the ghosts who would not let her sleep.

Phyro must not be allowed to launch an invasion on Unredeemed Dara. As much as the people already suffered, they would suffer ten times, a hundred times more in war. While Théra would take care of the Lyucu in their homeland, it was up to her, here, to save the people of Dara from the Lyucu hammer with the least amount of suffering.

"Just a little more time," she muttered. It was all she could say and would say aloud.

She would never be able to confess what she had done to anyone except the ghosts: Rin, Théca, Risana, Laughing Skeleton, and now Nazu Tei. What she had done and what she would do went against every Moralist principle, every ideal of honor and justice, every creed of the gods of Dara, every instinct she had as a mother.

She would be an exile among her own people, and yet it was the right thing to do.

With a soul-racking sob, tears spilled from her eyes.

Oh, how she wanted to sleep.

# CHAPTER TWENTY-EIGHT

# REFUGEES

SECRET AGON BASE IN KIRI VALLEY, IN THE
FOOTHILLS OF THE WORLD'S EDGE MOUNTAINS:
THE TWELFTH MONTH IN THE EIGHTH YEAR AFTER
THE DEPARTURE OF PRINCESS THÉRA FROM DARA
FOR UKYU-GONDÉ.

Kiri Valley was on fire.

Théra watched, stunned, as diving garinafins in the distance spit fire at the granaries, smokehouses, storage pits, cabins, and tents. All the supplies they had accumulated for the year, nay, for several years, had gone up in flames in just a few hours.

She, along with Thoryo and the children at the mat near them, about three dozen in total, had been rushed away in a daze as Agon garinafin riders took to the skies to try to fight off the aerial invaders, and Agon warriors and Dara soldiers scrambled to suit up in armor and grab weapons to fight off the equally brutal assault on the ground. All around was confusion, chaos, bewilderment. Pilots couldn't find their crew; soldiers couldn't locate their commanders; husband was separated from wife; children divided from their parents. Wailing, screams, cries for help, barked orders that couldn't be followed.

Takval's fiercest warriors and Commander Tipo Tho's personal guards had brought the group of escapees, disoriented and shocked into numbness, to this hideout up on one side of the valley.

While the children huddled in the rock shelter behind her, Théra stood defiantly outside, ignoring the pleas of everyone for her to hide.

Fiery trails streaking across the sky blotted out the stars, and the flickering torches of thousands of warriors snaked across the valley floor as two armies clashed in the darkness. Bones and limbs were crushed, guts and entrails spilled, screams of the dead and dying echoed in the distance.

And she was standing here, helpless, as everything she had built over the last seven years was consumed by the conflagration.

Gusts of wing turbulence whipped up the snow around Théra, and with a heavy thump, two wounded garinafins crashed through the trees on the mountainside and landed on the ledge before the rock shelter, panting in exhaustion.

The pilot of the garinafin in the lead was Takval. His hair had been half singed off, and across his face lay an ugly burn. Behind him, several charred and bloodied bodies hung from the netting of the garinafin, lifeless, and a few others groaned from their injuries. The second garinafin was piloted by Vara Ronalek, assisted by Radia and Toof, the adopted Lyucu riders. From the back of this second garinafin, protected and guarded by the first, Adyulek, Sataari, Gozofin, Tipo Tho, Razutana, Çami, and other high-ranking Agon and Dara climbed down.

"Why are there so few of you?" demanded Théra.

"Many refused to leave without their children," said Çami, her voice numb. "But we couldn't possibly carry all the children out . . . so they stayed to die with them."

Théra closed her eyes in grief. The large number of children in Kiri Valley had been one of her proudest accomplishments, a sign of hope for the Agon-Dara alliance. She could only imagine the heart-rending decision the parents down in the valley faced: Children who couldn't fight would weigh down the garinafins and possibly doom the whole crew, but how could they leave without them?

She turned to her husband. "Is it hopeless?" Her voice was hoarse, barely above a whisper.

Takval nodded reluctantly. Tears spilled from his eyes as he forced words past the lump in his throat. "There are too many of them."

"Where's your mother?" asked Théra.

"She . . . said she's done with running. She's leading a last stand as a . . . diversion and told me to get out no matter what happens. She said that I am your responsibility now."

Tears flowed down Théra's cheeks, unimpeded. Souliyan, who had wanted nothing more than a refuge from war, to live away from the Lyucu in peace, would run no more. Théra had not had the easiest of relationships with her mother-in-law, but she loved her; she was family.

*The aspen wishes to stand still, but the wind does not stop.*

Down in the valley, she could see that the few remaining Agon garinafins, completely surrounded by the Lyucu garinafins, were retreating into a tight circle in the air as the Lyucu pressed in. On the ground, the Lyucu forces had completely overrun the settlement, and only pockets of Agon and Dara resistance remained. The Lyucu were too well-prepared, too numerous, and they had the advantage of surprise. The outcome of the battle was never in doubt.

"How did this happen?" she asked, still hoping this was a nightmare that she could wake up from.

"We've been too careless," said Takval, his eyes filled with regret and shame and self-reprimand. "Too many hunting parties— someone must have been seen." After a moment, he croaked, "Volyu . . ." His voice trailed off.

For a moment Théra's mind interpreted Takval's invocation of his uncle as an accusation. "What? You think he betrayed us—"

But the horror and pain in Takval's eyes told her that she had made a mistake.

". . . and Sliyusa Ki," finished Takval, turning his face away.

Shame and understanding struck Théra's heart like twin hammers. Volyu had been risking his life and the lives of everyone who depended on him to pass them intelligence of the Lyucu. The Lyucu were supposed to be at Aluro's Basin right now, but there had been no warning from Volyu. This surprise attack meant that the Lyucu had also discovered Volyu's betrayal. Volyu was likely dead, and the Agon oasis was probably burning just like Kiri Valley now.

They truly had lost *everything*.

Though Takval didn't accuse her, she could feel the increasing weight of guilt pressing down on her, making it hard for her to breathe. She had pushed for seizing this opportunity to attack despite Souliyan's misgivings about striking the Lyucu when they were honoring the gods with sacrifices. She had pushed Volyu to spy for them, recklessly putting him and everyone at Sliyusa in danger. The sudden need to mobilize for an attack had then led to the risky move of sending out large numbers of hunting parties.

Worst of all, she had the nagging feeling that her insistence on delaying the attack until the Lyucu had gathered at Taten, motivated by the desire to destroy the city-ships, had contributed to the disaster. The extra time meant that Volyu had to disguise his clandestine activities for longer, that the Agon hunting parties grew complacent and reckless with their successes, that the settlement at Kiri Valley clamored for and indulged in the Winter Festival instead of remaining vigilant. It meant, above all, that the Lyucu had an opportunity to discover their preparations and retaliate. Had they decided to move against the Lyucu at Aluro's Basin, perhaps none of this would have happened.

*Arrogance, selfishness, and overconfidence,* she berated herself. *So many have died because of my error. We lost everything because I was so sure I knew what to do, because I wanted to have everything my way.*

"Votan," said Tipo Tho, gasping, "when will we launch the counterattack?" She leaned against a rock to support herself, her hands on her protruding belly.

Takval looked at her with pity in his eyes. "There won't be a counterattack."

"But Nméji is still down there! And my son and daughter!" Tipo said. "You said we would go back for them!"

"I lied," said Takval, his voice now steady. "Captain Gon asked me to lie to you to bring you out."

"We have to go back! He can't hold them off—"

"He's already dead," said Takval. "As are your children."

By the movement of the torches down in the valley, it was clear that the hastily assembled Agon defense lines had completely collapsed.

"No, he's not! They're not! They're waiting for us to go back!" Tipo pushed away from the rock, swaying unsteadily on her legs. She screamed, "You can't just abandon my husband and children!"

"We're all going to die if you don't come to your senses!" said Takval. "My mother is down there too!"

Tipo stared at him. She was straining so hard not to break down that her face convulsed.

"Your husband and my mother stayed down there to give us and our children, born and unborn, a chance. For the sake of your unborn child and these . . . orphans"—he swept his hand at the rock shelter, from which about a dozen pairs of terrified small eyes looked out—"don't let their sacrifices be in vain."

Tipo collapsed to the ground and wailed.

"What . . . what can we do next?" Théra asked. She hated how weak and helpless she sounded.

"We have to scatter and escape into the mountains while it's still dark."

"But everything we've built is here."

"Running is our only choice now," said Takval. "Remember what my mother said. We must get out no matter what happens. It's our only chance for vengeance."

"What are we going to do in the mountains?" asked Radia. "It's the middle of winter and we have no supplies."

"What makes you think you're coming with us?" asked Tipo. She didn't disguise the hatred as she stared at the two Lyucu. "Your people are the ones down there killing and burning. You should go back to them!"

Radia's face twisted in pain and fury, but before she could retort, Toof held her back. "Don't," he whispered.

"Toof and Radia are in my clan," said Vara Ronalek, her aged voice steady and cold. "Look at the wounds on their bodies. Toof blocked a spear meant for me; that's why he's limping. I would trust them with my life."

"This is no time to be fighting among ourselves," said Takval impatiently. "Radia and Toof have been with us for years, and there is no room for doubt."

Tipo Tho said nothing, but the stare she gave Toof and Radia did not soften.

Takval went back to Radia's question. "As hard as it will be in the mountains, we can't stay on the plains. There's no cover and every Lyucu garinafin rider will be looking for us. It'll be suicide."

"Are we going to climb over World's Edge Mountains?" asked Théra.

Takval shook his head. "That's impossible. The mountains are so tall that even garinafins cannot sustain their flight. We have to go deeper into the mountains and stay hidden in the valleys."

"Easier said than done," mused Radia. "To avoid being seen, I assume even the garinafins will have to hike."

Takval nodded. "We can fly at night. But during the day, yes, we should stay on the ground, under cover of the vegetation."

Toof glanced anxiously at the group of children in the rock shelter. "But if we have so many children with us . . . Maybe we could leave—"

"No!" said Théra. "Absolutely not. I won't be separated from my children."

It was the custom in the scrublands, she knew, for the lives of warriors be valued above all in desperate straits. Elders volunteered to die when food ran low, and children could be abandoned to escape a raid. A tribe that survived with its warriors could always have more children, but without healthy men and women in their prime fighting years, there would be no one to avenge the dead and seek victory another day.

But Théra could not think like that. Decades ago, during the Chrysanthemum-Dandelion War, Kuni Garu had abandoned Théra and Timu, when they were about Kunilo and Rokiri's ages, in the middle of a siege in order to escape. The decision turned out to be the right one for Kuni's eventual victory, but it left an irreparable breach in the bond between Kuni and Timu. Théra had no interest in repeating her father's mistake.

"That's not an option," said Takval. Théra gave him a grateful glance.

"But there may be a way to keep them safe without having them slow us down," Toof persisted. "We could—"

"No," said Takval resolutely. "If the Lyucu found Kiri Valley, how could any hiding place for the children escape their notice? We'll just have to manage the best we can with them in tow."

"The parents of many of these children have died tonight fighting against the Lyucu," said Théra. "We won't betray their trust by leaving their offspring behind." She didn't add that the children who they managed to save were only a minuscule portion of the total number of children at the settlement. The few survivors took on a symbolic meaning for her; saving them and keeping them close was the only way to assuage her guilt.

Radia and Toof looked at each other, sighed, but did not continue to object.

"We have to leave now," said Takval, glancing at the fire raging in the valley and the still-circling Lyucu garinafins. "The Lyucu are focused on destroying the base and haven't started looking for escapees."

Théra hesitated. The idea of becoming refugees, of leaving behind everything they'd built to start from scratch, frightened her.

"Too many have already died, Théra," said Takval. "If we don't leave, their deaths will be for nothing. As long as we remain alive, we can bide our time and find another opportunity."

Numbly, Théra nodded. She had to accept that her own chosen path had failed. She had no options.

While the others rushed about to prepare for the escape, she wondered if the Lyucu had realized that there was a way back to Dara. And if they had, would there be enough time to destroy the city-ships before they launched? Since the journey to Dara would take a year, the new invasion fleet would have to depart from Ukyu-Gondé a full twelve months before the reopening of the Wall of Storms. They had only seventeen months to prevent that future.

MEANWHILE, OUTSIDE TIRO COZO, EMPEROR MONADÉTU'S SECRET GARINAFIN TRAINING GROUNDS.

As soon as the messenger from the garrison finished speaking, Phyro jumped on the airship and rushed to the fortress beyond the ring of mountains. There, he found two riders surrounded by vigilant guards.

"*Rénga*," a smiling Ofluro called out as Phyro got out of the airship and approached on foot, "these guards of yours are really something.

They wouldn't let the two of us out of their sight for even a second. I was going to take a shit, but my sphincter just couldn't loosen with two of them staring at me the whole time as I squatted." His breath hovered in the cold winter air, not unlike the smoke of a garinafin.

Phyro laughed. "They're just doing their jobs the way I taught them."

He looked the pair over. The intervening two months had added some weariness to the corners of their eyes, but they looked well overall. Even under the bulky winter clothing, it was obvious that Lady Suca was due to give birth any day now.

"I hope the bumpy ride into the mountains hasn't wearied you or disturbed the baby!" Phyro exclaimed. He turned to summon his guards to bring over soft sitting cushions and a portable stove.

But Lady Suca laughed and patted her belly. "The baby and I aren't so delicate. I think the little one likes it when I ride. It kicks only when I'm sitting still—too boring."

Phyro grew concerned as he noticed that the pair didn't seem to have carried much in the way of luggage, considering they had come all the way from Faça.

"Did something happen?" he asked.

"Nothing went wrong," said Lady Suca. "Our papers got us where we wanted to be. We bought a ranch and prepared for winter. Some of our neighbors were kind and others were not. Some officials helped and others didn't."

Though she spoke in a light and carefree manner, Phyro could imagine the complicated truth that lay behind those words. Ofluro was Lyucu. It was impossible for the officials and the common people not to resent them, no matter what kind of papers they had been given.

"Were the locals in Faça harassing you? I shall write a letter to the governor—"

"No, *Rénga*, don't do that," said Ofluro.

"The magistrates were fair, but there is no refuge from hate within the four seas," said Lady Suca, holding Ofluro's hand. "The best you can do is to choose love."

"We know that being free to go where you like means others

already there are also free to resent you," said Ofluro. "We pay that price willingly. That's not why we came."

Phyro looked at them and nodded. "I see. Then why have you come?"

"To join you."

Phyro couldn't believe his ears. "What . . . How . . . Why did you change your mind?"

"On our way to Faça, we thought you were going to send assassins after us," said Ofluro. "We slept in our clothes at night, with horses ready outside the window. We tried to take obscure paths to shake off your spies—"

"I never sent any spies after you! I gave you my word that you were free."

"I know. But it took a while before we could verify that it was true."

"Why would you think I would come after you?" asked Phyro.

"In Ukyu and Ukyu-taasa, I was told that the people of Dara always lie."

Phyro had no response to that.

Ofluro went on. "After we realized that you weren't coming after us, we tried to settle down in Faça, but—"

"But he couldn't stay put," said Lady Suca. "He kept on telling me that we made a mistake."

Phyro looked at the Lyucu naro-votan, uncertain what to think. "What mistake was that?"

"On the scrublands, we have a saying: A garinafin picks the pilot as much as the pilot picks the garinafin. If you've shown trust in me, it's not the Lyucu way to not show trust in you. I erred in doubting you, and the only way to correct it is to come back."

"Besides, he'd be hopeless as a rancher," said Lady Suca, placing a hand affectionately on Ofluro's arm. "He has no tolerance for haggling and shoveling shit . . . at least not bull shit."

A powerful warmth surged in Phyro and formed a lump in his throat. The frigid winter wind no longer seemed so cold. He coughed and said, "I'm honored, Ofluro and Lady Suca. May I be a worthy pilot to you, now that you've picked me."

Ofluro shook his head. "Who said anything about you riding me?

You've misunderstood my comparison. I'm the pilot and *you* are the garinafin." A mischievous smile appeared on his face. "After all, that's why you wanted me back, right?"

Blood drained from Phyro's face. "What . . ."

"It's not very hard to figure out," said Ofluro. "I told you that I'd never reveal to you any military intelligence about Ukyu-taasa, and you still wanted me to join you. I'm no scholar or shaman, but even I can work out that if it's not military secrets you're after, then you must be in need of other knowledge—" He held up his hands, hooked the thumbs together, and flapped the fingers like the wings of a garinafin. "I don't know how you got them, but I imagine you want me and Suca to show you how to ride them."

Phyro was still in shock. "You . . . you knew? But you still—"

"Did you think I was going to run back to Tanvanaki and try to bargain this information into making me a wolf-thane?" asked Ofluro. "No, *Rénga*, I like you because you are trusting and straight-forward. I'm the same way. If someone looked down our throats, I bet they'd see straight out our asses, because neither of us has the twisty intestines needed to hold in shitty plots—"

Lady Suca burst out laughing, and Phyro's face turned red with suppressed mirth.

"In fact, I suspect you have the soul of a Lyucu."

Unable to hold back anymore, Phyro guffawed. "That's not a compliment you hear often around here."

"Get used to it. If you put in the work, I'll make a passable gari-nafin rider out of you yet. But I warn you yet again: I'll teach you all I know about these creatures and how to care for and ride them properly, but I'll never show you any underhanded tricks against my people or reveal the weaknesses of Ukyu-taasa."

"It's a deal."

A pack of wolves suddenly howled somewhere in the snow-draped mountains, the noise carrying for miles on the wind.

"Even the wolf, kin of the Lyucu, seems to approve of my deci-sion," said Ofluro.

"The wolf is also the *pawi* of Fithowéo, our god of war," said Phyro. "It's a good omen."

"Either way, I think there's been enough talking," said Ofluro. "Shall we go?"

"He's been bored out of his mind," said Lady Suca, giggling. "He's like his unborn child; he misses riding."

"As if you don't?" said Ofluro. "Life is too short to stay on the ground. The air is much more interesting. By the way, *Rénga*, since we've known your secret for two months and have been running about Dara without spilling it, maybe you can reconsider the rule about me and Suca not being allowed to leave? It would be nice to be able to go into town once in a while."

"We'll see about that," said Phyro, smiling. After a moment, he added, "My father would have enjoyed meeting the two of you. He always loved to gather interesting people of talent around him."

He led the way toward the airship that would bring them to Tiro Cozo, and Ofluro and Lady Suca followed.

MEANWHILE, SOMEWHERE TO THE NORTH OF THE BIG ISLAND.

*- Why do you meddle in what you don't understand, Tazu? Why do you pursue a refugee with relentless hate?*

*- Hate has nothing to do with it. It's in my nature to unleash storms for sport and toss ships from wave to wave in play.*

*- Then don't blame me if I reveal my nature.*

*- Did Kiji put you up to this, Rufizo? That featherbrain is such a push-over. Don't tell me he asked you to intervene just because Tanvanaki invoked his name? Remember, they hate us over there in Rui and Dasu now; they call us false gods!*

*- Then let me prove them wrong.*

One minute, the sky was perfectly calm.

The next minute, the stars and the moon were hidden behind roiling clouds, and sheets of rain drenched the sails and made the deck slick as though greased.

The pirate crew rushed about the deck, shouting for the heavy, waterlogged sails to be reefed. Savo, as green a sailor as the bile he vomited, tried to stay out of their way.

He hung on to the mast to prevent himself from being pitched into the water. And as he did, he seemed to hear two booming voices in the wind and the waves, contending against each other. One sounded like the beating of the wings of a thousand Mingén falcons, and the other sounded like a thousand sharks gnashing their teeth. How small was a ship, how insignificant the life of a man, how utterly helpless we all were when gripped by the power of great storms, whether natural or man-made.

And then a giant wave loomed over the ship like the curled tongue of a monster from the end of the Fifth Age, and he knew that all was lost.

# SUN-KISSED BOUGHS

# CHAPTER TWENTY-NINE

# THE GRAND EXAMINATION

PAN: THE THIRD MONTH IN THE NINTH YEAR OF
THE REIGN OF SEASON OF STORMS AND THE
REIGN OF AUDACIOUS FREEDOM (TWENTY-SIX
MONTHS UNTIL THE REOPENING OF THE WALL OF
STORMS).

Among the angular walls and steep roofs of the academic quarter of
the city, the cylindrical Examination Hall stuck out like a mushroom
sprouting from a pile of neatly cut lumber.

And at this moment, the simile seemed to have become literal as
the rioting scholars had torn the doors, window shutters, and wall
planks off the dormitories and shops nearby and built tall barricades
around the Examination Hall.

Standing atop the barricades, arm linked with arm, hundreds
of *cashima*, the most promising students from all over unconquered
Dara, had blocked off all access to the Examination Hall. Staring at
the soldiers facing off against them, the students chanted rhythmically under the direction of a woman named Réza Müi, a scholar
from Tunoa, the daughter of a soldier and a tenant farmer:

"*Are we afraid to go to prison?*"

"*No!*"

"*Are we going to yield?*"

"*Never!*"

"*What do we want?*"

"*A real test!*"

. . .

Normally, by now the Grand Examination essays should have already been scored, and the list of *firoa* posted so that the *pana méji*, the best of the best, could begin to prepare for the Palace Examination. However, this was anything but a normal Grand Examination.

At the beginning of the year, just as the *cashima* were gathering in Pan, Zomi Kidosu, the official in charge of the examination, had made the bold announcement that examinees this year would be prohibited from writing in Classical Ano, or even using logograms mixed with zyndari word-squares, as was sometimes done in drafts of official documents. Instead, the essays would have to be composed in the vernacular and written entirely using zyndari letters. As well, rather than being limited to citing to the Ano Classics, examinees were free to draw upon their own life experience in composing the essays.

(The old requirement to cite only the Ano Classics forced examinees into creative contortions to discuss their passions. Çami Phithadapu, for instance, had to begin her exam essay with a selection of quotes from Poti Maji and Üshin Pidaji on the role of whales in Ano life and the difficult trial of childbirth—as if these men would be the authority on that!—before pivoting, halfway through the essay, into actual evidence of midwifery being practiced among whales. Even then, she had to "support" the evidence from her own research with quotations from the Classics that barely applied.)

"No more forced appeals to the dubious authority of the Classics, no more compelled conformity to rigid logograms and archaic Classical Ano literary forms," proclaimed Zomi. "Let a new era of freethinking, where speech is matched to writing, begin!"

In disbelief, the *cashima* petitioned the court for clarification.

*There's nothing to clarify,* came the reply—written in brushed zyndari letters on silk scrolls bearing the official seal of the Farsight Secretary, as incongruous as a fishmonger's accounting records being carved in jade. *Any examinee using logograms will be summarily disqualified.*

The *cashima* demanded an audience with the Farsight Secretary, but the result of the meeting infuriated them even more.

"I've told schools and academies around Dara for years to

emphasize instruction in composition in zyndari letters," said Zomi Kidosu. "What exactly is the problem?"

"That's just intended to help students whose sights aren't set on lofty heights, so that they could keep a ledger book or write simple letters to business partners, servants, and tenant farmers," protested the representatives of the *cashima*. "No subject of consequence is taught in the vernacular."

"Then perhaps it's time for students who have been paying attention to the changes around them to succeed," said Zomi. "With the rise in commerce and travel, more and more people in Dara are writing in the vernacular."

The *cashima*, realizing that the Farsight Secretary was serious, left despondent and angry, and Zomi thought the matter was over.

However, on the morning the Grand Examination was scheduled to take place, a large contingent of examinees blocked the entrance and prevented anyone from entering, refusing to budge even when the Farsight Secretary arrived to administer the test. And when constables were dispatched to forcefully remove the protesters, a full riot broke out. By the time the city garrison was called to re-establish order, the *cashima* had chained themselves to the Examination Hall and proclaimed the start of a hunger strike.

Terrified of bloodshed, Cogo Yelu, the Prime Minister, came to the Examination Hall to ensure that the soldiers wouldn't resort to violence against these scholars, most of them youths with little experience of the world. As night fell, Zomi Kidosu was forced to announce that the Grand Examination would be delayed until the next day.

By next morn, the ranks of the protesters swelled as scholars teaching and pursuing research in the Imperial Academy and the laboratories, all of them past participants of the Grand Examination, joined the movement against the debasement of learning. Sympathetic residents of Pan brought food and drink to the protesters—the hunger strike was forgotten in the euphoria of having successfully resisted the Farsight Secretary, even for just one day. And vendors set up booths near the protests to serve the crowd of curious onlookers.

Zomi refused to back down. The next day, she again attempted to open the Grand Examination.

Once more, the protesters rebuffed her.

As the standoff continued into the fourth week, petitions from the College of Advocates denouncing the Farsight Secretary teetered in tall stacks on the desk of Empress Jia, storytellers began to describe the heroic protesters in dramatic performances filled with improbable details, governors and nobles from across the land sent envoys to the capital to plead for their *cashima*, and officials and ministers waited impatiently for the announcement of the next session of formal court so that they could point out to the empress how, this time, the Farsight Secretary had simply gone too far.

But there was no response from the palace except deafening silence.

Phyro stormed his way out of the Inner Council Chamber without bidding farewell to anyone except Than Carucono and Zomi Kidosu.

*Fools! Lily-livered cowards! Latrine rats with eyes only for the handbreadth of stinking mud in front of their noses!*

He strode straight for the western side gate of the palace, which would lead him to the airfield, ignoring the ladies-in-waiting and courtiers who shrank out of his way, frightened by his dark expression. He was sick of *talking*. He needed to get back to Tiro Cozo, where he could *do* things that needed to be done.

*O Mother, if only you were the Empress of Dara! You were by Father's side throughout his campaigns; you understood what it meant to have to stand up for the people groaning under the yoke of bloodthirsty tyrants; you would not have turned your back on the people of Unredeemed Dara. If you had been made regent and not died in such a freak accident, I would now be the true Emperor of Dara. And the people of Rui and Dasu would have hope.*

"Hudo-*tika*!"

He slowed down and saw that it was his little sister, Fara, standing by the winding path through the Palace Garden with a basket on her arm. Behind her stood Lady Soto.

"Ada-*tika*," he said, his face softening. Then, more stiffly, he nodded at his old governess. "Auntie Soto. What are you doing here?"

"I'm here to see you, of course," said Fara. "Aya and I told the Imperial kitchen to prepare rice balls with lotus paste and dates, your favorite. Do you want to come to Lake Tututika with us and Auntie Soto for a picnic? We have three new floral teas from Amu I want you to try. I've made a few logogram riddles that I think will stump you, and you should see what Aya has done with my airship—"

"Sorry, little sister, I can't. I've got to go back to work right away." Seeing her face fall at this, he sighed. "Thank you for the rice balls. I'll take them with me."

Fara gritted her teeth. "All right, there is another reason I want you to come. There is a crisis with the Grand Examination. I've secretly invited the leaders of the protesting scholars to join us. If you listen to them and successfully mediate in their dispute with Zomi, it will raise your standing among the ranked scholars. With them backing you, Gimoto won't have any chance, no matter how much he tries to please our aunt-mother."

"Listen to your sister," urged Lady Soto. "Surely the garinafins can wait an afternoon."

"The people of Rui and Dasu are suffering! How can I go out there and sip tea and munch on sweet snacks and chat with a bunch of bookworms about their inconsequential careers!?" Too late, he realized how much this sounded like a rebuke. "I don't mean . . . I know you mean well . . . I just can't."

"I take it your meeting with the Inner Council didn't go well?" asked Lady Soto.

Phyro sighed and said nothing.

He had come to Pan to report on his progress and to make a demand. Ofluro and Lady Suca had exceeded all his expectations. Under their tutelage, he was confident that he would have a powerful garinafin force in another year. With recent reports of instability in Rui and Dasu, he wanted the empress to authorize the immediate buildup of an invasion fleet to free the people of the conquered islands. Such an opportunity might not come again.

But other than Than and Zomi, everyone on the Inner Council argued against his proposal. Some pleaded the need for more funding for schools and cargo airships; some cautioned against provoking the Lyucu; some quoted from Kon Fiji's admonitions against war; some insisted that signs of instability in Kriphi were a Lyucu trap. Cogo Yelu was the worst, coming up with reason after reason for why more military funding was imprudent. The empress said little, but in the end she sided with the majority. There would be no funds for an invasion fleet.

"Jia hasn't forgotten the people of Rui and Dasu, you know?" Soto said. "But what you're asking for is too much."

"Too much?" Blood rushed into Phyro's face. "Back during the Reign of Four Placid Seas, when Dara was far less prosperous, we could field a grand fleet of airships equipped with silkmotic lances and bolts to repel the Lyucu at Zathin Gulf. And now, after eight years of peace and growth, we suddenly can't find the money to repeat the same feat?"

"Remember your aunt-mother is thinking of the long term, of what can happen when a state dedicates itself to war. Eight years ago, when the very survival of Dara was at stake, there was no choice but to devote all the resources of the nation to the stand at Zathin Gulf. But remember how quickly the empress discharged the veterans after the peace treaty, scuttled the expensive vessels and weapons so that components could be reappropriated for civilian use, took command away from the general and admirals—"

"I never understood why she did that. She seems to have an instinctive dislike for fighting men and women."

"She does," said Soto. "And as I told you once, it has to do with what she went through during your father's rise. But more important, she saw how devotion to war can ruin a nation. The Tiro states under the Hegemon kept large standing armies, and during the years of the Chrysanthemum-Dandelion War, they came to dominate political life in all the states. No general or admiral wanted to see their command shrink, and so every year came the demand for more naval vessels, more airships, more soldiers, more horses; those merchants and manufacturers who grew fat on military spending bribed court officials and petitioned the court for ever larger shares of the budget; all men and women of ambition saw tapping into the network of military influence as the path to move up in the world. The army eventually became the claw that choked the body of the state—"

"That may be what she tells you," said Phyro. "But I think there is a simpler explanation than that. My aunt-mother loves the Seal of Dara too much and views me as a threat."

Fara gasped at this and looked about to see if his rash comment had been overheard.

"You wrong her," said Soto, heat coming into her voice. "Have you forgotten the fate of Métashi, once the most powerful of the Tiro states? It was torn asunder by three generals, men whose ambitions were fed by the ever-growing army of a militarized state. When an army runs out of enemies, it will inevitably turn on its own people. She's trying to protect you—"

"You speak of distant dangers beyond the horizon and theoretical risks in the mists of time," said Phyro, uncaring who heard him. The frustration of the Inner Council meeting erupted to the surface. "A military buildup *now* is a matter of necessity. When the Wall of Storms opens in two years and the Lyucu are strengthened, it'll be too late then to counter their invasion. The time to prepare for a strike is now."

"Jia believes that Théra will succeed. There will be no reinforcements," said Soto.

Phyro laughed harshly, a disbelieving bark. "I have as much faith in my sister as anyone, but it's as absurd to trust our fate to her, far beyond the seas, as it would be to trust that the gods will come to our rescue because we're kind and pious. The gods help those who help themselves. Does my aunt-mother really believe that the Lyucu will give up and go home if we sit on our hands here doing nothing?"

"I don't know what Jia is planning either," confessed Soto. "She has always been subtle in her thinking. But if you would just trust her and give her more time—"

"The people of Rui and Dasu don't have more time!"

He bowed to her and embraced Fara quickly, whispering in her ear, "Take care of yourself. I know you mean well, but you can't force anyone to live a story that doesn't feel true to them."

Then he strode away, not looking back.

Silently, Fara watched her brother leave. Then she stomped her feet, angrily wiping away the tears of frustration.

"You can only offer counsel," said Soto, sighing. "It's up to him to take it."

"Forget it," said Fara, sniffling. "I'm done with politics. Maybe I'm done with this whole family!"

Neither of them paid any attention to the two large ravens, one black and one white, that took off from the bough overhead.

The ravens landed next to the pool in the large rock formation near the camera obscura. The golden carp came up to the surface.

- *If only Jia would work together with Phyro—*

*—instead of bickering with him like mortal enemies!*

- *Sisters, you can't force two mortals who have different ideals about where they want to go to walk the same path.*

- *So now you're an expert on mortal psychology?*

- *So are you going to enlighten us as to what Jia is up to?*

- *Wait, wait! Don't sound so offended, Kana and Rapa. I'm just pointing out that we can guide and nudge, but ultimately the mortals, like their children, go where they will.*

- *Tututika, if only your charge had done a better job of mediating between her brother and aunt-mother—*

*—we'd be closer to getting to where we need and want to be.*

- *But sisters, all you talk about is what you want. What about what I want? We don't all want the same things. Fithowéo wants to see Phyro at the head of a grand army, regardless of the consequences; the two of you want to see Dara triumph over the Lyucu, by strength or craft; Kiji wants to save the people of Rui and Dasu as well as the Lyucu but doesn't know how; Rufizo keeps himself busy by rescuing refugees; I just want everyone to get along and leave my favorite princess alone; and Tazu—*

- *Nobody knows what that maelstrom-minded fish-trap wants.*

- *Right. But if we can't even agree on where we want to go, how can we possibly hope to steer the mortals?*

- *We miss Lutho. He was the only one of us who always knew what to do.*

Zomi Kidosu crossed the small arched Bridge of Rules and entered the private section of the palace, where the Imperial family retired to be away from the public gaze. The early spring chill made her shiver in her formal court dress, embroidered with stylized scales weighing fish, the sign she had adopted for the farseers.

She hadn't wanted to come, not now, not when she was mired in an embarrassing stalemate, not when everyone doubted her competence. But there were things she needed: authority, clarity, direction—things that only the empress could provide.

Though she never called Jia *Rénga*, over the years of working with her, she had come to both fear and admire the empress. Jia was sometimes like a mother, like a teacher, like an adversary, like a friend, and sometimes none of these. She couldn't figure Jia out. The more she knew *about* the empress, the less she knew her.

Zomi needed her now.

She surveyed the Palace Garden. Her eyes lingered over a hothouse—covering the spot where Emperor Ragin had once stood in a taro patch while conversing with Luan Zyaji, her teacher; a field of diverse herbs—grown where Zato Ruthi had once walked through a hedge maze while debating Moralism with his favorite student, Timu; a patch of monkeyberries—planted where once Théra, her beloved Théra, had stopped Zomi to chat as she rushed to a meeting with Empress Jia that would change the fate of Gin Mazoti.

*Everything changes. The land belongs to the living, not the dead,* thought Zomi Kidosu. *But what of those who are alive but beyond our reach?*

Zomi glanced through the flowers, and she seemed to once again catch the slender figure of that girl who had once flitted through the garden like a graceful dyran to stop her on this path, babbling incoherently and blushing furiously; to once again hear the gentle laughter of that young woman who had once sat with her atop a cliff, holding her hand and gazing out at the rain-refreshed world; to once again feel the warmth of her breath against her own lips and the pounding of her heart against hers.

*O Théra, where are you now? Are you all right?*

Her reminiscence was broken by a sudden peal of masculine laughter. She frowned.

Two young men, barely out of their teens, dashed forth from behind the hothouse, giggling and shushing each other as they hid behind a clump of large planters. Zomi thought their handsome faces looked familiar but couldn't recall their names—the empress went through young playthings so quickly that it was rarely worth learning their names anyway.

"Whoever I catch first is going to have to sleep on the floor tonight," said an affectionate voice, a voice that decided the fate of millions with a single word.

Zomi stood very straight and bowed down in *jiri* in the direction of the voice. The bushes lining the garden path parted to reveal Jia Matiza Garu, Empress and Regent of Dara.

The empress was dressed in a crimson-and-gold water-silk robe cut in a classical style that would be at home on a scholar from her native Faça—though the color combination and the stylized embroidered dandelions around the collar and the cuffs of the long draping sleeves were reserved for members of the Imperial family. On her feet, she wore wooden clogs tied with leather strings that made treading through mud practical. These days, Jia often preferred masculine-style robes over feminine dresses when not at formal court, and her style had inspired many imitators in Pan, as grand ladies and women merchants craving to be seen and admired paraded about the capital in robes.

The empress's prominence as a fashion icon was not entirely unexpected. Now in her mid-fifties, her beauty was like that of the red maple and golden gingko in fall, more brilliant and magnificent than the raw budding verdure of spring and the effortlessly lush green of summer. Though her bright red hair was fading to a dull silver, her gaze had only grown sharper and more compelling, forcing all who dared to look directly into her eyes to shiver without being able to look away.

Jia looked around, searching for her young lovers. When her eyes fell on Zomi instead, she nodded, smiled, and beckoned Zomi closer.

"Réré and Momo, I can't play anymore. Go to the kitchen and ask for tea service to be brought to the Moon-Bathing Pavilion."

Zomi deepened her bow to hide the involuntary smile on her face. Evidently, even the empress herself didn't bother learning the names of her bedmates, instead choosing to give them appellations more appropriate for pet cats.

There was a constant supply of fresh men who thought they could win the favor of the most powerful person in the land with skills in the bedroom and thereby gain power for themselves and their families. However, though the empress showered her lovers with luxurious gifts and indulged their fancy, she never took a consort and always kept them strictly away from matters of state. The utter disregard for chastity on the part of the empress was a constant source of irritation to some of the older Moralist scholars, but Zomi found the situation merely amusing. Her own teacher, Luan Zyaji, had cared little for traditional Moralist proprieties, and she suspected that Jia engaged in the practice as much to flaunt her power as for pleasures of the flesh.

Zomi composed herself, straightened, and approached the empress. The pair strolled leisurely through the garden toward the Pellucid Cocoon Shrine, one of the highest structures in the palace. Next to it was a pavilion built on the shore of a lake fed by the small creek that Zomi had just crossed.

From time to time, Jia stopped to examine a leaf or to smell a flower, making notes to herself on a wax tablet tucked into her waistband.

Zomi, walking a few steps behind her, sorted through her tangled thoughts. She had several matters on which she needed to consult the empress. The Inner Council meeting earlier that day had been dominated by Phyro's demand for a military buildup, leaving no room for other discussions. However, she felt better about bringing up these in a private audience, without the distraction of bureaucratic jostling and the need to perform in front of others. She decided to start with the easiest matter.

"During the last month, we received thirty-five rafts of refugees from Rui and Dasu, more than double the amount from the month before."

"And what do they say is happening in the unredeemed lands?" asked the empress. She stopped by a trellis covered in vines, picked up a pair of shears, and began to prune the overgrown shoots.

Zomi sighed. The empress never asked after the welfare of the refugees, caring only about the information they brought. Though she always spoke of the welfare of the "people of Dara," she rarely focused on any *person* of Dara. It was a paradox.

"Many of them tell tales of atrocities," Zomi said, struggling to keep the emotion out of her voice. No matter how many times she had read similar accounts, they never lost the power to shock, to devastate, to haunt. "Entire villages are slaughtered on the smallest of offenses, and scholars have been particularly the focus of abuse. Death by garinafin fire—" Her voice cracked. Memories of the final moments of Aki Kidosu, her mother, came unbidden to her mind and made it impossible for her to finish her speech.

Jia said nothing.

Zomi waited until the rage and grief and hatred washed through herself like a surging and then ebbing tide. She swallowed the lump in her throat. "The details are in my report. There is no reliable news about Prince Timu, as the refugees are from small villages and know little of the goings-on at court."

She saw Jia's hands tremble for the briefest of moments before becoming steady again. "Did your interrogators interview the refugees before they'd had a chance to speak with refugees already resettled here?"

The unexpected question flustered Zomi. "I . . . I'm not certain. I believe in some cases the officials prioritized reuniting separated families before interviewing them. The refugees already resettled often also take part in the rescue operations."

The empress abruptly stopped her pruning, put the shears down, and walked away, her rustling sleeves a sign of her displeasure.

After a stunned second, Zomi hurried after her.

The empress walked rapidly for a while before taking a deep breath to speak in a calm tone. "Zomi, you are the Farsight Secretary. It's your job to gather intelligence, domestic and foreign. We have almost no way of getting true insight into the state of Lyucu politics other than the tribute visits and these refugees. How can you be so careless?"

"I'm afraid I don't understand."

"Each fresh raft of surviving refugees is an invaluable source of information about the Lyucu, and it's vital that they not be contaminated before extracting that intelligence. If they first speak with refugees already settled here, they may get an idea of the kind of stories that seem to elicit the most sympathy from the local officials, leading to exaggerations of Lyucu atrocities or repetitions of what we've already heard."

Zomi's face reddened and her voice rose. "I can't imagine that the refugees would lie—"

"I'm not accusing the refugees of deliberately *lying*. But I've read hundreds of these reports, and some of them are remarkably similar, even down to the details of particular gruesome methods of execution and what the Lyucu commanders supposedly said. It's human nature to want to maximize the sympathy one receives and to craft a narrative that one thinks the audience expects. By not isolating the refugees from potential coaching, you may inadvertently have allowed them to emphasize the stories they think we want to hear and omit details that may truly be new."

Though unsettled by Jia's calculating stance, Zomi had to admit that the empress had a point. "I apologize for my carelessness. I will refine the refugee-intake protocol to limit unsupervised contact between resettled refugees and newcomers still under observation."

"You're not deficient in acumen, Zomi," said Jia. "But you lack . . . the willingness to acknowledge the complexity of the human heart. You want the world to be black and white, evil and good, lies and truth. But working with people is far more complicated than working with machines."

Zomi wasn't sure if she agreed with this assessment. But there was no point in debating this throwaway sentiment. "The sudden flare-up in repression indicates that the shift away from accommodationist policies in Unredeemed Dara may be permanent, but we don't understand why."

The empress made some noncommittal noises, as though the question didn't interest her. In fact, she almost had to stifle a yawn, and her eyes looked tired. Zomi had heard that the empress was having trouble sleeping at night, and sometimes took naps during the day in the garden, surrounded by her young lovers. The Imperial doctors had discreetly hinted to the empress that perhaps she should moderate her amorous affairs, but Zomi wondered if that was the right diagnosis.

She went on. "During the spring tribute mission, Noda Mi again reiterated to Lady Ragi his hint concerning possible Lyucu-sponsored pirate raids for talent near Dimu and Dimushi. I think we need to do more than just passively watching and guarding to protect our people."

"What do you have in mind?" The two had reached the Moon-Bathing Pavilion, where servants had already laid out a tea service with a variety of snacks. Jia gestured for Zomi to sit opposite her. The empress folded her legs into *géüpa*, and the Farsight Secretary followed suit.

Zomi took a deep breath. This next order of business was more complicated.

"The best defense is an offense. I want a naval expedition to sweep the sea south of the Karo Peninsula and cleanse it of pirates. With the reduction in the naval budget in recent years, some bold pirates have even started to anchor near Écofi."

"Have you spoken to Than about it?" asked Jia. "He's always clamoring for more things to do."

"I have. He thinks he can spare the surface vessels and airships for such an expedition."

"Who does he want to lead it?"

"He was thinking of leading it himself, with . . . the emperor as monitor."

Zomi took advantage of the empress's silence to pour tea for both.

Jia, always suspicious of independent military commanders, had instituted a system of military monitors. Each commander of an army division, a fleet of ships, or a wing of airships had to share authority with a monitor appointed by the Throne. The monitors, civil officials rather than career military officers and dependent upon Imperial approval instead of the support of the soldiers for their authority, acted as a check on ambitious commanders. They were supposed to advise the commander on strategy, supervise training and logistics, and ensure that reports of battlefield accomplishments were accurate. Most importantly, major military maneuvers and deployments had to have the approval of both the commander and the monitor.

Jia was determined never to have a repeat of the rebellion of Théca Kimo or the horrors of generals turning on their sovereigns, rampant during the Tiro states era.

Given Than's vociferous support of the emperor's call for an invasion of the lost northern islands, he no doubt intended the anti-piracy expedition as a way for the emperor to gain combat experience and to develop a loyal base in the navy.

"No," said the empress, just as Zomi had expected. "The Dandelion Throne would be the laughingstock of the world if we have to dispatch the First Admiral of the Navy and the emperor himself to go after a few pirates. The very idea is ridiculous."

"I thought the same," said Zomi. Though politics did not come naturally to her, she *had* learned a few things in the years she had served the empress. "I have an alternative suggestion for the leadership of the expedition."

"Who?"

"Aya Mazoti, Imperial Princess."

Jia sipped her tea and absentmindedly cut a green-bean tea biscuit in halves with an ivory knife. Taking a half biscuit, she pushed the plate toward Zomi, cocking an eyebrow questioningly.

Zomi spoke hurriedly. "Though only eighteen, Aya has been steeped in the art of warfare since she was a child. Ever since the death of the Marshal, she has made it her life's goal to become as skilled in war as her mother. She excels at riding and shooting, and her swordsmanship instructors report constant progress. As the editor of the Marshal's treatise on war, she knows its teachings by heart—"

"I'm perfectly aware of her skills as a *student* of war—no thanks to your nonstop haranguing—but she has zero experience with actual fighting—"

"Which is why it's critical to take this opportunity to give her field experience. If you think about it, this is really the perfect—"

"Stop. Just stop."

With difficulty, Zomi swallowed the rest of her speech.

The empress regarded Zomi coolly. "What is this really about? Are you sure you're making this recommendation based on her merit? Or are you emotionally swayed by her parentage?"

*Isn't your suspicion of Aya also an emotional reaction to her parentage?* But Zomi clenched her teeth and choked off the retort just in time.

Truth be told, Zomi couldn't be sure that the empress was entirely wrong. Luan Zyaji, as her teacher, and Gin Mazoti, as her patron and benefactor, were like another pair of parents to her. It was natural that she would be devoted to their child. Moreover, Zomi was racked by guilt over her own role in Gin's disgrace, and she couldn't help but want to give the young woman every opportunity. After Aya was adopted into the Imperial household following her mother's death, Zomi had taken a particular interest in Aya's education, and the princess had tried to please her by focusing on military strategy and tactics.

"Aya's parentage can only add to her qualifications, not detract from them," said Zomi stubbornly. "She has her father's intelligence and her mother's instinct for victory."

Zomi paused. If she were entirely honest with herself, she would admit that this was overpraise. Aya was studious and hardworking, but she was no extraordinary scholar. Indeed, since Zomi had been such a quick student herself, she often lost her patience with Aya when the princess required more instruction to grasp a point. Their sessions often ended with the young woman in tears.

Gin Mazoti's treatise on war was supposed to have been posthumously completed by Aya, but in reality, much of the work had been done by Zomi without credit. Zomi sometimes thought the young princess showed far more interest in inconsequential pursuits like decorating cakes with Fara and designing comfortable furniture than tactics and the history of war, subjects she studied with more duty than passion. Still, Zomi comforted herself with the thought that Aya was probably just a late bloomer.

"It's in her nature to be a great tactician," she said to the empress.

"She also shows signs of her father's recklessness and her mother's arrogance," said Jia. "The more you tell her she's supposed to be a great general, the more it feeds her flaws."

"I don't agree with that assessment. And even if I did, the right solution would be to temper her with experience, not to keep her from—"

"We can argue like this all day and resolve nothing."

Zomi stared at the empress. Then, abruptly, she stood up, backed away from the table, knelt down in *mipa rari*, and then bowed until her forehead touched the ground.

"What is this?" asked Jia.

"I won't argue anymore," said Zomi meekly. "I've never begged you for anything, Your Imperial Majesty. So please, let me have this."

Jia was silent for a long time, and Zomi refused to sit up.

Finally, Jia sighed. "Fine. She can lead the expedition. I only hope this is as much a boon to her as you seem to think it is."

Zomi sat up, her eyes full of gratitude. Then she touched her forehead to the ground again.

"That's enough," said Jia. "Who do you suggest as the monitor?"

Zomi straightened and knee-walked to the table, settling back into *géüpa*. "How about Gori Ruthi?"

"Ragi's husband?"

Zomi nodded. "He's observant, competent, and open-minded—though he can be a little haughty at times. He's had some experience with the Lyucu as a farseer and can be an able aid to Aya." She didn't add that she thought his relationship to Lady Ragi would also likely allay the empress's suspicions, as she trusted Ragi completely.

"Fine. Let Than know of my decision and send Aya to Ginpen, the fleet base, to begin preparations for the expedition to the Karo Peninsula. Tell her to keep her journey there low-key. There's no reason to make the spies' jobs too easy by giving them advance warning."

Zomi nodded.

*What the emperor needs most of all are skilled young commanders who can share his vision,* thought Zomi. *If Aya can grow into who she's meant to be with this experience, it will be like giving the emperor another sword-wielding arm. Only then can my home island be freed; only then can my people be saved.*

"Are we finished?" The empress suppressed another yawn, and then sipped her tea.

Zomi clenched her jaw. Clearly the empress wasn't going to make this easy on her. "There is one more matter . . . the matter of the Grand Examination."

"Ah, I take it you have the list of *pana méji* for me?"

"I . . . do not. As you know, the protests have made it impossible to conduct the examination."

"Impossible? I was under the impression that you had it entirely under control, which is why you've not altered your approach for nearly a month."

Zomi blushed at this veiled rebuke. "I don't understand the intensity and persistence of the protests, or why they've been so . . . obstinate."

The empress chuckled. "It's all right, you can complain to me if you like. I know you feel wronged."

"I *do* feel wronged," Zomi said. "It's especially galling to see that some of the most vocal rioting *cashima* are from the poorest regions of Dara, where instruction in Classical Ano can never match the cram schools in places like Haan and Wolf's Paw. The leader of the protests, Réza Müi, is a tenant farmer's daughter, like me! These examinees would benefit the most from switching to the vernacular."

"Would they?" queried Jia. "I wonder. . . . The benefit of conducting the examinations in logograms and limiting the authorities cited to the Ano Classics is standardization. At least everyone, rich and poor alike, has to study the same books. Switching to the vernacular and opening up the essays to life experiences would actually benefit the wealthy and privileged more, as their children would have much richer lives to draw on: trips to faraway metropolises, art, music, exposure to elite society, and so forth."

Zomi was taken aback. "But . . . I hadn't intended . . . I was trying . . ."

"Sometimes what you intend and what you accomplish are different things. There may be other good reasons for the less privileged students to object to your reforms. Perhaps unlike students from Haan and Wolf's Paw, who feel a high rank in the Grand Examination is simply recognition for their already-proven brilliance, these other students fear that if they were to place among the *firoa* as a result of the switch to the vernacular, their accomplishments would be treated as debased and tainted, not quite the same as a real victory."

"That's ridiculous and shortsighted," said Zomi. "If that's how they think, it's also selfish. The switch to the vernacular written in zyndari letters isn't just about their individual advancement; it's for the benefit of all the impoverished people of Dara without access—"

"You don't need to—"

But having already launched into one of her impassioned tirades, Zomi would not be stopped. "The policy to encourage the use of the zyndari letters was something you supported, and I thought, after all these years, at least *some* of the teachers at the academies would understand my reasons. Use of zyndari letters promotes literacy in children and adults alike, and the use of vernacular documents by the government has allowed hundreds of thousands to no longer fear tax collectors and magistrates, and to be able to draft their own contracts and leases. Yet they continue to obsess over logograms in schools—"

"Reason and logic cannot answer every question," said Jia. "You've expounded upon the advantages of shifting to the vernacular in writing for years. No one disagrees with you on the evidence that can be measured, but you haven't accounted for the evidence of their hearts."

"What . . . do you mean?"

"Zomi, tell me, where are the latest census records of Géjira?"

"I suppose . . . they must be in the Imperial Treasury's record office somewhere. I don't know exactly."

"Then tell me where is *Gitré Üthu*?"

Zomi wasn't sure why the empress was bringing up Luan Zyaji's old notebook, in which he had recorded his observations about the Lyucu and the original calculations concerning the Wall of Storms. This entire line of questioning made no sense.

"It's at home, on the writing desk next to my bed."

"Interesting that you can only guess at the building one may be found in but know the precise location of the other by heart. . . . If Mount Kana and Mount Rapa were to erupt and Pan about to be destroyed, and you had only time to save one book, would you rush to the Imperial Treasury to save the census records or *Gitré Üthu*?"

"*Gitré Üthu*, of course."

"But why? The knowledge recorded in Luan's old book is all outdated and of no practical use, while the census records would be invaluable in the reconstruction effort. How do you justify your decision? Show me some evidence and facts. Justify your calculus."

Zomi said nothing.

The empress continued. "Years ago, Tanvanaki took from you and me all the jewelry on our persons as a tribute. I lost several priceless pieces of jade that way, and to this day at formal court I can't appear in the full regalia demanded by the protocols. If you could ask for only one piece of jewelry back from that day, which would it be?"

Almost reluctantly, she said, "The necklace of zomi berries that my teacher gave me."

"During the Battle of Zathin Gulf, we lost many valuable weapons and war engines. Some of the diamond-tipped silkmotic lances were worth as much as the annual tax revenue from a whole city. If you could recover only a single piece of weaponry from that battle, which would it be?"

"Na-aroénna, the Doubt-Ender, the blade wielded by the Marshal."

"And if I were to demand that you change the sign of the farseers to the zyndari spelling of the name so that it could be easily read by all, would you do so happily?"

Once again, Zomi was silent.

"In all of these decisions, you were guided by sentiment rather than reason, prizing that which is more meaningful over that which is measurably of more use and value. How can you fault the *cashima* for doing the same?"

"That isn't the same thing at all! You can't compare a personal connection with—"

"But it *is* the same. The Ano logograms are history. They connect us with our past, with the exploits of the hero Iluthan during the Diaspora Wars, and with the tales of the great Ano sages in the time before the Tiro states. The zyndari letters, on the other hand,

were invented to help merchants keep quick ledgers, to allow artisans to write down their measurements, and to make it possible for
government clerks to transcribe speeches in shorthand that would
then be converted into permanent logograms. They've always been
merely functional, uninvested with the beauty and prestige of the
logograms."

"I love the beauty of the logograms too, but that beauty comes
with a cost. Yes, I admit that the logograms make possible intricate visual puns and geometric poetry, riddles that erudite scholars
love to stump each other with, and endless games that the rich and
well-educated can play in idle moments. But these can't possibly be
worth as much as the benefits to the poor—"

"You keep on speaking *for* the poor, but the poor *cashima* have
already rebuked you," said Jia. "When was the last time you picked
up a hoe or a scythe? When was the last time you spent a day in the
ocean hauling in whitefish and eel? When was the last time you had
to beg a *toko dawiji* to write a letter for you? How long have you been
in Pan now? How long have you lived this life as one of the most
powerful people in the Islands?"

The empress's words felt like slaps to the face. Zomi had always
taken pride in the fact that she came from a poor family, as though
her low station at birth gave her a kind of moral authority that others
lacked. But now the empress was accusing her of being out of touch,
of being severed from her roots.

"I *know* what it's like to be poor! I could live here for a hundred
years and not forget the taste of pickled caterpillars. I *know* what's
good for them even if they don't!"

The empress sighed. "No one is accusing you of lack of knowledge or that you've forgotten your origins. Sometimes I wonder if
you're simply too smart to understand what is otherwise obvious to
everyone else."

"I don't understand what you're trying to say."

"Listen with your heart, Zomi, and don't slice apart everything I
say with your razor-sharp mind. Because you didn't grow up playing with blocks carved in the shapes of the logograms and you were
taught by a great teacher who despised conventions, your love for the

logograms tends toward the intellectual rather than the emotional. But think back to the time before you knew the logograms, and try to understand the perspective of those who disagree with you."

Zomi thought back to her childhood, before she had met Luan Zyaji, before she had even been given a formal name, and was known only as Mimi, the peasant girl. Her mother had always gone to the shrine dedicated to Kiji on the big holidays to ask for a fortune knot, a tiny wax logogram wrapped in the traditional knotwork of the Dasu peasants. The monks and nuns would then untie the knots and interpret the logogram for her mother, explaining its significance for the family in the coming season. Little Mimi had watched and listened to the explanations, completely rapt, thinking that the wax logograms held a powerful magic.

"You speak of the logograms as though they're only for the rich and powerful," said Jia, "but they are symbolic links to our collective story as a people, rich and poor alike. Even the poorest peasants of Dara prefer to see their ancestral graves marked with the logograms of their family names rather than zyndari word-squares. Destitute scholars recite with pride stories of how the ancient sages read with their finger in the dark because they couldn't afford candle and lamp oil. Illiterate villagers all over the Islands buy scrolls they can't read to hang in places of honor in their homes and carve folk logograms on doorframes to ward off bad luck. Merchants who deal with zyndari letters all day in their ledgers and inventory lists still sit down with a book written in logograms after dinner so that they can converse with the Ano sages, to experience a realm beyond the merely functional.

"You speak of usefulness and the future, but you neglect the past and the love we cherish for home, for where we came from and who we are, a love that needs no justification. To write with zyndari letters is only to freeze sound, to make speech visible. But to carve the Ano logograms is to relive our history and to *be* Dara.

"The logograms are not interchangeable functional units, but unique creations whose forms have evolved over time to adapt to the needs of the people. Mapidéré abolished the variant logograms in use in the Six States overnight, but even today, the people living in the territories of the old Tiro states cling to them because they speak to them in a way the standardized logograms cannot. When you learn calligraphy, you learn that each prominent style of calligraphy is the product of a great mind of the past: the severe, angular lines of seal script are associated with Aruano, the lawgiver; the stately, ornately decorated components of clerical script are associated with Kon Fiji, the One True Sage; the free-flowing, almost unrecognizable smooth surfaces and whimsical curves of wind script are associated with Ra Oji, the Fluxist gadfly; and the intricate, balanced composition of semantic roots and motive modifiers in fire script is the product of Lügo Crupo, Mapidéré's prized Incentivist Prime Minister. And so, as you learn to imitate the wax carving and shaping techniques of the great masters and develop your own style, you're also retracing the steps that they took to understand the world."

Reminded of her time studying under Luan Zyaji as a girl, Zomi felt her heart stir at this description. Her eyes moistened. The days in the company of her master had been among the happiest in her life.

"This is a time of crisis in Dara, Zomi. The Lyucu have placed our very survival in doubt. They despise the logograms; indeed, they despise all writing. Refugees from Unredeemed Dara speak of the killing of learned scholars and the desecration of ancestral graves to create more pastures for Lyucu cattle. They speak of the burning of books and the breaking of memorial tablets. The Lyucu are resculpting our gods and erasing our history, so is it any wonder that the people would feel even more protective of their past, of who they are?

"There has never needed to be a term for the people of Dara before, but now the pseudo–Classical Ano neologism *Anojiti* can be heard everywhere. For the people, the Ano logograms represent a bond with the past, with the very journey we've taken as a people.

"You think abolishing the logograms will help the poor, but the poor are more invested in them than the rich, as you've learned from the protesters. I spoke earlier too much like an Incentivist. The truth is, whether the tests are in the vernacular written with zyndari letters or Classical Ano written with logograms, the rich students will always have an advantage. *They* don't care.

"But because the scholars born poor have had to work so much harder to acquire knowledge of the logograms, they are even more attached to them. We love that which gives us heartache and difficulty, the same way parents love the wayward child. The logograms are the obstacle-laden paths they've trodden, the hopes and dreams of parents who sacrificed to give them that education, the futures they hope to win for their families. You may dismiss it as romantic nonsense, but it's that same impulse that keeps your heart tethered to the memory of Luan Zyaji, Gin Mazoti, your parents, and my daughter. Some of the most important decisions we make in life are not derived from reason, from weighing the fish, from an evaluation of the pros and cons—but from a simple leap of faith, of love that needs no evidence, apology, or argument."

Zomi could not help herself. She broke down in tears.

*I've been thinking of and speaking for the poor of Dara for so long as a collective that I've fallen out of touch with a woman like Réza Müi, with a woman like my mother, with the peasant girl named Mimi. It's a paradox.*

"I know you want to promote the zyndari letters because of their ease of use and the possibility of universal literacy, but trying to force changes through from the top without regard for the feelings of the people is rarely effective. And sometimes, such reforms are harmful and dangerous. The people most affected by change are also the ones who know best *how* to change.

"Watch what the people are doing. Haven't you seen the hybrid pamphlets in which the grammar follows the vernacular, but the words are written as logograms? Haven't you observed poets writing in classical forms inventing new pseudo-Ano logograms to represent concepts that didn't exist in the past? Haven't you noticed that many more shop signs now contain both logograms and zyndari letters?

"Let it evolve naturally. Lay the proper foundation, and the next generation, and the generation after that, may complete the work you started, but on their own terms."

It took a while before Zomi got control of herself. "I understand now that I was wrong. My shame is great."

"Who can claim to have never made mistakes?" The empress

sighed. "I've made many mistakes in my life. Didn't I have to go beg Gin to fight for the Dandelion Throne again? Didn't I have to rescind the decree that abolished paid litigators? Errors are inevitable when we're not all-knowing like the gods in the stories told by the priests."

"What should I do?"

"You must figure that out yourself," said the empress. "Your instinct is to push for radical changes, to eliminate injustices in one stroke. That isn't, in itself, wrong. But when you realize you've made a mistake that affects the lives of many, you must also bear the consequences."

The next day, the Farsight Secretary astounded everyone with the announcement that the Grand Examination would resume with the examinees having the option of composing either in the vernacular with zyndari letters or in Classical Ano using logograms—in fact, they could mix and match if they liked. The judges would endeavor, in their grading, to give no advantage to either.

Though phrased in the form of a proclamation, it was obviously a total capitulation to the demands of the protesters, and the *cashima* celebrated accordingly. Réza Müi was paraded through the streets of Pan on the shoulders of the other scholars, and the revelry continued long into the night. In the morning, as the examinees lined up outside the Examination Hall, there were many sleepy eyes and hungover faces.

However, the official who greeted the scholars at the hall to administer the exam was not Zomi Kidosu, but Cogo Yelu, the Prime Minister. Zomi had issued a second proclamation denouncing herself for dereliction of duty, causing a delay in the Grand Examination as well as the destruction of property in the academic quarter of Pan. She accepted all blame for the protests, and levied a large fine on herself to be paid out of her savings. She also applied to the empress for a reduction in her salary, which was summarily granted. Finally, she stripped herself of all honors accorded to one who administered the Grand Examination, and forbade herself from interfering in the tests in the future.

The people of Pan, including the scholars who had been shouting angrily at her but a few days ago, now sided with her in sympathy. Teahouse storytellers now told embellished accounts of her error and subsequent self-chastisement as a modern model of a good Moralist minister. (The phrase "teeth on the board" featured prominently in these tales.) Ranked scholars petitioned the court to reduce her punishment. The College of Advocates drafted many new proposals to promote the use of zyndari letters in even more areas of life.

But Zomi was content to accept her punishment. As part of the aftermath of her disgrace at the Grand Examination, she told Jia she thought it best for her to leave Pan for a while to devote herself to research at the Imperial laboratories in Ginpen.

*I've been at court for too long. I'm unsuited to the manipulation of opinions and backroom politics. I'll continue as Farsight Secretary, but in quieter places. Let me travel between the Imperial laboratories scattered about the Islands. Let me be back among my beloved machines and fellow engineers. Let me reacquaint myself with the excitement of discovery that Mimi knew.*

Empress Jia agreed.

"Remember your promise to me, Jia."

"I haven't forgotten, my old friend. I'm old, not senile."

"Then why do you thwart Phyro at every turn? Why do you not reason with him?"

"Reason cannot teach that which must be learned through failure. Everything comes to him too easily. He must learn through experience, the same as Zomi Kidosu."

"You have schemes within schemes, plots within plots. I no longer know what you truly think. Maybe I never did."

"Just give me a little more time, Soto. Just a little more time."

# CHAPTER THIRTY

# PIT

BY THE SHORES OF LAKE ARISUSO ON MOUNT
KIJI, RUI: THE THIRD MONTH IN THE NINTH YEAR
OF THE REIGN OF SEASON OF STORMS AND THE
REIGN OF AUDACIOUS FREEDOM (TWENTY-SIX
MONTHS UNTIL THE REOPENING OF THE WALL OF
STORMS).

The statue of Kiji had been toppled three days ago. It had taken the ensuing three days for teams of native laborers under the watchful eyes of Lyucu overseers to chop the wooden idol into pieces small enough to be dragged out here into the giant pit dug by the shore of the lake.

Teams of priests, monks, and nuns, their faces haunted and robes tattered, carried out boxes of books from the temple and dumped them into the pit. Once in a while, if one of them slowed down or faltered, a Lyucu overseer would step forward with a threatening gesture, and the poor wretch would flinch and hurry to complete the task.

Besides the holy revelations left by generations of priests and abbots, these books also contained detailed observation records, meticulously maintained for centuries, of the flight patterns and feeding habits of the Mingén falcons—thought to be an aid in divination and instrumental in the discovery of the secret of Mingén falcon flight by Kino Ye; the seasonal water levels in the two lakes on Mount Kiji; the number and species of fishes, shellfishes, birds, insects, flowers found in the environs. There were also meditations on the changing of the seasons, poems dating back to the earliest days of the Diaspora Wars, rare copies of the Ano Classics in the calligraphy of notable scribes, even letters written by members of the royal family during the Tiro states era. The temple was the repository of the culture of Xana, the old name for the islands of Rui and Dasu.

A Mingén falcon suddenly rose above the rim of the lake and flew toward the pit being fed by teams of ant-like members of Kiji's clergy. It soared overhead and circled the pit a few times, crying loudly.

Everyone stopped to watch, and even the Lyucu overseers stood with their mouths agape. The falcons, denizens of Lake Dako, rarely flew up to Lake Arisuso.

The massive bird dove down, swooped right over the heads of the humans, and glided back toward the lake, the gusts from its wings buffeting the upturned faces.

The priests and monastics knelt down and prayed fervently, for the falcon was the *pawi* of Lord Kiji, the patron of Xana.

The abbot, also one of the box-carriers, suddenly shouted, "Save us, Lord Kiji! Save us!"

Slowly, by ones and twos, other priests and monastics joined him. The pleas for help melded into a cacophony of lamentation, rising in volume by the minute.

Some of the Lyucu naros and culeks, amazed by the sight of the giant bird and the sudden defiance from the natives, looked at one another in confusion. Some began to kneel as well.

Flapping its mighty wings, the falcon slowly turned around over the lake and began to dive at the crowd gathered around the pit again.

Cutanrovo rushed forward and stood at the rim of the pit. She took off the bone war club on her back and raised it high overhead with both hands, staring at the diving falcon with unblinking eyes.

"Votan, duck down!"

"Votan, that's too dangerous!"

"The feathered beast doesn't know who you are!"

Cutanrovo ignored the frightened shouting of the Lyucu warriors behind her, ignored the cries and moans of the natives, ignored everything except the diving falcon aiming at her, talons forward, curved beak open like a giant sword.

"Votan-ru-taasa, votan-sa-taasa! What is the name of our pékyu-votan's axe?"

A few stunned voices answered her timidly, "Langiaboto."

The falcon was now closer, its wings covering up half the sky in Cutanrovo's vision. She didn't waver.

"Then have we forgotten who we are? We rely on no one but ourselves!" shouted Cutanrovo. "Dara-raaki must be destroyed! We fear no false gods!"

More voices now answered her, growing in confidence. "Dara-raaki must be destroyed!"

The falcon was now so close that Cutanrovo could smell the overwhelming, fishy stench. The sail-like wings blotted out the sun. Cutanrovo locked eyes with the giant creature's cold, emotionless orbs and gripped her club tighter.

"Dara-raaki must be destroyed! We will remake Ukyu-taasa into a paradise!"

Yet more voices shouted the response. "Dara-raaki must be destroyed!"

The Lyucu naros and culeks ran up to the pleading priests and monastics, and clubs and axes swung in quick arcs that ended with sickening thuds. Screams replaced the pleas, and the screams were then cut off abruptly in the middle.

Something flickered through the falcon's eyes. Despair? Pity? Horror?

Just as Cutanrovo was about to swing the club in a useless gesture of defiance against the gigantic bird, it swerved away. The powerful gust of wind tossed Cutanrovo off her feet. Screeching and screaming, the bird turned and flew away, disappearing beyond the rim of the lake.

Cutanrovo climbed up, dusted herself off, and laughed.

"Dara-raaki must be destroyed!" shouted the Lyucu warriors, voices cracking with bloodlust.

Cutanrovo strode up to the abbot, kneeling silently and trembling.

As the Lyucu thane approached, he abased himself and plunged his forehead against the ground again and again.

"Your god cannot save you," said Cutanrovo. She swung her bone club and bashed in his skull.

"Please, don't make me do this," begged Timu.

"You must," whispered Tanvanaki, standing behind him at the rim of the pit, blocking his retreat.

The pit was a scene unimaginable even in his nightmares. Broken pieces of the statue of Kiji lined the bottom. Over them lay scrolls and codices, a religious and cultural repository accumulated over more than a millennium. Besides the library of the temple, other books had been shipped in from Kriphi, ripped from the shelves of the palace library and the grand manors. And on top of these lay the headless bodies of the temple clergy, the abbot among them. Flammable oil had been poured over everything. Mixed with the odor of blood and brains and entrails, it gave off a macabre stench.

On the other side of the pit, the remaining members of Kiji's clergy knelt in neat rows. Behind them knelt the few ranked scholars still left in the surrounding countryside that Cutanrovo's roaming purification packs had captured. They had been wailing for so long that they had lost their voices or the will to continue. Most were as still as wooden mannequins. Beyond them, Cutanrovo exhorted the assembled Lyucu warriors to continue their chants of victory.

Timu turned around to face Tanvanaki. "Please. I can't."

Tanvanaki held out a lit torch.

Timu shook his head. He wanted to back up, but behind him was the yawning pit.

"If you don't do this," said Tanvanaki, "Cutanrovo will kill everyone on the other side of the pit. She has proof that they're all traitors. This is the best deal I've been able to make for you."

"How can you believe they're all traitors? Wira Pin and Noda Mi named them only to save their own hides!"

"It doesn't matter what I believe," said Tanvanaki, her voice full of weariness and anguish. "Do you hear the chants over there? Cutanrovo has the hearts of the warriors, and I cannot stop the tide."

"What happened to your empathy? To your ability to see what others see, feel what they feel? Do you not see what evil you're committing?"

For a moment he saw the cold determination in her eyes falter, saw a spark of the hope that he had once seen in her soul. Her lips quivered. But the light went out, and her face was again a mask of relentless resolve.

"I am my father's daughter," she said. "I cannot afford to be weak, to allow my own feelings to destroy the dream of my people. Neither can you. If you want to save the rest of *your* people, then you must do as I ask."

"You're asking me to call Lord Kiji a false god; you're asking me to denounce Kon Fiji as a liar. How can I do these things? Lord Kiji has been the patron of these islands from time immemorial, and the One True Sage is the teacher of teachers. You are asking me to desecrate my soul."

A strange glint came into his eyes.

"I've already compromised too much. You told me Cutanrovo's madness would burn itself out, but it has only grown and grown. First, it was Wira Pin and Noda Mi discovering six secret master-pupil relationships. Then, after a few rounds of torture, the six accused scholars named sixty coconspirators. Another few rounds of torture later, the sixty coconspirators named six hundred traitors in the temples and among the court-appointed tutors. And now you're asking me to legitimate all that has happened. I cannot. I cannot."

His right hand reached for his waist, and his fingers wrapped around the handle of his writing knife. Though useless against a sword or a club, the slender dagger was enough to end his life if plunged into the thick arteries pulsing in his neck.

Faster than a flash of lightning, Tanvanaki's fingers clamped around his wrist and kept it in place like a vise. She pulled him right up against her.

"Listen to me, Timu," she whispered into his ear. "You may think ending your life will end the conflagration, but it won't. Let me tell you what's going to happen next if you die. Cutanrovo will continue to find more traitors among the ranks of the officials and ministers and clerks and clergy until the entire state apparatus of Ukyu-taasa is in ruins. There will be no one to supervise the repairs to the irrigation system; there will be no one to distribute food to villages struck by plague or drought; there will be no one to stand up, however feebly, for natives subjected to another outrage from a Lyucu naro or culek. There will be rebellions, and more mass killings, until this carnage you see before you will seem like a mercy."

Timu struggled to free himself from her grip but could not.

"Cutanrovo doesn't care if that vision comes to pass. The more blood flows, the happier she is. But that isn't what I or Goztan or Vocu or even Wira Pin and Noda Mi want to see. Only you can stop that vision from coming true."

Timu continued to struggle. "How?"

"Right now the native villagers are frightened, uncertain, enraged. Right now the officials are terrified, vacillating, unsure if they can survive. But Wira Pin and Noda Mi and I have figured out a way to give Cutanrovo what she wants—the surrender of the soul of Dara—without killing everyone. If you denounce Kiji and Kon Fiji, your capitulation will tell the villagers that our gods are more powerful than yours and free the officials from guilt for abandoning their Moralist ideals. They'll convince themselves that they're only doing what their emperor is telling them to do, that they're just following orders. The people of Ukyu-taasa will be saved."

"You're asking me to become a symbol, to become an excuse for justifying compromises and a pretext to legitimate moral horrors."

"I'm asking you to do the right thing."

Timu stopped struggling. His face was scrunched into a mask of pain. "O gods, O gods," he muttered. "O Father, O Mother, O Master Ruthi, what should I do?"

Tanvanaki wrapped an arm around him. "You can do this. I know you're strong enough."

An expressionless Emperor Thaké stood at the rim of the pit.

He recited the proclamation drafted by Wira Pin, in which he acknowledged his errors in rebelling against the Lyucu in his heart, denounced the false histories in which the Lyucu liberators of Ukyu-taasa were maligned and defamed, proclaimed Lyucu the only speech fit for the people of Rui and Dasu, castigated the gods of Dara as false idols, and finally, vilified Kon Fiji as the Most Base Liar.

Then he tossed a lit torch into the fire pit, and watched as the erupting conflagration consumed everything.

Across the fire pit, the Lyucu warriors let out a deafening cheer. Cutanrovo smiled. Next to her stood Tanvanaki, who put her arms around the frightened and confused Todyu and Dyana. The kneeling scholars and monks and nuns watched the scene wordlessly, shuddering from time to time.

A storm more violent than any in memory raged over Ukyu-taasa for three days and three nights. In the torrential rain and typhoon-strength winds, houses caved in, mudslides buried villages, branches were torn from trees, and tides inundated coastal towns. Not even the great storm during the Reign of One Bright Heaven, when one of Mapidéré's sons was lost in the sea north of Rui, could compare.

But on the fourth morning, the storm abated. Based on reports by local officials across the two islands, if the villagers hurried to plant, the harvest would only be mildly affected. With the grain shipments from the core islands' tribute fleet, the people of Ukyu-taasa would survive.

Cutanrovo promptly proclaimed that the storm was a sign from the gods of Ukyu that they approved of the effort to purge Ukyu-taasa of Dara-raaki taint. Just as the storm washed away the old to make room for the new, the Lyucu would scorch away the scars of native accommodation and grow a new paradise. She ordered a feast among the Lyucu, with tolyusa distributed to aid the revelry.

"But the work has only begun," she warned. "Votan-ru-taasa and votan-sa-taasa, the work has only begun."

*A cackling noise ripped through the air as an old tree outside the Temple of Péa, weakened by the storm, finally broke and toppled.*

*- What happened there, Kiji? No vengeance? No wrath? No determination to see your plan through?*

*There was no response except the sighing of the wind and the screeching of faraway Mingén falcons.*

# CHAPTER THIRTY-ONE

# ESCAPE

SECRET AGON BASE IN KIRI VALLEY, IN THE
FOOTHILLS OF THE WORLD'S EDGE MOUNTAINS:
THE TWELFTH MONTH IN THE EIGHTH YEAR AFTER
THE DEPARTURE OF PRINCESS THÉRA FROM DARA
FOR UKYU-GONDÉ (SEVENTEEN MONTHS UNTIL
THE LYUCU MUST LAUNCH THEIR NEW INVASION
FLEET TO DARA).

"Let's load everyone up and get as far away as possible before sunrise," said Takval. The Lyucu were wiping up the few pockets of remaining resistance in the valley; they were certain to begin searching the surrounding mountains for escaped survivors soon.

With two garinafins for sixty-plus refugees from Kiri Valley, the first question was how best to distribute the weight.

"It's safer to have one garinafin crewed primarily for fighting and the other primarily for fleeing," Takval said. "In case they pursue us, the fighter can hold them off while the other one escapes."

Théra could already sense where Takval was going with this. But before she could object, another voice spoke up.

"It's a good plan," said Toof. "Alkir is stronger, faster, and more experienced. He should be the fighter garinafin. Ratopé should be the evader."

Alkir was Takval's personal mount, a bull garinafin in prime fighting shape. He had been bonded to Takval since he was a little calf, and Toof and Radia had helped the pékyu train him in advanced battle maneuvers. Ratopé was a young garinafin cow that belonged to Vara Ronalek's clan, though Toof was the pilot most familiar with her.

"I'll pilot Ratopé," continued Toof. "And all the children should be with me to free up the warriors to be on Alkir with the pékyu. Radia and I know more about knotwork than just about anyone. We can secure the children to the netting so that even with risky evasive maneuvers they won't fall off."

Théra had heard enough. "I'm *not* going to be separated from Tanto and Rokiri. Or Takval, either."

"If the princess is going to be on Ratopé, then I and my fighters will have to be mounted on her as well," said Tipo Tho. Grief for her children and husband strained her voice, but the determination came through loud and clear. "My husband and I both swore an oath to the House of Dandelion, and I won't be able to face Nméji in the afterlife if something should happen to her."

"It's only right that *you* should join the children," said Radia, who couldn't resist a dig at the Dara woman who had insulted her earlier. "You're certainly not going to be of much use in a fight and need to be strapped in."

"Even if I were on the verge of giving birth, I could take you without breaking a sweat." Tipo stood up and glared at Radia.

Takval ignored the bickering. He pulled Théra to face him. "My breath," he pleaded, "I know you want to save everyone, and so do I. But we have to be ready to make sacrifices to save the children. I'm the pékyu; I *have* to pilot the fighter and be ready to die. The children must not be on Alkir. Yet, if you and all the Dara go on Ratopé with the children, the weight will be too much. With so many people to carry, we're already pushing beyond the capacity of both garinafins . . . if you overload Ratopé, she won't be able to escape in a crisis, and we may lose her to exhaustion."

Théra hesitated. She had always wanted things her way, but her decisions had brought this disaster upon them. Maybe she needed to be less arrogant, less confident, less certain that she knew best.

But the idea of trusting Tanto and Rokiri to Toof while she rode with Takval felt unacceptable. The horrors of the evening made her crave to cling to her children, to keep them right next to her.

Something about the way the two former Lyucu kept on looking at each other bothered her too.

No matter how Takval reasoned and begged, Théra shook her head.

"*I* will pilot Ratopé with the children," said Vara Ronalek, looking at Théra. "Don't worry, Princess. I may be old, but I fly with a steady hand. Ratopé is young, but she's strong and fearless. We'll keep the children safe."

Radia and Toof looked at each other but made no objection.

Vara's intervention finally reassured Théra. Considering how much of a debt Radia and Toof owed her for adopting them into her clan, Vara was the only pilot she could entrust Tanto and Rokiri to if the Lyucu refugees would be riding with them. She nodded reluctantly.

The plan was settled on. Vara would pilot Ratopé as the evader, with Radia and Toof as slingshot scouts and lookouts. All the children, about forty in total, as well as some of the adults deemed to be liabilities rather than assets in a fight—Sataari and Razutana, for instance—would be strapped securely to the webbing on the garinafin for safety.

Takval would pilot Alkir as the fighter. Théra and the Agon and Dara warriors would act as Takval's crew. To not overburden Ratopé, the weapons and goods rescued from the valley, including a supply of firework powder and a few precious Dara instruments, would also be added to Alkir.

Çami Phithadapu, as the only Dara individual comfortable on the back of a garinafin, was handed a slingshot and asked to be a scout for Takval. Radia and Toof made another halfhearted bid to have Tipo Tho join them on Ratopé, which was summarily rebuffed. Adyulek, though not much of a fighter, insisted that her place was by the pékyu on Alkir. And Thoryo would not be parted from Théra, as she was almost catatonic from the shock of witnessing so many deaths in a single night. After some hesitation, Takval agreed to add her to his crew as well.

As the Agon warriors and Çami climbed into their harnesses and the rest of the crew were strapped to the webbing, Théra looked up at the moon, staring down at the carnage in the valley like the uncaring face of Nalyufin, and offered a silent prayer to the gods of Ukyu-Gondé.

*Keep the people I love safe, I beg of you. Thousands have already died, a fact that I cannot even comprehend. I was arrogant and didn't take to heart the most important lesson this land has to teach: Even a single moment of carelessness can be fatal.*

*I was greedy. I took unnecessary risks. I pushed people to gamble with the lives of their loved ones. I wanted to, in a single, decisive stroke, eliminate all possibility that the Lyucu would launch an invasion fleet in time for the yearlong sail to the opening of the Wall of Storms in Dara. Seized by the thirst for a quick and easy victory, I disregarded the need for caution, for circumspection, for counsel.*

*I was wrong, so reserve your punishments for me.*

Everyone was in their place. With a final sad look over at the fires still raging in the valley, Takval whistled, and Alkir took off. A few moments later, Vara's Ratopé also took off, following closely behind. The two garinafins, so heavily laden, flew clumsily and with difficulty, their breaths coming in strenuous pants.

Takval guided Alkir to the northeast, following the line of the Antler Range. Théra sat in the saddle right behind him, her arms wrapped around his waist. As they climbed higher, her face, unprotected by the thick furs she wore around her body, was whipped by cold winds. She leaned forward and pressed her face against Takval's back, and her husband's body heat seemed to warm more than just her cheeks as she cried silently.

A rising breeze caught them from behind. They flew fast and silent through the night air, and soon the valley was left far behind. She thought she should feel better with every additional flap of the wings, which took them farther away from the threat of Lyucu discovery. But somehow, the sense of unease grew.

She was missing something.

Théra turned around to look for Ratopé in the moonlight, to be sure that her children were all right.

"Takval!" she screamed.

On Ratopé, a fight had broken out. It was difficult to discern details in the dim glow of the moon, but she could see that Radia and Toof had climbed out of their harnesses and were struggling with Vara, the pilot. While Radia wrapped her arms about the upper body of the pilot, pulling her back and restraining her arms, Toof appeared to be shouting at Vara and trying to clamber over the two struggling women to get into the saddle. The children and the other adults, all tied securely against the webbing, could only watch helplessly.

The young garinafin was already tiring from the unusually heavy load and irritable. Without the guidance of a pilot and distracted by the fight on her back, she began to waver in her course erratically and fell farther behind Alkir with every passing moment.

"Go back! Go back!" Théra yelled at Takval.

Takval took one glance back and responded by squeezing the base of Alkir's neck with his knees. His face had turned ashen white.

Alkir's momentum—increased by the weight of all the passengers he was being asked to carry—made the turn excruciatingly slow, and as Théra strained her neck and watched, Toof and Radia wrestled Vara away from the saddle. As soon as Toof was in the saddle, he placed a bone trumpet against the base of Ratopé's neck and spoke to her reassuringly. The younger garinafin made a sharp turn back in the direction of Kiri Valley, speeding up as she did so. The promise of returning home, of rest, seemed to jolt her into a fresh burst of effort.

Meanwhile, Vara was still fighting Radia. Without the protection of safety harnesses, the two fought on top of the soaring garinafin like two sailors on the deck of a tempest-tossed ship. An agonizing eternity of a few seconds later, Vara succeeded in pushing Radia away, and the Lyucu woman fell, only managing to catch the netting dangling from the beast's shoulders at the last minute.

Théra's heart was in her throat, but she could do nothing except pray for Alkir to fly faster. In the distance, she could already see the burning valley coming into view again. Desperately, she hoped for Vara to take back the command of her garinafin before they drew the attention of the Lyucu garinafin riders circling over the valley.

As Radia hung on for dear life, Vara lunged at Toof, who seemed oblivious to the threat behind him. But at the very last possible moment, Toof ducked down, flattening his body against the garinafin's neck, and Vara plunged right past him, tumbling over the shoulder of the garinafin.

As Takval and Théra cried out in alarm, Toof reached out and grabbed the back of Vara's vest. He seemed to shout something at the thane, and Vara, dangling from Toof's arm, shook her head.

"Faster! Faster!" Théra screamed into Takval's ear.

Takval slapped his hand against Alkir's neck repeatedly, and Alkir strained to catch up to the younger garinafin. Now the two mounts were only about the lengths of three garinafins apart, and Théra could see everything happening on Ratopé, below and ahead of her, clearly in the pale glow of the moon.

Again, Toof seemed to ask something of Vara, who shook her head once more. Then, as her feet wheeled in the air for purchase against the slick hide of the garinafin's shoulder, she turned herself around and punched at Toof's face.

Toof let go.

With a scream that was instantly lost in the rushing wind, Vara plunged to her death hundreds of feet below.

Théra gasped in horror. But before she could even process the death, Ratopé had flown over the last ridge shielding Kiri Valley, with Alkir close behind. The burning remains of the settlement were in full view below them, with the shadows of Lyucu garinafins sweeping over it.

Ratopé flapped her wings and dove down, heading straight for the Lyucu riders.

Takval pressed his bone trumpet against the base of Alkir's neck and shouted into it. Théra held on tighter, preparing for the dive that was to come as they pursued the perfidious Lyucu who had stolen her children.

The view of the valley in Théra's eyes tilted, jerked, shifted, and swung away.

"What are you doing?" she shrieked in Takval's ear. "Why are we turning away?"

Takval turned around and looked into her eyes. She saw stars reflected in his glistening eyes. "It's too late, my breath. We can't be seen."

Then he turned his face away to look ahead as the garinafin flapped his wings hard, panting like the bellows of a blast furnace. With a sudden lurch, they were over the ridge, leaving the valley that had been their home for seven years forever behind.

Théra pounded Takval's back, demanding that he turn around. Tears poured down her face as she howled with rage and anguish. "Kunilu-*tika*! Jian-*tika*!"

Takval bore her abuse silently like a reef absorbing the rage of the pounding surf. Alkir kept to his course. The rest of the crew watched this tragic scene in complete silence, unable to do or say anything to help them. A few, like Gozofin, whose children were also on the other garinafin, either cried silently or gritted their teeth in despair.

When the pounding finally ceased, Takval reached back with one hand, grabbed Théra's hand, and squeezed it gently. She let her hand rest in his grip, feeling his anguish merge with hers. It was a long time before she squeezed him back.

In complete silence, the garinafin glided toward the sun, carrying them away from the bloodstained and charred valley that had once been full of hope.

As the sun rose, Cudyu Roatan, son of Tenryo Roatan, son of Toluroru Roatan, Pékyu of the Lyucu and the Voice of the Gods, surveyed the smoldering remains of the Agon camp in Kiri Valley as well as the bound captives kneeling before him, feeling very pleased.

He had achieved so much already, and there was no telling how much greater the victory would become yet.

It had not been easy for Tenryo, his father, to hold together the loose coalition of tribes that he had gathered under one banner. Every chief wanted to be given the rank of garinafin-thane, and every culek wanted to become a naro. The tribes squabbled incessantly over everything from the distribution of grazing rights to allotments of Agon and Dara slaves. Everyone wanted the pékyu to recognize and reward their contribution to the victory over the hated Agon and exaggerated their deeds during the war with the invaders from Dara.

*"The child of an Agon slave belongs to the tribe that owns the mother, not the father!"*

*"She killed my favorite Dara boy! I demand six heads of cattle in compensation!"*

*"Their herds consumed all the grazing that was reserved to the Tribe of the Finger Streams!"*

*"Why are both my neighbors wolf-thanes while I'm a mere ordinary thane? I saved the life of the mother of the second husband of the fifth daughter of your favorite nephew!"*

Sometimes Cudyu wondered if his father had not launched his mad scheme to sail over the endless ocean to conquer a new land as a way to escape the tedium of being pékyu. Preparing for and fighting wars were fun for the old man—not what came after the bodies of dead warriors strewn on the scrublands had been consumed by vultures and wolves. Even when Tenryo lived in Ukyu, he had often pleaded headaches and told Cudyu and Vadyu, mere children then, to face the long line of petitioners outside the Great Tent in his stead.

And then, Tenryo had taken Vadyu, not him, to go conquer Dara. It was Cudyu's duty to be the caretaker, to deal with the tedious squabbling chiefs by himself, to prepare additional ships to support his father. All the glories of war would belong to his father and sister, and all the drudgery of supporting that war fell to him.

*It was all so unfair.*

Had he not contributed just as much as "Tanvanaki" (oh, how he resented that nickname of hers—why couldn't he get a splashy moniker like that? Just because she was such a show-off?) to the scheme to trick Luan Zya into revealing the location of the Dara homeland? Had he not been just as skilled at chipping away the independence of the petty chiefs to build up the prestige and power of the Roatan clan? Had he not demonstrated just as much devotion to his father? He had. He had. *He had!*

Yet, when the moment came, his father had shown who was truly his favorite child.

Once the city-ships had disappeared beneath the horizon, however, he started to see things a different way.

It was foolish to pine after the love of a parent who didn't love you back. A wise wolf did not put all his hope into catching a single sheep—it was better to have the whole flock.

His father's departure had in fact been a blessing, he realized. Had Tenryo stayed in Ukyu, he would have ruled for many more years as pékyu, and when the time came to pick his successor, Cudyu would be past his prime, just one of many pékyus-taasa in contention.

But now, with his father gone, things were very different. Tenryo had taken with him his most loyal and powerful thanes—leaving behind some of the best grazing rights, the most prized slaves, the most coveted titles. There was a power vacuum that demanded to be filled. Most important of all, Tenryo had taken away Tanvanaki, the rival Cudyu had feared the most.

Yes, yes, his father had declared the arrangement to be temporary. Tenryo remained the pékyu, and would eventually either return in triumph or bring all the Lyucu to live with him in paradise. But the failed expeditions earlier had shown how dangerous the way to Dara was, and how remote the chance that they would succeed. It was very likely that Tenryo would never return.

And even if he did, why should Cudyu simply step aside? After all, Tenryo had not been the favored son of *his* father. He had cemented his position only by tossing Langiaboto, his battle axe, at Toluroru, Cudyu's grandfather.

Power was born from charred bone and spilled blood, not a parent's love.

Cudyu chuckled to himself. *You see, Father, I really should be your favorite child. I'm just like you.*

He set about his task with gusto. One by one, his remaining siblings died in mysterious circumstances, and his father's wives were sent back to their home tribes ("So that you may mourn the death of your child in peace," he told them). He picked out his most loyal followers—childhood playmates, men and women who had hunted with him in youth, seasoned warriors who nodded without question when he asked them to "take care" of his siblings—and made them into garinafin-thanes. He took notice of ambitious young naros-votan from lesser tribes and promoted them to tiger-thanes and wolf-thanes, bypassing those who had curried too much favor with his sister or father. He handed out lavish gifts to shamans who demonstrated a particular talent for retelling the old tales with an eye toward pleasing a new master. He assigned the best grazing rights and slaves to tribes whose elders demonstrated a keen sensitivity to the political winds, who understood that a fresh storm was about to tear through the scrublands.

One year after his father's departure, as directed by the plan based on Luan Zya's calculations, he prepared a fleet of reinforcements. He did this with much fanfare and piety, slaughtering many slaves in solemn sacrifice. But he was careful to staff the fleet with tribes who had been especially loyal to his father, with thanes and narosvotan that he knew he could never win over, with particularly recalcitrant Agon slaves—Cudyu wasn't going to worry overmuch if they should decide to stage an uprising on the high seas. He even came up with the idea of sending the second expedition with a bigger supply of garinafin eggs and fewer adult garinafins so that there would be more room to ship away the people he didn't want around.

*Let the old man have his fantasy of perpetual war. But I'll become the greatest pékyu the scrublands have ever known or will ever know. I'll crush the Agon until the very thought of rebellion has been erased from their minds; I'll bind the tribes to me until they stop thinking of themselves as anything but Lyucu; my name will live on in song and story like Kikisavo and Afir.*

In the spring of the fourth year after Pékyu Tenryo left for Dara, two things happened that would change the fate of the people of the scrublands forever.

The first was the discovery of wreckage along the coast of Ukyu, apparently from city-ships. Assuming that the broken spars and decking had come from the expeditions to conquer Dara, many began to mourn the deaths of their friends and beloved Pékyu Tenryo. Others, however, cautioned that it was error to underestimate the wily Tenryo, who had managed to overcome the jealousy of the gods and powerful mortal enemies many times.

One could be forgiven for thinking that news of the death of his father would be pleasing to Cudyu, but the fact was, the wreckage filled Cudyu with anxiety.

Always meticulous, Cudyu had ordered all the discovered pieces brought to Taten, where he studied them in secret. Because he had studied the language and culture of Dara from a young age, he could read the Ano logograms appearing in the debris, which appeared to most Lyucu as mere decoration.

What he found was that all the identifiable wreckage had come from the reinforcement expedition he had sent, not the original one carrying Tenryo.

Did the absence of wreckage from the first fleet mean that Tenryo, against all odds, had subdued Dara? Did the presence of wreckage from the second fleet mean that the Wall of Storms had defied Luan Zya's prediction and sealed off all routes to and from Dara?

Without more messages from beyond the sea, it was impossible to tell. And as long as the fate of Tenryo, beloved pékyu of the Lyucu people, was uncertain, he was stuck in his role as the caretaking pékyu-taasa.

While he was trying to decide what to do, a second event occurred: a wonder.

A large iceberg had drifted into Péa's Sea, the semi-enclosed body of water between the Upper and Lower Peninsulas on the western coast. This was where Admiral Krita had landed with the city-ships decades ago, and where Tenryo had established his site for Taten, the roaming tent-city of the Lyucu pékyu.

Every year, as spring arrived in the far north, Nalyufin's Pasture experienced something of a rebirth. As the ice sheet that covered the northern ocean during the winter cracked and retreated, stranding islands that had been of one piece with the ice during the winter, the few tribes that lived so far north (the "ice fleas")—including more than a few displaced Agon—ventured into the ocean to hunt sea-cows and seadogs, beasts yielding especially nourishing meat and thick, waterproof hides.

Even farther north, where the ice remained in place year-round, icebergs calved. These floating chunks of ice were so big that some of them rivaled the islands in Nalyufin's Pasture. Most of the icebergs drifted west, never to be seen again, but occasionally, perhaps once a decade, a lucky confluence of sea currents would seize one of them and carry it south, along the coast, until it drifted into Péa's Sea.

Traditionally, such icebergs were seen as curiosities, evidence of the capriciousness of the gods, but nothing more. But for Cudyu, the iceberg presented a perfect opportunity.

On the dry scrublands, access to fresh water was something that weighed constantly on the minds of everyone. Pékyu Toluroru, Cudyu's grandfather, had picked the shore of Aluro's Basin to be the site of his Taten for precisely this reason—the lake was the largest stable source of fresh water in all Ukyu-Gondé. Even so, every season, Toluroru had moved Taten to another part of the lake to avoid wearing out the grazing or fouling the water.

After Tenryo defeated the visitors from Dara, he moved Taten to the coast of Péa's Sea, where the city-ships were anchored, because these island-vessels now served as the most prominent symbols of his power. Taten stopped roaming.

However, there was a big problem with the new site: It lacked fresh water. Some shamans argued against the choice, claiming it wanted the favor of the gods; Tenryo, true to form, didn't think much of these objections. Patricide was something the gods despised, yet hadn't he achieved all his victories because he killed his father? The gods could only speak to the people through the shamans, and during his rise, he had found that the more power he possessed, the more the tales of the shamans changed to his liking.

Tenryo devised a system to have teams of Agon and Dara slaves haul water back to Taten from rivers and streams. And later, after most of the Dara slaves had died from overwork or the compelled combat sessions, their togaten children took up the task. Even so, it was impossible to keep large herds of long-haired cattle or sheep around, and Taten was forced to depend on a constant stream of tribute from all around Ukyu-Gondé.

The system, though functional, was always unstable. Though many of the shamans had muted their objections, there was an unceasing undercurrent of suspicion that the site of Taten wasn't "natural," that in overcoming their enemies, the corrupt Dara who didn't follow the will of the land or roam with the herds but tried to settle in one place, the Lyucu had become more like them.

The rare iceberg gave Cudyu an idea for moving out of the shadow of his father's legacy.

While groups of Lyucu warriors congregated on the shore to marvel at the floating island of ice and a few adventurous souls ventured forth on coracles to climb and play upon the slippery peaks, Cudyu gathered some of the shamans and garinafin-thanes he trusted the most in his personal tent. No one was allowed in for the rest of the day, and when the weary attendees finally emerged, they refused to tell anyone what had been discussed.

That night, a flotilla of coracles, apparently heavily laden, rowed to the iceberg. The warriors aboard belonged to the tribe of Tovo Tasaricu, Cudyu's most trusted thane. When they returned a few hours later, the coracles floated much higher in the water. The few naros and culeks who woke up in the middle of the night and saw the returning coracles dismissed them as night pleasure cruises by youths with too much energy and time on their hands.

In a few days, rumors began to spread that Cudyu Roatan had been plagued by a persistent dream since the spring.

In this dream, the pékyu-taasa saw his father, Tenryo Roatan, riding on the back of a pure black garinafin, heading into a raging storm over the seas. Three goddesses acted as his slingshot scout, lookout, and spearwoman, forming a triangle of gold, white, and blue: Cudyufin, the Well of Sunlight; Nalyufin, the Pillar of Ice; and Aluro, the Lady of a Thousand Streams. Just before the garinafin carrying the crew of four disappeared into the roiling clouds, Tenryo turned around and cried out to his son: "A gift!"

Cudyu, unable to make sense of this dream, had grown increasingly worried about the fate of his beloved father, the pékyu. He had become so anxious that he had trouble eating or sleeping.

As the rumors spread and mutated, drawing sympathy for the pékyu-taasa's predicament, three powerful shamans, representing the voices of the three goddesses in Cudyu's dream—Cudyufin, Nalyufin, and Aluro—came forward to explain that the pékyu had failed to understand the message from the gods.

The pékyu was dead, the shamans explained. The washed-up wreckage was proof, but Cudyu's refusal to accept the truth, though understandable from a loving son, was not helping the Lyucu people.

"It's time for you to assume your station as the pékyu of the

Lyucu, Cudyu," urged the shamans, "and to honor the gods properly. They've delivered you a gift to reveal the fitting course of
action, though you've been too consumed by filial care and anxiety to see it. That's why the spirit of your father had to come to
announce it."

The iceberg came from Nalyufin's Pasture in the far north, and
was converted by the Eye of Cudyufin's golden rays into the fresh,
life-giving water of Aluro. The message from the three goddesses
couldn't be any clearer.

"How dare you curse my father's fate in this manner?" shouted
an angry Cudyu. "Do you imagine that I fear you, just because you
claim to speak for the gods?"

He ordered the three shamans trussed up and carried by coracle
to the floating iceberg. There, they were abandoned on the ice.

"If you truly speak the will of the gods, let them keep you alive,"
announced Cudyu. "But if you lie, may you die in the most shameful way possible, despised by tribe, unacknowledged by kin, in full
view of the Eye of Cudyufin. The ice will keep her glare on you even
when you try to turn your faces away."

The thanes and warriors watched as the three shamans were
dragged away onto the mountain of ice. They whispered to one
another how devoted the young pékyu-taasa was to his father, in
clear contrast to the way Tenryo had treated his own father. This was
a worthy pékyu-taasa to carry on the legacy of not just his father, but
also his father's father.

The three shamans stayed on that iceberg for a full thirty days.
When Cudyu once again dispatched coracles to visit the iceberg,
everyone was astounded to find the three shamans alive. In fact,
they looked as hale and hearty as the day they had been left on the
ice a month ago.

(By now, no one could even recall Thane Tovo Tasaricu's heavily laden coracles, which had visited the iceberg to deposit hidden
caches of food and warm clothing during the night before the start
of this performance.)

"Forgive me, gods!" Cudyu fell onto the ice, prostrating himself.
"I will listen to your message with humility and patience."

"The pékyu is dead!" shouted Tovo Tasaricu. "Long live Pékyu Cudyu Roatan!"

The shamans joined Tovo, and soon, the other thanes and shamans did as well. Taten reverberated with the frenzied shouting of thousands of warriors proclaiming their love and fervor for the new pékyu.

And so, tearfully and reluctantly, Cudyu accepted the fact that his father really was dead and that the iceberg had been a gift from the goddesses. Despite the absence of a spirit portrait of Tenryo, no one challenged Cudyu's claim to be the new pékyu.

Cudyu heaved a sigh of relief. But his journey to surpass his father had only begun.

"You've done well," said Cudyu, breakfasting as he waved the pervasive smoke out of his eyes. He was chewing with relish, not at all bothered by the stench of charred human flesh all around him.

While Lyucu warriors walked about the battlefield, distributing a paste made from the segmented roots of cogon grass to help wounded comrades stanch their bleeding or tolyusa to dull the pain, shamans tended to the dead, praying to speed the journey of their souls to the cloud-garinafins.

Cudyu surveyed the carnage that was his handiwork with delight, tinged by a hint of boredom. He offered a piece of pemmican to the man genuflecting before him. "Hungry?"

"Thank you, Most Plenipotent Pékyu," said the man. "It's an honor to share a meal with you after the destruction of the faithless rebels." He looked up and held out his hands to accept the pemmican.

It was Volyu Aragoz.

# CHAPTER THIRTY-TWO

# THE PLAY

GINPEN: THE FOURTH MONTH IN THE NINTH YEAR OF
THE REIGN OF SEASON OF STORMS AND THE REIGN
OF AUDACIOUS FREEDOM (TWENTY-FIVE MONTHS
UNTIL THE REOPENING OF THE WALL OF STORMS).

The kitchen of the Splendid Urn, by consensus the best restaurant in all of Ginpen, was a long, one-story stone building separated from the restaurant itself to limit the risk of fire. The kitchen had its own yard that took up as much space as four ordinary residential plots, filled with smokehouses, bread kilns, open roasting pits, and other outdoor cooking stations. Serving guests who filled sixty-four tables spread across three stories took a lot of work.

Mati, the sous-chef, poked her head out of the back door of the kitchen and hollered, "Kinri! Come here!"

The young man she addressed was stacking firewood by the wall. He put down the bundle of logs in hand, wiped his sweaty face and neck with a towel draped over one shoulder, and rushed over.

"Look at this!" Mati held up a bunch of pipe scallions from a basket. Instead of standing up straight and proud like a pot of writing brushes, they dangled from her hand, limp and flat like seaweed. "I should have caught this earlier. We can't serve this to our guests tonight. Can you be a dear and run to the market for a fresh supply? Here's four coppers."

The Grand Mistress, owner of the Splendid Urn, was visiting this particular branch of her restaurant chain this month. Everyone was working extra hard to impress the boss.

"I'll be back before you know it," said Kinri. He turned to leave.

"Wait!" called Mati. "Striped monkeyberries are in season. Go get some." She handed him another two coppers.

"But that's not on the menu," said Kinri, puzzled.

"It's not for the guests," said Mati, smiling. "Didn't you say a month ago you've never had cold monkeyberry soup? I'll make you a pot."

As Kinri left the kitchen yard, his eyes were moist.

After being shipwrecked, Savo Ryoto had drifted with the waves for days, clinging on to a spar and subsisting on the occasional fish that he managed to catch. He didn't understand why he didn't die, as the icy sea should have numbed his limbs within minutes and brought him to the deadly embrace of Nalyufin, the hate-hearted (or perhaps the palace of Tazu, as the natives would have it). But somehow, a strange warmth suffused his limbs, keeping him afloat.

Nonetheless, by the time fishermen lifted him out of the Zathin Gulf, he was half-dead and delirious.

Given the decorative knots in the young castaway's clothing, the rescuers wondered if he might be from the old territories of Xana, up north. It was rare for lone refugees to make the hazardous journey, but not unheard of. By Imperial decree, refugees would have to be brought to the nearest intake center, where they could be interrogated to be sure that they weren't Lyucu spies.

But just as the rescuers were about to bring the young man to the refugee camp near Ginpen, a doctor passed by on the beach. He was a lanky young man in a green cape, and his kind face instantly made you want to trust him.

The doctor gently pulled away the thick blanket wrapped around the half-frozen castaway, lying prone on the sand. He gazed into Savo's eyes and whispered, "You've had a long journey."

Savo nodded, unsure what to say. His teeth chattered, but it wasn't just from the cold. The idea of being brought to a refugee camp terrified him. He had an instinctual terror of Dara officials, having heard many stories of the cruel tortures these Dara-raaki enforcers in the core islands inflicted on captured Lyucu. But he didn't know how to escape such a horrific fate.

The doctor put his ear on Savo's chest to listen to his breathing and heartbeat. Then he leaned over his face, shielding the young man from the view of onlookers. His hand reached inside Savo's robe, pressing against his racing heart.

"Before the sea, all men are brothers," the doctor whispered.

Then he pulled his hand out of Savo's robe and held up a folded square of silk. He opened it to reveal the tiny wax logograms written in precise clerical script.

"Ah, his name is Kinri Rito," announced the doctor. "This is an official passport issued by the authorities in Faça, giving him free passage all over Dara."

The onlookers sighed in sympathy. Such bad luck for a young man to have survived the arduous journey from Lyucu-occupied Dara, to have secured permission to make a life in Dara, only to be tossed into the sea again.

"Do you have anywhere you want to go?" asked the doctor.

Savo shook his head, amazed. How could the doctor have found such a document on him? And how did he know his Dara name, given to him by Master Nazu Tei and only used by her?

"Welcome to Ginpen, Kinri," said the doctor, smiling at him. "You have an auspicious name. May you find your own path."

The doctor pulled the thick blanket back around him. He pronounced the castaway physically fit—and Savo did feel a familiar warm strength, like the warmth he had felt when he was clinging to the spar, flow back into his limbs—though the effects of dehydration, starvation, and exposure would take time to heal.

"I'm certain the good deed you've done will be remembered by Lord Rufizo, healer of the sick and way-finder for the lost," the doctor said to the fishermen. He got up and strode down the beach without looking back, leaving Savo in the care of his rescuers.

The fishing boat that pulled Savo out of the sea turned out to belong to the Wasu clan, owner of the Splendid Urn. Grand Mistress Wasu—though many people still called her Widow Wasu out of her hearing—was a shrewd businesswoman who had managed, over the last thirty-some years, to grow a single tavern in the provincial Cocru city of Zudi into a vast business empire of restaurants, gambling parlors, and inns spread all over the Islands. Adding to the mystique, she was said to have been a friend and supporter of Emperor Ragin in his youth, back before anyone had foreseen his rise. The widow never confirmed the rumors, but only smiled and asked the curious questioners to enjoy themselves and order more wine.

At the time of Savo's rescue in the heart of winter, the Splendid Urn was doing a booming business. The Grand Examination was going to be held in Pan during the second and third months of the new year, and students from across Dara were gathering in Ginpen for a chance to attend cram sessions with famous *pana méji* at the various academies to gain any edge they could. This, in turn, meant lots of banquets and poetry-and-tea parties.

The manager of the restaurant, Teson Wasu, one of Widow Wasu's sons, took pity on the shipwrecked young man brought in by the fishing crew and allowed him to stay at the Urn, as he had nowhere to go. Once he felt better, Kinri explained that he was an orphan from Dasu who had made his way to the Big Island as a refugee. Since he had an official passport, Teson employed "Kinri" as a busboy, kitchen helper, and general errand runner in exchange for room and board plus a small salary.

The young man told no one the truth of his origins. Only late at night, when he was sure no one was listening, did he caress the turtle shell that he wore next to his skin and cry as he thought of his mother and wondered how she was doing. Since his fathers had all died early in battle, and they rarely paid any attention to him even when they were alive—he suspected it was in part because Goztan had never confirmed which of them had seeded her son—his mother was his only true parent, the person he felt closer to than anyone else.

The turtle shell had a map of Dara etched into the carapace, with a prominent dot on the shore of Dasu (perhaps marking the site where the turtle that once lived in this shell had been caught). The etching was done in the traditional Lyucu manner—with a native scorpion's caustic secretions in place of the juice of the gash cactus, which didn't exist in Dara. He knew that the map was a message from his mother, reminding him that Ukyu-taasa was his home, no matter how far he journeyed in Dara.

On the plastron was a portrait of five figures: a man, a woman, two younger men, and a baby in swaddling clothes decorated with the image of a tiny cat. All were dressed in native garb instead of Lyucu skins—a defiant hint of his mother's accommodationist views. He supposed that the older man represented his father, whose identity among his mother's five husbands remained a mystery. The two younger men were his mother's naros, here to guard the family. The baby, of course, was him. And the woman, standing strong and confident, was his mother, Goztan Ryoto. In her hand she held a war club-flail, and a fish dangled from the nonlethal end. Goztan had always enjoyed taking him hunting and fishing, and she was good at stunning the fish in the shallows with a blow from her war club before plucking them from the water with her bare hands.

He caressed the face of the woman. As tears silently welled in his eyes, his heart was full of questions with no answers.

*What did she mean that I could serve Ukyu-taasa outside of it?*

Kinri—for that was the name everyone here knew him by—hurried through the streets of Ginpen. Despite having lived in this city for almost four months, everything still felt so new and wondrous. He people-watched as he ran along. Though the natives of Haan were the most numerous, people from all across Dara congregated in this capital of learning and craft. He wasn't sure the great metropolis, many times the size and population of Kriphi, would ever exhaust his curiosity.

He turned a corner and headed down the broad central avenue toward the main food market, just beyond the Great Temple of Lutho.

There was an expansive plaza in front of the temple, filled with street performers and vendors of curios. As much as Kinri was focused on his errand, he couldn't help but slow down and gawk at the marvels on offer.

Here, two acrobats juggled flasks of beer as they each balanced on one leg on the ends of a bamboo pole raised high overhead by a third—making a visual pun for the Ano logogram for "laughter";

there, a woman dressed in the traditional cocoon-dress of Haan made a crowd of children squeal with delight as she handed them small Ogé jars that jolted with harmless shocks and guided them to put their hands on a silkmotic generator that made their hair stand on end. On one side, an old man promised to pay ten golds to anyone who could beat him in flicking the beads of an abacus to calculate the product of ten random numbers; on another, a couple sold sweet dough sculpted into the shapes of logograms in the customer's name.

In high-minded Haan, even the street vendors had to appeal to the intellectual side of the crowd.

*There's enough time to take in at least one performance*, Kinri thought.

He stopped next to one particular large ring of onlookers. He had to stand on tiptoe to see inside: An old woman sat in the middle of the ring on a chair.

"What's she doing?" he asked the man next to him.

"She's teaching animals to drive a cart through mazes."

Curiosity scratched at his heart like the claws of a cat. He pushed his way through the crowd, ignoring the grumbles, until he was near the front.

Loose bricks were piled to one side of the empty circle. Five or six children were busily arranging them into a maze, shouting instructions and debating with one another all the while.

The old woman, whose hair was so white that it shone in the sun, had a kind smile on her wrinkled face. A thin blanket in her lap hid her legs from view. She reminded Kinri of Nazu Tei, his teacher, and he instantly felt a liking for her. He noticed that, instead of posts, her chair was supported on two large wheels near the back and two smaller wheels in the front. A pair of long-handled levers on each side apparently allowed the occupant of the chair to propel herself forward with mechanical advantage by means of gear trains connected to the back wheels. There was a large box between the two back wheels, perhaps for storage.

"Now, make sure you build a complicated maze," said the old woman to the children. "Don't make this too easy on old Rati Yera. Now, gentle masters and mistresses, does anyone have a pet they'd like to see driving through this maze?"

A lady in a shimmering cocoon-dress, clearly from a prominent family, whispered to her maid. The maid giggled and came forward with a birdcage. Inside, a green siskin hopped from branch to branch on a crooked bough, twittering and trilling excitedly.

"This is our young mistress's favorite songbird," said the maid. "Zuzu is very clever, but I don't think he can drive a cart."

"Oh, anybody can learn to drive a cart," said Rati Yera, chuckling. "They just need to be taught."

The old woman gestured to a large, tall table a few paces away. "Would you bring Zuzu over there? I have to acquaint him with his new ride."

Alternately pushing the long handles on either side of the chair, Rati Yera wheeled herself over to the table and made herself comfortable. The long tablecloth draped over the top concealed most of her body from view. The maid placed the cage on the table, next to the small toy cart that was already there.

Kinri craned his neck to get a good look at the cart. It was triangular in shape, with two bigger wheels in the back and a tiny wheel in the front. About two feet in length and a foot across, it looked like a smaller version of the kind of hand carts that people used to haul heavy bags of rice or flour home. The platform of the cart was made of wood and a palm's width in thickness. The only distinctive feature about the cart was a bamboo pole sticking up near the back, about three feet tall and as thick as a forearm. Given the relatively small size of the cart, the oversized pole felt incongruous and unbalanced, like an oceangoing ship's mast stuck to a flat-bottomed riverboat.

Rati Yera leaned forward and began to talk to the siskin. "Zuzu, now let me introduce you to the spirit inside the cart, who'll listen to your chirps and steer the cart left or right. I'm sure the spirit will enjoy your singing. Why, I'm reminded of the story of Déa Su of old Amu, who was so handsome that he was nicknamed the Siskin Marquess! Déa used to ride on a cart just like this one through the streets of Dimushi, guiding his horses with his mellifluous voice. And all the grand ladies and their maids used to pant and swoon when they saw his handsome visage. They'd whistle and exclaim and toss fruits and flowers at the cart, hoping to catch his attention.

He got so much fruit that way that his family never had to buy any from the market. . . ."

While the rapt crowd locked their eyes on the old woman telling the story to the siskin in the cage, Kinri noticed that Rati kept her hands under the tablecloth and glanced surreptitiously from time to time at the growing maze.

Finally, the children had finished their construction. The old woman leaned forward and whispered inaudibly to the siskin.

The crowd grew impatient.

"O Granny, come on! Let's see the bird drive!"

"Don't tell me you were just boasting. I'm already late meeting my husband—"

"Just tell him that you saw the Siskin Marquess and had to check him out—"

"Shhh! I want to hear what she's whispering!"

Rati continued to murmur at the siskin, oblivious to the shouts and jeers. Then she pushed her chair back from the table and said to the maid, "Would you set the cage on the cart, secure it to the pole with a bit of twine, and place the cart at the entrance to the maze?"

The crowd quieted as the maid did what the old woman asked.

"Now pull up on that lever—that's for the brakes—and let's see how well Zuzu listened to his driving lessons."

The maid pulled up on a small lever that locked the back wheels of the cart.

As the crowd watched, holding their breath, the siskin hopped around inside the cage, chirping excitedly.

The cart jerked to life and rolled at a slow but steady pace forward into the maze.

At the first intersection, the cart stopped. The bird sat on the branch, twisting its head to look this way and that, completely silent.

"Zuzu, you can do it!" cried the lady in the shimmering cocoon-dress, her concern for her pet overcoming her shyness.

The bird hopped on the branch and trilled a few notes, and the cart jerked to life again, turning to the left as its left wheel spun backward and the right wheel spun forward.

The crowd cheered louder and louder as the cart, seemingly

guided by the songbird, navigated the maze. Coppers and even a few silvers clattered into the pot next to the old woman's wheeled chair, and she smiled and thanked her patrons.

Kinri was embarrassed that he didn't have any money to tip with. Without waiting until the end of the performance, he backed out of the crowd to continue with his shopping.

But the image of that cart gliding through the maze lingered in his mind. He was certain that the songbird had nothing to do with it. But what was Rati Yera's trick?

A mile from the city, a caravan of horse-drawn carriages and oxcarts stopped in the shade of a copse by the wide road leading up to the gates of Ginpen. At first glance, there seemed nothing remarkable about the caravan, but a careful observer would have been struck by the drivers in their seats and the servants and maids gathered around the carriages. All looked young and fit, and their eyes surveyed the road alertly. Not a single one was joking around or playing cards. There was an air about them that invoked the army rather than commerce.

Inside the largest carriage, two young women, both in their late teens, argued.

"Your brother and aunt-mother both told me to keep an eye on you," said one. Handsome and lithe, her dark skin and green eyes hinted at a heritage at least partly derived from Haan, though her accent was of the rolling plains of Cocru—the prestige topolect at the Dandelion Court, as Kuni Garu had been born and bred in that ancient Tiro state. She fidgeted with an ivory archer's thumb ring, revealing at least one source of her athletic figure, strong and slender like the trunk of a winter plum. "You're not leaving the protection of the farseers. Gori Ruthi will have my head if I let you go."

"But Aya, how am I supposed to have a good time with all this retinue around?" said the other young woman. Fair-skinned and flaxen-haired, she possessed an uncommon beauty. The harmony between her dress—plain pale yellow silk so skillfully cut and sewn that the seams were practically invisible—and her makeup—subtly applied gold powder with just a hint of lip rouge—evoked the nobility of the chrysanthemum and the vivacity of the dandelion. The overall effect was enhanced rather than belied by the colorful writing wax accumulated under her fingernails, giving her the air of an Imagist poet of old Amu, too consumed with the beauty of creation to care about perfection in personal appearance.

"If you want to have fun, I can send a few guards to accompany you around the city later in disguise."

"I don't think so. They may dress like merchants' clerks or drivers, but those stiff spines and threatening glares would tell everyone they're with the government. No one interesting would come anywhere near me."

"You mean no foolish boy would buzz over you like a bee drawn to a blooming rose." Aya Mazoti rolled her eyes. "This is exactly what I'm supposed to watch out for. Haven't you caused enough scandals? The scholars at court will bury the empress with their petitions again."

"Let them," said Fara carelessly. "As if the empress would care about fussy Moralists complaining to *her* about women behaving without virtue. Also, ahem, for your information, I'm here to collect folktales and interesting legends, not boys. Just because your mind is in the gutter—"

Aya sighed. "Fine, fine. I can never win an argument with you. But where are you going to stay in the city?"

"With an old family friend," said Fara. "I'll send you a message once I get settled."

"I'm here on official business, you know? Lyucu spies and pirates won't catch themselves, and a fleet won't be ready on its own. With so much to do before setting out to sea, I'm already a nervous wreck without having to worry about you—"

"I swear I'll stay out of trouble," said Fara. She placed her hands together placatingly. "My dear, dear sister, *pleeease*?"

Aya glared at her. "I knew it was a mistake to allow you to come."

"Oh, don't be so serious all the time," said Fara, the corners of her mouth gradually curling up in a sly smile. "Zomi and my brother aren't watching. Once I find the secret fun places to visit, I'll bring you along. Don't tell me you don't enjoy coming with me on these adventures. Why, those two boys at the theater last time—"

"Shush!" said Aya, blushing. "All right, I give up. If you promise to keep me updated on where you are, you may go by yourself. It's probably better to have you out of my hair anyway."

"Oh, thank you. I knew you'd be reasonable." Fara hugged Aya tightly before exiting the carriage. "Bring me a horse," she called to the grooms, her voice full of carefree joy.

Aya rubbed her temples and sighed again.

After buying the pipe scallions and monkeyberries, Kinri strolled leisurely back in the direction of the Splendid Urn. He was trying to find the old woman with her strange cart.

Of all the cities of Dara that Kinri could have ended up in, Ginpen was perhaps the best suited to his temperament. This was a city full of mechanical wonders and ingenious machinery: tide-driven water-wheels on the beaches, silkmotic mysteries in the temples, airships with kite-sails, workshops filled with master artisans, and of course, the many, many whirring, spinning, ticking, ratcheting, buzzing, clicking, creaking toys and gadgets offered for sale in the markets. Since he had no friends outside the Splendid Urn and no family in the city, he spent much of his time in his room taking apart such gadgets—most of his salary had gone to acquiring them—and putting them back together, trying to understand how they worked. He found peace in working with these machines, much as he had as a child playing with arucuro tocua.

The animal-steered cart lingered in his mind, and he wanted to see the performance again to see if he could divine its mystery. But the old woman was nowhere to be seen.

Disappointed, he stopped by a booth with a long line of customers, thinking one of them might be able to tell him where she had gone. From the ragged clothing of the customers, he guessed that most of them were unskilled laborers. Instead of a logogram, the sign in front of the booth showed only a picture of a tongue licking a lump of wax. Kinri had never seen a sign like that and wondered what trade the booth owner plied.

He took a closer look at the man in the booth. He was in his forties, with his long black hair tied up in the double scroll-bun of the *toko dawiji*, which clashed rather incongruously with his long handlebar mustache, typically associated with merchants of much cunning but little erudition. Instead of the plain, well-made-but-simply-cut robes in muted colors favored by almost all the scholars of Dara, he wore a bright blue hempen robe covered in patches of every color, shape, size, and material imaginable—the result reminded him of a map of Dara.

Intrigued, Kinri asked the man at the end of the line, "What's he selling?"

"He's not selling anything you can eat or wear," said the man. "Can't you see his sign? He's a 'knife-tongue,' a paid litigator."

Kinri had heard about paid litigators before, but only as villains in the Moralist classics. "I thought that was outlawed."

The man looked at him strangely. "Where have you been, little brother? Empress Jia made them legal again. Prime Minister Cogo Yelu issued the proclamation a few years ago."

Kinri searched through his memory for what little he knew about paid litigators. "Don't they charge their clients a lot of money just to lie?"

"Not this one. Widi Tucru only works for the poor, and he defends them from the lies of greedy tax collectors, bullying constables, and overweening landlords. That's why his sign isn't written in logograms or letters, because he knows most of us can't read."

"Has he helped many?"

"Has he! I was one of his clients last year. My landlord was going to raise my rent in retaliation because I refused to help him by lying to the tax collectors about how much I paid him. I was at my wit's end. But Widi convinced all the landlord's other tenant farmers to band with me and stop all work during planting season. Three days later, the landlord caved in, and now none of us are afraid of him."

"But how can poor tenant farmers afford to pay for his services?"

"He asks for what we can spare, and if we can't pay anything, he just asks us to do him a favor later. When Widi agrees to work for you, he cuts a patch from his robe and gets a patch from yours. There's no need for a contract."

Kinri was about to ask for more when a loud cheer drew his attention to a group of performers next to the knife-tongue's booth. They were putting on a play.

A man, around thirty years of age, wore a costume made of sheepskin that showed off his well-muscled chest and arms. On top of his head was strapped the skull of a deer, like a helmet. He was tossing and spinning a massive stone cylinder, the kind used to secure ships to docks at the harbor, as easily as a cook might twirl a rolling pin. The crowd oohed and aahed at this display of pure strength.

Opposite him stood a woman. She was dressed like a stage version of a Dara general, complete with flowing war cape and gleaming armor (though her set seemed to be made of paper). Her head was bald—Savo's heart clenched as he thought of his mother. The woman's face was leathery, scarred, and she held up a giant sword that was almost as long as she was tall. Pointing it at the man, she sang:

> The Four Placid Seas are as wide as the years are long.
> A wild goose flies over a pond, leaving behind a voice in the
>    wind.
> A man passes through this world, leaving behind a name.

The man jabbered at her in a string of nonsense syllables, tossed the stone pillar into the air and caught it again, and lifted it overhead like a massive war club or axe.

Kinri felt as though someone had punched him in the gut. He realized that he was looking at a caricature of Pékyu Tenryo, the greatest leader of the Lyucu and the architect of the conquest of Dara.

The woman opposite him—she was supposed to be Marshal Gin Mazoti, Kinri realized—didn't seem intimidated at all. "Tenryo," she said, her sonorous voice reverberating across Temple Square, "the gods of Dara have decreed three wards of protection for me: I shall not die as long as I can see the sky; I shall not die as long as I can see the earth; I shall not die as long as I'm faced with iron. I do not fear you, no matter how you howl and threaten. So long as my heart beats, you'll never enslave the *Anojiti* or succeed in your cruel plots. Come, let us decide who shall be the master of these Islands."

The man playing Tenryo rushed at her, holding the stone pillar like a battering ram. The woman playing Gin dodged easily out of the way, spun in place, and covered her face with her war cape.

When she stood still again and unveiled her face, she looked completely different. Her face was wrinkled and worn, there was a scraggly beard on her chin, and she had somehow sprouted a headful of straight black hair. The armor was woven leather (or leather-colored paper, rather). Instead of the gigantic sword, she now held a short sword in one hand and a war club studded with teeth in the other.

Kinri rubbed his eyes. If he hadn't seen it with his own eyes, he wouldn't have believed this was the same woman.

"Meet Biter and Simplicity," she called out, her voice that of a middle-aged man. She crossed her weapons. "I, Dafiro Miro, stand with the Marshal. You shall not leave this ship alive."

The audience exclaimed in amazement and applauded.

Tenryo roared and rushed at this new foe. Again, the woman dodged out of his way, spun in place with her cape held up about her face, and when she stood still, she looked like yet another person. This time, she was a beautiful court lady in martial dress, with impractical long sleeves that traced out graceful patterns in the air as she danced around.

"I, Consort Risana, will confuse and plant doubt . . ."

And on and on it went. As Tenryo charged at each new foe, the woman dodged out of the way and transformed into someone else. The applause of the audience grew louder and louder as they marveled at this wondrous display of stage skill.

*- Rufizo, did you make up those absurd rules for protecting Gin? I had no idea you had such a theatrical side!*

*- I assure you I did nothing of the sort, Tazu.*

*- The mortals love to make up their own stories about us. I wouldn't pay much attention to what she said.*

*- Oho, you certainly seem in a hurry to disclaim any responsibility, Kiji. Do you have a guilty conscience? It wouldn't be the first time you skirted the rules to interfere to save a mortal. . . . I'll wager all my teeth that feather-brain is behind those wards! Who wants to bet against me?*

*- I had absolutely nothing to do with those "rules."*

*- Put away your glittering jewels, you unpredictable fish-trap. No one is going to gamble with you.*

*- You're all just a bunch of no-fun statues. What did Dara do to deserve such boring deities? However . . . it's good to see that we've all decided to revert to our old forms. The Lyucu costumes were getting on my nerves. Wait, Rapa, you're looking awfully thoughtful. What's on your mind?*

*- . . .*

*- Don't tell me you've fallen in love with that muscleman. Sometimes I really question your taste—*

*- No one is falling in love, Tazu. I was just thinking that . . .*

*- What?*

*- That when Gin was in prison and Jia came to her, Gin was genuinely afraid.*

*- Oh, let me think. She couldn't see the sky or the earth because she was in a dank cell, and Jia didn't come at her with a weapon. . . . Are you telling me those wards were put in place by Kiji—*

*- I told you, I had nothing to do with them!*

*- Fine. Are you telling me those rules made up by the mortals really work?*

*- Even the gods don't know all the mysteries of fate. Shhh. Listen.*

Unnoticed by the enraptured crowd, Fara stopped her horse at the edge of the audience, intrigued by the performance. She had always loved to go into the streets without a retinue, sampling the entertainment of the commoners in disguise. But in the Harmonious City, too many people recognized her for the ploy to always be effective. She intended to fully take advantage of her freedom here in Ginpen.

Tenryo was slowing down. Despite his extraordinary strength, he couldn't keep up with enemies who appeared and disappeared like ghosts. His breathing was becoming labored, and sweat poured off his forehead in streams.

Abruptly, he stopped, planted the stone pillar on the ground, lifted his face to the heavens, and jabbered some gibberish. Then he pointed to the sky, pointed to the ground, pointed at his stone pillar, and laughed.

The woman opposite him spun once more and reappeared as the Marshal.

For the first time, fear clouded her face.

Her voice trembled as she spoke. "You're right, Tenryo. Smoke from the fires has obscured the sky; the deck of this ship and the sea are not the earth; that club in your hand is not made of iron."

The crowd quieted.

The expression on the woman's face shifted from fear to determination and then to one of peace. "Even if the gods no longer protect me, I am not afraid.

> "Will heroes be forgotten? Will faith be rewarded?
> Though stars tremble in the storm, our hearts do not waver.
> Our hair may turn white, but our blood remains crimson."

She ran at Tenryo with her giant sword lifted high overhead as Tenryo rushed at her with the pillar held level. The crowd gasped as that pillar was about to smash into her chest, but she leapt up at the last possible second, flipped through the air, and landed on the end of the pillar.

No matter how much Tenryo shook and swung and spun and twisted that pillar, Gin remained rooted to the tip, standing on one foot like a graceful crane.

The crowd erupted into wild applause at this extraordinary display of power and agility from both actors.

The woman leapt into the air again and aimed her sword for the man's chest like the beak of a diving Mingén falcon.

As the audience gasped, the sword plunged into the man's chest. He staggered back a few steps, dropped the pillar, and fell on his back. The woman landed next to him and leaned in to check on the dead pékyu.

The unmoving Lyucu suddenly exploded into motion—it was

a trick! He pulled the sword out of his own chest and plunged it into the heart of the Marshal. The woman stumbled but didn't fall. She wrapped her hands around the blade of the sword, and slowly pulled it out of her chest. Still holding on to the sword, she pushed back against the Lyucu.

"That sword is made of iron!" shouted someone in the audience. "The Marshal cannot die!"

The audience began to cheer, urging the Marshal to overcome the pékyu.

The two fought over the sword, neither giving an inch. But as the pékyu was holding the sword by the hilt while the Marshal had to grasp it by the blade, it was clear that she could not last long in this contest. Red liquid seeped from her fingers, and many members in the audience winced, even knowing that it was stagecraft.

"That's not a fair fight!" someone shouted.

"Give her the sword and fight with some honor!" someone else shouted.

"Shame! Shame!" more shouted from the crowd.

Tenryo looked about at the audience and snarled. Incredibly, even though he clearly had the advantage, Gin was pushing him back, step by step, toward the edge of the imaginary ship's deck.

Behind him lay the abandoned pillar he had wielded earlier. He took another step back and tripped over it, falling to the ground. He let go of the sword, his arms and legs splayed out.

As the audience cheered, Gin turned the sword around and held its grip in her bloody hands. She strode toward the fallen Tenryo.

Tenryo looked up at her and made pleading noises.

"Finish him! Finish him!" shouted the audience.

But Gin stopped. She looked about at the crowd. "Emperor Ragin always said that mercy was important, and he pardoned all who had followed the Hegemon after his defeat. Tenryo has yielded." She dropped the sword.

Tenryo got up and knelt before her, making grateful noises in his throat.

The crowd quieted, and though there were some dissenting voices, most seemed to approve of her action.

Gin spun in place again, letting her war cape flare out like the clouds at sunset. When she stopped again, she was surrounded by miniature models of the Islands of Dara. The models, made of silk or paper, seemed to undulate in the gentle breeze. They were covered by verdant fields and tiny cities, the colors and lines so vivid that one experienced the illusion of being able to hear the roosters crow in the villages and the noise of the crowd in the bustling towns. Gin stood in the middle of the islands like a goddess.

"*Anojiti*, we've overcome our foes. Let's bury the dead and mourn them, but don't forget why they died. We must never let despair and suspicion rule our hearts—"

As she spoke to the crowd, she was slowly turning in place. Her back was to Tenryo now.

"—but always look forward to a better future. We'll rebuild—"

A ferocious grin appeared on Tenryo's face as he dashed forward and pushed the pillar, which rolled toward the Islands of Dara like a giant tsunami.

The crowd shouted in surprise and rage. Gin turned about and saw what was happening. She jumped through the air like a breaching cruben and landed in front of the pillar.

She fell, and the pillar, far thicker than she, rolled over her body, slowed, and fell back.

Gin lay still. She had been crushed.

But the Islands were safe behind her.

A susurration of sighs from the audience. A few began to cry.

Tenryo laughed as the crowd cursed him. He pointed up at the sky, at the imaginary smoke that obscured the sky; he pointed down to his feet, at the sea that drowned the land; he pointed at the giant pillar that had crushed Gin, not made out of iron or steel. He taunted the crowd with insulting gestures—*even the gods of Dara cannot save Gin Mazoti. The gods of Dara are weak!*

He stepped over the pillar and the still body of the Marshal, striding toward the Islands like a colossus. He was going to grind the Islands into dust, to show the people of Dara who was their lord, to destroy all beauty and all life.

Behind him, Gin used all her remaining strength to raise one arm up at the heavens. She opened her fingers, and a tiny firework rocket flew into the sky. The crowd looked up in astonishment.

The rocket reached the apex of its flight and arced back down toward the earth, heading straight for the oblivious Tenryo. It exploded right over his head, sending a shower of sparks all around him like a veil of stars.

Tenryo collapsed to the ground and spasmed as though struck by lightning. He gurgled incoherently, kicked at the air, punched at ghosts, and finally, stopped moving.

Both the Marshal and the pékyu lay still.

But the Islands of Dara were safe.

Thunderous applause from the crowd. More than a few wiped tears from their faces.

Kinri's mind was in turmoil as the applause and cheers continued, and the two actors got up to bow to the audience. Their words drifted in and out of his consciousness.

"We're Mota Kiphi and Arona Taré, a pair of itinerant players . . . masters and mistresses, for allowing us to show you the deeds of heroes and villains . . . many veterans from the war haven't been taken care of . . ."

He had never seen this story told from the perspective of the natives, and a complex mix of emotions filled his mind: disbelief, disgust, anger, hatred, and a trace of doubt.

To him, Tenryo had always been a paragon of virtue: dauntless, resourceful, intent on liberating Dara from the clutches of the evil Ragin and Jia. He and his Lyucu warriors had suffered greatly at the hands of the dishonorable generals of Dara before winning over the support of the gods and the hearts of the natives. True, Ukyu-taasa still harbored traitors and rebels—mostly misguided natives who didn't understand the gift of freedom the Lyucu brought: a way of life that was not tied to digging food out of the exploited earth—but it was only a matter of time before everyone accepted the truth.

In this play, however, Tenryo was the villain, a babbling, incoherent force of destruction and chaos. Gin Mazoti was the perfect hero, a stand-in for native resistance to enslavers. The utter unfairness of the representation rankled and infuriated.

He recalled again the cryptic references to the truth from Master Nazu Tei. He had been sure that his master had been wrong, that she had been deceived by rebels and traitors. What had happened in Kigo Yezu was horrible, but it was an aberration, a crime committed by Cutanrovo Aga, contrary to the intent of Tenryo and Tanvanaki. The truth was that the Lyucu were much kinder, more honorable, and freer than most of the people of Dara.

But after living for so long in Dara proper, he was beginning to see that the people of Dara were not at all like the craven, selfish Dara-raaki he had known in stories told in Ukyu-taasa. The manager of the Splendid Urn had taken him in without hesitation, much as a tribe on the scrublands would adopt a wandering culek. Mati and Lodan had become his friends, and they were as faithful and caring as Vocu Firna and his own master Nazu Tei from back home. How could he be sure that nothing else was untrue in the stories he had been told?

Was this play mere native propaganda, or was there a hint of the truth in it?

Before he could sort through all the questions, a cry of alarm went up in the crowd around him.

- *What did you do that for, Tazu?*

　　*- Are you out of your mind, Tazu?*

　　*- Now wait just a minute, why do you two think I did it? I've been here the whole time, arguing with you about the play!*

　　*- It was I, brothers and sisters. I'm in charge of birds, remember?*

　　*- Kiji!*

　　*- Why?*

　　*- You sent a wild seed to the shores of Dara, Rufizo. You took a cultivated flower out of the hothouse of Pan, Tututika. Perhaps it's time to make both their lives more interesting. Didn't Tazu just call us boring? Let's prove him wrong.*

Zuzu the siskin looked at the door to his cage, puzzled. The latch was up, but no one was opening the door to feed him or change the bedding. Tentatively, he poked at it with his beak. It swung open.

His heart pounded. He had never done this before.

In another moment, he was outside the cage, swooping through and above the crowd. The surprised high-pitched yelps that followed him sounded like the trilling of two strange birds. He had not known his mistress and her maid were capable of such a musical vocal performance.

He dashed through the air, delighting in the freedom of flight through open space. The thrill of being unconfined for the first time in his life was intoxicating, and he chirped to show his joy.

Only too late did he realize that he was heading straight into the face of a gigantic creature, whose nostrils flared as he fluttered his wings in a desperate bid to avoid collision. He failed and smashed into the monster's wet, soft nose. Two eyes, each as large as the teacups that held his food and water in the cage, crossed to stare at him. A loud, startled snort later, the behemoth reared into the air.

*Is he about to take off in flight as well? But he has no wings,* Zuzu thought, awe and wonder suffusing his bird-sized brain.

Fara was still thinking about the folk play she had just seen.

She had always found the official accounts of Gin Mazoti's life wanting, dry and colorless, like a sketch that had been erased and redrawn too many times to show signs of life.

*But this play!*

Though the plot took liberty with the facts, though the language was crude, though the dramaturgy was unsophisticated, there was nevertheless a power in the performance, an authenticity of emotion conveyed by the actors, that moved her nearly to tears.

*Why doesn't the Imperial Troupe ever put on plays about the deeds of the Marshal? Why have I never seen any opera in the capital about the war against the Lyucu?*

Lost in thought, she had no chance to react when her steady mount suddenly turned into a barque in a stormy sea. Bucking, kicking, rearing, whinnying, the panicked horse turned the world around her into a blur. She fought to stay on, clinging to the reins and clasping the saddle with every ounce of strength.

It was all she could do; she didn't know if it was enough.

∿

Kinri saw the startled horse's hooves milling high in the air; he saw the surprised young woman struggling to stay in the saddle; he saw the crowd pushing and shoving to get away from the out-of-control creature.

He jumped into action. He had no plan. All he knew was that something had to be done.

In a few long strides, he was next to the horse. He reached for the reins and grabbed on. But the panicked beast was too powerful for him, and he was lifted into the air as the horse reared again and snorted, foaming at the mouth. He looked up and met the eyes of the rider.

The sound of his pounding heart filled his ears, and his vision narrowed into a tunnel. Even in her desperate condition, he saw no helpless desperation in her face, only a grim determination to survive, to bring order back from chaos.

She was the most beautiful woman he had ever seen.

He hung on, trying to calm the rampant beast. He barely dodged a kicking hoof. He was sure that he wouldn't survive the next kick, and the only thought going through his mind was that he didn't even know her name, and that, more than the possibility of death, felt like a tragedy.

And then all was still. His feet were on the ground. The rider's head was almost level with his own.

He looked down and saw that the horse was kneeling on the ground, still panting and foaming. Some weight seemed to be pressing it against the earth, forcing it to be still even as every corded muscle strained against the restraint. On the other side of the horse, he saw the actor who had played Tenryo holding a hand over the horse's neck. The muscles in his arms flexed and trembled, and he was staring at Kinri with a complicated expression—surprise mixed with curiosity mixed with wonder.

*This is no stagecraft*, he thought. *This man is stronger than a bucking horse.*

The woman took a deep breath, and, in a melodious voice that exuded authority and kindness at once, said, "Thank you, gentle masters."

His mind in a haze, he saw her climb down; he saw her stroking the horse's face until it stopped trembling; he saw her taking the reins out of his own hand.

"Would one of you direct me to the Splendid Urn, where I'm sure you'll both be rewarded for your courage?"

In Ginpen's Temple Square, four hushed voices whispered at one another.

"Are you sure?"

"The resemblance is uncanny. With my art, it'll be perfect."

"Do you really think this is our best chance?"

"Maybe it's a sign for us to meet him. Don't you want to see what's inside those cliffs before you die?"

"How are we going to get him to agree to this?"

"Let's begin by getting to know him."

# CHAPTER THIRTY-THREE

# TREASURE

MEANWHILE, IN KRIPHI.

Goztan came to see Vocu Firna at his tent.

The servant, an old native who kept his eyes on the ground, tried to convey in broken Lyucu the idea that his master was not home. The nervousness of facing a garinafin-thane made him stutter and lose command of the foreign tongue, and his whole body shook like a leaf in the wind.

"Where can I find him?" Goztan asked in Dara, trying to keep her voice gentle.

But instead of calming the old man, her effort only seemed to frighten him more. Without speaking, he sank to his knees and touched his forehead to the ground before Goztan again and again.

Goztan sighed. The old man must have thought she was trying to trick him. Cutanrovo's "purification packs," roaming bands of naros, culeks, and zealous native soldiers hoping to prove their loyalty to the Lyucu, were known to speak Dara to natives they accosted and then kill them on the spot if they answered back in the forbidden language.

She knelt down in front of him. "I think Thane Cutanrovo is a fool," she whispered to him, still in Dara. "You don't have to speak, just draw me a map of where to find your master."

The mention of a map brought to mind Savo, her son. She hoped that he was all right in his life among the pirates. In her desperation, she had prayed to the gods of Ukyu-taasa, and the idea of rescuing him and sending him into exile had come to her in a flash. She couldn't even articulate, to herself, why she had given him the turtle shell, except a vague sense that the shell's carver would perhaps protect the boy in his native land.

She shook the thought away. Savo was on his own; she had to focus on the present.

The old man touched his forehead to the ground a few more times. Then he drew a map in the earth with his finger.

Goztan had barely enough time to read the map before they were interrupted by loud childish voices.

In one quick motion, Goztan wiped away the map and turned around. A gang of children, most of them eight or nine years old, was marching through the street. They held bone clubs and axes that were far too large for them, and some of the younger children staggered as they tried to keep up. Before the gang strode two naros leading a string of shuffling native prisoners shackled to a chain. Some of the prisoners appeared to be peasants, while one or two looked like scholars, perhaps former court-appointed tutors.

The children chanted as they marched.

> We strengthen our limbs and hearts with the sweet blood of
>  our enemies.
> We purify our spirit with the lamentation of our prey.
> Dara-raaki must be destroyed!

The prisoners, their feet bare and bloody, shuffled along listlessly, their glassy eyes showing no expression, not even despair. The children, however, chanted every syllable with fervency and ardor, their eyes burning with a wild flame.

With a start, Goztan saw that Todyu Roatan, Tanvanaki's eldest, was among the children.

"Where are you taking them?" asked Goztan of the naros.

The naros, surprised to see her, stopped to salute. "We're taking them hunting, votan. Thane Cutanrovo thinks the children need more practice to prepare for war."

Goztan recognized many in the gang as children of prominent

thanes. A few faces were new to her, but based on their resemblance to others in the group, she realized that they must be previously unacknowledged fruit from unions between Lyucu thanes and native slaves or lovers. One of Cutanrovo's stated goals was to ensure that the togaten were brought up in as Lyucu a manner as possible, so these children had been taken away from their native parents to be brought up in Kriphi.

Since it was the custom of the scrublands for even very young children to learn to hunt, Goztan supposed that this hunting party was part of Cutanrovo's program of remedial education.

"Are you going for hare or geese?" asked Goztan. "This is a good time of the year, but you'll need slingshots."

"Oh no," said one of the naro, laughing. "We're bringing the prey along." She pointed at the chained prisoners.

A chill seized Goztan's heart. "What do you mean?"

"Thane Cutanrovo thinks the children have been coddled too much," said the other naro. "They'll grow up to be tanto-lyu-naro unless they get real experience. We'll release these Dara-raaki once we get outside the city and let the children have a go at them."

Goztan could hardly believe what she was hearing. "You are asking the children to kill defenseless prisoners?"

"Eventually we may allow the prisoners some weapons for realism," said the first naro. "But for a first practice session we don't want to risk injuring the kids. The prey are hobbled so that they can't outrun the children, and Thane Cutanrovo has promised extra servings of sheep sponge to whoever bashes in the first skull."

Fury and disgust rose in Goztan's heart. Cutanrovo's plan was a perversion of Lyucu custom. On the scrublands, young Lyucu learned to fight by defending the tribe against real enemies, not by murdering starved prisoners.

She grabbed the chain to which the prisoners were bound. "That isn't going to happen. I'm taking over these prisoners now."

The naros looked at each other and then turned back to her. "Votan, we'll have to report this to Thane Cutanrovo."

"Do whatever you have to," said Goztan. She turned back to the children. "If you want to learn to fight, come to me anytime and I'll teach you. But preying upon the defenseless teaches you nothing. It isn't the Lyucu way."

The map drawn by the old servant led to Vocu Firna's old mansion, the one he had had to vacate once Cutanrovo shamed all the Lyucu into abandoning native dwellings.

With the prisoners tagging along after her—Goztan had no idea what to do with them—she approached the naros guarding the door of the mansion. The naros had fought under Vocu Firna for years and knew of the friendship between their votan and Goztan. They nodded at her and allowed her in.

For a while, Goztan waited in the foyer, but Vocu didn't come to greet her. A constant thudding inside the mansion aroused her curiosity. Following the noise, she went into the cellar, taking the prisoners with her.

She found Vocu leaning against a spade in a pit in the middle of the cellar, along with several other naros and culeks.

Vocu was startled to have visitors, but his tense face relaxed as soon as he saw Goztan.

"I come to speak to you about Cutanrovo's destruction of native fields," said Goztan. As the unusual sight of a Lyucu thane with a farming implement finally sank in, she asked, "What are you doing? Digging . . . a well?"

Vocu chuckled bitterly. "Burying treasure."

"I never knew you to care for gold and jewels," said Goztan.

"Not that kind of treasure."

Vocu pointed at the boxes and crates stacked along the wall of the cellar. By the unsteady light of the torches, Goztan saw that the crates were filled with silk scrolls, paper codices, *zamaki* figurines, bronze ritual vessels, paintings, statuettes of native gods, and similar objects.

"I rescued these from the homes of the native officials denounced as traitors by Cutanrovo," explained Vocu.

Goztan browsed through the crates and held up a scroll with a wax seal imprinted with a stylized image of a Mingén falcon. She quirked an eyebrow at Vocu.

"All right," said Vocu. "Not everything is from the homes of the officials. Maybe a few of the objects are from the Temple of Kiji—er, of Péa."

"It's all right; Cutanrovo isn't around," said Goztan. "But this is forbidden! If she finds out what you've done—"

"I can't help it," protested Vocu. "That scroll contains the only known example of calligraphy by Lady Datha, Emperor Mapidéré's mother. The codex by your hand was one of the notebooks of Kino Ye, inventor of the Dara airship. These are irreplaceable treasures."

"These may be priceless treasures to the natives, but what do they have to do with you?" Goztan suppressed her growing impatience. "You know we cannot risk a confrontation with Cutanrovo right now. She's at the height of her powers, and all we can do is to stay out of her way until she overreaches. What if she brings you down with this act of disobedience the way she tried to bring me down with Savo? How can you—"

Vocu grabbed her hand and pointed at the prisoners cowering behind Goztan. "And is that your way of staying out of her way?"

Goztan sighed. "I just couldn't help myself. To see the defenseless die for no purpose, to hear her filling the heads of children with perverted traditions—"

"And now you know how I feel," said Vocu. "I may not be a native, but these scrolls and codices are no less sacred than our voice paintings and spirit portraits. Look, put your hand on them. Can't you hear a whisper of the voices of their ancestors or feel a tremor of their breath? It's evil to burn or desecrate these, as terrible as the killing of the defenseless."

Goztan recalled how, in her youth, as a captive of Captain Dathama, she had been so enraged to see the voice paintings abused by the Dara, and how much effort she had gone through to restore them to their families. She ran her hand over the scrolls and codices, and seemed to hear ancestral voices murmur in the dark.

"I got the idea to bury the treasure from the pirates we're always dealing with," said Vocu. "No one will think to look down here. Someday, if we're lucky, our children's children, who will be truly of Dara, will be glad to have these."

Goztan nodded. She picked up a spade and jumped into the pit to dig alongside Vocu and his followers.

"I get the feeling that you're also digging down here in part because you don't want to be outside," she said, pausing to wipe the sweat from her brow.

"It's a depressing sight out there, isn't it?" said Vocu. "Sometimes I just want to hole up down here and chew a few tolyusa berries. Forget about all the folly Cutanrovo is committing."

As tolyusa was important for military and ritual purposes, its recreational use was generally forbidden in Ukyu-taasa, but more than a few thanes were known to engage in the habit in secret.

"Don't give in to the urge," said Goztan. "You need a clear mind to face reality."

"There are times when I think you and I are the only ones sober."

They said no more as they put their backs into the digging.

Tanvanaki tore up the demand letter she had just written.

*No. To ask for more tribute is madness. It's like shouting at them how weak we are.*

But what else could she do? The storms had left pestilence and plague in their wake, and many heads of cattle had fallen sick. With so many naros and culeks drafted by Cutanrovo into her roaming purification packs to harass the natives, some cattle that could have been saved had died due to lack of care. And now Cutanrovo was leading troops in war games in farming fields, trampling crops and ruining the livelihoods of entire villages. There would be starvation in the fall if she didn't demand more food from the Big Island.

She had thought of having Cutanrovo assassinated. The nameless spy, for example, could cut her throat in her sleep. But the very idea of turning on a Lyucu, a thane who had given so much of her life for the hope of a better future for her people, revolted her. This wasn't a contest of succession; Cutanrovo was, in her own twisted way, trying to do what she thought was the best for the Lyucu, the same as Tanvanaki, the same as Tenryo.

*What would my father do if he were still alive? What would my brother do if he were here?*

In the old dance stories, Afir or Kikisavo had always known what to do. But she wasn't Afir or Kikisavo. She wished it were easier to discern the waybones leading to the right path.

Reluctantly, she picked up the writing knife and began to reheat the wax. She had to redraft the stern demand to Jia to increase the tribute, yet again.

<br>

# CHAPTER THIRTY-FOUR

# THE BLOSSOM GANG

GINPEN: THE FOURTH MONTH IN THE NINTH YEAR
OF THE REIGN OF SEASON OF STORMS AND THE
REIGN OF AUDACIOUS FREEDOM (TWENTY-FIVE
MONTHS UNTIL THE REOPENING OF THE WALL OF
STORMS).

"—one steamed carp, a plate of four-season dumplings, mashed taro with lotus seeds, and a flask of warm rice beer—"

"—honored masters and mistresses. Come back soon! And do remember the promotion—"

"—the sauce of the day is bean paste with pine nuts and crushed ice, with just a hint of honey—"

"—I'm so sorry, but we're out of wild goose eggs today. I can recommend—"

The Splendid Urn was a hubbub of activity at the height of lunch service. Even Kinri, whose Dasu-accented speech normally meant he could only help in the kitchen or perform clean-up duties, had to fill in as a temporary, extra waiter.

Even as he ran up and down the stairs, greeted and bowed to the guests, shuttled stacks of empty plates and bowls and trays filled with the fragrant, well-flavored-but-light-in-the-tummy fare the Urn was famous for between the steamy, hot kitchen, the cool, breeze-filled private suites on the third floor (merchants discussing business, wealthy patrons wishing to impress a date, and groups of students vying to impress a famous teacher), the four- and eight-person square tables and sitting mats on the second floor (families and friends), and the big round tables and benches on the ground floor (anyone in a hurry or who couldn't afford the prices charged on the upper floors), Kinri couldn't help but be consumed with thoughts of the rider on the startled horse.

Since the muscle-bound actor needed to stay behind to help his partner secure the equipment, Kinri had brought the young woman back to the Urn by himself. Upon arrival, she asked if she might see the Grand Mistress.

"The Grand Mistress rarely sees visitors," said Kinri apologetically.

"Would you bring her a message then?" said the woman. "Tell her . . . the daughter of an old friend is here."

"Who shall I say is the old friend?"

The young woman looked thoughtful. Then she smiled. "Fin Crukédori."

Then she waited with her horse under the parasol tree outside while Kinri went to deliver the message.

No one in the whole restaurant, not even Teson Wasu, the manager and Widow Wasu's son, could ever recall seeing the Grand Mistress run as fast as she did a few minutes later, heading straight for the parasol tree like a harpoon boat chasing after a dome-headed whale, leaving even her two maids far behind on the stairs. Kinri and the other staff members watched the unfolding scene with growing astonishment.

Widow Wasu bowed in such a deep *jiri* that she almost fell on her face. "Oh, it *is* you! I can see his face in yours—though you're much better looking. Prin—"

"Please call me Dandelion, Granny Wasu," said the young woman, hurrying to lift the old woman by her shoulders.

"How can I possibly—why, Your High—"

"No, no!" said Dandelion. "I insist. Please, just treat me like a granddaughter."

"That would never—"

Dandelion went up to the old woman and whispered in her ear. Widow Wasu's eyes widened and she tsked sympathetically, patting Dandelion's hands. "Oh, you poor thing—"

"Oh, there is one more thing," said Dandelion. "I believe my father left a tab unpaid at the Splendid Urn back in Zudi. As his daughter, I've decided to clear this family debt." She took out a heavy purse and stuffed it in Widow Wasu's hands.

"Oh . . ." Widow Wasu looked stunned. Then she laughed. "You may be his daughter, but I think I like you a lot more."

Widow Wasu tried to bow to the young woman several more times until Dandelion threatened to kneel down to her in front of everyone. Only then did Widow Wasu reluctantly straighten up. She barked orders for servants to clean out the best suite of rooms in the owner's residence for "Supreme Mistress Dandelion" and insisted that the kitchen prepare special meals for her six times a day.

"Er, please don't go to such trouble, Granny. A small guest room is more than adequate—"

"Nonsense! Look at how all the walls of my humble establishment are glowing just from your presence!"

After Dandelion told Widow Wasu what had happened at Temple Square, the old mistress thanked Kinri profusely for his bravery and for bringing honor to the Splendid Urn. She gave him a bonus equivalent to two months' wages, and dispatched a team of footmen to find the actor to give him his reward, and to invite him and his friends to come to the Splendid Urn for a meal.

All the waiters and waitresses clapped Kinri on the shoulders to congratulate him. Kinri blushed, muttering that it really was nothing, anyone would have done the same.

No one knew who Dandelion was, though there was plenty of speculation. Was she the daughter of some important official? Did her family once benefit Widow Wasu in some way lost in family lore? The young woman mentioned the name "Fin Crukédori," and the Crukédoris were once prominent jewelers in Zudi, but that family had long since fallen into ruin, and Dandelion didn't look like she was short on funds.

Kinri, unfamiliar with the history of the Wasu clan, had nothing to add to the gossip among the staff. All he wanted was to see that fearless face, to hear that heart-calming voice.

Kinri was awakened from his reverie by an impatient growl. "Waiter!"

The speaker was a man in his thirties, sitting at a table next to the window on the second floor. His expensive water-silk robe, bright blue with a thick border of golden threads, looked far too ostentatious for the tasteful, plain bamboo walls of the Splendid Urn. A pair of sharp, narrow eyes peeked out of an oily and fleshy face, and a thin excuse for a mustache curled above his lip like a fuzzy caterpillar. The overall effect was of an arrogant man who was used to having others cater to his whims. He curled a finger at Kinri.

Kinri rushed over. "How can I be of service, honored master?"

"This fish soup is absolutely horrid!" said Caterpillar Mustache in a booming voice. "Smell the pipe scallions: as rancid as cow-trampled grass!" Other customers turned to gawk, and the man, as though pleased with the attention, raised his voice even more. "Observe the bean curd cubes: falling apart as soon as my eating sticks touch them! Taste the broth, it's like your grand mistress's foot-bath water!"

Kinri stood there, stunned and embarrassed. Apologizing profusely, he took the soup away and promised a replacement.

Back at the kitchen, a rattled Kinri explained the situation to Mati, the sous-chef. "I thought for sure that I had gotten fresh pipe scallions. I'm so sorry."

Mati tasted the soup and made a face. She proceeded to examine the soup more carefully, her eyes gradually narrowing. "This isn't your fault. These aren't the scallions you bought."

"How can you tell?"

Mati picked out a piece of scallion and laid it on her palm to show it to Kinri. "See how the cuts are straight across the stem? I never chop them that way. A diagonal cut brings out more flavor. These bean curd cubes are also much too big, not the way we do it here in the kitchen. Something isn't right."

Mati handed Kinri a new bowl of soup and told him to alert the head waitress, Lodan, to keep an eye on Caterpillar Mustache.

A few moments after Kinri had brought the new bowl of soup to the customer, he heard another outraged roar.

"What is this!?" The man's face was now a dark purple as

engorged veins popped out of his forehead. The mustache threatened to fall off his trembling lips. He held his eating sticks up, and
from the tips dangled the pink, writhing body of a worm. "You serve
worm-ridden fish to your customers? Is your kitchen as filthy as
your waitstaff? *This* is considered the best eating establishment in
Ginpen? I think the Splendid Urn should be renamed the Splendid
Pisspot!"

Conversations at the other tables ceased as everyone gawked at
the angry man. Expressions of disgust appeared around the room as
a few customers turned back to their own dishes and poked at the
meat and fish suspiciously. A few tables called for the bill.

Observing from the corner near the staircase, Lodan cursed under
her breath. "I think we've got someone who wants to dine and bash.
This is going to be tricky—"

Kinri, standing next to her, could bear it no more. The Splendid
Urn was his tribe, and someone was trying to harm them. Before
Lodan could stop him, he strode up to Caterpillar Mustache. "There's
no way that came from our kitchen!" he said.

"Are you calling me a liar?" the man shouted.

Kinri looked at the man's billowing sleeves, an idea dawning.
"Shake those sleeves for me, please. I think you're hiding things that
you've been planting in the food."

"I see that Widow Wasu not only hires country bumpkins from
old Xana, but also teaches them to insult her customers!" the man
said. He turned around to the other customers and shook his sleeves
vigorously. Nothing came out. "Look at this! Look! A filthy kitchen
run by filthy minds! Accusing paying customers of being liars and
cheats! Are we going to let them get away with this?"

Lodan finally caught up to Kinri at the table, and she gently
pushed the young man, shaking with helpless rage, behind her. An
ingratiating smile was plastered over her face.

"Sir! Honored sir! I do most sincerely and humbly apologize for
this misunderstanding," she proclaimed in a loud voice, but kept her
tone calm and reassuring.

She bowed down to the man. As her face was brought close to his,
she said in a low whisper, "Some temples are too small for visiting

gods. But the monks are willing to do what's necessary to help the visitor depart in state."

Caterpillar Mustache finally lowered his voice, a cunning glint in his eyes. "Twenty golds."

"That's absurd!"

"You want me to keep on yelling? You'll lose a lot more than twenty golds once the name 'the Splendid Pisspot' sticks, I promise you that."

Lodan gritted her teeth. "All right. Let me speak to the manager."

She straightened up and turned to leave, but the man called her back. "Also have the kitchen prepare ten of your best dishes and bring them to me one by one. Since I'm such a valued customer, I think I'll have dinner here too."

A few tables away, the strong man who had saved Dandelion with Kinri gazed thoughtfully at the scene. He took out a few coins, left them on the table to pay for his food, and left.

Gentle spring breezes wafted through the second floor of the Splendid Urn. The lull between lunch and dinner service was generally the quietest time in the restaurant. But there were a few straggling customers.

"Aha!" said a woman triumphantly as she advanced her carriage to the last row. "Check and mate."

Her opponent, a man in his forties with a handlebar mustache and straight black hair pulled back with a sweatband, scrutinized the board like a field general desperately seeking a way out for his overmatched and surrounded army. Finally, he sighed and tipped his commander on the side. "I was distracted."

"Sure, if that makes you feel better," said the woman. She looked to be in her twenties, though traces of gray were already showing in her dark brown hair. Her fair, freckled face was dominated by a pair of lively, bright hazel eyes. "You shouldn't have used Lurusén's Lament in your middle game."

"But that's like my signature move!"

The woman rolled her eyes. "A *signature move*? Come on. You play to win in *zamaki*, not to show off like a fool on the dance floor.

You were down by two scholar-pawns, by Lutho's oracle bones. Sacrificing a minister is only worth it if you have positional advantage, which you didn't."

"You are good, I have to admit," said the man. "But now I think I really have your style down. Another game? Double or nothing?"

The woman shook her head. "You've already lost two. You owe me eight golds. Pay up."

Still looking longingly at the *zamaki* board, the man took out the money purse tucked into his waistband and reluctantly began counting the coins. He looked up. "I'm short."

"How much short?"

"I've got two silvers and fifteen coppers."

"Why did you agree to play if that's all you've got!?"

The man looked embarrassed. "I . . . uh . . . I've been playing since I was five. I can't get enough of this game. Also . . . I seldom lose. . . ."

"Well, I hope I've taught you a more realistic assessment of your skills. As your favorite, Lurusén, once said, 'Scaling each peak in the Wisoti Mountains only reveals another peak. Beating each opponent only shows more ways you may be beaten.'"

"I'd love to have you as my *zamaki* teacher—"

"No, no! Pay your debt first. This is how I make my living. I just wasted the whole lunch hour, usually my most profitable time of the day, with you."

The quiet game of *zamaki* at the table suddenly grew heated. Diners at the other tables in the Splendid Urn turned to look at the pair with interest.

The man flushed. "Please, don't make a scene. How about you stay here and I'll go home to get the money?"

"Oh, right, and leave me stranded here with the lunch bill? Do you take me for a fool?"

"I promise I'll be back before you know it. Here, let me leave my *zamaki* set with you as collateral."

The woman examined the playing pieces and the board critically. "The board is chipped, and these pieces don't look like gold or silver to me."

"Gah! Don't you see?" He gestured for the woman to lean closer.

Whispering so that other patrons of the Splendid Urn wouldn't overhear, he held up a few of the pieces and pointed out various features. She looked engrossed.

Some of the other patrons, bored that apparently there wasn't going to be a fight of some sort, turned back to their food and conversation. But Caterpillar Mustache, who had been enjoying his ongoing free late-post-lunch-early-pre-dinner for the last two hours, regarded the whispering pair with a thoughtful expression on his face.

"Anyway"—the man raised his voice—"this *zamaki* set is of great sentimental value to me. It was left to me by my father, and by his father before him. I'll never part ways with it, so you can be sure I'll be back."

The woman was still looking at him rather suspiciously, but she nodded her assent. Bowing and muttering thanks, the man backed up to the stairs, turned, and dashed down.

The woman sipped from her teacup, poked at the remaining dishes with her eating sticks, and began to arrange the playing pieces on the stone board. She seemed to be working through various scenarios as she pondered the pieces and moved them around, tapping her chin thoughtfully. Her nervousness could not be disguised, however, as she craned her neck to look out the window or at the staircase from time to time.

Caterpillar Mustache continued to eat and drink by himself, glancing at the woman now and then but not saying anything.

Kinri came by to serve him the next dish, steamed rockhopper crabs with spicy Dasu sauce. Rockhopper crabs were found only on remote isles near Crescent Island, far to the west, and didn't survive long after removal from their native habitat. Restaurants that wanted to serve them fresh had to make special arrangements to have them delivered by expensive cargo airships. It was one of the costliest dishes at the Splendid Urn, and Kinri hated to see the delicacy given for free to this dishonest cheat.

As he turned away, his eyes fell on the woman contemplating the *zamaki* board. She seemed familiar to him somehow, but he didn't recognize her face. He continued to walk away, his mind churning over why he thought he had seen her before.

The woman got up and went to the window, looking up and down the street. Her fingers nervously wrung her belt.

"You're never going to see him again," said Caterpillar Mustache.

The woman snapped around to gaze at him with narrowed eyes. "Mind your own business."

"I've been in this world a lot longer than you have," said the man confidently—despite the fact that he looked at most five years her senior. "I've seen many bad men in this world taking advantage of lovely young women like you."

The woman ignored the condescension. "I said, mind your own business. Unless you want to play *zamaki* for money, don't bother me again."

The man spread his hands placatingly. "All right. I'm just trying to be helpful. By the way your money purse is hanging limp and making no sound, I'm guessing when the waiter comes around with your bill, you won't be able to pay it."

The woman's face flushed, and she glared at him, but made no denial.

"*Tsk-tsk.* So sad to see the constables bring a lady to jail for trying to dine and dash. So very, very sad."

The woman's face grew even redder. "I'll give the restaurant this *zamaki* set if he doesn't show up soon."

"Fine." The man shrugged. "That sounds like a good plan." He returned to his food.

The woman gritted her teeth, clearly unwilling to engage this oily character. "If you have something to say, say it."

"What did he tell you about the *zamaki* set?"

"It's old and valuable."

"Anybody can make that kind of thing up. What did he say, exactly?"

"Why do you want to know?"

"Young mistress, you have to know who to trust and who not to trust. I happen to have quite a few friends who understand antiques, and I can tell you if what he told you is true or just a con. Don't you want to know?"

The woman bit her bottom lip, looking hesitant. But after a

moment, she went back to her table and gestured for the man to join her. Caterpillar Mustache gladly scooped up his bowl and eating sticks and went to sit at her table.

The woman leaned in and whispered, "He told me that this was a set from Rima, in King Crukizu's time, almost a century ago, which is why the pieces look a little odd. See this seal carved into the bottom of the red commander? That's the mark of the personal collection of King Crukizu's favorite consort, Lady Péthé. And look at the scholar-pawn: there's a line here that shows it was broken at one point and then patched back together. See how the adhesive they used oozed out a bit from the seam? If you lick it, you'll get a bitter, tingling sensation on your tongue. That's from the kind of wood glue they used in Rima back then. . . ."

The man listened and nodded. Meanwhile, his hands fondled the pieces as his eyes examined the set, committing every detail to memory.

"Let me go talk to my friends," said the man. "Can I take the red commander and the scholar-pawn with me?" Seeing a look of suspicion come into the woman's eyes, the man quickly changed his mind. "Never mind. I can just draw a few sketches to show them the seal. Who knows, maybe that man was telling the truth, and your faith will be rewarded." He beckoned at Kinri. "Keep on bringing the dishes you owe me to *this* table, but don't you dare charge her for it. Her meal is part of how you'll take care of me, too."

Kinri started to argue, but shut his mouth as Lodan shook her head emphatically from the other side of the room. He nodded reluctantly.

The woman, seemingly impressed by this act of generosity, gave Caterpillar Mustache a grateful smile as he left.

The woman continued to arrange and rearrange *zamaki* pieces on the board, humming to herself happily. When Kinri brought the next dish, a plate of fresh bamboo shoots pickled in honey-and-vinegar sauce, he decided he had to say something.

"Honored Mistress, that man in the blue robe . . . he's not who he seems. He's conning us for the meal."

The woman looked up at him and smiled. "I know."

Kinri was again seized with the feeling that he had seen her before, but he just couldn't recall where. Flustered by her answer, he retreated.

Tiphan Huto raced through the streets, careless of the spreading sweat stains in the pits of his expensive blue silk robe. He had to get back to the Splendid Urn before that fool with the handlebar mustache returned.

The Hutos were one of the largest trading clans from Wolf's Paw, but as his father's youngest son, Tiphan had always lived in the shadows of his older siblings and cousins. No one respected his suggestions for new trading opportunities or handed him the reins of responsibility, despite his precocious and keen business sense. Even as a teenager, he had suggested that the family buy up the land distributed to veterans from the Chrysanthemum-Dandelion War cheaply by first bankrupting the families with crop-destroying grubs secretly deposited into the soil. His eldest sister had summarily rejected that idea as immoral.

He was relegated to the least demanding tasks and cabined in with detailed instructions: verifying inventory at shipping yards, riding along with captains on trade routes as a "family representative" (with no more responsibility than glorified cargo), assisting his older siblings (or even Second Eldest Sister-in-Law, who had been a mere cashier before she married into the family!) as a clerk. It was as if everyone still treated him as a child, someone who couldn't be trusted to make the big decisions. Couldn't they see how brilliant he was? How original and unorthodox? How he could take the Huto clan to heights undreamed of?

After years of pleading and paying his dues, he was finally given a single ship of his own to trade with. But the gods seemed jealous of even this tiny glimmer of hope. The first time he sailed out on his own, taking a shipment of smoking herbs from Toaza to Dimushi, he saw a shoal of sharks frolicking around his ship as he approached the Silkworm Eggs. Deciding that this was an omen telling him to sail as fast as possible—*as though pursued by a shark*, as it was written in the saga of the hero Iluthan—he ordered his crew to make the passage through the Silkworm Eggs at night. The captain had objected, claiming that it was madness to try to sail through the treacherous channels at night, but Tiphan had overruled the seasoned sailor, reasoning that the night passage would allow him to get to Dimushi a day before his competitors and make more profit.

The result? He had run straight into a fleet of pirates at dawn, who boarded his ship, seized all the cargo, and held him for ransom.

He knew that his family was going to unfairly blame *him* for this bit of bad luck—but wasn't it obvious that it was actually his family's fault for not giving him a bigger fleet to command, which would have scared away the pirates?—and he would probably never get another chance. Thus, he decided to take the biggest gamble of his life, to propose to the pirates a bold deal that only his brilliant mind could have hatched.

*I have information. I can tell you the routes and cargos of the ships of my family's competitors and partners, and perhaps even the routes and cargos of the ships of my siblings and cousins. You'll be able to pick the most valuable goods and plan the safest attacks.*

*I can also help you find buyers for the goods you seize. There are plenty of customers who'd like to save on customs duties and who wouldn't ask too many questions about where things come from.*

*In exchange for these services, all you have to do is to pay me a percentage of your profits as a finder's fee, and to leave my ship—soon to be a fleet—unmolested. Doesn't this win-win seem so much better than just a little bit of ransom?*

The pirate leaders, stunned by this offer, went away to discuss among themselves. When they came back, they told him he had a partnership, but with one additional service required of him: from time to time, the pirates would ask him to acquire special goods: pig iron, saltpeter, smithing tools, manuals on the construction of various engines and machines, perhaps even men and women of skill: *toko dawiji* good with numbers, blacksmiths and bladesmiths, master fireworks makers, mechanics and engineers—preferably ones with records of inventions.

*You want me to help you acquire . . . people? What will happen to them?*

Even Tiphan Huto, who cared little about fussy so-called ethical rules of business—business was just like war, and what could be more ethical than winning?—hesitated at this. To abduct people was to enslave them, and that was a capital crime under the laws of Dara.

The pirate leaders had glared at him, contemptuous of his questions.

*People are no different from goods. We were about to hold you for ransom, and your family would have paid to buy you back. How is that any different from what we're asking you to do? Who are these strangers we want to acquire to you? Why do you care what's going to happen to them?*

But Tiphan Huto sensed something far more sinister behind the request than mere sophistry. Who would be interested in buying the raw materials for war and the skills necessary to make use of such materials? Whose interests did the pirates really serve beyond their own avarice? Why did some of the pirates dress in long-haired-cattle fur and wield bone weapons?

The answer was obvious, even to someone who had little use for patriotism or interest in politics beyond its effect on trading. Treason was not merely a capital crime, but would have led to the fall of the whole Huto clan.

The pirate leaders sneered at his hesitation.

*Because of your offer, we thought you had the flexibility and courage to achieve something extraordinary. But perhaps you're nothing but a runt, a timid man who has no killer instinct, no interest in winning.*

Just imagining the contempt his family would heap upon him if he were to return to Wolf's Paw in disgrace made his face glow hot from shame. He was not going to be like his foolish older siblings, afraid of seizing extraordinary opportunities. He gritted his teeth and nodded. And nodded again.

And then, almost in a trance, he watched the pirate leaders slaughter a rooster and drain its blood into several bowls. He then raised a bowl and swore an oath of brotherhood with the pirates, and drained the salty liquid in a single gulp. The gods had witnessed and sealed the partnership.

From that fateful day on, he prospered. While his ships found success after success, his siblings' and cousins' were met with repeated setbacks and pirate raids. Over time, his voice in the clan grew. Traders respected success; that was how they survived.

*How far I have come in such a short time!* mused Tiphan Huto as he huffed through the streets of Ginpen. Now that he was more confident, he had set his eyes on the Splendid Urn—but never mind that longer-term goal, when he had a short-term victory to secure. He had just returned from consulting one of Ginpen's antiques dealers, and he had learned something most interesting about the *zamaki* set back at the restaurant.

Everything the man with the handlebar mustache had told the woman was true, but he had lied by omission. The seal and repair technique only helped to date the set to when it had *entered* Lady Péthé's collection. The construction techniques and the details of the pieces showed that the set was far older than the reign of King Crukizu of Rima: What appeared to be oddly shaped airships were in fact cocoon-chariots with missing wheels; the funny-looking horses were in fact war elephants; the scholar-pawns had no scroll-buns. . . . In fact, the set had likely come into Lady Péthé's hands through grave robbers who had raided an ancient Rima tomb dating to many centuries earlier. Such an antique was worth thousands of gold pieces to a dedicated collector.

The woman *zamaki* player, despite her skill in the game, was apparently ignorant of the true worth of the figurines she held. And the current owner of the *zamaki* set either didn't understand the value of his father's legacy or had deliberately kept the woman in the dark. In any event, Tiphan had to hurry—*as though pursued by a shark*—before the opportunity fled.

Tiphan Huto came panting up the stairs onto the second floor of the Splendid Urn, wearing an expression about as disappointed as the one on Kinri's face at seeing him return.

By now, the second story of the restaurant was empty save for the woman *zamaki* player, and Kinri and Lodan standing near the stairs.

"Bad news?" asked the woman.

Keeping the relief of seeing the owner of the *zamaki* set still absent off his face, Tiphan went up to her table and said, "I'm afraid so. That man was lying to you. I described everything to my friend and showed him the sketches, but he explained that the seal is fake and the repair technique commonplace. In fact, he thought this set is likely a forgery designed to fool the gullible."

"A forgery!" the woman cried out.

"I really am sorry to hear about that," said Tiphan, wiping the sweat off his forehead with a sleeve.

Enraged, the woman swept all the *zamaki* pieces off the board onto the floor. "How could he! What a con man!"

Tiphan flinched but forced himself not to intervene. He couldn't give away the game now, and he prayed desperately that the playing pieces were unharmed.

The woman turned her face away, as though too angry to look anymore at the tokens scattered on the ground, taking the opportunity to wink at Lodan and Kinri, standing on the other side of the room. While Kinri became even more confused, the corners of Lodan's mouth suddenly curled up in a smile.

The woman looked back at the pieces on the ground and made a move to stomp on them.

"Ahhh!" cried out Tiphan. "Now, don't do *that*! Getting so angry over a con man isn't going to help." He rushed up as though trying to offer support to the woman, but managed in the process to gently steer her away from the fragile playing pieces.

"What am I going to do?" She wailed and stomped a foot impatiently. "I've just wasted a whole afternoon and made no money. And now I even owe you for my meal. This is the worst day ever."

"I'm offended that you'd think you owe me anything!" said Tiphan. "Gallantry is its own reward. But, although this *zamaki* set isn't worth much, it now belongs to you—"

The woman broke down and started to cry. "A *worthless* piece of forgery! I'll never understand how some men can pretend—"

"Oh, there are many, many terrible men in the world who would take advantage of hardworking, beautiful ladies trying to make it on their own in this terrible world," Tiphan said soothingly. He had put his arms around her, and now gently patted her on the back. She didn't pull away; instead, she leaned into him, as though seeking the comfort of his embrace.

He was very glad to see the woman cry; vulnerability could be very profitable. "Now I want you to be strong and smile for me. All right? There's nothing that can't be taken care of if you smile and remain grateful to the gods—"

"I simply adore men who tell me to smile," said the woman, blushing. "I hope that's not too bold?" she cooed as she looked up at him. With teardrops on her face, her smile gave her the air of a dew-bedecked safflower.

Her sudden swing in mood confused Tiphan, who began to feel that something wasn't quite right. But the prospect of profit made him press on. "No, no! To be thought of well by such a clever and elegant lady is every man's dream. So . . . about that *zamaki* set; though it's only a forgery, my friend thought it might make a decent teaching aid for his apprentices as they learn to identify real antiques. I was thinking—"

"Oh no! Absolutely not!" said the woman. "I know what you're doing."

Tiphan's heart pounded, uncertain how he had given himself away. "What . . . what am I doing?"

"You are still trying to cheer me up, silly!" Somehow, she had deftly gotten out of his embrace, though her attitude toward him remained grateful and trusting. "I'm touched that you're working *sooo* hard to make me think that I haven't been such a fool, that this worthless piece of forgery is worth something. No, I can't possibly allow you to take away the mark of my shame. I should keep this as a reminder of the price of being too trusting, and"—she batted her eyes at him—"of your kindness and masculine grace."

Tiphan cursed himself for playing the role of gallant hero too well. "No, please, I think my friend really does want—"

The woman's eyes focused on him, and a timid, hopeful look formed on her face. "How much do you think this *zamaki* set is worth?"

"Err . . . well, he really wasn't planning on reselling it, being a reputable antiques dealer and all. . . . Maybe . . . maybe five silvers?"

"Oh, that is perfect!" exclaimed the woman, clasping her hands together. "Now if there's one rule of life I follow, it's never a lender nor a borrower be—well, see how I was taken advantage of when I agreed to let that con man leave without paying me? Five silvers is just enough to cover my meal, and even the meal of that terrible fraud. I'll give this to the restaurant, and then I can leave with a clean conscience!"

"Wait! Don't—"

But it was too late. The woman beckoned at Lodan and Kinri. "This gentleman says the *zamaki* set is worth five silvers. Can I give it to you to discharge my debt fully?"

Lodan nodded. "Of course, Mistress."

While Tiphan's mouth gaped as he struggled to understand how things had gone so wrong, the woman jumped up, bowed to him in *jiri*, and headed straight for the stairs like a departing wild goose. As she passed Lodan, the two women stopped to bow at each other.

Kinri, who was standing next to Lodan, bowed also. The woman smiled at him again, and then he saw something slip from her hand into the hand of Lodan, which instantly disappeared up her sleeve.

A moment later, the woman was gone.

Tiphan's mouth finally closed. He turned to Lodan. "I'm sure you'd rather have cash than a silly *zamaki* set that you can't do anything with. I'll give you three silvers for it."

Lodan, who had turned her back to him as she watched the woman leave, seemed to be examining something. A few moments later, she turned back to him, her face set grimly. "I thought it was worth five," she said.

"You're in business too; surely you understand that I have to make a profit? Fine, based on the way you took care of me today, I'll generously yield up all profit and give you five silvers."

Lodan shook her head. "I think we'd better hold on to this. That man might return for his property. The Splendid Urn has a reputation to uphold, after all. We can't be known as a place where dirty deeds are done."

Tiphan's face darkened. "Speaking of dirty deeds, do you really want me to tell all Ginpen my dining experience today?"

"O Master Huto, I think we'd love to have your dining experience here today publicized."

Tiphan was taken aback. "How . . . I didn't tell you my name—"

"How can anyone not recognize the seal of the Huto clan?" Lodan said, pulling a small box out of her sleeve. The logograms for the Huto name were carved prominently into the lid. She opened it.

Kinri leaned in and saw the box was filled with earthworms, rotting bits of pipe scallions, hair, dead flies—"So this is where you kept the garbage you put into our food!" he blurted out.

Tiphan's eyes were as wide as beer cups.

"I think we should bring you to see the magistrate," said Lodan, her tone no longer breezy.

Tiphan berated himself for being so careless. Either he had dropped it in his hurry to see the antiques dealer or the waiters had stolen it from him. But it was too late to worry about that now. He gritted his teeth and put on a big smile. "I don't know how you got hold of my box of . . . err . . . herbal medicines. There's certainly been a lot of misunderstandings today. All right, why don't we just forget about all that unpleasantness. I'll pay you a gold piece for that *zamaki* set."

"A single gold piece? Come now, Master Huto, you're a businessman. Surely you understand we have to make a profit?"

Tiphan Huto returned to the owner's residence at his own restaurant, the Treasure Chest, which hadn't yet opened for business, rather pleased with himself. Sure, he hadn't quite accomplished everything he had set out to do today, and the plan to ruin the Splendid Urn's reputation would have to be put on hold. Still, buying a rare antique worth thousands of gold pieces for fifty was pretty good for a day's work.

Whistling, he entered the wide-open door of the residence and strode for the stairs with a swagger. A commotion in the back, in the direction of the small dining room, made him pause, and a moment later, a yelping puppy dashed out from the back, heading straight for him, pursued by a couple of angry servants.

"Watch it! Watch it!" He tried to hop out of the way, but it was too late. The puppy leapt on him, and as he tried to bat it away, the bag he was holding flew out of his hand and landed on the stone floor with a loud clatter.

Ignoring the servants, who were apologizing profusely, he scrambled across the floor to pick up the bag, opened it, and peeked in, hoping that the priceless antique *zamaki* pieces hadn't been broken.

His face froze as his shaking fingers closed around one of the playing pieces—which was now two half playing pieces. It was the scholar-pawn that had already been repaired once, nearly a hundred years ago. He only hoped that it could be patched up again without too much trouble.

But instead of the weathered wood grain he had been expecting, the broken surfaces revealed pure, fresh wood. Even he could tell now that the piece was modern, a rather crude forgery worth absolutely nothing.

The servants scattered, terrified, as the man in the stained blue silk robe screamed like a toddler throwing a tantrum.

"Thank you, masters and mistresses," said Mati, the sous-chef, as she lifted her cup of rice beer. "I don't know what we would have done without your aid."

Several days had passed since the incident with Tiphan Huto. Mati and her wife, Lodan, were hosting a private, early dinner in their quarters at the Splendid Urn to thank the heroes who had saved the day. It was still afternoon, long before the rush of dinner service. Mati had cooked some of her favorite dishes, many of which didn't even show up on the menu at the Splendid Urn.

"Not only did you save the restaurant from a scandal," said Lodan, also holding up her cup, "but you also saved Mati and the rest of us from a tongue-lashing from the Grand Mistress."

Mati chuckled. "You should hear her curse—even the sailors at the harbor would run blushing when she gets going."

"She didn't build the Splendid Urn into what it is today by being a wallflower, that's for sure," said Lodan.

Kinri, who had also been invited, raised his cup as well. He wasn't good at making speeches, but his gratitude for the heroes was deep and sincere.

The four strangers who had thwarted Tiphan Huto's plan smiled humbly and raised their cups as well.

Everyone drank. The beer was tasty but not strong like kyoffir. Kinri finished his in one gulp, but the spreading heat didn't assuage his aching heart. Seeing Lodan and Mati laugh and delight in their love for each other only heightened Kinri's sense of his own exiled status. Though Rapa marriages like theirs were unsanctioned among the Lyucu, the sense of easy affection reminded him of home. He wondered how Goztan was doing now.

"Try the monkeyberry soup," said Lodan, breaking into his reverie and filling his bowl with the cold and sweet concoction. "Mati made this just for you."

He nodded and smiled at her gratefully. Lodan and Mati had taken care of him ever since he arrived at the Splendid Urn, and he was already thinking of them as a kind of new family.

"Tell me again how you did it, masters and mistresses," said Mati. "I was in the kitchen when it happened. Mota, you were the first one to know Tiphan was up to no good."

"It really wasn't much," said Mota Kiphi, the actor who had saved Dandelion from the startled horse along with Kinri. He had observed Tiphan's shenanigans in the restaurant while having lunch at Widow Wasu's invitation.

Mota seemed a man of few words, and that was apparently all he felt comfortable saying. Lodan came to his rescue. "As soon as Master Mota saw what that rascal was trying to pull, he knew he had to do something about it. Since a restaurant can't accuse a customer of being a cheat without evidence, Master Mota knew a con artist like him had to be conned in turn."

Mota blushed and smiled, apparently confirming Lodan's account. "I knew my companions would enjoy the game," he added.

"You two put on a most amazing performance," said Kinri, looking in admiration at Arona Taré, the actress who could change faces and appearances in an instant—he still wasn't sure what she really looked like—and Widi Tucru, the paid litigator. The two of them had put on the performance with the *zamaki* set to ensnare Tiphan Huto.

"It's easy to trap a greedy man," said Arona. Chuckling, she turned to Lodan. "You could have asked for five hundred golds, I'll wager."

"Lodan took pity on the poor fool," said Widi. "Arona, you are worse than some of the tax collectors I have to deal with, I swear."

"I do it mostly for the challenge!" said Arona. "Let's also not forget about Rati." She put her arm around the old woman in the wheeled chair whose trick with the siskin and the magical cart had impressed Kinri—he was determined to ask her about her cart as soon as there was a good opportunity. "She's the one who made the 'antique' *zamaki* set."

"A simple trick," said Rati Yera modestly. "That sort of forgery is so crude that I'm embarrassed to be given credit for it, but it was the best I could do given so little time. You should have seen me and Gozogi Çadé years ago, when we managed to produce imitation antiques that fooled the most knowledgeable antiquarians of Dara. Later, when Gozogi went to work with Atharo Ye, Imperial scholar, I stayed to manage the gang, but I heard that Atharo was so impressed by our work that he said he wished he could be a thief! Sigh, my Gozogi is now beyond the River-on-Which-Nothing-Floats, and I'm not much farther behind. Time devours all."

To break up the suddenly morose atmosphere, Lodan and Mati urged everyone to drink and eat more. Kinri, on the other hand, was lost in thought as he tried to sort out his own conflicted feelings about these new friends: paid litigator, forger, actors who performed stories that denigrated Pékyu Tenryo—these were exactly the sort of crafty natives that the thanes back in Ukyu-taasa had warned him about. Didn't they demonstrate the hypocrisy and moral corruption of Dara? Yet, they had also helped him and his benefactors by conning the con artist. Was what they did really so bad?

He wished his master, Nazu Tei, were around to explain to him what he didn't understand about Dara. But that was impossible. He forced his attention back to the conversation around the table.

Widi Tucru, the paid litigator, was speaking. ". . . Rati, ingenious and inventive as the all-purpose bamboo; Mota, strong and steady as the stout-limbed pine; Arona, multifaceted like the many-hued safflower; and myself, striving for the integrity and faith of the common orchid—we think it must be the gods who brought us together to wander the isles as heart-oath companions."

"So do you drift around the isles like vagabonds with no steady abode? No grander ambition?" asked Lodan. She glanced at Mati fondly before continuing. "What about family?"

"Oh, some of us were rejected by our birth families," said Widi, "and others lost our loved ones to war or pestilence. But in one another, we found the mirrors of our souls, trusty companions with whom to weather the storms of this unpredictable world. There are as many different kinds of families as there are flowers, and a family of choice can be just as comforting as one by birth. We call ourselves the Blossom Gang, and we seek a life of clean conscience and constant learning."

"Constant learning?" Mati broke in. "Are you all scholars then?"

"I never got beyond the rank of *toko dawiji*," said Widi, "but there are more kinds of knowledge in the world than can be found in ancient tomes and lecture halls. Rati seeks the intoxication of the mechanical poetry of gears and levers—"

Rati's deep guffaws broke in. "Dear Widi, you're not making an argument before a magistrate. There's no need to make me sound more impressive than I am: a mere untaught tinkerer."

"There's nothing 'mere' about your skills," said Widi. "Mota wishes to become a living embodiment of Fithowéo's deadly dance of blades and cudgels—"

Mota blushed and shook his head at this.

"Arona studies the thousand faces worn by the human heart—"

"But not in learned histories or philosophical treatises," said Arona. "I'm only interested in vulgar plays that make the common housewife or gossip laugh and weep. The officials and grand scholars condemn folk theater for being sentimental and silly, but I think they just have a habit of accumulating too much shit in their bellies before going to the outhouse."

Everyone around the table exploded into laughter. It was some time before Widi could continue. "And I seek to understand the intricacies of practical and 'dirty' law—bribes for prison guards, trick clauses in contracts, loopholes in Imperial proclamations, arguments to twist *cashima* in knots—and how to use them to help the common people. As you can see, we don't care about the kind of learning that they test for in the Grand Examination, but our curiosity is ambition enough for the four of us."

Kinri was mesmerized. The members of the Blossom Gang were unlike anyone he had ever met. To wander the world seeking knowledge that wasn't found in logograms, to support each other and help the needy, to be a tribe unto themselves . . . that sounded like a life of freedom. He had not known that the people of Dara, bound to a life of digging food out of mud, tied to the land, were even capable of such freedom. They sounded . . . almost like the vagabond Lyucu.

A commotion outside Lodan and Mati's quarters broke his reverie. One of the kitchen maids rushed into the room, her face twisted in shock and panic. "The Grand Mistress is summoning everyone to the meeting hall. Tiphan Huto has challenged us to a contest for the title of Best Restaurant in Ginpen!"

# CHAPTER THIRTY-FIVE

# KNOW THY ENEMY

GINPEN: THE FOURTH MONTH IN THE NINTH YEAR
OF THE REIGN OF SEASON OF STORMS AND THE
REIGN OF AUDACIOUS FREEDOM (TWENTY-FIVE
MONTHS UNTIL THE REOPENING OF THE WALL OF
STORMS).

"The Hutos mean to humiliate us by making a big splash," declared Widow Wasu. "Their new restaurant, the Treasure Chest, hasn't even opened. But they're already acting as if they've taken the title from us. Well, I won't go down that easy."

Now in her seventies, her movements were slower, more deliberate; her spine was hunched over like a shrimp's; and her fingers trembled as she held up one hand to emphasize her words and leaned on a cane with the other. But her gaze was as sharp as it had been more than thirty years ago, when she had faced down Kuni Garu, the gangster, and her voice just as steady and assured. "There will be *three* contests."

Everyone in the meeting hall held their breath as all eyes focused on their Grand Mistress, standing on the dais at the front of the hall, flanked by two maids. The Wasus (the Grand Mistress's son Teson, two nephews, four nieces, their spouses, and children) stood near the front. Behind them were the assistant manager, the maitre d', the shift managers, the head chef, the head accountant, the head waitress, the entertainment booker, and other senior clerks. The waitstaff, kitchen staff, and low-level help like Kinri stood near the back. The Blossom Gang, as guests and outsiders, had not been invited to this assembly.

Widow Wasu continued. "The contests will be judged by a panel of the leading citizens of Ginpen, including representatives of the scholars, officials, indigo and scarlet houses, theaters, prominent merchants, and augurs and monks from the Great Temple of Lutho."

Excited whispers and murmurs filled the room. No one present had ever experienced anything like the proposed competition.

"I'll need all of you to put on your best effort. Needless to say, if we lose, we'll become the laughingstock of the city. Who's going to want to host a banquet or treat an honored guest to the *Second Best Restaurant in Ginpen*? I might as well shutter the doors of the Splendid Urn and slink back to Zudi."

The crowd sobered as they realized that their jobs and the very survival of the restaurant were on the line.

Widow Wasu held out her trembling right hand and counted off, one finger at a time. "The rules proposed by the Hutos are simple. The first contest will be a cooking competition. After all, the best restaurant *must* have the best food. We'll have a week to prepare."

The crowd turned to look at the head chef, an old man named Néfi Ézugo. He had served in the Grand Mistress's employ the longest, having opened the first iteration of the Splendid Urn, a noodle-and-dumplings stand in Temple Square, decades ago. The burden of this contest would obviously fall on his shoulders.

Néfi was breathing heavily, his white beard quivering as he kept his hands, clenched into tight fists, at his sides. His shoulders were hunched over and his neck tense, while his eyes strained wide open, not blinking at all.

"Uh-oh," whispered Lodan to Mati. "He reminds me of a rabbit stunned by a peal of thunder, unable to even bolt to the nearest hole for safety."

Kinri looked at the intense faces of everyone around and vowed to do whatever he could to help. He wasn't worried about losing his own job, but he wanted to make sure his friends were all right. It wasn't clear how he could help, though; while he helped out in the restaurant and enjoyed the special dishes Mati made for him from time to time, he knew nothing about fine cuisine. The idea of a cooking contest seemed both ridiculous and exciting to him, a far cry from the epic contests of strength and valor that he knew from Lyucu re-remembering and Dara history.

"The loser of the first contest will have the consolation prize of picking the subject of the next contest," said Widow Wasu. "And if necessary, the loser of *that* one will get to choose the format and content of the final contest to determine the ultimate winner. Now, are we ready to show the judges the best the Splendid Urn has to offer?"

Scattered murmurs of "Yes, Grand Mistress" and "Absolutely, ma'am" came from around the room.

Widow Wasu shook her head. "I'm old, but my ears still work pretty well. That was pathetic."

A few embarrassed chuckles.

"I once served my dumplings at the coronation of Emperor Ragin, and Empress Jia herself asked for seconds. Do you think after that I'm going to be afraid that our food won't impress the notables of Ginpen? Now, let me ask you again: Are you ready to show that the Splendid Urn is the best restaurant in Ginpen, and maybe all Dara?"

This time, the loud shouts of "Yes, we are!" "We'll get 'em!" rattled the shingles on the roof.

The head chef mouthed the words along with the others, but Kinri could tell that he wasn't actually shouting.

"You know, it's been a while since I've seen him cook," whispered Mati to Lodan. "I've been in charge of the menu for three seasons. But aged ginger has the sharpest bite, and I've learned a lot of good tricks from him. Can't wait to see what he comes up with."

Widow Wasu paused to survey the room, and then looked deliberately at Néfi Ézugo. "One more thing. Tiphan Huto has hired Mozo Mu as the head chef of the Treasure Chest."

Néfi's eyes rolled up into his skull as his lips flapped; a gurgling noise emerged from his throat. As the staff of the Splendid Urn cried out in alarm, he toppled backward and fell to the ground, unmoving.

Soon, the four best doctors in the neighborhood were summoned. One felt the comatose head chef's pulse with two fingers, looking thoughtful with his eyes shut; another listened to his heart and lungs with a bamboo trumpet; the third poked him with needles; and the last applied shocks to his hands and feet with Ogé jars.

This last diagnostic technique managed to awaken the head chef, who sputtered incoherently and hissed at anyone who dared to approach him. Soon, he was running about and bumping into walls, babbling all the while, "Impossible! Doomed!"

"My learned colleague has the touch of Rufizo!" exclaimed the doctor who liked quick pulses.

"What an amazing recovery!" blurted the doctor with the bamboo trumpet.

"Say, where did you get those jars?" asked the doctor with the needles, looking rather forlornly at his own outdated instruments. (Kinri actually had the same question. He knew almost nothing about silkmotic devices and was keen to find out more.)

"This isn't helpful at all," complained Lodan. "He's scaring everyone. We asked you to wake him, not make him raving mad. We need him to strategize! Do something!"

The four medical professionals conferred and agreed to go to an herbalist in the market. They returned with a packet of herbs, which they brewed into a bitter concoction. While Mati held the head chef's flailing arms, the four doctors directed Lodan to force the liquid down the head chef's throat with a funnel.

The head chef fell back into a deep sleep.

"Err . . ." said the doctor with the Ogé jars, "our fee?"

"We're right back where we started, and you want to be paid?" asked an incredulous Widow Wasu.

"Honored Grand Mistress," said the doctor with the Ogé jars, "is it not the case that after a customer has consumed one of your meals, he is hungry again six hours later? Is he not, as you put it, right back where he started? Do you think you should not be paid?"

"With that wagging tongue," muttered Widow Wasu, "you should be a paid litigator instead. At least give us a real diagnosis."

The doctors conferred again. "Delirium due to terror" was the consensus opinion, possibly the result of "overwork." The four competitors-cum-colleagues collected their fee from Widow Wasu and assured the Grand Mistress that her head chef would make a full recovery in time, though he would need plenty of rest during the next few weeks and should not be anywhere near the kitchen.

"I could have told them that myself!" said Widow Wasu. "Is it any wonder that people avoid going to the doctor's? All they do is prod you with their shiny toys and demand to be paid for their pleasure. Ah, may the Twins protect us."

Mati, as the most senior sous-chef, was now put in charge of the competition in a week. Looking terrified, she immediately canceled dinner service and took the senior staff with her to the Great Temple of Lutho to pray for good fortune. After giving Mati some extra money for incense at the temple, Widow Wasu secluded herself in her room to try to recover from the shock of this stroke of bad luck. The rest of the staff sat around the customerless tables, whispering in hushed voices and looking at one another with worried eyes. The Splendid Urn now had the look of a city under siege.

Since no one was telling him what to do, Kinri, rather puzzled by everyone's sudden loss of confidence, came into the street in front of the restaurant to escape the oppressive atmosphere inside.

He found the Blossom Gang waiting for him.

"What's with the hubbub?" asked Rati Yera, the old woman with the magical cart. "Everyone's running around like chickens with their heads chopped off. We thought we'd wait around to thank Mati and Lodan for hosting us, but they never even stopped as they ran by."

Kinri quickly explained what had happened.

"Did you say the Hutos have hired Mozo Mu as their head chef?" asked Rati.

Kinri nodded.

"Ah—" "Oh—" "Hmm—" "Aiya!"

Kinri looked at the four in consternation. Maybe they could explain to him what had so frightened Néfi and Mati.

*"Who exactly is this Mozo Mu?"*

That was indeed the question Kinri wanted to ask, but he couldn't figure out how his voice had suddenly turned so mellifluous. And . . . he was sure he hadn't spoken yet.

All five turned to the source of the question and saw the mysterious young woman Kinri and burly Mota Kiphi had rescued at Temple Square. But in contrast to the opulent outfit she'd worn on the day of her arrival, she was now sporting a decidedly more down-to-earth look: plain flaxen dress with a straw rope for a belt; no jewelry save for a few dandelions tucked into the rabbit-ear buns over her head.

Given how much respect Widow Wasu had shown the young woman, Kinri immediately bowed deeply. "Mistress . . . um—" Kinri felt strange calling her "Dandelion," which didn't seem like a real name at all.

"Didn't I tell you to just call me Dandelion? No 'Mistress'!" said the young woman impatiently. "What's wrong with people in Ginpen? Everyone at the teahouse was bowing and smiling and addressing me as 'Honored Mistress,' even though I'm dressed like a kitchen maid! How am I supposed to have any fun and hear all the good gossip?"

Arona, the actress, tried but didn't quite succeed in suppressing a chuckle.

"What's so funny?" asked Dandelion, her eyes narrowed suspiciously.

"You look like a scullery maid about as much as I look like the Empress of Dara right now," said Arona.

"What?" said an incredulous Dandelion. "I bought this dress from the kitchen maid sent to take care of me. And I saw plenty of country girls put wildflowers in their hair. I even painted these on!" She pointed at the streaks of soot on her cheeks. "My costume is *completely* authentic."

Arona burst out in laughter. And the rest of the Blossom Gang joined in.

Only Kinri didn't laugh. He didn't want to hurt Dandelion's feelings. He knew that she didn't look right as a maid, but he couldn't quite explain why.

"You're a terrible actress," said Arona, when she managed to get herself back under control. "I . . . oh, by Lutho's carapace, I haven't seen such a bad disguise in ages."

Instead of getting angry, Dandelion held up her hands in a sup- plicating gesture. "Please, big sister, teach me how to do this better!"

Back in Pan, Prince Gimoto had grown even more insolent, put- ting on airs as though it was only a matter of time before Empress Jia declared Phyro unfit to govern and made *him* the heir to the Dandelion Throne. At one of the palace tea parties, he lectured Fara about her habit of flirting with the young scholars of the College of Advocates and going to the theater with Aya to see ribald plays.

"It's indecorous for an Imperial princess to behave this way," he said, his features hardened in sententious disapproval. "You really need to reflect upon the wisdom of the sages and your duties as a role model for all the young noble ladies of the capital. Now, I can recommend several passages from Kon Fiji—"

"Who do you think you are?" said an incensed Fara. "You're not my father—"

"When the father isn't with the family, the eldest brother must step into his shoes," intoned Gimoto, quoting the Moralist adage piously. "If your brother is as neglectful of his private duty to instruct his younger sister as he is of his public duty as the sovereign-in-waiting, then I have no choice but to step up and do his job."

Oh, Fara would have liked to scratch his eyes out at that moment. But she knew blowing up publicly at him would only allow him to claim victory. Ever since she had vowed to stop meddling in politics, she had devoted herself to the theater, her art, and having fun. She wasn't going to let him spoil her mood.

So she retreated from that confrontation meekly. But then she asked one of the servants to gather some dead flies from the toilet stalls, which she dropped into Gimoto's teapot when he wasn't look- ing. For the rest of the evening, she smiled at him sweetly, pretend- ing to hang on his every word, as he consumed the oddly fragrant beverage.

She thought she would just stay out of his way in the future. But as the Adüans would say, *While the aspen wishes to stand still, the wind does not stop.*

Pleased with how compliantly Fara had submitted to him, Gimoto proceeded to write a petition to the empress listing all the ways Fara was "bringing disrepute to the Imperial name" and suggesting that he be appointed her tutor.

Empress Jia ignored the petition, but a scandal nonetheless erupted, with everyone tittering behind Fara's back. And when Fara wrote to Phyro and Zomi to gripe, instead of lending a sympathetic ear, they wrote back to censure her for "leading Aya astray."

Everyone was telling her what she must not do; Fara felt very alone in the world.

Only Lady Soto was supportive. "Your father would have understood you. He hated people like Gimoto too," she said. "Maybe you should try living away from the palace for a while."

Jia agreed to her request to go away from Pan, but only if she stayed in the care of someone she trusted. Fara begged Aya, who had just gotten her first military command, to take her to Ginpen and promised to be good.

She hoped that away from the rage-inducing presence of Gimoto, she would also be free from the frustrations and heartaches of being a daughter of the House of Dandelion. She was going to have a grand adventure and do things that Imperial Princess Fara never got to do.

Since Gimoto had wielded her status as a princess over her like a ferule, the more someone treated her as a "regular person," the more pleased Dandelion became. She took an instant liking to Arona.

"I swear I'll listen to you!" she pleaded. "What am I doing wrong?"

Arona composed herself and tried to look serious. She counted off on her fingers. "First of all, that dress is too clean. It might look plain to you, but it's the maid's temple-attending dress, and no one goes to a teahouse like that. Second, you're wearing those dandelions the same way noblewomen wear jeweled hairpins—in artfully arranged clusters, as though they're made of jade and precious stones. How are you supposed to get any work done in the kitchen if you wear your hair in such a fussy style? Third, you applied those bits of soot like makeup, with blending and balance—"

"I couldn't help it—" muttered Dandelion.

"You're obviously the daughter of a prominent family—no need to tell me who you are; I'm sure you have your reasons for wanting to keep your identity a secret. We who make a living in the turbulent sea that we call society all have our own secrets and respect the secrets of others."

"So if I fix my hair and get a dirtier dress, I'll be good?"

Arona shook her head. "No, no, no. Dress and makeup are the *least* important parts of a disguise. The biggest giveaway is the way you carry yourself and speak. First, there's your accent. Oi. I've known girls who, after years of elocution lessons, couldn't sound half as fancy as you."

Dandelion blushed self-consciously. "I . . . I could try to talk like my aunt—my mother's . . . maids. How's this? 'Mistress, what is your next command?' Was that better?"

"Better, but now you sound like you're from northern Faça," said Arona. "I thought your family was from Pan."

"Err . . . that's a long story. . . ."

To Kinri, Dandelion's regular accent actually sounded a lot like Widow Wasu's. This was no surprise, as the elevated accent of the Dandelion Court was based on the topolect of Central Cocru, where both Kuni Garu and Widow Wasu had grown up. But Kinri, not having been brought up in Dara proper, couldn't tell that Dandelion's accent showed the results of almost two decades of refinement the topolect had undergone in Pan. Certainly no one was going to call Widow Wasu's speech "fancy."

"I think you speak beautifully," blurted Kinri. He didn't like seeing Dandelion flustered. For some reason, he was blushing as much as Dandelion. He struggled to find some words to comfort her. "You sound like . . . like . . . the sun through the spiderweb in the morning, you know, with drops of dew . . . or . . . or like the Curved Mirrors of old Haan . . . glowing with the light of a thousand flames—"

Dandelion blushed even deeper and looked very annoyed. "Are you trying to say I sound like a fire-breathing spiderweb? Thanks a lot!"

"No, no! I just meant—"

The Blossom Gang laughed.

"Not sure you have much of a future as either a poet or a lover, kid," said Arona with a smirk. She patted Kinri on the arm before turning back to Dandelion. "Show me how you walked into that teahouse."

Dandelion took a deep breath to calm herself. Uncertain what was expected of her, she pretended to step through the door of a busy teahouse. She strode up to an imaginary table, sat down in *mipa rari*, and called out, "A dish of cored fresh lotus seeds, all flavors, and a pot of your best floral tea—but hold the osmanthus. Oh, wild honey and cacanut shavings if you have them." She deliberately tried to imitate Arona's own earthier accent.

Arona sighed. "You move about like you're used to having everyone get out of your way, and your tone tells me you're accustomed to being obeyed. Let's not even get started on your order—wanting cored fresh lotus seeds in *this* season . . . of course everyone at the teahouse knew you were a noblewoman out in common garb to have some fun."

"Ah . . ." said Dandelion, her face a deep crimson. "I had no idea there was so much to the art of disguise."

"You assume disguise is a matter of makeup and clothes, but that's the wrong way to think about it. A disguise is a role, and to inhabit the role, you must have a story."

Dandelion's eyes lit up at this. "I like stories. I can do stories."

Arona nodded. "When we put on a play, Mota and I have to construct stories for each of our characters: What does she want? How did he get here? Why is she speaking this way? When did he learn that trick?"

"That sounds like a lot of work." Dandelion bit her bottom lip. "And a lot of memorization."

"Acting *is* a lot of work," said Arona. "But memorization actually isn't the most important skill. Do you think Mota and I memorize all our lines? No. The audience for each of our performances is different, and we have to improvise based on the reactions of the crowd. When you play a role for a disguise, you must also be ready to adapt as conditions around you change. We don't write our plays out with inflexible logograms or dead letters; and neither should you memorize a set of canned answers."

Kinri found the discussion fascinating. The way Arona talked about the folk plays sounded a lot like how the shamans back home spoke of storytelling dances.

"Thank you for explaining, Mistress Taré," said Dandelion. "Maybe . . . you can be my teacher?"

The actress smiled. " 'Arona' will do. As for being your teacher . . . I fear that you are too high a branch for me to dare to perch on. However, I'm happy to give you a few pointers here and there. We all have to start somewhere. You've got potential if you are humble and want to learn."

"Thank you," said Dandelion, looking genuinely pleased. Then she seemed to remember why she had jumped into this conversation in the first place. "But . . . I want to hear all about this Mozo Mu. What manner of monster is he? Why's everyone so afraid of him?"

"Mozo Mu is the great-great-great-great-grandchild of Suda Mu, the greatest cook in all the Islands of Dara," said Widi Tucru, the litigator.

Long ago, when the Seven States schemed and fought against one another across land, air, and sea, the Tiro kings had not limited their competition to mere contests of arms, but also vied for dominance in every realm of art and culture.

With lavish gifts and promises of free rein to their visionary impulses, the Tiro kings recruited to their service scholars, artisans, artists, poets, tinkerers, and mystics and philosophers of every stripe. The Islands blossomed with a sudden burst of legendary creative thinkers in the last days of the Tiro states era, before the Xana Conquest.

Stories concerning the exploits of great philosophers like Gi Anji and his students, Tan Féuji and Lügo Crupo, crisscrossing the Islands and offering their services to whichever Tiro king was most willing to reshape the world according to their vision, were well known. But this was also the time of the great swordsman Médo, who taught Dazu Zyndu, the Hegemon's grandfather; the peerless bladesmith Suma Ji, who forged Na-aroénna; and Kino Ye, the Xana scholar-official who was willing to commit sacrilege to discover the secret of Mingén falcon flight, leading to the invention of the airships.

The Tiro kings competed even in fields such as music, architecture, painting, calligraphy—an extravagant palace built to monumental dimensions filled with imposing, never-before-seen artwork and soul-shattering music was seen as a direct reflection of the power and virtue of the king.

Xana, being at a remote distance from the other Tiro states and less wealthy, could not quite compete at the same level in traditional arts. Therefore, the kings of Xana sought to distinguish themselves in another realm: the culinary arts.

The court at Kriphi became, in the days when King Réon (the future Mapidéré) was but a mere babe, *the* destination for those who wished to explore beyond the known map of tastes into terra incognita. The master chefs employed by Xana were the first to systematically compile ancient recipes scattered in various worm-ridden scrolls and to evaluate their efficacy. They were also the first to attempt to cook the gigantic deep-sea-trench crabs, each the size of a full-grown man (steaming and frying both turned out to be good methods, after removal of the deadly poison found in the gills) and the minuscule wormglow truffle hearts, which were found deep underground and could only be safely consumed after the fungi had been eaten by rooting pigs and the bitter outer layer removed by passage through their digestive system. These culinary explorers dispatched ships to the remotest isles beyond Dasu and expeditions to the pristine, uninhabited valleys of Crescent Island to find exotic animals, plants, fungi, insects, fishes, spices, and even minerals that yielded new tastes. For a time, the Moralist philosophers working for other Tiro kings said, half in mockery and half in admiration, *Xana co i pha rétuthu ro ülo i copoüré phin mon ogi né loteré i rate, kinsén üçaü co ki mon ogi né loteré i ratedagira* ("The kings of Xana eat everything with four legs except tables and devour everything with two legs except humans").

The greatest of these Xana royal chefs was Suda Mu, a native of Haan. Mu had traveled around the Islands for thirty years to study the distinctive cuisine of each region of Dara before entering royal service, where he proceeded to fuse the best techniques from all the Tiro states. He distinguished himself not only by imagining inventive new dishes and boldly executing them, but also by elevating the ancient craft of fine cuisine into a true art.

"Mere cooks focus on taste alone," he said. "But great chefs are the only artists who engage all five senses."

His principles could be illustrated by one of his signature dishes: scorched rice cakes served with a variety of stews. Scorched rice, which formed as a crust against the bottom and sides of the pot when boiling rice over high heat, was a highly textured, crunchy substrate with a light toasted flavor that could be enhanced with a variety of sauces. In fact, when colorful sauces were poured over the dry scorched rice cakes, the rice snapped, crackled, and popped, both creating music and dispersing the sauce's aromas into the air, leading to a true feast of sensual delights for the diner.

Fine cooking in Dara had long subscribed to Yeruçado Maaji's Moralist dictum that it was uncouth to name the ingredients in a dish. A man of learning and virtue consumed the wondrous results from the kitchen but did not sully his mind with thoughts of bloody or raw ingredients, knives, dirty grease, or the hard labor of mere menials. Thus, every dish needed a poetic and allusive name. Suda Mu's scorched rice was therefore called "Stormy Dara."

Visitors to the Xana court who had the good fortune of sampling this legendary dish left with breathless accounts and poems celebrating its wonders. Gi Anji, who visited in his youth, wrote the following in his book of essays, *Pilgrim Among the Waves*:

*A deep blue jade platter was set before each of us in the Great Hall, the cerulean rectangle a representation of the endless sea. On it sat scorched rice cakes cut and sculpted in the shapes of the Islands of Dara. A servant knelt next to me with a tray filled with various stews. As I pointed my eating sticks at each scorched rice island, the servant ladled the sauce corresponding to that region over the cakes: fruitful Faça's lamb stew with dried monkeyberries; gleaming Gan's shark's fin soup flavored with seven types of fish and shellfish; castled Cocru's hearty vegetable medley, with bamboo shoots cut to resemble spear points; alluring Amu's fragrant lotus-seed mélange, where each seed is cored and filled with a different berry or* melon; high-minded Haan's turtle egg jumble, with bits of coconut carved to resemble augurs' oracle bones; ring-wooded Rima's mushroom pie, with pine nuts and wild roots cut in the shape of its legendary blades; and zealous Xana's poultry hash, garnished with wildflowers cut in the shapes of bird wings.

As each spoonful of sauce was poured over the scorched rice cakes, distinctive music arose from each part of the platter: spring rain beating against a thatched roof, pounding surf against a cliff-hung shore, rich grains of sorghum clattering against the threshing tray, rattling divination sticks and chips in an incense-shrouded temple, charcoal snapping in the bright flames of a forge, children chattering in a busy marketplace of floating platforms and flat-bottomed boats, bubbles popping in the pristine waters of Lake Dako. . . .

The Islands cracked, snapped, broke apart as the sauces soaked into the scorched rice, signaling cataclysmic changes that aroused our curiosity as well as our hunger. . . .

It was a painting richer in color than the work of jaded portraitists in money-blinded Dimushi, a symphony more pleasing than the vulgar din generated by the orchestras of traveling folk opera troupes, a tapestry of sensations and textures against the tongue more varied than the smooth silks and rough hempen clothes and nubbly woolen yarns found in Boama, a potpourri of aromas more intoxicating than the famed medicine shops of Çaruza, and a parade of tastes each more astounding than the last, a feast for the senses fit for the gods.

Later, after I retired to my guest room, I realized that this was the perfect dish for the Xana court. As each island disappeared into the chomping maw of the Xana king, he was enacting a gustatory metaphor for the boundless ambition of Kriphi. If anyone had doubts as to the danger of a rising Xana, they only had to come and share a meal—

"See, you have to know when to stop a story," Dandelion broke in. "You had a good setup and used allusions well, but going on too long will bore the audience."

Widi chuckled. "I appreciate the feedback. I take it Miss Dandelion is a connoisseur of stories?"

"I happen to have a keen interest in folktales and legends," said

Dandelion, declining to elaborate. "But how do you know so much about the history of cooking anyway? Did you also want to open your own restaurant?"

Rati and Arona laughed. "Widi's interest in food is purely from the consumption side," Arona said, her tone teasing but affectionate. "Though he's incapable of even frying an egg without burning it, he can describe for you in detail the one hundred and one ways to cook an egg in the culinary manuals of the old Cocru kings while wiping his drool."

"We all have our talents," said Widi, looking not at all embarrassed. "My talent happens to be art appreciation and criticism rather than creation."

"I'll give you this: You sure know how to talk up an appetite." Dandelion licked her lips and swallowed.

"My tongue is as skilled at talking as it is at tasting," said Widi. "Whereas the common orchid offers up a thousand sweet fragrances, I can conjure up ten thousand mouthwatering aromas—"

"All right! I get the picture. Where can I taste this Stormy Dara?"

"Alas, when King Dézan began his wars of conquest in earnest, Suda Mu destroyed all his recipe books, left Xana with his family, and retired to a hut in the Damu Mountains to live as a hermit. Stormy Dara was lost to history."

"No one knows how to make it anymore?" exclaimed Kinri. He felt an inexplicable sadness at hearing such a beautiful thing being lost forever.

"Well, maybe *someone* does," said Widi mysteriously. "After Suda Mu retired, many chefs visited his hut in the mountains, begging to be taught his secret recipes. In order to be left in peace, he swore an oath that he would never take a student who wasn't related to him by blood or marriage, and forbade his descendants from teaching anyone else either."

"I love stories like this!" Dandelion clapped her hands together excitedly. "Secret recipes! Mountain hermits! Vows to tie knowledge to blood. It's like a real-life folk opera."

Widi nodded. "It *is* a rather dramatic tale. There's a shrine in the Damu Mountains dedicated to the spirit of Suda Mu, and great chefs and restaurateurs continue to make pilgrimages there to pray for the master's blessing. The descendants of Suda Mu, however, continued to live in seclusion, and though many kings and nobles tried to entice them to come out and cook for them, no one has ever succeeded. Eventually, people just gave up."

"But now the Hutos have somehow managed to entice the seventh-generation descendant of the master chef to work for them," said Kinri, finally understanding. "I guess that must be why Chef Ézugo was terrified."

The four in the Blossom Gang nodded. Widi said, "I don't blame him. Imagine going up against a descendant of the renowned creator of Stormy Dara, the only one who knows all his secrets! That must be like a swordsman realizing he's about to duel with a fighter trained personally by the Hegemon."

"But who's to say that just because he bears the Mu name, he'd be any good at cooking?" asked Dandelion. "I've known . . . people like that. It's a lot of pressure to live under."

"Well, it is said that a cruben begets a cruben, a dyran begets a dyran, and an octopus's daughter can crack eight oysters at the same time," said Widi. "Considering Suda Mu's descendants have nothing to do up there in that mountain except practice recipes passed down the generations, I imagine they are all very skilled. Although no one has seen this Mozo Mu, rumors say that the Mu family considers him the greatest chef since Suda Mu. Even if he can't quite attain the heights of his illustrious ancestor, he'll be at least pretty good at replicating the legendary dishes."

"I just don't buy that theory," said Dandelion. "Skills don't pass down by blood alone. There's no point in being frightened by a reputation without testing out the substance behind it."

"Ah, so you're a believer in 'weighing the fish,'" said Widi. "I think we're going to get along very well."

Dandelion laughed. She had heard Zomi say that more than once. It was nice to hear such a familiar phrase among strangers.

"But how do we weigh the fish here?" she asked. "The Treasure Chest isn't open yet, so we can't judge Mozo Mu's cooking for ourselves."

No one raised an eyebrow at her use of the plural pronoun. Without realizing it, the Blossom Gang and Kinri were already treating her as one of them.

"You do pose an interesting question," said Widi. "But there may be more than one way to hook a fish—"

"I don't know what you're talking about," said Kinri, getting impatient with all this talk about fishing. "But I'm not going to sit by and watch my friends and benefactors at the Splendid Urn fret and worry over illusions. I'm going to sneak into the Treasure Chest and find out just what they're planning to cook for the competition."

The others looked at one another. "Err . . . just how do you plan on doing that?" asked Widi cautiously.

"I haven't thought that far," said Kinri, scratching his head. "I was just going to go to their restaurant and then figure out the next step."

"Are you always so impulsive?" asked Arona. "You do realize that the Hutos must have planned against spying from the Splendid Urn. They're one of the richest families in the Islands, and I'm sure they've hired plenty of mercenaries to guard their secrets."

"Things will work out. I jumped up to grab the reins of that panicked horse without knowing what I was going to do either."

While Mota grinned, Widi, Arona, and Rati laughed aloud.

"I like you, young man," said Rati. She tapped her fingers on the arms of the wheeled chair decisively. "I think we'll come along and help you."

"You will? Then you'll be saving the Urn a second time! I don't know how to thank you."

"Don't thank us until we succeed. Besides, a chance to learn the secret recipes of the greatest chef in history? We who hunger after knowledge wouldn't miss it for the world."

"Hey, don't forget me!" said Dandelion. Since her older siblings used to ditch her in the palace while they snuck out to have fun, she was extra sensitive to the possibility of being left out.

"Um, I don't think the Grand Mistress would like that—" began Kinri. He didn't think it was a good idea to bring along the daughter of some powerful family that even Widow Wasu seemed to defer to.

Besides, he didn't want to see her in any kind of danger, though just how dangerous could it be to go to a restaurant—

"Don't argue with me," said Dandelion imperiously, reverting to her courtly accent. "I am *not* letting another adventure go by without being part of it."

All Ginpen was abuzz with news of the contest between the Huto clan and the Wasu clan for the title of Best Restaurant in Ginpen. Honor and profit were both at stake.

As Tiphan Huto's trading successes grew, he wanted to expand into new lines of business, both to cement his reputation as the leader of the clan's next generation as well as to have a way to launder his rising profits from the illicit collaboration with pirates.

He settled on opening a restaurant in Ginpen. In this city of learning, high-class restaurants not only made a lot of money, but also served as venues for elite gatherings. In good restaurants, officials and scholars entertained friends, potential political allies, and business associates. He was certain that the information skimmed from overheard conversations among the customers would be of great value, both to him and his pirate partners.

The original plan had been to ruin the reputation of the Splendid Urn before the grand opening of the Treasure Chest, thereby creating a vacuum at the top that his restaurant could fill. The Blossom Gang, unfortunately, had quite ruined that plot.

It didn't matter. Through a judicious and selective recounting of his experience at the Splendid Urn, Tiphan Huto managed to convince all the elders of the Huto clan that what had happened to him was not merely a personal insult, but an attempt by upstart provincials from Zudi to challenge the supremacy of one of the oldest trading families in all the Islands. There was only one response possible: to absolutely crush Widow Wasu at her best business.

And with Mozo Mu as the Treasure Chest's head chef, victory was assured.

Tiphan Huto chuckled to himself as he admired his own boldness. The Treasure Chest, smelling of fresh paint and sawdust, was filled with workers and servants rushing about to get everything ready for the grand opening. He swaggered his way out of the building, intent on treating himself to an evening at the best indigo house in Ginpen.

How he was going to enjoy watching Widow Wasu and her arrogant servants grovel for mercy!

"So *that's* our competition," said Kinri.

The Treasure Chest was a five-story tower with sweeping roofs and wide-open balconies. From bottom to top, the relief carvings on the exterior friezes for the first four floors emphasized in turn one of the four elements. The ground floor represented the Realm of Fire, full of ferocious demons and toothy firebirds, as well as blind moles and worms gnawing on veins of gold and silver; the second floor was the Realm of Water, where fish, whales, crabs, and shrimp waged war from ramparts constructed of coral over chests overflowing with treasure; the third floor was the Realm of Earth, filled with peaceful bamboo groves and blooming orchid-laden boughs inhabited by colorful songbirds and cuddly furry creatures; the fourth floor was the Realm of Air, where wild geese and Mingén falcons flew in intricate patterns that presaged good fortune and health for the diners.

Around the top floor, the frieze showed immortals dining in fanciful palaces among the clouds and on the moon. This was where the most important customers would host their banquets and reserve private suites to entertain guests with music, dancing, riddle parties, and games of charades. On each corner of the upswept roof stood the statue of an ancient Ano sage: Kon Fiji lecturing from atop a roofless carriage, Ra Oji riding on his water buffalo, Poti Maji composing a book with a writing knife and a block of wax, Aruano the lawgiver drawing a map with a sword.

A large crowd gathered in the street, admiring the building.

"I think those veins are made of actual gold and silver!"

"Are those pearls in the centers of the orchids?"

"By Tazu! That coral must be the real thing."

. . .

"Well, the Hutos certainly know how to construct a temple to extravagance," said Rati Yera, leaning forward in her wheeled chair. "I feel richer just by looking at it."

"I can see why someone might pick this place to give a banquet over the Splendid Urn," said Widi.

Kinri looked a bit dejected.

"It's a little gaudy, in my opinion," said Dandelion, wrinkling her nose.

Kinri gave her a grateful smile, but she wasn't looking at him. He berated himself for not focusing on the task at hand. *What's wrong with me?*

"Let's figure out how to get inside," said Kinri. "It's not open for business yet, so we can't just walk in as customers."

Indeed, the doors and windows of the tower were shuttered, and it was impossible to see inside.

"Looks like that's where they're bringing in supplies," said Arona, pointing to the back of the tower.

Behind the tower was a wall-enclosed yard, where the stables, kitchen, and living quarters for the managers and staff were presumably located. In the wall was a gate through which passed a constant stream of oxcarts piled high with goods.

"They're pretty careful with the security of the place," said Widi.

The carts were all covered by large sheets of canvas that made it impossible to tell what exactly the cargo was. Guards at the gate asked the drivers for documents and pulled up the canvas to examine the goods before letting them in.

"Is there no way in then?" asked Kinri. This was turning out to be harder than he expected.

"Trust us, there's no vault or fortress that can stop the Blossom Gang," boasted Widi.

"Certainly not when delicious food is involved," said Dandelion. "I've seen you swallow your drool at least three times during the last minute. Maybe you can eat your way through the wall like a termite."

Arona giggled as Widi looked wounded.

"They built this place so quickly," said Kinri. His interest in Dara construction and machinery was piqued. "I wonder how they did it."

"If you're willing to throw money at a problem, a lot of them become not problems," said Rati. "I just hope they didn't take shortcuts. All that paint and gold leaf won't help if the frame is rotten."

"Wait!" said Kinri. "I have an idea!"

As the Blossom Gang and Dandelion gathered about him, Kinri explained his plan.

"Look at you," said Dandelion. "I thought you were the honest type, but this idea is rather deceptive. . . ." Her admiring tone, however, belied the censorious words.

"When you're dealing with a man like Tiphan Huto," said a grinning Arona, "deception *is* honesty. He already surveilled the Splendid Urn, so it's only fair for us to spy on the Treasure Chest."

"I think this just might work," said Widi. "But we'll need some preparation and a bit of . . . extra funds."

"I can buy you whatever you need," said Dandelion. "This is going to be *fun!*"

The guards at the gate of the Treasure Chest compound watched with interest as a sumptuous palanquin stopped next to the queue of oxcarts waiting to be inspected.

A *toko dawiji* walking next to the palanquin pulled open the curtain and bowed deferentially as a manservant and a maid helped a government official out of the palanquin and seated her in a wheeled chair.

"Banquets, banquets! All I've been doing every day since arriving in Ginpen is going to banquets. At least young Kita seems to know what he's doing . . ." the official, a distinguished-looking woman in her seventies, muttered.

The sharp-eared guards looked at one another. Could the old woman be talking about Archon Kita Thu, the head of the Imperial laboratories here in Ginpen? Her tone seemed to imply that Kita Thu was of a much lower rank compared to her. If so, she must be a very important person indeed.

A young woman who had been walking next to the palanquin— likely a high-ranking official herself, judging by her expensive water-silk dress and the jade-handled writing knife on her belt— approached the two guards, a *toko dawiji* following two steps behind with his head bowed submissively toward her. Paying no attention at all to the long line of oxcarts, the two cut right in front of a driver who was about to show the guards his papers.

"Do you have the agenda for the inspection?" the younger official demanded. Based on her crisp, courtly accent, the guards guessed she was either a highborn lady from Pan or at least had spent plenty of time at court to pick up the prestige topolect. Her imperious attitude made both possibilities equally likely.

"What inspection?" one of the guards asked in confusion.

He was still a bit unused to dealing with women officials and clerks. High-minded Haan, where learning was most revered, had long resisted Emperor Ragin's call for women to enter the civil service. While daughters of Haan were traditionally also taught to read the Ano Classics and compose in logograms, the purpose of such education was to make them good conversationalists during courtship and give them the wherewithal to help their husbands' careers later, not so they could make and execute official policy or run businesses independently.

But that didn't mean that the natives of Haan were spared women magistrates and bureaucrats from elsewhere. Empress Jia had continued the tradition begun by Mapidéré of dispatching officials who had qualified for civil service through the Imperial examinations across all Dara, regardless of their geographical origins. Not only did this prevent the kind of corruption and resistance to central rule that came from reliance on local elites and nobles to govern in each region, but it also promoted a sense among the literati of belonging to a single empire-wide elite. Magistrates and other officials were frequently transferred from one end of the empire to another to forestall them from forming factions and putting down roots among the local gentry. The empress and Prime Minister Cogo Yelu spoke often of an ideal bureaucracy that functioned efficiently based on roles in the system rather than who was occupying which role at that moment.

"Surely Magistrate Zuda told you to expect an inspection from Circuit Intendant Suti?" the young official asked impatiently. When the guards responded with blank looks, she gave them a withering stare. "Do you at least have the compliance paperwork? No? Nothing? Don't tell me you haven't been preparing at all? What have you been doing for the last week? Where's Tiphan Huto? He's going to have to answer for this—"

The guards felt like baby chicks dodging hailstones under this barrage of questions. This woman was clearly used to being obeyed. If the ground would split open now and present a crack wide enough, they would have happily jumped into it to avoid her.

The *toko dawiji*, evidently a bureaucrat of much lower rank, timidly approached. "Assistant Circuit Intendant Dadéluon, please don't let a little error by fools disturb your most sagacious tranquility. Would you allow me to speak to these mere menials?"

The young official harrumphed, swept her long sleeves abruptly through the air dismissively, and went back to the senior official in the wheeled chair. The two women whispered at each other, shaking their heads now and then as they looked disdainfully at the Treasure Chest.

The *toko dawiji* turned to the guards, an ingratiating smile on his face. "Masters, we're all just trying to do our jobs, right? I know this isn't your fault. Call me Diwi, and know that I'm in the same boat. As one of Magistrate Zuda's junior clerks, I've been assigned to take care of the circuit intendant." He put on a long-suffering look and wiped his sweaty brow. Then he whispered, "Between you and me, it's been rough."

The guards instantly felt a sense of camaraderie with this Diwi. Unlike the assistant circuit intendant, who was likely too highborn and highbred to understand the plight of the commoners, the liaison knew what it was like to be a working stiff dependent on the whims of higher-ups for that monthly salary. Considering Diwi was already in his forties and still working as a junior clerk, obviously he was stuck in a dead-end position and just trying to make it day to day without upsetting the boat.

"I can tell neither of those are easy cats to pet," said one of the guards sympathetically, jutting his chin at the circuit intendant and the assistant circuit intendant.

"Right you are," said Diwi. "They just arrived from Pan,

demanding this and that from Magistrate Zuda like mini empresses. Their charge is to inspect prominent local establishments to ensure they are compliant with Imperial codes regarding fire prevention, food safety, adequacy of drainage and hygiene, and so forth."

The guards looked at the old official in the wheeled chair and noticed the subtle stylized scales and fish embroidered into her robe. Now everything was falling into place. She was a farseer.

Empress Jia's chief innovation upon the system of bureaucracy across the Islands of Dara during her time as regent was the system of circuit intendants. These were generally junior officials selected from the College of Advocates and then sent around the Islands to ride circuit, investigating how local officials were carrying out Imperial decrees.

Zomi Kidosu, as a former advocate herself, had convinced the empress that the bureaucracy could not be relied on to watch itself. Since the advocates' primary responsibility was to attack policy proposals at court in an effort to discover potential pitfalls prior to implementation, it was natural to extend this duty to the post-implementation phase. Since their chances at being promoted were directly linked to the number of faults they could find with local officials, they owed their authority and allegiance directly to the Throne, and not to the tangled web of influence and power formed by the governors, magistrates, and their staff. Their incentive was aligned with promoting accountability in the vast bureaucracy.

Jia, of course, also saw Zomi's proposal as at least partially directed against Cogo Yelu. As the head of the Imperial bureaucracy, Cogo's power was great, and his refusal to support Phyro's push for war irked both Zomi and Phyro. Still, the empress saw a healthy amount of competition and mutual suspicion among her senior advisers as a good thing, so long as the rivalry promoted better governance.

After all, it was Empress Jia's habit to quote the adage, attributed to the Incentivist Lügo Crupo, *Sétolu pha, mocru co sétolu ça ago i ruüré cruthé i rucrudaéthu ingro ki thiéfi i dorathalo rofi ki nafé gipifi ki cathunés-moa*, or, in the vernacular, "A servant will only be honest when it profits another servant to catch him in a lie." This same principle had also finally convinced the empress to reintroduce the profession of paid litigators to give the common people an avenue to combat official abuse of power and corruption.

But the advocates, being relatively junior in rank and inexperienced with the many tricks that bureaucrats had developed over the centuries to promote their own interest, could not ferret out all instances of corruption. For this reason, Zomi suggested that Empress Jia also appoint, from time to time, special circuit intendants drawn from the ranks of the farseers. These professional spies had a great deal more investigative power and authority to mete out punishments to straying bureaucrats, and mere mention of them was enough to drain the blood from the faces of many magistrates.

"Magistrate Zuda should have sent a notice to your master a week ago, explaining that he should be expecting an inspection," said Diwi.

"I swear by all Lord Tazu's jewels that we don't know anything about an inspection," said one of the guards. "All we know is that Master Huto told us not to allow anyone in unless they're on the approved list and carrying exactly what the list says they should be carrying."

"Can't you summon Master Huto?"

"I would, but he's out."

"That's unfortunate," said Diwi, wiping the sweat from his brow again and struggling to keep his voice from shaking. "There must be a mix-up somewhere, but now that the circuit intendant is here, we've got to make this inspection happen." Diwi lowered his voice even further. "For both our bosses' sakes."

The guards examined the delegation again in light of the new information. The maid and the manservant pushing Circuit Intendant Suti's chair were obviously just hired help. Besides Circuit Intendant Suti, arrogant Assistant Circuit Intendant Dadéluon, and nervous Diwi, the only other member of the delegation worthy of notice was the powerfully built young man who hadn't said anything yet. He must be Suti's bodyguard and enforcer—probably a farseer himself and allowed to apply extraordinary interrogation techniques (still rumored to be legal for the dreaded farseers) to anyone who stood in the circuit intendant's way.

Listening between the lines, the guards understood from Diwi there was much pressure on Magistrate Zuda, which meant the magistrate expected their master, Tiphan Huto, to protect the magistrate's behind and assure these inspectors from the capital that there were no code violations at the Treasure Chest, the biggest private construction project approved by the magistrate.

The guards cursed under their breath that Tiphan had chosen this time to be away.

"Surely Master Huto would understand?" whispered one of the guards to the other.

The other guard nodded. "We're just trying to help him."

Shouting at the oxcart drivers to get out of the way, the two guards bowed deeply and invited Circuit Intendant Suti and her retinue to come right in and make themselves at home.

"I'd call that a pretty good bit of acting," said Dandelion, her nose turned up proudly. "Did you see how those guards scrambled at my word? I came up with a story for Dadéluon and everything."

One of the guards had run off to spread the news that the Treasure Chest was about to undergo a surprise code-compliance inspection. While "Circuit Intendant Suti" and her delegation waited in the courtyard for the manager, servants and maids rushed about in barely contained chaos.

"Considering you were pretty much playing yourself, I'd call that merely passable," said Arona, her tone teasing but friendly.

"Give her more credit than that," said Rati Yera. "I don't know how to sound fancy at all; we're lucky to have her doing most of the talking."

Dandelion beamed. "I think you have to make me an official member of the Blossom Gang."

"How so?" asked Arona.

"Hello! I'm called Dandelion! You each have a cool nickname that's a plant. I fit right in."

"I don't know about that," said Arona. "Our heart-oath isn't just because we happen to have thematic 'nicknames.' It's because we have similar ideals." Earlier, she had briefly explained to Dandelion why they were called the Blossom Gang without getting into details about what they each wanted.

"I'm very insightful, you know," said Dandelion. "I can guess your ideals."

"This, I have to hear," said Widi.

Dandelion put on a serious mien. "So Mistress Yera is Bamboo, since bamboos are flexible and useful in all kinds of machines."

Rati Yera chuckled. "Not bad."

Dandelion turned to Arona. "You're Safflower because . . . uh . . . safflower oil is good for the skin, and dried safflowers are used to make blush and rouge—"

"That is *not* why I prize the safflower! It's because I'm good at disguises and—"

But Dandelion would not be deterred. "That guy, who never talks, is Pine because he's really strong and . . . and always stands straight and tall, like a soldier—"

Mota Kiphi smiled and said nothing.

"And what about me?" asked Widi, grinning.

"You! Well, you're Orchid because . . . . orchid flowers have that hanging tongue-petal, and you are good at wagging your tongue, both for eating and talking."

Widi laughed. "I've never thought of it that way, but I rather like your explanation."

"And I'm a ray of sunshine, just like my namesake," said Dandelion. "So you see, I'm completely on theme."

"O Lady Kana, help me," said Arona. "You're insufferable. You can't be our heart-oath sister, but I can't stop you from following us around. I guess you *are* like the weed you are named after: It's impossible to get rid of you."

"So I'm a member of the *extended* Blossom Gang?" asked Dandelion.

Rati, Mota, and Widi nodded, laughing, and after a moment, Arona did as well.

"Hey, what about me?" asked Kinri.

"Of course you're an extended member," said Rati. "We came here to help you, didn't we?"

"Don't I need a flower, though?"

For some reason, everyone turned to Dandelion.

"Him?!" Dandelion, apparently still a bit miffed over the "fire-breathing spiderweb" comment earlier, looked at Kinri critically. Then her eyes lit up. "Since you're so awkward and gangly, you are . . . *Thasé-teki*."

Arona burst out laughing, and even Widi and Mota smiled. Rati, ever protective, said, "That's a little mean, Dandelion."

The *thasé-teki*, commonly known as "caterpillar grass," was a kind of caterpillar infected by a fungus. The caterpillar lived underground, and after infection by the fungus, the mycelia spread throughout the body of the host, eventually killing the caterpillar as the mycelia stiffened into a hard endosclerotium. A stroma then developed out of the dead caterpillar and sprouted aboveground in a grasslike spindly stalk in the spring. Though useful in medicine, it was not a very pretty "flower."

"Hey, don't just focus on appearance!" said Dandelion. "The caterpillar grass may look plain and taste bitter, but it is full of virtues that bring relief to the sick. Our Thasé-teki may be the opposite of handsome and eloquent, but it is *his* idea that got us in here."

Kinri blushed, torn between embarrassment and pride. Was Dandelion mocking or complimenting him? Or maybe a bit of both?

"Good thing that Tiphan Huto wasn't around," Kinri muttered. "We were lucky."

"Nah," said Widi, trying to change the topic to make Kinri feel less awkward. "Luck had nothing to do with it. Even if Tiphan were around, I could have gotten him to invite us to tea. The only thing I like better than food is talking about regulations and codes."

Kinri had been inspired by Magistrate Zuda's kitchen inspectors, who visited the Splendid Urn every month to make sure that the restaurant had plenty of filled water cisterns and sand buckets on hand and that the stairways and hallways were clear of obstructions. Prime Minister Cogo Yelu had promulgated a whole series of rules for crowded public establishments like restaurants, inns, indigo houses, gambling parlors, and so forth to ensure the safety of the patrons and to prevent disastrous city fires—though many business owners grumbled that the constant inspections were just an excuse to employ more clerks and to ensure tax compliance. Widi had taken Kinri's idea and run with it, leading to their elaborate ruse.

"Coming in here as the circuit intendant's delegation instead of sneaking in gives us lots of advantages," said Widi. "We can basically look anywhere we want to, and they wouldn't be able to say no."

"Still, it's risky," said Kinri. "Tiphan has seen you, me, and Arona—"

"Look in a mirror. I doubt even your mother would recognize you now. You have to trust Arona's makeup skills."

Kinri looked around at everyone—he did think of them now as the extended Blossom Gang—and had to admit that Widi was right. He wouldn't have recognized any of them.

Finally, a manager named Giphi emerged from the restaurant proper to greet them, apologizing profusely for making them wait, bowing with every other word. It was such an honor for the circuit intendant to deign to inspect their humble establishment! The management deeply regretted the mix-up at the door! The Treasure Chest was almost ready to be opened to the public, maybe as soon as next week, after the competition with the Splendid Urn.

"Oh?" Dandelion perked up at the mention of the competition. "I heard something about this. The Splendid Urn has been known as the Best Restaurant in Ginpen for years. Are you sure you'll be able to beat them?"

"Honorable circuit intendant and assistant circuit intendant, not to sound boastful, but our master has come prepared. The Wasus, after all, have only grown to prominence during the last few decades, whereas the Hutos have generations of wealth and connections to draw on. The outcome of the competition is like the Hegemon's famous sword, not in doubt. It's just a way to build up even more interest in our grand opening. If Your Honors will be around next week, you should be judges for the competition!"

"Circuit Intendant Suti" and "Assistant Circuit Intendant Dadéluon" made some noncommittal noises as Mota pushed the wheeled chair into the restaurant.

Giphi happily pointed out all the unique features of the first floor to the inspectors. As the theme of the floor was the Realm of Fire, most of the tables were set up with a charcoal brazier in the middle to grill meats and vegetables table side or to boil soup for hot pot. Hot pot and barbecue had always been popular in Rima and Faça, and the influx of refugees from Unredeemed Dara had made them even more popular since grilling was the Lyucu's favorite style of cooking, and the refugees' tales of Lyucu feasts made people curious. Hot pots and grilled platters were relatively affordable for large groups, and the best choice for middle-class families interested in dining out at an upscale place.

The ironwood tables and woven bamboo sitting mats would have been functional and attractive but for the fact that everything was painted a shade of gold. Combined with the chandeliers encrusted with fake emeralds and rubies, the effect was rather garish.

"Eating here is going to give me a headache," whispered Arona. "I feel like I'm inside a magpie's nest."

"I think whoever designed this place took the name of the restaurant too literally," whispered Dandelion.

Kinri shook his head in wonder. Some of the Lyucu thanes back home had decorated their houses in a similar manner, and he had learned from Nazu Tei that such ostentation was not considered "classy"—though quite appropriate for a man like Tiphan Huto.

"Most of these were taken from actual old forges in Rima," said Giphi, pointing at the hammers, clamps, tongs, and other implements of the blacksmithing trade hanging on the walls as decoration. The advent of more advanced furnaces capable of producing steel had rendered many old blacksmith shops obsolete, and Tiphan Huto had acquired the tools for scrap prices to add a touch of rustic charm to the place—which, again, would have been a good idea had the tools not also been painted in gleaming gold.

"How many bags of sand do you have stored per floor for fire suppression?" asked Dandelion, her tone superior and officious.

"Err, let me think. . . . Four bags are stored here, on the first floor."

"What?" Dandelion's eyebrows shot up (she was going for an imitation of Prince Gimoto, the inspiration for the role of "Dadéluon").

"Don't you remember what happened here during the Battle of Ginpen? Have you no respect for Kon Fiji's admonition to always prepare for the future with an eye on history?"

During that battle years ago, the Lyucu had assaulted the city with garinafin fire, and though most of the city residents had escaped harm due to the order to evacuate or to shelter in underground bunkers, the fire had spread to half the city as a result of poor construction and lack of fire prevention measures. Officials in Ginpen were thus extra vigilant about violations of the fire code.

"Imperial regulation requires at least one bag of sand on hand per twenty diners in capacity," said Widi. "And considering you're planning to have open flames right here in the dining hall, you should add even more. Fire suppression cannot be neglected."

"If you intend to become the leading restaurant in Ginpen," said Dandelion, her brows furrowed with concern, "you must take the duties of a role model seriously and set an example for the other restaurants in this city of learning to emulate. Follow the code down to every semantic root and inflection glyph!"

"Of course, of course! I'll get this remedied right away," promised Giphi.

"Take us upstairs," said Dandelion. "Let's see what other safety regulations have been violated. So far, this is not looking good, not good at all; you understand?"

Giphi bowed a few more times and showed the delegation to the stairs. He paused as he looked at Rati's wheeled chair. "Um . . . the honorable circuit intendant . . ."

"Don't you have a lift installed?" asked Rati.

Farsight Secretary Zomi Kidosu, who had once required a leg brace to move around, had pushed the empress to issue a proclamation to require all public-serving businesses beyond a certain size to make accommodations for patrons with mobility limitations. Unlike some of Zomi's more radical reform proposals, this particular measure had been supported by most Moralist scholars as being in line with the respect due the aged—who often needed wheeled chairs or other assistance to move around—and the large number of veterans who had lost limbs during the wars of the past decades.

"If Your Honor wouldn't mind, we could use the dumbwaiter at the back—"

"Surely you're not suggesting that your patrons be carried between the floors like platters of food!" reprimanded Dandelion. "Is this really how you intend to satisfy your code obligations? I'll have some choice words with Magistrate Zuda—"

"Most insightful and compassionate Assistant Circuit Intendant Dadéluon," broke in Widi. "I'm sure Manager Giphi made this suggestion only because construction at the restaurant isn't finished yet. A proper lift is most definitely part of the plans, right?"

Giphi wiped the sweat from his brow. "Y-yes! Master Diwi is absolutely correct. We have plans for a most comfortable lift for our honored customers who do not wish to use the stairs." Despite his valiant efforts, he couldn't quite disguise the horror of having to explain to his boss why the opening of his restaurant might have to be delayed in order to add in lifts.

"Meanwhile, it's a good thing that I've brought good help," said Rati Yera. She gestured to Mota Kiphi, who bent down and easily scooped her up and began to climb the stairs to the second floor, while Kinri and Arona collapsed and folded up the wheeled chair and carried it up behind them.

"Come on!" said Dandelion to Giphi. "Don't dawdle! We haven't got all day."

Giphi swallowed a sigh and ran up the stairs obediently. He only hoped that he'd still have a job by the end of the day.

After the conclusion of the inspection of the restaurant proper, Giphi had a long scroll of changes that had to be made for the Treasure Chest to open. Just thinking about presenting these demands to Tiphan Huto made his heart palpitate in terror. But his ordeal wasn't over yet.

"Now we need to inspect the kitchen and storage areas," said Widi Tucru. "Food safety is very important."

"But there are some . . . um . . . proprietary processes in the kitchen, intended for the upcoming competition—"

"So?" cut in Dandelion. "Are you suggesting that the circuit intendant is going to disclose your trade secrets? Are you trying to insult a government official?"

"Not at all!" pleaded Giphi. "It's just that . . . our chef is deeply engrossed in designing the menu for the competition and cannot be disturbed to accompany you on this inspection. I'm not sure any of the rest of us can explain the food safety measures that are in place, as the chef is an artist and quite particular about doing things the chef's own way."

"No matter," said Dandelion dismissively. "We are just here to inspect things for compliance with Imperial regulations, not to learn about cooking. As ladies of virtue and learning, we care nothing for culinary details involving dirty grease and unsightly blood."

Giphi sighed with relief. Tiphan Huto had repeatedly emphasized that the secrets of Chef Mozo Mu must be kept away from prying eyes. Most of the waitstaff hadn't even been allowed in the kitchen. At least he could assure his boss that the government inspectors weren't interested in cooking techniques.

The tour began with the kitchen.

Inside the long building, separated from the main restaurant, teams of cooks busied themselves at stoves along the two walls as well as at the island in the middle: chopping, shelling, peeling, coring, kneading, carving, stirring, boiling, frying, grilling, roasting, tasting, smelling, arguing. . . . The din of knife slamming against chopping block, spoon banging against pan, meat and vegetables sizzling in oil, sous-chefs shouting orders to assistants, was deafening. Despite the excellent ventilation of high windows, assisted by spinning fans operated by dogs running inside treadwheels, the air was permeated by steam and smoke, flavored with a thousand delicious spices and aromas.

"Oh, this is wonderful," said Widi. The bump in his throat moved up and down as he swallowed, and the fingers of his right hand wriggled as if already itching for a pair of eating sticks.

There was a high platform erected in the middle of the kitchen, on top of which a child of about twelve paced about, shouting directions to teams scattered around the enormous kitchen through a bamboo-and-silk trumpet that amplified her voice. With all the noise and hubbub around, she seemed like a general barking orders on a battlefield, or a foreman supervising one of the big manufacturing workshops in Dimu or Dimushi.

"Ha!" said Dandelion. "Look at that girl giving orders. So cute. Is she your master's daughter?"

"Uh . . . No, no! Our master has not yet found a suitable match," said Giphi.

"Who is she then?"

"Oh, just . . . just a helper. It's good luck in Faça to have a young girl in the kitchen to . . . you know, keep an eye on things."

Dandelion, whose mother was from Faça, had never heard of this custom. But she decided not to pursue the matter. "Where's the chef?" she asked.

The inspection team looked around. Everyone was curious to see this Mozo Mu, descendant of the legendary Suda Mu.

"The chef? . . . Not available."

Crushing disappointment.

"Is he too busy designing the menu?" asked Dandelion. "We need to ask him questions about hygiene practices."

"Uh, um, that is to say—"

Before he could answer, the child, who had seen the strangers coming into the kitchen, climbed down from the platform and ran over.

"What is this?" she demanded of Giphi. "Your instructions were not to disturb the kitchen staff while we're practicing for the competition."

"Oh . . ." Giphi bent down and whispered in her ear.

Kinri and his team examined the child with interest. She had the smooth black skin of a native of Haan, and thick, curled hair framed her handsome face. Her large green eyes surveyed the inspection team with suspicion.

When Giphi was done with his explanation, she reluctantly said, "We don't have time for questions. They can look around, but I want them to stay out of our way." She turned and began heading back to her platform.

"Can we taste some of the amazing creations here?" asked Widi.

"No," said the child, her tone brooking no argument. She didn't even slow down as she strode away.

"Who *is* she?" asked Dandelion again, her face turning red at the rudeness.

"Your Honor, don't waste your anger on a mere menial," begged Giphi. "She's just a child from the countryside unused to polite society."

"I bet she's related to Mozo Mu," whispered Dandelion to Kinri.

Kinri nodded. "Maybe we can get her to give us some hints of what Mozo Mu is planning. Should be easier to get a child to talk."

Rati noticed Widi's eyes roaming around the kitchen, the look of hunger and craving as obvious as a wolf's slobber. To be so close to such wonderful food without being able to taste was torture to him. There was no telling what he would do if they left him here.

"Why don't I go inspect the storage pantry and cellars?" said Rati. "Diwi, you come with me. Dadéluon, you stay here to inspect the kitchen."

Giphi apologized a few more times and led Rati Yera and Widi Tucru away, with Mota Kiphi pushing the wheeled chair. Widi looked back with every step, silently bidding farewell to the culinary wonders that fate refused to acquaint him with.

That left Dandelion, Kinri, and Arona in the kitchen.

"I guess we should at least pretend to be doing a compliance inspection," said Arona. The three of them began to stroll purposefully around the kitchen while staying out of the way of the cooks and servants buzzing about.

"I wish Widi were here," whispered Arona. "He'd probably be able to pick out a lot of interesting information just from all the smells and ingredients on display here. Still, I'm sure he can glean more knowledge from the pantry and cellar."

"You make it sound like he's the only one with eyes and nose," said Dandelion, clearly peeved. "Who says *we* can't figure out things on our own? Maybe I'm an expert on cooking too, and I just haven't told you."

Arona looked at her, amused. "Really? Then tell me, what sort of vegetable is that man chopping?"

Dandelion squinted at the green stalks, biting her bottom lip. "Are they . . . leeks? No, don't tell me. They must be . . . pipe scallions?"

Princess Fara had always prided herself on being a gourmet, having sampled all kinds of excellent dishes in Pan's most expensive restaurants, not to mention the Imperial kitchen. Indeed, she often designed the menus for her own dinner parties at the palace. But her knowledge of food was limited to ordering and consuming, having never set foot *inside* the kitchen herself or seen raw ingredients before they were transmuted through the art of cooking.

"Really? You think those are pipe scallions? I hope you never make me a soup. How about that fruit there? What's that?" Arona pointed at another cooking station.

"I . . . I'm pretty sure that's a winter melon? Wait, maybe winter melons aren't so small. Is that a . . . a kind of soft-shelled coconut?"

Arona covered her mouth with her hands as her body shook with silent laughter. Tears spilled from her eyes.

"All right, you've made your point," said a dejected Dandelion. "I know how to use the writing knife a lot better than the kitchen knife. Satisfied? I've never liked to read about cooking, and the em—my aunt wouldn't let me go into the kitchen anyway. So I don't know what anything looks like uncooked. But I *can* at least tell you what tastes good."

"I'm sure a girl like you has had a surfeit of fine dining," said Arona. "Whereas I'm plenty happy with a drumstick and a gourd of cheap beer. But to not know the difference between mountain chives and pipe scallions, or to confuse a winter melon with a sponge gourd . . ." Arona shook her head in amazement.

"Don't be so proud just because you can identify a few common ingredients," said Dandelion, her cheeks flushed. "How about I test *you* on a few things?"

"You're on," said Arona. "I can't claim to be a great cook either, but I know what food looks like."

Dandelion looked around the kitchen, trying to find something to stump Arona with. Suddenly, her eyes lit up. "What kind of fish is being cleaned over there?" She pointed to a woman standing by a wooden tub, scraping the scales from a fish with a flat, bony head and a slender tail that flared into long fins. "And what are those fruits over there?" She pointed to a bowl on the counter behind the woman.

Arona walked closer to the woman and pretended to be examining the cooking station for signs of accumulated grime. The actress's brows were furrowed in concentration.

Dandelion smiled. She had picked that particular fish because there was only one like it, and the woman seemed to be taking particular care. Similarly, the fruits were placed in an expensive-looking porcelain bowl instead of a wooden one. This probably meant that the ingredients were rare and precious. She hoped the actress wouldn't know what they were.

But when Arona walked back, she looked triumphant. "I have to admit, you *almost* got me. That fish is a moonbow trout, which is only found in Lake Toyemotika on Arulugi. The 'fruit' is actually a smooth-skinned taro, cultivated in Tan Adü."

"How do I know you aren't just making these up?"

Arona laughed. "You're welcome to ask the cook for confirmation. I recognize them only because we've traveled all over the Islands, and I enjoy going through markets to see what people in different places eat. To know something about the food of a place is to know something about its soul, and that helps when I have to portray people from there."

"You've been to Arulugi *and* Tan Adü?"

Arona nodded. "We like to learn all that the Islands have to teach us. The art of Arulugi's smokecrafters is perfect for the stage, and the Adüans can sing with their throats and lips at once, producing multiple notes."

Dandelion looked envious. "I've rarely been outside of Pan. . . ." Abruptly, her eyes narrowed. "Wait. The trout and the taros . . . those aren't local ingredients."

"So insightful, Miss Dandelion. I see that you're not only a master identifier of edible fauna and flora, but also a credible geographer—"

"Would you stop making fun of me for a moment?" Dandelion stomped her foot. "This is important."

"What's important? Of course Mozo Mu would source ingredients from all over Dara. The distinguishing characteristic of Suda Mu's style of cooking is fusion of many styles—"

"No! The point is that both of these ingredients spoil pretty fast."

"How do you know that? You didn't even know what they look like."

"But I read books! Nakipo of Amu has a poem in which she compares inconstant lovers to the eyes of the moonbow trout: 'Clouding over in a single hour.' And Luan Zyaji wrote of how quickly the smooth-skinned taro shriveled once pulled out of the ground. Can you tell how fresh they are?"

Arona looked. The fish had clear, bright eyes, and the mud on the taros appeared wet.

"That fish was probably alive this morning," said Arona. "And the taros . . . probably dug out no more than two days ago."

"Considering how far Arulugi and Tan Adü are from here, the only way they could get them this fresh is with airships," said Dandelion. "Even my house—um, I've heard that even the wealthiest restaurants in Pan can't afford to ship many ingredients fresh by airship."

With the only source of regular lift gas on Rui under Lyucu control, Dara had had to adapt by using airships powered by fermented manure gas. The flammability and reduced lift of these ships meant that air travel and transport were quite costly, and well out of the reach of even wealthy and noble households. The Splendid Urn did ship some ingredients in by airship, but very few.

"I see your point," said Arona. "But this isn't exactly a surprise either. We know the Hutos are rich, and that they're willing to spend to win this competition."

"It's more than that," said Dandelion. "Weren't you just telling me about the importance of stories? A contest, no less than a play or a disguise, is about a story."

"Stories? Where's the story here?"

"There are many ways to spend money, and the choices matter. There is a story that's being told by this restaurant: the use of gold paint everywhere; the ostentation of the jeweled friezes outside; the

lack of respect for the needs of the less mobile; the domineering attitude of a staff that thinks nothing of practicing with ingredients that
are out of reach for the kitchens of dukes—there's nothing graceful
about any of it. I don't quite know what it means yet, but knowing the story the enemy is trying to tell is the first step to defeating
them."

Arona now looked at Dandelion with a newfound respect. "I've
never quite thought of it that way, but I do believe you're right. Look
at you, already surpassing your not-quite-teacher."

They laughed. The two women then realized that Kinri hadn't
said anything for a while. They looked around and saw that he was
standing a little ways off, muttering to himself.

"What are you doing?" asked Dandelion, going up and elbowing
him in the ribs.

"Aw! What's that for?"

"Arona and I have been trying to learn all we can about this
place," said Dandelion. "What about you? Slacking off? This whole
thing was your idea."

"While you've been arguing, I've been listening to that girl."

"What *has* she been saying?" asked Dandelion with interest.

"Well, that's what's odd," said Kinri. "She's been quoting the Ano
Classics to herself."

"What?" Dandelion looked at Kinri, astounded. "You know the
Ano Classics?"

"I . . . I've picked up a few snippets here and there; anyway, that's
not important. She was shouting directions to the cooks—you know,
chop this, dice that, don't put in the fish until the bubbles in the oil
are as big as the nail on your pinkie, and so on—the sort of thing I
can't really make sense of. But once in a while, she'll stop and start
muttering to herself, almost like she's trying to remind herself of
something. Just now, I heard her say:

> *"A thousand scales fell at a single stroke.*
> *A thousand ships launched for a promise.*
> *A thousand pearls gazed at the fall*
> *Of the grandest walled treasure-hall.*

"I know I've heard those lines before, but I can't remember from where."

"Oh, *I* know where they come from," said Dandelion. "They're from Para's poem about Séraca, the hero who fought against Iluthan with a fleet of feather ships during the Diaspora Wars. Not one of my favorites, honestly. I'm not a big fan of these war-and-politics epics—"

"But the poems must be related to the dishes—"

"How?" asked Arona.

Kinri hesitated. "I think . . . they're kind of like logogram riddles."

Dandelion looked thoughtful at this.

"I don't know anything about cooking, but why would she be saying this to herself in the kitchen? Suda Mu wanted to keep his recipes secret, right? So it makes sense that he would only pass them down in the form of a code."

Dandelion and Arona thought about this. Then they both nodded.

"Can you tell me anything more about this Para?" asked Kinri.

"He was a court poet at Boama," said Dandelion. "He's often considered an important figure for the exuberance school of poetry, but I think he tends to write in an excessively decorative style. He taught three students of note—"

"No, no, I don't mean what he was like as a poet," said Kinri impatiently. "You said he was a court poet at Boama? When? During the time of the Xana Conquest or before?"

"Oh, long before. I'm not great with dates and wars, though. . . . Let me see, he studied under the Oyster Poet, who painted *Portrait of Three Ladies*, which was notable for capturing the expressions of the subjects vividly using just a few strokes, a restraint that Para himself lacked—"

Kinri tried to be patient. "Are these three ladies important? Did they fight in any wars?"

"I doubt it. But they were the wives of three prominent generals of the Tiro state—"

"Wait, you said three generals? Do you mean they were Ladies Faça, Rima, and Haan?"

Dandelion's face brightened. "Yes, that's it. Have you seen the painting?"

Kinri shook his head. "But if that's true, that means Para was a court poet in Boama right around the partitioning of the old Tiro state Métashi into Faça, Rima, and Haan. The court at Boama, prior to the partition, was reputed to be the wealthiest and most powerful in all Dara. Métashi fought many wars against the other Tiro states, and was thought to be on the path of conquering the whole Big Island before it fell apart."

Arona and Dandelion stared at him.

"What?" asked Kinri defensively. "I *like* history."

"I think you've got some interesting riddles of your own," said Dandelion, looking thoughtfully at him. From the moment she'd met him, she had felt an odd sense of familiarity and comfort with him. Indeed, she had to admit that she cared so much about the "fire-breathing spiderweb" comment only because *he* had said it.

*Someone who knows the history of the Tiro states and recognizes the Ano Classics is no ordinary busboy. Maybe* thasé-teki *really is the right flower for him, because he's got hidden depths under that gangly frame— which . . . actually can be pretty appealing in the right light.*

Kinri tried to head off more questions by focusing on the task at hand. "The court at Boama sounds a lot like the court at Kriphi at the time Suda Mu cooked there."

"*That* is interesting," said Dandelion. "Since extravagance seems to be the theme in this restaurant, it makes sense that they'd draw from the poet of an extravagant court for coded instructions."

"But how do we decode the instructions?" asked Arona.

"Let's just memorize the poems for now," said Kinri. "We don't know enough about cooking to understand what we're seeing in the kitchen, but we can try to figure out the riddle-poems later, just like how I take apart the gizmos I buy at the market."

"It's worth a try," said Dandelion.

The three "inspectors" continued to walk around the kitchen, pretending to look for fire suppression tools and evacuation routes, making notes about the cleanliness of the surfaces and the staff. But they kept their ears open and jotted down the poems recited by the child whenever she paused and muttered to herself.

Abruptly, Giphi ran up to them, his expression one of deep worry.

Giant drops of sweat beaded on his rotund, red face, making him resemble a dew-bedecked apple.

"Uh . . . we may have a problem. Circuit Intendant Suti is missing!"

The manager had taken the circuit intendant and her staff to the storehouse to inspect the supplies. This was a squat, medium-sized structure used for goods that could keep for a while, like bags of rice and beans, links of sausages, bundles of lotus leaves, and jars of rice beer. But the aboveground portion was only like the tip of an iceberg, for the storehouse sat on top of a giant ice cellar many times its size.

At first, the circuit intendant was content to allow Giphi to direct her around the vast ice cellar, pointing out the straw packed around the enormous blocks of ice, the system of ditches in the floor to drain the meltwater, the creation of different temperature zones for meats, vegetables, fruits, dairy, and so on. The aged official nodded non-committally in her wheeled chair, clearly bored by the presentation.

*Well, bored is good*, thought Giphi. *Bored means everything is in order.*

"What are those screens doing over there?" asked Rati. "They look a little crooked." She pointed to a set of silk-and-bamboo screens near the wall, which were normally used to give large parties of diners some privacy when they couldn't afford one of the private suites.

Giphi silently swore at the lazy servants who had done such a poor job of covering up what he was hoping the circuit intendant wouldn't see. He had whispered urgent directions to his staff before coming out to meet the inspection team and hadn't had time to check their work.

"Oh, nothing," said Giphi. "The restaurant hasn't opened yet, so we're just keeping the screens here."

"In an ice cellar?" asked Rati suspiciously. She gestured for Mota, who went over and moved the crooked screens out of the way to reveal the yawning opening of a tunnel leading into the darkness.

Rati looked up at Giphi, her eyes bright and cold as icicles.

"Oh . . . oh!" Giphi slapped his forehead. "How could I have forgotten! Master Huto intends to use this area as a vault to store some valuables and the earnings from the restaurant. He hasn't picked a bank yet, and he's very cautious about thieves and robbers, and . . . and potential raids by pirates. There's really nothing in there right now."

"Can we take a look?" said Rati, leaning forward in her chair to peer into the darkness.

"I really don't think we should—"

"Nonsense! What could possibly be the harm of having a government official look into a vault? Maybe I can offer some suggestions for increased security."

"It's private—"

"Private? Didn't you tell me that there's nothing in there?"

"Well, yes, but—"

"I insist! Tunneling under Ginpen can be very dangerous if you weaken the foundations of other buildings around you. This is definitely something we have to check out."

Giphi wasn't sure what had happened to the bored old woman from earlier. At that moment, the circuit intendant acted as eager as a child being told that she couldn't open the door to some forbidden room.

Before he could respond, Widi had grabbed one of the burning torches off the sconces in the wall and headed for the tunnel, with the burly Mota, pushing the circuit intendant's wheeled chair, following close behind.

"Wait!" called out Giphi. And when the three officials refused to slow down, he had no choice but to run after them, carrying a torch of his own.

Although a narrow line of windows near the ceiling allowed some dim light into the vast ice cellar, the tunnel was in complete darkness, and the flickering torches provided the only illumination. They soon came to a point in the tunnel where it forked, one branch opening to the left and another to the right. It was as if the four of them were spelunking in the legendary caves of the Shinané Mountains, or exploring the Mausoleum of Emperor Mapidéré.

"Which way?" asked Rati.

"Um . . . left," said Giphi weakly.

"Hmm . . . then I think we should go to the right," said Rati, a glint in her eyes.

Giphi followed, resigned to the fact that there was no way to stop the unfolding disaster.

A few twists and turns later, they arrived at another storage cellar, dry and cool. Inside, they saw shelves full of wooden boxes. Mota opened one of them without even bothering to ask Giphi for permission. The box was stuffed with soft moss, and when the moss was pushed aside, they saw something that resembled a small statue or a doll.

Rati reached in and took out the "doll." It was soft and dry to the touch, and when she held it under her nose, she detected a spicy fragrance. The doll wasn't made out of wood or stone, but some spongy material with wrinkled skin. Rootlike tendrils extended from the head and the ends of the limbs.

"Move the torches away," said Rati, the barest hint of an excited quaver in her voice.

Giphi and Widi complied. The statue glowed in the darkness with an inner light, a cold aquamarine much like jellyfish in the sea.

"This is a homunculus mushroom!" exclaimed Diwi, the junior clerk. "Look at the size! How perfect the features are!"

Homunculus mushrooms were important in herbal medicine and also considered a delicacy for many styles of Dara cuisine. The glowing mushrooms had a tendency to grow into human shapes, and those with the most perfect features and limbs could fetch hundreds of gold pieces on the market.

"Circuit Intendant Suti" exchanged looks with her staff, and then all three turned their gazes toward Giphi.

"Master Huto was willing to spend a lot for the best ingredients," Giphi said, his voice so weak that it was hard to imagine that even he believed what he was saying. "And he wanted to keep these here as . . . as a surprise—"

"The problem isn't the willingness to spend, but there being no legal market where the supply can be found," said Rati.

The best source of homunculus mushrooms was, in fact, the undersea tunnel connecting Rui with Dasu, where mushrooms had once been deliberately cultivated to provide a source of food for horses and men traveling that route. Ever since the Lyucu conquest of those two islands, however, high-quality homunculus mushrooms had been almost impossible to find for sale. A whole storeroom full of such mushrooms would have likely required access to smugglers or pirates.

"I can explain!" said Giphi. He ran to the shelf with his torch and pointed at the markings on the boxes. "See? See? These came on a shipment from Wolf's Paw, as you can tell from the shipping stamp. The supplier probably found a new source that he's keeping secret. Our master has always been meticulous about following the rules—"

He turned around and found that he was alone in the storage room.

Running into the dark tunnel, he shouted, "Circuit intendant! Where are you? Come back, please!"

But only darkness and silence answered him.

"Are you telling me that you managed to lose a senior court official in your cellar?" asked an incredulous Dandelion.

"It . . . it looks that way," said a terrified Giphi. "There are a lot of tunnels down . . . down there. I don't know all the routes. Honest! Only Master Huto knows where they . . . they lead to—"

"Your storage cellar is a *maze*? Why in the world would you build your cellar like that? What manner of vices are you concealing down there?" With each question, Dandelion took a step forward. Giphi backed up until he was against the wall, his hands scrabbling against the bricks helplessly for an escape that didn't exist.

Kinri was terrified as well. He hoped Rati Yera and the others were all right, but even if they were unharmed, they'd have to get the magistrate and the constables involved now, potentially revealing their identities and ruining the Splendid Urn's chances in the cooking competition.

"Get everyone into the maze and look for them!" he shouted. They had to find Rati and the others as soon as possible and get out.

The cooks in the kitchen stopped what they were doing and stared at him. The child on the platform looked extremely annoyed.

"What is all this commotion?" asked an old but forceful voice.

They turned around and saw Rati Yera coming into the kitchen in her wheeled chair. Mota was pushing her, with Widi following behind.

"Can't you move any faster?" Arona shouted at Mota. "The cellar is no place for the circuit intendant!"

Mota sped up until they were close together. Arona reached out and squeezed his hand, and he squeezed hers back. The gesture went unnoticed by the others, as Arona had covered their hands with her sleeve. They shared a quick, warm smile at each other.

"Oh, thank the gods that you're all right, Circuit Intendant!" cried out Giphi in relief.

"The air was stuffy down there, and we wanted to get out quickly," said Rati. "You've proven yourself quite untrustworthy, I must say."

"But how did you get out? I was looking for you—"

"We were taking a break in one of the storage rooms when you ran right by us like a fly with its head pinched off," said Rati Yera. "And then after we got out of the ice cellar, we waited for you. When you failed to show, we went off to look at the other parts of the restaurant some more."

"You were . . . not in the tunnels for long then?"

"No. We got right out. The good news is that other than some minor code violations, everything seems in order."

Giphi was amazed that she made no mention of the suspiciously sourced mushrooms, or any other surprises. He berated himself for missing the inspectors when he panicked in the tunnels, thinking they had wandered off.

But apparently the circuit intendant had gotten out without much trouble, and hadn't run into anything more incriminating than the homunculus mushrooms. Relief washed over him like warm bathwater. Thank Rufizo and Lutho for protecting Master Tiphan Huto!

"Would the honorable circuit intendant and her staff like to stay for dinner?" Giphi simpered at Rati. "We're not open yet, but I'm sure we can go to a nearby high-class establishment. . . ."

Rati looked at Kinri, Dandelion, and Arona. "I think our inspection is at an end. Don't you?"

"You have to know when to stop a story," Kinri whispered. Dandelion gave him a look—not unkind.

Everyone nodded.

"The circuit intendant is extremely busy," declared Dandelion. "We must move on to our next task posthaste. Make sure you remedy all the problems we've pointed out!"

With that, the inspection team left as abruptly as they had shown up, leaving a confused Giphi to celebrate the good fortune that Master Huto's many secrets seemed to have survived an unexpected official scrutiny.

As they made their way back to the Splendid Urn, the gang shared their findings about the Treasure Chest.

"This Tiphan Huto is no simple merchant," concluded Rati Yera. "That underground storage cellar was a warren of tunnels and secret rooms, filled with all kinds of strange goods that he shouldn't have access to at all. Not only was there cargo obviously from Unredeemed Dara, but we also found some strange accounting ledgers written in code, indicating deals that were not meant to be intelligible to anyone who didn't already know what they were about."

"There were also empty rooms that seemed intended to hold people, instead of goods," said Widi.

"You mean like prison cells?" exclaimed Dandelion.

Mota, Widi, and Rati nodded, their faces grim.

"Beyond the cells," said Widi, "there was another room with a sealed door. I went up to it, and the stench made me suspect it was a latrine—though the odor was a bit odd."

"Eww, you're an expert on latrine odors too?" asked Dandelion, her nose wrinkled in sympathy.

"I can't quite explain it, but it smelled . . . different. Anyway, it seemed odd to have holding cells in a food storage cellar, and also odd to have a smelly latrine without people in the cells."

There was tension in the air as everyone pondered the sinister implications of a private underground prison.

"At first, we got involved in this only because it seemed like fun," said Rati. "But now . . . the Blossom Gang isn't going to let evil go once we've caught a whiff of the stench."

"We'll have to figure out just what he's up to another time," said Widi. "It doesn't seem directly related to the competition."

Rati nodded. "It's prudent to take it step by step. I thought it best to get out of there before they decided that we must have seen too much and resorted to desperate measures."

"But how did you get out of there?" asked Kinri. "It sounds like the maze would have been hard to navigate without a map or guide."

Rati laughed and patted the arms of her wheeled chair. "The Blossom Gang has some secrets we'd rather keep. But a maze like that . . . ha! It's nothing."

Kinri was curious but decided to leave further questions for another time. The image of Rati Yera's magical maze-navigating cart surfaced in his mind, however.

He reported what they had learned in the kitchen. Widi was most excited by the poems they had copied down.

"I'm sure that with a little research we'll be able to crack these riddles," said Widi.

"And I'm sure we can figure out what kind of story they intend to tell," said Dandelion. "Once we know the story, we can come up with our own story to counter it."

The gang returned to the Splendid Urn ready to meet with Mati and to come up with a plan for the contest in a week.

# CHAPTER THIRTY-SIX

# TWO THANES

KIRI VALLEY, IN THE FOOTHILLS OF THE WORLD'S
EDGE MOUNTAINS: THE TWELFTH MONTH IN
THE EIGHTH YEAR AFTER THE DEPARTURE OF
PRINCESS THÉRA FROM DARA FOR UKYU-GONDÉ
(SEVENTEEN MONTHS UNTIL THE LYUCU MUST
LAUNCH THEIR NEW INVASION FLEET TO DARA).

Volyu Aragoz, Pé-Afir-tekten, was going home on the back of a great white garinafin.

Her hide was as smooth and flawless as the salt flats on the shores of the Sea of Tears. Her wingspan was easily three times as long as the wingspan of the largest garinafin the Agon were allowed to have these days. Her voice was as clear as the first thunderstorm of summer and as loud as the largest Péa pipes.

Volyu should be proud and joyful. He had achieved everything he wanted by betraying his nephew to the Lyucu, hadn't he? He was going home to Sliyusa Ki in style.

Except he wasn't riding the garinafin. Well, not exactly. He was on the back of the garinafin, to be sure, but enclosed inside a bone cage. And four Lyucu naros sat around him, spears at the ready to skewer him the moment he evinced any dissatisfaction with his fate.

He sighed quietly, keeping his face placid. With his eyes closed, he tried to imagine things working out better than they had.

On the way to Aluro's Basin with the caravan of winter tribute for the pékyu, Volyu seethed and muttered to himself.

If only Takval and Théra had agreed to share their glory with him, allowed him to play the hero for once in his life! But no, they had to hog all the honor and glory for themselves, and assigned him the most dangerous task of all, to act as a spy against Pékyu Cudyu. And even if he accomplished what they asked, what then? He would be given the title of pékyu-votan, a meaningless gesture, since all the Agon would view Takval and Théra as their saviors, while he would be despised, laughed at, mocked as no better than a tanto-lyu-naro. Because he had not led them to victory.

No, no, *no*. Volyu was too smart for that. He had to find a way to make things work out better for himself, as he always had.

The obvious thing to do was to report Takval and Théra to the Lyucu, as he had done so many times with other Agon rebels. But things were no longer that simple. He had helped hide Takval and Théra from the Lyucu for years, provided them support, given them information. He had even told them about the gathering at Aluro's Basin and Taten when he thought there was more to be gained from their rebellion and then continued to give them intelligence about Lyucu movements in order to stay in the couple's good graces. . . . How could he explain to Cudyu his own role in plotting against the Lyucu and this sudden change of heart? The pékyu would never forgive! Théra, years ago, had anticipated his vacillation by entangling him in their schemes, and the more time passed, the deeper he became ensnared in their rebellion.

Yet, he absolutely could not allow Takval and Théra to succeed. If he couldn't win the way he wanted to win, then they had to lose.

He reviewed that last discussion in Kiri Valley, fuming over the disrespect of the young couple. Théra had even shifted away from him, annoyed, when he had paid her a compliment. The nerve!

*Wait. Wait!*

He remembered something else that had bothered him. When he had suggested that they launch the attack on the Lyucu at Aluro's Basin, Théra had instantly objected. At the time he had believed her explanation for why Taten was the better choice, but her vehemence, in retrospect, was very suspicious.

He concentrated. *Why Taten? Why?*

～

The secret audience with Pékyu Cudyu had gone exactly the way he hoped.

He began his prepared speech: There was a vast and dangerous conspiracy against the great Lyucu, led by his traitorous nephew and his Dara barbarian bride.

Cudyu's eyes narrowed, but he said nothing.

He licked his lips and continued. He described how it all began with the perfidious Luan Zya, whose false prediction had led to the destruction of the reinforcement Lyucu fleet (Cudyu's breathing quickened at this); how the barbarians then sent their princess to Ukyu-Gondé, guided by Takval the Unfaithful, to seek the destruction of the noble Lyucu in order to save Dara from the peerless Tanvanaki (Cudyu set down his kyoffir bowl and leaned forward, hanging on every word); how he had tried his hardest to dissuade them from their fruitless endeavor, which would no doubt redound upon the Agon with ten times the misery; how they had threatened him and tortured him (here, he undressed to show Cudyu the scars on his back and shoulders, which his wives and shamans had helped him prepare with gash cactus juice); how he had nonetheless tried to thwart them at every opportunity, denying them goods and warriors, sending them false information, extracting from them as much food and furs and sinews and bones as possible to delay their preparations—

"Why did you wait until now to tell me this, old man?" demanded Cudyu, his voice low and threatening.

This was the question he had been waiting for. Volyu took a deep breath.

"Because I wanted to find out their deepest, darkest secret, Pékyu Cudyu, Pride of the Scrublands." He was proud of how he managed to apply the moniker of his own grandfather to this young whelp without even blushing.

He explained that he sensed that Théra and Takval were hiding something from him. Théra and her people had come to Ukyu-Gondé on diving ships, perversions of nature, which she had then destroyed. But a wily barbarian like that would of course not leave herself with no way to return to her den. She had a way back to Dara, and that was why he, Volyu Aragoz, loyal sheepdog of the Lyucu, had borne intolerable insults and suffered indescribable pain; he had worked to extract that valuable piece of information from the cunning Dara princess and his foolish nephew, beguiled by the seductive barbarian snake-witch.

Oh, how he had suffered their tortures in silence; how he had listened with boiling rage as they insulted the brave and honorable Lyucu; how he had matched wits and cunning with that slippery woman; how he had fought against his own guileless and open instincts to gain her trust; how he had to throw them snippets of intelligence—absolutely false, made-up, worthless information—to lull them into complacency, into thinking that he shared their ludicrous fantasy; how he had slowly, step by step, pieced together the clues; how he had—

Cudyu threw his kyoffir bowl at him, barely missing his head so that his ears felt the slicing wind as the projectile whipped by. "Get on with it, old man!"

"She is intent on seizing the city-ships at Taten, and soon." Words tumbled out of Volyu in a torrent. "I believe she wishes to murder you and your thanes in cold blood in your moment of sanctified celebration, as you honor the gods with fragrant sacrifices. And then, to escape divine anger at this sacrilege, she will board the city-ships during the ensuing chaos, as the Lyucu and Agon fight over mastery of the scrublands. There is going to be an opening in the Wall of Storms, I'm sure of it. That is why Théra is so insistent on being in Taten at the fatal moment!"

Cudyu looked thoughtful.

"For the sake of my people and the great Lyucu," pleaded Volyu, "I've brought you this hard-won information. I cannot sit idly by and allow Takval and Théra to plunge my people into pointless strife and warfare again. May you punish my traitorous nephew and his evil bride, so that Ukyu-Gondé may enjoy peace forever."

"Thank you, Volyu Aragoz," said Cudyu. "Your loyalty will be amply rewarded."

～

Volyu took one last look at the smoking ruins of Kiri Valley, disappearing behind the mountains as the garinafin carrying him flapped her wings to gain more height.

Everything had gone according to plan, hadn't it? He had given Cudyu the details of Kiri Valley's defenses, its number of warriors and garinafins, the enhanced equipment of the Agon rebels and their Dara allies. He had even led Cudyu's troops to the very opening of the valley. He had watched as the Lyucu surprise assault began in the dark and ended with the whole valley burning. He had cheered with the other thanes and even gotten to break pemmican with Cudyu in the morning.

And then he had, very carefully, hinted at the reward that Cudyu had promised him. He didn't dare to hope for any of the metal weapons or valuable barbarian treasure. But he was hoping Cudyu would give him Dara slaves—perhaps even Théra herself—and some of Takval's more docile warriors, which would vastly enhance his reputation among his own people. He had already worked out the story he would tell at home: of most base betrayal by Théra; of lack of foresight by Takval; of a most brutal and unanticipated assault by the Lyucu, of his own heroic intervention with Cudyu that saved the lives of the surrendered Agon warriors who would be joining Sliyusa Ki, of the many Dara slaves he had gained for his own people despite the tragedy; of the need to be patient and not reckless like the failed rebels.

In response to his query, Cudyu had shackled him inside this cage and informed him that he would be brought back to Sliyusa Ki under armed guard.

"You'll be handed over to the elders of your settlement," said Cudyu carelessly. "I'm sure they'll deal with you fairly once I tell them that you're responsible for the deaths of thousands of Agon."

Volyu's eyes bulged. "But . . . but I'm your loyal sheepdog! I—"

"There will be plenty of other sheepdogs to take your place," said Cudyu. "But you know what I can't stand? A cur who thinks he can use *me* for his own purposes."

"No! Nooo!!! Please, oh please listen to me, I can help—"

But Cudyu had already turned and walked away, having lost all interest in him.

Cudyu surveyed the bloody battlefield, strewn with corpses and shattered weapons, a deep frown creasing his brow.

The resistance in the valley had been fierce. Though surprised and overwhelmed, the Agon and their Dara allies had put up quite a fight. Even with crushed limbs and horrific wounds, many refused to yield and had to be killed.

In the end, most of the remaining fighters had been forced to retreat into a single Dara-style building with wooden walls, where they held the Lyucu at bay with arrows and slingshots. Cudyu surrounded the building with garinafins and demanded that they surrender or be consigned to flames. The leaders of the rebels, the Agon Souliyan Aragoz and a barbarian by the name of Nméji Gon, had then asked for Cudyu to come to the door to negotiate.

Suspecting a trick, Cudyu ordered one of the culeks to dress up in his own garinafin skull helmet, and then sent the decoy to negotiate. And as soon as the fake Cudyu and his escorts approached the entrance of the building, it had blown up in a fierce explosion. Limbs and heads and bloody torso pieces flew through the smoke and air; terrified garinafins took off; warriors within a hundred paces of the building all ended up with horrible injuries: blinded, maimed, some had their heads sheared off from shrapnel. Even Cudyu's own ears rang for a long time afterward.

*It's a victory. But why do I feel so unsatisfied?*

On the scrublands, nothing impressed like military victory. Even years after becoming pékyu, Cudyu couldn't secure the kind of respect his father and sister commanded due to the lack of pitched battles and grand conquests. He had almost been glad when Volyu told him about this rebellion, which provided him with the first great deed of his pékyuship worthy of being passed on in song and story.

*But . . . is it really worthy?*

Victories were measured by spoils, by slaves, by captured cattle and sheep.

The herds in the valley were so small that it was laughable. The supply of seized Dara weapons and artifacts, on the other hand, was sizable. It would strengthen his army and boost his reputation. But it wasn't enough.

To be sure, the Lyucu had taken many captives, both Dara and Agon. But most of these were wounded, or else too old, too young, too unskilled to be warriors—not the most impressive kinds of slaves. He had failed to crush the spirit of the fighters; they chose to die instead.

*Well, most of them, anyway.*

One of the Agon rebel leaders, a thane named Araten, came to the realization that their cause was lost soon after fighting began. He had quickly surrendered to Cudyu and led the Lyucu warriors to the underground hideouts and secret shelters where the non-fighters holed up like moonfur rats in their prairie tunnels. Thank the gods that Araten was there! Without him, the Lyucu might have missed at least some of the hiding spots and been deprived of these slaves. Grateful, Cudyu had promised not to enslave Araten and the surviving members of his family, and would instead reward him by adopting him into a Lyucu clan.

*The victory is incomplete. I have the body of a tusked tiger but not the head.*

He was morose because he had failed to catch Takval, the Agon pretender, and Théra, his Dara princess. Tovo Tasaricu was combing through the corpses with his naros, but Cudyu wasn't optimistic that the rebel leaders would be found among them. Based on the latest reports, at least one garinafin, perhaps even two, had escaped.

Crushing the rebellion was good, but not enough. He needed to have Takval; he needed to have Théra; he needed their secret. Only then could his name live on in song and story.

He hadn't been able to get a good night's sleep ever since Volyu revealed the possibility that the Wall of Storms could be breached.

*Dare I? Dare I follow my father and sister across the sea?*

Volyu had confirmed a truth that he had already guessed at, based on analysis of washed-up wreckage: Tenryo had conquered part of Dara; Tanvanaki now ruled the conquered land in their father's stead; the reinforcement fleet had been destroyed; the Dara were now in Ukyu.

If there were going to be another opening in the Wall in the future, it stood to reason that just as ships could sail through it *to* Dara, ships could also sail through it *from* Dara. What if Tanvanaki, having conquered Dara, decided that she would return to Ukyu to take away his hard-won title?

No, no, no. Such a thing must never be allowed to happen. If he were to go to Dara, he wouldn't be doing it to "support" Tanvanaki. He would be doing it to fulfill the prophecy of the gods.

*The pékyu is dead! Long live Pékyu Cudyu Roatan!*

Other than Tovo Tasaricu, he had shared his fears and hopes with absolutely no one. By torturing some of the Dara captives this morning, he had been able to confirm that Volyu's account of the political situation in Dara was accurate. But even as he tortured them to death, the captives told him nothing credible concerning the reopening of the Wall of Storms.

For a brief moment, he wondered if he had been played by Volyu. Could the sniveling coward have made up the story about reopening the Wall of Storms to further his own agenda?

Cudyu utterly despised people like Volyu. The problem with Volyu was that he was *too* clever and thought of others as fools, easily manipulated. Did the Agon slave really think that Cudyu would be taken in by his absurd story? He knew exactly what the political calculus of the old man had been. Volyu wasn't loyal to the Lyucu at all. How could he be? It wasn't in his nature.

Volyu had given aid and comfort to this rebellion, and he would have enjoyed seeing Cudyu killed and the Lyucu defeated so long as he got to have the largest share of the spoils afterward. But if he couldn't get the choicest cut of meat, he would rather piss on the whole roast instead.

And the man had dared to come to him to claim a reward, his beady eyes brimming with greedy anticipation. Cudyu had spared his life; that was reward enough. Let the Agon deal with this man who had betrayed their only hope for a turnabout. Cudyu wasn't going to dirty his own hands with the blood of such a feckless creature.

It wasn't entirely inconceivable for Volyu to have made up a fantasy about the Wall of Storms in order to deflect blame from his own role in the failed uprising. And if he had done so, Cudyu would not hesitate to turn on Sliyusa Ki next and kill every man, woman, child, and animal—even down to the last slisli maggot—to vent his fury!

But . . . the details in his account were so good, so vivid, so believable. Perhaps Takval and Théra had kept the secret even from their own people.

In that case, there was nothing he could do to resolve his doubt except by finding and capturing Takval and Théra. He had to have them. *Had to.*

He was about to give the order to abandon the valley and start the search for the escapees when a naro ran up to him, his helmet askew from excitement. "Votan! We caught a bunch of them!"

Cudyu was disappointed.

The new captives kneeling below the hill had been delivered by a pair of defectors. The two—Toof and Radia, no clan—were Lyucu naros who had been forced to serve the Agon but managed to seize their garinafin from the escapees. Their prisoners, mostly children, were surprisingly defiant. At first they even refused to kneel. It had taken a swing of the club to the back of the knees of a young shaman to get them to comply.

Théra and Takval weren't among them.

*There may still be someone useful among these captives.*

There was a barbarian man who looked at him with curiosity, evidently one of the "scholars" who obsessed over word-scars based on the implements found on his person; a young woman, the Agon shaman who had refused to kneel and who stared at him now balefully, muttering curses; and dozens of children, some Agon, some barbarian, and a few togaten spawn.

"You've done the Lyucu a great service," he announced to the two Lyucu warriors standing before him.

"Not at all, votan, we're just grateful to be rescued," said Toof.

"We're ashamed that we didn't fight off our captors earlier," said Radia.

"Oh, the things they did to us—" Toof's voice caught in his throat as he choked up.

"It's all right," said Radia, patting him on the back. "We're safe now in the protection of the pékyu."

"Liars! You dirty Lyucu liars!" shouted one of the kneeling boys. He struggled to get off his knees as his blazing eyes locked on Toof and Radia. "You were adopted into the family of Vara Ronalek, and we trusted you!"

A younger boy—by his looks, the older boy's brother—tried to emulate his older sibling. "Liar! Liar!" he shouted in support.

Several of the other children, seeing the pair of brothers being so defiant, also began to shout.

"Agon and barbarian children learn to lie from birth," said Toof awkwardly. "This Vara was the one who enslaved us and beat us daily."

"Those two are certainly feisty," said an amused Cudyu. "Do you know who they are? By the way they're dressed, they must be togaten or barbarian."

"I didn't see who was shouting," said Toof. He shaded his eyes and peered at the captives helplessly. "My eyes . . . the barbarians made me and Radia do hard labor in their smokehouse, and my sight is ruined."

"Surely you recognized the voices, though?" said Cudyu. "Maybe they are the children of that Nméji Gon, the despicable Dara fighter who cost me so many warriors near the end. Or . . ." His eyes suddenly lit up. "Volyu mentioned that Théra and Takval have two boys. Are they among these young rebel-spawn?"

"I'm . . . I'm not sure," said Toof. "There were many children in the settlement, and Radia and I . . . and I . . ."

Radia took over smoothly. "We were kept in shackles, away from the children, most of the time. The rebels thought we were dangerous. Even after they forced us to swear allegiance to the Agon, they didn't trust us."

"But Takval and Théra were very . . . um . . . they cared about . . ." Whether out of nervousness or fear, Toof couldn't stop the stutter.

"They were known for being extremely protective of their

children," said Radia. "They would certainly have taken their children with them during the escape—"

The older boy from earlier started yelling again. "Don't you dare to turn your faces away from me, Radia and Toof! You lying—"

A Lyucu guard standing next to the group of captives approached the boy menacingly, his club held at the ready. But he was undeterred.

"—scoundrels. My parents should have thrown you—"

His shouts were cut off as the young shaman clamped a hand over his mouth and pulled him back down to his knees. The boy continued to struggle, and the shaman finally removed her hand from his mouth and slapped him sharply across the face.

"You and your brother need to know when to shut up!" said the shaman in a loud, angry voice. "Your father and I have told you countless times that you need to learn to know when to yield."

"That's right." It was the barbarian scholar. "Taria and Riva, both of you need to listen to your mother and keep your mouths shut. Don't we have enough to worry about already?"

The shock of the slap finally quieted the older boy. He and his little brother seethed in silence, tears pouring down their faces. The other children looked at them and also at the shaman and the scholar, their faces contorted in confusion.

"Afir knew it was useless to stare at the Eye of Cudyufin directly," said the shaman. "Be like her and avert your gazes."

The shaman and the scholar adjusted their kneeling poses and kept their eyes on the ground. The children, though confused and terrified, latched onto this voice of adult authority and imitated them, keeping their eyes downcast as they knelt.

"Votan, we had to pretend to go along with them—" began Toof.

But Cudyu stopped him by holding up a hand. "It's all right. My father once also pretended to give in to the power of the Agon to bide his time. There's nothing shameful about what you did. You were captives of the rebel slaves, and only by pretending to submit could you have gotten this chance to escape. Moreover, you brought me these wayward calves—it's too bad that Théra and Takval's issue aren't among them. Still, I won't forget your contributions."

"Votan, you're most wise and merciful," said Radia and Toof together as they went to one knee, their heads bowed in submission.

"What do you think should be done with these children?" asked Cudyu, his tone casual.

Radia and Toof looked at each other.

"These pups may not be much of a threat now," ventured Toof in a low voice. "But once they've grown . . ."

"Speak up," said Cudyu.

Toof's face flushed and he seemed to have trouble getting his words out. Radia took over. "It would only be right to sacrifice these young rebels to the gods to bring a measure of peace to our brothers and sisters who lost their lives at sea due to Luan Zya's treachery."

"How are they responsible for the sins of Luan Zya?" asked Cudyu.

Radia glanced at the children kneeling at the foot of the hill. Then, her face full of hatred, she turned back to the pékyu. "All Dara barbarians are the same. The sins of one should be counted against all. That was the teaching of the pékyu-votan."

Time passed as Cudyu pondered the fate of the captives, while Toof and Radia remained on one knee, not daring to speak.

Cudyu found the eagerness of the two freed Lyucu to kill the children odd.

When he found out that Théra and Takval's sons weren't among the prisoners, he had lost interest in them, and his instinct had been to have the captives paraded to the various Agon settlements and then publicly slaughtered to instill fear and obedience. But Radia and Toof seemed to want the children killed immediately.

*Do the children know some secret about these two? Perhaps they did something shameful in their captivity, betrayed the Lyucu to curry favor with the Agon and Dara, or . . . adopted barbarian customs?*

He was, by nature, a suspicious pékyu. More than anything else, he hated to be *used*. The more eagerly someone wanted him to do something, the more likely there was some hidden agenda. He decided that he would keep the children alive after all.

Cudyu shook his head, as if emerging from a dream. "No. That's not the right thing to do. You're blinded by the thirst for vengeance.

It's likely that the parents of some of these children are among those who escaped with Takval and Théra. Since you don't recognize the children, we'll have to wait until they can be brought to the other captives and see if anyone among them knows who their parents are. By keeping the whelps alive, I'll have another way to bend their parents to my will. Just as we can compel obedience from the garinafins by holding their young ones hostage, I'm certain that these lambs will be worth more to us alive than dead."

"The pékyu is most wise," said Toof and Radia together.

"Votan," said Tovo, Cudyu's most trusted garinafin-thane, "we should go after the escaped Agon and Dara rebels before the trail grows cold." Tovo had grown up hunting with Cudyu, and the only thing he enjoyed more than bringing down a tusked tiger was hunting two-legged prey.

"Of course," said Cudyu. *I've been wasting my time here.* "Ready the garinafins and we'll leave immediately after lunch."

"What about the children?"

"What about them?"

"Araten already left. I'm afraid that if we leave them with the warriors assigned to clean up the valley, the situation might prove to be . . . too tempting."

Cudyu understood what Tovo was getting at. The attack on Kiri Valley, though successful, had also been costly. Nméji Gon's trick at the end, especially, had injured and killed many warriors. Leaving the children here would surely invite reprisals from the naros and culeks left behind, and by the time Cudyu and Tovo returned, the captives would likely all be dead. In fact, fear of such reprisals had been why the other captives, under guard by the surrendered Agon thane Araten, had been sent away to Taten with the wounded Lyucu warriors as soon as the battle was over.

Cudyu turned to Toof and Radia, a calculating look on his face. "These are your captives. Maybe your future slaves. How do you suggest we keep them safe?"

"Err . . ." Toof scratched his head and chin, and sweat beaded on his forehead.

Cudyu had to suppress the urge to laugh. The naro looked like he was devoting every fold of the fatty sponge in his skull to the effort of coming up with a solution for the puzzle his lord had posed. He found himself liking Toof. Stupid but loyal people were the best.

"Maybe you can send some trusted thanes to bring them back to Taten, like the other captives," suggested Toof, after much thinking.

"Are you volunteering then?" asked Cudyu, a smile curving up the corners of his lips.

Toof stared at the pékyu, looking confused. But Radia, who seemed much quicker of mind to Cudyu, immediately bowed her head. "Thank you, O great pékyu."

"But we're not thanes—" objected Toof.

Radia turned to him, looking incredulous. She punched him. "Shut up, you idiot! Thank the pékyu!"

"Aw!" Toof cried out. Then, a moment later, understanding finally dawned on his face. "Oh. Oh! OH!" He copied Radia's bow. "For a herdless naro like me to be elevated to a thane . . . oh, there are no words for my gratitude . . . no words . . . just no words . . ."

"From this day on, just think of me and Toof as your most obedient hounds," said Radia. "If you throw your signaling spear at a rock, the two of us will bite it. If you toss your signaling spear at our own children, we will tear them apart. If you but point your littlest finger at your enemy, be it man or beast or god, we will not hesitate to attack it with all—"

"All right, all right!" said Cudyu, waving his hand at the two freshly promoted thanes. "You really have spent too much time among the Dara slaves—you even grovel like them. Don't make me regret my decision."

"Never. Never!" Radia and Toof shook their heads like two rattle drums.

"It's settled then. You don't have proper clans, do you? Maybe I'll ask Tovo to adopt you later. . . . The shamans will mark you with your rank-scars tonight, and then the two of you will be in charge of escorting the prisoners to Taten."

Radia and Toof looked at him with anguish.

"But . . . but . . ."

"We've only just been made thanes! Shouldn't we be at the very vanguard, hounding down your enemies like the first storm of winter?"

Everyone knew that escorting prisoners when there was still more battle to be fought was a shameful task suitable only for the weak and infirm.

"No buts. Didn't you just claim that you would do whatever I wanted?" Cudyu's voice turned stern.

Inside, he was rather pleased at the reaction from these two. He didn't trust them, not completely, and it was better to have them out of the way. But the fact that they were so eager to serve their votan was a good sign. And by putting them together with the prisoners, he hoped that the young captives would be tempted to say something that would give away the shameful secret he was sure these two were hiding—even if it turned to be nothing more than speaking ill of Pékyu-votan Tenryo or allowing themselves to be adopted by some Agon clan. He liked knowing people's secrets; it made them easier to control. He'd tell the other guards to keep an eye on them.

"We'll do as you say, votan," said Radia as she and Toof bowed their heads, completely submissive.

Tanto, Rokiri, and the other children stared at the two new Lyucu thanes with utter hatred. They were glad to see that Radia and Toof stayed away from them the rest of the day.

For five days, the two garinafins and their passengers made their way northwest along the Blood River, one of the two rivers feeding into the Sea of Tears. This was the way to the site where Pékyu Tenryo had spent his childhood among the Agon, and was now an important military base from which Cudyu exerted control over the surrounding tribes.

"One more round, votan-ru-taasa and votan-sa-taasa?" asked Toof as he raised a small skin cup. Fashioned from a rim of four linked sheep ribs and a dangling piece of sheepskin, the skin cup was a portable substitute for the skull bowl favored in the scrublands for consuming kyoffir.

The eight other Lyucu guards on the prisoner transport mission, resting around the small fire, shook their heads. For the first few

nights of the journey, Toof and Radia had been subdued in the eve-
nings, claiming that they were still healing from the burn scars on
their backs that signified their new rank. None of the Lyucu guards
felt they knew the new thanes well yet.

"Already had too . . . too much," said one of the guards, her
speech slurring. She was a naro in her sixties, long beyond her prime
fighting years.

"We haven't had genuine Lyucu kyoffir for years!" said Radia.
"Come on, it would be most shameful for Toof and me to drink
alone." She grabbed the kyoffirskin and began to walk around the
circle, looking for empty skin cups.

"What are you so worried about?" asked Toof. "Do you think
you're going to find Agon rebels out here? Are you dreaming of a
commendation for valor?"

The old naro scoffed. Like the others in the guard detail, she was
from one of the tribes that happened to be closest to Kiri Valley,
drafted by Pékyu Cudyu at the last minute as support for the assault
on the secret base. Now that the attack was over and the pékyu was
off chasing after the escaped rebels, she had been relegated to this
thankless job. It was shameful to know that the pékyu thought so
little of her.

"If you're not going to be fighting," said Radia, "you might as
well enjoy yourself. That's why I loaded up on kyoffir before I left.
Now if only we had some good tolyusa leaves to smoke . . ."

"I . . . I guess I could have an-another cup," said the old naro. She
decided that the thane was right. What was the point of feeling sorry
for oneself at her age? Might as well try to drown her sorrows. She
held out her cup.

The other guards, equally demoralized, lifted their skin cups to
be refilled.

"Let's drink to the health of our pékyu," toasted Toof. "And may
we all rise to become garinafin-thanes!"

The Lyucu warriors laughed self-deprecatingly at this absurd
wish. They drained their cups, hoping to have better luck in their
dreams than they did in life.

Toof and Radia drank so enthusiastically that the kyoffir dripped down their necks—more intoxicating liquid probably went down their vests than into their bellies.

Beyond the circle of guards, some distance away, lay the trussed-up prisoners, and beyond them slept two garinafins. One of them was too old to even breathe fire because she had lost the canine teeth that were used to spark the flames, and the other was so young that he could barely fly a whole day and had to rest often. Like their human counterparts, they would not take part in the glorious hunt for the fugitives.

Tanto muttered curses as he stared at the drinking Lyucu guards in the flickering firelight. "If I ever get my hands on them, I'll make Toof's head into a bowl to piss in—"

"Shush," whispered Sataari. "The less you say, the better."

"How can you be so calm?" demanded Tanto. "Aren't you mad at them? They betrayed our trust."

"How is being angry going to help us when we are bound like this?" said Sataari, wiggling her toes, pretty much the only part of her body allowed such freedom. "Close your eyes and try to rest. We've still got a long journey ahead of us."

Tanto sighed and closed his eyes, thinking of his parents. He fell asleep while praying to the gods to keep them safe.

Toof and Radia knelt before him, and he felt the sweet pleasure of vengeance.

As the two cowered, he raised his war club. He was going to be like the heroes in those old stories, vanquishing his enemies and uplifting the spirits of all the dead friends and loved ones back in Kiri Valley—

Someone kicked him hard in the ribs.

"Aw!" he cried out, and woke up.

"Hurry!" whispered his brother. "We're leaving!"

"What? Where?"

But there was no time for answers. The entire campsite was in quiet tumult. The Lyucu guards were sprawled out around the fire, deep in their drunken slumber. Children were running toward the two garinafins, where Razutana and Sataari were strapping them in one by one.

And the two other adults helping them were . . . Toof and Radia.

Tanto growled and ran at Toof. The man was turned away from him, and the boy leapt to kick him hard in his behind. Grunting, the man fell down, his face slamming into the hard earth.

Tanto was about to go after the man again when Sataari grabbed him from behind and held him fast. "Stop it! No noises. He's helping us escape."

"What?" *Am I still in a dream?*

"Later!" whispered the shaman.

Sataari pushed him onto the back of the smaller garinafin, and Radia strapped him into the draped webbing. "Stay still. Don't spook the garinafin," the Lyucu whispered.

He watched, in a daze, as Toof got up and rushed to the head of the agitated garinafin, who seemed on the verge of crying out. Tanto's attack on Toof had alarmed him, making him think that something was wrong. If he did scream, some of the Lyucu guards would surely awaken.

Everyone held their breath.

The garinafin calmed down as Toof stroked his nose while cooing at him.

Within a few minutes, all the children were strapped onto the two garinafins. Sataari climbed into the saddle of the older one while Razutana climbed onto the younger one.

"I literally have no idea what I'm doing," said Razutana, his face ashen.

"I can't say I'm a master pilot myself," said Sataari. "I know just enough not to get us killed . . . I hope. I think your mount will follow mine."

Toof and Radia remained on the ground.

Tanto watched them mutely. Somehow they seemed so much *more* than they had ever seemed to him. He wondered if he would ever be able to tell true hearts apart from false ones.

"Are you sure about this?" asked Sataari.

Toof and Radia nodded.

"If we also disappear, our families up north will pay for it," said Radia. "At least there's a chance we'll muddle through if we stay."

"But you've got almost no supplies left," said Sataari. "Let me leave you at least more pemmican."

"No," said Toof. "We can find charred-bottom hares and dig for voles, even with all this snow. You'll need all the supplies on those garinafins out in the salt flats."

Sataari nodded. *Thank you* was inadequate for what the two Lyucu thanes had done, and so she did not bother saying it. She nudged the old garinafin with her knees to get her to take off.

"She didn't get a full night's rest," said Toof. "Don't push her too hard. Try to land before sunrise."

"I almost think that you care about the beasts more than you care about people," teased Sataari.

Toof chuckled and stepped back to stand with Radia.

The two garinafins took off. Sataari gently nudged her mount at the base of the neck with her heels until she was flying due east. The other garinafin, barely more than a juvenile, followed as he wasn't getting any clear instructions from his pilot—Razutana was doing all he could just to hang on to the saddle.

Rocked by the comforting thought of freedom and the garinafin's rhythmic undulation, Tanto and the other children fell asleep.

Toof and Radia watched until the garinafins had disappeared against the night sky. They turned to face each other.

"I don't know if we did the right thing," said Toof. "Takval and Théra . . . they must hate us."

"It was the only way," said Radia. "They can't possibly escape Cudyu with all those children slowing them down. My only regret is that we didn't lighten their load even more. And we managed to delay the pursuit by half a day with the gambit. Every second counts."

"I still shudder to think of that moment . . . when Cudyu asked us what to do about the children. We were gambling with their lives."

"Cudyu has always been like a bad-tempered yearling garinafin. You tell him to go east, he goes west. It was an easy bet to make." Radia tried to make herself sound casual, but her voice shook.

"If he had said yes, I would have had no choice but to die trying to save the kids."

"They're our tribe," said Radia, nodding. "Thank the gods it didn't come to that."

"Not all our gambles paid off," said Toof. "Vara . . ." His voice faded.

"There was no time to explain." Radia put a comforting arm around his shoulders. "You tried to save her. You tried."

Nothing was said for a while. The only sounds were the snores of the sleeping Lyucu guards and the howling of the wind across the scrubland. Maybe there were quiet sobs, but it was hard to tell.

"Do you think she's riding the cloud-garinafins now beyond the World's Edge?" asked Toof, picking up his club.

"I hope so," said Radia, also picking up hers. "But who can know what happens in the beyond? We'll have to carry on the Ronalek name ourselves and make it mean something. Do you want me to hit you first or the other way around?"

"I better go first," said Toof, sighing. "You don't have the gentlest hand, and I'm afraid that if you hit me first, I won't be able to hit back."

"Crybaby. All right, come get me."

"Remember, Razutana and Sataari aren't warriors—just a few light taps will do."

"Ha! They're stronger than you think. Besides, we have to make it convincing."

As the stars spun overhead, the two Lyucu thanes swung bone clubs against each other and grunted, spitting out the occasional loose tooth, until eventually both lay down where the garinafins had been sleeping earlier, hoping their bloody faces and bruised limbs would tell a good enough story.

# CHAPTER THIRTY-SEVEN

# THE FIRST CONTEST: PART I

GINPEN: THE FIFTH MONTH IN THE NINTH YEAR
OF THE REIGN OF SEASON OF STORMS AND THE
REIGN OF AUDACIOUS FREEDOM (TWENTY-FOUR
MONTHS UNTIL THE REOPENING OF THE WALL OF
STORMS).

*Masters and mistresses, lend me your ears—*
*Or even better, add your eyes, nose, tongue,*
*And eating-stick-wielding hands clapping cheers!*
*Bear witness to this magnificent war*
*Where kitchen boys are troops, chefs generals,*
*But the only fallen are albacore!*

With animated gestures and a musical cadence, Lolotika Tuné, head girl of the Aviary, Ginpen's most exclusive indigo house, worked the crowd in Temple Square as she paced the newly erected stage. It was a beautiful spring day in Ginpen, and thousands had turned out to attend this most unusual culinary event.

Girls at the Aviary were not sold to the house, but negotiated contracts of service that gave them choice over clients and a steady salary plus tips. Though traditional indigo houses still existed, their days were clearly numbered as Prime Minister Cogo Yelu continued to press for phasing out indentured servitude in as many industries as possible on the ground that such arrangements were incompatible with Moralist precepts. At the Aviary, girls who drew the most business had the opportunity to become full partners, which entitled them to a share of the profits and a say in the management of the house.

Lolotika—a stage name, though she went by "Lolo" to her friends—was widely acknowledged as the most beautiful woman in Ginpen and a talented poet, skilled in both comic vernacular song and tragic Classical Ano verse. Truth be told, she was almost as much a draw for the large crowd at this first contest between the Splendid Urn and the Treasure Chest as the cooking competition itself. That Tiphan Huto had suggested her as the hostess was a stroke of genius that had fanned even more interest.

As the crowd laughed and applauded, Séca Thu, Lolo's co-host and nephew of Kita Thu, the archon of the Imperial laboratories in Ginpen, stepped onto the stage and introduced the panel of judges sitting at the long, low table behind him and Lolo. Composed of monastics, scholars, nobles, prominent merchants, poets, artists, and leading foodies whose opinions on Ginpen's restaurant scene were avidly followed, the judges represented the cream of Ginpen society. Lolo and Séca had picked the judges, taking into account suggestions from the public.

Widow Wasu and Tiphan Huto, ensconced on two sitting mats at opposite ends of the stage, stared daggers at each other as the judges stood up one by one and bowed to the excited crowd.

That Magistrate Zuda himself had turned down the invitation was regretful, but neither Widow Wasu nor Tiphan Huto could fault the magistrate's concern that the government not be seen as tipping the scales in private competition. Given rumors that Widow Wasu had connections with the Imperial family in the past, Tiphan was actually glad that officials would play no part in this contest.

"We'll begin by explaining the rules to everyone," said Séca.

"First, since this is a cooking competition, food has to be the star of the show," said Lolo in her mellifluous voice. "Just because Séca is so handsome, judges, you can't let him steal the focus." She turned to wink at the judges.

The crowd laughed and hooted, and a few of the male judges who had been staring at Lolo in her diaphanous, curve-hugging cocoon-dress blushed and chuckled. Then they knelt up in *mipa rari* and stared solemnly at the empty table in front of them, as though they were scholars ready to tackle the essay question at the Grand Examination.

"Each side will present a full meal to the judges: an appetizer, meat and vegetable entrées, drinks, and a dessert," continued Lolo. "The only restriction is that the dishes must be cooked with the ingredients on hand and the people employed by the competitors— no running at the last minute to some other restaurant to pass off their work as your own."

"Second, although the judges only care about the final result," said Séca, "it's no fun for the rest of us if we just watch them eat, am I right?" The crowd murmured in approval. "That's why the cooking today is going to be done in the open here in Temple Square. Both restaurants have agreed to bring their equipment and prepare the meals right in front of us!" He pointed to the two smaller stages, one on each side of the big stage. Wild shouts and applause erupted from the crowd.

The staff of the Splendid Urn and the Treasure Chest had spent the last few days setting up their stoves, ovens, counters, and chopping blocks, and wagons full of ingredients and additional equipment waited next to the stages.

"Let's meet the contestants," said Lolo, a bright smile on her smooth, flawless face, the same hue as the black sands of Lutho Beach and just as alluring. She strode to the western end of the stage, struck a pose, and let her voice carry over the vast square.

"First, cooking for the challenger, the Treasure Chest, we have a true legend of loaves, *pana méji* of pies, sage of spices, maestro of marinades, genius of jams, philosopher of frying pans, scholar of stewpots, champion of chopping blocks, virtuoso of vittles—all right, I admit that last one is a bit of a stretch." She took a deep breath before continuing. "Hailing from the misty vales of the Damu Mountains, this seasoned chef made dumplings before walking or talking and is the heir to seven generations of culinary knowledge and secret techniques—can you imagine the gustatory delights lurking in that capacious familial mine of a mind? You should all count yourselves lucky, for this family has rebuffed invitations and enticements from the wealthiest households in Dara for generations, from Tiro kings and grand dukes, from pious priests and mindful ministers, from virtuous scholars and unscrupulous robber barons, preferring to cultivate their pure art in hermitic seclusion. The illustrious ancestor of this veteran culinary artist once slapped young Emperor Mapidéré's hand for daring to grab a cookie from the plate before the great chef considered it ready—yes, of course that story is true, for I once heard it from a drunk client. Let's give it up for the myth, the legend, the cruben of cooks, the dyran of dough-kneaders, MOHHHHH-ZO MUUUUUU!"

Amidst loud cheers and thunderous clapping, a figure bounded out of the covered wagon tethered next to the small stage on the west. She climbed up the steps, took her place, and surveyed the audience calmly. Then she clapped her hands, summoning a team of assistants onto the stage, and she began to direct them to their stations.

The crowd craned their necks to get a better look.

"She's just a kid!"

"What is she, eleven? Twelve?"

"How in the world can she lead a kitchen? What does she know about fine cooking?"

"Don't be so quick to judge. Remember how Lurusén wrote his first poem when he was just seven? Big talent can come in small packages."

As the crowd exclaimed and marveled at the youth of Mozo Mu, Kinri and Dandelion, peeking at the scene from a covered wagon next to the stage on the east, looked at each other in amazement.

Dandelion, along with the Blossom Gang, was here as Widow Wasu's guests. In fact, they were sitting inside the wagon originally meant for Teson Wasu, the manager. Teson had begged to be allowed to stay at the Splendid Urn to care for Head Chef Néfi Ézugo—but some of the servants whispered that the real reason was because Teson was too nervous to attend the competition in person.

"I *knew* there was something odd about her!" said Dandelion. "I have an extra sense about these things."

"As I recall, I was the one who said we should memorize her poems," said Kinri. "You were too busy arguing with Arona."

"Show-off," said Dandelion, sticking her tongue out at him. They had spent the better part of the past week together, sharing stories and working side by side.

The "seasoned" Mozo Mu was none other than the girl they had seen in the kitchen of the Treasure Chest on their spying mission.

"I don't know why everyone is so scared of her," said Kinri. "There's no way someone that young can outcook Mati."

"She's a tougher opponent than you realize," said Dandelion. "Pay attention to the way she's directing her assistants. She has them working in parallel on different parts of the same dish, but she's the only one who puts them together at the end."

Kinri looked. "All right, I see that. So?"

"She's making sure that none of the assistants get the whole recipe. Remember how we saw her muttering the recipes to herself in code, and only giving out isolated steps to the assistants? This way, she keeps the keys to Suda Mu's dishes secret. That's smart."

Kinri nodded. "That *is* clever."

Both Lolo and Séca were apparently stunned by the tender age of this heir to the great master chef, and there was a lull in the proceedings. Meanwhile, Tiphan Huto grinned like a quarter moon. The unveiling of his secret weapon had gone exactly as planned. The skepticism and wonder of the crowd would only add fuel to the flaring interest in his restaurant.

The hosts got the crowd back under control when Séca strode to the east side of the big stage and began to speak in a sonorous voice, as though delivering an oration to the professors at one of Haan's famed academies. He had, after all, just been added to the Imperial laboratories of Ginpen as a researcher, and the manners of the lecture hall came naturally to him.

"Cooking for the defending champion, the Splendid Urn, our second contestant is a last-minute replacement when the head chef suffered a health setback. But don't underestimate her because of her lack of fame. She began to cook for a whole family of twelve when she was five, when her mother became bedridden from a wasting disease and all her siblings had to labor in the fields. Instead of ancient tomes or celebrity chefs, she learned the art of traditional Cocru cuisine from that most unforgiving of teachers: rowdy patrons at beer-and-pot-sticker taverns. A loyal servant of the Wasu clan for over twenty years, let's give a warm welcome to Mati Phy!"

The applause this time was subdued, more out of politeness than delight. Though Séca had tried to make the most of the scant biography provided on Mati, he lacked Lolo's flair for drama and couldn't do much to compensate for Mati's rather unimpressive qualifications. Even the best cooks couldn't make a tasty meal without salt.

Mati climbed onto the stage on the east, looking nervous. The crowd couldn't help but contrast the sous-chef suddenly thrust into the spotlight against the confident young prodigy. Some began to wonder if the Splendid Urn had in fact earned its place as the premier restaurant of Ginpen or was merely coasting along on the reputation of Widow Wasu. True, Widow Wasu had once catered the pre-coronation meal of Emperor Ragin, but the emperor's qualification as a gourmet was rather suspect given his origins as a bandit, not a man of learning and refinement.

Even before the first dish had been served, it seemed that the Treasure Chest had already scored a victory.

"Ready?" asked Lolo, looking from one small stage to the other.

Mozo and Mati nodded.

"Begin!"

A dove landed on the giant screen at the back of the stage, behind the judges—what was a screen doing here?—along with a pair of ravens, one black, one white. At the edge of the crowd, a large dog—looking suspiciously like a wolf—circled around.

In the excitement of the competition, no one paid attention to the birds. The dog, despite his size, was quiet and friendly, and allowed the children in the audience to pet him without any sign of annoyance. Reassured, the parents turned their eyes back to the stages.

- *Why did you invite us here, Rufizo—*

*—when we have so many more important things to do?*

- *Don't you want to know how the competition turns out?*

- *This is silliness! Who cares about a bunch of cooks when there's a war to be fought and the lives of millions at stake?*

- *Sisters and brother, be patient. Even when a typhoon rages through the Islands, the shrimp continues to dance and court his mate in sheltered lagoons. Even when a snowstorm kills a thousand flowers, the buried* thasé-teki *dreams of summer bloom. Life goes on even in the midst of titanic war and all-consuming destruction. What is the point of plotting and fretting over the lives of millions if there is to be no warm spring of silliness, no restoring bath of zany hijinks, no salve of joy for wearied hearts and overtaxed spirits?*

　- *. . . What. Are. You. Talking. About?*

　- Sigh. *Let me try this another way. Don't you remember how Kuni started in a bar with his friends, comparing one another to flowers?*

　- *Are you suggesting these mechanics . . . these "Blossoms"—*

　—*can change the fate of Dara more than Jia?*

　- *Are you implying these cooks can pose a greater threat to the Lyucu than Phyro? What do you know that you aren't saying?*

　- *Are you—*

　- *Patience! I don't know the future any more than the rest of you. But I'm a god. I'm allowed to believe in omens.*

On the west stage, Mozo Mu was a blur of motion. She leapt from cooking station to cooking station like a determined woodpecker seeking the right perch, barking directions to assistant cooks, checking ingredients, and tasting sauces before returning to the central island, her command center. Half a dozen servants carried platters of partially-prepared ingredients to her, and she examined the work of her assistants with a critical eye, sometimes sending things back when they weren't done to her satisfaction. The whole kitchen stage ran as smoothly as a disciplined army camp, and everyone seemed to know exactly what to do.

Finally, when she was happy with the prep work, she climbed onto a stool next to the central island so that she could reach over the counter, picked up the polished steel knife, and wielded it with dazzling dexterity as she sliced, diced, chopped, carved, shaved, pierced, peeled, and cleaved. She moved with such ease and confidence that the mesmerized crowd was reminded of a sword dancer of Cocru.

Lolo and Séca walked around the big stage, looking first at one of the side stages and then the other. With them was one of the judges, Lady Gina Cophy, a plump noblewoman in her forties widely reputed to be a fine foodie. She had founded a dining club composed of noblewomen from Ginpen's oldest families, and they dined once a week at one of the restaurants in Ginpen, after which they made their judgment known at poetry-and-tea parties and in private conversation. It was said that a word from Gina's club could make or break a new restaurant in the city.

"Lady Cophy, can you tell us what's happening in the Treasure Chest kitchen?" asked Lolo. She held a silk-and-bamboo speaking trumpet to Gina's mouth so that her rather soft voice could be heard by the crowd above the din from both kitchens.

"Hmm, I have to say I'm a little confused." Although at first unused to speaking into a trumpet, Gina Cophy soon grew comfortable with the instrument. It was nice to have everyone hanging on her every word. "The knife-work is exceptional, of course, but I'm not sure I know what dish Mozo is preparing. Those ebony quails are quite rare, as you know, and prized for their medicinal bones and tender flesh."

"It's really impressive that the Treasure Chest has supplied dozens of them, isn't it?"

"Oh, definitely. I don't think I've ever heard of a restaurant obtaining more than five at a time. When my husband, the baron, was alive, the Cavorting Cruben would always reserve one for him when they got some."

"But it looks like Mozo is discarding most of the bird!" Lolo cried.

Indeed, the audience could see that Mozo was picking up each plucked bird, about the size of a fist, and making a few precise cuts in the flesh. After something plopped into a porcelain bowl, she tossed the rest of the bird into the refuse bin.

"That's why I'm confused," said Gina. "To cook ebony quail *without* using the bone or much of the flesh is most unusual—oh, wait!" She leaned over the edge of the big stage and shaded her eyes with a hand to get a better look. "These birds are all male. She's harvesting their testicles!"

At this, Séca winced, along with many of the men in the crowd. Some of the women laughed.

Although rooster testicles were often served at pubs in Cocru and Faça, they were not part of traditional Haan cuisine.

"A most . . . most unusual choice," said Séca weakly.

"Oh, this makes me even more excited," gushed Gina. "Over in that corner, you can also see one of the sous-chefs picking out the roe from deep-sea jade crabs. And beyond the island, they're slicing the seedpods from dyran's-tail seaweed fronds—as you know, you have to look through a thousand fronds before finding even one pod. The sheer expense that is going into this dish is breathtaking!"

"All right, I think we've been over here long enough. Let's take a look at the other kitchen, shall we?" asked Lolo. She and Séca guided Lady Cophy away from the western edge of the stage, though the lady looked back with every step, clearly reluctant to go.

Instead of the hubbub of activity on the Treasure Chest stage, Mati was working with only two assistants. The three of them were squeezed into one corner of the stage, their backs to the audience, almost as if they were afraid to show them what they were doing.

"Oh, listen to that oil sizzle! Look at how flat they're rolling that dough!" said Lolo. She was doing her best to focus Lady Cophy's attention on the Splendid Urn.

Certainly, Lolo had a soft spot for Widow Wasu. Back when she was still a low-ranking girl indentured to another indigo house, she often had her clients take her to the Splendid Urn because the widow told her staff to step in whenever one of the girls seemed to have trouble with a drunk or violent client. Later, after she had paid back her debts to the house and bought her freedom, Widow Wasu had lent her the money for dance and elocution lessons to further her career. "We girls in business need to invest in one another," the widow had told her.

Naturally, Lolo would like to see the Splendid Urn keep its title. But more than that, it simply didn't make for a good show if the commentary were too lopsided.

Lady Cophy, however, didn't seem to understand basic show business. She took one look at what Mati was doing and frowned. "It looks like the team from the Splendid Urn is making dumplings . . . and frying them . . . They're making pot stickers." Her voice faded, and then stopped.

"Err, could you say a few more words to give our audience a

better sense of these delicious treats?" prodded Lolo. "Maybe comment a bit on the technique? The team's movements?"

"Well, I don't know if they're delicious," said Lady Cophy. "As far as I can tell, they're just standard pot stickers: pork filling, some pipe scallions for flavoring, hundred-fold dough. I didn't even realize that pot stickers were on the menu at the Urn."

"Also a most . . . most unusual choice, wouldn't you say?" Séca chimed in.

"Honestly, I'm not sure that kind of peasant fare—"

"Hey, I think they're doing something new over at the Treasure Chest again!" said Lolo, and she and Séca gently ushered the commentator back to the other side.

Mati's face was bright red. She had heard every word.

A week earlier, when Kinri, Dandelion, and the Blossom Gang told Mati what they had found at the Treasure Chest, she had been overwhelmed.

As the six of them surrounded her in the kitchen courtyard, vying to recount their adventures, all she heard was a flood of names of exotic ingredients she had never touched, cooking techniques she had never tried, Classical Ano poetry that she had never studied—"Stop." She held up her hands. "Just stop. This is my contest, not yours."

She had always found the people of Ginpen a bit too full of themselves and their school-taught knowledge. "High-minded," as the poets would say. Even after a decade in Ginpen, she found the city's elite customers not entirely welcoming. In a way, the capital of old Haan felt to her not unlike Tiphan's fancy new restaurant: all golden glitter on the outside and a cold, icy cellar on the inside. She was afraid that she didn't belong.

"But we can help," said Dandelion. "These are very sophisticated dishes they're attempting. You'll need someone who can decipher their poetry and get at the heart of their story."

Mati had no idea what Dandelion was talking about. She knew that big-spending diners who hosted parties at the Splendid Urn with girls from the Aviary were not just there for the food and drinks; she knew that Lodan didn't always understand the riddles and poems recited by the scholars toasting each other; she knew that the splendid restaurant she had helped to build in Ginpen was nothing like the tavern she had run back in Zudi. But what did poetry and story have to do with cooking?

"Let us help," said Widi Tucru. "The judges will be impressed by what Mozo Mu has planned. You'll need to elevate your game too."

Defiance arose in her. No one liked to be looked down upon. Sure, she didn't know how to read logograms or recite poetry, and she wasn't sophisticated like Dandelion and Widi. But no matter how fancy a restaurant tried to be, the foundation was food, wasn't it? And though she didn't know poetry and story, she knew food.

"I've kept the Splendid Urn in business with my artless hands for three years," she said, her tone more wounded than she meant to make it. "I reckon I can keep the game at *my* level a little longer."

The others looked at one another.

"We didn't mean it like that," said Dandelion contritely.

Kinri tried to persuade her. "Mati, I really think—"

She waved at them decisively.

"My mind is made up. I'll handle this Mozo Mu myself."

Of the ten dishes head chef Néfi Ézugo was most proud of, Mati knew how to make eleven—that's right, she had been quietly improving the menu on her own. She hadn't worked her way up from a scullery maid to the sous-chef of the greatest restaurant in Ginpen without learning a few tricks along the way.

Some of these dishes that had earned the Splendid Urn its reputation required rare ingredients that the restaurant didn't keep in stock in large quantities. Truth be told, like most established restaurants, the Splendid Urn had been coasting a bit as the years went on, and the patrons no longer requested these signature dishes as often.

Mati sent Kinri and the other kitchen servants to the market right away for supplies. She wanted to practice.

They came back with empty baskets. None of the things she needed could be found.

Cursing her bad luck, she sent them out of the city, to towns and farms all over Haan, hoping that the Twins would aid her. Even after so many years in Haan, she still trusted Rapa and Kana, patrons of old Cocru, more than Lutho, the god of this region. But the shop-keepers told the staff that men from Ginpen had come a few days earlier with bags of gold and bought up all the spices and preserves she needed, offering prices several times higher than what they were used to.

Mati knew this to be the work of Tiphan Huto. He had not only filled the pantries of the Treasure Chest with exotic ingredients, but also sought to deprive the Splendid Urn of the resources required to make their signature dishes. Finding out what his competition needed to make their best dishes was, in part, why he had dined at the Splendid Urn on that fateful day.

Mati prayed to the Twins, the goddesses of her home; to Lutho, the patron of this land; to Rufizo, who always came to the aid of the needy; even to Fithowéo, the god of war—why not? She had seen the *cashima* heading to the Grand Examination pray to him as well. A war was a war, whether one wielded sword and shield or spatula and frying pan.

But no matter how much she prayed, the ingredients she needed could not be found.

Kinri came to her again, explaining that he and his friends had some ideas for how to help her. She tried to keep an open mind this time and listened to them, but they were not cooks, and the sugges-tions they gave were preposterous, involving the use of complicated machines and strange devices, the sort of ideas outsiders who knew nothing about cooking would come up with.

No, panicking and putting one's hope in well-meaning but unskilled friends was not the answer. The right answer, as she had learned since she was a little girl, was to go back to the basics.

Back in Cocru, she had kept to the ancient practice of putting away a cup of rice every week, despite the other young women in the village laughing at her old-fashioned ways. That extra store was what kept her family fed when the harvest was late. When she had first started to work for Widow Wasu, the Splendid Urn was just a tavern in Zudi, but it had a menu three hundred items long, the result of successive chefs chasing after different fads in an attempt to make the place appealing to a trendier crowd. She had tossed all those new dishes away and returned to greasy pot stickers and cheap, strong sorghum liquor. The old ways were the best, for they had survived the test of time. The way you got ahead was by sticking to what you knew, working hard, and ignoring the noise.

And so now Mati stubbornly rolled and cut the dough in the show kitchen onstage, mixed the filling with fatty pork and a dash of salted shrimp paste (because people always liked fat and salt, no matter what they said), made the dumplings the way her mother had shown her (a simple pinch to seal the dough and no fancy knot-work), and fried them in the saucepan exactly the way her father had shown her (gently dropping the dumplings into the sizzling oil, at a slight angle away from her so they wouldn't splash, but also not shrinking from the heat).

She would not listen to the noise.

"Looks like the Splendid Urn is the first to be ready to serve the appetizer!" Lolo called out.

Mati climbed up onto the main stage. Lodan followed right behind with a platter covered by banana leaves, and Kinri came last with a thin, narrow-necked amphora. Mati had asked them to be the servers because, despite her bravado, she was feeling nervous, and she wanted people who she trusted to, as she put it, "carry me off the stage if I collapse."

"Oh, that smells good!" said Lolo. Despite years of dining at the finest restaurants with sophisticated clients, she still enjoyed hearty pub fare the most. The tastes of one's youth had a special pull.

"Yes, I'm looking forward to getting reacquainted with pepper-and-cacanut sauce," said Séca politely. "It's been a while, I must admit."

Lady Cophy said nothing at all but wrinkled her nose slightly.

Lodan lifted the banana leaves to reveal rows of golden pot stickers bulging with rich, savory filling, fried to perfection.

As Mati and Lodan walked along the long, low table, Mati used a pair of serving sticks almost as long as her arm to pick up a pot sticker and put it on the plate in front of each of the twelve judges. Then she spooned a bit of hot pepper-and-cacanut sauce onto each plate. Kinri, coming after them, tipped the amphora to fill the cup before each judge with hard sorghum liquor from Mati's home still. Like the pot stickers, this sort of strong, peasant liquor had not been served at the Urn in ages.

The judge sitting at one end of the table, a boy of ten, declined the liquor in favor of tea. After Mati and Lodan had finished serving all the other judges, he called out, "May I have another?"

"Of course," said Mati.

The boy's name was Pimié, a *cüpa* prodigy. Pimié's request made Mati feel a lot better. Children were often the most honest of critics.

Mati reserved the last pot stickers for Lolo and Séca, the hosts.

"Thank you, chef," said Lolo. The crowd watched her, mesmerized. Even the way she held the pot sticker between her eating sticks and dabbed it in sauce seemed as elegant as a scholar practicing calligraphy. Lifting a long draping sleeve to half cover her face, she took a dainty bite with her pearly teeth. "Mmm," she declared, setting down the sleeve and closing her eyes, her elaborate Müning-spire hairdo bobbing like the elegant neck of a crane. "I could eat this all day." Her face glowed with the pleasure of the food, and her whole pose oozed joy.

Many in the audience sighed. No wonder clients paid a fortune just to have a meal with her.

Then she took a sip of sorghum liquor. Instantly her face turned red and her eyes bulged. She covered her mouth again as she was seized by a fit of coughing, tears spilling from her eyes.

"There's that bite," said Séca, who had politely declined the drink when Kinri offered.

It took a few moments for Lolo to recover. In a slightly raspy voice, she said, "I had heard that hard sorghum liquor was something the Hegemon enjoyed, and now I know why it's a drink for heroes."

Mati smiled at the young woman, grateful for her game attempt at elevating the presentation of her homely cooking. But she was growing more confident by the minute as each judge bit into the pot sticker, chewed, and nodded.

"Though it's been a long time since I've had such plebeian food, I have to confess I'm rather won over by the rustic charm," declared Lady Cophy. "The quotidian ingredients, rather common by themselves, have been given a new life. The filling is hearty, rich, and seasoned with simplicity and boldness; the dough is smooth, slippery, and shaped with a primitive candor. The dumplings are cooked to perfection, and the tongue-stinging pepper-and-cacanut sauce really complements the flavors well. The best touch is the sorghum liquor, which is so strong and biting that it comes like a rebellion against the taste regime of the pot stickers, completely unexpected and yet perfectly reasonable."

"Lady Cophy, listening to you talk about food is almost as good as eating it," said Lolo.

"I imagine this was why the Splendid Urn chose to make this dish for the judges," said Séca. "It's an homage to the humble origins of Emperor Ragin and the way he and his friend, the Hegemon, had rebelled against tyranny."

The crowd oohed and aahed at Séca's free association. Mati beamed.

Seriatim, the other judges also offered their words of praise, concluding with young Pimié, who said, "These are almost as good as the ones made by my mom."

Everyone laughed, especially Mati. Of all the praise her cooking had received today, this was the one she would remember.

While Mati was serving the judges the Splendid Urn's appetizer, Mozo Mu was still cooking in the Treasure Chest kitchen. From her central island, she coordinated and commanded helpers at eight workstations. Jumping from oven to stove, from frying pan to sink, from chopping block to mortar and pestle, she was a whirl of motion as she ladled, dripped, spun, stirred, poked, kneaded, tasted, flipped—the audience sometimes wasn't sure if they were watching just a single person or a whole battalion.

Finally, just as Mati bowed and retired from the center stage amidst the applause of the judges, Mozo Mu wiped off the last plate and nodded at the host and hostess, indicating that she was ready.

"Let's see this wondrous dish that the heir of Suda Mu has prepared—" said Séca, but he was interrupted by Mozo, who began to sing in a voice that seemed far older than her age.

> *"Your voice lingers*
> *Like a scab I can't stop picking.*
>
> *"Your laughter*
> *An itch in my heart that I can't scratch.*
>
> *"Cruel Lady Rapa!*
> *To have made you so beautiful.*
>
> *"Heartless Lady Kana!*
> *To deny me armor against you.*
>
> *"Don't speak, my darling*
> *My sweet, my every-moment wakeful weakness.*
> *Words lie, but not the music of your limbs*
> *Sweeping over me, moonlit ocean waves."*

As a long line of assistants followed her, each carrying a carefully plated dish of food, the singing Mozo climbed onto the main stage, passed by the stunned Séca and Lolo, and then, when she had reached the middle of the stage, turned dramatically to the crowd and declared, "I present a dish from my great-great-great-great-grandfather, Suda Mu, one that hasn't been seen in public since the time of the old Xana kings: Music of the Limbs."

"Incredible," whispered Dandelion from her perch inside the covered wagon.

"What are you exclaiming about?" asked Kinri, slightly irked. "You haven't even seen her offering."

"Didn't you listen to the poem and the name?" asked Dandelion. "Those lines are from the great Imagist poet Suzaré."

"I kind of skipped over the Imagists," admitted Kinri. "They're all sappy love poems, aren't they?"

"Typical," muttered Dandelion. "You were clearly not a very diligent student."

"Oh, you should talk. You didn't remember much about the partitioning of Métashi—"

"Fine! So we have different interests." Dandelion enjoyed arguing with Kinri. Other than Aya, no one her age had ever treated her as an equal. She adopted a more professorial tone. "You're going to miss out on a lot life has to offer if you focus only on wars and politics. Suzaré was Nakipo's student, and she wrote several cycles of poems to a mysterious woman she loved at the Xana court, who we only know by the name of Jito of White Sleeves. Although only fragments have survived, she pushed Nakipo's practice of constructing intricate, elaborate visual puns with Ano logograms to a new height. A rare woman of high culture in remote Kriphi, she was also an accomplished musician and the first to invent the system of musical notation—"

"Please," begged Kinri. "What does all of this have to do with cooking? Unless you tell me you've finally cracked their code, stories and poems about love aren't useful right now."

"You sound just like my sister," said Dandelion critically. She sighed. "Well, she might not have liked love stories, but she lived a great romance herself—I'm sure she would have loved Suzaré—"

"Cooking, please, focus on cooking."

"All right! In fine cuisine, the key is to invoke all five senses. But the best dishes must draw upon a sixth sense, often described as 'mind-pleasure.' This means that the dish should engage the intellect as well as the body by drawing upon literary and artistic allusions to complement the experience of the other senses."

"You're saying this Music of the Limbs has tickled your mind-pleasure? This all sounds like a lot of nonsense. I hope the judges aren't as easily swayed."

"Vulgarian!"

"Pretentious!"

The two went on bickering as the presentation on the stage continued.

"What a stunning work of art!" exclaimed Séca.

Lolo had to agree. She was so amazed by the vision presented by Mozo's dish that she had quite forgotten to banter with Séca or to describe what she was seeing for the benefit of the audience.

Luckily, she was saved from having to talk by a new contraption. For years, natural philosophers in Haan, especially those following the Patternist school, had investigated the use of mirrors and lenses to manipulate light—even the great Luan Zyaji had made some contributions in this area. One recent invention consisted of a set of lenses and mirrors ingeniously placed over an object on a table so that an image of the object, many times the original size, could be projected onto a hanging screen. This was used as a teaching aid in the lecture halls of Ginpen so that even students sitting in the nose-bleed seats could see the demonstrations by the lecturer in the pit clearly.

Such enlarger-projectors were now set up on the big stage as well as over the various cooking stations on the kitchen stages. As Mozo's assistants served the judges, an extra plate was brought over to a small white pedestal, called a specimen stage. Several mirrors were angled to bathe the dish in strong sunlight, much as such mirrors were used to spotlight actors in a theater, and instantly, a gigantic image of the dish appeared on the white screen hanging behind the judges (with the dove and the ravens from earlier perched on top, trying to appear unobtrusive).

The crowd hushed.

Eight edible sculptures sat around the edge of the plate, each an abstract representation of one of the gods of Dara. The bulk of the plate, on the other hand, was taken up by a delicate mosaic of glutinous rice and seaweed that invoked the orderly grid of farms, ponds, forests, and fields of Dara seen from the air. This was a dish that functioned similarly to Stormy Dara, but far more refined. Whereas Stormy Dara felt ambitious and unrestrained—a little insecure—Music of the Limbs gave off an air of confident peace and self-assured harmony.

As the crowd gazed at the screen and the judges admired the plates in front of them, all mouths agape, Séca and Lolo huddled with Mozo to get some chef's notes. Eventually, Lolo and Séca returned to the enlarger-projector and began to explain the dish to the assembled.

"Music of the Limbs celebrates a love made immortal through Suzaré's poem," said Séca. "Music is the theme, and the immortal gods are the players. This is an appetizer where the rice and seaweed at the center are to be enjoyed to the accompaniment of a divine orchestra composed of eight sections."

"As you can see," said Lolo, "there are eight seasoning stations arranged around the plate, representing the eight musical instrument families and their respective patron gods. First, at the north point, we have the silk family of stringed instruments, paying homage to Tazu, who rules over the briny waves as well as waves along vibrating strings."

She pointed to an ethereal confection of spun sugar: fine caramelized strands wound into a filigree whirlwind that glistened in the sunlight.

"When you bite into it, the strings vibrate against your palate and tongue, creating an internal music of sweet delight," said Séca.

"And the sugar here is no ordinary cane sugar," said Lolo. "It's ice sugar, to give the resulting music a truly divine quality."

The crowd gasped in appreciation. White sugar, an expensive delicacy by itself, was cane sugar purified and bleached white with bone char. Ice sugar, in contrast with ordinary white sugar, further required the bone char from the sacrificial animals used at the temples.

"Next, we move to the northeast corner, where the bamboo instruments pay homage to Kiji, Lord of Air and connoisseur of the breathing pipes," said Séca. "The tubes you see are hollowed bamboo shoots pickled in cider vinegar, and they are arranged in the shape of the famed Mingén falcon flutes, which were invented by Na Moji and carried aloft on kites to be played by the divine winds."

"The workmanship on these miniature flutes is already breath-taking," said Lolo, "but you'll be even more amazed to know that the bamboo shoots are from Mount Kiji itself. Suda Mu himself praised the bamboo shoots from Mount Kiji for possessing an airiness not found anywhere else."

The crowd murmured in confusion. How could the Treasure Chest have obtained ingredients from Unredeemed Dara?

On the stage, Tiphan Huto looked as pleased as a cat who had just swallowed a platter of moonbow trout strips. The bamboo shoots had made an impression. The Treasure Chest wasn't just wealthy, it was able to obtain ingredients that no one else could. Tiphan Huto's restaurant offered diners extraordinary culinary experiences impossible to replicate.

In this manner, Séca and Lolo continued around the plate, explaining each exquisite seasoning station: the wood instruments represented by glowing homunculus mushroom limbs arranged by length like a xylophone; the stone instruments represented by ebony quail testicles, each hollowed to resemble an echo bowl and filled with a dab of sea cucumber roe; the clay instruments represented by the ocarina-shaped pellets of edible clay from the foothills of Mount Rapa, long said to possess healing powers and beneficial effects for women in pregnancy; the gourd and vine instruments represented by those rare pods from dyran's-tail seaweed and coconut shavings; the hide and leather instruments represented by fried boar rinds—at least fifty varieties—from Crescent Island; and the metal family of instruments represented by the heavy, golden roe of deep-sea-trench jade crabs.

The audience and judges gazed at Mozo Mu with awe. No one thought of her as a mere child any longer.

"How can mushrooms represent the wood family? That doesn't even make sense," fumed Kinri.

"The ancient Ano believed that mushrooms, being grown from dead wood, take on their essence," said Dandelion.

"What about the crab roe then? Where's the metal in that?"

"Crab roe is golden, and gold is a metal," said Dandelion. "Also, the 'golden roe' logogram is written with a metal semantic root—"

"That's stretching the theme beyond the breaking point. If you're going to try to replicate the instrument families with food, then you have to—"

"It's a metaphor! Why do you have to be so literal-minded about everything?"

"Whose side are you on anyway?"

"As if you know *anything* about fine cuisine!"

The two glared at each other, their eyes as round as teacups, until, finally, both burst out laughing.

"I admit the dish does look and sound very impressive," said Kinri at length.

"And I admit the dish's interpretation of 'stones' is a bit . . . um . . ." Dandelion blushed. Then she turned serious. "The real problem with the appetizer, though, is that it's so impersonal. Suzaré's love of Jito of White Sleeves is about one woman's yearning for another, not this grand, bombastic piece of political propaganda for Mapidéré."

Kinri shook his head. "I think the real problem is the taste. I don't know what they're doing to flavor the clay, but I can't imagine it will taste better than freshly made pepper-and-cacanut sauce on golden pot stickers."

"The judges look plenty impressed to me."

"Music of the Limbs seems to awe and shock the diner with the rarity of the ingredients and the skill of the chef. But actual taste has to be the key in a cooking competition. What was that thing you and Widi were saying . . . oh, right, to 'weigh the fish' here, you have to *taste* the fish."

On the main stage, pairs of eating sticks hovered over the dishes hesitantly. The judges looked awkwardly at one another, none willing to be the first to destroy the amazing objects of art in front of them.

In the end, little Pimié was the first to dig in. He broke the puffy whirl of spun sugar on his plate, and, without even bothering to place the broken strands on top of a piece of glutinous rice, stuffed the sugar right into his mouth. A moment later, his face broke into a wide grin.

"Who says children can't cook?" he yelled at Mozo Mu, and gave her a thumbs-up. Mozo smiled back at him.

Chuckling, the other judges began to eat as well. Soon, sounds of praise erupted from every part of the long table.

"The homunculus is seasoned to perfection! It's a dish fit to offer to Lord Lutho himself."

"I've never had such tasty bamboo shoots! The pickle sauce brings out the flavor of the mountains as ably as Lurusén once served the kings of Cocru!"

"Oh, by the Twins! This clay is to die for—"

"No, no, you haven't tried the fried boar rinds yet. The texture is simply exquisite, like caressing the ancient books of the Ano sages with your tongue—"

"The dyran's-tail pods are unbelievable. Just biting into one gives me visions of the moonlit seas by which Lady Suzaré walked with Jito of White Sleeves—"

"Have you tried to play music on the sugar strings? Listen, just lean your ear in, real close, and tap on the strands with an eating stick. Be careful that you don't tap too hard. Can you hear that?"

"Oh, do I hear it! But have you tapped the strands against your teeth yet? There's another level of heavenly music that comes right through your bones—"

"Try this! Try this! Tap the strands against *different* teeth. Do you hear the distinctive pitches? Incredible! This dish captures the sensual beauty of Suzaré's poem with such ingenuity! And look at the way the rice has been carved: Doesn't it remind you of the limbs of a great beauty?"

Lolo and Séca stood by, slack-jawed. There was really no need to provide any banter when the judges themselves had taken over the entertainment duties.

"Are the judges in their own competition to see who can offer the most ridiculous, over-the-top praise?" whispered Kinri in disgust.

Dandelion swallowed her retort. Somehow "I told you so" didn't feel so satisfying when she noticed how dejected Widow Wasu and Mati both looked. As the crowd salivated at the beautiful dish on the screen and the judges vied with one another to exclaim their enjoyment, Mati was literally wilting in her kitchen, trying to find some way to make herself invisible.

"I just don't believe it. Tapping sugar strands against your teeth to make music? Come on, that's not even believable," muttered Kinri.

"Your problem is that you think *weighing* the fish is the same as *tasting* the fish," said Dandelion.

"How do you mean?"

"Weighing the fish requires only a fair scale, but there is no fairness when it comes to taste. The senses are governed by mind-pleasure. If you love a man, you think him handsome; if you hear a song from your childhood, you think it pleasant; if a smell or taste reminds you of home, then you feel its tickling caress in your heart."

"But surely you aren't suggesting that a mouthful of clay can be delicious—"

"Why not? I once played a trick on my father's friends. They had come to have a private meal with the Imp—my family, and my father was going to serve them a special jar of rice beer brewed from the dew-fed rice in Faça, next to the Rufizo Falls. I stole the jar—well, mainly because my brother wanted a taste—poured out the beer into another flask, and refilled the jar with the common rice beer I found in the servants' quarters. You should have heard how my father's friends complimented that beer! 'So pure!' 'So gut-warming!' 'Worth every gold!'"

"Maybe your father's friends didn't know anything about beers."

"Quite a few of them were connoisseurs and collectors."

"So you think they were lying to make your father happy?"

"Not at all. I think they really did taste the difference. Like I said, taste isn't something like weight. It's more about how you feel, the memories and associations the sensations draw up. Before you can taste something with the tongue, you season your mind with flavor-expectations."

"And you think that's what's happening with these judges?"

"Exactly. The kind of dishes made by Mozo Mu may not taste any better than Mati's pot stickers to someone who doesn't know the allusions behind the name and are given bites blindfolded. But that's not how we approach fine cuisine. Everything about Music of the Limbs is designed to engage mind-pleasure. Before you've even had that first bite, your mind is already awash with the beauty of the plating; the care and effort shown in the ingredients and the preparation; the romance of the story of Lady Suzaré and her lover; layers of refinement, culture, and history."

"But . . . those are imagined pleasures. They aren't real."

"Of course they're real. Despite all the wonderful dishes the cooks at my home can make, I've never tasted anything as delicious as fresh lotus seeds picked from Lake Tututika because my sister once took me there on a special outing when I was a little girl, and I think about her every time I bite into a lotus seed. Mind-pleasure comes from love, Kinri, love of sister, parent, friend, country, literature, beauty itself. A great lady I met at Lake Tututika on that outing taught me that. Love allows us to taste the fish, not just to weigh it.

"And so, the best way to evoke mind-pleasure is to tell a story about love. That's what all great art, fine cooking included, is about."

By the time Lolo and Séca returned to the front of the stage to announce the results of the appetizer portion of the competition, there was little doubt as to the outcome.

"The final tally is . . . eleven votes for the Treasure Chest, and one vote for the Splendid Urn!"

Widow Wasu sat tight-lipped and stony-faced. And if Tiphan Huto's grin were any wider, the top of his head would have fallen off.

Mati looked gratefully at young Pimié, who had cast the lone vote for the Urn, and he nodded back at her, an encouraging smile on his face.

The crowd clapped, approving the judges' decision. Mozo Mu marched back to her kitchen stage, proud as a victorious general. Mati, on the other hand, quietly descended from the back of her kitchen stage, averting her face from the audience. Many in the crowd assumed that she was so embarrassed by the result that she needed some time by herself to recover, and they felt sorry for her.

Lodan hugged Mati, and the two whispered together for a moment. Then Lodan patted Mati on the back and let her go.

Mati climbed into the first covered wagon, where Kinri and Dandelion were hiding. The two stayed quiet, uncertain how to comfort her.

To their surprise, Mati didn't look dejected at all. Instead, she appeared to have had a great weight lifted off her shoulders. "To keep on going the way I had planned would mean total loss. Let's try it your way."

"Are you sure?" asked Kinri, unwilling to injure the pride of the sous-chef.

Mati nodded determinedly. "There's a time to stick to what you know best, and a time to throw away everything and begin anew. I can't beat them the only way I know, so I'm going to learn some new tricks."

# CHAPTER THIRTY-EIGHT

# OBEDIENCE

MEANWHILE, IN KRIPHI.

Tanvanaki stared at the kneeling figure of Noda Mi. "You are certain?"

Noda Mi touched his forehead to the ground. "I am. Dasu will run out of food in about two months, before the harvest. The villages were dependent on the granaries in Daye."

"You may leave," Tanvanaki said.

"Thank you, votan." The native minister held his forehead against the ground for another beat before climbing up. Still keeping his upper body bowed, he backed away from Tanvanaki until he was at the entrance to the Great Tent. He turned and disappeared.

The purification campaign had essentially paralyzed the native bureaucracy of Ukyu-taasa. By this point, the native deputy ministers were little more than heralds who reported on the world crumbling around them without the power to do anything about it.

Tanvanaki turned her attention back to the three Lyucu thanes left in the Great Tent: Cutanrovo Aga, who looked unconcerned, Goztan Ryoto, whose face was unreadable, and Vocu Firna, who looked worried.

"If we institute rationing right away," said Vocu Firna, "we may be able to last until the harvest."

"Rationing will tell the natives that we're running out of food," said Goztan. "When people believe they're going to starve to death, nothing will stop them from a rebellion. Not even the threat of more reprisals."

Tanvanaki turned to Cutanrovo. "Why did you burn down the granaries in Daye?"

A week ago, Cutanrovo's purification packs had descended on Daye, the biggest city in Dasu, where they proceeded to smash temples and shrines and to tear down the old palace that had once housed Kuni Garu. To maintain the frenzied mood of destruction, Cutanrovo had distributed tolyusa to the Lyucu members of the pack (the natives were forbidden from consuming tolyusa). Nowadays, she did this sort of thing often, justifying the practice by arguing that the purification of native taint was a celebration and the tolyusa allowed everyone to feel more connected to the gods.

But Daye was not a prosperous city, and the small temples and modest palace didn't take long to be reduced to rubble. Unsatisfied with the extent of the destruction, one of the tolyusa-frenzied naros then suggested that the packs go to the graveyards outside the city and continue their demolition frenzy.

At this, the native members of the purification packs balked. It was one thing to tear down old palaces and temples: The common people's attachment to the houses of silk-garbed grand lords and greasy-lipped priests and monks was attenuated; besides, many of the natives who joined the purification packs secretly kept tiny figurines of the gods and prayed to them for forgiveness at night. But to desecrate the graves of ordinary people, to disturb the rest of the dead, to defile the bodies of ancestors—that proved to be too much to ask of her native followers.

So, of course, Cutanrovo insisted on having them smash the gravestones, dig up the bodies of their families, and toss the bones into outhouses. When the natives refused, she ordered random executions to compel obedience. This led to a sudden rebellion by the native purification pack members, which Cutanrovo suppressed harshly. In the end, the remaining rebels retreated to the granaries and threatened to destroy the food supply in an effort to negotiate a surrender. Cutanrovo laughed and set the granaries on fire herself, killing all the rebels in the process.

"I did it to make a point," said Cutanrovo.

"What point, exactly?" demanded Tanvanaki.

"That there is no choice except to submit to the Lyucu, no virtue except obedience," said Cutanrovo. She spoke forcefully, with little deference to Tanvanaki, as though she were giving a speech before a crowd.

These days, wherever Cutanrovo went, she was welcomed as though she were the living embodiment of Pékyu Tenryo himself. Naros and culeks praised her for making the Lyucu feel powerful again, and natives who wished to demonstrate their loyalty vied with one another to show how much they loved this terrifying living goddess. They built shrines to Cutanrovo, named children after Cutanrovo, accused their enemies of insulting the aura of Cutanrovo.

The thane continued. "Nothing, not their word-scars, not their language, not their ancestors, not their gods—nothing must stand in the way of obedience!"

Goztan flinched. She seemed to have been thrown back to that moment from decades ago, a moment she had tried so hard to forget.

*She was kneeling next to a Dara-style raised bed. She kept her eyes lowered so that she didn't have to look at the face of the vile man who thought he possessed her, the man who sat on the edge of the bed. All she could see were his feet.*

*The feet were resting on a Dara-style footstool, but it had been wrapped in a spirit portrait.*

*Oh, how she wanted to smash those feet, to break every bone in every toe, to hear him howl and beg for mercy for defiling the most sacred object of a Lyucu family, a portrait of the last breaths of an ancestor.*

*But she couldn't. She had to kneel there and endure the caresses of this man; every touch from him made her skin crawl, but she had to keep the revulsion from her face. Had to. Had to.*

*The man caressed her head like he would pet a dog. He coughed, and she stiffened, dreading what he was going to say in his intolerably harsh language, a language she had to learn if she wanted to defeat him.*

*"I think I'll call you Obedience," said Captain Dathama. "Do you like the name? Tell me."*

"This isn't the Lyucu way," croaked Goztan.

Tanvanaki, Vocu, and Cutanrovo turned to her.

"This isn't right," said Goztan in a more steady voice. "If your aim is to make the natives into Lyucu, this will utterly fail."

"Who says I'm interested in making them Lyucu?" said Cutanrovo, her voice full of contempt. "If they don't have Lyucu blood, they can never become Lyucu."

"Then what exactly is your aim?"

"I've told you: obedience. Once they've submitted completely, they'll become acururo tocua, living bones who move only by the winds of our will."

Goztan closed her eyes. The vision painted by Cutanrovo was repulsive. Everything was wrong with this comparison between, on the one hand, the art of children at play and the craft that lay behind the mysteries of the shamans, and on the other hand, slaves with their souls crushed through desecration.

"We're going to have an island full of living bones soon enough," said Vocu Firna, "if we don't find more food."

"Just ask for more from that coward Jia," said Cutanrovo.

"I've already asked for more food barely two months ago," said Tanvanaki. "To do so again now will leave no room to disguise our weakness. What if she says no?"

"She won't say no," said Cutanrovo confidently. "Does a sheep ever refuse to be sheared or milked? There is no courage in the heart of the Dara-raaki."

"Even if you're right, what do you want all the obedient natives to do?" demanded Vocu Firna. "The harvest this year is already ruined because you've trampled so many fields with your military and hunting exercises, and many young natives who should have been working were pulled into your purification packs. You've already destroyed just about all the temples and shrines on both islands, so there's nothing left for your followers to even smash—"

"Don't be so certain of that," said Cutanrovo. "I'm sure I can find more ways to test them: ancestral graves, their customs and morals, family bonds. . . . There's no end to what I can make them destroy, and the more they destroy, the more soulless and obedient they'll become."

"But there must be a purpose to this," said Vocu Firna, his

voice anguished. "The gods did not send us here only to break and destroy!"

"Of course there is a purpose," said Cutanrovo. "Once they've been sufficiently purified, they can join the Lyucu army. They will never be Lyucu, but it doesn't mean they can't fight for us."

"You think we're going to invade the core islands with a bunch of emaciated peasants whose spirits have been broken?" asked Tanvanaki in disbelief. "You are deluded!"

There was more than a touch of madness in Cutanrovo, Tanvanaki had to admit. Once again, she wondered whether killing the thane might be the safest thing to do. The fervor Cutanrovo had inspired among the naros and culeks was burning out of control, and she was beginning to fear for the very survival of the Lyucu in Ukyu-taasa.

Cutanrovo looked her right in the eyes. "Votan, do you really think that's the war you should be concerned about?"

Tanvanaki locked eyes with Cutanrovo. Vocu Firna and Goztan looked from one to the other.

Shifting emotions flitted through the four faces: arrogant confidence, total bewilderment, gradual understanding, shock of recognition, disgusted contempt.

"I see," said Tanvanaki, looking somber and resigned. "I see."

In two years, when the Wall of Storms reopened, a new wave of Lyucu reinforcements would arrive, possibly led by Cudyu, Tanvanaki's brother. It was hard to imagine that Cudyu would submit to Tanvanaki's authority meekly, and so a contest for succession was almost inevitable. In such a contest, Tanvanaki's position would be significantly strengthened if she could count on the support of native "arucuro tocua" who obeyed only Cutanrovo. A touch of madness or not, Cutanrovo's understanding of the flow of power was impeccable.

As Vocu Firna and Goztan came to the same realization, they shared a look of despair.

Heart aching, Goztan recalled something Pékyu Tenryo had said. *"In war, we become more like our enemies, whether we want to or not."*

# CHAPTER THIRTY-NINE

# THE FIRST CONTEST: PART II

GINPEN: THE FIFTH MONTH IN THE NINTH YEAR
OF THE REIGN OF SEASON OF STORMS AND THE
REIGN OF AUDACIOUS FREEDOM (TWENTY-FOUR
MONTHS UNTIL THE REOPENING OF THE WALL OF
STORMS).

Even though Mati had rejected their offer to help, the Blossom Gang had not been idle during the previous week.

Right after their spying mission to the Treasure Chest, Dandelion begged the gang, "for fun," to show her some ideas for cooking.

"I never get to go in the kitchen back home," she said, eagerness written all over her face.

"Err, the way we cook isn't very orthodox," said Rati. "I doubt you'd find what we do in any kitchen in Dara."

"Do we do *anything* the orthodox way?" asked Widi.

"If we did things by the book, we wouldn't be wandering around the Islands, vagabonds in both spirit and body," said Arona.

"That just makes it *more* fun," said Dandelion. "Come on, show me!"

So the Blossom Gang took her and Kinri to their rented house and demonstrated some of their cooking techniques. Dandelion squealed in delight at each before peppering the gang with questions. Since cuisine à la Blossom Gang tended to involve Rati Yera's impractical and bizarre inventions, the demonstrations also piqued Kinri's interest—though, he had to admit to himself, he was hanging around mainly because he got to spend more time in Dandelion's company.

Widow Wasu had closed the Splendid Urn for the week to give

Mati more time to prepare. This allowed Kinri to come visit the gang
with Dandelion every day. The two of them interrupted the demonstrations with so many questions that it took a few days to show
them everything. While Kinri was entranced by the designs of the
novel kitchen implements, Dandelion sat around with a wax tablet
and a writing knife, looking thoughtful as she scribbled notes or
drew pictures.

After the first few days, while Kinri continued to examine the
Blossom Gang's machines to teach himself the basics of Dara engineering, Dandelion turned her attention to the poems they had
copied from the Treasure Chest. Working with the assumption that
they were encoded recipes, Dandelion tried to break the code with
the help of Widi, the Blossom with the most knowledge about food
as well as poetry. The two spent hours picking the poems apart,
trying substitutions, anagrams, semantic root shifts, philology and
etymology, aural and visual puns, acrostics, structural analysis, close
reading, deconstruction . . . but made little progress. Dandelion even
dressed up as a scholar and went to several of Ginpen's leading
academies so that she could access their libraries for research, but
she returned with her brows furrowed, only shaking her head when
asked about her findings.

Since the poems turned out to be a dead end, they went back to
studying cooking.

Rati, in particular, enjoyed showing off her inventions to these
two. She had never had students, and she found teaching enjoyable.
Sometimes a stray remark from Kinri or an insightful question from
Dandelion would cause her mind to spin off in dozens of new directions, revealing new possibilities to tinker and experiment with. But
occasionally, out of sight of Dandelion and Kinri, she would also
sigh with melancholy, knowing that she would never be able to take
a formal student.

Mati, on the other hand, was much less welcoming to Kinri's and
Dandelion's ad-hoc apprenticeships. She was nervous about the competition and had little time or patience with two amateurs bothering
her. So Dandelion and Kinri observed her rehearsing in the kitchen
from a distance. Dandelion also interviewed Lodan and Widow

Wasu. But much to Kinri's bafflement, Dandelion asked few concrete question about kitchen practices, instead concentrating her queries around Mati's personal history and the history of the Splendid Urn.

Finally, Dandelion asked Kinri to go with her on sightseeing tours all over Ginpen. Kinri readily agreed, having had little chance to explore the city at large. Dandelion took on the disguise of a lady of means—an easier role for her than a kitchen maid—while Kinri went as her servant. The pair went to many of Ginpen's teahouses—both fashionable establishments and holes-in-the-wall—where Dandelion sat for hours, listening to storytellers and observing the scholars, merchants, nobles, and laborers around her. Kinri grew concerned that these tours had nothing to do with the competition, but Dandelion assured him that it was all part of her plan.

As Dandelion and Kinri learned about cooking and Ginpen, they also shared stories about each other's lives. While Dandelion told Kinri funny tales from her childhood in a large manor in Pan, surrounded by loving siblings and stern tutors, he sensed that she was holding something back. A trace of anguish seeped from her words now and then, and sometimes she stared into the distance, her brows knitted.

He, on the other hand, told her edited stories about his own childhood. Since he couldn't reveal to her his true identity, he tried to stick with stories that were consistent with his current guise as a refugee from Unredeemed Dara. He told her about studying the Ano Classics with Master Nazu Tei, his home village's schoolmaster, arguing with her and guessing logogram riddles; about preparing for Lyucu feasts with other native servants, butchering and dressing cattle the Lyucu way and stepping back from roasting pits as garinafin fire breath sealed in the flavor in the beef; about watching the winged beasts take off at sunset, performing maneuvers against the twilight sky like aerial whales breaching in a fiery cloud-sea.

He even tapped on older, half-forgotten memories, from the time when he had been a mere child in Ukyu. He spoke of old Oga, his mother's faithful slave—in the version he told Dandelion, Oga was recast as a family friend in Unredeemed Dara—who had told him stories about Mapidéré and Dazu Zyndu, and cooked Dasu dishes for him in garinafin-stomach pots. He had loved Oga, who had cared for him when his mother was away at war and his fathers were too absorbed in bickering and fighting with one another to pay any attention to him. And a lump came into his throat as he spoke of him.

"What was his full name?" asked Dandelion. "Did Oga come from a prominent native family?"

"I . . . don't know," he said, embarrassed. Dara slaves in Ukyu, as war captives, were not referred to by their full names. The man had always just been "old Oga" to him. For a moment he was terrified that Dandelion would realize that Oga was no family friend and see through his ruse.

Mercifully, she didn't pursue that line of questioning.

He wished he could tell her about his mother, about the adventures of Kikisavo and Afir, about how the people of Dara misunderstood the Lyucu. But he knew she had grown up thinking of the Lyucu as monsters—like in that play Arona and Mota had put on—and he understood there was a gulf between them that could never be bridged, that he could never reveal to her his true self.

Sometimes, Kinri wondered if Dandelion sensed that he was holding back, that he dared not tell her the truth about himself. Perhaps that was why she didn't allow him to really know her, either. He didn't know how to comfort her, how to assure her that it was safe to confide in him, because he couldn't assure himself that it was safe to confide in her.

But meanwhile, it was enough to be with her, to learn about novel engines designed for the kitchen, to watch the people of Ginpen live their multitude of individual lives full of laughter and tears, to work together for a common goal.

In the end, Kinri, impressed by the devices of the Blossom Gang, went to Mati, who was having trouble locating ingredients for the fancy dishes taught by Head Chef Néfi Ézugo, to see if she could be convinced to let the gang help. But when Rati and the others tried to explain their ideas, they seemed to Mati just a parade of amateur kitchen toys of little practical use.

Kinri was dejected, but Dandelion told him to cheer up. "Good food takes time," she said, "as do good stories."

～

Despite Tiphan Huto's vociferous protests, Lolo and Séca approved the Splendid Urn's request for a slight delay before the start of the entrée portion of the contest. As Mozo and her staff rested in their kitchen, watching the other stage with curiosity, the team from the Splendid Urn rushed about to dismantle their kitchen, replacing the standard equipment with boxes and a jumble of unrecognizable equipment taken from the covered wagons. Mota alone was doing the work of four men, carrying giant chests two at a time onto the stage as though they were nothing more than toy blocks, eliciting exclamations of admiration from the crowd.

Earlier, when Mati had announced the change of direction in competition strategy to Widow Wasu, the old matriarch had been surprised—she had no idea that Mati had prepared a backup plan. When she heard that the plan involved the Blossom Gang and Dandelion, however, she began to shake her head. But then she saw the look in Mati's eyes, and she sighed and patted her sous-chef on the shoulder. "Even if the pig is already dead, it's better to act like it's still alive. Sometimes Lord Rufizo grants miracles."

Widow Wasu was full of these old Cocru proverbs that made no sense if you thought too hard about them. Mati figured the Grand Mistress meant to be reassuring.

The Blossom Gang climbed onto the kitchen stage and surveyed their half-assembled machines.

"Are you sure we can do this?" asked Kinri, nervously pulling Mota Kiphi aside. Unlike the rest of the gang, Mota was a man of few words, but for that reason, Kinri also felt the most confidence in whatever he had to say.

Mota shrugged. "A great general once said that armies are never as prepared for battle as they'd like to be, but you go to war anyway when you have no choice."

"We really have to start," said Lolo to Mati apologetically. "Tiphan Huto has complained multiple times, and the judges may deduct points if you delay any longer."

Mati looked at the confusing jumble of equipment around her, none of which she knew how to use. Nonetheless, she nodded reso-lutely. *I must act like the pig is still alive.*

"Let the entrée portion of the contest begin!" announced Séca. The crowd, which was growing restless, refocused their eyes on the two kitchen stages.

As before, Mozo methodically marched around the worksta-tions, checking over everything and shouting directions to make sure the assistants were kept apprised of one another's progress. Moreover, as some sharp-eyed observers among the crowd pointed out, when the sous-chefs were nearly finished with one stage of the preparation, Mozo would often lean over and shield the cooking station from the enlarger-projector with her body as she completed the step.

"What do you think she's doing?" someone in the crowd whis-pered.

"Probably adding her family's secret sauce," answered her friend.

"Secret sauce?"

"You didn't think Mozo Mu would reveal *all* the secrets of her ancestor onstage, did you? It was said that Suda Mu had developed a whole array of secret sauces that performed miracles. One sauce could turn bland water into chicken soup, and another could revive old, stringy vegetables into crunchy young shoots!"

"Oh, to be able to see such secret magic at work!"

. . .

Over on the Splendid Urn's side, however, a wholly different scene prevailed. People kept on bumping into one another; servants and maids tripped over the bizarre contraptions; strangely dressed cooks—one of them was an old lady who wheeled herself around in a chair!—bickered as they fought over what to do.

The crowd grew uneasy. Things were not looking good for the Splendid Urn. Was the contest going to be so lopsided?

Kinri rushed up to Mati. "You have to get everyone to work together."

"But I have no idea what you're planning on cooking!"

Kinri felt sweat pouring off his forehead and back. Since they hadn't been sure Mati would call on them for help, the Blossom

Gang had never worked out which specific dishes to cook and what order to prepare them in. He felt adrift, completely at a loss.

"You need a story," whispered Dandelion.

Kinri looked at her like a man about to drown who saw a bit of straw floating past. He clutched her by the shoulders. "You have an idea?"

"Oh, do I have ideas. I've been thinking about this nonstop since the day we got back. But there's no time to explain everything. You have to listen and do exactly what I say," she said, looking from Kinri to the rest of the Blossom Gang.

Everyone nodded.

"All right," said Dandelion. "The good news is: We're going to work off what Mati already prepared. So the first dish we'll cook is . . ." She lowered her voice and whispered the name.

The Blossom Gang, Mati, Lodan, and Kinri stared at Dandelion, dumbfounded.

"Dandelion," began Mati helplessly, "I'm afraid you've exceeded my meager knowledge of fine cuisine. I don't think I've ever heard the name—"

"What *is* she talking about?" asked Kinri. He turned to the Blossom Gang's gourmet, who he thought might have a clue. "Widi, have you heard of such a dish?"

Widi shook his head. But he was looking at Dandelion with an amused expression rather than one of confusion.

"Some codes don't need to be broken to be useful," said Widi.

Dandelion smiled back and nodded.

"Will you two stop grinning and let the rest of us in on the secret?" pleaded Kinri.

"You are the one who actually helped me come up with the idea for this dish," said Dandelion, continuing to smile in that mysterious and confident way that made Kinri's heart race. "You just don't understand the power of what you already know."

Kinri's face flushed. "But what—"

Dandelion held up a hand imperiously. "All in good time. First, Rati and Arona, set up the sun stoves . . ."

"There she goes, playing her favorite character," muttered Arona Taré, "the Boss." But she and Rati Yera complied.

The sun stoves were invented by Rati Yera during a time when the gang had played a trick on a wealthy landlord who had tormented his tenant farmers with deceptive leases and demands for free labor akin to corvée. After emptying his treasury and distributing the funds to the tenant farmers, the gang had escaped into the mountains to hide from the local garrison, summoned by the landlord to catch the "stonehearted robbers." In order to conceal their location, the gang had not dared to light fires. Rati therefore invented a cooking device designed to draw upon the power of the sun itself, without needing any smoking fuel.

The Blossom Gang brought out an umbrella-shaped lattice frame constructed from supple bamboo. Into this lattice, they began to fit bright glass mirrors. Kinri, familiar with the machine, went to help, but Dandelion pulled him back.

"I've got to direct the work here in the kitchen," said Dandelion to him, "but we also have to prep the judges and the audience to buy us some time. I can't be in two places at once, so you have to act as my messenger."

"No problem," said Kinri. "I'll do whatever to help."

Dandelion whispered instructions to Kinri as he nodded, silently memorizing. Then he ran up to the main stage and repeated them to the host and the hostess.

Lolo and Séca looked at each other and smiled. This was going to be a really good show.

Séca coughed, and Lolo cleared her throat.

"Oh, my dear Séca, are we in for a treat today! Can you tell our judges and audience what's happening in the Splendid Urn kitchen?"

"Certainly. The first entrée prepared by the Splendid Urn is called 'Shattered Oracle,' inspired by an episode in the history of our illustrious province. . . ."

Back when the conquering armies of King Réon of Xana had ranged across Dara, striking terror into the hearts of all the Tiro kings, high-minded Haan had not been exempt. One time, a large fleet of ships and airships sailed into Zathin Gulf, and Xana messengers delivered to Ginpen an ultimatum: surrender or be destroyed.

As the people of Haan ran through the streets in a panic and merchants began to hoard and profiteer, the king and his ministers went to the Great Temple of Lutho to seek the advice of the god.

The chief augur brought out the oldest turtle shell stored in the inner sanctum, a carapace the size of a banquet table, so aged and caked with wisdom that it had turned as black as the sands of Lutho Beach. As the king and his ministers, having fasted for days, knelt before the statue of Lutho in the incense-filled great hall, muttering and chanting in delirium, the chief augur raised his iron divining staff, heated it in a bellows-pumped furnace until the tip glowed bright yellow, and pressed it against the ancient turtle shell.

The shell didn't just crack. It disintegrated on contact. Small fragments, each no bigger than a child's hand, scattered across the floor. The acrid stench of charred bone filled the hall, shocking the king and his ministers out of their incense-trance.

"We must surrender," cried one of the terrified ministers. "Lord Lutho has spoken. We will crumble before the might of Xana like a rotten shell. Only a fool would resist!"

The king looked hesitant. Spies had spoken of strangers whose accents evoked the shores of Xana sneaking into that minister's residence in the middle of the night. But what he said seemed wise. Haan was not like Cocru or Faça. Its people had always been more comfortable with the writing knife than the killing sword.

He stared at the scattered, smoking shell fragments on the floor. Was the god telling him to yield?

The chief augur's son, a youngster named Luan Zya, had been hiding behind the statue of Lutho. He chose that moment to run out. Pointing at the fragments, he shouted, "The pattern! It's like a sea wall."

He was right. The fragments had fallen in two long, symmetrically curved lines that resembled the remnants of a coral atoll that had eroded away. The hidden tensions within the worn shell must have been quite balanced for it to shatter in this manner.

The ministers and the king tried to ignore this childish outburst. The already-terrible oracle was made even worse by association with the imagery of broken walls, atolls sinking into the sea, ruins unable to withstand the powerful tides.

"Surrender won't save us," said one of the king's generals. "The Duke of Tacü surrendered, and the city was slaughtered anyway since Réon believed the inhabitants disrespected him because a child looked up into his face as he rode into the city instead of keeping his forehead on the ground. A tyrant like that shows no mercy."

"I'm confident that if we surrender immediately and offer the Xana army free passage to Rima, we'll not only be spared but perhaps even gain—"

"How can you think of betraying the lives of others to profit yourself? The gods won't—"

"I speak of the only way to save lives! The tides of history have turned against the independent Tiro states. Xana is—"

"The tides of history are made by those willing to brave the ocean. The words of the Ano sages tell us—"

"Enough!" cried out the king. "Let's hear what the chief augur has to say."

The chief augur, who had been staring at the shell fragments on the floor, like so many islands dotting the sea, finally looked up. "From the mouths of little children come great truths. Lord Lutho's will is clear: Haan will be protected by curved walls."

"What nonsense are you spouting—" began the minister advocating surrender.

But he was cut off by the eager king. "Speak more, Chief Augur Zya. What hope does Lord Lutho offer? Does he mean that the Xana fleet will founder on the hidden reefs of Zathin Gulf? Or does he mean that we should hide behind the curved walls of Ginpen like a turtle retreating into its shell?"

"The omen is difficult to interpret," said the chief augur. "I ask that you give me three days and all the resources of the royal workshops. I shall meditate in seclusion to understand the obscure meaning of the God of Wisdom."

"I knew all your knowledge of wars and heroes would come in handy," whispered Dandelion to Kinri, "even if you did call me a fire-breathing spiderweb. Séca and Lolo are doing a great job of set-ting up the audience."

"I told you that's not what I meant!" said Kinri, rather irked. "But what's the point of telling a story like that? I still don't know *what we're making*."

Dandelion laughed. "Patience! Just stay out of the way and try to help out when someone calls on you."

"Mota and I won't need him," said Arona. "We already worked out our part of the show."

"You *are* fast," said Dandelion.

"We've had a lot of practice with improvising on short notice," said Arona. She smiled at Mota and touched him affectionately on the arm. He smiled back, but as usual, said nothing.

"Widi and I won't need him either," said Rati.

Mati and Lodan were huddled to the side, examining the assem-bled kitchen equipment. They didn't seem to need him either.

"Why does everyone have a job except me?" asked Kinri, getting anxious.

Arona chortled. "Maybe someone is worried about tiring you out." She threw a meaningful glance Dandelion's way.

"I have to go now," said Dandelion, her cheeks flushed. "All of our dishes have to be cooked in two places at once: the kitchen stage and the main stage. Mati and the Blossoms will cook the food while I stir-fry the audience."

Before Kinri could ask more questions, Dandelion glided away toward the main stage, as attention-grabbing in her bright, flowing water-silk dress as a fluttering butterfly.

Kinri looked about and was a bit disappointed to see that the lat-tice bowl, filled with small mirrors, had already been turned into a highly reflective parabolic mosaic—putting the mirrors together was a task he had looked forward to. A metal pole protruded from the center of the concave bowl to end in a flat ring hovering above the mirror. He had seen this device in operation, but he wasn't sure it made food taste any better.

Carefully, Rati turned the contraption to aim the parabolic surface at the sun, while Arona and Mota left the stage.

Widi saw that Kinri looked lost.

"I have to talk to Chef Mati to get her ready," Widi said to Kinri. "Can you help me and get all the eggs you can find in the wagon? And I do mean *all* the eggs."

Kinri ran to the wagon and found a stack of straw-packed crates in the back. Although buyers from the Treasure Chest had emptied the markets of more exotic ingredients, they couldn't deprive them of the basics.

He sifted through the straw and retrieved goose eggs, duck eggs, chicken eggs, quail eggs, pheasant eggs, pigeon eggs. . . . Carefully, he carried the laden basket back onto the kitchen stage.

Dandelion climbed onto the main stage and introduced herself as a sous-chef, here to explain the unfamiliar cooking techniques of the Splendid Urn to the audience.

Lolo and Séca, who had been entertaining the crowd with the story of the Shattered Oracle, welcomed the new presenter. Dandelion was vivacious, pretty, and clearly not shy about speaking in public.

"Masters and mistresses, honored judges." Dandelion held up the trumpet and spoke into it with a natural confidence. She was used to talking like this at the parties she organized in the palace, and since there were no officials present, she wasn't afraid of anyone revealing her true identity.

"Remember that cooking and eating are about more than sustenance. Food is a language of its own. Chewing up tough meat and vegetables to feed us one mouthful at a time was how parents spoke to us before we had grown teeth or learned our first words; making their favorite dishes and leaving them on the ancestral altar is how we tell our parents that we love them when they can no longer hear us. We honor our past and hope for the future when we cook and eat.

"From Zudi to Ginpen, from a tavern to a famed hall of hospitality, from the palates of day laborers to the tastes of great lords and ladies, Grand Mistress Wasu and Chef Mati have never been afraid to experiment for the future while carrying on our proud traditions. And today, you'll see that tradition of innovation on display.

"But since we're competing for the title of Best Restaurant in

Ginpen, it only makes sense to cook dishes that honor Ginpen's history.

"When the chief augur emerged from the Great Temple of Lutho three days later, he held the plans for a new kind of machine.

"'These are the curved walls spoken of in the oracle,' he told the king. 'Do you recall how the two lines of shell fragments curved toward each other, like a pair of arms open in embrace, one a mirror image of the other? That is Lord Lutho's clue!'

"Constructed in a manner similar to the batten-supported rigid sails of oceangoing vessels, the bamboo lattices designed by the chief augur resembled the skeletons of sails, before canvas had been stretched over them. These gigantic sails were erected all along the coast of Haan, and the chief augur assigned a team of workers to each sail. They'd be responsible for turning the sail in accordance with directions from the capital.

"'How are these sails going to protect us?' protested the king. 'They are not curved at all. And they don't even have canvas stretched over them!'

"'A little more faith, Your Majesty,' said the chief augur.

"Instead of stretching canvas over the sail towers, the chief augur asked every family in Haan to donate their mirrors: big polished bronze mirrors for dressing at home; small glass mirrors carried by ladies who must travel long distances; new mirrors found in bars and indigo houses; ancient mirrors found in temples and lecture halls—the mirrors were attached to the sail towers, turning all of them into gleaming, gigantic, dew-bedecked spiderwebs. . . ."

Back on the kitchen stage, Kinri found Widi talking to a hyperventilating Mati, with Lodan trying to calm her down.

"Chef," said Widi, "you have to do this. None of the rest of us are actually good cooks. You don't want to eat an omelette made by me."

"But I've never cooked with the power of the sun!" protested Mati.

"Nothing to it! Like Dandelion said, you'll be cooking the dishes you're already comfortable with. It's just like a regular stove, except instead of fire—"

"Wait," said Lodan, who had her arms around her wife's

shoulders protectively. "Did you say that you want Mati to make an omelette? With the very survival of the restaurant on the line, with us already behind from the appetizer round, you are suggesting that we cook *an omelette*, something that even a mediocre line cook could make blindfolded—"

"Shhh!" whispered Widi. "Not so loud! Of course we're not just making 'an omelette'! Mati, you had the right idea when you wanted to return to the basics, but here's what you'll do different. . . ."

Mati placed a dark, flat-bottom pan into the ring suspended above the mirrored surface and brushed the inside with oil—a special concoction Arona had prepared.

The crowd and judges divided their attention between the Splendid Urn kitchen, where Chef Mati, after some apparently intense pep talk with her staff, had reappeared, and the main stage, where Dandelion continued to weave a mesmerizing tale.

*When the first invading Xana airship peeked over the horizon, the chief augur gave the order. Teams composed of soldiers, scholars, and even peasants pulled together to turn the great mirror sails so that the beams of sunlight reflecting from their gleaming surfaces converged on the Xana airship.*

*This was how the curved walls were made: by concentrating the power of the many into one.*

In the kitchen, all the rays of the sun collected by the mirrors in the parabolic bowl were reflected onto the bottom of the black pan.

Widi Tucru and Rati Yera played the coconut lute and the bamboo flute like the orchestra of a small traveling folk opera troupe. Using one foot, Widi tapped a rhythm stick against a box on the ground to keep the beat. Widi also sang in a guttural style that was at once otherworldly and deeply intimate, evoking the sounds of sun-dappled ocean waves, grunting airship rowers, the rage of the gods in the winds, and the pride of a people under attack.

A young woman in the audience was startled to hear Widi sing. Blond-haired and blue-eyed, with bronze skin covered in dark blue tattoos, she was a native of Tan Adü who had come to Ginpen to study the arts of Dara. Her eyes teared up at the throat-singing of her homeland, something she hadn't heard in a long while.

As the oil in the pan began to sizzle, billowing smoke seemed to come out of nowhere and soon filled the stage. It was a strange smoke that stayed near the surface of the stage, obscuring Mati's legs but leaving her upper body and the sun stove visible above its roiling folds. The effect was as if Mati was floating in a sea of clouds.

Those well-traveled among the audience recognized the signs of Arulugi smokecraft, a rare sight here in Ginpen.

A slender figure in flowing robes suddenly popped out of the smoke on one side of the sun stove. A moment later, another figure, this one much taller and with much broader shoulders, appeared on the opposite side of the sun stove, wearing stage armor.

The crowd gasped, and then a wave of applause broke out. The two characters were dressed in period costume as the chief augur of Haan (as portrayed by Arona Taré) and an invading Xana general (as portrayed by Mota Kiphi).

The two glared at each other, their bodies tense, ready to battle.

Mati stood between them, trying very hard to block out their distracting performance and the smoke billowing around her as she nodded at Kinri, waiting to the side with his basket of eggs.

The crowd and the judges were mesmerized. They had never seen a kitchen literally turned into a theater. Séca and Lolo said nothing, now part of the audience. Tiphan Huto and Widow Wasu had both gotten out of their seats to get a closer look at the Splendid Urn kitchen. Even Mozo Mu couldn't help glancing over from time to time as she urged her team to stay focused on their work.

*The chief augur's invention was an unprecedented way to make war with the power of the sun, just as the sun stove we've erected in the kitchen to honor that episode is an unprecedented way to cook. Just as Chief Augur Zya once called upon the fire from the heavens to aid the defense of Haan, today we call upon that divine flame to prepare a sumptuous feast fit for all your refined senses!*

*But back to that time, decades ago, when the people of Haan worked together to resist the tyrant Mapidéré. The airship moved fast, and so the mirror sails had to be turned constantly to keep it in their focus. Would there be enough time for the sun to do its work?*

In the kitchen, Kinri jumped into motion at Mati's sign. Basket in hand, he stayed out of the audience's view and crawled through the smoke to the feet of Mota Kiphi, who stooped and picked up a large goose egg and lifted it into the smoke over the sizzling pan.

As the music from the orchestra changed, Mota gently "flew" the large egg through the smoke. In the eyes of the crowd, the egg seemed to turn into the streamlined shape of a powerful Xana airship, slowly winging its way toward the coast of Haan, full of menace.

*The chief augur rallied the people not to give up hope. "Just a little longer!" he cried. "Let's concentrate the power of the sun as we concentrate our love of home and faith in ourselves."*

Arona held up a pair of delicate silver egg mallets and danced around the sun stove, trying to strike at the fleeing egg-airship. The orchestra added to the tension with their music and singing, now fast, now slow, now loud, now soft. . . .

The audience had their hearts in their throats. Would the bold invention of the chief augur work? Would the egg be cooked? What a marvelous show! Already they could tell this was going to be a dish the likes of which they had never experienced.

*The people's hearts were tired. They couldn't help the growing doubt. They pulled and pushed, trying to keep their gazes and the gaze of the sun upon that approaching airship. But the airship stubbornly refused to be stopped by the curved mirrors of the oracle.*

Widi tapped his rhythm stick so rapidly that is sounded like a drumroll; Rati's bamboo flute rose to a crescendo. Widi's throat-singing sounded like the desperate pleas of a hundred thousand hearts yearning after one wish.

Mota stopped moving as the goose egg stopped directly over the pan. Arona spun like a whirlwind, her two circling egg mallets a glowing ring in the bright sun.

Widi suddenly ceased singing, and Rati stopped the flute. The gongs strapped to Widi's knees slammed against each other as Arona's mallets struck the goose egg.

The crash from the gongs reverberated in the audience's ears as the contents of the cracked egg spilled out. Mati easily caught the egg and began to cook. Arona and Mota dropped out of view into the smoke.

*And just like that! The airship burst into flames. Slowly, it plunged toward the sea.*

The crowd erupted into wild cheers and applause.

"Widow Wasu should be selling tickets to her kitchen if this is what happens every night!"

"Cooking with the sun . . . Have you ever envisioned such a thing? Imagine the taste!"

"What a great way to honor the memory of the chief augur. The Splendid Urn really knows what makes Haan Haan."

More eggs, representing different Imperial airships and naval ships, were cracked and dropped into the sizzling oil. Mati was getting into the spirit of the performance now as she wielded the spatula and pan, flipping, tossing, even spinning in place as an omelette tumbled through the air, catching it just in time to more cheers and applause.

Dandelion, over on the main stage, continued her speech.

"Inspired by the wise chief augur, the Shattered Oracle of Haan also shattered the myth of the invincibility of Xana might, and it reminded the people that gathering the scattered light from individuals can form an unstoppable force.

"Chief Augur Zya, of course, wasn't the only one to contribute to the defense of Haan. Because so many of the men were serving in the army and navy of Haan at the time, most of the laborers who built the light sails and hauled the cables that turned them were women, children, and the elderly. Many were silk makers from Haan's innumerable workshops.

"Silk is the foundation of Haan's distinctive cocoon-dress and the star of so many interesting inventions coming out of Ginpen's great academies and laboratories. But let's not forget that silk comes from the labor of women, many of them poor and illiterate, who toil in anonymity for a beauty they themselves cannot afford.

> *"My child, I saw many jade-tempered lords*
> *And honey-voiced ladies dressed in fine silk.*
> *How many know that they are wearing shrouds?*
> *Or silk makers only have hempen shawls?*

*Pick the cocoons, soak, boil, stir, reel.*
*Spin the wheel, sister, spin that wheel!*

"So as we celebrate the victory of the Curved Mirrors of Haan, let's also pay respect to the sacrifices of the women who, like the worms they harvest, devote their youth and health to beautifying the world. They, along with the waitresses, indigo-house girls, maids, fishwives, and farmwives of Haan, spin threads of love that make up the weft and warp of our fair city, a web of connections worth defending against tyranny!"

Reverently, Mati opened jars of pickled caterpillars and added the contents to the omelettes. The eyes of many in the crowd moistened as they watched this peasant food being transformed into a symbol of the indomitable spirit of Haan's people, scholar and illiterate peasant alike, high-minded all.

Wiping the sweat dripping from her brow, Mozo Mu presented several entrées to the judges. A quick sketch of a couple would suffice to yield a sense of the overall approach.

"Tututika's Loom" was made by steaming a piece of bean curd with several different varieties of living loaches and eels—all of them rare and hard to obtain—in the same pot. As the pot heated up, the loaches and eels, seeking shelter from the fire, burrowed into the bean curd and were cooked inside. The bean curd was then sliced into thin slices, and the cross-sections of the fish inside formed colorful patterns that brought to mind clouds at sunset, late-retiring immortals in the dawn sky, extravagant court dresses of noble ladies studded with jewels, or a reef filled with sea stars and resting fish.

"Sovereign of the Seas" was centered around a steamed lobster tail carved to resemble a cruben. Around it were arranged a variety of shellfish and fish shaped and garnished to remind the viewer of court dress worn by civil and military officials: Moonbow trout's long tail fins stood in for the minister of rituals' long sleeves; starglow oyster shells brought to mind the ceremonial armor of a marshal; aged sea cucumbers with fermented "beards" referenced wise court tutors; and so on. The "officials" presented to the cruben many gifts of exotic delicacies: stone's ear and homunculus mushrooms; platters of "pearls" that were in fact flying-fish eyes; hundred-year preserved lotus seeds so pitted and shriveled that they resembled corals; coulis of wild flowers collected from no-man's-cliffs on distant isles; fried rice flavored with all sixty of the herbs listed in the ancient medical manual, *Secrets of Rufizo*; and so on.

Every dish was made from expensive ingredients meticulously prepared and seasoned to perfection. Mozo Mu made sure to taste everything before it was plated, and only food that passed her exacting standards was allowed out. Despite her youth, she ran her kitchen with military precision. Every assistant knew exactly what to do, and mise en place was always maintained and followed.

In contrast, all of Mati's dishes were prepared in a manner better described as improvisational than professional. Rati and Widi herded the Urn's staff to set up new equipment and taught them how to operate it at the last minute; to fill the time during these preparatory steps, Dandelion told stories about the unfamiliar cooking techniques; Mota and Arona performed skits to entertain the audience and the judges, changing costumes and masks in quick succession; Lodan and Kinri served the food to the judges, trying to keep up a lighthearted banter to disguise their nervousness; Mati strove to cook while everything around her teetered on the verge of chaos.

Besides "Shattered Oracle," Mati's other entrées were also themed around the history and people of Haan. First, there was "The Grand Examination," a traditional vegetable-and-beef stew.

Mati enjoyed making this hearty dish, which was simple but had a lot of potential for flavors. Though not one of Head Chef Néfi Ézugo's signature dishes, it was popular at the Urn, especially among the not-so-wealthy scholars, who believed that the stew was good for providing brain fuel during the brutal cram sessions before the Imperial examinations. Mati often had the waitresses ask the scholars where they were from so that she could flavor the stew to give them a taste of home, knowing that many of them missed their mothers' cooking. The only problem with the dish was the long cooking time needed to extract the flavors and to tenderize the meat, and Mati wasn't sure there was enough time at the competition to make it.

However, Dandelion assured her it was no problem. She had
Mati switch to a special cast-iron pot developed by the Blossom
Gang, which looked rather intimidating. It was heavy and bulky,
and required a roaring fire underneath. After Mati added the ingredients, Rati and Mota placed a thick domed lid on top and screwed
it securely to the rim. A narrow conical vent protruded out of the top,
plugged by a tower of stackable iron weights.

"Everyone knows how much pressure the scholars are under
when preparing for the Grand Examination," Dandelion said into
the speaking trumpet.

The judges and many in the audience nodded and murmured
their agreement. Scholars from all around Dara were intimately
familiar with test anxiety, as performance in the Grand Examination
literally determined the careers and fortunes of families.

But perhaps nowhere else was this pressure felt as acutely as in
Ginpen. Since Haan was historically considered the most learned
region of Dara, scholars here felt a heavy burden to excel not just
for their own advancement, but also to maintain the reputation of
their homeland. The fact that session after session, Haan always produced more examinees on the *firoa* than anywhere else only added
to that pressure (even Dasu's Zomi Kidosu, first-place examinee a
few sessions back, was claimed by Haan as an adopted daughter
due to her having studied under Ginpen's own Luan Zyaji). Ginpen
had the highest concentration of *cashima* in Dara, but it also had the
largest number of critics of the examination system, who lamented
the pressure on young students and argued that the focus on the Ano
Classics produced smart fools who didn't do much to advance the
state of civilization.

"That pressure has driven many scholars to drink or dream
herbs," continued Dandelion. "But the pressure has also driven parents to make enormous sacrifices for the education of their children,
and made Haan the most literate province in all Dara."

The crowd beamed with pride.

"Do you know what happens to water under pressure?" asked
Dandelion.

Séca, who had actually studied the effects of steam pressure in a laboratory in an effort to improve the propulsion of mechanical crubens, answered, "The water can be heated to a higher temperature when placed under pressure."

"That's right," said Dandelion, "and with this pressure cooker, the temperature inside—"

She was interrupted by a shrill whistle as steam hissed out of the vent in the lid of the massive black pot, pushing up the weights. Mati, assisted by Mota and Widi, placed more weights on top with a long-handled fork to keep the vent plugged.

"The pressure in this cooker can be adjusted by placing different weights over the release valve. Due to the higher temperature, even tough meat and stringy vegetables quickly become tender. Food inside cooks faster and thus retains more flavors, in this manner echoing the way Haan's scholars mature faster and develop sharper insights due to the competitive atmosphere and all-pervasive pressure to excel."

The crowd and judges nodded vigorously at this affirmation of their culture.

Rati looked on, pleased. Though she had invented the device to make tough meat more palatable for her aged teeth, she hadn't ever thought it would be of interest to others, much less be turned into a metaphor for the education-first culture of Ginpen.

Next to Rati, Kinri, who was helping to push her wheeled chair, was amazed. Rati had explained the principles of the pressure cooker to him and Dandelion, and he had found the device fascinating. But he could never have spun such a fine web of associations around the engineering details. The more he got to know Dandelion, the more he admired her.

As Dandelion continued her presentation, her tone shifted from nostalgic recounting to professorial lecture. ". . . Every ordinary cook knows that different types of cooking—boiling, frying, poaching, baking, grilling, steaming, and so on—are distinguished by the ways in which heat is applied to the food. Is it through water, oil, air, steam, radiation, or direct conduction? But the ancient cooking techniques, inherited from our ancestors, cannot be the entirety of the culinary arts. Just as the laboratories of Ginpen are the engines of industrial innovation, cooks who represent Ginpen must also lead the Islands in invention and change.

"You've already seen how the power of the sun, once harnessed for the defense of Haan, can also be used to satisfy the palate. But we aim to show you even more ingenious ways of preparing familiar foods in unfamiliar ways, to generate new tastes that celebrate the uniqueness of Haan."

Next, the Splendid Urn presented another dumpling dish, though this was unlike any dumpling the judges had ever seen.

Instead of wrapping dough around filling and boiling or frying the dumplings, here, the dough was cooked in thick strips separately, almost like noodles. Over this layer of "thick noodles" were deposited round balls of pork filling fried to a crisp. Then a red-pepper-and-cacanut sauce was poured over the top.

It had taken some convincing from Dandelion to get Mati, who was so proud of her dumplings that she decided to make them twice for the competition, to agree to modify them this way. A bowl of dumpling soup was the cheapest item on the Urn's menu and mostly consumed by patrons who ate on the first floor. But just because they didn't represent much profit for the restaurant didn't mean that Mati took shortcuts. She always tried to make them as full of filling as possible to give the price-conscious customers their money's worth. ("If you make them my way, you can put even more filling in without worrying about wrapping," said Dandelion, and that finally convinced Mati to try this unorthodox approach.)

"This dish, 'Inside Out,' represents a deconstructed version of the traditional dumpling," explained Dandelion on the main stage. Mota and Arona, dressed as scholars in the Imperial laboratories, posed over the dish on the enlarger-projector, chin in hand, looking deep in thought. "Just as we seek to understand nature by deconstructing the whole into its constituent parts, dissecting the garinafin to reveal its secrets, so does this dish of noodles and meatballs slathered in red sauce seek to give us a new understanding of the traditional dumpling's charms."

The final dish presented by the Splendid Urn was "Alchemical Beast," a fresh carp seasoned with pipe scallions and ginger. A favorite among wealthy and not-so-wealthy patrons alike, fresh carp was always on the Urn's menu. Though the population of Ginpen, a coastal city, generally favored saltwater fish in their cuisine, the carp was a notable exception. It represented good luck to the scholars, who hoped to achieve greatness in the Imperial examinations much as the carp of legend turned into dyrans by leaping over Rufizo Falls. Mati, no scholar herself, had to learn to score the flesh of the fish into a semblance of the logogram for "wisdom," a gesture much appreciated by the scholar customers.

But today, instead of steaming or frying, Dandelion asked Mati to cook the carp in a special way. In fact, the Blossom Gang had devised the technique within the last week, based on an idea from Dandelion.

First, the fish and seasoning were sealed inside a pouch made from a cow bladder from which as much air was pumped out as possible. The pouch was then immersed inside a water bath whose temperature was precisely controlled and monitored via a gauge made of mercury sealed inside a glass tube.

"Temperature control is a method of alchemical preparation known to many in the laboratories," said Dandelion, "but the idea of cooking food inside a sealed pouch, separated from water, is inspired by Lyucu practice."

The audience became agitated at this, and surprised murmurs and whispers passed through the crowd.

Dandelion went on, seemingly oblivious to the reaction. "In the unredeemed islands to the north, many of our compatriots have been enslaved by the invaders. But we do them an injustice to think that they are *only* victims. Even in the harshest conditions, they have held on to the beacon of hope and found ways to express the love and vitality of their inviolable inner character. Just as many scholars in Rui and Dasu have continued to compose great poetry and create art, transforming the drossy circumstances of their oppression into valuable gold, great cooks in the far north have learned to adapt the cooking techniques of their conquerors into novel ways to express the essence of Dara."

The crowd quieted, rapt with attention. The refugees from Unredeemed Dara often aroused pity (and sometimes resentment and annoyance), but rarely had anyone thought of their courage, of what it took to remain human in inhumane conditions.

"I've learned recently that the people of Unredeemed Dara cook traditional Dara dishes with vessels made from the tough stomachs and intestines of the garinafin, a beast uniquely adapted to live with fire. We don't have access to garinafin body parts, but the principle can be adapted to other materials available to us. After all, it is the way of the people of Haan to always seek to understand first and then to improve, to take inspiration wherever found, to tinker and experiment until something completely new is realized."

Rati nodded and smiled. Though Dandelion spoke of "the people of Haan," she knew the young woman was really talking about her. She had really enjoyed developing this method of "stomach cook-ing" with her—one of the best things about teaching, she reflected, was learning something new from the student.

"By cooking food in sealed cow or sheep bladders immersed in a temperature-controlled water bath, we can achieve novel flavors undreamed of before. Here, the food is cooked in its own juices, with-out drying out or dilution by water, and we can control the applica-tion of heat with laboratory precision. While traditional cuisine relies on the experience of the chef and a great deal of luck, this method of alchemical preparation melds modern invention with ancient tech-nique, and transforms the weapons of our enemies into new ways of producing beauty."

Kinri was startled. Tears welled up in his eyes. He had not believed that his stories would make such an impression on Dandelion. She had taken the insignificant details he had dared to share from his life in Ukyu and Ukyu-taasa and woven them into something as warm and beautiful as herself.

"Lady Cophy, what do you think of the entrées?" asked Lolo.

Some of the judges were chewing slowly with their eyes closed, savoring every bite. Others, Lady Cophy among them, had given up the pretense of maintaining decorum and wielded their eating sticks as though waging war against an edible foe, spearing, stabbing, picking, hoisting, scissoring, wolfing down the food with gusto.

"Mmm—um—" Lady Cophy swallowed a mouthful, and, remembering that she was under the gaze of an audience of thousands, blushed and wiped her mouth daintily with a napkin. "The Splendid Urn's dishes are simply divine—"

"Could we start with some comments on the Treasure Chest?" asked Séca. He was worried that Lolo's obvious favoritism might lead to complaints from Tiphan Huto later.

"Eh? Oh, right. The Treasure Chest's dishes are well-seasoned and professionally prepared. And they look . . . very . . ." Lady Cophy seemed to be struggling to come up with the right word. ". . . extravagant," she finished rather weakly.

Séca was about to probe for more, but Lady Cophy's eyes brightened as she plunged on. "The Splendid Urn's dishes, on the other hand, have taken the culinary arts to a new height. Take 'Shattered Oracle,' for instance. The divine heat of the sun seems to have imparted into the eggs a flavor that is at once bright and dark, terrifying and wholesome, more the hand of gods than mere humans. 'The Grand Examination' has some of the most tender beef and bamboo shoots I've ever tasted—the ingredients practically melt in the mouth—but the texture is nonetheless sophisticated and layered. 'Inside Out' has given me a new appreciation of the components of a dumpling, and I now wish we would see more of these 'deconstructed' dishes on the Urn's menu in the future. But it is 'Alchemical Beast' that gives me the most enjoyment. I've never seen a fish more evenly cooked or with such thorough flavoring. The carp tastes like . . . like it isn't carp at all, but a dyran that has been lifted straight from Tazu's realm, tenderly infused with seasoning from Rufizo's woodlands, and then blessed in the heat of Mount Kana."

Recalling Lady Cophy's earlier rather lukewarm reception of the Splendid Urn's "plebeian" appetizer, Lolo asked a follow-up question. "But don't you think the Treasure Chest had more impressive ingredients? Certainly more befitting haute cuisine, wouldn't you say?"

"Ingredients are not *everything*," said Lady Cophy severely. "The skill of a cook is in elevating plebeian ingredients to nobility, much as knowledge elevates the pedestrian mind to rarified heights. Haven't you been paying attention to Sous-Chef"—the grand lady stumbled over the rather plebeian name of this young chef—"Dandelion's insightful lecture? *That* is what Ginpen is all about! To summarize my feelings about the dishes made by Chef Mati and her crew in one line: We've been blessed with food stolen from a feast of the gods."

The Splendid Urn had bought a whole basket of carp for "Alchemical Beast." There was one left, curled up in the bottom of the straw basket at the side of the stage kitchen. As the afternoon sun cast its slanted rays into the basket, the scales glinted with gold.

The Adüan woman in Temple Square squinted at the sun and hoped the crew from the Splendid Urn would do more throat-singing. Around her neck she wore a necklace of shark's teeth, which glinted as she stood on tiptoes, straining to see.

- *Ah, little sister! Glad you could join us.*

- *Hello to you, too, Tazu.*

- *Is that all of us? Let's see: Kiji the oversized chicken hawk can't make it because he's sulking over there about how the Lyucu don't love him anymore. Lutho the old slippery turtle has gone off to sleep with Agon maidens. So that leaves Kana and Rapa, the jabbering ravens who can't seem to get anything done or understand Jia, their pet mortal; Rufizo, my fine feathered brother with a dovish heart, hoping to save everybody one by one and therefore saving absolutely no one; Fithowéo, a wolf in dog's clothing panting for blood; Tututika, whose favorite mortal princess just cooked her in a cow stomach; and of course me, Tazu, the handsomest, brightest, bestest god of all. I alone am sober while the world is drunk—*

- *I swear I'm going to wring your neck. My promise to our parents be damned—*

- *Don't fall for that, Fithowéo. He loves it when you argue with him. He thrives on discord and chaos. Just ignore him.*

- *Fine, fine, fine. I'll be good. So what do we think of this cooking contest?*

- *I really wish we could serve—*

- *—such dishes at our feasts.*

- *O sisters, surely you know the woman is exaggerating. How can an omelette made with the sun's heat be any better than one cooked over a fire? Heat is heat.*

- Even if she's exaggerating, the sauce of these mortals' stories is better—

—than that stale brine you keep on using instead of proper salt out of laziness.

- Now I'm hurt! See if I cook for you again the next time we get together.

- If you never cooked again, it would be a relief.

- Stop bickering. Look! I haven't seen our little sister smile so happily in ages.

- Why shouldn't I smile? My Fara is winning!

- Hey, did you do something with that fish? You're not supposed to interfere.

- I'm not . . . answering that. Look, Fara cooked that audience at least as well as the mechanics cooked the food.

- All the more reason that we're mad that your charge is wasting her talents on this nonsense—

—instead of war and politics. If only she would devote her mind to serious things!

- Let her live the life she wants to according to her nature and self-sought nurture. So few of us get to do so, even among the gods.

- I don't always agree with our little sister, but I will say this: Having attended this contest, even I'm a little envious of being a mortal—but only in Dara proper, not Ukyu-taasa. What a grand sovereign Jia is that the people of Dara can live like this under her reign, freely cultivating their natures.

- . . .

- Tazu, if I didn't know any better, I'd say that, for once, you made a good point.

"By our judges' votes, the Treasure Chest came out ahead in the appetizer portion," said Séca.

"But the Splendid Urn answered with a victorious blow in the entrée round!" said Lolo.

Over on the Treasure Chest kitchen stage, Mozo Mu looked stricken. Tiphan Huto, who had marched over to the kitchen, leaned down to the child and whispered something in her ear, his face a mask of rage. Tears pooled in Mozo Mu's eyes and threatened to spill out.

Even the team over on the Splendid Urn kitchen stage felt sorry for her.

But there was no time for pity. The competition had to go on.

"It all comes down to the dessert now," whispered Kinri.

Mozo rallied her staff and fought valiantly. "Tiro Tiro" was a fruit tart constructed from sixteen varieties of berries and melons gathered from all across Dara set on a golden, fluffy pastry shell, glazed all over with the rare honey from the swollen bee. This species of bee nested in high cliff caves in the Wasoti Mountains. Certain workers in the hive dangled from cave ceilings and were fed nectar by others until their abdomens expanded into giant, translucent pouches filled with honey. After stunning the bees with smoke, brave villagers collected these "honeypots" much as one plucked grapes from the vine. The task was dangerous, and each year, villagers died from frenzied bee attacks or by losing their footing on the sheer cliffs.

"Love-Me-Not" was a variation of the traditional thousand-layer cake made up of alternating tiers of glutinous rice and sweet pastes of lotus seeds, green bean, crushed dates, honey-pickled rose petals, coconut shavings, and so on. The name was supposedly derived from an ancient Xana princess who was forbidden from seeing her lover, and who then passed him her love notes in the layers of the cake she prepared for the royal feasts. The version Mozo Mu presented glittered on the judges' plates, having been dusted with real gold flakes.

In response, Mati and the Blossom Gang offered two desserts, again made from quotidian ingredients available to the Splendid Urn.

The first, "Lady Rapa's Feast," was made from cream flavored with different pureed fruits poured into spheres formed by screwing two copper bowls together, rim to rim. The bowls were then immersed in tubs of crushed ice and spun in place. Salt was sprinkled into the ice to lower the temperature. When the spheres were opened at the end, the cream had turned into a fluffy, icy substance that melted against the tongue, and produced exclamations of wonder from the judges. Young Pimié finished his portion so quickly that Mati teased him for performing a magic trick. He then asked for seconds, thirds, fourths . . . until he lay behind the judging table, groaning from a stomachache.

"I was just going to make crushed ice with fruit juices," said an admiring Mati.

"I know," said Dandelion with a smile. "I watched you all week. These are still your ideas, just sharpened and enhanced."

However, the last dessert, "Lady Kana's Feast," almost ended the competition prematurely.

Mati began by preparing small, shallow dishes of red bean custard, a standard dessert, and then sprinkling a layer of sugar on top.

"Hmm, that seems to be the kind of thing you could get at any street vendor," said Lady Cophy, squinting at the kitchen stage.

"You sound disappointed," said Lolo. "We've seen that the Splendid Urn doesn't seem to be relying on any expensive ingredients today."

"After the entrées, I was really hoping to be blown away," admitted Lady Cophy. "They've elevated my expectations as much as they've elevated their previous ingredients."

"Oh, I think you'll be blown away by this last step," said a smiling Dandelion. "You might want to find something to hold on to."

Rati and Widi directed their crew to clear the kitchen stage of other equipment, and then placed the shallow dishes of custard on a metal rack. The enlarger-projector was set up to show the magnified custards to the audience. Cautiously, Mota wheeled out a large bag connected to a long tube with a nozzle.

A few in the crowd, somewhat knowledgeable about the weapons deployed by Marshal Gin Mazoti during the war, began to whisper excitedly.

"What's in the bag?" asked Lady Cophy.

"Fermented gas," said Dandelion. "The same substance used to keep airships aloft," she added, for clarification. "Would you like a clearer view of this next step? I promise you'll enjoy it."

Lady Cophy nodded excitedly. Dandelion led her, Séca, and Lolo to the Splendid Urn kitchen stage.

While Mota held the long tube, Arona brought a torch and placed it in front of the nozzle. The two smiled at each other. Rati wheeled herself next to the bag, and then slowly opened a valve in the bag.

"Wait," said Lady Cophy, "isn't fermented gas highly flammable?"

"That's the idea," said Dandelion. "With this dish, we again celebrate the inventiveness of Haan's laboratories. Marshal Mazoti once used a similar contraption, refined here in Ginpen, to simulate garinafin fire in the invasion of Rui by ghost airships—"

With a loud *fwuuump*, a long tongue of fire shot out of the nuzzle. It hissed and flared, and the flame appeared as bright as the sun on the screen of the enlarger-projector.

The crowd gasped with surprise and delight, while Lady Cophy screamed, grabbed onto Séca, and tried to position him between herself and the flickering flame-tongue.

Unperturbed, Mota shuffled closer to the rack of custards and ran the tongue of fire over them. The sugar sprinkled on top melted under the intense heat and turned into a brown caramelized shell.

As Kinri watched, he wondered if this technique could be adopted in Ukyu-taasa. Perhaps real garinafin fire breath could be used instead of a mere simulation. He was sure his mother would enjoy a caramel-glazed roast. *How much better it would be,* he thought, *to use garinafin fire to make sweetness instead of death.*

"Would anyone else like to try?" asked Dandelion.

Lolo volunteered. Mota showed her how to hold the flamethrower steady and then let go. She ran it over the custards and laughed. "This is really fun, Lady Cophy and Séca! You have to try it!"

Lady Cophy shook her head resolutely and held on to Séca's sleeve, refusing to let him go. A few of the other judges, however, climbed onto the kitchen stage to give it a go. Even young Pimié somehow recovered from his stomachache and had a turn.

While Lady Cophy turned down the chance to wield fire breath, she was the first to taste the result. Sinking her spoon through the crispy shell and digging into the warm, soft custard underneath was a sensation that she would rave about to her friends for days afterward.

The crowd waited with bated breath.

On the main stage, the judges were preparing to cast their votes. Some whispered amongst themselves; others looked thoughtful as they read over their own notes. Only Pimié wasn't in his seat; instead, he tarried on the Splendid Urn's kitchen stage, admiring the flame-throwing apparatus that had created such wonders.

The covered wagons next to the kitchen stage had been pulled together and the cloth covers linked so that the whole caravan resembled a large tent. Inside, the Splendid Urn's team gathered around Widow Wasu.

"I can't thank you enough for what you've done," she said to Mati. "You rallied from a position of weakness and saved the reputation of my restaurant."

Then she turned to the Blossom Gang, Dandelion, and Kinri, and bowed to each in turn. "And we all know that Mati couldn't have accomplished this feat without your help. I owe all of you a debt of gratitude that cannot be repaid."

Everyone returned the bow. "Grand Mistress, it was a pleasure to put our knowledge in the service of a true Ginpen institution," said Rati Yera.

"It would be outrageous for a lying scoundrel like Tiphan Huto to win the title of Best Restaurant in Ginpen," chimed in Arona.

"Granny, it was fun!" added Dandelion.

Widow Wasu smiled, sighed, picked up a bamboo shoot from "Music of the Limbs" with her eating sticks, and took a bite. Dishes from each team had also been served to the head of the other team as a gesture of courtesy.

She chewed thoughtfully. "This really *is* very good, you know. The flavors are so complex and layered. Look at the knife-work on these bamboo shoots! Though only three or four ingredients are used, in the mouth it tastes like a hundred different things are happening, a true symphony of tastes. Mozo is a worthy heir to her ancestor."

Mati and Lodan also each took a bite. Their eyes widened in amazement.

"I'm impressed," said Mati, grudging admiration in her tone. "It isn't just a pretty name and expensive ingredients. I can never make something this tasty."

"Don't let the opponent's skill blind you to your own worth," said Lodan. "I think we have a real chance."

Widi said nothing, lost in the sensual delight of the dish. Finally, after so much strife and strain, he got to sample the legacy of Suda Mu.

"That was one of the most amazing shows I've ever seen," said Widow Wasu, but she didn't look assured of victory. "What do you think?" She turned to Dandelion. She spoke reverently, as though the young woman's opinion counted far more than anyone else's.

"In every competition where human judging is involved, it's the story that matters the most," said Dandelion.

Widi clapped his hands together and chuckled. "Spoken like a true paid litigator."

Dandelion grinned at him. "I'm afraid that's one art I'll never pick up."

"Such wasted talent," said Widi, shaking his head sadly.

"How does story matter the most?" asked Kinri. "You told stories that engaged the mind-pleasure of the judges—'cooking' the audience, as you put it—but is there more than that?"

"Of course," said Dandelion. "A story isn't told just in words, but in the selection of ingredients, the methods of preparation, the presentation of the food on the plate, and the kind of audience that is implied. Above all, however, a story requires heart."

"Maybe you'll be better suited as a teacher in the academies," teased Arona. "You certainly enjoy lectures."

Dandelion blushed self-consciously.

"Go on," urged Rati Yera. "Ignore Arona. She loves to talk herself."

Dandelion took a deep breath to sort her thoughts before she continued. "Mozo Mu is a skilled technician, and I think we can all agree that she was the more technically proficient chef." She turned to Mati. "No disrespect meant."

"Oh, I *know* she's the better cook," said Mati. Truth be told, Mati didn't think she deserved to win. She had tried her best, but the focus on theater and the unfamiliar equipment had flustered her and forced her into making compromises. For instance, Dandelion, not being a cook herself, had choreographed "Shattered Oracle" without accounting for the need to scramble the eggs properly for the omelettes, and Mati hadn't been able to improvise a solution in time. Those omelettes were definitely not her best work.

Even if she *had* been able to cook her best, however, Mati doubted she could have approached a tenth of the technical virtuosity of Mozo.

She took a bite of "Tututika's Loom" and savored the flavors. "Even I want to go to her restaurant. To think she's so young! I can only imagine what she'll be capable of in ten, twenty years."

"True, but let's put aside her expensive ingredients and technical virtuosity for the moment," said Dandelion, "and focus instead on the story her dishes told. She wasn't telling her own story, but a story handed to her, a story unsuited for the occasion."

While Widi nodded vigorously at this, the rest looked confused.

Dandelion went on. "The story Mozo Mu told through her cooking was first told by her ancestor, Suda Mu. Before I could come up with a counter-story, I had to first understand Suda Mu."

Kinri's eyes lit up. "That was why you were away at the libraries."

Dandelion nodded. "The poems we memorized gave us hints about the recipes, but they acted as mnemonics, impossible to fully decipher by anyone who didn't already know how to make the dishes."

"How do you mean?"

"Take, as an example, the poem you first heard at the Treasure Chest:

> *"A thousand scales fell at a single stroke.*
> *A thousand ships launched for a promise.*
> *A thousand pearls gazed at the fall*
> *Of the grandest walled treasure-hall.*

"It wasn't until today, after seeing Mozo Mu's dishes, that I understood how the poems worked. This is a part of the recipe for 'Sovereign of the Seas.' The first line refers to a cruben with its armor removed." Dandelion pointed to the lobster tail in the middle of the dish, still mostly intact. "That is to say: an unshelled lobster tail carved to resemble a cruben. The third line refers to a mound of pearls." She pointed to the pile of whitish globules near the edge of the plate. "That is to say: a heap of flying-fish eyes."

Widi laughed. "Ah, I see. It's a riddle impossible to decipher without already knowing the recipe. It makes sense only after seasoning by the secret knowledge in the chef's head."

"They're all like that. So Kinri's first idea wasn't wrong: The poems *are* coded recipes. But the code is a shorthand that cannot be read without already knowing the answer. However, when we couldn't break the code, I realized that the poems also served a second purpose: They could be woven into a picture of Suda Mu's state of mind."

Kinri was reminded of the shaman knots and storytelling dances of his own people. The voice paintings left after the dances were impossible to decipher by anyone who didn't already know the stories, but they provided a reflection of the dance itself, of the conversation between audience and shaman that produced the picture.

Dandelion went on. "As Kinri noted, I've never been very interested in history independent of art. But since every story is rooted in history, I decided to go to the libraries to study the time Suda Mu invented these dishes. Back then, rivalry between the Tiro states impeded trade. The only way to obtain all the ingredients Suda needed was to have the resources of a powerful Tiro king behind the chef. Thus, in order to develop his art, Suda Mu had to place himself under the patronage of the Xana court. Since Xana was planning to conquer all of Dara, he had to please the ambition of the Xana kings in his cooking. Look at the names, 'Tiro, Tiro,' 'Sovereign of the Seas,' 'Tututika's Loom'—they either speak explicitly to the intended audience's hunger for power, or reference it indirectly by suggesting divine justification for Xana's growing ambition. Everything is power, glory, manifest destiny."

"What about the dishes based on . . . love?" asked Kinri.

"Even the dishes based on classical poems about love eschewed the specific for the abstract, leaving the realm of mortals for the magnificence of divinely sanctioned empire. A dish called 'Music of the Limbs' ought to be sensual and intimate, celebrating one of the greatest love stories of all time. But Suda's dish interprets the theme of music literally, not metaphorically, and presents the music of the gods as a kind of servile praise to the sovereign from all corners of Dara. This kind of forced fusion that betrays the very idea of love even as it celebrates it was seen in every aspect of art from the Xana court of that time."

"I thought you weren't interested in war and politics," said Kinri.

Dandelion laughed, a trace of melancholy in her eyes. "Much as I wish love conquered all, it's impossible to understand love or the art inspired by it without seeing the ugliness of politics and war. War is love corrupted."

"War is love corrupted?"

Dandelion nodded. "That's how I see it. War comes from hatred, but hatred is always based on a selfish love, a love that seeks to confine rather than to expand—love of home can turn into hatred of strangers; love of country can turn into arrogance toward other states; love of fellow travelers can turn into a desire to suppress anyone with a different opinion."

"Why did Suda Mu put his skill in the service of tyrants in Xana?"

"Also out of love. Suda was a great artist who needed resources to complete his vision. He allowed his love of beauty, of his art, to be corrupted by that need. Perhaps he thought he could wield the power of the Xana kings to serve his own purposes, but in the end, his art was co-opted by his patrons. He regretted it, which was why he retired to the mountains and kept his recipes from the world. That extravagance, that naked need to display to an abstract multitude, was what appealed to grand lords like King Dézan and Emperor Mapidéré, and continues to appeal to men like Tiphan Huto. When you eat these dishes, you sense power, ambition, opulence, strength. But there is no love. No intimacy of the chef's heart."

"And that is what we have," said Mati. "I cooked everything with love."

Lodan reached out and held her hand, and the two looked warmly into each other's eyes. To the side, Arona smiled at Mota, who smiled back.

"That's right," said Dandelion solemnly. "After I understood the story told by Mozo Mu's dishes, I went to observe Chef Mati and the staff at the Splendid Urn. From these observations, I discovered the perfect counter-story. The abstract should be countered by the concrete, the multitudes with the one, and war with love. Chef Mati's dishes were plain and homely, but suffused with the love of a woman cooking for her children, a man cooking for his dying parents, a couple sharing their first meal together in their new home, a child waking up to make breakfast for the whole family before a day of labor in the fields."

"A return to the basics," whispered Mati.

Dandelion nodded. "You and your staff told the story of love each time you gave a scholar away from home a taste of her mother's kitchen, each time you ladled an extra dumpling into the bowl of a hungry laborer, each time you put a smile on a child's face with crushed ice flavored in fruit juices, each time you made something special for a refugee from distant shores. The story told by the Splendid Urn today is the story of Mati and Lodan and your staff, laid out on a plate. All the Blossoms and I had to do was to elevate the food with a performance that told the story, that allowed the judges to see the ordinary in a new light."

"You did far more than that," chided Widow Wasu, her tone affectionate.

"True. We also had to connect your story to the story of the audience, to make them see how your personal story is also the story of a people. We turned Mati's food into a morality play about Haan's past, when the Zyas led the people to resist Xana aggression; about Haan's present, when scholars flock to Ginpen for knowledge and advancement; and about Haan's future, where the endless search for knowledge and understanding of the world means that we can learn even from our enemies.

"But all of it was tethered to the basics, to the love that can be held in a single heart. A great lady once taught me that there's nothing abstract about love: It requires the specific and the quotidian.

"The four great pleasures in life, she said, are sitting by a cozy fire in winter while snow falls outside the window; climbing onto a high place after a spring rain to admire a revitalized world; eating crabs with freshly brewed tea next to the fall tides; and dipping your feet into a cool lotus-covered lake in the middle of summer. Moreover, each is better with a friend, with love that makes hearts vibrate in sympathy. The rarest ingredient of all is love, and it elevates the feast of life, whether you must cook with duck eggs or deep-sea jade crab.

"Mati cooks not only to make a living, but because cooking is how she expresses her love. The Zyas fought not because they hated Xana, but because they loved the people of Haan, with all their ordinary flaws and quotidian virtues. The best scholars spend so much time studying the Classics that they forget to eat not because they wish to exercise power as high officials, but because they love the smell of writing knife carving into hot wax and the mind-pleasure of debating the wisdom of the sages with a friend. The tinkerers and wanderers who invent and create do so not to pursue profit, but because they love the freedom they experience when they make a thing: something imperfect, silly, perhaps even useless, but theirs and wholly new."

Members of the Blossom Gang nodded at this, their eyes moist.

"But couldn't it also be said that you simply flattered the people of Ginpen?" asked Widi.

"That's the Skeptics' view, yes," acknowledged Dandelion. "But the Splendid Urn *is* part of the fabric of Ginpen, and your story *is* connected to the city's story. The stories we love the most aren't stories about who we are, but who we could become. That was why I ended our story with a hope for turning the weapons of war into sweetness and light.

"You can say they are stories about our self-love—and perhaps that is what the judges responded to—yet, what's wrong with that? We're never as good as we'd like to think we are, but that doesn't mean we shouldn't strive to be closer to the realm of the gods. That is the point of stories, and the point of fine cuisine and all art."

Widow Wasu sighed. "You're every bit as good a talker as your father. In fact, I think your stories are more interesting."

Dandelion laughed softly. "Thank you, Granny. I didn't know him well, and it's always wonderful to speak to someone who knew him . . . as an ordinary person. I'd love to hear more stories about him as a young man."

"I promise to tell you every—"

A timid, childish voice interrupted from outside the covered wagon. "Grand Mistress Wasu, may I speak with you?"

"Maybe Séca and Lolo are ready to announce the winner!" said Arona.

Widow Wasu nodded at Lodan, who went to the flap of the covered wagon. "Ah!" She let out a cry of surprise.

A moment later, Mozo Mu entered. Still wearing her kitchen apron, she showed the strain of a struggle to maintain composure in her face. The child walked to the middle of the tent, faced Widow Wasu, and knelt down, placing her forehead against the floor.

"What is this?" asked a surprised Widow Wasu. "Please, sit up. Please!"

Mozo Mu refused to budge. "Grand Mistress," she said, her voice trembling with barely suppressed sobs, "please save my family."

With many pauses to collect herself and to wipe away tears, Mozo Mu finally managed to tell her story.

For years, the Mu clan lived in their hermitage in the Damu Mountains, secluded from the world. Suda Mu's directions to his children had been clear: The art he had devised would be reserved for the pleasure of the gods, not mankind. Any of his descendants could choose to remain and study his secrets or leave the hermitage with nothing, not even the Mu name. Both choices would be permanent. Those who wanted to learn to cook his recipes swore never to leave the mountain compound.

From time to time, women and men escaping trouble at home and seeking a life away from the world came to the hermitage. The Mu family gave them shelter and food, but kept them away from the inner compound, where Suda Mu's recipes were kept and studied, much like the holy scriptures of various temples. Some of these outsiders became servants of the family and ran errands for them; some even married into the family. But even so, they were kept away from Suda Mu's recipes.

From a very young age, Mozo showed unusual talent. Barely a few months old, she pointed at and reached for the kitchen from her nanny's arms. Before she had learned to talk, she was already wrapping perfect dumplings. Before she had learned to walk, she could already pull noodles from dough. At age five, she successfully made "Moon Over Lake Dako," a technically challenging dish that even skilled chefs feared to attempt. In fact, since Mozo was too young to know how to read more than a few logograms, she had managed her feat entirely by looking at drawings in the recipe book and by observing her teenaged older brother try and fail multiple times.

By the time she was ten, she had mastered all eighty-one dishes in Suda Mu's magnum opus, *A Gourmet's Atlas of Dara*. This was a collection of the old master's proudest inventions over his illustrious career, and some of the dishes were so difficult to make that no one in the family could even remember what they tasted like. The elders considered Mozo the answer to their prayers, a seventh-generation descendant of Suda who had the potential to take the Mu family legacy to new heights.

The wealthy and the powerful, hearing rumors of the young culinary prodigy, came with platters of rare pearls and chests filled with gold, trying to entice her to come and cook for them—even if it was just one meal. Always, these messengers were politely but firmly turned away.

"Let not desire for fame or riches corrupt your art" was Suda Mu's final instruction to his family as he lay dying, and these words were carved into the wall of the ancestral hall.

But then, one night, while the whole family was asleep, the compound was surrounded by a group of men wielding torches and fearful weapons. They pounded on the gates and woke everyone up. When the gates were opened, they rushed in like a pack of wolves and bound everyone inside with thick ropes.

Seeing their tattered clothes—many wore fur—and mismatched weaponry—some were even fashioned out of animal bones—the Mu matriarch thought they were desperate bandits seeking treasure. She told them to take whatever of value they found in the compound.

But the bandits laughed in her face. They demanded to be taken to the secret recipe books of Suda Mu.

The matriarch, Mozo Mu's great-grandmother, refused to yield. They killed her in front of the whole family.

Mozo Mu's father then offered to lead the bandits to the books. But he managed to evade the bandits escorting him, entered the secret storage cellar, barred the doors, and then set fire to the old scrolls. By the time the bandits broke down the cellar doors, all the recipe books had been burned to ashes, and the man himself was severely burned.

"There's nothing for you to take now," said Mozo's father.

"Don't think you can get out of this that easily," said the leader of the bandits, a burly man with a nasty smile. "The dead books may be gone, but there are still living ones."

The young Mozo Mu was pulled in front of the man and told that she could either agree to cook for the bandits' master or watch her family be executed in front of her, one each hour.

Mozo agreed.

The bandits, as it turned out, were working for Tiphan Huto. Some took the rest of the Mu family away as hostages, while the rest took Mozo to Ginpen, where she was told to prepare for a cooking competition. Victory was the only outcome allowed if she wanted to see her family alive.

"Please," said a weeping Mozo Mu, "save my family."

Everyone in the tent stared at the young girl, dumbfounded by this sudden turn of events.

Lodan stepped forward. "Grand Mistress, there's no proof that what she's saying is true. This could be a trick to get us to concede. There's nothing Tiphan wouldn't resort to."

Mozo looked at Widow Wasu, tears streaming down her face. "I know that you have bested me on this day. And as the vanquished, I have no claim on your sympathy. But my family . . . I have nothing to bargain with, but I will pray for Lady Kana to shorten my life and give the extra years to you; I will teach you all the secret sauces passed down in my family, including the essence of vegetable youth and the crystals of seaweed extract—"

Widow Wasu sighed, shuffled forward, and held the young girl by her arms. "Child, stand up."

"Not unless you agree to save my family."

"Of course I'll concede," said Widow Wasu. "And you don't need to give me anything."

Kinri and Dandelion looked at each other.

"Grand Mistress," said Kinri. "If we concede this round, we'll be competing the rest of the way from a position of weakness. Even if she's telling the truth, we can't let them blackmail us into submission."

"Why don't we report this to the magistrate?" said Dandelion. "Surely the officials will be able to rescue her family?"

"No!" cried out Mozo. "The bandits took my family away on ships. Tiphan said that he'll keep them in the Silkworm Eggs. If you tell the magistrate here, Tiphan will surely send word by messenger pigeon. My family will be dead by the time rescuers get there, and the bandits will be gone!"

Widow Wasu patted her arm in comfort. "Don't worry. We won't do anything to endanger your family." Then she turned to the rest of the team. "I know that you don't feel we should concede, but the truth is, I don't think we're winning this the right way. Mati, without the benefit of Dandelion's stories and the performances of the heroes of the Blossom Gang, you know her food tastes better than yours."

Mati nodded as tears spilled from her eyes. Lodan hugged her.

Widow Wasu continued. "Besides, the rules say that we can't rely on the help of anyone who's not already a member of the Splendid Urn's staff."

"Oh!" exclaimed Dandelion.

Everyone's heart sank. Widow Wasu was right. In their eagerness to help, they had forgotten about this part of the rules.

"You can hire us right now!" cried Widi.

Widow Wasu shook her head. "It's too late. Tiphan will say that you had to be on staff at the time the competition was first announced—"

"I think that's arguable—"

Widow Wasu held up a hand. "Litigator, this isn't a court. I felt uneasy earlier when I accepted your help, but I tried to convince myself that the pig wasn't already dead. But now I know: To win this way isn't fair."

"How can it possibly be unfair when Tiphan is playing all kinds of dirty tricks?" cried Kinri. "Taking Mozo's family hostage, buying up all the ingredients—"

"We can't sink to his level," said Widow Wasu calmly. "There was a time, when I was younger, when I didn't care about such scruples. But the gods are always watching, and deceit and lies never yield true victory. You spoke of good stories, Dandelion. Well, I built the Splendid Urn out of love of good food and good company, but love has no place for lies."

After a moment, Dandelion bowed. "Granny, your grandness of spirit humbles me. You're right. Love has no place for lies."

For some reason, both Kinri and Dandelion chose that moment to look at each other. As if struck by lightning, they both instantly looked away.

The rest of the team hung their heads in dejection. To have victory come so close, only to have it snatched away, felt worse than losing outright.

Widow Wasu hugged Mozo. "You are a brave girl to have done what you did. I'll go to the judges now."

The young girl knelt down again and touched her forehead to the floor. "Grand Mistress, I'm in your debt forever."

"You may call me Granny if you wish," said Widow Wasu. "It is I who should thank you for showing me and everyone here just what is possible with food. You're a real artist, Mozo. I only wish that in the future you'll create your own dishes instead of replicating the creations of your ancestor. You have a talent, and you deserve to wield it to tell your own story."

When Lolo and Séca announced the Splendid Urn's concession, the crowd and the judges alike were shocked. Competing rumors offering outrageous explanations began to fly around Ginpen before the kitchen stages in Temple Square had even been dismantled. Some claimed that the Urn had tried to cheat and was caught; others said that they saw the Urn's chef break down in tears when she tasted the amazing food cooked by the Chest's prodigy.

Inside his covered wagon, Tiphan handed a few local wastrels small bags of coins. "Thank you, good sirs and madams. Keep those lips flapping."

Back at the Splendid Urn, Widow Wasu seemed to have aged in just a few hours. Her back was even more bent, and her steps had lost their spring.

"The one thing I can do to remedy my mistake is to add you to the staff of the Splendid Urn," said Widow Wasu to Dandelion and the Blossom Gang. "If you're still willing to help me for the next round."

Everyone nodded.

"What's the next contest?" asked Dandelion.

"Since we're the loser, we get to pick," said Widow Wasu. "I proposed a competition on service."

"When?" asked Lodan.

"They'll need a few weeks—apparently the Treasure Chest has to do some reconstruction to be compliant with Imperial building code. But no matter how much money they have, there's no way they can compete against our service. Even when the Urn was just a simple pub, we always made every guest feel at home and made sure they left with satisfied bellies and glad hearts."

- *Little sister, were you the great lady who taught Fara all about love?*

- *I only planted a seed, Rufizo. She has cultivated it into a magnificent flower. And what's more: I was aiming for her sister, not her.*

- *That's the thing about mortals. They always surprise us.*

- *Sometimes I think the greatest pleasure of being a god is to learn something new from a favorite mortal.*

# CHAPTER FORTY

# LETTERS

DIMUSHI: THE SIXTH MONTH IN THE NINTH YEAR
OF THE REIGN OF SEASON OF STORMS AND THE
REIGN OF AUDACIOUS FREEDOM (TWENTY-THREE
MONTHS UNTIL THE REOPENING OF THE WALL OF
STORMS).

*To Her Most August Imperial Majesty,*

*Following my last dispatch, Princess Aya has launched another expedition against the pirates operating in Amu Strait. A full evaluation of the results of the expedition will follow in a more detailed account, but heeding your command to highlight the most salient points of lengthy reports, I shall offer a description of one engagement here to give a flavor of the expedition as a whole.*

*On the morning of the full moon, after having been at sea for a week without any signs of piracy, lookouts reported sighting a merchantman being attacked by two ships flying the Banner of the Broken Tooth, the sign of the notorious pirate-king Dozy Mémén, also known as One-Eyed Shark.*

*Princess Aya and I conferred and agreed to engage the pirates immediately. All hands were roused, and the fleet of four castle ships and two flying barques sailed toward the troubled merchantman.*

*The two pirate ships abandoned the merchantman and turned to engage us. I advised Princess Aya to switch to oars and ram the pirate ships, to be followed by boarding and a marine assault, should the pirate ships survive the initial attack. My advice was founded* on standard naval tactics: We outnumber the enemy, possess the weather gage, and the castle ships are hardened for ramming.

Princess Aya, however, disagreed.

"Instead of running away, the pirates are attacking us. This suggests a plot. We should assume a defensive posture."

I explained that pirates, being desperadoes, always attack in the hope of intimidating a foe, no matter how overmatched.

"Not so," said Princess Aya. "'A foolhardy general is contemptuous of his opponent; a prudent general thinks his opponent is his equal; a brilliant general respects and honors his opponent as his teacher.' Do you know who said that?"

I confessed that I did not.

"My mother, in The Mazoti Way of War, Book II, chapter seventeen, 'Mindset of the General.' Are you claiming to be a more brilliant general than my mother?"

I explained that I in no way thought myself the Marshal's equal. However, it seemed to me that the Marshal's words shouldn't be interpreted to mean we should always act like turtles. The task, after all, is to eliminate the piracy threat and find evidence of pirate collaboration with the Lyucu, not merely to avoid harm to ourselves.

"Did you win more battles or did my mother?"

I conceded that I had, in fact, not won any battles, though I did serve as staff observer on several anti-piracy and anti-banditry missions and have some experience.

"I shall report you for obstructing military planning and putting the lives of our sailors and marines at risk."

Meanwhile, the pirate ships were getting closer with each passing minute.

Despite the majority of the captains agreeing with me, I acceded to Princess Aya's decision. However, instead of the standard naval defensive formation of placing the castle ships in a line with the flying barques on the wings, Princess Aya ordered the heavy castle ships be chained together into a square, with the flying barques kept inside this floating fortress.

I objected to this most unorthodox defensive formation, which sacrificed all mobility for dubious gains.

"Do you not recognize the Box Formation that achieved so much success at the Battle of Zathin Gulf? I suggest you read my mother's treatise, especially Book IV, chapters one through eight. I've studied this formation in detail and described it at length in a note to chapter eight."

I pointed out that the Marshal's use of the Box Formation with interlocking airships was a response to garinafin attack patterns. There seemed little reason to force an aerial tactic against a different foe into the present naval engagement.

"'An inflexible general uses cavalry to counter cavalry, infantry to oppose infantry, siege weaponry to answer siege weaponry; a flexible general sees the commonality between all realms of war and knows that infantry may sometimes employ cavalry tactics, that cavalry may sometimes take cities, that siege weaponry may sometimes devastate infantry in the field.' Do you know who said that?"

I ventured a guess that it was the Marshal.

"Exactly! Your mind is so inflexible that you view naval and aerial battles as entirely separate realms. Gori Ruthi, you remind me of your uncle, who was so bound by the foolish words of Kon Fiji that he lost to my mother's much smaller force three times. Now, will you let me fight this battle or will you keep on yapping like an annoying lapdog?"

I wished to point out that it isn't the words of the sages that are foolish, but the foolish manner in which we interpret the words of our teachers. However, given the proximity of the pirate ships, I once again yielded.

The pirate ships, rather stunned by our floating fortress, hesitated at first, uncertain what to do. They cruised around the squared fleet cautiously while our archers watched them vigilantly from the castle ship ramparts.

"You see how brilliantly my plan has worked out? You need to know to defer to the daughter of the most—"

At that point, a pirate leader wearing an eye patch climbed onto the crow's nest of the lead ship and identified himself as One-Eyed Shark. He shouted many unspeakable insults at us and mocked our formation, enraging Princess Aya. But he was too far away for our arrows to reach.

Princess Aya then gave the order to assemble and make ready the stone-throwers. Archers had to evacuate the castles to join the effort. But while most of our crew was occupied in this endeavor, One-Eyed Shark ordered his ships to approach and launched a volley of burning tar buckets at one castle ship before pulling away. By the time archers scrambled back into the castles to repel the attack, the fire had spread into the riggings, and it took the entire crew's effort to keep the fire from consuming the ship.

Meanwhile, One-Eyed Shark's ships were heading back to the disabled merchantman again.

Princess Aya demanded that we give chase to the despicable knaves, the first of her decisions that I fully agreed with. However, since our castle ships were chained together and the flying barques blocked within, it took a considerable amount of time before the ships could be untangled. By the time the fleet—minus the castle ship dealing with the fire—arrived at the merchantman, the pirates had taken all the loot and hostages and escaped, leaving the raided merchantman a floating wreck.

At this point, the only thing left to do was to search the merchantman for survivors. I urged sending a small boarding party out of caution, for One-Eyed Shark has a reputation for being cruel and wily, but Princess Aya wanted every able-bodied seaman to board the ship immediately in order to search the ship in the shortest amount of time.

"The pirates have already run away, fearful of our might. 'Beware cowardice dressed up in the garb of prudence.'"

A few more quotations from the Marshal later, I once again lost the argument.

Unfortunately, with so many searchers onboard, they got in one another's way and duplicated effort. It took much longer to search the whole ship than anticipated, and about half an hour later, there was an explosion in one of the compartments below the waterline, likely the result of a booby trap by Dozy. We had to evacuate the merchantman before it sank, and several sailors were injured in the chaotic stampede.

In all, as a result of this engagement, one castle ship had to be sent back to Dimushi for repairs, and a total of twenty sailors and marines *were wounded, though none of the injuries were life-threatening. We captured no pirates.*

*My overall assessment of Princess Aya's performance is . . . unfavorable. She is reckless when she should be cautious, timid when she should be bold. She eschews standard tactics but her innovations are not effective. She ignores counsel and subsists on pride. She knows every line of her mother's treatise by heart, but doesn't appear to know how to apply the lessons of the Marshal to life. In short, I would heartily recommend her to play the part of a general onstage, but would think thrice—and thrice more—before entrusting her with another command.*

> *Your Loyal Servant,*
> *Gori Ruthi*

*P.S. I have just been informed that One-Eyed Shark has sent us the ransom demands for his hostages. As I noted in my last letter, there is no evidence that any of the pirates of Amu Strait are working with the Lyucu, or that any abductions are for more than ransom. I recommend that we pay the ransom to ensure the safe return of the merchantman's crew. It will be cheaper and more effective than sending Princess Aya again.*

MEANWHILE, IN GINPEN.

*My Dearest Aya,*

*I'm sorry to hear that you've been having so much trouble with that stuffy Gori Ruthi. No doubt he'll be waxing eloquent in his reports to our aunt-mother, casting the few setbacks you've suffered in the worst light possible. Moralists like him are always so good at pointing out the faults of others while excusing themselves. If he's so clever and smart, why didn't he present his arguments to you in a more convincing manner? Hmm?*

*Chin up! What great general doesn't suffer a few defeats in her career? I'm sure even your mother didn't win every battle. I can imagine the pressures you're under, and I know that you're doing your best. I wish I knew how to help you, but I really know nothing about war. So please, just remember that I believe in you.*

*Now, on to more pleasant matters. I've been keeping my promise and not getting into any trouble, of that you may be sure. Indeed, Granny Wasu takes exceptionally good care of me, and I have eaten so much good food that I daresay by the time you see me next I shall be as plump as an airship. I spend all day working on my art, my only companions harmless denizens of the garden, such as the pine, the orchid, the safflower, the bamboo, and . . . even some* thasé-teki. *I'm sure Aunt-Mother will be happy to hear that I've taken an interest in the domestic arts of cooking, hostessing, herb gardening. So if you're going to write her a report about what's happening with me, mention that.*

*(I can already see your skeptical look—so suspicious!—I swear every word I've written is true. Look at how neat my logograms are!)*

*Anyway, I hope you finish your anti-piracy mission soon and come home. I may (or may not, you'll just have to remain in suspense) have some good gossip to share. By the way, have you thought about designing comfortable furniture for restaurants? I bet you'd be good at it. It's something we can explore when we're back in Pan. I know Granny Wasu will appreciate it.*

*One last thing: When you're on your way back, would you mind swinging by the Silkworm Eggs? I have fairly reliable information— don't ask me how I got it, for I will never reveal my sources—that there is a group of pirates holding hostages at the private shipyard of the Huto clan in those isles. Please do all you can to rescue the hostages safely. Note the use of red wax in the last sentence: VERY IMPORTANT.*

*Your sister,*
*Fara*

～

MEANWHILE, IN TIRO COZO, EMPEROR
MONADÉTU'S SECRET GARINAFIN TRAINING
GROUNDS.

*Dear Zomi,*

*I'm convinced that Ofluro and Lady Suca have been sent by the gods to aid us. With their help, I've made more progress with the garinafins in the last six months than I did in all the years previous.*

*For the first time, I really do believe we can build up a garinafin force to challenge the Lyucu. The next time we meet on the battlefield, we'll be able to send up garinafin riders of our own. No longer will we have to watch helplessly as the deadly beasts lay waste to our cities; no longer will we have to mourn heroes lost because airships cannot match winged crubens for speed and firepower. Can you imagine what Auntie Gin would have done if she had what I have?*

*The world may not be fair, but we've taken a huge stride to make it more so.*

*That brings me to the purpose of my letter. As you know, without money, garinafins alone cannot change the tides of war. To win, I must have weapons, vehicles, soldiers, riders, logistics corps, transportation, naval and ground support, and a thousand other things besides.*

*Based on intelligence gathered from the latest wave of refugees and the last tribute trade mission, the Lyucu have found out about the reopening of the Wall of Storms and are preparing for the arrival of a second wave of reinforcements, at which point they'll launch a general invasion of the core islands. But the Inner Council and the empress act like toddlers who believe that when they cover their eyes, the world disappears. Repeated requests for funding to strengthen Dara against this invasion have been rebuffed, and Aunt-Mother tells me that any mobilization for war on our part will risk provoking the Lyucu, which must be avoided at all costs. Besides, she tells* me, we must not raise taxes, for farmers already live a hard life, and what money we do have must be spent on education, roads, irrigation, civil engineering, and the like. I am not ignorant of the benefits of these projects, but what is the point of building roads and harbors if you cannot protect them when the Lyucu invade?

I believe Aunt-Mother is too indulgent of the demands of peace. The people grow indolent and forgetful, losing the sobriety of our ancient virtues in a drunken stupor of greed and vanity. I hear that in some of the metropolises, merchants vie with one another in conspicuous displays of wealth—this one burns candles in furnaces instead of firewood; that one stacks silk handkerchiefs next to toilets instead of tissue grass. Private academies boast about the tuition they charge; restaurants compete to put out the most expensive, ostentatious menu. How could this be the Dara that Father and the Marshal died to save?

No. I don't just want to defend the core islands; I want to take back Rui and Dasu. I want the people to live again with a purpose in their hearts, not merely the accumulation of wealth and status. The stories of the refugees from Unredeemed Dara haunt me. I cannot abandon those islands; I cannot allow the Lyucu to continue their reign of terror.

Aunt-Mother is correct that I want to provoke war. Isn't it a sovereign's duty to preserve and defend his people, to fight for them?

As I am not at court, I have no resources to draw on. Can you find a way to secure me funding by other means? This is of critical importance.

As well, I need you to find me men and women of talent. I don't mean military commanders—I can train them myself. But a war isn't fought only by soldiers. Auntie Gin achieved what she did only because you, Théra, and the other engineers devised the silkmotic lances and bolts that carried the day. But those weapons from a decade ago cannot be mounted on garinafins, and they are, in any event, far too expensive to produce in sufficient quantities to be of use without access to the public treasury. I therefore need you to help me bring together a second team to repeat the miracle of Zathin Gulf, composed of skilled engineers who can build me new weapons for a new war.

*I know that to privately fund an army, when the empress has denied public funding, verges on treason. Yet, does not* mutagé *require more than obedience to the holder of the Seal of Dara? When the Islands are under the threat of annihilation, is it treason to try to save the people using whatever means one has? I believe my sister, the true sovereign of Dara, would emphatically answer yes to the first question and no to the second. I hope you will agree.*

    *I remain, as always,*

*Your friend,*
*Phyro*

PAN.

Jia got to the point right away. "How is the harvest?"

"Not great," said Wi. She and Shido had just returned from Mount Rapa. "The sisters at the site said there were few flowers, and we ended up with only about five baskets' worth of usable yield."

Jia sighed. Since the plant flowered in winter, she had only been able to get one crop in this year before it became too warm. She had hoped that planting a second crop near the icebound peak of Mount Rapa would lead to similar results as a true winter, but the plant's nature likely sensed the difference in daylight length and refused to cooperate.

"For the next crop, I'll ask the sisters to climb higher on the peak, where it's colder," said Wi. "I'm sorry I didn't—"

"It isn't your fault," said Jia. "Don't ask the other Dyran Fins to climb higher either; it won't do any good, and sustained exposure to such frigid conditions will damage their joints. Actually, get them all back here. They've lived in the cold for too long as it is. I'll make them a homunculus mushroom soup to heal their bodies."

"Thank you, Mistress," said Wi and Shido, a grateful quaver in their voices.

Jia waved dismissively. "I'll think of another way to grow them in summer and autumn. You may go."

Wi and Shido bowed and melted away into the night.

Instead of going to sleep—and the unwelcome visits by ghosts—Jia stayed up to think about the problem of growing a winter-flowering plant in summer.

*All living things know the world through their senses, and senses can be fooled. Perhaps there is a way to give them the sensation of winter. . . . I remember my teacher mentioning a way to make winter plums bloom in summer. . . . Icehouses, shading parasols, the essence of rotting leaves . . .*

She paced and muttered to herself. From time to time she sat down to sketch in her experimental notebook and to write notes to herself in code for leads to follow up in the library in the morning.

It would be easier if she had a partner with whom she could discuss her ideas, to help her think. But this had to be her task alone.

At length, satisfied with her progress, she stopped, put the notebooks away, and turned to the stack of official reports and petitions. She had been delegating as much as possible to the Inner Council, not just so that she could focus on the few matters that truly needed her attention, but also to make sure that they were used to making decisions on their own. It might become necessary.

There was a petition from Prince Gimoto. She broke the seal, unfolded it, but didn't bother reading the contents before dripping a clump of red wax at the end and carving *DENIED*. She tossed it to the side.

There was also a petition from Phyro. She read it carefully, twice. Instead of demanding more money for his army, it requested funding to build a temple to Gin Mazoti so that her heroic deeds might be remembered by the people; it proposed a system of pensions and honors to be given to veterans of the war against the Lyucu; it urged the establishment of a holiday to honor the sacrifices of those who fought for Dara and gave their lives and limbs; it spoke of collecting and publishing the horrifying tales of the refugees from Unredeemed Dara.

*You want to change the hearts of the people. You want to rouse them from the slumber of peace to the frenzy of war. You want to force my hand.*

*But you haven't thought it through. You don't understand the consequences, and the consequences of the consequences.*

She dripped a clump of red wax at the end and carved *DENIED*.

There was a letter from Gori Ruthi. Like most letters from Moralists, it was prolix and tedious. Forcing herself to be patient, Jia read all the way through.

There were two things of interest. The first concerned Aya Mazoti. As she had suspected, the princess was no military genius, but that didn't make her useless. Despite all of Gori Ruthi's attempts to slant the narrative, Jia could discern the truth between the lines. Yes, Aya was insecure and burdened with the weight of her lineage, but even so, she cared about the lives of the people she was charged with leading. Despite multiple errors, no one had died under her command. Her first instinct wasn't to gain herself the greatest glory by capturing pirates, but to rescue the survivors of the pirate raid on the wrecked ship—certainly Gori Ruthi neglected to mention the precautions she must have taken so that the booby trap didn't kill anyone. All in all, she was rather satisfied with the young woman's performance.

The second was the point about no evidence of pirate abductions of people of skill near Dimu and Dimushi. This required more thinking. Tanvanaki could not be underestimated. She had to figure out what was going on . . . not just because the Lyucu must not be allowed to steal Dara's people and knowledge, but also because the answer could be the solution to another problem that had been plaguing her.

She sat by the desk, lost in thought, until dawn peeked through the window.

## CHAPTER FORTY-ONE

# A CURSE

GINPEN: THE SIXTH MONTH IN THE NINTH YEAR
OF THE REIGN OF SEASON OF STORMS AND THE
REIGN OF AUDACIOUS FREEDOM (TWENTY-THREE
MONTHS UNTIL THE REOPENING OF THE WALL OF
STORMS).

Sixteen-year-old Pénozy yawned and pushed opened the doors of the Splendid Urn just as the sun peeked over the walls of Ginpen.

Though she still had the physique of a healthy peasant girl used to heavy labor, she was already finding it difficult to get up as early as she had a few months ago, before she left her parents in the village to take this job her cousin had found for her. There were just so many more fun things to do in the city, and she and her friends had once again stayed out late last night for drinks and street snacks after ogling the gaudy edifice that was the Treasure Chest.

Pénozy smiled at the memory. Laborers were trying to install a strange kind of lamps in the restaurant—*silkmotic torches*, she heard others say—very expensive and delicate. Tiphan Huto, the boss of the Treasure Chest, had been screaming at the workmen to be careful. Through the open windows of the restaurant, she and her friends had giggled at the sight of the rotund man jumping up and down like a spooked rooster, his face bright red and his voice so high-pitched that the neighborhood dogs barked.

She sighed, hoping that Grand Mistress Wasu would figure out a way to beat that nasty man and his palace-like restaurant—though it did look so impressive.

The early morning summer air was pleasantly cool, and the clean tables and benches behind her gleamed in the dawn light. Time to get to work.

Pénozy squinted against the bright sun and bowed. "Welcome to the Splendid Urn, masters and mistresses."

Breakfast service wasn't a big moneymaker for the Urn, as most wealthy patrons didn't hold parties or schedule meetings in the morning. In fact, most of the breakfast patrons who came to the Urn tended to be poor scholars who wanted to get an early start on a long day of studying and unmarried laborers in the neighborhood on their way to work. Living in cramped tenements with communal kitchens meant that breakfast was always a chaotic affair, requiring one to get up early to secure a place in the crowded kitchen and then cook under the impatient gazes of latecomers. Those who preferred to avoid the stress sometimes went hungry.

Widow Wasu had always insisted that her restaurants all across Dara serve this clientele with affordable options. Besides having a natural sympathy for men and women who reminded her of her own humble origins—("The lonely stevedores and morning-soil maids especially need someone to hand them a warm bowl of bean milk with a smile")—she also thought it was smart business to be in the good graces of neighborhood residents. One never knew when the restaurant might need to call on those same laborers and poor scholars to help put out a fire or to sign a petition to the magistrate in support of the restaurant's application for a bigger carriage parking lot and guest stable.

Thus, although most of the Urn's breakfast patrons wouldn't dream of paying the kind of prices charged for lunch and dinner, they were happy to stop by the Urn for a bowl of sweet bean milk and a couple of hot knot fritters before going off to work. Mati always made the bean milk smell so good with a sprinkling of Cocru herbs and flowers, and the knot fritters were so crisp that they cheered you right up when they crunched against your teeth. Lodan also made sure that the waiters and waitresses treated these one-copper customers with just as much respect as they did the twenty-gold customers later in the day.

Pénozy straightened up and realized that no one was lined up in front of the restaurant. Surprised and confused, she stepped out into the street and looked around. A group of laborers and scholars stood around the large parasol tree that shaded the entrance to the Splendid Urn, pointing up and chatting amongst themselves anxiously.

"... not a good sign ..."

"... never seen anything like it ... only on this tree ..."

"... a curse, I heard. Didn't believe it at first ..."

Gingerly, Pénozy shuffled closer and shaded her eyes to get a clearer look. The parasol tree did look a bit odd. There was a kind of haze that softened the clean outlines of the leaves and branches. . . .

*And what are those dangling strands that look like tassels at the rim of a real parasol? Oh, wasn't that a pretty parasol Tasana and I saw at Temple Square the other day? That lady was so elegant. Anyway, let me take a closer look at these strands. They're so silky and thick. . . . I didn't know parasol trees had flowers or fruits like that. . . . Huh, something heavy, like beads, seem to hang from the end of each. There's a breeze passing through now. Feels so nice . . . wait, are the beads wiggling on their own? Oops, I think one of them just fell on me—*

She screamed. The creature that fell on her neck was as long as a finger, and covered by fuzz. Frantically, she tried to brush it away, and it ended up on her arm. Wherever it touched, she felt as though she had been pricked, and then a burning sensation spread across the skin.

Hundreds, thousands, tens of thousands of caterpillars dangled on silk strands from the parasol tree. The entire tree was covered in a gauzy gossamer cocoon.

By the time the torches had singed away most of the caterpillars and hired laborers had trimmed off most of the silk-choked branches, it was long past time for lunch service. Mota Kiphi had led the workers, fearlessly lopping off thick branches with a single swing of the axe. Without his example, it was doubtful if the others would have dared to approach the evil-looking cocoons.

Lots of caterpillars still remained on the tree, but short of cutting the tree down, it would be hard to completely eliminate them.

Lodan paid the laborers—several of whom had suffered painful, ugly rashes from caterpillars falling on them—and called a stop to the extermination effort. A crowd had gathered around the Splendid Urn to witness this horrific sight, though few came in to eat.

"This is the third day something strange has happened at the restaurant," fretted Widow Wasu. She sat in her bedroom, and a young maid gently massaged her tense shoulders.

"It could just be coincidences," offered Mati, though she didn't sound at all convinced. Lodan, who sat next to her, held her hand.

Since Teson Wasu, the manager, was busy dealing with the crowd of onlookers and trying to reassure spooked staff, and Néfi Ézugo, the head chef, was still too weak to get out of bed, Widow Wasu was convening this meeting with Mati and Lodan, who she thought of as her two generals in this war. Just as Mati was in charge of the food competition, Lodan would be in charge of the service competition.

"I don't think so," said the widow. "The day before yesterday, two vegetable vendors' carts had their axles break just as they turned the corner for our delivery door. Yesterday, a pack of feral dogs just happened to surround the restaurant around dinnertime, barking up a storm and leaving their shit everywhere. And today, caterpillars ruined that old parasol tree and breakfast. How could so many unfortunate things be happening all at once?"

"Grand Mistress, do you think Tiphan Huto is behind this?" asked Lodan.

"Of course he is!" said Widow Wasu. "It's just . . . we can't prove it. That man is slimy but careful."

"But what does he hope to accomplish?" asked Mati. "Sure, he's disturbing our customers, but that's not going to help him win."

The Treasure Chest's renovations were almost complete, and the second round of the competition was scheduled to be held in a week. In order to isolate the competition to service and remove food from consideration, Lolotika Tuné and Séca Thu had drawn up rules that dictated that the two restaurants would serve the same dishes to capacity crowds. The judges—a different panel from the last time and whose identities were secret—would be divided between the two venues. Mixed in with the customers, they would observe the staff to determine which was most worthy of the title of Best Restaurant in Ginpen in the manner they took care of their diners.

"I'll talk to Kinri and the Blossom Gang about some ways to keep watch and prevent more sabotage," said Mati.

Mati was confident of victory. As much as the kitchen crew liked working for her and Head Chef Néfi Ézugo, she knew that the waitstaff respected and liked Lodan. The Splendid Urn's turnover was low because a job there was coveted. Not only did Teson Wasu pay well, but there were generous bonuses at New Year and High Autumn, and Widow Wasu even loaned money to former staff members who wanted to start their own businesses or learn a trade. To be part of the Splendid Urn was to be part of a family.

Lodan took the time to train her staff, and everyone knew what to do when it got busy. Teson, the manager, had also always followed his mother's direction to keep standards high and to make sure every customer felt like they were welcome and got the best service, no matter how much or how little they bought. To be sure, for the competition, the staff would have to learn a new menu. But considering how often Néfi and Mati changed the menu throughout the year based on the availability of ingredients—both of them believed in buying local as much as possible to ensure the freshest taste—it shouldn't be a big deal.

The Treasure Chest, on the other hand, was working with a green crew who hadn't been together long enough to develop trust and routine, and Tiphan Huto seemed to have a reputation as an impatient manager who liked to meddle in things he didn't understand. The soft opening of the Treasure Chest a few weeks earlier, a sort of trial run for the competition, had been a disaster. The place had been filled with curious diners who wanted to sample the amazing dishes that had defeated the Splendid Urn at the first round of the competition, but Mozo's kitchen couldn't keep up, and the waitstaff, many of them hired because they asked for the lowest salaries, was unfamiliar with the complicated menu and got many orders wrong. An enraged Tiphan had fired the shift manager on the spot and threw a tantrum in the middle of the restaurant, ending dinner service rather ignominiously.

"If these weird disruptions really were planned by Tiphan," said Lodan hesitantly, "then they might be having an effect already."

Widow Wasu sighed. "I was worried about that."

"What do you mean?" asked Mati.

"There are rumors that the Splendid Urn is cursed, which is why we're being plagued with unclean dogs and bad accidents," said Lodan. "A lot of the staff are worried and think we should ask the monks at the Temple of Lutho for an exorcism."

Mati was surprised. She had never believed in curses and evil spirits. Her attitude wasn't too unusual in the big cities. The scholars who studied the Ano Classics generally followed Kon Fiji's precept that the learned should respect gods and spirits but not rely on them to explain everything. *Ocara ça pihu ügi i adinagacaü phi ki crudiçadi i ané co caça-ga ki radotré lunagaü* ("Keep the gods at arm's length lest you yield your free will"), as the One True Sage put it in his *Meditations*. Or, as Poti Maji glossed in a less diplomatic manner later, "Studying Moralism will yield a thousand times the benefit of burning incense and chanting mystical nonsense."

Mati, not being a scholar herself, had come to reject superstition by another path. Her family, poor tenant farmers in Cocru, had lost everything due to drought, heavy taxes, and constant warfare. Repeated prayers to the gods had yielded no discernible benefit, and Mati had come to the conclusion that the gods were no more likely to help an ordinary person than to actively seek their destruction. It was simply too arrogant to presume that the gods would bother with cursing or blessing mere commoners. If the gods cared about people at all, they only cared about the grand lords and ladies.

Upon reflection, Mati realized that many of the waitstaff had come from poor but pious families particularly susceptible to superstition. They had neither the scholars' privilege of wealth and status nor her experience of losing everything despite prayers. To them, the idea that prayers to the gods could offer some influence over the vicissitudes of daily life was a source of comfort.

"I'll go to the Great Temple of Lutho right away," said Mati. "Maybe an exorcism will restore the faith of the staff and get them to focus on preparing for the competition."

"No!" said Widow Wasu, shaking her head vigorously. "That is the one thing we *must* not do."

"But why?" asked Lodan and Mati together.

Widow Wasu didn't get to answer their question because Pénozy rushed into the room at that moment. "The monks are here!"

Kinri and Dandelion stood on the side of the street in front of the restaurant, slack-jawed at the spectacle.

Eight nuns dressed in somber black robes were dancing and chanting in front of the Splendid Urn, holding ritual implements that invoked the power of Lutho. Behind them, a team of novitiates played wooden instruments, which were dedicated to Lutho: clappers, rhythm sticks, xylophones, singing casks filled with different amounts of water. And behind them, a still larger team of lay assistants held aloft incense braziers on bamboo poles, saturating the street with fragrant, thick smoke.

The crowd murmured.

"That's an impressive exorcism team!"

"How much do you think Widow Wasu paid to get *eight* nuns to come?"

"Do you see how many turtle-patches are on that one's robes? She must be very senior in the temple."

"Why did the temple send nuns instead of monks?"

"Have you forgotten that the owner of the Urn is a widow? It would be improper for monks to enter her private quarters, should that become necessary."

The nuns chanted louder, their voices eerie and strident, careening all over the musical scale. Several in the large crowd that had gathered to watch the exorcism shivered and held their hands together as they prayed.

*Go éphy othé kri-é-ga-mu-a*
*Patemé po gé tha pa-pi-za-ü!*

*Go éphy othé kri-é-ga-mu-a*
*Patemé po gé tha pa-pi-za-ü!*

"Do you have any idea what they're chanting?" whispered Kinri. "Something something wild seas? Something praise something begone?"

Dandelion shrugged. "No idea. I'm not even sure it's really Classical Ano. But I'm no expert on temple rituals."

Through the smoke, the nuns danced toward the parasol tree—which now resembled less a parasol than a fork, as most of the branches had been pruned away.

Four of the nuns carried a large machine in the shape of a turtle by its four feet. The machine appeared to be fashioned out of some dark-colored wood, and the features of the turtle were carefully carved to be lifelike but also to display an august wisdom. As the nuns carried the turtle through the smoky fog, dancing three steps forward before pulling back two, it seemed to be swimming through a turbulent sea.

"An aunt of mine would have enjoy watching this," whispered Dandelion. "She was a smokecrafter and knew all about how to stage good shows with vapor and fumes."

Kinri was about to ask for more, but the team of nuns had reached the parasol tree. While the four nuns holding up the turtle swayed and rocked in place, one of the other nuns ducked under the turtle, inserted the snake-shaped staff in her hand into a hole in the plastron, and began to crank it rapidly.

The eyes of the turtle glowed with a strange blue light. The crowd grew more excited.

"Is that really magic?" whispered Kinri.

"Maybe," said Dandelion. "But . . . let's just watch."

The three other nuns danced near the head of the turtle, waving their ritual implements, which resembled long-handled whips or short flails. Then, as they sped up their chant, they attached the "whips" to the turtle's head—the tips of the thin, soft thongs went into the turtle's mouth, while the nuns held on to the handles.

Then, waving the long handles like wands, the nuns quickened their chants, now sounding like war cries. As they twirled the wands about, they peered through the thick smoke in every direction, searching for evil spirits.

With a loud cry, one of the nuns leapt at the parasol tree. She reached into the lapel of her robe with her left hand and sprinkled something on the trunk of the parasol tree, then she touched the wand, still connected to the giant turtle, to the same spot.

A blinding explosion lit up that part of the trunk. Through the thick incense smoke, it looked like the eruption of a tiny volcano. The crowd gasped, and some of the young children began to cry as their mothers tried to reassure them.

"Oh baby, don't be scared. Their Holinesses will get all the evil spirits!"

"They're channeling Lord Lutho's powers!"

The wooden orchestra played louder; the incense-carriers hoisted even more braziers; the turtle-carrying nuns danced about the parasol tree, and more explosive eruptions lit up the haze.

Dandelion frowned.

"You look skeptical," said Kinri.

"I'm trying to figure out how they're doing it," said Dandelion. "Zo—err, a friend always said that the universe is knowable."

"Even the mysteries of the gods?" asked Kinri.

"*Especially* the mysteries of the gods," said Dandelion stubbornly.

"I can tell you how they did it," came a low voice behind them.

They turned and saw that it was Rati Yera, wheeling herself along, Mota Kiphi close behind her.

"It's very simple," said the old woman, rather pleased with herself. "That turtle is a silkmotic generator. I bet if you opened it up you'd find a spinning glass disk and a silk-encased rubber. The glowing eyes are probably mercury-vapor lamps. As for the explosions, I imagine they're sprinkling firework powder on the remaining caterpillars. And then, when they touch the wands, charged with silkmotic force, to the caterpillars, the sparks set off an explosion."

"How do you know that?" challenged Dandelion.

"Well, these nuns and I are basically in the same profession," said

Rati. "Temple magic is no different from street magic. That's how I would do it."

"You can't compare street entertainment with religious ritual!" said a shocked Kinri.

Rati shrugged. "Suit yourself. I'm just telling you what I know."

"But then . . . you're saying this is all fake."

"No," said Rati, shaking her head. "Remember what Dandelion said about mind-pleasure? There *is* a deeper meaning to ritual that goes beyond the incense and the wooden turtle and the spectacle. That part is what matters."

Kinri wanted to ask for elaboration, but he was interrupted by Widow Wasu, who had emerged from the restaurant with Lodan and Mati in tow.

Widow Wasu went directly to the orchestra and gestured for them to stop playing. The ethereal music ground to a halt, and the nuns stopped dancing.

"Your Holiness," said Widow Wasu to an old nun standing behind the orchestra, who appeared to be in charge. In fact, she had also been one of the judges at the cooking round of the competition a few weeks earlier. "I'm grateful for your presence. But . . . who asked you to come? We didn't ask for an exorcism."

"I was wondering about that," whispered Dandelion to Kinri.

"How did you know the Grand Mistress didn't ask for the exorcism?" whispered Kinri.

"Because she's too smart to make a mistake like that," said Dandelion.

"How do you mean?"

"The moment she goes to the temple, she as good as admits that the curse is real."

Before the old nun could answer Widow Wasu, a rotund and oleaginous man stepped out from behind her, a smile on his face that didn't reach his eyes.

"I did," said Tiphan Huto.

*- The old turtle's disciples certainly are quick to adopt new machines. Did they, perhaps, feel the absence of their god?*

*- The rest of us have been trying to answer their queries, but Lutho had his own way of speaking truths. It's not easy to imitate.*

*- As long as they put on a good show.*

Widow Wasu stared at Tiphan Huto.

"O Grand Mistress Wasu," said Tiphan, bowing slightly, hands held together in front. "As a fellow restaurateur, I'm great troubled by reports of evil spirits plaguing one of my distinguished colleagues. Greatly!"

"Your concern is noted," said Widow Wasu, her tone as cold as the bowls of Rapa's Feast served a few weeks ago.

"Even though we're in the middle of a competition, I couldn't imagine winning as a result of you forfeiting because your place is cursed. I was down at the temple to pray for good fortune, and my staff convinced me that I had to help you."

"Your staff?"

"Here she comes," said Tiphan, pointing at an ox-drawn cart clattering down the street.

The cart approached the Splendid Urn, stopped, and Mozo Mu jumped out. "Granny Wasu! Is everything all right? I heard that strange things have been happening at the Urn, and when I was down at the Grand Temple to pray to Lord Lutho for guidance, they said no one from your place has come yet." She lowered her voice as she leaned in to Widow Wasu's ear. "I overheard two of Tiphan's men say that customers were staying away from the Urn because . . . because of what happened last time. They were speculating maybe that was why you couldn't afford to pay for an exorcism."

Widow Wasu looked into the earnest face of the young woman. "You overheard, did you? Were those two men following you around at the temple?"

"Now that you mention it . . . they were," said a surprised Mozo. "So . . . I begged Tiphan to pay for an exorcism out of a sense of fair play."

"And I'm guessing he didn't protest too much."

"He did at first."

"Oh?"

"So I pointed at the statue of Lord Lutho and said that the gods wouldn't think it right for us to win under these circumstances because it would be against the rules."

"How is that against the rules?"

"The rules say that only those already on the staffs of the restaurants could participate in the competition. So if we won because of the help of evil spirits, then either the evil spirits are in his employment—and surely he wouldn't want to be known to consort with such characters—or he must be cheating by using them as late-addition contractors. In either case, the only way to redeem his good name is by helping you get rid of them."

Widow Wasu chuckled. "That's clever."

"So he agreed to pay for the exorcism. Maybe he's not as bad as I thought."

Widow Wasu sighed. "Child, you grew up away from the world of schemes and plots, and though you may know all about how to dress a chicken or clean a fish, you know little of the darkness inside people's hearts . . . never mind."

Mozo Mu tried to conceal her disappointment that her effort at helping Widow Wasu didn't seem to be as welcome as she had hoped. "I made some snacks for the nuns and your staff. It's not much, but my father"—she paused and took a deep breath, swallowing the lump in her throat—"my father always said he felt better after eating one of these if he was anxious."

She took out a large platter of steamed buns from the cart. They were beautifully sculpted, and it was clear that she had spent a lot of time on them.

Widow Wasu's face softened. "Thank you, child."

Mozo leaned in again. "The ones with a red dot on them have homunculus mushroom filling. They're beneficial for the elderly." She smiled mischievously at Widow Wasu. "Since Tiphan gave me access to such expensive ingredients, I thought I might as well do some good with them."

Widow Wasu smiled and patted Mozo's hand. She turned to Mati and Lodan. "Have the kitchen prepare lunch for everyone."

Teson Wasu, who had joined his mother during this conversation, pulled Widow Wasu aside. "Shouldn't we get rid of them as soon as possible? Such a public exorcism will only confirm and fan the rumors that the Urn is cursed."

"I know that!" whispered Widow Wasu. "But do you want to make a scene and chase the nuns away? That's not going to help things. They're just being used by Tiphan, and we can't shirk our obligation as hosts."

Teson wanted to argue, but Widow Wasu had already turned away.

"We'll hold a street banquet to thank Their Holinesses and . . . Master Huto for his generosity."

"Oh, don't mention it," said Tiphan Huto, still grinning in that mirthless manner he had. "I've brought along some dipping sauce too. Let's have lunch together to celebrate the end of the curse on the Splendid Urn and prove to everyone that even in competition, we can still be good friends."

Widow Wasu's face twitched, but she said nothing.

The "celebratory" feast didn't last very long. Although the food, combining the efforts of both the Splendid Urn and the Treasure Chest, was uniformly deemed excellent, the chill between Widow Wasu and Tiphan Huto cast a pall over the whole affair. Tiphan left after just a few drinks, saying that he had other business to attend to, and Mozo had to go with him.

While the nuns ate, Rati Yera and Mota Kiphi approached to ask if they might be allowed to examine the magical turtle. The senior nuns summarily denied this request; so Mota and Rati resorted to wandering around the turtle in a wide circle, looking at it and whispering to each other as the novitiates and lay assistants glared at them, keeping them at a distance. Kinri, always curious about machines, went to help Mota push Rati's wheeled chair. Though she got around just fine on her own, thanks to the clever gear trains and long-handled levers, the old street magician appreciated a helping hand from her friends when she requested it. Kinri listened intently as Rati and Mota speculated on the turtle's operation.

"The silkmotic force is a most wondrous phenomenon," said Rati. "It's too bad that the temples like to hoard their knowledge."

"It's also a dangerous force," said Mota. "I've seen what it can do when deployed as a weapon."

"Anything useful is like that," said Rati. After a pause, she added, "Can you imagine the experiments in the Imperial laboratory at Last Bite?"

Mota made no response, which only piqued Kinri's interest. But as Rati and Mota continued their discussion of the turtle, they said no more about the mysterious Imperial laboratory.

By the time Kinri got back to the feast, all the steamed buns were gone. He had to content himself with trying out the dipping sauces with leaves of lettuce. They were still tasty, though.

Widi and Arona, on the other hand, said they weren't hungry from the start of the feast.

"We'll go investigate the sites of the misfortunes that have befallen the Splendid Urn over the last few days," Widi said to Widow Wasu.

"Wait, take me with you!" said Dandelion. "I've never investigated a mystery before. That sounds fun!"

"Eat a few buns before you go," said Widow Wasu. "Mozo made them."

Dandelion grabbed a steamed bun and ran after Widi and Arona.

"Wait!" called Widow Wasu. "They're better with the dipping sauces!"

"Too messy!" said Dandelion, stuffing the bun into her mouth as she ran. "Mmm!"

Widow Wasu shook her head, smiling affectionately.

The three went to the intersection where the vegetable carts had broken down, the trails left by the feral dogs, and the now-bare trunk of the parasol tree, looking for clues that the events were the result of sabotage.

"Do you do this sort of thing a lot?" asked Dandelion.

"What, investigating mysteries?" said Widi. He gathered some dead caterpillars from the parasol tree, wrapped them in a piece of cloth, and put the packet away. "Well, as a paid litigator, I do get called on sometimes to solve suspicious cases. The magistrates, even when they mean well, just want cases resolved quickly. They make mistakes."

"He's being modest," said Arona. "I'll tell you about the time he found a bunch of children kidnapped by a bandit named Laughing Skeleton. . . ."

Back at the Urn, having zapped the remaining caterpillars on the tree with their magical turtle, the nuns, refreshed by the snacks and drinks, carried the turtle into the restaurant itself and danced through all three floors. They left only as dinner service was about to start.

"Well, that was probably the most expensive extermination effort in the history of Ginpen," muttered Widow Wasu.

"At least we didn't have to pay for it," said Mati.

"And the staff will be assured that the curse has been lifted," said Lodan. "Mozo is a kindhearted girl, and she's done us a good deed."

Widow Wasu shook her head, looking not nearly as reassured. "Keep an eye out for more trouble. I have a bad feeling about this."

About an hour into dinner service, the first problems started.

Pénozy was climbing the stairs to bring a bowl of dumpling soup to a customer on the second floor when she suddenly felt a sharp pain in her stomach. She faltered, and the soup spilled onto her hands.

"What's wrong?" asked Lodan, standing at the top of the staircase.

"I'm not sure," said Pénozy. Sweat beaded on her forehead. "I . . . I have to go to the toilet."

Lodan took over as the young girl ran off to the bathroom in the back.

When she came out, she felt weak and swayed unsteadily on her feet. A wave of nausea bowed her over. As she threw up, several more waiters and waitresses emerged from the restaurant, running toward the bathroom.

The situation in the kitchen wasn't much better. Several line cooks experienced stomach cramps and excused themselves, but once they sat down on the toilet, they couldn't even get up.

As orders backed up in the kitchen and customers waited impatiently for the waitstaff to return, Lodan met Mati in the kitchen.

"We have to shut the kitchen down," said Lodan, panting and sweating. "I've lost most of my servers, and I'm not feeling so great myself."

"I don't know what's wrong," said Mati, holding a hot-water pouch to her stomach. "I've never felt like this before. We're lucky that none of the customers seem to be affected yet."

Widow Wasu agreed with the decision to end dinner service. To have the restaurant's service disrupted for three days in a row was a terrible blow financially, but there really was no choice.

But by then even Widow Wasu was feeling ill. Lodan and Mati struggled to apologize to the customers and handed out vouchers for future meals. Some of the customers saw the long line of cooks and waitstaff outside the bathroom in the back, and their faces blanched. Soon, rumors began to spread that something was wrong with the food.

As the last customers were leaving, sudden, loud screams came from in front of the restaurant.

Lodan and Mati rushed out, and they were greeted by the sight of hundreds of rats screeching and running through the street, all in a panic. It was as though the neighborhood had been set on fire, or the buildings around them were ships sinking into the sea. The rats dashed about aimlessly, shrieking and clawing at everything. Many of the customers huddled together, terrified by the sight.

Lodan and Mati wanted to help, but they felt so weak that they could barely remain standing. In the end, it fell to Rati, Mota, Arona, and Widi, who seemed unaffected by the strange plague that had afflicted the restaurant staff, to disperse the rodents with their flamethrower, and Dandelion and Kinri, also healthy, hailed hired carriages to bring the terrified customers home.

By morning, whispers of the very real curse afflicting the Splendid Urn could be heard everywhere in Ginpen.

～

TWO DAYS LATER.

Lodan handed Pénozy her wages. "It's a long way home," she said. "Remember to pack something for the road." She pointed to a table of pancakes and knot fritters.

Like the other cooks, maids, kitchen boys, waiters, and waitresses who had left the Splendid Urn during the last couple of days, the young girl thanked Lodan but didn't take any food.

"I'm sorry," she said, not meeting Lodan's gaze. She walked to the door, stopped, turned around. "I'm really sorry. But my mother sent word saying that my father is ill, I—"

"It's all right," said Lodan. "I understand."

The girl bit her bottom lip, ashamed, and left. She climbed onto an oxcart and, a moment later, was gone.

Lodan sighed and returned to Widow Wasu's sitting room.

"How many are left?" asked the widow.

"I have two waitresses willing to stay," said Lodan.

"Brave of them," said the widow.

"They say that they're without parents or children, and the Urn is their home. They don't care if the curse gets them."

The widow sighed and nodded. She turned to Mati. "What about you?"

"I've got one cook, one busboy, and a scullery maid," said Mati.

"That would be Munapo, Kinri, and Ruthé, right?"

Mati nodded.

"All of them orphans too," said the widow. "I guess everyone with a choice has decided to leave."

"Cowards," said Teson angrily. "After all you've done for these people, Mother, for them to abandon you—"

"Don't blame them," said the widow. "They're scared. If senior nuns from the Grand Temple can't even chase the evil spirits away, why would they stay?"

"But we know this is because Tiphan did something with the food he brought," said Teson heatedly. "We should go to the magistrate—"

"We have no proof," said the widow. "The people he brought also fell sick that evening, including Tiphan himself. How are we going to prove our accusations to the magistrate?"

Teson had no answer.

Mati and Lodan couldn't contribute to this debate, as they had little understanding of courts and litigators. But they were both certain that everyone had gotten sick because of the food Tiphan and Mozo brought. It was both painful and maddening to think that the young girl could plot against them after the Urn had forfeited the first match to save her family.

"We haven't been able to hire anyone new, either," said Teson. "Everyone we've spoken to is too afraid to come work at the Urn after everything that's happened."

Widow Wasu shook her head. "That wouldn't have worked anyway. The rules are that we can only use people already on staff on the day each new round of the competition is announced. We can't just hire a new crew."

"As if following the rules is something Tiphan Huto cares about," scoffed Teson.

"We don't have enough people to put on a dinner service at all," said the widow, her brows knitted with worry. "What about the Treasure Chest's people?"

"Those who came to the Urn with Tiphan fell sick that night, but they were better by morning, just like us. A few decided to quit, saying that they didn't want to have anything to do with the Urn, whether working for or against us. But Tiphan hired the monks at the temple to do a cleansing ritual for them."

"If the cleansing didn't work on us, why would it work for them?" asked Lodan.

"Apparently Tiphan received an oracle at the temple: 'Treasure pleasure; burn urn.' Most of the staff then agreed to stay," said Teson.

"I wonder how much of a donation Tiphan promised the monks before that oracle," said the widow with a sigh. She closed her eyes. At length, she said, "We'll have to concede."

"No!" shouted Lodan. "I'll serve all the customers myself if I have to."

"How are you going to serve two hundred customers all by your-self? Have you developed the art of dividing yourself into twenty people?"

Lodan had no response to that. Mati hugged her sympathetically.

"Let's spend the rest of the time settling our accounts and paying off our bills," said the widow.

Teson looked alarmed. "Mother . . . you're not thinking—"

"We can't run a restaurant if no one wants to work for us," said the widow.

Teson lowered his head. "I'm sorry. I should have insisted that they leave when they came to us in such suspicious circumstances. . . ."

Widow Wasu shook her head. "Of course it's not your fault. I was the one who invited them to stay. . . . Maybe it's a sign. We've had a good run in Ginpen, but nothing lasts forever."

Teson looked devastated. "We've always done the right thing and treated our customers with respect. Why?"

"I know you've put a lot of sweat and tears into building up the Urn here in Ginpen," said Widow Wasu, laying a hand gently over her son's shoulder. "The race goes not always to the swift. Why don't you go home to Zudi and look for another opportunity to invest the funds once we've sold this place? I'll stay to handle the concession and wrap up affairs here."

Lodan and Mati were too shocked to speak as they clung to each other.

Kinri and Dandelion came to see the Blossom Gang.

"Have you figured out how they did it?" asked Kinri.

Widi shook his head. "I've met with Mozo in secret, and she's devastated. She swore that she prepared all the buns herself, and she even tasted everything ahead of time. If someone had tampered with the food in the kitchen, she would have fallen sick before anyone else."

"And as it happened, one of the cooks saved a few buns from the feast for her children," said Arona. "After everyone got sick, no one touched them. We fed the leftover buns to feral dogs and rats we caught. They were fine after eating them."

"But we *know* something was wrong with the food," said Kinri. He pounded the nearest wall, frustrated.

"I agree with your theory," said Widi. "None of us ate the food, and none of us fell sick that night. But we can't figure out how Tiphan did it."

"Wait," said Dandelion. "That's not true. I ate food from the feast, and I didn't get sick."

"Me too," said Kinri. "I just figured I didn't eat whatever was spoiled."

"You did?" asked Widi, perking up. "Tell me exactly what you ate and how."

After much questioning, Widi determined that while Dandelion had been in such a hurry that she had eaten only a bun without any dipping sauce, Kinri had gotten to the feast so late that he didn't eat any of the buns, only some sauce with lettuce.

"That must be it!" said Dandelion. "Tiphan did something with *both* the sauces and the buns. But it's only if the two are put together that you get sick. That explains why Mozo didn't get sick earlier, when she tasted the buns in the kitchen."

"That does seem possible," mused Widi. "But how do you know this?"

"My . . . aunt is a skilled herbalist," said Dandelion. "I remember her explaining this technique for assassination by poison. The Tiro kings employed teams of food tasters, but if you divided the poison into two portions, each of which was harmless by itself, you could apply one portion to the appetizer and another to the dessert. For a long feast, two different tasters would be used, which would allow the poison to remain undetected until it was too late."

Widi nodded. "That must be the trick Tiphan used. Except he didn't want to murder us, only to add to the impression of a curse."

"What about the other strange events?" asked Dandelion. "Have you made any progress on the caterpillars, the feral dogs, and the rats?"

Widi shook his head. "The feral dogs could have been collected from anywhere around the city. The caterpillars weren't from around here, but no one has been able to tell me their origins. The rats were definitely from the neighborhood, since all the cellars around here now are rat-free, but I don't know what they were so terrified of on that night—though I detected some suspicious smells. . . . I know that's not much, but there are still a few leads I want to check."

Kinri sat down, dejected. "It doesn't matter anyway. All the cooks and waitstaff have left. It really is over, like the Grand Mistress said."

"You just need servers, right?" said Dandelion. "I can pitch in."

Rati shook her head. "Even with all of us helping, we don't have enough people to handle a full restaurant—assuming the customers and judges even dare to show up after all these rumors of curses and spoiled food. Besides, what do we know about efficient service? There's an art to every profession."

Kinri closed his eyes.

*We don't have enough servers and can't hire new ones or train them in time. If only there were some way to allow the people we do have to work as though they were many more . . . Lodan mentioned something about wishing she could divide herself into twenty people. . . .*

*- If only Lutho were around—*

*—he'd be able to come up with something!*

*- Sisters, I thought you weren't that interested in this minor spat among a few cooks and waitresses!*

*- The thing about the mortals is that—*

*—there's always drama, even in the most unlikely of places.*

*- Just like a hurricane starts out as the eddies around the tips of a butterfly's wings, small scuffles far from the centers of power may have big consequences.*

The next day, Dandelion returned to the Splendid Urn in the evening to find Kinri sitting by the door, staring into space.

"What are you doing here?" she asked.

Kinri jumped up, shaken out of his reverie. "I've been thinking about . . . how to turn Lodan into twenty people."

Dandelion laughed. "That would be a neat trick. If you could figure that out, you'd be as great an inventor as Na Moji."

Kinri blushed. "I know it's unrealistic. But . . . Anyway, where did you go?"

Dandelion was dressed again like a kitchen maid, though this time her disguise was far more convincing. The lessons with Arona were paying off.

"Mota and Arona took me to the refugee camp to help unload the food Granny Wasu donated," said Dandelion.

With such a reduced staff, the Urn couldn't run its regular lunch or dinner service. Rather than having the food in the storehouse spoil, Widow Wasu had asked Magistrate Zuda whether she could donate it to the refugee camp outside the city. Mota and Arona volunteered to drive the goods, and asked Kinri to come along, but Kinri had turned them down, afraid that one of the refugees from Rui might recognize him and reveal his true identity.

Dandelion had apparently taken up the offer in his stead.

"Are . . . the refugees doing well?" he asked cautiously.

"They seem well," said Dandelion. "After we unloaded the supplies, I got to spend some time with the children, telling them stories and teaching them songs I learned as a little girl. The parents are hopeful that their interrogations will soon end so that they'll be allowed to leave and make their way in Dara."

She kept her tone upbeat and light, and Kinri knew she was doing so for his benefit. He was also supposed to be a refugee from Ukyu-taasa, after all. But he could tell there was a trace of melancholy in her expression.

"What's wrong?" he asked. "Something is troubling you."

She tried to deny it, but gave up the effort with a sigh. "I chatted a little bit with the parents, and they told me what had happened to them back home. It was horrible. I can't imagine real people, not villains from the old sagas, being so cruel. I'm going to have nightmares, I'm sure."

Kinri said nothing. He did have nightmares still from what he had seen in Kigo Yezu.

"I don't understand why the Lyucu are like that. Do they really want to kill everyone who's not Lyucu?" She shuddered in disbelief and terror. "My brother . . . he always said he wants to fight the Lyucu, and I think I understand how he feels now, at least a little bit."

Kinri tried to keep his face expressionless. Her words reverberated in his head like thunderclaps. *How will she react when she finds out who I am?*

"Maybe they're not all like that," he said weakly. "I . . . I knew some Lyucu culeks and naros, and even thanes, who . . . didn't want to kill everyone. . . ."

His voice drifted off because he didn't know how to defend his people. If the refugees were all telling tales of atrocities, then he had to contemplate the possibility that Cutanrovo wasn't the only monster. He didn't know how to square what he had seen in Kigo Yezu with the re-remembered tales of Tenryo's compassion and courage; he didn't know how to accept that what he had seen was true, that what the refugees had told Dandelion was true, that what Master Nazu Tei had hinted at was true, without questioning Emperor Thaké's dream of the Lyucu living together in harmony with the natives, without distrusting his mother's insistence that he learn as much as possible about the culture of Dara, without doubting the very ideal of the Lyucu conquest being an effort at freeing the natives from the bondage of their tyrants.

It was growing ever more difficult to believe what he had been taught by the court-appointed tutors back in Kriphi. The contrast between Ukyu-taasa and Dara proper was simply too great. The compassion, love, joy, silliness, exuberance, and even pettiness he had experienced among the people of Dara under the regency of Empress Jia—Lodan and Mati, Grand Mistress Wasu, the Blossom Gang, Dandelion, even Tiphan Huto—all pointed him to one undeniable truth: This was not a society in bondage, not a people under the yoke of a tyrant.

He loved Ukyu-taasa, his homeland, but Dara was *free*.

*Is this what Master Nazu Tei meant by learning from experience?*

He forced the thought away. That couldn't be the truth. *Couldn't.* He had to be wrong; he had to be missing *something*.

He had to hold on to the possibility that Cutanrovo and the others who agreed with her were aberrations, that they did not represent the true Lyucu spirit. *Had to.*

Dandelion looked at him strangely. "Maybe you're right," she said. "After all, I didn't live in Unredeemed Dara. I don't know what it's really like there." After a pause, she added, "I also feel terrible because of what Mota and Arona said on the way back. They told me that even after they leave the camp, the refugees have a hard time. A lot of people don't trust them, thinking that they are cowards for submitting to the Lyucu or that they've become tainted, no longer true members of the people of Dara. They have trouble finding steady work or practicing their trades. Some of them end up going to Crescent Island, trying to scrape out new farmland in the wilderness; others end up joining criminal gangs or pirates—which makes people even more mistrustful of the refugees; still others try to find shelter at temples and shrines deep in the mountains, where monks and nuns are more compassionate. Even though they're free to move around Dara, they never feel at home."

Kinri nodded, unable to offer any words of comfort because his heart was a tangled mess.

"Arona and Mota said Granny Wasu and Uncle Teson are very special because they took you in without any questions," said Dandelion.

"I'm lucky," said Kinri. "I can't imagine what would have happened if I hadn't been rescued by them."

"If only there were a way to turn them each into twenty people!" said Dandelion. She smiled in a way that made Kinri's heart ache. But the light soon dimmed in her face. "Only . . . it looks like the Urn won't survive much longer."

Kinri seized on Dandelion's last thought. He was powerless in the grand clash between the Lyucu and the natives, but focusing on the specific problem of how to survive the next round in the competition made him feel not so helpless.

"You've read a lot more books than I have," he said. "Do you remember any stories about . . . contraptions that could behave like people?" It was a wild, desperate idea, but he had nothing better.

Dandelion looked thoughtful. "My education is a bit of a mess, since I didn't like my first tutor that much—never mind, that's a long story. The point is I *have* read a lot of books of romance and adventure with fantastical machines. . . . Let me see . . . Oh, I remember an account of Na Moji building the King of Xana a team of mechanical men who could play the *moaphya* with great skill."

Na Moji was the founder of the Patternist school, and possibly the greatest engineer in Dara's history. Kinri's heart sped up. "Do you remember if the book explained how the mechanical men worked?"

Dandelion shook her head. "Na Moji didn't write down detailed instructions for many of the wonders he built, and even when he did, most of the instructions were lost. The account I read was from a noble at the court who witnessed one of the performances. But the writer provided only a general description of the mechanical orchestra, with few details. He was mainly concerned with the king's reactions, who was present on that day, and what they discussed during the concert. To him, war and politics were far more important, while Na Moji's invention was just a piece of entertainment."

"That's a pity."

Still, Dandelion said that the noble had recorded that the team of wooden musicians were mounted on a platform in front of the *moaphya*, with a separate wooden man standing before each hanging bronze slab. A team of assistants had to crank a mechanism concealed under the platform. As the assistants turned the crank, the wooden men came to life in a coordinated dance, each striking its mallet against his bronze slab when the song called for that particular note.

"Did the musicians play a single song or did they play different songs?"

Dandelion struggled to remember. "I think the orchestra played the same song several times. When the king was tired of it, Na Moji had to call for a short intermission to adjust the mechanism. After waiting long enough to boil a new pot of tea, the musicians played a different song."

"Adjustments? Did Na Moji have to take the musicians or the platform apart?"

Dandelion shook her head. "That wasn't in the account. But I imagine not. If they had to take everything apart, it wouldn't have been nearly as interesting to the king. The orchestra seems like a magic act, and a magician never reveals his secrets."

To Kinri, this suggested that the mechanical orchestra could be "taught" to play a new song within a short period of time. But exactly how this was done eluded him.

"Did Emperor Ragin ever have anything like that at his court?" asked Kinri.

Dandelion shook her head. "No." Then, as though realizing something, she added quickly, "Not that someone like me would ever know." A grin appeared on her face. "Now that you mention it, I suppose Emperor Ragin would have enjoyed an orchestra like that."

Arona Taré, who happened to be passing through the ground floor of the restaurant at that moment, stopped at this exchange. Quietly, she ducked down and crept closer to the front door. Staying out of sight behind some tables, she listened intently.

"Why?" asked Kinri. "Was Ragin very musical?"

Dandelion nodded. "Emperor Ragin played the coconut lute and sang, and though he wasn't the most skilled performer, he was never self-conscious about entertaining his friends and family, and that made it fun for those who listened to him." She chuckled. "I'm sure he would have liked to see mechanical musicians and perhaps even challenged them to a music competition."

"I had no idea the bandit-emperor could be so . . . amiable," said Kinri. It was odd to learn about this aspect of the butcher of Naza Pass. Somehow, the tyrant no longer seemed to him just an embodiment of villainy, but more like a real person.

"Emperor Ragin was known to have a silly side," said Dandelion. "In fact, even his Imperial name was a bit of a joke."

"How so?" Kinri had always understood Ragin's Imperial name to be a Classical Ano allusion that disguised his base origins and unsavory past.

"Well, most scholars say that 'Ragin' is an allusion from a passage in Kon Fiji's *Treatise on Moral Relations*, in which a robber debates the One True Sage, but that's just the Moralists trying to comfort themselves. My . . . uh, Ragin wasn't interested in making the Moralists happy. It's true that most Imperial names are supposed to be very serious. For example, Mapidéré's name means literally 'the first to try.'"

Kinri nodded. Master Nazu Tei had explained this to him.

"'*Ragin*,' on the other hand, is an onomatopoeia that literally means 'banging' or 'ringing' in Classical Ano, and the emperor definitely intended no connection to Kon Fiji trying to 'ring the bell of moral clarity in the face of a stonehearted robber,' as the Moralists claim. In reality, when the emperor was young and a bit of a lazy layabout, his sister-in-law used to bang an empty pot when he came home to show that there was no more rice for him to eat. The emperor decided to reference that episode of his life to show that he never forgot the music of his humble origins."

Kinri was amazed. "Are the other Imperial names also jokes?"

"No, no one can get away with a joke the way Ragin could," said Dandelion. "But his children did continue with a musical theme in their Imperial names, as was proper for children honoring their parent. Though the names are all proper Classical Ano allusions, they also have a second meaning that is more private. Empress Üna, also known as Grand Princess Théra, picked her Imperial name to reference the humming of the zither, for she believed the sympathetic vibration of heartstrings was an ideal in romance as well as in the relation between sovereign and subject."

A blush came into her face as she looked at Kinri. She composed herself and continued.

"And the current emperor, Monadétu, picked his Imperial name to allude to the thumping of martial drums calling an army to battle."

"What about Thaké?" asked Kinri.

Dandelion gave Kinri a strange look. Timu's Imperial name was almost never mentioned in Dara proper, as he was not seen as a legitimate emperor by most. "I . . . I can't be sure. But I suspect by naming himself after the pitter-patter of gentle rain, he was giving a nod to his formal name as 'Gentle Ruler' and showing both obedience to his father—for he also picked an onomatopoetic name—and some measure of defiance—for the sound is the very opposite of the loud banging of an empty pot."

"I never knew there was so much embedded in the names," said Kinri admiringly. "You must have had a very erudite master."

It was Dandelion's turn to be flustered. "Oh . . . this is common knowledge . . . here. You just didn't know because you grew up in Rui."

Impulsively, Kinri said, "I lacked music in my education . . . but I've always wanted to learn. Would you teach me to play the zither?" The zither was the most common instrument in Dara, and practically all scholars were expected to know how to play it. In Kinri's case, however, his real motivation wasn't the throbbing strings.

Dandelion regarded him, and a smile curved up the corners of her mouth as a light blush colored her cheeks. "Of course, Thaséteki. I'd be delighted to."

Behind her, a thoughtful look appeared on Arona's face.

For the rest of the evening, Kinri couldn't get the image of the mechanical orchestra out of his mind. Men made of wood being taught to play music felt like the key to some puzzle, but he just couldn't seem to fit the key anywhere.

His mind was a jumble. The happy days he spent in the company of Dandelion and the Blossom Gang turned into visions of the deserted Splendid Urn, its doors shut forever and its staff dismissed. The mechanical men swinging their mallets against the bronze slabs turned into images of Cutanrovo slamming her war club down on the skull of the despairing mother whose baby had just been tortured and drowned. The logograms from Master Nazu Tei's lessons turned into slippery fish that he tried to lift onto a scale, only to have them flop out of his hands at the last minute. Memories of natives and Lyucu thronging the streets of Kriphi turned into scenes of bloody battles, with him yelling, crying, pleading for everyone to stop.

Of all that he had been taught as a child about the Lyucu and Dara, what portions were true? Of all that he had learned from Master Nazu Tei, what portions were true? Of all that he had seen and heard in Dara, what portions were true?

*Besides, I cannot teach you the truth. Experience is the only teacher that will convince you.*

He saw Dandelion's face, filled with anguish at the suffering described by the refugees. He saw her turning toward him, her features twisted by rage and hatred. *My brother . . . he always said he wants to fight the Lyucu, and I think I understand how he feels now.*

He cradled his head in his hands, stifling a scream. *But how can I experience the truth when I must live a lie?*

He saw the face of his mother, trying to comfort him in the cold winter wind above a swaying pirate ship's deck. *I told her I was sorry that you couldn't serve her well in Ukyu-taasa. But that doesn't mean you can't serve her, or serve all of us, outside of it.*

He pounded his head with his fists. *How am I supposed to serve my people? I can't even find a way to help my benefactors to save their restaurant. I can't even figure out what to do with myself.*

Teaching, learning, mechanical men, living refugees, truth, lies, the contest between the Splendid Urn and the Treasure Chest, the contest between the Lyucu and Dara. Everything was connected; everything was disconnected.

He felt trapped inside a maze. No matter what direction he turned in, he bumped into a wall.

*Perhaps you'll even have a chance to see the core islands. That's what you've always wanted, isn't it? To see the strange machines you've heard so much about.*

The words seemed a ray of light in the darkness, a strand of hope he clung to. He followed it and saw . . . Rati Yera's maze-running cart, glowing brightly in the jumble of his doubts.

# CHAPTER FORTY-TWO

# THE SECOND CONTEST

GINPEN: THE SIXTH MONTH IN THE NINTH YEAR
OF THE REIGN OF SEASON OF STORMS AND THE
REIGN OF AUDACIOUS FREEDOM (TWENTY-THREE
MONTHS UNTIL THE REOPENING OF THE WALL OF
STORMS).

"The Treasure Chest is going to have their hands full tonight," announced Lolotika Tuné to the giant crowd assembled outside the restaurant.

If anything, this crowd was even bigger than the one that had shown up several weeks ago for the cooking competition. Magistrate Zuda dispatched constables to keep order, and two lines of barricades were set up to hold the crowd of onlookers back from the entrance like dikes holding back a surging sea. The long line of diners waiting to get into the restaurant snaked between the barricades, pleased that they had been able to secure a place for tonight.

"The key will be whether Tiphan Huto can rally his inexperienced staff to rise to the occasion. They may be ahead in the competition, one to nothing, but efficient service is a totally different game from cooking impressive dishes. I don't think they've ever seen a house this full.

"Are you excited?"

Onlookers as well as prospective diners cheered as they looked up at Lolo, standing at the top of a bamboo tower right next to the five-story Treasure Chest. The tower had been constructed just for the occasion and was as tall as the restaurant itself. By climbing up and down the tower, Lolo could look in on each of the restaurant's five floors and comment on the service. A carriage stood at the foot of the tower, ready to whisk her to the kitchen in the back should she wish to observe the kitchen crew and update the audience on their performance.

"I can't hear you," shouted Lolo into the speaking trumpet, and cupped her ear for the response. "*Are you excited?*"

Tonight she was in a water-silk cocoon-dress of bright yellow, the color of old Haan. In the last rays of dusk, hundreds of blazing torches and whale-oil lamps lit up the Treasure Chest like the old palace at the Lantern Festival, and in their combined light, the sheen of her dress changed with mesmerizing fluidity with every step and gesture, as though she were wearing liquid gold.

The crowd erupted into thunderous cheers that rattled the bamboo tower. The constables manning the barricades had to push the crowd back lest they spill into the entryway, but they did so with wide grins on their faces. The festive mood was infectious.

The extravagance and opulence of the Treasure Chest were on full display for the occasion. The bright lamps and torches showed off the shiny interior to good effect, and the sitting cushions, made of golden silk stuffed with soft downy wild-goose feathers, gleamed like miniature thrones. It was said that Tiphan had tried to get some of the newfangled silkmotic torches installed at the Treasure Chest to add to the sense of luxury, but the plan had to be scrapped because the gadgets proved too temperamental. In any case, the whale-oil lamps and torches seemed to be doing the job just fine.

Lolo nodded, satisfied. "Then let the dinner service at the Treasure Chest, the would-be best restaurant in all of Ginpen, begin!"

A trace of worry furrowed her brows. She knew that she had by far the easier job of hosting tonight. In truth, she had asked to be posted at the Treasure Chest because she didn't have the heart to witness the Splendid Urn's certain humiliation.

From atop her bamboo tower, she gazed across the rooftops and twisting streets of Ginpen, across the faint lamps in the crowded tenements and the bright lights in the grand manors, across the still-busy Temple Square and the deserted workshops, wondering what was happening at the other competition site.

∽

A similar tower of bamboo had been constructed next to the Splendid Urn, but the crowd here was much smaller. Rumors of the curse kept most would-be onlookers away, and those who had gathered here were more trepidatious than celebratory. Many were residents of the neighborhood, here to offer their support to the kind Teson Wasu and Widow Wasu. To them, the Splendid Urn was a neighborhood institution.

Earlier, a group of local wastrels had shown up at the Urn with banners of disgusting furry caterpillars, rats with tangled tails, and piles of steaming dog shit. The idle youths and ne'er-do-wells chanted things like "Cheater!" "Bad food!" "Dirty kitchen!" at the waiting diners, clearly an attempt at scaring some away. The local residents here to support the Urn shouted back angrily, and the two sides started shoving each other.

The constables struggled to break up the fight, and the captain of the constables met with Widow Wasu to propose that dinner service be delayed in order to restore order.

"No, no," said Widow Wasu. "Let me try."

Leaning on a cane and never raising her voice, the tiny woman talked to the gang of disruptive youths. Within minutes, she had reduced them to tears.

"My mother *would* be so ashamed of me," one of the youths sniffled.

"My grandmother said the same thing, Granny," said another youth. "I'll do better."

"Please don't tell my teacher I was here, Granny, please!" pleaded a third.

Widow Wasu patted them on the hand in reassurance and asked them if they'd like some soup. The youths cried even harder. They furled their banners and slunk away, concealing their faces behind long sleeves.

"Impressive!" whispered Dandelion when the widow returned, shutting the door of the restaurant behind her.

"That Tiphan never stops. . . . He probably doesn't know I'm used to handling gangs like that," said the widow. "Why, back in Zudi, your father . . . heh . . ."

The waiting diners got back in line, but they looked unsettled. Some in the small group of spectators, Widow Wasu's supporters, tried to tell them about the virtues of the Splendid Urn, though the diners were clearly in no mood to be pitched.

From atop the tower, Séca tried gamely to rally this crowd. "Masters and mistresses, if you're just joining us, welcome to this unprecedented contest for the title of Best Restaurant in Ginpen!"

He was dressed in a dark blue water-silk robe that matched Lolo's dress for opulence, but, given its subdued colors and conservative cut, the costume seemed to underscore the general lack of faith in the Splendid Urn.

Despite the rather scattered applause, Séca continued to shout into the trumpet. "The test diners at both restaurants are recruited from noble households, scholars of renown, merchants with a record of public works and civic service, learned monks and nuns from the temples, other individuals of note, as well as some lucky members of the public selected by lottery."

The lack of an enthusiastic response from the diners, however, showed that they didn't share this assessment of their luck.

In fact, the Splendid Urn didn't even look like it was open for business, much less ready for the battle for its life. The front door was closed; the windows were shuttered; the upper stories were completely dark. Only a few faint flickering lights showed through the paper-covered windows on the ground floor. The building actually seemed deserted.

The crowd whispered among themselves.

"I heard that they didn't have enough people working for them to serve lunch the last couple of days!"

"My cousin told me Teson Wasu isn't even here—he got too scared and ran away, leaving his mother to deal with the embarrassment by herself."

"Don't stand so close to that parasol tree! I think it's still got evil spirits in it."

Séca tried to shout over the restless crowd. "The diners have been divided between the two restaurants by lot, and mixed with the diners will be our esteemed judges, whose identities are secret.

They'll score the service of the two staffs on a combination of speed, accuracy, orderliness, and friendliness. To focus the judging on service alone, the two restaurants will be cooking from the same standard menu of appetizers, entrées, soups, and desserts."

He didn't add that assigning the diners to the two restaurants by lot had been necessary because more than a few, especially those more inclined to superstition, had been afraid to eat at the Splendid Urn. In addition to the constables, Magistrate Zuda had asked a team of monks and nuns to come to the Splendid Urn and stand watch down the street in order to reassure the skittish customers.

*It's unfortunate to see the Splendid Urn come to such a sorry end,* Séca reflected. He had many fond memories of the beef-and-vegetable stew here as a poor student, and then later, of attending logogram riddle parties thrown by senior archons and administrators at the laboratory. But there was little Séca could do about the restaurant's fate now.

He sighed, lifted the trumpet, and shouted, "Let the dinner service begin!"

The latticed doors of the Treasure Chest swung open, and the crowd had to shield their eyes at the brilliant light that spilled out, as though a piece of the sun had been caught inside.

Mirrors, crystals, whale-oil lamps, and candles turned the inside of the Treasure Chest bright as day, and rows and rows of waiters and waitresses, dressed in golden uniforms, stood ready. As they were revealed to the waiting diners, they began to clap rhythmically and chant:

> *Welcome, welcome to the Treasure Chest, we vaunt,*
> *The most perfect and excellent restaurant.*
> *Service here is the best;*
> *Let your limbs and teeth rest.*
> *We'll feed you, even chew for you, if you want.*

Lolo had to suppress her giggles with some effort. She had heard that Tiphan Huto had devised a "fight song" for his staff that he insisted they sing every morning before the restaurant opened. The man, who had studied with a tutor for only two years before claiming that he knew all he needed to know for the family business, was evidently quite proud of his own literary skills and did not want to be edited.

After a moment of stunned silence, diners began to file through the door, where they were greeted by two handsome young men wearing the double scroll-bun of the *toko dawiji*. The young men bowed to the diners, quoted a few lines of Classical Ano poetry relating to good health and good wealth to each customer as they consulted a chart, and then assigned parties to waiters and waitresses, who brought them to their tables.

Lolo climbed down the observation tower and beckoned for Gina Cophy, serving as Lolo's co-hostess and assistant tonight. Cophy was posted inside the entrance to get an up-close look at this phase of the service.

"Very impressive work by the Treasure Chest so far," said Lady Cophy as she approached Lolo. "I was worried that they'd have people stuck in the stairways with so many coming in at once, but it looks like they have a system."

Indeed, it seemed that the two *toko dawiji* were dispatching dining parties to the different floors in such a way that they didn't get in each other's way or the way of the servers rushing to bring out drinks and menus. Moreover, those who looked to be of higher social rank were being brought to the upper floors and private suites, while those of lower social rank were brought to the less desirable seats closer to the stairways. Clearly some kind of seating chart coded to the appearance of the diners had long been worked out ahead of time. The Treasure Chest *was* prepared.

"Why does Tiphan Huto have two scholars who passed the first level of the Imperial examinations working for him as door greeters?" Lolo asked.

"That *is* a little strange," said Lady Cophy. "But I have to say it is nice to have such cultured and well-educated greeters. Look at that young man on the left. So handsome and limber . . . and such long fingers!—"

Lolo broke in before Lady Cophy could embarrass herself by

drooling. "No, no! That's not what I meant. The scholars stand out, but they're just part of a pattern. There are way too many servers here. The Treasure Chest can't possibly keep all of them on staff."

"Maybe Tiphan Huto likes to have a large team. Many hands make light work, right? I *do* think he's got a good team. Look at the waitresses and waiters. Every one of them is as pretty and delectable as one of Mozo Mu's—"

"That's just it! I don't remember anyone commenting on the size of the staff at the Treasure Chest or their attractiveness before tonight, and they've been operating after their soft opening for a few weeks now. The rules are that no one is allowed to hire extra staff but must rely on people already employed by the competitors at the time the service round was announced."

"Oh . . . I see," said Lady Cophy. "Let me find Tiphan Huto and ask some questions."

Although the staff of the Treasure Chest appeared unused to working as a team under pressure, the fact that there were so many of them at least took a lot of the pressure off individual servers. With minimal confusion, the diners were directed to their seats, and drinks and menus were being brought out.

Gina Cophy returned. "It seems that Tiphan has flown in hand-picked people from the Huto clan's businesses all around Dara. Those *toko dawiji*, for example, work for Tazu's Palace, one of the newest casinos in Dimushi, and are experts at making sure celebrities and high-stakes gamblers are satisfied."

"Then why are they here?" asked Lolo.

"Err . . . Tiphan said that since the Huto clan has invested in each of these businesses, they are all in fact already employed by him by proxy."

"But they don't work for the Treasure Chest!"

"The rules only say that the staff must already be employed by one of the competitors. And Tiphan says that the competitors are the Wasu clan and the Huto clan. I'm no paid litigator, so I figure . . ."

*Of course Tiphan Huto would find every possible loophole!* Lolo seethed as she climbed up the bamboo tower. But they weren't in court, and if the judges all thought like Lady Cophy, Tiphan might actually get away with it. She took a deep breath and put a smile on her face as she turned back to the crowd below. Cheating or no cheating, the show had to go on.

The doors to the Splendid Urn slid open noiselessly. The queued-up diners and onlookers craned their necks, unsure what they were going to see.

Lodan, Dandelion, and Kinri stepped out, bowed to the waiting customers, and stood to the side of the entryway.

Behind them, through the yawning door, the restaurant remained mostly dark and silent.

The diners waited, uncertain what to do.

Young Pimié, the *cüpa* prodigy, was serving as Séca's assistant and co-host at the Splendid Urn tonight. He ran from the foot of the observation tower to Lodan. Timidly, he asked, "Err, are you expecting more staff?"

"Oh, no," said Lodan, "we've got everyone working already. It's all hands on deck tonight."

The diners stared at the three standing before them in disbelief. Were they really expecting to serve almost two hundred customers with three servers?

"Come in!" said Dandelion. "Welcome to the dining experience of a lifetime!"

The diners looked at one another, shrugged, and stepped into the dark restaurant.

All at once, lights came on, and the whole place was bathed in a bright bluish glow given off by spinning glass spheres placed at every table. The light was nothing like the light from torches or whale-oil lamps. Somehow, it was at once colder but also brighter.

The gasps of admiration from the crowd brought Séca down from the tower. He and Pimié examined the glowing globes closest to the door.

The globes were in fact glass bowls placed upside down in a dish of mercury. Protruding up through the mercury and into the bowl was a small bamboo tube, at the top of which was mounted a fixed ring of wool. Through the center of the hollow bamboo tube rose a spindle that ended in a disk of amber. The spindle was turning rapidly, rubbing the amber disk against the woolen ring around it, and it was this action that generated the bright light that filled the glass globe and lit up the restaurant.

Looking below the globe, Séca and Pimié saw that the whole apparatus—glass globe, mercury bath, bamboo tube, and spindle—was mounted atop a latticed bamboo stand. Inside the stand, some creature was running rapidly inside a treadwheel, and it was this motor, through a series of belts and gears, that powered the spindle.

"What *is* that?" asked Pimié.

"That is a leaf-dancer cicada," said Dandelion. "They love to run. In fact, if you remember, Mitahu Piati, the early Tiro-period Rima memoirist, wrote a lovely prose poem about his childhood experience of observing thousands of these cicadas emerging from the ground, running across the Ring-Woods—"

"No, no! I don't mean *that*," said Pimié. "I've raced leaf-dancer cicadas myself. I know all about them. You can get them to fun faster by feeding them a bit of pungent pipe scallion—anyway, that's not the point. I mean *this*! What is this glowing thing?"

"Ah, well, I'm not entirely sure," said Dandelion. "Rati Yera calls these silkmotic candles, and their advantage lies in the fact that they don't need to be lit, trimmed, refilled, or taken care of by anyone all night. We are a bit shorthanded, as you might have noticed, so lighting that doesn't require much work is much appreciated."

"I definitely made the right decision to come here tonight," said Pimié, his face a wide grin in the bright silkmotic glow. "I want one of these for myself."

"Talk to Rati later," said Dandelion. "She told me she was inspired by the equipment used by the nuns from the Great Temple of Lutho."

"I've seen other designs for silkmotic lamps, but none so compact or effective," said Séca, his voice full of admiration. "Does the bowl inverted over mercury create a partial vacuum? And is it the case that when the silkmotic force is discharged by the amber-wool assembly inside, the mercury vapor—"

"Don't ask me to explain anything," said a grinning Dandelion. "I just work here."

"Are all the silkmotic candles powered by cicadas?" asked Pimié, his boyish interest piqued by the creatures in other cages.

"Not all. We started off using pet mice and squirrels, but we couldn't find enough—"

Pimié eyes widened at this. "But the poor squirrels—"

"Don't worry, when the animals get tired, they can just stop; there's a flywheel that keeps the spindle going until they recover. The cicadas are much easier to work with, anyway." She didn't add that she also liked the cicadas because there seemed to her a kind of poetic justice in drawing on the aid of an insect in response to the terrifying caterpillars that had been partially responsible for the Urn's present predicament.

"I can't believe Rati Yera thought of that," said Séca. "She should come and work at the Imperial laboratories with me."

"Oh, she would hate to have to dress up every day and report to an official. She did tell me that she got the idea for this motor from the dog-powered treadwheel fans at the Treasure Chest—she insists on not taking credit for other people's good ideas."

By now, the restaurant's first floor was filled with diners standing around tables, admiring the glowing silkmotic candles. The devices proved to be good conversation pieces, and the test customers, at first nervous and fearful, were now laughing and happily chatting. Some of the gawkers outside, sensing the shift in mood, ran to summon others to come and join the fun.

"Just pick a table you like and sit down," hollered Lodan. "Trust me, all the tables are equally good tonight. Your servers will be with you shortly."

While Lodan continued to usher the diners in, and Dandelion walked around with a bunch of pipe scallions to encourage a few recalcitrant cicadas to brighten their silkmotic candles, Kinri went from table to table, making sure that everyone had a menu.

"Are you planning on taking all our orders tonight?" asked some of the customers. Despite the impressive lighting display, they still weren't sure how the Splendid Urn was going to pull off the logistics of taking orders and serving food to more than two hundred people with such a tiny staff.

"Oh, absolutely not," said Kinri with a mysterious smile. "But your servers will be coming. In fact, I think I hear them now."

"It looks like the Treasure Chest's appetizer service is running into some headwinds," Lolo said into the trumpet.

Despite the large number of servers—or because of it—appetizer service in the Treasure Chest was backed up.

The problem wasn't the kitchen. The crew of cooks and assistants produced the two appetizers on the menu with little trouble: "Bounty of the Sea" (a hot seafood stew served with a side of crispy fried noodles to represent the net) and "Gifts of the Land" (a platter of delicately carved fruits-and-nuts hors d'oeuvres served with eight dipping sauces).

The servers, on the other hand, often got the orders wrong and had trouble carrying large trays of hot soup and elegant food sculptures. Rushing up and down the narrow staircases and through the busy door to the kitchen, they often collided with one another, and plates and bowls crashed to the ground, requiring cleanup and further slowing down the service.

Tiphan Huto's face turned as red as a lantern chili pepper. He stood outside the door leading to the kitchen and berated the servers.

"How hard can it be to remember the orders?" he yelled at two hapless waitresses. "There are literally just two dishes on the menu. That table asked for five stews and three platters, and you brought them three stews and five platters instead. Now the whole table has to wait while you fix your mistake because no one can start eating until all the elders have gotten their stews, and the elders won't start until the youngsters have gotten their platters. Why are you dawdling? By the time you get back, the stews will be cold and you'll have to bring new ones out again!"

"We're not waitresses at all," said one of the young women, a wronged expression on her face. "I'm a sparrow tiles dealer at Tazu's Palace, and she's a flautist at the Fool's Mirror Theater. We're here only because our bosses told us we *had* to be here. What do we know about memorizing orders and carrying trays?"

"And there are so many people here," said the other waitress.

"We can't even get to the kitchen because you have too many people working tonight."

"Especially with you standing in our way," said the first waitress. "You have a very large . . . um . . . personality."

"It doesn't help to have you yelling in our faces, you know," said the second waitress. "Now I've forgotten what table sixteen ordered."

"Dare to mock me, do you?" shouted Tiphan Huto, panting and sweating. Since he was shorter than the two statuesque waitresses, he had to jump up with every word to be sure that he was staring into their eyes. "Look, it's easy! I'll let you in on a tip. . . ."

Lolo, who had quietly approached from behind to witness this confrontation, took note of Tiphan Huto's impromptu lecture on table-serving tips. Silently thanking Dophino, the protective spirit of indigo-house girls, she tiptoed away, returned to the tower, and gave the audience outside an update.

"Masters and mistresses, we have just discovered a most ingenious aspect of the Treasure Chest's system. Let me recite for you a quote from the inimitable Tiphan Huto:

"'To memorize orders, just connect the order in your mind with some striking aspect of the customer's physical appearance. For example, if the man is bald and orders stew, picture him as a smooth reef poking out of the sea. But if he orders the platter of hors d'oeuvres, picture him as a rock in the woods sticking out of a carpet of moss. If the woman is ugly and orders the stew, imagine her as a seacow. But if the woman is ugly and orders the platter, imagine her as a cow mooing. For instance, the table you just came from could be memorized as:

> *Seacow, seahorse, moo-moo, bare reef;*
> *Moss, boss, hot sauce, a hunk of beef.*

'See how easy that was?'"

The crowd erupted into riotous laughter and angry groans. A few daring youths went up to the restaurant and repeated the ditty to patrons sitting near windows on the first floor. Soon, the faces of the table of diners blazoned by this most talented restaurateur-poet flushed, and all got up and left the restaurant in a huff.

Lolo tried to suppress her grin of victory. She didn't feel she was tilting the scales of the competition unfairly. After all, if this was how Tiphan Huto thought of his customers, then she felt no compunction about publicizing it.

Still, as dinner service went on, the new waitstaff grew used to the demands of their unfamiliar job, and orders were coming out of the kitchen to the tables with some regularity. Most of the servers made it a point, however, to say to the table that they did not employ their boss's mnemonic technique, and Tiphan Huto hid in the back, too angry and embarrassed to come out.

It sounded like hundreds of wooden beads being dropped into a temple collection tray, like a caravan of miniature horse-drawn carriages clattering through the streets, like a flock of woodpeckers had landed inside the Splendid Urn and were looking for caterpillars in the walls.

As customers watched in disbelief, dozens of little triangular carts emerged from the service tunnel on the first floor and filed into the restaurant. Some headed straight for the tables, while others lined up at the elevator for Kinri or Dandelion to crank them to the upper floors.

At the tip of each cart was a little animal: a cat, a puppy, a pet mouse, a parrot, a monkey, or some other equally appealing creature. All the animals wore little hats in the shape of an inverted urn.

Lodan stood in the middle of the first floor and hollered, making sure that her voice carried to all the corners. "Honored guests! Tonight we're a little shorthanded, as you can see. So we've borrowed some helpers. The drivers will guide the carts to your table, and there, you'll see a stack of wax tablets and a writing knife, with which you can indicate your order. Once you've recorded your choices, just load the tablets into the receptacle at the back of the cart, and our animal servers will guide the carts back to the kitchen to bring you your dishes."

As she spoke, the carts separated and headed to the tables, stopping next to the perplexed customers. The monkeys, cats, puppies, birds, and other animals looked around, bowed, flipped, meowed, licked their paws, and put on a show that delighted the children at the tables and astounded the elders.

"Oh, look, look! The monkey is imitating you!"

"That is the *cutest* cat ever. Look at that hat!"

"Did you hear the crested mynah asking me how I'm doing? What a delightful waiter!"

"Such an adorable mouse! Are you working hard, little fella? Are they paying you in sunflower seeds?"

Pimié went around the tables, ostensibly to gather feedback on this unorthodox method of service but really to pet the adorable drivers. While most of the animals seemed very excited by their unusual jobs, he noticed one particular green siskin who perched in his cage lazily, head cocked jauntily to one side. The bird seemed to survey the other animals with a bored haughtiness.

"That little guy looks like he owns this place," said Pimié, laughing. "He's stretching out his claws like he's sitting in *thakrido*!"

"Oh, Zuzu is a veteran driver," said Dandelion with a wink. "He had a pretty harrowing experience the last time he drove one of the carts, and Rati had to make him a cast for his wings. But he's all better now, and his mistress was gracious enough to lend him to us for the night."

Pimié looked at her suspiciously, uncertain how much of this outrageous tale was true. But he was quickly distracted by an upturned turtle driver who was having trouble flipping back onto her belly.

Séca stared at the scene as if his eyes were about to pop out.

"This is impossible," he muttered to himself. He turned to Kinri and Dandelion. "How are you doing this?"

"Mistress Yera is a very skilled trainer," said Kinri, a cryptic smile on his face. "You should have seen her maze act in Temple Square."

"Oh, come on!" said Séca.

"The world is full of wonders," said Dandelion piously. "Maybe Lord Lutho saw fit to help us tonight."

FOUR DAYS EARLIER.

Kinri barged into the rented house of the Blossom Gang. Everyone was there, including Dandelion. The furrowed brows and discarded sketches on the tables showed that everyone was still trying, but fail-ing, to come up with a way to save the Splendid Urn.

He addressed himself to Rati. "I think I have a plan. Tell me if you think this will work."

He had everyone's attention.

"We don't have enough people to run dinner service," Kinri said, "not unless we find a way to allow one person to do the work of ten, of twenty."

"That's obvious," said Dandelion.

"So I thought of a way. We have to make more of your maze-running cart, and teach the self-driving carts to be waiters," said Kinri.

"Self-driving carts?" Rati Yera said the phrase slowly, her expres-sion unreadable. "I don't know anything about self-driving carts."

"I saw your act in Temple Square, and I just couldn't figure out how animals could be driving a cart through a maze," said Kinri. "But when I saw you come out of the cellar maze in the Treasure Chest with no trouble, I knew that the two had to be connected. The trick must be in the cart and the wheeled chair. The cart, not the ani-mals, can be taught."

The rest of the Blossom Gang stayed silent.

"Why? What is it?" asked Kinri. "Is this a secret? But you've taught me the principles behind so many of your other machines. Why not this one?"

"Rati has never taught anyone the art of the maze-running cart," said Widi Tucru. He didn't elaborate. All street magicians had secrets that they were not willing to share with anyone else, not even part-ners as close as brothers and sisters.

"The maze-running cart is my most . . . unusual invention. To study its secrets, a student must first formally take on the obligations of having me as their teacher," said Rati Yera. She gazed at Kinri, hope and doubt warring on her face.

"I'm willing," said Kinri. He had admired Rati Yera's proficiency with machines for as long as he had known her. If the price of saving the business of his benefactor was to become the student of this master engineer, he thought he was coming out way ahead in the deal. Besides, there was another reason that he wanted to study with Rati, but it was a reason that he couldn't reveal.

"That's not fair!" said Dandelion. "How come you're willing to take him as a student but not me?"

Arona gave her a look. "Rati has never taken a student. This is a serious matter."

"Sorry," Dandelion whispered.

"You really want this?" asked Rati, a quaver in her voice. "To be my student is to agree to carry on my legacy, to honor me as a parent. Are you certain?"

"I've had a master teacher before," said Kinri. "I understand the obligations. I would consider it a great honor to call you master."

He knelt down and got ready to perform the ritual bows that would bind them as student and teacher.

"Wait," said Rati Yera. She took a deep breath to calm herself and looked around at the others in the room. "Please leave me with Kinri. I'll explain to him certain truths that he must know."

Long ago, before Mapidéré was known as Mapidéré, before the title of "Hegemon" had been lifted out of dusty history books, a girl was born to a poor Amu couple making a living by fishing the eastern coast of Arulugi.

Though the Xana Conquest had yet to come, the armies of the various kings fought fiercely in the waning days of the Tiro states, vying for honor and glory. As the King of Amu and the King of Cocru fought over dominion of the Amu Strait, Arulugi's poorest were like the straw on top of a thatched roof: the first to be drenched by thunderstorms and the first to be broken by winter ice. They were considered disposable by the great lords, not worthy of protection.

A long naval blockade took away their source of living. A village delegation went to Müning to beg for help, and they returned with the message that the king had no resources to spare.

"Shall we leave and seek better fortune elsewhere?" asked the villagers. "Perhaps we can go to Müning."

"No." The messengers explained that the king wanted everyone to stay exactly where they were lest refugees drain the resources of the capital and the other refined cities of the Beautiful Island.

Starvation was followed by plague, and now there was even more reason for the king to make sure that the villagers stayed put. Soldiers behind barricades shot arrows at anyone found on the roads leading out of the village, and naval ships patrolled the coast, sinking fishing boats and rafts. One by one, families in the village fell ill. The girl's family wasn't the first to succumb to the plague, but they weren't the last either. Seized by fever and delirium, both parents crawled into bed and never left it again. Miraculously, the girl herself, barely a toddler, seemed immune to the wasting disease, but she wasn't going to last much longer, unfed and with no one to care for her.

A passing gang of laborers took whatever was valuable in the plague-ridden village, buried the dead bodies, and carried the toddling child away with them.

The laborers were able to roam through a quarantined village because they were *raye*, descendants of prisoners of war. They weren't slaves, but they were forbidden from farming, cultivating silk, learning to read, or any of the other professions open to ordinary citizens. The only paths left to them were to beg for a living or to take up unclean tasks: tanning leather; carting away night soil; grave digging and handling corpses, especially bodies that others did not dare to touch, such as executed criminals and plague victims.

The gang of *raye* who took the orphaned girl with them didn't know her name—everyone who knew her nursing name was dead. So they named her Rati Yera. Her given name was also the name of a wild weed that grew on graves, life that derived its nourishment from decaying bodies. Her "family name," based on reversing the syllables in *raye*, was nothing more than a hope, hope that she would reverse her cascade of misfortunes.

Because respectable professions were closed to them, many *raye*, unwilling to live in poverty, were drawn to an opportunity few others would contemplate: robbing graves. The wealthy in Dara loved to collect antiques to show off their taste and culture, but time had a merciless habit of breaking down the treasures of the past. There was an obvious source to satisfy the cravings of the collectors: the graves of ancient lords and ladies, filled with goods that were meant to accompany them beyond the River-on-Which-Nothing-Floats. But few dared to tap into this supply. The taboo against disturbing the rest of the ancients, possibly ancestors of those who still lived near their graves, was strong. Moreover, most graves were sealed by monks and nuns with powerful curses against the intrusion of grave robbers.

But when you were already living at the very bottom of the pit that was the war-torn world, curses did not scare you as much.

And so the bold among the *raye* became like the rati grass, robbing the dead to satisfy the greed of the living. Risking life and limb, they dug into ancient tombs, braved plagues, poisons, deadly mechanisms meant to secure the peace of the afterlife, and sold the antiquities they dug up for a pittance to dealers who turned around and resold them to collectors for a hundred- or thousandfold markup. The collectors could pretend that what they touched came from the inheritances of living descendants of great families fallen on hard times, and the lies allowed everyone to sleep peacefully at night.

Grave robbing was a dangerous profession that required great skill in practical geography and mechanical engineering. Underground passages of the tombs of great lords and ladies were filled with traps and dangers, and constructed like mazes to confuse intruders. The Mausoleum of Emperor Mapidéré, a project that consumed the lives of countless corvée laborers, was only an extreme version of this.

As Rati Yera grew up, she learned the craft of grave robbing from the gang who had adopted her, and because she was clever and nimble with her hands, soon she became a builder of novel tools and new gadgets that allowed her to become the most skilled robber of them all.

The Xana Conquest and the subsequent rebellion during the time of Emperor Erishi transformed the landscape of Dara. Many had their household registration records destroyed and took on new identities. Ancient noble lines faded into obscurity, and condemned criminals became dukes and marquesses overnight. Rati Yera herself became at first a rebel and then a thief, and joined the gang of Gozogi

Çadé, the master forger. Rati and Gozogi became as close as sisters, a legendary pair of master thieves whose exploits left magistrates and constables scratching their heads and became the standard by which all heists were measured. There seemed to be no vault their gang couldn't breach, no armed guards they couldn't evade, no fortress that they couldn't walk in and out of as easily as reaching into a purse left on the table. Some said they could fly as easily as Mingén falcons, and tunnel through the earth as quickly as star-eared moles. Others said that they had the aid of Lord Lutho's own fantastical machines.

After the death of Gozogi, Rati also left the life of heists. In her old age, gold and baubles no longer moved her; rather, she realized that she craved the understanding, skill, and craft that led to ingenious machines. By chance, she met Widi Tucru, Mota Kiphi, and Arona Taré, who shared with her that thirst for the treasure of knowledge, albeit the branch of knowledge they each sought was different. They became for her a new adopted family as they wandered about the Islands.

Throughout her time with Gozogi and later, the Blossom Gang, Rati never revealed to them her origins as a *raye*. Though Emperor Ragin had abolished all the legal restrictions placed on castes originating from the Tiro states era, the stigma around them persisted. Just as a writing knife cut against the tender skin of a sapling would grow into a long, deep scar in the bark of the towering tree, the shame and humiliation one learned in childhood didn't go away with a simple Imperial proclamation.

She was afraid of how those she loved would look at her if they knew the truth of how she had first learned her skills, and though she was free and open about the machines and techniques she invented, teaching anyone who wanted to learn with generosity, she kept from all the secret of her maze-running cart, believing its origin too shameful to be accepted.

When she thought that the beauty of these carts, perhaps her proudest invention, might have to die with her, she felt pangs of anguish. Never having had children of her own, she was gripped from time to time by the idea of taking on a student to carry on her legacy. But a formal student was also like a child, and they would inherit her shame. She couldn't bear the thought of saddling anyone with the taint of the *raye*, inseparable from the knowledge of the maze-running—no, self-driving, cart.

"I was a grave robber." Rati Yera paused, not daring to look at Kinri, not wanting to see the look of admiration and respect turn into revulsion or disapproval.

She waited for him to shuffle uncomfortably, to make an excuse, to bolt for the door.

Nothing.

She looked up. The admiration and respect remained on the young man's face, now mixed with an intense curiosity.

Surprised and hopeful, Rati went on.

"The most important tenet of the profession of grave robbing is discretion. In many ways, robbing a grave is a lot like carrying out a heist. We rely on small teams and leave the site as undisturbed— on the surface—as possible. Drawing the attention of competitors or officialdom had to be avoided at all costs.

"Therefore, the best way to rob a grave is to tunnel into it, similar to a bank vault. After the initial shaft has been dug, a scout needs to go in to explore. But graves are underground mazes full of danger, and it's easy to get lost in the twisting, branching passages and never make one's way back to the surface. Every robber has found the bodies of those who had tunneled into the same tomb before them but never left.

"Some robbers use a ball of rope or string as a safety line back to the exit, but a ball of rope unwound and rewound in this manner has no memory of paths already taken. The key isn't just to get in and get out, but to map out all the underground chambers and passageways. The richest tombs are much too large for human memory to accomplish such a task. Drawing a map during exploration is impractical, for the scout often has to work by touch and feel alone, in complete darkness."

"Can't a map be produced by having the scout take notes in some . . . tangible form?" asked Kinri.

Rati nodded, pleased. "Very good. Some clever souls came up

with the idea of rope-writing. A length of rope is used to track paths taken and not taken. At every fork in the tunnel, a knot is made. One kind of knot indicates a turn to the left, another a turn to the right, and yet another that the person has turned around and is retracing their steps. Knots can be made and read in the darkness, by touch alone, and simply by running one's hands down the rope it's possible to obtain a complete record of the paths explored."

"It's like a map," said Kinri. "A map that records and represents only changes in direction, not distance or position."

Rati nodded again. "You catch on quick. The rope-map was something my grave-robbing masters taught me. I refined it and then invented the self-driving cart on my own, but ultimately this entire line of invention consists of the fruit of breaking a taboo. So, knowing that my art derives from one of the most despised professions in the world, do you still wish to become my student?"

"Of course," said Kinri. "I don't care if your knowledge comes from grave robbing. The spirits of the departed are no longer trapped within those tombs, and I do not see why you should be reviled any more than the collectors who profit from your work."

A growing sense of excitement gripped him. The knot-writing of grave robbers reminded him of the memory knots of Lyucu shamans. *This must be a sign that I'm on the right path.* Yet, a trace of unease also crept into his heart. *If only you knew that you're teaching your secrets to a Lyucu barbarian, you'd be horrified.*

Rati laughed, shook her head, and laughed again. "You think ... so differently. Perhaps the gods have already bound our fates together. All right, I will be your teacher, and you my student."

Kinri knelt and touched his forehead to the ground three times. "Master Yera," he said.

Rati nodded, so happy that she couldn't stop smiling. "Let's start with more understanding of mapping. In my youth, my small size and agility made me the ideal tomb scout, and I grew to be the best mapper on my gang. But one time, a stone trap crushed my legs, rendering them useless. Many thought my grave robbing days over, but I devised a way to scout in a wheeled chair. Come, I'll show you. Let's take apart my chair."

Kinri helped Rati out of her wheeled chair onto a sitting mat. Then, under her direction, Kinri took off the back panel from the box under the chair. Inside, he could see a rope tightly wound on a spool, with the free end disappearing into a complicated nest of gears and levers.

"The rope runs between two spools, under tension," explained Rati. "The spool you see is driven by the back wheels of my chair, and it winds the rope unwound from the other spool, concealed behind those gears."

Kinri nodded. So far, it was easy to follow the explanation.

"Do you see that pair of irregularly-shaped gears with razor-edged teeth, one on each side of the rope?" asked Rati. "Those are driven independently by the two back wheels. As the chair progresses, the rope is slowly pulled between them from one spool to the other. But every quarter turn of one of the wheels, the corresponding razor-edged gear cuts a notch in the rope. This chair is a more comfortable version of my grave-robbing device, which was just the box on wheels, with me sitting on top, legs strapped to the box. I would propel myself through the tight passageways in a grave with my hands, and then emerge with a movement rope-map."

Kinri was impressed by the intricate mechanism but uncertain how it made a map.

"The best way to understand it is to see it in operation," said Rati. "Why don't you set up a maze on the floor? You can use sitting cushions and pillows as walls."

Kinri complied and quickly set up a simple maze on the floor.

"Now, push my chair through it. When you're done, lift the small green-handled lever at the side to disengage the mapping mechanism, and bring it back to me."

Kinri did so. Rati reached into the back of the box under the wheeled chair, manipulated a few mechanisms, and retrieved a length of rope.

"As you moved the chair through the maze, the mechanism you saw recorded spins of the back wheels in notches. When the wheels were spinning in sync, which was when the chair was moving straight ahead, the notches on both sides were regularly spaced. But when you made a turn, one wheel would spin faster than the other, and that was also recorded on the rope in mismatched notches. So just by running your hand down this rope, you can read a map of the journey the chair took, including both distances and turns. Try it."

Kinri closed his eyes and did as Rati instructed. Carefully, he felt for the small notches along the length of the rope. In several places, the notches along one side were more closely spaced than the other, showing that one wheel traveled a longer distance than the other. He could picture the turns of the chair in his head, and imagined his master navigating the lightless passageways of a tomb in the same way.

"This was how you navigated the maze in the cellar of the Treasure Chest!" he blurted.

Rati nodded, beaming.

"But . . . how does mapping relate to self-driving carts?"

"Patience. I've only shown you one half of the puzzle. Now for the other half."

Rati Yera had Kinri retrieve a small cart from a large chest in the corner. It looked like a cruder version of the cart used in her animal maze performances, with a triangular base and a large bamboo mast. She held it in her lap and pried open the cover panel, revealing the mechanism within.

Each of the back wheels, where the driving force of the cart came from, was mounted on a separate axle that spun independently of the other. A thin cable was wrapped a few turns around each axle, and the two cables were then pulled together at the base of the mast. There, a pulley kept the cables under tension as they ran up a groove in the side of the mast until they disappeared into the top of the tube.

"The cables are attached to a heavy weight resting on the sand— sometimes I use rice—filling the inside of the mast. The sand drains out at a constant rate through a hole at the bottom of the mast, much like the sand in an hourglass," explained Rati. "Here, try it so you can see."

She had Kinri place the cart on the floor and showed him how to pull out the plug in the base of the mast. Kinri looked in. As sand silently fell out of the bottom, the weight fell, pulling on the two cables attached to the axles; the cables unwound and turned the axles; the cart slowly moved forward.

"When all this mechanism is concealed, I can see how it would appear as if the cart is moving on its own," said Kinri slowly. Certainly the trick was neat, but it also seemed so simple. "But how do you get the cart to turn or move backward?"

"That is why we have two separate axles," said Rati, a pleased grin on her face. She was delighted to finally be explaining the mechanism to someone.

She asked Kinri to refill the mast with sand while she began to wind the cables around the axles again. This time, however, after wrapping the cable several turns counter-sundial-wise around the left axle, she pointed out to Kinri the series of small holes drilled down the length of the axle. Into one of these holes she pushed a short peg, wrapped the cable around this peg, and then wound the cable around the axle in the opposite direction (i.e., sundial-wise) two more turns. She placed another peg into the next hole, wrapped the cable around this peg, and then wound the rest of the cable around the axle counter-sundial-wise again. For the right axle, she wound the cable in the same direction all the way through.

This time, when Kinri set the cart free, it moved forward a short distance and stopped. The cable on the left axle had unwound to the last peg she had pushed into the axle, and now the cable, wound around the axle in reverse, began to drive the wheel to spin in the opposite direction. As the left wheel spun backward, the right wheel continued to spin forward so that the cart turned to the left in place. By now, the cable had unwound to the first peg Rati pushed into the axle, and the left wheel began to spin forward again. The cart moved in the new direction a short distance and stopped.

"It moves like a living creature!" exclaimed Kinri. "It can be taught!"

"Now comes the most important step. If you already have a map of the tomb or maze"—she indicated the rope-map made by the chair earlier—"can you think of a way to teach the cart to repeat the same journey you just took?"

Kinri caressed the rope-map and looked at the disassembled

self-driving cart on the floor. He strained his mind against the problem.

"The rope map and the cables around the axles represent the same information . . ." he said tentatively.

"Go on," said Rati, leaning forward eagerly.

"They are like two sentences describing the same road in two languages: past and future. One is about the path taken, and the other is about the way forward; one uses notches cut into two sides of the rope, and the other uses turns around two axles. . . . You have to translate from one to the other." As he continued, the vision in his head grew clearer, and his voice became more confident. "All you have to do is to encode the rope-map into different ways of winding the cables around the axles. The pegs allow you to change the direction in which the cables wind around the axle, and thus alter the direction the wheels spin. The number of turns you wind the cables around the axles controls how far the wheels move!"

Rati clapped her hands together. "You have it! I can even add empty loops in the cable, not wound around the axles at all, to allow the wheels to idle for a certain period of time. And by changing the speed at which sand flows out of the bottom of the mast, I can alter the speed at which the cart moves.

"From these primitives, it's possible to build up a set of basic operations such as moving forward a full turn of the wheels, backing up, turning left a quarter, turning right a quarter, wiggle, and so forth. These make it easier to translate the route in the rope-map into a sequence of basic operations that can be taught to the cart."

While she talked, Rati wound the cables around the axles and pushed in pegs. She paused to show Kinri that she had to translate the directions on the notched rope from her wheeled chair into loops on the axles in reverse order because the last instruction encoded by the cables would actually be the first action performed by the cart.

Kinri set the cart on the floor at the opening of the pillow maze and removed the plug at the base of the mast. He watched, rapt, as the machine navigated through the maze as though it had a will of its own.

"In my grave-robbing days, after I mapped out a tomb by rope,

I extracted the most direct routes to the treasure chambers and then encoded the instructions into multiple carts. The carts drove themselves to the treasure chambers and back out without issue. A few of my fellow thieves stationed themselves at the treasure chambers to catch the carts as they arrived, put the brakes on, load the carts, and then send them back out. At the opening, the rest of the gang unloaded the carts while I re-instructed the carts and sent them in again. I timed the carts so that they didn't bump into each other in the cramped passageways. I called the carts mechanical oxen, for they ferried the goods out of the graves just like obedient, tireless oxen with minds that could be trained. With their help, my gang could empty a grave faster than anyone else."

Finally, Kinri understood how Rati Yera had been able to pull off her magic act in Temple Square.

Rati elaborated. "The carts I use for the performance are more refined—for instance, a wind-up spring attached to an escapement is used in place of the falling weight and sand to drive the wheels— but the principle is the same. With my hands under the tablecloth, I would navigate the maze with my eyes and encode the instructions into the axles."

"You'd have to wind the cables and push the pegs in really fast."

"Quite easily done with practice. And with a cute mouse or bird on top, viewers are distracted by our interaction. Much of stage magic is about misdirecting the audience's attention."

Knowing the secret didn't detract from Kinri's admiration of the trick. The way the cart turned and clattered through the maze was one of the most amazing sights he had ever seen, akin to watching a young garinafin take flight for the first time. Some wonders were more magnificent when enhanced with knowledge.

"I think this solves our problem with servers," said Kinri. "We just need a few bigger versions of the maze-running cart." In his mind, he pictured an army of mechanical oxen, each instructed by Lodan to perform the duties of a member of the waitstaff—

Rati broke into his reverie. "I'm fast, but I'm not *that* fast. Each cart forgets what it has been taught as soon as the cables are unwound, and must be re-instructed again after every journey. I can't wind cables quickly enough to instruct a few carts to go to all the different tables on the night of the service."

"What if we built a separate cart for each table, and instructed them ahead of time?"

Rati thought about it and shook her head. "First of all, even if the whole Blossom Gang worked nonstop, we don't have enough time to build a cart for each table. Even if we could, there's not enough space at the Urn. They'd just all run into each other on the floor. We need a small number of carts, but also a way to teach them how to go to different tables quickly. I don't see how it can be done."

Kinri stared at the maze-running cart. *There has to be a way to solve this problem. Has to be.*

The problem of building a small number of enlarged carts turned out to be the easier one to solve.

A year earlier, a group of carpenters had been accused of negligent homicide when a bridge they built collapsed, killing the driver of an oxcart. Widi Tucru, the knife-tongue, defended them and produced proof that the bridge had collapsed not from faulty construction, but sabotage by a rival builder who had lost the bid for the bridge. The carpenters had exhausted most of their funds while the case was pending, and so couldn't pay Widi his fee. But they gave him patches for his robe, promising to come to his aid in the future.

When Widi explained what he needed, the carpenters came with friends, apprentices, and even masters. Taking inspiration from Mozo Mu's tricks for maintaining secrecy, Rati produced drawings of the components of the cart and gave them to different teams of carpenters without revealing how the components would be put together.

"Do you think you can get everything done in time?" asked Widi anxiously.

The leader of the carpenters, a man named Lutuma, nodded confidently. "We're a bit shorthanded since Master Dina is missing. But we'll be fine."

"What happened to Master Dina?" asked Widi. Dina was Lutuma's teacher, and probably one of the most inventive carpenters in the city. It was said that he had been a lead designer on Marshal Mazoti's transforming airships nearly a decade ago.

"He went to a job at the docks three days ago and never came home. Magistrate Zuda has posted his portrait at all the city gates and sent the constables out to look for him." A look of concern clouded Lutuma's face. "I worry that it's too late. He's the third master craftsman who's disappeared this month."

"The third!"

Lutuma nodded. "Earlier in the month, Master Go, the blacksmith, left home in the evening to go to a pub near the docks to meet with friends. He never showed up. Then a week later, Master Raa, the architect, went to visit a new client near the Temple of Fithowéo and never returned. We're all a little scared. My wife won't even let me go meet new clients without taking at least four assistants with me."

Widi looked thoughtful. He left Arona in charge of the carpenters and departed with Mota.

"Where are you going?" asked Arona.

"Just taking a stroll around the city," said Widi. "We'll stop around the docks, and maybe . . . the Temple of Fithowéo."

"I've never known you to pray to Fithowéo," said Arona. The Temple of Fithowéo in Ginpen was frequented by scholars preparing for the Imperial examinations rather than soldiers, but since Widi had no interest in the examinations, he never visited.

"It can't hurt to ask for the god's help in this contest," said Widi vaguely.

While Lutuma and his crew worked on the carts, Rati went to Temple Square to speak to other performers with animal acts and patrons who had enjoyed her act. Many of them agreed to lend her their animal assistants or pets for the night of the competition, so that the carts would have misdirecting "drivers."

Meanwhile, Kinri struggled with the problem of how to instruct so many carts within a short period of time.

After tossing and turning for half the evening, thinking about cables and pegs, he finally fell asleep. In his dream he was back home in Ukyu with his mother as a young boy again, and he was watching a storytelling dance about Kikisavo and Afir. While the dancing shaman spun and slammed her staff against the cactus drums, the storytelling shaman held a long leather string in his hand, on which were knots and shells and bones of various sizes. Each was a reminder of an important scene, and as the storyteller finished improvising and chanting each scene, he moved to the next. . . .

The dream shifted to a beach in Ukyu-taasa. There was a set of Péa pipes on the sand, the garinafin bladder already blown up. Goztan stood next to the pipes, beckoning him closer.

He ran up to her, his heart racing and a lump in his throat. He had so many questions he wanted to ask her, but all he could get out was a quavering "Mother!"

Goztan smiled at him. "You are looking well, my son."

He hesitated, but then screwed up the courage. "Are things as terrible at home as the refugees say?"

The smile disappeared from Goztan's face. "I think you already know the answer to that."

Kinri's heart ached. He hadn't realized how much he wanted his mother to deny it until she didn't.

"I . . . I don't know what to do," he said. "I don't know how to help everyone in Ukyu-taasa from here."

"You have some ideas, though," she said. "Tell me what you think I and the pékyu want you to do."

"You . . . want me to study the arts of Dara. The pékyu thinks I can learn about the engines of war and help Ukyu-taasa resist an invasion from Dara."

"Is that what you want to do?"

"No!" His vehemence surprised even himself. "But I will do it if that is what you want."

"I can't tell you that," said Goztan, "because I'm not really here. You're speaking to me in your heart. I can't tell you anything you don't already know."

Disappointment struck him like a blow from a war club. He staggered but remained upright.

"Tell me what *you* want to do," said Goztan, when he had recovered.

"I . . . I want to be with Dandelion."

His mother laughed. "Besides that. I know you care about her and your friends. But what else do you want?"

He decided to tell her the thoughts he hadn't dared to say aloud before. "There are engines of peace here in Dara too, many more. I want to study them and help Ukyu-taasa. I think it's possible the arts of peace can let us live in harmony with the natives."

"How will they do that?"

"I don't know." He shook his head in frustration. "But we don't have to do as Cutanrovo advocates. Your ideas are better. They're what the pékyu-votan wanted."

He didn't voice his doubts on that last point.

"Is that why you're studying with Master Rati Yera?"

"Yes."

Goztan nodded. "We all have to do as our nature dictates. But it can take a lifetime to discover what that nature is."

He was about to ask her to explain when she held up a hand. "We don't have much time. Come, let me teach you how to play the Péa pipes."

"Why?"

"Dara is a world full of beautiful sights," his mother said. "But you must always remember that the Lyucu prize above all the voice. Life comes from breath, from speaking and listening. To play the Péa pipes well, you must first listen to your heart and sing the song that is within. The pipes amplify your inner breath much as this dream amplifies your inner doubts."

Goztan showed him how to manipulate the pilot pipe as he blew into it, almost singing into it from his throat. In real life, Kinri had seen the Péa pipes played at great festivals, though he had never tried to work them himself. But on this dream beach, he picked up the technique with little effort, almost as if he had been doing it all his life or as if the pilot pipe was a part of himself. Perhaps his first zither lesson with Dandelion helped. Music was music.

He took a deep breath and let it out, singing of his general doubts about the truth; his specific longing for home and fire pit; his thrill each time he saw Dandelion or heard her voice; his worry about

Lodan, Mati, Widow Wasu, and the Splendid Urn; his excitement as he learned about each element of Rati's machines.

As he played the pilot pipe, his mother stood to the side and pushed against the pumped-up bladder, and a powerful, magnificent music boomed from the horde. It was a bone-rattling song felt as much as heard, and he sensed his whole body vibrating in sympathy, as though he were being borne on the wings of garinafins.

The look of pleasure on his mother's face at seeing him perform seasoned his thrilling joy with melancholy and longing.

Looking down, he noticed the way the skin around the pilot pipe vibrated and changed as he pushed and pulled on the tube. The pilot pipe, being fashioned from an antler, was full of thick knobs, with thinner segments between. The skin of the bladder stretched and relaxed around the tube by turns, and the sight reminded him of the knotted rope going through the hands of the storyteller as well as the rope running between the razor-edged gears in Rati's mapping chair. . . .

### NIGHT OF THE SERVICE COMPETITION.

Kinri hurried back into the kitchen to see how things were going.

Carts lined up next to a counter filled with plates of appetizers like a queue of oxen waiting at the well for water. As each cart came to the end of the counter, it stopped. Mati greeted the cat, dog, monkey, bird, or mouse driving the cart, fed them a treat, and then examined the stack of wax tablets in the back. Each tablet showed stylized icons of the two appetizers—courtesy of Dandelion—with the customer indicating the one they preferred with a mark in the wax under the appropriate image. Mati fulfilled the order by loading the appetizers onto the cart, and then pushed it to Rati, waiting at the next station.

Here, Rati looked at the wax tablets again to see which table the order had come from, and then went to the wall behind her, where long, thick ropes dangled from nails labeled with the different table numbers.

She found the rope corresponding to the table that the order should be sent to, and then threaded one end of the rope through a hole in the side of the cart, turned a hand crank until the end of the rope emerged from the other side of the cart, and pulled it through.

The rope was full of bumps, with a few different-sized knots and many nicked notches spaced irregularly along its length. Each rope, in actuality, represented a map of the path that the cart must take to go from the kitchen to a specific table and back. Different knots represented turns in different directions, while the notches counted off turns of the wheels.

As each rope was pulled through the cart, it engaged a pair of gears pressed against the rope by springs. The notched rope served as a kind of toothed rack that turned the pair of gears, which wound the cables around the independent axles. As they passed the gears, the large knots pushed one of the gears or the other away from the resting position, which engaged levered arms that deposited pegs into the axles and toggled the direction by which the cables were wound around the axles.

In other words, the system of gears "read" the map off the rope as it was pulled through, and then encoded the instructions into cable-winding patterns on the axles.

"Looks like things are working," said a relieved Kinri. He rushed to help his master by refilling the sand bucket in the cart that revived the gravity-driven engine.

"I've been working with these carts for years, and I've never thought of making the cart teach itself by reading," said Rati, laughing. "You've already taken my invention further than my original vision."

Several days earlier, when Kinri had first proposed the idea to Rati, the old woman had been skeptical. Kinri couldn't explain everything that had led to his epiphany—it would have revealed to the Blossom Gang too much of his real identity. But his dream had given him the last pieces of the puzzle: The Lyucu shamans' memory-aid knots reminded him of the notched rope that recorded a route; the Péa pipes inspired him to imagine a mechanical opening that could be manipulated by running a series of notches and bumps through it. . . .

Instead, he had convinced the old woman with a series of models. And once the idea was proven, they had scrambled to teach Widi's carpenters to build copies of the necessary mechanism and to create the rope-maps to the different tables.

After Rati finished instructing each cart, it was sent back into the restaurant proper to bring the dishes to the ordering table. There, the cart stopped when it bumped against the table, as the bumper temporarily closed off the opening through which the sand fell. After customers unloaded the dishes from the cart and verified their order (optionally feeding the animal driver a treat), they stacked the wax tablets into the receptacle at the back of the cart to indicate that everything was in order. Unbeknownst to them, the weight of the stack of tablets activated a switch that started the flow of sand again, and the cart clattered its way back to the kitchen, ready to be instructed to go to a different table.

From time to time, the carts got stuck in grooves in the floor or bumped against each other. But Kinri, Lodan, and Dandelion were on hand to resolve these minor traffic mishaps with relative ease.

Séca went around the Splendid Urn, asking the diners for their opinions. A few of the diners expressed reservations about the fact that they had to mark down their orders for the animal servers and take the dishes off the carts on their own—and a few were unhappy over the cheeky monkey who seemed to be mocking them with impressions—but most were ecstatic over the marvelous service. They thought the cute animals added to the fun atmosphere, and rumors of the curse that supposedly had struck the Urn were forgotten.

Séca returned to the tower. Now that he had plenty of material to work with, he sounded a lot more confident as he waxed poetic about the unorthodox service at the Splendid Urn.

As the onlookers listened to Séca and admired the silkmotic candles and mechanical oxen, more sent word to their friends. The crowd outside the restaurant swelled, and Séca and Pimié soon had an audience that rivaled the one outside the Treasure Chest.

~

With looks of panic on their faces, the two *toko dawiji* told Tiphan Huto that the entrée service of the Treasure Chest was on the verge of total collapse.

It wasn't the fault of the waitstaff this time. The servers— whether they were sparrow tiles dealers, dancers, musicians, stevedores, shipping accountants, or warehouse managers in real life—got better at their new jobs as the evening went on (Tiphan's interference notwithstanding). They figured out how to take notes and work together to carry heavy trays, and the earlier chaos had subsided.

The problem was the kitchen.

Since food wasn't supposed to be the focus of the contest this time, diners at both restaurants were limited to a menu of four choices, all fine dishes that could be prepared by a moderately skilled chef. Mozo, however, claimed to be a perfectionist who found these choices too pedestrian for her tastes. During the week before the competition, she came to Tiphan multiple times with suggestions for how to elevate the dishes, vociferously advocating that he go to the judges to alter the menu.

"I am an *artist*!" said Mozo, stomping her foot like the child that she was. "I *cannot* work like this. You must explain to the judges that we must not serve common stone's ear mushrooms when we have homunculus! And why are we giving our esteemed judges monkeyberry compote when we can delight them with Lady Rapa's Feast instead?"

Tiphan tried to reason with her. "Both restaurants must cook with the same menu, my dear Mozo. Where will Widow Wasu get homunculus mushrooms? And where will you get the equipment to make that frozen cream concoction of theirs?"

"I don't care!" Mozo was now in full tantrum mode. She grabbed a plate and smashed it against the ground, making Tiphan jump. "Give them homunculus mushrooms if you have to! You have so much anyway. And you should buy the equipment for Lady Rapa's Feast from them!"

The idea of giving anything to Widow Wasu was utterly absurd.

"Come now, Mozo. This round isn't about food. Just make whatever is on the menu."

"'Just make whatever is on the menu'?" Mozo smashed another plate. "Oh I'm feeling faint. To think that *I*, a descendant of Suda Mu, am being told to throw things together in the kitchen like some army camp gruel stirrer! I . . . I think I cannot breathe. Doctor! I need a doctor! Maybe two or three!"

For a moment, he thought about forcing Mozo to comply with more threats against her family, but then he thought better of it. Why was he wasting time with trying to bring a recalcitrant chef to heel when food wasn't even important to this round? He had already gotten what he needed from Mozo with those steamed buns. . . . So he told Mozo that she wouldn't be cooking for the service round at all.

A smile flitted across Mozo's face so quickly that Tiphan wasn't sure he had seen it. But as Mozo continued to smash plates and stomp about the kitchen ("A true artist would *never* cave in to demands to do *vulgar* work. . . . I am Lurusén, striving alone in a crowd of boors. . . ."), he had a sneaking suspicion that this histrionic display was more feigned than real.

In any event, the Treasure Chest was operating tonight without its head chef. Tiphan hadn't thought this would be an issue, since the dishes on the menu didn't require, in his opinion, a great deal of skill. However, without Mozo acting as facilitator and sovereign of the kitchen, the chefs de partie refused to yield to or support one another. Each considering themselves the hegemon in Mozo's absence, they fell to war with one another like the mighty Tiro kings of old. Tempers flared and arguments erupted as the chefs fought over assistants, territories, pots and pans, even priority access to the dogs running the treadwheels for the fans.

So, while the waitstaff tried their best to placate the impatient diners with pots of tea, no entrées emerged from the kitchen. Several diners were beginning to grumble to the staff that they were thinking of heading over to the Splendid Urn.

The longer the *toko dawiji*'s explanation went on, the redder grew Tiphan Huto's face. He huffed and puffed, and turned in the direction of the kitchen, ready to launch another tirade, but the two *toko dawiji* pulled him back.

"Master Huto," one of them said. "Have you forgotten? Lolotika may be watching!"

Memory of his latest humiliation by the hostess sobered Tiphan. He might have a very high opinion of himself, but he wasn't completely blind to his own faults. Gritting his teeth, he whispered to the *toko dawiji*.

The *toko dawiji* looked at each other, shrugged, and went into the kitchen to pass on the master's orders.

Slowly, dishes began to come out of the kitchen. But customers only grew more restless.

"Hey, that table placed their order long after us. Why are they getting their food before us?"

"Waiter! Waiter! Right here . . . *Hey!* Where are you going with *our* food?"

"Where's Tiphan? Get him out here! I demand to know why six servers went by with the food I ordered as if I didn't exist!"

Lady Cophy, the co-hostess, stopped one of the waiters. "Why are customers being served out of order? I saw that table by the stairs place their order first."

"I was told to serve that table by the window first," said the waiter. "I just work here. Whatever Master Huto wants, he gets, right?"

Lady Cophy returned to Lolo to share her findings. Lolo climbed up the tower and peeked in at each floor. It was true: Only the tables in the upper floors and near the windows were being served. She squinted and recognized some of the patrons seated near the windows.

With rising indignation, Lolo realized what was happening.

Tiphan had told the *toko dawiji* to prioritize the orders of the people on a certain list. Although the identities of the judges for this round were supposed to be a secret, Tiphan must have bribed one of Lolo's or Séca's servants to steal that particular list ahead of time.

This was such a blatant violation of the rules of fair play that it took Lolo a few seconds to recover her breath. Her instinct was to shout about the cheating from the top of the tower . . . but a moment's reflection stopped her. She had only suspicion, not proof. If she confronted him now, he would surely seize the opportunity to claim that Lolo was working with Widow Wasu. Since she couldn't prove the accusation, the result would be disrepute for both the Splendid Urn and the Aviary.

She had to swallow her knowledge of Tiphan's treachery and pretend everything was fine. The show had to go on.

Hidden behind a window curtain, Tiphan took in Lolo's looks of shock, rage, and eventual resignation. He chuckled to himself.

"Business is war," he muttered. "'Know thy enemy,' as Marshal Mazoti would say." Tiphan thought of himself as a man of many talents, including warfare, and he enjoyed deploying martial language when handling battle-like scenarios such as berating employees, plotting the destruction of competitors, and counting money.

He had indeed obtained the list of judges from one of Séca's servants with a bribe—a pity that even a government researcher like Séca Thu couldn't afford to pay his servants enough to place them beyond temptation, which just went to show that it was better to be a clever man of business than a bookworm.

With the list in hand, Tiphan had been able to devise a seating chart that placed the judges at tables with the best views and the best airflow, a subtle attempt to gain the Treasure Chest an advantage. The manipulation had been discreet because Tiphan didn't want to make the cheating too obvious. Now, however, the situation had turned desperate, and Tiphan had made the decision to serve the judges first. After all, the Splendid Urn had, during the last round, tried to appeal to the judges by setting up those flamethrowers that they could play with; Tiphan thought it was only fair that he would now get a chance to appeal to the judges directly by giving them special treatment.

He was also prepared for the customer complaints that would follow this favoritism. The *toko dawiji* went to the waiters and waitresses waiting around for their orders and explained Master Huto's new orders.

"Master Huto says that—um." One of the *toko dawiji* paused, embarrassed by what he was about to say. "Let me just quote him:

'Giggle, touch their arms, offer to massage their backs, lean over their tables—do whatever you have to do to take the customers' minds off the food.'"

"You mean you want us to flirt with the patrons," said one of the waiters, a handsome dock foreman. He pursed his lips in disgust. "I have a husband and two kids! I'm *not* doing any of that."

"Look, I'm not opposed to the idea of entertaining the hungry customers," said the waitress who was a sparrow tiles dealer. "But if I wanted to work in an indigo house, I would have asked for a *lot* more money. I noticed that Tiphan hasn't actually brought in anyone from an indigo house, probably because he's too cheap."

"Aren't you ashamed of yourselves?" a waitress who was a dress-maker in one of the Huto clan's shops asked the *toko dawiji*. "And how is this a good idea? My customers are here with their families. If I did as Tiphan demanded, there would be distractions all right, just not the kind he wanted."

"We're just repeating what he told us," protested the other *toko dawiji*. "I don't like this any more than you do. But even we've been told to do the same."

"Well, he can forget it," said the sparrow tiles dealer. "If he really likes flirting so much, let him come out here and do a striptease. I guarantee you customers will lose their appetites, and then they won't demand their food. Problem solved."

"He says if you don't distract the customers, he's going to fire the lot of you," said the *toko dawiji*.

"Fine by me. I'm not a waitress anyway."

"No, from your real jobs! And he says he'll go to the magistrates in your cities and accuse you of being thieves."

The waitstaff sobered at this threat.

"I *hate* that man," said the dock foreman.

"We'll distract the customers," said the sparrow tiles dealer, throwing a contemptuous glance in the direction of the hidden Tiphan Huto. "But we'll do this *our* way."

The waiters and waitresses went out among the foodless tables. Some offered to host a game of sparrow tiles at the table while the diners were waiting for their meals. Some gave tips on the latest fashion trends in the Harmonious City. Some told stories about the strangest goods they had seen being shipped into the docks of Dimushi.

"I'm no good at any of that," said one of the waiters, a good-looking boy who was so shy that he looked nervous even saying that much.

"Then ask your customers what they do and what they're most proud of," said the sparrow tiles dealer. "And sympathize if they complain about their work. There's nothing people love more than talking about themselves."

As conversation and laughter filled the Treasure Chest, Tiphan Huto, peeking at the scene from a service hallway, nodded in satisfaction.

"Looks like the friendly staff at the Treasure Chest is having a positive effect on the diners," announced Lolo from her perch up in the tower outside the restaurant. "As the ancient poets said, 'Conversation is the best spice for a good meal.'"

"See, I knew it would work," Tiphan muttered to himself. "I amaze myself sometimes. Such command of the developing battle-field! Such resolution in the face of adversity! Such knowledge of strategyration and tacticalisthenics! I am the very model of a modern managerial maestro—"

And that was when he was interrupted by messengers he had dispatched to the Splendid Urn to observe the competition. As they whispered into his ears about what was happening there, his face changed.

He left for the backyard, muttering to himself, "So Widow Wasu has some tricks up her sleeves, after all. We'll see about that."

Séca and Pimié moved into the Splendid Urn's kitchen to gather material for their commentary.

To the two observers, Rati Yera's "teaching" of the carts appeared as no more than a way to impel motive force to the carts, perhaps through a kind of wind-up mechanism. Séca was sure more was involved in these self-driving carts, but no matter how he probed and pried, Rati Yera smiled and pointed at the animal drivers.

"Sorry," she said at length. "I've got a whole furry and feathered team to run. Maybe you can focus on the cooking instead."

Indeed, the cooks did present a much more exciting sight. Mati had at her command only the kitchen boy Munapo and the scullery maid Ruthé, but the whole kitchen bustled as though there were twenty people working in it.

That was because the kitchen had been rearranged into twenty identical workstations: chopping block, stove, oven, mixing bowls, kneading boards. Every vessel or board was fixed in place, on supporting blocks with nails and clamps. A series of crisscrossing beams hung overhead, to which were affixed pulleys, levers, gears, and dangling wooden arms. Attached to the ends of the arms were various implements like cleavers, paddles, pot covers, spatulas, and so on. Once again, Lutuma and his crew had come through.

Mati stood at the head station and guided the knife held in a mechanical hand—the way a parent would teach a child to cook—as she chopped a winter melon into equal-sized chunks. The motion of the cleaver she guided was transmitted up the mechanical arm into the beam overhead, and through a series of gears and strings, replicated by the nineteen other cleavers held in nineteen other mechanical hands, against nineteen other winter melons (carefully picked to be of equal size) lying on nineteen other chopping blocks.

She was the puppet master for twenty puppets moving in sync. When she chopped, twenty knifes hacked. When she lifted a lid, twenty lids released steam. When she stirred, twenty spoons twirled.

The kitchen boy and the scullery maid ran between the stations, handling tasks that were simply too complicated for the mechanical hands to replicate: laying out ingredients, picking out wilted pipe scallions, cleaning up the inevitable mess when Mati moved too fast and the mechanical arms couldn't quite keep up.

"More magic!" exclaimed Pimié.

"The principles on display here are ancient," said Rati Yera. She addressed herself to Séca. "I'm sure you've seen something similar when you were at the academy. Did you ever take a class in architecture, where you had to enlarge a smaller drawing? You probably used a 'copying machine,' said to have been invented by Na Moji. It's a mechanical linkage between a tracing brush that you guide over the lines on an existing drawing and an inking brush that produces a bigger version of the drawing on another sheet of paper."

"I do recall such a machine," said Séca. "But the scale of this . . . is beyond imagining."

"Oh, anything that can be imagined can be reduced to practice with enough effort," said Rati Yera. "This is also the same technique used by street performers in Boama to demonstrate the veil dance with one dancer and a dozen mechanical puppets all copying her movements in perfect synchrony."

"She makes it sound so easy," grumbled Mati as she continued working. "I've had to practically break my brain to reduce the recipes down to a series of clear steps with simple motions so that the mindless mechanical drudges can keep up. It's such an unnatural way to think! But this was the only way to cook all the entrées as we're so short-staffed."

"What did I tell you?" declared Rati with pride. "Anything you can do, my machines can be taught to do. The trick is to decompose your motion into its most basic constituent pieces."

The Splendid Urn was having one of the best dinner services in memory. Carts shuttled back and forth between the tables like fantastic carriages in a city where animals had gained intelligence. The silkmotic candles produced a cool and bright light that enveloped everything in a dreamlike, romantic haze. Dandelion and Kinri went between the tables to take care of customer needs that the carts couldn't handle. Widow Wasu happily went from table to table, asking after the well-being of the customers and telling funny stories.

The judges struggled to come up with enough superlatives in their heads to describe this most unreal dining experience later to their colleagues at the other restaurant.

As Kinri brushed by Dandelion, he said, "You holding up all right?"

"Better than all right. I never get to have this much fun at home! Widi, Mota, and Arona are missing the best part."

"Let's hope they were just paranoid and don't have to do anything."

"I hope they end up doing exactly what they proposed to do."

A carriage rattled through the heart of Ginpen, keeping to small streets and dark alleys, winding its way toward the Splendid Urn.

Inside the carriage, Tiphan Huto muttered to himself angrily. From time to time, he poked his head out of the window and told the driver to go faster.

Suddenly, the driver of the carriage, Manager Giphi, pulled on the reins. The horses whinnied, and Tiphan almost tumbled out of his seat.

"What's wrong with you?" he growled.

"There's a roadblock," said Giphi.

Tiphan stuck his head out of the window, and sure enough, there was a barricade in the middle of the street. A tall and broad-shouldered soldier stood behind it, holding up a hand.

"Err, Captain, what's going on?" asked Giphi carefully.

"A routine security check," said the soldier. "The magistrate wants to put a stop to the random disappearances of Ginpen's citizens. Step out of the carriage, please."

"We're in a hurry," said Giphi. "Is there any way . . ." He got down from the driver's seat, reached into his sleeves for his money purse, and approached the soldier. "Wait . . . Don't I know you?"

Mota swore to himself under his breath. To save time, Arona had simply reused the makeup from the spying mission to the Treasure Chest for both Mota and Widi. They hadn't counted on meeting Giphi, who had spent the most time with "Circuit Intendant Suti" and her retinue.

Widi emerged from behind the barricade. "Ah, it's you!"

"Master Diwi!" said a surprised Giphi. "Why are you dressed like a soldier as well? Has Magistrate Zuda pressed his clerks into traffic inspection duty?"

Widi laughed awkwardly. "Er—"

Arona, also dressed as a soldier, stepped out from behind the barricade. "Circuit Intendant Suti asked that we investigate potential corruption in the army. So we're embedding ourselves in the garrison as they perform their duties around the city."

"Exactly," said Widi, nodding vigorously. Then he approached Giphi and winked. "The things we have to do while the bosses drink tea and take naps, eh?"

Giphi took note of the furtive glances between the three soldiers. But at Diwi's ingratiating wink, he relaxed. Most likely, he guessed that the three low-level officials had set up an unauthorized checkpoint to extort bribes from passing merchants. While Empress Jia paid the Imperial bureaucracy well and the layers of mutual monitoring by the College of Advocates and the system of circuit intendants prevented most corruption, low-level members of the bureaucrats' private staffs, like Diwi the clerk and Circuit Intendant Suti's maid and bodyguard, probably *would* scheme to make some extra cash by abusing their power.

If reported to Magistrate Zuda, all three would be in big trouble. But Tiphan Huto was in a hurry and didn't want more delays. Giphi went back to his master and explained the situation.

"You say they work for the circuit intendant?"

Giphi nodded. "I know that clerk, Diwi, well."

Tiphan looked thoughtful for a moment. "Pay whatever toll these three clowns demand so we can be on our way."

Giphi went back and discreetly held out the money purse. But to his surprise, Widi refused to take it. "We *have* to inspect the carriage. Not that we don't trust Master Huto, but orders are orders."

Giphi was about to argue more when Tiphan Huto climbed out of the carriage. "Let them inspect."

Widi climbed into the carriage and began to look around. He wrinkled his nose at a strong stench. The odor evidently came from several covered buckets in the back of the carriage.

"What are in these?" Widi asked.

"Just some . . . unclean things," said Tiphan, standing next to the carriage and looking in. "I have a sick child at home, and I wanted to get rid of the vomit and excrement somewhere outside the city to avoid contaminating the water supply."

"That's very civic-minded of you," said Widi. He climbed deeper into the carriage, toward the covered buckets.

"Wait!" cried out Tiphan Huto. "You don't want to open those!" He clambered into the carriage after Widi.

Widi pulled the cover off one of the buckets.

The overwhelming odor made him gag, but in that moment he also realized what he was smelling—it was a stench he had encountered thrice before: in the cellar of the Treasure Chest, beyond a sealed door; in an alley near the Splendid Urn, the day after everyone fell sick; and at the Temple of Fithowéo, where the monks kept a few of the god's *pawi*.

He was smelling the urine of wolves.

"That's it!" he cried out. "We have the proof!"

At that moment, Tiphan Huto also exploded into motion. He pushed Widi aside, grabbed one of the buckets and a ladle, and scrambled out of the carriage. Before anyone could react, he tossed ladlefuls of the foul liquid toward the other two soldiers. When Widi climbed out after Tiphan, Tiphan treated him to the same fragrant shower.

Arona screamed, Widi gagged, and Mota cursed. Taken by surprise, all three were drenched in the fetid liquid. They hurried to wipe their noses and mouths with their sleeves to avoid having to swallow any of the urine.

The makeup also came off their faces.

"Just as I thought," said Tiphan Huto coldly. "Who are you? I've seen at least one of you working for Widow Wasu."

The conversation between Giphi and Widi earlier had aroused his suspicion. The story they told of being embedded with the garrison, which happened to be setting up checkpoints around the city, made no sense at all. If Magistrate Zuda, spooked by the disappearing craftspeople, really were setting up security checkpoints, Tiphan would have heard something about it. Also, there was something unnatural about the way the three kept looking at one another. He had been on guard the whole time.

"We do work for Widow Wasu," said Widi, realizing there was no longer any point to keeping up the pretense. "And now we know everything about your little plot against the Splendid Urn. Not only will the judges for the competition force you to forfeit, but Magistrate Zuda will also enjoy hearing about all the ways you've endangered public health."

"I don't know what you're talking about," said Tiphan.

"Using predator pee is how you were able to drive all the rats in the neighborhood into a frenzy around the Splendid Urn," said Widi. "We used animals in dinner service tonight at the Splendid Urn for two reasons. One is because they're cute and add to the atmosphere, but the other is to act as bait. We figured that once you heard about our success, you'd try to sabotage it. Of all the tricks you've used, panicking animals with wolf urine is the easiest to replicate, and we've caught you red-handed."

"You have no proof for anything," said Tiphan. "A bucket of pee? Maybe I used it to keep the Treasure Chest rat-free."

"That's not all the evidence we have," said Widi. "The *raye* gang who empty the night soil from your toilets will tell Magistrate Zuda that they had to get rid of buckets of dog shit from your premises on the day when the feral dogs disturbed the customers at the Splendid Urn. You caught the dogs and kept them there."

Tiphan flinched but he said nothing.

"The doctors on Coconut Lane will also testify that on the night when the parasol tree in front of the Splendid Urn was covered by caterpillars, they had to treat several workers from the Treasure Chest for caterpillar rashes, the exact same rash that the workers we hired to get rid of caterpillars contracted."

Tiphan continued to look defiant.

"All of this, added together, will be enough to convince the magistrate that there's probable cause to search the Treasure Chest. Who knows what they'll find there?"

Tiphan's face ran through a range of emotions: shock, embarrassment, fear, and then, a nasty grin.

"You've clearly been doing a lot of work to entrap me. But this is all circumstantial, and competition is no crime. In competition, people get hurt and businesses get shuttered. Why would the magistrate be interested?"

"Not when the competition is unfair," said Widi. "Prime Minister Cogo Yelu's pronouncements are clear. Even though competition among businesses is encouraged, techniques that rely on fraud or deceit, or threaten the public health, are against the law. I think you'll have a fine time trying to explain all this to Magistrate Zuda."

"Ah, you've clearly seen too many folk plays about paid litigators. But you've forgotten one thing: No convicted felon can testify against a gentleman of good reputation."

"We're not felons," said Arona, looking perplexed.

"Oh, but you will be, when I report to Magistrate Zuda that you've been impersonating Imperial officials and members of the city garrison."

Arona, Widi, and Mota looked at one another, dismayed. Tiphan was right. They had indeed been caught doing something much worse in the eyes of officialdom.

"I'm sorry," whispered Arona to Widi and Mota. "I shouldn't have been lazy about the disguises."

Mota sighed and said nothing.

"The best thing, it seems," said Widi to Tiphan, "is for both of us to head back the way we came. You won't bother the Urn tonight, and we won't go to the magistrate."

Tiphan laughed. "You have a deal. But even with your little circus performance, I'm sure the Treasure Chest will come out on top."

As Tiphan's carriage clattered away, Arona made sure that Mota wasn't within hearing and turned to Widi, whispering, "Maybe it's time for us to invoke our secret weapon. You know, *her*."

Widi shook his head. "Not yet. We'll save her for another occasion. Remember where we ultimately want to go."

As the night wore on, the chefs de partie at the Treasure Chest achieved a temporary truce in their contest for territory and dominance. But the dishes were still coming out slower than expected.

The waitstaff's efforts at entertaining the hungry diners flagged, as there were only so many rounds of sparrow tiles you could play and so many stories that you could tell before growling stomachs could no longer be ignored.

Servants from some of the more prominent families ran into the restaurant and discreetly whispered into the ears of their masters and mistresses. Soon, diners were getting up and demanding the bill.

"Why be in such a hurry?" asked Giphi, his habitual ingratiating smile even more cloying than usual. He did try to stand a little farther away from the customers than usual. Though he had changed his outfit from head to toe, he couldn't get rid of the feeling that the scent of wolf urine spilled onto his robe lingered on his person.

"Err . . . I'm told that there are marvels at the Splendid Urn that I should see before they finish for the night."

Tiphan gritted his teeth. Still, he was confident of victory because the judges on the list he had obtained from Séca's servant were being taken care of. He even made sure they got free extra portions, taking from the food meant for the other patrons.

By the time the evening came to an end, the crowd outside both restaurants had grown tenfold. The streets and nearby park lots were packed. Carriages from all over Ginpen streamed to and fro between the two competitors to take in the handsome waitstaff and the opulence of the Treasure Chest as well as the ingenious mechanical contrivances that allowed a tiny staff to serve a full house at the Splendid Urn.

As diners finished at the Treasure Chest, Lady Cophy and Lolo went around to hand out small boxes filled with pebbles of different colors. Over at the Splendid Urn, on the other hand, Séca and Pimié decided to ask Lodan to distribute the voting pebbles with the magical carts. The diners were delighted to have another chance at seeing the cute animals parade around on their vehicles.

"When you leave, you'll see Lolo with a jar by the door," said Lady Cophy. "Drop in a red pebble if you think the service tonight was top-rate, a white one if you think it was lacking, and a blue one if you think it was just all right. Patrons who already left will be deemed to have deposited a white pebble."

After watching patrons dropping pebbles into Lolo's jar for a while, Tiphan Huto could no longer hold himself back. He went up to Lolo and whispered, "How will you and Séca tell the winner?"

Lolo looked at him, a smirk on her face. "Why, Master Huto,

we're going to get together, sort the pebbles in each jar by color, and then count them."

"Are the pebbles given to the judges marked in some way? Is that how you'll tell the votes that matter apart from the votes that don't?"

Lolo looked at him, her grin growing wider. "All the votes matter, Master Huto. Whatever gave you the idea that we were only going to count *some* of the votes? The secret to this round's panel is that all the patrons are judges."

"But . . . but . . . but I got that list from Séca's servant—" Tiphan couldn't help himself. His face grew red at the thought that he might have been fooled.

"A list? Do you mean the list with 'Judges' at the top?"

Tiphan just stared at her.

"That is a list of people Séca and I want to talk to about starting a dining club next month. We are going to call it 'The Judges.'"

"A . . . a dining club?"

"Yes! Would you like to join? Since this restaurant competition is such a success, we're thinking of making it a regular thing in Ginpen. You do have to pay a membership fee—"

Tiphan turned and left in a huff without hearing the end of her speech, much less the peals of her laughter. The notion that he had been bested on the business battlefield by an indigo-house girl was absolutely intolerable.

The Splendid Urn's victory in the second round was overwhelming. Whereas its jar looked like it was full of ripe monkeyberries, the Treasure Chest's jar looked like it was filled with lotus seeds.

Tiphan Huto fell sick from the humiliation. When he finally managed to get out of bed a few days later, he proposed the subject for the third and decisive round of the competition, something that no Best Restaurant in Ginpen could be without: entertainment.

# CHAPTER FORTY-THREE

# THE SEA OF TEARS

THE SALT FLATS SOUTH OF THE SEA OF TEARS,
UKYU-GONDÉ: THE TWELFTH MONTH IN THE
EIGHTH YEAR AFTER THE DEPARTURE OF
PRINCESS THÉRA FROM DARA FOR UKYU-GONDÉ
(SEVENTEEN MONTHS UNTIL THE LYUCU MUST
LAUNCH THEIR NEW INVASION FLEET TO DARA).

The two garinafins flew through the night. By the time the sun rose, the land below them was pure white, as though covered by snow.

They were in the wasteland south of the Sea of Tears. It was said that the great salt lake had once been far bigger in extent, and as it shrank, the retreating water left behind a salt-encrusted landscape in which few things grew.

Sataari and Razutana guided the two garinafins to land near a small hill, though perhaps it would be more accurate to say that Razutana's mount guided the pilot rather than the other way around. In the lee of the hill, once an island in the salt lake, they released the children from their netting.

The two adults coaxed the garinafins under a shallow overhang so that they couldn't be spotted from the air. Then they directed the children to gather the sparse, feathery tumble fern, the only vegetation hardy enough to subsist in the salty soil, as garinafin feed.

Normally, in the scrublands, garinafins could graze on just about any cactus and bush, no matter how adorned with protective thorns, by singeing off the barbs with fire breath, but there was literally nothing here for them except salt and the wispy fern that provided little nourishment. They would not be able to last long in this wasteland, but there wasn't much the refugees could do about the situation.

Tanto worked alongside the other children, but his heart was full of rage and confusion. He went up to Razutana.

"Can I ask you a question?"

The scholar paused. "Of course."

"Did Toof and Radia really mean to let us go?"

"Yes."

"Why now?"

Razutana looked thoughtful. "They had to find a way to get us away from Cudyu's main forces before helping us escape. This maximizes our chances to get far away before the Lyucu come after us."

"I don't mean that! I mean . . . why did they change their minds?"

"They didn't change their minds. This was their plan all along." The scholar sighed. "It's incredibly risky. If their plot is discovered, they'll surely be killed."

"But . . . but then why did they betray us to Cudyu in the first place?"

Razutana looked at him and softened his tone. "To save your parents."

"What?"

"Look at all of us," said Razutana, sweeping his arm around. "Sataari and I are useless in a fight, and the rest of you are children. If we had escaped with your parents and their fighters, we'd be nothing but burdens slowing them down and consuming their supplies."

Tanto wanted to protest, but he knew that Razutana was right.

"The princess, your mother, is a great leader," said Razutana. He paused and sighed again. "But she lacks your grandfather's ability to be ruthless when necessary. She would never have left any of us behind, and that would have meant certain death for all. Toof and Radia had no choice but to take us away from her."

Tanto wanted to find some way, any way, to allow himself to continue to hate the two. "They killed Vara!"

"It was an accident. I was closest to the struggle on Ratopé, and I heard Toof yell for Vara to yield. 'We have a plan,' he said. But she kept fighting and there was no time to explain."

"But . . . they also told Cudyu to have us sacrificed to the gods!"

"It was a gamble they had to make. They needed to keep you alive without revealing your identity. Your granduncle Volyu often said that Cudyu was suspicious by nature. He wouldn't have trusted two Lyucu captives who had lived with the Agon and the Dara for so long. If Toof and Radia had begged him to keep you alive, he would have naturally suspected a plot and decided that the safer thing was to have you killed. By advocating that you be killed immediately, on the other hand, Toof and Radia pushed Cudyu into thinking that it was more prudent to keep you alive, at least for a while, until he figured out who you were."

"Why couldn't they have just told us their plan ahead of time?"

"Because if you knew, you wouldn't have been able to convincingly show your hatred for them in front of the Lyucu pékyu. This was the only way to get you to play your part, to assuage Cudyu's doubts."

Tanto was silent with shame. He thought of himself as a brave fighter like his father and a great leader like his mother. To be treated as a burden, a mere child who had to be left behind and deceived into doing the right thing . . . he didn't have the words for how he felt.

"Staying alive right now is the best thing you can do to help your parents," said Razutana gently.

Tanto nodded, but he vowed to do more to change their fate as soon as he found a chance. He was a pékyu-taasa of the Agon people, and he would not be denied the chance to prove his mettle.

Two large rivers fed into the Sea of Tears. One, the Blood River, began in the hills just north of Lurodia Tanta and flowed northwest into the southern shore of the giant salt lake. The river was so named for its reddish water, which had to be left to settle and then filtered before it could be drunk. The color was likely the result of the ochre silt in the hills.

The second river, called the Ghost River, came out of the Foot Range (also known as the Wing among the Agon) and entered the lake (generally) in the east. The river's bed was so shallow that its course changed unpredictably. Some years, when the spring melt was inadequate, the river even dried up altogether.

Because of its unpredictable nature, few tribes relied on the Ghost River as a source of water, but its ephemeral course wasn't the reason for the river's ominous name.

By sleeping during the day—with the garinafins concealed in whatever camouflage was on hand—and flying during the night, the group of escapees gradually made their way east and north, away from the Blood River.

Heading into the heart of the salt flats made pursuit less likely, but at the same time, it also made it harder to find water and food. The bone-chilling cold didn't help. The riders shivered practically every moment they were awake, buffeted by the constant wintry wind.

The salt-stained landscape below was so white that it sometimes seemed as though they were tiny flies cruising above a gigantic vat of milk, or the stretched vellum skin atop the cactus drums for storytelling dances before any colored dust had been scattered over it. The monotonous view was beautiful in an austere way, but it also made the riders and their two mounts anxious. Since nothing changed, it was as if they were making no progress at all.

Food and water both ran low.

Sataari allowed her mount to pick the direction now, hoping that the garinafins would, by instinct, fly them to a source of potable water.

On the evening of the fifth day after their escape, something new appeared in the endless white earth: tiny dots, medium squares, triangles that resembled shark's teeth, big circles with spiraling arms that seemed to stretch all the way to the horizon.

Each of the geometric shapes, ochre red, earthen brown, charcoal black, and dark clay gray, was composed from piles of rocks carefully placed in the empty landscape. Together, they formed gigantic images: birds, fish, beasts, humans, and strange structures that even Sataari, who had been memorizing lore since she was a little girl, had never seen in a voice painting or heard in a storytelling dance.

But the shapes could only be grasped and comprehended from high up in the air. The amount of labor and organization that would be required to construct them was unimaginable. This could not have been the work of a single tribe. Even if the Pékyu of the Lyucu had conceived of such a vision, it would have taken generations of backbreaking labor to construct it.

The riders fell silent with awe, and even the garinafins seemed stunned. They hesitated and circled in the air at the edge of the gigantic designs, refusing to cross into the air above them.

Sataari sighed and signaled for the garinafins to land.

"What are these things?" asked Razutana. He was staring at a pile of red rocks twice his height and as wide as the biggest tent back in Kiri Valley. It was the eye of a single bird in the grand design, and not even a very big bird by comparison with the rest.

Sataari seemed not to hear his question. "The garinafins will go no farther, and we should be safe from pursuit beyond this point. Let them go. We could make the water last longer if we didn't have to share it with the beasts also."

They watched as the two passengerless garinafins took off and headed south. Whether they would be able to make their way out of the salt flats before they fell from the sky, mad with thirst, was something that the refugees would never know.

Sataari pointed north, and the group began to march through the landscape of fantastic stone piles and walls, mere ants in a gigantic painting.

"Where are we going?" asked Nalu, Gozofin's son and Tanto's close friend.

Sataari made no response but simply trudged on.

The mounds first rose in the distance like outsized prairie voles poking out of their holes.

As they continued to march, the mounds grew steadily, until they became small mountains that loomed in their way, stretching from horizon to horizon. Even in the middle of winter, it was obvious that there was something odd about this region. Though much of the salt flats was inhospitable to any form of life, between the mounds could be seen the husks of leafless shrubs as well as a carpet of dry, dead grass and leaves.

"Hey, we could take shelter in those hills!" said Razutana. "And there's the lake!"

After many days through the salt flats, they had finally reached the shore of the inland sea, which lay just west of the mounds. Just the thought of building a shelter against the relentless cold wind and nestling in a blanket of soft, dry hay was enough to get the children to quicken their steps.

But Sataari stopped, gazed at the mounds, and knelt down.

Razutana and the children looked at her, confused. For the first time that they could remember, they saw fear in the young shaman's eyes.

Sataari closed her eyes and began to pray, rocking back and forth rhythmically. Though the children didn't understand what she was doing, they stopped and knelt along with her.

The young shaman took out a set of bone tiles from a leather pouch and scattered them on the ground. She stared at them intently, muttering to herself. Then she got up, unsheathed her bone knife, and sliced it decisively across her left palm. Instantly, the cut filled with blood, and bright red drops fell onto the white, salted ground.

Tanto cried out in alarm and tried to get up to rush to her aid, but the young shaman held out her right hand in warning and shook her head without speaking, indicating with her eyes that the pékyu-taasa was to remain still.

The young shaman chanted and danced around the group. As she passed each kneeling figure, she pressed her bloody left hand against their face, leaving behind a smeared streak of blood.

She did this three times around the group, painting three bloody streaks across the forehead, nose, and chin of each person.

Some of the other children, finally realizing where they were, began to sob quietly. They lowered their heads and began to pray.

Razutana, Tanto, and Rokiri looked at one another, confused and more than a little frightened.

After Sataari had completed her three rounds, she knelt down again and prayed some more. She pressed her wounded hand against the salted ground and winced as the salt stung her. Gradually, the white earth around her hand turned into a dark patch of crimson.

Finally, she opened her eyes and looked at Razutana and the two pékyus-taasa.

"Where are we?" asked Razutana in a hushed voice.

"Taten-ryo-alvovo," said Sataari. *The City of Ghosts.* "The Every-Mother demands that we survive winter in this forbidden place—it's up to us to see how many of us will make it."

# CHAPTER FORTY-FOUR

# THE THIRD CONTEST

Mota was falling.

Above him, the silk-clad frame of the Imperial airship *Spirit of Kiji* was in flames. The burning wreckage buckled and undulated gently in the air, covering half the sky like a crimson sail, like clouds at sunset, like the war cape of the Hegemon flapping in the cold wind as he made his last stand by the seashore opposite Tunoa, the homeland he would never return to.

Mota fell faster. The sound of the wind whipping by filled his ears.

*How can something so beautiful die?* thought Mota. His heart clenched, not because he was about to perish, but because victory had yet to be won.

A dark shadow interposed itself between the fiery wreckage and his eyes: a sleek, serpentine neck and tail, two large triangular wings like the fins of a skate gliding over the bloodred coral reef that was the doomed *Spirit of Kiji*. And another. And yet another.

The garinafins, he remembered. The garinafins had destroyed the ship and killed Captain Atamu. He and his fellow aviators were supposed to stop the garinafins from assaulting Dara, and they had failed.

His perspective shifted vertiginously as his body turned and the sea swung into view. Below him were other figures also plummeting through the air, plunging toward the sea as their arms and legs flapped helplessly, unable to slow their descent.

The voices of his comrades came to his mind.

> The Four Placid Seas are as wide as the years are long.
> A wild goose flies over a pond, leaving behind a voice in the
>     wind.
> A man passes through this world, leaving behind a name.

"Captain, do you think they'll remember us in the future like they remember the Hegemon?"

"Probably not. Most soldiers who die are quickly forgotten. But we don't fight to leave a name; we fight because it's the right thing to do."

The garinafins swooped through the air, slicing apart the tumbling women and men with their talons or skewering them on their menacing antlers. Many screams were cut off abruptly.

Mota howled with rage. He waved his arms and kicked, as though trying to swim in this all-too-thin medium, but gravity didn't relent. They did not deserve to die this way. They should die with their feet planted on the ground, staring into the faces of their enemies, weapons in hand. Like the Hegemon. Like the heroes of old.

The sea was so much closer now. He closed his eyes. His would not be a heroic death; his would be a death full of regrets.

Abruptly, something powerful slammed against his torso and halted his fall. His organs felt in disarray, flung against his rib cage and spine. His head and legs throbbed in agony, having come close to being ripped off. His arms were pinned against his sides by shackles that squeezed and tightened. Overwhelming waves of pain stunned him.

By the time he recovered, he was looking into the malevolent eyes of a garinafin. The giant beast turned slowly in the air, its wings blocking out all light. Its talons wrapped around his body like iron hoops, and he couldn't breathe. He was sure several ribs or worse were broken.

The garinafin pulled him closer for a good look, like a cat wanting to play with a mouse.

He squirmed and twisted, until he managed to free one arm, which shot straight for the short sword at his hip. A searing stab of pain from his ribs almost made him black out. But finally, he pulled the weapon out of its sheath and slashed against the talons locked around his torso. He knew it would be useless, like an ant trying to sting a man who had pinched it between his fingers. But he didn't care.

The talons tightened in response, and the tips of the sharp claws dug into his back, slicing through muscle and sinew like a set of butchering axes. He opened his mouth to scream, but nothing came out because his lungs had no air. The sword dropped from his grasp. His vision narrowed to a tunnel as he teetered on the verge of consciousness.

The beast's eyes loomed closer, but he didn't look away. He couldn't punch, kick, scream, spit, speak, or show defiance in any other way except by fighting to stay conscious so he could stare back into those eyes.

*I do not surrender*, he screamed in his mind. *I do not yield.*

Mota started awake, drenched in sweat and gasping for breath.

Arona held him. He was too big and heavy for her to lift his head into her lap, so she was curled up against him, her face pressed against his cheek, her cool hands resting soothingly against his temples.

She did not speak. Neither did he. This was an old nightmare, and she knew that he didn't like to talk about it.

On that fateful day in Zathin Gulf, Mota had been one of the few survivors of the destroyed airships. He had lost consciousness when the garinafin finally let go of his broken body, and it was only out of sheer luck that a mangled spar had kept him afloat long enough for rescuers to pluck him out of a sea filled with the carcasses of exploded garinafins and the bodies of dead airship crew.

He, like the other survivors of the Battle of Zathin Gulf, didn't become a hero.

At first, it was a matter of choice. He refused the offer of the captain of the ship that had rescued him to bring him to Admiral Than Carucono, claiming that he felt too weak from his injuries. In truth, what he felt was a complicated tangle that festered: guilt, self-loathing, shame. The looks of admiration and the reverent manner in which sailors spoke to him made him avert his eyes, his cheeks burning. He was not braver than Captain Atamu. He had not done more than his crewmates. Had he survived because he didn't fight hard enough? Was he alive because the gods had found him unworthy to be invited to join the Hegemon and the heroes of old?

And after all, why should the survivors of the destroyed airships be treated as heroes? They weren't responsible for defeating the Lyucu. Based on the accounts of the sailors later, it had been the Marshal who confronted Pékyu Tenryo and bested him in personal combat. She had stood at the prow of the Lyucu flagship after killing their leader and waved the banner of Dara to rally the fleet into one final assault that drove back the invaders.

Having given all she had to defend the people of Dara, the Marshal had then passed beyond the River-on-Which-Nothing-Floats.

But the Lyucu were still there on Rui and Dasu, still waiting to invade. Their garinafins grew stronger by the day, craving for a chance to do to all what they had done to him and his dead comrades.

"Dandelions are blooming everywhere," said Arona. "Can you see the drifting seeds? They always remind me of jellyfish swimming through the air." She ran her hands gently across his back, not shying away from the ugly, deep scars there.

Still curled on his side and shivering, he opened his eyes and looked beyond the window. It was true. White tufts gently floated through the breeze, as carefree as children at play.

Her voice calmed him. She knew that talking about the present, about the everyday beauty of the world, about the reality of living breathing moving eating, was what he needed in moments like this.

He didn't answer, but simply wrapped an arm around her, resting one of his strong, broad hands against her back.

The Battle of Zathin Gulf was not a victory, at least not for Mota. He wasn't a hero like his comrades, like Captain Atamu, like Marshal

Mazoti. They had stopped the Lyucu onslaught by paying the ultimate price, while he had been deemed too cowardly for even a garinafin to finish him properly. Guilt racked him every waking moment. He was content to be discharged, to take the last of his wages and fade into obscurity.

Like the Hegemon, who had refused to go home to Tunoa because he couldn't bear the shame of facing the elders, widows, and orphans who had entrusted their sons, husbands, and fathers to him, Mota couldn't bear the thought of going home to Tunoa and having to explain why he had survived. He decided to wander the Islands, entertaining patrons at markets with feats of physical strength. *It's all I'm good for,* he thought. *A clown, a brute, a failure.*

But though the aspen wished to stand still, the wind didn't stop. The aftermath of the war shocked him. A peace treaty was signed. The new Empress Üna, Emperor Ragin's daughter and chosen successor, led an assault against the Lyucu reinforcements coming through the Wall of Storms. She died in the attempt, though the Wall defeated the reinforcements as well.

And then it seemed that everyone was in a hurry to forget about the war, to forget about Rui and Dasu, to forget about how Emperor Ragin, Marshal Mazoti, and Empress Üna had died. The humiliating peace treaty, which required Dara to pay the Lyucu tribute every season, was celebrated as a trade pact that preserved the peace. There were no commemorative monuments erected to the memory of the Battle of Zathin Gulf. Efforts to recover the bodies and bones of the dead from that terrible day were called off. There was no recruitment drive to build up the army, the navy, or the air force. There was no talk from Empress Jia, the regent, of seizing the first opportunity to free the people in the conquered islands.

The men and women who had fought and died to drive back the Lyucu had been erased. Their names were recorded on tablets in the Hall of Mutagé, but there were no plays by the Imperial Troupe celebrating their lives, no poems commissioned by the Throne to memorialize their bravery, no proclamations by Empress Jia on the day of the Grave-Mending Festival urging everyone to remember what they had done.

Even the name of Marshal Mazoti was seldom brought up by the regent, as though the Marshal were not a hero at all, but an embarrassment, a death as inconsequential as a feather in the wind.

With the example set by the regent, officials, scholars, and even folk storytellers followed suit. After a brief burst of interest in stories about Marshal Mazoti and the band of fighters she had rallied around her in Zathin Gulf, the performances petered out. The storytellers grew concerned that Jia's attitude was a signal of the official judgment of the Marshal.

*She was a traitor who barely redeemed herself in that battle,* whispered the people, *best not to mention her.*

"There should be fresh lotus seeds as well," said Arona. "We'll go get some in the market, and I'll make you a cold, sweet soup. You always like that."

He patted her back to show that he was listening, and he was grateful to think about sweet, cold lotus-seed soup rather than the bitter bile of rage, rage at a throne that seemed to treat those who had fought for faith and love as disposable, as inconvenient sacrifices best consigned to oblivion.

And the official indifference and forgetfulness weren't limited to the dead. While the emperor virtually disappeared from Pan, doing gods knew what on his own, the regent did everything in her power to make the people forget about the ongoing suffering in Rui and Dasu. The refugees from Unredeemed Dara were at first sequestered in camps and then quietly released, their harrowing tales of enslavement and slaughter under the Lyucu given little publicity. Empress Jia and Prime Minister Cogo Yelu focused on commerce, agriculture, the promotion of learning and scholarship in what remained of Dara, as if fattening purses and indigo houses full of song and dance could drown out the cries of the people abandoned in the conquered lands.

There were no special pensions or honors given to sailors, marines, soldiers, and aviators who had fought in the Battle of Zathin Gulf. Being a soldier, a warrior who fought for the survival of Dara, was treated as a career unworthy of recognition. Veterans who wanted to return to civilian life retired with nothing more than their wages and the promise of a plot of land in remote corners of Dara. Many veterans sold their land and turned the money into drink or gambled it away, too disappointed with the coldness with which the empress regarded their service.

He could live with the guilt of having survived, with the shame of not being able to live up to the ideals of his own heroes. But what he could not bear was the thought that his comrades had died in vain, that the name of Captain Atamu would be forgotten, that Marshal Mazoti would be thought of as a traitor who had barely redeemed herself. He could not tolerate the idea that the Lyucu were allowed to put their roots down in Rui and Dasu, to enslave and slaughter while growing fat from tribute from the rest of Dara.

Empress Jia was a tyrant, Mota realized. Her distrust of men and women who took up arms to defend the homeland was based on her love of power.

"Come," said Arona. "I'm hungry. You may be strong enough to skip meals whenever you please, but I become short-tempered when I'm hungry. We have a lot of plotting and thinking to do for the final round of the competition, and Rati, Widi, and I haven't forgotten what you want. We may just have a way to win the competition *and* go *there.*"

"Thank you, Rona," Mota said. Only he could call her by the diminutive, just like how only she could touch the scars on his back.

Mota squeezed his arm around her gratefully, affectionately. She kept him anchored to the present, to hope for the future. He was sorry that he could not devote himself wholly to her, to the life that she wanted.

*O Gods of Dara, aid me in my task.*

He might not be a hero, but he was going to make sure that true heroes would not be forgotten.

And then, perhaps, he would finally be at peace, would finally be able to be the man Arona deserved.

Since great restaurants in Dara were often chosen for official banquets and gatherings of the notable—victory celebrations for triumphant admirals returning after cleansing the sea of pirates, receptions for circuit intendants, poetry contests, logogram riddle competitions, debates between philosophers, the introduction of a prominent singer or artist, and so on—they were expected not only to provide great service and cook delicious food, but also to supply suitable entertainment when called on to do so.

In addition, because prominent restaurants were city institutions, the public expected them to sponsor shows at big holidays like New Year and the Lantern Festival. Tiphan Huto's proposed contest was focused on this last aspect of restaurateurship. The Treasure Chest and the Splendid Urn were each going to put on a production for the judges, one that would live up to the title of Best Restaurant in Ginpen.

"Why can't we just do the same thing we do for New Year?" asked Widow Wasu. "The fireworks display is always a hit."

"You can't just repeat what you've always done," said Dandelion. "People are expecting something new, something spectacular."

"Like what?"

"I can come up with lots of ideas," said Dandelion. "But unlike food and service, entertainment is a much more open arena, with limitless potential. It may be hard to beat them without knowing their plan."

"It won't be hard."

Everyone paused. The speaker was Mota, who so rarely talked that sometimes Dandelion and Kinri forgot about him. Indeed, Dandelion looked a bit stunned at Mota's contradiction.

"Everyone tends to rely on their strength," said Mota. "Even when it fails them. The Lyucu were so proud of their garinafins that even after they received hints that Marshal Mazoti was working on weapons that could counter them, they didn't adopt any new fighting techniques."

Kinri's face burned at this, but he forced himself to focus on the matter at hand. "How does that help us here?"

Dandelion broke in. "Are you saying that Tiphan Huto will also stick with his strength, even if it didn't bring him victory in the past?"

Mota nodded.

"It's like a story about yourself that you can't escape," mused

Dandelion. "Even when you don't like the story, you can't stop retelling it."

Now it was Mota's turn to look a bit stunned.

"So what do we think is the strength of Tiphan Huto?" asked Kinri.

A cacophony of voices. "Deviousness." "Lack of morals." "Cheating!" "Not playing fair!"

"No, no," said Dandelion. "I don't think that's what Mota meant at all. We might think all these terrible things about Tiphan, but that's not how he sees himself. We're never the villains in our own stories."

Mota nodded. He held up a hand and made the gesture of lifting something heavy in his palm.

"Gold?" asked Widow Wasu.

"Right," said Dandelion. "Though he would probably phrase it as 'power,' 'command of resources,' 'generosity,' or something like that."

"That makes sense to me," said Mati. "During the first round, he used the most expensive ingredients and prepared them in the most lavish ways."

"And during the second round, he devoted his resources to decorations, lamps, and picking and flying in staff from all over the Islands," said Lodan.

"He's impressed by things that you can buy if you have a lot of money," said Widow Wasu, catching on. "So he thinks everyone else will be impressed the same way. And since for this round, we're allowed to use outside contractors during the performance, he's going to pay the performers most impressive to him."

"That's the story he keeps on telling," said Kinri. "But since we know his story, we can craft our own story to counter it." He and Dandelion shared a smile.

Mota fell silent again, thinking over Dandelion's words.

*It's like a story about yourself that you can't escape.*

Kinri came upon Dandelion painting in the kitchen yard.

The place was bustling. Many members of the restaurant staff had returned to work after victory in the second round, confident that the supposed curse on the Splendid Urn was nonsense. As the cooks and their helpers rushed about the bread kilns and curved-mirror sun stoves, carrying water and firewood, plucking chickens and cleaning fish, retrieving ingredients from the cellar, setting out custards on racks for flame-tongues, Dandelion stood behind her easel in the middle of the hubbub, examining the commotion around her with deep concentration. Once in a while, she made a few decisive strokes on the paper.

He approached her quietly from behind, unwilling to disturb her, thinking that he would just catch a quick peek of her work before resuming his duties. Lodan and Mati were running a busy dinner service and needed every pair of hands.

The painting she was working on was not large, about four feet square. It was no recognizable portrait of the scene before her. Dandelion had used only black ink, and the sheet was dominated by irregularly shaped splotches of various sizes, interspersed with wispy strokes that curved and swirled between them. Occasionally, she dipped her brush into the inkwell at her feet, stood back, and flung the brush at the paper from a distance so that tiny dots of ink splattered across the sheet. She was working so energetically that her dress was covered in splattered ink, and even her face had a few stray brushstrokes.

Kinri stood before the painting, slack-jawed. He had seen plenty of Dara-style paintings, both in Ukyu-taasa and here in Ginpen's markets, but never had he seen anything like this. All at once, it resembled the wild strokes and irregular logograms of wind-script calligraphy, footprints of terns on a beach at low tide, gossamer dew-bedecked spiderwebs at dawn, ropy strands of frozen lava in frost-bearded winter.

What it most reminded him of, he realized, were the voice paintings of the Lyucu.

Abruptly, Dandelion stepped back, brush reared over her shoulder as she prepared for another flick. Kinri, mesmerized, couldn't get out of her way in time, and the ink-drenched brush stabbed him directly in the nose.

Yelps and mutual apologies later, the two stood looking at each other. Dandelion giggled at the black splotch covering the entirety of Kinri's nose and much of the rest of his face.

"I suppose this is one way to become part of my painting," said Dandelion. "But in general, my advice to my subjects is to sit in front of me, not sneak up behind me."

Kinri chuckled and rubbed his nose. "I think that painting is beautiful."

Dandelion was used to boys praising her painting (well, except for that loathsome Gimoto). She knew that most of the time, they weren't really commenting on the painting at all, much like the boys who held tea-tasting parties in indigo houses would write poetry about the fragrance of the beverage while keeping their eyes on the girls doing the brewing. She resented this sort of false praise, and was disappointed to hear it from Kinri. So, mischievously, she cocked her head. "Do you really think so?"

"I . . . I do," he stammered. He was rather intimidated by the way she looked at him, and didn't dare to meet her gaze.

"Tell me then," she said, biting the end of the handle of her brush and pointing at a bread kiln, "where is that kiln in my painting?"

Kinri furrowed his brows. "It's in the painting and also not in the painting."

"Oh? How do you mean?"

Kinri walked closer to the painting. "This blob right here has the weight of the kiln; that swirl over there has the lightness of the smoke; these wisps capture the gooey dough that goes inside; those long strokes evoke the energy of the baker as she runs into the kitchen with the hot bread; and the dots on top . . . I can taste the way the crust crumbles in my mouth as I look at them. . . . Yet there's nothing that looks like a kiln in the painting at all. You've painted the spirit of the kiln but not its body; I've never seen anyone do that, at least not in Ginpen—" He stopped when he saw Dandelion's expression. "I'm sorry. I don't know what I'm talking about. I know nothing about art."

Dandelion blinked away the tears that welled in her eyes. "No, you didn't say anything wrong. . . . I just . . . no one has ever understood my painting, not even my brother."

"It's . . . very beautiful," said Kinri awkwardly. "It looks like the trails left by snails on banana leaves . . . just before the sun goes down, you know, with glowing arcs in the grooves like little golden rainbows; they tell you how hard the snail worked for every inch and make you wonder what the snail was thinking. . . ." He swallowed and added nervously, "Don't get mad because I'm comparing your painting to snail slime . . . I don't really have the words."

"I'm not going to get mad," she said softly. "You're speaking from the heart, and anything true is beautiful and should be treasured."

*Is that true?* he wondered. *Can I tell you the truth about me and still have you think it beautiful?*

"You mentioned that you've never seen anyone paint like this in Ginpen," Dandelion said. "Does that mean you've seen it elsewhere?"

He shook his head. "No, not in brush painting, but it reminds me of the voice paintings back home."

So he told her about storytelling dances and cactus drums, and the way shamans painted with their voice and music. "A voice painting captures the spirit of the story, not the word-scars," he said, unconsciously falling back to a translated version of the Lyucu kenning. As he spoke, his eyes misted over from the longing ache for home, while Dandelion listened intently, trying to imagine the scene.

When he was finished, she said, "I wish I could see such a voice painting being made one day. . . . Even if the shaman is Lyucu and I am Dara, I'm sure we can talk about our art. . . ."

Kinri's heart clenched at the impossibility of that vision.

"Do a lot of servants get to go to the storytelling dances?" asked Dandelion.

Kinri shook his head. "No. The storytelling dances are sacred"— only too late did he realize that he was supposed to be a native servant himself—"most . . . most of the time," he finished feebly.

Luckily, Dandelion didn't seem to notice. "Do you remember any of the stories they painted at the storytelling dances?"

Glad to have the change of topic, Kinri told her the story of Afir and Kikisavo. Dandelion was delighted and hung on every word. In the end, she said, "It's too bad that they couldn't remain friends after all they went through. Reminds me of the way Emperor Ragin and the Hegemon fell out after everything they went through together."

It was odd for Kinri to hear the great heroes of the people of the scrublands being compared to two cruel tyrants of Dara, but after having lived in Dara for so long, the stories of the court-appointed tutors no longer felt like the absolute truth.

"How did you come up with this way of painting?" he asked Dandelion.

"I was inspired by Lady Mira, my favorite hero," she said.

"Lady Mira? The Hegemon's consort?" Kinri was startled. He couldn't think of anything that was heroic about the Hegemon's lover.

Dandelion nodded. "Everyone knows about her killing herself for the Hegemon, but she was also a great artist. She embroidered portraits of the Hegemon composed from geometric figures and simple, bold dashes. I think they're better than all the portraits of him by classically trained court painters."

Kinri, uninterested in the history of art, had no knowledge of these portraits. Dandelion pulled the painting off the easel and re-created for Kinri sketches of the embroidered portraits on a fresh sheet of paper.

"But how is she heroic?"

"While everyone cowered before the Hegemon, she stood up to him and told him the truth. While everyone else fled from the Hegemon, she dared to love him and saw him the way he wanted to be seen, not the way others expected him to be. She was the only one who ever understood him."

Kinri was silent. *While everyone cowered . . . she dared to love him.*

"My sister didn't think much of Mira. 'She devoted her life to someone else, and her greatest accomplishment was to have loved a man!' As if somehow dying for romance was worse than dying for a king, as if prizing love was less than prizing some other ideal!

"But I think Mira was misjudged. Just as she was the only one who ever understood the Hegemon, the Hegemon was the only one who ever understood *her*. No one at the time comprehended her embroideries, except him. He prized her work more than gold and jewels, more than legendary swords and the seals of the Tiro kings. She was the last person he shed tears for before he died, and from his body, they recovered nothing except a handkerchief embroidered by Mira. In those bold lines and the defiant refusal to *represent*, he recognized her grand spirit. He cherished the way she glimpsed and grasped the world, made it hers.

"For an artist, the work, the way she sees the world, is more precious than the self. She saw him the way he wanted to be seen, but he saw her *vision* the way she wanted her vision to be seen.

"Kon Fiji said that men should be willing to die for great lords who recognize their talent. But I think the word usually rendered as 'talent' has been mistranslated from the original Classical Ano. A better word would be 'nature,' or capacity, tendency, quality of spirit. The Hegemon recognized Mira's nature; he was the mirror of her soul. That was why she died, no less heroically than Ratho Miro or Mün Çakri."

Kinri was stunned. He couldn't help but think that there was something more to Dandelion's speech than a lesson on art. They looked into each other's eyes.

*Can we see each other the way we want to be seen? Can we recognize our souls in each other's vision? Should I—*

"Kinri! Where's that block of ice?" Mati shouted from the door of the kitchen.

Kinri made his excuses and rushed away, but the words and painting of Dandelion lingered long in his mind.

"Welcome, welcome to the final and decisive round of the battle between the Treasure Chest and the Splendid Urn!" said Séca.

"I have a feeling we're all going to witness something spectacular today," said Lolo. "This is it: one last bout, and winner takes all! Will the Splendid Urn defend their crown? Or will the Treasure Chest unseat the champion? After today, I think even the next New Year's is going to be a bit of a letdown."

The two were speaking again from on top of a stage constructed in Temple Square, with a panel of judges sitting behind a low table. The judges for this round had also been picked from the notable ranks of Ginpen society, but with special emphasis on theater and indigo-house managers, playwrights and critics, leaders of performing troupes, actors and actresses, firework designers, and other experts on entertainment and spectacle.

For weeks now, the contest between the two restaurants had dominated all conversation in the city. Storytellers in teahouses and in market squares served up vivid descriptions of Mozo Mu's culinary creations and the Urn's animal-driven serving carts, with liberal helpings of exaggeration, and the listeners who hadn't been able to witness these rounds of the competition sighed with regret and vowed to make it to the final round.

Meanwhile, the secondary competition to be selected as one of the judges, seen as the most desirable prize in Ginpen high society at the moment, was so intense that numerous plots were hatched and many friendships sundered. In the end, Lolo and Séca literally had to pick logograms out of a jar to establish the final panel.

A huge crowd, many times the one that had shown up for the first round, filled the square. So many had come out to watch the shows put on by the two restaurants that vendors were doing a lively business serving the crowd ice water, chilled sour plum soup, and even imitation Rapa's Feast.

Séca and Lolo glanced at Widow Wasu and Manager Giphi, seated on opposite ends of the stage. Tiphan Huto claimed that he had too much work to do for the show itself and had sent the loyal Giphi in his stead.

"Are you ready, Grand Mistress Wasu and Master Giphi?" asked Séca.

They nodded grimly.

"Then may the most interesting restaurant win!" declared Lolo.

As the loser of the last round, the Treasure Chest had the choice to go first or last this time. Tiphan Huto, a believer in the military adage that it was better to strike first, chose to present before Widow Wasu.

"People of Ginpen," declared Giphi, dressed for the occasion in a somber robe in a classical cut that had been popular perhaps fifty years earlier. The crowd quieted. "Ginpen is a city rich in history, and your reactions from the cooking competition told me how much history matters to all of you."

"Sounds like they're going to try to steal from us," whispered Dandelion to Kinri. They were standing at the foot of the stage, near the front of the crowd.

Kinri nodded, his heart speeding up. If the Treasure Chest had learned from Dandelion's weaving of history and the present into a compelling story during the cooking competition, that would make them formidable opponents.

Giphi took a deep breath and shouted so that he could be heard all over the square. "Today, we're going to relive one of the greatest scenes in the annals of this city and the chronicles of Dara!"

As the loud trumpet blasts neared, accompanied by thunderous drumming, the crowd on the western edge of Temple Square divided like the ocean being parted by the prow of a city-ship. Soon, a wide avenue opened through the middle of the square.

Into this void came a parade. At the head of the parade were seven elephants from Écofi, draped in the colors of the seven ancient Tiro states. Beautiful young women and men—the staff from the Treasure Chest on the night of the service competition—scattered beach-rose petals and sprayed rose-scented water at the crowd, providing much-welcomed relief from the hot sun.

"By the Twins," whispered Widow Wasu, who stood up onstage with Lodan supporting her. "I think I know where he's going with this. I saw the model of this parade when I was a young woman in Zudi."

Behind the elephants came a phalanx of marching men, their upper bodies bared to show bronzed and oiled muscles. They twirled swords so that they spun like steel-blue chrysanthemums in bloom.

"Cocru sword dancers!" whispered Dandelion to Kinri, leaning down so that she could be heard. She was sitting on his shoulders so that she could see over the heads of the crowd before them. "I've never even seen this many all at once."

"I don't know how they can twirl swords like that without hurting themselves," whispered Kinri.

Behind the sword dancers came a group of young women, all of them exactly the same height and dressed in the same diaphanous silk that revealed their lithe curves. Gyrating seductively, they waved their long sleeves through the air, tracing spirals and arches that echoed the billowing fog shrouding the craggy cliff-walls of Boama.

More excited whispers throughout the crowd.

"Faça veil dancers!"

"I thought the art had been lost. I've only seen puppet versions. . . ."

"The last time . . . was when Mapidéré passed through here. . . ."

Phalanx after phalanx of dancers, musicians, jugglers, animal trainers, acrobats . . . marched through the square. Some displayed their skills on floats that displayed miniature scenes of the wonders around Dara: a fountain that was a scale model of the Rufizo Falls; Mount Rapa and Mount Kana constructed out of painted dough, with an ice-sculpted palace on one and a flame-limned castle on the other; actors and actresses dressed up as gods and goddesses drinking mead in a valley in the Wisoti Mountains, pointing into the distance and arguing as though they were debating the future of Dara; scholars on stilts walking and chanting passages from ancient Ano Classics. . . .

Finally, near the end of the parade, came a giant bamboo-and-silk palanquin. Carried on the shoulders of fifty men holding crisscrossed bamboo poles, the palanquin itself was shaped like a smaller version of the Treasure Chest itself: divided into five stories, the lower four each painted to resemble one of the realms of Fire, Water, Earth, and Air. At the top, leaning back on a sitting cushion in *thakrido* like an august sovereign, Tiphan Huto waved at the crowd confidently. Around and below him, singers chorused the famous lines of Lügo Crupo, Prime Minister to the dread Emperor Mapidéré:

> *To the north: Fruitful Faça, green as the eyes of kind Rufizo,*
> *Pastures ever kissed by sweet rain, craggy highlands shrouded*
> *in mist.*

*To the west: Alluring Amu, the jewel of Tututika,*
  *Luminous elegance, filigreed cities surround two blue lakes.*

  . . .

"He's *literally* re-creating Emperor Mapidéré's victory parade
through Ginpen," muttered Widow Wasu. "How can he *possibly*
think this a good idea?"

The older observers among the crowd were mostly silent, gazing
at the parade with complicated expressions. A few looked furious
and shouted at this display that seemed to make a mockery of the
heroes of the rebellion who had resisted Xana tyranny both before
and after the unification.

But they were quickly shushed by the younger audience members, who were, for the most part, impressed by the spectacle. They
cheered and gawked and clapped and talked excitedly about the
wonders before them.

Dandelion's eyebrows furrowed.

"Mapidéré was a despot, wasn't he?" asked Kinri. At least this
aspect of the court-appointed tutors' teaching seemed to be generally accepted in Dara. He was confused by the way so many in the
crowd cheered and hooted, with some shouting, "Long Live Tiphan
Huto!" It sounded like they all thought they were participating in a
joke, part of some farcical play.

"Tiphan is more clever than I thought," said Dandelion softly. She
climbed down from Kinri's shoulders. "I knew he would go all out
and try to overwhelm the crowd with a display of power and wealth,
but I hadn't counted on how he would tap into an old story and
breathe new life into it."

"What do you mean?"

"Listen to the singing. Huto changed the words."

*You bow down, bow down, bow down to Dara, Zenith, Ruler*
  *of Air,*
  *Why resist, why persist against Anojiti in strife you can't*
  *bear?*

"So he's turned Xana into Dara . . ." muttered Kinri. "But it's still a song praising a tyrant."

Widi, who had been listening to the exchange, broke in. "Emperor Mapidéré has always been a figure of controversy. The House of Dandelion began as rebels against Xana tyranny over the Tiro states, but when the rebellion succeeded, instead of restoring the world to separate Tiro states as the Hegemon had wanted, Emperor Ragin re-created the Xana empire under a different name, albeit a much gentler and well-ordered version."

"He did it to avoid the trap of the warring Tiro states again, and because he thought he could continue those aspects of Mapidéré's grand task that benefited the people while avoiding aspects that were bad," said Dandelion, sounding a bit defensive.

"Of course," said Widi. "I'm not saying Emperor Ragin was wrong. I'm just pointing out that the House of Dandelion couldn't condemn the whole of the legacy of Mapidéré, and that left an opening for Tiphan."

"How can so many people celebrate a parade that hearkens back to a tyrant?"

"There's always a tendency for those who didn't personally experience suffering to romanticize aspects of the past that seem better than the present," said Widi. "Under Mapidéré, Dara was united and powerful. Indeed, Dara could send out an expedition to look for legendary immortals beyond the Wall of Storms. Compare that with today, when two of the Islands are under barbarous Lyucu occupation, when the empress maintains the peace by paying tribute—"

"When veterans from the wars, especially the war against the Lyucu, are forgotten," said Mota, standing nearby.

Kinri remained studiously silent through this exchange. Mapidéré and the horrors he had unleashed upon the Lyucu in the form of Admiral Krita were at the very core of Pékyu Tenryo's heroic legends.

Widi nodded. "Yes. The empress regent seems to disdain all military institutions and martial strength. After comparing the strength displayed by Mapidéré then and the weakness shown by the empress now, it's easy for people to become nostalgic for him and everything else associated with him, more so if you have no memory of his reign or only vague recollections from childhood. Tiphan is clever to evoke the time of Mapidéré as a proxy for the people's yearning for a strong Dara."

As if in response to this, a new float appeared after the throne-pagoda of Tiphan Huto. On a large wheeled platform with papier-mâché fencing, rows of men knelt with their arms bound behind them, stand-ins for war captives. They were dressed in furs and skins, and around them were heaps of axes, spears, and clubs made of bone, apparently the spoils of war.

More loud cheering from the crowd, with cries of "Great Dara!" "Long Live the *Anojiti*!" "Save Dasu and Rui!"

Kinri looked away, unable to gaze upon this caricature of his own people's defeat. His hands balled into fists at his sides. *Tenryo fought to free the Lyucu from a tyrant, and he came to Dara to free you from more tyranny!* he wanted to shout. But the sentiment felt hollow, and he dared not make a sound. Rage, hatred, doubt, and the pain of being misunderstood warred within his breast.

But then he snapped his eyes back to the "prisoner wagon." Something about those weapons . . .

"They're real!" he blurted.

Dandelion turned to him. "What?"

Kinri took a moment to compose himself. "The bone clubs and axes . . . they look genuine. I've seen many bone weapons in . . . Unredeemed Dara, and I know that each has a distinct design based on the clan and tribe of the owner. Those bone weapons aren't props; they're real."

"They may still be props," said Widi, "just well-made props."

"Why would Tiphan spend the resources to make authentic-looking Lyucu weapons?" asked Dandelion. "No one—except Thasé-teki here—would even know the difference. Tiphan doesn't strike me as someone too concerned with accuracy."

"That's true . . . and thus out of character," Widi mused. "Maybe it's not him . . . rather, he hired as his designer a refugee from Unredeemed Dara who is familiar with Lyucu weaponry." But he didn't look too convinced by his own explanation.

"We need to look into this," insisted Dandelion. Then, frowning, she returned to the larger theme of the parade. "History is always a story retold through the present. And now Tiphan has told a story that the people of Ginpen, especially the young, crave—"

The rest of what she had to say was drowned out in an eruption of deafening cheers as a fleet of sleek airships decked out for war appeared overhead.

In reality, these airships were used for transporting quick-spoiling freight for the Tiphan clan's commercial empire, and had only been painted to resemble military ships. Still, they evoked legends and memories of a time when Dara had flown massive airships, powered by pure lift gas that came out of pristine Lake Dako, striking fear into all who dared to attack her; instead of today, when airships were modest vessels suitable only for transporting time-critical cargo and ferrying wealthy passengers, powered by weak, flammable fermented manure gas, posing a danger to anyone who wanted to fly.

Indeed, ever since the core islands had lost access to the sole source of lift gas in Rui, old Imperial airships were grounded or had to be retrofitted and weakened to use the new manure gas. Empress Jia apparently considered military airships a potential provocation to the Lyucu; therefore, she and the Inner Council refused to allocate funding for the construction of new airships and starved the air force of the funds needed to maintain old airships. It was rumored that Than Carucono had been forced to reduce Imperial air force drills to an absolute minimum, and aviators had to practice maneuvers in models on the ground, with no chance to take to the air.

Everyone from the Splendid Urn looked up at the painted mock warships. It couldn't have been cheap to repaint and redecorate so many freight vessels in such a short time, or to pull them away from their commercial routes for this show. Tiphan Huto had clearly been given free rein by the elders of the Huto clan to do whatever it took to win.

The painted freight airships didn't fly as high, as far, or as fast as the old military airships, and they looked far more clumsy due to all the safety features needed for civilian use. Still, to people who hadn't seen the glory of Imperial airships in ages, the sight of these imitations elicited sighs of wonder and admiration. Many in the crowd wiped their eyes and swallowed the lumps in their throats. A few whispered words of complaint against the timid empress and yearned for bold Emperor Ragin and fearless Marshal Gin Mazoti.

"Well, that kind of ruins a key part of our show," said Rati Yera.

"Yes," said Widi Tucru. "We knew they would go for ostentation, but tapping into the people's emotions ... I have to admit that's smart."

"Every story has a counter-story," said Dandelion. "We just have to tweak our story to be better."

Kinri looked at her, and the two locked eyes as an unspoken understanding passed between them.

He took a deep breath. Dandelion calmed him. Whatever his feelings about Tiphan Huto and the crowd that cheered on the defeat of the Lyucu, Dandelion's smile was always a ray of sunshine.

"Kinri and I will rewrite the script," said Dandelion, and at this Kinri was startled. "Rati, how much time do you need to modify the machines to suit?"

Because putting on a spectacle for the public required many disruptions to city traffic, Magistrate Zuda had asked that the two competitors produce their shows on different days lest Ginpen come to a complete standstill.

Since the Treasure Chest had chosen to go first, this gave the Splendid Urn an extra week to prepare.

On the day of the Splendid Urn's presentation, excited crowds once again streamed into Temple Square. Some speculated that fifty folk opera troupes had been hired to put on a grand pageant; some thought there would be a fireworks show the likes of which had never been seen in all the Islands; some thought Widow Wasu would finally use her connections with the Imperial family to bring in a member of the House of Dandelion for a surprise appearance. Rumors piled on rumors, and expectations were at the highest ...

... until they saw what the Splendid Urn had actually built.

There was a tent in Temple Square, about the size of a lecture hall in one of Ginpen's academies and shaped like a cylinder with a cone top. Around the tent was a wide circular fence of bamboo and silk that concealed the base and the entrance from view, keeping the crowd at a distance.

The tent was large, to be sure, but it was hard to imagine what kind of wonder could be shown inside an enclosed space that could hold no more than one of Ginpen's old theaters. It was clear that there would be no fireworks, no airships, no parade of thousands. Amidst scattered groans of disappointment, memories of the grand pageant put on by the Treasure Chest a week ago seemed even more vivid, and many wondered aloud if the Splendid Urn had given up and was about to concede.

"The entertainment provided by the Splendid Urn today requires a stout heart and a steady mind," announced Lolo. "Grand Mistress Wasu expresses her regret that, for your own safety, you must be at least this tall to view the show." She held up a stick with a red line marked three-quarters of the way up.

"Wait," said one of the judges, a famous scholar of *Morality*. "That would exclude most children. . . . Don't tell me that Widow Wasu has put on a show that relies on titillation and vulgarity! That would be contrary to the admonition of the One True Sage—"

"I promise that this isn't about appealing to prurient interests," said Widow Wasu. "Due to the time constraints, we couldn't get it to work for wheeled chair users or those who are not tall enough. But we'll definitely make the attraction more accessible so that it can be experienced by everyone who wants to in the near future."

Widow Wasu's confident tone and mysterious words got the crowd excited again.

Séca announced that the show could accommodate fifty visitors at a time. The judges and members of the public would line up outside the screen fence and be admitted in waves.

Pimié couldn't suppress the excitement as he finally stepped through the gate in the long fence—he was just tall enough to reach the red mark on the stick (helped by the fact that Lolo was too distracted to notice he was on tiptoes).

Inside, he saw a team of workers with carpentry tools, buckets of paint, silkmotic generators, and other implements. It looked like they had finished building whatever was inside the tent at the last minute and were kept around for repairs.

Nervously, he peeked in at the dark opening of the tent, hesitating. Dandelion, noticing his trepidation, came over.

"Scared?" she teased.

"No," he said, swallowing uneasily. Earlier visitors had emerged from the tent with dazed expressions, and when pressed for details by those waiting outside, they shook their heads and told them that they just had to wait and see for themselves.

"Sometimes it's fun to be scared," said Dandelion.

Along with the other visitors in his cohort, Pimié was guided into the tent, where they were directed to climb up a very long ladder. It was so dark inside that he could barely see anything. By the time his eyes had adjusted, he realized that the spacious interior of the tent was filled with a bamboo lattice, and partitioned into large compartments with hanging silk curtains. There was a long rail constructed from wooden beams that wound its way through the lattice, rising and falling like the body of a serpent. The rail reminded him of the kind of tracks used in mines to bring carts in and out without having to grade roads.

At the very top of the ladder, Pimié found himself and the others standing on a platform with railings. They were very high from the ground, up near the ceiling of the tent. Before them was a cart with rows of seats riding atop the long rail.

Kinri showed everyone how to get into one of the seats and to secure themselves into the harness. Once tightened, the harness pressed Pimié against the seat and made it impossible to get up and move about. The chatter among the riders turned apprehensive.

"Whatever you do, don't try to loosen the harness," said Kinri. "I promise you that you'll be safe."

Pimié was about to ask a question, but Kinri had already stepped away from the cart, and he nodded at one of the workers standing by a tall lever next to the rail. The worker pulled the lever, and the cart began to slide forward.

As it followed the rail on a downward slant, the cart picked up speed. The riders gasped. In the darkness, the sensation of falling and accelerating was both thrilling and terrifying.

A loud voice boomed overhead. It was the voice of Kinri, speaking into a system of tubes that resonated and carried his speech throughout the tent, much like the tubes on Pékyu Tenryo's city-ship.

*Long ago, before there were people who called themselves people, before there were gods or oceans or islands or volcanoes, the world was a milky soup, where light was not separated from darkness, nor life from not-life.*

The steady voice took away some of the terror. As the wind whipped their hair behind them, the riders focused on the voice in the darkness, the voice that accompanied them as they accelerated toward the unknown.

*One day, a long-haired cow, the eldest of giants and monsters, drank the milk of the universe. The milk curdled and broke apart, and the first spark of life, the wolf, came into being.*

There was a thunderous howl overhead, and lightning bolts arced through the darkness, momentarily illuminating the space around the cart with bright flashes.

Dimly, Pimié wondered just how powerful a silkmotic generator was needed to create lightning bolts like the one he had seen, but then, like everyone else in the cart, he screamed, as he saw that the cart was plunging toward a barrier, a smooth, featureless sheer cliff like the face of the moon.

He closed his eyes and contracted his body as much as the unyielding harness allowed, expecting to be flattened on impact. . . .

. . . They broke right through the cliff, which turned out to be just a silk curtain, and emerged into a space of swirling white mist. The mist was lit up brightly—Pimié suspected by sunlight directed into this partitioned-off section of the tent via mirrors—and through it they could glimpse the outlines of mountains, scrublands, gleaming lakes.

The mist softened everything so that the world appeared newly formed, still solidifying, like the translucent body of a freshly exuviated cicada.

The cart slowed down and rattled along the rail, suspended in the mist. The scenery around them was painted at such a scale that it created the illusion of them being very high up in the air. Sprays of water from hidden nozzles added to the illusion.

The voice continued, speaking of shape-shifting gods and powerful monsters with shark teeth and wolf claws, about humans huddled on the scrublands without the means to obtain heat or food. As the cart progressed along the rail, the scenes around them also continued to change, illustrating the story told by the voice.

Then, some force seemed to seize the cart like a giant hand, and the cart began to ascend up a steep incline, toward another barrier up near the ceiling of the tent.

Pimié held on. . . .

. . . The world around them now was a deep aquamarine, and giant dark shadows swam gracefully through the simulated sea, concealing and revealing themselves among the towering papier-mâché corals.

The voice told them about the fight between Kikisavo and Afir and the great whale that was Péten. The cart tilted, twisted, dove, rose through this imitation ocean, re-creating the thrill of the mythical struggle against the trickster god.

A massive maw loomed up at the left, intent on swallowing the riders. The cart took a sharp turn, rose, and looped through the sea as the riders realized they were upside down, held in their seats only by the force of the cart's acceleration and the harnesses. Along with the other riders, Pimié screamed and covered his eyes as the cart careened along the rail.

*For ten days and ten nights Kikisavo and Afir fought the great whale, neither yielding an inch. The waves from their struggle wrecked the coast and innumerable denizens of the sea were tossed ashore, providing a bounty for the tribes living by the shore.*

Despite his terror, Pimié couldn't help opening his eyes again to take in the incredible scene around him. His heart was in his throat, and he wanted the experience both to end as quickly as possible and to last forever.

. . .

Hurtling through one space after another, Pimié and his fellow riders lived the creation story of the Lyucu and the Agon. They soared on the back of a garinafin and struggled against sleet and rain on the open scrublands. They trudged through the deadly heat of the end-less desert in the south and shivered against the bone-chilling cold of the ice fields in the north. They witnessed the cruel deception of the gods as well as the endlessly inventive courage of the two mortal companions. They cheered with joy; they screamed out of fright.

They didn't merely hear the story; they felt it through their bodies as the cart followed the plot's rises and falls, twists and turns, plunged them into the depths of despair before lifting them to the heights of ecstasy, allowed them to relax through peaceful episodes of sightseeing and banter before corkscrewing them through narrow escapes and literal cliff-hangers. As the cart traveled the rail, all their senses were assaulted, and they experienced the sensations of being larger-than-life heroes in a living myth.

By the time the cart rattled into the safety of the dock at the start of the journey and came to a gentle stop, Pimié understood the looks of awe and confusion on the faces of all the other passengers from earlier. This was indeed an experience he couldn't put into words.

He wanted to get on the ride immediately again, to re-experience the story. But Dandelion smiled and shook her head no matter how much he pleaded. He had to give the other passengers a chance.

Kinri watched the young boy leave before turning to Dandelion.

"You're amazing," he said. "The paintings . . . the garinafins . . . the water . . . they're beautiful."

Dandelion had stayed up two nights to design and sketch much of the scenery for the ride, which had then been magnified by Rati Yera with an enlarger-projector for the hired artisans to reproduce inside the tent.

What Kinri really wanted to articulate was the beauty of the story she had crafted based on his retelling, but a lump in his throat made him croak instead.

She smiled at him. "It's easy to paint when you have a good story. But . . . perhaps we'll be ready to tell each other our own true stories soon?"

His heart raced. He didn't know what to say.

She pressed a folded-up handkerchief into his hand. "Read this when you're ready to tell." A look of trepidation. "It may be that I am more scared to tell you than you are to tell me. But I see you the way you wish to be seen, and I hope you see me the way I wish to be seen."

Long after she had turned and left, Kinri stood rooted to the spot. He squeezed the silk handkerchief gently and felt the hard wax logograms inside. Holding it up to his nose, he breathed in the fragrance of fresh dandelions, mixed with a hint of beach rose.

The announcement of the final result was anticlimactic.

Tiphan Huto refused to even show up for the humiliation as Lolo and Séca presented the logogram sign, "First in Ginpen," written by Magistrate Zuda himself, to Widow Wasu. Teson supported his mother as she climbed onto the stage on unsteady legs. The old woman, overcome with emotion, called for Lodan, Mati, Dandelion, Kinri, and the Blossom Gang to all come onto the stage and accept the sign with her.

"Without the inventions and skills of my friends," said Widow Wasu, "the Splendid Urn would not have survived, let alone stand here today victorious. All of us in the Wasu family vow to live up to the promise of this sign and keep the Urn the pride of Ginpen."

To be sure, not everyone in Ginpen was enamored of the Splendid Urn's entry in the final contest. Quite a few discharged veterans grumbled that the ride seemed to resemble Lyucu propaganda— how could glorifying the myths of the enemy even be contemplated when Dasu and Rui remained unredeemed? More than a few scholars threatened to organize a boycott of the Splendid Urn to express their displeasure.

"People are free to speak their minds," said Widow Wasu. "*I* know that there is no disloyalty in my heart, and that is enough." Still, she gave the order to donate a month's profits from the Urn to healing monks at the Temple of Rufizo, known to tend to impoverished veterans and their families.

There was a grand celebration at the restaurant that night. All the staff of the Splendid Urn had returned, and Head Chef Nézi Ézugo went into the kitchen and cooked his best dishes. The judges for the contests, along with the cream of Ginpen society, came to congratulate Teson and Widow Wasu. Even Magistrate Zuda agreed to come as the guest of honor—now that the contest was over, he no longer had to worry about the appearance of impropriety for a government official to interfere in private competition.

But, as always happened when a government official was invited to a banquet, a speech had to be made. Magistrate Zuda, a voluble and learned Moralist, made the mutually reinforcing benefits of good governance and private enterprise his theme. As he droned on and on, he flitted from topic to topic like a cow browsing patches of tender clover: the beneficence of Empress Jia, the wisdom of Prime Minister Cogo Yelu, the lessons we could all learn from the words of the One True Sage, the special place the Splendid Urn held in the life of the city, the importance of studying history and economics, the pitfalls of being a magistrate for a bustling metropolis like Ginpen, an anecdote about his favorite restaurant in Boama when he studied there as a young man, two more anecdotes about his dining experiences at the Splendid Urn. . . .

The other important guests on the top floor watched their mugs of rice beer grow cold and felt their stomachs growl. But they had no choice but to sit in *mipa rari*, stifle their yawns, and listen attentively. Until the magistrate was done with his speech, they couldn't pick up eating sticks or put their lips to the mugs.

The Blossom Gang and Dandelion had the foresight to request to be seated on the ground floor, away from the magistrate and the other high-ranking guests. Kinri was glad he had listened to them and declined Widow Wasu's kind offer to be seated at the head table. He and his friends were now crowded around a large round table and happily enjoying the excellent food and warm rice beer.

"It was a risk to center the entertainment on a story about the Lyucu," said Rati Yera. "I still can't quite believe we pulled it off."

The original idea the gang had settled on was to create an experience around the fateful assassination attempt on Emperor Mapidéré by Luan Zyaji, Haan's favorite son. That act of heroism, which inspired the young Kuni Garu, seemed a surefire way to tap into patriotic sentiments for old Haan, thereby giving the Splendid Urn an advantage in the competition.

But after getting a sense of the conflicting emotions the people of Ginpen felt about Mapidéré, Dandelion and Kinri had suggested changing the story to be something completely different.

At first, the Blossom Gang, especially Mota, were vehemently opposed to the proposed change. How could a story about the Lyucu, the enemy of Dara, appeal to the people of the city?

"The Lyucu are our enemy, but we know so little about them," said Dandelion. "People are curious. Kinri told me a story, and I can't stop thinking about it. I know the people of Ginpen will be moved."

"Curiosity isn't enough to overcome the revulsion they feel after what the Lyucu have done," objected Mota. "And why should we try to tell one of their stories anyway?"

"Why did Emperor Ragin allow the cult of the Hegemon to flourish?" asked Dandelion. "He and many people of Dara were certainly revolted by what the Hegemon had done."

Mota had no answer to this.

"I think it's because the Hegemon was not the villain in his own story, but the hero, and a powerful hero at that. Any story of heroism, of someone who risked his life for an ideal he believed in, inspires," said Dandelion. "It is the same reason why we love stories about Marshal Gin Mazoti, though she was a traitor to the Dandelion Throne. She put her life on the line when Dara teetered on the edge of an abyss."

Mota said nothing.

"Tiphan Huto's parade is a caricature about what it means to be Dara and what it means to be Lyucu," said Dandelion. "But I think the most powerful stories are not caricatures, but truths, or at least aspects of the truth. Caricaturing your enemy inevitably involves caricaturing yourself. Why not tell a true story of the Lyucu? A story that inspires?"

"But the Lyucu!" Mota swallowed a lump in his throat. "They . . ."

Dandelion's voice was gentle. "I'm not saying that the story of the Lyucu is *the* truth; rather, it's the story they tell themselves about who they are, their foundation myth. Just as understanding the myth of the Hegemon doesn't mean forgiving him, understanding the foundational myth of the Lyucu doesn't mean forgetting about the refugees, the people who suffered and still suffer."

Kinri looked at Dandelion with a complicated expression. He had not expected her to take the story of Afir and Kikisavo so deeply to heart. When she had told him what she had in mind, he had been of two minds about it: both trepidation that a story that mattered to him so deeply would be told right and hope that she would be grand-spirited enough for him to finally tell her the truth.

"But there's a power in the foundational myth of any people," said Dandelion, "and in these foundational myths, the tellers are always heroes, not villains. Emperor Ragin believed that only by empathizing with our enemies, understanding why they are the heroes in their own stories, which is also why they fight, can we defeat them. That was why he was able to avoid slaughtering the rest of the Hegemon's army at Rana Kida by sending in the women of Cocru. Only by understanding the story of the Lyucu can we cease to view them as caricatures, and thereby elevate ourselves as well."

Arona stroked Mota's back gently. Gradually, he calmed down. At length, he nodded and bowed to Dandelion.

"So let's try to tell a powerful story that the people don't expect," said Dandelion. "After all, it was Luan Zyaji who spoke of an 'empathy that encompasses the world' as an ideal to strive for. I believe that if we tell the story of the Lyucu with empathy, with grandness of spirit, it will inspire the people of Ginpen to a new craving, not for mere strength, but grandness of spirit, sea-wide, sky-high, earth-deep. It will . . . allow us to recognize our nature."

As she spoke, Dandelion looked at Kinri, and Kinri couldn't help but feel that her eyes were speaking as well.

*I see you. I know.*

Kinri looked away, berating himself for imagining things.


"After this competition, I feel like I've gained three years of wisdom," boasted Dandelion, her cheeks already red from rice beer, "even though it hasn't even been three months."

"Only someone as young as you can think that a good thing," said Rati Yera.

"I'm really glad I came to the Splendid Urn," said Dandelion. "I got to be a waitress, a storyteller, a playwright, an Imperial official ... Master Lutuma even allowed me to swing the hammer a few times and Mati showed me how to make an omelette, so I think I can pull off carpenter and cook too. I think there's no role that I can't play in this world. Just imagine the adventures I'll have—"

"You need to learn the role of 'Humble Student' first," said Arona, laughing. "If having made one omelette makes you a cook, then I'm an Imperial Princess, since I played one onstage!"

"We've certainly seen a lot of wonders," said Kinri, coming to the rescue of the blushing Dandelion. "Surely we've seen everything there is to be seen in Ginpen, if not all of Dara."

"But not the most interesting wonder of them all," said Widi. He and the rest of the Blossom Gang exchanged glances.

"What do you mean?" asked Dandelion.

"Are you sure you want to hear this?" asked Arona, but her eyes were on Kinri, not Dandelion.

Mota took another sip of beer, not speaking, but his hand trembled so that some of the beer spilled.

"Now I *really* have to hear this," said Dandelion.

"Yes, do tell us," said Kinri.

Widi took a deep drink of his beer and looked mysteriously around the table. He lowered his voice. "What I'm going to say are only rumors, mind you. . . ."

Outside Ginpen, a short ride away by carriage, was a bluff that jutted into the ocean. Because of its resemblance to a giant shark's tooth stuck into the shoreline, the locals called it "Last Bite."

Waves had crashed against the sheer face of the bluff for countless millennia, and the action of the waves, as well as water seeping through the porous rock, drip by drip, had carved out a large cave at the foot of the bluff and a system of tunnels and smaller caves above. The local children liked to take rafts and paddle their way into the big cave at low tide to explore for treasure and secret hideouts where they could stage pirate adventures or catch lovers trying to evade vigilant chaperones and parents.

But a decade ago, in the midst of the Lyucu invasion of the Islands, change came to Last Bite. Soldiers took over the bluff and sealed off all roads leading to it, and local fishing boats were told not to go anywhere near the cliffs. The few fishing and farming families who lived nearby were told that they had to move, though the Imperial family paid for their land handsomely to minimize any fuss. The chief administrator of the Imperial laboratories in Ginpen, Archon Kita Thu, informed the locals that dangerous research would be performed there, and people should stay away out of prudence.

Gradually, the bluff grew into a small town of sorts. Farmers and beachgoers passing at a distance—for land within a radius of several miles around the bluff was declared to be a protected Imperial garden off-limits to the common people—could see huts, windmills, and other structures being erected on top of the bluff. Fishing boats returning to villages along the shore could see ladders and paths being carved into the sheer cliff face, leading to cave mouths that dotted Last Bite. The giant cave at the foot of the cliff was covered by a massive gate that hid what was within from prying eyes.

Rumors had it that this was where Imperial scholars had devised the silkmotic machines that led to the triumph at Zathin Gulf. But even in the years after the war, security at the site remained as tight as ever, though some of the huts on top of the bluff fell into disrepair. Fisherfolk and farmers still saw occasional Imperial ships or carriages visiting the bluff, as though research continued there, albeit at a slower pace.

"You want to go to Last Bite?" asked Dandelion in disbelief. "That's an Imperial research facility forbidden to all except authorized researchers."

"We're not going to steal anything," protested Arona. "But I heard that there's a library there too, with all kind of books not seen anywhere else."

"We're just going to look," said Rati Yera. "Can you imagine the secrets that must be hidden there? The kind of wonders that must be on display? Silkmotic engines that would make the work of the monks and nuns at the Great Temple of Lutho look like child's play."

"It is said that some of the rarest books in all Dara are stored there," said Widi. "Emperor Mapidéré ordered the burning of old books, but a few copies were kept in the Imperial Library in Pan before it was burned down. Supposedly, Prime Minister Cogo Yelu saved the books but felt it would be safer to store them away from Pan. I think Last Bite may be the chosen site."

"And there may be documents there about the Marsh—" Mota stopped when Arona put a calming hand on his shoulder. He took a deep breath, seemingly keeping his emotions in check with great effort. ". . . about what happened during the war," he finished.

Dandelion looked at him oddly but said nothing.

Kinri's heart leapt wildly. *Is this my chance to do what both Tanvanaki and my mother wanted? Is this a way to find out the secrets of Dara's war engines?*

He didn't know which of Dara's secrets, if any, he would take back to Ukyu-taasa. He didn't want to see the armies of Dara overrun Ukyu-taasa, and his mother a captive like the ones in Tiphan Huto's parade. But he also didn't want to see this city that he had come to love consigned to the flames of war. He wasn't sure what to do.

"But this is all beside the point," said Dandelion. "How can we possibly get in there?"

Arona looked at Kinri and smiled. "We've been planning this for a long time."

Kinri was about to ask a question when a waiter came to their table. "Mistress Rati Yera and Master Widi Tucru?"

Rati and Widi nodded.

"There's an urgent message for you."

## CHAPTER FORTY-FIVE

# ALONE

WORLD'S EDGE MOUNTAINS: THE TWELFTH MONTH
IN THE EIGHTH YEAR AFTER THE DEPARTURE OF
PRINCESS THÉRA FROM DARA FOR UKYU-GONDÉ
(SEVENTEEN MONTHS UNTIL THE LYUCU MUST
LAUNCH THEIR NEW INVASION FLEET TO DARA).

Théra had never felt so alone.

Takval scouted; Adyulek prayed; Çami improved her garinafin-piloting skills; Tipo Tho and Gozofin hunted and led the other warriors in daily drills. Even Thoryo, traumatized by the experience in Kiri Valley, occupied herself by learning the names of the animals and plants they saw in the valleys they bivouacked in every day.

But there was nothing for Théra to do. For years, she had given orders and listened to counsel and planned and plotted, but now, she didn't want to do any of those things. And, she thought, no one wanted her to do those things.

*I am useless. I've ruined everything.*

*I trusted Radia and Toof, and now our children are in the clutches of the Lyucu. Takval and Tipo and Gozofin and the other parents haven't uttered a word of recrimination against me, but I know. I know.*

*I thought I had the perfect plan to destroy the city-ships and overthrow the Lyucu, and now Sliyusa Ki and Kiri Valley are both gone. Thousands are dead because of me. The few survivors grieve because of me. Because of me.*

*I thought I could start a revolution, to change the lives of the people of the scrublands for the better, to save Dara. I can't do any of these things. I can't even protect my children. I'm a failure.*

*I am named Dissolver of Sorrows, but I've multiplied the sorrows of the people I love a hundred hundredfold.*

*I'm not strong enough. Look at Gozofin and Tipo, still fighting and drilling, despite having lost spouse and children and aged parents. Look at Thoryo, still learning and exploring. Look at Takval, still leading and hoping. I can't even get up from where I sit without someone's help.*

*I can't sleep; I can't eat; I can't speak. I do what people tell me to do. I climb onto the garinafin at night and let them strap me in, putting my arms around Takval like a marionette. I climb off the garinafin in the morning and eat what they put in front of me, and pretend to sleep so they'll leave me alone.*

*I can't even pray. O gods of Dara, are you even here? O gods of Gondé, do you even hear me?*

*If I could end it all, I would.*

*Only I know that even death will bring no peace. Even though I am of no help, they still look to me as their princess. My death will bring yet more pain to the people I love.*

*"As long as you're with me, my breath, I know there is hope," says Takval.*

*"As long as you're with us, Rénga, I know we'll avenge my family and save the children," says Tipo Tho.*

*"As long as you're with us, Princess, I know we'll get out of this," says Çami Phithadapu.*

*"As long as you're with us, Princess, I know we'll triumph over the Lyucu," says Gozofin.*

*They mean to make me feel better. But they can't. No one can.*

*Was this how Princess Kikomi felt on the eve of Kindo Marana's invasion of Arulugi? Was this how King Jizu felt as Tanno Namen's army surrounded Na Thion? I am a symbol of hope but I have no hope myself. I am helpless to help.*

*How much longer until sunset? How much longer until sunrise? How many more days must I go on like this?*

She wept with her face turned away toward the wall of the cave they were sheltering in, silently so that no one would hear. She wept so that neither Cudyufin nor Nalyufin would see her shame. She wept until her eyes had run as dry as the Ghost River in winter.

Outside, clouds roiled over the peaks of the World's Edge Mountains, as uncertain as the will of the gods of the scrublands.

# CHAPTER FORTY-SIX

# LAST BITE

GINPEN: THE SEVENTH MONTH IN THE NINTH
YEAR OF THE REIGN OF SEASON OF STORMS AND
THE REIGN OF AUDACIOUS FREEDOM (TWENTY-
TWO MONTHS UNTIL THE REOPENING OF THE
WALL OF STORMS).

"How did your master find out about us?" asked Arona.

The Blossom Gang, along with Kinri and Dandelion, were riding inside a fast carriage pulled by a team of four horses, heading toward the docks of Ginpen.

"My master attended the contest between the Splendid Urn and the Treasure Chest, and he was most impressed by the ingenuity of the Splendid Urn's designs. When the widow—er, Grand Mistress Wasu announced that the Blossom Gang was responsible for the victory, he just knew he had found his saviors."

Kinri smiled. Hearing that his friends' accomplishments and talents were being recognized pleased him immensely. He found it odd, therefore, that Rati and Widi looked tense as they stared out the window, paying no attention to the banter between Arona and the man who had invited them on this midnight outing. Mota was his usual quiet self, sitting as steady as a pine tree with his eyes closed, meditating and oblivious to his surroundings. Dandelion, on the other hand, listened to the conversation between Arona and the driver with interest, though from time to time she looked over at him and grinned.

"And your master said he had to have this taken care of tonight?" asked Arona.

"Yes, yes! This lowly servant wouldn't have dared to bother the masters and mistresses otherwise. My master is in desperate straits. Since its appearance ten days ago, the ghost has been returning every night, making noise and moving boxes in the warehouse. Sometimes there are mysterious lights and strange smells that make people ill. It left a note that our master must give it an offering of ten thousand golds and not go to the magistrate or his family would be harmed. The deadline is tomorrow."

"And you've already asked for an exorcism and it hasn't helped."

"Exactly. Our master is terrified, but we haven't been able to catch the ghost or keep it away, even with everyone standing watch all night. The master suspects that the ghost may not be real, but is a plot from his competitor. He thought only the brilliant Blossom Gang could figure out how the haunting is done and catch the culprits."

Just from listening to the story, Kinri was certain that there was no ghost. It had to be a bunch of tricks akin to street magic. This kind of "haunting" was exactly the kind of mystery that the Blossom Gang loved to solve, and he could see why they had departed from the banquet, eager to help.

"Oh, your poor master," said Arona sympathetically. "I can only imagine how much stress he's under. Your master's competitor sounds like a very evil man, almost as unscrupulous as . . . that Tiphan Huto."

The driver nodded and chuckled at this, but Kinri could sense more than a little awkwardness and nervousness. He attributed the reaction to Tiphan's general bad reputation in the city after some of his dirty tricks against the Splendid Urn had leaked and became the topic of much derisive gossip.

As Arona went on chatting with the man, the carriage neared the docks. This late at night, the area was deserted. As the carriage wended its way between giant warehouses, the clattering of the horses' hooves seemed particularly loud.

"Ooh, I hope the horses don't scare away the ghost!" exclaimed Arona. "They sure are loud. Hey, isn't this where Master Go, the blacksmith, disappeared a few weeks back? Maybe . . . he's the ghost haunting your master! Now, if that's the case, we may have to turn back, because Master Go is a powerful man, and he'll only be even more powerful as an incorporeal being—"

"No, no! The ghost can't possibly be Master Go. He's still—" The man choked back the rest of his sentence.

"You know Master Go's whereabouts?" Arona's eyes were wide as teacups.

"Oh, I . . . uh . . . I don't. I'm just saying that it's bad luck to think he's dead, right?" Sweat beaded on the man's forehead. "Hey, look, we're almost there! Whoa! Whoa! What happened here!?"

He pulled hard on the reins and the carriage rattled to a stop. An overturned cart blocked their way, its cargo spilled everywhere. There were no signs of the horses or the driver.

"What happened here?" asked Kinri. "Bandits in the middle of Ginpen?"

But neither Widi nor Rati seemed the least bit surprised. In fact, they visibly relaxed when they saw the roadblock. Mota's eyes snapped open, and he looked as ready as a drawn bow for action.

"Do you think that's the ghost's doing too?" asked Arona, a teasing tone in her voice.

"Er? Uh . . . masters and mistresses, please stay put. Let me just go down to see what happened, and I'll be right back."

"How thoughtful of you!" said Arona. "Maybe you'll make a friend out of the ghost, hmm?"

The driver laughed nervously at this, and, uncertain what to say, bowed, hopped down from the seat, and ran to the upturned cart. Instead of investigating the accident, however, he continued running and disappeared down a side alley.

"Hey!" Kinri cried out. "Where are you going?"

Arona looked at him. "You didn't know he was going to do that?"

"What are you talking about?"

"This is a trap," said Dandelion. But instead of looking scared, she looked positively giddy.

As if on cue, men dressed in black clothes and with scarves covering the bottom halves of their faces emerged from the alleys and surrounded the carriage. In the light of suddenly lit torches, their unsheathed swords and polished staffs gleamed.

"Only thirty people," said Widi, shaking his head. "Disappointing."

"I feel insulted," said Arona. "I was expecting maybe double this number."

"You knew this was going to happen?" Kinri looked around at the Blossom Gang. They nodded.

"I imagine this was how Master Go the blacksmith and the other mechanics were abducted," said Widi.

"You're going to have to be a lot more attentive if you want to become a true Blossom," chided Rati, but her tone was affectionate.

"Come out of that carriage and drop your weapons now unless you want to die!" the leader of the black-garbed men shouted.

Kinri instantly moved to the front of the carriage, keeping Rati and Dandelion behind him. "Master, you can't move as well as the rest of us, so please stay inside. Dandelion and Arona, can you protect her? Widi, can you take the reins and break out of this ambush? Mota and I will stay to fight and slow them down."

Dandelion gave him a look composed of equal parts joy and frustration. "Who needs you to play the hero? You're the only fool who didn't know what was going on! I'm not missing out on this adventure."

"I'm not pl-playing the hero!" Kinri felt himself vibrating with anxiety. "You and Master Yera must make it out so someone can tell the magistrate what happened here."

Before Dandelion could retort, several black-garbed fighters had leapt forward and cut loose the harnesses of the horses. While a few attackers waved their weapons to keep the occupants of the carriage from interfering, two others led the horses away.

"And now we're stuck," said Kinri, feeling desperate. "Mota, can you carry Master Yera out of here if I clear a path for you? Dandelion, stay close to the others and get out!"

Without waiting for an answer, he jumped out of the carriage, grabbing a carrying pole lying near the footboard as he did so. As he landed, he growled like a wolf, and went at the nearest black-garbed fighter.

He had trained with his mother and some of her naros since he was a little boy in the use of the bone club and the spear. Though he had no combat experience, at least he knew what to do with a weapon. The carrying pole was too short for a spear and too long for a club, and wasn't the right weight for either, but since he fought as though he didn't care about his life at all, the black-garbed men were forced to back up a few steps as he swung the unwieldy weapon about in wide arcs.

But they soon regrouped and pushed back, weaving their deadly blades and long staffs into an impenetrable wall. Kinri had to step back.

He heard Dandelion shouting behind him, "Come back! You'll get hurt!"

Instantly, a warmth coursed through his body. He felt strong enough to take on all the swordsmen of Dara by himself. "Ukyu-kyo," he shouted, the instinctive patterns instilled by the story-dancing shamans taking over. He raised the carrying pole and rushed at the masked men again.

The man in front met his eyes and, apparently startled by what he saw there—Kinri hoped it was a fearless look of bloodlust worthy of Tenryo himself—stumbled back. With a triumphant cry, Kinri pressed forward, hoping to finally force an opening in the encirclement.

But the stumbling man turned out to be only feinting. As Kinri thrust his carrying pole forward, the man dropped his sword and grabbed the pole, pulling hard. Combined with Kinri's forward momentum, the move threw him off balance, and he tripped, falling flat on his face. Before he could get up, he felt the tips of multiple swords land against his back, piercing through his clothes to draw blood against his skin. "Yield!" someone yelled.

Shame, terror, and regret flooded him. He hadn't even gotten a chance to read Dandelion's handkerchief message, and now perhaps he never would. But the idea of dying without letting her know who he really was seemed worse than death.

*Love has no place for lies.*

He decided to make his last words a stirring speech about how the Lyucu never yielded, but when he looked up defiantly, the words died in his throat. Two of the black-garbed men held bone war clubs.

*They are Lyucu.*

It was an impossible idea. *How can the Lyucu be here on the Big Island?* And as he watched the men strutting about, waving their clubs, he became even more confused. The way they held the clubs was all wrong; they swung them like ill-balanced blunt swords. No naro or culek would treat their weapon in such a careless manner.

As innumerable questions ran through his mind, a bright explosion of light erupted behind him, illuminating the area around the carriage as though the noon sun had suddenly burst upon the scene.

The enemy fighters squinted and drew back, shielding their eyes. Several cried out in pain and surprise. The light was blinding, a thousand times brighter than the flickering glow of the torches.

Kinri felt the swords against his back slacken. With a kick and roll, he got out from under them. As the source of the bright light was behind him, his vision was unaffected. Keeping himself flat against the ground to not draw attention, he turned himself around. Carefully shielding his eyes with one hand, he peeked out from between his fingers to check on the carriage.

A hissing, sparkling orb, like a shooting star in reverse, was slowly rising into the sky. It really was as bright as the sun, and could be seen for miles around.

"You idiots! I told you to grab them as quickly as possible! Don't let them call for help!"

The speaker stood beyond the circle of black-garbed swordsmen, and he was shaking with rage. In the glow of the powerful signaling rocket, Kinri recognized the face of Tiphan Huto.

"Get them! Get them now!" Tiphan screamed, jumping up and down for emphasis.

But before the blinded fighters could carry out his orders, a figure leapt out of the carriage like a Mingén falcon diving off a cliff. The figure landed in front of the carriage, raised an arm, and slammed a palm like an axe against one of the thick shafts of the carriage, between which the horses had been harnessed. The shaft, though thicker than Kinri's thigh, snapped like an eating stick.

As Kinri watched, jaw hanging, the figure—Kinri really wasn't sure if it was a person or Diasa-Fithowéo incarnate—picked up the massive broken shaft and swept it around in a wide arc, instantly flattening the dozen attackers standing before Kinri, to the accompaniment of pained howls. The warrior brandished the unwieldy makeshift weapon as easily as Kinri might have swung a bone club.

Mota Kiphi.

Stupefied by this inhuman display of strength, Kinri didn't move as Mota took a few steps forward and swung the shaft again. Though already lying prone, Kinri pressed his face to the ground, feeling the gusts of turbulence from the weapon tingling the back of his neck. The screams and moans behind him told him that Mota had leveled another group of attackers.

Gingerly, Kinri looked up.

Mota stood in front of him. Holding the heavy shaft aloft with one hand, Mota offered his other hand.

Almost as in a dream, Kinri allowed himself to be pulled up.

"Get him! Get him now before the garrison shows up!" Tiphan Huto shouted.

A few black-garbed men, having recovered from the flash bomb, rushed at Mota's back.

"Careful!" Kinri shouted.

Without even looking back, Mota swung the shaft, one-handed, behind him. There was no technique to it. The beam moved as slowly and as clumsily as a falling tree. But there was no dodging or deflecting its irresistible power. The men fell to the ground with dull thuds, moaning piteously, their resistance as ineffective as grass trying to stand up against the swinging scythe.

Realizing that there was no way to overcome this inhuman warrior, Tiphan Huto decided that discretion was the better part of valor. "Tight wind! Tough marks!" Without waiting for any of his followers, he ran for one of the alleys.

"Too late for that," Widi Tucru shouted from the carriage.

Indeed, Tiphan Huto staggered back into the light a moment later, as streams of soldiers rushed out of the alleys to surround him and the remaining black-garbed fighters.

As soldiers forced Tiphan and the others to their knees and bound their arms behind them, a smiling Magistrate Zuda strode into view. "Thank you for your selfless assistance, heroes of the Blossom Gang!"

Magistrate Zuda's ornate carriage clattered through the main road leading away from Ginpen toward the sea. Soon, the lights of the metropolis faded into the darkness. The only sounds that accompanied the rattling of the carriage were the hooting of owls and the rustling of invisible creatures through the underbrush on the sides of the road.

Inside, the Blossom Gang, Kinri, and Dandelion talked as Arona worked on Kinri's disguise, having already finished everyone else's makeup.

". . . Remember Tiphan Huto's underground prison?" Widi asked. "As soon as I heard about the disappearing mechanics and engineers, I realized the two might be connected."

"When Widi mentioned his suspicions, I told him that I'd heard that pirates were abducting skilled workers to sell them to the Lyucu as slaves," said Dandelion. Arona had made her up to be as plain and unnoticeable as possible, but Kinri still found her appearance breathtaking. "However, the news I heard was that the pirates were operating near Dimu and Dimushi, not here in Ginpen."

"How did you hear this?" Kinri was horrified that the pékyu would resort to such a tactic. "I don't believe it!"

"I . . . have my sources," said Dandelion, looking away.

"Why do you sound so shocked?" Widi asked. "The Lyucu are capable of any outrage."

Kinri said nothing.

"There were other clues that Tiphan Huto was working with the pirates and the Lyucu," said Arona, as though unaware of any awkwardness in the air. "Mozo Mu said that the men who had come to kidnap her family had bone weapons, and we saw such weapons in Tiphan Huto's parade. You told me that they looked genuine, not mere props designed to frighten or sow confusion."

"Not to mention the goods we saw in the cellar of the Treasure Chest," said Rati Yera, "which could only come from dealings with pirates who traded with the Lyucu."

"I confirmed our guesses later by talking to the *raye* crew cleaning the toilets at the Treasure Chest," said Widi. "We swapped patches last year when I helped them win a case against a vindictive noble who didn't like having the *raye* camp near his estate. They told me that servants at the Treasure Chest were complaining about having to deal with the night soil buckets of 'guests' in the cellar, and the servants' mocking description of one of the 'guests' matched Master Go, the blacksmith."

Kinri didn't know what to think. He had not realized that the Blossom Gang had been conducting an extensive investigation while helping the Splendid Urn. Had he been too involved in the competition to notice it, or had they deliberately kept him in the dark? "Did you go to the magistrate right away?"

"Stay still," said Arona as she began painting Kinri's eyebrows. "We would have, but we weren't sure we had enough evidence to convince Magistrate Zuda to move against such a prominent family. And if we didn't land a decisive blow, Tiphan would have moved the prisoners elsewhere, erased all the evidence, and then accused us of impersonating Imperial officials."

"So that's why you set a trap for him!" said Dandelion.

Widi nodded, looking smug. "We asked Grand Mistress Wasu to make a big deal about us onstage, which we knew would make Tiphan hate us even more than he already did. But by emphasizing our skills as engineers, a greedy and vindictive man like him would think it more satisfying to abduct us and sell us to the pirates than to turn us in to the magistrate."

"Before we left the Urn, we told Magistrate Zuda to alert the garrison around the docks because we were going to help him catch the criminals behind all the recent disappearances," said Rati Yera. "He was skeptical, but he did as we asked."

"Of course he did," said Dandelion. "Catching the culprits would be a major administrative accomplishment and add to his chances the next time an opening for a governorship came up."

"And the rest, as you know, pretty much went down as planned," said Widi. "Except you gave us quite a scare back there, rushing at the kidnappers like that."

Kinri was embarrassed by his ineffectual intervention, but Dandelion said, "You reminded me of the *thasé-teki* sprouting in spring."

"Is that . . . a compliment?" said Arona, laughing. "A caterpillar turning into a stout stalk . . ."

Dandelion, though cheeks reddening, ignored her. "I think you were very brave, Kinri. Your transformation was more impressive than any Arona performed onstage."

Kinri felt much better.

By now, Magistrate Zuda's soldiers had surely surrounded the Treasure Chest and broken in, and the place was likely being turned upside down. He hoped that the kidnapped victims would be rescued without harm.

The carriage bumped down a small, unmarked side road. The tall grass in the dirt path indicated that though the road was wide and well-graded, it was seldom used.

Kinri's mind drifted, seized by conflicting emotions.

After Tiphan's capture, when the Blossom Gang explained that they didn't have a way of getting back to the Splendid Urn, Magistrate Zuda, grateful for their assistance, had lent them the use of his own carriage.

Kinri had been surprised to see that instead of heading back to the Splendid Urn, Mota was driving the carriage toward the city gates.

"This is the best part," said Arona. "We're going to Last Bite, right now. The magistrate's own vehicle is the last missing piece." She explained the plan to him.

It sounded absurd, impossible, dependent on too many things going just right to work. Yet, hadn't that always been the case with the Blossom Gang?

This was his chance to complete the mission that his mother had risked so much to send him on. Yet, why was he so hesitant? It wasn't just out of fear that the plan would fail.

The familiar sight of the magistrate's carriage led the guards at the city gates to wave them through without checking their traveling documents, though it was long past the free passage curfew. No one knew that the Blossom Gang was no longer in Ginpen.

Mota slowed down. Flickering torches appeared far ahead in the distance.

"That's the checkpoint," whispered Arona, examining Kinri's face one last time. "Don't worry." She squeezed Kinri's hand reassuringly. "I've done my best work."

"I can confirm that," said Dandelion. "I always thought you looked a bit . . . familiar. But now, you really *do* look like her."

The Blossom Gang looked at her strangely. Dandelion looked flustered. "I . . . I'm from Pan, and I've seen her . . . a few times."

Kinri's heart raced like crazy and he could feel his back grow clammy. The expensive silk dress on him felt unfamiliar, confining.

Getting out of the city without anyone noticing was one thing; fooling an Imperial security detachment serving the farseers with a false identity was something else entirely.

"We've been studying this place for months," said Arona. "We know that she's been coming here more often—but she's not here now. The timing is perfect."

"But I don't know anything about how she acts!" protested Kinri. "How can I possibly pass for someone I've never met?" The very idea of impersonating one of the most famous people in Dara seemed to him utter madness.

"You have an advantage that even the most well-trained actors don't have: your true self."

"What do you mean?"

"Though I'm very good with disguises, the most convincing impersonators bear a natural resemblance to the subject that can be heightened. If I use a mask instead of mere makeup, detailed facial expressions won't come through. In fact, your appearance was why we first paid attention to you."

"What?" The revelation was too surprising for Kinri to process right away. After a pause, he asked in a trembling voice, "You've been using me?"

"No! That's not . . . not what I meant." Kinri could not recall Arona being so at a loss for words. "I should . . . should have . . ."

"Stop the carriage," said Kinri. "I won't be a scholar-pawn in someone else's *zamaki* game."

Mota stopped the carriage. "I was the one who first suggested that we get to know you. I met the person you're impersonating when I was young, and the resemblance between the two of you struck me right away."

"You!?" Of all the members of the Blossom Gang, Mota, who always seemed to be without guile or scheme, was the last one Kinri would have suspected of taking advantage of him.

"I needed your help, Kinri," said Mota. "But I should have been plain with you. I'm sorry."

Kinri waited.

Mota took a deep breath. "I survived the Battle of Zathin Gulf, and there's no one in this world I respect more than Marshal Gin Mazoti, who died to keep Tenryo from overrunning these Islands."

Kinri recalled the play he had seen from Mota and Arona.

Mota went on. "But the Marshal has been forgotten by the people of Dara. While everyone seems to know the latest gossip about the head girl of the Aviary or the actor who charges three hundred golds just to show up at a banquet, no one cares about the Marshal. The official histories still declare her a traitor, and the people are content to accept that, not to question the story they've been told."

Kinri's stony face softened as he thought of Master Nazu Tei and the stories of the court-appointed tutors.

He had almost been relieved by Arona's revelation; it was an excuse to avoid having to carry out his mission. But Mota was trying to find out the truth. Wasn't it the same quest he was on? There were other truths—the truths behind stories—far more important than the secrets of Dara's war machines.

"That's why Rona and I put on our play; to remind the people that they're alive today because she died! I don't believe the Marshal was ever a traitor to the Throne, and I want to find the proof. I believe the fortress at Last Bite is where the court keeps documents it doesn't want anyone to ever see. Yes, it is a place of wonders and secret research, and that does make it enticing to Rati, Widi, and Rona—but all of them are really only doing this to help me, because redeeming the Marshal's name has been my dream."

"One should always be ready to stick knives between one's ribs if that would help a friend," said Widi.

"And when you saw me . . ." Kinri's voice trailed off.

"We thought it was a sign," said Mota. "Out of all the acts in Temple Square, you stopped to see our play about the Marshal; out of all the people gathered there, you and I saved Dandelion together and our eyes met. All these coincidences . . . they mean something. We thought the gods wanted us to come together.

"I never thought of using you, Kinri. After these last few months, I've come to know you. You're courageous, clever, and loyal. I'm grateful that you're my friend."

Kinri didn't know what to say, neither did he have names for the conflicting emotions in his chest. Memories of the last few months flitted through his mind: Master Rati Yera's patient instruction; Mota's quiet, plain dependability; Arona's teasing laughter; Widi's outrageous schemes; and above all . . . Dandelion.

They were his friends. Though away from home and fire pit, these had been among the happiest times of his life.

Yet there was the countervailing claim of his mother and the pékyu. Ukyu-taasa must be in desperate straits for the pékyu to resort to abduction of skilled engineers from the core islands.

*How bad are things at home? How can I not carry out my mission?*

To steal the secrets of Dara would be to betray his friends. To not do so would be to betray his homeland.

"But it isn't right to base friendship on deception," said Mota. "So I won't lie anymore. What we're planning isn't a fun adventure or a pleasant jaunt. Breaking into a secured Imperial facility to find out the knowledge I need is likely a capital crime. But nonetheless, I'm asking for your help because I sense we're kindred spirits, my friend."

Kinri closed his eyes and thought.

*Was it indeed a sign for us to meet? Did the gods want us to come together? How does one know the will of the gods?*

Yet, Mota's words moved him deeply. *To find out the truth about the past, to redeem the names of our heroes—aren't these the very things I want? Last Bite may hold the plans for terrifying engines of war, but it may also hold the truth about Pékyu Tenryo and Kuni Garu.*

*Only the truth can guide my actions.*

He opened his eyes. "You *are* my friend. We must know the truth."

"The Marshal . . . I had no idea . . ." said Dandelion. Her voice grew resolute. "Yes, let's find out the truth."

Relief flooded the faces of the Blossom Gang. Mota coaxed the horses into moving again.

As they approached the checkpoint in the darkness, Arona whispered into Kinri's ear. "Even if things don't work out exactly as planned, I think we'll be safe."

"Why?" asked Kinri.

Arona tilted her chin at the figure of Dandelion, looking thoughtful on the other side of the carriage, and then she said no more.

"Halt!" a voice shouted in the darkness.

The checkpoint was staffed by a squad of at least ten Imperial soldiers. They weren't part of the army, but under the direct command of the farseers, who were responsible both for spying and catching spies. Widi handed over the documents Rati had forged, and the soldiers examined them under the torchlight.

"They're taking a long time," fretted Kinri.

"Stay calm," said Arona, peeking through the curtains at the front of the carriage.

The soldiers continued to scrutinize the documents, and two of them seemed to be arguing and looking back and forth from the documents to the carriage.

Widi, again disguised as a city clerk, went up to the group. "Is there a problem, officers?"

"We didn't receive any notice of a visit," one of the soldiers said. "Messenger pigeons usually send the preclearance list ahead of time."

"The secretary is visiting with Magistrate Zuda in the city," said Widi. "But she has received some important intelligence concerning Lyucu-sponsored piracy that must be analyzed tonight in Last Bite. That's why the magistrate lent us the use of his carriage."

"But the secretary made the rules for preclearance herself."

Inside the carriage, Arona whispered to Kinri, who nodded. Then

Arona dropped her makeup case on the floor of the carriage, making a ruckus.

The soldiers by the torches looked up at the sound and saw a hand with slender fingers pull back the curtain at the side of the carriage. The hand rested on the window, showing the sleeve of an expensive silk dress. The face that looked out at them was cold, severe, and authoritative.

Farsight Secretary Zomi Kidosu's visage was not known by many, as she preferred to keep a low profile despite her great power, but these soldiers were used to seeing her. They bowed.

"Her absence from Ginpen isn't supposed to be known," Widi hissed.

Despite the skill of Arona's disguise, the Blossom Gang thought it prudent as well as more effective to make Kinri's appearance a surprise, with the implication that the soldiers were interfering with an unannounced, secretive visit to Last Bite. Surprised guards fearful of offending a powerful figure usually didn't look too closely.

But these soldiers were too well-trained for that. "Always a pleasure to have you here, Secretary Kidosu," one of the guards said, his tone respectful but not fearful. "However, the documents don't describe everyone in your group."

Kinri waved his hand impatiently, indicating that he was in a hurry.

"I'm sorry, but we must interview every member of your retinue if they're not precleared," said the soldier. "That's the rule. Can you give us an overview of everyone's qualifications and names now to speed up the process?"

The group froze. This was unexpected, and all eyes were on Kinri.

Kinri almost fainted. The idea of speaking to these guards was absolutely out of the question. He was no actor and didn't know how to imitate the voice of anyone, much less the voice of a woman, much less the voice of a Lord of Dara.

Just as Widi was about to step forward to try to salvage the disaster, Dandelion, disguised as an official, strode up to the guards and stood imperiously before them.

"Thank Tututika . . . she's so good at that," whispered Arona.

Dandelion pulled something out of her sleeve and showed it to the guards. Instantly, the faces of the guards changed, and they bowed deeply.

"The secretary is here pursuant to a direct Imperial order," intoned Dandelion. "This group of special . . . experts must not be delayed."

The soldiers rushed to clear the roadblocks.

Dandelion returned to the carriage. "Let's go," she said to Mota, her tone effortlessly commanding.

Mota lifted the reins. "*Ka! Ka!*" he called, and snapped the whip through the air.

Kinri allowed the curtain to drop back and let out a held breath, his back cold with sweat. The carriage rolled forward.

"I told you we'd be fine as long as we have her," whispered Arona to Kinri.

He looked at her questioningly, but Arona held up a finger against her lips.

The carriage climbed the gentle slope to the top of the bluff, where another group of soldiers checked the documents again, and the team exited the carriage.

Guided by a torch-carrying guard, they descended a narrow set of steps that stitched back and forth across the face of the cliff. The pounding surf below grew louder with every turn, and the smell of the sea became stronger.

At the bottom of the cliff, they got into a small boat that was oared into the yawning mouth of the giant cavern. The incessant sound of waves breaking against rocks reverberated in the enclosed space.

Dandelion broke the silence among the passengers.

"What a big cave!" she exclaimed.

Arona tried to tell her to be quiet with a severe look, but it was too late.

"I'm new," Dandelion, sitting nearest the stern, said to the man holding the tiller. "This cave looks big enough for a warship to sail right in. Ever seen anything interesting pass through here? Like a pirate ship?"

The man seemed taken aback, but was disarmed by Dandelion's

obvious enthusiasm. "I'll never forget the day when the garinafin carcasses were pulled in here," he said.

"Garinafin carcasses!"

"That's right." The man glanced discreetly at Kinri, sitting silently at the bow of the boat, and then lowered his voice. "Didn't you know? I guess you really haven't been working for her for long. This was where she and Grand Princess Théra first learned the secrets of how the beasts flew."

"Oh! I had no idea this was the dissection site."

The rest of the group tried to look dignified and nonchalant, as befitting "special experts" invited here by the Farsight Secretary. But every heart was beating faster. Just imagining the gigantic creatures being hauled through the same waterway they were oaring over now seemed to bring them closer to that legendary time.

The boat docked at a small wharf, and the team, escorted by more torch-carrying guards, climbed up long sets of steps carved into the stone wall of the large cavern. Mota carried Rati on his back while Widi carried the wheeled chair.

They reached a platform halfway up the cave wall. The captain of the guards asked, "Is the Farsight Secretary here to make use of the laboratories or the library?"

The team looked at one another.

"My work will require a visit to the laboratories," Rati Yera said.

Kinri, knowing that his master's request was motivated by the fact that she couldn't read and wouldn't be able to take advantage of the library, nodded. Widi set up the wheeled chair, and the old woman wheeled herself after one of the guards toward an opening at the side of the platform.

The rest of the team continued the climb up the long stone steps.

"An attendant will be with you shortly," said the guard. He bowed and left.

Rati found herself inside a small, circular room whose wall was fashioned from vertical wooden planks like the side of a barrel. The wall wasn't very high—about the height of a tall man—which added to the impression of sitting inside a large barrel with the top cut off.

Beyond the wooden planks, she could see the rocky interior of the mountain a short gap away. She looked up and realized that there was no roof to the room. Her wheeled chair was in fact at the bottom of a long shaft inside the bluff. Every few yards, glowing glass globes protruding from the wall of the shaft provided illumination, until the contracting rings of lights disappeared far above her in the murk. She was like the proverbial frog at the bottom of a well looking up.

A woman in her thirties, dressed in a scholar's robe, entered the barrel-room and bowed awkwardly to Rati. Recalling Widi's admonition to act as haughty as possible to discourage questions, Rati kept a severe mien and only nodded slightly in acknowledgment.

Evidently the socially awkward type, the woman gave Rati a nervous grimace, shut the door, shuffled around the wheeled chair to a long wooden handle on the opposite side, and pulled it down.

A clanging noise began far above, and with a slight jerk, the room began to rise.

A startled Rati soon realized that her original impression of a well had been quite close to the mark. The "room" she was in was a low-walled bucket at the bottom of the well, and by flipping that switch, the scholar had engaged some kind of mechanism that allowed the whole room to rise up, much like a giant version of the elevator at the Urn, used by waitstaff carrying heavy loads and customers with mobility needs.

The silent ride made Rati uncomfortable. Her personality was unsuited to the role Widi had designed for her, and so she decided she would try to be more like herself.

"I haven't been here before," she said tentatively. "Is this . . . an invention by Secretary Kidosu?"

Being given a chance to skip small talk and discuss something concrete visibly relaxed the young scholar. She nodded. "In her youth, the Farsight Secretary needed the assistance of crutches and braces. To be sure that people of talent aren't kept out of the laboratories because of such mobility needs, she installed this elevator. It's also convenient for bringing larger pieces of equipment to the labs."

Rati gave a thoughtful nod. Though she didn't know much about

Zomi Kidosu's personal life, this detail endeared her to the old woman.

"How is it powered?" asked Rati, more to keep the conversation going than out of real interest. She figured it was just a standard piece of mechanical engineering. "Is there a windmill far above us? With a flywheel perhaps to store energy and to regulate the speed? Or . . . maybe it's driven by a waterwheel powered by the tides below?"

The scholar, taking Rati's interest to be professional, beamed with pride. "Common engines aren't reliable or flexible enough for the needs of this facility. Like many other machines here, the elevator is powered by the silkmotic force."

"The silkmotic force!" Rati was astounded. The silkmotic force was a relatively new addition to the repertoire of the engineer in Dara. In her experience, its main applications were limited to warfare and enhancements to stage and temple magic. Some adventurous inventors not associated with one of the Imperial laboratories also tried to use it for illumination, but the general consensus was that silkmotic lamps were too dangerous and difficult to maintain. Even her own silkmotic candles had fallen out of use at the Urn, as the staff were nervous around them and found leaf-dancer cicadas too troublesome to keep night after night. Rati had never envisioned that the silkmotic force could be used to do real work, to drive anything as impressive as this elevator. "How!?"

"If you're interested, I can take you to see the engine." The scholar's smile was as wide as it was genuine. She had evidently been worried that a surprise visitor brought by the Farsight Secretary was here to investigate some security breach or dictate additional laboratory procedure, but the old woman's obvious interest in machinery meant that they could speak as fellow engineers. "Last Bite was where much of the research on modern silkmotic engineering was first conducted, and we have some wonders not seen in the rest of Dara. Oh, do forgive me for my lack of social graces—we don't get too many visitors. I'm Kisli Péro, junior researcher, ranked *cashima* two sessions ago."

Rati smiled wryly at Kisli's attempt to be smooth. It was the habit of Dara scholars to mention their own achievements at the Imperial examinations as a way to establish hierarchy and precedence when

meeting unfamiliar fellow scholars—and also a way to build camaraderie by recalling the grueling the examination process. Rati, however, lacked both the interest and capital to participate in such rituals. "I'd love to see the engine. I'm Rati Yera."

Kisli waited, and when it was obvious that Rati would not reveal
more about herself, nodded deferentially, apparently taking Rati's
refusal to disclose her rank as a sign that she considered herself too
important to try to impress a junior researcher.

As the elevator approached the level of the laboratories, Kisli
reached for the large wooden handle and flipped it to the neutral
position. The elevator slowed down and then stopped.

Kisli opened the door to the elevator. "May I?" she asked, gesturing at Rati's chair. "I imagine your trip here has been quite taxing."
Rati nodded, consenting to be helped.

Kisli pushed Rati Yera's wheeled chair out into the corridor. The
research compound was a warren of caves and branching passageways, all lit by silkmotic globes. Rati wondered if these globes were
closer in principle to the dangerous "burning wick"–style lamps she
had seen from other inventors, or the silkmotic candles of her own
creation.

"Your chair is very well-designed," said Kisli. "I've never seen handles or gear trains like that . . . and the wheels glide so smoothly. . . .
Ah, it shifts between gears to take advantage of the terrain! Is it your
own invention? You must be an extremely accomplished artificer."

Rati couldn't help but grin with pleasure. Nothing made her glow
like praise from a fellow engineer.

"I tinker," she said modestly.

"I'd love to be given a tutorial on the mechanism."

"It would be a pleasure."

Now evidently feeling entirely at ease with Rati, Kisli grew more
voluble. "Master Yera, do you require the use of a visitor's laboratory for your work?" In the absence of a clear signal of rank from
Rati Yera, she defaulted to the common courtesy title of a teacher.
"I hope you aren't expected to start right away, after traveling all
day . . . though I hear Secretary Kidosu can be quite demanding on
her staff! Or . . . perhaps you'd like a bath first?"

"A bath?" Rati Yera was confused.

"I find that after a tiring journey, a hot bath is the best way to clean off the grime of the road as well as to restore mental tranquility. In fact, I do some of my best thinking in the bath barrel or tub! Here at Last Bite, we've installed some state-of-the-art bathing facilities, including a heated wave tub powered by the silkmotic force! It feels exactly like swimming in the pools near Rufizo Falls—"

"That's all right," said Rati Yera, chuckling. She liked the enthusiastic young woman. In her experience, anyone who could get so excited about something so mundane as a bath was all right. "I'm not that tired. My work can wait. I prefer to see the engine for the elevator first."

"As you wish."

After a few twists and turns through the winding tunnels, they stopped on a platform hanging over the side of a vast cavern. Rati peeked out over the edge and felt a wave of vertigo—it was a long way down into the darkness. A persistent, deep humming filled the air.

"The elevator we came up on is over there," said Kisli, pointing along the wall of the cavern. "The shaft is behind that seam in the rock; up above you can see the silkmotic mill that drives it."

Rati peered across the cavern and saw a giant spinning vaned wheel embedded in the cave wall. That was the source of the humming noise. Located above and below the wheel were two massive cylinders, each the size of a large house in Ginpen.

"Those are two of the largest Ogé jars in the compound, though we have multiple sets scattered throughout the compound," explained Kisli. "They are kept charged by a bank of silkmotic generators, which are indeed powered by windmills on the bluff above us. In addition, Secretary Kidosu has installed some Fithowéo's Needles on the bluff to channel lightning strikes into underground silkmotic reservoirs modeled on the coiled garinafin-gut Ogé jars that powered the Imperial airships during the Battle of Zathin Gulf. The reservoirs release their dammed-up silkmotic force into the rest of the system when wind power proves insufficient."

Rati imagined the power of lightning being stored in bottles in cellars like so much fine wine and smiled. Zomi Kidosu really had an extraordinary mind.

"The silkmotic force pent up in the large Ogé jars is used for all sorts of applications in the compound, including powering the silkmotic mill—that's the spinning wheel you see up there. The wheel is attached to a main shaft connected to a series of different gear trains to drive various pieces of machinery in the laboratory, such as the elevator."

Rati examined the gigantic engine from afar. She still had many questions, but she was starting to get an inkling of how it functioned. "Is there some way to inspect it up close?"

"It's not safe to get too close to the Ogé jars," replied Kisli. "But I can show you a model that will make the functioning of the silkmotic mill clearer."

"Please do!" said Rati, giddy as a child who has been promised a visit to a fireworks factory.

Kisli pushed Rati through more corridors until they emerged into the main Imperial laboratory cavern ("This was where they dissected the garinafin carcasses during the war," said Kisli). The cavern was illuminated by shafts of light coming through openings in the ceiling, which Rati guessed were provided by mirror-bent sunlight during the day and probably silkmotic globes at night.

Kisli pushed Rati into one of the smaller lab rooms at the side of the cavern.

"Welcome to my office, Master Yera," said Kisli. "Let me set up the model."

She reached up to a shelf and took down a bamboo stick about the size of a painting brush—except that instead of hairs at the end, it was tipped with a sharp needle. She inserted this stick into a stand on the desk, needle up. Then she took down an extremely thin and delicate ceramic plate with strips of silver foil radiating from its edge like the spokes of a wheel. At the center of the wheel was a slight depression. Carefully, she balanced the plate on top of the needle so that it went into the depression, and the plate was free to spin over the tip.

"This is similar to the wheel in the mill you saw," said Kisli. "Except that one is much larger and spins on bearings."

Rati nodded, gazing at the model intently.

"Next, these drive the wheel," said Kisli. She took down from the shelf two small ceramic Ogé jars, coated on the inside and outside with silver foil. A large metal pole poked out of the center of each and ended in a sphere. The heights of the jars were such that the spheres just reached the level of the strips of foil on the spinning plate.

"Finally, we charge up the Ogé jars," said Kisli. She took down a glass rod and began to rub it vigorously with a piece of silk. After she felt sufficient charge had been produced, she touched the rod to the outside of the Ogé jar on the left. "We charge this one with the Rapa variety of the silkmotic force." Then she rubbed the rod again and picked up the jar on the right, touching the rod to the pole inside the jar. "We charge this one, on the other hand, with the Kana variety of the silkmotic force."

Kisli placed the two jars on opposite sides of the plate, just out of the reach of the metal foil strips. And as though moved by a gust of wind, the plate began to spin between the two Ogé jars.

"As you know, the motes carrying the silkmotic force always move from the Rapa pole toward the Kana pole—" began Kisli, but she didn't need to go on, as Rati had already discerned the principle.

"The silkmotic mill works analogously to a water mill," said Rati. "These"—she pointed to the strips of foil radiating from the spinning plate—"function similar to the blades of a waterwheel. The motes carrying the silkmotic force move from the Rapa pole here onto the blade closest to it, thereby charging it with the Rapa force and repelling it away from the pole. And as the foil blade approaches the Kana pole, it is pulled toward it as the two opposing polarities of the silkmotic force hold an irresistible attraction for each other. As the foil moves past the Kana pole, the motes jump into this other Ogé jar, and the foil itself becomes charged with the Kana variety of the force so that it is repelled away from the Kana pole back toward the Rapa pole, and the cycle begins anew. So long as the two Ogé jars retain this differential in charges—much as there is a height differential between the headrace and tailrace of a waterwheel—the mill will keep on spinning."

"That is exactly right!" said Kisli in admiration. "Secretary Kidosu cited the waterwheel as her inspiration for the invention. Are you an expert of the silkmotic force as well?"

"Hardly an expert," said Rati. "I dabble. But it is wondrous to see the silkmotic force being harnessed to perform the task of elevating the lowly into high places. I'm very glad I got to see this today."

Outside, the wind suddenly picked up, and the sound of more energetic waves lapping against the seaside cavern entrance of Last Bite reverberated, as though a thousand tongues were speaking inside the mountain's mouth.

Soldiers carried the small boats inside the sea entrance cave to higher ground. They retreated and barred the doors to the tunnels and honeycombed passageways against a flood.

A caravan on its way to Ginpen stopped. The drivers got out to examine the sky, hesitating. It looked like an unanticipated storm was developing, and Ginpen was still some distance away. After the drivers conferred with the occupant of the largest carriage, the caravan turned down a side road and headed for Last Bite.

- *What are you doing, Tazu? Why are you leading her here?!*

- *Isn't that the entire point of our improvised schemes, of this intricate closet drama, of a temporary respite from armies clashing by night, little sister? It's best for all the secrets to be bared in a chaotic whirl, the same way I reveal my treasure at the bottom of a whirlpool.*

- *Are you with him in this mad scheme, Rapa and Kana?*

- *Yes. That boy has knowledge that would greatly aid Jia and Phyro—*

— *and craves knowledge that would greatly aid Tanvanaki and Goztan. It's time to bring everything to a head.*

- *But the boy . . . he hesitates . . . he doubts . . . will he aid the Lyucu or Dara? What is his destiny? What will happen to him and Fara?*

- *Little sister, love untested is love unvalued. You must weigh the fish.*

They reached the library. The guards doused their torches before pushing open the two sets of heavy doors that led inside. "Zomi Kidosu's retinue" looked at one another, took deep breaths, and stepped through.

The library was constructed inside a large natural cavern several hundred yards long and fifty yards across. Shelves full of boxed scrolls and codices lined all the walls, reaching up to four or five stories above the cave floor. Shafts of white light spilled from wells in the ceiling, making the enclosed space bright as day.

"Whale-oil lamps?" Arona asked one of the guards. She couldn't fathom how they kept the place so well lit at night.

The guard shook his head, confused by the ignorance of one of Secretary Kidosu's attendants. "Open flames would be a bad idea with so many books around—and back when we used to work with fermented gas in the labs, they were positively life-threatening. Secretary Kidosu has always preferred mirror-directed sunlight or sealed silkmotic globes."

Kinri looked up at the light wells, amazed. He had not thought Rati's candles could be scaled up to be as bright as the sun.

"Good, very good," said Widi, trying to cover up Arona's error. "The secretary wanted to be sure that everyone still remembers the reasons behind the regulations."

"We should not be disturbed while the secretary conducts her research," Arona hurried to add.

The guards nodded and exited the library, closing the doors behind them.

"Let's split up," Widi said. "Everyone can look for the documents they're most interested in."

"I'll go with Mota," said Dandelion. "I have some experience with Imperial filing systems. Besides, I'm curious about the Marshal too."

Mota smiled at her gratefully. He couldn't read, and he didn't want to deprive his friends of the opportunity to explore this treasure trove to pursue their own interests.

Kinri hesitated. By coming up to the library instead of going to the laboratories with his master, he had already given up a chance to find out more secrets of Dara's war engines. His sense of duty as a thane-taasa told him that he should head to the section of the library devoted to weapons research, but he couldn't bear the thought of betraying his friends. He loved them; he loved Dara; he needed to know the truth about Ukyu-taasa.

In his vacillation, he walked around the library—cautiously, as he was unused to the feminine dress and shoes, not to mention the care that needed to be taken not to damage the makeup or prosthetics Arona had used to complete his disguise.

Widi had already climbed up one of the long ladders in the corner and was strolling along a bamboo catwalk as he exclaimed over the objects on the shelf next to him.

"Look at these!" he said, awe evident in every syllable. "Prime Minister Cogo Yelu did us all a service by saving them."

Curious, Kinri gingerly climbed up the ladder and joined him. He surveyed the objects on the shelf, confused. "They look like animal bones . . . And what are those? Bundles of bamboo?"

Though Master Nazu Tei had owned few physical books, he had seen many books since coming to Ginpen. Most books in Dara were written in wax logograms on silk scrolls, folded or rolled to fit inside a protective case; some were codices of sheets of paper sewn along a spine, usually filled with quick notes in zyndari letters or the short-hand that reduced the three-dimensional logograms to flat symbols. But the objects Widi was admiring were unlike any book he had ever seen.

"Books haven't always been made out of silk or paper," said Widi reverently. "It was said that at the time of the Ano's arrival in the Islands, they wrote by carving logograms into animal bones or clay tablets—so that's what you see here. And later, some began to etch logograms into strips of bamboo that were then tied together and then rolled up into a scroll—this was before silk had become popular or even been invented, perhaps. You can imagine how much more effort it took to write by carving bone or etching bamboo, compared to soft, malleable wax. That was why the earliest Ano books were so short. Every logogram had to say so much. Or, as the poet Nakipo put it, when reminiscing about the ancients older than the Ancient philosophers: 'a logogram, a thousand breaths, a lifetime of contemplative solitude.'"

Kinri tried to imagine what it was like to have to write every word with so much exertion. He was used to laying down a vertical column of wax blobs and then carving out the logograms he needed with quick, practiced strokes of the writing knife. Many writing knives were made of soft wood or even ivory, which would have been useless against these earlier writing mediums.

The Lyucu derisively called Ano logograms "word-scars" because of their similarity to ugly scabs left on the bodies of warriors, but Kinri wondered if the name was more appropriate than his people realized. The logograms were indeed born as scars left in the mind, a crystallization of intense concentration and effort, of war against the vicissitudes of fickle time, against the ephemerality of life.

He climbed down the ladder and strode over to Arona, who was in a section of the library devoted to silk scrolls yellow from age.

"What are these?" he asked.

"Scripts for plays," said Arona.

"Plays? But they're so short."

Indeed, some of the scrolls were so short that they barely folded over half a dozen times in their boxes.

"Oh, back then, they didn't write down everything that actors said in a play," explained Arona. "Mostly, we folk troupes still don't. Classical drama was an earthy, oral art—very different from the modern plays and operas they put on in fancy theaters in Pan, based on scripts by famous playwrights that require extensive memorization by actors. Remember how I told you that when Mota and I put on a play, we never write out every word we're going to say? Here, let me show you."

She unfolded one of the ancient books carefully. Bamboo battens had been added between the columns of logograms at the folding seams as reinforcement to prevent the delicate wax logograms from rubbing against one another. Kinri had always thought that this was done in imitation of the sails found on large ships in Dara, but now he realized that the practice was probably derived from old books made of strips of bamboo.

The unfurled scroll revealed columns of cracked wax logograms, many of them in very old forms that Kinri found difficult to read. Some logograms were damaged or had fallen away, making the text even harder to decipher.

Arona pointed at the book. "This is the script for a play called *The Queen's Lament*. It's about Queen Tho-zu, the loyal wife of far-ranging hero Xadi and mother of the compassionate King Dacan."

Kinri knew the vague outline of the story, which took place during the pre-Tiro Diaspora Wars. King Xadi of Aké was a wily hero who tried his best to preserve his band of warriors against utter annihilation in the bloody battles between the heroes Iluthan and Séraca, as well as the gods who intervened on both sides. For ten years he was away from home, adventuring all across Dara as he stayed one step ahead of deadly pursuits by furious Tazu and scorned Kana. Meanwhile, his wife, chaste Tho-zu, ruled his kingdom wisely and prudently as regent, fending off waves of suitors who coveted the throne through clever stratagems and contests, until he returned safely. Thoughtful Tho-zu, the Lady of Ten Thousand Excuses, was often invoked in Moralist treatises and poetry as a model of womanhood.

Kinri's teacher, Master Nazu Tei, had suggested to Kinri that the story might be read allegorically, with the struggles of Xadi and Tho-zu seen as reflections of the wisdom-seeking soul overcoming external threats and internal temptation in the journey home to Aké, the isle of true philosophical enlightenment.

"There are only sixteen columns of logograms here," continued Arona, "and they specify four acts with an intermission. As you can see, the text describes the scenes in broad terms: 'Ologa debates Tho-zu on the best virtue of a woman'; 'Tho-zu proposes three contests for the suitors: Rice, Beer, Salt; she declares no winner'; 'Tho-zu announces Xadi is dead and ascends the throne'; 'Invasion by Séraca and Dacan'; 'the queen rallies the people'; and so on. There are bits of poetry that should be worked into the performance, but for the most part the actors improvise from stock characters built around the skeletal outline, guided by formulaic speeches and responsive to audience input. This is worlds away from the impossible-to-perform monstrosities that some modern scholars compose to satisfy their vanity, called closet dramas—"

"Wait, wait!" said Kinri. It had taken him a few seconds to confirm Arona's reading of the unfamiliar ancient logograms, so different in form from the Mapidéré-Xana standard Nazu Tei had taught him. "What do you mean 'Tho-zu announces Xadi is dead and ascends the throne'? That never happened."

"Ah, you are talking about the standard rendition of the story," said Arona. "But as with most legends of the Diaspora Wars, there are many versions. In this one, Tho-zu takes over as the monarch after the death of her husband, usurping the throne from her son. She then has to defend Aké against an invasion led by Dacan, her son and the rightful heir."

"When was this written?"

Arona shook her head. "I'm not as good at dating ancient manuscripts as Widi, but I'd guess it's at least a few hundred years old."

"Was this version not very popular then? I've never heard of it."

"That's hard to say," said Arona. "The plot twist you noticed would not have found favor with the Moralists, so very few copies of the script survived. But that doesn't tell us much about how audiences reacted. Mota and I, for example, put on plays about Marshal Gin Mazoti that don't involve her being a traitor as described in the official histories, and they're very popular."

Kinri nodded. The discussion reminded him of the many versions of the deeds of the gods of Ukyu. *Does every story exist in multiple versions? Which version is the truest?*

"Are you looking for a specific play?"

"I am! Actually, Lolotika was the one who told me about it. Among indigo-house girls, there's a long tradition of praying to Dophino, their protective spirit. But Dophino wasn't just a story. He was in fact one of Kon Fiji's students. Brought up as a girl, he preferred to go about the world as a man, and he led a rebellion of prostitutes that terrorized the early Tiro kings. There's a play about him that survives only in fragments. I want to find the full script."

Leaving Arona to her search, Kinri wandered off again. He saw Mota and Dandelion searching in one corner of the library, hunched over, bodies tense. He realized that they had likely located where the historical records were kept. He took a few steps to join them, but stopped himself. Now that the truth was within reach, he suddenly grew even more trepidatious.

He wanted, no, *needed*, to stave off the moment of reckoning just a little bit longer.

He found himself in the opposite corner of the library, as far from the historical records as possible. Bookcases here were arranged around a central cubby like the three walls of a room, leaving only one side open. The cases here were relatively open and not packed with books, as in the rest of the library.

Inside the cubby, the stone floor was carpeted with sheepskin against the chill, and there was a thin sleeping mat, a small desk, and sitting cushions around it. Kinri noticed that the sleeping mat was woven out of pig's-bristle grass, commonly found on seaside dunes. The rough material was familiar to him. It was popular among the peasantry of Rui and Dasu, and Master Nazu Tei had used it in her hut as well, but he had not seen it in houses in Ginpen.

There were multiple stands placed around the desk to hold up scrolls for reading and reference, fashioned out of bronze, ivory, or coral, clearly antiques or at least very refined, skillfully-made modern imitations. A writing set sat on the desk, consisting of an ivory-handled writing knife, a bronze wax-heating brazier, several blocks of orchid-infused whale wax, a dozen wolf's-hair inking brushes in a bamboo brush pot, and three jade ink pots. Though Kinri was no connoisseur of fine writing implements, he could tell these were rare instruments of great beauty.

The cubby was like a pool of tranquility that calmed his tumultuous heart. It was good to be curious about something small, insignificant; it allowed him to ignore the waves of questions pounding at the very foundational myth of his being.

A tea set on the desk stuck out. In contrast to the finely crafted reading and writing instruments, the porcelain teapot and two ceramic cups were clearly crude pieces cheaply fired in a kiln for mass consumption. The teapot showed a garden scene, depicting flowers in a repetitive pattern that was meant to make life easier for the artisans who probably had to paint hundreds of the same pictures every day. One of the butterflies had a wing that was incomplete, as though the painter had been in such a hurry to finish their quota that they couldn't be bothered to fix an obvious error.

Kinri picked up one of the teacups and turned it over. On the bottom was a crude drawing: a trapezoid with three curved lines coming out of the top.

He shivered. The design reminded him of the stylized representation of a garinafin common among the Lyucu, often carved into the handles of weapons or woven in decorative sinew patterns on kilts and vests. It was abstracted from the view of a garinafin's head from above, and the three curving lines represented the two antlers and a sinuous tongue of flames.

*How did a Lyucu design come to be on the bottom of a teacup in Dara?*

He grabbed the cup, exited the cubby, and showed it to Arona.

"Do you know this sign?" asked Kinri. "What does it mean?"

Arona gave him an odd look and examined the cup closely, looking at it from every direction before handing it back. "Do you never go to pubs?"

Kinri shook his head. He had stayed away from pubs out of concern that he might inadvertently get into a fight or say something that gave away his identity when inebriated. He had even turned down invitations from Dandelion, who wanted to go to pubs for racier stories than the ones told at the teahouses.

"That explains it," said Arona.

"What?"

"That design is called a three-legged jug. Trapezoidal jugs are drinking vessels dating from the early days of the Tiro states, reserved for nobles. No one uses them now except at big ceremonial occasions. Some pubs put pictures of them on their signs to give themselves a bit of class. The workmanship on that one, for example, is so poor that it must be from a very mediocre place." Arona turned the cup so that the three curved lines were at the bottom of the inverted trapezoid. "See? The three-legged variety, also called a *kunikin*, is the most common. There are also jugs with four legs, five legs, six legs. . . ."

Kinri sighed in relief. So it had been a case of mistaken identity. A drawing of a *kunikin* just happened to look exactly like the Lyucu sign for a garinafin.

He thanked her and returned to the cubby, setting the teacup back down. Arona's explanation only added to the sense of mystery about the place. If the tea set had come from a common tavern or pub, it was completely incongruous with the rest of the equipment on the desk.

The cubby didn't look like a storage area for books, like the rest of the library, but a place where someone could *live* among the books. In fact, it reminded Kinri of a poor scholar's dormitory as Master Nazu Tei had described such places to him, where a common hall would be partitioned by thin screens into dozens of tiny cubbies to house the many impoverished scholars who went to the regional capitals to take the Provincial Examinations in hopes of attaining the rank of *cashima*.

*What is this place? And who uses it?*

Kinri couldn't reconcile the contrasts in styles and class. The occupant of this space clearly loved writing and reading and had the resources to afford the best, and yet they slept on a peasantlike bed and used a tea set acquired or "borrowed" from a lowly pub.

He looked around at the bookcases that served as walls to the space, hoping to discover more clues.

In the middle of the largest shelf, a place of honor, there were two memorial tablets to the dead. These were common in Dara home shrines, stand-ins for the souls of revered ancestors and venerated lords, in front of which offerings of incense and food could be placed.

Both mourning tablets were of rough-hewn wood, adorned with large wax logograms, and then painted over in black. Instead of the creation of eminent monks at a large temple, these were homemade, as befitting objects of veneration in a private shrines meant for only one person.

On the first tablet: *Beloved parents: Oga and Aki*. There was no family name, and the logograms were written with some of the knife strokes omitted. Kinri was familiar with this custom in Dasu. It was considered improper and disrespectful for a child to write the logograms in family elders' names in full; by omitting a few strokes, the child expressed their gratitude and commitment toward the ancestors.

His mother's old slave back in Ukyu surfaced in his mind. He whispered a prayer for the old man's soul. Regretfully, he had never known much about the man's life, or how he had come to be in Ukyu and ended up serving the pékyu-votan and his mother. "Oga" was a common name, but perhaps this tablet would nonetheless pass on the prayer to the right Oga.

On the second tablet: *Beloved teacher: Luan.*

*The great Luan Zyaji?* His heart leapt in momentary excitement before settling down. He berated his own overactive imagination. *What are the chances of that?*

The items on the rest of the shelves confused him even more.

There was a piece of faded rough silk on which the phrase "weigh the fish" had been written several times. The rightmost column consisted of beautifully proportioned logograms, done by a classically trained calligrapher. Next to it were zyndari word-squares providing a translation, brushed in a neat, if childish, script. The left half of the page, however, was filled with misshapen copies of the logograms on the right, with ill-proportioned semantic roots and motive modifiers, or even blobs of wax where the writer had clearly given up. It looked, in fact, as though a master had provided a template for a student to duplicate and practice.

There was a bundle of sticks that seemed to form some kind of brace for an arm or leg. Judging by its size, it was also meant for a child.

A massive codex with stained and wrinkled pages. The logograms on the cover read *Gitré Üthu.*

A jar of pickled caterpillars.

A painting of a young woman of great beauty. Garbed in a light pink dress with long, flowing sleeves, she stood on a dais in the form of a giant lily pad, making her resemble a lotus flower. Her features, arranged in a slightly crooked smile, reminded Kinri of Dandelion. His heart quickened and his face glowed at the thought.

A vague sense of unease seized him. Why would he find a painting of a woman resembling Dandelion here, in this most secretive Imperial research facility?

*No,* he decided, *this painting can't have anything to do with Dandelion.*

I just care about her so much that I'm imagining that I could see her every-where, like the silly poets who claimed to detect the beloved's visage in the dappled shadows of the pagoda tree and to hear the beloved's voice in the patter of eave-dripping rain.

Below the painting was a poem composed in wax logograms. Though the calligraphy wasn't masterful, the carving was precise and the inking applied with great care.

> Green green green the thili grass, swell swell swell the endless
>> sea.
> Only in the land of dreams, my beloved, you I see.
> Our fingers twine and lips touch, but the dawn takes you
>> away.
> In a strange land you fight, helpless am I even to pray.
> A withered branch still remembers the caress of the wind;
> The salty main still recounts the dance of departed fins.
> Skiffs and barges and rafts and ships leap over each wave
> To fetch news of every kind except what I truly crave.
>
> Last night, I dreamed that I bought a fish from a market stall.
> The vendor tried to weigh it but the scale would not hold still.
> She sliced it open;
> We found a silk scroll.
>
> I knelt in mipa rari and caressed each logogram,
> From the opening line asking how well I've been eating
> And sleeping, to accounts of journeying, building, changing,
> To gazing at a lithe willow and thinking of my frame,
> Until the very last hasty wax drip of your signed name.
> I knelt in mipa rari and caressed each logogram.

He was silent for a while as the longing in the words, melancholy yet celebratory, filled his heart.

On the shelf next to the painting were several small turtle shells. He picked them up, and he saw that the plastrons were carved with some artificial-seeming patterns.

As he brought them closer to his eyes to get a better look, his body shuddered as though struck by lightning: a sketch of a three-legged jug, a *kunikin*.

But the pattern wasn't etched with a knife or chisel. It went smoothly into the bone, as though grown there naturally.

This was done in the Lyucu fashion, he was certain of it. He had seen enough of these at home to know. Either scorpion blood or gash cactus juice would do the trick.

Which also meant that the patterns had to be Lyucu: not the sign of the *kunikin*, but the sign of the garinafin.

His mind was again in utter turmoil. How did turtle shells carved with the sign of the garinafin come to be in the possession of an official working in a secret Dara Imperial facility? And why did a tea set with the same sign appear in the same place? There were too many inexplicable coincidences here, too many strange things for him to hold in his mind.

*It's a sign, but of what?*

Mota's loud exclamation reverberated throughout the library. "We've found them!"

Kinri exited the cubby and hurried over to the corner where Mota and Dandelion had been searching. The others were already there.

"These are the official interrogation records from Marshal Gin Mazoti's trial for treason," said Mota. "And also contemporaneous court petitions and debates in the College of Advocates."

Kinri looked at the scrolls lying in the sandalwood boxes, which protected the contents from bookworms and moths. There was a wax seal across the lips of the scrolls that prevented them from being unfolded, stamped with a simple crest: a round flower composed of densely packed, slender, radiating rays, like a cluster of swords.

Mota placed a finger against the seal, ready to rip it away.

"Wait!" implored Arona. She placed a hand over his and looked into his eyes. "Let her do this." She gestured at Dandelion.

"Me!?" asked Dandelion, her face drained of blood.

Arona ignored her. "Everything we've done up to this point . . . is wrong but perhaps still salvageable if we're caught. But if you break that seal, there will be no way out."

Mota shook his head. "I have to." He didn't raise his voice, but there was a quiet strength in his words, like an unyielding pine in the storm.

Kinri looked from one to the other. "I don't understand." He couldn't fathom what could possibly be so taboo about breaking a seal.

Dandelion answered him in a trembling voice. "That's the seal of the Dandelion Throne. It is applied to documents intended only for the sovereign's eyes. To break the seal is to attack the person of the sovereign, to commit treason." She turned to Arona. "It doesn't matter who you are."

Kinri was still confused. The significance attached to the symbol felt to him a little like the superstitions Master Nazu Tei had told him about the logograms in graves. It was as if the wax seal itself were endowed with magic.

"I'll break it," he said.

Dandelion looked even more terrified at this. "No! You and I . . . especially you and I, must not touch it!"

"As if you are really afraid," said Arona.

"I am!" said Dandelion. "I thought we were going to have an adventure . . . but this isn't what I wanted at all. It's one thing to pretend to be an Imperial official; to commit treason . . . absolutely not!"

"Do you think I don't know your secret?" said Arona. "Why do you think we brought you with us? You're the only one who can do this with impunity!"

Dandelion's eyes widened. "You . . ." A look of anguish came onto her face. "You don't understand. I'm not . . . I can't . . ."

Kinri stepped protectively before her. "What's going on here?" he demanded of Arona. "Why are you threatening her? I thought we were friends."

Widi and Arona looked at each other. Widi sighed. "Dandelion, do you really want to keep this charade going? Arona and I figured out your real identity a while ago. We brought you precisely for a moment like this, to protect Mota."

"Then no one else knows?" asked Dandelion.

Widi and Arona shook their heads.

"Please don't tell anyone," said Dandelion. But the way she looked at Kinri made it clear that she meant only him.

"Then break that seal!" said Arona. "Break it or I will tell him."

"What is the secret? Who are you?" Kinri's heart pounded. He couldn't imagine what sort of secret Dandelion had that would be worse than his own. "There's nothing that I can know about you that would change how I . . . feel . . ."

Dandelion shook her head, tears welling in her eyes.

"This isn't right," said Mota.

Everyone turned to him.

Mota looked at Arona. "Rona, don't." He paused, and when he spoke again, his voice was tender. "I know why you did this. But . . . love is no excuse to treat others as instruments to obtain what we desire. Kinri and Dandelion came to us because the gods willed us to know one another. I know you consider them soul-baring friends; you've merely been blinded by your feelings for me. Don't you see how they look at each other? How can you contemplate sacrificing another pair in love for us?"

Widi sighed. "But they . . . he doesn't even know who she is."

"Do any of us really know who *we* are?" asked Mota. "Until the moment we die, each of us is striving to find out our nature, to improvise upon the unreadable script etched in our souls by fate. He knows her in a way that transcends name, rank, and title; they recognize each other's souls. The secret you refer to is hers to keep and hers to reveal."

After a moment, Widi nodded. He turned to Dandelion. "I'm sorry. After all we've been through together . . . I am ashamed."

Arona dropped her face into her hands. Her shoulders heaved, though she made no sound.

Still facing her, Mota spoke gently. "This is my quest, and I must pay the price. You've always known that."

Arona said nothing, but at length, she nodded.

Kinri and Dandelion huddled to the side. He wrapped his arms about her, and she wept against his shoulder. He didn't ask; she didn't answer.

Mota took a deep breath and ripped away the first seal. Hearing the sound, Dandelion choked back a pained yelp.

Mota turned to her and said kindly, "It's just a wax seal. *Mutagé* is more than a logogram; it's to be shown through actions. The empress may hold the Seal of Dara, but she doesn't dictate our stories of loyalty and faith. I don't consider it treason to find proof of the Marshal's *mutagé*, to find the truth. Do you?"

Dandelion held his gaze. Then she shook her head.

Mota turned back, unfolded the scroll, revealing dense columns of logograms. He turned pleadingly to Widi.

Widi stepped forward, and, extending a finger down to the scroll to help keep his place, began to read the logograms aloud to Mota.

Arona put down her hands, wiped away her tears, and stepped up as well.

"Rona, you don't have to—" said Mota.

"I want to," said Arona. She leaned against Mota and listened as Widi read.

"Do you want to listen?" whispered Kinri to Dandelion.

Dandelion shook her head. "I think the story of the Marshal can wait. There is something else . . . you should see."

She led him to a different shelf. The scrolls here looked quite new, all likely written within the last decade, some probably in this year.

"We spoke about the stories of the refugees. . . . We spoke about the stories of the Lyucu. . . ." She stopped.

He waited with an aching heart. *What does she suspect? What does she know?*

Almost carelessly, he glanced at the scrolls. His heart sped up as he realized what he was reading.

These were notes from the interrogation records of refugees from Ukyu-taasa.

Knowing that he needed to be alone, Dandelion went away.

He began to read.

The most recent records spoke of further atrocities by Cutanrovo and her cleansing squads. He shuddered as he read accounts that brought to mind that fateful day in Kigo Yezu. Students forced to reveal and accuse their masters; native, togaten, and Lyucu youths being organized into purification packs in Kriphi and elsewhere to practice the art of killing on scholars and accused traitors; destruction of native books and temples; desecration of ancestral graves; enslavement of children after the executions of parents and grandparents; mass slaughters, castrations, disembowelments, crushed skulls, hobblings, systematic rapes.

He closed his eyes. Cutanrovo's betrayal of the ideals of Pékyu Tenryo made him physically ill, and it felt as if a dagger had been plunged into his heart and was being twisted again and again.

He turned to some of the older records, hoping to find evidence of the peace that had reigned under Tanvanaki and Tenryo, before the madness of Cutanrovo's hard-liners had turned the world upside down.

But . . . the earlier testimony from the refugees told much the same story: the arbitrary execution of natives on the flimsiest of evidence; the enslavement of entire villages for the acts of a single individual; the slaughter of hundreds when a Lyucu naro or culek was injured by natives who resisted some outrage; the declaration by Pékyu Tenryo that mass rape was to be practiced as a tactic of war.

*Lies! Lies!* he shouted in his heart. *The mass executions were of dangerous rebels! There were no rapes! The natives wanted to be Lyucu concubines! In Kriphi, they were happy!*

But then he remembered the way Master Nazu Tei seemed to always change the subject when the recent history of Ukyu-taasa came up, and the way his own mother gave vague answers when he asked what the prisoners being executed en masse in the market square had done. All the stories he had heard about seductive native concubines . . . had he ever really known any of them? All those happy natives in Kriphi . . . were they bowing to him out of respect or out of fear?

He remembered how sad Emperor Thaké had always looked when he made the proclamations on New Year's to thank Pékyu Tenryo for establishing the state of Ukyu-taasa. He recalled the grim look on Tanvanaki's face when she watched her husband at these public functions.

*What if . . . Cutanrovo isn't an aberration? What if . . . the refugees aren't liars, but Emperor Thaké, Tanvanaki, and even my mother are?*

He realized he had to go back earlier. He was afraid to, but he couldn't stop himself.

Lying at the end of the shelf were the earliest records of refugees, from the time when Pékyu Tenryo had fought and overcome the tyrant Ragin to establish Ukyu-taasa, his homeland.

One name caught his eye: the account of Zomi Kidosu, special adviser to Princess Théra.

He had not realized that the woman he was impersonating had been a refugee from Ukyu-taasa as well. With trembling hands, he unfolded the scroll containing her testimony.

*"I intend to keep you as my guest a little longer," shouted Tenryo. "If you really must leave, I'll have to enjoy the entertainment all by myself."*

*One of the garinafins lumbered over and crouched next to the crowd of civilians. The men and women and children shied away from the beast, but their ankles were chained together, and the panicked moves only caused them to fall down into a heap.*

*"Emperor, please come off that ladder," said a smiling Tenryo.*

*"Don't listen to him!" shouted Mün Çakri. "Go! Go!"*

*The emperor hesitated. He looked at the crying, screaming men and women and children, and his hands and legs seemed stuck to the ladder.*

*Tenryo waved his arm decisively, and the pilot on the back of the garinafin stuck the speaking trumpet into the base of her mount's neck and shouted into it.*

*The beast lowered its head to the ground and closed its mouth.*

*"No!" Emperor Ragin screamed, and he let go, falling from the ladder.*

*The beast snapped its mouth open, and a red glowing tongue of flames emerged from its maw and swept across the crowd before it.*

*Where a hundred people had scrambled and struggled for life a moment ago, now only a hundred smoldering pyres remained. The charred but still sizzling bodies maintained the poses of the last moments of their lives: a mother shielding the body of her child, a husband interposing himself before his wife, a son and daughter trying to cover the body of their mother—all three were now fused into one smoldering corpse.*

*My mother was among the victims.*

*Forgive me. I cannot write anymore.*

Lies! Lies!

Kinri screamed inside his head.

This story of how Pékyu Tenryo had overcome the cruel bandit-emperor Kuni Garu was perhaps the story Kinri loved the most in childhood. Outnumbered, overmatched, the indomitable pékyu-votan nonetheless slipped out of a trap set for him by Kuni Garu the betrayer and managed to surround *him* instead. And then the native tyrant, in his rush to get to his airship so that he could escape, had ordered his men to burn innocent civilians to death with flamethrowers in order to clear a way. Only then was Tenryo forced to rally his exhausted garinafin riders to put up a heroic fight until *Grace of Kings* was forced to land so that Kuni Garu could face justice for the crimes he had committed against his own people.

*The version told by Zomi Kidosu must be a lie! The stories told by the refugees must all be lies! Crafty Dara-raaki propaganda!*

But then he realized that he had never heard the story of Tenryo from his mother or Nazu Tei. The only people who had told him that story were the court-appointed tutors, and they always told it the same way. As a child, he had begged them to tell that story over and over, and they had always indulged him, never varying in any detail.

*What story doesn't change from telling to telling? No story-dance from the shamans ever told the same story the same way.*

A chill came into his heart. *A dead story doesn't change: a made-up story that must be told exactly the same way each time lest it is revealed for the lie it is.*

The stories from the refugees concerning Cutanrovo had the ring of truth because he could compare them against his own experience at Kigo Yezu. If he believed those stories by refugees, why wouldn't he believe the stories from refugees about life under Tenryo? Why wouldn't he believe this account by Zomi Kidosu?

*There never was a paradise in Ukyu-taasa. Cutanrovo is doing exactly what Pékyu Tenryo wanted. My mother, Emperor Thaké, and Tanvanaki were all lying.*

He dropped the scroll and cradled his head in pain. That the play by Mota and Arona was closer to the truth than the heroic figure of Pékyu Tenryo he had constructed in his head was intolerable.

Had he encountered these texts, these stories, before he had come to Ginpen, before he had lived among the people of Dara, before he had fallen in love with their breast-hoard and lungsong, he could have easily dismissed them all as fabrications, as propaganda. But such refuge was no longer possible. Beneath the words lay something as self-affirming as the dances of the shamans, as hard to doubt as the power of the garinafin: experience, the only teacher that convinced.

He staggered away from the shelf, unable to bear the horrors that it forced him to confront.

The lights went out, plunging everything into darkness. The darkness was more complete than any he had experienced. Because they were inside a cave, there wasn't even starlight or moonlight to alleviate the complete absence of light.

Screams. Shouts. Curses echoing from all around the library. It was too chaotic to make out what anyone was saying. Instinctively, he shouted too, adding to the cacophony. The noise of ladders and racks and who knew what else crashing to the floor. The grinding of metal against metal. More screams and grunts and barked orders.

Stumbling, crawling, shuffling, he made his way toward the last place he had seen Dandelion, a few bookcases away.

As quickly as they had gone out, the lights flooded back on, forcing him to squint against the blinding brightness. He crouched down and waited until his eyes no longer throbbed with pain. Far too many people were talking all at once for him to understand what was going on. Peeking cautiously around the shelf he was hiding behind, he realized that soldiers had taken over the library.

Widi was on the ground, bound hand and foot.

Mota, the invincible Mota, was kneeling quietly by a pile of scattered books, his hands bound behind him. A sword rested against his throat. His eyes were on Arona, kneeling opposite him, also with a sword against her throat. A line of blood trickled down her neck as she held very still, and the soldier wielding the sword stared at her grimly. Soldiers around them barked question after question, but they kept their lips tightly sealed.

*Where's Dandelion?*

He heard her voice, as clear through the hubbub as a siskin's song among the clucking of chickens. Frantically, he looked around and finally located her near the entrance, where two soldiers held her by the arms, and a third was trying to bind her legs. Angrily, Dandelion kicked and writhed against her captors, shouting all the while.

"Just let me wipe off my makeup! You'll be very sorry once you see my face!"

Her eyes looked as imperious and commanding as ever. But the soldiers were unmoved.

A woman, dressed in the formal robes of a high-ranking court official, stood near Dandelion. She held up a hand and said something, and the clamor in the library died down. Her back was to Kinri.

"Let her go!" Kinri shouted.

The official snapped around, and dozens of soldiers instantly ran at Kinri, ready to take down this last intruder. Kinri grabbed a long and heavy book box and ran at the official, heedless of the soldiers rushing at him from every direction.

The soldiers slowed down when they saw that the intruder, shouting in the voice of a man, was in fact a woman. They pulled up in amazement, however, when they saw the intruder's face. As the soldiers skidded to a stop, they looked back and forth between Kinri and the official in command, unsure what to do.

Kinri raised his book box like a war club and grunted a threat. Grim-faced, the official strode toward him, showing no fear. He opened his mouth to shout some more, but the breath caught in his throat as he got close enough to see her face clearly.

It was the same face that he had seen earlier when he looked into the mirror in Arona's hand, right after she had finished his makeup.

# CHAPTER FORTY-SEVEN

# FAMILY

LAST BITE: THE SEVENTH MONTH IN THE NINTH
YEAR OF THE REIGN OF SEASON OF STORMS AND
THE REIGN OF AUDACIOUS FREEDOM (TWENTY-
TWO MONTHS UNTIL THE REOPENING OF THE
WALL OF STORMS).

Inside the library cubby used as Zomi Kidosu's office and bedroom, Fara knelt in *mipa rari* on a sitting cushion, looking defiant. She had finally taken off her makeup, and Zomi had almost fainted at the sight.

Agitated, Zomi paced back and forth in the cubby.

"What is your explanation for this, Fara?"

"I wanted to have a bit of fun."

"A bit of fun! This is one of the most secure facilities in all of Dara. And you decided that it would be all right to help a bunch of spies break in—"

"They're not spies! They're just people curious about the truth."

"How can you be so naive! Look at how well planned this whole operation is. They even managed to find a look-alike to impersonate me. Does that sound like idle curiosity to you?"

"I never said it was 'idle' curiosity. It's purposeful!"

"Yes, exactly. Did they know who you are? Were you targeted?"

"No . . . Yes . . . It's . . . complicated."

Zomi let out a deep sigh. "Oh, I'm sure it's complicated. I cannot believe Aya has been covering for you this whole time—"

"Aya doesn't know anything! Leave her out of it!"

"You are going back to Pan, and you're not going to set foot out-side the palace for a *long* time. I have half a mind to tell the empress to keep you under lock and key in your bedroom—"

"O Rata-*tika*!" Tears burst out of Fara's eyes and streamed down her face. "Oh if . . . if only . . . if only you could see—"

Zomi sighed. The manipulation was so transparent yet effective. The young princess did look a lot like Théra at that age. "Stop bawl-ing! And leave your sister out of this. I'm going to interrogate your 'friends' and find out just what they're after. You better hope they're not Lyucu spies."

She was about to turn away, but the flitting look of terror on Fara's face made her pause. *No, it can't be.* A chill seized her heart.

"Look at me, Fara."

Fara locked eyes with her.

"Is there something you want to tell me?"

Fara shook her head.

"Even if you're an Imperial princess," said Zomi slowly, enunci-ating every word, "treason is a capital crime. Do you understand? This isn't a game."

Fara looked away.

"Is it the old woman? Is it the tall man? . . ." As Zomi went through each of the captives, she kept her eyes on the young woman's face.

Fara looked annoyed, twisting her face away from Zomi's gaze and muttering impatiently.

"Is it the young man who looks like me?"

Fara continued to look annoyed. Almost reflexively, she swal-lowed.

Zomi's eyes narrowed.

"Stay here," she said. "I'll deal with you after I've gotten the truth out of him."

Farsight Secretary Zomi Kidosu, charged with defending Dara against Lyucu espionage, stared coldly at the young man kneeling in front of her, held in place by two guards.

This young man who inexplicably looked like her, she felt, was the key.

From his companions, she had received a preliminary account of what the "extended Blossom Gang" had been up to the last few months. It was obvious to her that while the gang thought they were using the young man, *he* had instead been using *them* to get close to Fara and to acquire knowledge of Dara engineering. The mastermind's elaborate ruse and depth of planning was breathtaking, and the fact that he had not only seduced Fara but even revealed to her that he was connected with the Lyucu—judging by her reaction—showed a streak of boldness that verged on recklessness. That gamble had apparently paid off.

His papers were a sham, as one would expect of a spy for the Lyucu. But even worse, based on the extent of his knowledge of Lyucu lore and an apparent sympathy for the Lyucu cause—as shown by his role in the third contest between the Splendid Urn and the Treasure Chest—Zomi suspected that the young man wasn't even an *Anojiti* from Unredeemed Dara, but a *Lyucu* operative.

*How could he speak our tongue so well? How could he know so much of our customs and history? If Tanvanaki has more spies like him, how can we possibly ferret them out?*

Zomi's mind returned again to Fara's look of terror.

*The little princess is inexperienced but clever. . . . Did this man tell her that he's a Lyucu, or did she figure it out on her own? In any event, how could she show such poor judgment!*

Fara's foolishness aside, this was without a doubt the worst security disaster in Zomi's time as Farsight Secretary, and she was even more incensed by the disguise the spy had chosen: It felt like a deliberate slap in the face.

Yet, instead of cunning and arrogance, she saw only bewilderment and confusion in the young man's face.

"Why do you look like that?" he muttered.

The same question was on Zomi's mind. Even with his makeup removed, the resemblance between them, once highlighted, was impossible to ignore. The very idea that the gods would choose to make a Lyucu look so much like her was unsettling.

"What is your name?" Zomi asked, keeping her voice emotionless.

"Kinri Rito," he said.

"A lie. Where are you from?"

"I'm a refugee from Rui."

"Another lie. You may be from Unredeemed Dara, but you're no refugee," said Zomi. "There is no record of such a name in any of the refugee camps, and your claimed parentage is pure fiction. You're a Lyucu spy, aren't you?"

He flinched, but he gave no denial.

"What is your mission?"

He laughed bitterly. "If only I knew."

"What do you mean by that?"

He closed his eyes and turned his face away.

Zomi sighed. In some ways it was too bad that she had caught him only now. Under Empress Jia's regency, torture and collective punishment had been steadily reduced and phased out of both the domains of the Minister of Justice and the Farsight Secretary. The kinds of interrogation techniques that had once made the farseers so feared in the Islands of Dara were no longer practiced. Had the young man been caught by one of her underlings in years past, no doubt his confession would have long been completed.

*No matter,* she thought. *Torture is neither reliable nor always effective. There are other ways to weigh the fish.*

She turned to the objects recovered from the young man's person. There wasn't much: a little money in a knotwork purse; a few pieces of polished bone—one was apparently in the process of being carved into a hairpin with a dandelion-shaped knob at the end; a silk handkerchief with a sappy message—clearly Fara's hand; and a turtle shell etched in the style of the scrubland tribes.

The turtle shell caught Zomi's interest. Such objects of Lyucu handicraft, due to their rarity in Dara, were prized by smugglers and collectors, and Zomi was familiar with them from contraband seized from pirates as well as the turtle-shell messages sent by her beloved from beyond the Wall of Storms.

But instead of the three-legged kunikin, the carapace of Kinri's shell showed a map of Dara. She shook her head, puzzled. *Perhaps a rough guide used by the spy to find out where to go once he arrived in core Dara?*

She flipped the shell over to look at the plastron.

Time seemed to stop; what she was seeing was impossible.

There was a portrait of a family: a father, a mother, two older boys, and a baby. The figures were dressed in the style of fisherfolk from Dasu, familiar from Zomi's childhood. The figures were outlined roughly and devoid of distinctive features except for the woman, holding a scale from which a fish dangled, and the baby, swaddled in clothes decorated with the image of a tiny cat.

The woman was weighing the fish.

Zomi spun the shell around again and examined the carapace closely. Yes, there was a dot in the coastline of Dasu on the map, marking the location of her home village.

How could this be? This was a picture of her own family shortly after she had been born. Her mother always spoke of weighing the fish to understand the truth of the world, and she had been named "Mimi" because the way she rooted for milk and mewled reminded her mother of a kitten.

"My family," she croaked. "How did you . . ."

The shell fell from her hand, clattering against the table.

"Secretary Kidosu!"

"Are you all right?"

"Summon the doctor!"

As her aides and guards fussed about her, Zomi locked eyes with the young man, and the same expression of overwhelming shock at a nascent, impossible truth appeared on both faces.

It took time for the stories to be told.

But in the end, Kinri and Zomi had to face the truth: They were brother and sister, votan-sa-taasa, both children of Oga Kidosu, though born on two shores separated by an ocean.

Zomi was thirty-two, Kinri nineteen. They were only thirteen years apart in age, yet the gap felt like many lifetimes.

"All that time that old Oga lived with us, I never knew he was my father," said Kinri in wonder and sorrow.

"He might not even have known the truth himself," said Zomi.

Kinri thought back to the way her mother had always kept his paternity vague. He thought back to the conflicted manner in which his mother had treated old Oga—kind one moment, impatient and demanding the next. He could see why his mother had done such a thing—the best way to keep her fractious husbands in line was to dangle before them the hope that any of them *could* be Kinri's father while ensuring in reality that the hope would always be illusory. It was a stroke of luck that Oga was from Dasu, whose inhabitants tended to be lighter in complexion than much of the rest of Dara, and so the ruse that Kinri was pure Lyucu could be maintained. He could also see why his mother, torn between the myth of a visionary pékyu-votan who wished to integrate the natives into Lyucu society, a myth she had helped to cultivate, and the reality of a Tenryo who saw no future for the natives except enslavement and death, a reality that he was only reluctantly coming to accept, would vacillate and keep the truth of his paternity from everyone, including himself and Oga.

"What was he like?" asked Zomi. "I never knew him except near the moment of his death."

And so Kinri shared with Zomi his memories of Oga. He spoke of the old man's tales about the heroes of Dara, his songs about his lost homeland, the times when he had reminisced about his family: the sons who had gone off to fight for Xana and never returned, the baby daughter he had known for only a few days before long-lasting exile, the wife whose struggles and sufferings he wished to share but could not.

"But why did he . . ." Zomi could not finish. "And how did you . . ." Her voice trailed off.

Kinri understood what she wanted to ask, but he could offer no insight. He had been too young to know if Goztan had taken Oga to bed often, the nature and origin of their bond, or even if it had been a bond of affection and love or something darker and involuntary. After reading the testimonies of the refugees, the smiles he had seen on the faces of the native concubines he had known growing up in Kriphi took on a far more sinister shade. Could there ever be love between a Lyucu and a Dara, when the difference in power was always so stark and the re-rememberings between their peoples so knotty?

Unbidden, Dandelion's face surfaced in his mind. He pushed it away resolutely.

And he was not yet ready to tell the story of how he had truly come to be in Ginpen.

"I never knew I had a sister," said Kinri, because there was nothing else to say. He didn't know her at all, yet he could see shades of himself in her: the shape of the chin, the tilt of the brow, the look of concentration when contemplating a puzzle. He felt drawn to her— she *was* family—yet she also frightened him.

"I never knew I had another brother," said Zomi. "How much you must have suffered in Unredeemed Dara!"

Tears flowed down both their faces as they embraced each other. So much pain and regret had been visited upon their family because of the whims of Mapidéré's mad schemes and Tenryo's boundless ambition.

"I'm glad you could tell me something about his life," said Zomi at length. "Even on the other side of the River-on-Which-Nothing-Floats, I'm sure he's smiling to see the two of us."

Kinri nodded, but his mind was all confusion. Zomi had spoken sympathetically of his suffering—but had he actually suffered at all as a thane-taasa of the Lyucu? All along, he had thought of himself as a descendant of the conquerors; should knowing that he was togaten, that the blood of Dara also flowed in his veins, change the nature of his experiences?

He realized that he had not asked Zomi about Aki, Oga's wife in Dasu, and Zomi had not asked after Goztan, his own mother. Though they were siblings, there was also a wall that divided them, a wall that he feared was as impenetrable as the Wall of Storms.

"What is this place?" he asked, his arm sweeping in an arc to indicate the bookcases that formed the walls of the cubby, more to fill the silence than because he was interested in the answer. He needed time to come to terms with the many, many revelations of Last Bite.

"This is where I come to think," said Zomi. As her gaze lingered on each object on the shelves and the table, her eyes softened. "My work in Pan is full of darkness and strife, but Last Bite is a refuge. These objects bring me comfort because they remind me of people who I love and love me."

"Tell me about them," said Kinri. It felt odd to connect "love" with the name "Zomi Kidosu." In the official accounts of the court historians of Kriphi, Zomi Kidosu was a dangerous witch, whose devious mind the resourceful Tanvanaki had to overcome to protect the paradise that was Ukyu-taasa—a false myth did not lose its power overnight.

"This scroll is from my teacher," said Zomi, caressing the silk scroll filled with childish copies of the model logograms. "He taught me much about books and philosophy, but the most important lesson of all"—she moved her hand to the bundle of sticks next to it—"was how I was in charge of the path I walked, not the starting place the gods assigned me at birth."

"I, too, had a teacher in Ukyu-taa—in Rui."

"Had?"

"She was killed . . . by Pékyu Vadyu after a false accusation of treason."

Zomi looked at him strangely. "False?"

Kinri didn't know how to explain. Certainly Nazu Tei was no loyal hound of Tanvanaki, but she had acquiesced to Lyucu supremacy and showed no defiance until the very end. He realized that his old master's passivity and acceptance of the Lyucu conquest would bring her nothing but contempt in the eyes of his sister. "She was a learned scholar," he said feebly, as if that explained everything.

Zomi waited. And when it was clear that Kinri would say no more, she said, in a hard-edged voice, "Tanvanaki is her father's daughter," as if that explained everything.

*It is impossible for us to speak even of our loves with open hearts,* he thought, and the agony of that realization made him gasp.

To cover up the truth, he added in a rush, "She also taught me much about the beauty of the culture of Dara, and to look beyond the stories told by the thanes and court historians."

"A great teacher is the shaper of our mind, as much as our parents are the shapers of our bodies," said Zomi reverently. "What was her name?"

He gave it.

Zomi nodded. "I know the name, which is listed in the Hall of Mutagé. To be truthful, I had not thought her worthy based on the little I knew of her official record. You must tell me some of her deeds of courageous resistance and defiance against the Lyucu so that we can properly commemorate her at the next Grave-Mending Festival."

There seemed to be no topic on which they could converse without bumping into awkward, invisible fences. He tried again. "What about these?" he asked, pointing to the turtle shells lining a shelf. "Why do they have the sign of the garinafin? And what about those?" He pointed to the teacups on the desk. "Why do they have the same design?"

A gentle, longing smile softened Zomi's face. "That tea set is taken from a pub, the Three-Legged Jug."

Kinri nodded. Just as Arona had explained.

"That pub was where I first met the woman I love," said Zomi, "and also the place where we spent a very special night."

"What happened to her?"

A melancholy shadow fell over Zomi's face like a veil. "She left to be the bride of another."

"I'm sorry to hear that," said Kinri. He searched his mind for some suitable words of comfort. "But the heart breaks and heals, much as the tides wane and wax." It sounded false even to his ears.

Despite her sorrow, Zomi smiled at this. "You sound like a doddering matchmaker. What do you know of heartbreak at your age?" A look of sudden understanding flitted across her face as she stared intently at Kinri, who turned away, flustered.

Zomi took a deep breath. "Anyway, it's not like that. She didn't leave me because her feelings changed; she went beyond the Wall of Storms because she needed to do grand deeds."

"Beyond the Wall of Storms?" asked Kinri, shocked. "You mean she is—"

"Yes," said Zomi, her voice full of pride. "My teacher, Luan Zyaji, was the first man of Dara to go beyond the Wall of Storms with determined purpose, and my lover, Grand Princess Théra, was the first woman of Dara to do so." She looked over at the painting hanging on the shelf across from her.

Kinri looked at the portrait that resembled Dandelion, and a terrifying realization threatened to break through his consciousness. He turned away from the implications of that understanding with all his strength, like a man closing his eyes before a looming tidal wave. *It's impossible. It can't be.*

"And you didn't go with her?" he croaked, to distract himself.

"No, I stayed because I had other dreams I wanted to make real here."

"Dreams grander than being with the woman you loved?" He pressed a hand against the handkerchief she had given him, now pinned securely over his heart. He couldn't think of being apart from her—as long as she could see beyond his Lyucu heritage once she found out, as long as she wasn't . . . no, he refused to think of it.

Zomi sighed. "I suppose the love poets would call ours a tragedy of ambition and vanity, for in their verses there is nothing grander than romance. But Théra and I both understood that there are other grand ideals in this universe worth pursuing, and being apart is not the end of a love that is true."

Kinri wondered if Zomi truly believed what she was saying or if she was merely trying to comfort herself, but either way he held his tongue. He knew that Grand Princess Théra died in the Wall crossing; everyone knew.

After a moment, Zomi went on. "Later, I bought the tea set from the owners to remind me of her because I was too foolish to ask for something of hers before she left."

"It's possible that you didn't ask for anything because you didn't quite believe that she was going to be gone forever," said Kinri, thinking of how he had not asked for something from Master Nazu Tei before they parted for the last time.

"You may be right about that," said Zomi. "But the gods have taken pity on me. She isn't gone forever."

"What?"

"Though Théra is on the other side of the Wall of Storms, she isn't beyond the River-on-Which-Nothing-Floats." She pointed to the turtle shells. "These have arrived from Ukyu and Gondé, and I know they're from her because the sign of the *kunikin*, the three-legged jug, holds a special meaning between us."

The idea that Théra had not died but managed to invade Ukyu

was another shocking revelation, but by now Kinri was feeling numb from the barrage of surprises. He felt himself stiffening, like the *thasé-teki* caterpillar after the fungus had ramified within the body. Dimly, he wondered if Tanvanaki and his mother had seen similar turtle shells from beyond the Wall and understood what they really meant.

"The princess is clever," said Zomi. "She must have carved the signs into the carapaces of dozens of turtles, if not more, and sent them into the great circular belt current, hoping that a few at least would make it through the Wall of Storms. And even then, in order to avoid detection by the Lyucu invaders, she wrote her messages in an ambivalent way. Only I would know why the turtles carry the three-legged jug."

Kinri tried to imagine what Tanvanaki would make of the signs. Would the pékyu think the garinafin a cry for help from the Lyucu in Ukyu? Or would she think they signified another reinforcement fleet?

A new, growing sense of unease gnawed at him. What Zomi was telling him were state secrets, the very kind of information his mother and the pékyu were desperately in need of. That Zomi was telling him these things freely, the way family members would confide in one another, showed that she had no doubt about his loyalty, thought of him as one of the people of Dara. She believed the claim of blood was clear, the tenor of his allegiance obvious. But did he share her feelings?

Worse, what would happen to him if he didn't want to be a subject of the Dandelion Throne, one of the people of Dara? What would she do if he refused to take her side?

"I'd like to add this one to the others," said Zomi, holding up the shell on which Oga had carved his family and the map of Dara. "This place, if you like, can be your refuge as well, filled with love." In her voice was the yearning for kin and hearth, for the consolation of family.

Kinri stared as Zomi placed his shell next to the other shells bearing the messages from Grand Princess Théra. His mind was blank. Oga's family portrait contained Zomi but not him—did that mean that Zomi had the better claim to the shell? But the shell was also the last thing his mother had given him, and he could not bear not to have it next to his heart, the same place where he kept the handkerchief from Dandelion.

"When you've recovered, I shall bring you to see the empress and the emperor, and the intelligence you have of the Lyucu will be most welcome."

Was he really going to see the empress and tell her everything he knew about the Lyucu? Was he really going to betray the pékyu and his mother? What about his mission, the mission he thought Goztan and Tanvanaki had assigned to him?

"I'd like to hold on to the shell a little longer," he croaked.

She looked at him oddly, but soon, the frown relaxed. "Of course. You've only just found out he's your father. It's natural to want to spend more time with him."

She handed him the shell; he accepted it without contradicting her.

"I need some time by myself," he said. "I think I'd like to stay here and read."

Zomi nodded sympathetically. "You haven't explained to me how you escaped from the clutches of your cruel mother and the wily Tanvanaki, but I can already tell it's a tale of great trauma and suffering. Time will soothe your scarred heart." Pride came into her voice, as though she were imagining Kinri's brave escape from the Lyucu. "Know that you've already shown great courage in making your way here, and that they'll never be able to get their hands on you again—"

Kinri broke in because Zomi's misdirected patter was proving intolerable. "May I . . . see Dandelion?"

Zomi chuckled. "So that's the name you know her by? . . . Ah, how the gods love to play jokes . . . putting the two of you together." She shook her head and turned serious. "Do you really not know who she is?"

He shook his head. *There is no avoiding the inevitable.*

"And your feelings for her are sincere?"

He nodded, harder than he had ever assented to any query.

The last trace of concern fled from Zomi's face. "The young woman you've been wooing is Fara, Imperial Princess of the House of Dandelion. She is . . . a bold and free spirit, and gives everyone who loves her plenty of headaches. I'm certain she'll be relieved to know that you're not actually a Lyucu. I have a feeling she's been fretting over that."

Long after Zomi was gone, Kinri sat in the cubby, the shell in one hand and the handkerchief in the other, as still as a reef buffeted by too many waves of unexpected truths.

Over the next few days, Zomi interrogated the other members of the Blossom Gang in depth. Although Princess Fara vouched for them strenuously, Zomi did not quite trust them. Still, knowing that they had not, in fact, been duped by a Lyucu spy, but had befriended and given aid to her brother, softened her toward them considerably.

After she had gone over the competition between the Splendid Urn and the Treasure Chest in detail, she came to see the gang in a different light. The curiosity that drove them was not so different, after all, from her own thirst for knowledge as a simple fishing-farming girl of Dasu.

"Secretary Kidosu," said Rati Yera, "now that you know Tiphan Huto to be a traitor working with pirates to abduct engineers and skilled workers for the Lyucu, can you also send people to rescue Mozo Mu's family? I'm afraid that—"

Zomi held up a hand. "That, you don't need to worry about. On my way here, I received a report from the empress's expedition against the pirates. They raided Tiphan Huto's shipyard in the Silkworm Eggs and rescued numerous hostages. I'm sure your friend's family are among them."

Fara clapped her hands in joy. "I knew Aya would come through!"

Zomi lifted an eyebrow. "More schemes? I really need to keep a closer eye on you."

She asked Fara, Rati Yera, Widi Tucru, Arona Taré, and Mota Kiphi to explain the inventions, stratagems, and performances, walking through the trickier parts with models.

Fara was glad to show off her accomplishments, and the gang, though uncertain of the intent behind Zomi's interest, obliged. Rati did explain that she could not reveal the details of the self-driving carts, and Zomi, well aware of the custom of secrecy among street magicians, did not press the point.

Delving into these wondrous machines gave her much mind-pleasure. So long had she been surrounded by the deafening noise of pushing and pulling the levers of power in bureaucratic competition, the piercing screeching and grinding of the gears of plots and conspiracies in espionage and counterespionage, that she had almost forgotten how much she loved the clean, calming poetry of engineering, the first language she had learned from Luan Zyaji, her beloved teacher.

"All these inventions are ingenious, but I am most impressed by the teachable carts, even if I'm not privy to the principles of their operation," said Zomi. "Do you realize what you've done?"

"We . . . won the contest?" offered Rati Yera timidly. She was still awed to be speaking to one of the most powerful—perhaps *the* most powerful—official of the empire as well as an inventor of great renown, and the idea that a *raye* woman could offer anything valuable to the government besides labor and suffering was unimaginable.

"No!" said Zomi, chuckling. "Well, yes, you did, but that's not what I mean. You've invented a way to record and play back a precise sequence of movements."

Her mind raced as she imagined the possibilities. Machines amenable to instruction, which could replicate the motion of experts, presented a breakthrough that could transform the very way that work was done in Dara.

"In the kitchen, you had machines copying the cook's moves," said Zomi. "In the restaurant itself, you taught machines to follow a particular path. Could you have combined the two principles to instruct the machines in the kitchen to cook the dishes on their own, *without* a cook to hold their hand?"

Rati considered this. "In theory, perhaps. But that would require a great deal of precision and refinement. I would have to experiment and tinker—"

"I'm not asking if you can make it work right now, but only what is possible in principle," said Zomi, her voice rising in excitement.

"Assuming we can overcome the engineering challenges, you could take a dish that has to be prepared by a master chef by feel and instinct and reduce it to a precise sequence of instructions carried out by dozens of machines, multiplying the work of one adept a hundredfold."

Rati still looked doubtful, but her eyes also began to glow with the excitement of imagined possibilities. "This is a process that could be extended to the making of all kinds of things: the weaving of complex patterns, the painting and glazing of china for the kiln—"

Zomi joined her. "The hammering of steel and iron, the fashioning of uniform rings and scales for armor, the transportation of goods through no-man's-land—"

*I need you to find me men and women of talent.*

Abruptly, she stopped. Had she, by happenstance, stumbled upon exactly the people Phyro needed?

She had been fretting over Phyro's letter ever since she received it. Much as she sympathized with the emperor's frustration, much as she wished for the empress to take a harder line against the Lyucu, what the emperor was asking for was treason. She could not condone it. Jia's reasoning was sound; her system worked; Dara had never prospered as it had under her reign. People of talent must serve the Throne, not a private army founded in defiance of the Throne, however just the cause. She pushed the intruding thought away.

"Luan Zyaji, my teacher, spoke of engineering as a kind of poetry. What you've done is to devise an entire new way to compose mechanical poems. The ability to record a master craftsman's transitory movements and to replay them back exactly is akin to the invention of writing to record ephemeral speech, and no less momentous!"

"I . . . never thought in such grand patterns," said Rati Yera, bewildered by Zomi's breathtaking vision. "We're simple men and women who only wanted to pursue knowledge that we loved."

As her mind continued to churn, Zomi spoke with each of the gang in turn about their inventions: Widi's legal and investigative tricks that allowed the poor to have some protection against the powerful; Arona and Mota's performances that entertained and illuminated, much as Consort Risana's smokecraft; Rati's mechanical wonders that echoed the creations of the academies but also broke new ground.

As Farsight Secretary, besides espionage and counterespionage, she was also charged with discovering men and women of talent so that they could serve the Dandelion Throne and the people of Dara. Outrage and gratitude both filled her heart as she realized how the Blossom Gang would never have come to her attention except for this fortuitous encounter.

"You should all be working for the Imperial Academy and the Imperial laboratories, or as officials in the civil service!" said Zomi. "How can men and women of your talent live in obscurity, like pearls hidden in the sea?"

"Are you suggesting that we should take the Imperial examinations?" asked Arona in disbelief.

Zomi thought she understood the source of Arona's objection. "The examinations no longer must be conducted solely in logograms. You may write in zyndari letters—"

"That's quite an assumption to make!" objected a red-faced Arona. "I'll have you know, Secretary Kidosu, that I can certainly read and write, and I probably know more about ancient drama than most of your *firoa*. I just don't care much about the words of the sages."

"And I am a *toko dawiji*," said Widi. "Yet I have no desire to advance further in the examinations at all. Essays that don't say anything practical bore me. I much prefer to wield the writing knife and my sharp tongue to achieve practical results for my clients."

"If the objection is to the format of the exams," said Zomi, "we can reform them further. You can help! Though I can no longer meddle in the examinations, I can pass your ideas on to the officials in charge. Instead of essays on general topics, perhaps the tests can also probe for knowledge in specific subjects like mathematics and engineering. You could write about your passions and real problems you've solved—"

"That wouldn't help me," muttered Rati Yera. "I don't know how to write at all."

"Then we can devise ways to allow you to demonstrate your practical skills in building and crafting—"

Widi shook his head. "No, Most Honorable Secretary Kidosu, you're not listening. We have no interest in the examinations because we don't view service to the government as the greatest of all goals."

Arona, Mota, and Rati nodded at this.

"How can you say such a thing?" exclaimed Zomi. "It's a blessing from the gods to have a great talent, and talent must not be wasted in obscurity."

"You view our lives as obscure and wasted," said Widi. "But that isn't our view. There is much more mind-pleasure in living a life that has little prestige or wealth, but which is free."

Zomi was stumped. She had not considered the possibility that the one thing scholars desired above all else, to be recognized for their talent and to be *useful* to the court, held no appeal for these wild Blossoms.

She turned to Rati, whose service she desired most of all, and tried another tack. "You speak of the love of knowledge. Don't you think you would enjoy working in an Imperial laboratory like this one, where you'll have access to materials and equipment that you cannot afford on your own, where you'll be stimulated by conversation with learned colleagues equally in love with knowledge, where your research will change the lives of millions?"

Rati thought about her conversation with Kisli Péro and the incredible energy humming through the massive Ogé jars that powered the lab. She felt the stirring of a longing that she didn't even know she had.

But then her face fell. "But . . . how can an illiterate *raye* woman ever be accepted among the ranks of the *cashima* and *firoa*?"

Zomi was silent. She could well imagine the kind of contempt Rati would face among researchers who took great pride in their own erudition and saw folk tinkerers as beneath their notice. Was there no way to harness the talents of all who loved the pursuit of knowledge without regard to birth, station, status, and erudition in the Ano Classics?

"Besides, there is a cost to bowing to the Throne," said Rati. "I will no longer be able to work on problems of my choosing, to pursue avenues not aligned with another's vision, to be beholden to no master save my own curiosity."

"Ambition does not rule all of us," said Arona. "We don't wish to become kites dancing to the currents of power, to soar high only by paying the price of being tethered to the hands of the mighty. Widi spoke of freedom, and the freedom to glide where we please, to be accepted by our friends for who we are, is more precious than gold and titles."

"And some of us wish to effect change from outside the Dandelion Court because there will always be things that cannot be done unless you stand apart from the institutions that channel and collect power," said Widi. "The Fluxists, among others, advocate heeding the example of the free-flowing streams. Not all water should be collected in buckets and ladled out among the fields, or be harnessed by a waterwheel."

"Then are you determined not to serve the Dandelion Throne?" asked Zomi, her voice hardening. To waste the potential of these talented individuals was unacceptable. The empress had set up a system that served the people of Dara. Once recognized, talent must be harnessed, tamed, channeled. She would have to force them into the system, into buckets and waterwheels.

The gang shook their heads resolutely.

"Then let me explain to you what you've done," said Zomi Kidosu, her voice low and dispassionate, the very model of how she thought a Farsight Secretary should speak. "You impersonated Imperial officials multiple times; you gained entry into a secure Imperial research facility under false pretenses; you broke the seal of the Dandelion Throne, committing an outrage upon the embodiment of the sovereign. Each of these crimes can be prosecuted as a category of treason, a capital offense."

The gang looked at her, surprised by the sudden change in demeanor.

"Are you . . . threatening us?" asked Widi.

"But you know we aren't spies," said Arona. "We helped you catch Tiphan Huto, the real traitor."

"And you know we didn't do anything to harm the Throne,"

said Rati. "We came here out of curiosity, out of love of truth and knowledge."

Zomi held up a hand. "I'm simply laying out your options. You may choose to serve the Throne or to be charged as traitors. There is no other choice."

Looks of outrage appeared on the faces of Widi, Arona, and Rati, but before any of them could speak, Mota, who had not spoken so far, stepped forward.

"Why are you doing this?" he asked. "The Lyucu are abducting people of talent to serve their schemes of slaughter and enslavement. Your goals may be nobler, but by forcing us to serve the Throne at the threat of imprisonment or worse, are you not, at least in some measure, emulating them?"

Zomi's eyes widened. "I . . . that's not . . . how can you . . ."

Mota did not relent. "I've read the transcripts of the trial of Marshal Gin Mazoti. You were once also forced to serve a power against your conscience. Do you wish to emulate the empress or the Marshal?"

The words struck Zomi like thunder. She staggered back, and her lips moved voicelessly as she searched in vain for words to defend herself.

In the end, she said nothing and fled from their presence.

Fara came to see Kinri.

Zomi had given him an empty office to stay in. He could go about the compound, but not leave. He was not exactly a prisoner, but he was watched and kept under guard.

Fara found him in the library, browsing. It was obvious that his heart wasn't in reading.

"I have some good news," she blurted. It seemed too hard to talk about what she really wanted to talk about, so she chose to tell him about how her friend, Princess Aya Mazoti, had rescued Mozo Mu's family; how the pirates collaborating with the Lyucu had all been caught; how Magistrate Zuda had rescued the abducted mechanics in the cellar prison; how Tiphan Huto was going to be tried for treason—

"You knew I was not Dara," he said, interrupting her.

Quietly, Fara nodded. "The stories you told me . . . you couldn't have told them with such love unless you were Lyucu. It was the same way Arona and Widi figured out who I was: No matter how much I tried to hide my identity, my stories gave me away."

Kinri pondered this. *Are we defined by the stories we know and love?*

"You weren't worried that I was a spy, just using you?"

She shook her head. "Never. You love Dara too much, love . . . your friends too much. I thought you were like that defector who joined my brother . . . a good Lyucu."

He closed his eyes. *Is that what I am? A "good" Lyucu?*

"Yet, you were afraid to tell me who you were," he said.

"I didn't know how you truly felt about me," she said. "I want you to . . . like me because I'm Dandelion, not because I'm an Imperial princess. I suppose it's a kind of vanity . . . but I wanted to be *seen*."

He recalled their conversation about art, about Lady Mira and the Hegemon. It seemed a lifetime ago.

"Also," she said, hesitating, "I was afraid that if you were a Lyucu warrior and I a Dara princess, then there would be no possibility for us to ever be together. It would be too scandalous. I chose not to confirm the truth, to delay. It would have been too hard."

*Like me*, he thought.

"Has that really changed?" he asked reflexively.

"Of course it has!" said Fara. "The gods pitied us, and you're not Lyucu at all! You're Dara, and Zomi's brother!"

"Does that mean I've changed in your eyes?" asked Kinri. "Does that mean you are *seeing* me differently?"

"I don't understand . . ." Fara's voice trailed off.

Kinri's eyes landed on the thick, water-stained book titled *Gitré Üthu*.

*Know thyself. That's the problem. I don't know myself at all.*

"I think," he said, swallowing a lump in his throat, "that I prefer to be alone."

There were tears and shouts, and then, in the silence she left behind, his trembling fingers reached for the still-unopened handkerchief. The fragrance of dandelions and beach rose brought to mind helpless ships on storm-tossed seas and drifting seeds caught in gales too powerful to be resisted.

Kinri sent word through the guards that he wished to see Zomi.

In the estimation of the Lyucu in Ukyu-taasa, books and writing, as inventions of the crafty natives of Dara, whose nature was to lie, could not be trusted. Kinri now wondered if perhaps this distrust was a case of the robber raising a hue and cry when he was robbed: The entire court of Kriphi, from Tanvanaki and his mother to the court historians, seemed dedicated to the task of lying.

But he still harbored hope that some shred of the truth could be salvaged from the stories of his childhood. The Lyucu shamans justified distrust of books by pointing out that unlike living witnesses, they could not be interrogated and made to defend their accounts. In this instance, however, Kinri had access to at least one of the authors of the re-rememberings he had read.

"Was this the truth?" he asked his sister, pointing at her account of the Battle of Naza Pass.

Zomi's eyes grew hard. "No."

Kinri's heart leapt with excitement.

*Can it be? Was Pékyu Tenryo falsely vilified?*

"Then what was the truth?"

"The truth was not something that could be captured by words," said Zomi. "I watched as my mother was incinerated by garinafin breath at the command of Tenryo. How I felt at that moment was the most important part of the truth, but I had no words for it. I had a duty to report to the empress what could be ascertained: the number of people killed, the manner in which the deaths took place, the words spoken by those on the battlefield.

"Would all of these, added up together, be the truth?"

Kinri was silent.

*I cannot teach you the truth. Experience is the only teacher that will convince you.*

"I heard many other accounts of great atrocities committed by the Lyucu during the conquest of Dasu and Rui," said Zomi, "but since I was not the witness, I could not include them in my report. I wanted to be sure that my words were dispassionate, unimpeachable, so that the empress could decide on the conduct of the war based on facts, not passions."

"But why?" asked Kinri. "Why leave out the most important part of the truth: experience?"

"Because experience cannot be . . . reduced to symbols," said Zomi. "Words are slippery, frail things, and powerless to carry the weight of the truth. I can tell you that my Théra is the most beautiful woman in the world or that Aki Kidosu is the best mother anyone can have, but you cannot experience my love through these words. I can tell you that Tenryo is the cruelest conqueror and that Tanvanaki is a most merciless foe, but you cannot feel my hatred through these syllables. Eyewitness accounts have always been subject to doubt, for it is in our nature to want stories but also to be disappointed by how they fall short of the irreducible qualia of lived reality.

"And so the accounts of the survivors and refugees of Unredeemed Dara, by the time they reach the empress, are reduced to names of villages razed; numbers of the missing, wounded, and dead; tables of figures summarizing rapes, mutilations, and executions. No, they're not the truth, because the truth of the Lyucu in Dara is darkness unspeakable."

Kinri's heart clenched. He had confronted his sister to try to redeem Tenryo and his own love for the dead pékyu-votan; but there was no salvation, only more darkness.

Obsessively, Kinri went back to the eyewitness accounts of the creation of Ukyu-taasa: Lyucu thanes killing infants and babies in front of parents; forced labor and torture; massacres of unresisting civilians in order to instill fear; a policy of rape to break the will of the resistance. . . .

Every time he wanted to doubt the stories, to defend the innocence of the Lyucu, images of Cutanrovo Aga's troops slaughtering the village of Kigo Yezu came to mind. Denial was impossible. Atrocities were in fact the very foundation of the life of comfort and learning that he had experienced in Ukyu-taasa.

⁓

He woke up from nightmares in which Dandelion and Rati Yera and Nazu Tei and Lodan and Mati and Grand Mistress Wasu turned to cinders in the flame breath of garinafins piloted by his mother and Cutanrovo Aga. The dying screams of those he had come to love lingered in his mind long after he sat up panting, his body drenched in sweat.

He recoiled from his own reflection in the mirror, afraid to see shades of his mother.

He stared at the writing knife on the table, imagining opening his own veins with it so that the self-loathing, the weight of inherited sin, could be released along with the blood, to propitiate unrelenting fate.

He wept silently for the deaths and suffering that gave birth to his homeland, for the destruction of a myth that had sustained him.

He caressed the turtle shell given to him by his mother. It encapsulated, in miniature, all the turmoil in his mind. He had interpreted the portrait on the shell one way in Ukyu-taasa, only to be shown an entirely new reading in Dara proper.

*Something to guide you back to family and home.*

The family on the shell wasn't his, but Zomi's. In that light, everything had to be re-examined. Was the shell a kind of confession from his mother, wordlessly hinting at the truth?

She showed him how to wield a hunting spear and a fishing club; she bandaged his wounds and wiped away his tears; she told him that Ukyu-taasa was his home; she answered his questions about life on the scrublands; she told him stories about Admiral Krita's cruel rule and Pékyu Tenryo's brilliant rebellion; she sang him songs about the deeds of Afir and Kikisavo; she asked old Oga to teach him to speak the language of Dara; she begged Master Nazu Tei to become his teacher. . . .

Always, there was a look of anguish in her eyes that he had not known how to interpret when he asked about the founding of Ukyu-taasa. She had not wanted to lie, he understood now, though the silence of omission ate away at her inside.

He didn't know what she had done in the past, and what kind

of atrocities she had committed to make Ukyu-taasa possible. But after all the words and eyewitness accounts and real horrors and fantasized nightmares, there was one truth that remained steadfast against the onslaught of waves of revelations, one experience that he could not doubt: his mother loved him, and he loved his mother.

He loved her, no matter what she had done. And that knowledge was both sweeter and more painful than anything else in the world.

When the Blossom Gang came to visit, he almost wanted to plead some illness and turn them away. Now that they knew the truth about him, that the blood of the hated Lyucu flowed through his veins, would they see him differently?

But Rati, Widi, Arona, and Mota did not speak to him of his identity at all.

At first, he was grateful because he thought they were looking past his heritage and seeing him as their friend, the man they had come to know as Kinri Rito. But then, as they made casual references to his good fortune, he realized that they were simply assuming that he was glad to be reunited with his Dara heritage, that he had rejected his Lyucu mother as easily as someone who had seen the truth would embrace it and cast away falsehoods.

He felt the gulf of experience between them, always present, yawning wider. How much wider still then, he wondered, was the gulf between him and Dan—no, Fara, Princess of Dara?

Similar to Kinri's state, Zomi had not placed restrictions on where the gang members could go, so long as they made no effort to leave Last Bite. Thus, Rati spoke of the wonders they had seen in the laboratories and experimental galleries; Widi spoke of various proposals and reforms that had been rejected by the empress over the years and sealed away in the archives of Last Bite, many of which would have led to a Dara very different from the one they were living in; Arona spoke of the lost plays and songs from the days of the Tiro states and from the reign of Emperor Mapidéré, most of which she had known only by reputation; and Mota spoke of his investigation into Marshal Mazoti's trial.

"She was not a traitor to Dara at all," said Mota. And there was a joy in his voice and a glow in his face that Kinri couldn't remember ever seeing.

"How do you know this?" he asked, to avoid having to talk about himself.

"Come; let me show you."

The seals on the scrolls remained broken. Zomi had not yet decided whether to use them as evidence in a new treason trial.

So Kinri read through the voluminous records of Gin Mazoti's trial for treason: the court historian's transcript of the first dialogue between Empress Jia and Princess Fara (only a little girl back then, who had no awareness of the political storm brewing around her); Prime Minister Cogo Yelu's pleas for evidence; Zomi Kidosu's testimony that Gin Mazoti was plotting rebellion; the Marshal's own angry denunciation of the charges against her; Farsight Secretary Rin Coda's suicide note confessing his role in Empress Jia's schemes; the confessions from Doru Solofi and Noda Mi substantiating Rin Coda's account; Zomi Kidosu's retraction of her accusation; the empress's own confession of her trumped-up charges; and finally, the long dialogue between Emperor Ragin and the Marshal, recorded by the emperor himself, at the end of which Gin broke her sword to show that she would not bend the truth for the sake of political stability, to give in to Jia's lies.

The Dandelion Court was exactly as ugly and as full of deceit as he had always been taught to believe in Ukyu-taasa.

But such confirmation brought him little joy.

Inexplicably, there was nothing in the record to explain why, after Kuni Garu had been captured by Pékyu Tenryo, Gin Mazoti had suddenly reversed herself and accepted the falsehoods staining her reputation while taking up the sword to defend Dara. She had fought for Jia, the woman who tried to destroy her, and even praised her as a worthy Empress of Dara.

"Some truths," said Mota, "are forever lost to history."

Kinri put away the last scroll; his heart was all ashes.

If learning the truth of the Lyucu atrocities during the conquest made him wish he had never been born Lyucu, the ugliness of court politics in Dara made him question why he had ever seen beauty and hope in the pretty words of the Ano sages.

The nature of all humankind was corrupt and there was nothing new under the sun.

"Why are these books sealed away?" he demanded of Zomi. "Why are they not open to all who wish to study the truth?"

"Because the truth is sometimes not what the world needs to be better," said Zomi, looking weary.

"What do you mean?"

"When the Hegemon swept through Dara on his war steed, Réfiroa, he was driven by the memories of the slaughter of his family at the hands of Mapidéré. He rallied his troops by reminding them of the truth that the conquering Xana armies had once buried alive tens of thousands of surrendered Cocru soldiers, and so his followers did not object when he engineered the drowning of tens of thousands of Xana prisoners.

"Emperor Ragin, on the other hand, granted clemency to the Xana Empire's bureaucrats and soldiers when he was king of Dasu, and later, when he became emperor, relieved the taxes of those who had supported the Hegemon. He did not seek vengeance or remind the populace of the cruelties of Mapidéré, nor did he build monuments to all the innocents who had died for Mata Zyndu's ambition. He kept the truth sealed away in these hidden archives, and in fact, allowed the people to romanticize the Hegemon's legacy.

"Which of these, do you think, was the better course?"

Kinri was silent. He could see that insisting on justice for the Marshal would have destabilized the Dandelion Court at the moment when it needed the support of the people the most, when the Lyucu were threatening to overrun the Islands, but why were the records of the atrocities of the Lyucu also sealed away?

"The truth can sometimes be a confirmation for falsehoods," said Zomi.

Kinri was startled, confused.

"There are enough tales of the atrocities committed by the Lyucu spreading from mouth to mouth already," said Zomi, "and a book of eyewitness accounts would have confirmed the tales and made even more bloody exaggerations believable."

Kinri thought this over. He himself had believed the worst tales about Kuni Garu's character after hearing confirmation of the bandit-king's betrayal of the Hegemon at Rana Kida.

"The empress believed that after the Battle of Zathin Gulf, peace, not further warfare, was what was needed. Accounts of the atrocities committed by the Lyucu would only whip up frenzy among the common people for war, and she concluded that had to be avoided at all costs. While she never actively suppressed the stories, she decided that official testimony of such atrocities had to be sealed away until it could be spoken of without the desire for bloodlust."

There was a weariness to Zomi's voice; unexpectedly, Kinri felt pity for her. His sister, he saw, was like a wild goose who had been charged for so long by her mate to tend to the nest, protecting it and repairing it, patching and securing it, that she no longer knew how to fly away from the placid lake, leaving behind nothing but a cry and a shadow.

Deep into the night, Zomi sat alone, thinking.

Kinri remained morose and withdrawn, and she worried about him. Having grown up in the household of a high-ranking Lyucu thane, he would no doubt have much useful intelligence to share. But she was coming to realize that perhaps she had been too hasty in assuming his state of mind. A child did not abandon a lifetime of love for a mother upon finding out that she was a killer, a rapist, a warrior for an unjust cause. A man did not abandon a lifetime of indoctrination in devotion to tribe, homeland, an imagined myth upon finding out that all was not as he had been told.

*The most important decisions we make in life are not derived from reason, from weighing the fish, from an evaluation of the pros and cons— but from a simple leap of faith, of love that needs no evidence, apology, or argument.*

She decided that it was best to wait until she had brought him back to Pan, where she could seek out healers and wise counselors at the court to help Kinri adjust to his new Dara identity, before asking him many questions.

The more pressing problem was what to do about the Blossom Gang.

Mota's questions had rattled her deeply. The empress had accused Gin Mazoti of treason to achieve her own political goals, and Zomi, to her lasting regret, had aided in that effort. But at least formally, the empress's accusation wasn't baseless. Gin, believing Empress Jia was going down the wrong path, *had* harbored fugitive rebels against the Throne as evidence against the empress, an action she believed befitting the ideal of *mutagé*. It was treason on paper, but not in substance.

The Blossom Gang had broken the seal of the Dandelion Throne in order to find out the truth about Gin Mazoti's trial, a goal they believed to be in harmony with *mutagé*. By threatening them with accusations of treason in order to get them to comply with her own wishes, was she merely repeating what the empress had done?

She believed her goal was grand, was *right*. But did that justify suppressing truth for power, for adopting the methods of the Lyucu—at least in form—to press the Blossoms into service?

She thought about Théra's parting words, asking her to help Phyro be the steward of Dara; she thought about Phyro's request, asking for her help to build up an army to free the people of Unredeemed Dara; she thought about Empress Jia's stern reminder that Zomi had taken an oath to serve the holder of the Seal of Dara; she thought about Luan Zyaji's instruction to her, the first time she thought he was going to die: *Sometimes you must do the right thing even if it hurts you. Actions reify ideals.*

Did *mutagé* mean loyalty to the wishes of whoever held the Seal of Dara, or did it mean something *more*?

For years, she had done as the empress demanded of her, believing that Jia was trying to do the right thing for Dara. But what if she was wrong? What if Phyro's private army was the only hope for Dara? Empress Jia had been wrong once before; she could be wrong again. She had always tried to work within the elaborate system of bureaucracy set up by Jia, to follow the rules, but what if there was no way to achieve what was right unless she was willing to cut the strings, to no longer soar as a kite, but to dive freely as one of Luan's mechanical Mingén falcons?

Gin Mazoti had harbored fugitives because it was *mutagé*; she had refused to confess to treason because it was *mutagé*; she had ultimately accepted the judgment of treason to protect the Throne and took up arms to fight for Dara despite her stained name, also because it was *mutagé*.

Could she do any less?

*After you have reasoned through the thicket, you must still rely on the compass of the passion-pumped heart. Once you have worked out all the odds, you still have to toss the dice, to take that leap of faith.*

Doubt subsided in her heart. She knew what she must do.

It was a sunny morning a week later. A large caravan sat on the road out of Last Bite, ready to bring Zomi Kidosu and Princess Fara back to Pan.

Usually, for a trip this long, Zomi would have opted for an airship. But for this occasion, Zomi had loads of interesting goods to haul and a secret destination she wanted to detour to before returning to Pan. Travel by land was the best choice, and so Aya Mazoti, who had disembarked in Ginpen after her anti-pirate raids, had been summoned to provide escort.

The carts were packed with prototypes, models, and drawings of the Blossom Gang's inventions. A similar set had been left at Last Bite, while most of the rest would be brought back to Pan, where scholars at the Imperial Academy would examine them and elucidate their principles. Zomi was very excited about their potential.

But a small subset of the plans and models would never make it to Pan. Zomi was going to make a special trip to the Wisoti Mountains, taking the Blossom Gang with her.

Zomi had finally divulged to the gang an astonishing secret: Emperor Monadétu, long absent from the veiled throne, had been preparing for an invasion of Unredeemed Dara.

"I intend to help the emperor in whichever way I can," said Zomi. "And the first step is to bring him people of talent. There will be no examinations, no abstract essays, no grand titles and impressive salaries. You will not be part of the system. All I can promise you is a great deal of hard work and endless danger."

"Danger?" asked Arona, confused. "You're not expecting us to fight the Lyucu ourselves, are you?"

"Not unless you want to," said Zomi. She glanced at Mota, who looked ready to pick up a sword right then and there.

"She means that we'll be treated as traitors to the Throne," said Widi, "because this invasion, if I understand correctly, isn't authorized by Empress Jia." He eyed Zomi warily.

Zomi didn't deny it. "That is true. Even by suggesting this plan to you, I could be argued to have committed treason. What happened to the Marshal could easily happen to me and to all of you. You must understand the risks."

"What if we don't want to?" asked Widi.

"Then you may go on to live your lives of freedom," said Zomi. "There will be no charges, no threats, no punishment. If you do join the emperor and me, you do so of your own free will."

The gang looked at one another. Other than Mota, all seemed hesitant.

"You've all seen the latest refugee accounts, and some of you have spoken to refugees themselves," said Zomi. "So you know the truth of what is happening in Unredeemed Dara. The empress, I fear, believes that the peace and prosperity we have in Dara proper is too precious to risk a war, and she will never authorize an invasion, even after the peace treaty expires."

"How can a private army, not backed by the wealth of the empire, have a chance against the might of the Lyucu?" asked Widi.

"That is why I'm asking for your help. The emperor will not have much in the way of resources or manpower, and he cannot re-create the magnificent fleet that stood against the Lyucu at Zathin Gulf nearly a decade ago. While the Lyucu have grown stronger in the interim, the power the emperor can wield will be much weaker. Yes, he does have a few surprises that I'll reveal to you when we see him, but they aren't enough. What he needs are ingenious inventions, power-amplifiers to overcome a far superior foe."

"Like how the Splendid Urn overcame the Treasure Chest," muttered Rati Yera.

Zomi nodded. "But there is a graver threat on the horizon. What you do not know—indeed, what very few in Dara know—is that the Wall of Storms will reopen in less than two years, possibly bringing reinforcements for the Lyucu."

The gang exclaimed in consternation.

"The empress has kept this information extremely secret out of fear of panicking the general public, but she seems to put all her hope in continued appeasement of the Lyucu rather than risking a war. The emperor and I, on the other hand, believe that preparing an invasion force is not only required to rescue the people of Unredeemed Dara, but a matter of Dara's survival."

Mota, who had been silent until now, finally spoke. "The Marshal could have stayed in her house, refusing to bear the name of being a traitor, while the Lyucu overran the Islands. We could also remain uninvolved, living as we have been while the darkness descends over Dara. But how can that be a life of freedom? The Marshal chose to walk out of her house, bear the burden of being called a traitor, and take up the sword for Dara. Now that we know the truth of her life, can we do any less?"

"If we must become traitors to save Dara, then so be it," said Widi.

The rest of the gang nodded.

And so Rati Yera worked for days to repair the broken seals on the scrolls, while her companions retrieved their possessions from Ginpen and bid friends farewell. There would be no trial for treason—not when a far grander scheme was being plotted.

While Zomi was giving her final instructions to Kita Thu, the archon of the Imperial laboratories of Ginpen, the Blossom Gang inspected the carts to be sure their inventions and artifacts were secure.

"Let me get a few men to carry you into your cart, Master Yera," Kita Thu called out, seeing Rati Yera straining to move her wheeled chair over the uneven ground. Even with the long handles and the gear trains, she had to exert great effort to make any progress. The chair seemed heavier than its appearance.

Rati Yera waved him away. "No, no. Mota will carry me just fine.

I prefer his steady hand." Mota Kiphi came over and easily pushed her chair over a rut as the gang continued their inspection, chatting among themselves.

They were nervous and excited. Zomi had devised roles for each of them suited to their skills, and it promised to be the start of a new grand adventure.

Carts holding the prisoners formed the last part of the caravan. The pirate leaders—both those captured at sea and those caught at the Treasure Chest—were packed into several cage carts guarded by soldiers. Tiphan Huto, looking despondent, had a cage all to himself. Because they were accused of piracy, kidnapping, offering aid and comfort to the Lyucu, and multiple other capital offenses, the prisoners had to be brought back to the capital, where they would be tried by a special tribunal overseen by the Inner Council.

At this moment, Tiphan was rather glad that he was in this cage cart; he really couldn't imagine facing his furious siblings, cousins, and family elders, who could lose practically everything because of his bad decisions. Much of the clan's assets had already been frozen. Once he was convicted at trial, most of the Hutos' businesses and properties, essentially everything Tiphan had touched, would escheat to the state.

"Where's Kinri?" asked Princess Fara. She was standing next to Aya Mazoti at the head of the procession, waiting impatiently for the caravan to get underway.

"Look at you!" said Aya Mazoti. "You can't even talk to me for ten minutes without bringing him up."

"It's not like that," said a blushing Fara. "I haven't seen him all morning, that's all."

"Relax, he's not some child prone to getting lost. I'll go fetch him—but I warn you, you can't ride next to him."

"Why not?"

"I'm supposed to be your chaperone! So I'll have to sit between the two of you all the way back to Pan—"

"Oh, you're asking for it now—"

But a giggling Aya had already run away to search the caravan for the boy.

Fara sighed. Ever since returning from the pirate mission, Aya had seemed morose and dejected, as though her experiences at sea had changed her, made her seem more "grown up" but also doubt who she was. She supposed that it was the same way with her—these months spent in Ginpen had shown her much about the lives of the people as well as about her own heart, and she felt like a different person. It was good to have a few moments with Aya where they could be as carefree and silly as they used to be.

Aya returned a little later, looking puzzled. "I can't find him anywhere."

Fara, feeling trepidatious, went toward Zomi.

They found him on top of the bluff, legs dangling over the cliffs that jutted into the waters of Zathin Gulf.

For a moment, Zomi felt as though she had slipped back in time to that day years ago when she and Théra had sat in this same spot, when they had first confessed their feelings for each other. A temporary dizziness seized her, and she swayed unsteadily upon her feet. She looked up at the sun and whispered *I love you*, hoping that the bright orb, like a mirror, would reflect her message beyond the Wall of Storms, to the edge of the world where her beloved was.

*But there are other matters in the here and now,* she reminded herself.

He didn't turn around as the two women approached.

"Kinri," Fara said, her voice gentle. "It's time to go."

At first, he said nothing. A seagull flying overhead cried in the silence as it dove for fish in the distant sea below.

"My name is Savo Ryoto."

Though the sun continued to shine brightly, Fara seemed to sense a shadow overhead and a cold gust around her heart.

"That may be the name you were given at birth," said Zomi Kidosu, her voice even, "but that isn't a name that belongs in Dara. To those who love you, you're Kinri Kidosu."

"A sign," he muttered, gazing out at the sea. "I've been looking for a sign from the gods to tell me what to do, but there hasn't been any."

"What sign do you need?" asked Zomi. "I stand here, as does

Fara. We're your family. Is the love of a princess and the most powerful minister of these Islands not enough of a sign?"

"There are others who love me. My mother, Goztan Ryoto, Thane of the Five Tribes of the Antler."

Zomi flinched, and her eyes glowed with hate, but she kept her voice calm. "You were born from an act of dominance, but the sins of your mother do not stain you. You are innocent, as all the children of Dara are."

"How can you judge her when you don't know her? She gave me the shell that he had carved as a memento before I went into exile. Can you say she didn't care for him, or that he didn't care for her—"

"They were *not* equals!" Zomi shouted, unable to hold back her rage anymore. "She was the conqueror, and he the enslaved. How can you speak of anything other than injustice and vengeance?"

"In Ukyu, he was the conqueror, and she the enslaved."

Zomi trembled with fury. "How dare you make such false equivalencies—"

"Neither of us knows the truth!" said the young man. After a pause, he added, "You call me a child of Dara, but I am just as much a child of Ukyu. My teacher, Master Nazu Tei, gave me my Dara name, but my mother gave me my name in Lyucu. I am both. I cannot simply deny who I am."

"What are you saying?" asked an increasingly anxious and confused Fara.

He looked at her, his face full of sorrow. "I'm sorry. I wish you could remain Dandelion, and I Kinri. But you're not Dandelion, and I'm not Kinri."

"But you *are*, and I *am*. Nothing has changed."

"Everything has changed."

Zomi, who had finally gotten her emotions under control, broke in. "What do you intend to do?"

He shook his head. "I don't know. Zomi, you told me that once I'm brought to Pan, I'll have to tell you everything I know about the Lyucu court and military to help you and the empress plot against Kriphi, to aid Emperor Monadétu in his invasion plans. But I can no more do that than I can go back to Rui and tell them all the secrets

I've learned about Dara, to help them defeat you." His voice cracked. "How can I help my sister kill my mother? How can I help my mother kill my sister?"

"But not choosing is also a choice," said Zomi. "You were born Savo Ryoto, and now you have a chance to become Kinri Kidosu. By not seizing that chance, you'll be choosing a legacy of barbarism and death, rather than a living future with people who love you. Is that what you really want?"

"What I really want," said the young man, "is to not know what I know, to not feel what I feel, to not have experienced what I've experienced, to not be who I am. But even the gods cannot grant me that wish. The terrible things that my mother and her people did, they did so in the name of Ukyu-taasa, which is also my name. The terrible things that my master and my father and their people suffered, they suffered in the name of Ukyu-taasa, which is also my name. I can no more cut away either part of these truths than I can cut out my heart.

"But I never knew my father as my father, while I know my mother has risked life and limb for me, for my future. I cannot deny her. I am called Savo Ryoto, son of Goztan Ryoto, daughter of Dayu Ryoto. I serve Ukyu-taasa as Thane-taasa of the Five Tribes of the Antler."

With a long and heart-wrenching wail, Fara turned and ran down the mountain.

"You've made your choice, and so I'll make mine," said Zomi tonelessly. "I'll bring you back to Pan not as my brother, but as a Lyucu spy. If you insist on being a thane-taasa of the Lyucu, then I must carry out the duties of the Farsight Secretary of Dara."

Savo Ryoto nodded.

He traveled in darkness.

Instead of a cage cart, Zomi had chosen to put him inside a regular carriage with all the curtains drawn. Perhaps she hoped that isolation would make him change his mind.

A flash of bright light as a curtain lifted and settled; the fragrance of dandelions and beach rose; a warm body pressed up against his.

"I don't care if you are Lyucu, Dara, a busboy or a spy," said Fara. "You'll always be my Kinri, and I'll always be your Dandelion. Isn't that enough?"

*It should be enough*, he thought, *it should be*.

"But that isn't the truth," he croaked. "And love has no place for lies."

"Forget about the past; forget about history. Let's be like the Fluxists of old, who lived individual lives of freedom, buoyed up by love and not weighed down by anything."

He closed his eyes. What a beautiful scene she sketched. What lovely visions.

"But we're not characters in epic romances," he said. "You love your brothers, your sister, your aunt-mother, your parents. I love my mother, my sister, my playmates from childhood, the naros who taught me how to wrestle and ride. Yet your brother and my sister wish to drive my mother's people, who are also my people, into the sea, and take pleasure in their cries of lamentation.

"We are embedded in strands of love and hatred, a web that glows in the sunlight of history, bedecked in pearls of blood and fragments of bone. How can we truly *see* each other the way we deserve to be seen without acknowledging the truth?"

Her hand felt cold against his. She was shaking. "Then this is the end?"

His vision grew blurry, and the lump in his throat refused to go down. He reached inside his robe and took out the handkerchief that she had given him.

Pressing it into her hand, he said, "I never opened it."

As if that would salve her pain, as if that would make her whole. She pulled her hand away.

"Love, once given, cannot be rescinded."

A bright flash, and she was gone. Her heat and perfume lingered in the air.

He curled his fingers, and the handkerchief was still there, soft against the palm of his hand.

Tears flowed noiselessly down his face.

Another flash, this time lasting longer. Several figures were in the carriage with him. He clutched the handkerchief protectively to his chest and looked up at them fearfully.

Had the farseers already come? Would he ever make it to Pan, the mystical Harmonious City?

It was evening before Zomi decided to look in on her brother. A whole day alone in the dark interior of a sealed carriage, accompanied by nothing but his own thoughts, should have a salutary effect on that stubborn attitude.

She opened the curtain, left it furled, and climbed in.

"Kinri," she began. "I've been—"

She stopped because it was a smiling Widi Tucru who greeted her.

"What . . . why . . . how . . ." she sputtered.

Her mind jumped back to earlier today, when Widi, Mota, and Arona had claimed that they were tired of riding in carriages and requested horses to ride ahead and get some fresh air. Preoccupied, she had granted their request without much thought. It was obvious what had happened. The "Widi" who had ridden away was not Widi at all, and he had not returned.

"Don't blame the Blossoms," a voice said behind her.

Zomi whipped around. Fara.

There were tear stains on her face, but she defiantly jutted out her chin. "*I* was the mastermind."

"How could you just let him go!? He refuses to be Dara! Don't you understand the risk—"

"He will *not* harm Dara. He loves the Islands. He loves us."

"And how do you know this?"

"Because I can tell true stories apart from false ones."

Zomi sighed. She swallowed the order to give chase.

*Love makes us do strange things.*

*- That did not work out the way it should have, at all. We gave the boy so many signs! So many!*

*- To be fair, even I have trouble reading your signs.*

*- That's because whether we realize it or not, we've all been doing as Lutho asked before he left. We've stopped relying on mysteries—*

—*But we nudged! We tweaked! We tickled the wings of coincidence and blew on the sails of fortune!*

- *Even a mortal mathematician with the skill of Luan Zya wouldn't know with certainty when an occurrence has crossed from the realm of random chance into the purview of an oracle. Chance, after all, is inherent in the nature of the universe. Let this be a lesson to all of you on the futility of meddling.*

- *I never thought I'd see the day, Tazu, when you'd be advocating the same thing as Lutho!*

- *You misunderstand me, brother. The old turtle and I may both want the gods to step back, but we do so for completely different reasons. The more mortals understand the universe—or "weigh the fish," as they so crudely put it—the less room there is for divine wonder and the greater the role assigned to pure chance. I'm delighted to see my domain increase at the expense of the rest of you.*

- *Why, you selfish, conceited trap of fish, you cold-blooded, obdurate demon of chaos—*

- *Enough, brothers and sisters! This bickering gets us nowhere. What next? What's our plan?*

- *Did anyone really think that the fate of Dara would be decided by a romance? That hate-hearted factions would lay down their swords and beat them into weaving hooks and shepherd's staffs just because two youngsters are in love? That sort of softheaded wishful thinking belongs to teahouse storytellers and hack playwrights, not reality!*

- *Wait!* That *was* never the plan. *I thought we were trying to give useful intelligence—*

- *I thought we were trying to assemble a team of talented advisers—*

- *I thought we were going to teach a lesson of experience—*

- *I thought we just wanted good food?*

- *Are you blaming me?*

- *I think we have to accept—*

- *Back up! Back up! Who died and made you the arbiter of reality?*

- *Well, I hate to point this out, but actually none of us can die, that's kind of the point—*

- *Unbelievable. So we've been stumbling about at cross-purposes? None of us even shared the same plan?*

- *You can see now why it's hard for the mortals to know what we want, when we don't even know what we want. But you don't see me getting upset over—*

- *Of course you are happy, Tazu. You love it when we fall to strife and mutual recrimination—*

So much noise. So much confusion. It was impossible to tell who said what when where why how.

At length, the rhetorical waves subsided, the argumentative eruptions flared out, the grandiloquent storms calmed.

- *The only thing we've accomplished, it seems, is furnishing a little drama while the mortals did what they always wanted. To think that we thought we were supposed to be the puppet masters . . .*

- *Why do we bother meddling in their affairs? It never goes the way we want—*

—*But how can we stop trying to save this land, which is as much our home as theirs? It's in our nature, my sister, my other self.*

- *Therein lies the source of all our sorrow.*

- *Not all of us are melancholy, though. Little sister, why do you look so tranquil? Your pair of lovebirds have flown apart.*

- *I can't say I'm pleased that they've parted ways, but neither am I disheartened. The boy was right: The mortals are not lonely reefs, each a bare rock stranded in a vast, empty sea, but knots in a messy web woven from gossamer strands of love extending across time and space, at once confining as well as supportive. For Savo and Fara to do otherwise than they have done would be to deny their natures. A life isn't and shouldn't be a single grand romance.*

- *That is a surprising sentiment from a goddess of love.*

- *Who says that teachers cannot learn from students, or gods from mortals? Just as the mortals must entangle themselves in conflicting loves for one another as they stumble through their all-too-brief span, no matter how much pain it brings them, we must enmesh ourselves in love for this land, no matter how futile the effort sometimes appears.*

- *Are you saying . . . that we should keep on meddling, in spite of our failures?*

- *I think . . . we should each aid our charge as best we're able. But we can all try to be a bit more humble and listen more than talk, observe more than press. Since we cannot seem to come to one unified plan by council and debate, let's rather trust in the individual inclinations of our favorite mortals. They cannot act other than as demanded by their nature, and neither can we. Maybe that is the point Lutho was trying to make.*

The gods of Dara pondered this mystery.

One thing was sure: There would be far fewer meetings like this in the future, far fewer attempts to align, confine, define.

The freedom for each individual to choose their own tale moved the gods as much as the mortals.

# GLOSSARY

## DARA

ANOJITI: a neologism formed from Classical Ano roots to describe the people of Dara, created in response to the Lyucu invasion.

CASHIMA: a scholar who has passed the second level of the Imperial examinations. The Classical Ano word means "practitioner." A *cashima* is allowed to wear his or her hair in a triple scroll-bun and carry a sword. *Cashima* can also serve as clerks for magistrates and mayors.

CRUBEN: a scaled whale with a single horn protruding from its head; symbol of Imperial power.

CÜPA: a game played with black and white stones on a grid.

DYRAN: a flying fish, symbol of femininity and sign of good fortune. It is covered by rainbow-colored scales and has a sharp beak.

FIROA: a *cashima* who places within the top one hundred in the Grand Examination is given this rank. The Classical Ano word means "a (good) match." Based on their talents, the *firoa* are either given positions in Imperial administration, assigned to work for various enfeoffed nobles, or promoted to engage in further study or research with the Imperial Academy.

GÉÜPA: an informal sitting position where the legs are crossed and folded under the body, with each foot tucked under the opposite thigh.

JIRI: a woman's bow where the hands are crossed in front of the chest in a gesture of respect.

KUNIKIN: a large, three-legged drinking vessel.

MINGÉN FALCON: a species of extraordinarily large falcon native to the island of Rui.

MIPA RARI: a formal kneeling position where the back is kept straight and weight is evenly distributed between the knees and toes.

MOAPHYA: an ancient Ano instrument of the "metal" class, consisting of rectangular bronze slabs of various thicknesses suspended from a frame and struck with a mallet to produce different pitches.

MUTAGÉ: variously translated as "faith-mercy" or "loyalty-benefaction," one of the most important virtues to the ancient Ano. It refers to a dedication to the welfare of the people as a whole, one that transcends self-interest or concern for family and clan.

OGÉ: drops of sweat. The Ogé Islands were supposedly formed from drops of sweat from the god Rufizo.

PANA MÉJI: a scholar who has done especially well in the Grand Examination and is given the chance to participate in the Palace Examination, where the emperor himself assesses the qualities of the candidates and assigns them a rank. The Classical Ano phrase means "on the list."

PAWI: animal aspects of the gods of Dara.

RAYE: descendants of prisoners of war, the lowest social caste in the days of the Tiro states.

RÉNGA: honorific used to address the emperor.

THAKRIDO: an extremely informal sitting position where one's legs are stretched out in front; used only with intimates or social inferiors.

THASÉ-TEKI: literally "winter worm, summer grass," a hybrid organism consisting of a fungus and a particular species of underground caterpillar that the fungus infects. The mycelia slowly spread throughout the body of the caterpillar, eventually killing it to sprout aboveground in a grasslike stroma. Called "caterpillar grass" in the vernacular, it has many uses in herbal medicine.

-TIKA: suffix expressing endearment toward younger family members.

TOKO DAWIJI: a scholar who has passed the first level of the Imperial examinations. The Classical Ano phrase means "the elevated." A *toko dawiji* is allowed to wear his or her hair in a double scroll-bun.

TUNOA: grapes.

ZAMAKI: a game of war between opposing armies composed of tokens representing pieces such as the king, consort, ship, adviser, assassin, horse, kite, and so on.

## LYUCU/AGON

ARUCURO SANA: literally "talking bones"; logograms constructed from animal parts using principles derived from arucuro tocua as well as Classical Ano.

ARUCURO TOCUA: literally "living bones"; articulated creations made from bones, sinew, horn, antler, and other animal parts.

GARINAFIN: the flying, fire-breathing beast that is the core of Lyucu culture. Its body is about the size of three elephants, with a long tail, two clawed feet, a pair of great, leathery wings, and a slender, snakelike neck topped with a deerlike, antlered head.

KYOFFIR: an alcoholic drink made from fermented garinafin milk.

PÉDIATO SAVAGA: literally "stomach journey," the scrublands funeral practice of leaving a body exposed to the elements and scavenging animals.

PÉKYU: title given to the leader of the Lyucu or Agon.

PÉKYU-TAASA: title given to the children of pékyus; sometimes translated into Dara as "prince" or "princess."

TANTO-LYU-NARO: tribeless wanderers of Ukyu-Gondé who do not follow the ways of either the Lyucu or the Agon and who renounce all war-making. Literally "warriors who do not make war."

TOGATEN: literally "runt"; a slur used against those of mixed Lyucu and native Dara ancestry.

TOLYUSA: a plant with hallucinogenic properties; the berries are essential for the garinafins to breed successfully.

VOTAN-RU-TAASA: "older-and-younger"; brothers.

VOTAN-SA-TAASA: "older-and-younger"; sisters (or siblings).

# LIST OF SELECTED
# ARTIFACTS AND MOUNTS

CRUBEN'S THORN: a dagger made from a cruben's tooth and therefore undetectable to lodestone detectors, a favorite weapon of assassins. A rebel from Gan first attempted to kill King Réon of Xana with it. It was later wielded by Princess Kikomi against Phin Zyndu, and finally by Consort Mira on herself.

NA-AROÉNNA, THE DOUBT-ENDER: an extraordinarily heavy sword constructed by the master bladesmith Suma Ji for Dazu Zyndu, Marshal of Cocru. With a heart of bronze and a coat of thousand-hammered steel, it was quenched in the blood of a wolf. Later, it became the weapon, successively, of Mata Zyndu, Gin Mazoti, and Phyro Garu.

GOREMAW: an ironwood cudgel made more fearsome with rings of teeth embedded in the strike-head. Wielded by Mata Zyndu, it was the companion to Na-aroénna.

RÉFIROA: Mata Zyndu's war steed, the "Well-Matched."

GITRÉ ÜTHU: the Classical Ano title means "Know Thyself." Legend has it that Luan Zyaji received it as a gift from the gods. The book supposedly showed divine revelations, but only of what the user already knew. Luan carried it with him beyond the Wall of Storms, and later gave it to his disciple, Zomi Kidosu.

BITER: a toothed war club given to Dafiro Miro by Huluwen of Tan Adü.

SIMPLICITY: once the sword of Mocri Zati, champion of Gan. When Mata Zyndu defeated him, the sword was gifted to Ratho Miro, the Hegemon's personal guard.

LANGIABOTO: a war axe fashioned from garinafin rib and talon, it had been in the hands of the Aragoz clan, the ruling family of the Agon, for generations. The name means "self-reliance" in the language of the scrublands. Later, it was seized by Tenryo Roatan and became the symbol of Lyucu domination.

GASLIRA-SATA, THE PEACE-BITE: Goztan Ryoto's war axe, made from a tusked tiger's fang and four baby garinafin ribs bound together with horrid-wolf sinew.

# NOTES

The Veiled Throne and Speaking Bones were conceived of as one continuous narrative, and should be read as such.

(Speaking Bones will be coming soon!)

A few notes specific to this book:

It is believed that the camera obscura was originally invented by Mohists.

Rati Yera's instructible machines are based on the mobile carts of Hero of Alexandria and the pattern looms of Han Dynasty China. For more on these wondrous machines, see, *inter alia*, Sharkey, Noel. "A programmable robot from 60 AD 2611." *New Scientist* (2007) and Zhao, Feng, et al. "The earliest evidence of pattern looms: Han Dynasty tomb models from Chengdu, China." *Antiquity* 91.356 (2017): 360–374. Incidentally, the Chinese character for "machine," 機, is based on the stylized form of a pattern loom.

The silkmotic mill of Dara is based on the same principles that moved Ben Franklin's electric wheel of 1748.

For more generally on orality and literacy, see Ong, Walter J. *Orality and Literacy*. Routledge, 2013.

Zomi's poem for Théra is in part reworked from the anonymous Han Dynasty poem 《飲馬長城窟行》.

Ro Taça of Rima's actions during the legendary *cüpa* game are inspired by a dialogue in 《禮記·檀弓上》, in which the following quote appears: 「謀人之軍師，敗則死之；謀人之邦邑，危則亡之。」("A military adviser should die with the army in defeat; a sovereign's counselor should die when the country is put in peril").

I'm deeply grateful to the following individuals for their help in the production of this book: Joe Monti (editor extraordinaire); Russell Galen (bestest of agents); Danny Baror and Heather Baror-Shapiro (foreign rights); Angela Cheng Caplan (media rights); John Vairo and Lisa Litwack (art direction); Sam Weber (cover); Robert Lazzaretti (map); Valerie Shea and Alexandre Su (copyediting); Lauren Truskowski and Kayleigh Webb (marketing and publicity); Madison Penico (manuscript assistance); Caroline Pallotta, Kaitlyn Snowden, Kathryn Kenney-Peterson, Alexis Alemao (managing editorial and production).

I also wish to thank the many people who helped me during the drafting of this book, whether by reading drafts, giving me ideas, providing research assistance, or keeping up my spirits: Anatoly Belilovsky, Dario Ciriello, Elodie Coello, Elías Combarro, Kate Elliott, Nathan Faries, Barbara Hendrick, Crystal Huff, Emily Jin, Allison King, Leticia Lara, Anaea Lay, Felicia Low-Jimenez, John P. Murphy, Erica Naone, Tochi Onyebuchi, Emma Osborne, Bridget Pupillo, Achala Upendran, Alex Shvartsman, Carmen Yiling Yan, Christie Yant, Florina Yezril, Caroline Yoachim, Hannah Zhao.

Above all, I couldn't have done this without my family. Lisa, Esther, Miranda, I love you.

Thank you, reader, for having journeyed so far with me to Dara and Ukyu-Gondé. The story of Dara isn't over. I'll see you in *Speaking Bones*, the last Dandelion Dynasty book.

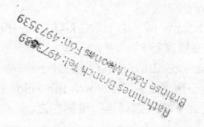